PENGUIN BOOKS

COLLECTED STORIES

William Trevor was born in 1928 at Mitchelstown, County Cork, and he spent his childhood in provincial Ireland. He attended a number of Irish schools and later Trinity College, Dublin. He is a member of the Irish Academy of Letters. He has written many novels, including *The Old Boys* (1964), winner of the Hawthornden Prize; *The Children of Dynmouth* (1976) and *Fools of Fortune* (1983), both winners of the Whitbread Fiction Award; *The Silence in the Garden* (1988), winner of the Yorkshire Post Book of the Year Award; *Two Lives* (1991), which was shortlisted for the *Sunday Express* Book of the Year Award and includes the Booker shortlisted novella *Reading Turgenev*; *Felicia's Journey* (1994), which won both the Whitbread Book of the Year and the *Sunday Express* Book of the Year awards; and *Death in Summer* (1998). A celebrated short-story writer, his most recent collection is *After Rain* (1996). He is also the editor of *The Oxford Book of Irish Short Stories* (1989). He has written plays for the stage and for radio and television; several of his television plays have been based on his short stories. Most of his books are published in Penguin.

In 1976 William Trevor received the Allied Irish Banks' Prize, and in 1977 was awarded an honorary CBE in recognition of his valuable services to literature. In 1992 he received the *Sunday Times* Award for Literary Excellence and in 1999 he was awarded the prestigious David Cohen British Literature Prize in recognition of a lifetime's literary achievement. Many critics and writers have praised his work: he is to Hilary Mantel he 'one of the contemporary writers I most admire' and to Carol Shields 'a worthy chronicler of our times'. In the *Spectator* Anita Brookner wrote 'These novels will endure. And in every beautiful sentence there is not a word out of place,' and John Banville believes William Trevor's to be 'among the most subtle and sophisticated fiction being written today'.

PENGUIN BOOKS

in association with The Bodley Head

WILLIAM TREVOR

COLLECTED STORIES

PENG

Published in

Penguin Books Ltd, 27
Penguin Putnam Inc., 375
Penguin Books
Penguin Books Canada Ltd,
Penguin Books (NZ)

Penguin Books L

The Ballroom of R

The Day We Got Dr

Angels at the Ritz and O
Published in
Copyright ⊙ Wil

Lovers of Their Time and Other St
Published in
Copyright ⊙ Wil

Beyond the Pale and Other Stories first pu
Published in Penguin Books 1
Copyright ⊙ William Tr

The News from Ireland and Other Stories first publi
Published in Penguin Books 1
Copyright ⊙ William Trevor, 198

Family Sins and Other Stories first published by The Bod
Published in Penguin Books 1991
Copyright ⊙ William Trevor, 1990

This collected edition first published by Viking, in association with The Bod
Published in Penguin Books 1993
9 10 8

All rights reserved

The moral right of the author has been asserted

Printed in England by Clays Ltd, St Ives plc

Contents

Contents

Contents

A Meeting in Middle Age

'I am Mrs da Tanka,' said Mrs da Tanka. 'Are you Mr Mileson?'

The man nodded, and they walked together the length of the platform, seeking a compartment that might offer them a welcome, or failing that, and they knew the more likely, simple privacy. They carried each a small suitcase, Mrs da Tanka's of white leather or some material manufactured to resemble it, Mr Mileson's battered and black. They did not speak as they marched purposefully: they were strangers one to another, and in the noise and the bustle, examining the lighted windows of the carriages, there was little that might constructively be said.

'A ninety-nine years' lease,' Mr Mileson's father had said, 'taken out in 1862 by my grandfather, whom of course you never knew. Expiring in your lifetime, I fear. Yet you will by then be in a sound position to accept the misfortune. To renew what has come to an end; to keep the property in the family.' The property was an expression that glorified. The house was small and useful, one of a row, one of a kind easily found; but the lease when the time came was not renewable – which released Mr Mileson of a problem. Bachelor, childless, the end of the line, what use was a house to him for a further ninety-nine years?

Mrs da Tanka, sitting opposite him, drew a magazine from an assortment she carried. Then, checking herself, said: 'We could talk. Or do you prefer to conduct the business in silence?' She was a woman who filled, but did not overflow from, a fair-sized, elegant, quite expensive tweed suit. Her hair, which was grey, did not appear so; it was tightly held to her head, a reddish-gold colour. Born into another class she would have been a chirpy woman; she guarded against her chirpiness, she disliked the quality in her. There was often laughter in her eyes, and as often as she felt it there she killed it by the severity of her manner.

'You must not feel embarrassment,' Mrs da Tanka said. 'We are beyond the age of giving in to awkwardness in a situation. You surely agree?'

Mr Mileson did not know. He did not know how or what he should feel. Analysing his feelings he could come to no conclusion. He supposed he was excited but it was more difficult than it seemed to track down the emotions. He was unable, therefore, to answer Mrs da Tanka. So he just smiled.

Mrs da Tanka, who had once been Mrs Horace Spire and was not likely to forget it, considered those days. It was a logical thing for her to do, for they were days that had come to an end as these present days were coming to an end. Termination was on her mind: to escape from Mrs da Tanka into Mrs Spire was a way of softening the worry that was with her now, and a way of seeing it in proportion to a lifetime.

'If that is what you want,' Horace had said, 'then by all means have it. Who shall do the dirty work – you or I?' This was his reply to her request for a divorce. In fact, at the time of speaking, the dirty work as he called it was already done: by both of them.

'It is a shock for me,' Horace had continued. 'I thought we could jangle along for many a day. Are you seriously involved elsewhere?'

In fact she was not, but finding herself involved at all reflected the inadequacy of her married life and revealed a vacuum that once had been love.

'We are better apart,' she had said. 'It is bad to get used to the habit of being together. We must take our chances while we may, while there is still time.'

In the railway carriage she recalled the conversation with vividness, especially that last sentence, most especially the last five words of it. The chance she had taken was da Tanka, eight years ago. 'My God,' she said aloud, 'what a pompous bastard he turned out to be.'

Mr Mileson had a couple of those weekly publications for which there is no accurate term in the language: a touch of a single colour on the front – floppy, half-intellectual things, somewhere between a journal and a magazine. While she had her honest mags. *Harper's*. *Vogue*. Shiny and smart and rather silly. Or so thought Mr Mileson. He had opened them at dentists' and doctors', leafed his way through the ridiculous advertisements and aptly titled model girls, unreal girls in unreal poses, devoid it seemed of sex, and half the time of life. So that was the kind of woman she was.

'Who?' said Mr Mileson.

'Oh, who else, good heavens! Da Tanka I mean.'

Eight years of da Tanka's broad back, so fat it might have been padded beneath the skin. He had often presented it to her.

'I shall be telling you about da Tanka,' she said. 'There are interesting facets to the man; though God knows, he is scarcely interesting in himself.'

It was a worry, in any case, owning a house. Seeing to the roof; noticing the paint cracking on the outside, and thinking about damp in mysterious places. Better off he was, in the room in Swiss Cottage; cosier in winter. They'd pulled down the old house by now, with all the others in the road.

Flats were there instead: bulking up to the sky, with a million or so windows. All the gardens were gone, all the gnomes and the Snow White dwarfs, all the winter bulbs and the little paths of crazy paving; the bird-baths and bird-boxes and bird-tables; the miniature sandpits, and the metal edging, ornate, for flower-beds.

'We must move with the times,' said Mrs da Tanka, and he realized that he had been speaking to her; or speaking aloud and projecting the remarks in her direction since she was there.

His mother had made the rockery. Aubrietia and sarsaparilla and pinks and Christmas roses. Her brother, his uncle Edward, bearded and queer, brought seaside stones in his motor-car. His father had shrugged his distaste for the project, as indeed for all projects of this nature, seeing the removal of stones from the seashore as being in some way disgraceful, even dishonest. Behind the rockery there were loganberries: thick, coarse, inedible fruit, never fully ripe. But nobody, certainly not Mr Mileson, had had the heart to pull away the bushes.

'Weeks would pass,' said Mrs da Tanka, 'without the exchange of a single significant sentence. We lived in the same house, ate the same meals, drove out in the same car, and all he would ever say was: "It is time the central heating was on." Or: "These windscreen-wipers aren't working."'

Mr Mileson didn't know whether she was talking about Mr da Tanka or Mr Spire. They seemed like the same man to him: shadowy, silent fellows who over the years had shared this woman with the well-tended hands.

'He will be wearing city clothes,' her friend had said, 'grey or non-descript. He is like anyone else except for his hat, which is big and black and eccentric.' An odd thing about him, the hat: like a wild oat almost.

There he had been, by the tobacco kiosk, punctual and expectant; gaunt of face, thin, fiftyish; with the old-fashioned hat and the weekly papers that somehow matched it, but did not match him.

'Now would you blame me, Mr Mileson? Would you blame me for seeking freedom from such a man?'

The hat lay now on the luggage-rack with his carefully folded overcoat. A lot of his head was bald, whitish and tender like good dripping. His eyes were sad, like those of a retriever puppy she had known in her childhood. Men are often like dogs, she thought; women more akin to cats. The train moved smoothly, with rhythm, through the night. She thought of da Tanka and Horace Spire, wondering where Spire was now. Opposite her, he thought about the ninety-nine-year lease and the two plates, one from last night's supper, the other from breakfast, that he had left unwashed in the room at Swiss Cottage.

'This seems your kind of place,' Mr Mileson said, surveying the hotel from its ornate hall.

'Gin and lemon, gin and lemon,' said Mrs da Tanka, matching the words with action: striding to the bar.

Mr Mileson had rum, feeling it a more suitable drink, though he could not think why. 'My father drank rum with milk in it. An odd concoction.'

'Frightful, it sounds. Da Tanka is a whisky man. My previous liked stout. Well, well, so here we are.'

Mr Mileson looked at her. 'Dinner is next on the agenda.'

But Mrs da Tanka was not to be moved. They sat while she drank many measures of the drink; and when they rose to demand dinner they discovered that the restaurant was closed and were ushered to a grill-room.

'You organized that badly, Mr Mileson.'

'I organized nothing. I know the rules of these places. I repeated them to you. You gave me no chance to organize.'

'A chop and an egg or something. Da Tanka at least could have got us soup.'

In 1931 Mr Mileson had committed fornication with the maid in his parents' house. It was the only occasion, and he was glad that adultery was not expected of him with Mrs da Tanka. In it she would be more experienced than he, and he did not relish the implication. The grill-room was lush and vulgar. 'This seems your kind of place,' Mr Mileson repeated rudely.

'At least it is warm. And the lights don't glare. Why not order some wine?'

Her husband must remain innocent. He was a person of importance, in the public eye. Mr Mileson's friend had repeated it, the friend who knew Mrs da Tanka's solicitor. All expenses paid, the friend had said, and a little fee as well. Nowadays Mr Mileson could do with little fees. And though at the time he had rejected the suggestion downright, he had later seen that friend – acquaintance really – in the pub he went to at half past twelve on Sundays, and had agreed to take part in the drama. It wasn't just the little fee; there was something rather like prestige in the thing; his name as co-respondent – now *there* was something you'd never have guessed! The hotel bill to find its way to Mrs da Tanka's husband, who would pass it to his solicitor. Breakfast in bed, and remember the face of the maid who brought it. Pass the time of day with her, and make sure she remembered yours. Oh very nice, the man in the pub said, very nice Mrs da Tanka was – or so he was led to believe. He batted his eyes at Mr Mileson; but Mr Mileson said it didn't matter, surely, about Mrs da Tanka's niceness. He knew his duties: there was nothing personal about them. He'd do it himself, the man in the pub explained, only he'd never be able to keep his hands off an attractive middle-aged woman. That was the trouble about finding someone for the job.

'I've had a hard life,' Mrs da Tanka confided. 'Tonight I need your sympathy, Mr Mileson. Tell me I have your sympathy.' Her face and neck had reddened: chirpiness was breaking through.

In the house, in a cupboard beneath the stairs, he had kept his gardening boots. Big, heavy army boots, once his father's. He had worn them at weekends, poking about in the garden.

'The lease came to an end two years ago,' he told Mrs da Tanka. 'There I was with all that stuff, all my gardening tools, and the furniture and bric-à-brac of three generations to dispose of. I can tell you it wasn't easy to know what to throw away.'

'Mr Mileson, I don't like that waiter.'

Mr Mileson cut his steak with care: a three-cornered piece, neat and succulent. He loaded mushroom and mustard on it, added a sliver of potato and carried the lot to his mouth. He masticated and drank some wine.

'Do you know the waiter?'

Mrs da Tanka laughed unpleasantly; like ice cracking. 'Why should I know the waiter? I do not generally know waiters. Do *you* know the waiter?'

'I ask because you claim to dislike him.'

'May I not dislike him without an intimate knowledge of the man?'

'You may do as you please. It struck me as a premature decision, that is all.'

'What decision? What is premature? What are you talking about? Are you drunk?'

'The decision to dislike the waiter I thought to be premature. I do not know about being drunk. Probably I am a little. One has to keep one's spirits up.'

'Have you ever thought of wearing an eye-patch, Mr Mileson? I think it would suit you. You need distinction. Have you led an empty life? You give the impression of an empty life.'

'My life has been as many other lives. Empty of some things, full of others. I am in possession of all my sight, though. My eyes are real. Neither is a pretence. I see no call for an eye-patch.'

'It strikes me you see no call for anything. You have never lived, Mr Mileson.'

'I do not understand that.'

'Order us more wine.'

Mr Mileson indicated with his hand and the waiter approached. 'Some other waiter, please,' Mrs da Tanka cried. 'May we be served by another waiter?'

'Madam?' said the waiter.

'We do not take to you. Will you send another man to our table?'

'I am the only waiter on duty, madam.'

'It's quite all right,' said Mr Mileson.

'It's not quite all right. I will not have this man at our table, opening and dispensing wine.'

'Then we must go without.'

'I am the only waiter on duty, madam.'

'There are other employees of the hotel. Send us a porter or the girl at the reception.'

'It is not their duty, madam –'

'Oh nonsense, nonsense. Bring us the wine, man, and have no more to-do.'

Unruffled, the waiter moved away. Mrs da Tanka hummed a popular tune.

'Are you married, Mr Mileson? Have you in the past been married?'

'No, never married.'

'I have been married twice. I am married now. I am throwing the dice for the last time. God knows how I shall find myself. You are helping to shape my destiny. What a fuss that waiter made about the wine!'

'That is a little unfair. It was you, you know –'

'Behave like a gentleman, can't you? Be on my side since you are with me. Why must you turn on me? Have I harmed you?'

'No, no. I was merely establishing the truth.'

'Here is the man again with the wine. He is like a bird. Do you think he has wings strapped down beneath his waiter's clothes? You are like a bird,' she repeated, examining the waiter's face. 'Has some fowl played a part in your ancestry?'

'I think not, madam.'

'Though you cannot be sure. How can you be sure? How can you say you think not when you know nothing about it?'

The waiter poured the wine in silence. He was not embarrassed, Mr Mileson noted; not even angry.

'Bring coffee,' Mrs da Tanka said.

'Madam.'

'How servile waiters are! How I hate servility, Mr Mileson! I could not marry a servile man. I could not marry that waiter, not for all the tea in China.'

'I did not imagine you could. The waiter does not seem your sort.'

'He is your sort. You like him, I think. Shall I leave you to converse with him?'

'Really! What would I say to him? I know nothing about the waiter except what he is in a professional sense. I do not wish to know. It is not my habit to go about consorting with waiters after they have waited on me.'

'I am not to know that. I am not to know what your sort is, or what your personal and private habits are. How could I know? We have only just met.'

'You are clouding the issue.'

'You are as pompous as da Tanka. Da Tanka would say issue and clouding.'

'What your husband would say is no concern of mine.'

'You are meant to be my lover, Mr Mileson. Can't you act it a bit? My husband must concern you dearly. You must wish to tear him limb from limb. Do you wish it?'

'I have never met the man. I know nothing of him.'

'Well then, pretend. Pretend for the waiter's sake. Say something violent in the waiter's hearing. Break an oath. Blaspheme. Bang your fist on the table.'

'I was not told I should have to behave like that. It is against my nature.'

'What is your nature?'

'I'm shy and self-effacing.'

'You are an enemy to me. I don't understand your sort. You have not got on in the world. You take on commissions like this. Where is your self-respect?'

'Elsewhere in my character.'

'You have no personality.'

'That is a cliché. It means nothing.'

'Sweet nothings for lovers, Mr Mileson! Remember that.'

They left the grill-room and mounted the stairs in silence. In their bedroom Mrs da Tanka unpacked a dressing-gown. 'I shall undress in the bathroom. I shall be absent a matter of ten minutes.'

Mr Mileson slipped from his clothes into pyjamas. He brushed his teeth at the wash-basin, cleaned his nails and splashed a little water on his face. When Mrs da Tanka returned he was in bed.

To Mr Mileson she seemed a trifle bigger without her daytime clothes. He remembered corsets and other containing garments. He did not remark upon it.

Mrs da Tanka turned out the light and they lay without touching between the cold sheets of the double bed.

He would leave little behind, he thought. He would die and there would be the things in the room, rather a number of useless things with sentimental value only. Ornaments and ferns. Reproductions of paintings. A set of eggs, birds' eggs he had collected as a boy. They would pile all the junk together and probably try to burn it. Then perhaps they would light a couple of those fumigating candles in the room, because people are insulting when other people die.

'Why did you not get married?' Mrs da Tanka said.

'Because I do not greatly care for women.' He said it, throwing caution to the winds, waiting for her attack.

'Are you a homosexual?'

The word shocked him. 'Of course I'm not.'

'I only asked. They go in for this kind of thing.'

'That does not make me one.'

'I often thought Horace Spire was more that way than any other. For all the attention he paid to me.'

As a child she had lived in Shropshire. In those days she loved the country, though without knowing, or wishing to know, the names of flowers or plants or trees. People said she looked like Alice in Wonderland.

'Have you ever been to Shropshire, Mr Mileson?'

'No. I am very much a Londoner. I lived in the same house all my life. Now the house is no longer there. Flats replace it. I live in Swiss Cottage.'

'I thought you might. I thought you might live in Swiss Cottage.'

'Now and again I miss the garden. As a child I collected birds' eggs on the common. I have kept them all these years.'

She had kept nothing. She cut the past off every so often, remembering it when she cared to, without the aid of physical evidence.

'The hard facts of life have taken their toll of me,' said Mrs da Tanka. 'I met them first at twenty. They have been my companions since.'

'It was a hard fact the lease coming to an end. It was hard to take at the time. I did not accept it until it was well upon me. Only the spring before I had planted new delphiniums.'

'My father told me to marry a good man. To be happy and have children. Then he died. I did none of those things. I do not know why except that I did not care to. Then old Horry Spire put his arm around me and there we were. Life is as you make it, I suppose. I was thinking of homosexual in relation to that waiter you were interested in downstairs.'

'I was not interested in the waiter. He was hard done by, by you, I thought. There was no more to it than that.'

Mrs da Tanka smoked and Mr Mileson was nervous; about the situation in general, about the glow of the cigarette in the darkness. What if the woman dropped off to sleep? He had heard of fires started by careless smoking. What if in her confusion she crushed the cigarette against some part of his body? Sleep was impossible: one cannot sleep with the thought of waking up in a furnace, with the bells of fire brigades clanging a death knell.

'I will not sleep tonight,' said Mrs da Tanka, a statement which frightened Mr Mileson further. For all the dark hours the awful woman would be there, twitching and puffing beside him. *I am mad. I am out of my mind to have brought this upon myself.* He heard the words. He saw them on paper, written in his handwriting. He saw them typed, and repeated again as on a telegram. The letters jolted and lost their order. The words were confused, skulking behind a fog. 'I am mad,' Mr Mileson said, to establish the thought completely, to bring it into the open. It was a habit of his; for a moment he had forgotten the reason for the thought, thinking himself alone.

'Are you telling me now you are mad?' asked Mrs da Tanka, alarmed. 'Gracious, are you worse than a homo? Are you some sexual pervert? Is that what you are doing here? Certainly that was not my plan, I do assure you. You have nothing to gain from me, Mr Mileson. If there is trouble I shall ring the bell.'

'I am mad to be here. I am mad to have agreed to all this. What came over me I do not know. I have only just realized the folly of the thing.'

'Arise then, dear Mileson, and break your agreement, your promise and your undertaking. You are an adult man, you may dress and walk from the room.'

They were all the same, she concluded: except that while others had some passing superficial recommendation, this one it seemed had none. There was something that made her sick about the thought of the stringy limbs that were stretched out beside her. What lengths a woman will go to to rid herself of a horror like da Tanka!

He had imagined it would be a simple thing. It had sounded like a simple thing: a good thing rather than a bad one. A good turn for a lady in need. That was as he had seen it. With the little fee already in his possession.

Mrs da Tanka lit another cigarette and threw the match on the floor.

'What kind of a life have you had? You had not the nerve for marriage. Nor the brains for success. The truth is you might not have lived.' She laughed in the darkness, determined to hurt him as he had hurt her in his implication that being with her was an act of madness.

Mr Mileson had not before done a thing like this. Never before had he not weighed the pros and cons and seen that danger was absent from an undertaking. The thought of it all made him sweat. He saw in the future further deeds: worse deeds, crimes and irresponsibilities.

Mrs da Tanka laughed again. But she was thinking of something else.

'You have never slept with a woman, is that it? Ah, you poor thing! What a lot you have not had the courage for!' The bed heaved with the raucous noise that was her laughter, and the bright spark of her cigarette bobbed about in the air.

She laughed, quietly now and silently, hating him as she hated da Tanka and had hated Horace Spire. Why could he not be some young man, beautiful and nicely mannered and gay? Surely a young man would have come with her? Surely there was one amongst all the millions who would have done the chore with relish, or at least with charm?

'You are as God made you,' said Mr Mileson. 'You cannot help your shortcomings, though one would think you might by now have recognized them. To others you may be all sorts of things. To me you are a frightful woman.'

'Would you not stretch out a hand to the frightful woman? Is there no temptation for the woman's flesh? Are you a eunuch, Mr Mileson?'

'I have had the women I wanted. I am doing you a favour. Hearing of your predicament and pressed to help you, I agreed in a moment of generosity. Stranger though you were I did not say no.'

'That does not make you a gentleman.'

'And I do not claim it does. I am gentleman enough without it.'

'You are nothing without it. This is your sole experience. In all your clerkly subservience you have not paused to live. You know I am right, and as for being a gentleman – well, you are of the lower middle classes. There has never been an English gentleman born of the lower middle classes.'

She was trying to remember what she looked like; what her face was like, how the wrinkles were spread, how old she looked and what she might pass for in a crowd. Would men not be cagey now and think that she must be difficult in her ways to have parted twice from husbands? Was there a third time coming up? Third time lucky, she thought. Who would have her, though, except some loveless Mileson?

'You have had no better life than I,' said Mr Mileson. 'You are no more happy now. You have failed, and it is cruel to laugh at you.'

They talked and the hatred grew between them.

'In my childhood young men flocked about me, at dances in Shropshire that my father gave to celebrate my beauty. Had the fashion been duels, duels there would have been. Men killed or maimed for life, carrying a lock of my hair on their breast.'

'You are a creature now, with your face and your fingernails. Mutton dressed as lamb, Mrs da Tanka!'

Beyond the curtained windows the light of dawn broke into the night. A glimpse of it crept into the room, noticed and welcomed by its occupants.

'You should write your memoirs, Mr Mileson. To have seen the changes in your time and never to know a thing about them! You are like an occasional table. Or a coat-rack in the hall of a boarding-house. Who shall mourn at your grave, Mr Mileson?'

He felt her eyes upon him; and the mockery of the words sank into his heart with intended precision. He turned to her and touched her, his hands groping about her shoulders. He had meant to grasp her neck, to feel the muscles struggle beneath his fingers, to terrify the life out of her. But she, thinking the gesture was the beginning of an embrace, pushed him away, swearing at him and laughing. Surprised by the misunderstanding, he left her alone.

The train was slow. The stations crawled by, similar and ugly. She fixed her glance on him, her eyes sharpened; cold and powerful.

She had won the battle, though technically the victory was his. Long before the time arranged for their breakfast Mr Mileson had leaped from bed. He dressed and breakfasted alone in the dining-room. Shortly afterwards, after sending to the bedroom for his suitcase, he left the hotel, informing the receptionist that the lady would pay the bill. Which in time she had done, and afterwards pursued him to the train, where now, to disconcert him, she sat in the facing seat of an empty compartment.

'Well,' said Mrs da Tanka, 'you have shot your bolt. You have taken the only miserable action you could. You have put the frightful woman in her place. Have we a right,' she added, 'to expect anything better of the English lower classes?'

Mr Mileson had foolishly left his weekly magazines and the daily paper at the hotel. He was obliged to sit bare-faced before her, pretending to observe the drifting landscape. In spite of everything, guilt gnawed him a bit. When he was back in his room he would borrow the vacuum cleaner and give it a good going over: the exercise would calm him. A glass of beer in the pub before lunch; lunch in the ABC; perhaps an afternoon cinema. It was Saturday today: this, more or less, was how he usually spent Saturday. Probably from lack of sleep he would doze off in the cinema. People would nudge him to draw attention to his snoring; that had happened before, and was not pleasant.

'To give you birth,' she said, 'your mother had long hours of pain. Have you thought of that, Mr Mileson? Have you thoughts of that poor woman crying out, clenching her hands and twisting the sheets? Was it worth it, Mr Mileson? You tell me now, was it worth it?'

He could leave the compartment and sit with other people. But that would be too great a satisfaction for Mrs da Tanka. She would laugh loudly at his going, might even pursue him to mock in public.

'What you say about me, Mrs da Tanka, can equally be said of you.'

'Are we two peas in a pod? It's an explosive pod in that case.'

'I did not imply that. I would not wish to find myself sharing a pod with you.'

'Yet you shared a bed. And were not man enough to stick to your word. You are a worthless coward, Mr Mileson. I expect you know it.'

'I know myself, which is more than can be said in your case. Do you not think occasionally to see yourself as others see you? An ageing woman, faded and ugly, dubious in morals and personal habits. What misery you must have caused those husbands!'

'They married me, and got good value. You know that, yet dare not admit it.'

'I will scarcely lose sleep worrying the matter out.'

It was a cold morning, sunny with a clear sky. Passengers stepping from the train at the intermediate stations muffled up against the temperature, finding it too much after the warm fug within. Women with baskets. Youths. Men with children, with dogs collected from the guard's van.

Da Tanka, she had heard, was living with another woman. Yet he refused to admit being the guilty party. It would not do for someone like da Tanka to be a public adulterer. So he had said. Pompously. Crossly. Horace Spire, to give him his due, hadn't given a damn one way or the other.

'When you die, Mr Mileson, have you a preference for the flowers on your coffin? It is a question I ask because I might send you off a wreath. That lonely wreath. From ugly, frightful Mrs da Tanka.'

'What?' said Mr Mileson, and she repeated the question.

'Oh well – cow-parsley, I suppose.' He said it, taken off his guard by the image she created; because it was an image he often saw and thought about. Hearse and coffin and he within. It would not be like that probably. Anticipation was not in Mr Mileson's life. Remembering, looking back, considering events and emotions that had been at the time mundane perhaps – this kind of thing was more to his liking. For by hindsight there was pleasure in the stream of time. He could not establish his funeral in his mind; he tried often but ended up always with a funeral he had known: a repetition of his parents' passing and the accompanying convention.

'Cow-parsley?' said Mrs da Tanka. Why did the man say cow-parsley?

Why not roses or lilies or something in a pot? There had been cow-parsley in Shropshire; cow-parsley on the verges of dusty lanes; cow-parsley in hot fields buzzing with bees; great white swards rolling down to the river. She had sat among it on a picnic with dolls. She had lain on it, laughing at the beautiful anaemic blue of the sky. She had walked through it by night, loving it.

'Why did you say cow-parsley?'

He did not know, except that once on a rare family outing to the country he had seen it and remembered it. Yet in his garden he had grown delphiniums and wallflowers and asters and sweet-peas.

She could smell it again: a smell that was almost nothing: fields and the heat of the sun on her face, laziness and summer. There was a red door somewhere, faded and blistered, and she sat against it, crouched on a warm step, a child dressed in the fashion of the time.

'Why did you say cow-parsley?'

He remembered, that day, asking the name of the white powdery growth. He had picked some and carried it home; and had often since thought of it, though he had not come across a field of cow-parsley for years.

She tried to speak again, but after the night there were no words she could find that would fit. The silence stuck between them, and Mr Mileson knew by instinct all that it contained. She saw an image of herself and him, strolling together from the hotel, in this same sunshine, at this very moment, lingering on the pavement to decide their direction and agreeing to walk to the promenade. She mouthed and grimaced and the sweat broke on her body, and she looked at him once and saw words die on his lips, lost in his suspicion of her.

The train stopped for the last time. Doors banged; the throng of people passed them by on the platform outside. They collected their belongings and left the train together. A porter, interested in her legs, watched them walk down the platform. They passed through the barrier and parted, moving in their particular directions. She to her new flat where milk and mail, she hoped, awaited her. He to his room; to the two unwashed plates on the draining board and the forks with egg on the prongs; and the little fee propped up on the mantelpiece, a pink cheque for five pounds, peeping out from behind a china cat.

Access to the Children

Malcolmson, a fair, tallish man in a green tweed suit that required pressing, banged the driver's door of his ten-year-old Volvo and walked quickly away from the car, jangling the keys. He entered a block of flats that was titled – gold engraved letters on a granite slab – The Quadrant.

It was a Sunday afternoon in late October. Yellow-brown leaves patterned grass that was not for walking on. Some scurried on the steps that led to the building's glass entrance doors. Rain was about, Malcolmson considered.

At three o'clock precisely he rang the bell of his ex-wife's flat on the third floor. In response he heard at once the voices of his children and the sound of their running in the hall. 'Hullo,' he said when one of them, Deirdre, opened the door. 'Ready?'

They went with him, two little girls, Deirdre seven and Susie five. In the lift they told him that a foreign person, the day before, had been trapped in the lift from eleven o'clock in the morning until teatime. Food and cups of tea had been poked through a grating to this person, a Japanese businessman who occupied a flat at the top of the block. 'He didn't get the hang of an English lift,' said Deirdre. 'He could have died there,' said Susie.

In the Volvo he asked them if they'd like to go to the Zoo and they shook their heads firmly. On the last two Sundays he'd taken them to the Zoo, Susie reminded him in her specially polite, very quiet voice: you got tired of the Zoo, walking round and round, looking at all the same animals. She smiled at him to show she wasn't being ungrateful. She suggested that in a little while, after a month or so, they could go to the Zoo again, because there might be some new animals. Deirdre said that there wouldn't be, not after a month or so: why should there be? 'Some old animals might have died,' said Susie.

Malcolmson drove down the Edgware Road, with Hyde Park in mind.

'What have you done?' he asked.

'Only school,' said Susie.

'And the news cinema,' said Deirdre. 'Mummy took us to a news cinema. We saw a film about how they make wire.'

'A man kept talking to Mummy. He said she had nice hair.'

'The usherette told him to be quiet. He bought us ice-creams, but Mummy said we couldn't accept them.'

'He wanted to take Mummy to a dance.'

'We had to move to other seats.'

'What else have you done?'

'Only school,' said Susie. 'A boy was sick on Miss Bawden's desk.'

'After school stew.'

'It's raining,' said Susie.

He turned the windscreen-wipers on. He wondered if he should simply bring the girls to his flat and spend the afternoon watching television. He tried to remember what the Sunday film was. There often was something suitable for children on Sunday afternoons, old films with Deanna Durbin or Nelson Eddy and Jeanette MacDonald.

'Where're we going?' Susie asked.

'Where d'you want to go?'

'*A Hundred and One Dalmatians*.'

'Oh, please,' said Susie.

'But we've seen it. We've seen it five times.'

'Please, Daddy.'

He stopped the Volvo and bought a *What's On*. While he leafed through it they sat quietly, willing him to discover a cinema, anywhere in London, that was showing the film. He shook his head and started the Volvo again.

'Nothing else?' Deirdre asked.

'Nothing suitable.'

At Speakers' Corner they listened to a Jehovah's Witness and then to a woman talking about vivisection. 'How horrid,' said Deirdre. 'Is that true, Daddy?' He made a face. 'I suppose so,' he said.

In the drizzle they played a game among the trees, hiding and chasing one another. Once when they'd been playing this game a woman had brought a policeman up to him. She'd seen him approaching the girls, she said; the girls had been playing alone and he'd joined in. 'He's our daddy,' Susie had said, but the woman had still argued, claiming that he'd given them sweets so that they'd say that. 'Look at him,' the woman had insultingly said. 'He needs a shave.' Then she'd gone away, and the policeman had apologized.

'The boy who was sick was Nicholas Barnet,' Susie said. 'I think he could have died.'

A year and a half ago Malcolmson's wife, Elizabeth, had said he must choose between her and Diana. For weeks they had talked about it; she knowing that he was in love with Diana and was having some kind of an affair with her, he caught between the two of them, attempting the impossible in his effort not to hurt anyone. She had given him a chance to get over Diana, as she put it, but she couldn't go on for ever giving him a chance, no woman could. In the end, after the shock and the tears and the period of reasonableness, she became bitter. He didn't blame her: they'd been in the middle of a happy marriage, nothing was wrong, nothing was lacking.

He'd met Diana on a train; he'd sat with her, talking for a long time, and after that his marriage didn't seem the same. In her bitterness Elizabeth said he was stupidly infatuated: he was behaving like a murderer: there was neither dignity nor humanity left in him. Diana she described as a flat-chested American nymphomaniac and predator, the worst type of woman in the world. She was beautiful herself, more beautiful than Diana, more gracious, warmer, and funnier: there was a sting of truth in what she said; he couldn't understand himself. In the very end, after they'd been morosely drinking gin and lime-juice, she'd suddenly shouted at him that he'd better pack his bags. He sat unhappily, gazing at the green bottle of Gordon's gin on the carpet between his chair and hers. She screamed; tears poured in a torrent from her eyes. 'For God's sake go away!' she cried, on her feet, turning away from him. She shook her head in a wild gesture, causing her long fair hair to move like a horse's mane. Her hands, clenched into fists, beat at his cheeks, making bruises that Diana afterwards tended.

For months after that he saw neither Elizabeth nor his children. He tried not to think about them. He and Diana took a flat in Barnes, near the river, and in time he became used to the absence of the children's noise in the mornings, and to Diana's cooking and her quick efficiency in little things, and the way she always remembered to pass on telephone messages, which was something that Elizabeth had always forgotten to do.

Then one day, a week or so before the divorce was due, Diana said she didn't think there was anything left between them. It hadn't worked, she said; nothing was quite right. Amazed and bewildered, he argued with her. He frowned at her, his eyes screwed up as though he couldn't properly see her. She was very poised, in a black dress, with a necklace at her throat, her hair pulled smooth and neatly tied. She'd met a man called Abbotforth, she said, and she went on talking about that, still standing.

'We could go to the Natural History Museum,' Deirdre said.

'Would you like to, Susie?'

'Certainly not,' said Susie.

They were sitting on a bench, watching a bird that Susie said was a yellow-hammer. Deirdre disagreed: at this time of year, she said, there were no yellow-hammers in England, she'd read it in a book. 'It's a little baby yellow-hammer,' said Susie. 'Miss Bawden said you see lots of them.'

The bird flew away. A man in a raincoat was approaching them, singing quietly. They began to giggle. '*Sure, maybe some day I'll go back to Ireland,*' sang the man, '*if it's only at the closing of my day.*' He stopped, noticing that they were watching him.

'Were you ever in Ireland?' he asked. The girls, still giggling, shook their heads. 'It's a great place,' said the man. He took a bottle of VP wine from his raincoat pocket and drank from it.

'Would you care for a swig, sir?' he said to Malcolmson, and Malcolmson thanked him and said he wouldn't. 'It would do the little misses no harm,' suggested the man. 'It's good, pure stuff.' Malcolmson shook his head. 'I was born in County Clare,' said the man, 'in 1928, the year of the Big Strike.' The girls, red in the face from containing their laughter, poked at one another with their elbows. 'Aren't they the great little misses?' said the man. 'Aren't they the fine credit to you, sir?'

In the Volvo on the way to Barnes they kept repeating that he was the funniest man they'd ever met. He was nicer than the man in the news cinema, Susie said. He was quite like him, though, Deirdre maintained: he was looking for company in just the same way, you could see it in his eyes. 'He was staggering,' Susie said. 'I thought he was going to die.'

Before the divorce he had telephoned Elizabeth, telling her that Diana had gone. She hadn't said anything, and she'd put the receiver down before he could say anything else. Then the divorce came through and the arrangement was that the children should remain with Elizabeth and that he should have reasonable access to them. It was an extraordinary expression, he considered: reasonable access.

The Sunday afternoons had begun then, the ringing of a doorbell that had once been his own doorbell, the children in the hall, the lift, the Volvo, tea in the flat where he and Diana had lived and where now he lived on his own. Sometimes, when he was collecting them, Elizabeth spoke to him, saying in a matter-of-fact way that Susie had a cold and should not be outside too much, or that Deirdre was being bad about practising her clarinet and would he please speak to her. He loved Elizabeth again; he said to himself that he had never not loved her; he wanted to say to her that she'd been right about Diana. But he didn't say anything, knowing that wounds had to heal.

Every week he longed more for Sunday to arrive. Occasionally he invented reasons for talking to her at the door of the flat, after the children had gone in. He asked questions about their progress at school, he wondered if there were ways in which he could help. It seemed unfair, he said, that she should have to bring them up single-handed like this; he made her promise to telephone him if a difficulty arose; and if ever she wanted to go out in the evenings and couldn't find a babysitter, he'd willingly drive over. He always hoped that if he talked for long enough the girls would become so noisy in their room that she'd be forced to ask him in so that she could quieten them, but the ploy never worked.

In the lift on the way down every Sunday evening he thought she was more beautiful than any woman he'd ever seen, and he thought it was amazing that once she should have been his wife and should have borne him children, that once they had lain together and loved, and that he had let her go. Three weeks ago she had smiled at him in a way that was like the old way. He'd been sure of it, positive, in the lift on the way down.

He drove over Hammersmith Bridge, along Castelnau and into Barnes High Street. No one was about on the pavements; buses crept sluggishly through the damp afternoon.

'Miss Bawden's got a black boyfriend,' Susie said, 'called Eric Mantilla.'

'You should see Miss Bawden,' murmured Deirdre. 'She hasn't any breasts.'

'She has lovely breasts,' shouted Susie, 'and lovely jumpers and lovely skirts. She has a pair of earrings that once belonged to an Egyptian empress.'

'Flat as a pancake,' said Deirdre.

After Diana had gone he'd found it hard to concentrate. The managing director of the firm where he worked, a man with a stout red face called Sir Gerald Travers, had been sympathetic. He'd told him not to worry. Personal troubles, Sir Gerald had said, must naturally affect professional life; no one would be human if that didn't happen. But six months later, to Malcolmson's surprise, Sir Gerald had suddenly suggested to him that perhaps it would be better if he made a move. 'It's often so,' Sir Gerald had said, a soft smile gleaming between chubby cheeks. 'Professional life can be affected by the private side of things. You understand me, Malcolmson?' They valued him immensely, Sir Gerald said, and they'd be generous when the moment of departure came. A change was a tonic; Sir Gerald advised a little jaunt somewhere.

In reply to all that Malcolmson said that the upset in his private life was now over; nor did he feel, he added, in need of recuperation. 'You'll easily find another berth,' Sir Gerald Travers replied, with a wide, confident smile. 'I think it would be better.'

Malcolmson had sought about for another job, but had not been immediately successful: there was a recession, people said. Soon it would be better, they added, and because of Sir Gerald's promised generosity Malcolmson found himself in a position to wait until things seemed brighter. It was always better, in any case, not to seem in a hurry.

He spent the mornings in the Red Lion, in Barnes, playing dominoes with an old-age pensioner, and when the pensioner didn't turn up owing to bronchial trouble Malcolmson would borrow a newspaper from the landlord. He slept in the afternoons and returned to the Red Lion later. Occasionally when he'd had a few drinks he'd find himself thinking about his children and their mother. He always found it pleasant then, thinking of them with a couple of drinks inside him.

'It's *The Last of the Mohicans*,' said Deirdre in the flat, and he guessed that she must have looked at the *Radio Times* earlier in the day. She'd known they'd end up like that, watching television. Were they bored on Sundays? he often wondered.

'Can't we have *The Golden Shot*?' demanded Susie, and Deirdre pointed out that it wasn't on yet. He left them watching Randolph Scott and Binnie Barnes, and went to prepare their tea in the kitchen.

On Saturdays he bought meringues and brandy-snaps in Frith's Patisserie. The elderly assistant smiled at him in a way that made him wonder if she knew what he wanted them for; it occurred to him once that she felt sorry for him. On Sunday mornings, listening to the omnibus edition of *The Archers*, he made Marmite sandwiches with brown bread and tomato sandwiches with white. They loved sandwiches, which was something he remembered from the past. He remembered parties, Deirdre's friends sitting around a table, small and silent, eating crisps and cheese puffs and leaving all the cake.

When *The Last of the Mohicans* came to an end they watched *Going for a Song* for five minutes before changing the channel for *The Golden Shot*. Then Deirdre turned the television off and they went to the kitchen to have tea. 'Wash your hands,' said Susie, and he heard her add that if a germ got into your food you could easily die. 'She kept referring to death,' he would say to Elizabeth when he left them back. 'D'you think she's worried about anything?' He imagined Elizabeth giving the smile she had given three weeks ago and then saying he'd better come in to discuss the matter.

'Goody,' said Susie, sitting down.

'I'd like to marry a man like that man in the park,' said Deirdre. 'It'd be much more interesting, married to a bloke like that.'

'He'd be always drunk.'

'He wasn't drunk, Susie. That's not being drunk.'

'He was drinking out of a bottle –'

'He was putting on a bit of flash, drinking out of a bottle and singing his little song. No harm in that, Susie.'

'I'd like to be married to Daddy.'

'You couldn't be married to Daddy.'

'Well, Richard then.'

'Ribena, Daddy. Please.'

He poured drops of Ribena into two mugs and filled them up with warm water. He had a definite feeling that today she'd ask him in, both of them pretending a worry over Susie's obsession with death. They'd sit together while the children splashed about in the bathroom; she'd offer him gin and lime-juice, their favourite drink, a drink known as a Gimlet, as once he'd told her. They'd drink it out of the green glasses they'd bought, years ago, in Italy. The girls would dry themselves and come to say good-night. They'd go to bed. He might tell them a story, or she would. 'Stay to supper,' she would say, and while she made risotto he would go to her and kiss her hair.

'I like his eyes,' said Susie. 'One's higher than another.'

'It couldn't be.'

'It is.'

'He couldn't see, Susie, if his eyes were like that. Everyone's eyes are —'

'He isn't always drunk like the man in the park.'

'Who?' he asked.

'Richard,' they said together, and Susie added: 'Irishmen are always drunk.'

'Daddy's an Irishman and Daddy's not always —'

'Who's Richard?'

'He's Susie's boyfriend.'

'I don't mind,' said Susie. 'I like him.'

'If he's there tonight, Susie, you're not to climb all over him.'

He left the kitchen and in the sitting-room he poured himself some whisky. He sat with the glass cold between his hands, staring at the grey television screen. 'Sure, maybe some day I'll go back to Ireland,' Deirdre sang in the kitchen, and Susie laughed shrilly.

He imagined a dark-haired man, a cheerful man, intelligent and subtle, a man who came often to the flat, whom his children knew well and were already fond of. He imagined him as he had imagined himself ten minutes before, sitting with Elizabeth, drinking Gimlets from the green Italian glasses. 'Say good-night to Richard,' Elizabeth would say, and the girls would go to him and kiss him good-night.

'Who's Richard?' he asked, standing in the kitchen doorway.

'A friend,' said Deirdre, 'of Mummy's.'

'A nice friend?'

'Oh, yes.'

'I love him,' said Susie.

He returned to the sitting-room and quickly poured himself more whisky. Both of his hands were shaking. He drank quickly, and then poured and drank some more. On the pale carpet, close to the television set, there was a stain where Diana had spilt a cup of coffee. He hated now this memory of her, he hated her voice when it came back to him, and the memory of her body and her mind. And yet once he had been rendered lunatic with the passion of his love for her. He had loved her more than Elizabeth, and in his madness he had spoilt everything.

'Wash your hands,' said Susie, close to him. He hadn't heard them come into the room. He asked them, mechanically, if they'd had enough to eat. 'She hasn't washed her hands,' Susie said. 'I washed mine in the sink.'

He turned the television on. It was the girl ventriloquist Shari Lewis, with Lamb Chop and Charley Horse.

Well, he thought under the influence of the whisky, he had had his fling. He had played the pins with a flat-chested American nymphomaniac and predator, and he had lost all there was to lose. Now it was Elizabeth's turn: why shouldn't she have, for a time, the dark-haired Richard who took another man's children on to his knee and kissed them good-night? Wasn't it better that the score should be even before they all came together again?

He sat on the floor with his daughters on either side of him, his arms about them. In front of him was his glass of whisky. They laughed at Lamb Chop and Charley Horse, and when the programme came to an end and the news came on he didn't want to let his daughters go. An electric fire glowed cosily. Wind blew the rain against the windows, the autumn evening was dark already.

He turned the television off. He finished the whisky in his glass and poured some more. 'Shall I tell you,' he said, 'about when Mummy and I were married?'

They listened while he did so. He told them about meeting Elizabeth in the first place, at somebody else's wedding, and of the days they had spent walking about together, and about the wet, cold afternoon on which they'd been married.

'February the 24th,' Deirdre said.

'Yes.'

'I'm going to be married in summer-time,' Susie said, 'when the roses are out.'

His birthday and Elizabeth's were on the same day, April 21st. He reminded the girls of that; he told them of the time he and Elizabeth had discovered they shared the date, a date shared also with Hitler and the Queen. They listened quite politely, but somehow didn't seem much interested.

They watched *What's in a Game?* He drank a little more. He wouldn't be able to drive them back. He'd pretend he couldn't start the Volvo and then he'd telephone for a taxi. It had happened once before that in a depression he'd begun to drink when they were with him on a Sunday afternoon. They'd been to Madame Tussaud's and the Planetarium, which Susie had said frightened her. In the flat, just as this time, while they were eating their sandwiches, he'd been overcome with the longing that they should all be together again. He'd begun to drink and in the end, while they watched television, he'd drunk quite a lot. When the time came to go he'd said that he couldn't find the keys of the Volvo and that they'd have to have a taxi. He'd spent five minutes brushing his teeth so that Elizabeth wouldn't smell the alcohol when she opened the door. He'd smiled at her with his well-brushed teeth but she, not then being over her bitterness, hadn't smiled back.

The girls put their coats on. Deirdre drank some Ribena; he had another small tot of whisky. And then, as they were leaving the flat, he suddenly felt he couldn't go through the farce of walking to the Volvo, putting the girls into it and then pretending he couldn't start it. 'I'm tired,' he said instead. 'Let's have a taxi.'

They watched the Penrhyn Male Voice Choir in *Songs of Praise* while they waited for it to arrive. He poured himself another drink, drank it slowly, and then went to the bathroom to brush his teeth. He remembered the time Deirdre had been born, in a maternity home in the country because they'd lived in the country then. Elizabeth had been concerned because she'd thought one of Deirdre's fingers was bent and had kept showing it to nurses who said they couldn't see anything the matter. He hadn't been able to see anything the matter either, nor had the doctor. 'She'll never be as beautiful as you,' he'd said and quite soon after that she'd stopped talking about the finger and had said he was nice to her. Susie had been born at home, very quickly, very easily.

The taxi arrived. 'Soon be Christmas,' said the taxi man. 'You chaps looking forward to Santa Claus?' They giggled because he had called them chaps. 'Fifty-six more days,' said Susie.

He imagined them on Christmas Day, with the dark-haired Richard explaining the rules of a game he'd bought them. He imagined all four of them sitting down at Christmas dinner, and Richard asking the girls which they liked, the white or the brown of the turkey, and then cutting them small slices. He'd have brought, perhaps, champagne, because he was that kind of person. Deirdre would sip from his glass, not liking the taste. Susie would love it.

He counted in his mind: if Richard had been visiting the flat for, say, six weeks already and assuming that his love affair with Elizabeth had begun two weeks before his first visit, that left another four months to go, allowing the affair ran an average course of six months. It would therefore come to an end at the beginning of March. His own affair with Diana had lasted from April until September. 'Oh darling,' said Diana, suddenly in his mind, and his own voice replied to her, caressing her with words. He remembered the first time they had made love and the guilt that had hammered at him and the passion there had been between them. He imagined Elizabeth naked in Richard's naked arms, her eyes open, looking at him, her fingers touching the side of his face, her lips slightly smiling. He reached forward and pulled down the glass shutter. 'I need cigarettes,' he said. 'There's a pub in Shepherd's Bush Road, the Laurie Arms.'

He drank two large measures of whisky. He bought cigarettes and lit one, rolling the smoke around in his mouth to disguise the smell of the alcohol. As he returned to the taxi, he slipped on the wet pavement and almost lost his balance. He felt very drunk all of a sudden. Deirdre and Susie were telling the taxi man about the man in Hyde Park.

He was aware that he walked unsteadily when they left the taxi and moved across the forecourt of the block of flats. In the hall, before they got into the lift, he lit another cigarette, rolling the smoke about his mouth. 'That poor Japanese man,' said Deirdre.

He rang the bell, and when Elizabeth opened the door the girls turned to him and thanked him. He took the cigarette from his mouth and kissed them. Elizabeth was smiling: if only she'd ask him in and give him a drink he wouldn't have to worry about the alcohol on his breath. He swore to himself that she was smiling as she'd smiled three weeks ago. 'Can I come in?' he asked, unable to keep the words back.

'In?' The smile was still there. She was looking at him quite closely. He released the smoke from his mouth. He tried to remember what it was he'd planned to say, and then it came to him.

'I'm worried about Susie,' he said in a quiet voice. 'She talked about death all the time.'

'Death?'

'Yes.'

'There's someone here actually,' she said, stepping back into the hall. 'But come in, certainly.'

In the sitting-room she introduced him to Richard who was, as he'd imagined, a dark-haired man. The sitting-room was much the same as it always had been. 'Have a drink,' Richard offered.

'D'you mind if we talk about Susie?' Elizabeth asked Richard. He said he'd put them to bed if she liked. She nodded. Richard went away.

'Well?'

He stood with the familiar green glass in his hand, gazing at her. He said:

'I haven't had gin and lime-juice since –'

'Yes. Look, I shouldn't worry about Susie. Children of that age often say odd things, you know –'

'I don't mind about Richard, Elizabeth, I think it's your due. I worked it out in the taxi. It's the end of October now –'

'My due?'

'Assuming your affair has been going on already for six weeks –'

'You're drunk.'

He closed one eye, focusing. He felt his body swaying and he said to himself that he must not fall now, that no matter what his body did his feet must remain firm on the carpet. He sipped from the green glass. She wasn't, he noticed, smiling any more.

'I'm actually not drunk,' he said. 'I'm actually sober. By the time our birthday comes round, Elizabeth, it'll all be over. On April the 21st we could have family tea.'

'What the hell are you talking about?'

'The future, Elizabeth. Of you and me and our children.'

'How much have you had to drink?'

'We tried to go to *A Hundred and One Dalmatians*, but it wasn't on anywhere.'

'So you drank instead. While the children –'

'We came here in a taxi-cab. They've had their usual tea, they've watched a bit of *The Last of the Mohicans* and a bit of *Going for a Song* and all of *The Golden Shot* and *The Shari Lewis Show* and –'

'You see them for a few hours and you have to go and get drunk –'

'I am not drunk, Elizabeth.'

He crossed the room as steadily as he could. He looked aggressively at her. He poured gin and lime-juice. He said:

'You have a right to your affair with Richard, I recognize that.'

'A *right*?'

'I love you, Elizabeth.'

'You loved Diana.'

'I have never not loved you. Diana was nothing – nothing, nothing at all.'

'She broke our marriage up.'

'No.'

'We're divorced.'

'I love you, Elizabeth.'

'Now listen to me –'

'I live from Sunday to Sunday. We're a family, Elizabeth; you and me and them. It's ridiculous, all this. It's ridiculous making Marmite sandwiches with brown bread and tomato sandwiches with white. It's ridiculous buying meringues and going five times to *A Hundred and One Dalmatians* and going up the Post Office Tower until we're sick of the sight of it, and watching drunks in Hyde Park and poking about at the Zoo –'

'You have reasonable access –'

'Reasonable access, my God!' His voice rose. He felt sweat on his forehead. Reasonable access, he shouted, was utterly no good to him; reasonable access was meaningless and stupid; a day would come when they wouldn't want to go with him on Sunday afternoons, when there was nowhere left in London that wasn't an unholy bore. What about reasonable access then?

'Please be quiet.'

He sat down in the armchair that he had always sat in. She said:

'You might marry again. And have other children.'

'I don't want other children. I have children already. I want us all to live together as we used to –'

'Please listen to me –'

'I get a pain in my stomach in the middle of the night. Then I wake up and can't go back to sleep. The children will grow up and I'll grow old. I couldn't begin a whole new thing all over again: I haven't the courage. Not after Diana. A mistake like that alters everything.'

'I'm going to marry Richard.'

'Three weeks ago,' he said, as though he hadn't heard her, 'you smiled at me.'

'Smiled?'

'Like you used to, Elizabeth. Before –'

'You made a mistake,' she said, softly. 'I'm sorry.'

'I'm not saying don't go on with your affair with this man. I'm not saying that, because I think in the circumstances it'd be a cheek. D'you understand me, Elizabeth?'

'Yes, I do. And I think you and I can be perfectly good friends. I don't feel sour about it any more: perhaps that's what you saw in my smile.'

'Have a six-month affair –'

'I'm in love with Richard.'

'That'll all pass into the atmosphere. It'll be nothing at all in a year's time –'

'No.'

'I love you, Elizabeth.'

They stood facing one another, not close. His body was still swaying. The liquid in his glass moved gently, slopping to the rim and then settling back again. Her eyes were on his face: it was thinner, she was thinking. Her fingers played with the edge of a cushion on the back of the sofa.

'On Saturdays,' he said, 'I buy the meringues and the brandy-snaps in Frith's Patisserie. On Sunday morning I make the sandwiches. Then I cook sausages and potatoes for my lunch, and after that I come over here.'

'Yes, yes –'

'I look forward all week to Sunday.'

'The children enjoy their outings, too.'

'Will you think about it?'

'About what?'

'About all being together again.'

'Oh, for heaven's sake!' She turned away from him. 'I wish you'd go now,' she said.

'Will you come out with me on our birthday?'

'I've told you.' Her voice was loud and angry, her cheeks were flushed. 'Can't you understand? I'm going to marry Richard. We'll be married within a month, when the girls have had time to get to know him a little better. By Christmas we'll be married.'

He shook his head in a way that annoyed her, seeming in his drunkenness to deny the truth of what she was saying. He tried to light a cigarette; matches dropped to the floor at his feet. He left them there.

It enraged her that he was sitting in an armchair in her flat with his eyelids drooping through drink and an unlighted cigarette in his hand and his matches spilt all over the floor. They were his children, but she wasn't his wife: he'd destroyed her as a wife, he'd insulted her, he'd left her to bleed and she had called him a murderer.

'Our birthday,' he said, smiling at her as though already she had agreed to join him on that day. 'And Hitler's and the Queen's.'

'On our birthday if I go out with anyone it'll be Richard.'

'Our birthday is beyond the time –'

'For God's sake, there is no beyond the time. I'm in love with another man –'

'No.'

'On our birthday,' she shouted at him, 'on the night of our birthday

Richard will make love to me in the bed you slept in for nine years. You have access to the children. You can demand no more.'

He bent down and picked up a match. He struck it on the side of the empty box. The cigarette was bent. He lit it with a wobbling flame and dropped the used match on to the carpet. The dark-haired man, he saw, was in the room again. He'd come in, hearing her shouting like that. He was asking her if she was all right. She told him to go away. Her face was hard; bitterness was there again. She said, not looking at him:

'Everything was so happy. We had a happy marriage. For nine years we had a perfectly happy marriage.'

'We could –'

'Not ever.'

Again he shook his head in disagreement. Cigarette ash fell on to the green tweed of his suit. His eyes were narrowed, watching her, seemingly suspicious.

'We had a happy marriage,' she repeated, whispering the words, speaking to herself, still not looking at him. 'You met a woman on a train and that was that: you murdered our marriage. You left me to plead, as I am leaving you to now. You have your Sunday access. There is that legality between us. Nothing more.'

'Please, Elizabeth –'

'Oh for God's sake, stop.' Her rage was all in her face now. Her lips quivered as though in an effort to hold back words that would not be denied. They came from her, more quietly but with greater bitterness. Her eyes roved over the green tweed suit of the man who once had been her husband, over his thin face and his hair that seemed, that day, not to have been brushed.

'You've gone to seed,' she said, hating herself for saying that, unable to prevent herself. 'You've gone to seed because you've lost your self-respect. I've watched you, week by week. The woman you met on a train took her toll of you and now in your seediness you want to creep back. Don't you know you're not the man I married?'

'Elizabeth –'

'You didn't have cigarette burns all over your clothes. You didn't smell of toothpaste when you should have smelt of drink. You stand there, pathetically, Sunday after Sunday, trying to keep a conversation going. D'you know what I feel?'

'I love –'

'I feel sorry for you.'

He shook his head. There was no need to feel sorry for him, he said, remembering suddenly the elderly assistant in Frith's Patisserie and remembering also, for some reason, the woman in Hyde Park who peculiarly had said that he wasn't shaved. He looked down at his clothes and saw the burn marks she had mentioned. 'We think it would be better', said the voice of Sir Gerald Travers unexpectedly in his mind.

'I'll make some coffee,' said Elizabeth.

She left him. He had been cruel, and then Diana had been cruel, and now Elizabeth was cruel because it was her right and her instinct to be so. He recalled with vividness Diana's face in those first moments on the train, her eyes looking at him, her voice. 'You have lost all dignity,' Elizabeth had whispered, in the darkness, at night. 'I despise you for that.' He tried to stand up but found the effort beyond him. He raised the green glass to his lips. His eyes closed and when he opened them again he thought for a drunken moment that he was back in the past, in the middle of his happy marriage. He wiped at his face with a handkerchief.

He saw across the room the bottle of Gordon's gin so nicely matching the green glasses, and the lime-juice, a lighter shade of green. He made the journey, his legs striking the arms of chairs. There wasn't much gin in the bottle. He poured it all out; he added lime-juice, and drank it.

In the hall he could hear voices, his children's voices in the bathroom, Elizabeth and the man speaking quietly in the kitchen. 'Poor wretch,' Elizabeth was saying. He left the flat and descended to the ground floor.

The rain was falling heavily. He walked through it, thinking that it was better to go, quietly and without fuss. It would all work out; he knew it; he felt it definitely in his bones. He'd arrive on Sunday, a month or so before their birthday, and something in Elizabeth's face would tell him that the dark-haired man had gone for ever, as Diana had gone. By then he'd be established again, with better prospects than the red-faced Sir Gerald Travers had ever offered him. On their birthday they'd both apologize to one another, wiping the slate clean: they'd start again. As he crossed the Edgware Road to the public house in which he always spent an hour or so on Sunday nights, he heard his own voice murmuring that it was understandable that she should have taken it out on him, that she should have tried to hurt him by saying he'd gone to seed. Naturally, she'd say a thing like that; who could blame her after all she'd been through? At night in the flat in Barnes he watched television until the programmes closed down. He usually had a few drinks, and as often as not he dropped off to sleep with a cigarette between his fingers: that was how the burns occurred on his clothes.

He nodded to himself as he entered the saloon bar, thinking he'd been wise not to mention any of that to Elizabeth. It would only have annoyed her, having to listen to a lot of stuff about late-night television and cigarettes. Monday, Tuesday, Wednesday, he thought, Thursday, Friday. On Saturday he'd buy the meringues and brandy-snaps, and then it would be Sunday. He'd make the sandwiches listening to *The Archers*, and at three o'clock he'd ring the bell of the flat. He smiled in the saloon bar, thinking of that, seeing in his mind the faces of his children and the beautiful face of their mother. He'd planted an idea in Elizabeth's mind and even though she'd been a bit shirty she'd see when she thought about it that it was what she wanted, too.

He went on drinking gin and lime-juice, quietly laughing over being so upset when the children had first mentioned the dark-haired man who took them on to his knee. Gin and lime-juice was a Gimlet, he told the barmaid. She smiled at him. He was celebrating, he said, a day that was to come. It was ridiculous, he told her, that a woman casually met on a train should have created havoc, that now, at the end of it all, he should week by week butter bread for Marmite and tomato sandwiches. 'D'you understand me?' he drunkenly asked the barmaid. 'It's *too* ridiculous to be true – that man will go because none of it makes sense the way it is.' The barmaid smiled again and nodded. He bought her a glass of beer, which was something he did every Sunday night. He wept as he paid for it, and touched his cheeks with the tips of his fingers to wipe away the tears. Every Sunday he wept, at the end of the day, after he'd had his access. The barmaid raised her glass, as always she did. They drank to the day that was to come, when the error he had made would be wiped away, when the happy marriage could continue. 'Ridiculous,' he said. 'Of course it is.'

The General's Day

General Suffolk pulled on two grey knitted socks and stood upright. Humming a marching air, he walked to the bathroom, intent upon his morning shave. The grey socks were his only apparel and he noticed as he passed the mirror of his wardrobe the white spare body of an elderly man reflected without flattery. He voiced no comment nor did he ponder, even in passing, upon this pictured nakedness. He was used to the sight; and had, over the years, accepted the changes as they came. Still humming, he half filled the wash-basin with water. It felt keenly warm on his fingers, a circumstance he inwardly congratulated himself on.

With deft strokes the General cleared his face of lather and whisker, savouring the crisp rasp of razor upon flesh. He used a cut-throat article and when shorn to his satisfaction wiped it on a small absorbent pad, one of a series he had collected from the bedrooms of foreign hotels. He washed, dressed, set his moustache as he liked to sport it, and descended to his kitchen.

The General's breakfast was simple: an egg poached lightly, two slices of toast and a pot of tea. It took him ten minutes to prepare and ten to consume. As he finished he heard the footsteps of the woman who daily came to work for him. They were slow, dragging footsteps implying the bulk they gracelessly shifted. The latch of the door rose and fell and Mrs Hinch, string bags and hairnet, cigarette cocked from the corner of her mouth, stood grinning before him. 'Hullo,' this woman said, adding as she often did, 'my dear.'

'Good morning, Mrs Hinch.'

Mrs Hinch stripped herself of bags, coat and cigarette with a single complicated gesture. She grinned again at the General, replaced her cigarette and set to clearing the table.

'I shall walk to the village this morning,' General Suffolk informed her. 'It seems a pleasant morning to dawdle through. I shall take coffee at the brown café and try my luck at picking up some suitable matron.'

Mrs Hinch was accustomed to her employer's turn of speech. She laughed shrilly at this sally, pleased that the man would be away for the morning. 'Ah, General, you'll be the death of us,' she cried; and planned for his absence a number of trunk calls on his telephone, a leisurely bath and the imbibing of as much South African sherry as she considered discreet.

'It is Saturday if I am not mistaken,' the General went on. 'A good morning for my plans. Is it not a fact that there are stout matrons in and out of the brown café by the score on a Saturday morning?'

'Why, sure, General,' said Mrs Hinch, anxious to place no barrier in his way. 'Why, half the county goes to the brown café of a Saturday morning. You are certain to be successful this time.'

'Cheering words, Mrs Hinch, cheering words. It is one thing to walk through the campion-clad lanes on a June morning, but quite another to do so with an objective one is sanguine of achieving.'

'This is your day, General. I feel it in my bones. I said it to Hobson as I left. "This is a day for the General," I said. "The General will do well today," I said.'

'And Hobson, Mrs Hinch? Hobson replied?'

Again Mrs Hinch, like a child's toy designed for the purpose, shrilled her merriment.

'General, General, Hobson's my little bird.'

The General, rising from the table, frowned. 'Do you imagine I am unaware of that? Since for six years you have daily informed me of the fact. And why, pray, since the bird is a parrot, should the powers of speech be beyond it? It is not so with other parrots.'

'Hobson's silent, General. You know Hobson's silent.'

'Due to your lethargy, Mrs Hinch. No bird of his nature need be silent: God does not intend it. He has taken some pains to equip the parrot with the instruments of speech. It is up to you to pursue the matter in a practical way by training the animal. A child, Mrs Hinch, does not remain ignorant of self-expression. Nor of the ability to feed and clean itself. The mother teaches, Mrs Hinch. It is part of nature. So with your parrot.'

Enthusiastic in her own defence, Mrs Hinch said: 'I have brought up seven children. Four girls and three boys.'

'Maybe. Maybe. I am in no position to question this. But indubitably with your parrot you are flying in the face of nature.'

'Oh, General, never. Hobson's silent and that's that.'

The General regarded his adversary closely. 'You miss my point,' he said drily; and repeating the remark twice he left the room.

In his time General Suffolk had been a man of more than ordinary importance. As a leader and a strategist in two great wars he had risen rapidly to the heights implied by the title he bore. He had held in his hands the lives of many thousands of men; his decisions had more than once set the boundaries of nations. Steely intelligence and physical prowess had led him, in their different ways, to glories that few experience at Roeux; and at Monchy-le-Preux he had come close to death. Besides all that, there was about the General a quality that is rare in the ultimate leaders of his army: he was to the last a rake, and for this humanity a popular figure. He had cared for women, for money, for alcohol of every sort; but in the end he had found himself with none of these commodities. In his modest cottage he was an elderly man with a violent past; with neither wife nor riches nor cellar to help him on his way.

Mrs Hinch had said he would thrive today. That the day should be agreeable was all he asked. He did not seek merriness or reality or some moment of truth. He had lived for long enough to forgo excitement; he had had his share; he wished only that the day, and his life in it, should go the way he wished.

In the kitchen Mrs Hinch scoured the dishes briskly. She was not one to do things by halves; hot water and detergent in generous quantities was her way.

'Careful with the cup handles,' the General admonished her. 'Adhesive for the repair of such a fracture has apparently not yet been perfected. And the cups themselves are valuable.'

'Oh they're flimsy, General. So flimsy you can't watch them. Declare to God, I shall be glad to see the last of them!'

'But not I, Mrs Hinch. I like those cups. Tea tastes better from fine china. I would take it kindly if you washed and dried with care.'

'Hoity-toity, General! Your beauties are safe with me. I treat them as babies.'

'Babies? Hardly a happy analogy, Mrs Hinch – since five of the set are lost for ever.'

'Six,' said Mrs Hinch, snapping beneath the water the handle from the cup. 'You are better without the bother of them. I shall bring you a coronation mug.'

'You fat old bitch,' shouted the General. 'Six makes the set. It was my last remaining link with the gracious life.'

Mrs Hinch, understanding and wishing to spite the General further, laughed. 'Cheery-bye, General,' she called as she heard him rattling among his walking sticks. He banged the front door and stepped out into the heat of the day. Mrs Hinch turned on the wireless.

'*I walked entranced,*' intoned the General, '*through a land of morn. The sun in wondrous excess of light ...*' He was seventy-eight: his memory faltered over the quotation. His stick, weapon of his irritation, thrashed through the campions, covering the road with broken blooms. Grasshoppers clicked; bees darted, paused, humming in flight, silent in labour.

The road was brown with dust, dry and hot in the sunlight. It was a day, thought the General, to be successfully in love; and he mourned that the ecstasy of love on a hot summer's day was so far behind him. Not that he had gone without it; which gave him his yardstick and saddened him the more.

Early in his retirement General Suffolk had tried his hand in many directions. He had been, to start with, the secretary of a golf club; though in a matter of months his temper relieved him of the task. He was given to disagreement and did not bandy words. He strode away from the golf club, red in the face, the air behind him stinging with insults. He lent his talents to the business world and to a military academy: both were dull and in both he failed. He bought his cottage, agreeing with himself that retirement was retirement and meant what it suggested. Only once since moving to the country had he involved himself with salaried work: as a tennis coach in a girls' school. Despite his age he was active still on his legs and managed well enough. Too well, his grim and beady-eyed headmistress avowed, objecting to his method of instructing her virgins in the various stances by which they might achieve success with the serve. The General paused only to level at the headmistress a battery of expressions well known to him but new to her. He went on his way, his cheque in his wallet, his pockets bulging with small articles from her study. The girls he had taught pursued him, pressing upon him packets of cheap cigarettes, sweets and flowers.

The General walked on, his thoughts rambling. He thought of the past; of specific days, of moments of shame or pride in his life. The past was his hunting ground; from it came his pleasure and a good deal of everything else. Yet he was not proof against the moment he lived in. The present could snarl at him; could drown his memories so completely that when they surfaced again they were like the burnt tips of matches floating on a puddle, finished and done with. He walked through the summery day, puzzled that all this should be so.

The brown café, called 'The Cuppa', was, as General Suffolk and Mrs Hinch had anticipated, bustling with mid-morning traffic. Old men and their wives sat listening to the talk about them, exchanging by the way a hard comment on their fellows. Middle-aged women, outsize in linen dresses, were huddled three or four to a table, their great legs battling for room in inadequate space, their feet hot and unhappy in unwise shoes. Mothers passed unsuitable edibles towards the searching mouths of their young. Men with girls sipped at the pale creamy coffee, thinking only of the girls. Crumbs were everywhere; and the babel buzzed like a clockwork wind.

The General entered, surveyed the scene with distaste, and sat at a table already occupied by a youth engrossed in a weekly magazine. The youth, a fat bespotted lad, looked up and immediately grinned. General Suffolk replied in kind, stretching the flesh of his face to display his teeth in a smile designed to promote goodwill between them, for the pair were old friends.

'Good morning, Basil. And how is youth and vigour today?'

'Oh well, not so bad, General. My mum's in the family way again.'

'A cause for joy,' murmured General Suffolk, ordering coffee with Devonshire cream and the fruit pie he favoured. 'Your mother is a great one for babies, is she not?'

'My dad says the same. He don't understand it neither. Worried, is Dad. Anyone can see that.'

'I see.'

'Well, it is a bit fishy, General. Dad's not the man to be careless. It's just about as fishy as hell.'

'Basil, your mother needs all the support she can get at a time like this. Talk about fishiness is scarcely going to help her in her ordeal.'

'Mum's had five. Drops 'em like hot bricks so she says. Thing is, if this one's fishy what about the others?'

The General placed a portion of pie in his mouth. Crumbs of pastry and other matter lingered on his moustache. 'You are thinking of yourself, Basil.'

'Wouldn't you? I mean to say.'

'I would attach no importance to such a doubt, I do assure you. Basil, what do you say we spend this afternoon at some local fête? It is just an afternoon for a fête. I will stand you lunch.'

The plumpness of Basil's face sharpened into suspicion. He moved his large hams uneasily on his chair and avoided his companion's gaze. 'It's Mum really, General. I've got to tend her a bit, like you say it's a hard time for her. And with Dad so snappish and the kids all over the place I don't think she'd take it kindly if I was to go going off to fêtes and that. Not at a time like this like.'

'Ah, filial duty. I trust your mother appreciates your sacrifices.'

But Basil, not anxious to prolong the conversation in this direction, was on his feet, his right hand hovering for the General's grasp. And then, the handshake completed, he moved himself clumsily between the tables and passed through the open doorway.

General Suffolk stirred sugar into his coffee and looked about him. A lanky schoolmistress from the school he had taught tennis at sat alone at a corner table. She was a woman of forty or so, the General imagined; and he recalled having seen her by chance once, through an open window, in her underclothes. Since then he had often considered her in terms of sex, though now, when he might have explored the possibility, he found himself unable to remember her name. He watched her, trying to catch her glance, but either she did not recognize him or did not wish to associate with so reprobate a character. He dismissed her mentally and surveyed the room again. There was no one with whom he could fall into casual conversation, except perhaps a certain Mrs Consitine, known in her youth as Jumbo Consitine because of her size, and whose freakish appearance repelled him always to the point of physical sickness. He dodged the lady's predatory stare and left the café.

It was a quarter to twelve. If the General walked through the village he would be just in time for a morning drink with Frobisher. Frobisher always drank – sometimes considerably – before lunch. On a day like this a drink was emphatically in order.

Mrs Hinch, the General reflected, would be settling down to his South African sherry about now. 'You thieving old bitch,' he said aloud. 'Fifty years in Their Majesties' service and I end up with Mrs bloody Hinch.' A man carrying a coil of garden hose tripped and fell across his path. This man, a weekend visitor to the district, known to the General by sight and disliked by him, uttered as he dropped to the ground a series of expletives of a blasphemous and violent nature. The General, since the man's weight lay on his shoes, stooped to assist him. 'Oh, buzz off,' ordered the man, his face close to the General's. So the General left him, conscious not so much of his dismissal as of the form of words it had taken. The sun warmed his forehead and drops of sweat glistened on his nose and chin.

The Frobishers' house was small and vaguely Georgian. From the outside it had the feeling of a town house placed by some error in the country. There were pillars on either side of the front door, which was itself dressed in a grey and white canvas cover as a protection against the sun. Door and cover swung inwards and Mrs Frobisher, squat and old, spoke from the hall.

'It's General Suffolk,' she said.

'Yes,' said the General. 'That old soldier.'

'You've come to see Frob. Come in a minute and I'll fetch him. What a lovely day.'

The General stepped into the hall. It was cool and smelt rather pleasantly of floor polish. Daggers, swords, Eastern rugs, knick-knacks and novelties hung in profusion everywhere. 'Frob! Frob!' Mrs Frobisher called, climbing the stairs. There had been a day, a terrible sultry day in India all of fifty years ago, when the General – though then not yet a general – had fought a duel with a certain Major Service. They had walked together quietly to a selected spot, their seconds, carrying a pair of *kukris*, trailing behind them. It had been a quarrel that involved, surprisingly, neither man's honour. In retrospect General Suffolk could scarcely remember the cause: some insult directed against some woman, though by whom and in what manner escaped him. He had struck Major Service on the left forearm, drawing a considerable quantity of blood, and the duel was reckoned complete. An excuse was made for the wound sustained by the Major and the affair was successfully hushed up. It was the nearest that General Suffolk had ever come to being court-martialled. He was put in mind of the occasion by the presence of a *kukri* on the Frobishers' wall. A nasty weapon, he reflected, and considered it odd that he should once have wielded one so casually. After all, Major Service might easily have lost his arm or, come to that, his life.

'Frob! Frob! Where are you?' cried Mrs Frobisher. 'General Suffolk's here to see you.'

'Suffolk?' Frobisher's voice called from another direction. 'Oh my dear, can't you tell him I'm out?'

The General, hearing the words, left the house.

In the saloon bar of the public house General Suffolk asked the barman about the local fêtes.

'Don't think so, sir. Not today. Not that I've heard of.'

'There's a fête at Marmount,' a man at the bar said. 'Conservative fête, same Saturday every year.'

'Ah certainly,' said the barman, 'but Marmount's fifteen miles away. General Suffolk means a *local* fête. The General doesn't have a car.'

'Of course, of course,' said the man. 'Marmount's not an easy spot to reach. Even if you did have a car, sir.'

'I will have a sandwich, Jock,' said General Suffolk. 'Chop me a cheese sandwich like a good man.' He was beginning to feel low; the day was not good; the day was getting out of control. Fear filled his mind and the tepid beer was no comfort. He began to pray inwardly, but he had little faith now in this communication. 'Never mind,' he said aloud. 'It is just that it seems like a day for a fête. I won a half guinea at a summer fête last year. One never knows one's luck.' He caught sight of a card advertising the weekly films at the cinema of the nearby town.

'Have you seen *The Guns of Navarone*?' he questioned the barman.

'I have, sir, and very good it is.'

The General nodded. 'A powerful epic by the sound of it.'

'That's the word, General. As the saying goes, it had me riveted.'

'Well, hurry the sandwiches then. I can catch the one-ten bus and achieve the first performance.'

'Funny thing, sir,' said the barman. 'I can never take the cinema of an afternoon. Not that it isn't a time that suits me, the hours being what they are. No, I go generally on my night off. Can't seem to settle down in the afternoon or something. Specially in the good weather. To me, sir, it seems unnatural.'

'That is an interesting point of view, Jock. It is indeed. And may well be shared by many – for I have noticed that the cinemas are often almost empty in the afternoon.'

'I like to be outside on a good afternoon. Taking a stroll by a trout stream or in a copse.'

'A change is as good as a cure, or whatever the adage is. After all, you are inside a good deal in your work. To be alone must be quite delightful after the idle chatter you have to endure.'

'If you don't mind my saying it, General, I don't know how you do it. It would kill me to sit at the pictures on an afternoon like this. I would feel – as it were, sir – guilty.'

'Guilty, Jock?'

'Looking the Great Gift Horse in the mouth, sir.'

'The –? Are you referring to the Deity, Jock?'

'Surely, sir. I would feel it like an unclean action.'

'Maybe, Jock. Though I doubt that God would care to hear you describe Him as a horse.'

'Oh but, General –'

'You mean no disrespect. It is taken as read, Jock. But you cannot be too careful.'

'Guilt is my problem, sir.'

'I am sorry to hear it. Guilt can often be quite a burden.'

'I am never free of it, sir. If it's not one thing it's another.'

'I know too well, Jock.'

'It was not presumptuous of me to mention that thing about the cinema? I was casting no stone at you, sir.'

'Quite, quite. It may even be that I would prefer to attend an evening house. But beggars, you know, cannot be choosers.'

'I would not like to offend you, General.'

'Good boy, Jock. In any case I am not offended. I enjoy a chat.'

'Thank you, sir.'

'Not at all. But now I must be on my way. Consider your problem closely: you may discover some simple solution. There are uncharted regions in the human mind.'

'Sir?'

'You are a good fellow, Jock. We old soldiers must stick together.'

'Ha, ha,' said Jock, taking the remark as a joke, since he was in the first place a young man still, and had never been in the army.

'Well, cheerio then.'

'Cheerio, sir.'

How extraordinary, thought the General, that the man should feel like that: guilty about daytime cinema attendance. As Mrs Hinch would have it, it takes all sorts.

The thought of Mrs Hinch depressed the General further and drove him straight to a telephone booth. He often telephoned his cottage at this time of day as a check on her time-keeping. She was due to remain at work for a further hour, but generally the telephone rang unanswered. Today he got the engaged signal. As he boarded his bus, he wondered how much it was costing him.

Taurus. 21 April to 20 May. Financial affairs straighten themselves out. Do not make decisions this afternoon: your judgement is not at its best.

The General peeped around the edge of the newspaper at the woman who shared his table. She was a thin, middle-aged person with a face like a faded photograph. Her hair was inadequately dyed a shade of brown, her face touched briefly with lipstick and powder. She wore a cream-coloured blouse and a small string of green beads which the General assumed, correctly, to be jade. Her skirt, which the General could not see, was of fine tweed.

'How thoughtless of me,' said the General. 'I have picked up your paper. It was on the chair and I did it quite automatically. I am so sorry.'

He knew the newspaper was not hers. No one places a newspaper on the other chair at a café table when the other chair is so well out of reach. Unless, that is, one wishes to reserve the place, which the lady, since she made no protest at his occupying it, was clearly not interested in doing. He made the pretence of offering the paper across the tea-table, leaning forward and sideways to catch a glimpse of her legs.

'Oh but,' said the lady, 'it is not my newspaper at all.'

Beautiful legs. Really beautiful legs. Shimmering in silk or nylon, with fine firm knees and intoxicating calves.

'Are you sure? In that case it must have been left by the last people. I was reading the stars. I am to have an indecisive afternoon.' She belongs to the upper classes, General Suffolk said to himself; the upper classes are still well-bred in the leg.

The lady tinkled with laughter. I am away, the General thought. 'When is your birthday?' he asked daringly. 'And I will tell you what to expect for the rest of today.'

'Oh, I'm Libra, I think.'

'It is a good moment for fresh associations,' lied the General, pretending to read from the paper. 'A new regime is on its way.'

'You can't believe a thing they say.'

'Fighting words,' said the General, and they laughed and changed the subject of conversation.

In the interval at the cinema, when the lights had gone up and the girls with ice-cream began their sales stroll, the General had seen, two or three rows from the screen, the fat unhealthy figure of his friend Basil. The youth was accompanied by a girl, and it distressed General Suffolk that Basil should have made so feeble an excuse when earlier he had proposed an excursion to a fête. The explanation that Basil wished to indulge in carnal pleasures in the gloom of a picture house would naturally have touched the General's sympathy. Basil was an untrustworthy lad. It was odd, the General reflected, that some people are like that: so addicted to the lie that to avoid one, when the truth is in order, seems almost a sin.

'General Suffolk,' explained the General. 'Retired, of course.'

'We live in Bradoak,' said the lady. 'My name actually is Mrs Hope-Kingley.'

'Retired?'

'Ha, ha. Though in a way it's true. My husband is not alive now.'

'Ah,' said the General, delighted. 'I'm sorry.'

'I am quite over it, thank you. It is all of fifteen years since last I saw him. We had been divorced some time before his death.'

'Divorce and death, divorce and death. You hear it all the time. May I be personal now and say I am surprised you did not remarry?'

'Oh, General Suffolk, Mr Right never came along!'

'*Attention! Les étoiles!*'

'Ha, ha.' And to her own surprise, Mrs Hope-Kingley proceeded to reveal to this elderly stranger the story of her marriage.

As he listened, General Suffolk considered how best to play his cards. It was a situation he had found himself in many times before, but as always the game must vary in detail. He felt mentally a little tired as he thought about it; and the fear that, in this, as in almost everything else, age had taken too great a toll struck at him with familiar ruthlessness. In his thirties he had played superbly, as good at love as he was at tennis. Now arrogant, now innocent, he had swooped and struck, captured and killed; and smiled over many a breakfast at the beauty that had been his prize.

They finished their tea. 'I am slipping along to the County for a drink,' said the General. 'Do join me for a quick one.'

'How kind of you. I must not delay though. My sister will expect me.' And they climbed into Mrs Hope-Kingley's small car and drove to the hotel. Over their gins the General spoke of his early days in the army and touched upon his present life, naming Mrs Hinch.

'What a frightful woman! You must sack her.'

'But who would do for me? I need my bed made and the place kept clean. Women are not easy to find in the country.'

'I know a Mrs Gall who lives in your district. She has the reputation of being particularly reliable. My friends the Boddingtons use her.'

'Well, that is certainly a thought. D'you know, I had become quite reconciled to Hinch. I never thought to change her really. What a breath of life you are!'

After three double gins Mrs Hope-Kingley was slightly drunk. Her face flushed with pleasure. Compliments do not come your way too often these days, thought the General; and he ambled off to the bar to clinch the matter with a further drink. How absurd to be upset by the passing details of the day! What did it all matter, now that he had found this promising lady? The day and its people, so directed against him, were balanced surely by this meeting? With her there was strength; from her side he might look out on the world with power and with confidence. In a panic of enthusiasm he almost suggested marriage. His hands were shaking and he felt again a surge of the old arrogance. There is life in the old dog yet, he thought. Handing her her drink, he smiled and winked.

'After this I must go,' the lady said.

'Come, come, the night is younger than we are. It is not every day I can pick up a bundle of charms in a teashop.'

'Ha, ha, ha.' Mrs Hope-Kingley purred, thinking that for once her sister would simply have to wait, and wondering if she should dare to tell her that she had been drinking with an elderly soldier.

They were sitting at a small table in a corner. Now and again, it could have been an accident, the General's knee touched hers. He watched the level of gin lower in her glass. 'You are a pretty lady,' murmured the General, and beneath the table his hand stroked her stockinged knee and ventured a little beyond it.

'My God!' said Mrs Hope-Kingley, her face like a beetroot. The General lowered his head. He heard her snatch her handbag from the seat beside him. When he looked up she was gone.

*

'When were you born?' General Suffolk asked the man in the bus.

The man seemed startled. 'Well,' he said, 'nineteen-oh-three actually.'

'No, no, no. What month? When does your birthday fall?'

'Well, October the 21st actually.'

'Libra by a day,' the General informed him, consulting his newspaper as he spoke. 'For tomorrow, there are to be perfect conditions for enjoying yourself; though it may be a little expensive. Don't gamble.'

'I see,' said the man, glancing in embarrassment through the window.

'Patrelli is usually reliable.'

The man nodded, thinking: The old fellow is drunk. He was right: the General was drunk.

'I do not read the stars every day,' General Suffolk explained. 'It is only when I happen upon an evening paper. I must say I find Patrelli the finest augur of the lot. Do you not agree?'

The man made an effort to smile, muttering something incomprehensible.

'What's that, what's that? I cannot hear you.'

'I don't know at all. I don't know about such matters.'

'You are not interested in the stars?'

The man shook his head.

'In that case, I have been boring you.'

'No, no –'

'If you were not interested in my conversation you should have said so. It is quite simple to say it. I cannot understand you.'

'I'm sorry –'

'I do not like to offend people. I do not like to be a nuisance. You should have stopped me, sir.'

The man made a gesture vague in its meaning.

'You have taken advantage of an old warrior.'

'I cannot see –'

'You should have halted me. It costs nothing to speak.'

'I'm sorry.'

'Think nothing of it. Think nothing of it at all. Here is my village. If you are dismounting, would you care to join me in a drink?'

'Thank you, no. I am –'

'I swear not to speak of the stars.'

'I go on a bit. This is not my stop.'

The General shook his head, as though doubting this statement. The bus stopped and, aided by the conductor, he left it.

'Did you see *The Guns*, General?' Jock shouted across the bar.

Not hearing, but understanding that the barman was addressing him, General Suffolk waved breezily. 'A large whisky, Jock. And a drop of beer for yourself.'

'Did you see *The Guns* then?'

'The guns?'

'The pictures, General. *The Guns of Navarone.*'

'That is very kind of you, Jock. But we must make it some other time. I saw that very film this afternoon.'

'General, did you like it?'

'Certainly, Jock. Certainly I liked it. It was very well done. I thought it was done very well indeed.'

'Two gins and split a bottle of tonic,' a man called out.

'I beg your pardon,' said the General, 'I think I am in your way.'

'Two gins and a split tonic,' repeated Jock.

'And something for our friend,' the man added, indicating the General.

'That is kind of you. Everyone is kind tonight. Jock here has just invited me to accompany him to the pictures. Unfortunately I have seen the film. But there will be other occasions. We shall go together again. May I ask you when you were born, the month I mean?'

The man, whose attention was taken up with the purchasing and transportation of his drinks, said: 'Some time in May, I think.'

'But exactly? When is your birthday, for instance?' But the man had returned to a small table against the wall, where a girl and several packets of unopened crisps awaited him.

'Jock, do you follow the stars?'

'D'you mean telescopes and that?'

'No, no, my boy.' The General swayed, catching at the bar to balance himself. He had had very little to eat all day: the old, he maintained, did not need it. 'No, no, I mean the augurs. Capricorn, Scorpio, Gemini, you know what I mean.'

'Lord Luck in the *Daily Express?*'

'That's it. That's the kind of thing. D'you take an interest at all?'

'Well, General, now, I don't.'

'When's your birthday, Jock?'

'August the 15th.'

'A Leo, by Harry! It is quite something to be a Leo, Jock. I would never have guessed it.'

Jock laughed loudly. 'After all, General, it is not my doing.'

'Fill up our glasses. Let me see what tomorrow holds for you.' But examining the paper, he found it difficult to focus. 'Here Jock, read it yourself.'

And Jock read aloud:

'*You will gain a lot by mingling with friends old and new. Late evening particularly favours entry into new social circles.*'

'Hark at that then! Remember the words, my friend. Patrelli is rarely wrong. The best augur of the bunch.' The General had become dishevelled. His face was flushed and his eyelids drooped intermittently and uncontrollably. He fidgeted with his clothes, as though nervous about the positioning of his hands. 'A final whisky, Jock boy; and a half bottle to carry home.'

On the road from the village to his cottage the General felt very drunk indeed. He lurched from one grass verge to the other, grasping his half bottle of whisky and singing gently under his breath. He knocked on the Frobishers' door with his stick, and scarcely waiting for a reply knocked loudly again.

'For God's sake, man,' Frobisher demanded, 'what's the matter with you?'

'A little drink,' explained General Suffolk. 'You and me and Mrs Frob, a little drink together. I have brought some with me. In case you had run out.'

Frobisher glared at him. 'You're drunk, Suffolk. You're bloody well drunk.'

General Suffolk loosed a peal of laughter. 'Ha, ha, the old man's drunk. Let me in, Frob, and so shall you be.'

Frobisher attempted to close the door, but the General inserted his stick. He laughed again, and then was silent. When he spoke his voice was pleading.

'One drink, Frob. Just one for you and me. Frob, when were you born?'

Frobisher began to snort with anger: he was a short-tempered man, he saw no reason to humour this unwelcome guest. He kicked sharply at the General's stick, then opening the door widely he shouted into his face: 'Get the hell off my premises, you bloody old fool! Go on, Suffolk, hop it!'

The General did not appear to understand. He smiled at Frobisher. 'Tell me the month of your birth and I shall tell you in return what the morrow holds –'

'God damn it, Suffolk –'

'One little drink, and we'll consult the stars together. They may well be of interest to Mrs –'

'Get off my premises, you fool! You've damaged my door with your damned stick. You'll pay for that, Suffolk. You'll hear from my solicitors. I promise you, if you don't go immediately I won't hesitate to call for the police.'

'One drink, Frob. Look, I'm a little lonely —'

Frobisher banged the door. 'Frob, Frob,' General Suffolk called, striking the door with his stick. 'A nightcap, my old friend. Don't refuse a drink now.' But the door remained closed against him. He spoke for a while to himself, then made his way unsteadily homewards.

'General Suffolk, are you ill?'

The General narrowed his eyes, focusing on the couple who stood before him; he did not recognize them; he was aware of feeling guilty because of it.

'We are returning home from a game of cards,' the woman of the two told him. 'It is a balmy evening for a stroll.'

The General tried to smile. Since leaving the Frobishers' house he had drunk most of the whisky. The people danced a bit before him, like outsize puppets. They moved up and down, and from side to side. They walked rapidly, silently, backwards. 'Ha, ha, ha,' laughed the General. 'What can I do for you?'

'Are you ill? You don't seem yourself.'

The General smiled at some little joke. 'I have not been myself for many years. Today is just another day.'

The people were moving away. He could hear them murmuring to each other.

'You have not asked me about the stars,' he shouted after them. 'I could tell you if you asked.' But they were already gone, and uncorking the bottle he drained the remains and threw it into a ditch.

As he passed Mrs Hinch's cottage he decided to call on her. He had it on his mind to play some joke on the woman, to say that she need not again attend to his household needs. He banged powerfully on the door and in a moment Mrs Hinch's head, rich in curling pins, appeared at a window to his right.

'Why, General dear,' said Mrs Hinch, recognizing immediately his condition. 'You've been on the razzle.'

'Mrs Hinch, when is your birthday?'

'Why, my dear? Have you a present for little Hinchie?'

'Give me the information and I will let you know what tomorrow brings.'

'May the 3rd. I was born at two o'clock in the morning.'

But in his walk he had somewhere mislaid the newspaper and could tell her nothing. He gripped the doorstep and seemed about to fall.

'Steady now,' said Mrs Hinch. 'I'll dress myself and help you home.' The head was withdrawn and the General waited for the company of his unreliable servant.

She, in the room, slipped out of her nightdress and buttoned about her her everyday clothes. This would last her for months. 'Ho ho, my dear,' she would say, 'remember that night? Worse for wear you were. Whatever would you have done without your little Hinchie?' Chortling and crowing, she hitched up her skirts and paraded forth to meet him.

'Oh General, you're naughty! You shouldn't be allowed out.'

The General laughed. Clumsily he slapped her broad buttocks. She screamed shrilly, enjoying again the position she now held over him. 'Dirty old General! Hinchie won't carry her beauty home unless he's a good boy tonight.' She laughed her cackling laugh and the General joined in it. He dawdled a bit, and losing her patience Mrs Hinch pushed him roughly in front of her. He fell, and in picking him up she came upon his wallet and skilfully extracted two pounds ten. 'General would fancy his Hinchie tonight,' she said, shrieking merrily at the thought. But the General was silent now, seeming almost asleep as he walked. His face was gaunt and thin, with little patches of red. 'I could live for twenty years,' he whispered. 'My God Almighty, I could live for twenty years.' Tears spread on his cheeks. 'Lor' love a duck!' cried Mrs Hinch; and leaning on the arm of this stout woman the hero of Roeux and Monchy-le-Preux stumbled the last few yards to his cottage.

Memories of Youghal

He did not, he said, remember the occasion of his parents' death, having been at the time only five months old. His first memory was of a black iron gate, of his own hand upon a part of it, and of his uncle driving through the gateway in a Model-T Ford. These images, and that of his uncle's bespectacled face perspiring, were all in sunshine. For him, so he said to Miss Ticher, the sunlight still glimmered on the dim black paint of the motor-car; his uncle, cross and uncomfortable on hot upholstery, did not smile.

He remembered also, at some later time, eating tinned tomato soup in a house that was not the house of his aunt and uncle; he remembered a tap near a greenhouse; he remembered eating an ice-cream outside Horgan's Picture House while his aunt engaged another woman in conversation. Pierrots performed on the sands; a man who seemed to be a priest gave him a Fox's Glacier Mint.

'The gate was tarred, I think,' he said. 'A tarred black gate. That memory is the first of all.'

The elderly woman to whom he spoke smiled at him, covering with the smile the surprise she experienced because a stout, untidy stranger spoke to her so easily about his memories.

'I recall my uncle eating the tomato soup,' the man said, 'and my aunt, who was a severe woman, giving him a disapproving glance because of the row he was kicking up with it. The tap near the greenhouse came from a pipe that rose crookedly out of the ground.'

'I see,' she said, smiling a little more. She added that her own earliest memory, as far as she could remember, was of a papier-mâché spotted dog filled with sweets. The man didn't comment on that.

'Horgan's Picture House,' he said. 'I wonder is it still going strong?'

She shook her head. She said she didn't know if Horgan's Picture House was still standing, since she had never been to the town he spoke of.

'I first saw Gracie Fields there,' he revealed. 'And Jack Hulbert in a funny called *Round the Washtub*.'

They were reclining in deck-chairs on a terrace of the Hôtel Les Galets in Bandol, looking out at the Mediterranean. Mimosa and bougainvillaea bloomed around them, oranges ripened, palm trees flapped in a small breeze, and on a pale-blue sky the sun pushed hazy clouds aside. With her friend Miss Grimshaw, Miss Ticher always came to Bandol in late April, between the mistral and the season, before the noise and the throbbing summer heat. They had known one another for more than thirty years and when, next year, they both retired at sixty-five they planned to live in a bungalow in Sevenoaks, not far from St Mildred's School for Girls, where Miss Ticher taught history and Miss Grimshaw French. They would, they hoped, continue to travel in the spring to Bandol, to the quiet Mediterranean and the local bouillabaisse, their favourite dish.

Miss Ticher was a thin woman with a shy face and frail, thin hands. She had been asleep on the upper terrace of Les Galets and had wakened to find the untidy man standing in front of her. He had asked if he might sit in the deck-chair beside hers, the chair that Miss Grimshaw had earlier planned to occupy on her return from her walk. Miss Ticher felt she could not prevent the man from sitting down, and so had nodded. He was not staying in the hotel, he said, and added that his business was that of a detective. He was observing a couple who were at present in an upstairs room: it would facilitate his work if Miss Ticher would kindly permit him to remain with her and perhaps engage in a casual conversation while he awaited the couple's emergence. A detective, he told Miss Ticher, could not be obvious: a detective must blend with the background, or at least seem natural. 'The So-Swift Investigation Agency', he said. 'A London firm'. As he lowered himself into the chair that Miss Grimshaw had reserved for herself he said he was an exiled Irishman. 'Did you ever hear of the Wild Geese?' he enquired. 'Soldiers of fortune? I often feel like that myself. My name is Quillan.'

He was younger than he looked, she thought: forty-five, she estimated, and seeming to be ten years older. Perhaps it was that, looking older than he was, or perhaps it was the uneasy emptiness in his eyes, that made her feel sorry for him. His eyes apologized for himself, even though he attempted to hide the apology beneath a jauntiness. He wouldn't be long on the terrace, he promised: the couple would soon be checking out of the hotel and on behalf of the husband of the woman he would discreetly follow them, around the coast in a hired Renault. It was work he did not much care for, but it was better than other work he had experienced: he'd drifted about, he added with a laugh, from pillar to post. With his eyes closed in the warmth he talked about his childhood memories while Miss Ticher listened.

'Youghal,' he said. 'I was born in Youghal, in County Cork. In 1934 my mother went in for a swim and got caught up with a current. My dad went out to fetch her and they both went down.'

He left his deck-chair and went away, and strangely she wondered if perhaps he was going to find a place to weep. An impression of his face remained with her: a fat red face with broken veins in it, and blue eyes beneath dark brows. When he smiled he revealed teeth that were stained and chipped and not his own. Once, when laughing over a childhood memory, they had slipped from their position in his jaw and had had to be replaced. Miss Ticher had looked away in embarrassment, but he hadn't minded at all. He wasn't a man who cared about the way he struck other people. His trousers were held up with a tie, his pale stomach showed through an unbuttoned shirt. There was dandruff in his sparse fluff of sandy hair and on the shoulders of a blue blazer: yesterday's dandruff, Miss Ticher had thought, or even the day before's.

'I've brought you this,' he said, returning and sitting again in Miss Grimshaw's chair. He proffered a glass of red liquid. 'A local aperitif.'

Over pots of geraniums and orange-tiled roofs, across the bay and the green sea that was ruffled with little bursts of foam, were the white villas of Sanary, set among cypresses. Nearer, and more directly below, was the road to Toulon and beyond it a scrappy beach on which Miss Ticher now observed the figure of Miss Grimshaw.

'I was given over to the aunt and uncle,' said Quillan, 'on the day of the tragedy. Although, as I'm saying to you, I don't remember it.'

He drank whisky mixed with ice. He shook the liquid in his glass, watching it. He offered Miss Ticher a cigarette, which she refused. He lit one himself.

'The uncle kept a shop,' he said.

She saw Miss Grimshaw crossing the road to Toulon. A driver hooted; Miss Grimshaw took no notice.

'Memories are extraordinary,' said Quillan, 'the things you'd remember and the things you wouldn't. I went to the infant class at the Loreto Convent. There was a Sister Ita. I remember a woman with a red face who cried one time. There was a boy called Joe Murphy whose grandmother kept a greengrocer's. I was a member of Joe Murphy's gang. We used to fight another gang.'

Miss Grimshaw passed from view. She would be approaching the hotel, moving slowly in the warmth, her sunburnt face shining as her spectacles shone. She would arrive panting, and already, in her mind, Miss Ticher could hear her voice. 'What on earth's that red stuff you're drinking?' she'd demand in a huffy manner.

'When I was thirteen years old I ran away from the aunt and uncle,' Quillan said. 'I hooked up with a travelling entertainments crowd that used to go about the seaside places. I think the aunt must have been the happy female that day. She couldn't stand the sight of me.'

'Oh surely now –'

'Listen,' said Quillan, leaning closer to Miss Ticher and staring intently into her eyes. 'I'll tell you the way this case was. You'd like to know?'

'Well –'

'The uncle had no interest of any kind in the bringing up of a child. The uncle's main interest was drinking bottles of stout in Phelan's public house, with Harrigan the butcher. The aunt was a different kettle of fish: the aunt above all things wanted nippers of her own. For the whole of my thirteen years in that house I was a reminder to my aunt of her childless condition. I was a damn nuisance to both of them.'

Miss Ticher, moved by these revelations, did not know what to say. His eyes were slightly bloodshot, she saw; and then she thought it was decidedly odd, a detective going on about his past to an elderly woman on the terrace of an hotel.

'I wasn't wanted in that house,' he said. 'When I was five years old she told me the cost of the food I ate.'

It would have been 1939 when he was five, she thought, and she remembered herself in 1939, a girl of twenty-four, just starting her career at St Mildred's, a girl who'd begun to feel that marriage, which she'd wished for, might not come her way. 'We're neither of us the type,' Miss Grimshaw later said. 'We'd be lost, my dear, without the busy life of school.'

She didn't want Miss Grimshaw to arrive on the terrace. She wanted this man who was a stranger to her to go on talking in his sentimental way. He described the town he spoke of: an ancient gateway and a main street, and a harbour where fishing boats went from, and the strand with wooden breakwaters where his parents had drowned, and seaside boarding-houses and a promenade, and short grass on a clay hill above the sea.

'Near the lighthouse in Youghal,' said Quillan, 'there's a shop I used buy Rainbow Toffees in.'

Miss Grimshaw appeared on the terrace and walked towards them. She was a small, plump woman with grey hair, and short legs and short arms. Generations of girls at St Mildred's had likened her to a dachshund and had, among themselves, named her appropriately. She wore now a flowered dress and carried in her left hand a yellow plastic bag containing the fruits of her morning's excursion: a number of shells.

'At a later time,' said Quillan, 'I joined the merchant navy in order to get a polish. I knocked about the world a bit, making do the best way I could. And then a few years back I entered the investigation business.'

Miss Grimshaw, annoyed because an unprepossessing man in a blazer was sprawling in her chair, saw that her friend was holding in her hand a glass of red liquid and was further annoyed because of this: they pooled their resources at the beginning of each holiday and always consulted each other before making a purchase. Ignoring the sprawling man, she asked Miss Ticher what the glass contained, speaking sharply to register her disapproval and disappointment. She stood, since there was no chair for her to sit on.

'I never went back to Youghal,' the man said before Miss Ticher could reply to Miss Grimshaw's query. 'I only have the childhood memories of it now. Unhappy memories,' said the man to Miss Grimshaw's amazement. 'Unhappy memories of a nice little place. That's life for you.'

'It's an aperitif,' said Miss Ticher, 'that Mr Quillan kindly bought for me. Mr Quillan, this is Miss Grimshaw, my friend.'

'We were discussing memories,' said Quillan, pushing himself out of the deck-chair. 'Miss Ticher and myself were going down Memory Lane.' He laughed loudly, causing the teeth to move about in his mouth. His shoes were scuffed, Miss Grimshaw noted; the blue scarf that was stuck into the open neck of his shirt seemed dirty.

Again he walked abruptly away. He offered Miss Grimshaw no greeting and Miss Ticher no farewell. He moved along the terrace with the glass in his hand and a cigarette in his mouth. His trousers bagged at the back, requiring to be hitched up.

'Who on earth's that?' demanded Miss Grimshaw. 'You never let him pay for that stuff you're drinking?'

'He's a detective,' said Miss Ticher. 'He's watching a couple for a husband. He followed them here.'

'Followed?'

'He's in the investigation business.'

Miss Grimshaw sat in the chair the man had been sitting in. Her eyes returned to the glass of red intoxicant her friend was still holding. She thought to herself that she had gone out alone, looking for shells because Agnes Ticher had said she was tired that morning, and the next thing was Agnes Ticher had got herself involved with a bore.

'He smelt,' said Miss Grimshaw. 'I caught a most unwelcome little whiff.'

'His whisky,' Miss Ticher began. 'Whisky has a smell –'

'You know what I mean, Agnes,' said Miss Grimshaw quietly.

'Did you enjoy your walk?'

Miss Grimshaw nodded. She said it was a pity that Miss Ticher hadn't accompanied her. She felt much better after the exercise. She had an appetite for lunch, and the salt of the sea in her nostrils. She looked again at the glass in Miss Ticher's hand, implying with her glance that the consumption of refreshment before lunch could serve only to fatigue whatever appetite Miss Ticher had managed to gain in the course of her idle morning.

'My God,' said Miss Grimshaw, 'he's coming back.'

He was coming towards them with another deck-chair. Behind him walked a waiter bearing on a tin tray three glasses, two containing the red liquid that Miss Ticher was drinking, the third containing ice and whisky. Without speaking, he set up the deck-chair, facing both of them. The waiter moved an ornamental table and placed the glasses on it.

'A local aperitif,' said Quillan. 'I wouldn't touch it myself, Miss Grimshaw.'

He laughed and again had difficulty with his teeth. Miss Ticher looked away when his fingers rose to his mouth to settle them back into place, but Miss Grimshaw was unable to take her eyes off him. False teeth were common enough today, she was thinking: there was no need at all for them to come leaping from the jaw like that. Somehow it seemed typical of this man that he wouldn't bother to have them attended to.

'Miss Ticher and Miss Grimshaw,' said Quillan slowly, as though savouring the two names. He drank some whisky. 'Miss Ticher and Miss Grimshaw,' he said again. 'You're neither of you a married woman. I didn't marry myself. I was put off marriage, to tell you the truth, by the aunt and uncle down in Youghal. It was an unnatural association, as I saw from an early age. And then of course the investigation business doesn't exactly encourage a fellow to tie up his loose ends with a female. My mother swam into the sea,' he said, addressing Miss Grimshaw and seeming to be pleased to have an opportunity to retail the story again. 'My dad swam in to get her back. They went down to the bottom like a couple of pennies. I was five months old.'

'How horrible,' said Miss Grimshaw.

'If it hadn't happened I'd be a different type of man today. Would you believe that? Would you agree with me, Miss Grimshaw?'

'What?'

'Would I be a different type of man if the parents had lived? When I was thirteen years of age I ran away with an entertainments crowd. I couldn't stand the house a minute more. My uncle never said a word to me, the aunt used look away when she saw me coming. Meals were taken in silence.' He paused, seeming to consider all that. Then he said: 'Youghal's a place like this place, Miss Grimshaw, stuck out on the sea. You know what I mean?'

Miss Grimshaw said she did know what he meant. He talked a lot, she thought, and in a most peculiar way. Agnes Ticher was keeping herself quiet, which no doubt was due to her embarrassment at having involved them both with such a character.

'I have another memory,' said Quillan, 'that I can't place at all. It is a memory of a woman's face and often it keeps coming and going in my mind when I'm trying to sleep in bed. Like the black iron gate, it's always been there, a vague type of face that I can discern and yet I can't. D'you know what I mean?'

'Yes,' said Miss Ticher.

Miss Grimshaw shook her head.

'I told a nun about it one time, when I was a little lad, and she said it was maybe my mother. But I don't believe that for an instant. Will I tell you what I think about that face?'

Miss Ticher smiled, and seeing the smile and noting as well a flush on her friend's cheeks, it occurred to Miss Grimshaw that Agnes Ticher, having been imbibing a drink that might well have been more intoxicating than it seemed, was by now a little tipsy. There was an expression in Agnes Ticher's eyes that suggested such a condition to Miss Grimshaw; there was a looseness about her lips. In a playful way, she thought, she would tell the story in the common-room when they returned to St Mildred's: how Agnes Ticher had been picked up by a ne'er-do-well Irishman and had ended up in a squiffy condition. Miss Grimshaw wanted to laugh, but prevented herself.

'What I think is this,' said Quillan. 'The face is the face of a woman who tried to steal me out of my pram one day when the aunt left the pram outside Pasley's grocer's shop. A childless woman heard about the tragedy and said to herself that she'd take the child and be a mother to it.'

'Did a woman do that?' cried Miss Ticher, and Miss Grimshaw looked at her in amusement.

'They'd never bother to tell me,' said Quillan. 'I have only the instinct to go on. Hi,' he shouted to the waiter who was hovering at the distant end of the terrace. '*Encore, encore! Trois verres, s'il vous plaît.*'

'Oh no,' murmured Miss Ticher.

Miss Grimshaw laughed.

'An unmarried woman like yourselves,' said Quillan, 'who wanted a child. I would be a different man today if she had succeeded in doing what she wanted to do. She would have taken me away to another town, maybe to Cork, or up to Dublin. I would have different memories now. D'you understand me, Miss Grimshaw?'

The waiter came with the drinks. He took away the used glasses.

'If I close my eyes,' said Quillan, 'I can see the whole episode: the woman bent over the pram and her hands going out to the orphan child. And then the aunt comes out of Pasley's and asks her what she thinks she's doing. I remember one time the aunt beating me on the legs with a bramble stick. I used eat things from the kitchen cupboard. I used bite into Chivers' jellies, I well remember that.' He paused. He said: 'If ever you're down that way, go into Youghal. It's a great place for fresh fish.'

Miss Grimshaw heard voices and looked past Miss Ticher and saw a man and a woman leaving the hotel. They stood for a moment beside the waiter at the far end of the terrace. The woman laughed. The waiter went away.

'That's the pair,' said Quillan. 'They're checking out.'

He tilted his glass, draining a quantity of whisky into his mouth.

The man, wearing dark glasses and dressed in red trousers and a black leather jacket, lit his companion's cigarette. His arm was on the woman's shoulder. The waiter brought them each a drink.

'Are they looking this way, Miss Grimshaw?'

He crouched in the deck-chair, anxious not to be observed. Miss Grimshaw said the man and the woman seemed to be absorbed in one another.

'A right couple to be following around,' Quillan said with sarcasm and a hint of bitterness. 'A right vicious couple.'

Suddenly and to Miss Grimshaw's discomfiture, Miss Ticher stretched out an arm and touched with the tips of her fingers the back of the detective's large hand. 'I'm sorry,' Miss Ticher said quietly. 'I'm sorry your parents were drowned. I'm sorry you don't like the work you do.'

He shrugged away the sympathy, although he seemed not surprised to have received it. He said again that if his parents had not drowned he would not be the man they saw in front of them. He was obsessed by that idea, Miss Grimshaw considered. If the woman had succeeded in taking him from the pram he would not be the man he was either, he said: he'd had no luck in his childhood. 'It's a nice little seaside resort and yet I can never think of it without a shiver because of the bad luck that was there for me. When I think of the black iron gate and the uncle sweating in the Ford car I think of everything else as well. The woman wanted a child, Miss Ticher. A child needs love.'

'A woman too,' whispered Miss Ticher.

'But the woman's a figment of Mr Quillan's imagination,' Miss Grimshaw said with a laugh. 'He made up the story to suit some face in his mind. Couldn't it be, Mr Quillan, that the woman's face was the face of any woman at all?'

'Ah, of course, of course,' agreed Quillan, glancing surreptitiously at the couple he was employed to glance at. 'You can never know certainly about a business like that.'

The couple, having finished their two drinks, descended a flight of stone steps that led from the terrace to the terrace below, and then went on down to the courtyard of the hotel. The waiter followed them, carrying their luggage. Quillan stood up.

Miss Ticher imagined ironing his blazer. She imagined his face as a child. For a moment, affected as she afterwards thought by the red aperitif, it seemed that Miss Grimshaw was the stranger: Miss Grimshaw was a round woman, unknown to either of them, who had materialized suddenly, looking for a chat. Having no one's blazer to iron herself, Miss Grimshaw was jealous, for in her life she had known only friendship.

'In 1934,' said Miss Ticher, 'when you were five months old, Mr Quillan, I was still hopeful of marriage. A few years later I would have understood the woman who wished to take you from your pram.'

Miss Ticher's face was crimson as she spoke those words. She saw Miss Grimshaw looking at it. She saw her looking at her as she clambered to her feet and held a hand out to the detective. 'Goodbye,' Miss Ticher said. 'It was nice to hear your childhood memories.'

He went away in his abrupt manner. They watched him walking the length of the terrace. Miss Ticher watched his descent to the courtyard.

'My dear,' said Miss Grimshaw with her laugh, 'he bowled you over.' The story for the common-room was even better now. 'A fat man,' Miss Grimshaw heard herself saying on the first evening of term, 'who talked to Agnes about his childhood memories in a place called Youghal. He had fantasies as well, about some woman pilfering him from his pram, as though a woman would. In her tipsiness Agnes entered into all of it. I thought she'd cry.'

Miss Ticher sat down and sipped the drink the man had bought her. Miss Grimshaw said:

'Thank heavens he's not staying here.'

'You shouldn't have said he made up that story.'

'Why ever not?'

'You hurt him.'

'Hurt him?' cried Miss Grimshaw.

'He's the victim of his wretched childhood –'

'You're tipsy, Agnes.'

Miss Ticher drank the last of her red aperitif, and Miss Grimshaw glared through her shining spectacles, thinking that her friend looked as if she'd just put down a cheap romantic novel.

'It's time for lunch,' announced Miss Grimshaw snappishly, rising to her feet. 'Come on now.'

Miss Ticher shook her head. 'Near the lighthouse there's a shop,' she said, 'that sold in those days Rainbow Toffees. A woman like you or me might have seen there a child who ran away from loneliness.'

'Lunch, dear,' said Miss Grimshaw.

'How very cruel the world is.'

Miss Grimshaw, who in reply had been about to say with asperity that no one must let emotional nonsense play tricks on the imagination, instead said nothing at all. Three unnamed drinks and the conversation of a grubby detective had taken an absurd toll of Agnes Ticher in the broad light of day. Miss Grimshaw no longer wished to think about the matter; she did not wish to recall the words that Agnes Ticher in her tipsiness had spoken, nor ever now to retail the episode in the common-room; it was better not to dwell on any of it. They were, after all, friends and there could remain unspoken secrets between them.

'It is all second best,' said the voice of Agnes Ticher, but when Miss Grimshaw looked at her friend she knew that Miss Ticher had not spoken. Miss Grimshaw went away, jangling the shells in the yellow plastic bag and screening from her mind the thoughts that were attempting to invade it. There was a smell of garlic on the air, and from the kitchen came the rich odour of the local bouillabaisse, the favourite dish of both of them.

The Table

In a public library, looking through the appropriate columns in a business-like way, Mr Jeffs came across the Hammonds' advertisement in *The Times*. It contained a telephone number which he noted down on a scrap of paper and which he telephoned later that same day.

'Yes,' said Mrs Hammond vaguely, 'I think this table is still for sale. Let me just go and look.'

Mr Jeffs saw her in his mind's eye going to look. He visualized a fattish, middle-aged woman with light-blue hair, and shapely legs coming out of narrow shoes.

'It is my husband's affair, really,' explained Mrs Hammond. 'Or I suppose it is. Although strictly speaking the table is my property. Left to me by my grandmother. Yes, it's still there. No one, I'm sure, has yet made an offer for this table.'

'In that case –' said Mr Jeffs.

'It was foolish of me to imagine that my husband might have had an offer, or that he might have sold it. He would naturally not have done so without consultation between us. It being my table, really. Although he worded the advertisement and saw to putting it in the paper. I have a daughter at the toddling stage, Mr Jeffs. I'm often too exhausted to think about the composition of advertisements.'

'A little daughter. Well, that is nice,' said Mr Jeffs, looking at the ceiling and not smiling. 'You're kept busy, eh?'

'Why not come round if the table interests? It's completely genuine and is often commented upon.'

'I will do that,' announced Mr Jeffs, naming an hour.

Replacing the receiver, Mr Jeffs, a small man, a dealer in furniture, considered the voice of Mrs Hammond. He wondered if the voice belonged to a woman who knew her p's and q's where antique furniture was concerned. He had been wrong, quite clearly, to have seen her as middle-aged and plumpish. She was younger if she had a toddling child, and because she had spoken of exhaustion he visualized her again, this time in soft slippers, with a strand of hair across her forehead. 'It's a cultured voice,' said Mr Jeffs to himself and went on to believe that there was money in the Hammond house, and probably a maid or two, in spite of the protest about exhaustion. Mr Jeffs, who had made his small fortune through his attention to such nagging details, walked on the bare boards of his Victorian house, sniffing the air and considering afresh. All about him furniture was stacked, just purchased, waiting to be sold again.

Mrs Hammond forgot about Mr Jeffs almost as soon as his voice ceased to echo in her consciousness. Nothing about Mr Jeffs remained with her because as she had conversed with him no image had formed in her mind, as one had in his. She thought of Mr Jeffs as a shop person, as a voice that might interrupt a grocery order or a voice in the jewellery department of Liberty's. When her *au pair* girl announced the presence of Mr Jeffs at the appointed hour, Mrs Hammond frowned and said: 'My dear Ursula, you've certainly got this name wrong.' But the girl insisted. She stood with firmness in front of her mistress repeating that a Mr Jeffs had called by appointment. 'Heavens!' cried Mrs Hammond eventually. 'How extraordinarily stupid of me! This is the new man for the windows. Tell him to go at them immediately. The kitchen ones first so that he gets them over with while he's still mellow. They're as black as your boot.'

So it was that Mr Jeffs was led into the Hammonds' kitchen by a girl from central Switzerland and told abruptly, though not intentionally so, to clean the windows.

'What?' said Mr Jeffs.

'Start with the kitchen, Mrs Hammond says, since they have most filth on them. There is hot water in the tap.'

'No,' said Mr Jeffs. 'I've come to see a table.'

'I myself have scrubbed the table. You may stand on it if you place a newspaper underneath your feet.'

Ursula left Mr Jeffs at this juncture, although he had already begun to speak again. She felt she could not stand there talking to window-cleaners, since she was not employed in the house to do that.

'He is a funny man,' she reported to Mrs Hammond. 'He wanted to wash the table too.'

'My name is Jeffs,' said Mr Jeffs, standing at the door, holding his stiff black hat. 'I have come about the console table.'

'How odd!' murmured Mrs Hammond, and was about to add that here indeed was a coincidence since at that very moment a man called Jeffs was cleaning her kitchen windows. 'Oh my God!' she cried instead. 'Oh, Mr Jeffs, what a terrible thing!'

It was this confusion, this silly error that Mrs Hammond quite admitted was all her fault, that persuaded her to let Mr Jeffs have the table. Mr Jeffs, standing with his hat, had recognized a certain psychological advantage and had pressed it imperceptibly home. He saw that Mrs

Hammond, beneath the exterior of her manner, was concerned lest he might have felt himself slighted. She is a nice woman, he thought, in the way in which a person buying meat decides that a piece is succulent. She is a nice person, he assured himself, and will therefore be the easier and the quicker to deal with. He was correct in his surmise. There was a prick of guilt in Mrs Hammond's face: he saw it arrive there as the explanation dawned on her and as she registered that he was a dealer in antiques, one with the features and the accents of a London Jew. She is afraid I am thinking her anti-Semitic, thought Mr Jeffs, well pleased with himself. He named a low price, which was immediately accepted.

'I've been clever,' said Mrs Hammond to her husband. 'I have sold the console table to a little man called Mr Jeffs whom Ursula and I at first mistook for a window-cleaner.'

Mr Jeffs put a chalk mark on the table and made a note of it in a notebook. He sat in the kitchen of his large house, eating kippers that he had cooked in a plastic bag. His jaws moved slowly and slightly, pulping the fish as a machine might. He didn't pay much attention to the taste in his mouth: he was thinking that if he sold the table to Sir Andrew Charles he could probably rely on a hundred per cent profit, or even more.

'An everyday story of country folk,' said a voice on Mr Jeffs' old wireless, and Mr Jeffs rose and carried the plate from which he had eaten to the sink. He wiped his hands on a tea-cloth and climbed the stairs to the telephone.

Sir Andrew was in Africa, a woman said, and might not be back for a month. It was far from certain when he would return, but it would be a month at least. Mr Jeffs said nothing more. He nodded to himself, but the woman in Sir Andrew Charles' house, unaware of this confirmation, reflected that the man was ill-mannered not to acknowledge what she was saying.

Mr Jeffs made a further note in his notebook, a reminder to telephone Sir Andrew in six weeks' time. As it happened, however, this note was unnecessary, because three days later Mr Jeffs received a telephone call from Mrs Hammond's husband, who asked him if he still had the table. Mr Jeffs made a pretence of looking, and replied after a moment that he rather thought he had.

'In that case,' said Mrs Hammond's husband, 'I rather think I would like to buy it back.'

Mr Hammond announced his intention of coming round. He contradicted himself by saying that it was really a friend of his who wanted the table and that he would bring his friend round too, if that was all right with Mr Jeffs.

'Bring whomsoever you wish,' said Mr Jeffs. He felt awkward in advance: he would have to say to Mr Hammond or to Mr Hammond's friend that the price of the table had doubled itself in three days. He would not put it like that, but Mr Hammond would recognize that that was what it amounted to.

Mr Jeffs was in the kitchen, drinking tea, when they called. He blew at the mug of tea, not wishing to leave it there, for he disapproved of waste. He drank most of it and wiped his lips with the tea-cloth. The door-bell sounded again and Mr Jeffs hastened to answer it.

'I am the nigger in the woodpile,' said a Mrs Galbally, who was standing with Hammond. 'It is I who cause all this nonsense over a table.'

'Mrs Galbally hasn't ever seen it,' Hammond explained. 'She, too, answered our advertisement, but you, alas, had snaffled the treasure up.'

'Come into the house,' said Mr Jeffs, leading the way to the room with the table in it. He turned to Mrs Galbally, pointing with one hand. 'There it is, Mrs Galbally. You are quite at liberty to purchase it, though I had earmarked it for another, a client in Africa who has been looking for that very thing and who would pay an exceedingly handsome price. I am just warning you of that. It seems only fair.'

But when Mr Jeffs named the figure he had in mind neither Mrs Galbally nor Hammond turned a hair. Hammond drew out a cheque-book and at once inscribed a cheque. 'Can you deliver it?' he asked.

'Oh yes,' said Mr Jeffs, 'provided it is not too far away. There will be a small delivery charge to cover everything, insurance in transit, etcetera. Four pounds four.'

Mr Jeffs drove his Austin van to the address that Hammond had given him. On the way, he reckoned what his profit on this journey of three-quarters of an hour would be: a quarter of a gallon of petrol would come to one and three; subtracting that from four guineas, he was left with four pounds two and ninepence. Mr Jeffs did not count his time: he considered it of little value. He would have spent the three-quarters of an hour standing about in his large house, or moving himself to keep his circulation going. It was not a bad profit, he decided, and he began to think of Mrs Galbally and Hammond, and of Mrs Hammond who had mistaken him for a window-cleaner. He guessed that Hammond and Mrs Galbally were up to something, but it was a funny way in which to be up to something, buying antique tables and having them delivered.

'They are conducting an affair,' said Mr Jeffs to himself. 'They met because the table was up for sale and are now romantic over it.' He saw the scene clearly: the beautiful Mrs Galbally arriving at the Hammonds' house, explaining that she had come about the table. Perhaps she had made a bit of a scene, reminding the Hammonds that she had previously telephoned and had been told to come. 'And now I find the table is already disposed of,' said Mrs Galbally in Mr Jeffs' imagination. 'You should have telephoned me back, for God's sake! I am a busy creature.'

'Come straight in, Mrs Galbally and have a glass of brandy,' cried Hammond in Mr Jeffs' mind. 'How can we make amends?'

'It is all my fault,' explained Mrs Hammond. 'I've been quite hopelessly scatty, placing our beautiful table in the hands of a Jewish trader. A Mr Jeffs whom Ursula in her foreign ignorance ordered to wash down the kitchen windows.'

'The table has brought nothing but embarrassment,' said Hammond, pouring out a fair quantity of brandy. 'Have this, Mrs Galbally. And have a nut or two. Do.'

'I had quite set my heart on that table,' said Mrs Galbally in Mr Jeffs' mind. 'I am disappointed unto tears.'

'A table for Mrs Galbally,' said Mr Jeffs to a woman with a shopping basket who was leaving the block of flats.

'Oh yes?' said the woman.

'Which floor, please? I have been given this address.'

'No one of that name at all,' said the woman. 'I never heard of no Galbally.'

'She may be new here. Is there an empty flat? It tells you nothing on these bells.'

'I'm not at liberty,' said the woman, her voice striking a high pitch. 'I'm not at liberty to give out information about the tenants in these flats. Not to a man in a closed van. I don't know you from Adam.'

Mr Jeffs recognized the woman as a charwoman and thereafter ignored her, although she stood on the steps, close to him, watching his movements. He rang one of the bells and a middle-aged woman opened the door and said, when Mr Jeffs had inquired, that everyone was new in the flats, the flats themselves being new. She advised him quite pleasantly to ring the top bell, the one that connected apparently with two small attic rooms.

'Ah, Mr Jeffs,' said the beautiful Mrs Galbally a moment later. 'So you got here.'

Mr Jeffs unloaded the table from the van and carried it up the steps. The charwoman was still about. She was saying to Mrs Galbally that she would clean out the place for six shillings an hour whenever it was suitable or desired.

Mr Jeffs placed the table in the smaller of the two attic rooms. The room was empty except for some rolled-up carpeting and a standard lamp.

The door of the second room was closed: he imagined it contained a bed and a wardrobe and two brandy glasses on a bedside table. In time, Mr Jeffs imagined, the whole place would be extremely luxurious. 'A love-nest,' he said to himself.

'Well, thank you, Mr Jeffs,' said Mrs Galbally.

'I must charge you an extra pound. You are probably unaware, Mrs Galbally that it is obligatory and according to the antique dealers' association to charge one pound when goods have to be moved up a staircase. I could be struck off if I did not make this small charge.'

'A pound? I thought Mr Hammond had –'

'It is to do with the stairs. I must honour the rules of the antique dealers' association. For myself, I would easily waive it, but I have, you understand, my biennial returns to make.'

Mrs Galbally found her handbag and handed him a five-pound note. He gave her back three pounds and sixteen shillings, all the change he claimed to have.

'Imagine it!' exclaimed Mrs Galbally. 'I thought that cleaning woman must be your wife come to help you carry the thing. I couldn't understand why she was suddenly talking about six shillings an hour. She's just what I'm looking for.'

Mr Jeffs thought that it was rather like Mrs Hammond's *au pair* girl making the mistake about the window-cleaner. He thought that but he did not say it. He imagined Mrs Galbally recounting the details of the episode at some later hour, recounting them to Hammond as they lay in the other room, smoking cigarettes or involved with one another's flesh. 'I thought she was the little Jew's wife. I thought it was a family business, the way these people often have. I was surprised beyond measure when she mentioned about cleaning.'

Naturally enough, Mr Jeffs thought that he had seen the end of the matter. A Louis XVI console table, once the property of Mrs Hammond's grandmother, was now the property of her husband's mistress, or the joint property of husband and mistress, Mr Jeffs was not sure. It was all quite interesting, Mr Jeffs supposed, but he had other matters to concern him: he had further furniture to accumulate and to sell at the right moment; he had a living to make, he assured himself.

But a day or two after the day on which he had delivered the table to Mrs Galbally he received a telephone call from Mrs Hammond.

'Am I speaking to Mr Jeffs?' said Mrs Hammond.

'Yes, this is he. Jeffs here.'

'This is Mrs Hammond. I wonder if you remember, I sold you a table.'

'I remember you perfectly, Mrs Hammond. We were amused at an error.' Mr Jeffs made a noise that he trusted would sound like laughter. He was looking at the ceiling, without smiling.

'The thing is,' said Mrs Hammond, 'are you by any chance still in possession of that table? Because if you are I think perhaps I had better come round and see you.'

There rushed into Mr Jeffs' mind the vision of further attic rooms, of Mrs Hammond furnishing them with the table and anything else she could lay her hands on. He saw Mrs Hammond walking down a street, looking at beds and carpets in shop windows, her elbow grasped by a man who was not her husband.

'Hullo, Mr Jeffs,' said Mrs Hammond. 'Are you there?'

'Yes, I am here,' said Mr Jeffs. 'I am standing here listening to you, madam.'

'Well?' said Mrs Hammond.

'I'm sorry to disappoint you about the table.'

'You mean it's sold? Already?'

'I'm afraid that is the case.'

'Oh God in heaven!'

'I have other tables here. In excellent condition and keenly priced. You might not find a visit here a waste of time.'

'No, no.'

'I do not as a rule conduct my business in that way: customers coming into my house and that. But in your case, since we are known to one another –'

'It wouldn't do. I mean, it's only the table I sold you I am possibly interested in. Mr Jeffs, can you quickly give me the name and address of the person who bought it?'

This question caught Mr Jeffs off his guard, so he at once replaced the telephone receiver. Mrs Hammond came through again a moment or so later, after he had had time to think. He said:

'We were cut off, Mrs Hammond. There is something the matter with the line. Sir Andrew Charles was twice cut off this morning, phoning from Nigeria. I do apologize.'

'I was saying, Mr Jeffs, that I would like to have the name and address of the person who bought the table.'

'I cannot divulge that, Mrs Hammond. I'm afraid divulgences of that nature are very much against the rules of the antique dealers' association. I could be struck off for such a misdemeanour.'

'Oh dear. Oh dear, Mr Jeffs. Then what am I to do? Whatever is the answer?'

'Is this important? There are ways and means. I could, for instance, act as your agent. I could approach the owner of the table in that guise and attempt to do my best.'

'Would you, Mr Jeffs? That is most kind.'

'I would have to charge the customary agent's fee. I am sorry about that, Mrs Hammond, but the association does not permit otherwise.'

'Yes, yes, of course.'

'Shall I tell you about that fee, how it's worked out and what it may amount to? It's not much, a percentage.'

'We can fix that up afterwards.'

'Well, fine,' said Mr Jeffs, who meant when he spoke of a percentage thirty-three and a third.

'Please go up to twice the price you paid me. If it seems to be going higher I'd be grateful if you'd telephone for instructions.'

'That's the usual thing, Mrs Hammond.'

'But do please try and keep the price down. Naturally.'

'I'll be in touch, Mrs Hammond.'

Walking about his house, shaking his body to keep his circulation in trim, Mr Jeffs wondered if tables nowadays had a part to play in lovers' fantasies. It was in his interest to find out, he decided, since he could accumulate tables of the correct kind and advertise them astutely. He thought for a while longer and then entered his van. He drove it to Mrs Galbally's attic room, taking a chance on finding her there.

'Why, Mr Jeffs,' said Mrs Galbally.

'Yes,' said Mr Jeffs.

She led him upstairs, trailing her curiosity behind her. She is thinking, he thought, that I have come to sell her another thing or two, but she does not care to order me out in case she is wrong, in case I have come to blackmail her.

'Well, Mr Jeffs, what can I do for you?'

'I have had a handsome offer for the Louis XVI table. Or a fairly handsome offer. Or an offer that might be turned into an exceedingly handsome offer. Do you take my meaning?'

'But the table is mine. Are you telling me you wish to buy it back?'

'I am saying something of the kind. I received hint of this offer and thought I should let you know at once. "I will act as Mrs Galbally's agent," I said to myself, "in case she is at all tempted to dispose of the article at one and a half times what she paid for it."'

'Oh, but no, Mr Jeffs.'

'You are not interested?'

'Not at all, I'm afraid.'

'Suppose my client goes up to twice the price? How would you feel about that? Or how would Mr Hammond feel about that?'

'Mr Hammond?'

'Well, I am not quite certain who owns the article. That is why I mention the gentleman. Perhaps I should have contacted him. It was Mr Hammond who gave me the cheque.'

'The table is mine. A gift. I would rather you didn't contact Mr Hammond.'

'Well, that is that, then. But since I have acted in your interest in this matter, Mrs Galbally, thinking that I should report the offer to you without delay and involving myself in travelling expenses etcetera, I'm afraid I shall have to charge you the usual agent's fee. It is the ruling of the antique dealers' association that a fee be charged on such occasions. I feel you understand?'

Mrs Galbally said she did understand. She gave him some money, and Mr Jeffs took his leave.

In his house Mr Jeffs considered for a further hour. Eventually he thought it wise to telephone Mrs Hammond and ascertain her husband's office telephone number. He went out on to the street with a piece of paper in his hand which stated that he was deaf and dumb and wished urgently to have a telephone call made for him. He handed this to an elderly woman, pointing to a telephone booth.

'May I know your husband's office telephone number?' said the woman to Mrs Hammond. 'It's a matter of urgency.'

'But who are you?'

'I am a Mrs Lacey, and I am phoning you on behalf of Sir Andrew Charles of Africa.'

'I've heard that name before,' said Mrs Hammond, and gave the telephone number of her husband's office.

'You say you have been to see Mrs Galbally,' said Hammond. 'And what did she say?'

'I don't believe she fully understood what was at stake. I don't think she got the message.'

'The table was a gift from me to Mrs Galbally. I can hardly ask for it back.'

'This is an excellent offer, Mr Hammond.'

'Oh, I don't dispute that.'

'I was wondering if you could use your influence with Mrs Galbally, that's all. If you happen to be seeing her, that is.'

'I'll ring you back, Mr Jeffs.'

Mr Jeffs said thank you and then telephoned Mrs Hammond. 'Negotiations are under way,' he said.

But two days later negotiations broke down. Hammond telephoned Mr Jeffs to say that the table was to remain the property of Mrs Galbally. Mr Jeffs, sorrowfully, decided to drive round to tell Mrs Hammond, so that he could collect what little was owing him. He would tell her, he decided, and that would surely now be the end of the matter.

'I'm afraid I have come up against a stone wall,' he reported. 'I'm sorry, Mrs Hammond, about that, and I would trouble you now only for what is owing.'

He mentioned the sum, but Mrs Hammond seemed not to hear clearly. Tears rolled down her cheeks and left marks on the powder on her face. She took no notice of Mr Jeffs. She sobbed and shook, and further tears dropped from her eyes.

In the end Mrs Hammond left the room. Mr Jeffs remained because he had, of course, to wait for the money owing to him. He sat there examining the furniture and thinking it odd of Mrs Hammond to have cried so passionately and for so long. The *au pair* girl came in with a tray of tea for him, blushing as she arranged it, remembering, he imagined, the orders she had given him as regards the windows. He poured himself some tea and ate two pieces of shortbread. It was very quiet in the room, as though a funeral had taken place.

'Whoever are you?' said a child, a small girl of five.

Mr Jeffs looked at her and endeavoured to smile, forcing his lips back from his teeth.

'My name is Mr Jeffs. What is your name?'

'My name is Emma Hammond. Why are you having tea in our house?'

'Because it was kindly brought to me.'

'What is the matter with your mouth?'

'That is how my mouth is made. Are you a good little girl?'

'But why are you waiting here?'

'Because I have to collect something that your mother has arranged to give me. A little money.'

'A little money? Are you poor?'

'It is money owing to me.'

'Run along, Emma,' said Mrs Hammond from the door, and when the child had gone she said:

'I apologize, Mr Jeffs.'

She wrote him a cheque. He watched her, thinking of Hammond and Mrs Galbally and the table, all together in the attic rooms at the top of the big block of flats. He wondered what was going to happen. He supposed

Mrs Hammond would be left with the child. Perhaps Mrs Galbally would marry Hammond then; perhaps they would come to this house and bring the table back with them, since Mrs Galbally was so attached to it, and perhaps they would take on the same *au pair* girl, and perhaps Mrs Hammond and the child would go to live in the attic rooms. They were all of a kind, Mr Jeffs decided: even the child seemed tarred with her elders' sophistication. But if sides were to be taken, he liked Mrs Hammond best. He had heard of women going berserk in such circumstances, taking their lives even. He hoped Mrs Hammond would not do that.

'Let me tell you, Mr Jeffs,' said Mrs Hammond.

'Oh now, it doesn't matter.'

'The table belonged to my grandmother, who died and left it to me in her will.'

'Do not fret, Mrs Hammond. It's all perfectly all right.'

'We thought it ugly, my husband and I, so we decided to be rid of it.'

'Your husband thought it was ugly?'

'Well, yes. But I more than he. He doesn't notice things so much.'

Mr Jeffs thought that he had noticed Mrs Galbally all right when Mrs Galbally had walked into this house. Mrs Hammond was lying her head off, he said to himself, because she was trying to save face: she knew quite well where the table was, she had known all along. She had wept because she could not bear the thought of it, her grandmother's ugly table in the abode of sin.

'So we put in an advertisement. We had only two replies. You and a woman.'

Mr Jeffs stood up, preparatory to going.

'You see,' said Mrs Hammond, 'we don't have room in a place like this for a table like that. It doesn't fit in. Well, you can see for yourself.'

Mr Jeffs looked hard at her, not into her eyes or even at her face: he looked hard and seriously at the green wool of her dress. The woman said:

'But almost as soon as it had gone I regretted everything. I remember the table all my life. My grandmother had left it to me as an act of affection as well as generosity.'

Mr Jeffs reckoned that the table had stood in the grandmother's hall. He reckoned that Mrs Hammond as a child had been banished from rooms and had been bidden to stand by the table in the hall, crying and moaning. The table had mocked her childhood and it was mocking her again, with silent watching in an attic room. He could see the two of them, Mrs Galbally and Hammond, placing their big bulbous brandy glasses on the table and marching toward one another for a slick kiss.

'Once I had sold it to you I couldn't get it out of my mind. I remembered that my grandmother had always promised it to me. She was the only one who was kind to me as a child, Mr Jeffs. I felt that truly I had thrown all her love back at her. Every night since I sold it to you I've had wretched dreams. So you see why I was so very upset.'

The grandmother was cruel, thought Mr Jeffs. The grandmother punished the child every hour of the day, and left the table as a reminder of her autocratic soul. Why could not Mrs Hammond speak the truth? Why could she not say that the spirit of the old dead grandmother had passed into the table and that the spirit and the table were laughing their heads off in Mrs Galbally's room? Imagine, thought Mr Jeffs, a woman going to such lengths, and a woman whom he had passingly respected.

'I'm sorry I've burdened you with all this, Mr Jeffs. I'm sorry it's been such a bother. You have a kindly face.'

'I am a Jewish dealer, madam. I have a Jewish nose; I am not handsome; I cannot smile.'

He was angry because he thought that she was patronizing him. She was lying still, and all of a sudden she was including him in her lies. She was insulting him with her talk of his face. Did she know his faults, his weaknesses? How dare she speak so?

'The table should have passed from me to my daughter. It should have stayed in the family. I didn't think.'

Mr Jeffs allowed himself to close his eyes. She can sit there telling those lies, he thought, one after another, while her own child plays innocently in the next room. The child will become a liar too. The child in her time will grow to be a woman who must cover up the humiliations she has suffered, who must put a face on things, and make the situation respectable with falsehoods.

With his eyes closed and his voice speaking in his mind, Mr Jeffs saw the figure of himself standing alone in his large Victorian house. Nothing was permanent in the house, not a stick of furniture remained there month by month. He sold and bought again. He laid no carpets, nor would he ever. He owned but the old wireless set because someone once had told him it was worthless.

'Why are you telling me lies?' shouted Mr Jeffs. 'Why can't you say the truth?'

He heard his voice shouting those words at Mrs Hammond and he saw the image of himself, standing quietly on the bare boards of his house. It was not his way to go shouting at people, or becoming involved, or wishing for lies to cease. These people were a law unto themselves; they did not concern him. He cooked his own food; he did not bother people.

'Your grandmother is dead and buried,' said Mr Jeffs to his amazement.

'It is Mrs Galbally who is alive. She takes her clothes off, Mrs Hammond, and in comes your husband and takes off his. And the table sees. The table you have always known. Your childhood table sees it all and you cannot bear it. Why not be honest, Mrs Hammond? Why not say straight out to me: "Jew man, bargain with this Mrs Galbally and let me have my childhood table back." I understand you, Mrs Hammond. I understand all that. I will trade anything on God's earth, Mrs Hammond, but I understand that.'

There was a silence again in the room, and in it Mr Jeffs moved his eyes around until their gaze alighted on the face of Mrs Hammond. He saw the face sway, gently, from side to side, for Mrs Hammond was shaking her head. 'I did not know any of that,' Mrs Hammond was saying. Her head ceased to shake: she seemed like a statue.

Mr Jeffs rose and walked through the deep silence to the door. He turned then, and walked back again, for he had left behind him Mrs Hammond's cheque. She seemed not to notice his movements and he considered it wiser in the circumstances not to utter the sounds of farewell. He left the house and started up the engine of his Austin van.

He saw the scene differently as he drove away: Mrs Hammond hanging her head and he himself saying that the lies were understandable. He might have brought Mrs Hammond a crumb of comfort, a word or two, a subtle shrug of the shoulder. Instead, in his clumsiness, he had brought her a shock that had struck her a blow. She would sit there, he imagined, just as he had left her, her face white, her body crouched over her sorrow; she would sit like that until her husband breezily arrived. And she would look at him in his breeziness and say: 'The Jewish dealer has been and gone. He was there in that chair and he told me that Mrs Galbally has opened up a love-nest for you.'

Mr Jeffs drove on, aware of a sadness but aware as well that his mind was slowly emptying itself of Mrs Hammond and her husband and the beautiful Mrs Galbally. 'I cook my own food,' said Mr Jeffs aloud. 'I am a good trader, and I do not bother anyone.' He had no right to hope that he might have offered comfort. He had no business to take such things upon himself, to imagine that a passage of sympathy might have developed between himself and Mrs Hammond.

'I cook my own food,' said Mr Jeffs again. 'I do not bother anyone.' He drove in silence after that, thinking of nothing at all. The chill of sadness had left him, and the mistake he had made appeared to him as a fact that could not be remedied. He noticed that dusk was falling; and he returned to the house where he had never lit a fire, where the furniture loomed and did not smile at him, where nobody wept and nobody told a lie.

A School Story

Every night after lights-out in the dormitory there was a ceremonial story-telling. One by one we contributed our pieces, holding the stage from the gloom for five or six minutes apiece. Many offerings were of a trite enough order: the Englishman, the Irishman and the Scotsman on a series of desert islands, and what the drunk said to the Pope. But often the stories were real: reminiscences from a short past, snippets of overheard conversation, descriptions of the naked female body in unguarded moments. Only Markham deliberately repeated himself, telling us again and again, and by unanimous demand, about the death of his mother. On a night when no one had much to say, Markham would invariably be called upon; and none of us ever expected to hear anything new. We were satisfied that it was so; because Markham told his story well and it was, to us, a fascinating one.

'It was like this, you see. One Sunday morning my father and I were walking up Tavistock Hill and I asked him to tell me about my mother. It was a good sunny morning in early May and my father looked up at the sky and started on about how beautiful she'd been. So then, when I could get a word in, I asked him about how she'd died and that. Well, he took an extra breath or two and said to prepare myself. I assured him I was well prepared, and then he told me about how they had been staying with these friends in Florence and how they had set out to the hills to do some shooting. They rode out in a great Italian shooting-brake and soon they were slaying the birds like nobody's business. But in the middle of everything there was this accident and my mother was lying in a pool of blood and all the Italians were throwing up their hands and saying "Blessed Mother of Jesus, what a terrible thing!" I said: "Did her gun go off by accident? Was she not carrying it correctly or what?" And my father said it wasn't like that at all, it was his gun that went off by accident and what a shocking thing it was to be the instrument of one's wife's slaughter. Well, sharp as a knife I could see the lie in his face and I said to myself: "Accident, forsooth! Murder more like." Or, anyway, words to that effect. You'll understand with a discovery like that fresh on the mind one is in an emotional tizzy and apt to forget the exact order of thinking. Why was I certain? I'll tell you, boys, why I was certain: because within a six-month the father had married the dead mother's sister. My stepmother to this day. And I'll tell you another thing: I have plans laid to wipe out those two with a couple of swoops of a butcher's knife. Am I not, when all's said and done, a veritable pocket Hamlet? And isn't it right that I should dream at night of the sharpening of the knife?'

Markham had a long, rather serious face; deeply set, very blue eyes; and smooth fair hair the colour of yellow terracotta. People liked him, but nobody knew him very well. His stories about his family and the threats they exposed were taken only half seriously; and when he talked in this way he seemed to be speaking outside his role. Markham was too quiet, too pleasant, too attractive to be mixed up in this way. There was something wrong, not so much with what he said – which we quite understood, whether we thought of it as fact or not – as with Markham's saying it. That at least is how it appears in retrospect, to me and to the others with whom I have since discussed it. Then, we scarcely analyzed our feelings; after all, we were only fifteen at the time of the Markham affair.

'I've got some bread from Dining Hall,' Williams said. 'Let's toast it in the boilerhouse.' He drew from beneath his jacket four rounds of hard-looking bread and a couple of pieces of straightened wire. His small red-rimmed eyes darted about my face as though seeking some minute, mislaid article. He held out a piece of wire and I took it from him, already recognizing its utter uselessness for the task in hand. One had to open the top of the boiler and toast from above, guiding the bread far into the bowels of the ironwork until it was poised neatly above the glowing coke. It was a business of expertise, and a single length of wire in place of an expanding toasting fork indicated rudimentary disaster.

It was mid-afternoon and, recovering from a cold, I was 'off games'. Williams, who suffered from asthma, was rarely seen on the games field. He disliked any form of physical exercise and he used his disability as an excuse to spend solitary afternoons hanging around the classrooms or enjoying a read and a smoke in the lavatories. He was despised for his laziness, his unprepossessing appearance, and his passion for deception. I said I would join him on his expedition to the boilerhouse.

'I've snitched some jam,' he said, 'and a pat or two of butter.'

We walked in silence, Williams occasionally glancing over his shoulder in his customary furtive manner. In the boilerhouse he laid the bread on the seat of the boilerman's chair and extracted the jam and butter from the depths of his clothes. They were separately wrapped in two sheets of paper torn from an exercise book. The jam was raspberry and contact with the paper had caused the ruled lines to run. Fearing the effects of this, I said at once that as far as I was concerned the addition of butter was quite sufficient.

The toast was badly burnt and tasted of smoke. Williams ate his ravenously, wiping his fingers on his trouser pockets. I nibbled at mine and eventually threw it into the corner. At this Williams expostulated, picked up the discarded piece, wiped it and smeared on the remains of the jam. He made a crunching noise as he ate, and explained that his inordinate appetite was due to the presence of worms in his body.

There was a footfall on the steps outside and a moment later a figure appeared, sharply silhouetted in the doorway. We could not at first establish its identity, and Williams, speaking loudly, said to me: 'It has been well worth while. The knowledge we have gained of our school's heating system will stand us in good stead. It is well to put a use to one's time in this way.' The figure advanced, and Williams, seeing that it was not the headmaster, sniggered. 'It's only bloody Markham,' he said. 'I thought it was Bodger at least.'

'I have come to smoke,' Markham announced, offering each of us a small, thin cigar.

'When I am fully grown and equipped for life,' Williams said, 'I intend to pursue a legal career. As well, I shall smoke only the most expensive cigars. One can well afford such a policy if one makes a success of the law.'

Markham and I, concerned with the lighting of our tobacco, heard this pronouncement in silence.

'It may be,' Williams went on, 'that I shall learn in time to roll the leaves together myself. The female thigh, I understand, is just the instrument for such a chore.'

'Williams will make an excellent lawyer,' Markham remarked.

'Certainly he will be splendid beneath his wig,' I said.

'And what,' Williams asked, 'do you intend to do with your years, Markham?'

'Oh, they are well numbered. I shall hang quite soon for the slaughter of my father.'

'Would you not wait a while that I might defend you?'

'It is not an action you could readily defend surely? I am guilty already. I would prefer not to die, but I would not wish to dissociate myself from my crime.'

Williams, puffing hard and with the cigar clamped in the centre of his teeth, said:

'Markham's a bloody madman, eh?'

'Damn it, isn't it correct that I should be hatching schemes of vengeance? Wasn't it my own mother? Would you do less, Mr Williams? Answer me now, would you do less?'

'Ah Markham, I wouldn't go about with the noose around my neck before it was time for it. I'd hold my peace on that account.'

'Puny, Williams, puny.'

'But wise, none the less.' He kicked a piece of coke across the floor, following it with his glance. He said: 'Anyway, Markham will never do it. Markham is all talk.'

'This is a good cigar,' Markham said. 'May we enjoy many another.'

'Yes,' said Williams agreeably enough. 'A fine drag.'

We smoked in silence. Looking back on it, it seems certain that it all began that afternoon in the boilerhouse. Had I not met Williams on the way to his toasting session, had Markham not later shared his cigars with us, how different the course of events might have been. My friendship with Markham might never have come about; Williams might never have been transformed from a cunning nonentity into a figure of mystery and power; and Markham, somehow, might have dodged the snare he had already set for himself.

Becoming friends with Markham was an odd thing, he being so silent, so unforthcoming on any subject except the death of his mother. Yet he was sunny rather than sullen; thoughtful rather than brooding. We walked together on the hills behind the school, often without exchanging more than a dozen words. In spite of this our friendship grew. I discovered that Markham's father and stepmother were now in Kenya. Markham saw them only once a year, during the summer holidays; he spent Easter and Christmas with a grandmother on the south coast.

The other odd aspect of this new relationship between Markham and me was the attitude of Williams. He hung around us. Often, uninvited, he accompanied us on our walks. He took to sidling up to us and whispering: 'Markham will never do it. Markham's just a madman, eh?' Markham rarely replied. He stared at Williams with a puzzled expression and smiled.

When he came on walks with us Williams would ask Markham to tell us about the shooting accident in Florence, and this of course Markham never tired of doing. He didn't seem to resent Williams. I think he was more generous than the rest of us about people like Williams. Certainly he was more generous than I was. Frankly, Williams used to set my teeth on edge. I found him alone one day and asked him bluntly what he was up to. He sniffed at me and asked me what I meant.

'Why do you follow Markham and me around?' I said. 'Why don't you leave Markham alone?'

Williams laughed. 'Markham's an interesting bird.'

'What are you up to, Williams?'

But he wouldn't tell me. He said: 'I'm an unhealthy personage.' He laughed again and walked away.

This exchange had no effect on Williams. He still haunted our movements, chattering of his future in the legal world or retailing the fruits of an hour's eavesdropping. When we were alone together Markham no longer repeated his famous story or made any allusion to this particular aspect of life. I came to realize that although he truly hated his father it had become a joke with him to talk about it. I was the first close friend Markham had known, and he was quite unused to the communication that such a relationship involved. It was only very gradually that new topics of conversation developed between us.

But there was always Williams, devotedly determined, it seemed, to wrap Markham and his story closer and closer together. We formed, I suppose, an odd kind of triangle.

At the beginning of the autumn term the headmaster, Bodger, addressed us at length about this and that, announcing the names of the new prefects and supplying us with fresh items of school routine. When he had finished this part of his peroration he paused for a suitable moment and then he said:

'There are times, boys, in the lives of us all when we must display the ultimate bravery. When we must face the slings and arrows with a fortitude we may perhaps have never had call to employ before. Such a fearful moment has come to one of our number. I would ask you to show him kindness and understanding. I would ask you this term to help him on his way; to make that way as easy as you may. For us it is a test as it is for him. A test of our humanity. A test of our Christian witness. It is with the greatest grief, boys, that I must report to you the sudden and violent death of Ian Markham's father and stepmother.'

Markham had not yet returned. During the fortnight of his absence speculation and rumour ran high. Neither Bodger nor his henchmen seemed to know about the threats he had been wont to issue. Only we who were in their care questioned the accuracy of the facts as they had been presented to us: that a Mau Mau marauder armed with a heavy knife had run berserk through the Markham farm in Kenya. Was not the coincidence too great? Was it not more likely that Markham had finally implemented his words with action?

'Markham's a madman, eh?' Williams said to me.

When he did return, Markham was changed. He no longer smiled. Waiting expectantly in the dormitory for a new and gory story, his

companions received only silence from Markham's bed. He spoke no more
of his mother; and when anyone sympathized with him on his more recent
loss he seemed not to know what was being spoken of. He faded into
the background and became quite unremarkable. Pointedly rejecting my
companionship, he ended our brief friendship. Instead, he and Williams
became inseparable.

It was, I remember, a particularly beautiful autumn. Red, dead leaves
gleamed all day in the soft sunlight. On warm afternoons I walked alone
through the gorse-covered hills. I did not make friends easily; and I missed
the company of Markham.

As the weeks passed it became clear the murder of Markham's parents
by the Mau Mau was now generally accepted. It might be thought that
against a background of Markham's stories and avowed intentions a
certain fear would have developed; an uneasiness about sharing one's daily
existence with such a character. It was not so. Markham seemed almost
dead himself; he was certainly not a figure to inspire terror. The more one
noticed him the more unlikely it appeared that he could possibly have had
any hand in the events in Kenya, although he had been in the house at the
time and had himself escaped undamaged.

I thought that only I must have been aware of the ominous nature of
Markham's association with Williams. Williams, I knew, was up to no
good. He whispered constantly to Markham, grinning slyly, his small eyes
drilling into Markham's face. I didn't like it and I didn't know what to do.

One afternoon I walked into the town with a boy called Block. We went
to a café with the intention of passing an hour over tea and cakes and, if
the coast seemed clear, a surreptitious smoke.

'This is an uncivilized place,' Block remarked as we sat down. 'I cannot
imagine why we came here.'

'There is nowhere else.'

'It is at least too revolting for the Bodger or any of his band. Look,
there's our dreaded Williams. With Markham.'

They were sitting at a table in an alcove. Williams, talking as usual, was
fiddling with the spots on his face. As I watched him, he picked a brightly
coloured cake from the plate between them. It looked an uninviting article,
indeed scarcely edible. He nibbled at one corner and replaced it on the
plate.

'Whatever does Markham see in him?' Block asked.

I shook my head. Block was a simple person, but when he next spoke
he revealed a depth I had not before had evidence of. He cocked his head
to one side and said: 'Williams hates Markham. You can see it easily

enough. And I believe Markham's terrified of him. You used to know Markham rather well. D'you know why?'

Again I shook my head. But there was no doubt about it, Block was quite right.

The nub of the relationship was William's hatred. It was as though hatred of some kind was essential to Markham; as though, since he had no father to hate now, he was feeding on this unexplained hatred of himself. It all seemed a bit crazy, but I felt that something of the kind must be true.

'I feel I should do something about it all,' I said. 'Williams is a horribly untrustworthy fellow. God knows what his intentions are.'

Did Williams know something we others were ignorant of? Something of the double death in Kenya?

'What can you do?' Block said, lighting the butt of a cigarette.

'I wonder if I should talk to Pinshow?'

Block laughed. Pinshow was a fat, middle-aged master who welcomed the personal problems of his pupils. He was also a bit of an intellectual. It was enough to tell Mr Pinshow that one had an ambition to become a writer or an actor to ensure endless mugs of black coffee in Mr Pinshow's room.

'I often wonder if we don't underestimate Pinshow,' I said. 'There's lots of goodwill in the man. And good ideas quite often originate in unexpected quarters. He just might be able to suggest something.'

'Perhaps. You know more about Markham than I do. I mean, you probably know more about what the matter is. He doesn't seem much good at anything any more, does he?'

I looked across the room at his sad, lost-looking face. 'No, I'm afraid he doesn't.'

Block suddenly began to laugh. 'Have you heard Butler's one about the sick budgerigar?'

I said I didn't think I had, and he leaned forward and told me. Listening to this obscene account of invalid bird-life, I made up my mind to see Pinshow as soon as possible.

The evening light faded and Mr Pinshow continued to talk. I tried in the gloom to take some biscuits without his observing my action. He pushed the box closer to me, oblivious, or so I hoped, of my deceit. '*Out of the slimy mud of words,*' said Mr Pinshow, '*out of the sleet and hail of verbal imprecisions, approximate thoughts and feelings . . . there spring the perfect order of speech and the beauty of incantation.*' Mr Pinshow often said this. I think it may have been his favourite quotation. I drained my coffee mug, filling my mouth with bitter sediment as I did so.

I said: 'There is a land of the living and a land of the dead and the bridge is love.'

'Ah, Wilder.' Mr Pinshow drew a large coloured handkerchief from his trouser pocket and blew his nose.

'The only survival,' I added, 'the only meaning.'

Mr Pinshow replaced his handkerchief. He scratched a match along the side of its box and held the flame to his pipe. 'Love,' he said, puffing, 'or love? One sort or the other sort?'

'The other sort, sir?'

'You question such a division? Good. Good.'

I said: 'I wanted to speak to you, sir.'

'Quite right. Fire away, then.'

'In confidence, sir, I think Williams is a bad influence on Markham.'

'Ah.'

'I think Markham may be very upset about his parents' death, sir. Williams is the last person . . .'

'Come now, in what way a bad influence? Speak freely, my friend. We must straightway establish the facts of the case.'

I knew then that the whole thing was going to be useless. It had been a mistake to come to Pinshow. I could not reveal to him the evidence on which my fears were based. I said nothing, hoping he would not press me.

'I see,' he said.

'Perhaps I am making a mountain out of a molehill, sir.'

Mr Pinshow, however, did not think so at all. 'This is a serious business,' he said. 'Though it is unusual in these matters, I am glad you came to me.'

Clearly, I had given the man a completely false impression. I attempted to rectify this, but Mr Pinshow waved me to silence.

'Say no more, my friend. Leave the matter with me. You can rely on me to speak with discretion in the right directions.'

'Sir, I hope I have not misled you.'

'No, no, no.'

'It is not a *serious* thing, sir. It is just that Markham was once a friend of mine and I am sure that now he . . .'

Mr Pinshow held up his hand. He smiled. 'You are a good fellow. Do not despair. All will be well.'

God knows, I thought, what damage I have done.

'Mind your own bloody business,' Williams muttered to me. 'Any more of this kind of stuff to Pinshow and I'll have you for slander. Don't you know that man's a menace?'

'Go to hell, Williams.' And Williams, seeming a fit candidate for such a destination, shuffled angrily away.

After that, I decided to forget about Markham and Williams. After all, it had nothing to do with me; and in any case I appeared to have no option. I settled down to concentrating a little harder on my work and then, when I really had forgotten all about this strange alliance, I was summoned from class one day by the headmaster.

He stood by the window of his study, a terrible, sickly figure of immense height. He remained with his back to me when I entered the room and spoke to me throughout the interview from this position. 'You will tell me what you know about Markham and the boy Williams,' he said. 'Do not lie, boy. I know a lie. I feel a lie on its utterance. Likewise, do not exaggerate. You will repeat to me simply and honestly all that is apposite. Unburden yourself, boy, that you may leave the room with your duty well done.'

I did not intend to lie. To conceal three-quarters of the story was not to lie. I said: 'The whole truth, sir, is that ...' I paused not knowing how to go on. The headmaster said:

'Well, boy, let us have haste with the whole truth.'

'I can tell you nothing, sir.'

'Nothing?'

'Yes, sir. I know nothing of Markham and Williams.'

'They are boys in this school. You know that, I presume? You have associated with them. You have spoken to Mr Pinshow of these boys. If their relationship is an illicit one I wish to know it. You will achieve little by reticence.'

'There is nothing illicit, sir, in their friendship. I spoke to Mr Pinshow merely because I felt Williams to be the wrong sort of friend for Markham at this particular time.'

'That is a presumptuous decision for you to make, boy.'

'Yes, sir.'

'Why, then, did you so perversely make it?'

'I like Markham, sir.'

'Why, then, did you not see to it that his days were made easier by persuading him personally against an ill influence?'

'Markham no longer wished for my companionship, sir.'

'You had harmed him in some manner?'

'No, sir. At least not that I know of.'

'Yes or no, boy? Do not leave yourself a cowardly loophole.'

'No, sir. I had not harmed him.'

'Well then, why did he not wish to converse with you?'

'I'm afraid I don't know.'

'You do not know. It is unnecessary to be afraid as well.'

'Yes, sir.'

'You see, boy, that you have placed me in an intolerable position with your wild irresponsibilities? I am the fount of authority in this school. You have made me uneasy in my mind. You have forced me to pursue a course I see no good reason for pursuing. Yet because there may be one tittle of reality in your guarded suspicions I must act as I do not wish to act. Have you ever placed yourself in a headmaster's shoes?'

'No, sir.'

'No, sir. I had sensed as much. They are shoes that pinch, boy. It is well to remember that.'

'Yes, sir.'

'Walk forward to my desk, boy, and press the bell you see there. We will order this affair one way or the other.'

Markham and Williams were summoned. When they entered, the headmaster turned from the window and faced us. He said to them:

'Your friendship is in dispute. Your accuser stands beside you. Do not lie, boys. I know a lie. I can feel a lie on its utterance. Have you reason for shame?'

Williams, whose eyes were fastened on the legs of the headmaster's desk, shook his head. Markham replied that he had no cause to be ashamed.

'On what then is your relationship based? Have you like interests? Of what do you speak together?'

'Of many things, sir,' Williams said. 'Politics and affairs of state. Of our ambitions, sir. And our academic progress as the term passes.'

'We talk of one subject only, sir,' Markham said. 'The death of my father and stepmother.'

'Yet you, boy,' the headmaster said to Williams, 'would claim a wider conversational field. The air is blackened with the lie. Which boy are we to believe?'

'Markham is ill, sir. He is not at all himself. I give him what help I can. He does not recall the full extent of our conversation.'

'We speak of one subject,' Markham repeated.

'Why, boy, do you speak of this subject to the exclusion of all others?'

'Because I killed my father, sir. And my stepmother too.'

'Markham is ill, sir. He . . .'

'Leave the room, you boys. Markham, you shall remain.'

Neither Williams nor I spoke as we walked away from the headmaster's door. Then, as our ways were about to divide, I said:

'You know he didn't. You know it is not true.'

Williams did not look at me. He said: 'That's right. Why didn't you tell Bodger that?'

'You've made him believe he did it, Williams.'

'Markham's all talk. Markham's a madman, eh?'

'You're an evil bastard, Williams.'

'That's right. I'm an unhealthy personage.'

He went on his way and I stood where he had left me, looking back at the closed door of the headmaster's study. The little red light which indicated that for no reason whatsoever should the headmaster be disturbed gleamed above it. Within, I guessed that the curtains were by now closely drawn, since to do so was the headmaster's practice on all grave occasions.

Suddenly I had the absurd notion of returning to this darkened room and demanding to be heard, since now I was free to speak. I felt for the moment that I could put his case more clearly, more satisfactorily than Markham himself. I felt that I knew everything: the horror of the thought that had leapt in Markham's mind when first his father told him of the accident in Florence; the game he had made of it, and the later fears that Williams had insidiously played upon. But as I paused in doubt I heard the urgent chiming of a bell, and, like the object of some remote control, I answered the familiar summons.

That same evening Markham was driven away. He was seen briefly in the headmaster's hall, standing about in his overcoat, seeming much as usual.

'They've sent him up to Derbyshire,' said Mr Pinshow when later I attempted to elicit information. 'Poor lad; so healthy in the body, too.' He would say no more, but I knew what he was thinking; and often since I have thought of Markham, still healthy in his body, growing up and getting older in the place they had found for him in Derbyshire. I have thought of Williams too, similarly growing older though in other circumstances, marrying perhaps and begetting children, and becoming in the end the man he had said he would one day be.

The Penthouse Apartment

'Flowers?' said Mr Runca into his pale blue telephone receiver. 'Shall we order flowers? What's the procedure?' He stared intently at his wife as he spoke, and his wife, eating her breakfast grapefruit, thought that it would seem to be her husband's intention to avoid having to pay for flowers. She had become used to this element in her husband; it hardly ever embarrassed her.

'The procedure's quite simple,' said a soft voice in Mr Runca's ear. 'The magazine naturally supplies the flowers. If we can just agree between us what the flowers should be.'

'Indeed,' said Mr Runca. 'It's to be remembered that not all blooms will go with the apartment. Our fabrics must be allowed to speak for themselves, you know. Well, you've seen. You know what I mean.'

'Indeed I do, Mr Runca –'

'They came from Thailand, in fact. You might like to mention that.'

'So you said, Mr Runca. The fabrics are most beautiful.'

Mr Runca, hearing this statement, nodded. He said, because he was used to saying it when the apartment was discussed:

'It's the best-dressed apartment in London.'

'I'll come myself at three,' said the woman on the magazine. 'Will someone be there at half past two, say, so that the photographers can set up their gear and test the light?'

'We have an Italian servant,' said Mr Runca, 'who opened the door to you before and who'll do the same thing for the photographers.'

'Till this afternoon then,' said the woman on the magazine, speaking lightly and gaily, since that was her manner.

Mr Runca carefully replaced the telephone receiver. His wife, a woman who ran a boutique, drank some coffee and heard her husband say that the magazine would pay for the flowers and would presumably not remove them from the flat after the photography had taken place. Mrs Runca nodded. The magazine was going to devote six pages to the Runcas' flat: a display in full colour of its subtleties and charm, with an article about how the Runcas had between them planned the décor.

'I'd like to arrange the flowers myself,' said Mrs Runca. 'Are they being sent round?'

Mr Runca shook his head. The flowers, he explained, were to be brought to the house by the woman from the magazine at three o'clock, the photographers having already had time to deploy their materials in the manner they favoured.

'But how ridiculous!' cried Mrs Runca. 'That's completely hopeless. The photographers with their cameras poised for three o'clock and the woman arriving then with the flowers. How long does the female imagine it'll take to arrange them? Does she think it can be done in a matter of minutes?'

Mr Runca picked up the telephone and dialled the number of the magazine. He mentioned the name of the woman he had recently been speaking to. He spoke to her again. He said:

'My wife points out that none of this is satisfactory. The flowers will take time to arrange, naturally. What point is there in keeping your photographers waiting? And I myself haven't got all day.'

'It shouldn't take long to arrange the flowers.'

Mrs Runca lit her first cigarette of the day, imagining that the woman on the magazine was saying something like that. She had a long, rather thin face, and pale grey hair that had the glow of aluminium. Her hands were long also, hands that had grown elegant in childhood, with fingernails that now were of a fashionable length, metallically painted, a reflection of her hair. Ten years ago, on money borrowed from her husband, she had opened her boutique. She had called it St Catherine, and had watched it growing into a flourishing business with a staff of five women and a girl messenger.

'Very well then,' said the woman on the magazine, having listened further to Mr Runca. 'I'll have the flowers sent round this morning.'

'They're coming round this morning,' reported Mr Runca to his wife.

'I have to be at St Catherine at twelve,' she said, 'absolutely without fail.'

'My wife has to be at her business at midday,' said Mr Runca, and the woman on the magazine cursed silently. She promised that the flowers would be in the Runcas' penthouse apartment within three-quarters of an hour.

Mr Runca rose to his feet and stood silently for a minute. He was a rich, heavily jowled man, the owner of three publications that appealed to those involved in the clothing trade. He was successful in much the same way as his wife was, and he felt, as she did, that efficiency and a stern outlook were good weapons in the business of accumulating wealth. Once upon a time they had both been poor and had recognized certain similar qualities in one another, had seen the future as a more luxurious time, as in fact it had become. They were proud that once again their penthouse apartment was to be honoured by photographs and a journalist. It was the symbol of their toil; and in a small way it had made them famous.

Mr Runca walked from the spacious room that had one side made entirely of glass, and his feet caused no sound as he crossed a white carpet of Afghanistan wool. He paused in the hall to place a hat on his head and gloves on his hands before departing for a morning's business.

At ten to ten the flowers arrived and by a quarter past eleven Mrs Runca had arranged them to her satisfaction. The Runcas' Italian maid, called Bianca, cleaned the flat most carefully, seeking dust in an expert way, working with method and a conscience, which was why the Runcas employed her. Mrs Runca warned her to be in at half past two because the photographers were coming then. 'I must go out now then,' replied Bianca, 'for shopping. I will make these photographers coffee, I suppose?' Mrs Runca said to give the men coffee in the kitchen, or tea, if they preferred it. 'Don't let them walk about the place with cups in their hands,' she said, and went away.

In another part of the block of flats lived Miss Winton with her Cairn terrier. Her flat was different from the Runcas'; it contained many ornaments that had little artistic value, was in need of redecoration, and had a beige linoleum on the floor of the bathroom. Miss Winton did not notice her surroundings much; she considered the flat pretty in its way, and comfortable to live in. She was prepared to leave it at that.

'Well,' remarked Miss Winton to her dog in the same moment that Mrs Runca was stepping into a taxi-cab, 'what shall we do?'

The dog made no reply beyond wagging its tail. 'I have eggs to buy,' said Miss Winton, 'and honey, and butter. Shall we go and do all that?'

Miss Winton had lived in the block of flats for fifteen years. She had seen many tenants come and go. She had heard about the Runcas and the model place they had made of the penthouse. It was the talk of London, Miss Winton had been told by Mrs Neck, who kept a grocer's shop near by; the Runcas were full of taste, apparently. Miss Winton thought it odd that London should talk about a penthouse flat, but did not ever mention that to Mrs Neck, who didn't seem to think it odd in the least. To Miss Winton the Runcas were like many others who had come to live in the same building: people she saw and did not know. There were no children in the building, that being a rule; but animals, within reason, were permitted.

Miss Winton left her flat and walked with her dog to Mrs Neck's shop. 'Fresh buns,' said Mrs Neck before Miss Winton had made a request. 'Just in, dear.' But Miss Winton shook her head and asked for eggs and honey and butter. 'Seven and ten,' said Mrs Neck, reckoning the cost before reaching a hand out for the articles. She said it was shocking that food should cost so much, but Miss Winton replied that in her opinion two shillings wasn't exorbitant for half a pound of butter. 'I remember it ninepence,' said Mrs Neck, 'and twice the stuff it was. I'd sooner a smear of Stork than what they're turning out today.' Miss Winton smiled, and agreed that the quality of everything had gone down a bit.

Afterwards, for very many years, Miss Winton remembered this conversation with Mrs Neck. She remembered Mrs Neck saying: 'I'd sooner a smear of Stork than what they're turning out today,' and she remembered the rather small, dark-haired girl who entered Mrs Neck's shop at that moment, who smiled at both of them in an innocent way. 'Is that so?' said the Runcas' maid, Bianca. 'Quality has gone down?'

'Lord love you, Miss Winton knows what she's talking about,' said Mrs Neck. 'Quality's gone to pieces.'

Miss Winton might have left the shop then, for her purchasing was over, but the dark-haired young girl had leaned down and was patting the head of Miss Winton's dog. She smiled while doing that. Mrs Neck said:

'Miss Winton's in the flats too.'

'Ah, yes?'

'This young lady,' explained Mrs Neck to Miss Winton, 'works for the Runcas in the penthouse we hear so much about.'

'Today they are coming to photograph,' said Bianca. 'People from a magazine. And they will write down other things about it.'

'Again?' said Mrs Neck, shaking her head in wonderment. 'What can I do for you?'

Bianca asked for coffee beans and a sliced loaf, still stroking the head of the dog.

Miss Winton smiled. 'He has taken to you,' she said to Bianca, speaking timidly because she felt shy of people, especially foreigners. 'He's very good company.'

'Pretty little dog,' said Bianca.

Miss Winton walked with Bianca back to the block of flats, and when they arrived in the large hallway Bianca said:

'Miss Winton, would you like to see the penthouse with all its fresh flowers and fruits about the place? It is at its best in the morning sunlight as Mr Runca was remarking earlier. It is ready for the photographers.'

Miss Winton, touched that the Italian girl should display such thoughtfulness towards an elderly spinster, said that it would be a pleasure to look at the penthouse flat but added that the Runcas might not care to have her walking about their property.

'No, no,' said Bianca, who had not been long in the Runcas' employ.

'Mrs Runca would love you to see it. And him too. "Show anyone you like," they've said to me. Certainly.' Bianca was not telling the truth, but time hung heavily on her hands in the empty penthouse and she knew she would enjoy showing Miss Winton the flowers that Mrs Runca had so tastefully arranged, and the curtains that had been imported specially from Thailand, and the rugs and the chairs and the pictures on the walls.

'Well,' began Miss Winton.

'Yes,' said Bianca and pressed Miss Winton and her dog into the lift.

But when the lift halted at the top and Bianca opened the gates Miss Winton experienced a small shock. 'Mr Morgan is here too,' said Bianca. 'Mending the water.'

Miss Winton felt that she could not now refuse to enter the Runcas' flat, since to do so would be to offend the friendly little Italian girl, yet she really did not wish to find herself face to face with Mr Morgan in somebody else's flat. 'Look here,' she said, but Bianca and the dog were already ahead of her. 'Come on, Miss Winton,' said Bianca.

Miss Winton found herself in the Runcas' small and fastidious hall, and then in the large room that had one side made of glass. She looked around her and noted all the low furniture and the pale Afghanistan carpet and the objects scattered economically about, and the flowers that Mrs Runca had arranged. 'Have coffee,' said Bianca, going quickly off to make some, and the little dog, noting her swift movement and registering it as a form of play, gave a single bark and darted about himself, in a small circle. 'Shh,' whispered Miss Winton. 'Really,' she protested, following Bianca to the kitchen, 'don't bother about coffee.' 'No, no,' said Bianca, pretending not to understand, thinking that there was plenty of time for herself and Miss Winton to have coffee together, sitting in the kitchen, where Mrs Runca had commanded coffee was to be drunk. Miss Winton could hear a light hammering and guessed it was Mr Morgan at work on the water-pipes. She could imagine him coming out of the Runcas' bathroom and stopping quite still as soon as he saw her. He would stand there in his brown overall, large and bulky, peering at her through his spectacles, chewing, probably, a piece of his moustache. His job was to attend to the needs of the tenants when the needs were not complicated, but whenever Miss Winton telephoned down to his basement and asked for his assistance he would sigh loudly into the telephone and say that he mightn't manage to attend to the matter for a day or two. He would come, eventually, late at night but still in his brown overall, his eyes watering, his breath rich with alcohol. He would look at whatever the trouble was and make a swift diagnosis, advising that experts should be summoned the following morning. He didn't much like her, Miss Winton thought; no doubt he considered her a poor creature, unmarried at sixty-four, thin and weak-looking, with little sign that her physical appearance had been attractive in girlhood.

'It's a lovely place,' said Miss Winton to Bianca. 'But I think perhaps we should go now. Please don't bother with coffee; and thank you most awfully.'

'No, no,' said Bianca, and while she was saying it Mr Morgan entered the kitchen in his brown overall.

One day in 1952 Miss Winton had mislaid her bicycle. It had disappeared without trace from the passage in the basement where Mr Morgan had said she might keep it. 'I have not seen it,' he had said slowly and deliberately at that time. 'I know of no cycle.' Miss Winton had reminded him that the bicycle had always had a place in the passage, since he had said she might keep it there. But Mr Morgan, thirteen years younger then, had replied that he could recall none of that. 'Stolen,' he had said. 'I dare say stolen. I should say the coke men carted it away. I cannot always be watching the place, y'know. I have me work, madam.' She had asked him to inquire of the coke men if they had in error removed her bicycle; she had spoken politely and with a smile, but Mr Morgan had repeatedly shaken his head, pointing out that he could not go suggesting that the coke men had made off with a bicycle, saying that the coke men would have the law on him. 'The wife has a cycle,' Mr Morgan had said. 'A Rudge. I could obtain it for you, madam. Fifty shillings?' Miss Winton had smiled again and had walked away, having refused this offer and given thanks for it.

'Was you wanting something, madam?' asked Mr Morgan now, his lower lip pulling a strand of his moustache into his mouth. 'This is the Runcas' flat up here.'

Miss Winton tried to smile at him. She thought that whatever she said he would be sarcastic in a disguised way. He would hide his sarcasm beneath the words he chose, implying it only with the inflection of his voice. Miss Winton said:

'Bianca kindly invited me to see the penthouse.'

'It is a different type of place from yours and mine,' replied Mr Morgan, looking about him. 'I was attending to a tap in the bathroom. Working, Miss Winton.'

'It is to be photographed today,' said Bianca. 'Mr and Mrs Runca will return early from their businesses.'

'Was you up here doing the flowers, madam?'

He had called her madam during all the years they had known one another, pointing up the fact that she had no right to the title.

'A cup of coffee, Mr Morgan?' said Bianca, and Miss Winton hoped he would refuse.

'With two spoons of sugar in it,' said Mr Morgan, nodding his head and adding: 'D'you know what the Irish take in their coffee?' He began to laugh rumbustiously, ignoring Miss Winton and appearing to share a joke with Bianca. 'A tot of the hard stuff,' said Mr Morgan. 'Whisky.'

Bianca laughed too. She left the kitchen, and Miss Winton's dog ran after her. Mr Morgan blew at the surface of his coffee while Miss Winton, wondering what to say to him, stirred hers.

'It's certainly a beautiful flat,' said Miss Winton.

'It would be too large for you, madam. I mean to say, just you and the dog in a place like this. You'd lose one another.'

'Oh, yes, of course. No, I meant –'

'I'll speak to the authorities if you like. I'll speak on your behalf, as a tenant often asks me to do. Put a word in, y'know. I could put a word in if you like, madam.'

Miss Winton frowned, wondering what Mr Morgan was talking about. She smiled uncertainly at him. He said:

'I have a bit of influence, knowing the tenants and that. I got the left-hand ground flat for Mr Webster by moving the Aitchesons up to the third. I got Mrs Bloom out of the back one on the first –'

'Mr Morgan, you've misunderstood me. I wouldn't at all like to move up here.'

Mr Morgan looked at Miss Winton, sucking coffee off his moustache. His eyes were focused on hers. He said:

'You don't have to say nothing outright, madam. I understand a hint.'

Bianca returned with a bottle of whisky. She handed it to Mr Morgan, saying that he had better add it to the coffee since she didn't know how much to put in.

'Oh, a good drop,' said Mr Morgan, splashing the liquor on to his warm coffee. He approached Miss Winton with the neck of the bottle poised towards her cup. He'll be offended, she thought; and because of that she did not, as she wished to, refuse his offering. 'The Irish are heavy drinkers,' said Mr Morgan. 'Cheers.' He drank the mixture and proclaimed it good. 'D'you like that, Miss Winton?' he asked, and Miss Winton tasted it and discovered to her surprise that the beverage was pleasant. 'Yes,' she said. 'I do.'

Mr Morgan held out his cup for more coffee. 'Just a small drop,' he said, and he filled the cup up with whisky. Again he inclined the neck of the bottle towards Miss Winton, who smiled and said she hadn't finished. He held the bottle in the same position, watching her drinking her coffee.

She protested when Bianca poured her more, but she could sense that Bianca was enjoying this giving of hospitality, and for that reason she accepted, knowing that Mr Morgan would pour in more whisky. She felt comfortably warm from the whisky that was already in her body, and she experienced the desire to be agreeable – although she was aware, too, that she would not care for it if the Runcas unexpectedly returned.

'Fair enough,' said Mr Morgan, topping up Bianca's cup and adding a further quantity to his own. He said:

'Miss Winton is thinking of shifting up here, her being the oldest tenant in the building. She's been stuck downstairs for fifteen years.'

Bianca shook her head, saying to Miss Winton: 'What means that?'

'I'm quite happy,' said Miss Winton, 'where I am.' She spoke softly, with a smile on her face, intent upon being agreeable. Mr Morgan was sitting on the edge of the kitchen table. Bianca had turned on the wireless. Mr Morgan said:

'I come to the flats on March the 21st, 1951. Miss Winton here was already in residence. Riding about on a cycle.'

'I was six years old,' said Bianca.

'D'you remember that day, Miss Winton? March the 21st?'

Miss Winton shook her head. She sat down on a chair made of an ersatz material. She said:

'It's a long time ago.'

'I remember the time you lost your cycle, Miss Winton. She come down to me in the basement,' said Mr Morgan to Bianca, 'and told me to tick off the coke deliverers for thieving her bicycle. I never seen no cycle, as I said to Miss Winton. D'you understand, missy?' Bianca smiled, nodding swiftly. She hummed the tune that was coming from the wireless. 'Do you like that Irish drink?' said Mr Morgan. 'Shall we have some more?'

'I must be going,' said Miss Winton. 'It's been terribly kind of you.'

'Are you going, madam?' said Mr Morgan, and there was in his tone a hint of the belligerency that Miss Winton knew his nature was imbued with. In her mind he spoke more harshly to her, saying she was a woman who had never lived. He was saying that she might have been a nun the way she existed, not knowing anything about the world around her; she had never known a man's love, Mr Morgan was saying; she had never borne a child.

'Oh, don't go,' said Bianca. 'Please, I'll make you a cold cocktail, like Mr Runca showed me how. Cinzano with gin in it, and lemon and ice.'

'Oh, no,' said Miss Winton.

Mr Morgan sighed, implying with the intake of his breath that her protest was not unexpected. There were other women in the block of flats,

Miss Winton imagined, who would have a chat with Mr Morgan now and again, who would pass the time of day with him, asking him for racing tips and suggesting that he should let them know when he heard that a flat they coveted was going to be empty. Mr Morgan was probably a man whom people tipped quite lavishly for the performance of services or favours. Miss Winton could imagine people – people like the Runcas maybe – saying to their friends: 'We greased the caretaker's palm. We gave him five pounds.' She thought she'd never be able to do that.

Bianca went away to fetch the ingredients for the drink, and again the dog went with her.

Miss Winton stood still, determined that Mr Morgan should not consider that she did not possess the nerve to receive from the Runcas' Italian maid a midday cocktail. Mr Morgan said:

'You and me has known one another a number of years.'

'Yes, we have.'

'We know what we think of a flat like this, and the type of person. Don't we, Miss Winton?'

'To tell the truth, I don't really know the Runcas.'

'I'll admit it to you: the whisky has loosened my tongue, Miss Winton. You understand what I mean?'

Miss Winton smiled at Mr Morgan. There was sweat, she noticed, on the sides of his face. He said with vehemence: 'Ridiculous, the place being photographed. What do they want to do that for, tell me?'

'Magazines take an interest. It's a contemporary thing. Mrs Neck was saying that this flat is well-known.'

'You can't trust Mrs Neck. I think it's a terrible place. I wouldn't be comfortable in a place like this.'

'Well –'

'You could report me for saying a thing like that. You could do that, Miss Winton. You could tell them I was intoxicated at twelve o'clock in the day, drinking a tenant's liquor and abusing the tenant behind his back. D'you see what I mean, madam?'

'I wouldn't report you, Mr Morgan. It's no business of mine.'

'I'd like to see you up here, madam, getting rid of all this trash and putting in a decent bit of furniture. How's about that?'

'Please, Mr Morgan, I'm perfectly happy –'

'I'll see what I can do,' said Mr Morgan.

Bianca returned with glasses and bottles. Mr Morgan said:

'I was telling Miss Winton here that she could report me to the authorities for misconduct, but she said she never would. We've known one another a longish time. We was never drinking together though.'

Bianca handed Miss Winton a glass that felt cold in Miss Winton's hand. She feared now what Mr Morgan was going to say. He said:

'I intoxicate easily.' Mr Morgan laughed, displaying darkened teeth. He swayed back and forth, looking at Miss Winton. 'I'll put in a word for you,' he said, 'no bother at all.'

She was thinking that she would finish the drink she'd been given and then go away and prepare lunch. She would buy some little present to give Bianca, and she would come up to the Runcas' flat one morning and hand it to her, thanking her for her hospitality and her thoughtfulness.

While Miss Winton was thinking that, Mr Morgan was thinking that he intended to drink at least two more of the drinks that the girl was offering, and Bianca was thinking that it was the first friendly morning she had spent in this flat since her arrival three weeks before. 'I must go to the WC,' said Mr Morgan, and he left the kitchen, saying he would be back. 'It's most kind of you,' said Miss Winton when he had gone. 'I do hope it's all right.' It had occurred to her that Bianca's giving people the Runcas' whisky and gin was rather different from her giving people a cup of coffee, but when she looked at Bianca she saw that she was innocently smiling. She felt light-headed, and smiled herself. She rose from her chair and thanked Bianca again and said that she must be going now. Her dog came to her, wishing to go also. 'Don't you like the drink?' said Bianca, and Miss Winton finished it. She placed the glass on the metal draining-board and as she did so a crash occurred in the Runcas' large sitting-room. 'Heavens!' said Miss Winton, and Bianca raised a hand to her mouth and kept it there. When they entered the room they saw Mr Morgan standing in the centre of it, looking at the floor.

'Heavens!' said Miss Winton, and Bianca widened her eyes and still did not take her hand away from her mouth. On the floor lay the flowers that Mrs Runca had earlier arranged. The huge vase was smashed into many pieces. Water was soaking into the Afghanistan carpet.

'I was looking at it,' explained Mr Morgan. 'I was touching a flower with my fingers. The whole thing gave way.'

'Mrs Runca's flowers,' said Bianca. 'Oh, Mother of God!'

'Mr Morgan,' said Miss Winton.

'Don't look at me, ma'am. Don't blame me for an instant. Them flowers was inadequately balanced. Ridiculous.'

Bianca, on her hands and knees, was picking up the broken stalks. She might have been more upset, Miss Winton thought, and she was glad that she was not. Bianca explained that Mrs Runca had stayed away from her boutique specially to arrange the flowers. 'They'll give me the sack,' she said, and instead of weeping she gave a small giggle.

The gravity of the situation struck Miss Winton forcibly. Hearing Bianca's giggle, Mr Morgan laughed also, and went to the kitchen, where Miss Winton heard him pouring himself some more of the Runcas' gin. Miss Winton realized then that neither Bianca nor Mr Morgan had any sense of responsibility. Bianca was young and did not know any better; Mr Morgan was partly drunk. The Runcas would return with people from a magazine and they would find that their property had been damaged, that a vase had been broken and that a large damp patch in the centre of their Afghanistan carpet would not look good in the photographs. 'Let's have another cocktail,' said Bianca, throwing down the flowers she had collected and giggling again. 'Oh, no,' cried Miss Winton. 'Please, Bianca. We must think what's best to do.' But Bianca was already in the kitchen, and Miss Winton could hear Mr Morgan's rumbustious laugh.

'I tell you what,' said Mr Morgan, coming towards her with a glass in his hand. 'We'll say the dog done it. We'll say the dog jumped at the flowers trying to grip hold of them.'

Miss Winton regarded him with surprise. 'My dog?' she said. 'My dog was nowhere near the flowers.' Her voice was sharp, the first time it had been so that morning.

Mr Morgan sat down in an armchair, and Miss Winton, about to protest about that also, realized in time that she had, of course, no right to protest at all.

'We could say,' said Mr Morgan, 'that the dog went into a hysterical fit and attacked the flowers. How's about that?'

'But that's not true. It's not the truth.'

'I was thinking of me job, madam. And of the young missy's.'

'It was an accident,' said Miss Winton, 'as you have said, Mr Morgan.'

'They'll say what was I doing touching the flowers? They'll say to the young missy what was happening, was you giving a party? I'll have to explain the whole thing to the wife.'

'Your wife?'

'What was I doing in the Runcas' flat with the young one? The wife will see through anything.'

'You were here to mend a water-pipe, Mr Morgan.'

'What's the matter with the water-pipes?'

'Oh really, Mr Morgan. You were repairing a pipe when I came into the flat.'

'There was nothing the matter with the pipes, ma'am. Nor never has been, which is just the point. The young missy telephones down saying the pipes is making a noise. She's anxious for company. She likes to engage in a chat.'

'I shall arrange what flowers we can salvage,' said Miss Winton, 'just as neatly as they were arranged before. And we can explain to the Runcas that you came to the flat to mend a pipe and in passing brushed against Mrs Runca's flowers. The only difficulty is the carpet. The best way to get that damp stain out would be to lift up the carpet and put an electric fire in front of it.'

'Take it easy,' said Mr Morgan. 'Have a drink, Miss Winton.'

'We must repair the damage –'

'Listen, madam,' said Mr Morgan, leaning forward, 'you and I know what we think of a joint like this. Tricked out like they've got it –'

'It's a question of personal taste –'

'Tell them the dog done the damage, Miss Winton, and I'll see you right. A word in the ear of the authorities and them Runcas will be out on the street in a jiffy. Upsetting the neighbours with noise, bringing the flats into disrepute. I'd say it in court, Miss Winton: I seen naked women going in and out of the penthouse.'

Bianca returned, and Miss Winton repeated to her what she had said already to Mr Morgan about the drying of the carpet. Between them, they moved chairs and tables and lifted the carpet from the floor, draping it across two chairs and placing an electric fire in front of it. Mr Morgan moved to a distant sofa and watched them.

'I used not to be bad with flowers,' said Miss Winton to Bianca. 'Are there other vases?' They went together to the kitchen to see what there was. 'Would you like another cocktail?' said Bianca, but Miss Winton said she thought everyone had had enough to drink. 'I like these drinks,' said Bianca, sipping one. 'So cool.'

'You must explain,' said Miss Winton, 'that Mr Morgan had to come in order to repair the gurgling pipe and that he brushed against the flowers on the way across the room. You must tell the truth: that you had invited me to have a look at the beautiful flat. I'm sure they won't be angry when they know it was an accident.'

'What means gurgling?' said Bianca.

'Hey,' shouted Mr Morgan from the other room.

'I think Mr Morgan should go now,' said Miss Winton. 'I wonder if you'd say so, Bianca? He's a very touchy man.' She imagined Mr Runca looking sternly into her face and saying he could not believe his eyes: that she, an elderly spinster, still within her wits, had played a part in the disastrous proceedings in his flat. She had allowed the caretaker to become drunk, she had egged on a young foreign girl. 'Have you no responsibility?' shouted Mr Runca at Miss Winton in her imagination. 'What's the matter with you?'

'Hey,' shouted Mr Morgan. 'That carpet's burning.'

Miss Winton and Bianca sniffed the air and smelt at once the tang of singed wool. They returned at speed to the other room and saw that the carpet was smoking and that Mr Morgan was still on the sofa, watching it. 'How's about that?' said Mr Morgan.

'The fire was too close,' said Bianca, looking at Miss Winton, who frowned and felt afraid. She didn't remember putting the fire so close to the carpet, and then she thought that she was probably as intoxicated as Mr Morgan and didn't really know what she was doing.

'Scrape off the burnt bit,' advised Mr Morgan, 'and tell them the dog ate it.'

They unplugged the fire and laid the carpet flat on the floor again. Much of the damp had disappeared, but the burnt patch, though small, was eye-catching. Miss Winton felt a weakness in her stomach, as though a quantity of jelly were turning rhythmically over and over. The situation now seemed beyond explanation, and she saw herself asking the Runcas to sit down quietly, side by side with the people from the magazine, and she heard herself trying to tell the truth, going into every detail and pleading that Bianca should not be punished. 'Blame me,' she was saying, 'if someone must be blamed, for I have nothing to lose.'

'I'll tell you what,' said Mr Morgan, 'why don't we telephone for Mrs Neck? She done a carpet for her hearth, forty different wools she told me, that she shaped with a little instrument. Ring up Mrs Neck, missy, and say there's a drink for her if she'll oblige Mr Morgan with ten minutes of her time.'

'Do no such thing,' cried Miss Winton. 'There's been enough drinking, Mr Morgan, as well you know. The trouble started with drink, when you lurched against the flowers. There's no point in Mrs Neck adding to the confusion.'

Mr Morgan listened to Miss Winton and then rose from the sofa. He said:

'You have lived in these flats longer than I have, madam. We all know that. But I will not stand here and be insulted by you, just because I am a working man. The day you come after your cycle –'

'I must go away,' cried Bianca in distress. 'I cannot be found with a burnt carpet and the flowers like that.'

'Listen,' said Mr Morgan, coming close to Miss Winton. 'I have a respect for you. I'm surprised to hear myself insulted from your lips.'

'Mr Morgan –'

'You was insulting me, madam.'

'I was not insulting you. Don't go, Bianca. I'll stay here and explain everything to the Runcas. I think, Mr Morgan, it would be best if you went off to your lunch now.'

'How can I?' shouted Mr Morgan very loudly and rudely, sticking his chin out at Miss Winton. 'How the damn hell d'you think I can go down to the wife in the condition I'm in? She'd eat the face off me.'

'Please, Mr Morgan.'

'You and your dog: I have respect for the pair of you. You and me is on the same side of the fence. D'you understand?'

Miss Winton shook her head.

'What d'you think of the Runcas, ma'am?'

'I've said, Mr Morgan: I've never met the Runcas.'

'What d'you think of the joint they've got here?'

'I think it's most impressive.'

'It's laughable. The whole caboodle is laughable. Did you ever see the like?' Mr Morgan pointed at objects in the room. 'They're two tramps,' he shouted, his face purple with rage at the thought of the Runcas. 'They're jumped-up tramps.'

Miss Winton opened her mouth in order to speak soothingly. Mr Morgan said:

'I could put a match to the place and to the Runcas too, with their bloody attitudes. I'm only a simple caretaker, madam, but I'd see their bodies in flames.' He kicked a chair, his boot thudding loudly against pale wood. 'I hate that class of person, they're as crooked as a corkscrew.'

'You're mistaken, Mr Morgan.'

'I'm bloody not mistaken,' shouted Mr Morgan. 'They're full of hate for a man like me. They'd say I was a beast.'

Miss Winton, shocked and perturbed, was also filled with amazement. She couldn't understand why Mr Morgan had said that he and she belonged on the same side of the fence, since for the past fifteen years she had noted the scorn in his eyes.

'We have a thing in common,' said Mr Morgan. 'We have no respect whatever for the jumped-up tramps who occupy this property. I'd like to see you in here, madam, with your bits and pieces. The Runcas can go where they belong.' Mr Morgan spat into the chair which he had struck with his boot.

'Oh, no,' cried Miss Winton, and Mr Morgan laughed. He walked about the room, clearing his throat and spitting carelessly. Eventually he strolled away, into the kitchen. The dog barked, sensing Miss Winton's distress. Bianca began to sob and from the kitchen came the whistling of Mr Morgan, a noise he emitted in order to cover the sound of gin being poured into his glass. Miss Winton knew what had happened: she had read of men who could not resist alcohol and who were maddened by its presence in their bloodstream. She considered that Mr Morgan had gone mad in the Runcas' flat; he was speaking like an insane person, saying he had respect for her dog.

'I am frightened of him,' said Bianca.

'No,' said Miss Winton. 'He's a harmless man, though I wish he'd go away. We can clean up a bit. We can make an effort.'

Mr Morgan returned and took no notice of them. He sat on the sofa while they set to, clearing up the pieces of broken vase and the flowers. They placed a chair over the burnt area of carpet so that the Runcas would not notice it as soon as they entered the room. Miss Winton arranged the flowers in a vase and placed it where the other one had been placed by Mrs Runca. She surveyed the room and noticed that, apart from the presence of Mr Morgan, it wasn't so bad. Perhaps, she thought, the explanation could be unfolded gradually. She saw no reason why the room shouldn't be photographed as it was now, with the nicely arranged flowers and the chair over the burnt patch of carpeting. The damp area, greater in size, was still a little noticeable, but she imagined that in a photograph it mightn't show up too badly.

'You have let me get into this condition,' said Mr Morgan in an aggressive way. 'It was your place to say that the Runcas' whisky shouldn't be touched, nor their gin neither. You're a fellow-tenant, Miss Winton. The girl and I are servants, madam. We was doing what came naturally.'

'I'll take the responsibility,' said Miss Winton.

'Say the dog done it,' urged Mr Morgan again. 'The other will go against the girl and myself.'

'I'll tell the truth,' said Miss Winton. 'The Runcas will understand. They're not monsters that they won't forgive an accident. Mrs Runca –'

'That thin bitch,' shouted Mr Morgan, and added more quietly: 'Runca's illegitimate.'

'Mr Morgan –'

'Tell them the bloody dog done it. Tell them the dog ran about like a mad thing. How d'you know they're not monsters? How d'you know they'll understand, may I ask? "The three of us was boozing in the kitchen," are you going to say? "Mr Morgan took more than his share of the intoxicant. All hell broke loose." Are you going to say that, Miss Winton?'

'The truth is better than lies.'

'What's the matter with saying the dog done it?'

'You would be far better off out of this flat, Mr Morgan. No good will come of your raving on like that.'

'You have always respected me, madam. You have never been familiar.'

'Well –'

'I might strike them dead. They might enter that door and I might hit them with a hammer.'

Miss Winton began to protest, but Mr Morgan waved a hand at her. He sniffed and said: 'A caretaker sees a lot, I'll tell you that. Fellows bringing women in, hypocrisy all over the place. There's those that slips me a coin, madam, and those that doesn't bother, and I'm not to know which is the worse. Some of them's miserable and some's boozing all night, having sex and laughing their heads off. The Runcas isn't human in any way whatsoever. The Runcas is saying I was a beast that might offend their eyes.' Mr Morgan ceased to speak, and glared angrily at Miss Winton.

'Come now,' she said.

'A dirty caretaker, they've said, who's not fit to be alive –'

'They've never said any such thing, Mr Morgan. I'm sure of it.'

'They should have moved away from the flats if they hated the caretaker. They're a psychological case.'

There was a silence in the room, while Miss Winton trembled and tried not to show it, aware that Mr Morgan had reached a condition in which he was capable of all he mentioned.

'What I need,' he said after a time, speaking more calmly from the sofa on which he was relaxing, 'is a cold bath.'

'Mr Morgan,' said Miss Winton. She thought that he was at last about to go away, down to his basement and his angry wife, in order to immerse his large body in cold water. 'Mr Morgan, I'm sorry that you should think badly of me –'

'I'll have a quick one,' said Mr Morgan, walking towards the Runcas' bathroom. 'Who'll know the difference?'

'No,' cried Miss Winton. 'No, please, Mr Morgan.'

But with his glass in his hand Mr Morgan entered the bathroom and locked the door.

When the photographers arrived at half past two to prepare their apparatus Mr Morgan was still in the bathroom. Miss Winton waited with Bianca, reassuring her from time to time, repeating that she would not leave until she herself had explained to the Runcas what had happened. The photographers worked silently, moving none of the furniture because they had been told that the furniture was on no account to be displaced.

For an hour and twenty minutes Mr Morgan had been in the bathroom. It was clear to Miss Winton that he had thrown the vase of flowers to the ground deliberately and in anger, and that he had placed the fire closer to the carpet. In his crazy and spiteful condition Miss Winton imagined that he was capable of anything: of drowning himself in the bath maybe, so that the Runcas' penthouse might sordidly feature in the newspapers. Bianca had been concerned about his continued presence in the bathroom, but Miss Winton had explained that Mr Morgan was simply being unpleasant since he was made like that. 'It is quite disgraceful,' she said, well aware that Mr Morgan realized she was the kind of woman who would not report him to the authorities, and was taking advantage of her nature while involving her in his own. She felt that the Runcas were the victims of circumstance, and thought that she might use that very expression when she made her explanation to them. She would speak slowly and quietly, breaking it to them in the end that Mr Morgan was still in the bathroom and had probably fallen asleep. 'It is not his fault,' she heard herself saying. 'We must try to understand.' And she felt that the Runcas would nod their heads in agreement and would know what to do next.

'Will they sack me?' said Bianca, and Miss Winton shook her head, repeating again that nothing that had happened had been Bianca's fault.

At three o'clock the Runcas arrived. They came together, having met in the hallway downstairs. 'The flowers came, did they?' Mr Runca had inquired of his wife in the lift, and she had replied that the flowers had safely been delivered and that she had arranged them to her satisfaction. 'Good,' said Mr Runca, and reported to his wife some facts about the morning he had spent.

When they entered their penthouse apartment the Runcas noted the presence of the photographers and the photographers' apparatus. They saw as well that an elderly woman with a dog was there, standing beside Bianca, that a chair had been moved, that the Afghanistan carpet was stained, and that some flowers had been loosely thrust into a vase. Mr Runca wondered about the latter because his wife had just informed him that she herself had arranged the flowers; Mrs Runca thought that something peculiar was going on. The elderly woman stepped forward to greet them, announcing that her name was Miss Winton, and at that moment a man in a brown overall whom the Runcas recognized as a Mr Morgan, caretaker and odd-job man, entered the room from the direction of the bathroom. He strode towards them and coughed.

'You had trouble with the pipes,' said Mr Morgan. He spoke urgently and it seemed to Mr and Mrs Runca that the elderly woman with the dog was affected by his speaking. Her mouth was actually open, as though she had been about to speak herself. Hearing Mr Morgan's voice, she closed it.

'What has happened here?' said Mrs Runca, moving forward from her husband's side. 'Has there been an accident?'

'I was called up to the flat,' said Mr Morgan, 'on account of noise in the pipes. Clogged pipes was on the point of bursting, a trouble I've been dealing with since eleven-thirty. You'll discover the bath is full of water. Release it, sir, at five o'clock tonight, and then I think you'll find everything OK. Your drain-away was out of order.'

Mrs Runca removed her gaze from Mr Morgan's face and passed it on to the face of Miss Winton and then on to the bowed head of Bianca. Her husband examined the silent photographers, sensing something in the atmosphere. He said to himself that he did not yet know the full story: what, for instance, was this woman with a dog doing there? A bell rang, and Bianca moved automatically from Miss Winton's side to answer the door. She admitted the woman from the magazine, the woman who was in charge of everything and was to write the article.

'Miss Winton,' said Mr Morgan, indicating Miss Winton, 'occupies a flat lower down in the building.' Mr Morgan blew his nose. 'Miss Winton wished,' he said, 'to see the penthouse, and knowing that I was coming here she came up too and got into conversation with the maid on the doorstep. The dog dashed in, in a hysterical fit, knocking down a bowl of flowers and upsetting an electric fire on the carpet. Did you notice this?' said Mr Morgan, striding forward to display the burnt patch. 'The girl had the fire on,' added Mr Morgan, 'because she felt the cold, coming from a warmer clime.'

Miss Winton heard the words of Mr Morgan and said nothing. He had stood in the bathroom, she reckoned, for an hour and twenty minutes, planning to say that the girl had put on the fire because, being Italian, she had suddenly felt the cold.

'Well?' said Mr Runca, looking at Miss Winton.

She saw his eyes, dark and intent, anxious to draw a response from her, wishing to watch the opening and closing of her lips while his ears listened to the words that relayed the explanation.

'I regret the inconvenience,' she said. 'I'll pay for the damage.'

'Damage?' cried Mrs Runca, moving forward and pushing the chair further away from the burnt area of carpet. 'Damage?' she said again, looking at the flowers in the vase.

'So a dog had a fit in here,' said Mr Runca.

The woman from the magazine looked from Mr Morgan to Bianca and then to Miss Winton. She surveyed the faces of Mr and Mrs Runca and glanced last of all at the passive countenances of her photographers. It seemed, she reflected, that an incident had occurred; it seemed that a dog had gone berserk. 'Well now,' she said briskly. 'Surely it's not as bad as all that? If we put that chair back who'll notice the carpet? And the flowers look most becoming.'

'The flowers are a total mess,' said Mrs Runca. 'An animal might have arranged them.'

Mr Morgan was discreetly silent, and Miss Winton's face turned scarlet.

'We had better put the whole thing off,' said Mr Runca meditatively. 'It'll take a day or two to put everything back to rights. We are sorry,' he said, addressing himself to the woman from the magazine. 'But no doubt you see that no pictures can be taken?'

The woman, swearing most violently within her mind, smiled at Mr Runca and said it was obvious, of course. Mr Morgan said:

'I'm sorry, sir, about this.' He stood there, serious and unemotional, as though he had never suggested that Mrs Neck might be invited up to the Runcas' penthouse apartment, as though hatred and drink had not rendered him insane. 'I'm sorry, sir,' said Mr Morgan. 'I should not have permitted a dog to enter your quarters, sir. I was unaware of the dog until it was too late.'

Listening to Mr Morgan laboriously telling his lies, Miss Winton was visited by the thought that there was something else she could do. For fifteen years she had lived lonesomely in the building, her shyness causing her to keep herself to herself. She possessed enough money to exist quite comfortably; she didn't do much as the days went by.

'Excuse me,' said Miss Winton, not at all knowing how she was going to proceed. She felt her face becoming red again, and she felt the eyes of everyone on her. She wanted to explain at length, to go on talking in a manner that was quite unusual for her, weaving together the threads of an argument. It seemed to Miss Winton that she would have to remind the Runcas of the life of Mr Morgan, how he daily climbed from his deep basement, attired invariably in his long brown overall. 'He has a right to his resentment,' was what she might say; 'he has a right to demand more of the tenants of these flats. His palm is greased, he is handed a cup of tea in exchange for a racing tip; the tenants keep him sweet.' He had come to consider that some of the tenants were absurd, or stupid, and that others were hypocritical. For Miss Winton he had reserved his scorn, for the Runcas a share of his hatred. Miss Winton had accepted the scorn, and understood why it was there; they must seek to understand the other. 'The ball is in your court,' said Miss Winton in her imagination, addressing the Runcas and pleased that she had thought of a breezy expression that they would at once appreciate.

'What about Wednesday next?' said Mr Runca to the woman from the magazine. 'All this should be sorted out by then, I imagine.'

'Wednesday would be lovely,' said the woman.

Miss Winton wanted to let Mr Morgan see that he was wrong about these people. She wanted to have it proved here and now that the Runcas were human and would understand an accident, that they, like anyone else, were capable of respecting a touchy caretaker. She wished to speak the truth, to lead the truth into the open and let it act for itself between Mr Morgan and the Runcas.

'We'll make a note of everything,' Mrs Runca said to her, 'and let you have the list of the damage and the cost of it.'

'I'd like to talk to you,' said Miss Winton. 'I'd like to explain if I may.'

'Explain?' said Mrs Runca. 'Explain?'

'Could we perhaps sit down? I'd like you to understand. I've been in these flats for fifteen years. Mr Morgan came a year later. Perhaps I can help. It's difficult for me to explain to you.' Miss Winton paused, in some confusion.

'Is she ill?' inquired the steely voice of Mrs Runca, and Miss Winton was aware of the woman's metallic hair, and fingernails that matched it, and the four shrewd eyes of a man and a woman who were successful in all their transactions. 'I might hit them with a hammer,' said the voice of Mr Morgan in Miss Winton's memory. 'I might strike them dead.'

'We must try to understand,' cried Miss Winton, her face burning with embarrassment. 'A man like Mr Morgan and people like you and an old spinster like myself. We must relax and attempt to understand.' Miss Winton wondered if the words that she forced from her were making sense; she was aware that she was not being eloquent. 'Don't you see?' cried Miss Winton with the businesslike stare of the Runcas fixed harshly upon her.

'What's this?' demanded Mrs Runca. 'What's all this about understanding? Understanding what?'

'Yes,' said her husband.

'Mr Morgan comes up from his basement every day of his life. The tenants grease his palm. He sees the tenants in his own way. He has a right to do that; he has a right to his touchiness –'

Mr Morgan coughed explosively, interrupting the flow of words. 'What are you talking about?' cried Mrs Runca. 'It's enough that damage has been done without all this.'

'I'm trying to begin at the beginning.' Ahead of her Miss Winton sensed a great mound of words and complication before she could lay bare the final truth: that Mr Morgan regarded the Runcas as people who had been in some way devoured. She knew that she would have to progress slowly, until they began to guess what she was trying to put to them. Accepting that they had failed the caretaker, as she had failed him too, they would understand the reason for his small revenge. They would nod their heads guiltily while she related how Mr Morgan, unhinged by alcohol, had spat at their furniture and had afterwards pretended to be drowned.

'We belong to different worlds,' said Miss Winton, wishing the ground would open beneath her, 'you and I and Mr Morgan. Mr Morgan sees your penthouse flat in a different way. What I am trying to say is that you are not just people to whom only lies can be told.'

'We have a lot to do,' said Mrs Runca, lighting a cigarette. She was smiling slightly, seeming amused.

'The bill for damage must be paid,' added Mr Runca firmly. 'You understand, Miss Winter? There can be no shelving of that responsibility.'

'I don't do much,' cried Miss Winton, moving beyond embarrassment now. 'I sit with my dog. I go to the shops. I watch the television. I don't do much, but I am trying to do something now. I am trying to promote understanding.'

The photographers began to dismantle their apparatus. Mr Runca spoke in a whisper to the woman from the magazine, making some final arrangement for the following Wednesday. He turned to Miss Winton and said more loudly: 'Perhaps you had better return to your apartment, Miss Winter. Who knows, that little dog may have another fit.'

'He didn't have a fit,' cried Miss Winton. 'He never had a fit in the whole of his life.'

There was a silence in the room then, before Mr Runca said:

'You've forgotten, Miss Winter, that your little dog had a bout of hysteria and caused a lot of trouble. Come now, Miss Winter.'

'My name is not Miss Winter. Why do you call me a name that isn't correct?'

Mr Runca threw his eyes upwards, implying that Miss Winton was getting completely out of hand and would next be denying her very existence. 'She's the Queen Mother,' whispered Mrs Runca to one of the photographers, and the photographer sniggered lightly. Miss Winton said:

'My dog did not have a fit. I am trying to tell you, but no one bothers to listen. I am trying to go back to the beginning, to the day that Mr Morgan first became caretaker of these flats –'

'Now, madam,' said Mr Morgan, stepping forward.

'I am going to tell the truth,' cried Miss Winton shrilly. Her dog began to bark, and she felt, closer to her now, the presence of Mr Morgan. 'Shall we be going, madam?' said Mr Morgan, and she was aware that she was being moved towards the door. 'No,' she cried while the movement continued. 'No,' whispered Miss Winton again, but already she was on the landing and Mr Morgan was saying that there was no point whatsoever in attempting to tell people like the Runcas the truth. 'That type of person,' said Mr Morgan, descending the stairs with Miss Winton, his hand beneath her left elbow as though she required aid, 'that type of person wouldn't know the meaning of the word.'

I have failed, said Miss Winton to herself; I have failed to do something that might have been good in its small way. She found herself at the door of her flat, feeling tired, and heard Mr Morgan saying: 'Will you be all right, madam?' She reflected that he was speaking to her as though she were the one who had been mad, soothing her in his scorn. Mr Morgan began to laugh. 'Runca slipped me a quid,' he said. 'Our own Runca.' He laughed again, and Miss Winton felt wearier. She would write a cheque for the amount of the damage, and that would be that. She would often in the future pass Mr Morgan on the stairs and there would be a confused memory between them. The Runcas would tell their friends, saying there was a peculiar woman in one of the flats. 'Did you see their faces,' said Mr Morgan, 'when I mentioned about the dog in a fit?' He threw his head back, displaying all his teeth. 'It was that amusing,' said Mr Morgan. 'I nearly smiled.' He went away, and Miss Winton stood by the door of her flat, listening to his footsteps on the stairs. She heard him on the next floor, summoning the lift that would carry him smoothly to the basement, where he would tell his wife about Miss Winton's dog having a fit in the Runcas' penthouse, and how Miss Winton had made a ridiculous fuss that no one had bothered to listen to.

In at the Birth

Once upon a time there lived in a remote London suburb an elderly lady called Miss Efoss. Miss Efoss was a spry person, and for as long as she could control the issue she was determined to remain so. She attended the cinema and the theatre with regularity; she read at length; and she preferred the company of men and women forty years her junior. Once a year Miss Efoss still visited Athens and always on such visits she wondered why she had never settled in Greece: now, she felt, it was rather too late to make a change; in any case, she enjoyed London.

In her lifetime, nothing had passed Miss Efoss by. She had loved and been loved. She had once, even, given birth to a child. For a year or two she had known the ups and downs of early family life, although the actual legality of marriage had somehow been overlooked. Miss Efoss's baby died during a sharp attack of pneumonia; and shortly afterwards the child's father packed a suitcase one night. He said goodbye quite kindly to Miss Efoss, but she never saw him again.

In retrospect, Miss Efoss considered that she had run the gamut of human emotions. She settled down to the lively superficiality of the everyday existence she had mapped for herself. She was quite content with it. And she hardly noticed it when the Dutts entered her life.

It was Mr Dutt who telephoned. He said: 'Ah, Miss Efoss, I wonder if you can help us. We have heard that occasionally you babysit. We have scoured the neighbourhood for a reliable babysitter. Would you be interested, Miss Efoss, in giving us a try?'

'But who are you?' said Miss Efoss. 'I don't even know you. What is your name to begin with?'

'Dutt,' said Mr Dutt. 'We live only a couple of hundred yards from you. I think you would find it convenient.'

'Well –'

'Miss Efoss, come and see us. Come and have a drink. If you like the look of us perhaps we can arrange something. If not, we shan't be in the least offended.'

'That is very kind of you, Mr Dutt. If you give me your address and a time I'll certainly call. In fact, I shall be delighted to do so.'

'Good, good.' And Mr Dutt gave Miss Efoss the details, which she noted in her diary.

Mr and Mrs Dutt looked alike. They were small and thin with faces like greyhounds. 'We have had such difficulty in finding someone suitable to sit for us,' Mrs Dutt said. 'All these young girls, Miss Efoss, scarcely inspire confidence.'

'We are a nervous pair, Miss Efoss,' Mr Dutt said, laughing gently as he handed her a glass of sherry. 'We are a nervous pair and that's the truth of it.'

'There is only Mickey, you see,' explained his wife. 'I suppose we worry a bit. Though we try not to spoil him.'

Miss Efoss nodded. 'An only child is sometimes a problem.'

The Dutts agreed, staring intently at Miss Efoss, as though recognizing in her some profound quality.

'We have, as you see, the television,' Mr Dutt remarked. 'You would not be lonely here of an evening. The radio as well. Both are simple to operate and are excellent performers.'

'And Mickey has never woken up,' said Mrs Dutt. 'Our system is to leave our telephone behind. Thus you may easily contact us.'

'Ha, ha, ha.' Mr Dutt was laughing. His tiny face was screwed into an unusual shape, the skin drawn tightly over his gleaming cheekbones.

'What an amusing thing to say, Beryl! My wife is fond of a joke, Miss Efoss.'

Unaware that a joke had been made, Miss Efoss smiled.

'It would be odd if we did *not* leave our telephone behind,' Mr Dutt went on. 'We leave the telephone *number* behind, Beryl. The telephone number of the house where we are dining. You would be surprised, Miss Efoss, to receive guests who carried with them their telephone receiver. Eh?'

'It would certainly be unusual.'

' "We have brought our own telephone, since we do not care to use another." Or: "We have brought our telephone in case anyone telephones us while we are here." Miss Efoss, will you tell me something?'

'If I can, Mr Dutt.'

'Miss Efoss, have you ever looked up the word *joke* in the *Encyclopaedia Britannica*?'

'I don't think I have.'

'You would find it rewarding. We have the full *Encyclopaedia* here, you know. It is always at your service.'

'How kind of you.'

'I will not tell you now what the *Encyclopaedia* says on the subject. I will leave you to while away a minute or two with it. I do not think you'll find it a wasted effort.'

'I'm sure I won't.'

'My husband is a great devotee of the *Encyclopaedia*,' Mrs Dutt said. 'He spends much of his time with it.'

'It is not always pleasure,' Mr Dutt said. 'The accumulation of information on many subjects is part of my work.'

'Your work, Mr Dutt?'

'Like many, nowadays, Miss Efoss, my husband works for his living.'

'You have some interesting job, Mr Dutt?'

'Interesting, eh? Yes, I suppose it is interesting. More than that I cannot reveal. That is so, eh, Beryl?'

'My husband is on the secret list. He is forbidden to speak casually about his work. Alas, even to someone to whom we trust our child. It's a paradox, isn't it?'

'I quite understand. Naturally, Mr Dutt's work is no affair of mine.'

'To speak lightly about it would mean marching orders for me,' Mr Dutt said. 'No offence, I hope?'

'Of course not.'

'Sometimes people take offence. We have had some unhappy occasions, eh, Beryl?'

'People do not always understand what it means to be on the secret list, Miss Efoss. So little is taken seriously nowadays.'

Mr Dutt hovered over Miss Efoss with his sherry decanter. He filled her glass and his wife's. He said:

'Well, Miss Efoss, what do you think of us? Can you accept the occasional evening in this room, watching our television and listening for the cry of our child?'

'Naturally, Miss Efoss, there would always be supper,' Mrs Dutt said.

'With sherry before and brandy to finish with,' Mr Dutt added.

'You are very generous. I can quite easily have something before I arrive.'

'No, no, no. It is out of the question. My wife is a good cook. And I can be relied upon to keep the decanters brimming.'

'You have made it all so pleasant I am left with no option. I should be delighted to help you out when I can manage it.'

Miss Efoss finished her sherry and rose. The Dutts rose also, smiling benignly at their satisfactory visitor.

'Well then,' Mr Dutt said in the hall, 'would Tuesday evening be a time you could arrange, Miss Efoss? We are bidden to dine with friends near by.'

'Tuesday? Yes, I think Tuesday is all right. About seven?'

Mrs Dutt held out her hand. 'Seven would be admirable. Till then, Miss Efoss.'

On Tuesday Mr Dutt opened the door to Miss Efoss and led her to the sitting-room. His wife, he explained, was still dressing. Making conversation as he poured Miss Efoss a drink, he said:

'I married my wife when she was on the point of entering a convent, Miss Efoss. What d'you think of that?'

'Well,' Miss Efoss said, settling herself comfortably before the cosy-stove, 'it is hard to know what to say, Mr Dutt. I am surprised, I suppose.'

'Most people are surprised. I often wonder if I did the right thing. Beryl would have made a fine nun. What d'you think?'

'I'm sure you both knew what you were doing at the time. It is equally certain that Mrs Dutt would have been a fine nun.'

'She had chosen a particularly severe order. That's just like Beryl, isn't it?'

'I hardly know Mrs Dutt. But if it is like her to have made that choice, I can well believe it.'

'You see my wife as a serious person, Miss Efoss? Is that what you mean?'

'In the short time I have known her, yes I think I do. Yet you also say she relishes a joke.'

'A joke, Miss Efoss?'

'So you remarked the other evening. In relation to a slip in her speech.'

'Ah yes. How right you are. You must forgive me if my memory is often faulty. My work is wearing.'

Mrs Dutt, gaily attired, entered the room. 'Here, Miss Efoss,' she said, proffering a piece of paper, 'is the telephone number of the house we are going to. If Mickey makes a sound please ring us up. I will immediately return.'

'Oh, but I'm sure that's not necessary. It would be a pity to spoil your evening so. I could at least attempt to comfort him.'

'I would prefer the other arrangement. Mickey does not take easily to strangers. His room is at the top of the house, but please do not enter it. Were he to wake suddenly and catch sight of you he might be extremely frightened. He is quite a nervous child. At the slightest untoward sound do not hesitate to telephone.'

'As you wish it, Mrs Dutt. I only suggested –'

'Experience has taught me, Miss Efoss, what is best. I have laid you a tray in the kitchen. Everything is cold, but quite nice, I think.'

'Thank you.'

'Then we will be away. We should be back by eleven fifteen.'

'Do have a good evening.'

The Dutts said they intended to have a good evening, whispered for a moment together in the hall and were on their way. Miss Efoss looked critically about her.

The room was of an ordinary kind. Utrillo prints on plain grey walls. Yellowish curtains, yellowish chair-covers, a few pieces of simple furniture on a thick grey carpet. It was warm, the sherry was good and Miss Efoss was comfortable. It was pleasant, she reflected, to have a change of scene without the obligation of conversation. In a few moments, she carried her supper tray from the kitchen to the fire. As good as his word, Mr Dutt had left some brandy. Miss Efoss began to think the Dutts were quite a find.

She had dropped off to sleep when they returned. Fortunately, she heard them in the hall and had time to compose herself.

'All well?' Mrs Dutt asked.

'Not a sound.'

'Well, I'd better change him right away. Thank you so much, Miss Efoss.'

'Thank you. I have spent a very pleasant evening.'

'I'll drive you back,' Mr Dutt offered. 'The car is still warm.'

In the car Mr Dutt said: 'A child is a great comfort. Mickey is a real joy for us. And company for Beryl. The days hangs heavy when one is alone all day.'

'Yes, a child is a comfort.'

'Perhaps you think we are too careful and fussing about Mickey?'

'Oh no, it's better than erring in the other direction.'

'It is only because we are so grateful.'

'Of course.'

'We have much to be thankful for.'

'I'm sure you deserve it all.'

Mr Dutt had become quite maudlin by the time he delivered Miss Efoss at her flat. She wondered if he was drunk. He pressed her hand warmly and announced that he looked forward to their next meeting. 'Any time,' Miss Efoss said as she stepped from the car. 'Just ring me up. I am often free.'

After that, Miss Efoss babysat for the Dutts many times. They became more and more friendly towards her. They left her little bowls of chocolates and drew her attention to articles in magazines that they believed might be of interest to her. Mr Dutt suggested further words she might care to look up in the *Encyclopaedia* and Mrs Dutt wrote out several of her recipes.

One night, just as she was leaving, Miss Efoss said: 'You know, I think it might be a good idea for me to meet Mickey some time. Perhaps I could come in the daytime once. Then I would no longer be a stranger and could comfort him if he woke.'

'But he *doesn't* wake, Miss Efoss. He has never woken, has he? You have never had to telephone us.'

'No. That is true. But now that I have got to know you, I would like to know him as well.'

The Dutts took the compliment, smiling at one another and at Miss Efoss. Mr Dutt said: 'It is kind of you to speak like this, Miss Efoss. But Mickey is rather scared of strangers. Just at present at any rate, if you do not mind.'

'Of course not, Mr Dutt.'

'I fear he is a nervous child,' Mrs Dutt said. 'Our present arrangement is carefully devised.'

'I'm sorry,' Miss Efoss said.

'No need. No need. Let us all have a final brandy,' Mr Dutt said cheerfully.

But Miss Efoss was sorry, for she feared she had said something out of place. And then for a week or so she was worried whenever she thought of the Dutts. She felt they were mistaken in their attitude about their child; and she felt equally unable to advise them. It was not her place to speak any further on the subject, yet she was sure that to keep the child away from people just because he was nervous of them was wrong. It sounded as though there was a root to the trouble somewhere, and it sounded as though the Dutts had not attempted to discover it. She continued to babysit for them about once every ten days and she held her peace. Then, quite unexpectedly, something happened that puzzled Miss Efoss very much indeed.

It happened at a party given by some friends of hers. She was talking about nothing in particular to an elderly man called Summerfield. She had known him for some years but whenever they met, as on this occasion, they found themselves with little to say beyond the initial courteous greetings. Thinking that a more direct approach might yield something of interest, Miss Efoss, after the familiar lengthy silence, said: 'How are you coping with the advancing years, Mr Summerfield? I feel I can ask you, since it is a coping I have to take in my own stride.'

'Well, well, I think I am doing well enough. My life is simple since my wife died, but there is little I complain of.'

'Loneliness is a thing that sometimes strikes at us. I find one must regard it as the toothache or similar ailment, and seek a cure.'

'Ah yes. I'm often a trifle alone.'

'I babysit, you know. Have you ever thought of it? Do not shy off because you are a man. A responsible person is all that is required.'

'I haven't thought of babysitting. Not ever, I think. Though I like babies and always have done.'

'I used to do quite a lot. Now I have only the Dutts, but I go there very often. I enjoy my evenings. I like to see the TV now and again and other people's houses are interesting.'

'I know the Dutts,' said Mr Summerfield. 'You mean the Dutts in Raeburn Road? A small, weedy couple?'

'They live in Raeburn Road, certainly. They are small too, but you are unkind to call them weedy.'

'I don't particularly mean it unkindly. I have known Dutt a long time. One takes liberties, I suppose, in describing people.'

'Mr Dutt is an interesting person. He holds some responsible position of intriguing secrecy.'

'Dutt? 25 Raeburn Road? The man is a chartered accountant.'

'I feel sure you are mistaken –'

'I cannot be mistaken. The man was once my colleague. In a very junior capacity.'

'Oh, well . . . then I must be mistaken.'

'What surprises me is that you say you babysit for the Dutts. I think you must be mistaken about that too.'

'Oh no, I am completely certain about that. It is for that reason that I know them at all.'

'I cannot help being surprised. Because, Miss Efoss – and of this I am certain – the Dutts have no children.'

Miss Efoss had heard of the fantasy world with which people, as they grow old, surround themselves. Yet she could not have entirely invented the Dutts in this way because Mr Summerfield had readily agreed about their existence. Was it, then, for some other reason that she visited them? Did she, as soon as she entered their house, become so confused in her mind that she afterwards forgot the real purpose of her presence? Had they hired her in some other capacity altogether? A capacity she was so ashamed of that she had invented, even for herself, the euphemism of babysitting? Had she, she wondered, become some kind of servant to these people – imagining the warm comfortable room, the sherry, the chocolates, the brandy?

'We should be back by eleven, Miss Efoss. Here is the telephone number.' Mrs Dutt smiled at her and a moment later the front door banged gently behind her.

It is all quite real, Miss Efoss thought. There is the sherry. There is the television set. In the kitchen on a tray I shall find my supper. It is all quite real: it is old Mr Summerfield who is wandering in his mind. It was only when she had finished her supper that she had the idea of establishing her role beyond question. All she had to do was to go upstairs and peep at the child. She knew how to be quiet: there was no danger of waking him.

The first room she entered was full of suitcases and cardboard boxes. In the second she heard breathing and knew she was right. She snapped on the light and looked around her. It was brightly painted, with a wallpaper with elves on it. There was a rocking horse and a great pile of coloured bricks. In one of the far corners there was a large cot. It was very large and very high and it contained the sleeping figure of a very old man.

When the Dutts returned Miss Efoss said nothing. She was frightened and she didn't quite know why she was frightened. She was glad when she was back in her flat. The next day she telephoned her niece in Devon and asked if she might come down and stay for a bit.

Miss Efoss spoke to nobody about the Dutts. She gathered her strength in the country and returned to London at the end of a fortnight feeling refreshed and rational. She wrote a note to the Dutts saying she had decided to babysit no more. She gave no reason, but she said she hoped they would understand. Then, as best she could, she tried to forget all about them.

A year passed and then, one grey cold Sunday afternoon, Miss Efoss saw the Dutts in a local park. They were sitting on a bench, huddled close together and seeming miserable. For a reason that she was afterwards unable to fathom Miss Efoss approached them.

'Good afternoon.'

The Dutts looked up at her, their thin, pale faces unsmiling and unhappy.

'Hullo, Miss Efoss,' Mr Dutt said. 'We haven't seen you for a long time, have we? How are you this nasty weather?'

'Quite well, thank you. And you? And Mrs Dutt?'

Mr Dutt rose and drew Miss Efoss a few yards away from his wife. 'Beryl has taken it badly,' he said. 'Mickey died. Beryl has not been herself since. You understand how it is?'

'Oh, I am sorry.'

'I try to cheer her up, but I'm afraid my efforts are all in vain. I have taken it hard myself too. Which doesn't make anything any easier.'

'I don't know what to say, Mr Dutt. It's a great sadness for both of you.'

Mr Dutt took Miss Efoss's arm and led her back to the seat. 'I have told Miss Efoss,' he said to his wife. Mrs Dutt nodded.

'I'm very sorry,' Miss Efoss said again.

The Dutts looked at her, their sad, intent eyes filled with a pathetic desire for comfort. There was something almost hypnotic about them.

'I must go,' Miss Efoss said. 'Goodbye.'

'They have all died, Miss Efoss,' Mr Dutt said. 'One by one they have all died.'

Miss Efoss paused in her retreat. She could think of nothing to say except that she was sorry.

'We are childless again,' Mr Dutt went on. 'It is almost unbearable to be childless again. We are so fond of them and here we are, not knowing what to do on a Sunday afternoon because we are a childless couple. The human frame, Miss Efoss, is not built to carry such misfortunes.'

'It is callous of me to say so, Mr Dutt, but the human frame is pretty resilient. It does not seem so at times like this I know, but you will find it is so in retrospect.'

'You are a wise woman, Miss Efoss, but, as you say, it is hard to accept wisdom at a moment like this. We have lost so many over the years. They are given to us and then abruptly they are taken away. It is difficult to understand God's infinite cruelty.'

'Goodbye, Mr Dutt. Goodbye, Mrs Dutt.'

They did not reply, and Miss Efoss walked quickly away.

Miss Efoss began to feel older. She walked with a stick; she found the cinema tired her eyes; she read less and discovered that she was bored by the effort of sustaining long conversations. She accepted each change quite philosophically, pleased that she could do so. She found, too, that there were compensations; she enjoyed, more and more, thinking about the past. Quite vividly, she re-lived the parts she wished to re-live. Unlike life itself, it was pleasant to be able to pick and choose.

Again by accident, she met Mr Dutt. She was having tea one afternoon in a quiet, old-fashioned teashop, not at all the kind of place she would have associated with Mr Dutt. Yet there he was, standing in front of her.

'Hullo, Miss Efoss,' he said.

'Why, Mr Dutt. How are you? How is your wife? It is some time since we met.'

Mr Dutt sat down. He ordered some tea and then he leaned forward and stared at Miss Efoss. She wondered what he was thinking about: he had the air of someone who, through politeness, makes the most of a moment but whose mind is busily occupied elsewhere. As he looked at her, his face suddenly cleared. He smiled, and when he spoke he seemed to be entirely present.

'I have great news, Miss Efoss. We are both so happy about it. Miss Efoss, Beryl is expecting a child.'

Miss Efoss blinked a little. She spread some jam on her toast and said:

'Oh, I'm so glad. How delightful for you both! Mrs Dutt will be pleased. When is it – when is it due?'

'Quite soon. Quite soon.' Mr Dutt beamed. 'Naturally Beryl is beside herself with joy. She is busy preparing all day.'

'There is a lot to see to on these occasions.'

'Indeed there is. Beryl is knitting like a mad thing. It seems as though she can't do enough.'

'It is the biggest event in a woman's life, Mr Dutt.'

'And often in a man's, Miss Efoss.'

'Yes, indeed.'

'We have quite recovered our good spirits.'

'I'm glad of that. You were so sadly low when last I saw you.'

'You gave us some wise words. You were more comfort than you think, you know.'

'Oh, I was inadequate. I always am with sorrow.'

'No, no. Beryl said so afterwards. It was a happy chance to have met you so.'

'Thank you, Mr Dutt.'

'It's not easy always to accept adversity. You helped us on our way. We shall always be grateful.'

'It is kind of you to say so.'

'The longing for a child is a strange force. To attend to its needs, to give it comfort and love – I suppose there is that in all of us. There is a streak of simple generosity that we do not easily understand.'

'The older I become, Mr Dutt, the more I realize that one understands very little. I believe one is meant not to understand. The best things are complex and mysterious. And must remain so.'

'How right you are! It is often what I say to Beryl. I shall be glad to report that you confirm my thinking.'

'On my part it is instinct rather than thinking.'

'The line between the two is less acute than many would have us believe.'

'Yes, I suppose it is.'

'Miss Efoss, may I do one thing for you?'

'What is that?'

'It is a small thing but would give me pleasure. May I pay for your tea? Beryl will be pleased if you allow me to.'

Miss Efoss laughed. 'Yes, Mr Dutt, you may pay for my tea.' And it was as she spoke this simple sentence that it dawned upon Miss Efoss just what it was she had to do.

Miss Efoss began to sell her belongings. She sold them in many directions, keeping back only a few which she wished to give away. It took her a long time, for there was much to see to. She wrote down long lists of details, finding this method the best for arranging things in her mind. She was sorry to see the familiar objects go, yet she knew that to be sentimental about them was absurd. It was for other people now to develop a sentiment for them; and she knew that the fresh associations they would in time take on would be, in the long run, as false as hers.

Her flat became bare and cheerless. In the end there was nothing left except the property of the landlord. She wrote to him, terminating her tenancy.

The Dutts were watching the television when Miss Efoss arrived. Mr Dutt turned down the sound and went to open the door. He smiled without speaking and brought her into the sitting-room.

'Welcome, Miss Efoss,' Mrs Dutt said. 'We've been expecting you.'

Miss Efoss carried a small suitcase. She said: 'Your baby, Mrs Dutt. When is your baby due? I do hope I am in time.'

'Perfect, Miss Efoss, perfect,' said Mr Dutt. 'Beryl's child is due this very night.'

The pictures flashed silently, eerily, on the television screen. A man dressed as a pirate was stroking the head of a parrot.

Miss Efoss did not sit down. 'I am rather tired,' she said. 'Do you mind if I go straight upstairs?'

'Dear Miss Efoss, please do.' Mrs Dutt smiled at her. 'You know your way, don't you?'

'Yes,' Miss Efoss said. 'I know my way.'

The Introspections of J. P. Powers

J. P. Powers, big, forty-three, his face a mass of moustache, said: 'You must depress the clutch, Miss Hobish. It is impossible to change from one gear to another without you depress the clutch.'

J. P. Powers was aware of his grammatical lapse. *It is impossible to change from one gear to another unless you depress the clutch. It is impossible to change from one gear to another without depressing the clutch.* Either variant would have done: both were within his idiom. *Without you depress* was foreign to him, the way the Irish talk. Despite the Celtic ring of his name, Justin Parke Powers was not Irish.

Miss Hobish drove the Austin in a jagged manner down Cave Crescent and into Mortimer Road. Ahead lay Putney Hill and an awkward right turn, across both streams of traffic. Powers prepared himself for the moment, feet ready for the dual controls, fingers poised to jab the starter when the engine stalled.

'Slowing down signal,' said J. P. Powers. Then: 'Change to second, hand signal, indicator. Always the old hand signal: never rely on the indicator, Miss Hobish.'

Miss Hobish edged the car forward, aiming at a bus.

'Wait for a gap, Miss Hobish. All that traffic has the right of way.'

He had said *without you depress* just for the novelty sound of it, because he had become so used to the usual patter of words, because his tongue grew tired of forming them.

'Now, Miss Hobish.' He seized the steering wheel and swung it, giving the engine a spurt of petrol.

The Austin bore to the left at the traffic lights, along Upper Richmond Road, and later turned right, into the quiet roads of Barnes Common. Powers relaxed then, telling her to take it calmly. Miss Hobish was always happy on Barnes Common.

He lit a cigarette and lowered the window so that the smoke would be carried away. He sat in silence, watching the road. Occasionally he glanced at Miss Hobish and occasionally at parts of himself. He saw his fingernails splayed on his two thick knees. He was not a particularly clean man, and this was a fact he now thought about. He visualized his grey-brown underclothes and the tacky yellow on the underarms of his shirts. Once his wife had commented on this yellow, saying he was a dirty man, running baths for him and pushing deodorants at him. She did all this no longer, only sighing when by chance she came upon his socks, stiff like little planks, in the big cardboard carton she used as a laundry basket. A complaint had come in one summer from a fastidious man called Hopker. Roche had had him in and told him about it, with the typing girl still in the room. 'Wash out your armpits, old son. Get Lifebuoy and Odo-ro-no or Mum.' Roche was a little fellow; it was easy for Roche, there wasn't an ounce of sweat in him. Powers was fifteen stone: rolls of fat and muscle, grinding out the perspiration, secreting it in fleshy caches. To keep himself sweet he'd have to take a shower every two hours.

During his daily periods of boredom J. P. Powers was given to thought. It was thought of a depressing quality, being concerned with his uselessness. Fifty years ago there were no driving instructors in the world: what would he have done fifty years ago, how would he have made a living? The truth was he brought no skill to the job, he had no interest in it. How could one be interested in so unnecessary an occupation as teaching people to drive motor-cars? People could walk, they had legs. People could avail themselves of public transport. He gave no real service; better to be a booking clerk for British Railways. Not that people weren't grateful to him. They waved to him afterwards, implying that he had helped them on their way. But J. P. Powers was thinking of himself; there was nothing expert in what he did, anyone could teach the gears and the knack.

'Well, that was nice,' said Miss Hobish. 'I do enjoy it, Mr Powers. Now, will you take a cup of tea with me?'

Miss Hobish had been learning to drive for five years. It was an outing for her: Miss Hobish was seventy-three.

There was a job that was waiting for J. P. Powers, preserved for him by Ransome, with whom he had served in the Royal Air Force. 'Any time you're ready, J. P.,' was how Ransome put it. Ransome with an amber pint in his paw, down at the Saracen's Head on a Sunday morning. Ransome was sorry for him, remembering how he had driven a Spitfire during the war, thinking of him being driven by inept drivers now. Ransome felt he owed him something, some vague debt incurred in 1945. 'Your day's your own,' said Ransome. 'We supply the car.' The task was to sell baby requisites from door to door: gripe water and talcum powder, disinfectant and baby oil. Ransome was expanding: he'd just bought up a concern that manufactured nappies; he was taking a look at the plastic toy business. 'Let me ask you a question,' said Ransome. 'Doesn't it send you up the wall hawking these learner drivers about?' Ransome had a nice little patch keeping warm for Powers out Kingston way. 'Look at the commission,' said Ransome. 'You won't find commissions like that in your front garden.'

Justin Parke Powers, a man unclean and not entirely satisfied with himself, said yes to Miss Hobish; said yes, he would take the cup of tea, and held the car door open for her and followed her into her small house. Miss Hobish paid for her lessons in advance, by the quarter, but each lesson lasted only twenty minutes instead of the full hour: Miss Hobish at seventy-three could not sustain more.

Darker than the strands that crossed his scalp, softer than the bristle of moustache, was the mat of hair beneath the arms of J. P. Powers. 'A growth that traps, a growth that sours', said Roche, referring to the twin clumps and Powers' perspiration. The hair overflowed from the armpits like stuffing from a mattress – yet his chest was naked as a girl's. Smooth and white; a suggestion of breasts; pitted, if you cared to look, with blackheads. Earlier in his life J. P. Powers had been concerned about it: a big man like him with so unmanly an expanse. He had turned his back on the company in changing rooms, whistling to cover the gesture.

In the bath on Sunday mornings he washed this body with passing diligence, watching the milky scum form on the water, lathering himself with Lifebuoy as Roche had counselled. As he bathed he could hear the cry of the radio in the kitchen and the quarrelling sounds of his two small daughters. It was a Sunday ritual, accepted by his wife who took no part in it; ritual that the geyser should snarl and the water flow, that scum should form, radio play, daughters quarrel; ritual that at midday precisely J. P. Powers should emerge from the bathroom temporarily cleansed, should leave his rented house by the back door and board a bus to the Saracen's Arms. It was ritual too that he should later return with four pints of beer in his barrel stomach and eat a lunch that had been kept for him in a low oven.

When he got going he couldn't stop himself. The images of himself, of his daily work and of his body, rose often and unbidden before him. They bloomed in Mortimer Road and Cave Crescent, among the similar houses, detached or partly so. They hovered, then, over conversation and instruction; they were there in the Austin, like fog. He saw houses and roads being built and wished he had the courage to join a labour gang. He saw his big hands on the steering wheel and considered afresh their function.

On Tuesday September the 21st, Justin Parke Powers gave Miss Hobish her next driving lesson, her two hundred and forty-first. He sat beside her, feet and hands alerted.

'We've had no summer, Mr Powers.' She sighed, settling herself. 'One, two, three, four, up and back for reverse. Are we ready, Mr Powers?'

She drove raggedly from Cave Crescent to Amervale Avenue.

'Hand signals,' said Powers, and Miss Hobish extended a scrawny arm and waved it arbitrarily about.

He fancied the typing girl in Roche's office. When the weather was cold she wore knitted jumpers that shaped her breasts. They quivered as she typed, but there was nothing he could do about them now. Probably she'd giggled with Roche afterwards, about what fastidious Hopker had said, about Roche so bold as to recommend Odo-ro-no or Mum.

'You're forgetting those hand signals,' said Powers.

'So difficult,' murmured Miss Hobish.

'Come and have a drink,' a woman had said to him once, at the end of a lesson; and his heart had fluttered in his naked chest, for he had heard from the other men of such approaches made. Nothing had come of it though, because with the drink in his hand he had laughed and been himself, had told her a few jokes and moved around the room so that he was positioned to give her an exploratory slap on the bottom. All this the woman had not welcomed, and had requested a different tutor for future lessons.

'Slow down for the crossing,' Powers said.

'I beg your pardon?' said Miss Hobish, turning to look at him, jerking the Austin onwards, missing a woman with a pram.

'Turn right. We'll go up Mortimer Road. Hand signal, indicator. Draw out to the centre of the road.'

Excited, Miss Hobish allowed the car to stall.

'More gas, more gas,' cried J. P. Powers, apologizing to the traffic.

'Tell me about the RAF,' said Miss Hobish in Mortimer Road. 'I love to hear your tales.'

'We must concentrate on our driving, Miss Hobish.'

'Shall we have a cup of coffee afterwards and shall you tell me then?'

'Yes, Miss Hobish; a coffee would be nice.'

He closed his eyes and within seconds Miss Hobish had driven the Austin into the back of a stationary van.

'Oh dear, oh dear,' said Miss Hobish.

Powers got out and examined the damage. Both wings and the radiator grill had suffered considerably. The bumper had folded like a length of cardboard.

'I'd better drive,' said Powers. 'The steering may be wonky.'

He drove in silence, reflecting upon what the incident would cost in terms of himself. Then he wondered idly, as he often did, what it would be like to be a solicitor or a bank manager. He couldn't fit himself into either role; he couldn't hear himself advising on the purchase of a house, or lending money, or retailing the details of the divorce laws. It seemed a truth that his tasks were destined to be expendable; only in war had he established himself.

'Coffee now?' Miss Hobish asked with meekness.

He looked at the front of the car again. Both headlights were smashed.

'I'm going to give you a cheque,' said Miss Hobish. She handed him coffee, and biscuits with icing on them. 'For that damage to your motor. I suppose it would be two hundred pounds?'

'Two hundred,' said Powers, falling in with the plan. 'J. P. the initials are.'

'Now we'll forget about it?' She was anxious, and he nodded, tucking the cheque away and thinking about it.

Ransome would be at the Saracen's Head at lunchtime. He'd park the Austin round at the back where Ransome wouldn't see it and wouldn't guess anything. Two hundred: he could make it last a long time, nice to have it by him, nice to be able to draw on it now and again.

'Lovely biscuits, Miss Hobish.'

'So forgiving, Mr Powers! I thought you mightn't speak to me, your beautiful motor broken up.'

'Not at all –'

'Have another of those biscuits, I know you like them. I get them at Sainsbury's.'

He dunked the biscuit in his coffee and sucked off the coloured icing. It was a comfortable room. The armchair he sat in was large and soft. Once he had fallen asleep in it. Once Miss Hobish, recognizing his fatigue, had invited him to take off his shoes.

'Goodbye, Miss Hobish.'

'More coffee? Biscuits?'

'I fear I must make my way, Miss Hobish.'

'Goodbye then, Mr Powers.' They shook hands as they always did.

It was the boredom, he thought; it was that that prevented him from being the easy extrovert he was born to be. The boredom of repeating, the boredom of talking in simple terms. Hand signals and gear changes: the boredom gave him time to think, it made him think. Powers did not employ these words in his survey of his trouble, but that was the meaning he arrived at. Thoughts ran around in his brain like hares. He didn't know how to catch them.

'I couldn't be happier,' said Ransome.

Powers examined the beer in his tankard. He nodded, smiling to display enthusiasm.

'Do you know,' queried Ransome, 'what I'm going to do next?'

In three months' time Powers knew he'd be beginning to think Ransome a swine. Ransome had the makings of another Roche; probably he was worse.

'I'm going to fire Jack Clay,' said Ransome.

It was one thing knowing the man in the Saracen's Head, talking over a beer about their days in the RAF; it was rather different having him in charge of one's daily life. *I'm going to fire J. P. Powers*. He could hear the man saying it, in this very bar, to some youthful figure who might make a better hand of distributing the requisites.

'I'm going to fire Jack Clay and put J. P. Powers in his car. What d'you think of that, a big Consul?'

'Fine,' said J. P. Powers. 'Fine, fine, a Consul's lovely.'

'I've got a concern making rubber sheets and hot-water bottles shaped like a bunny rabbit. I'd like to have the lot, you know; carry-cots, everything, a full service. I've got a fellow in Hoxton working on a wee-control.'

The old, tired thoughts began all over again. He couldn't see himself clearly; he couldn't see how his pattern was cut or what he was meant to do, or had ever been meant to do. He began to worry and he hated himself for it; because he didn't want to worry, because the thoughts were forced upon him.

'A pregnant woman,' Ransome was going on, 'will buy anything. Apples off a tree, old boy. Two days out and by God, you'll *know* you never had it so good.'

Powers nodded.

'Two pints,' Ransome said to the barmaid.

If he worked on the public transport he'd be a cog in a big machine, getting people to work in the morning, taking them home at night. Otherwise they'd have to walk. He'd seen them during a transport strike, walking from Regent Street to Wimbledon. You couldn't do that more than once a week.

'Will I be all right?'

'Old boy?'

'Will I fit the bill?'

'Haven't I said so? Haven't I been plaguing you to come in for years? I mean what I say, old boy.'

It occurred to him that Ransome, far from being kind, was deliberately being cruel. Ransome was pointing the moral. They had walked out of the RAF together on the same day. They had gone their separate ways, he to teach learner drivers, Ransome to set up in business. And now Ransome was going to employ him. For years, all those Sunday mornings in the pub, Ransome's persuasive talk had been designed to needle him. He had been Ransome's superior in the RAF.

'Drink to it.'

He raised his tankard to meet Ransome's.

'Get a nice new suit,' suggested Ransome, smiling. 'Spick and span, with a polish on the shoes. They'll love you, old boy.'

He sat in the Austin, thinking about the last three hours. The pints of beer had darkened the hue of his face. He could feel them in his stomach, thick and comforting – a moat against Roche who was talking in his mind. He saw his flat mouth open and close, and the words lay between them, above Roche's tidy desk, eavesdroppings for the typing girl. So that was that: Powers must nod and understand, and go away and never return, must be forgotten by Roche, and by the typist whose breasts he had so much desired. Already he was a man of another trade, a good-hearted man who talked to the pregnant woman about what was to come, taking an interest and selling a requisite.

The sun was hot on his face as he sat in the Austin. His skin relaxed, that part of him happy in the heat. He closed his eyes and gave himself up to the tiny moment. The sun touched his hands on the steering wheel and warmed them too. Beer in his stomach, sun on his skin: he had felt such cosseting before. He had lain in bed, stretched and at peace, warmly covered. The warmth of his wife had welcomed him and given him another version of simple sensuality. Blearily, an awareness stirred in J. P. Powers. He did not think in so many words that the excuse for his life lay in moments like these: only in what he received, since he contributed nothing. He did not think it because it was absurd when it was put like that, clarified and clinical. The feeling hammered at his brain but no tendril stretched out to fashion it into thought. A cloud obscured the shaft of sunlight and the feeling evaporated, giving way to an afternoon depression. He switched on the ignition and drove the Austin for the last time, past Cave Crescent and Mortimer Road, out on to Putney Hill and into the stream of traffic.

The Day We Got Drunk on Cake

Garbed in a crushed tweed suit, fingering the ragged end of a tie that might have already done a year's service about his waist, Swann de Lisle uttered a convivial obscenity in the four hundred cubic feet of air they euphemistically called my office. I had not seen him for some years: he is the kind of person who is often, for no reason one can deduce, out of the country. In passing, one may assume that his lengthy absences are due in some way to the element of disaster that features so commandingly in his make-up.

I should have known when I saw him standing there that I must instantly be on my guard. In my prevailing condition of emotional delicacy I could not hope to cope with whatever entertainment Swann had in mind for me. For, to give him his due, Swann never came empty-handed. Swann was a great one for getting the best out of life; and he offered one, invariably, a generous part of his well-laid plans. This time, he explained, he was offering me an attractive afternoon. In turn, I explained that I did not feel like an attractive afternoon, that I was too busy to gild the hours in the manner he was suggesting. But Swann was sitting down, well entrenched; and in the end he talked me into it.

I wrote a note and put it on my typewriter: *Tuesday p.m. Am under surgeon's knife.* Then I made a telephone call.

'Lucy?'

'Hullo, Mike.'

'How are you?'

'Very well, Mike. How are you?'

'Very well, too. Just thought I'd ring –'

'Thank you, Mike.'

'We must meet again soon.'

'Yes, we must.'

'I'd invite you to lunch only an old and valued friend has just transpired.'

'That's nice for you.'

'Well, yes.'

'Thanks for ringing, Mike.'

'Goodbye, Lucy.'

'Goodbye, Mike.'

Swann was drawing designs on the varnish of my desk with a straightened-out paper-clip.

'That wasn't your wife,' he said.

'Wife? Far from it.'

'You haven't married or anything?'

'No.'

'Good. I've got a couple in a hostelry. They tell me they know you.' We sauntered out into the September sun to meet them.

I have always wanted to invent pert shorthand typists with good figures and pretty lips whose heads may easily be turned by the crisp jingle of money, jolly girls who have done the stint at Pitman's and do not believe in anticipating marriage. It might quite easily have been such companions with whom we found ourselves wasting away that afternoon. As it happened, it was Margo and Jo, a smart pair who drew pictures for the glossy magazines.

'When I was eleven,' Jo told me, 'I wrote this children's book and drew all the pictures. Somebody published it, and that of course made me unpopular with everyone.'

'You must have been hugely clever.'

'No, honestly. It was terribly bad, as you can imagine. Just chance that it got published.'

'Words,' said Margo, 'mean a lot to Jo. She has a real sense.'

'She's bonkers,' said Swann.

'For God's sake, Swann,' said Margo.

Jo and Swann moved together. Swann was bored and he began to tell Jo a joke. Margo said, specifically to me: 'Jo is the most talented person I've ever met.' I nodded, not caring one way or the other. The bar was full of uniformed men: dark grey suits, waistcoats, white shirts, striped ties of some club or school.

'Have a drink, Margo?'

Margo said that was a good idea and I squeezed through to the wet counter and floated a ten-shilling note on a pool of beer. When I returned to her Margo said:

'Tell me straight, what do you think of Nigel?'

Nigel? Playing for time I sipped my beer, wondering why I drank the stuff since I disliked it so much. I said:

'Oh, I like Nigel.'

'Do you *really*?'

'Well, he's all right. I mean –'

'Sometimes, Mike, I think Nigel is the most awful bore.'

I remembered. Nigel was plump and talkative. Nigel would tell you anything you might ever wish to know. When Nigel got going there was, in truth, no stopping Nigel. Nigel was Margo's husband.

I drank some more beer. It was cold and tasteless. I said nothing.

'Nigel and I had a barney last night.'

'Oh God!'

Margo told me about the barney. I listened dejectedly. Then I bought some more drink, and this time I changed mine to whisky. Someone had once told me that Jo had a husband too. Both marriages were considered to be heading for the rocks.

Suddenly Margo stopped about Nigel. She leered at me and said something I didn't catch. From the next few sentences, I realized she was telling me I'd make a good husband.

'I suppose I would,' I said.

'I'm not in love with you or anything,' Margo said, swaying.

'Of course not.'

After the pub we went off to have some lunch. All the way in the taxi I thought about Lucy.

We went to an Italian place in Soho that was too expensive and not particularly good. Swann told us the history of his life and ate only series of cassatas. I found a telephone on the stairs and rang up Lucy.

'Hullo, Lucy. What are you doing?'

'What d'you mean, what am I doing? I'm standing here talking to you on the telephone.'

'I'm getting drunk with people in Soho.'

'Well, that's nice for you.'

'Is it? Wish you were here.'

Lucy would be bored by this. 'I've been reading *Adam Bede*,' she said.

'A good story.'

'Yes.'

'Have you had lunch?'

'I couldn't find anything. I had some chocolate.'

'I telephoned to see how you were.'

'I'm fine, thanks.'

'I wanted to hear your voice.'

'Oh come off it. It's just a voice.'

'Shall I tell you about it?'

'I'd rather you didn't. I don't know why.'

'Shall we meet some time?'

'I'm sure we shall.'

'I'll ring you when I'm sober.'

'Do that. I must get back to *Adam Bede*.'

'Goodbye.'

'Goodbye.'

I replaced the receiver and stood there looking down the steep stairs. Then I descended them.

'What on earth shall we do now?' Swann said. 'It's four o'clock.'

'I want to talk to Mike,' Margo announced. 'Nobody's to listen.'

I sat beside her and she began to speak in a limping whisper. 'I want your advice about Nigel, Mike.'

'Honestly, I scarcely know him.'

'Doesn't matter. Look, I think there's something the matter with Nigel.'

I asked her to be specific. Instead she turned her assertion into a question. 'Mike, do *you* think there's something wrong with Nigel?'

'Well –'

'Be frank now.'

'I tell you, I don't know him. For all I know he may have an artificial stomach.'

'Nigel hasn't an artificial stomach, actually.'

'Good.'

'I don't know why you should think that about him. He doesn't even have trouble with his stomach.'

'Well, then, what's the mat·er with the man?'

'I think he's probably mental.'

'Well, for God's sake get him attended to, Margo.'

'You think I should?'

'Certainly I do. Unless you like his being mental.'

Margo giggled. She said:

'He's taken to doing such odd things. I mean, I don't know where this is going to stop.'

'Odd things like what?'

'Like bringing home elderly women. He comes in with these women, explaining that he has been attending some meeting with them and has brought them back for coffee. It's quite alarming – Nigel with four or five old ladies trailing behind him. They stay for ages. I've no idea where he gets them from. I think he imagines he's being kind.'

'What does Nigel say?'

'He says they haven't finished their meeting. They just sit around writing little notes. Nobody *says* anything.'

'I think it's all very interesting. I'm sure there's some quite simple explanation. I don't think you've really investigated the matter, Margo.'

'Let's leave this place,' Swann said.

We went to another place, called the Blue Goat. It was one of those clubs where you can drink in the afternoon without having to watch strip-tease. Margo tried to go on about Nigel, but I said firmly that I didn't want to hear anything more about Nigel. I talked to Jo.

'Jo,' I said, 'do you know a girl called Lucy Anstruth?'

'Small, plump, balding a little?'

'No. Lucy is a very beautiful person.'

'Not the same girl.'

'Tall, fair, very blue eyes. Moves like a cat.'

'Don't know her.'

'She says unexpected things. She's half Swedish or something.'

'Mike, would you guess I was half Welsh?'

'No. I want to ask you about Lucy –'

'But I don't know her.'

'I don't know what to do about Lucy.'

'You sound like Margo. Margo doesn't know what to do about Nigel. Nobody knows what to do about anyone else. God! May I have some more vodka?'

'Yes. As I say –'

'I want a triple vodka.'

I ordered the vodka. Beside us, Swann and Margo were sitting in preoccupied silence; they weren't even listening to what we were saying. Margo caught my eye and opened her mouth to speak. I turned my back and handed Jo her drink.

'Something's the matter with Margo's husband,' Jo said. 'Poor Margo's terribly worried.'

'Yes, I know all about it. Margo has been telling me.'

'I like Nigel, you know.'

'Perhaps you can help him straighten himself out. We were talking about something else. I was telling you –'

'Seems Nigel brings women home.'

'Yes I know, Jo.'

'Bit rough on Margo.'

Margo heard this. She shouted: 'What's rough on Margo?' and then the conversation became general. I went away to telephone Lucy.

'Lucy?'

'Hullo. Is that Mike?'

'Yes.'

'Hullo, Mike.'

'Hullo, Lucy.'

'How are you?'

'I'm feeling funny. But Lucy?'

'Yes?'

'I'm not trying to *be* funny. I'm not being amusing.'

'Where are you?'

'In the Blue Goat.'

'Wherever's that?'

'It's lined with leopard skin. Jo and Margo and Swann are here too.'

'Who are they?'

'Just other people.'

'Nice of you to ring, Mike.'

'Margo's husband Nigel brings women home. I wondered perhaps if you had a word of advice I could give her. She's worried about the women. They come in groups.'

'Oh, Mike, I don't know about things like that. I wouldn't know what to do. Honestly.'

'Sorry, Lucy; I just thought you might.'

'The doorbell's ringing. Goodbye, Mike. If I were you I'd go home.'

Swann said he wanted tea. We left the Blue Goat and walked in dazzling sunshine towards Floris.

Margo began again about Nigel.

Swann said he knew a man who would do Nigel a world of good. He couldn't remember the treatment this man offered, but he said it was highly thought of.

I went away to telephone Lucy.

'Lucy?'

A man's voice answered. I said: 'May I speak to Lucy? Is that the right number?'

The man didn't reply and in a moment Lucy came on. 'Is that Mike again?'

'Hullo, Lucy. How are you?'

'I'm fine, Mike.'

'Good.'

'Mike, you telephoned me at four fifteen. Do you know what time it is now?'

'What time is it now?'

'Four thirty-five.'

'Am I being a nuisance, is that it?'

'No, no. Just, is there anything I can do for you? I mean, do you want something and feel unable to express yourself?'

'I'm bored. I'm with these people. Lucy.'

'Yes?'

'Who's that in your flat?'

'A friend called Frank. You don't know him.'

'What's he doing there?'

'What d'you mean, what's he doing?'

'Well –'

'Look, I'll ask him. Frank, what are you doing?'

'What's he say?'

'He says he's making a cup of tea.'

'I'm having tea too. In Floris. I wish you were here.'

'Goodbye, Mike.'

'Don't go, Lucy.'

'Goodbye, Mike.'

'Goodbye, Lucy.'

When I got back to the others I found them laughing in an uproarious manner. Swann said the cake they were eating was making them drunk. 'Smell it,' he said. It smelt of rum. I tasted some: it tasted of rum too. We all ate a lot of the cake, laughing at the thought of getting drunk on cake. We ordered some more, and told the waitress it was delicious. When the enthusiasm had melted a bit Swann said:

'Mike, we want your advice about Margo's husband.'

'I've told Margo –'

'No, Mike – seriously now. You know about these things.'

'Why do you think I know about these things? I do not know about these things.'

'All right, Mike, I'll tell you. Margo's husband Nigel keeps turning up with groups of old females. Margo's worried in case the thing develops a bit – you know, tramps, grocers, one-legged soldiers. What d'you think she should do?'

'I don't know what Margo should do. Margo, I don't know what you should do. Except perhaps ask Nigel what he's up to. In the meantime, have some more cake.'

'Now there's an idea,' Swann shouted excitedly. 'Margo love, why don't you ask old Nigel what he's up to?'

Jo hacked affectionately at my face with her great spiked fingers. I guessed it was an expression of admiration rather than attack because she smiled as she did so.

'But all Nigel says,' Margo said, 'is that they haven't finished their meeting.'

'Ah yes,' said Swann, 'but you don't press him. You don't say: "What meeting?" You don't indicate that you are in the dark as to the nub of their business. Nigel may well imagine that you accept the whole state of affairs without question and expect little else of married life. When you were at the Gents,' Swann said to me, 'Margo confessed she was worried.'

'She had previously confessed as much to me. I wasn't at the Gents. I was making a telephone call.'

'Shall *I* do that?' Margo said. 'Shall I ring up Nigel and ask him to explain everything?'

We all nodded. Margo rose, hesitated, and sat down again. She said she couldn't. She explained she was too shy to telephone her husband in this way. She turned to me.

'Mike, would you do it?'

'Me?'

'Mike, would you telephone?'

'Are you asking me to telephone your husband and inquire about his relationship with some elderly women who are entirely unknown to me?'

'Mike, for my sake.'

'Think of the explanations it would involve me in. Think of the confusion. Nigel imagining I was the husband of one of these women. Nigel imagining I was the police. Nigel asking me question after question. For goodness' sake, how do you think I would get some kind of answer out of *him*?'

Swann said: 'All you have to do is to say: "Is that Nigel? Now look here, Nigel, what's all this I hear about these women who come to your house at all hours of the day and night?" Say you represent the Ministry of Pensions.'

'I can't address the man as Nigel and then say I'm from the Ministry of Pensions.'

'Mike, Margo's husband's name *is* Nigel. He'll be expecting you to address him as Nigel. If you don't address him as Nigel, he'll simply tell you to go to hell. He'll say you've got a wrong number.'

'So I say: "Hullo, Nigel, this is the Ministry of Pensions." The man'll think I'm crazy.'

Margo said: 'Mike, you just do it your own way. Take no notice of Swann. Swann's been eating too much cake. Come on, you know where the telephone is.' She gave me a piece of paper with a number on it.

'Oh God,' I said; and unable to bear it any longer I borrowed fourpence and marched off to the telephone.

'Hullo?' said the voice at the other end.

'Hullo. Can I speak to Lucy? Please.'

'Hullo,' Lucy said.

'Hullo, Lucy.'

'Well?' said Lucy.

'It's Mike.'

'I know it's Mike.'

'They wanted me to telephone this man I was telling you about, but I can't go telephoning people in this way –'

'Why don't you go home to bed?'

'Because I wouldn't sleep. Remember the man with the elderly women? Well, they wanted me to telephone him and ask him what he's up to. Lucy, I can't do that, can I?'

'No, quite honestly I don't believe you can.'

'They told me to pose as the Ministry of Pensions.'

'Goodbye, Mike.'

'Just a – Lucy?'

'Yes?'

'Isn't that man still there?'

'Which man is this?'

'The man in your flat.'

'Frank. He's still here.'

'Who is he, Lucy?'

'He's called Frank.'

'Yes, but what does he do?'

'I don't know what he does. Frank, what do you do? For a living? He says he's a – what, Frank? A freight agent, Mike.'

'A freight agent.'

'Goodbye.'

'Goodbye, Lucy.'

When I arrived back at the tea-table everyone was very gay. Nobody asked me what Nigel had said. Swann paid the bill and said he was anxious to show us a display of Eastern horrors somewhere in Euston and would afterwards take us to a party. In the taxi Margo said:

'What did Nigel say?'

'He was out.'

'Was there no reply?'

'A woman answered. She said I was interrupting the meeting. I said "What meeting?" but she wanted to know who I was before she would answer that. I said I was the Ministry of Pensions and she said "Oh my God", and rang off.'

We were hours early for the party, but nobody seemed to mind. I helped a woman in slacks to pour bottles of wine into a crock. Swann, Margo and Jo played with a tape-recorder, and after a time the woman's husband arrived and we all went out to eat.

About eight, people began to arrive. The place filled with tobacco smoke, music and fumes; and the party began to swing along at a merry enough pace. A girl in ringlets talked to me earnestly about love. I think she must have been feeling much the same as I was, but I didn't fancy her as a soulmate, not even a temporary one. She said: 'It seems to me that everyone has a quality that can get the better of love. Is stronger, you see. Like pride. Or honesty. Or moral – even intellectual, even emotional – integrity. Take two people in love. The only thing that can really upset things is this personal quality in one of them. Other people don't come into it at all. Except in a roundabout way – as instruments of jealousy, for instance. Don't you agree?'

I wasn't sure about anything, but I said yes.

'Another thing about love,' the girl with the ringlets said, 'is its extraordinary infection. Has it ever occurred to you that when you're in love with someone you're really wanting to be loved yourself? Because that, of course, is the natural law. I mean, it would be odd if every time one person loved another person the first person wasn't loved in return. There's only a very tiny percentage of that kind of thing.'

An aggressive young man, overhearing these remarks, began to laugh. He went on laughing, looking at the girl in ringlets and looking at me.

I went away and filled my glass from the crock, and asked a pretty middle-aged woman what she did. Her answer was coy; I smiled and passed on. Margo caught my arm and dragged me off to a corner. 'Mike, you'll ring Nigel again?'

'I've been thinking about that,' I said. 'Honestly, I don't think I can interfere.'

'Oh but, dear, you promised.'

'Promised? I didn't promise anything.'

'Oh Mike.'

'Really, the whole affair – oh all right.'

'Now, Mike?'

'All right. Now.'

'Lucy?'

'Is that Mike?'

'Who else?'

'Who indeed? Where are you now?'

'I'm at a party.'

'A good party?'

'Yes, I suppose so. Why don't you come along?'

'I can't, Mike. I'm doing things.'

'With the bloody freight agent, I suppose.'

'The what agent?'

'Freight. Your friend the freight agent. Frank.'

'He's not a freight agent. He's in publishing.'

'What'd he say he was a freight agent for?'

A lengthy explanation followed. Calling himself a freight agent was a sample of Frank's humour. I thought about this as I made my way back to Margo.

'What'd he say, Mike?'

'A woman said Nigel wasn't in.'

'Is that all?'

'I said the house was being watched. I said the local authorities weren't at all happy.'

'What'd she say?'

'She began to moan, so I said "I mean it," and rang off.'

'Thank you, Mike.'

'That's all right. Any time.'

Swann joined us and Margo said: 'Mike's been on to Nigel again. Mike's being wonderful.'

Swann patted me on the back and said: 'Any joy?'

Margo started to tell him. I went away.

Jo was pretending to listen to a couple of men who were between them retailing a complicated story. She said to me in a low voice: 'Don't worry about Margo. I'll see she comes through the other side.'

I stared at her, wondering why she should imagine I was worried about Margo. 'I'm sure you will, Jo,' I said.

'Trust Jo,' she whispered.

I said I considered her a trustworthy person. I began to elaborate on the thought. One of the men said: 'D'you mind, old boy?'

I shrugged and pushed a path back to the telephone. I dialled three times to be certain, but on each occasion there was no reply.

A ragged form of dancing was now taking place. Pausing by the crock, I found myself once again in the company of the girl with the ringlets. She smiled at me and in a boring way I said: 'Do you know a girl called Lucy Anstruth?'

The girl with the ringlets shook her head. 'Should I?'

'I suppose not,' I said. The girl examined me closely and passed on.

I went upstairs and discovered a quiet room with a bed in it. A lamp on a dressing-table gave out a weak light. The bed, which looked comfortable, was almost in darkness. I stretched out on it, welcoming the gloom. In a few moments I dropped off to sleep. When I awoke the luminous dial of my watch indicated that I had been asleep for two hours. Two girls were tidying their faces at the dressing-table. They drew head-scarves with horses on them from their handbags and placed them about their heads. They spoke in a whisper and left the room. I lay there considering the events of the day and wondering how I was going to feel about them at breakfast. How one feels at breakfast about the preceding day has always seemed to be important to me.

A man with a glass in his hand entered the room and placed himself before the mirror on the dressing-table. He combed his hair and tightened his tie. Then he took a handkerchief from his pocket and wrapped it around his right forefinger. He inserted this into each ear, twisting his forefinger back and forth. He remarked to himself on the outcome of this operation, examining his handkerchief. I closed my eyes; when I opened them he was gone. I lit a cigarette and set off to the telephone again.

'What is it?' a voice said. It was the publishing man. I asked to speak to Lucy.

'Hullo, Lucy.'

'Oh, Mike, really –'

'Lucy, that man's there again.'

'I know, Mike.'

'It's two o'clock in the morning.'

'Two o'clock in the morning. I'm sorry, Mike.' Her voice was so gentle that I said:

'Stop trying not to hurt me.'

'I think I'd better ring off.'

'I'll ring off, damn it.'

I stood by the telephone, considering, and feeling sick. I felt something between my fingers and looked down at the piece of paper with Nigel's telephone number on it. I lifted the receiver and dialled it.

I waited almost a minute and then a woman's voice said: 'Yes? Who is that please?'

I think I said: 'I want to know what's going on.'

The woman said quickly: 'Who is that speaking? You haf the wrong number.'

'I do not,' I retaliated briskly. 'Please bring Nigel to the phone.'

'Nigel is in the Chair. You are interrupting our meeting with this demand. There is much on the agenda. I cannot attend to you, sir.'

'This is the Ministry of Pensions,' I said, and I heard the woman breathing laboriously. Then she cut me off.

I walked back through the party and looked for the front door. I was thinking that everything had been more or less resolved. Margo's grievance had had its airing; she felt the better for it, and all anyone had to do now was to ask Nigel what he was up to and press the point until a satisfactory answer was achieved. As for me, time would heal and time would cure. I knew it, and it was the worst thing of all. I didn't want to be cured. I wanted the madness of my love for Lucy to go on lurching at me from dreams; to mock me from half-empty glasses; to leap at me unexpectedly. In time Lucy's face would fade to a pin-point; in time I would see her on the street and greet her with casualness, and sit with her over coffee, quietly discussing the flow beneath the bridges since last we met. Today – not even that, for already it was tomorrow – would slide away like all the other days. Not a red-letter day. Not the day of my desperate bidding. Not the day on which the love of my life was snaffled away from me. I opened the front door and looked out into the night. It was cold and uncomforting. I liked it like that. I hated the moment, yet I loved it because in it I still loved Lucy. Deliberately I swung the door and shut away the darkness and drizzle. As I went back to the party the sadness of all the forgetting stung me. Even already, I thought, time is at work; time is ticking her away; time is destroying her, killing all there was between us. And with time on my side I would look back on the day without bitterness and without emotion. I would remember it only as a flash on the brittle surface of nothing, as a day that was rather funny, as the day we got drunk on cake.

Miss Smith

One day Miss Smith asked James what a baby horse was called and James couldn't remember. He blinked and shook his head. He knew, he explained, but he just couldn't remember. Miss Smith said:

'Well, well, James Machen doesn't know what a baby horse is called.'

She said it loudly so that everyone in the classroom heard. James became very confused. He blinked and said:

'Pony, Miss Smith?'

'Pony! James Machen says a baby horse is a pony! Hands up everyone who knows what a baby horse is.'

All the right arms in the room, except James's and Miss Smith's, shot upwards. Miss Smith smiled at James.

'Everyone knows,' she said. 'Everyone knows what a baby horse is called except James.'

James thought: I'll run away. I'll join the tinkers and live in a tent.

'What's a baby horse called?' Miss Smith asked the class and the class shouted:

'Foal, Miss Smith.'

'A foal, James,' Miss Smith repeated. 'A baby horse is a foal, James dear.'

'I knew, Miss Smith. I knew but –'

Miss Smith laughed and the class laughed, and afterwards nobody would play with James because he was so silly to think that a baby horse was a pony.

James was an optimist about Miss Smith. He thought it might be different when the class went on the summer picnic or sat tightly together at the Christmas party, eating cake and biscuits and having their mugs filled from big enamel jugs. But it never was different. James got left behind when everyone was racing across the fields at the picnic and Miss Smith had to wait impatiently, telling the class that James would have to have his legs stretched. And at the party she heaped his plate with seed-cake because she imagined, so she said, that he was the kind of child who enjoyed such fare.

Once James found himself alone with Miss Smith in the classroom. She was sitting at her desk correcting some homework. James was staring in front of him, admiring a fountain pen that the day before his mother had bought for him. It was a small fountain pen, coloured purple and black and white. James believed it to be elegant.

It was very quiet in the classroom. Soundlessly Miss Smith's red pencil ticked and crossed and underlined. Without looking up, she said: 'Why don't you go out and play?'

'Yes, Miss Smith,' said James. He walked to the door, clipping his pen into his pocket. As he turned the handle he heard Miss Smith utter a sound of irritation. He turned and saw that the point of her pencil had broken. 'Miss Smith, you may borrow my pen. You can fill it with red ink. It's quite a good pen.'

James crossed the room and held out his pen. Miss Smith unscrewed the cap and prodded at the paper with the nib. 'What a funny pen, James!' she said. 'Look, it can't write.'

'There's no ink in it,' James explained. 'You've got to fill it with red ink, Miss Smith.'

But Miss Smith smiled and handed the pen back. 'What a silly boy you are to waste your money on such a poor pen!'

'But I didn't –'

'Come along now, James, aren't you going to lend me your pencil-sharpener?'

'I haven't got a pencil-sharpener, Miss Smith.'

'No pencil-sharpener? Oh James, James, you haven't got anything, have you?'

When Miss Smith married she stopped teaching, and James imagined he had escaped her for ever. But the town they lived in was a small one and they often met in the street or in a shop. And Miss Smith, who at first found marriage rather boring, visited the school quite regularly. 'How's James?' she would say, smiling alarmingly at him. 'How's my droopy old James?'

When Miss Smith had been married for about a year she gave birth to a son, which occupied her a bit. He was a fine child, eight pounds six ounces, with a good long head and blue eyes. Miss Smith was delighted with him, and her husband, a solicitor, complimented her sweetly and bought cigars and drinks for all his friends. In time, mother and son were seen daily taking the air: Miss Smith on her trim little legs and the baby in his frilly pram. James, meeting the two, said: 'Miss Smith, may I see the baby?' But Miss Smith laughed and said that she was not Miss Smith any more. She wheeled the pram rapidly away, as though the child within it might be affected by the proximity of the other.

'What a dreadful little boy that James Machen is,' Miss Smith reported to her husband. 'I feel so sorry for the parents.'

'Do I know him? What does the child look like?'

'Small, dear, like a weasel wearing glasses. He quite gives me the creeps.'

Almost without knowing it, James developed a compulsion about Miss Smith. At first it was quite a simple compulsion: just that James had to talk to God about Miss Smith every night before he went to sleep, and try to find out from God what it was about him that Miss Smith so despised. Every night he lay in bed and had his conversation, and if once he forgot it James knew that the next time he met Miss Smith she would probably say something that might make him drop down dead.

After about a month of conversation with God James discovered he had found the solution. It was so simple that he marvelled he had never thought of it before. He began to get up very early in the morning and pick bunches of flowers. He would carry them down the street to Miss Smith's house and place them on a window-sill. He was careful not to be seen, by Miss Smith or by anyone else. He knew that if anyone saw him the plan couldn't work. When he had picked all the flowers in his own garden he started to pick them from other people's gardens. He became rather clever at moving silently through the gardens, picking flowers for Miss Smith.

Unfortunately, though, on the day that James carried his thirty-first bunch of blooms to the house of Miss Smith he was observed. He saw the curtains move as he reached up to lay the flowers on the window-sill. A moment later Miss Smith, in her dressing-gown, had caught him by the shoulder and pulled him into the house.

'James Machen! It would be James Machen, wouldn't it? Flowers from the creature, if you please! What are you up to, you dozy James?'

James said nothing. He looked at Miss Smith's dressing-gown and thought it was particularly pretty: blue and woolly, with an edging of silk.

'You've been trying to get us into trouble,' cried Miss Smith. 'You've been stealing flowers all over the town and putting them at our house. You're an underhand child, James.'

James stared at her and then ran away.

After that, James thought of Miss Smith almost all the time. He thought of her face when she had caught him with the flowers, and how she had afterwards told his father and nearly everyone else in the town. He thought of how his father had had to say he was sorry to Miss Smith, and how his mother and father had quarrelled about the affair. He counted up all the things Miss Smith had ever said to him, and all the things she had ever done to him, like giving him seed-cake at the Christmas party. He hadn't meant to harm Miss Smith as she said he had. Giving people flowers wasn't unkind; it was to show them you liked them and wanted them to like you.

'When somebody hurts you,' James said to the man who came to cut the grass, 'what do you do about it?'

'Well,' said the man, 'I suppose you hurt them back.'

'Supposing you can't,' James argued.

'Oh, but you always can. It's easy to hurt people.'

'It's not, really,' James said.

'Look,' said the man, 'all I've got to do is to reach out and give you a clip on the ear. That'd hurt you.'

'But I couldn't do that to you because you're too big. How d'you hurt someone who's bigger than you?'

'It's easier to hurt people who are weaker. People who are weaker are always the ones who get hurt.'

'Can't you hurt someone who is stronger?'

The grass-cutter thought for a time. 'You have to be cunning to do that. You've got to find the weak spot. Everyone has a weak spot.'

'Have you got a weak spot?'

'I suppose so.'

'Could I hurt you on your weak spot?'

'You don't want to hurt me, James.'

'No, but just could I?'

'Yes, I suppose you could.'

'Well then?'

'My little daughter's smaller than you. If you hurt her, you see, you'd be hurting me. It'd be the same, you see.'

'I see,' said James.

All was not well with Miss Smith. Life, which had been so happy when her baby was born, seemed now to be directed against her. Perhaps it was that the child was becoming difficult, going through a teething phase that was pleasant for no one; or perhaps it was that Miss Smith recognized in him some trait she disliked and knew that she would be obliged to watch it develop, powerless to intervene. Whatever the reason, she felt depressed. She often thought of her teaching days, of the big square schoolroom with the children's models on the shelves and the pictures of kings on the walls. Nostalgically, she recalled the feel of frosty air on her face as she rode her bicycle through the town, her mind already practising the first lesson of the day. She had loved those winter days: the children stamping their feet in the playground, the stove groaning and crackling, so red and so fierce that it had to be penned off for safety's sake. It had been good to feel tired, good to bicycle home, shopping a bit on the way, home to tea and the wireless and an evening of reading by the fire. It wasn't that she regretted anything; it was just that now and again, for a day or two, she felt she would like to return to the past.

'My dear,' Miss Smith's husband said, 'you really will have to be more careful.'

'But I am. Truly I am. I'm just as careful as anyone can be.'

'Of course you are. But it's a difficult age. Perhaps, you know, you need a holiday.'

'But I've had difficult ages to deal with for years –'

'Now now, my dear, it's not quite the same, teaching a class of kids.'

'But it shouldn't be as difficult. I don't know –'

'You're tired. Tied to a child all day long, every day of the week, it's no joke. We'll take an early holiday.'

Miss Smith did feel tired, but she knew that it wasn't tiredness that was really the trouble. Her baby was almost three, and for two years she knew she had been making mistakes with him. Yet somehow she felt that they weren't her mistakes: it was as though some other person occasionally possessed her: a negligent, worthless kind of person who was cruel, almost criminal, in her carelessness. Once she had discovered the child crawling on the pavement beside his pram: she had forgotten apparently to attach his harness to the pram hooks. Once there had been beads in his pram, hundreds of them, small and red and made of glass. A woman had drawn her attention to the danger, regarding curiously the supplier of so unsuitable a plaything. 'In his nose he was putting one, dear. And may have swallowed a dozen already. It could kill a mite, you know.' The beads were hers, but how the child had got them she could not fathom. Earlier, when he had been only a couple of months, she had come into his nursery to find an excited cat scratching at the clothes of his cot; and on another occasion she had found him eating a turnip. She wondered if she might be suffering from some kind of serious absent-mindedness, or blackouts. Her doctor told her, uncomfortingly, that she was a little run down.

'I'm a bad mother,' said Miss Smith to herself; and she cried as she looked at her child, warm and pretty in his sleep.

But her carelessness continued and people remarked that it was funny in a teacher. Her husband was upset and unhappy, and finally suggested that they should employ someone to look after the child. 'Someone else?' said Miss Smith. 'Someone *else*? Am I then incapable? Am I so wretched and stupid that I cannot look after my own child? You speak to me as though I were half crazy.' She felt confused and sick and miserable. The marriage teetered beneath the tension, and there was no question of further children.

Then there were two months without incident. Miss Smith began to feel better; she was getting the hang of things; once again she was in control of her daily life. Her child grew and flourished. He trotted nimbly beside her, he spoke his own language, he was wayward and irresponsible, and to Miss Smith and her husband he was intelligent and full of charm. Every day Miss Smith saved up the sayings and doings of this child and duly reported them to her husband. 'He is quite intrepid,' Miss Smith said, and she told her husband how the child would tumble about the room, trying to stand on his head. 'He has an aptitude for athletics,' her husband remarked. They laughed that they, so unathletic in their ways, should have produced so physically lively an offspring.

'And how has our little monster been today?' Miss Smith's husband asked, entering the house one evening at his usual time.

Miss Smith smiled, happy after a good, quiet day. 'Like gold,' she said.

Her husband smiled too, glad that the child had not been a nuisance to her and glad that his son, for his own sake, was capable of adequate behaviour. 'I'll just take a peep at him,' he announced, and he ambled off to the nursery.

He sighed with relief as he climbed the stairs, thankful that all was once again well in the house. He was still sighing when he opened the nursery door and smelt gas. It hissed insidiously from the unlit fire. The room was sweet with it. The child, sleeping, sucked it into his lungs.

The child's face was blue. They carried him from the room, both of them helpless and inadequate in the situation. And then they waited, without speaking, while his life was recovered, until the moment when the doctor, white-coated and stern, explained that it had been a nearer thing than he would wish again to handle.

'This is too serious,' Miss Smith's husband said. 'We cannot continue like this. Something must be done.'

'I cannot understand –'

'It happens too often. The strain is too much for me, dear.'

'I cannot understand it.'

Every precaution had been taken with the gas-fire in the nursery. The knob that controlled the gas pressure was a key and the key was removable. Certainly, the control point was within the child's reach but one turned it on or off, slipped the key out of its socket and placed it on the mantelpiece. That was the simple rule.

'You forgot to take out the key,' Miss Smith's husband said. In his mind an idea took on a shape that frightened him. He shied away, watching it advance, knowing that he possessed neither the emotional nor mental equipment to fight it.

'No, no, no,' Miss Smith said. 'I never forget it. I turned the fire off and put the key on the mantelpiece. I remember distinctly.'

He stared at her, drilling his eyes into hers, hopelessly seeking the truth. When he spoke his voice was dry and weary.

'The facts speak for themselves. You cannot suggest there's another solution?'

'But it's absurd. It means he got out of his cot, turned the key, returned to bed and went to sleep.'

'Or that you turned off the fire and idly turned it on again.'

'I couldn't have; how could I?'

Miss Smith's husband didn't know. His imagination, like a pair of calipers, grasped the ugly thought and held it before him. The facts were on its side, he could not ignore them: his wife was deranged in her mind. Consciously or otherwise she was trying to kill their child.

'The window,' Miss Smith said. 'It was open when I left it. It always is, for air. Yet you found it closed.'

'The child certainly could not have done that. I cannot see what you are suggesting.'

'I don't know. I don't know what I am suggesting. Except that I don't understand.'

'He's too much for you, dear, and that's all there is to it. You must have help.'

'We can't afford it.'

'Be that as it may, we must. We have the child to think of, if not ourselves.'

'But one child! One child cannot be too much for anyone. Look, I'll be extra careful in future. After all, it is the first thing like this that has happened for ages.'

'I'm sorry, dear. We must advertise for a woman.'

'Please –'

'Darling, I'm sorry. It's no use talking. We have talked enough and it has got us nowhere. This is something to be sensible about.'

'Please let's try again.'

'And in the meanwhile? In the meanwhile our child's life must be casually risked day in, day out?'

'No, no.'

Miss Smith pleaded, but her husband said nothing further. He pulled hard on his pipe, biting it between his jaws, unhappy and confused in his mind.

Miss Smith's husband did indeed advertise for a woman to see to the needs of their child, but it was, in fact, unnecessary in the long run to employ one. Because on his third birthday, late in the afternoon, the child disappeared. Miss Smith had put him in the garden. It was a perfectly safe garden: he played there often. Yet when she called him for his tea he did not come; and when she looked for the reason she found that he was not there. The small gate that led to the fields at the back of the house was open. She had not opened it; she rarely used it. Distractedly, she thought he must have managed to release the catch himself. 'That is quite impossible,' her husband said. 'It's too high and too stiff.' He looked at her oddly, confirmed in his mind that she wished to be rid of her child. Together they tramped the fields with the police, but although they covered a great area and were out for most of the night they were unsuccessful.

When the search continued in the light of the morning it was a search without hope, and the hopelessness in time turned into the fear of what discovery would reveal. 'We must accept the facts,' Miss Smith's husband said, but she alone continued to hope. She dragged her legs over the wide countryside, seeking a miracle but finding neither trace nor word of her child's wanderings.

A small boy, so quiet she scarcely noticed him, stopped her once by a sawmill. He spoke some shy salutation, and when she blinked her eyes at his face she saw that he was James Machen. She passed him by, thinking only that she envied him his life, that for him to live and her child to die was proof indeed of a mocking Providence. She prayed to this Providence, promising a score of resolutions if only all would be well.

But nothing was well, and Miss Smith brooded on the thought that her husband had not voiced. *I released the gate myself. For some reason I have not wanted this child. God knows I loved him, and surely it wasn't too weak a love? Is it that I've loved so many other children that I have none left that is real enough for my own?* Pathetic, baseless theories flooded into Miss Smith's mind. Her thoughts floundered and collapsed into wretched chaos.

'Miss Smith,' James said, 'would you like to see your baby?'

He stood at her kitchen door, and Miss Smith, hearing the words, was incapable immediately of grasping their meaning. The sun, reflected in the kitchen, was mirrored again in the child's glasses. He smiled at her, more

confidently than she remembered, revealing a silvery wire stretched across
his teeth.

'What did you say?' Miss Smith asked.

'I said, would you like to see your baby?'

Miss Smith had not slept for a long time. She was afraid to sleep because
of the nightmares. Her hair hung lank about her shoulders, her eyes were
dead and seemed to have fallen back deeper into her skull. She stood
listening to this child, nodding her head up and down, very slowly, in a
mechanical way. Her left hand moved gently back and forth on the smooth
surface of her kitchen table.

'My baby?' Miss Smith said. 'My baby?'

'You have lost your baby,' James reminded her.

Miss Smith nodded a little faster.

'I will show you,' James said.

He caught her hand and led her from the house, through the garden and
through the gate into the fields. Hand in hand they walked through the
grass, over the canal bridge and across the warm, ripe meadows.

'I will pick you flowers,' James said and he ran to gather poppies and
cow-parsley and blue, beautiful cornflowers.

'You give people flowers,' James said, 'because you like them and you
want them to like you.'

She carried the flowers and James skipped and danced beside her,
hurrying her along. She heard him laughing; she looked at him and saw
his small weasel face twisted into a merriment that frightened her.

The sun was fierce on Miss Smith's neck and shoulders. Sweat gathered
on her forehead and ran down her cheeks. She felt it on her body, tightening
her clothes to her back and thighs. Only the child's hand was cool, and
beneath her fingers she assessed its strength, wondering about its history.
Again the child laughed.

On the heavy air his laughter rose and fell; it quivered through his body
and twitched lightly in his hand. It came as a giggle, then a breathless
spasm; it rose like a storm from him; it rippled to gentleness; and it pounded
again like the firing of guns in her ear. It would not stop. She knew it
would not stop. As they walked together on this summer's day the laughter
would continue until they arrived at the horror, until the horror was
complete.

The Hotel of the Idle Moon

The woman called Mrs Dankers placed a rose-tipped cigarette between her lips and lit it from the lighter on the dashboard. The brief spurt of light revealed a long, handsome face with a sharpness about it that might often have been reminiscent of the edge of a chisel. In the darkness a double funnel of smoke streamed from her nostrils, and she gave a tiny gasp of satisfaction. On a grass verge two hundred miles north of London the car was stationary except for the gentle rocking imposed by the wind. Above the persistent lashing of the rain the radio played a popular tune of the thirties, quietly and without emotion. It was two minutes to midnight.

'Well?'

The car door banged and Dankers was again beside her. He smelt of rain; it dripped from him on to her warm knees.

'Well?' Mrs Dankers repeated.

He started the engine. The car crept on to the narrow highway, its wipers slashing at the rain, its powerful headlights drawing the streaming foliage startlingly near. He cleared the windscreen with his arm. 'It'll do,' he murmured. He drove on slowly, and the sound of the engine was lost in a medley of wind and rain and the murmur of music and the swish of the wipers.

'It'll do?' said Mrs Dankers. 'Is it the right house?'

He twisted the car this way and that along the lane. The lights caught an image of pillars and gates, closed in upon them and lost them as the car swung up the avenue.

'Yes,' he murmured. 'It's the right house.'

Within that house, an old man lying stiffly in bed heard the jangle of the bell at the hall door and frowned over this unaccustomed sound. At first he imagined that the noise had been caused by the wind, but then the bell rang again, sharply and in a peremptory manner. The old man, called Cronin, the only servant in the house, rose from his bed and dragged a coat on to his body, over his pyjamas. He descended the stairs, sighing to himself.

The pair outside saw a light go on in the hall, and then they heard the tread of Cronin's feet and the sound of a bar being pulled back on the door. Dankers threw a cigarette away and prepared an expression for his face. His wife shivered in the rain.

'It's so late,' the old man in pyjamas said when the travellers had told him their tale. 'I must wake the Marstons for guidance, sir. I can't do this on my own responsibility.'

'It's wet and cold as well,' Dankers murmured, smiling at the man through his widely spread moustache. 'No night to be abroad, really. You must understand our predicament.'

'No night to be standing on a step,' added Mrs Dankers. 'At least may we come in?'

They entered the house and were led to a large drawing-room. 'Please wait,' the man invited. 'The fire is not entirely out. I'll question the Marstons as you warm yourselves.'

The Dankerses did not speak. They stood where the man had left them, staring about the room. Their manner one to the other had an edge of hostility to it, as though they were as suspicious in this relationship as they were of the world beyond it.

'I am Sir Giles Marston,' said another old man. 'You've sustained some travelling difficulty?'

'Our car has let us down – due, I suppose, to some penetration of the weather. We left it by your gates. Sir Giles, we're at your mercy. Dankers the name is. The lady is my good wife.' Dankers stretched his arm towards his host in a manner that might have suggested to an onlooker that he, and not Sir Giles, was the welcomer.

'Our need is simple,' said Mrs Dankers. 'A roof over our heads.'

'Some outhouse maybe,' Dankers hazarded, overplaying his part. He laughed. 'Anywhere we can curl up for an hour or two. We cannot be choosers.'

'I'd prefer a chair,' his wife interceded sharply. 'A chair and a rug would suit me nicely.'

'I'm sure we can do better than that. Prepare two beds, Cronin; and light our guests a fire in their room.'

Sir Giles Marston moved into the centre of the room and in the greater light the Dankerses saw a small, hunched man, with a face like leather that has been stretched for a lifetime and is suddenly slackened; as lined as a map.

'Oh, really,' Dankers protested in his soft voice, 'you mustn't go to such trouble. It's imposition enough to rouse you like this.'

'We'll need sheets,' Cronin said. 'Sheets and bedding: God knows where I shall find them, sir.'

'Brandy,' Sir Giles suggested. 'Am I right, Mrs Dankers, in thinking that strong refreshment would partly answer the situation?'

Cronin left the room, speaking to himself. Sir Giles poured the brandy. 'I'm ninety years of age,' he told his guests, 'But yet aware that inhospitality is a sin to be ashamed of. I bid you good-night.'

'Who are they?' Lady Marston asked in the morning, having heard the tale from her husband.

'My dear, they are simply people. They bear some unpleasant name. More than that I do not really wish to know.'

'It's a sunny day by the look of it. Your guests will have breakfasted and gone by now. I'm sorry in a way, for I would welcome fresh faces and a different point of view. We live too quiet a life, Giles. We are too much thrown in upon each other. It's hardly a healthy manner in which to prepare for our dying.'

Sir Giles, who was engaged in the drawing up of his trousers, smiled. 'Had you seen these two, my dear, you would not have said they are the kind to make our going any easier. The man has a moustache of great proportions, the woman you would describe as smart.'

'You're intolerant, love. And so high-handed that you didn't even discover the reason for this visit.'

'They came because they could move in neither direction. Trouble with their motor-car.'

'They've probably left with all our little bits and pieces. You're a sitting bird for a confidence trick. Oh, Giles, Giles!'

Sir Giles departed, and in the breakfast-room below discovered the pair called Dankers still at table.

'Your man has been most generous,' Dankers said. 'He's fed us like trenchermen: porridge, coffee, bacon and eggs. Two for me, one for my good wife. And toast and marmalade. And this delicious butter.'

'Are you trying to say that an essential commodity was lacking? If so, I fear you must be more precise. In this house we are now past subtlety.'

'You've made a fool of yourself,' Mrs Dankers said to her husband. 'Who wishes to know what two strangers have recently digested?'

'Pardon, pardon,' murmured Dankers. 'Sir Giles, forgive a rough diamond!'

'Certainly. If you have finished, please don't delay on my account. Doubtless you are anxious to be on your way.'

'My husband will attend to the car. Probably it's necessary to send for help to a garage. In the meantime I'll keep you company if I may.'

Dankers left the room, passing on the threshold an elderly lady whom he did not address, wishing to appear uncertain in his mind as to her identity.

'This is the woman who came in the night,' Sir Giles said to his wife. 'Her husband is seeing to their motor-car so that they may shortly be on their way. Mrs Dankers, my wife, Lady Marston.'

'We're more than grateful, Lady Marston. It looked as though we were in for a nasty night.'

'I hope Cronin made you comfortable. I fear I slept through everything. "My dear, we have two guests," my husband said to me this morning. You may imagine my surprise.'

Cronin entered and placed plates of food before Sir Giles and Lady Marston.

Conversationally, Mrs Dankers said: 'You have a fine place here.'

'It's cold and big,' Sir Giles replied.

The Marstons set about their breakfast, and Mrs Dankers, unable to think of something to say, sat in silence. The smoke from her cigarette was an irritation to her hosts, but they did not remark on it, since they accepted its presence as part of the woman herself. When he returned Dankers sat beside his wife again. He poured some coffee and said: 'I am no mechanic, Sir Giles. I would like to use your phone to summon help.'

'We are not on the telephone.'

'Not?' murmured Dankers in simulated surprise, for he knew the fact already. 'How far in that case is the nearest village? And does it boast a garage?'

'Three miles. As to the presence of a garage, I have had no cause to establish that point. But I imagine there is a telephone.'

'Giles, introduce me please. Is this man Mrs Dankers' husband?'

'He claims it. Mr Dankers, my wife, Lady Marston.'

'How d'you do?' Dankers said, rising to shake the offered hand. 'I'm afraid we're in a pickle.'

'You should walk it in an hour,' Sir Giles reminded him.

'There's no way of forwarding a message?'

'No.'

'The postman?'

'He hardly ever comes. And then brings only a circular or two.'

'Perhaps your man?'

'Cronin's days as Hermes are over. You must see that surely for yourself?'

'In that case there's nothing for it but a tramp.'

This conclusion of Dankers' was received in silence.

'Walk, Mr Dankers,' Lady Marston said eventually, and added to her husband's dismay, 'and return for lunch. Afterwards you can leave us at your leisure.'

'How kind of you,' the Dankerses said together. They smiled in unison too. They rose and left the room.

Cronin watched and listened to everything. 'Prepare two beds,' his master had said, and from that same moment Cronin had been on his guard. He had given them breakfast in the morning, and had hoped that once they had consumed it they would be on their way. He took them to be commercial travellers, since they had the air of people who were used to moving about and spending nights in places. 'You have a fine place here,' Mrs Dankers had said to the Marstons, and Cronin had narrowed his eyes, wondering why she had said it, wondering why she was sitting there, smoking a cigarette while the Marstons breakfasted. He had examined their motor-car and had thought it somehow typical of the people. They were people, thought Cronin, who would know what to do with all the knobs and gadgets on the motor-car's dashboard; they would take to that dashboard like ducks to water.

For forty-eight years Cronin had lived in the house, serving the Marstons. Once, there had been other servants, and in his time he had watched over them and over the house itself. Now he contented himself with watching over the Marstons. 'Some outhouse maybe,' Dankers had said, and Cronin had thought that Dankers was not a man who knew much about outhouses. He saw Dankers and Mrs Dankers sitting together in a café connected with a cinema, a place such as he had himself visited twenty-odd years ago and had not cared for. He heard Dankers asking the woman what she would take to eat, adding that he himself would have a mixed grill with chips, and a pot of strong tea, and sliced bread and butter. Cronin observed these people closely and memorized much of what they said.

'Clearly,' Dankers remarked at lunch, 'we're not in training. Or perhaps it was the fascination of your magnificent orchard.'

'Are you saying you didn't walk to the village?' Sir Giles inquired, a trifle impatiently.

'Forgive these city folk,' cried Dankers loudly. 'Quite frankly, we got no distance at all.'

'What are you to do then? Shall you try again this afternoon? There are, of course, various houses on the route. One of them may have a telephone.'

'Your orchard has greatly excited us. I've never seen such trees.'

'They're the finest in England.'

'A pity,' said Mrs Dankers, nibbling at fish on a fork, 'to see it in such rack and ruin.'

Dankers blew upwards into his moustache and ended the activity with a smile. 'It is worth some money, that orchard,' he said.

Sir Giles eyed him coolly. 'Yes, sir; it is worth some money. But time is passing and we are wasting it in conversation. You must see to the affair of your motor-car.'

The storm had brought the apples down. They lay in their thousands in the long grass, damp and glistening, like immense, unusual jewels in the afternoon sun. The Dankerses examined them closely, strolling through the orchard, noting the various trees and assessing their yield. For the purpose they had fetched Wellington boots from their car and had covered themselves in waterproof coats of an opaque plastic material. They did not speak, but occasionally, coming across a tree that pleased them, they nodded.

'A lot could be done, you know,' Dankers explained at dinner. 'It is a great orchard and in a mere matter of weeks it could be set on the road to profit and glory.'

'It has had its glory,' replied Sir Giles, 'and probably its profit too. Now it must accept its fate. I cannot keep it up.'

'Oh, it's a shame! A terrible shame to see it as it is. Why, you could make a fortune, Sir Giles.'

'You didn't get to the village?' Lady Marston asked.

'We could not pass the orchard!'

'Which means,' Sir Giles said, 'that you'll be with us for another night.'

'Could you bear it?' Mrs Dankers smiled a thin smile. 'Could you bear to have us all over again?'

'Of course, of course,' said Lady Marston. 'Perhaps tomorrow you'll feel a little stronger. I understand your lethargy. It's natural after an unpleasant experience.'

'They have been through neither flood nor fire,' her husband reminded her. 'And the village will be no nearer tomorrow.'

'Perhaps,' Dankers began gently, 'the postman will call in the morning –'

'We have no living relatives,' Sir Giles cut in, 'and most of our friends are gone. The circulars come once a month or so.'

'The groceries then?'

'I have inquired of Cronin about the groceries. They came yesterday. They will come again next week.'

'The daily milk is left at the foot of the avenue. Cronin walks to fetch it. You could leave a message there,' Lady Marston suggested. 'It is the arrangement we have for emergencies, such as summoning the doctor.'

'The doctor? But surely by the time he got here —?'

'In greater emergency one of the three of us would walk to the nearest house. We do not,' Sir Giles added, 'find it so difficult to pass one leg before the other. Senior though we may be.'

'Perhaps the milk is an idea,' Lady Marston said.

'Oh no, we could never put anyone to so much trouble. It would be too absurd. No, tomorrow we shall have found our feet.'

But tomorrow when it came was a different kind of day, because with something that disagreed with him in his stomach Sir Giles died in the night. His heart was taxed by sharp little spasms of pain and in the end they were too much for it.

'We're going to see to you for a bit,' Mrs Dankers said after the funeral. 'We'll pop you in your room, dear, and Cronin shall attend to all your needs. You can't be left to suffer your loss alone; you've been so kind to us.'

Lady Marston moved her head up and down. The funeral had been rather much for her. Mrs Dankers led her by the arm to her room.

'Well,' said Dankers, speaking to Cronin with whom he was left, 'so that's that.'

'I was his servant for forty-eight years, sir.'

'Indeed, indeed. And you have Lady Marston, to whom you may devote your whole attention. Meals in her room, Cronin, and pause now and then for the occasional chat. The old lady'll be lonely.'

'I'll be lonely myself, sir.'

'Indeed. Then all the more reason to be good company. And you, more than I, understand the business of being elderly. You know by instinct what to say, how best to seem soothing.'

'Your car is repaired, sir? At least it moved today. You'll be on your way? Shall I pack some sandwiches?'

'Come, come, Cronin, how could we leave two lonely people so easily in the lurch? Chance has sent us to your side in this hour of need: we'll stay to do what we can. Besides, there are Sir Giles's wishes.'

What's this? thought Cronin, examining the eyes of the man who had come in the night and had stayed to see his master buried. They were eyes he would not care to possess himself, for fear of what went with them. He said:

'His wishes, sir?'

'That his orchard should again be put in use. The trees repaired and pruned. The fruit sold for its true value. An old man's dying wish won't go unheeded.'

'But, sir, there's so much work in it. The trees run into many hundreds —'

'Quite right, Cronin. That's observant of you. Many men are needed to straighten the confusion and waste. There's much to do.'

'Sir Giles wished this, sir?' said Cronin, playing a part, knowing that Sir Giles could never have passed on to Dankers his dying wish. 'It's unlike him, sir, to think about his orchard. He watched it failing.'

'He wished it, Cronin. He wished it, and a great deal else. You who have seen some changes in your time are in for a couple more. And now, my lad, a glass of that good brandy would not go down amiss. At a time like this one must try to keep one's spirits up.'

Dankers sat by the fire in the drawing-room, sipping his brandy and writing industriously in a notebook. He was shortly joined by his wife, to whom he handed from time to time a leaf from this book so that she might share his plans. When midnight had passed they rose and walked through the house, measuring the rooms with a practised eye and noting their details on paper. They examined the kitchens and outhouses, and in the moonlight they walked the length of the gardens. Cronin watched them, peeping at them in all their activity.

'There's a pretty little room next to Cronin's that is so much sunnier,' Mrs Dankers said. 'Cosier and warmer, dear. We'll have your things moved there, I think. This one is dreary with memories. And you and Cronin will be company for one another.'

Lady Marston nodded, then changing her mind said: 'I like this room. It's big and beautiful and with a view. I've become used to it.'

'Now, now, my dear, we mustn't be morbid, must we? And we don't always quite know what's best. It's good to be happy, dear, and you'll be happier there.'

'I'll be happier, Mrs Dankers? Happier away from all my odds and ends, and Giles's too?'

'My dear, we'll move them with you. Come, now, look on the bright side. There's the future too, as well as the past.'

Cronin came, and the things were moved. Not quite everything though, because the bed and the wardrobe and the heavy dressing-table would not fit into the new setting.

In the orchard half a dozen men set about creating order out of chaos. The trees were trimmed and then treated, paths restored, broken walls rebuilt. The sheds were cleared and filled with fruit-boxes in readiness for next year's harvest.

'There's a wickedness here,' Cronin reported to Lady Marston. 'There's a cook in the kitchen, and a man who waits on them. My only task, they tell me, is to carry your food and keep your room in order.'

'And to see to yourself, Cronin, to take it easy and to watch your rheumatics. Fetch a pack of cards.'

Cronin recalled the house as it once had been, a place that was lively with weekend guests and was regularly wallpapered. Then there had come the years of decline and the drifting towards decay, and now there was a liveliness of a different order; while the days passed by, the liveliness established itself like a season. Mrs Dankers bustled from room to room, in tune with the altered world. Dankers said: 'It's good to see you seeming so sprightly, Cronin. The weather suits you, eh? And now that we've made these few little changes life is easier, I think.' Cronin replied that it was certainly true that he had less to do. 'So you should have less to do,' said Dankers. 'Face the facts: you cannot hope to undertake a young chap's work.' He smiled, to release the remark of its barb.

Cronin was worried about the passive attitude of Lady Marston. She had gone like a lamb to the small room, which now served as her sitting-room and bedroom combined. She had not stirred from the top of the house since the day of the move; she knew nothing save what he told her of all that was happening.

'The builders are here,' he had said; but quite often, midway through a game of cards, she would pause with her head a little to one side, listening to the distant sound of hammering. 'It is the noise of the builders,' he would remind her; and she would place a card on the table and say: 'I did not know that Sir Giles had ordered the builders.' In the mornings she was well aware of things, but as the day passed on she spoke more often of Sir Giles; of Sir Giles's plans for the orchard and the house. Cronin feared that, day by day, Lady Marston was sinking into her dotage; the morning hours of her clarity were shrinking even as he thought about it.

One afternoon, walking to the foot of the avenue to stretch his legs, Cronin found a small, elegantly painted board secured to one of the pillars. It faced the road, inviting those who passed to read the words it bore. He read them himself and expostulated angrily, muttering the words, repeating them as he made his way back to the house.

'M'lady, this cannot happen. They've turned your house into an hotel.'

Lady Marston looked at Cronin, whom she had known for so many years, who had seen with her and her husband a thousand details of change and reconstruction. He was upset now, she could see it. His white, sparse hair seemed uncombed, which was unusual for Cronin. There was a blush of temper on his cheeks; and in his eyes a wildness one did not associate with so well-trained a servant.

'What is it, Cronin?'

'There's a notice at the gate announcing "The Hotel of the Idle Moon".'

'Well?'

'The Dankerses –'

'Ah, the Dankerses. You talk so much about the Dankerses, Cronin. Yet as I remember them they are surely not worth it. Sir Giles said the man had repeated to him every mouthful of his breakfast. In the end he had to make short shrift of the pair.'

'No, no –'

'Yes, Cronin: they tried his patience. He gave them their marching orders, reminding them that the night was fine and the moon was full. There was a coolness between us, for I believed he had gone too far.'

'No, no. You must remember: the Dankerses are still here. They've tidied up the orchard and now have turned your house into an hotel.'

Lady Marston made her impatient little shaking of the head. 'Of course, of course. Cronin, I apologize. You must find me very trying.'

'It has no meaning: The Hotel of the Idle Moon. Yet I fear, m'lady, it may in time mean much to us.'

Lady Marston laughed quite gaily. 'Few things have meaning, Cronin. It is rather much to expect a meaning for everything.'

They played three games of cards, and the matter was not again referred to. But in the night Lady Marston came to Cronin's bedside and shook him by the shoulder. 'I'm upset,' she said, 'by what you tell me. This isn't right at all. Cronin, listen carefully: tomorrow you must inform Sir Giles. Tell him of our fears. Beg him to reconsider. I'm far too old to act. I must leave it all to you.'

The house was busy then with visitors, and cars up and down the avenue. It thrived as the orchard thrived; it had a comfortable and sumptuous feel, and Cronin thought again of the past.

'Ah, Cronin,' Mrs Dankers said, pausing on the back stairs one day. 'Tell me, how is poor Lady Marston? She does not come down at all, and we're so on the go here that it's hard to find time to make the journey to the top of the house.'

'Lady Marston is well, madam.'

'She's welcome in the lounges. Always welcome. Would you be good enough to tell her, Cronin?'

'Yes, madam.'

'But keep an eye on her, like a good man. I would not like her upsetting the guests. You understand?'

'Yes, madam. I understand. I don't think Lady Marston is likely to make use of the lounges.'

'She would find the climb up and down too much, I dare say.'

'Yes, madam. She would find it too much.'

Cronin made many plans. He thought that one day when Dankers was away he would approach the orchard with Sir Giles's rifle and order the men to cut down the trees. That at least would bring one part of the sadness to an end. He saw the scene quite clearly: the trees toppling one against the other, their branches webbed as they hung in the air above the fresh stumps. But when he searched for the rifle he could not find it. He thought that he might wreak great damage in the house, burning carpets and opening up the upholstery. But for this he found neither opportunity nor the strength it demanded. Stropping his razor one morning, he hit upon the best plan of all: to creep into the Dankerses' bedroom and cut their throats. It had once been his master's bedroom and now it was theirs; which made revenge the sweeter. Every day for forty-eight years he had carried to the room a tray of tea-cups and a pot of Earl Grey tea. Now he would carry his sharpened razor; and for the rest of his life he would continue his shaving with it, relishing every scrape. The idea delighted him. Sir Giles would have wished to see the last of them, to see the last of all these people who strayed about the house and grounds, and to see the orchard settle down again to being the orchard he had left behind. And was not he, Cronin, the living agent of the dead Sir Giles? Was he not now companion to his wife? And did she not, in an occasional moment of failure, address him as she had her husband? Yet when he shared his plans with Lady Marston she did not at all endorse them.

'Take the will for the deed, Cronin. Leave these people be.'

'But they are guilty. They may have killed Sir Giles.'

'They may have. And does it matter this way or that – to chop off a few dwindling years?'

Cronin saw no reason in her words. He pitied her, and hardened himself in his resolve.

'I am sorry to speak to you like this, Cronin,' Dankers said, 'but I cannot, you know, have you wandering about the house in this manner. There have been complaints from the guests. You have your room, with Lady Marston to talk to; why not keep more to the region we have set aside for you?'

'Yes, sir.'

'Of late, Cronin, you've become untidy in your appearance. You have a dishevelled look and often seem – well, frankly, Cronin, dirty. It's not good for business. Not good at all.'

The moon shall not be idle, Cronin thought. The moon shall be agog to see. The moon shall clear the sky of clouds that the stars may ponder on the pillows full of blood.

'Mr Dankers, sir, why is this place called the Idle Moon?'

Dankers laughed. 'A foible of my good wife's. She liked the sound of it. Quite telling, don't you think?'

'Yes, sir.' The moon shall like the sound of her. A shriek in a severed throat, a howl of pain.

'See to it, Cronin, eh?'

'Yes, sir.'

So Cronin kept to his room, descending the back stairs only for his food and Lady Marston's. The weeks passed, and more and more he sat entranced with the duty he had set himself. Sometimes, as though drunk with it, he found himself a little uncertain as to its exactitudes. That was when he felt tired; when he dropped off into a doze as he sat by his small window, staring at the sky and listening to the faraway hum from the house below.

Then one morning Cronin discovered that Lady Marston had died in her sleep. They carried her off, and he put away the pack of cards.

'It's a sad day for us all,' Dankers said, and in the distance Cronin could hear Mrs Dankers giving some brisk order to a servant. He returned to his room and for a moment there was an oddness in his mind and he imagined that it was Sir Giles who had said that the day was sad. Then he remembered that Sir Giles was dead too and that he was the only one left.

In the months that followed he spoke to no one but himself, for he was concentrating on the details of his plan. They kept slipping away, and increasingly he had a struggle to keep them straight.

When the razor was there the faces on the pillows were vague and empty, and he could not remember whose he had planned they should be. There was the pattern of moonlight, and the red stain on the bed-clothes, but Cronin could not often now see what any of it meant. It made him tired, thinking the trouble out. And when, in the end, the shreds of his plan came floating back to him he smiled in some astonishment, seeing only how absurd it had been that late in his life he should have imagined himself a match for the world and its conquerors.

Nice Day at School

Eleanor lay awake, thinking in advance about the day. The face of Miss Whitehead came into her mind, the rather pointed nose, eyes set wide apart, a mouth that turned up at the corners and gave the impression that Miss Whitehead was constantly smiling, although it was a widely held view among the girls whom she taught that Miss Whitehead had little to smile over, having missed out. The face of Liz Jones came into Eleanor's mind also, a pretty, wild face with eyes that were almost black, and black hair hanging prettily down on either side of it, and full lips. Liz Jones claimed to have gypsy blood in her, and another girl, Mavis Temple, had once remarked to Eleanor that she thought Liz Jones's lips were negroid. 'A touch of the tar brush,' Mavis Temple had said. 'A seaman done her mum.' She'd said it three years ago, when the girls had all been eleven, in Miss Homber's class. Everything had been different then.

In the early morning gloom Eleanor considered the difference, regretting, as always, that it had come about. It had been nice in Miss Homber's class, the girls' first year at Springfield Comprehensive: they'd all had a crush on Miss Homber because Miss Homber, who'd since become Mrs George Spaxton and a mother, had been truly beautiful and intelligent. Miss Homber told them it was important to wash all the parts of the body once per day, including you knew where. Four girls brought letters of complaint after that and Miss Homber read them out to the class, commenting on the grammar and the spelling errors and causing the girls to become less carefree about what they repeated to their mums. 'Remember, you can give birth at thirteen,' Miss Homber warned, and she added that if a boy ever said he was too embarrassed to go into a chemist's for preventatives he could always get them in a slot machine that was situated in the Gents at the filling station on the Portsmouth Road, which was something her own boyfriend had told her.

It had been nice in those days because Eleanor didn't believe that any boy would try stuff like that on when she was thirteen, and the girls of the first year all agreed that it sounded disgusting, a boy putting his thing up you. Even Liz Jones did, although she was constantly hanging about the boys of the estate and twice had had her knickers taken down in the middle of the estate playground. There were no boys at Springfield Comprehensive, which was just as well, Eleanor had always considered, because boys roughened up a school so.

But in spite of their physical absence boys had somehow penetrated, and increasingly, as Eleanor passed up through the school, references to them infiltrated all conversation. At thirteen, in Miss Croft's class, Liz Jones confessed that a boy called Gareth Swayles had done her in the corner of the estate playground, at eleven o'clock one night. She'd been done standing up, she reported, leaning against the paling that surrounded the playground. She said it was fantastic.

Lying in bed, Eleanor remembered Liz Jones saying that and saying a few months later that a boy called Rogo Pollini was twice as good as Gareth Swayles, and later that a boy called Tich Ayling made Rogo Pollini seem totally laughable. Another girl, Susie Crumm, said that Rogo Pollini had told her that he'd never enjoyed it with Liz Jones because Liz Jones put him off with all her wriggling and pinching. Susie Crumm, at the time, had just been done by Rogo Pollini.

By the time they reached Class 2 it had become the fashion to have been done and most of the girls, even quiet Mavis Temple, had succumbed to it. Many had not cared for the experience and had not repeated it, but Liz Jones said that this was because they had got it from someone like Gareth Swayles, who was no better on the job than a dead horse. Eleanor hadn't ever been done nor did she wish to be, by Gareth Swayles or anyone else. Some of the girls said it had hurt them: she knew it would hurt her. And she'd heard that even if Gareth Swayles, or whoever it was, went to the slot machine in the filling station it sometimes happened that the preventative came asunder, a disaster that would be followed by weeks of worry. That, she knew, would be her fate too.

'Eleanor's prissy,' Liz Jones said every day now. 'Eleanor's prissy like poor prissy Whitehead.' Liz Jones went on about it all the time, hating Eleanor because she still had everything in store for her. Liz Jones had made everyone else think that Eleanor would grow into a Miss Whitehead, who was terrified of men, so Liz Jones said. Miss Whitehead had hairs on her chin and her upper lip that she didn't bother to do anything about. Quite often her breath wasn't fresh, which was unpleasant if she was leaning over you, explaining something.

Eleanor, who lived on the estate with her parents, hated being identified with Miss Whitehead and yet she felt, especially when she lay awake in the early morning, that there was something in Liz Jones's taunting. 'Eleanor's waiting for Mr Right,' Liz Jones would say. 'Whitehead waited forever.' Miss Whitehead, Liz Jones said, never had a fellow for long because she wouldn't give herself wholly and in this day and age a girl had to be sensible and natural over a matter like that. Everyone agreed that this was probably so, because there was no doubt about it that in her time Miss Whitehead had been pretty. 'It happens to you,' Liz Jones said, 'left solitary like that: you grow hairs on your face; you get stomach trouble that makes your breath bad. Nervous frustration, see.'

Eleanor gazed across her small bedroom, moving her eyes from the pink of the wall to her school uniform, grey and purple, hanging over the back of a chair. In the room there was a teddy-bear she'd had since she was three, and a gramophone, and records by the New Seekers and the Pioneers and Diana Ross, and photographs of such performers. In her vague, uninterested manner her mother said she thought it awful that Eleanor should waste her money on these possessions, but Eleanor explained that everyone at Springfield Comprehensive did so and that she herself did not consider it a waste of money.

'You up?' Eleanor heard her mother calling now, and she replied that she was. She got out of bed and looked at herself in a looking-glass on her dressing-table. Her night-dress was white with small sprigs of violets on it. Her hair had an auburn tinge, her face was long and thin and was not afflicted with spots, as were a few of the faces of her companions at Springfield Comprehensive. Her prettiness was delicate, and she thought as she examined it now that Liz Jones was definitely right in her insinuations: it was a prettiness that could easily disappear overnight. Hairs would appear on her chin and her upper lip, a soft down at first, later becoming harsher. 'Your sight, you know,' an oculist would worriedly remark to her, and tell her she must wear glasses. Her teeth would lose their gleam. She'd have trouble with dandruff.

Eleanor slipped her night-dress over her head and looked at her naked body. She didn't herself see much beauty in it, but she knew that the breasts were the right size for the hips, that arms and legs nicely complemented each other. She dressed and went into the kitchen, where her father was making tea and her mother was reading the *Daily Express*. Her father hadn't been to bed all night. He slept during the day, being employed by night as a doorman in a night-club called Daisy's, in Shepherd Market. Once upon a time her father had been a wrestler, but in 1961 he'd injured his back in a bout with a Japanese and had since been unfit for the ring. Being a doorman of a night-club kept him in touch, so he claimed, with the glamorous world he'd been used to in the past. He often saw familiar faces, he reported, going in and out of Daisy's, faces that once had been his audience. Eleanor felt embarrassed when he talked like that, being unable to believe much of what he said.

'You're in for a scorcher,' he said now, placing a pot of tea on the blue formica of the table. 'No end to the heatwave, they can't see.'

He was a large, red-faced man with closely cut grey hair and no lobe to his right ear. He'd put on weight since he'd left the wrestling ring and although he moved slowly now, as though in some way compensating for years of nimbleness on the taut canvas, he was still, in a physical sense, a formidable opponent, as occasional troublemakers at the night-club had painfully discovered.

Eleanor knocked Special K into a dish and added milk and sugar.

'That's a lovely young girl,' her father said. 'Mia Farrow. She was in last night, Eleanor.'

His breakfast-time conversation was always the same. Princess Margaret had shaken him by the hand and Anthony Armstrong-Jones had asked if he might take his photograph for a book about London he was doing. The Burtons came regularly, and Rex Harrison, and the Canadian Prime Minister whenever he was in London. Her father had a way of looking at Eleanor when he made such statements, his eyes screwed up, almost lost in the puffed red flesh of his face: he stared unblinkingly and beadily, as if defying her to reply that she didn't for a moment accept that Princess Margaret's hand had ever lain in his or that Anthony Armstrong-Jones had addressed him.

'Faceful of innocence,' he said. 'Just a faceful of innocence, Eleanor. "Good-night, Miss Farrow," I said, and she turned the little face to me and said to call her Mia.'

Eleanor nodded. Her mother's eyes were fixed on the *Daily Express,* moving from news item to news item, her lips occasionally moving also as she read. 'Liz Jones,' Eleanor wanted to say. 'Could you complain to the school about Liz Jones?' She wanted to tell them about the fashion in Class 2, about Miss Whitehead, and how everyone was afraid of Liz Jones. She imagined her voice speaking across the breakfast table, to her father who was still in his doorman's uniform and her mother who mightn't even hear her. There'd be embarrassment as her father listened, her own face would be as hot as fire. He'd turn his head away in the end, like the time she'd had to ask him for money to buy sanitary towels.

'Lovely little fingers,' he said, 'like a baby's fingers, Eleanor. Little wisps of things. She touched me with the tips.'

'Who?' demanded her mother, suddenly sharp, looking up. 'Eh, then?'

'Mia Farrow,' he said. 'She was down in Daisy's last night. Sweetest thing; sweetest little face.'

'Ah, yes, *Peyton Place,*' her mother said, and Eleanor's father nodded.

Her mother had spectacles with swept-up, elaborately bejewelled frames.

The jewels were made of glass, but they glittered, especially in strong sunlight, just like what Eleanor imagined diamonds must glitter like. Her mother, constantly smoking, had hair which she dyed so that it appeared to be black. She was a thin woman with bones that stuck out awkwardly at the joints, seeming as though they might at any moment break through the surface of taut, anaemic skin. In Eleanor's opinion her mother had suffered, and once she had had a dream in which her mother was fat and married to someone else, a man, as far as Eleanor could make out, who ran a vegetable shop.

Her mother always had breakfast in her night-dress and an old fawn-coloured dressing-gown, her ankles below it as white as paper, her feet stuck into tattered slippers. After breakfast, she would return to bed with Eleanor's father, obliging him, Eleanor knew, as she had obliged him all her life. During the school holidays, and on Saturdays and Sundays when Eleanor was still in the flat, her mother continued to oblige him: in the bedroom he made the same kind of noise as he'd made in the wrestling ring. The Prince of Hackney he'd been known as.

Her mother was a shadow. Married to a man who ran a vegetable shop or to any other kind of man except the one she'd chosen, Eleanor believed she'd have been different: she'd have had more children, she'd have been a proper person with proper flesh on her bones, a person you could feel for. As she was, you could hardly take her seriously. She sat there in her night-clothes, waiting for the man she'd married to rise from the table and go into their bedroom so that she might follow. Afterwards she cleared up the breakfast things and washed them, while he slept. She shopped in the Express Dairy Supermarket, dropping cigarette ash over tins of soup and peas and packets of crisps, and at half past eleven she sat in the corner of the downstairs lounge of the Northumberland Arms and drank a measure of gin and water, sometimes two.

'Listen to this,' her mother said in her wheezy voice. She quoted a piece about a fifty-five-year-old woman, a Miss Margaret Sugden, who had been trapped in a bath for two days and three nights. '*It ended*,' read Eleanor's mother, '*with two burly policemen – eyes carefully averted – lifting her out. It took them half an hour of gentle levering, for Miss Sugden, a well-rounded sixteen stone, was helplessly stuck.*'

He laughed. Her mother stubbed her cigarette out on her saucer and lit a fresh one. Her mother never ate anything at breakfast-time. She drank three cups of tea and smoked the same number of cigarettes. He liked a large breakfast, eggs and bacon, fried bread, a chop sometimes.

'*History's longest soak*,' her mother said, still quoting from the *Daily Express*. Her father laughed again.

Eleanor rose and carried the dish she'd eaten her Special K out of to the sink, with her cup and her saucer. She rinsed them under the hot tap and stacked them on the red, plastic-covered rack to dry. Her mother spoke in amazed tones when she read pieces out of the newspaper, surprised by the activities of people and animals, never amused by them. Some part of her had been smashed to pieces.

She said goodbye to both of them. Her mother kissed her as she always did. Winking, her father told her not to take any wooden dollars, an advice that was as regular and as mechanical as her mother's embrace.

'Netball is it?' her mother vaguely asked, not looking up from the newspaper. There wasn't netball, Eleanor explained, as she'd explained before, in the summer term: she wouldn't be late back.

She left the flat and descended three flights of concrete stairs. She passed the garages and then the estate's playground, where Liz Jones had first of all been done. 'Good-morning, Eleanor,' a woman said to her, an Irish woman called Mrs Rourke. 'Isn't it a great day?'

Eleanor smiled. The weather was lovely, she said. Mrs Rourke was a lackadaisical woman, middle-aged and fat, the mother of eight children. On the estate it was said that she was no better than she should be, that one of her sons, who had a dark tinge in his pallor, was the child of a West Indian railway porter. Another of Mrs Rourke's children and suspect also, a girl of Eleanor's age called Dolly, was reputed to be the daughter of Susie Crumm's father. In the dream Eleanor had had in which her own mother was fat rather than thin it had seemed that her mother had somehow become Mrs Rourke, because in spite of everything Mrs Rourke was a happy woman. Her husband had a look of happiness about him also, as did all the Rourke children, no matter where they'd come from. They regularly went to Mass, all together in a family outing, and even if Mrs Rourke occasionally obliged Susie Crumm's father and others it hadn't taken the same toll of her as the obliging of Eleanor's father by her mother had. For years, ever since she'd listened to Liz Jones telling the class the full facts of life, Eleanor had been puzzled by the form the facts apparently took when different people were involved. She'd accepted quite easily the stories about Mrs Rourke and had thought no less of the woman, but when Dolly Rourke had said, about a month ago, that she'd been done by Rogo Pollini, Eleanor had felt upset, not caring to imagine the occasion, as she didn't care to imagine the occasion that took place every morning after breakfast in her parents' bedroom. Mrs Rourke didn't matter because she was somehow remote, like one of the people her mother read about in the *Daily Express* or one of the celebrities her father told lies about: Mrs Rourke didn't concern her, but Dolly Rourke and Rogo Pollini did because they were close to her, being the same as she was and of the same generation. And her parents concerned her because they were close to her also. You could no longer avoid any of it when you thought of Dolly Rourke and Rogo Pollini, or your parents.

She passed a row of shops, Len Parrish the baker, a dry cleaner's, the Express Dairy Supermarket, the newsagent's and post office, the off-licence attached to the Northumberland Arms. Girls in the grey-and-purple uniform of Springfield Comprehensive alighted in numbers from a bus. A youth whistled at her. 'Hi, Eleanor,' said Gareth Swayles, coming up behind her. In a friendly manner he put his hand on her back, low down, so that, as though by accident, he could in a moment slip it over her buttocks.

There's a new boy in Grimes the butcher's, Liz Jones wrote on a piece of paper. *He's not on the estate at all.* She folded the paper and addressed it to Eleanor. She passed it along the row of desks.

'*Je l'ai vu qui travaillait dans la cour,*' said Miss Whitehead.

I saw him in Grimes, Eleanor wrote. *Funny-looking fish.* She passed the note back and Liz Jones read it and showed it to her neighbour, Thelma Joseph. *Typical Eleanor,* Liz Jones wrote and Thelma Joseph giggled slightly.

'*Un anglais qui passait ses vacances en France,*' said Miss Whitehead.

Miss Whitehead lived in Esher, in a bed-sitting-room. Girls had some-times visited her there and those who had done so described for others what Miss Whitehead's residence was like. It was very clean and comfortable and neat. White paint shone on the window ledges and the skirting-boards, lace curtains hung close to sparkling glass. On the mantelpiece there were ornaments in delicate ceramic, Highland sheep and cockerels, and a chimney sweep with his brushes on his back. A clock ticked on the mantelpiece, and in the fireplace – no longer used – Miss Whitehead had stood a vase of dried flowers. Her bed was in a recess, not at all obtrusive in the room, a narrow divan covered in cheerful chintz.

'*Le pêcheur,*' said Miss Whitehead, '*est un homme qui* . . . Eleanor?'

'*Pêche?*'

'*Très bien. Et la blanchisseuse est une femme qui* . . .?'

'*Lave le linge.*'

Liz Jones said it must be extraordinary to be Miss Whitehead, never to have felt a man's hand on you. *Gareth Swayles said he'd give it to her,* she'd written on one of the notes she was constantly passing round the class. *Imagine Swayles in bed with Whitehead!*

'*La mère n'aime pas le fromage,*' said Miss Whitehead, and Liz Jones passed another note to Eleanor. *The new boy in Grimes is called Denny Price*, it said. *He wants to do you.*

'Eleanor,' said Miss Whitehead.

She looked up from the elaborately looped handwriting of Liz Jones. In their bedroom her father would be making the noises he used to make in the wrestling ring. Her mother would be lying there. Once, when she was small, she'd gone in by mistake and her father had been standing without his clothes on. Her mother had pulled a sheet up to cover her own nakedness.

'Why are you writing notes, Eleanor?'

'She didn't, Miss Whitehead,' Liz Jones said. 'I sent her −'

'Thank you, Elizabeth. Eleanor?'

'I'm sorry, Miss Whitehead.'

'Were you writing notes, Eleanor?'

'No, I −'

'I sent her the note, Miss Whitehead. It's a private matter −'

'Not private in *my* class, Elizabeth. Pass me the note, Eleanor.'

Liz Jones was sniggering: Eleanor knew that she'd wanted this to happen. Miss Whitehead would read the note out, which was her rule when a note was found.

'The new boy in Grimes is called Denny Price,' Miss Whitehead said. 'He wants to do you.'

The class laughed, a muffled sound because the girls' heads were bent over their desks.

'He wants to have sexual relations with Eleanor,' Liz Jones explained, giggling more openly. 'Eleanor's a −'

'Thank you, Elizabeth. The future tense, Elizabeth: *s'asseoir*.'

Her voice grated in the classroom. Her voice had become unattractive also, Eleanor thought, because she'd never let herself be loved. In her clean bed-sitting-room she might weep tonight, recalling the insolence of Liz Jones. She'd punish Liz Jones when the bell went, the way she always inflicted punishment. She'd call her name out and while the others left the room she'd keep the girl longer than was necessary, setting her a piece of poetry to write out ten times and explaining, as if talking to an infant, that notes and conversation about sexual matters were not permitted in her classroom. She'd imply that she didn't believe that the boy in Grimes' had said what Liz Jones had reported he'd said. She'd pretend it was all a fantasy, that no girl from Springfield Comprehensive had ever been done in the playground of the estate or anywhere else. It was easy for Miss Whitehead, Eleanor thought, escaping to her bed-sitting-room in Esher.

'It's your bloody fault,' Liz Jones said afterwards in the washroom. 'If you weren't such a curate's bitch –'

'Oh, for heaven's sake, shut up about it!' Eleanor cried.

'Denny Price wants to give you his nine inches –'

'I don't want his bloody nine inches. I don't want anything to do with him.'

'You're under-sexed, Eleanor. What's wrong with Denny Price?'

'He's peculiar-looking. There's something the matter with his head.'

'Will you listen to this!' Liz Jones cried, and the girls who'd gathered round tittered. 'What's his head got to do with it for God's sake? It's not his head that's going to –' She broke off, laughing, and all the girls laughed also, even though several of them didn't at all care for Liz Jones.

'You'll end like Whitehead,' Liz Jones said. 'Doing yourself in Esher.' The likes of Whitehead, she added, gave you a sickness in your kidneys. Eleanor had the same way of walking as Whitehead had, which was a way that dried-up virgins acquired because they were afraid to walk any other way in case a man touched their dried-up bottoms.

Eleanor went away, moving through the girls of other classes, across the washroom.

'Liz Jones is a nasty little tit,' a girl called Eileen Reid whispered, and Joan Moate, a fair-haired girl with a hint of acne, agreed. But Liz Jones couldn't hear them. Liz Jones was still laughing, leaning against a washbasin with a cigarette in her mouth.

For lunch that day at Springfield Comprehensive there was stew and processed potatoes and carrots, with blancmange afterwards, chocolate and strawberry.

'Don't take no notice,' Susie Crumm said to Eleanor. The way Liz Jones went on, she added, it wouldn't suprise her to hear that she'd contracted syphilis.

'What's it like, Susie?' Eleanor asked.

'Syphilis? You get lesions. If you're a girl you can't tell sometimes. Fellas get them all over their equipment –'

'No, I mean what's it like being done?'

''Sall right. Nice really. But not like Jones goes for it. Not all the bloody time.'

They ate spoonfuls of blancmange, sucking it through their teeth.

''Sall right,' Susie Crumm repeated when she'd finished. ''Sall right for an occasion.'

Eleanor nodded. She wanted to say that she'd prefer to keep it for her wedding night, but she knew that if she said that she'd lose Susie Crumm's sympathy. She wanted it to be special, not just a woman lying down waiting for a man to finish taking his clothes off; not just a fumbling in the dark of the estate playground, or something behind the North-umberland Arms, where Eileen Reid had been done.

'My dad said he'd gut any fella that laid a finger on me,' Susie Crumm said.

'Jones's said the same.'

'He done Mrs Rourke. Jones's dad.'

'They've all done Mrs Rourke.' For a moment she wanted to tell the truth: to add that Susie Crumm's dad had done Mrs Rourke also, that Dolly Rourke was Susie's half-sister.

'You've got a moustache growing on you,' Liz Jones said, coming up behind her and whispering into her hair.

The afternoon of that day passed without incident at Springfield Comprehensive, while on the estate Eleanor's father slept. He dreamed that he was wrestling again. Between his knees he could feel the ribs of Eddie Rodriguez; the crowd was calling out, urging him to give Eddie Rodriguez the final works. Two yards away, in the kitchen, Eleanor's mother prepared a meal. She cut cod into pieces, and sliced potatoes for chips. He liked a crisply fried meal at half past six before watching a bit of television. She liked cod and chips herself, with tinned peas, and bread and butter and apricot jam, and Danish pastries and tea, and maybe a tin of pears. She'd bought a tin of pears in the Express Dairy: they might as well have them with a tin of Carnation cream. She'd get everything ready and then she'd run an iron over his uniform, sponging off any spots there were. She thought about *Crossroads* on the television, wondering what would happen in the episode today.

'I'd remind you that the school photographs will be taken on Tuesday,' Miss Whitehead said. 'Clean white blouses, please.'

They would all be there: Eleanor, Liz Jones, Susie Crumm, Eileen Reid, Joan Moate, Mavis Temple, and all the others: forty smiling faces, and Miss Whitehead standing at the end of the middle row. If you kept the photograph it would be a memory for ever, another record of the days at Springfield Comprehensive. 'Who's that with the bow legs?' her father had asked a few years ago, pointing at Miss Homber.

'Anyone incorrectly dressed on Tuesday,' Miss Whitehead said, 'will forfeit her place in the photo.'

The bell rang for the end of school. 'Forfeit her bloody knickers,' said Liz Jones just before Miss Whitehead left the classroom.

The girls dispersed, going off in twos and threes, swinging the briefcases that contained their school books.

'Walk with you?' Susie Crumm suggested to Eleanor, and together they left the classrooms and the school. 'Baking, innit?' Susie Crumm remarked.

They walked slowly, past concrete buildings, the Eagle Star Insurance Company, Barclays Bank, the Halifax Building Society. Windows were open, the air was chalky dry. Two girls in front of them had taken off their shoes but now, finding the pavement too hot to walk on, had paused to put them on again. The two girls shrieked, leaning on one another. Women pushed prams around them, irritation in their faces.

'I want to get fixed in a Saxone,' Susie Crumm said. 'Can't wait to leave that bloody place.'

An *Evening Standard* van swerved in front of a bus, causing the bus-driver to shout and blow his horn. In the cab of the van the driver's mate raised two fingers in a gesture of disdain.

'I fancy selling shoes,' Susie Crumm said. 'Fashion shoes type of thing. You get them at cost if you work in a Saxone.'

Eleanor imagined the slow preparation of the evening meal in her parents' flat, and the awakening of her father. He'd get up and shave himself, standing in the bathroom in his vest, braces hanging down, his flies half open. Her mother spent ages getting the evening meal, breaking off to see to his uniform and then returning to the food. He couldn't bear not being a wrestler any more.

'What you going to do, Eleanor?'

She shook her head. She didn't know what she was going to do. All she wanted was to get away from the estate and from Springfield Comprehensive. She wondered what it would be like to work in the Eagle Star Insurance Company, but at the moment that didn't seem important. What was important was the exact present, the afternoon of a certain day, a day that was like others except for the extreme heat. She'd go home and there the two of them would be, and in her mind there'd be the face of Miss Whitehead and the voice of Liz Jones. She'd do her homework and then there'd be *Crossroads* on the TV and then the fried meal and the washing-up and more TV, and then he'd go, saying it was time she was in bed. 'See you in the morning,' he'd say and soon after he'd gone they'd both go to bed, and she'd lie there thinking of being married in white lace in a church, to a delicate man who wouldn't hurt her, who'd love the virginal innocence that had been kept all these years for him alone. She'd go away in a two-piece suit on an autumn afternoon when the leaves in London were yellow-brown. She'd fly with a man whose fingers were long and thin and gentle, who'd hold her hand in the aeroplane, Air France to Biarritz. And afterwards she'd come back to a flat where the curtains were the colour of lavender, the same as the walls, where gas-fires glowed and there were rugs on natural-wood floors, and the telephone was pale blue.

'What's matter?' Susie Crumm asked.

'Nothing.'

They walked past Len Parrish the baker, the dry cleaner's, the Express Dairy Supermarket, the newsagent's and post office, the off-licence attached to the Northumberland Arms.

'There's that fella,' Susie Crumm said. 'Denny Price.'

His head was awkwardly placed on his neck, cocked to one side. His hair was red and long, his face small in the midst of it. He had brown eyes and thick, blubbery lips.

'Hullo,' he said.

Susie Crumm giggled.

'Like a fag?' he said, holding out a packet of Anchor. 'Smoke, do you, girls?'

Susie Crumm giggled again, and then abruptly ceased. 'Oh God!' she said, her hand stretched out for a cigarette. She was looking over Denny Price's shoulder at a man in blue denim overalls. The man, seeing her in that moment, sharply called at her to come to him.

'Stuff him,' she said before she smiled and obeyed.

'Her dad,' said Denny Price, pleased that she had gone. 'You want a fag, Eleanor?'

She shook her head, walking on. He dropped into step with her.

'I know your name,' he said. 'I asked Liz Jones.'

'Yes.'

'I'm Denny Price. I work in Grimes'.'

'Yes.'

'You're at the Comprehensive.'

'Yes.'

She felt his fingers on her arm, squeezing it just above the elbow. 'Let's go for a walk,' he said. 'Come down by the river, Eleanor.'

She shook her head again and then, quite suddenly, she didn't care what happened. What harm was there in walking by the river with a boy from Grimes'? She looked at the fingers that were still caressing her arm. All day long they had handled meat; the fingernails were bitten away, the flesh was red from scouring. Wasn't it silly, like an advertisement, to imagine that a man would come one day to marry her in white lace in a church and take her, Air France, to Biarritz?

'We'll take a bus to the bridge,' he said. 'A thirty-seven.'

He sat close to her, paying her fare, pressing a cigarette on her. She took it and he lit it for her. His eyes were foxy, she noticed; she could see the desire in them.

'I saw you a week back,' he said.

They walked by the river, away from the bridge, along the tow-path. He put his arm around her, squeezing a handful of underclothes and flesh. 'Let's sit down here,' he said.

They sat on the grass, watching barges going by and schoolboys rowing. In the distance traffic moved, gleaming, on the bridge they'd walked from. 'God,' he said, 'you have fantastic breasts.'

His hands were on them and he was pushing her back on to the grass. She felt his lips on her face, and his teeth and his tongue, and saliva. One hand moved down her body. She felt it under her skirt, on the bare flesh of her thigh, and then on her stomach. It was like an animal, a rat gnawing at her, prodding her and poking. There was no one about; he was muttering, his voice thickly slurred. 'Take down your knickers,' he said.

She pushed at him and for a moment he released his hold, imagining she was about to undo some of her clothing. Instead she ran away, tearing along the tow-path, saying to herself that if he caught up with her she'd hit him with the briefcase that contained her school books.

But he didn't follow her and when she looked back he was lying where she had left him, stretched out as though wounded on the grass.

Her father talked of who might come that night to Daisy's. He mentioned Princess Margaret. Princess Margaret had seen him wrestling, or if it hadn't been Princess Margaret it had been a face almost identical to hers. The Burtons might come tonight; you never knew when the Burtons were going to pop in.

Her mother placed the fried fish, with chips and peas, in front of him. She never really listened to him when he went on about the night-club because her mind was full of what had happened on *Crossroads*. She put her cigarette on a saucer on the draining-board, not extinguishing it. She remembered the news items she'd read at breakfast-time and wondered about them all over again.

Tomorrow would be worse, Eleanor thought. Even at this very moment Denny Price's blubber lips might be relating the incident to Liz Jones, how Eleanor had almost let him and then had drawn back. 'I went down by the river with a boy,' she wanted to say. 'I wanted to get done because it's the Class 2 fashion. I'm tired of being mocked by Liz Jones.' She could say it with her eyes cast down, her fork fiddling with a piece of cod on her plate. She wouldn't have to see the embarrassment in her father's face, like she'd seen it when she'd asked for money for sanitary towels. Her mother wouldn't hear at first, but she'd go on saying it, repeating herself until her mother did hear. She longed for the facts to be there in the room, how it disgusted her to imagine her father taking off his uniform in the mornings, and Rogo Pollini doing Dolly Rourke. She wanted to say she'd been disgusted when Denny Price had told her to take down her knickers.

'Extraordinary, that woman,' her mother said. 'Fancy two days stuck in a bath.'

Her father laughed. It could be exaggerated, he said: you couldn't believe everything you read, not even in the newspapers.

'Extraordinary,' her mother murmured.

Her mother was trapped, married to him, obliging him so that she'd receive housekeeping money out of which she could save for her morning glass of gin. He was trapped himself, going out every night in a doorman's uniform, the Prince of Hackney with a bad back. He crushed her mother because he'd been crushed himself. How could either of them be expected to bother if she spoke of being mocked, and then asked them questions, seeking reassurance?

They wouldn't know what to say – even if she helped them by explaining that she knew there was no man with delicate hands who'd take her away when the leaves in London were yellow-brown, that there were only the blubber lips of Denny Price and the smell of meat that came off him, and Susie Crumm's father doing Mrs Rourke, and Liz Jones's father doing her also, and the West Indian railway porter, and Mr Rourke not aware of a thing. They wouldn't know what she was talking about if she said that Miss Whitehead had divorced herself from all of it by lying solitary at night in a room in Esher where everything was clean and neat. It was better to be Miss Whitehead than a woman who was a victim of a man's bad back. In her gleaming room Miss Whitehead was more successful in her pretence than they were in theirs. Miss Whitehead was complete and alone, having discarded what she wished to discard, accepting now that there was no Mr Right.

'Nice day at school?' her mother inquired suddenly in her vague manner, as though mistily aware of a duty.

Eleanor looked up from her fish and regarded both of them at once. She smiled, forcing herself to, feeling sorry for them because they were trapped by each other; because for them it was too late to escape to a room in which everything was clean.

The Original Sins of Edward Tripp

Edward Tripp had often noticed Mrs Mayben at her sitting-room window, putting bread on the window-sills for the birds. Her hair was white and she was dressed always in the same way, in several shades of grey. She had, he considered, the kindest face in all Dunfarnham Avenue, and when she saw him she would nod at him in a dignified manner, befitting a woman of her years. He had never rung the bell of Mrs Mayben's house as he had rung the bells of the other houses; he had never held her in conversation on her doorstep, but he knew that the day would come when his sister would ask him to cross the road and speak to the old woman. Edward was notorious in Dunfarnham Avenue, yet he felt whenever he considered the fact that Mrs Mayben, who kept herself to herself and did not gossip with the other people, was perhaps – just possibly – unaware of his notoriety. He thought, too, that when the time came, when eventually he found himself face to face with Mrs Mayben, he would tell her the truth: he would speak to her bluntly, and Edward guessed that an old woman with Mrs Mayben's dignity, who was a Christian and who never forgot the birds, would listen to him and would say a word or two of comfort. He imagined how things would be after that visit, he himself passing by Mrs Mayben's house and the truth hanging between them, she nodding with a smile from her window and he giving thanks to God for her understanding heart.

On Sunday August 26th Edward Tripp's sister, Emily, spoke of Mrs Mayben and Edward knew that on this morning he would hear himself protesting in a familiar way and that in the end he would cross the road to Mrs Mayben's house.

'We have watched the neighbourhood go down,' said Emily. 'Mrs Mayben was the last who was a decent sort of person. And now she's gone too. In cold blood.'

Edward, slicing some ham that he had purchased the day before in Lipton's, had been thinking to himself that the piece of gammon was not as satisfactory as usual: there was, for instance, a certain stringiness and a confusion about the direction of the grain. Before his sister had mentioned Mrs Mayben he had been allowing his thoughts to consider the meat as once it had been, an area of living flesh on the thigh of a pig. He imagined that something might have troubled that pig, some physical disorder that caused it to wriggle and dash about its sty, banging itself against the concrete sides and causing the stringiness to develop in its flesh.

'In cold blood,' said Emily again.

Edward looked up and regarded her back. He stared at the blackness of the material of which her long, old-fashioned dress was composed and at the roll of her hair, neat and formal on her neck.

'No, no,' said Edward. 'Not dead, dear. Not dead.'

But his sister nodded, denying his denial, and Edward shook his head with firmness.

'I remember when she came,' said Emily. 'Fourteen years ago. Her husband with her.'

Edward agreed with that. 'Her husband,' he said, 'died in 1955.'

'Death again,' murmured Emily, and Edward sighed. His sister was standing by their dining-room window, observing through it the house of Mrs Mayben opposite. Her left hand gripped the grey curtain that had flanked the window for almost thirty years, her right hung limply by her side. Edward guessed what was in her mind and did not care to consider it, since soon, he knew, he would be obliged to consider it whether he wished to or not. Attempting to keep the workings of his sister's brain at bay, he cut deeply into the ham. The image of the living animal appeared again before him. He said:

'After lunch why don't we try to repair the sitting-room carpet? It gets worse, you know. Quite a hole has worn through. It seems a pity.'

'The carpet?' said Emily, and Edward added:

'Father used to talk about that carpet, d'you remember? About its quality. The years have proved him right.'

Emily, continuing to stare through the window, made no comment.

'It's lasted a couple of lifetimes,' Edward said quickly. 'It's a shame to let it go.' His eyes again travelled over his sister's back, moving upwards, to the roll of her hair. Emily said:

'There was a man here yesterday. Looking at Mrs Mayben's windows.'

'A robber,' suggested Edward, again slicing the ham, and in an automatic way beginning to feel sick in his stomach. He said, in a slow, low voice, that Mrs Mayben was probably now in church, or else within her house, cooking a simple lunch for herself.

'She hasn't been about,' said Emily. 'I haven't seen Mrs Mayben for four days.'

'I thought I saw her yesterday. I'm sure, you know.'

'He came,' said Emily, 'in a light-blue motor-car. The kind that's called a tourer, is it? Out of that he stepped at a quarter to four and stood on the pavement gazing up at her house – returning to his scene, God knows. He was indecently dressed, Edward: canvas shoes and light-weight trousers that matched the blue paintwork of his motor-car, and nothing at all where a shirt should have been. He was like a lunatic, I'll tell you that, walking on the edge of the pavement in the August sunshine, his eyes uplifted to the house. And I said to myself: "There's evil there".'

'Mrs Mayben's in church,' repeated Edward, 'or maybe home already, doing her Sunday chores.'

His sister shook her head. 'It's past her time for returning from church. She hasn't returned today, for I have watched at the window, being worried about her. Mrs Mayben, as well you know, Edward, is by now in two places at once.'

Edward imagined old Mrs Mayben delayed in a traffic jam in the hired car that called for her every Sunday at half past eleven to take her to church. He imagined the chauffeur, the sallow-faced man who always came, with a green peaked cap, apologizing to her about the delay, apologizing about all the traffic, since she was the kind of woman who inspired apology, he imagined. Emily said.

'You know what I mean, don't you, when I say she's in two places at once? In heaven and in some cupboard, Edward; strung to a hook.'

There was a look, Edward knew, that must be there by now in his sister's eyes as she stared through the glass, ready to inflict her punishment. He thought, as he had thought before on similar occasions, that she was like a woman entering a fit.

'Now, now,' said Edward softly.

'Read the papers,' cried his sister, turning about to face him and speaking with emotion. 'A man has killed eight nurses in Chicago.'

'Oh no,' began Edward.

'Prize-fighters turn on their children. Mothers go out with the tide.'

Edward placed the ham knife on the polished mahogany of the dining-room table. Slowly, he raised his eyes to meet his sister's.

'An old woman living alone,' said Emily.

Edward watched her tongue moving over her lips, begining at one corner and returning to it. The tip of her tongue protruded at that corner for a moment and was then withdrawn. Again he raised his eyes to hers and they looked at one another in silence for a while, a brother and a sister who had lived all their lives in this house in Dunfarnham Avenue, Number Seventeen. Edward remembered the past and he knew that his sister was remembering it too. In the past were the children they had been, two other people, a different relationship: a girl thin and tall, four years older than the brother, he a boy who had laughed and had had his way, who had grown to be a man of slight build, permitting a small moustache to accumulate on his upper lip. The house that had been the house of their parents had changed only a little over the years. Wallpaper, the colour of good oatmeal, had hung all over it for three decades, placed there one spring when Emily was fourteen. Large engravings that featured the bridges of London decorated the hall and the stairs, and in dark bookcases, dustless behind glass, were volumes by Sapper, and *The Life of a Bengal Lancer*, and poems by Austin Dobson, and the collected works of Kipling and Scott. Edward often felt strange in the house now, feeling the present dominated by the past, remembering everything. From her own private flowerbed he had pulled her pansies, roots and all, when he was five years old; and with a pair of scissors he had cut through the centre of the buds of her roses. 'I have played a trick on you,' he used to say, sidling close to her. He had given two of her books away to an old woman who came seeking alms at the door. He had lit a fire in a fireplace of her doll's house, and had been punished because it was, so they said, a dangerous thing to do. He had taken one of her guinea-pigs and put it in her bed, where by mischance it had died. 'I have played a trick on you': he had said it repeatedly, bringing out her temper and her tears and running away himself. In middle age Emily was still taller than her brother, and had a hint of beauty about her features that was not reflected in his. Edward had developed a stoop in early manhood, and the child who had been bright with darting mischief became, in his own opinion, a shrimpish creature, fond of the corners of rooms.

On that Sunday morning, August 26th, Emily continued to speak about the man who had loitered in Dunfarnham Avenue in the sunshine. She spoke of the baldness of his head and the evil that she had recognized in the pupils of his eyes. He had worn no shirt, she repeated, emphasizing the fact, and she said again that his shoes, placed over bare feet, had been of light-blue canvas, the same colour as his trousers and his car.

Listening to his sister's voice, Edward prayed in his mind. He prayed that she might turn from the window and walk away from the room, saying that she was going to the kitchen to make mustard, since mustard would be necessary with the ham. But his sister only stood before him, strange and thin as she had been as a child.

'I wish you could have seen him,' said Emily. 'I think I dreamed of him last night. The man is on my mind.'

'Why not sit down, my dear? Why not rest and try to forget?' As he spoke, Edward prayed for a day that was to come, a day that God, he felt, had promised him. His sister said:

'Perhaps on Wednesday night it was, or early on Thursday morning, that he slipped into the old woman's house to do what he had to do. And in his madness, Edward, he could not resist returning later to the scene of all the violence. I have read of this kind of thing. It has happened with other men.'

'Come along now –'

'Not at all unusual,' said Emily. 'Criminal history is not being made in Dunfarnham Avenue, if that's what you're thinking. He came and acted and returned, as others have in a similar way. D'you understand? D'you follow me?'

What was there to follow? Edward thought. What was there to understand except the facts from the past? – the quiet child of four and the son who was suddenly born in the house and allowed to go his way. The son growing up and his sport becoming the game he played with her, until her days were filled to the brim with his cunning smile and the baby tricks that everyone excused. Wasn't the simple truth that those cruelties in their thousands had fallen like a blight upon her nature in the end, wrenching some bit of it out of shape, embittering the whole?

When Edward was seventeen their parents had died, one after the other within a month. He remembered still standing at his mother's funeral, the second funeral of the pair, and seeing on his sister's face the look that by now he had become familiar with, a look of reproach and sorrow. They had returned together to the dark house with the oatmeal wallpaper and Emily had said: 'There was a woman in a red coat, Edward. Did you see her? I thought it odd, you know, a woman dressed in red at the grave of another woman.' Edward had seen no woman in red and had said so at once, but Emily, making tea, had continued about this figure, and then had ceased to make tea and had stood quite still, gazing at him and talking at length, on and on, about the woman. 'What should we do?' she said. 'Shouldn't we try to find out a thing or two?' And then, in a moment, she had seemed to forget about the woman and had poured boiling water into a china teapot that both of them had known as a family possession all their lives. Afterwards, in the back garden, Edward had examined in detail his early sins against his sister, and he had closed his eyes and prayed to God. He prayed for forgiveness and he prayed that she in turn might forgive him and he prayed that the damage might not mark her for ever. From the garden, that day, he returned to the house, having found his duty, to live there with her, in that cool and silent place, to keep an eye on her for ever, and to atone as best he might. God had spoken harshly to Edward in the garden, and God had spoken harshly since. Every morning and evening Edward Tripp prayed at length, kneeling by his bed, and during the day he prayed as well, seeing her before him, she who never now walked out into Dunfarnham Avenue, who dressed herself in black and forgot her beauty. No longer children, they were reticent now in what they said one to another; they were polite in their relationship as their thoughts filled the rooms of the house and were not spoken. She played her game in a vengeful way, acting a madness and saying to him in silence that this was the state she should be in, warning him that her bitter nature needed his tenderness. And Edward prayed and often wept, accepting the punishment as his due.

'There's nothing to worry about,' said Edward now. 'Mrs Mayben is quite all right.'

'You have a callous mind,' murmured Edward's sister, looking at him. 'You can know of a thing like this and stand there cutting ham and saying it doesn't matter that a lunatic has walked in Dunfarnham Avenue and brought an old woman to a grim full-stop. It doesn't matter what's in that house this morning, is that it? Edward, she has not come back from church because today she's never been there; because she's been dead and rotting for eighty-four hours. We have buried our parents: we know about the deceased. They're everywhere, Edward. Everywhere.'

'Please,' muttered Edward. 'Please now, my dear.'

'Death has danced through Dunfarnham Avenue and I have seen it, a man without socks or shirt, a man who shall fry in the deep fat of Hell. For you, Edward, must put a finger on him.'

'There's nothing I can do,' said Edward, feeling his size, five foot four, as his sister towered in the room with him.

'Cross the road,' said Emily, 'and go to the back of Mrs Mayben's house. Climb through some small window and walk through the rooms until you come to the woman.'

Edward sighed. He would cross the road, he knew, as he had known when first she mentioned Mrs Mayben, and he would tell Mrs Mayben the truth because she had a face that was kind. He would not stand on her doorstep and make some lame excuse, as he had with all the others. He would not today prevaricate and pretend; he would not dishonour the woman by meting out dishonest treatment to her. 'I will ease your mind,' he said to his sister. 'I'll go and see that Mrs Mayben's quite all right.'

'Carry that ham knife with you, that you may cut her down. It's wrong, I think, don't you, that we should leave her as she is?'

'Stand by the window,' said Edward, already moving to the door, 'and watch me as I cross the road to ring her bell. You'll see her appear, my dear, and if you strain your ears you may even hear her voice.'

Emily nodded. She said:

'Telephone the police when you have cut the cord. Dial 999 and ask to speak to a sergeant. Tell him the honest truth.'

Edward walked from the room and descended the stairs of the house. He opened the front door and crossed Dunfarnham Avenue, to the house of Mrs Mayben. He rang the bell, standing to one side so that his sister, from the dining-room window, would be able to see the old woman when she opened the door.

'I was trying to repair this thing,' said Mrs Mayben, holding out an electric fuse, 'with a piece of silver paper. You've been sent to me, Mr Tripp. Come in.'

Edward entered the house of Mrs Mayben, carrying the ham knife. 'I'm sorry,' he said, 'to bother you.' But Mrs Mayben seemed not to question his presence on her property. 'My husband could mend a fuse,' she said, 'with silver paper; yet I can make no hand of this.' Edward placed the ham knife on a table in the hall and took the ineffective fuse from her hand. He said there was stuff called fuse wire, and Mrs Mayben led him to a cupboard where the electric meters were and in which he discovered the wire he sought. 'I was cooking a chop,' said Mrs Mayben, a woman of eighty-two, 'when all the heat went off.'

'I was cutting ham,' said Edward, 'and I was interrupted too.' He repaired the fuse and replaced it in its socket. 'Let's go and see,' said Mrs Mayben, and led the way to her kitchen. They watched the chop for a moment, still and uninviting in the centre of a frying pan on the electric stove. In a moment a noise came from it, a spurt of sizzling that indicated to them that Edward had been successful with the fuse. 'You must take a glass of sherry,' said Mrs Mayben. 'I have one always myself, on Sundays.'

Edward followed the old woman to her sitting-room and sat down, since she wished that he should, in a comfortable armchair. She poured two glasses of Dry Fly sherry and then, holding hers formally in the air, she reminded Edward that she had lived in Dunfarnham Avenue for fourteen years and had never actually spoken to him before.

'I see you feeding the birds,' said Edward, 'from your sitting-room window.'

'Yes, I feed the local sparrows,' said Mrs Mayben. 'I do my bit.'

A silence fell between them, and then Mrs Mayben said:

'It is odd to have lived opposite you for all these years and yet not to have spoken. I have seen you at the windows, as you have seen me. I have seen the lady too.'

Edward felt the blood moving into his face. He felt again a sickness in his stomach and thought his hands were shivering.

'You have heard of me,' he casually said. 'I dare say you have. I am notorious in Dunfarnham Avenue.'

'I know your name is Tripp,' said Mrs Mayben. 'I know no more.'

'She is my sister, the woman you see in that house. She and I were born there, and now she never leaves it. I go out to do the shopping – well, you've seen me.'

'I have seen you, certainly,' said Mrs Mayben, 'returning from the shops with a string bag full of this and that, potatoes and tins, lettuces in season. I do not pry, Mr Tripp, but I have seen you. Have more sherry?'

Edward accepted another glass. 'I am known to every house in the road,' he said. 'Parents warn their children to cross to the other side when they see me coming. Men have approached me to issue rough warnings, using language I don't much care to hear. Women move faster when Edward Tripp's around.'

Mrs Mayben said that she was not deaf but wondered if she quite understood what Edward was talking about. 'I don't think I follow,' she said. 'I know nothing of all this. Like your sister, I don't go out much. I've heard nothing from the people of Dunfarnham Avenue about you, Mr Tripp, or how it is you have become notorious.'

Edward said he had guessed that might be so, and added that one person at least in Dunfarnham Avenue should know the truth, on this Sabbath day.

'It's very kind of you to have repaired my fuse,' said Mrs Mayben a little loudly. 'I'm most obliged to you for that.' She rose to her feet, but did not succeed in drawing her visitor to his. Edward sat on in the comfortable armchair holding his sherry glass. He said:

'It is a hell for me, Dunfarnham Avenue, walking down it and feeling all eyes upon me. I have rung the bells of the houses. I have trumped up some story on the doorsteps, even on the doorsteps she cannot see from the dining-room window. She always knows if I have talked to someone and have been embarrassed: I come back in a peculiar state. I suffer from nerves, Mrs Mayben.'

'Thank you,' said Mrs Mayben more loudly still. 'And how nice to meet you after all these years.'

'I am going to tell you the truth,' explained Edward, 'as I have never told a soul in my life. It is an ugly business, Mrs Mayben. Perhaps you should sit down.'

'But, Mr Tripp,' protested the old woman, greatly puzzled, 'what on earth is all this?'

'Let me tell you,' said Edward, and he told her of his sister standing at the top of the stairs while their mother broke to her the news that her two coloured story-books had been handed out to a beggar at the front door. 'He's only little,' their mother had explained to Edward's sister. 'Forgive an imp, my dear.' But Emily had not found it in her heart to forgive him and he had sniggered at the time.

'I see,' said Mrs Mayben.

'I knew you would,' cried Edward, smiling at her and nodding his head several times. 'Of course you see. You have a kindly face; you feed the birds.'

'Yes, but –' said Mrs Mayben.

'No,' said Edward. 'Listen.'

He told her about the woman in red at the funeral of their mother, the woman his sister had seen, and how he afterwards prayed in the back garden and had been sternly answered by Almighty God. He explained how he had come upon his duty then and had accepted all that was required of him.

'It has nothing to do with the present,' said Edward. 'Do not see my sister and myself as we stand today, but as two children playing in that house across the road. I sinned against my sister, Mrs Mayben, every hour of my early life. She was stamped into the ground; she was mocked and taunted.'

'I'm sorry,' said Mrs Mayben. 'I'm sorry there have been these troubles in your life. It's difficult to accept adversity and unhappiness, I know that.'

'I was cutting ham,' repeated Edward, 'when my sister turned to me and said you had been murdered by a man in canvas shoes.'

'Murdered?' repeated Mrs Mayben, opening the door of her sitting-room and appearing to be nervous.

'She's affected by the past,' said Edward. 'You understand it?'

Mrs Mayben did not reply. Instead she said:

'Mr Tripp, you have been most gallant. I wish you would now return to your home. I have my lunch to prepare and eat.'

' "I saw a dog today," my sister said, "a vicious dog abroad in Dunfarnham Avenue. Go to the houses, Edward, and tell the mothers to look to their children until the dog is captured and set to rest." She talked for seven hours, Mrs Mayben, about that dog, one day in 1951, and in the end she watched me move from house to house ringing the bells and warning the people about a vicious animal.'

'This is no concern of mine. If your sister is unwell –'

'My sister is not unwell. My sister pretends, exacting her revenge. God has told me, Mrs Mayben, to play my part in her pretended fantasies. I owe her the right to punish me, I quite understand that.'

Mrs Mayben shook her head. She said in a quiet voice that she was an old woman and did not understand much of what went on in the world. She did not mind, she said, Edward ringing her doorbell, but she wished now that he would leave her house since she had much to do.

'I have never told anyone else,' said Edward. 'Years ago I said to myself that when I had to come to your house I would tell you the truth about everything. How I have grown up to be an understanding man, with the help of God. How the punishment must be shared between us – well, she has had hers. D'you see?'

Mrs Mayben shook her head and was about to speak again. Edward said:

'"There's a smell of burning," my sister said to me in 1955. "It comes from the house with the three Indian women in it." She had woken me up to tell me that, for it was half past two in the morning. "They are women from the East," she said. "They do not understand about precautions against fire as we do." In my dressing-gown, Mrs Mayben, I walked the length of Dunfarnham Avenue and rang the bell of that house. "May I use your telephone?" I said to the Indian woman who opened the door, for I could think of nothing else to say to her. But she said no, I could not; and rightly pointed out that she could not be expected to admit into her house a man in pyjamas at half past two in the morning. I have never told anyone because it seemed to be a family thing. I have never told the truth. It is all pretence and silence between my sister and myself. We play a game.'

'I must ask you to go now. I really must. An old woman like me can't be expected to take a sudden interest. You must do the best you can.'

'But I am telling you terrible things,' cried Edward. 'I killed my sister's guinea-pig, I pulled her pansies by the roots. Not an hour passed in my early childhood, Mrs Mayben, but I did not seek to torment her into madness. I don't know why I was given that role, but now I have the other since I've been guided towards it. She is quite sane, you know. She plays a part. I am rotten with guilt.'

Mrs Mayben clapped her hands sharply together. 'I cannot have you coming here,' she said, 'telling me you are rotten with guilt, Mr Tripp. You are a man I have seen about the place with a string bag. I do not know you. I do not know your sister. It's no concern of mine. Not at all.'

'You have a kind face to live up to,' said Edward, bowing and smiling in a sad way. 'I have seen you feeding the sparrows, and I've often thought you have a kind face.'

'Leave me alone, sir. Go from this house at once. You speak of madness and death, Mr Tripp; you tell me I've been murdered: I am unable to think about such things. My days are simple here.'

'Since I was seventeen, Mrs Mayben, since the day of my mother's funeral, I have lived alone with all this horror. Dunfarnham Avenue is the theatre of my embarrassment. You feed the sparrows, Mrs Mayben, yet for me it seems you have no crumb of comfort.'

'I cannot be expected –' began Mrs Mayben.

'I am forty-one this month. She is four years older. See us as children, Mrs Mayben, for it's absurd that I am here before you as a small man in a weekend suit. We are still children in that house, in our way: we have not grown up much. Surely you take an interest?'

'You come here saying you are notorious, Mr Tripp –'

'I am notorious, indeed I am, for God is a hard master. The house is dark and unchanged. Only the toys have gone. We eat the same kind of food.'

'Go away,' cried Mrs Mayben, her voice rising. 'For the sake of God, go away from me, Mr Tripp. You come here talking madly and carrying a ham knife. Leave my house.'

Edward rose to his feet and with his head bowed to his chest he walked past Mrs Mayben into her hall. He picked up the ham knife from the table and moved towards the front door.

'I'm sorry I can't interest myself in you and your sister,' said Mrs Mayben. 'I am too old, you see, to take on new subjects.'

Edward did not say anything more. He did not look at Mrs Mayben, but into his mind came the picture of her leaning from her sitting-room window putting crumbs of bread on the window-sills for the birds. He walked from her house with that picture in his mind and he heard behind him the closing of her hall door.

Edward crossed Dunfarnham Avenue and entered the house he had always known, carrying the ham knife in his left hand. He moved slowly to the dining-room and saw that the table was neatly laid for lunch. The sliced ham had been placed by his sister on two blue-and-white plates. Salt and pepper were on the table, and a jar of pickles that he himself had bought, since they both relished them. She had washed a lettuce and cut up a few tomatoes and put chives and cucumber with the salad. 'I've made the mustard,' said Emily, smiling at him as he sat down, and he saw, as he expected, that the look had gone from her face. 'We might repair the sitting-room carpet this afternoon,' said Emily, 'before that hole becomes too large. We could do it together.'

He nodded and murmured, and then, although he was awake and eating his lunch, Edward dreamed. It seemed to him that he was still in Mrs Mayben's sitting-room and that she, changed in her attitude, was murmuring that of course she understood, and all the better because she was old. She placed a hand on Edward's shoulder and said most softly that he had made her feel a mother again. He told her then, once more, of the pansies plucked from the flowerbed, and Mrs Mayben nodded and said he must not mind. He must suffer a bit, she said in a gentle way, since that was his due; he must feel his guilt around him and know that it was rightly there. In Edward's dream Mrs Mayben's voice was soothing, like a cool balm in the sunshine that came prettily through her sitting-room window. 'My dear, do not weep,' said the voice. 'Do not cry, for soon there is the Kingdom of Heaven.' The birds sang while the sun illuminated the room in which Mrs Mayben stood. 'I will go now,' said Edward in his dream, 'since I have mended your fuse and had my sherry. We've had a lovely chat.' He spoke in a peculiar voice and when he rose and walked away his feet made little sound as they struck the floor. 'Come when you wish,' invited Mrs Mayben with tears in her eyes. 'Cross the road for comfort. It's all you have to do.'

Edward chewed lettuce and ham and a piece of tomato, staring over his sister's shoulder at the grey curtains that hung by the window. His eyes moved to his sister's face and then moved downwards to the table, towards the knife that lay now on the polished wood. He thought about this knife that he had carried into a neighbour's house, remembering its keen blade slicing through the flesh of a pig. He saw himself standing with the knife in his hand, and he heard a noise that might have been a cry from his sister's throat. 'I have played a trick on you,' his own voice said, tumbling back to him over the years.

'A pity if that carpet went,' said Emily.

Edward looked at her, attempting to smile. He heard her add:

'It's always been there. All our lives, Edward.' And then, without meaning to say it, Edward said:

'She was harsh in how she looked. Too old to take on new subjects: she was making excuses.'

'What?' murmured Emily, and Edward sighed a little, eating more of the food she had prepared. Vaguely, he told her not to worry, and as he spoke he imagined them that afternoon, sitting on the floor of the other room stitching the carpet they had always known, not saying much except to comment perhaps upon the labour and upon the carpet. And as they worked together, he knew that he would go on praying, praying in his mind for the day to come: a day when old Mrs Mayben and all the people of Dunfarnham Avenue would see his sister walking lightly in the Kingdom of Heaven. In their presence she would smile as once she had smiled as a child, offering him her forgiveness while saying she was sorry too, and releasing in sumptuous glory all the years of imprisoned truth.

The Forty-seventh Saturday

Mavie awoke and remembered at once that it was Saturday. She lay for a while, alone with that thought, considering it and relishing it. Then she thought of details: the ingredients of a lunch, the cleaning of the kitchen floor, the tidying of her bedroom. She rose and reached for her dressing-gown. In the kitchen she found a small pad of paper and wrote in pencil these words: *mackerel, parmesan cheese, garlic*. Then she drew back the curtains, placed a filled kettle over a gas-jet and shook cornflakes on to a plate.

Some hours later, about midday, Mr McCarthy stood thoughtfully in a wine shop. He sighed, and then said:

'*Vin rosé*. The larger size. Is it a litre? I don't know what it's called.'

'Jumbo *vin rose*,' the assistant murmured, ignoring the demands of the accented word. 'Fourteen and seven.'

It was not a wine shop in which Mr McCarthy had ever before made a purchase. He paused, his hand inside his jacket, the tips of his fingers touching the leather of his wallet.

'Fourteen and seven?'

The assistant, perceiving clearly that Mr McCarthy had arrested the action with which he had planned to draw money from within his clothes, took no notice. He blew on the glass of the bottle because the bottle was dusty. Whistling thickly with tongue and lips, he tore a piece of brown paper and proceeded to wrap with it. He placed the parcel in a carrier bag.

'I thought it was ten shillings that size,' Mr McCarthy said. 'I have got it in another place for ten shillings.'

The assistant stared at him, incredulous.

'I buy a lot of *vin rosé*,' Mr McCarthy explained.

The assistant, a man of thirty-five with a face that was pock-marked, spoke no word but stared on. In his mind he was already retailing the incident to his superior when, an hour or so later, that person should return. He scrutinized Mr McCarthy, so that when the time came he might lend authority to his tale with an accurate description of the man who had demanded *vin rosé* and then had argued about the charged price. He saw before him a middle-aged man of medium height, with a hat and spectacles and a moustache.

'Well, I haven't time to argue.' Mr McCarthy handed the man a pound note and received his change. 'Threepence short, that is,' he said; and the assistant explained:

'The carrier bag. It's necessary nowadays to charge. You understand?'

But Mr McCarthy lifted the wine out of the bag, saying that the brown paper wrapping was quite sufficient, and the assistant handed him a threepenny piece.

'I take a taxi,' Mr McCarthy explained. 'It's no hardship to carry.'

In the flat Mavie laid two mackerel on the smoking fat of the frying pan and sniffed the air. A plastic apron covered her navy-blue, well-worn suit. Her fair hair, recently released from curling-pins, quivered splendidly about her head; her bosom heaved as she drew the tasty air into her lungs. She walked from the stove to the kitchen table, seeking a glass of medium dry sherry that a minute or two previously she had poured and placed somewhere.

'Ta-ra-ta-ta-ta-ta-ta-ta, ta-ta-ta-ta-ta-ta,' tuned Mr McCarthy in his taxi-cab, trying to put from his mind the extra four and sevenpence that he had been obliged to spend on the wine. 'A basement place,' he called to the driver. 'You'll know it by a motor-cycle and side-car parked outside.' The driver made no response.

'Motor-bike and side-car,' repeated Mr McCarthy. 'Parked by a lamp-post, number twenty-one. D'you understand?'

'Twenty-one, Roeway Road,' said the driver. 'We'll endeavour.'

Mr McCarthy closed his eyes and stretched his legs stiffly in front of him. He thought of Mavie, as was suitable at that moment. He saw her standing by the edge of the kitchen table, with a cigarette protruding from the left-hand extremity of her mouth, and the thumb and forefinger of her right hand grasping a glass which contained sherry and which bore, painted around it on the outside, two thin lines, one in red, the other in gold. It was the forty-seventh time that Mr McCarthy had made this midday journey, in a taxi-cab with a bottle of wine.

'Doesn't he want you to dress up?' the girls had asked when first she had told them. 'Pith helmets, chukka boots?' Mavie had found that funny. She had laughed and said: 'Dress up? Rather the opposite!' But that was at the very beginning of the affair, before she had fallen so deeply in love with him.

'Hullo.' Mavie, holding the sherry glass before her, struck a pose in the basement kitchen. She had taken off her plastic apron.

'Hullo, Mavie.' He held out the bottle, his hat still upon his head, his soft raincoat creased and seeming unclean. 'I've brought some wine. A little wine. I thought it would cheer us up.' He had let himself in, for the door was always on the latch. He had clicked the Yale catch behind him, as he had long since learned she liked him to do, so that no disturbances might later take place. 'I don't care for disturbances,' Mavie had said on the fifth occasion: an embarrassing time, when a coal-heaver, mistaking the basement for the basement next door, had walked into her bedroom with a sack on his back to find Mr McCarthy and herself playing about on the covers of her bed.

'My, my, you're looking sweet.' He removed his hat and overcoat and cast his eye about for a corkscrew. It was his policy on these visits to prime himself beforehand with two measures of brandy and, having made his entry, to take an immediate glass of *vin rosé*. He did not care for Mavie's sherry. *British sherry* was how the label described it; a qualification that put Mr McCarthy off.

'I love that costume.' He had said this before, referring to Mavie's navy-blue coat and skirt. In reply she had once or twice pointed out that it had been, originally, the property of her sister Linda.

Mr McCarthy could smell the fish. He could sense the atmosphere rich with mackerel and the perfumed mist with which Mavie had sprayed the room.

'I'm doing a nice fresh mackerel in a custard sauce,' Mavie announced, moving towards the stove. She had been closely embraced by Mr McCarthy, who was now a little shaken, caught between the promise of the embrace and the thought of mackerel in a sauce. He imagined he must have heard incorrectly: he could not believe that the sauce was a custard one. 'Custard!' he said. 'Custard?'

Mavie stirred the contents of a bowl. She remembered the first time: she had made an omelette; the mushrooms with which she had filled it had not cooked properly and Mr McCarthy had remarked upon the fact. She could have wept, watching him move the mushrooms to the side of his plate. 'Have them on toast,' she had cried. 'I'll cook them a bit more, love, and you can have them on a nice piece of toast.' But he had shaken his head, and then, to show that all was well, he had taken her into his arms and had at once begun to unzip her skirt.

'Custard?' said Mr McCarthy again, aware of some revulsion in his bowels.

'A garlic custard sauce. I read it in that column.'

'My dear, I'd as soon have a lightly boiled egg. This wretched old trouble again.'

'Oh, you poor thing! But fish is as easy to digest. A small helping. I'd have steamed had I known. You poor soul. Sit down, for heaven's sake.'

He was thinking that he would vomit if he had to lift a single forkful of mackerel and garlic custard sauce to his lips. He would feel a retching at the back of his throat and before another second passed there would be an accident.

'Love, I should have told you: I am off fish in any shape or form. The latest thing, I am on a diet of soft-boiled eggs. I'm a terrible trouble to you, Mavie love.'

She came to where he was sitting, drinking his way through the wine, and kissed him. She said not to worry about anything.

Mr McCarthy had told Mavie more lies than he had ever told anyone else. He had invented trouble with his stomach so that he could insist upon simple food, even though Mavie, forgetfully or hopefully, always cooked more elaborately. He had invented a Saturday appointment at four o'clock every week so that no dawdling would be required of him after he had exacted what he had come to look upon as his due. He had invented a wife and two children so that Mavie might not get ideas above her station.

'Brush your teeth, Mavie, like a good girl.' Mr McCarthy was being practical, fearful of the garlic. He spoke with confidence, knowing that Mavie would see it as reasonable that she should brush her teeth before the moments of love.

While she was in the bathroom he hummed a tune and reflected on his continuing good fortune. He drank more wine and when Mavie returned bade her drink some, too. It could only happen on Saturdays because the girl whom Mavie shared the flat with, Eithne, went away for the weekends.

'Well, this is pleasant,' said Mr McCarthy, sitting her on his knee, stroking her navy-blue clothes. She sat there, a little heavy for him, swinging her legs until her shoes slipped off.

This Saturday was Mavie's birthday. Today she was twenty-seven, while Mr McCarthy remained at fifty-two. She had, the night before and for several other nights and days, considered the fact, wondering whether or not to make anything of it, wondering whether or not to let Mr McCarthy know. She had thought, the Saturday before, that it might seem a little pushing to say that it was her birthday in a week; it might seem that her words contained the suggestion that Mr McCarthy should arm himself with a present or should contrive to transform the day into a special occasion. She thought ecstatically of his arriving at the house with a wrapped box and sitting down and saying: 'What lovely mackerel!' and putting it to her then that since this was her twenty-seventh birthday he would arrange to spend the whole afternoon and the night as well. 'We shall take to the West End later on,' Mr McCarthy had said in Mavie's mind, 'and shall go to a show, that thing at the Palladium. I have the tickets in my wallet.'

'What terrible old weather it is,' said Mr McCarthy. 'You wouldn't know whether you're coming or going.'

Mavie made a noise of agreement. She remembered other birthdays: a year she had been given a kite, the time that her cake, its flavour chosen by her, had not succeeded in the oven and had come to the table lumpy and grey, disguised with hundreds and thousands. She had cried, and her mother had picked up a teaspoon and rapped her knuckles. 'After the show,' said Mr McCarthy, 'what about a spot of dinner in a little place I've heard of? And then liqueurs before we return in style to your little nest.' As he spoke Mr McCarthy nuzzled her neck, and Mavie realized that he was, in fact, nuzzling her neck, though he was not speaking.

'Today is a special day,' said Mavie. 'It's a very special November day.'

Mr McCarthy laughed. 'Every Saturday is a special day for me. Every Saturday is outlined in red on my heart.' And he initiated some horseplay, which prevented Mavie from explaining.

Born beneath the sign of Scorpio, she was meant to be strong, fearless and enterprising. As a child she had often been in trouble, not because of naughtiness but because she had been dreamy about her work. She dreamed now, dominated by an image of Mr McCarthy rushing out for flowers. She saw him returning, blooms everywhere, saying he had telephoned to put off his Saturday appointment and had telephoned his home to say he had been called away on vital business. She felt his hands seeking the outline of her ribs, a thing he liked to do. They lay in silence for a while, and increasingly she felt low and sad.

'How lovely you are,' murmured Mr McCarthy. 'Oh, Mavie, Mavie.'

She squeezed the length of pale flesh that was Mr McCarthy's arm. She thought suddenly of the day the coal-heaver had arrived and felt her neck going red at the memory. She remembered the first day, rolling down her stockings and seeing her lover watching her, he already naked, standing still and seeming puzzled, near the electric fire. She had not been a virgin that day, but in the meanwhile she had not once been unfaithful to him.

'Tell me you love me,' Mavie cried, forgetting about her birthday, abruptly caught up in a new emotion. 'Tell me now; it worries me sometimes.'

'Of course it does. Of course I do. I'm all for you, Mavie, as I've said a thousand times.'

'It's not that I doubt you, honey, only sometimes between one Saturday and another I feel a depression. It's impossible to say. I mean, it's hard to put into words. Have you got a fag?'

Mr McCarthy shook his head on the pillow. She knew he did not smoke: why did she ask? It was like the custard sauce all over again. When he went to the trouble of inventing stomach trouble, you'd think she'd take the trouble to remember it.

'You don't smoke. I always ask and you always don't say anything and I always remember then. Am I very irritating to you, honey? Tell me you love me. Tell me I'm not irritating to you.'

'Mavie.'

'You don't like me today. I feel it. Jesus, I'm sorry about the mackerel. Tell the truth now, you don't like me today.'

'Oh yes, I do. I love you. I love you.'

'You don't like me.' She spoke as though she had not heard his protestations; she spaced the words carefully, giving the same emphasis to each.

'I love you,' said Mr McCarthy. 'Indeed I do.'

She shook her head, and rose and walked to the kitchen, where she found cigarettes and matches.

'My Mavie,' said Mr McCarthy from the bed, assuring himself that he was not finished yet, that he had not fully exacted his pleasurable due. 'Mavie, my young heart,' he murmured, and he began to laugh, thinking that merriment in the atmosphere would cheer matters up. 'Shall I do a little dance for you?'

Mavie, cigarette aglow, pulled the sheets around her as Mr McCarthy vacated the bed and stood, his arms outstretched, on the centre of the floor. He began to dance, as on many occasions before he had danced, swaying about without much tempo. When first he had performed in this way for her he had explained that his dance was an expression of his passion, representing, so he said, roses and presents of jewellery and lamé gowns. Once Mr McCarthy had asked Mavie to take the braces off his trousers and strike him with them while he acted out his dance. He was guilty, he said, because in their life together there were neither roses nor jewels, nor restaurant dinners. But Mavie, shocked that he should feel like that, had refused his request, saying there was no cause for punishment. Sulkily, he had maintained otherwise, though he had not ever again suggested chastisement.

'How's that?' said Mr McCarthy, ending with a gesture. Mavie said nothing. She threw back the bed-clothes and Mr McCarthy strode jauntily towards her, a smile shaping beneath his moustache.

'I often wonder about her,' Mavie said a moment later. 'It's only natural. You can't help that.'

Mr McCarthy said: 'My wife's a hard case. She's well able to take care of herself. I'm on a leash where the wife is concerned.'

'I don't even know her name.'

'Oh, Mavie, Mavie. Isn't Mrs McCarthy enough?'

'I'm jealous. I'm sorry, honey.'

'No bother, Mavie. No bother, love.'

'I see her as a black-haired woman. Tall and sturdy. Would you rather we didn't speak of her?'

'It would be easier, certainly.'

'I'm sorry, honey.'

'No bother.'

'It's only jealousy. The green-eyed monster.'

'No need to be jealous, Mavie. No need at all. There's no love lost between Mrs McCarthy and myself. We never go together nowadays.'

'What sign is she under?'

'Sign, love?'

'Sagittarius? Leo? When's her birthday?'

Mr McCarthy's small eyes screwed up.

He looked through the lashes. He said:

'The 29th of March.'

'You make an occasion of it, do you? In the home, with the children around? You all give her presents, I suppose. Is there a special cake?'

'The wife likes a jam-roll. She buys one at Lyons.'

'And the children get her little gifts? Things from Woolworth's?'

'Something like that.'

'When I was little I used to buy presents in Woolworth's. My dad used to take me by the hand. I suppose you did, too. And your wife.'

'Yes, love, I suppose so.'

'I often think of your wife. I can't help it. I see her in my mind's eye.'

'She's a big woman,' said Mr McCarthy meditatively. 'Bigger than you, Mavie. A big, dark woman – more than that I won't say.'

'Oh, honey, I never meant to pry.'

'It's not prying I mind, Mavie. No, you're not prying. It's just that I don't wish to soil the hour.'

When Mr McCarthy had said that, he heard the words echoing in his mind as words occasionally do. *I don't wish to soil the hour*. Mavie was silent, feeling the words to be beautiful. *I don't wish to soil the hour*, she thought. She drew her fingernails along the taut skin of Mr McCarthy's thigh. 'Oh God,' said Mr McCarthy.

She knew that when he left, at twenty to four, she would sit alone in her dressing-gown and weep. She would wash the dirty dishes from lunch and she would wash his lovingly: she would wash and dry his egg-cup and be aware that it was his. She knew that that was absurd, but she knew that it would happen because it had happened before. She did not think it odd, as Mr McCarthy had often thought, that she, so pretty and still young, should love so passionately a man of fifty-two. She adored every shred of him; she longed for his presence and the touch of his hand. 'Oh, my honey, my honey,' cried Mavie, throwing her body on the body of Mr McCarthy and wrapping him up in her plump limbs.

At half past three Mr McCarthy, who had dropped into a light doze, woke to the awareness of a parched throat and a desire for tea. He sighed and caressed the fair hair that lay on the pillow beside him.

'I'll make a cup of tea,' said Mavie.

'*Merci*,' whispered Mr McCarthy.

They drank tea in the kitchen while Mr McCarthy buttoned his waistcoat and drew on his socks. 'I've bought a bow tie,' he confided, 'though I'm still a little shy in it. Maybe next week I'll try it out on you.'

'You could ask me anything under the sun and I'd do it for you. You could ask me anything, I love you that much.'

Hearing this, Mr McCarthy paused in the lacing of a boot. He thought of his braces, taut now about his shoulders; he thought of a foot fetish he had read about in the public library.

'I love you that much,' whispered Mavie.

'And I you,' said Mr McCarthy.

'I dream of you at nights.'

'I dream of you, my dear.'

Mavie sighed and looked over her shoulder, ill at ease. 'I cannot think of you dreaming of me.'

'I dream of you in my narrow twin bed, with that woman in the twin beside it.'

'Don't speak like that. Don't talk to me of the bedroom.'

'I'm sorry.'

'I can't bear the thought of the twin beds in that room. I've told you before, honey.'

'Oh, Mavie, Mavie, if we could be together.'

'I love you that much.'

For a moment there was silence in the kitchen. Then, having tilted his cup to drain it of tea, Mr McCarthy rose to go.

As he crossed the floor his eyes fell on a birthday card propped up on the mantelshelf. It registered with him at once that the day was Mavie's birthday, and for a moment he considered remarking on that fact. Then he remembered the time and he kissed her on the head, his usual form of farewell. 'The forty-seventh time,' he murmured. 'Today was the forty-seventh.'

She walked with him along the passage to the door of the flat. She watched him mount the basement steps and watched his legs move briskly by the railings above. His footsteps died away and she returned to the kitchen and poured herself a cup of tea. She thought of him keeping his Saturday appointment, a business appointment he had always called it, and afterwards returning on a bus to his suburb. She saw him entering a door, opening it with a latchkey, being greeted by a dog and two children and the big, dark woman who was his wife. The dog barked loudly and the woman shrilled abuse, upbraiding her husband for a misdemeanour or some piece of forgetfulness or some small deceit discovered. Marie could feel his tiredness as he stood in his own hall, the latchkey still poised between his fingers, like a man at bay. Her eyes closed as she held that image in her mind; tears slipped from beneath their lids.

The bus let Mr McCarthy down at an Odeon cinema. He moved rapidly, checking his watch against a brightly lit clock that hung out over a shop. He was reckoning as he walked that there was time to have another cup of tea, with a Danish pastry perhaps, because he felt quite peckish. Afterwards, as always on a Saturday, he'd go to the pictures.

The Ballroom of Romance

On Sundays, or on Mondays if he couldn't make it and often he couldn't, Sunday being his busy day, Canon O'Connell arrived at the farm in order to hold a private service with Bridie's father, who couldn't get about any more, having had a leg amputated after gangrene had set in. They'd had a pony and cart then and Bridie's mother had been alive: it hadn't been difficult for the two of them to help her father on to the cart in order to make the journey to Mass. But two years later the pony had gone lame and eventually had to be destroyed; not long after that her mother had died. 'Don't worry about it at all,' Canon O'Connell had said, referring to the difficulty of transporting her father to Mass. 'I'll slip up by the week, Bridie.'

The milk lorry called daily for the single churn of milk, Mr Driscoll delivered groceries and meal in his van, and took away the eggs that Bridie had collected during the week. Since Canon O'Connell had made his offer, in 1953, Bridie's father hadn't left the farm.

As well as Mass on Sundays and her weekly visits to a wayside dance-hall Bridie went shopping once every month, cycling to the town early on a Friday afternoon. She bought things for herself, material for a dress, knitting wool, stockings, a newspaper, and paper-backed Wild West novels for her father. She talked in the shops to some of the girls she'd been at school with, girls who had married shop-assistants or shopkeepers, or had become assistants themselves. Most of them had families of their own by now. 'You're lucky to be peaceful in the hills,' they said to Bridie, 'instead of stuck in a hole like this.' They had a tired look, most of them, from pregnancies and their efforts to organize and control their large families.

As she cycled back to the hills on a Friday Bridie often felt that they truly envied her her life, and she found it surprising that they should do so. If it hadn't been for her father she'd have wanted to work in the town also, in the tinned-meat factory maybe, or in a shop. The town had a cinema called the Electric, and a fish-and-chip shop where people met at night, eating chips out of newspaper on the pavement outside. In the evenings, sitting in the farmhouse with her father, she often thought about the town, imagining the shop-windows lit up to display their goods and the sweet-shops still open so that people could purchase chocolates or fruit to take with them to the Electric cinema. But the town was eleven miles away, which was too far to cycle, there and back, for an evening's entertainment.

'It's a terrible thing for you, girl,' her father used to say, genuinely troubled, 'tied up to a one-legged man.' He would sigh heavily, hobbling back from the fields, where he managed as best he could. 'If your mother hadn't died,' he'd say, not finishing the sentence.

If her mother hadn't died her mother could have looked after him and the scant acres he owned, her mother could somehow have lifted the milk-churn on to the collection platform and attended to the few hens and the cows. 'I'd be dead without the girl to assist me,' she'd heard her father saying to Canon O'Connell, and Canon O'Connell replied that he was certainly lucky to have her.

'Amn't I as happy here as anywhere?' she'd say herself, but her father knew she was pretending and was saddened because the weight of circumstances had so harshly interfered with her life.

Although her father still called her a girl, Bridie was thirty-six. She was tall and strong: the skin of her fingers and her palms were stained, and harsh to touch. The labour they'd experienced had found its way into them, as though juices had come out of vegetation and pigment out of soil: since childhood she'd torn away the rough scotch grass that grew each spring among her father's mangolds and sugar beet; since childhood she'd harvested potatoes in August, her hands daily rooting in the ground she loosened and turned. Wind had toughened the flesh of her face, sun had browned it; her neck and nose were lean, her lips touched with early wrinkles.

But on Saturday nights Bridie forgot the scotch grass and the soil. In different dresses she cycled to the dance-hall, encouraged to make the journey by her father. 'Doesn't it do you good, girl?' he'd say, as though he imagined she begrudged herself the pleasure. 'Why wouldn't you enjoy yourself?' She'd cook him his tea and then he'd settle down with the wireless, or maybe a Wild West novel. In time, while still she danced, he'd stoke the fire up and hobble his way upstairs to bed.

The dance-hall, owned by Mr Justin Dwyer, was miles from anywhere, a lone building by the roadside with treeless boglands all around and a gravel expanse in front of it. On pink pebbled cement its title was painted in an azure blue that matched the depth of the background shade yet stood out well, unfussily proclaiming *The Ballroom of Romance*. Above these letters four coloured bulbs – in red, green, orange and mauve – were lit at appropriate times, an indication that the evening rendezvous was open for business. Only the façade of the building was pink, the other walls being a more ordinary grey. And inside, except for pink swing-doors, everything was blue.

On Saturday nights Mr Justin Dwyer, a small, thin man, unlocked the metal grid that protected his property and drew it back, creating an open mouth from which music would later pour. He helped his wife to carry crates of lemonade and packets of biscuits from their car, and then took up a position in the tiny vestibule between the drawn-back grid and the pink swing-doors. He sat at a card-table, with money and tickets spread out before him. He'd made a fortune, people said: he owned other ball-rooms also.

People came on bicycles or in old motor-cars, country people like Bridie from remote hill farms and villages. People who did not often see other people met there, girls and boys, men and women. They paid Mr Dwyer and passed into his dance-hall, where shadows were cast on pale-blue walls and light from a crystal bowl was dim. The band, known as the Romantic Jazz Band, was composed of clarinet, drums and piano. The drummer sometimes sang.

Bridie had been going to the dance-hall since first she left the Presentation Nuns, before her mother's death. She didn't mind the journey, which was seven miles there and seven back: she'd travelled as far every day to the Presentation Nuns on the same bicycle, which had once been the property of her mother, an old Rudge purchased originally in 1936. On Sundays she cycled six miles to Mass, but she never minded either: she'd grown quite used to all that.

'How're you, Bridie?' inquired Mr Justin Dwyer when she arrived in a new scarlet dress one autumn evening. She said she was all right and in reply to Mr Dwyer's second query she said that her father was all right also. 'I'll go up one of these days,' promised Mr Dwyer, which was a promise he'd been making for twenty years.

She paid the entrance fee and passed through the pink swing-doors. The Romantic Jazz Band was playing a familiar melody of the past, 'The Destiny Waltz'. In spite of the band's title, jazz was not ever played in the ballroom: Mr Dwyer did not personally care for that kind of music, nor had he cared for various dance movements that had come and gone over the years. Jiving, rock and roll, twisting and other such variations had all been resisted by Mr Dwyer, who believed that a ballroom should be, as much as possible, a dignified place. The Romantic Jazz Band consisted of Mr Maloney, Mr Swanton, and Dano Ryan on drums. They were three middle-aged men who drove out from the town in Mr Maloney's car, amateur performers who were employed otherwise by the tinned-meat factory, the Electricity Supply Board and the County Council.

'How're you, Bridie?' inquired Dano Ryan as she passed him on her way to the cloakroom. He was idle for a moment with his drums, 'The Destiny Waltz' not calling for much attention from him.

'I'm all right, Dano,' she said. 'Are you fit yourself? Are the eyes better?' The week before he'd told her that he'd developed a watering of the eyes that must have been some kind of cold or other. He'd woken up with it in the morning and it had persisted until the afternoon: it was a new experience, he'd told her, adding that he'd never had a day's illness or discomfort in his life.

'I think I need glasses,' he said now, and as she passed into the cloakroom she imagined him in glasses, repairing the roads, as he was employed to do by the County Council. You hardly ever saw a road-mender with glasses, she reflected, and she wondered if all the dust that was inherent in his work had perhaps affected his eyes.

'How're you, Bridie?' a girl called Eenie Mackie said in the cloakroom, a girl who'd left the Presentation Nuns only a year ago.

'That's a lovely dress, Eenie,' Bridie said. 'Is it nylon, that?'

'Tricel actually. Drip-dry.'

Bridie took off her coat and hung it on a hook. There was a small wash-basin in the cloakroom above which hung a discoloured oval mirror. Used tissues and pieces of cotton-wool, cigarette-butts and matches covered the concrete floor. Lengths of green-painted timber partitioned off a lavatory in a corner.

'Jeez, you're looking great, Bridie,' Madge Dowding remarked, waiting for her turn at the mirror. She moved towards it as she spoke, taking off a pair of spectacles before endeavouring to apply make-up to the lashes of her eye. She stared myopically into the oval mirror, humming while the other girls became restive.

'Will you hurry up, for God's sake!' shouted Eenie Mackie. 'We're standing here all night, Madge.'

Madge Dowding was the only one who was older than Bridie. She was thirty-nine, although often she said she was younger. The girls sniggered about that, saying that Madge Dowding should accept her condition – her age and her squint and her poor complexion – and not make herself ridiculous going out after men. What man would be bothered with the like of her anyway? Madge Dowding would do better to give herself over to do Saturday-night work for the Legion of Mary: wasn't Canon O'Connell always looking for aid?

'Is that fellow there?' she asked now, moving away from the mirror. 'The guy with the long arms. Did anyone see him outside?'

'He's dancing with Cat Bolger,' one of the girls replied. 'She has herself glued to him.'

'Lover boy,' remarked Patty Byrne, and everyone laughed because the person referred to was hardly a boy any more, being over fifty it was said, a bachelor who came only occasionally to the dance-hall.

Madge Dowding left the cloakroom rapidly, not bothering to pretend she wasn't anxious about the conjunction of Cat Bolger and the man with the long arms. Two sharp spots of red had come into her cheeks, and when she stumbled in her haste the girls in the cloakroom laughed. A younger girl would have pretended to be casual.

Bridie chatted, waiting for the mirror. Some girls, not wishing to be delayed, used the mirrors of their compacts. Then in twos and threes, occasionally singly, they left the cloakroom and took their places on upright wooden chairs at one end of the dance-hall, waiting to be asked to dance. Mr Maloney, Mr Swanton and Dano Ryan played 'Harvest Moon' and 'I Wonder Who's Kissing Her Now' and 'I'll Be Around'.

Bridie danced. Her father would be falling asleep by the fire; the wireless, tuned in to Radio Eireann, would be murmuring in the background. Already he'd have listened to *Faith and Order* and *Spot the Talent*. His Wild West novel, *Three Rode Fast* by Jake Matall, would have dropped from his single knee on to the flagged floor. He would wake with a jerk as he did every night and, forgetting what night it was, might be surprised not to see her, for usually she was sitting there at the table, mending clothes or washing eggs. 'Is it time for the news?' he'd automatically say.

Dust and cigarette smoke formed a haze beneath the crystal bowl, feet thudded, girls shrieked and laughed, some of them dancing together for want of a male partner. The music was loud, the musicians had taken off their jackets. Vigorously they played a number of tunes from *State Fair* and then, more romantically, 'Just One of Those Things'. The tempo increased for a Paul Jones, after which Bridie found herself with a youth who told her he was saving up to emigrate, the nation in his opinion being finished. 'I'm up in the hills with the uncle,' he said, 'labouring fourteen hours a day. Is it any life for a young fellow?' She knew his uncle, a hill farmer whose stony acres were separated from her father's by one other farm only. 'He has me gutted with work,' the youth told her. 'Is there sense in it at all, Bridie?'

At ten o'clock there was a stir, occasioned by the arrival of three middle-aged bachelors who'd cycled over from Carey's public house. They shouted and whistled, greeting other people across the dancing area. They smelt of stout and sweat and whiskey.

Every Saturday at just this time they arrived, and, having sold them their tickets, Mr Dwyer folded up his card-table and locked the tin box that held the evening's takings: his ballroom was complete.

'How're you, Bridie?' one of the bachelors, known as Bowser Egan, inquired. Another one, Tim Daly, asked Patty Byrne how she was. 'Will we take the floor?' Eyes Horgan suggested to Madge Dowding, already pressing the front of his navy-blue suit against the net of her dress. Bridie danced with Bowser Egan, who said she was looking great.

The bachelors would never marry, the girls of the dance-hall considered: they were wedded already, to stout and whiskey and laziness, to three old mothers somewhere up in the hills. The man with the long arms didn't drink but he was the same in all other ways: he had the same look of a bachelor, a quality in his face.

'Great,' Bowser Egan said, feather-stepping in an inaccurate and inebriated manner. 'You're a great little dancer, Bridie.'

'Will you lay off that!' cried Madge Dowding, her voice shrill above the sound of the music. Eyes Horgan had slipped two fingers into the back of her dress and was now pretending they'd got there by accident. He smiled blearily, his huge red face streaming with perspiration, the eyes which gave him his nickname protuberant and bloodshot.

'Watch your step with that one,' Bowser Egan called out, laughing so that spittle sprayed on to Bridie's face. Eenie Mackie, who was also dancing near the incident, laughed also and winked at Bridie. Dano Ryan left his drums and sang. 'Oh, how I miss your gentle kiss,' he crooned, 'and long to hold you tight.'

Nobody knew the name of the man with the long arms. The only words he'd ever been known to speak in the Ballroom of Romance were the words that formed his invitation to dance. He was a shy man who stood alone when he wasn't performing on the dance-floor. He rode away on his bicycle afterwards, not saying good-night to anyone.

'Cat has your man leppin' tonight,' Tim Daly remarked to Patty Byrne, for the liveliness that Cat Bolger had introduced into foxtrot and waltz was noticeable.

'I think of you only,' sang Dano Ryan. 'Only wishing, wishing you were by my side.'

Dano Ryan would have done, Bridie often thought, because he was a different kind of bachelor: he had a lonely look about him, as if he'd become tired of being on his own. Every week she thought he would have done, and during the week her mind regularly returned to that thought. Dano Ryan would have done because she felt he wouldn't mind coming to live in the farmhouse while her one-legged father was still about the place. Three could live as cheaply as two where Dano Ryan was concerned because giving up the wages he earned as a road-worker would be balanced by the saving made on what he paid for lodgings. Once, at the end of an evening, she'd pretended that there was a puncture in the back wheel of her bicycle and he'd concerned himself with it while Mr Maloney and Mr Swanton waited for him in Mr Maloney's car. He'd blown the tyre up with the car pump and had said he thought it would hold.

It was well known in the dance-hall that she fancied her chances with Dano Ryan. But it was well known also that Dano Ryan had got into a set way of life and had remained in it for quite some years. He lodged with a widow called Mrs Griffin and Mrs Griffin's mentally affected son, in a cottage on the outskirts of the town. He was said to be good to the affected child, buying him sweets and taking him out for rides on the crossbar of his bicycle. He gave an hour or two of his time every week to the Church of Our Lady Queen of Heaven, and he was loyal to Mr Dwyer. He performed in the two other rural dance-halls that Mr Dwyer owned, rejecting advances from the town's more sophisticated dance-hall, even though it was more conveniently situated for him and the fee was more substantial than that paid by Mr Dwyer. But Mr Dwyer had discovered Dano Ryan and Dano had not forgotten it, just as Mr Maloney and Mr Swanton had not forgotten their discovery by Mr Dwyer either.

'Would we take a lemonade?' Bowser Egan suggested. 'And a packet of biscuits, Bridie?'

No alcoholic liquor was ever served in the Ballroom of Romance, the premises not being licensed for this added stimulant. Mr Dwyer in fact had never sought a licence for any of his premises, knowing that romance and alcohol were difficult commodities to mix, especially in a dignified ballroom. Behind where the girls sat on the wooden chairs Mr Dwyer's wife, a small stout woman, served the bottles of lemonade, with straws, and the biscuits, and crisps. She talked busily while doing so, mainly about the turkeys she kept. She'd once told Bridie that she thought of them as children.

'Thanks,' Bridie said, and Bowser Egan led her to the trestle table. Soon it would be the intermission: soon the three members of the band would cross the floor also for refreshment. She thought up questions to ask Dano Ryan.

When first she'd danced in the Ballroom of Romance, when she was just sixteen, Dano Ryan had been there also, four years older than she was, playing the drums for Mr Maloney as he played them now. She'd hardly noticed him then because of his not being one of the dancers: he was part of the ballroom's scenery, like the trestle table and the lemonade bottles,

and Mrs Dwyer and Mr Dwyer. The youths who'd danced with her then
in their Saturday-night blue suits had later disappeared into the town, or
to Dublin or Britain, leaving behind them those who became the middle-
aged bachelors of the hills. There'd been a boy called Patrick Grady whom
she had loved in those days. Week after week she'd ridden away from the
Ballroom of Romance with the image of his face in her mind, a thin face,
pale beneath black hair. It had been different, dancing with Patrick Grady,
and she'd felt that he found it different dancing with her, although he'd
never said so. At night she'd dreamed of him and in the daytime too, while
she helped her mother in the kitchen or her father with the cows. Week by
week she'd returned to the ballroom, delighting in its pink façade and
dancing in the arms of Patrick Grady. Often they'd stood together drinking
lemonade, not saying anything, not knowing what to say. She knew he
loved her, and she believed then that he would lead her one day from the
dim, romantic ballroom, from its blueness and its pinkness and its crystal
bowl of light and its music. She believed he would lead her into sunshine,
to the town and the Church of Our Lady Queen of Heaven, to marriage
and smiling faces. But someone else had got Patrick Grady, a girl from the
town who'd never danced in the wayside ballroom. She'd scooped up
Patrick Grady when he didn't have a chance.

Bridie had wept, hearing that. By night she'd lain in her bed in the
farmhouse, quietly crying, the tears rolling into her hair and making the
pillow damp. When she woke in the early morning the thought was still
naggingly with her and it remained with her by day, replacing her daytime
dreams of happiness. Someone told her later on that he'd crossed to Britain,
to Wolverhampton, with the girl he'd married, and she imagined him there,
in a place she wasn't able properly to visualize, labouring in a factory, his
children being born and acquiring the accent of the area. The Ballroom of
Romance wasn't the same without him, and when no one else stood out
for her particularly over the years and when no one offered her marriage,
she found herself wondering about Dano Ryan. If you couldn't have love,
the next best thing was surely a decent man.

Bowser Egan hardly fell into that category, nor did Tim Daly. And it
was plain to everyone that Cat Bolger and Madge Dowding were wasting
their time over the man with the long arms. Madge Dowding was already
a figure of fun in the ballroom, the way she ran after the bachelors; Cat
Bolger would end up the same if she wasn't careful. One way or another
it wasn't difficult to be a figure of fun in the ballroom, and you didn't have
to be as old as Madge Dowding: a girl who'd just left the Presentation
Nuns had once asked Eyes Horgan what he had in his trouser pocket
and he told her it was a penknife. She'd repeated this afterwards in the

cloakroom, how she'd requested Eyes Horgan not to dance so close to her because his penknife was sticking into her. 'Jeez, aren't you the right baby!' Patty Byrne had shouted delightedly; everyone had laughed, knowing that Eyes Horgan only came to the ballroom for stuff like that. He was no use to any girl.

'Two lemonades, Mrs Dwyer,' Bowser Egan said, 'and two packets of Kerry Creams. Is Kerry Creams all right, Bridie?'

She nodded, smiling. Kerry Creams would be fine, she said.

'Well, Bridie, isn't that the great outfit you have!' Mrs Dwyer remarked. 'Doesn't the red suit her, Bowser?'

By the swing-doors stood Mr Dwyer, smoking a cigarette that he held cupped in his left hand. His small eyes noted all developments. He had been aware of Madge Dowding's anxiety when Eyes Horgan had inserted two fingers into the back opening of her dress. He had looked away, not caring for the incident, but had it developed further he would have spoken to Eyes Horgan, as he had on other occasions. Some of the younger lads didn't know any better and would dance very close to their partners, who generally were too embarrassed to do anything about it, being young themselves. But that, in Mr Dwyer's opinion, was a different kettle of fish altogether because they were decent young lads who'd in no time at all be doing a steady line with a girl and would end up as he had himself with Mrs Dwyer, in the same house with her, sleeping in a bed with her, firmly married. It was the middle-aged bachelors who required the watching: they came down from the hills like mountain goats, released from their mammies and from the smell of animals and soil. Mr Dwyer continued to watch Eyes Horgan, wondering how drunk he was.

Dano Ryan's song came to an end, Mr Swanton laid down his clarinet, Mr Maloney rose from the piano. Dano Ryan wiped sweat from his face and the three men slowly moved towards Mrs Dwyer's trestle table.

'Jeez, you have powerful legs,' Eyes Horgan whispered to Madge Dowding, but Madge Dowding's attention was on the man with the long arms, who had left Cat Bolger's side and was proceeding in the direction of the men's lavatory. He never took refreshments. She moved, herself, towards the men's lavatory, to take up a position outside it, but Eyes Horgan followed her. 'Would you take a lemonade, Madge?' he asked. He had a small bottle of whiskey on him: if they went into a corner they could add a drop of it to the lemonade. She didn't drink spirits, she reminded him, and he went away.

'Excuse me a minute,' Bowser Egan said, putting down his bottle of lemonade. He crossed the floor to the lavatory. He too, Bridie knew, would have a small bottle of whiskey on him. She watched while Dano Ryan, listening to a story Mr Maloney was telling, paused in the centre of the ballroom, his head bent to hear what was being said. He was a big man, heavily made, with black hair that was slightly touched with grey, and big hands. He laughed when Mr Maloney came to the end of his story and then bent his head again, in order to listen to a story told by Mr Swanton.

'Are you on your own, Bridie?' Cat Bolger asked, and Bridie said she was waiting for Bowser Egan. 'I think I'll have a lemonade,' Cat Bolger said.

Younger boys and girls stood with their arms still around one another, queuing up for refreshments. Boys who hadn't danced at all, being nervous because they didn't know any steps, stood in groups, smoking and making jokes. Girls who hadn't been danced with yet talked to one another, their eyes wandering. Some of them sucked at straws in lemonade bottles.

Bridie, still watching Dano Ryan, imagined him wearing the glasses he'd referred to, sitting in the farmhouse kitchen, reading one of her father's Wild West novels. She imagined the three of them eating a meal she'd prepared, fried eggs and rashers and fried potato-cakes, and tea and bread and butter and jam, brown bread and soda and shop bread. She imagined Dano Ryan leaving the kitchen in the morning to go out to the fields in order to weed the mangolds, and her father hobbling off behind him, and the two men working together. She saw hay being cut, Dano Ryan with the scythe that she'd learned to use herself, her father using a rake as best he could. She saw herself, because of the extra help, being able to attend to things in the farmhouse, things she'd never had time for because of the cows and the hens and the fields. There were bedroom curtains that needed repairing where the net had ripped, and wallpaper that had become loose and needed to be stuck up with flour paste. The scullery required white-washing.

The night he'd blown up the tyre of her bicycle she'd thought he was going to kiss her. He'd crouched on the ground in the darkness with his ear to the tyre, listening for escaping air. When he could hear none he'd straightened up and said he thought she'd be all right on the bicycle. His face had been quite close to hers and she'd smiled at him. At that moment, unfortunately, Mr Maloney had blown an impatient blast on the horn of his motor-car.

Often she'd been kissed by Bowser Egan, on the nights when he insisted on riding part of the way home with her. They had to dismount in order to push their bicycles up a hill and the first time he'd accompanied her he'd contrived to fall against her, steadying himself by putting a hand on her shoulder. The next thing she was aware of was the moist quality of his lips and the sound of his bicycle as it clattered noisily on the road. He'd suggested then, regaining his breath, that they should go into a field.

That was nine years ago. In the intervening passage of time she'd been kissed as well, in similar circumstances, by Eyes Horgan and Tim Daly. She'd gone into fields with them and permitted them to put their arms about her while heavily they breathed. At one time or another she had imagined marriage with one or other of them, seeing them in the farmhouse with her father, even though the fantasies were unlikely.

Bridie stood with Cat Bolger, knowing that it would be some time before Bowser Egan came out of the lavatory. Mr Maloney, Mr Swanton and Dano Ryan approached, Mr Maloney insisting that he would fetch three bottles of lemonade from the trestle table.

'You sang the last one beautifully,' Bridie said to Dano Ryan. 'Isn't it a beautiful song?'

Mr Swanton said it was the finest song ever written, and Cat Bolger said she preferred 'Danny Boy', which in her opinion was the finest song ever written.

'Take a suck of that,' said Mr Maloney, handing Dano Ryan and Mr Swanton bottles of lemonade. 'How's Bridie tonight? Is your father well, Bridie?'

Her father was all right, she said.

'I hear they're starting a cement factory,' said Mr Maloney. 'Did anyone hear talk of that? They're after striking some commodity in the earth that makes good cement. Ten feet down, over at Kilmalough.'

'It'll bring employment,' said Mr Swanton. 'It's employment that's necessary in this area.'

'Canon O'Connell was on about it,' Mr Maloney said. 'There's Yankee money involved.'

'Will the Yanks come over?' inquired Cat Bolger. 'Will they run it themselves, Mr Maloney?'

Mr Maloney, intent on his lemonade, didn't hear the questions and Cat Bolger didn't repeat them.

'There's stuff called Optrex,' Bridie said quietly to Dano Ryan, 'that my father took the time he had a cold in his eyes. Maybe Optrex would settle the watering, Dano.'

'Ah sure, it doesn't worry me that much –'

'It's terrible, anything wrong with the eyes. You wouldn't want to take a chance. You'd get Optrex in a chemist, Dano, and a little bowl with it so that you can bathe the eyes.'

Her father's eyes had become red-rimmed and unsightly to look at. She'd gone into Riordan's Medical Hall in the town and had explained what the trouble was, and Mr Riordan had recommended Optrex. She told this to Dano Ryan, adding that her father had had no trouble with his eyes since. Dano Ryan nodded.

'Did you hear that, Mrs Dwyer?' Mr Maloney called out. 'A cement factory for Kilmalough.'

Mrs Dwyer wagged her head, placing empty bottles in a crate. She'd heard references to the cement factory, she said: it was the best news for a long time.

'Kilmalough won't know itself,' her husband commented, joining her in her task with the empty lemonade bottles.

"Twill bring prosperity certainly,' said Mr Swanton. 'I was saying just there, Justin, that employment's what's necessary.'

'Sure, won't the Yanks –' began Cat Bolger, but Mr Maloney interrupted her.

'The Yanks'll be in at the top, Cat, or maybe not here at all – maybe only inserting money into it. It'll be local labour entirely.'

'You'll not marry a Yank, Cat,' said Mr Swanton, loudly laughing. 'You can't catch those fellows.'

'Haven't you plenty of homemade bachelors?' suggested Mr Maloney. He laughed also, throwing away the straw he was sucking through and tipping the bottle into his mouth. Cat Bolger told him to get on with himself. She moved towards the men's lavatory and took up a position outside it, not speaking to Madge Dowding, who was still standing there.

'Keep a watch on Eyes Horgan,' Mrs Dwyer warned her husband, which was advice she gave him at this time every Saturday night, knowing that Eyes Horgan was drinking in the lavatory. When he was drunk Eyes Horgan was the most difficult of the bachelors.

'I have a drop of it left, Dano,' Bridie said quietly. 'I could bring it over on Saturday. The eye stuff.'

'Ah, don't worry yourself, Bridie –'

'No trouble at all. Honestly now –'

'Mrs Griffin has me fixed up for a test with Dr Cready. The old eyes are no worry, only when I'm reading the paper or at the pictures. Mrs Griffin says I'm only straining them due to lack of glasses.'

He looked away while he said that, and she knew at once that Mrs Griffin was arranging to marry him. She felt it instinctively: Mrs Griffin was going to marry him because she was afraid that if he moved away from her cottage, to get married to someone else, she'd find it hard to replace him with another lodger who'd be good to her affected son. He'd become a father to Mrs Griffin's affected son, to whom already he was kind. It was a natural outcome, for Mrs Griffin had all the chances, seeing him every night and morning and not having to make do with weekly encounters in a ballroom.

She thought of Patrick Grady, seeing in her mind his pale, thin face. She might be the mother of four of his children now, or seven or eight maybe. She might be living in Wolverhampton, going out to the pictures in the evenings, instead of looking after a one-legged man. If the weight of circumstances hadn't intervened she wouldn't be standing in a wayside ballroom, mourning the marriage of a road-mender she didn't love. For a moment she thought she might cry, standing there thinking of Patrick Grady in Wolverhampton. In her life, on the farm and in the house, there was no place for tears. Tears were a luxury, like flowers would be in the fields where the mangolds grew, or fresh whitewash in the scullery. It wouldn't have been fair ever to have wept in the kitchen while her father sat listening to *Spot the Talent*: her father had more right to weep, having lost a leg. He suffered in a greater way, yet he remained kind and concerned for her.

In the Ballroom of Romance she felt behind her eyes the tears that it would have been improper to release in the presence of her father. She wanted to let them go, to feel them streaming on her cheeks, to receive the sympathy of Dano Ryan and of everyone else. She wanted them all to listen to her while she told them about Patrick Grady who was now in Wolverhampton and about the death of her mother and her own life since. She wanted Dano Ryan to put his arm around her so that she could lean her head against it. She wanted him to look at her in his decent way and to stroke with his road-mender's fingers the backs of her hands. She might wake in a bed with him and imagine for a moment that he was Patrick Grady. She might bathe his eyes and pretend.

'Back to business,' said Mr Maloney, leading his band across the floor to their instruments.

'Tell your father I was asking for him,' Dano Ryan said. She smiled and she promised, as though nothing had happened, that she would tell her father that.

She danced with Tim Daly and then again with the youth who'd said he intended to emigrate. She saw Madge Dowding moving swiftly towards the man with the long arms as he came out of the lavatory, moving faster than Cat Bolger. Eyes Horgan approached Cat Bolger. Dancing with her, he spoke earnestly, attempting to persuade her to permit him to ride part of the way home with her. He was unaware of the jealousy that was coming from her as she watched Madge Dowding holding close to her the man with the long arms while they performed a quickstep. Cat Bolger was in her thirties also.

'Get away out of that,' said Bowser Egan, cutting in on the youth who was dancing with Bridie. 'Go home to your mammy, boy.' He took her into his arms, saying again that she was looking great tonight. 'Did you hear about the cement factory?' he said. 'Isn't it great for Kilmalough?'

She agreed. She said what Mr Swanton and Mr Maloney had said: that the cement factory would bring employment to the neighbourhood.

'Will I ride home with you a bit, Bridie?' Bowser Egan suggested, and she pretended not to hear him. 'Aren't you my girl, Bridie, and always have been?' he said, a statement that made no sense at all.

His voice went on whispering at her, saying he would marry her tomorrow only his mother wouldn't permit another woman in the house. She knew what it was like herself, he reminded her, having a parent to look after: you couldn't leave them to rot, you had to honour your father and your mother.

She danced to 'The Bells Are Ringing', moving her legs in time with Bowser Egan's while over his shoulder she watched Dano Ryan softly striking one of his smaller drums. Mrs Griffin had got him even though she was nearly fifty, with no looks at all, a lumpish woman with lumpish legs and arms. Mrs Griffin had got him just as the girl had got Patrick Grady.

The music ceased, Bowser Egan held her hard against him, trying to touch her face with his. Around them, people whistled and clapped: the evening had come to an end. She walked away from Bowser Egan, knowing that not ever again would she dance in the Ballroom of Romance. She'd been a figure of fun, trying to promote a relationship with a middle-aged County Council labourer, as ridiculous as Madge Dowding dancing on beyond her time.

'I'm waiting outside for you, Cat,' Eyes Horgan called out, lighting a cigarette as he made for the swing-doors.

Already the man with the long arms – made long, so they said, from carrying rocks off his land – had left the ballroom. Others were moving briskly. Mr Dwyer was tidying the chairs.

In the cloakroom the girls put on their coats and said they'd see one another at Mass the next day. Madge Dowding hurried. 'Are you OK, Bridie?' Patty Byrne asked and Bridie said she was. She smiled at little Patty Byrne, wondering if a day would come for the younger girl also, if one day she'd decide that she was a figure of fun in a wayside ballroom.

'Good-night so,' Bridie said, leaving the cloakroom, and the girls who were still chatting there wished her good-night. Outside the cloakroom she paused for a moment. Mr Dwyer was still tidying the chairs, picking up empty lemonade bottles from the floor, setting the chairs in a neat row.

His wife was sweeping the floor. 'Good-night, Bridie,' Mr Dwyer said. 'Good-night, Bridie,' his wife said.

Extra lights had been switched on so that the Dwyers could see what they were doing. In the glare the blue walls of the ballroom seemed tatty, marked with hair-oil where men had leaned against them, inscribed with names and initials and hearts with arrows through them. The crystal bowl gave out a light that was ineffective in the glare; the bowl was broken here and there, which wasn't noticeable when the other lights weren't on.

'Good-night so,' Bridie said to the Dwyers. She passed through the swing-doors and descended the three concrete steps on the gravel expanse in front of the ballroom. People were gathered on the gravel, talking in groups, standing with their bicycles. She saw Madge Dowding going off with Tim Daly. A youth rode away with a girl on the crossbar of his bicycle. The engines of motor-cars started.

'Good-night, Bridie,' Dano Ryan said.

'Good-night, Dano,' she said.

She walked across the gravel towards her bicycle, hearing Mr Maloney, somewhere behind her, repeating that no matter how you looked at it the cement factory would be a great thing for Kilmalough. She heard the bang of a car door and knew it was Mr Swanton banging the door of Mr Maloney's car because he always gave it the same loud bang. Two other doors banged as she reached her bicycle and then the engine started up and the headlights went on. She touched the two tyres of the bicycle to make certain she hadn't a puncture. The wheels of Mr Maloney's car traversed the gravel and were silent when they reached the road.

'Good-night, Bridie,' someone called, and she replied, pushing her bicycle towards the road.

'Will I ride a little way with you?' Bowser Egan asked.

They rode together and when they arrived at the hill for which it was necessary to dismount she looked back and saw in the distance the four coloured bulbs that decorated the façade of the Ballroom of Romance. As she watched, the lights went out, and she imagined Mr Dwyer pulling the metal grid across the front of his property and locking the two padlocks that secured it. His wife would be waiting with the evening's takings, sitting in the front of their car.

'D'you know what it is, Bridie,' said Bowser Egan, 'you were never looking better than tonight.' He took from a pocket of his suit the small bottle of whiskey he had. He uncorked it and drank some and then handed it to her. She took it and drank. 'Sure, why wouldn't you?' he said, surprised to see her drinking because she never had in his company before. It was an unpleasant taste, she considered, a taste she'd experienced only twice before, when she'd taken whiskey as a remedy for toothache. 'What harm would it do you?' Bowser Egan said as she raised the bottle again to her lips. He reached out a hand for it, though, suddenly concerned lest she should consume a greater share than he wished her to.

She watched him drinking more expertly than she had. He would always be drinking, she thought. He'd be lazy and useless, sitting in the kitchen with the *Irish Press*. He'd waste money buying a secondhand motor-car in order to drive into the town to go to the public houses on fair-days.

'She's shook these days,' he said, referring to his mother. 'She'll hardly last two years, I'm thinking.' He threw the empty whiskey bottle into the ditch and lit a cigarette. They pushed their bicycles. He said:

'When she goes, Bridie, I'll sell the bloody place up. I'll sell the pigs and the whole damn one and twopence worth.' He paused in order to raise the cigarette to his lips. He drew in smoke and exhaled it. 'With the cash that I'll get I could improve some place else, Bridie.'

They reached a gate on the left-hand side of the road and automatically they pushed their bicycles towards it and leaned them against it. He climbed over the gate into the field and she climbed after him. 'Will we sit down here, Bridie?' he said, offering the suggestion as one that had just occurred to him, as though they'd entered the field for some other purpose.

'We could improve a place like your own one,' he said, putting his right arm around her shoulders. 'Have you a kiss in you, Bridie?' He kissed her, exerting pressure with his teeth. When his mother died he would sell his farm and spend the money in the town. After that he would think of getting married because he'd have nowhere to go, because he'd want a fire to sit at and a woman to cook food for him. He kissed her again, his lips hot, the sweat on his cheeks sticking to her. 'God, you're great at kissing,' he said.

She rose, saying it was time to go, and they climbed over the gate again. 'There's nothing like a Saturday,' he said. 'Good-night to you so, Bridie.'

He mounted his bicycle and rode down the hill, and she pushed hers to the top and then mounted it also. She rode through the night as on Saturday nights for years she had ridden and never would ride again because she'd reached a certain age. She would wait now and in time Bowser Egan would seek her out because his mother would have died. Her father would probably have died also by then. She would marry Bowser Egan because it would be lonesome being by herself in the farmhouse.

A Happy Family

On the evening of Thursday, May 24th 1962, I returned home in the usual way. I remember sitting in the number 73 bus, thinking of the day as I had spent it and thinking of the house I was about to enter. It was a fine evening, warm and mellow, the air heavy with the smell of London. The bus crossed Hammersmith Bridge, moving quite quickly towards the leafy avenues beyond. The houses of the suburbs were gayer in that evening's sunshine, pleasanter abodes than often they seemed.

'Hullo,' I said in the hall of ours, speaking to my daughter Lisa, a child of one, who happened to be loitering there. She was wearing her night-dress, and she didn't look sleepy. 'Aren't you going to bed?' I said, and Lisa looked at me as if she had forgotten that I was closely related to her. I could hear Anna and Christopher in the bathroom, talking loudly and rapidly, and I could hear Elizabeth's voice urging them to wash themselves properly and be quick about it. 'She's fourteen stone, Miss MacAdam is,' Christopher was saying. 'Isn't she, Anna?' Miss MacAdam was a woman who taught at their school, a woman about whom we had come to know a lot. 'She can't swim,' said Anna.

Looking back now, such exchanges come easily to my mind. Bits of conversations float to the surface without much of a continuing pattern and without any significance that I can see. I suppose we were a happy family: someone examining us might possibly have written that down on a report sheet, the way these things are done. Yet what I recall most vividly now when I think of us as a family are images and occasions that for Elizabeth and me were neither happy nor unhappy. I remember animals at the Zoo coming forward for the offerings of our children, smelling of confinement rather than the jungle, seeming fierce and hard done by. I remember birthday parties on warm afternoons, the figures of children moving swiftly from the garden to the house, creatures who might have been bored, with paper hats on their heads or in their hands, seeking adventure in forbidden rooms. I remember dawdling walks, arguments that came to involve all of us, and other days when everything went well.

I used to leave the house at half past eight every morning, and often during the day I imagined what my wife's day must be like. She told me, of course. She told me about how ill-tempered our children had been, or how tractable; about how the time had passed in other ways, whom she had met and spoken to, who had come to tea or whom she had visited. I imagined her in summer having lunch in the garden when it was warm, dozing afterwards and being woken up by Lisa. In turn, she would ask me how the hours had gone for me and I would say a thing or two about their passing, about the people who had filled them. 'Miss Madden is leaving us,' I can hear myself saying. 'Off to Buenos Aires for some reason.' In my memory of this, I seem to be repeating the information. 'Off to Buenos Aires,' I appear to be saying. 'Off to Buenos Aires. Miss Madden.' And a little later I am saying it again, adding that Miss Madden would be missed. Elizabeth's head is nodding, agreeing that that will indeed be so. 'I fell asleep in the garden,' Elizabeth is murmuring in this small vision. 'Lisa woke me up.'

My wife was pretty when I married her, and as the years passed it seemed to me that she took on a greater beauty. I believed that this was some reflection of her contentment, and she may even have believed it herself. Had she suddenly said otherwise, I'd have been puzzled; as puzzled as I was, and as she was, on the evening of May 24th, when she told me about Mr Higgs. She sat before me then, sipping at a glass of sherry that I'd poured her and remembering all the details: all that Mr Higgs had said and all that she had said in reply.

She had been listening to a story on the radio and making coffee. Christopher and Anna were at school; in the garden Lisa was asleep in her pram. When the telephone rang Elizabeth walked towards it slowly, still listening to the wireless. When she said 'Hullo' she heard the coins drop at the other end and a man's voice said: 'Mrs Farrel?'

Elizabeth said yes, she was Mrs Farrel, and the man said: 'My name is Higgs.'

His voice was ordinary, a little uneducated, the kind of voice that is always drifting over the telephone.

'A very good friend,' said Mr Higgs.

'Good-morning,' said Elizabeth in her matter-of-fact way. 'Are you selling something, Mr Higgs?'

'In a sense, Mrs Farrel, in a sense. You might call it selling. Do I peddle salvation?'

'Oh, I am not religious in the least –'

'It may be your trouble, Mrs Farrel.'

'Yes, well –'

'You are Elizabeth Farrel. You have three children.'

'Mr Higgs –'

'Your father was a Captain Maugham. Born 1892, died 1959. He lost an arm in action and never forgave himself for it. You attended his funeral, but were glad that he was dead, since he had a way of upsetting your children. Your mother, seventy-four a week ago, lives near St Albans and is unhappy. You have two sisters and a brother.'

'Mr Higgs, what do you want?'

'Nothing. I don't want anything. What do you want, Mrs Farrel?'

'Look here, Mr Higgs –'

'D'you remember your tenth birthday? D'you remember what it felt like being a little girl of ten, in a white dress spotted with forget-me-not, and a blue ribbon tying back your hair? You were taken on a picnic. "You're ten years old," your father said. "Now tell us what you're going to do with yourself." "She must cut the chocolate cake first," your mother cried, and so you cut the cake and then stood up and announced the trend of your ambitions. Your brother Ralph laughed and was scolded by your father. D'you remember at all?'

Elizabeth did remember. She remembered playing hide-and-seek with her sisters after tea; she remembered Ralph climbing a tree and finding himself unable to get down again; she remembered her parents quarrelling, as they invariably did, all the way home.

'Do I know you, Mr Higgs? How do you manage to have these details of my childhood?'

Mr Higgs laughed. It wasn't a nasty laugh. It sounded even reassuring, as if Mr Higgs meant no harm.

On the evening of May 24th we sat for a long time wondering who the odd individual could be and what he was after. Elizabeth seemed nervously elated and naturally more than a little intrigued. I, on the other hand, was rather upset by this Mr Higgs and his deep mine of information. 'If he rings again,' I said, 'threaten him with the police.'

'Good-morning, Mrs Farrel.'

'Mr Higgs?'

'My dear.'

'Well then, Mr Higgs, explain.'

'Ho, ho, Mrs Farrel, there's a sharpness for you. Explain? Why, if I explained I'd be out of business in no time at all. "So that's it," you'd say, and ring off, just like I was a salesman or a Jehovah's Witness.'

'Mr Higgs –'

'You was a little girl of ten, Mrs Farrel. You was out on a picnic. Remember?'

'How did you know all that?'

'Why shouldn't I know, for heaven's sake? Listen now, Mrs Farrel. Did you think then what you would be today? Did you see yourself married to a man and mothering his children? Have you come to a sticky end, or otherwise?'

'A sticky end?'

'You clean his house, you prepare his meals, you take his opinions. You hear on the radio some news of passing importance, some bomb exploded, some army recalled. Who does the thinking, Mrs Farrel? You react as he does. You've lost your identity. Did you think of that that day when you were ten? Your children will be ten one day. They'll stand before you at ten years of age, first the girl, then the boy. What of their futures, Mrs Farrel? Shall they make something of themselves? Shall they fail and be miserable? Shall they be unnatural and unhappy, or sick in some way, or perhaps too stupid? Or shall they all three of them be richly successful? Are you successful, Mrs Farrel? You are your husband's instrument. You were different at ten, Mrs Farrel. How about your children? Soon it'll be your turn to take on the talking. I'll listen like I was paid for it.'

I was aware of considerable pique when Elizabeth reported all this to me. I protested that I was not given to forcing my opinions on others, and Elizabeth said I wasn't either. 'Clearly, he's queer in the head,' I said. I paused, thinking about that, then said: 'Could he be someone like a window-cleaner to whom you once perhaps talked of your childhood? Although I can't see you doing it.'

Elizabeth shook her head; she said she didn't remember talking to a window-cleaner about her childhood, or about anything very much. We'd had the same window-cleaners for almost seven years, she reminded me: two honest, respectable men who arrived at the house every six weeks in a Ford motor-car. 'Well, he must be someone,' I said. 'Someone you've talked to. I mean, it's not guesswork.'

'Maybe he's wicked,' said Elizabeth. 'Maybe he's a small wicked man with very white skin, driven by some force he doesn't understand. Perhaps he's one of those painters who came last year to paint the hall. There was a little man –'

'That little man's name was Mr Gipe. I remember that well. "Gipe," he said, walking into the hall and saying it would be a long job. "Gipe, sir; an unusual name."'

'He could be calling himself Higgs. He could have read through my letters. And my old diaries. Perhaps Mr Gipe expected a tip.'

'The hall cost ninety pounds.'

'I know, but it didn't all go to Mr Gipe. Perhaps nobody tips poor Mr Gipe and perhaps now he's telephoning all the wives, having read through their letters and their private diaries. He telephones to taunt them and to cause trouble, being an evil man. Perhaps Mr Gipe is possessed of a devil.'

I frowned and shook my head. 'Not at all,' I said. 'It's a voice from the past. It's someone who really did know you when you were ten, and knows all that's happened since.'

'More likely Mr Gipe,' said Elizabeth, 'guided from Hell.'

'Daddy, am I asleep?'

I looked at her wide eyes, big and blue and clear, perfect replicas of her mother's. I loved Anna best of all of them; I suppose because she reminded me so much of Elizabeth.

'No, darling, you're not asleep. If you were asleep you couldn't be talking to me, now could you?'

'I could be dreaming, Daddy. Couldn't I be dreaming?'

'Yes, I suppose you could.'

'But I'm not, am I?'

I shook my head. 'No, Anna, you're not dreaming.'

She sighed. 'I'm glad. I wouldn't like to be dreaming. I wouldn't like to suddenly wake up.'

It was Sunday afternoon and we had driven into the country. We did it almost every Sunday when the weather was fine and warm. The children enjoyed it and so in a way did we, even though the woods we went to were rather tatty, too near London to seem real, too untidy with sweet-papers to be attractive. Still, it was a way of entertaining them.

'Elizabeth.'

She was sitting on a tree-stump, her eyes half-closed. On a rug at her feet Lisa was playing with some wooden beads. I sat beside her and put my arm about her shoulders.

'Elizabeth.'

She jumped a little. 'Hullo, darling. I was almost asleep.'

'You were thinking about Mr Higgs.'

'Oh, I wasn't. My mind was a blank; I was about to drop off. I can do it now, sitting upright like this.'

'Anna asked me if she was dreaming.'

'Where is she?'

'Playing with Christopher.'

'They'll begin to fight. They don't play any more. Why do they perpetually fight?'

I said it was just a phase, but Elizabeth said she thought they would always fight now. The scratching and snarling would turn to argument as they grew older and when they became adults they wouldn't ever see one another. They would say that they had nothing in common, and would admit to others that they really rather disliked one another and always had. Elizabeth said she could see them: Christopher married to an unsuitable woman, and Anna as a girl who lived promiscuously and did not marry at all. Anna would become a heavy drinker of whisky and would smoke slim cigars at forty.

'Heavens,' I said, staring at her, and then looking at the small figure of Anna. 'Why on earth are you saying all that?'

'Well, it's true. I mean, it's what I imagine. I can see Anna in a harsh red suit, getting drunk at a cocktail party. I can see Christopher being miserable –'

'This is your Mr Higgs again. Look, the police can arrange to have the telephone tapped. It's sheer nonsense that some raving lunatic should be allowed to go on like that.'

'Mr Higgs! Mr Higgs! What's Mr Higgs got to do with it? You've got him on the brain.'

Elizabeth walked away. She left me sitting there with her frightening images of our children. Out of the corner of my eye I saw that Lisa was eating a piece of wood. I took it from her. Anna was saying: 'Daddy, Christopher hurt me.'

'Why?'

'I don't know. He just hurt me.'

'How did he hurt you?'

'He pushed me and I fell.' She began to cry, so I comforted her. I called Christopher and told him he mustn't push Anna. They ran off to play again and a moment later Anna was saying: 'Daddy, Christopher pushed me.'

'Christopher, you mustn't push Anna. And you shouldn't have to be told everything twice.'

'I didn't push her. She fell.'

Anna put her thumb in her mouth. I glanced through the trees to see where Elizabeth had got to, but there was no sign of her. I made the children sit on the rug and told them a story. They didn't like it much. They never did like my stories: Elizabeth's were so much better.

'I'm sorry.' She stood looking down on us, as tall and beautiful as a goddess.

'You look like a goddess,' I said.

'What's a goddess?' Anna asked, and Christopher said: 'Why's Mummy sorry?'

'A goddess is a beautiful lady. Mummy's sorry because she left me to look after you. And it's time to go home.'

'Oh, oh, oh, I must find Mambi first,' Anna cried anxiously. Mambi was a faithful friend who accompanied her everywhere she went, but who was, at the moment of departure, almost always lost.

We walked to the car. Anna said: 'Mambi was at the top of an old tree. Mambi's a goddess too. Daddy, do you *have* to be beautiful to be a goddess?'

'I suppose so.'

'Then Mambi can't be.'

'Isn't Mambi beautiful?'

'Usually she is. Only she's not now.'

'Why isn't she now?'

'Because all her hair came off in the tree.'

The car heaved and wobbled all the way home as Christopher and Anna banged about in the back. When they fought we shouted at them, and then they sulked and there was a mile or so of peace. Anna began to cry as I turned into the garage. Mambi, she said, was cold without her hair. Elizabeth explained about wigs.

I woke up in the middle of that night, thinking about Mr Higgs. I kept seeing the man as a shrimpish little thing, like the manager of the shop where we hired our television set. He had a black moustache – a length of thread stuck across his upper lip. I knew it was wrong, I knew this wasn't Mr Higgs; and then, all of a sudden, I began to think about Elizabeth's brother, Ralph.

A generation ago Ralph would have been called a remittance man. Just about the time we were married old Captain Maugham had packed him off to a farm in Kenya after an incident with a hotel receptionist and the hotel's account books. But caring for nothing in Kenya, Ralph had made his way to Cairo, and from Cairo on the long-distance telephone he had greeted the Captain with a request for financial aid. He didn't get it, and then the war broke out and Ralph disappeared. Whenever we thought of him we imagined that he was up to the most reprehensible racket he could lay his hands on. If he was, we never found out about it. All we did know was that after the war he again telephoned the Captain, and the odd thing was that he was still in Cairo. 'I have lost an arm,' Captain Maugham told him testily. 'And I,' said Ralph, 'have lost the empire of my soul.' He was given to this kind of decorated statement; it interfered so much with his conversation that most of the time you didn't know what he was talking about. But the Captain sent him some money and an agreement was drawn up by which Ralph, on receipt of a monthly cheque, promised not to return to England during his father's lifetime. Then the Captain died and Ralph was back. I gave him fifty pounds and all in all he probably cleaned up quite well. Ralph wasn't the sort of person to write letters; we had no idea where he was now. As a schoolboy, and even later, he was a great one for playing practical jokes. He was certainly a good enough mimic to create a Mr Higgs. Just for fun, I wondered? Or in some kind of bitterness? Or did he in some ingenious way hope to extract money?

The following morning I telephoned Elizabeth's sisters. Chloe knew nothing about where Ralph was, what he was doing or anything about him. She said she hoped he wasn't coming back to England because it had cost her fifty pounds the last time. Margaret, however, knew a lot. She didn't want to talk about it on the telephone, so I met her for lunch.

'What's all this?' she said.

I told her about Mr Higgs and the vague theory that was beginning to crystallize in my mind. She was intrigued by the Higgs thing. 'I don't know why,' she said, 'but it rings a queer sort of bell. But you're quite wrong about Ralph.' Ralph, it appeared, was being paid by Margaret and her husband in much the same way as he had been paid by the Captain; for the same reason and with the same stipulation. 'Only for the time being,' Margaret said a little bitterly. 'When Mother dies Ralph can do what he damn well likes. But it was quite a serious business and the news of it would clearly finish her. One doesn't like to think of an old woman dying in that particular kind of misery.'

'But whatever it was, she'd probably never find out.'

'Oh yes, she would. She reads the papers. In any case, Ralph is quite capable of dropping her a little note. But at the moment I can assure you that Ralph is safe in Africa. He's not the type to take any chances with his gift horses.'

So that was that. It made me feel even worse about Mr Higgs that my simple explanation had been so easily exploded.

'Well,' I said, 'and what did he have to say today?'

'What did who say?'

'Higgs.'

'Nothing much. He's becoming a bore.'

She wasn't going to tell me any more. She wasn't going to talk about Mr Higgs because she didn't trust me. She thought I'd put the police on him, and she didn't want that, so she said, because she had come to feel sorry for the poor crazed creature or whatever it was he happened to be. In fact, I thought to myself, my wife has become in some way fascinated by this man.

I worked at home one day, waiting for the telephone call. There was a ring at eleven-fifteen. I heard Elizabeth answer it. She said: 'No, I'm sorry; I'm afraid you've got the wrong number.' I didn't ask her about Mr Higgs. When I looked at her she seemed a long way away and her voice was measured and polite. There was some awful shaft between us and I didn't know what to do about it.

In the afternoon I took the children for a walk in the park.

'Mambi's gone to stay in the country,' Anna said. 'I'm lonely without her.'

'Well, she's coming back tonight, isn't she?'

'Daddy,' Christopher said, 'what's the matter with Mummy?'

I'm not very sure when it was that I first noticed everything was in rather a mess. I remember coming in one night and stumbling over lots of wooden toys in the hall. Quite often the cornflakes packet and the marmalade were still on the kitchen table from breakfast. Or if they weren't on the table the children had got them on to the floor and Lisa had covered most of the house with their mixed contents. Elizabeth didn't seem to notice. She sat in a dream, silent and alone, forgetting to cook the supper. The children began to do all the things they had ever wanted to do and which Elizabeth had patiently prevented, like scribbling on the walls and playing in the coal-cellar. I tried to discuss it with Elizabeth, but all she did was to smile sweetly and say she was tired.

'Why don't you see a doctor?'

She stared at me. 'A doctor?'

'Perhaps you need a tonic.' And at that point she would smile again and go to bed.

I knew that Elizabeth was still having her conversations with Mr Higgs even though she no longer mentioned them. When I asked her she used to laugh and say: 'Poor Mr Higgs was just some old fanatic.'

'Yes, but how did he –'

'Darling, you worry too much.'

I went to St Albans to see old Mrs Maugham, without very much hope. I don't know what I expected of her, since she was obviously too deaf and too senile to offer me anything at all. She lived with a woman called Miss Awpit who was employed by the old woman's children to look after her. Miss Awpit made us tea and did the interpreting.

'Mr Farrel wants to know how you are, dear,' Miss Awpit said. 'Quite well, really,' Miss Awpit said to me. 'All things being equal.'

Mrs Maugham knew who I was and all that. She asked after Elizabeth and the children. She said something to Miss Awpit and Miss Awpit said: 'She wants you to bring them to her.'

'Yes, yes,' I shouted, nodding hard. 'We shall come and see you soon. They often,' I lied, 'ask about Granny.'

'Hark at that,' shouted Miss Awpit, nudging the old lady, who snappishly told her to leave off.

I didn't quite know how to put it. I said: 'Ask her if she knows a Mr Higgs.'

Miss Awpit, imagining, I suppose, that I was making conversation, shouted: 'Mr Farrel wants to know if you know Mr Higgs.' Mrs Maugham smiled at us. 'Higgs,' Miss Awpit repeated. 'Do you know Mr Higgs at all, dear?'

'Never,' said Mrs Maugham.

'Have you ever known a Mr Higgs?' I shouted.

'Higgs?' said Mrs Maugham.

'Do you know him?' Miss Awpit asked. 'Do you know a Mr Higgs?'

'I do not,' said Mrs Maugham, suddenly in command of herself, 'know anyone of such a name. Nor would I wish to.'

'Look, Mrs Maugham,' I pursued, 'does the name mean anything at all to you?'

'I have told you, I do not know your friend. How can I be expected to know your friends, an old woman like me, stuck out here in St Albans with no one to look after me?'

'Come, come,' said Miss Awpit, 'you've got me, dear.'

But Mrs Maugham only laughed.

A week or two passed, and then one afternoon as I was sitting in the office filing my nails the telephone rang and a voice I didn't recognize said: 'Mr Farrel?'

I said 'Yes', and the voice said: 'This is Miss Awpit. You know, Mrs Maugham's Miss Awpit.'

'Of course. Good afternoon, Miss Awpit. How are you?'

'Very well, thank you. I'm ringing to tell you something about Mrs Maugham.'

'Yes?'

'Well, you know when you came here the other week you were asking about a Mr Higgs?'

'Yes, I remember.'

'Well, as you sounded rather anxious about him I just thought I'd tell you. I thought about it and then I decided. I'll ring Mr Farrel, I said, just to tell him what she said.'

'Yes, Miss Awpit?'

'I hope I'm doing the right thing.'

'What did Mrs Maugham say?'

'Well, it's funny in a way. I hope you won't think I'm being very stupid or anything.'

I had the odd feeling that Miss Awpit was going to die as she was speaking, before she could tell me. I said:

'I assure you, you are doing the right thing. What did Mrs Maugham say?'

'Well, it was at breakfast one morning. She hadn't had a good night at all. So she said, but you know what it's like with old people. I mean, quite frankly I had to get up myself in the night and I heard her sleeping as deep and sweet as you'd wish. Honestly, Mr Farrel, I often wish I had her constitution myself –'

'You were telling me about Mr Higgs.'

'I'm sorry?'

'You were telling me about Mr Higgs.'

'Well, it's nothing really. You'll probably laugh when you hear. Quite honestly I was in two minds whether or not to bother you. You see, all Mrs Maugham said was: "It's funny that man suddenly talking about Mr Higgs like that. You know, Ethel, I haven't heard Mr Higgs mentioned for almost thirty years." So I said "Yes", leading her on, you see. "And who was Mr Higgs, dear, thirty years ago?" And she said: "Oh nobody at all. He was just Elizabeth's little friend!"'

'Elizabeth's?'

'Just what I said, Mr Farrel. She got quite impatient with me. "Just someone Elizabeth used to talk to," she said, "when she was three. You know the way children invent things."'

'Like Mambi,' I said, not meaning to say it, since Miss Awpit wouldn't understand.

'Oh dear, Mr Farrel,' said Miss Awpit, 'I knew you'd laugh.'

I left the office and took a taxi all the way home. Elizabeth was in the garden. I sat beside her and I held her hands. 'Look,' I said. 'Let's have a holiday. Let's go away, just the two of us. We need a rest.'

'You're spying on me,' Elizabeth said. 'Which isn't new, I suppose. You've got so mean, darling, ever since you became jealous of poor Mr Higgs. How could you be jealous of a man like Mr Higgs?'

'Elizabeth, I know who Mr Higgs is. I can tell you –'

'There's nothing to be jealous about. All the poor creature does is to ring me up and tell me about the things he read in my diaries the time he came to paint the hall. And then he tries to comfort me about the children. He tells me not to worry about Lisa. But I can't help worrying because I know she's going to have this hard time. She's going to grow big and lumpy, poor little Lisa, and she's not going to be ever able to pass an exam, and in the end she'll go and work in a post office. But Mr Higgs –'

'Let me tell you about Mr Higgs. Let me just remind you.'

'You don't know him, darling. You've never spoken to him. Mr Higgs is very patient, you know. First of all he did the talking, and now, you see, he kindly allows me to. Poor Mr Higgs is an inmate of a home. He's an institutionalized person, darling. There's no need to be jealous.'

I said nothing. I sat there holding her two hands and looking at her. Her face was just the same; even her eyes betrayed no hint of the confusion that held her. She smiled when she spoke of Mr Higgs. She made a joke, laughing, calling him the housewife's friend.

'It was funny,' she said, 'the first time I saw Christopher as an adult, sitting in a room with that awful woman. She was leaning back in a chair, staring at him and attempting to torture him with words. And then there was Anna, half a mile away across London, in a house in a square. All the lights were on because of the party, and Anna was in that red suit, and she was laughing and saying how she hated Christopher, how she had hated him from the first moment she saw him. And when she said that, I couldn't remember what moment she meant. I couldn't quite remember where it was that Anna and Christopher had met. Well, it goes to show.' Elizabeth paused. 'Well, doesn't it?' she said. 'I mean, imagine my thinking that poor Mr Higgs was evil! The kindest, most long-suffering man that ever walked on two legs. I mean, all I had to do was to remind Mr Higgs that I'd forgotten and Mr Higgs could tell me. "They met in a garden," he could say, "at an ordinary little tea-party." And Lisa was operated on several times, and counted the words in telegrams.'

Elizabeth talked on, of the children and of Mr Higgs. I rang up our doctor, and he came, and then a little later my wife was taken from the house. I sat alone with Lisa on my knee until it was time to go and fetch Christopher and Anna.

'Mummy's ill,' I said in the car. 'She's had to go away for a little.' I would tell them the story gradually, and one day perhaps we might visit her and she might still understand who we were. 'Ill?' they said. 'But Mummy's never ill.' I stopped the car by our house, thinking that only death could make the house seem so empty, and thinking too that death was easier to understand. We made tea, I remember, the children and I, not saying very much more.

The Grass Widows

The headmaster of a great English public school visited every summer a village in County Galway for the sake of the fishing in a number of nearby rivers. For more than forty years this stern, successful man had brought his wife to the Slieve Gashal Hotel, a place, so he said, he had come to love. A smiling man called Mr Doyle had been for all the headmaster's experience of the hotel its obliging proprietor: Mr Doyle had related stories to the headmaster late at night in the hotel bar, after the headmaster's wife had retired to bed; they had discussed together the fruitfulness of the local rivers, although in truth Mr Doyle had never held a rod in his life. 'You feel another person,' the headmaster had told generations of his pupils, 'among blue mountains, in the quiet little hotel.' On walks through the school grounds with a senior boy on either side of him he had spoken of the soft peace of the riverside and of the unrivalled glory of being alone with one's mind. He talked to his boys of Mr Doyle and his unassuming ways, and of the little village that was a one-horse place and none the worse for that, and of the good plain food that came from the Slieve Gashal's kitchen.

To Jackson Major the headmaster enthused during all the year that Jackson Major was head boy of the famous school, and Jackson Major did not ever forget the paradise that then had formed in his mind. 'I know a place,' he said to his fiancée long after he had left the school, 'that's perfect for our honeymoon.' He told her about the heathery hills that the headmaster had recalled for him, and the lakes and rivers and the one-horse little village in which, near a bridge, stood the ivy-covered bulk of the Slieve Gashal Hotel. 'Lovely, darling,' murmured the bride-to-be of Jackson Major, thinking at the time of a clock in the shape of a human hand that someone had given them and which would naturally have to be changed for something else. She'd been hoping that he would suggest Majorca for their honeymoon, but if he wished to go to this other place she didn't intend to make a fuss. 'Idyllic for a honeymoon,' the headmaster had once remarked to Jackson Major, and Jackson Major had not forgotten. *Steady but unimaginative* were words that had been written of him on a school report.

The headmaster, a square, bald man with a head that might have been carved from oak, a man who wore rimless spectacles and whose name was Angusthorpe, discovered when he arrived at the Slieve Gashal Hotel in the summer of 1968 that in the intervening year a tragedy had occurred. It had become the custom of Mr Angusthorpe to book his fortnight's holiday by saying simply to Mr Doyle: 'Till next year then,' an anticipation that Mr Doyle would translate into commercial terms, reserving the same room for the headmaster and his wife in twelve months' time. No letters changed hands during the year, no confirmation of the booking was ever necessary: Mr Angusthorpe and his wife arrived each summer after the trials of the school term, knowing that their room would be waiting for them, with sweet-peas in a vase in the window, and Mr Doyle full of welcome in the hall. 'He died in Woolworth's in Galway,' said Mr Doyle's son in the summer of 1968. 'He was buying a shirt at the time.'

Afterwards, Mr Angusthorpe said to his wife that when Mr Doyle's son spoke those words he knew that nothing was ever going to be the same again. Mr Doyle's son, known locally as Scut Doyle, went on speaking while the headmaster and his small wife, grey-haired, and bespectacled also, stood in the hall. He told them that he had inherited the Slieve Gashal and that for all his adult life he had been employed in the accounts department of a paper-mill in Dublin. 'I thought at first I'd sell the place up,' he informed the Angusthorpes, 'and then I thought maybe I'd attempt to make a go of it. "Will we have a shot at it?" I said to the wife, and, God bless her, she said why wouldn't I?' While he spoke, the subject of his last remarks appeared behind him in the hall, a woman whose appearance did not at all impress Mr Angusthorpe. She was pale-faced and fat and, so Mr Angusthorpe afterwards suggested to his wife, sullen. She stood silently by her husband, whose appearance did not impress Mr Angusthorpe either, since the new proprietor of the Slieve Gashal, a man with shaking hands and a cocky grin, did not appear to have shaved himself that day. 'One or other of them, if not both,' said Mr Angusthorpe afterwards, 'smelt of drink.'

The Angusthorpes were led to their room by a girl whose age Mr Angusthorpe estimated to be thirteen. 'What's become of Joseph?' he asked her as they mounted the stairs, referring to an old porter who had always in the past been spick-and-span in a uniform, but the child seemed not to understand the question, for she offered it no reply. In the room there were no sweet-peas, and although they had entered by a door that was familiar to them, the room itself was greatly altered: it was, to begin with, only half the size it had been before. 'Great heavens!' exclaimed Mr Angusthorpe, striking a wall with his fist and finding it to be a partition. 'He had the carpenters in,' the child said.

Mr Angusthorpe, in a natural fury, descended the stairs and shouted in the hall. 'Mr Doyle!' he called out in his peremptory headmaster's voice. 'Mr Doyle! Mr Doyle!'

Doyle emerged from the back regions of the hotel, with a cigarette in his mouth. There were feathers on his clothes, and he held in his right hand a half-plucked chicken. In explanation he said that he had been giving his wife a hand. She was not herself, he confided to Mr Angusthorpe, on account of it being her bad time of the month.

'Our room,' protested Mr Angusthorpe. 'We can't possibly sleep in a tiny space like that. You've cut the room in half, Mr Doyle.'

Doyle nodded. All the bedrooms in the hotel, he told Mr Angusthorpe, had been divided, since they were uneconomical otherwise. He had spent four hundred and ten pounds having new doorways made and putting on new wallpaper. He began to go into the details of this expense, plucking feathers from the chicken as he stood there. Mr Angusthorpe coldly remarked that he had not booked a room in which you couldn't swing a cat.

'Excuse me, sir,' interrupted Doyle. 'You booked a room a year ago: you did not reserve a specific room. D'you know what I mean, Mr Angusthorpe? I have no note that you specified with my father to have the exact room again.'

'It was an understood thing between us –'

'My father unfortunately died.'

Mr Angusthorpe regarded the man, disliking him intensely. It occurred to him that he had never in his life carried on a conversation with a hotel proprietor who held in his right hand a half-plucked chicken and whose clothes had feathers on them. His inclination was to turn on his heel and march with his wife from the unsatisfactory hotel, telling, if need be, this unprepossessing individual to go to hell. Mr Angusthorpe thought of doing that, but then he wondered where he and his wife could go. Hotels in the area were notoriously full at this time of year, in the middle of the fishing season.

'I must get on with this for the dinner,' said Doyle, 'or the wife will be having me guts for garters.' He winked at Mr Angusthorpe, flicking a quantity of cigarette ash from the pale flesh of the chicken. He left Mr Angusthorpe standing there.

The child had remained with Mrs Angusthorpe while the headmaster had sought an explanation downstairs. She had stood silently by the door until Mrs Angusthorpe, fearing a violent reaction on the part of her husband if he discovered the child present when he returned, suggested that she should go away. But the child had taken no notice of that and

Mrs Angusthorpe, being unable to think of anything else to say, had asked her at what time of year old Mr Doyle had died. 'The funeral was ten miles long, missus,' replied the child. 'Me father wasn't sober till the Monday.' Mr Angusthorpe, returning, asked the child sharply why she was lingering and the child explained that she was waiting to be tipped. Mr Angusthorpe gave her a threepenny-piece.

In the partitioned room, which now had a pink wallpaper on the walls and an elaborate frieze from which flowers of different colours cascaded down the four corners, the Angusthorpes surveyed their predicament. Mr Angusthorpe told his wife the details of his interview with Doyle, and when he had talked for twenty minutes he came more definitely to the conclusion that the best thing they could do would be to remain for the moment. The rivers could hardly have altered, he was thinking, and that the hotel was now more than inadequate was a consequence that would affect his wife more than it would affect him. In the past she had been wont to spend her days going for a brief walk in the morning and returning to the pleasant little dining-room for a solitary lunch, and then sleeping or reading until it was time for a cup of tea, after which she would again take a brief walk. She was usually sitting by the fire in the lounge when he returned from his day's excursion. Perhaps all that would be less attractive now, Mr Angusthorpe thought, but there was little he could do about it and it was naturally only fair that they should at least remain for a day or two.

That night the dinner was well below the standard of the dinners they had in the past enjoyed in the Slieve Gashal. Mrs Angusthorpe was unable to consume her soup because there were quite large pieces of bone and gristle in it. The headmaster laughed over his prawn cocktail because, he said, it tasted of absolutely nothing at all. He had recovered from his initial shock and was now determined that the hotel must be regarded as a joke. He eyed his wife's plate of untouched soup, saying it was better to make the best of things. Chicken and potatoes and mashed turnip were placed before them by a nervous woman in the uniform of a waitress. Turnip made Mrs Angusthorpe sick in the stomach, even the sight of it: at another time in their life her husband might have remembered and ordered the vegetable from the table, but what he was more intent upon now was discovering if the Slieve Gashal still possessed a passable hock, which surprisingly it did. After a few glasses, he said:

'We'll not come next year, of course. While I'm out with the rod, my dear, you might scout around for another hotel.'

They never brought their car with them, the headmaster's theory being that the car was something they wished to escape from. Often she had thought it might be nice to have a car at the Slieve Gashal so that she could drive around the countryside during the day, but she saw his argument and had never pressed her view. Now, it seemed, he was suggesting that she should scout about for another hotel on foot.

'No, no,' he said. 'There is an excellent bus service in Ireland.' He spoke with a trace of sarcasm, as though she should have known that no matter what else he expected of her, he did not expect her to tramp about the roads looking for another hotel. He gave a little laugh, leaving the matter vaguely with her, his eyes like the eyes of a fish behind his rimless spectacles. Boys had feared him and disliked him too, some even had hated him; yet others had been full of a respect that seemed at times like adoration. As she struggled with her watery turnips she could sense that his mind was quite made up: he intended to remain for the full fortnight in the changed hotel because the lure of the riverside possessed him too strongly to consider an alternative.

'I might find a place we could move to,' she said. 'I mean, in a day or so.'

'They'll all be full, my dear.' He laughed without humour in his laugh, not amused by anything. 'We must simply grin and bear it. The chicken,' he added, 'might well have been worse.'

'Excuse me,' Mrs Angusthorpe said, and quickly rose from the table and left the dining-room. From a tape-recorder somewhere dance music began to play.

'Is the wife all right?' Doyle asked Mr Angusthorpe, coming up and sitting down in the chair she had vacated. He had read in a hotelier's journal that tourists enjoyed a friendly atmosphere and the personal attention of the proprietor.

'We've had a long day,' responded the headmaster genially enough.

'Ah well, of course you have.'

The dining-room was full, indicating that business was still brisk in the hotel. Mr Angusthorpe had noted a familiar face or two and had made dignified salutations. These people would surely have walked out if the hotel was impossible in all respects.

'At her time of the month,' Doyle was saying, 'the wife gets as fatigued as an old horse. Like your own one, she's gone up to her bed already.'

'My wife —'

'Ah, I wasn't suggesting Mrs Angusthorpe, was that way at all. They have fatigue in common tonight, sir, that's all I meant.'

Doyle appeared to be drunk. There was a bleariness about his eyes that suggested inebriation to Mr Angusthorpe, and his shaking hands might well be taken as a sign of repeated over-indulgence.

'She wakes up at two a.m. as lively as a bird,' said Doyle. 'She's keen for a hug and a pat –'

'Quite so,' interrupted Mr Angusthorpe quickly. He looked unpleasantly at his unwelcome companion. He allowed his full opinion of the man to pervade his glance.

'Well, I'll be seeing you,' said Doyle, rising and seeming to be undismayed. 'I'll tell the wife you were asking for her,' he added with a billowing laugh, before moving on to another table.

Shortly after that, Mr Angusthorpe left the dining-room, having resolved that he would not relate this conversation to his wife. He would avoid Doyle in the future, he promised himself, and when by chance they did meet he would make it clear that he did not care to hear his comments on any subject. It was a pity that the old man had died and that all this nastiness had grown up in his place, but there was nothing whatsoever that might be done about it and at least the weather looked good. He entered the bar and dropped into conversation with a man he had met several times before, a solicitor from Dublin, a bachelor called Gorman.

'I was caught the same way,' Mr Gorman said, 'only everywhere else is full. It's the end of the Slieve Gashal, you know: the food's inedible.'

He went on to relate a series of dishes that had already been served during his stay, the most memorable of which appeared to be a rabbit stew that had had a smell of ammonia. 'There's margarine every time instead of butter, and some queer type of marmalade in the morning: it has a taste of tin to it. The same mashed turnip,' said Gorman, 'is the only vegetable he offers.'

The headmaster changed the subject, asking how the rivers were. The fishing was better than ever he'd known it, Mr Gorman reported, and he retailed experiences to prove the claim. 'Isn't it all that matters in the long run?' suggested Mr Gorman, and Mr Angusthorpe readily agreed that it was. He would refrain from repeating to his wife the information about the marmalade that tasted of tin, or the absence of variation where vegetables were concerned. He left the bar at nine o'clock, determined to slip quietly into bed without disturbing her.

In the middle of that night, at midnight precisely, the Angusthorpes were awakened simultaneously by a noise from the room beyond the new partition.

'Put a pillow down, darling,' a male voice was saying as clearly as if its possessor stood in the room beside the Angusthorpes' bed.

'Couldn't we wait until another time?' a woman pleaded in reply. 'I don't see what good a pillow will do.'

'It'll lift you up a bit,' the man explained. 'It said in the book to put a pillow down if there was difficulty.'

'I don't see –'

'It'll make entry easier,' said the man. 'It's a well-known thing.'

Mrs Angusthorpe switched on her bedside light and saw that her husband was pretending to be asleep. 'I'm going to rap on the wall,' she whispered. 'It's disgusting, listening to this.'

'I think I'm going down,' said the man.

'My God,' whispered Mr Angusthorpe, opening his eyes. 'It's Jackson Major.'

At breakfast, Mrs Angusthorpe ate margarine on her toast and the marmalade that had a taste of tin. She did not say anything. She watched her husband cutting into a fried egg on a plate that bore the marks of the waitress's two thumbs. Eventually he placed his knife and fork together on the plate and left them there.

For hours they had lain awake, listening to the conversation beyond the inadequate partition. The newly wed wife of Jackson Major had wept and said that Jackson had better divorce her at once. She had designated the hotel they were in as a frightful place, fit only for Irish tinkers. 'That filthy meal!' the wife of Jackson Major had cried emotionally. 'That awful drunk man!' And Jackson Major had apologized and had mentioned Mr Angusthorpe by name, wondering what on earth his old headmaster could ever have seen in such an establishment. 'Let's try again,' he had suggested, and the Angusthorpes had listened to a repetition of Mrs Jackson's unhappy tears. 'How can you rap on the wall?' Mr Angusthorpe had angrily whispered. 'How can we even admit that conversation can be heard? Jackson was head boy.'

'In the circumstances,' said Mrs Angusthorpe at breakfast, breaking the long silence, 'it would be better to leave.'

He knew it would be. He knew that on top of everything else the unfortunate fact that Jackson Major was in the room beyond the partition and would sooner or later discover that the partition was far from soundproof could be exceedingly embarrassing in view of what had taken place during the night. There was, as well, the fact that he had enthused so eloquently to Jackson Major about the hotel that Jackson Major had clearly, on his word alone, brought his bride there. He had even said, he recalled, that the Slieve Gashal would be ideal for a honeymoon. Mr Angusthorpe considered all that, yet could not forget his forty years' experience of the surrounding rivers, or the information of Mr Gorman that the rivers this year were better than ever.

'We could whisper,' he suggested in what was itself a whisper. 'We could whisper in our room so that they wouldn't know you can hear.'

'Whisper?' she said. She shook her head.

She remembered days in the rain, walking about the one-horse village with nothing whatsoever to do except to walk about, or lie on her bed reading detective stories. She remembered listening to his reports of his day and feeling sleepy listening to them. She remembered thinking, once or twice, that it had never occurred to him that what was just a change and a rest for her could not at all be compared to the excitements he derived from his days on the river-bank, alone with his mind. He was a great, successful man, big and square and commanding, with the cold eyes of the fish he sought in mountain rivers. He had made a firm impression on generations of boys, and on parents and governors, and often on a more general public, yet he had never been able to give her children. She had needed children because she was, compared with him, an unimportant kind of person.

She thought of him in Chapel, gesturing at six hundred boys from the pulpit, in his surplice and red academic hood, releasing words from his throat that were as cold as ice and cleverly made sense. She thought of a time he had expelled two boys, when he had sat with her in their drawing-room waiting for a bell to ring. When the chiming had ceased he had risen and gone without a word from the room, his oaken face pale with suppressed emotion. She knew he saw in the crime of the two boys a failure on his part, yet he never mentioned it to her. He had expelled the boys in public, castigating them with bitterness in his tone, hating them and hating himself, yet rising above his shame at having failed with them: dignity was his greatest ally.

She sat with him once a week at the high table in the dining-hall, surrounded by his prefects, who politely chatted to her. She remembered Jackson Major, a tall boy with short black hair who would endlessly discuss with her husband a web of school affairs. 'The best head boy I remember,' her husband's voice said again, coming back to her over a number of years: 'I made no mistake with Jackson.' Jackson Major had set a half-mile record that remained unbroken to this day. There had been a complaint from some child's mother, she recalled, who claimed that her son had been, by Jackson Major, too severely caned. *We must not forget*, her husband had written to that mother, *that your son almost caused another boy to lose an eye. It was for that carelessness that he was punished. He bears no resentment: boys seldom do.*

Yet now this revered, feared and clever man was suggesting that they should whisper for a fortnight in their bedroom, so that the couple next door might not feel embarrassment, so that he himself might remain in a particularly uncomfortable hotel in order to fish. It seemed to Mrs Angusthorpe that there were limits to the role he had laid down for her and which for all her married life she had ungrudgingly accepted. She hadn't minded being bored for this fortnight every year, but now he was asking more than that she could continue to feel bored; he was asking her to endure food that made her sick, and to conduct absurd conversations in their bedroom.

'No,' she said, 'we could not whisper.'

'I meant it only for kindness. Kindness to them, you see –'

'You have compensations here. I have none, you know.'

He looked sharply at her, as at an erring new boy who had not yet learnt the ways of school.

'I think we should leave at once,' she said. 'After breakfast.'

That suggestion, he pointed out to her, was nonsensical. They had booked a room in the hotel: they were obliged to pay for it. He was exhausted, he added, after a particularly trying term.

'It's what I'd like,' she said.

He spread margarine on his toast and added to it some of the marmalade. 'We must not be selfish,' he said, suggesting that both of them were on the point of being selfish and that together they must prevent themselves.

'I'd be happier,' she began, but he swiftly interrupted her, reminding her that his holiday had been spoilt enough already and that he for his part was intent on making the best of things. 'Let's simply enjoy what we can,' he said, 'without making a fuss about it.'

At that moment Jackson Major and his wife, a pretty, pale-haired girl called Daphne, entered the dining-room. They stood at the door, endeavouring to catch the eye of a waitress, not sure about where to sit. Mrs Jackson indicated a table that was occupied by two men, reminding her husband that they had sat at it last night for dinner. Jackson Major looked towards it and looked impatiently away, seeming annoyed with his wife for bothering to draw his attention to a table at which they clearly could not sit. It was then, while still annoyed, that he noticed the Angusthorpes.

Mrs Angusthorpe saw him murmuring to his wife. He led the way to their table, and Mrs Angusthorpe observed that his wife moved less eagerly than he.

'How marvellous, sir,' Jackson Major said, shaking his headmaster by the hand. Except for a neat moustache, he had changed hardly at all, Mrs Angusthorpe noticed; a little fatter in the face, perhaps, and the small pimples that had marked his chin as a schoolboy had now cleared up completely. He introduced his wife to the headmaster, and then he turned to Mrs Angusthorpe and asked her how she was. Forgetfully, he omitted to introduce his wife to her, but she, in spite of that, smiled and nodded at his wife.

'I'm afraid it's gone down awfully, Jackson,' Mr Angusthorpe said. 'The hotel's changed hands, you know. We weren't aware ourselves.'

'It seems quite comfortable, sir,' Jackson Major said, sitting down and indicating that his wife should do the same.

'The food was nice before,' said Mrs Angusthorpe. 'It's really awful now.'

'Oh, I wouldn't say awful, dear,' Mr Angusthorpe corrected her. 'One becomes used to a hotel,' he explained to Jackson Major. 'Any change is rather noticeable.'

'We had a perfectly ghastly dinner,' Daphne Jackson said.

'Still,' said Mr Angusthorpe, as though she had not spoken, 'we'll not return another year. My wife is going to scout around for a better place. You've brought your rod, Jackson?'

'Well, yes, I did. I thought that maybe if Daphne felt tired I might once or twice try out your famous rivers, sir.'

Mrs Angusthorpe saw Mrs Jackson glance in surprise at her new husband, and she deduced that Mrs Jackson hadn't been aware that a fishing-rod had comprised part of her husband's luggage.

'Capital,' cried Mr Angusthorpe, while the waitress took the Jacksons' order for breakfast. 'You could scout round together,' he said, addressing the two women at once, 'while I show Jackson what's what.'

'It's most kind of you, sir,' Jackson Major said, 'but I think, you know –'

'Capital,' cried Mr Angusthorpe again, his eyes swivelling from face to face, forbidding defiance. He laughed his humourless laugh and he poured himself more tea. 'I told you, dear,' he said to Mrs Angusthorpe. 'There's always a silver lining.'

In the hall of the Slieve Gashal Doyle took a metal stand from beneath the reception desk and busied himself arranging picture postcards on it. His wife had bought the stand in Galway, getting it at a reduced price because it was broken. He was at the moment offended with his wife because of her attitude when he had entered the hotel kitchen an hour ago with a number of ribs of beef. 'Did you drop that meat?' she had said in a hard voice, looking up from the table where she was making bread. 'Is that dirt on the suet?' He had replied that he'd been obliged to cross the village street hurriedly, to avoid a man on a bicycle. 'You dropped the meat on the road,' she accused. 'D'you want to poison the bloody lot of them?' Feeling hard done by, he had left the kitchen.

While he continued to work with the postcards, Mr Angusthorpe and Jackson Major passed before him with their fishing-rods. 'We'll be frying tonight,' he observed jollily, wagging his head at their two rods. They did not reply: weren't they the queer-looking eejits, he thought, with their sporty clothes and the two tweed hats covered with artificial flies. 'I'll bring it up, sir,' Jackson Major was saying, 'at the Old Boys' Dinner in the autumn.' It was ridiculous, Doyle reflected, going to that much trouble to catch a few fish when all you had to do was to go out at night and shine a torch into the water. 'Would you be interested in postcards, gentlemen?' he inquired, but so absorbed were Mr Angusthorpe and Jackson Major in their conversation that again neither of them made a reply.

Some time later, Daphne Jackson descended the stairs of the hotel. Doyle watched her, admiring her slender legs and the flowered dress she was wearing. A light-blue cardigan hung casually from her shoulders, its sleeves not occupied by her arms. Wouldn't it be great, he thought, to be married to a young body like that? He imagined her in a bedroom, taking off her cardigan and then her dress. She stood in her underclothes; swiftly she lifted them from her body.

'Would you be interested in postcards at all?' inquired Doyle. 'I have the local views here.'

Daphne smiled at him. Without much interest, she examined the cards on the stand, and then she moved towards the entrance door.

'There's a lovely dinner we have for you today,' said Doyle. 'Ribs of beef that I'm just after handing over to the wife. As tender as an infant.'

He held the door open for her, talking all the time, since he knew they liked to be talked to. He asked her if she was going for a walk and told her that a walk would give her a healthy appetite. The day would keep good, he promised; he had read it in the paper.

'Thank you,' she said.

She walked through a sunny morning that did little to raise her spirits. Outside the hotel there was a large expanse of green grass, bounded on one side by the short village street. She crossed an area of the grass and then passed the butcher's shop in which earlier Doyle had purchased the ribs of beef. She glanced in and the butcher smiled and waved at her, as though he knew her well. She smiled shyly back. Outside a small public house a man was mending a bicycle, which was upturned on the pavement: a child pushing a pram spoke to the man and he spoke to her. Farther on, past a row of cottages, a woman pumped water into a bucket from a green pump at the road's edge, and beyond it, coming towards her slowly, she recognized the figure of Mrs Angusthorpe.

'So we are grass widows,' said Mrs Angusthorpe when she had arrived at a point at which it was suitable to speak.

'Yes.'

'I'm afraid it's our fault, for being here. My husband's, I mean, and mine.'

'My husband could have declined to go fishing.'

The words were sour. They were sour and icy, Mrs Angusthorpe thought, matching her own mood. On her brief walk she had that morning disliked her husband more than ever she had disliked him before, and there was venom in her now. Once upon a time he might at least have heard her desires with what could even have been taken for understanding. He would not have acted upon her desires, since it was not in his nature to do so, but he would not have been guilty, either, of announcing in so obviously false a way that they should enjoy what they could and not make a fuss. There had been a semblance of chivalry in the attitude from which, at the beginning of their marriage, he had briefly regarded her; but forty-seven years had efficiently disposed of that garnish of politeness. A week or so ago a boy at the school had been casual with her, but the headmaster, hearing her report of the matter, had denied that what she stated could ever have occurred: he had moulded the boy in question, he pointed out, he had taken a special interest in the boy because he recognized in him qualities that were admirable: she was touchy, the headmaster said, increasingly touchy these days. She remembered in the first year of their marriage a way he had of patiently leaning back in his chair, puffing at the pipe he affected in those days and listening to her, seeming actually to weigh her arguments against his own. It was a long time now since he had weighed an argument of hers, or even devoted a moment of passing consideration to it. It was a long time since he could possibly have been concerned as to whether or not she found the food in a hotel unpalatable. She was angry when she thought of it this morning, not because she was unused to these circumstances of her life but because, quite suddenly, she had seen her state of resignation as an insult to the woman she once, too long ago, had been.

'I would really like to talk to you,' Mrs Angusthorpe said, to Daphne Jackson's surprise. 'It might be worth your while to stroll back to that hotel with me.'

On her short, angry walk she had realized, too, that once she had greatly disliked Jackson Major because he reminded her in some ways of her husband. A priggish youth, she had recalled, a tedious bore of a boy who had shown her husband a ridiculous respect while also fearing and resembling him. On her walk she had remembered the day he had broken the half-mile record, standing in the sports field in his running clothes, deprecating his effort because he knew his headmaster would wish him to act like that. What good was winning a half-mile race if he upset his wife the first time he found himself in a bedroom with her?

'I remember your husband as a boy,' said Mrs Angusthorpe. 'He set an athletic record which has not yet been broken.'

'Yes, he told me.'

'He had trouble with his chin. Pimples that wouldn't go away. I see all that's been overcome.'

'Well, yes –'

'And trouble also because he beat a boy too hard. The mother wrote, enclosing the opinion of a doctor.'

Daphne frowned. She ceased to walk. She stared at Mrs Angusthorpe.

'Oh yes,' said Mrs Angusthorpe.

They passed the butcher's shop, from the doorway of which the butcher now addressed them. The weather was good, the butcher said: it was a suitable time for a holiday. Mrs Angusthorpe smiled at him and bowed. Daphne, frowning still, passed on.

'You're right,' Mrs Angusthorpe said next, 'when you say that your husband could have declined to go fishing.'

'I think he felt –'

'Odd, I thought, to have a fishing-rod with him in the first place. Odd on a honeymoon.'

They entered the hotel. Doyle came forward to meet them. 'Ah, so you've palled up?' he said. 'Isn't that grand?'

'We could have sherry,' Mrs Angusthorpe suggested, 'in the bar.'

'Of course you could,' said Doyle. 'Won't your two husbands be pegging away at the old fish for the entire day?'

'They promised to be back for lunch,' Daphne said quickly, her voice seeming to herself to be unduly weak. She cleared her throat and remarked to Doyle that the village was pretty. She didn't really wish to sit in the hotel bar drinking sherry with the wife of her husband's headmaster. It was all ridiculous, she thought, on a honeymoon.

'Go down into the bar,' said Doyle, 'and I'll be down myself in a minute.'

Mrs Angusthorpe seized with the fingers of her left hand the flowered material of Daphne's dress. 'The bar's down here,' she said, leading the way without releasing her hold.

They sat at a table on which there were a number of absorbent mats that advertised brands of beer. Doyle brought them two glasses of sherry, which Mrs Angusthorpe ordered him to put down to her husband's account. 'Shout out when you're in need of a refill,' he invited. 'I'll be up in the hall.'

'The partition between our bedrooms is far from soundproof,' said Mrs Angusthorpe when Doyle had gone. 'We were awakened in the night.'

'Awakened?'

'As if you were in the room beside us, we heard a conversation.'

'My God!'

'Yes.'

Blood rushed to Daphne Jackson's face. She was aware of an unpleasant sensation in her stomach. She turned her head away. Mrs Angusthorpe said:

'People don't speak out. All my married life, for instance, I haven't spoken out. My dear, you're far too good for Jackson Major.'

It seemed to Daphne, who had been Daphne Jackson for less than twenty-four hours, that the wife of her husband's headmaster was insane. She gulped at the glass of sherry before her, unable to prevent herself from vividly recalling the awfulness of the night before in the small bedroom. He had come at her as she was taking off her blouse. His right hand had shot beneath her underclothes, pressing at her and gripping her. All during their inedible dinner he had been urging her to drink whiskey and wine, and drinking quantities of both himself. In bed he had suddenly become calmer, remembering instructions read in a book.

'Pack a suitcase,' said Mrs Angusthorpe, 'and go.'

The words belonged to a nightmare and Daphne was aware of wishing that she were asleep and dreaming. The memory of tension on her wedding-day, and of guests standing around in sunshine in a London garden, and then the flight by plane, were elements that confused her mind as she listened to this small woman. The tension had been with her as she walked towards the altar and had been with her, too, in her parents' garden. Nor had it eased when she escaped with her husband on a Viscount: it might even have increased on the flight and on the train to Galway, and then in the hired car that had carried her to the small village. It had certainly increased while she attempted to eat stringy chicken at a late hour in the dining-room, while her husband smiled at her and talked about intoxicants. The reason he had talked so much about whiskey and wine, she now concluded, was because he'd been aware of the tension that was coiled within her.

'You have made a mistake,' came the voice of Mrs Angusthorpe, 'but even now it is not too late to rectify it. Do not accept it, reject your error, Mrs Jackson.'

Doyle came into the bar and brought to them, without their demanding it, more sherry in two new glasses. Daphne heard him remarking that the brand of sherry was very popular in these parts. It was Spanish sherry, he said, since he would stock nothing else. He talked about Spain and Spaniards, saying that at the time of the Spanish Armada Spanish sailors had been wrecked around the nearby coast.

'I love my husband,' Daphne said when Doyle had gone again.

She had met her husband in the Hurlingham Club. He had partnered her in tennis and they had danced together at a charity dance. She'd listened while he talked one evening, telling her that the one thing he regretted was that he hadn't played golf as a child. Golf was a game, he'd said, that must be started when young if one was ever to achieve championship distinction. With tennis that wasn't quite so important, but it was, of course, as well to start tennis early also. She had thought he was rather nice. There was something about his distant manner that attracted her; there was a touch of arrogance in the way he didn't look at her when he spoke. She'd make him look at her, she vowed.

'My dear,' said Mrs Angusthorpe, 'I've seen the seamy side of Jackson Major. The more I think of him the more I can recall. He forced his way up that school, snatching at chances that weren't his to take, putting himself first, like he did in the half-mile race. There was cruelty in Jackson Major's eye, and ruthlessness and dullness. Like my husband, he has no sense of humour.'

'Mrs Angusthorpe, I really can't listen to this. I was married yesterday to a man I'm in love with. It'll be all right —'

'Why will it be all right?'

'Because,' snapped Daphne Jackson with sudden spirit, 'I shall ask my husband as soon as he returns to take me at once from this horrible hotel. My marriage does not concern you, Mrs Angusthorpe.'

'They are talking now on a riverside, whispering maybe so as not to disturb their prey. They are murmuring about the past, of achievements on the sports field and marches undertaken by a cadet force. While you and I are having a different kind of talk.'

'What our husbands are saying to one another, Mrs Angusthorpe, may well make more sense.'

'What they are not saying is that two women in the bar of this hotel are unhappy. They have forgotten about the two women: they are more relaxed and contented than ever they are with us.'

Mrs Angusthorpe, beady-eyed as she spoke, saw the effect of her words reflected in the uneasy face of the woman beside her. She felt herself carried away by this small triumph, she experienced a headiness that was blissful.

She saw in her mind another scene, imagining herself, over lunch, telling her husband about the simple thing that had happened. She would watch him sitting there in all his dignity: she would wait until he was about to pass a forkful of food to his mouth and then she would say: 'Jackson Major's wife has left him already.' And she would smile at him.

'You walked across the dining-room at breakfast,' said Mrs Angusthorpe. 'An instinct warned me then that you'd made an error.'

'I haven't made an error. I've told you, Mrs Angusthorpe –'

'Time will erode the polish of politeness. One day soon you'll see amusement in his eyes when you offer an opinion.'

'Please stop, Mrs Angusthorpe. I must go away if you continue like this –'

' "This man's a bore," you'll suddenly say to yourself, and look at him amazed.'

'Mrs Angusthorpe –'

'Amazed that you could ever have let it happen.'

'Oh God, please stop,' cried Daphne, tears coming suddenly from her eyes, her hands rushing to her cheeks.

'Don't be a silly girl,' whispered Mrs Angusthorpe, grasping the arm of her companion and tightening her fingers on it until Daphne felt pain. She thought as she felt it that Mrs Angusthorpe was a poisonous woman. She struggled to keep back further tears, she tried to wrench her arm away.

'I'll tell the man Doyle to order you a car,' said Mrs Angusthorpe. 'It'll take you into Galway. I'll lend you money, Mrs Jackson. By one o'clock tonight you could be sitting in your bed at home, eating from a tray that your mother brought you. A divorce will come through and one day you'll meet a man who'll love you with a tenderness.'

'My husband loves me, Mrs Angusthorpe –'

'Your husband should marry a woman who's keen on horses or golf, a woman who might take a whip to him, being ten years older than himself. My dear, you're like me: you're a delicate person.'

'Please let go my arm. You've no right to talk to me like this –'

'He is my husband's creature, my husband moulded him. The best head boy he'd ever known, he said to me.'

Daphne, calmer now, did not say anything. She felt the pressure on her arm being removed. She stared ahead of her, at a round mat on the table that advertised Celebration Ale. Without wishing to and perhaps, she thought, because she was so upset, she saw herself suddenly as Mrs Angusthorpe had suggested, sitting up in her own bedroom with a tray of food on her knees and her mother standing beside her, saying it was all right. 'I suddenly realized,' she heard herself saying. 'He took me to this awful hotel, where his old headmaster was. He gave me wine and whiskey, and then in bed I thought I might be sick.' Her mother replied to her, telling her that it wasn't a disgrace, and her father came in later and told her not to worry. It was better not to be unhappy, her father said: it was better to have courage now.

'Let me tell Doyle to order a car at once.' Mrs Angusthorpe was on her feet, eagerness in her eyes and voice. Her cheeks were flushed from sherry and excitement.

'You're quite outrageous,' said Daphne Jackson.

She left the bar and in the hall Doyle again desired her as she passed. He spoke to her, telling her he'd already ordered a few more bottles of that sherry so that she and Mrs Angusthorpe could sip a little as often as they liked. It was sherry, he repeated, that was very popular in the locality. She nodded and mounted the stairs, not hearing much of what he said, feeling that as she pushed one leg in front of the other her whole body would open and tears would gush from everywhere. Why did she have to put up with talk like that on the first morning of her honeymoon? Why had he casually gone out fishing with his old headmaster? Why had he brought her to this terrible place and then made her drink so that the tension would leave her body? She sobbed on the stairs, causing Doyle to frown and feel concerned for her.

'Are you all right?' Jackson Major asked, standing in the doorway of their room, looking to where she sat, by the window. He closed the door and went to her. 'You've been all right?' he said.

She nodded, smiling a little. She spoke in a low voice: she said she thought it possible that conversations might be heard through the partition wall. She pointed to the wall she spoke of. 'It's only a partition,' she said.

He touched it and agreed, but gave it as his opinion that little could be heard through it since they themselves had not heard the people on the other side of it. Partitions nowadays, he pronounced, were constructed always of soundproof material.

'Let's have a drink before lunch,' she said.

In the hour that had elapsed since she had left Mrs Angusthorpe in the bar she had changed her stockings and her dress. She had washed her face in cold water and had put lipstick and powder on it. She had brushed her suede shoes with a rubber brush.

'All right,' he said. 'We'll have a little drink.'

He kissed her. On the way downstairs he told her about the morning's fishing and the conversations he had had with his old headmaster. Not asking her what she'd like, he ordered both of them gin and tonic in the bar.

'I know her better than you do, sir,' Doyle said, bringing her a glass of sherry, but Jackson Major didn't appear to realize what had happened, being still engrossed in the retailing of the conversations he had had with his old headmaster.

'I want to leave this hotel,' she said. 'At once, darling, after lunch.'

'Daphne –'

'I do.'

She didn't say that Mrs Angusthorpe had urged her to leave him, nor that the Angusthorpes had lain awake during the night, hearing what there was to hear. She simply said she didn't at all like the idea of spending her honeymoon in a hotel which also contained his late headmaster and the headmaster's wife. 'They remember you as a boy,' she said. 'For some reason it makes me edgy. And anyway it's such a nasty hotel.'

She leaned back after that speech, glad that she'd been able to make it as she'd planned to make it. They would move on after lunch, paying whatever money must necessarily be paid. They would find a pleasant room in a pleasant hotel and the tension inside her would gradually relax. In the Hurlingham Club she had made this tall man look at her when he spoke to her, she had made him regard her and find her attractive, as she found him. They had said to one another that they had fallen in love, he had asked her to marry him, and she had happily agreed: there was nothing the matter.

'My dear, it would be quite impossible,' he said.

'Impossible?'

'At this time of year, in the middle of the season? Hotel rooms are gold dust, my dear. Angusthorpe was saying as much. His wife's a good sort, you know –'

'I want to leave here.'

He laughed good-humouredly. He gestured with his hands, suggesting his helplessness.

'I cannot stay here,' she said.

'You're tired, Daphne.'

'I cannot stay here for a fortnight with the Angusthorpes. She's a woman who goes on all the time; there's something the matter with her. While you go fishing –'

'Darling, I had to go this morning. I felt it polite to go. If you like, I'll not go out again at all.'

'I've told you what I'd like.'

'Oh, for God's sake!' He turned away from her. She said:

'I thought you would say yes at once.'

'How the hell can I say yes when we've booked a room for the next fortnight and we're duty-bound to pay for it? Do you really think we can just walk up to that man and say we don't like his hotel and the people he has staying here?'

'We could make some excuse. We could pretend –'

'Pretend? Pretend, Daphne?'

'Some illness. We could say my mother's ill,' she hurriedly said. 'Or some aunt who doesn't even exist. We could hire a car and drive around the coast –'

'Daphne –'

'Why not?'

'For a start, I haven't my driving licence with me.'

'I have.'

'I doubt it, Daphne.'

She thought, and then she agreed that she hadn't. 'We could go to Dublin,' she said with a fresh burst of urgency. 'Dublin's a lovely place, people say. We could stay in Dublin and –'

'My dear, this is a tourist country. Millions of tourists come here every summer. Do you really believe we'd find decent accommodation in Dublin in the middle of the season?'

'It wouldn't have to be decent. Some little clean hotel –'

'Added to which, Daphne, I must honestly tell you that I have no wish to go gallivanting on my honeymoon. Nor do I care for the notion of telling lies about the illness of people who are not ill, or do not even exist.'

'I'll tell the lies. I'll talk to Mr Doyle directly after lunch. I'll talk to him now.' She stood up. He shook his head, reaching for the hand that was nearer to him.

'What's the matter?' he asked.

Slowly she sat down again.

'Oh, darling,' she said.

'We must be sensible, Daphne. We can't just go gallivanting off –'

'Why do you keep on about gallivanting? What's it matter whether we're gallivanting or not so long as we're enjoying ourselves?'

'Daphne –'

'I'm asking you to do something to please me.'

Jackson Major, about to reply, changed his mind. He smiled at his bride. After a pause, he said:

'If you really want to, Daphne –'

'Well, I do. I think perhaps it'll be awkward here with the Angusthorpes. And it's not what we expected.'

'It's just a question,' said Jackson Major, 'of what we could possibly do. I've asked for my mail to be forwarded here and, as I say, I really believe it would be a case of out of the frying pan into nothing at all. It might prove horribly difficult.'

She closed her eyes and sat for a moment in silence. Then she opened them and, being unable to think of anything else to say, she said:

'I'm sorry.'

He sighed, shrugging his shoulders slightly. He took her hand again. 'You do see, darling?' Before she could reply he added: 'I'm sorry I was angry with you. I didn't mean to be: I'm very sorry.'

He kissed her on the cheek that was near to him. He took her hand. 'Now tell me,' he said, 'about everything that's worrying you.'

She repeated, without more detail, what she had said already, but this time the sentences she spoke did not sound like complaints. He listened to her, sitting back and not interrupting, and then they conversed about all she had said. He agreed that it was a pity about the hotel and explained to her that what had happened, apparently, was that the old proprietor had died during the previous year. It was unfortunate too, he quite agreed, that the Angusthorpes should be here at the same time as they were because it would, of course, have been so much nicer to have been on their own. If she was worried about the partition in their room he would ask that their room should be changed for another one. He hadn't known when she'd mentioned the partition before that it was the Angusthorpes who were on the other side of it. It would be better, really, not to be in the next room to the Angusthorpes since Angusthorpe had once been his headmaster, and he was certain that Doyle would understand a thing like that and agree to change them over, even if it meant greasing Doyle's palm. 'I imagine he'd fall in with anything,' said Jackson Major, 'for a bob or two.'

They finished their drinks and she followed him to the dining-room. There were no thoughts in her mind: no voice, neither her own nor Mrs Angusthorpe's, spoke. For a reason she could not understand and didn't want to bother to understand, the tension within her had snapped and was no longer there. The desire she had felt for tears when she'd walked away from Mrs Angusthorpe was far from her now; she felt a weariness, as though an ordeal was over and she had survived it. She didn't know why she felt like that. All she knew was that he had listened to her: he had been patient and understanding, allowing her to say everything that was in her mind and then being reassuring. It was not his fault that the hotel had turned out so unfortunately. Nor was it his fault that a bullying old man had sought him out as a fishing companion. He couldn't help it if his desire for her brought out a clumsiness in him. He was a man, she thought: he was not the same as she was: she must meet him half-way. He had said he was sorry for being angry with her.

In the hall they met the Angusthorpes on their way to the dining-room also.

'I'm sorry if I upset you,' Mrs Angusthorpe said to her, touching her arm to hold her back for a moment. 'I'm afraid my temper ran away with me.'

The two men went ahead, involved in a new conversation. 'We might try that little tributary this afternoon,' the headmaster was suggesting.

'I sat there afterwards, seeing how horrid it must have been for you,' Mrs Angusthorpe said. 'I was only angry at the prospect of an unpleasant fortnight. I took it out on you.'

'Don't worry about it.'

'One should keep one's anger to oneself. I feel embarrassed now,' said Mrs Angusthorpe. 'I'm not the sort of person –'

'Please don't worry,' murmured Daphne, trying hard to keep the tired-ness that possessed her out of her voice. She could sleep, she was thinking, for a week.

'I don't know why I talked like that.'

'You were angry –'

'Yes,' said Mrs Angusthorpe.

She stood still, not looking at Daphne and seeming not to wish to enter the dining-room. Some people went by, talking and laughing. Mr Gorman, the solicitor from Dublin, addressed her, but she did not acknowledge his greeting.

'I think we must go in now, Mrs Angusthorpe,' Daphne said.

In her weariness she smiled at Mrs Angusthorpe, suddenly sorry for her because she had so wretched a marriage that it caused her to become emotional with strangers.

'It was just,' said Mrs Angusthorpe, pausing uncertainly in the middle of her sentence and then continuing, 'I felt that perhaps I should say something. I felt, Mrs Jackson –'

'Let's just forget it,' interrupted Daphne, sensing with alarm that Mrs Angusthorpe was about to begin all over again, in spite of her protestations.

'What?'

'I think we must forget it all.'

Daphne smiled again, to reassure the woman who'd been outrageous because her temper had run away with her. She wanted to tell her that just now in the bar she herself had had a small outburst and that in the end she had seen the absurdity of certain suggestions she had made. She wanted to say that her husband had asked her what the matter was and then had said he was sorry. She wanted to explain, presumptuously perhaps, that there must be give and take in marriage, that a bed of roses was something that couldn't be shared. She wanted to say that the tension she'd felt was no longer there, but she couldn't find the energy for saying it.

'Forget it?' said Mrs Angusthorpe. 'Yes, I suppose so. There are things that shouldn't be talked about.'

'It's not that really,' objected Daphne softly. 'It's just that I think you jumped to a lot of wrong conclusions.'

'I had an instinct,' began Mrs Angusthorpe with all her previous eagerness and urgency. 'I saw you at breakfast-time, an innocent girl. I couldn't help remembering.'

'It's different for us,' said Daphne, feeling embarrassed to have to converse again in this intimate vein. 'At heart my husband's patient with me. And understanding too: he listens to me.'

'Of course,' agreed Mrs Angusthorpe, slowly nodding her head and moving at last towards the dining-room.

The Mark-2 Wife

Standing alone at the Lowhrs' party, Anna Mackintosh thought about her husband Edward, establishing him clearly for this purpose in her mind's eye. He was a thin man, forty-one years of age, with fair hair that was often untidy. In the seventeen years they'd been married he had changed very little: he was still nervous with other people, and smiled in the same abashed way, and his face was still almost boyish. She believed she had failed him because he had wished for children and she had not been able to supply any. She had, over the years, developed a nervous condition about this fact and in the end, quite some time ago now, she had consulted a psychiatrist, a Dr Abbatt, at Edward's pleading.

In the Lowhrs' rich drawing-room, its walls and ceiling gleaming with a metallic surface of ersatz gold, Anna listened to dance music coming from a tape-recorder and continued to think about her husband. In a moment he would be at the party too, since they had agreed to meet there, although by now it was three-quarters of an hour later than the time he had stipulated. The Lowhrs were people he knew in a business way, and he had said he thought it wise that he and Anna should attend this gathering of theirs. She had never met them before, which made it more difficult for her, having to wait about, not knowing a soul in the room. When she thought about it she felt hard done by, for although Edward was kind to her and always had been, it was far from considerate to be as late as this. Because of her nervous condition she felt afraid and had developed a sickness in her stomach. She looked at her watch and sighed.

People arrived, some of them kissing the Lowhrs, others nodding and smiling. Two dark-skinned maids carried trays of drinks among the guests, offering them graciously and murmuring thanks when a glass was accepted. 'I'll be there by half past nine,' Edward had said that morning. 'If you don't turn up till ten you won't have to be alone at all.' He had kissed her after that, and had left the house. I'll wear the blue, she thought, for she liked the colour better than any other: it suggested serenity to her, and the idea of serenity, especially as a quality in herself, was something she valued. She had said as much to Dr Abbatt, who had agreed that serenity was something that should be important in her life.

An elderly couple, tall twig-like creatures of seventy-five, a General

Ritchie and his wife, observed the lone state of Anna Mackintosh and reacted in different ways. 'That woman seems out of things,' said Mrs Ritchie. 'We should go and talk to her.'

But the General suggested that there was something the matter with this woman who was on her own. 'Now, don't let's get involved,' he rather tetchily begged. 'In any case she doesn't look in the mood for chat.'

His wife shook her head. 'Our name is Ritchie,' she said to Anna, and Anna, who had been looking at the whisky in her glass, lifted her head and saw a thin old woman who was as straight as a needle, and behind her a man who was thin also but who stooped a bit and seemed to be cross. 'He's an old soldier,' said Mrs Ritchie. 'A general that was.'

Strands of white hair trailed across the pale dome of the old man's head. He had sharp eyes, like a terrier's, and a grey moustache. 'It's not a party I care to be at,' he muttered, holding out a bony hand. 'My wife's the one for this.'

Anna said who she was and added that her husband was late and that she didn't know the Lowhrs.

'We thought it might be something like that,' said Mrs Ritchie. 'We don't know anyone either, but at least we have one another to talk to.' The Lowhrs, she added, were an awfully nice, generous couple.

'We met them on a train in Switzerland,' the General murmured quietly.

Anna glanced across the crowded room at the people they spoke of. The Lowhrs were wholly different in appearance from the Ritchies. They were small and excessively fat, and they both wore glasses and smiled a lot. Like jolly gnomes, she thought.

'My husband knows them in a business way,' she said. She looked again at her watch: the time was half past ten. There was a silence, and then Mrs Ritchie said:

'They invited us to two other parties in the past. It's very kind, for we don't give parties ourselves any more. We live a quiet sort of life now.' She went on talking, saying among other things that it was pleasant to see the younger set at play. When she stopped, the General added:

'The Lowhrs feel sorry for us, actually.'

'They're very kind,' his wife repeated.

Anna had been aware of a feeling of uneasiness the moment she'd entered the golden room, and had Edward been with her she'd have wanted to say that they should turn round and go away again. The uneasiness had increased whenever she'd noted the time, and for some reason these old people for whom the Lowhrs were sorry had added to it even more. She would certainly talk this over with Dr Abbatt, she decided, and then, quite absurdly, she felt an urge to telephone Dr Abbatt and tell him at once about the feeling she had. She closed her eyes, thinking that she would keep them like that for only the slightest moment so that the Ritchies wouldn't notice and think it odd. While they were still closed she heard Mrs Ritchie say:

'Are you all right, Mrs Mackintosh?'

She opened her eyes and saw that General Ritchie and his wife were examining her face with interest. She imagined them wondering about her, a woman of forty whose husband was an hour late. They'd be thinking, she thought, that the absent husband didn't have much of a feeling for his wife to be as careless as that. And yet, they'd probably think, he must have had a feeling for her once since he had married her in the first place.

'It's just,' said Mrs Ritchie, 'that I had the notion you were going to faint.'

The voice of Petula Clark came powerfully from the tape-recorder. At one end of the room people were beginning to dance in a casual way, some still holding their glasses in their hands.

'The heat could have affected you,' said the General, bending forward so that his words would reach her.

Anna shook her head. She tried to smile, but the smile failed to materialize. She said:

'I never faint, actually.'

She could feel a part of herself attempting to bar from her mind the entry of unwelcome thoughts. Hastily she said, unable to think of anything better:

'My husband's really frightfully late.'

'You know,' said General Ritchie, 'it seems to me we met your husband here.' He turned to his wife. 'A fair-haired man – he said his name was Mackintosh. Is your husband fair, Mrs Mackintosh?'

'Of course,' cried Mrs Ritchie. 'Awfully nice.'

Anna said that Edward was fair. Mrs Ritchie smiled at her husband and handed him her empty glass. He reached out for Anna's. She said:

'Whisky, please. By itself.'

'He's probably held up in bloody traffic,' said the General before moving off.

'Yes, probably that,' Mrs Ritchie said. 'I do remember him well, you know.'

'Edward did come here before. I had a cold.'

'Completely charming. We said so afterwards.'

One of the dark-skinned maids paused with a tray of drinks. Mrs Ritchie explained that her husband was fetching some. 'Thank you, madam,' said the dark-skinned maid, and the General returned.

'It isn't the traffic,' Anna said rather suddenly and loudly. 'Edward's not held up like that at all.'

The Ritchies sipped their drinks. They can sense I'm going to be a nuisance, Anna thought. 'I'm afraid it'll be boring,' he had said. 'We'll slip away at eleven and have dinner in Charlotte Street.' She heard him saying it now, quite distinctly. She saw him smiling at her.

'I get nervous about things,' she said to the Ritchies. 'I worry unnecessarily. I try not to.'

Mrs Ritchie inclined her head in a sympathetic manner; the General coughed. There was a silence and then Mrs Ritchie spoke about episodes in their past. Anna looked at her watch and saw that it was five to eleven. 'Oh God,' she said.

The Ritchies asked her again if she was all right. She began to say she was but she faltered before the sentence was complete, and in that moment she gave up the struggle. What was the point, she thought, of exhausting oneself being polite and making idle conversation when all the time one was in a frightful state?

'He's going to be married again,' she said quietly and evenly. 'His Mark-2 wife.'

She felt better at once. The sickness left her stomach; she drank a little whisky and found its harsh taste a comfort.

'Oh, I'm terribly sorry,' said Mrs Ritchie.

Anna had often dreamed of the girl. She had seen her, dressed all in purple, with slim hips and a purple bow in her black hair. She had seen the two of them together in a speedboat, the beautiful young creature laughing her head off like a figure in an advertisement. She had talked for many hours to Dr Abbatt about her, and Dr Abbatt had made the point that the girl was simply an obsession. 'It's just a little nonsense,' he had said to her kindly, more than once. Anna knew in her calmer moments that it was just a little nonsense, for Edward was always kind and had never ceased to say he loved her. But in bad moments she argued against that conclusion, reminding herself that other kind men who said they loved their wives often made off with something new. Her own marriage being childless would make the whole operation simpler.

'I hadn't thought it would happen at a party,' Anna said to the Ritchies. 'Edward has always been decent and considerate. I imagined he would tell me quietly at home, and comfort me. I imagined he would be decent to the end.'

'You and your husband are not yet separated then?' Mrs Ritchie inquired.

'This is the way it is happening,' Anna repeated. 'D'you understand? Edward is delayed by his Mark-2 wife because she insists on delaying him. She's demanding that he should make his decision and afterwards that he and she should come to tell me, so that I won't have to wait any more. You understand,' she repeated, looking closely from one face to the other, 'that this isn't Edward's doing?'

'But, Mrs Mackintosh – '

'I have a woman's intuition about it. I have felt my woman's intuition at work since the moment I entered this room. I know precisely what's going to happen.'

Often, ever since the obsession had begun, she had wondered if she had any rights at all. Had she rights in the matter, she had asked herself, since she was running to fat and could supply no children? The girl would repeatedly give birth and everyone would be happy, for birth was a happy business. She had suggested to Dr Abbatt that she probably hadn't any rights, and for once he had spoken to her sternly. She said it now to the Ritchies, because it didn't seem to matter any more what words were spoken. On other occasions, when she was at home, Edward had been late and she had sat and waited for him, pretending it was a natural thing for him to be late. And when he arrived her fears had seemed absurd.

'You understand?' she said to the Ritchies.

The Ritchies nodded their thin heads, the General embarrassed, his wife concerned. They waited for Anna to speak. She said:

'The Lowhrs will feel sorry for me, as they do for you. "This poor woman," they'll cry, "left in the lurch at our party! What a ghastly thing!" I should go home, you know, but I haven't even the courage for that.'

'Could we help at all?' asked Mrs Ritchie.

'You've been married all this time and not come asunder. Have you had children, Mrs Ritchie?'

Mrs Ritchie replied that she had had two boys and a girl. They were well grown up by now, she explained, and among them had provided her and the General with a dozen grandchildren.

'What did you think of my husband?'

'Charming, Mrs Mackintosh, as I said.'

'Not the sort of man who'd mess a thing like this up? You thought the opposite, I'm sure: that with bad news to break he'd choose the moment elegantly. Once he would have.'

'I don't understand,' protested Mrs Ritchie gently, and the General lent his support to that with a gesture.

'Look at me,' said Anna. 'I've worn well enough. Neither I nor Edward would deny it. A few lines and flushes, fatter and coarser. No one can escape all that. Did you never feel like a change, General?'

'A change?'

'I have to be rational. I have to say that it's no reflection on me. D'you understand that?'

'Of course it's no reflection.'

'It's like gadgets in shops. You buy a gadget and you develop an affection for it, having decided on it in the first place because you thought it was attractive. But all of a sudden there are newer and better gadgets in the shops. More up-to-date models.' She paused. She found a handkerchief and blew her nose. She said:

'You must excuse me: I am not myself tonight.'

'You mustn't get upset. Please don't,' Mrs Ritchie said.

Anna drank all the whisky in her glass and lifted another glass from a passing tray. 'There are too many people in this room,' she complained. 'There's not enough ventilation. It's ideal for tragedy.'

Mrs Ritchie shook her head. She put her hand on Anna's arm. 'Would you like us to go home with you and see you safely in?'

'I have to stay here.'

'Mrs Mackintosh, your husband would never act like that.'

'People in love are cruel. They think of themselves: why should they bother to honour the feelings of a discarded wife?'

'Oh, come now,' said Mrs Ritchie.

At that moment a bald man came up to Anna and took her glass from her hand and led her, without a word, on to the dancing area. As he danced with her, she thought that something else might have happened. Edward was not with anyone, she said to herself: Edward was dead. A telephone had rung in the Lowhrs' house and a voice had said that, *en route* to their party, a man had dropped dead on the pavement. A maid had taken the message and, not quite understanding it, had done nothing about it.

'I think we should definitely go home now,' General Ritchie said to his wife. 'We could be back for *A Book at Bedtime*.'

'We cannot leave her as easily as that. Just look at the poor creature.'

'That woman is utterly no concern of ours.'

'Just look at her.'

The General sighed and swore and did as he was bidden.

'My husband was meant to turn up,' Anna said to the bald man. 'I've just thought he may have died.' She laughed to indicate that she did not really believe this, in case the man became upset. But the man seemed not to be interested. She could feel his lips playing with a strand of her hair. Death, she thought, she could have accepted.

Anna could see the Ritchies watching her. Their faces were grave, but it came to her suddenly that the gravity was artificial. What, after all, was she to them that they should bother? She was a wretched woman at a party, a woman in a state, who was making an unnecessary fuss because her husband was about to give her her marching orders. Had the Ritchies been mocking her, she wondered, he quite directly, she in some special, subtle way of her own?

'Do you know those people I was talking to?' she said to her partner, but with a portion of her hair still in his mouth he made no effort at reply. Passing near to her, she noticed the thick, square fingers of Mr Lowhr embedded in the flesh of his wife's shoulder. The couple danced by, seeing her and smiling, and it seemed to Anna that their smiles were as empty as the Ritchies' sympathy.

'My husband is leaving me for a younger woman,' she said to the bald man, a statement that caused him to shrug. He had pressed himself close to her, his knees on her thighs, forcing her legs this way and that. His hands were low on her body now, advancing on her buttocks. He was eating her hair.

'I'm sorry,' Anna said. 'I'd rather you didn't do that.'

He released her where they stood and smiled agreeably: she could see pieces of her hair on his teeth. He walked away, and she turned and went in the opposite direction.

'We're really most concerned,' said Mrs Ritchie. She and her husband were standing where Anna had left them, as though waiting for her. General Ritchie held out her glass to her.

'Why should you be concerned? That bald man ate my hair. That's what people do to used-up women like me. They eat your hair and force their bodies on you. You know, General.'

'Certainly, I don't. Not in the least.'

'That man knew all about me. D'you think he'd have taken his liberties if he hadn't? A man like that can guess.'

'Nonsense,' said Mrs Ritchie firmly. She stared hard at Anna, endeavouring to impress upon her the errors in her logic.

'If you want to know, that man's a drunk,' said the General. 'He was far gone when he arrived here and he's more so now.'

'Why are you saying that?' Anna cried shrilly. 'Why are you telling me lies and mocking me?'

'Lies?' demanded the General, snapping the word out. 'Lies?'

'My dear, we're not mocking you,' murmured Mrs Ritchie.

'You and those Lowhrs and everyone else, God knows. The big event at this party is that Edward Mackintosh will reject his wife for another.'

'Oh now, Mrs Mackintosh –'

'Second marriages are often happier, you know. No reason why they shouldn't be.'

'We would like to help if we could,' Mrs Ritchie said.

'Help? In God's name, how can I be helped? How can two elderly strangers help me when my husband gives me up? What kind of help? Would you give me money – an income, say? Or offer me some other husband? Would you come to visit me and talk to me so that I shouldn't be lonely? Or strike down my husband, General, to show your disapproval? Would you scratch out the little girl's eyes for me, Mrs Ritchie? Would you slap her brazen face?'

'We simply thought we might help in some way,' Mrs Ritchie said. 'Just because we're old and pretty useless doesn't mean we can't make an effort.'

'We are all God's creatures, you are saying. We should offer aid to one another at every opportunity, when marriages get broken and decent husbands are made cruel. Hold my hands then, and let us wait for Edward and his Mark-2 wife. Let's all three speak together and tell them what we think.'

She held out her hands, but the Ritchies did not take them.

'We don't mean to mock you, as you seem to think,' the General said. 'I must insist on that, madam.'

'You're mocking me with your talk about helping. The world is not like that. You like to listen to me for my entertainment value: I'm a good bit of gossip for you. I'm a woman going on about her husband and then getting insulted by a man and seeing the Lowhrs smiling over it. Tell your little grandchildren that some time.'

Mrs Ritchie said that the Lowhrs, she was sure, had not smiled at any predicament that Anna had found herself in, and the General impatiently repeated that the man was drunk.

'The Lowhrs smiled,' Anna said, 'and you have mocked me too. Though perhaps you don't even know it.'

As she pushed a passage through the people, she felt the sweat running on her face and her body. There was a fog of smoke in the room by now, and the voices of the people, struggling to be heard above the music, were louder than before. The man she had danced with was sitting in a corner with his shoes off, and a woman in a crimson dress was trying to persuade him to put them on again. At the door of the room she found Mr Lowhr. 'Shall we dance?' he said.

She shook her head, feeling calmer all of a sudden. Mr Lowhr suggested a drink.

'May I telephone?' she said. 'Quietly somewhere?'

'Upstairs,' said Mr Lowhr, smiling immensely at her. 'Up two flights, the door ahead of you: a tiny guest-room. Take a glass with you.'

She nodded, saying she'd like a little whisky.

'Let me give you a tip,' Mr Lowhr said as he poured her some from a nearby bottle. 'Always buy Haig whisky. It's distilled by a special method.'

'You're never going so soon?' said Mrs Lowhr, appearing at her husband's side.

'Just to telephone,' said Mr Lowhr. He held out his hand with the glass of whisky in it. Anna took it, and as she did so she caught a glimpse of the Ritchies watching her from the other end of the room. Her calmness vanished. The Lowhrs, she noticed, were looking at her too, and smiling. She wanted to ask them why they were smiling, but she knew if she did that they'd simply make some polite reply. Instead she said:

'You shouldn't expose your guests to men who eat hair. Even unimportant guests.'

She turned her back on them and passed from the room. She crossed the hall, sensing that she was being watched. 'Mrs Mackintosh,' Mr Lowhr called after her.

His plumpness filled the doorway. He hovered, seeming uncertain about pursuing her. His face was bewildered and apparently upset.

'Has something disagreeable happened?' he said in a low voice across the distance between them.

'You saw. You and your wife thought fit to laugh, Mr Lowhr.'

'I do assure you, Mrs Mackintosh, I've no idea what you're talking about.'

'It's fascinating, I suppose. Your friends the Ritchies find it fascinating too.'

'Look here, Mrs Mackintosh –'

'Oh, don't blame them. They've nothing left but to watch and mock, at an age like that. The point is, there's a lot of hypocrisy going on tonight.' She nodded at Mr Lowhr to emphasize that last remark, and then went swiftly upstairs.

'I imagine the woman's gone off home,' the General said. 'I dare say her husband's drinking in a pub.'

'I worried once,' replied Mrs Ritchie, speaking quietly, for she didn't wish the confidence to be heard by others. 'That female, Mrs Flyte.'

The General roared with laughter. 'Trixie Flyte,' he shouted. 'Good God, she was a free-for-all!'

'Oh, do be quiet.'

'Dear girl, you didn't ever think –'

'I didn't know what to think, if you want to know.'

Greatly amused, the General seized what he hoped would be his final drink. He placed it behind a green plant on a table. 'Shall we dance one dance,' he said, 'just to amuse them? And then when I've had that drink to revive me we can thankfully make our way.'

But he found himself talking to nobody, for when he had turned from his wife to secrete his drink she had moved away. He followed her to where she was questioning Mrs Lowhr.

'Some little tiff,' Mrs Lowhr was saying as he approached.

'Hardly a tiff,' corrected Mrs Ritchie. 'The woman's terribly upset.' She turned to her husband, obliging him to speak.

'Upset,' he said.

'Oh, there now,' cried Mrs Lowhr, taking each of the Ritchies by an arm. 'Why don't you take the floor and forget it?'

They both of them recognized from her tone that she was thinking the elderly exaggerated things and didn't always understand the ways of marriage in the modern world. The General especially resented the insinuation. He said:

'Has the woman gone away?'

'She's upstairs telephoning. Some silly chap upset her apparently, during a dance. That's all it is, you know.'

'You've got the wrong end of the stick entirely,' said the General angrily, 'and you're trying to say we have. The woman believes her husband may arrive here with the girl he's chosen as his second wife.'

'But that's ridiculous!' cried Mrs Lowhr with a tinkling laugh.

'It is what the woman thinks,' said the General loudly, 'whether it's ridiculous or not.' More quietly, Mrs Ritchie added:

'She thinks she has a powerful intuition when all it is is a disease.'

'I'm cross with this Mrs Mackintosh for upsetting you two dear people!' cried Mrs Lowhr with a shrillness that matched her roundness and her glasses. 'I really and truly am.'

A big man came up as she spoke and lifted her into his arms, preparatory to dancing with her. 'What could anyone do?' she called back at the Ritchies as the man rotated her away. 'What can you do for a nervy woman like that?'

There was dark wallpaper on the walls of the room: black and brown with little smears of muted yellow. The curtains matched it; so did the bedspread on the low single bed, and the covering on the padded headboard. The carpet ran from wall to wall and was black and thick. There was a narrow wardrobe with a door of padded black leather and brass studs and an ornamental brass handle. The dressing-table and the stool in front of it reflected this general motif in different ways. Two shelves, part of the bed, attached to it on either side of the pillows, served as bedside tables: on each there was a lamp, and on one of them a white telephone.

As Anna closed and locked the door, she felt that in a dream she had been in a dark room in a house where there was a party, waiting for Edward to bring her terrible news. She drank a little whisky and moved towards the telephone. She dialled a number and when a voice answered her call she said:

'Dr Abbatt? It's Anna Mackintosh.'

His voice, as always, was so soft she could hardly hear it. 'Ah, Mrs Mackintosh,' he said.

'I want to talk to you.'

'Of course, Mrs Mackintosh, of course. Tell me now.'

'I'm at a party given by people called Lowhr. Edward was to be here but he didn't turn up. I was all alone and then two old people like scarecrows talked to me. They said their name was Ritchie. And a man ate my hair when we were dancing. The Lowhrs smiled at that.'

'I see. Yes?'

'I'm in a room at the top of the house. I've locked the door.'

'Tell me about the room, Mrs Mackintosh.'

'There's black leather on the wardrobe and the dressing-table. Curtains and things match. Dr Abbatt?'

'Yes?'

'The Ritchies are people who injure other people, I think. Intentionally or unintentionally, it never matters.'

'They are strangers to you, these Ritchies?'

'They attempted to mock me. People know at this party, Dr Abbatt; they sense what's going to happen because of how I look.'

Watching for her to come downstairs, the Ritchies stood in the hall and talked to one another.

'I'm sorry,' said Mrs Ritchie. 'I know it would be nicer to go home.'

'What can we do, old sticks like us? We know not a thing about such women. It's quite absurd.'

'The woman's on my mind, dear. And on yours too. You know it.'

'I think she'll be more on our minds if we come across her again. She'll turn nasty, I'll tell you that.'

'Yes, but it would please me to wait a little.'

'To be insulted,' said the General.

'Oh, do stop being so cross, dear.'

'The woman's a stranger to us. She should regulate her life and have done with it. She has no right to bother people.'

'She is a human being in great distress. No, don't say anything, please, if it isn't pleasant.'

The General went into a sulk, and at the end of it he said grudgingly:

'Trixie Flyte was nothing.'

'Oh, I know. Trixie Flyte is dead and done for years ago. I didn't worry like this woman if that's what's on your mind.'

'It wasn't,' lied the General. 'The woman worries ridiculously.'

'I think, you know, we may yet be of use to her: I have a feeling about that.'

'For God's sake, leave the feelings to her. We've had enough of that for one day.'

'As I said to her, we're not entirely useless. No one ever can be.'

'You feel you're being attacked again, Mrs Mackintosh. Are you calm? You haven't been drinking too much?'

'A little.'

'I see.'

'I am being replaced by a younger person.'

'You say you're in a bedroom. Is it possible for you to lie on the bed and talk to me at the same time? Would it be comfortable?'

Anna placed the receiver on the bed and settled herself. She picked it up again and said:

'If he died, there would be a funeral and I'd never forget his kindness to me. I can't do that if he has another wife.'

'We have actually been over this ground,' said Dr Abbatt more softly than ever. 'But we can of course go over it again.'

'Any time, you said.'

'Of course.'

'What has happened is perfectly simple. Edward is with the girl. He is about to arrive here to tell me to clear off. She's insisting on that. It's not Edward, you know.'

'Mrs Mackintosh, I'm going to speak firmly now. We've agreed between us that there's no young girl in your husband's life. You have an obsession, Mrs Mackintosh, about the fact that you have never had children and that men sometimes marry twice –'

'There's such a thing as the Mark-2 wife!' Anna cried. 'You know there is. A girl of nineteen who'll delightedly give birth to Edward's sons.'

'No, no –'

'I had imagined Edward telling me. I had imagined him pushing back his hair and lighting a cigarette in his untidy way. "I'm terribly sorry," he would say, and leave me nothing to add to that. Instead it's like this: a nightmare.'

'It is not a nightmare, Mrs Mackintosh.'

'This party is a nightmare. People are vultures here.'

'Mrs Mackintosh, I must tell you that I believe you're seeing the people at this party in a most exaggerated light.'

'A man —'

'A man nibbled your hair. Worse things can happen. This is not a nightmare, Mrs Mackintosh. Your husband has been delayed. Husbands are always being delayed. D'you see? You and I and your husband are all together trying to rid you of this perfectly normal obsession you've developed. We mustn't complicate matters, now must we?'

'I didn't run away, Dr Abbatt. I said to myself I mustn't run away from this party. I must wait and face whatever was to happen. You told me to face things.'

'I didn't tell you, my dear. We agreed between us. We talked it out, the difficulty about facing things, and we saw the wisdom of it. Now I want you to go back to the party and wait for your husband.'

'He's more than two hours late.'

'My dear Mrs Mackintosh, an hour or so is absolutely nothing these days. Now listen to me please.'

She listened to the soft voice as it reminded her of all that between them they had agreed. Dr Abbatt went over the ground, from the time she had first consulted him to the present moment. He charted her obsession until it seemed once again, as he said, a perfectly normal thing for a woman of forty to have.

After she had said goodbye, Anna sat on the bed feeling very calm. She had read the message behind Dr Abbatt's words: that it was ridiculous, her perpetually going on in this lunatic manner. She had come to a party and in no time at all she'd been behaving in a way that was, she supposed, mildly crazy. It always happened, she knew, and it would as long as the trouble remained: in her mind, when she began to worry, everything became jumbled and unreal, turning her into an impossible person. How could Edward, for heaven's sake, be expected to live with her fears and her suppositions? Edward would crack as others would, tormented by an impossible person. He'd become an alcoholic or he'd have some love affair with a woman just as old as she was, and the irony of that would be too great. She knew, as she sat there, that she couldn't help herself and that as long as she lived with Edward she wouldn't be able to do any better. 'I have lost touch with reality,' she said. 'I shall let him go, as a bird is released. In my state how can I have rights?'

She left the room and slowly descended the stairs. There were framed prints of old motor-cars on the wall and she paused now and again to examine one, emphasizing to herself her own continued calmness. She was thinking that she'd get herself a job. She might even tell Edward that Dr Abbatt had suggested their marriage should end since she wasn't able to live with her thoughts any more. She'd insist on a divorce at once. She didn't mind the thought of it now, because of course it would be different: she was doing what she guessed Dr Abbatt had been willing her to do for quite a long time really: she was taking matters into her own hands, she was acting positively – rejecting, not being rejected herself. Her marriage was ending cleanly and correctly.

She found her coat and thanked the dark-skinned maid who held it for her. Edward was probably at the party by now, but in the new circumstances that was neither here nor there. She'd go home in a taxi and pack a suitcase and then telephone for another taxi. She'd leave a note for Edward and go to a hotel, without telling him where.

'Good-night,' she said to the maid. She stepped towards the hall door as the maid opened it for her, and as she did so she felt a hand touch her shoulder. 'No, Edward,' she said. 'I must go now.' But when she turned she saw that the hand belonged to Mrs Ritchie. Behind her, looking tired, stood the General. For a moment there was a silence. Then Anna, speaking to both of them, said:

'I'm extremely sorry. Please forgive me.'

'We were worried about you,' said Mrs Ritchie. 'Will you be all right, my dear?'

'The fear is worse than the reality, Mrs Ritchie. I can no longer live with the fear.'

'We understand.'

'It's strange,' Anna said, passing through the doorway and standing at the top of the steps that led to the street. 'Strange, coming to a party like this, given by people I didn't know and meeting you and being so rude. Please don't tell me if my husband is here or not. It doesn't concern me now. I'm quite calm.'

The Ritchies watched her descend the steps and call out to a passing taxi-cab. They watched the taxi drive away.

'Calm!' said General Ritchie.

'She's still in a state, poor thing,' agreed his wife. 'I do feel sorry.'

They stood on the steps of the Lowhrs' house, thinking about the brief glance they had had of another person's life, bewildered by it and saddened, for they themselves, though often edgy on the surface, had had a happy marriage.

'At least she's standing on her own feet now,' Mrs Ritchie said. 'I think it'll save her.'

A taxi drew up at the house and the Ritchies watched it, thinking for a moment that Anna Mackintosh, weak in her resolve, had returned in search of her husband. But it was a man who emerged and ran up the steps in a manner which suggested that, like the man who had earlier misbehaved on the dance-floor, he was not entirely sober. He passed the Ritchies and entered the house. 'That is Edward Mackintosh,' said Mrs Ritchie.

The girl who was paying the taxi-driver paused in what she was doing to see where her companion had dashed away to and observed two thin figures staring at her from the lighted doorway, murmuring to one another.

'Cruel,' said the General. 'The woman said so: we must give her that.'

'He's a kind man,' replied Mrs Ritchie. 'He'll listen to us.'

'To us, for heaven's sake?'

'We have a thing to do, as I said we might have.'

'The woman has gone. I'm not saying I'm not sorry for her –'

'And who shall ask for mercy for the woman, since she cannot ask herself? There is a little to be saved, you know: she has made a gesture, poor thing. It must be honoured.'

'My dear, we don't know these people; we met the woman quite in passing.'

The girl came up the steps, settling her purse into its right place in her handbag. She smiled at the Ritchies, and they thought that the smile had a hint of triumph about it, as though it was her first smile since the victory that Anna Mackintosh had said some girl was winning that night.

'Even if he'd listen,' muttered the General when the girl had passed by, 'I doubt that she would.'

'It's just that a little time should be allowed to go by,' his wife reminded him. 'That's all that's required. Until the woman's found her feet again and feels she has a voice in her own life.'

'We're interfering,' said the General, and his wife said nothing. They looked at one another, remembering vividly the dread in Anna Mackintosh's face and the confusion that all her conversation had revealed.

The General shook his head. 'We are hardly the happiest choice,' he said, in a gentler mood at last, 'but I dare say we must try.'

He closed the door of the house and they paused for a moment in the hall, talking again of the woman who had told them her troubles. They drew a little strength from that, and felt armed to face once more the Lowhrs' noisy party. Together they moved towards it and through it, in search of a man they had met once before on a similar occasion. 'We are sorry for interfering,' they would quietly say; and making it seem as natural as they could, they would ask him to honour, above all else and in spite of love, the gesture of a woman who no longer interested him.

'A tall order,' protested the General, pausing in his forward motion, doubtful again.

'When the wrong people do things,' replied his wife, 'it sometimes works.' She pulled him on until they stood before Edward Mackintosh and the girl he'd chosen as his Mark-2 wife. They smiled at Edward Mackintosh and shook hands with him, and then there was a silence before the General said that it was odd, in a way, what they had to request.

An Evening with John Joe Dempsey

In Keogh's one evening Mr Lynch talked about the Piccadilly tarts, and John Joe Dempsey on his fifteenth birthday closed his eyes and travelled into a world he did not know. 'Big and little,' said Mr Lynch, 'winking their eyes at you and enticing you up to them. Wetting their lips,' said Mr Lynch, 'with the ends of their tongues.'

John Joe Dempsey had walked through the small town that darkening autumn evening, from the far end of North Street where he and his mother lived, past the cement building that was the Coliseum cinema, past Kelly's Atlantic Hotel and a number of shops that were now closed for the day. 'Go to Keogh's like a good boy,' his mother had requested, for as well as refreshments and stimulants Keogh's public house sold a variety of groceries: it was for a pound of rashers that Mrs Dempsey had sent her son.

'Who is there?' Mr Lynch had called out from the licensed area of the premises, hearing John Joe rapping with a coin to draw attention to his presence. A wooden partition with panes of glass in the top half of it rose to a height of eight feet between the grocery and the bar. 'I'm here for rashers,' John Joe explained through the pebbly glass. 'Isn't it a stormy evening, Mr Lynch? I'm fifteen today, Mr Lynch.'

There was a silence before a door in the partition opened and Mr Lynch appeared. 'Fifteen?' he said. 'Step in here, boy, and have a bottle of stout.'

John Joe protested that he was too young to drink a bottle of stout and then said that his mother required the rashers immediately. 'Mrs Keogh's gone out to Confession,' Mr Lynch said. 'I'm in charge till her ladyship returns.'

John Joe, knowing that Mr Lynch would not be prepared to set the bacon machine in action, stepped into the bar to await the return of Mrs Keogh, and Mr Lynch darted behind the counter for two bottles of stout. Having opened and poured them, he began about the Piccadilly tarts.

'You've got to an age,' Mr Lynch said, 'when you would have to be advised. Did you ever think in terms of emigration to England?'

'I did not, Mr Lynch.'

'I would say you were right to leave it alone, John Joe. Is that the first bottle of stout you ever had?'

'It is, Mr Lynch.'

'A bottle of stout is an acquired taste. You have to have had a dozen bottles or maybe more before you do get an urge for it. With the other matter it's different.'

Mr Lynch, now a large, fresh-faced man of fifty-five who was never seen without a brown hat on his head, had fought for the British Army during the Second World War, which was why one day in 1947 he had found himself, with companions, in Piccadilly Circus. As he listened, John Joe recalled that he'd heard boys at the Christian Brothers' referring to some special story that Mr Lynch confidentially told to those whom he believed would benefit from it. He had heard boys sniggering over this story, but he had never sought to discover its content, not knowing it had to do with Piccadilly tarts.

'There was a fellow by the name of Baker,' said Mr Lynch, 'who'd been telling us that he knew the ropes. Baker was a London man. He knew the places, he was saying, where he could find the glory girls, but when it came to the point of the matter, John Joe, we hardly needed a guide.'

Because, explained Mr Lynch, the tarts were everywhere. They stood in the doorways of shops showing off the stature of their legs. Some would speak to you, Mr Lynch said, addressing you fondly and stating their availability. Some had their bosoms cocked out so that maybe they'd strike a passing soldier and entice him away from his companions. 'I'm telling you this, John Joe, on account of your daddy being dead. Are you fancying that stout?'

John Joe nodded his head. Thirteen years ago his father had fallen to his death from a scaffold, having been by trade a builder. John Joe could not remember him, although he knew what he had looked like from a photograph that was always on view on the kitchen dresser. He had often wondered what it would be like to have that bulky man about the house, and more often still he listened to his mother talking about him. But John Joe didn't think about his father now, in spite of Mr Lynch's reference to him: keen to hear more about the women of Piccadilly, he asked what had happened when Mr Lynch and his companions finished examining them in the doorways.

'I saw terrible things in Belgium,' replied Mr Lynch meditatively. 'I saw a Belgian woman held down on the floor while four men satisfied themselves on her. No woman could be the same after that. Combat brings out the brute in a man.'

'Isn't it shocking what they'd do, Mr Lynch? Wouldn't it make you sick?'

'If your daddy was alive today, he would be telling you a thing or two in order to prepare you for your manhood and the temptations in another country. Your mother wouldn't know how to tackle a matter like that, nor would Father Ryan, nor the Christian Brothers. Your daddy might have sat you down in this bar and given you your first bottle of stout. He might have told you about the facts of life.'

'Did one of the glory girls entice yourself, Mr Lynch?'

'Listen to me, John Joe.' Mr Lynch regarded his companion through small blue eyes, both of which were slightly bloodshot. He lit a cigarette and drew on it before continuing. Then he said: 'Baker had the soldiers worked up with his talk of the glory girls taking off their togs. He used to describe the motion of their haunches. He used to lie there at night in the dug-out describing the private areas of the women's bodies. When the time came we went out with Baker and Baker went up to the third one he saw and said could the six of us make arrangements with her? He was keen to strike a bargain because we had only limited means on account of having remained in a public house for four hours. Myself included, we were in an intoxicated condition.'

'What happened, Mr Lynch?'

'I would not have agreed to an arrangement like that if it hadn't been for drink. I was a virgin boy, John Joe. Like yourself.'

'I'm that way, certainly, Mr Lynch.'

'We marched in behind the glory girl, down a side street. "Bedad, you're fine men," she said. We had bottles of beer in our pockets. "We'll drink that first," she said, "before we get down to business."'

John Joe laughed. He lifted the glass of stout to his lips and took a mouthful in a nonchalant manner, as though he'd been drinking stout for half a lifetime and couldn't do without it.

'Aren't you the hard man, Mr Lynch!' he said.

'You've got the wrong end of the stick,' replied Mr Lynch sharply. 'What happened was, I had a vision on the street. Amn't I saying to you those girls are no good to any man? I had a vision of the Virgin when we were walking along.'

'How d'you mean, Mr Lynch?'

'There was a little statue of the Holy Mother in my bedroom at home, a little special one my mother gave me at the occasion of my First Communion. It came into my mind, John Joe, when the six of us were with the glory girl. As soon as the glory girl said we'd drink the beer before we got down to business I saw the statue of the Holy Mother, as clear as if it was in front of me.'

John Joe, who had been anticipating an account of the soldiers' pleasuring, displayed disappointment. Mr Lynch shook his head at him.

'I was telling you a moral story,' he said reprovingly. 'The facts of life is one thing, John Joe, but keep away from dirty women.'

John Joe was a slight youth, pale of visage, as his father had been, and with large, awkward hands that bulged in his trouser pockets. He had no friends at the Christian Brothers' School he attended, being regarded there, because of his private nature and lack of interest in either scholastic or sporting matters, as something of an oddity – an opinion that was strengthened by his association with an old, simple-minded dwarf called Quigley, with whom he was regularly to be seen collecting minnows in a jam jar or walking along the country roads. In class at the Christian Brothers' John Joe would drift into a meditative state and could not easily be reached. 'Where've you gone, boy?' Brother Leahy would whisper, standing above him. His fingers would reach out for a twist of John Joe's scalp, and John Joe would rise from the ground with the Brother's thumb and forefinger tightening the short hairs of his neck, yet seeming not to feel the pain. It was only when the other hand of Brother Leahy gripped one of his ears that he would return to the classroom with a cry of anguish, and the boys and Brother Leahy would laugh. 'What'll we make of you?' Brother Leahy would murmur, returning to the blackboard while John Joe rubbed his head and his ear.

'There is many a time in the years afterwards,' said Mr Lynch ponderously, 'when I have gone through in my mind that moment in my life. I was tempted in bad company: I was two minutes off damnation.'

'I see what you mean, Mr Lynch.'

'When I came back to West Cork my mother asked me was I all right. Well, I was, I said. "I had a bad dream about you," my mother said. "I had a dream one night your legs were on fire." She looked at my legs, John Joe, and to tell you the truth of it she made me slip down my britches. "There's no harm there," she said. 'Twas only afterwards I worked it out: she had that dream in the very minute I was standing on the street seeing the vision in my brain. What my mother dreamed, John Joe, was that I was licked by the flames of Hell. She was warned that time, and from her dream she sent out a message that I was to receive a visit from the little statue. I'm an older man now, John Joe, but that's an account I tell to every boy in this town that hasn't got a father. That little story is an introduction to life and manhood. Did you enjoy the stout?'

'The stout's great stuff, Mr Lynch.'

'No drink you can take, John Joe, will injure you the way a dirty woman would. You might go to twenty million Confessions and you wouldn't relieve your heart and soul of a dirty woman. I didn't marry myself, out of shame for the memory of listening to Baker making that bargain. Will we have another bottle?'

John Joe, wishing to hear in further detail the bargain that Baker had made, said he could do with another drop. Mr Lynch directed him to a crate behind the counter. 'You're acquiring the taste,' he said.

John Joe opened and poured the bottles. Mr Lynch offered him a cigarette, which he accepted. In the Coliseum cinema he had seen Piccadilly Circus, and in one particular film there had been Piccadilly tarts, just as Mr Lynch described, loitering in doorways provocatively. As always, coming out of the Coliseum, it had been a little strange to find himself again among small shops that sold clothes and hardware and meat, among vegetable shops and tiny confectioners' and tobacconists' and public houses. For a few minutes after the Coliseum's programme was over the three streets of the town were busy with people going home, walking or riding on bicycles, or driving cars to distant farms, or going towards the chip-shop. When he was alone, John Joe usually leaned against the window of a shop to watch the activity before returning home himself; when his mother accompanied him to the pictures they naturally went home at once, his mother chatting on about the film they'd seen.

'The simple thing is, John Joe, keep a certain type of thought out of your mind.'

'Thought, Mr Lynch?'

'Of a certain order.'

'Ah, yes. Ah, definitely, Mr Lynch. A young fellow has no time for that class of thing.'

'Live a healthy life.'

'That's what I'm saying, Mr Lynch.'

'If I hadn't had a certain type of thought I wouldn't have found myself on the street that night. It was Baker who called them the glory girls. It's a peculiar way of referring to the sort they are.'

'Excuse me, Mr Lynch, but what kind of an age would they be?'

'They were all ages, boy. There were nippers and a few more of them had wrinkles on the flesh of their faces. There were some who must have weighed fourteen stone and others you could put in your pocket.'

'And was the one Baker made the bargain with a big one or a little one?'

'She was medium-sized, boy.'

'And had she black hair, Mr Lynch?'

'As black as your boot. She had a hat on her head that was a disgrace to the nation, and black gloves on her hands. She was carrying a little umbrella.'

'And, Mr Lynch, when your comrades met up with you again, did they tell you a thing at all?'

Mr Lynch lifted the glass to his lips. He filled his mouth with stout and savoured the liquid before allowing it to pass into his stomach. He turned his small eyes on the youth and regarded him in silence.

'You have pimples on your chin,' said Mr Lynch in the end. 'I hope you're living a clean life, now.'

'A healthy life, Mr Lynch.'

'It is a question your daddy would ask you. You know what I mean? There's some lads can't leave it alone.'

'They go mad in the end, Mr Lynch.'

'There was fellows in the British Army that couldn't leave it alone.'

'They're a heathen crowd, Mr Lynch. Isn't there terrible reports in the British papers?'

'The body is God-given. There's no need to abuse it.'

'I've never done that thing, Mr Lynch.'

'I couldn't repeat,' said Mr Lynch, 'what the glory girl said when I walked away.'

John Joe, whose classroom meditations led him towards the naked bodies of women whom he had seen only clothed and whose conversations with the town's idiot, Quigley, were of an obscene nature, said it was understandable that Mr Lynch could not repeat what the girl had said to him. A girl like that, he added, wasn't fit to be encountered by a decent man.

'Go behind the counter,' said Mr Lynch, 'and lift out two more bottles.'

John Joe walked to the crate of stout bottles. 'I looked in at a window one time,' Quigley had said to him, 'and I saw Mrs Nugent resisting her husband. Nugent took no notice of her at all; he had the clothes from her body like you'd shell a pod of peas.'

'I don't think Baker lived,' said Mr Lynch. 'He'd be dead of disease.'

'I feel sick to think of Baker, Mr Lynch.'

'He was like an animal.'

All the women of the town – and most especially Mrs Taggart, the wife of a postman – John Joe had kept company with in his imagination. Mrs Taggart was a well-built woman, a foot taller than himself, a woman with whom he had seen himself walking in the fields on the Ballydehob road. She had found him alone and had said that she was crossing the fields to where her husband had fallen into a bog-hole, and would he be able to come with her? She had a heavy, chunky face and a wide neck on which the fat lay in encircling folds, like a fleshy necklace. Her hair was grey and black, done up in hairpins. 'I was only codding you,' she said when they reached the side of a secluded hillock. 'You're a good-looking fellow, Dempsey.' On the side of the hillock, beneath a tree, Mrs Taggart commenced to rid herself of her outer garments, remarking that it was hot.

'Slip out of that little jersey,' she urged. 'Wouldn't it bake you today?' Sitting beside him in her underclothes, Mrs Taggart asked him if he liked sunbathing. She drew her petticoat up so that the sun might reach the tops of her legs. She asked him to put his hand on one of her legs so that he could feel the muscles; she was a strong woman, she said, and added that the strongest muscles she possessed were the muscles of her stomach. 'Wait till I show you,' said Mrs Taggart.

On other occasions he found himself placed differently with Mrs Taggart: once, his mother had sent him round to her house to inquire if she had any eggs for sale and after she had put a dozen eggs in a basket Mrs Taggart asked him if he'd take a look at a thorn in the back of her leg. Another time he was passing her house and he heard her crying out for help. When he went inside he discovered that she had jammed the door of the bathroom and couldn't get out. He managed to release the door and when he entered the bathroom he discovered that Mrs Taggart was standing up in the bath, seeming to have forgotten that she hadn't her clothes on.

Mrs Keefe, the wife of a railway official, another statuesque woman, featured as regularly in John Joe's imagination, as did a Mrs O'Brien, a Mrs Summers, and a Mrs Power. Mrs Power kept a bread-shop, and a very pleasant way of passing the time when Brother Leahy was talking was to walk into Mrs Power's shop and hear her saying that she'd have to slip into the bakery for a small pan loaf and would he like to accompany her? Mrs Power wore a green overall with a belt that was tied in a knot at the front. In the bakery, while they were chatting, she would attempt to untie the belt but always found it difficult. 'Can you aid me?' Mrs Power would ask and John Joe would endeavour to loose the knot that lay tight against Mrs Power's stout stomach. 'Where've you gone, boy?' Brother Leahy's voice would whisper over and over again like a familiar incantation and John Joe would suddenly shout, realizing he was in pain.

'It was the end of the war,' said Mr Lynch. 'The following morning myself and a gang of the other lads got a train up to Liverpool, and then we crossed back to Dublin. There was a priest on the train and I spoke to him about the whole thing. Every man was made like that, he said to me, only I was lucky to be rescued in the nick of time. If I'd have taken his name I'd have sent him the information about my mother's dream. I think that would have interested him, John Joe. Wouldn't you think so?'

'Ah, it would of course.'

'Isn't it a great story, John Joe?'

'It is, Mr Lynch.'

'Don't forget it ever, boy. No man is clear of temptations. You don't have to go to Britain to get temptations.'

'I understand you, Mr Lynch.'

Quigley had said that one night he looked through a window and saw the Protestant clergyman, the Reverend Johnson, lying on the floor with his wife. There was another time, he said, that he observed Hickey the chemist being coaxed from an armchair by certain activities on the part of Mrs Hickey. Quigley had climbed up on the roof of a shed and had seen Mrs Sweeney being helped out of her stockings by Sweeney, the builder and decorator. Quigley's voice might continue for an hour and a half, for there was hardly a man and his wife in the town whom he didn't claim to have observed in intimate circumstances. John Joe did not ever ask how, when there was no convenient shed to climb on to, the dwarf managed to make his way to so many exposed upstairs windows. Such a question would have been wholly irrelevant.

At Mass, when John Joe saw the calves of women's legs stuck out from the kneeling position, he experienced an excitement that later bred new fantasies within him. 'That Mrs Moore,' he would say to the old dwarf, and the dwarf would reply that one night in February he had observed Mrs Moore preparing herself for the return of her husband from a County Council meeting in Cork. From the powdered body of Mrs Moore, as described by Quigley, John Joe would move to an image that included himself. He saw himself pushing open the hall door of the Moores' house, having been sent to the house with a message from his mother, and hearing Mrs Moore's voice calling out, asking him to come upstairs. He stood on a landing and Mrs Moore came to him with a red coat wrapped round her to cover herself up. He could smell the powder on her body; the coat kept slipping from her shoulders. 'I have some magazines for your mother,' she said. 'They're inside the bedroom.' He went and sat on the bed while she collected a pile of magazines. She sat beside him then, drawing his attention to a story here and there that might be of particular interest to his mother. Her knee was pressed against his, and in a moment she put her arm round his shoulders and said he was a good-looking lad. The red coat fell back on to the bed when Mrs Moore took one of John Joe's large hands and placed it on her stomach. She then suggested, the evening being hot, that he should take off his jersey and his shirt.

Mrs Keogh, the owner of the public house, had featured also in John Joe's imagination and in the conversation of the old dwarf. Quigley had seen her, he said, a week before her husband died, hitting her husband with a length of wire because he would not oblige her with his attentions. 'Come down to the cellar,' said Mrs Keogh while Brother Leahy scribbled on the blackboard. 'Come down to the cellar, John Joe, and help me with a barrel.' He descended the cellar steps in front of her and when he looked back he saw her legs under her dark mourning skirt. 'I'm lost these days,' she said, 'since Mr Keogh went on.' They moved the barrel together and then Mrs Keogh said it was hot work and it would be better if they took off their jerseys. 'Haven't you the lovely arms!' she said as they rolled the barrel from one corner of the cellar to another. 'Will we lie down here for a rest?'

'We'll chance another bottle,' suggested Mr Lynch. 'Is it going down you all right?'

'My mother'll be waiting for the rashers, Mr Lynch.'

'No rasher can be cut, boy, till Mrs Keogh returns. You could slice your hand off on an old machine like that.'

'We'll have one more so.'

At the Christian Brothers', jokes were passed about that concerned grisly developments in the beds of freshly wedded couples, or centred around heroes who carried by chance strings of sausages in their pockets and committed unfortunate errors when it came to cutting one off for the pan. Such yarns, succeeding generally, failed with John Joe, for they seemed to him to be lacking in quality.

'How's your mammy?' Mr Lynch asked, watching John Joe pouring the stout.

'Ah, she's all right. I'm only worried she's waiting on the rashers –'

'There's honour due to a mother.'

John Joe nodded. He held the glass at an angle to receive the dark, foaming liquid, as Mr Lynch had shown him. Mr Lynch's mother, now seventy-nine, was still alive. They lived together in a house which Mr Lynch left every morning in order to work in the office of a meal business and which he left every evening in order to drink bottles of stout in Keogh's. The bachelor state of Mr Lynch was one which John Joe wondered if he himself would one day share. Certainly, he saw little attraction in the notion of marriage, apart from the immediate physical advantage. Yet Mr Lynch's life did not seem enviable either. Often on Sunday afternoons he observed the meal clerk walking slowly with his mother on his arm, seeming as lost in gloom as the married men who walked beside women pushing prams. Quigley, a bachelor also, was a happier man than Mr Lynch. He lived in what amounted to a shed at the bottom of his niece's garden. Food was carried to him, but there were few, with the exception of John Joe, who lingered in his company. On Sundays, a day which John Joe, like Mr Lynch, spent with his mother, Quigley walked alone.

'When'll you be leaving the Brothers?' Mr Lynch asked.

'In June.'

'And you'll be looking out for employment, John Joe?'

'I was thinking I'd go into the sawmills.'

Mr Lynch nodded approvingly. 'There's a good future in the sawmills,' he said. 'Is the job fixed up?'

'Not yet, Mr Lynch. They might give me a trial.'

Mr Lynch nodded again, and for a moment the two sat in silence. John Joe could see from the thoughtful way Mr Lynch was regarding his stout that there was something on his mind. Hoping to hear more about the Piccadilly tarts, John Joe patiently waited.

'If your daddy was alive,' said Mr Lynch eventually, 'he might mention this to you, boy.'

He drank more stout and wiped the foam from his lips with the back of his hand. 'I often see you out with Quigley. Is it a good thing to be spending your hours with a performer like that? Quigley's away in the head.'

'You'd be sorry for the poor creature, Mr Lynch.'

Mr Lynch said there was no need to feel sorry for Quigley, since that was the way Quigley was made. He lit another cigarette. He said:

'Maybe they would say to themselves up at the sawmills that you were the same way as Quigley. If he keeps company with Quigley, they might say, aren't they two of a kind?'

'Ah, I don't think they'd bother themselves, Mr Lynch. Sure, if you do the work well what would they have to complain of?'

'Has the manager up there seen you out with Quigley and the jam jars?'

'I don't know, Mr Lynch.'

'Everything I'm saying to you is for your own good in the future. Do you understand that? If I were in your shoes I'd let Quigley look after himself.'

For years his mother had been saying the same to him. Brother Leahy had drawn him aside one day and had pointed out that an elderly dwarf wasn't a suitable companion for a young lad, especially since the dwarf was not sane. 'I see you took no notice of me,' Brother Leahy said six months later. 'Tell me this, young fellow-me-lad, what kind of a conversation do you have with old Quigley?' They talked, John Joe said, about trees and the flowers in the hedgerows. He liked to listen to Quigley, he said, because Quigley had acquired a knowledge of such matters. 'Don't tell me lies,' snapped Brother Leahy, and did not say anything else.

Mrs Keogh returned from Confession. She came breathlessly into the bar, with pink cheeks, her ungloved hands the colour of meat. She was a woman of advanced middle age, a rotund woman who approached the proportions that John Joe most admired. She wore spectacles and had grey hair that was now a bit windswept. Her hat had blown off on the street, she said: she'd nearly gone mad trying to catch it. 'Glory be to God,' she cried when she saw John Joe. 'What's that fellow doing with a bottle of stout?'

'We had a man-to-man talk,' explained Mr Lynch. 'I started him off on the pleasures of the bottle.'

'Are you mad?' shouted Mrs Keogh with a loud laugh. 'He's under age.'

'I came for rashers,' said John Joe. 'A pound of green rashers, Mrs Keogh. The middle cut.'

'You're a shocking man,' said Mrs Keogh to Mr Lynch. She threw off her coat and hat. 'Will you pour me a bottle,' she asked, 'while I attend to this lad? Finish up that now, Mr Dempsey.'

She laughed again. She went away and they heard from the grocery the sound of the bacon machine.

John Joe finished his stout and stood up.

'Good-night, Mr Lynch.'

'Remember about Quigley like a good fellow. When the day will come that you'll want to find a girl to marry, she might be saying you were the same type as Quigley. D'you understand me, John Joe?'

'I do, Mr Lynch.'

He passed through the door in the partition and watched Mrs Keogh slicing the bacon. He imagined her, as Quigley had said he'd seen her, belabouring her late husband with a length of wire. He imagined her as he had seen her himself, taking off her jersey because it was hot in the cellar, and then unzipping her green tweed skirt.

'I've sliced it thin,' she said. 'It tastes better thin, I think.'

'It does surely, Mrs Keogh.'

'Are you better after your stout? Don't go telling your mammy now.' Mrs Keogh laughed again, revealing long, crowded teeth. She weighed the bacon and wrapped it, munching a small piece of lean. 'If there's parsley in your mammy's garden,' she advised, 'chew a bit to get the smell of the stout away, in case she'd be cross with Mr Lynch. Or a teaspoon of tea-leaves.'

'There's no parsley, Mrs Keogh.'

'Wait till I get you the tea then.'

She opened a packet of tea and poured some on to the palm of his hand. She told him to chew it slowly and thoroughly and to let the leaves get into all the crevices of his mouth. She fastened the packet again, saying that no one would miss the little she'd taken from it. 'Four and two for the rashers,' she said.

He paid the money, with his mouth full of dry tea-leaves. He imagined

Mrs Keogh leaning on her elbows on the counter and asking him if he had a kiss for her at all, calling him Mr Dempsey. He imagined her face stuck out towards his and her mouth open, displaying the big teeth, and her tongue damping her lips as the tongues of the Piccadilly tarts did, according to Mr Lynch. With the dryness in his own mouth and a gathering uneasiness in his stomach, his lips would go out to hers and he would taste her saliva.

'Good-night so, Mrs Keogh.'

'Good-night, Mr Dempsey. Tell your mother I was asking for her.'

He left the public house. The wind which had dislodged Mrs Keogh's hat felt fresh and cold on his face. The pink wash on a house across the street seemed pinker than it had seemed before, the ground moved beneath his feet, the street lighting seemed brighter. Youths and girls stood outside the illuminated windows of the small sweet-shops, waiting for the Coliseum to open. Four farmers left Regan's public house and mounted four bicycles and rode away, talking loudly. *Your Murphy Dealer* announced a large coloured sign in the window of a radio shop. Two boys he had known at school came out of a shop eating biscuits from a paper bag. 'How're you, John Joe?' one of them said. 'How's Quigley these days?' They had left the school now: one of them worked in Kilmartin's the hardware's, the other in the Courthouse. They were wearing blue serge suits; their hair had been combed with care, and greased to remain tidy. They would go to the Coliseum, John Joe guessed, and sit behind two girls, giggling and whispering during the programme. Afterwards they would follow the girls for a little while, pretending to have no interest in them; they would buy chips in the chip-shop before they went home.

Thursday, Friday, Saturday, announced the sign outside the Coliseum: *His Girl Friday*. As John Joe read them, the heavy black letters shifted, moving about on green paper that flapped in the wind, fixed with drawing-pins to an unpainted board. Mr Dunne, the owner of the grey Coliseum, arrived on his bicycle and unlocked his property. *Sunday Only: Spencer Tracy in Boom Town*. In spite of the sickness in his stomach and the unpleasant taste of tea-leaves in his mouth, John Joe felt happy and was aware of an inclination to loiter for a long time outside the cinema instead of returning to his mother.

'It's great tonight, John Joe,' Mr Dunne said. 'Are you coming in?'

John Joe shook his head. 'I have to bring rashers home to my mother,' he said. He saw Mrs Dunne approaching with a torch, for the small cinema was a family business. Every night and twice on Sundays, Mr Dunne sold the tickets while his wife showed the customers to their seats. 'I looked in a window one time,' Quigley had said, 'and she was trying to put on her underclothes. Dunne was standing in his socks.'

A man and a girl came out of a sweet-shop next to the cinema, the girl with a box of Urney chocolates in her hand. She was thanking the man for them, saying they were lovely. 'It's a great show tonight, John Joe,' Mrs Dunne said, repeating the statement of her husband, repeating what she and he said every day of their lives. John Joe wagged his head at her. It looked a great show definitely, he said. He imagined her putting on her underclothes. He imagined her one night, unable because of a cold to show the customers to their seats, remaining at home in bed while her husband managed as best he could. 'I made a bit of bread for Mrs Dunne,' his mother said. 'Will you carry it down to her, John Joe?' He rang the bell and waited until she came to the door with a coat over her night-dress. He handed her the bread wrapped in creased brown paper and she asked him to step into the hall out of the wind. 'Will you take a bottle, John Joe?' Mrs Dunne said. He followed her into the kitchen, where she poured them each a glass of stout. 'Isn't it shocking hot in here?' she said. She took off her coat and sat at the kitchen table in her night-dress. 'You're a fine young fellow,' she said, touching his hand with her fingers.

John Joe walked on, past Blackburn's the draper's and Kelly's Atlantic Hotel. A number of men were idling outside the entrance to the bar, smoking cigarettes, one of them leaning on a bicycle. 'There's a dance in Clonakilty,' a tall man said. 'Will we drive over to that?' The others took no notice of this suggestion. They were talking about the price of turkeys.

'How're you, John Joe?' shouted a red-haired youth who worked in the sawmills. 'Quigley was looking for you.'

'I was up in Keogh's for my mother.'

'You're a decent man,' said the youth from the sawmills, going into the bar of Kelly's Hotel.

At the far end of North Street, near the small house where he lived with his mother, he saw Quigley waiting for him. Once he had gone to the Coliseum with Quigley, telling his mother he was going with Kinsella, the boy who occupied the desk next to his at the Christian Brothers'. The occasion, the first and only time that Quigley had visited the Coliseum, had not been a success. Quigley hadn't understood what was happening and had become frightened. He'd begun to mutter and kick the seats in front of him. 'Take him off out of here,' Mr Dunne had whispered, flashing his wife's torch. 'He'll bring the house down.' They had left the cinema after only a few minutes and had gone instead to the chip-shop.

'I looked in a window last night,' said Quigley now, hurrying to his friend's side, 'and, God, I saw a great thing.'

'I was drinking stout with Mr Lynch in Keogh's,' said John Joe. He might tell Quigley about the glory girls that Mr Lynch had advised him against, and about Baker who had struck a bargain with one of them, but it wouldn't be any use because Quigley never listened. No one held a conversation with Quigley: Quigley just talked.

'It was one o'clock in the morning,' said Quigley. His voice continued while John Joe opened the door of his mother's house and closed it behind him. Quigley would wait for him in the street and later on they'd perhaps go down to the chip-shop together.

'John Joe, where've you been?' demanded his mother, coming into the narrow hall from the kitchen. Her face was red from sitting too close to the range, her eyes had anger in them. 'What kept you, John Joe?'

'Mrs Keogh was at Confession.'

'What's that on your teeth?'

'What?'

'You've got dirt on your teeth.'

'I'll brush them then.'

He handed her the rashers. They went together to the kitchen, which was a small, low room with a flagged floor and a dresser that reached to the ceiling. On this, among plates and dishes, was the framed photograph of John Joe's father.

'Were you out with Quigley?' she asked, not believing that Mrs Keogh had kept him waiting for more than an hour.

He shook his head, brushing his teeth at the sink. His back was to her, and he imagined her distrustfully regarding him, her dark eyes gleaming with a kind of jealousy, her small wiry body poised as if to spring on any lie he should utter. Often he felt when he spoke to her that for her the words came physically from his lips, that they were things she could examine after he'd ejected them, in order to assess their truth.

'I talked to Mr Lynch,' he said. 'He was looking after the shop.'

'Is his mother well?'

'He didn't say.'

'He's very good to her.'

She unwrapped the bacon and dropped four rashers on to a pan that was warming on the range. John Joe sat down at the kitchen table. The feeling of euphoria that had possessed him outside the Coliseum was with him no longer; the floor was steady beneath his chair.

'They're good rashers,' his mother said.

'Mrs Keogh cut them thin.'

'They're best thin. They have a nicer taste.'

'Mrs Keogh said that.'

'What did Mr Lynch say to you? Didn't he mention the old mother?'

'He was talking about the war he was in.'

'It nearly broke her heart when he went to join it.'

'It was funny all right.'

'We were a neutral country.'

Mr Lynch would be still sitting in the bar of Keogh's. Every night of his life he sat there with his hat on his head, drinking bottles of stout. Other men would come into the bar and he would discuss matters with them and with Mrs Keogh. He would be drunk at the end of the evening. John Joe wondered if he chewed tea so that the smell of the stout would not be detected by his mother when he returned to her. He would return and tell her some lies about where he had been. He had joined the British Army in order to get away from her for a time, only she'd reached out to him from a dream.

'Lay the table, John Joe.'

He put a knife and a fork for each of them on the table, and found butter and salt and pepper. His mother cut four pieces of griddle bread and placed them to fry on the pan. 'I looked in a window one time,' said the voice of Quigley, 'and Mrs Sullivan was caressing Sullivan's legs.'

'We're hours late with the tea,' his mother said. 'Are you starving, pet?'

'Ah, I am, definitely.'

'I have nice fresh eggs for you.'

It was difficult for her sometimes to make ends meet. He knew it was, yet neither of them had ever said anything. When he went to work in the sawmills it would naturally be easier, with a sum each week to add to the pension.

She fried the eggs, two for him and one for herself. He watched her basting them in her expert way, intent upon what she was doing. Her anger was gone, now that he was safely in the kitchen, waiting for the food she cooked. Mr Lynch would have had his tea earlier in the evening, before he went down to Keogh's. 'I'm going out for a long walk,' he probably said to his mother, every evening after he'd wiped the egg from around his mouth.

'Did he tell you an experience he had in the war?' his mother asked, placing the plate of rashers, eggs and fried bread in front of him. She poured boiling water into a brown enamel teapot and left it on the range to draw.

'He told me about a time they were attacked by the Germans,' John Joe said. 'Mr Lynch was nearly killed.'

'She thought he'd never come back.'

'Oh, he came back all right.'

'He's very good to her now.'

When Brother Leahy twisted the short hairs on his neck and asked him what he'd been dreaming about he usually said he'd been working something out in his mind, like a long-division sum. Once he said he'd been trying to translate a sentence into Irish, and another time he'd said he'd been solving a puzzle that had appeared in the *Sunday Independent*. Recalling Brother Leahy's face, he ate the fried food. His mother repeated that the eggs were fresh. She poured him a cup of tea.

'Have you homework to do?'

He shook his head, silently registering that lie, knowing that there was homework to be done, but wishing instead to accompany Quigley to the chip-shop.

'Then we can listen to the wireless,' she said.

'I thought maybe I'd go out for a walk.'

Again the anger appeared in her eyes. Her mouth tightened, she laid down her knife and fork.

'I thought you'd stop in, John Joe,' she said, 'on your birthday.'

'Ah, well now –'

'I have a little surprise for you.'

She was telling him lies, he thought, just as he had told her lies. She began to eat again, and he could see in her face a reflection of the busyness that had developed in her mind. What could she find to produce as a surprise? She had given him that morning a green shirt that she knew he'd like because he liked the colour. There was a cake that she'd made, some of which they'd have when they'd eaten what was in front of them now. He knew about this birthday cake because he had watched her decorating it with hundreds and thousands: she couldn't suddenly say it was a surprise.

'When I've washed the dishes,' she said, 'we'll listen to the wireless and we'll look at that little thing I have.'

'All right,' he said.

He buttered bread and put a little sugar on the butter, which was a mixture he liked. She brought the cake to the table and cut them each a slice. She said she thought the margarine you got nowadays was not as good as margarine in the past. She turned the wireless on. A woman was singing.

'Try the cake now,' she said. 'You're growing up, John Joe.'

'Fifteen.'

'I know, pet.'

Only Quigley told the truth, he thought. Only Quigley was honest and straightforward and said what was in his mind. Other people told Quigley to keep that kind of talk to himself because they knew it was the truth, because they knew they wanted to think the thoughts that Quigley thought. 'I looked in a window,' Quigley had said to him when he was nine years old, the first time he had spoken to him, 'I saw a man and woman without their clothes on.' Brother Leahy would wish to imagine as Quigley imagined, and as John Joe imagined too. And what did Mr Lynch think about when he walked in gloom with his mother on a Sunday? Did he dream of the medium-sized glory girl he had turned away from because his mother had sent him a Virgin Mary from her dreams? Mr Lynch was not an honest man. It was a lie when he said that shame had kept him from marrying. It was his mother who prevented that, with her dreams of legs on fire and her First Communion statues. Mr Lynch had chosen the easiest course: bachelors might be gloomy on occasion, but they were untroubled men in some respects, just as men who kept away from the glory girls were.

'Isn't it nice cake?'

'Yes,' he said.

'This time next year you'll be in the sawmills.'

'I will.'

'It's good there's work for you.'

'Yes.'

They ate the two pieces of cake and then she cleared away the dishes and put them in the sink. He sat on a chair by the range. The men who'd been loitering outside Kelly's Hotel might have driven over to Clonakilty by now, he thought. They'd be dancing with girls and later they'd go back to their wives and say they'd been somewhere else, playing cards together in Kelly's maybe. Within the grey cement of the Coliseum the girl who'd been given the box of chocolates would be eating them, and the man who was with her would be wanting to put his hands on her.

Why couldn't he say to his mother that he'd drunk three bottles of stout in Keogh's? Why couldn't he say he could see the naked body of Mrs Taggart? Why hadn't he said to Mr Lynch that he should tell the truth about what was in his mind, like Quigley told the truth? Mr Lynch spent his life returning to the scenes that obsessed him, to the Belgian woman on the ground and the tarts of Piccadilly Circus. Yet he spoke of them only to fatherless boys, because it was the only excuse for mentioning them that he'd been able to think up.

'I have this for you,' she said.

She held towards him an old fountain pen that had belonged to his father, a pen he had seen before. She had taken it from a drawer of the dresser, where it was always kept.

'I thought you could have it on your fifteenth birthday,' she said.

He took it from her, a black-and-white pen that hadn't been filled with ink for thirteen years. In the drawer of the dresser there was a pipe of his father's, and a tie-pin and a bunch of keys and a pair of bicycle clips. She had washed and dried the dishes, he guessed, racking her mind to think of something she might offer him as the surprise she'd invented. The pen was the most suitable thing; she could hardly offer him the bicycle clips.

'Wait till I get you the ink,' she said, 'and you can try it out.' From the wireless came the voice of a man advertising household products. 'Ryan's Towel Soap', urged the voice gently. 'No better cleanser.'

He filled the pen from the bottle of ink she handed him. He sat down at the kitchen table again and tried the nib out on the piece of brown paper that Mrs Keogh had wrapped round the rashers and which his mother had neatly folded away for further use.

'Isn't it great it works still?' she said. 'It must be a good pen.'

It's hot in here, he wrote. *Wouldn't you take off your jersey?*

'That's a funny thing to write,' his mother said.

'It came into my head.'

They didn't like him being with Quigley because they knew what Quigley talked about when he spoke the truth. They were jealous because there was no pretence between Quigley and himself. Even though it was only Quigley who talked, there was an understanding between them: being with Quigley was like being alone.

'I want you to promise me a thing,' she said, 'now that you're fifteen.'

He put the cap on the pen and bundled up the paper that had contained the rashers. He opened the top of the range and dropped the paper into it. She would ask him to promise not to hang about with the town's idiot any more. He was a big boy now, he was big enough to own his father's fountain pen, and it wasn't right that he should be going out getting minnows in a jam jar with an elderly affected creature. It would go against his chances in the sawmills.

He listened to her saying what he had anticipated she would say. She went on talking, telling him about his father and the goodness there had been in his father before he fell from the scaffold. She took from the dresser the framed photograph that was so familiar to him and she put it into his hands, telling him to look closely at it. It would have made no difference, he thought, if his father had lived. His father would have been like the others; if ever he'd have dared to mention the nakedness of Mrs Taggart his father would have beaten him with a belt.

'I am asking you for his sake,' she said, 'as much as for my own and for yours, John Joe.'

He didn't understand what she meant by that, and he didn't inquire. He would say what she wished to hear him say, and he would keep his promise to her because it would be the easiest thing to do. Quigley wasn't hard to push away, you could tell him to get away like you'd tell a dog. It was funny that they should think that it would make much difference to him now, at this stage, not having Quigley to listen to.

'All right,' he said.

'You're a good boy, John Joe. Do you like the pen?'

'It's a lovely pen.'

'You might write better with that one.'

She turned up the volume of the wireless and together they sat by the range, listening to the music. To live in a shed like Quigley did would not be too bad: to have his food carried down through a garden by a niece, to go about the town in that special way, alone with his thoughts. Quigley did not have to pretend to the niece who fed him. He didn't have to say he'd been for a walk when he'd been drinking in Keogh's, or that he'd been playing cards with men when he'd been dancing in Clonakilty. Quigley didn't have to chew tea and keep quiet. Quigley talked; he said the words he wanted to say. Quigley was lucky being how he was.

'I will go to bed now,' he said eventually.

They said good-night to one another, and he climbed the stairs to his room. She would rouse him in good time, she called after him. 'Have a good sleep,' she said.

He closed the door of his room and looked with affection at his bed, for in the end there was only that. It was a bed that, sagging, held him in its centre and wrapped him warmly. There was ornamental brass-work at the head but not at the foot, and on the web of interlocking wire the hair mattress was thin. John Joe shed his clothes, shedding also the small town and his mother and Mr Lynch and the fact that he, on his fifteenth birthday, had drunk his first stout and had chewed tea. He entered his iron bed and the face of Mr Lynch passed from his mind and the voices of boys telling stories about freshly married couples faded away also. No one said to him now that he must not keep company with a crazed dwarf. In his iron bed, staring into the darkness, he made of the town what he wished to make of it, knowing that he would not be drawn away from his dreams by the tormenting fingers of a Christian Brother. In his iron bed he heard again only the voice of the town's idiot and then that voice, too, was there no more. He travelled alone, visiting in his way the women of the town, adored and adoring, more alive in his bed than ever he was at the Christian Brothers' School, or in the grey Coliseum, or in the chip-shop, or Keogh's public house, or his mother's kitchen, more alive than ever he would be at the sawmills. In his bed he entered a paradise: it was grand being alone.

Kinkies

'Look,' said Mr Belhatchet in the office one Thursday afternoon, 'want you back in Trilby Mews.'

'Me, Mr Belhatchet?'

'Whole stack new designs. Sort them out.'

A year ago, when Eleanor had applied for the position at Sweetawear, he'd walked into Mr Syatt's office, a young man with a dark bush of hair. She'd been expecting someone much older, about the age of Mr Syatt himself: Mr Belhatchet, a smiling, graceful figure, was in his mid-twenties. 'Happy to know you,' he'd said in an American manner but without any trace of an American accent. He'd been sharply dressed, in a dark grey suit that contained both a blue and a white pinstripe. He wore a discreetly jewelled ring on the little finger of his left hand. 'Mr Belhatchet,' Mr Syatt had explained, 'will be your immediate boss. Sweetawear, of which he is in command, is one small part of our whole organization. There is, as well, Lisney and Company, Harraps, Tass and Prady Designs, Swiftway Designs, Dress-U, etcetera, etcetera.' There was a canteen in the basement, Mr Syatt had added; the Christmas bonus was notably generous. Mr Syatt spoke in a precise, rather old-fashioned manner, punctuating his sentences carefully. 'Use these?' Mr Belhatchet had more casually offered, holding out a packet of Greek cigarettes, and she, wearing that day a high-necked blouse frilled with lace, had smilingly replied that she didn't smoke.

'All righty, Eleanor?' pursued Mr Belhatchet a year later, referring to his suggestion that she should help him sort out dress designs in Trilby Mews. 'Okayie?'

'Yes, of course, Mr Belhatchet.'

Trilby Mews was where Mr Belhatchet lived. He'd often mentioned it and Eleanor had often imagined it, seeing his flat and the mews itself as being rather glamorous. Occasionally he telephoned from there, saying he was in bed or in the bath. He couldn't bear a room that did not contain a telephone.

They left the office at a quarter past six, having finished off what work there was. Eleanor was wearing a pale blue suit in tweed so fine that it might have been linen, and a pale blue blouse. Around her neck there was a double row of small cultured pearls. Her shoes, in darker blue, were square-toed, as current fashion decreed.

That evening she was due to attend the night-school where, once a week, she learned Spanish. It wouldn't matter missing a class because she never had in the past. Several of the other girls missed classes regularly and it never seemed to matter much. They'd be surprised not to see her all the same.

In the taxi Mr Belhatchet lit a Greek cigarette and remarked that he was exhausted. He'd had an exhausting week, she agreed, which was true, because he'd had to fly to Rome in order to look at designs, and then to Germany. In the taxi he said he'd spent all of Tuesday night examining the Italian designs, discussing them with Signor Martelli.

'Dog's Head,' he suddenly ordered the taxi-driver, and the taxi-driver, who appeared to know Mr Belhatchet personally, nodded.

'Join us, Bill?' Mr Belhatchet invited as he paid the fare, but the taxi-driver, addressing Mr Belhatchet with equal familiarity, declined to do so on the grounds that the delay would cost him some trade.

'Two gin, tonic,' Mr Belhatchet ordered in the Dog's Head. 'Large, Dorrie,' he said to the plump barmaid. 'How keeping?'

The barmaid smiled at Eleanor even though the bar was full and she was busy. She was keeping well, she told Mr Belhatchet, whom she addressed, as the taxi-driver had, as Andy.

A Mr Logan, who taught golf at the night-school, had asked Eleanor to have a drink a few times and he'd taken her to a place that wasn't unlike the Dog's Head. She'd quite liked Mr Logan at first, even though he was nearly thirty years older than she was. On the third occasion he'd held her hand as they sat in a corner of a lounge bar, stroking the back of it. He'd confessed then that he was married – to a woman who'd once dropped, deliberately, a seven-pound weight on his foot. He wanted to leave her, he said, and had then suggested that Eleanor might like to accompany him to Bury St Edmunds the following Saturday. They could stay in a hotel called the Queen's Arms, he suggested, which he'd often stayed in before and which was comfortable and quiet, with excellent food. Eleanor declined, and had since only seen Mr Logan hurrying through the corridors of the night-school. He hadn't invited her to have another drink with him.

Mr Belhatchet consumed his gin and tonic very quickly. He spoke to a few people in the bar and at one point, while speaking to a man with a moustache, he put his arm round Eleanor's shoulders and said that Eleanor was his secretary. He didn't introduce her to any of the others, and he didn't reveal her name to the man with the moustache.

'Feel better,' he said when he'd finished his drink. He looked at hers and she drank the remainder of it as quickly as she could, finding it difficult because the ice made her teeth cold. She wanted to say to Mr Belhatchet that she was just an ordinary girl – in case, later on, there should be any misunderstanding. But although she formed a sentence to that effect and commenced to utter it, Mr Belhatchet didn't appear to be interested.

'I just thought –' she said, smiling.

'You're fantastic,' said Mr Belhatchet.

They walked to Trilby Mews, Mr Belhatchet addressing familiarly a newsvendor on the way. The flat was much as she had imagined it, a small, luxuriously furnished apartment with green blinds half drawn against the glare of the evening sun. The sitting-room was full of small pieces of Victorian furniture and there was a large sofa in purple velvet, fashionably buttoned. The walls were covered with framed pictures, but in the green gloom Eleanor couldn't see what any of them were of.

'Want loo?' suggested Mr Belhatchet, leading her down a short passage, the walls of which also bore framed pictures that couldn't be properly seen. ''Nother drink,' he said, opening the lavatory door and ushering her into it. She said she'd better not have another drink, not really if she was to keep a clear head. She laughed while she spoke, realizing that her head was far from clear already. 'Fix you one,' said Mr Belhatchet, closing the door on her.

The lavatory had a telephone in a nook in the wall and the seat was covered in brown-and-white fur. There were framed picture postcards on the walls, seaside cards with suggestive messages. They didn't seem the kind of thing that should be so expensively framed, Eleanor considered, and was surprised to see them there, especially in such numbers. One or two, she noticed, were in German.

'Same 'gain,' said Mr Belhatchet in the sitting-room. 'Sit yourself, Ellie.'

She couldn't see the designs he'd spoken of: she'd imagined they'd be spread all over the place, propped up on chairs, even on the walls, because that was the way he liked to surround himself with designs when he was making a selection in the office. She couldn't even see a pile anywhere, but she put this down to the gloom that pervaded the sitting-room. It surprised her, though, that he'd addressed her as Ellie, which he'd never done before. Nobody, in fact, had ever called her Ellie before.

'Know Nick's?' asked Mr Belhatchet. 'Nick's Diner? Okayie?'

He smiled at her, blowing out Greek cigarette smoke.

'What about the designs?' she asked, smiling at him also.

'Eat first,' he said, and he picked up a green telephone and dialled a number. 'Belhatchet,' he said. 'Andy. Table two, nine-thirty. All righty?'

She said it was very kind of him to invite her to dinner, thinking that it couldn't be more than half past seven and that for almost two hours apparently they were going to sit in Trilby Mews drinking gin and tonic. She hoped it was going to be all right.

Besides Mr Logan, many men – most of them much younger than Mr Logan – had taken Eleanor out. One, called Robert, had repeatedly driven her in his yellow sportscar to a country club on the London–Guildford road called The Spurs. At half past three one morning he'd suggested that they should walk in the wood behind the country club: Eleanor had declined. Earlier that evening he'd said he loved her, but he never even telephoned her again, not after she declined to walk in the woods with him.

Other men spoke of love to her also. They kissed her and pressed themselves against her. Occasionally she felt the warm tip of a tongue exploring one of her ears and she was naturally obliged to wriggle away from it, hastily putting on lipstick as a sign that the interlude was over. She was beautiful, they said, men she met at the night-school or men employed in Sweetawear or Lisney and Company or Dress-U. But when she resisted their ultimate advances they didn't again say she was beautiful; more often than not they didn't say anything further to her at all. She'd explained a few times that she didn't want to anticipate marriage because she believed that marriage was special. But when it came to the point, although stating that they loved her, not one of them proposed marriage to her. Not that any of them had ever been right, which was something she felt most strongly after they'd made their ultimate advances.

'Use grass?' inquired Mr Belhatchet and for a moment, because of his economical manner of speech, she didn't know what he was talking about: use grass for what? she wondered, and shook her head.

'Mind?' asked Mr Belhatchet, breaking open a fresh cigarette and poking what looked like another kind of tobacco among the leaves that were already there. He fiddled around for some time, adding and taking away, and then placed the untidy-looking cigarette between his lips. She asked again about the designs, but he didn't seem to hear her.

Eleanor didn't enjoy the next two hours, sipping at her drink while Mr Belhatchet smoked and drank and asked her a series of economically framed questions about herself. Later, while they waited for a taxi, he said he felt marvellous. He put his arm round her shoulders and told her that the first day he saw her he'd thought she was fabulous.

'Fabulous,' he said in Nick's Diner, referring to a bowl of *crudités* that had been placed in front of them. He asked her then if she liked him, smiling at her again, smoking another Greek cigarette.

'Well, of course, Mr Belhatchet.'

'Andy. What like 'bout me?'

'Well –'

'Ha, ha, ha,' said Mr Belhatchet, hitting the table with the palm of his left hand. He was smiling so much now that the smile seemed to Eleanor to be unnatural. Nevertheless, she tried to keep smiling herself. None of the girls at Sweetawear had ever told her that there was anything the matter with Mr Belhatchet. She'd never thought herself that there might be something the matter with him: apart from his mode of speech he'd always seemed totally normal. His mother had set him up in Sweetawear, people said, occasionally adding that he'd certainly made a go of it.

'Fabulous,' said Mr Belhatchet when a waiter served them with fillet steak encased in pastry.

They drank a red wine that she liked the taste of. She said, making conversation, that it was a lovely restaurant, and when he didn't reply she said it was the best restaurant she'd ever been in.

'Fabulous,' said Mr Belhatchet.

At eleven o'clock she suggested that perhaps they should return to Trilby Mews to examine the designs. She knew, even while she spoke, that she shouldn't be going anywhere that night with Mr Belhatchet. She knew that if he was anyone else she'd have smiled and said she must go home now because she had to get up in the morning. But Mr Belhatchet, being her office boss, was different. It was all going to be much harder with Mr Belhatchet.

'Age you now, Ellie?' he asked in the taxi, and she told him she'd become twenty-seven the previous Tuesday, while he'd been in Rome.

'Lovely,' he said. 'Fabulous.'

He was still smiling and she thought he must be drunk except that his speech was in no way slurred.

'It's really so late,' she said as the taxi paused in traffic. 'Perhaps we should leave the designs for tonight, Mr Belhatchet?'

'Andy.'

'Perhaps, Andy –'

'Take morning off, Ellie.'

As they entered the flat he asked her again if she'd like to use the lavatory and reminded her where it was. While she was in there the telephone in the nook beside her rang, causing her to jump. It rang for only a moment, before he picked up one of the other extensions. When she entered the sitting-room he was speaking into the receiver, apparently to Signor Martelli in Rome. 'Fabulous,' he was saying. 'No, truly.'

He'd turned several lights on and pulled the green blinds fully down. The pictures that crowded the walls were more conventional than those in the lavatory, reproductions of drawings mainly, limbs and bones and heads scattered over a single sheet, all of them belonging to the past.

"*vederci*,' said Mr Belhatchet, replacing his green telephone.

In the room there was no pile of designs and she said to herself that in a moment Mr Belhatchet would make a suggestion. She would deal with it as best she could; if the worst came to the worst she would naturally have to leave Sweetawear.

'Fancy drop brandy?' offered Mr Belhatchet.

'Thanks awfully, but I really think I'd better –'

'Just get designs,' he said, leaving the sitting-room.

He returned with a stack of designs which he arrayed around the room just as he would have done in the office. He asked her to assess them while he poured both of them some orange juice.

'Oh, lovely,' she said, because she really felt like orange juice.

The designs were of trouser-suits, a selection of ideas from four different designers. One would be chosen in the end and Sweetawear would manufacture it on a large scale and in a variety of colours.

'Fancy that,' he said, returning with the orange juice and pointing at a drawing with the point of his right foot.

'Yes. And that, the waistcoat effect.'

'Right.'

She sipped her juice and he sipped his. They discussed the designs in detail, taking into consideration the fact that some would obviously be more economical to mass-produce than others. They whittled them down to three, taking about half an hour over that. He'd come to a final decision, he said, some time tomorrow, and the way he said it made her think that he'd come to it on his own, and that his choice might even be one of the rejected designs.

She sat down on the buttoned sofa, feeling suddenly strange, wondering if she'd drunk too much. Mr Belhatchet, she saw, had pushed a few of the designs off an embroidered arm-chair and was sitting down also. He had taken the jacket of his suit off and was slowly loosening his tie.

'Okayie?' he inquired, and leaned his head back and closed his eyes.

She stood up. The floor was peculiar beneath her feet, seeming closer to her, as though her feet had become directly attached to her knees. It moved, like the deck of a ship. She sat down again.

'Fantastic,' said Mr Belhatchet.

'I'm afraid I've had a little too much to drink.'

'God, those days,' said Mr Belhatchet. 'Never 'gain. Know something, Ellie?'

'Mr Belhatchet –'

'Mother loved me, Ellie. Like I was her sweetheart, Mother loved me.'

'Mr Belhatchet, what's happening?'

She heard her own voice, as shrill as a bird's, in the bright, crowded room. She didn't want to move from the sofa. She wanted to put her feet up but she felt she might not be able to move them and was frightened to try in case she couldn't. She closed her eyes and felt herself moving upwards, floating in the room, with a kaleidoscope in each eyelid. 'Mr Belhatchet!' she cried out. 'Mr Belhatchet! Mr Belhatchet!'

She opened her eyes and saw that he had risen from his chair and was standing above her. He was smiling; his face was different.

'I feel,' she cried, but he interrupted her before she could say what she felt.

'Love,' he murmured.

He lifted her legs and placed them on the sofa. He took her shoes off and then returned to the chair he'd occupied before.

'You made us drunk,' she heard her own voice crying, shrill again, shrieking almost in the room. Yet in another way she felt quite tranquil.

'We're going high,' he murmured. 'All righty? We had it in our orange juice.'

She cried out again with part of her. She was floating above the room, she said. The colours of the trouser-suits that were all around her were vivid. They came at her garishly from the paper; the drawn heads of the girls were strange, like real people. The purple of the buttoned sofa was vivid also, and the green of the blinds. All over the walls the pictures of limbs and bones were like glass cases containing what the pictures contained, startling on a soft background. Bottles gleamed, and silver here and there, and brass. There was polished ebony in the room, and ivory.

'You're riding high, Ellie,' Mr Belhatchet said and his voice seemed a long way away, although when she looked at him he seemed nearer and more beautiful than before. He was insane, she thought: there was beauty in his insanity. She never wanted to leave the vivid room above which and through which she floated, depending on the moment. She closed her eyes and there were coloured orchids.

Eleanor slept, or seemed to sleep, and all through her dreams Mr Belhatchet's voice came to her, speaking about his mother. At the same time she herself was back at school, at Springfield Comprehensive, where Miss Whitehead was teaching Class 2 French. The clothes of Miss Whitehead were beautiful and the hairs on her face were as beautiful as the hair on her head, and the odour of her breath was sweet.

'Mother died,' said Mr Belhatchet. 'She left me, Ellie.'

He talked about a house. His voice described a house situated among hills, a large house, remote and rich, with an exotic garden where his mother walked in a white dress, wearing dark glasses because of the sunshine.

'She left me the little business,' he said. 'The pretty little business. Flair: she had flair, Ellie.'

He said he could remember being in his mother's womb. She'd taught him to remember, he said. They read novels together. His mother's hand took his and stroked the flesh of her arm with it.

He took off his shirt and sat in the embroidered chair with the upper half of his body naked. His feet, she saw, were naked also.

'I loved her too,' he said. 'She's back with me now. I can taste her milk, Ellie.'

He was like a god in the embroidered chair, his bushy hair wild on his head, his pale flesh gleaming. His eyes seemed far back in his skull, gazing at her from the depths of caverns. Time did not seem to be passing.

In the house among the hills there were parties, he said, and afterwards quiet servants gathered glasses from the lawns. Cars moved on gravel early in the morning, driving away. Couples were found asleep beneath trees.

She wanted to take some of her own clothes off as Mr Belhatchet had, but her arms were heavy and in time, she guessed, he would take them off for her and that would be beautiful too. His eyes were a rare blue, his flesh was like the flesh of flowers. The room was saturated with colours that were different now, subtly changing: the colours of the trouser-suits and the purple of the sofa and the coloured threads of the embroidered chair and the green blinds and telephone. The colours were liquid in the room, gently flowing, one into another. People stood on banks of foliage, people at Mrs Belhatchet's parties. Mrs Belhatchet stood with her son.

She would like to have children, Eleanor said; she would like to be married. She'd noticed a house once, in Gwendolyn Avenue in Putney, not far from where her bed-sitting-room was: she described it, saying she'd once dreamed she lived there, married to a man with delicate hands.

'I love you,' she said, knowing that she was speaking to that man, a man she had always imagined, who would marry her in a church and take her afterwards to Biarritz for a honeymoon.

'I love you,' she said again, with her eyes closed. 'I've waited all my life.'

She wanted him to come to her, to lie beside her on the sofa and gently to take her clothes off. In the room they would anticipate marriage because marriage was certain between them, because there was perfection in their relationship, because in every detail and in every way they understood each other. They were part of one another; only death could part them now.

'Come to me,' she said with her eyes still closed. 'Oh, come to me now.'

'Mother,' he said.

'No, no –'

'Up here you can be anyone, Ellie. Up here where everything is as we wish it.'

He went on speaking, but she couldn't hear what he said, and it didn't matter. She murmured, but she didn't hear her own words either. And then, a long time later it seemed, she heard a voice more clearly.

'The truth is in this room,' Mr Belhatchet was saying. 'I couldn't ravish anyone, Mother.'

She opened her eyes and saw Mr Belhatchet with his bushy hair, still looking like a god.

'My friend,' she said, closing her eyes again.

She spoke of her bed-sitting-room in East Putney and the posters she'd bought to decorate its walls, and the two lamps with pretty jade-coloured shades that she'd bought in the British Home Stores. She'd said to her landlady that she was determined to make a home of her bed-sitting-room and the landlady said that that sounded a first-class idea. Her landlady gave her a brass gong she didn't want.

In the room their two voices spoke together.

'I put my arms around her,' he said. 'With my arms around her and hers round me, it is beautiful.'

'It is beautiful here,' she said. 'The foliage, the leaves. It is beautiful in the garden of your mother's house.'

'Yes,' he said.

'I am waiting here for a tender man who wouldn't ever hurt me.'

'That's beautiful too,' he said. 'Your clothes are beautiful. Your blue clothes and the pearls at your neck, and your shoes. We are happy in this present moment.'

'Yes.'

'We have floated away.'

They ceased to speak. Time, of which as they dreamed and imagined neither of them was aware, passed normally in the room. At half past six Eleanor, still feeling happy but by now more in control of her limbs, slowly pushed herself from the sofa and stood up. The floor swayed less beneath her feet; the colours in the room, though vivid still, were less so than they had been. Mr Belhatchet was asleep.

Eleanor went to the lavatory and when she returned to the sitting-room she did not lie down on the sofa again. She stood instead in the centre of the room, gazing around it, at Mr Belhatchet with bare feet and a bare chest, asleep in his embroidered chair, at the designs of trouser-suits and the pictures of limbs and bones. 'Mother,' murmured Mr Belhatchet in his sleep, in a voice that was a whisper.

She left the flat, moving slowly and gently closing the door behind her. She descended the stairs and stepped out into Trilby Mews, into fresh early-morning air.

Police Constable Edwin Lloyd found Eleanor an hour later. She was lying on the pavement outside a betting-shop in Garrad Street, W.1. He saw the still body from a distance and hurried towards it, believing he had a death on his hands. 'I fell down,' Eleanor explained as he helped her to rise again. 'I'm tired.'

'Drugs,' said Police Constable Lloyd in Garrad Street police station, and another officer, a desk sergeant, sighed. 'Cup of tea, miss?' Constable Lloyd offered. 'Nice hot tea?'

A middle-aged policewoman searched Eleanor's clothing in case there were further drugs on her person.

'Pretty thing like you,' the woman said. 'Shame, dear.'

They brought her tea and Eleanor drank it, spilling some over her pale blue suit because her hands were shaking. Constable Lloyd, returning to his beat, paused by the door.

'Will she be OK?' he asked, and his two colleagues said that they considered she would be.

In the police station the colours were harsh and ugly, not at all like the colours there'd been in Mr Belhatchet's flat. And the faces of the desk sergeant and the policewoman were unpleasant also: the pores of their skin were large, like the cells of a honeycomb. There was something the matter with their mouths and their hands, and the uniforms they wore, and the place they occupied. The wooden seat was uncomfortable, the pages of a book in front of the desk sergeant were torn and grubby, the air stank of stale cigarette smoke. The man and the woman were regarding her as skeletons might, their teeth bared at her, their fingers predatory, like animals' claws. She hated their eyes. She couldn't drink the tea they'd given her because it caused nausea in her stomach.

The noise in the room, a distant fuzziness, was her voice. It spoke of what her mind was full of: Mrs Belhatchet and her son in the garden he had described. Servants collected glasses that were broken and jagged; their hands had blood on them. Couples were found dead beneath trees. The garden was all as ugly as the room she was in now, as dirty and as unpleasant.

And then it was different. In the garden they came at her, Mr Logan of the night-school, Robert in his yellow sportscar, and all the others. The touch of their hands was hard, like metal; she moaned in distress at their nakedness. They laughed because of that, pressing her apart, grunting with the passion of beasts. Through blood she screamed, and the voices of the men said that her tortured face was ecstasy to them. They longed for her cries of pain. They longed to wrap her in the filth of their sweat.

Their voices ceased and she heard the fuzziness again, and then it ceased also.

'Eh now,' murmured the desk sergeant soothingly.

'I can't help it,' she said, weeping. 'I'm frightened of it, and disgusted. I can't help it; I don't know why I'm like this.'

'Just drink your tea and stop quiet, dear,' the policewoman suggested. 'Best to stop quiet, dear.'

Eleanor shook her head and for a moment her vision was blurred. She closed her eyes and forgot where she was. She opened them and found that her vision had cleared: she saw that she was in a grimy police station with two ugly people. Tea was spilt over her suit and there were drops of tea on her shoes. Her office boss had given her a drug in orange juice: she had experienced certain dreams and fantasies and had conducted with him a formless conversation. She'd never be able to return to the offices of Sweetawear.

'He floats away,' she heard a voice crying out and realized that it was her own. 'He lies there entranced, floating away from his fear and his disgust. "The truth's in this room," he says – when what he means is the opposite. Poor wretched thing!'

She wept and the policewoman went to her and tried to help her, but Eleanor struck at her, shrieking obscenities. 'Everywhere there's ugliness,' she cried. 'His mother loved him with a perverted passion. He floats away from that.'

Tears fell from her eyes, dripping on to her clothes and on to the floor by her feet. She wanted to be dead, she whispered, to float away for ever from the groping hands. She wanted to be dead, she said again.

They took her to a cell; she went with them quietly. She lay down and slept immediately, and the desk sergeant and the policewoman returned to their duties. 'Worse than drink,' the woman said. 'The filth that comes out of them; worse than a navvy.'

'She's hooked, you know,' the desk sergeant remarked. 'She's hooked on that floating business. That floating away.'

The policewoman sighed and nodded. They sounded like two of a kind, she commented: the girl and the chap she'd been with.

'Kinkies,' said the desk sergeant. 'Extraordinary, people getting like that.'

'Bloody disgraceful,' said the policewoman.

Going Home

'Mulligatawny soup,' Carruthers said in the dining-car. 'Roast beef, roast potatoes, Yorkshire pudding, mixed vegetables.'

'And madam?' murmured the waiter.

Miss Fanshawe said she'd have the same. The waiter thanked her. Carruthers said:

'Miss Fanshawe'll take a medium dry sherry. Pale ale for me, please.'

The waiter paused. He glanced at Miss Fanshawe, shaping his lips.

'I'm sixteen and a half,' Carruthers said. 'Oh, and a bottle of Beaune. 1962.'

It was the highlight of every term and every holiday for Carruthers, coming like a no man's land between the two: the journey with Miss Fanshawe to their different homes. Not once had she officially complained, either to his mother or to the school. She wouldn't do that; it wasn't in Miss Fanshawe to complain officially. And as for him, he couldn't help himself.

'Always Beaune on a train,' he said now, 'because of all the burgundies it travels happiest.'

'Thank you, sir,' the waiter said.

'Thank *you*, old chap.'

The waiter went, moving swiftly in the empty dining-car. The train slowed and then gathered speed again. The fields it passed through were bright with sunshine; the water of a stream glittered in the distance.

'You shouldn't lie about your age,' Miss Fanshawe reproved, smiling to show she hadn't been upset by the lie. But lies like that, she explained, could get a waiter into trouble.

Carruthers, a sharp-faced boy of thirteen, laughed a familiar harsh laugh. He said he didn't like the waiter, a remark that Miss Fanshawe ignored.

'What weather!' she remarked instead. 'Just look at those weeping willows!' She hadn't ever noticed them before, she added, but Carruthers contradicted that, reminding her that she had often before remarked on those weeping willows. She smiled, with false vagueness in her face, slightly shaking her head. 'Perhaps it's just that everything looks so different this lovely summer. What will you do, Carruthers? Your mother took you to Greece last year, didn't she? It's almost a shame to leave England, I always think, when the weather's like this. So green in the long warm days –'

'Miss Fanshawe, why are you pretending nothing has happened?'

'Happened? My dear, what has happened?'

Carruthers laughed again, and looked through the window at cows resting in the shade of an oak tree. He said, still watching the cows, craning his neck to keep them in view:

'Your mind is thinking about what has happened and all the time you're attempting to make ridiculous conversation about the long warm days. Your heart is beating fast, Miss Fanshawe; your hands are trembling. There are two little dabs of red high up on your cheeks, just beneath your spectacles. There's a pink flush all over your neck. If you were alone, Miss Fanshawe, you'd be crying your heart out.'

Miss Fanshawe, who was thirty-eight, fair-haired and untouched by beauty, said that she hadn't the foggiest idea what Carruthers was talking about. He shook his head, implying that she lied. He said:

'Why are we being served by a man whom neither of us likes when we should be served by someone else? Just look at those weeping willows, you say.'

'Don't be silly, Carruthers.'

'What has become, Miss Fanshawe, of the other waiter?'

'Now please don't start any nonsense. I'm tired and –'

'It was he who gave me a taste for pale ale, d'you remember that? In your company, Miss Fanshawe, on this train. It was he who told us that Beaune travels best. Have a cig, Miss Fanshawe?'

'No, and I wish you wouldn't either.'

'Actually Mrs Carruthers allows me the odd smoke these days. Ever since my thirteenth birthday, May the 26th. How can she stop me, she says, when day and night she's at it like a factory chimney herself?'

'Your birthday's May the 26th? I never knew. Mine's two days later.' She spoke hastily, and with an eagerness that was as false as the vague expression her face had borne a moment ago.

'Gemini, Miss Fanshawe.'

'Yes: Gemini. Queen Victoria –'

'The sign of passion. Here comes the interloper.'

The waiter placed sherry before Miss Fanshawe and beer in front of Carruthers. He murmured deferentially, inclining his head.

'We've just been saying,' Carruthers remarked, 'that you're a new one on this line.'

'Newish, sir. A month – no, tell a lie, three weeks yesterday.'

'We knew your predecessor.'

'Oh yes, sir?'

'He used to say this line was as dead as a doornail. Actually, he enjoyed not having anything to do. Remember, Miss Fanshawe?'

Miss Fanshawe shook her head. She sipped her sherry, hoping the waiter would have the sense to go away. Carruthers said:

'In all the time Miss Fanshawe and I have been travelling together there hasn't been a solitary soul besides ourselves in this dining-car.'

The waiter said it hardly surprised him. You didn't get many, he agreed, and added, smoothing the tablecloth, that it would just be a minute before the soup was ready.

'Your predecessor,' Carruthers said, 'was a most extraordinary man.'

'Oh yes, sir?'

'He had the gift of tongues. He was covered in freckles.'

'I see, sir.'

'Miss Fanshawe here had a passion for him.'

The waiter laughed. He lingered for a moment and then, since Carruthers was silent, went away.

'Now look here, Carruthers,' Miss Fanshawe began.

'Don't you think Mrs Carruthers is the most vulgar woman you've ever met?'

'I wasn't thinking of your mother. I will not have you talk like this to the waiter. Please now.'

'She wears a scent called "In Love", by Norman Hartnell. A woman of fifty, as thin as fuse wire. My God!'

'Your mother –'

'My mother doesn't concern you – oh, I agree. Still you don't want to deliver me to the female smelling of drink and tobacco smoke. I always brush my teeth in the lavatory, you know. For your sake, Miss Fanshawe.'

'Please don't engage the waiter in conversation. And please don't tell lies about the waiter who was here before. It's ridiculous the way you go on –'

'You're tired, Miss Fanshawe.'

'I'm always tired at the end of term.'

'That waiter used to say –'

'Oh, for heaven's sake, stop about that waiter!'

'I'm sorry.' He seemed to mean it, but she knew he didn't. And even when he spoke again, when his voice was softer, she knew that he was still pretending. 'What shall we talk about?' he asked, and with a weary cheerfulness she reminded him that she'd wondered what he was going to do in the holidays. He didn't reply. His head was bent. She knew that he was smiling.

'I'll walk beside her,' he said. 'In Rimini and Venice. In Zürich maybe.

By Lake Lugano. Or the Black Sea. New faces will greet her in an American Bar in Copenhagen. Or near the Spanish Steps – in Babbington's English Tea-Rooms. Or in Bandol or Cassis, the Ritz, the Hotel Excelsior in old Madrid. What shall we talk about, Miss Fanshawe?'

'You could tell me more. Last year in Greece –'

'I remember once we talked about guinea-pigs. I told you how I killed a guinea-pig that Mrs Carruthers gave me. Another time we talked about Rider Minor. D'you remember that?'

'Yes, but let's not –'

'McGullam was unpleasant to Rider Minor in the changing-room. McGullam and Travers went after Rider Minor with a little piece of wood.'

'You told me, Carruthers.'

He laughed.

'When I first arrived at Ashleigh Court the only person who spoke to me was Rider Minor. And of course the Sergeant-Major. The Sergeant-Major told me never to take to cigs. He described the lungs of a friend of his.'

'He was quite right.'

'Yes, he was. Cigs can give you a nasty disease.'

'I wish you wouldn't smoke.'

'I like your hat.'

'Soup, madam,' the waiter murmured. 'Sir.'

'Don't you like Miss Fanshawe's hat?' Carruthers smiled, pointing at Miss Fanshawe, and when the waiter said that the hat was very nice Carruthers asked him his name.

Miss Fanshawe dipped a spoon into her soup. The waiter offered her a roll. His name, he said, was Atkins.

'Are you wondering about us, Mr Atkins?'

'Sir?'

'Everyone has a natural curiosity, you know.'

'I see a lot of people in my work, sir.'

'Miss Fanshawe's an undermatron at Ashleigh Court Preparatory School for Boys. They use her disgracefully at the end of term – patching up clothes so that the mothers won't complain, packing trunks, sorting out laundry. From dawn till midnight Miss Fanshawe's on the trot. That's why she's tired.'

Miss Fanshawe laughed. 'Take no notice of him,' she said. She broke her roll and buttered a piece of it. She pointed at wheat ripening in a field. The harvest would be good this year, she said.

'At the end of each term,' Carruthers went on, 'she has to sit with me on this train because we travel in the same direction. I'm out of her authority really, since the term is over. Still, she has to keep an eye.'

The waiter, busy with the wine, said he understood. He raised his eyebrows at Miss Fanshawe and winked, but she did not encourage this, pretending not to notice it.

'Imagine, Mr Atkins,' Carruthers said, 'a country house in the mock Tudor style, with bits built on to it: a rackety old gymn and an art-room, and changing-rooms that smell of perspiration. There are a hundred and three boys at Ashleigh Court, in narrow iron beds with blue rugs on them, which Miss Fanshawe has to see are all kept tidy. She does other things as well: she wears a white overall and gives out medicines. She pours out cocoa in the dining-hall and at eleven o'clock every morning she hands each boy four *petit beurre* biscuits. She isn't allowed to say Grace. It has to be a master who says Grace: "For what we're about to receive ..." Or the Reverend T. L. Edwards, who owns and runs the place, T.L.E., known to generations as a pervert. He pays boys, actually.'

The waiter, having meticulously removed a covering of red foil from the top of the wine bottle, wiped the cork with a napkin before attempting to draw it. He glanced quickly at Miss Fanshawe to see if he could catch her eye in order to put her at her ease with an understanding gesture, but she appeared to be wholly engaged with her soup.

'The Reverend Edwards is a law unto himself,' Carruthers said. 'Your predecessor was intrigued by him.'

'Please take no notice of him.' She tried to sound bracing, looking up suddenly and smiling at the waiter.

'The headmaster accompanied you on the train, did he, sir?'

'No, no, no, no. The Reverend Edwards was never on this train in his life. No, it was simply that your predecessor was interested in life at Ashleigh Court. He would stand there happily listening while we told him the details: you could say he was fascinated.'

At this Miss Fanshawe made a noise that was somewhere between a laugh and a denial.

'You could pour the Beaune now, Mr Atkins,' Carruthers suggested.

The waiter did so, pausing for a moment, in doubt as to which of the two he should offer a little of the wine to taste. Carruthers nodded to him, indicating that it should be he. The waiter complied and when Carruthers had given his approval he filled both their glasses and lifted from before them their empty soup-plates.

'I've asked you not to behave like that,' she said when the waiter had gone.

'Like what, Miss Fanshawe?'

'You know, Carruthers.'

'The waiter and I were having a general conversation. As before, Miss Fanshawe, with the other waiter. Don't you remember? Don't you remember my telling him how I took forty of Hornsby's football cards? And drank the Communion wine in the Reverend's cupboard?'

'I don't believe –'

'And I'll tell you another thing. I excused myself into Rider Minor's gum-boots.'

'Please leave the waiter alone. Please let's have no scenes this time, Carruthers.'

'There weren't scenes with the other waiter. He enjoyed everything we said to him. You could see him quite clearly trying to visualize Ashleigh Court, and Mrs Carruthers in her awful clothes.'

'He visualized nothing of the sort. You gave him drink that I had to pay for. He was obliged to listen to your fantasies.'

'He enjoyed our conversation, Miss Fanshawe. Why is it that people like you and I are so unpopular?'

She didn't answer, but sighed instead. He would go on and on, she knew, and there was nothing she could do. She always meant not to protest, but when it came to the point she found it hard to sit silent, mile after mile.

'You know what I mean, Miss Fanshawe? At Ashleigh Court they say you have an awkward way of walking. And I've got no charm: I think that's why they don't much like me. But how for God's sake could any child of Mrs Carruthers have charm?'

'Please don't speak of your mother like that –'

'And yet men fancy her. Awful men arrive at weekends, as keen for sex as the Reverend Edwards is. "Your mother's a most elegant woman," a hard-eyed lecher remarked to me last summer, in the Palm Court of a Greek hotel.'

'Don't drink too much of that wine. The last time –'

' "You're staggering," she said the last time. I told her I had flu. She's beautiful, I dare say, in her thin way. D'you think she's beautiful?'

'Yes, she is.'

'She has men all over the place. Love flows like honey while you make do with waiters on a train.'

'Oh, don't be so *silly*, Carruthers.'

'She snaps her fingers and people come to comfort her with lust. A woman like that's never alone. While you –'

'Will you please stop talking about me!'

'You have a heart in your breast like anyone else, Miss Fanshawe.'

The waiter, arriving again, coughed. He leaned across the table and placed a warmed plate in front of Miss Fanshawe and a similar one in front of Carruthers. There was a silence while he offered Miss Fanshawe a silver-plated platter with slices of roast beef on it and square pieces of Yorkshire pudding. In the silence she selected what she wanted, a small portion, for her appetite on journeys with Carruthers was never great. Carruthers took the rest. The waiter offered vegetables.

'Miss Fanshawe ironed that blouse at a quarter to five this morning,' Carruthers said. 'She'd have ironed it last night if she hadn't been so tired.'

'A taste more carrots, sir?'

'I don't like carrots, Mr Atkins.'

'Peas, sir?'

'Thank you. She got up from her small bed, Mr Atkins, and her feet were chilly on the linoleum. She shivered, Mr Atkins, as she slipped her night-dress off. She stood there naked, thinking of another person. What became of your predecessor?'

'I don't know, sir. I never knew the man at all. All right for you, madam?'

'Yes, thank you.'

'He used to go back to the kitchen, Mr Atkins, and tell the cook that the couple from Ashleigh Court were on the train again. He'd lean against the sink while the cook poked about among his pieces of meat, trying to find us something to eat. Your predecessor would suck at the butt of a cig and occasionally he'd lift a can of beer to his lips. When the cook asked him what the matter was he'd say it was fascinating, a place like Ashleigh Court with boys running about in grey uniforms and an undermatron watching her life go by.'

'Excuse me, sir.'

The waiter went. Carruthers said:

' "She makes her own clothes," the other waiter told the cook. "She couldn't give a dinner party the way the young lad's mother could. She couldn't chat to this person and that, moving about among *décolletée* women and outshining every one of them." Why is she an undermatron at Ashleigh Court Preparatory School for Boys, owned and run by the Reverend T.L. Edwards, known to generations as a pervert?'

Miss Fanshawe, with an effort, laughed. 'Because she's qualified for nothing else,' she lightly said.

'I think that freckled waiter was sacked because he interfered with the passengers. "Vegetables?" he suggested, and before he could help himself he put the dish of cauliflowers on the table and put his arms around a woman. "All tickets please," cried the ticket-collector and then he saw the waiter and the woman on the floor. You can't run a railway company like that.'

'Carruthers –'

'Was it something like that, Miss Fanshawe? D'you think?'

'Of course it wasn't.'

'Why not?'

'Because you've just made it up. The man was a perfectly ordinary waiter on this train.'

'That's not true.'

'Of course it is.'

'I love this train, Miss Fanshawe.'

'It's a perfectly ordinary —'

'Of course it isn't.'

Carruthers laughed gaily, waiting for the waiter to come back, eating in silence until it was time again for their plates to be cleared away.

'Trifle, madam?' the waiter said. 'Cheese and biscuits?'

'Just coffee, please.'

'Sit down, why don't you, Mr Atkins? Join us for a while.'

'Ah no, sir, no.'

'Miss Fanshawe and I don't have to keep up appearances on your train. D'you understand that? We've been keeping up appearances for three long months at Ashleigh Court and it's time we stopped. Shall I tell you about my mother, Mr Atkins?'

'Your mother, sir?'

'Carruthers —'

'In 1960, when I was three, my father left her for another woman: she found it hard to bear. She had a lover at the time, a Mr Dalacourt, but even so she found it hard to forgive my father for taking himself off.'

'I see, sir.'

'It was my father's intention that I should accompany him to his new life with the other woman, but when it came to the point the other woman decided against that. Why should she be burdened with my mother's child? she wanted to know: you can see her argument, Mr Atkins.'

'I must be getting on now, sir.'

'So my father arranged to pay my mother an annual sum, in return for which she agreed to give me house room. I go with her when she goes on holiday to a smart resort. My father's a thing of the past. What d'you think of all that, Mr Atkins? Can you visualize Mrs Carruthers at a resort? She's not at all like Miss Fanshawe.'

'I'm sure she's not —'

'Not at all.'

'Please let go my sleeve, sir.'

'We want you to sit down.'

'It's not my place, sir, to sit down with the passengers in the dining-car.'

'We want to ask you if you think it's fair that Mrs Carruthers should round up all the men she wants while Miss Fanshawe has only the furtive memory of a waiter on a train, a man who came to a sticky end, God knows.'

'Stop it!' cried Miss Fanshawe. 'Stop it! Stop it! Let go his jacket and let him go away –'

'I have things to do, sir.'

'He smelt of fried eggs, a smell that still comes back to her at night.'

'You're damaging my jacket. I must ask you to release me at once.'

'Are you married, Mr Atkins?'

'Carruthers!' Her face was crimson and her neck blotched with a flushing that Carruthers had seen before. 'Carruthers, for heaven's sake behave yourself!'

'The Reverend Edwards isn't married, as you might guess, Mr Atkins.'

The waiter tried to pull his sleeve out of Carruthers' grasp, panting a little from embarrassment and from the effort. 'Let go my jacket!' he shouted. 'Will you let me go!'

Carruthers laughed, but did not release his grasp. There was a sound of ripping as the jacket tore.

'Miss Fanshawe'll stitch it for you,' Carruthers said at once, and added more sharply when the waiter raised a hand to strike him: 'Don't do that, please. Don't threaten a passenger, Mr Atkins.'

'You've ruined this jacket. You bloody little –'

'Don't use language in front of the lady.' He spoke quietly, and to a stranger entering the dining-car at that moment it might have seemed that the waiter was in the wrong, that the torn sleeve of his jacket was the just result of some attempted insolence on his part.

'You're mad,' the waiter shouted at Carruthers, his face red and sweating in his anger. 'That child's a raving lunatic,' he shouted as noisily at Miss Fanshawe.

Carruthers was humming a hymn. 'Lord, dismiss us,' he softly sang, 'with Thy blessing.'

'Put any expenses on my bill,' whispered Miss Fanshawe. 'I'm very sorry.'

'Ashleigh Court'll pay,' Carruthers said, not smiling now, his face all of a sudden as sombre as the faces of the other two.

No one spoke again in the dining-car. The waiter brought coffee, and later presented a bill.

The train stopped at a small station. Three people got out as Miss Fanshawe and Carruthers moved down the corridor to their compartment. They walked in silence, Miss Fanshawe in front of Carruthers, he drawing his right hand along the glass of the windows. There'd been an elderly man in their compartment when they'd left it: to Miss Fanshawe's relief he was no longer there. Carruthers slid the door across. She found her book and opened it at once.

'I'm sorry,' he said when she'd read a page.

She turned the page, not looking up, not speaking.

'I'm sorry I tormented you,' he said after another pause.

She still did not look up, but spoke while moving her eyes along a line of print. 'You're always sorry,' she said.

Her face and neck were still hot. Her fingers tightly held the paper-backed volume. She felt taut and rigid, as though the unpleasantness in the dining-car had coiled some part of her up. On other journeys she'd experienced a similar feeling, though never as unnervingly as she experienced it now. He had never before torn a waiter's clothing.

'Miss Fanshawe?'

'I want to read.'

'I'm not going back to Ashleigh Court.'

She went on reading and then, when he'd repeated the statement, she slowly raised her head. She looked at him and thought, as she always did when she looked at him, that he was in need of care. There was a barrenness in his sharp face; his eyes reflected the tang of a bitter truth.

'I took the Reverend Edwards' cigarette-lighter. He's told me he won't have me back.'

'That isn't true, Carruthers –'

'At half past eleven yesterday morning I walked into the Reverend's study and lifted it from his desk. Unfortunately he met me on the way out. Ashleigh Court, he said, was no place for a thief.'

'But why? Why did you do such a silly thing?'

'I don't know. I don't know why I do a lot of things. I don't know why I pretend you were in love with a waiter. This is the last horrid journey for you, Miss Fanshawe.'

'So you won't be coming back –'

'The first time I met you I was crying in a dormitory. D'you remember that? Do you, Miss Fanshawe?'

'Yes, I remember.'

' "Are you missing your mummy?" you asked me, and I said no. I was crying because I'd thought I'd like Ashleigh Court. I'd thought it would be heaven, a place without Mrs Carruthers. I didn't say that; not then.'

'No.'

'You brought me to your room and gave me liquorice allsorts. You made me blow my nose. You told me not to cry because the other boys would laugh at me. And yet I went on crying.'

In the fields men were making hay. Children in one field waved at the passing train. The last horrid journey, she thought; she would never see the sharp face again, nor the bitterness reflected in the eyes. He'd wept, as others occasionally had to; she'd been, for a moment, a mother to him. His own mother didn't like him, he'd later said – on a journey – because his features reminded her of his father's features.

'I don't know why I'm so unpleasant, Miss Fanshawe. The Reverend stared at me last night and said he had a feeling in his bones that I'd end up badly. He said I was a useless sort of person, a boy he couldn't ever rely on. I'd let him down, he said, thieving and lying like a common criminal. "I'm chalking you up as a failure for Ashleigh," he said. "I never had much faith in you, Carruthers."'

'He's a most revolting man.' She said it without meaning to, and yet the words came easily from her. She said it because it didn't matter any more, because he wasn't going to return to Ashleigh Court to repeat her words.

'You were kind to me that first day,' Carruthers said. 'I liked that holy picture in your room. You told me to look at it, I remember. Your white overall made a noise when you walked.'

She wanted to say that once she had told lies too, that at St Monica's School for Girls she'd said the King, the late George VI, had spoken to her when she stood in the crowd. She wanted to say that she'd stolen two rubbers from Elsie Grantham and poured ink all over the face of a clock, and had never been found out.

She closed her eyes, longing to speak, longing above all things in the world to fill the compartment with the words that had begun, since he'd told her, to pound in her brain. All he'd ever done on the train was to speak a kind of truth about his mother and the school, to speak in their no man's land, as now and then he'd called it. Tormenting her was incidental; she knew it was. Tormenting her was just by chance, a thing that happened.

His face was like a flint. No love had ever smoothed his face, and while she looked at it she felt, unbearably now, the urge to speak as he had spoken, so many times. He smiled at her. 'Yes,' he said. 'The Reverend's a most revolting man.'

'I'm thirty-eight,' she said and saw him nod as though, precisely, he'd guessed her age a long time ago. 'Tonight we'll sit together in the bungalow by the sea where my parents live and they'll ask me about the term at Ashleigh. "Begin at the beginning, Dora," my mother'll say and my father'll set his deaf-aid. "The first day? What happened the first day, Dora?" And

I shall tell them. "Speak up," they'll say, and in a louder voice I'll tell them about the new boys, and the new members of staff. Tomorrow night I'll tell some more, and on and on until the holidays and the term are over. "Wherever are you going?" my mother'll say when I want to go out for a walk. "Funny time," she'll say, "to go for a walk." No matter what time it is.'

He turned his head away, gazing through the window as earlier she had gazed through the window of the dining-car, in awkwardness.

'I didn't fall in love with a freckled waiter,' he heard her say, 'but God knows the freckled waiter would have done.'

He looked at her again. 'I didn't mean, Miss Fanshawe –'

'If he had suddenly murmured while offering me the vegetables I'd have closed my eyes with joy. To be desired, to be desired in any way at all ...'

'Miss Fanshawe –'

'Born beneath Gemini, the sign of passion, you said. Yet who wants to know about passion in the heart of an ugly undermatron? Different for your mother, Carruthers: your mother might weep and tear away her hair, and others would weep in pity because of all her beauty. D'you see, Carruthers? D'you understand me?'

'No, Miss Fanshawe. No, I don't think I do. I'm not as –'

'There was a time one Christmas, after a party in the staff-room, when a man who taught algebra took me up to a loft, the place where the Wolf Cubs meet. We lay down on an old tent, and then suddenly this man was sick. That was in 1954. I didn't tell them that in the bungalow: I've never told them the truth. I'll not say tonight, eating cooked ham and salad, that the boy I travelled with created a scene in the dining-car, or that I was obliged to pay for damage to a waiter's clothes.'

'Shall we read now, Miss Fanshawe?'

'How can we read, for God's sake, when we have other things to say? What was it like, d'you think, on all the journeys to see you so unhappy? Yes, you'll probably go to the bad. He's right: you have the look of a boy who'll end like that. The unhappy often do.'

'Unhappy, Miss Fanshawe? Do I seem unhappy?'

'Oh, for God's sake, tell the truth! The truth's been there between us on all our journeys. We've looked at one another and seen it, over and over again.'

'Miss Fanshawe, I don't understand you. I promise you, I don't understand –'

'How could I ever say in that bungalow that the algebra teacher laid me down on a tent and then was sick? Yet I can say it now to you, a thing I've never told another soul.'

The door slid open and a woman wearing a blue hat, a smiling, red-faced woman, asked if the vacant seats were taken. In a voice that amazed Carruthers further Miss Fanshawe told her to go away.

'Well, really!' said the woman.

'Leave us in peace, for God's sake!' shrieked Miss Fanshawe, and the woman, her smile all gone, backed into the corridor. Miss Fanshawe rose and shut the door again.

'It's different in that bungalow by the sea,' she then quite quietly remarked, as though no red-faced woman had backed away astonished. 'Not like an American Bar in Copenhagen or the Hotel Excelsior in Madrid. Along the walls the coloured geese stretch out their necks, the brass is polished and in its place. Inch by inch oppression fills the air. On the chintz covers in the sitting-room there's a pattern of small wild roses, the stair-carpet's full of fading lupins. *To W.J. Fanshawe on the occasion of his retirement*, says the plaque on the clock on the sitting-room mantelpiece, *from his friends in the Prudential*. The clock has a gold-coloured face and four black pillars of ersatz material: it hasn't chimed since 1958. At night, not far away, the sea tumbles about, seeming too real to be true. The seagulls shriek when I walk on the beach, and when I look at them I think they're crying out with happiness.'

He began to speak, only to speak her name, for there was nothing else he could think of to say. He changed his mind and said nothing at all.

'Who would take me from it now? Who, Carruthers? What freckled waiter or teacher of algebra? What assistant in a shop, what bank-clerk, postman, salesman of cosmetics? They see a figure walking in the wind, discs of thick glass on her eyes, breasts as flat as paper. Her movement's awkward, they say, and when she's close enough they raise their hats and turn away: they mean no harm.'

'I see,' he said.

'In the bungalow I'm frightened of both of them: all my life I've been afraid of them. When I was small and wasn't pretty they made the best of things, and longed that I should be clever instead. "Read to us, Dora," my father would say, rubbing his hands together when he came in from his office. And I would try to read. "Spell *merchant*," my father would urge as though his life depended upon it, and the letters would become jumbled in my mind. Can you see it, Carruthers, a child with glasses and an awkward way of walking and two angry figures, like vultures, unforgiving? They'd exchange a glance, turning their eyes away from me as though in shame. "Not bright," they'd think. "Not bright, to make up for the other."'

'How horrid, Miss Fanshawe.'

'No, no. After all, was it nice for them that their single child should be a gawky creature who blushed when people spoke? How could they help themselves, any more than your mother can?'

'Still, my mother —'

' "Going to the pictures?" he said the last time I was home. "What on earth are you doing that for?" And then she got the newspaper which gave the programme that was showing. "*Tarzan and the Apemen*", she read out. "My dear, at your age!" I wanted to sit in the dark for an hour or two, not having to talk about the term at Ashleigh Court. But how could I say that to them? I felt the redness coming in my ·face. "For children surely," my father said, "a film like that." And then he laughed. "Dora's made a mistake," my mother explained, and she laughed too.'

'And did you go, Miss Fanshawe?'

'Go?'

'To *Tarzan and the Apemen*?'

'No, I didn't go. I don't possess courage like that: as soon as I enter the door of the bungalow I can feel their disappointment and I'm terrified all over again. I've thought of not going back but I haven't even the courage for that: they've sucked everything out of me. D'you understand?'

'Well —'

'Why is God so cruel that we leave the ugly school and travel together to a greater ugliness when we could travel to something nice?'

'Nice, Miss Fanshawe? *Nice*?'

'You know what I mean, Carruthers.'

He shook his head. Again he turned it away from her, looking at the window, wretchedly now.

'Of course you do,' her voice said, 'if you think about it.'

'I really —'

'Funny our birthdays being close together!' Her mood was gayer suddenly. He turned to look at her and saw she was smiling. He smiled also.

'I've dreamed this train went on for ever,' she said, 'on and on until at last you stopped engaging passengers and waiters in fantastic conversation. "I'm better now," you said, and then you went to sleep. And when you woke I gave you liquorice allsorts. "I understand," I said: "it doesn't matter." '

'I know I've been very bad to you, Miss Fanshawe. I'm sorry —'

'I've dreamed of us together in my parents' bungalow, of my parents dead and buried and your thin mother gone too, and Ashleigh Court a thing of the nightmare past. I've seen us walking over the beaches together, you growing up, me cooking for you and mending your clothes and knitting you pullovers. I've brought you fresh brown eggs and made you apple dumplings. I've watched you smile over crispy chops.'

'Miss Fanshawe –'

'I'm telling you about a dream in which ordinary things are marvellous. Tea tastes nicer and the green of the grass is a fresher green than you've ever noticed before, and the air is rosy, and happiness runs about. I would take you to a cinema on a Saturday afternoon and we would buy chips on the way home and no one would mind. We'd sit by the fire and say whatever we liked to one another. And you would no longer steal things or tell lies, because you'd have no need to. Nor would you mock an unpretty undermatron.'

'Miss Fanshawe, I – I'm feeling tired. I think I'd like to read.'

'Why should they have a child and then destroy it? Why should your mother not love you because your face is like your father's face?'

'My mother –'

'Your mother's a disgrace,' she cried in sudden, new emotion. 'What life is it for a child to drag around hotels and lovers, a piece of extra luggage, alone, unloved?'

'It's not too bad. I get quite used to it –'

'Why can He not strike them dead?' she whispered. 'Why can't He make it possible? By some small miracle, surely to God?'

He wasn't looking at her. He heard her weeping and listened to the sound, not knowing what to do.

'You're a sorrowful mess, Carruthers,' she whispered. 'Yet you need not be.'

'Please. Please, Miss Fanshawe –'

'You'd be a different kind of person and so would I. You'd have my love, I'd care about the damage that's been done to you. You wouldn't come to a bad end: I'd see to that.'

He didn't want to turn his head again. He didn't want to see her, but in spite of that he found himself looking at her. She, too, was gazing at him, tears streaming on her cheeks. He spoke slowly and with as much firmness as he could gather together.

'What you're saying doesn't make any sense, Miss Fanshawe.'

'The waiter said that you were mad. Am I crazy too? Can people go mad like that, for a little while, on a train? Out of loneliness and locked-up love? Or desperation?'

'I'm sure it has nothing to do with madness, Miss Fanshawe –'

'The sand blows on to my face, and sometimes into my eyes. In my bedroom I shake it from my sandals. I murmur in the sitting-room. "Really,

Dora," my mother says, and my father sucks his breath in. On Sunday mornings we walk to church, all three of us. I go again, on my own, to Evensong: I find that nice. And yet I'm glad when it's time to go back to Ashleigh Court. Are you ever glad, Carruthers?'

'Sometimes I have been. But not always. Not always at all. I –'

' "Let's go for a stroll," the algebra teacher said. His clothes were stained with beer. "Let's go up there," he said. "It's nice up there." And in the pitch dark we climbed to the loft where the Wolf Cubs meet. He lit his cigarette-lighter and spread the tent out. I don't mind what happens, I thought. Anything is better than nothing happening all my life. And then the man was sick.'

'You told me that, Miss Fanshawe.'

' "You're getting fat," my mother might have said. "Look at Dora, Dad, getting fat." And I would try to laugh. "A drunk has made me pregnant," I might have whispered in the bungalow, suddenly finding the courage for it. And they would look at me and see that I was happy, and I would kneel by my bed and pour my thanks out to God, every night of my life, while waiting for my child.' She paused and gave a little laugh. 'They are waiting for us, those people, Carruthers.'

'Yes.'

'The clock on the mantelpiece still will not chime. "Cocoa," my mother'll say at half past nine. And when they die it'll be too late.'

He could feel the train slowing, and sighed within him, a gesture of thanksgiving. In a moment he would walk away from her: he would never see her again. It didn't matter what had taken place, because he wouldn't ever see her again. It didn't matter, all she had said, or all he had earlier said himself.

He felt sick in his stomach after the beer and the wine and the images she'd created of a life with her in a seaside bungalow. The food she'd raved about would be appalling; she'd never let him smoke. And yet, in the compartment now, while they were still alone, he was unable to prevent himself from feeling sorry for her. She was right when she spoke of her craziness: she wasn't quite sane beneath the surface, she was all twisted up and unwell.

'I'd better go and brush my teeth,' he said. He rose and lifted his overnight case from the rack.

'Don't go,' she whispered.

His hand, within the suitcase, had already grasped a blue sponge-bag. He released it and closed the case. He stood, not wishing to sit down again. She didn't speak. She wasn't looking at him now.

'Will you be all right, Miss Fanshawe?' he said at last, and repeated the question when she didn't reply. 'Miss Fanshawe?'

'I'm sorry you're not coming back to Ashleigh, Carruthers. I hope you have a pleasant holiday abroad.'

'Miss Fanshawe, will you –'

'I'll stay in England, as I always do.'

'We'll be there in a moment,' he said.

'I hope you won't go to the bad, Carruthers.'

They passed by houses now; the backs of houses, suburban gardens. Posters advertised beer and cigarettes and furniture. *Geo. Small. Seeds*, one said.

'I hope not, too,' he said.

'Your mother's on the platform. Where she always stands.'

'Goodbye, Miss Fanshawe.'

'Goodbye, Carruthers. Goodbye.'

Porters stood waiting. Mail-bags were on a trolley. A voice called out, speaking of the train they were on.

She didn't look at him. She wouldn't lift her head: he knew the tears were pouring on her cheeks now, more than before, and he wanted to say, again, that he was sorry. He shivered standing in the doorway, looking at her, and then he closed the door and went away.

She saw his mother greet him, smiling, in red as always she was. They went together to collect his luggage from the van, out of her sight, and when the train pulled away from the station she saw them once again, the mother speaking and Carruthers just as he always was, laughing his harsh laugh.

A Choice of Butchers

The upper landing of our house had brown linoleum on it and outside each of the bedroom doors there was a small black mat. From this square landing with its three mats and its window overlooking the backyard there rose a flight of uncarpeted steps that led to the attic room where Bridget, who was our maid, slept. The stairs that descended to the lower landing, where the bathroom and lavatory were and where my mother and father slept, were carpeted with a pattern of red flowers which continued downwards to a hall that also had brown linoleum on its floor. There was a hall-stand in the hall and beside it a high green plant in a brass pot, and a figure of the Holy Mother on a table, all by itself. The walls of the landings, and of the hall and the staircase, were papered gloomily in an oatmeal shade that had no pattern, only a pebbly roughness that was fashionable in my childhood in our West Cork town. On this hung two brown pictures, one of oxen dragging a plough over rough ground at sunrise, the other of a farmer leading a working horse towards a farmyard at the end of the day. It was against a background of the oatmeal shade and the oxen in the dawn that I, through the rails of the banisters on the upper landing, saw my father kissing Bridget at the end of one summer holiday.

I had come from my room on that warm September evening to watch for Henry Dukelow, who came up every night to say good-night to me. I had knelt down by the banisters, with my face against them, pressing hard so that I might be marked, so that Mr Dukelow would laugh when he saw me. 'God, you're tip-top,' my father said in a whisper that travelled easily up to me, and then he put his arms round her shoulders and roughly hugged her, with his lips pressed on to her lips.

I was seven years of age, the afterthought of the family, as my father called me. My brothers and sisters were all grown up, but I didn't feel then, not yet, that my parents had given so much to them that there wasn't a lot left to give me. Once upon a time they had all been a family like any other family: the children in turn had left home, and then, when my mother should have been resting and my father finding life less demanding, I had arrived. I did not ever doubt my parents' concern for me, but for the six months that he was in our house I felt that Mr Dukelow loved me as much as they did. 'Say good-night to him for me,' I often heard my mother calling out to him as he mounted the stairs to tell me my night-time story, and I grew up thinking of my mother as a tired person because that was what she was. Her hair was going grey and her face bore a fatigued look: Mr Dukelow said she probably didn't sleep well. There were a lot of people who didn't sleep well, he told me, sitting on my bed one night when I was seven, and I remember he went on talking about that until I must have fallen asleep myself.

Mr Dukelow, who occupied the room next to mine, taught me to play marbles on the rough surface of our backyard. He made me an aeroplane out of heavy pieces of wood he found lying about, and he explained to me that although a star could fall through the sky it would never land on the earth. He told me stories about Columbus and Vasco da Gama, and about the great emperors of Europe and the Battle of the Yellow Ford. He had a good memory for what had interested him at school, but he had forgotten as easily the rest: he had been a poor scholar, he said. He told me the plots of films he'd seen and of a play called *Paddy the Next Best Thing*. He spoke very quietly and he always answered my questions: a small man, as thin as a willow, bony and pale-faced and supposed to be delicate, different from my father. He was fifty-seven; my father was fifty-nine.

In the middle of the night that my father kissed Bridget Mr Dukelow came to my room again. He switched the light on and stood there in grey-striped pyjamas that were badly torn.

'I could hear you crying,' he said. 'What's the trouble with you?'

He wore spectacles with fine wire rims, and all his face seemed to have gone into his nose, which was thin and tapering. His greased hair was black, his hands were like a skeleton's. The first night Mr Dukelow arrived in our house my father brought him into the kitchen, where my mother was reading the *Irish Press* at the table and Bridget was darning one of her black stockings. 'I've employed this man,' my father said, and as he stepped to one side of the doorway the bent figure of Mr Dukelow appeared suddenly and silently, and my father gestured in the manner of a ringmaster introducing a circus act. Mr Dukelow was carrying a cardboard suitcase that had too many clothes in it. I remember seeing the flannel material of a shirt protruding, for the case was not fastened as it was meant to be.

'What are you crying for?' he asked me on that later occasion. 'What's up with you?'

'Go away, Mr Dukelow.'

A frown appeared on his white forehead. He went away, leaving the light on, and he returned within a minute carrying a packet of cigarettes and a cigarette-lighter. He always smoked Craven A, claiming that they were manufactured from a superior kind of tobacco. He lit one and sat on my bed. He talked, as often he did, about the moment of his arrival at our house and how he had paused for a moment outside it.

Looking at our house from the street, you saw the brown hall door, its paintwork grained to make it seem like mahogany. There was a brass knocker and a letter-box that every morning except Sunday were cleaned with Brasso by Bridget. To the right of the hall door, and dwarfing it, were the windows of my father's butcher shop, with its sides of mutton hanging from hooks, tripe on a white enamel dish, and beef and sausages and mince and suet.

Afterwards, when he became my friend, Mr Dukelow said that he had stood on the street outside the shop, having just got off the Bantry bus. With his suitcase weighing him down, he had gazed at the windows, wondering about the shop and the house, and about my father. He had not come all the way from Bantry but from a house in the hills somewhere, where he had been employed as some kind of manservant. He had walked to a crossroads and had stood there waiting for the bus: there had been dust on his shoes that night when first he came into our kitchen. 'I looked at the meat in the window,' he told me afterwards, 'and I thought I'd rather go away again.' But my father, expecting him, had come out of the shop and had told him to come on in. My father was a big man; beside Mr Dukelow he looked like a giant.

Mr Dukelow sat on my bed, smoking his Craven A. He began to talk about the advertisement my father had placed in the *Cork Examiner* for an assistant. He repeated the words my father had employed in the advertisement and he said he'd been nervous even to look at them. 'I had no qualifications,' Mr Dukelow said. 'I was afraid.'

That night, six months before, there'd been that kind of fear in his face. 'Sit down, Mr Dukelow,' my mother had said. 'Have you had your tea?' He shook hands with my mother and myself and with Bridget, making a great thing of it, covering up his shyness. He said he'd had tea, although he confessed to me afterwards that he hadn't. 'You'll take a cup, anyway,' my mother offered, 'and a piece of fruit-cake I made?' Bridget took a kettle from the range and poured boiling water into a teapot to warm it. 'Errah, maybe he wants something stronger,' my father said, giving a great gusty laugh. 'Will we go down to Neenan's, Henry?' But my mother insisted that, first of all, before strong drink was taken, before even Mr Dukelow was led to his room, he should have a cup of tea and a slice of fruit-cake. 'He's hardly inside the door,' she said chidingly to my father, 'before you're lifting him out again.' My father, who laughed easily, laughed again. 'Doesn't he have to get to know the people of the town?' he demanded. 'It's a great little town,' he informed Mr Dukelow. 'There's tip-top business here.' My father had only six fingers and one thumb: being a clumsy man, he had lost the others at different moments, when engaged in his trade. When he had no fingers left he would retire, he used to say, and he would laugh in his roaring way, and add that the sight of a butcher with no fingers would be more than customers could tolerate.

'I often think back,' said Mr Dukelow, 'to the kindness of your mother that first time.'

'He kissed Bridget in the hall,' I said. 'He said she was looking great.'

'Ah, no.'

'I saw him through the banisters.'

'Is it a nightmare you had? Will I get your mammy up?'

I said it wasn't a nightmare I had had: I said I didn't want my mother. My mother was sleeping beside him in their bed and she didn't know that he'd been kissing the maid.

'She'd go away,' I said. 'My mother would go away.'

'Ah no, no.'

'He was kissing Bridget.'

Once, saying good-night to me, Mr Dukelow had unexpectedly given me a kiss, but it was a kiss that wasn't at all like the kiss I had observed in the hall. Mr Dukelow had kissed me because my mother was too tired to climb the stairs; he had kissed me in case I felt neglected. Another time, just as unexpectedly, he had taken a florin from his waistcoat pocket and had put it under my pillow, telling me to buy sweets with it. 'Where d'you get that from?' my father had demanded the next day, and when I told him he hit the side of his leg with his fist, becoming angry in a way that puzzled me. Afterwards I heard him shouting at my mother that Henry Dukelow had given me a two-bob bit and had she anything to say to that? My father was sometimes so peculiar in his behaviour that I couldn't make him out. My mother's quietness was always more noticeable when he was present; I loved her for her quietness.

'He had a few jars in tonight.'

'Was he drunk, Mr Dukelow?'

'I think he was.'

'My mother —'

'Will I tell you a story?'

'No, no.'

I imagined Bridget, as I had been imagining her while I lay awake, thinking to herself that she'd give my mother her marching orders. I imagined, suddenly, my mother doing Bridget's work in the kitchen and Bridget standing at the door watching her. She was a plump girl, red-cheeked, with black curly hair. She had fat arms and legs, and she wasn't as tall as my mother. She must have been about twenty-five at the time; Mr Dukelow had told me that my mother was fifty-one. Bridget used to bring me the green glass balls that fishermen use for floating their nets, because she lived by the sea and often found them washed up on the strand. She didn't tell me stories like Mr Dukelow did, but sometimes she'd read to me out of one of the romances she borrowed from a library that the nuns ran. All the books had brown paper covers on them to keep them from getting dirty, with the titles written in ink on the front. I couldn't remember a time that Bridget hadn't been in the house, with those brown-covered volumes, cycling back from her Sunday afternoon off with fish and vegetables in a basket. I had always liked her, but she was different from my mother: I was fonder of my mother.

'If my mother died,' I said, 'he would be married to Bridget. She didn't mind it when he kissed her.'

Mr Dukelow shook his head. She might have been taken unawares, he pointed out: she might have minded it and not been able to protest owing to surprise. Maybe she'd protested, he suggested, after I'd run back to bed.

'She's going out with the porter in the Munster and Leinster Bank,' he said. 'She's keen on that fellow.'

'My father's got more money.'

'Don't worry about your father now. A little thing like that can happen and that's the end of it. Your father's a decent man.'

It was typical of Mr Dukelow to say that my father was a decent man, even though he knew my father didn't like him. In the shop Mr Dukelow outclassed him: after he'd recovered from his initial nervousness, he'd become neater with the meat than my father was, and it was impossible to imagine Mr Dukelow banging through his thin fingers with the cleaver, or letting a knife slip into his flesh. My father said Mr Dukelow had a lot to learn, but it was my father really who had a lot to learn, since he hadn't been able to learn properly in the first place. Once, a woman called Mrs Tighe had returned a piece of meat to the shop, complaining that it had a smell. 'Will you watch that, Henry?' my father expostulated after Mrs Tighe had left the shop, but Mrs Tighe hadn't said it was Mr Dukelow who had sold her the meat. I was there myself at the time and I knew from the expression on Mr Dukelow's face that it was my father who had sold the bad meat to Mrs Tighe. 'Any stuff like that,' my father said to him, 'mince up in the machine.' I could see Mr Dukelow deciding that he intended to do no such thing: it would go against his sensitivity to mince up odorous meat, not because of the dishonesty of the action but because he had become a more prideful butcher than my father, even though he was only an assistant. Mr Dukelow would throw such a piece of meat away, hiding it beneath offal so that my father couldn't accuse him of wasting anything.

In my bedroom, which had a yellow distemper on the walls and a chest of drawers painted white, with a cupboard and wash-stand to match, Mr Dukelow told me not to worry. There was a little crucifix on the wall above my bed, placed there by my mother, and there was a sacred picture opposite the bed so that I could see the face of Our Lady from where I lay. 'Say a prayer,' urged Mr Dukelow, indicating with a thin hand the two reminders of my Faith. 'I would address St Agnes on a question like that.'

Slowly he selected and lit another cigarette. 'Your father's a decent man,' he repeated, and then he must have gone away because when I woke up the light had been switched off. It was half past seven and the first thing I thought was that the day was the last day of the summer holidays. Then I remembered my father kissing Bridget and Mr Dukelow talking to me in the night.

We all had our breakfast together in the kitchen, my mother at one end of the table, my father at the other, Bridget next to me, and Mr Dukelow opposite us. We always sat like that, for all meals, but what I hadn't paid any attention to before was that Bridget was next to my father.

'Two dozen chops,' he said, sitting there with blood on his hands. 'Did I tell you that, Henry? To go over to Mrs Ashe in the hotel.'

'I'll cut them so,' promised Mr Dukelow in his quiet way.

My father laughed. 'Errah, man, haven't I cut them myself?' He laughed again. He watched while Bridget knelt down to open the iron door of the oven. 'There's nothing like cutting chops,' he said, 'to give you an appetite for your breakfast, Bridget.'

My eyes were on a piece of fried bread on my plate. I didn't lift them, but I could feel Mr Dukelow looking at me. He knew I felt jealous because my father had addressed Bridget instead of my mother. I was jealous on my mother's behalf, because she couldn't be jealous herself, because she didn't know. Mr Dukelow sensed everything, as though there was an extra dimension to him. The chops for Mrs Ashe would have been more elegantly cut if he had cut them himself; they'd have been more cleverly cut, with less waste and in half the time.

'Ah, that's great,' said my father as Bridget placed a plate of rashers and sausages in front of him. She sat down quietly beside me. Neither she nor my mother had said anything since I'd entered the kitchen.

'Is there no potato-cakes?' my father demanded, and my mother said she'd be making fresh ones today.

'The last ones were lumpy.'

'A little,' agreed my mother. 'There were a few little lumps.'

He held his knife and fork awkwardly because of the injuries to his hands. Often he put too much on his fork and pieces of bacon would fall off. Mr Dukelow, when he was eating, had a certain style.

'Well, mister-me-buck,' said my father, addressing me, 'it's the final day of your holidays.'

'Yes.'

'When I was the age you are I had to do work in my holidays. I was delivering meat at six and a half years.'

'Yes.'

'Don't the times change, Bridget?'

Bridget said that times did change. My father asked Mr Dukelow if he had worked during the holidays as a child and Mr Dukelow replied that he had worked in the fields in the summertime, weeding, harvesting potatoes and making hay.

'They have an easy time of it these days,' my father pronounced. He had addressed all of us except my mother. He pushed his cup towards Bridget and she passed it to my mother for more tea.

'An easy time of it,' repeated my father.

I could see him eyeing Mr Dukelow's hands as if he was thinking to himself that they didn't look as if they would be much use for harvesting potatoes. And I thought to myself that my father was wrong in this estimation: Mr Dukelow would collect the potatoes speedily, having dug them himself in a methodical way; he would toss them into sacks with a flick of the wrist, a craftsman even in that.

The postman, called Mr Dicey, who was small and inquisitive and had squinting eyes, came into the kitchen from the yard. When he had a letter for the household he delivered it in this manner, while we sat at breakfast. He would stand while the letter was opened, drinking a cup of tea.

'That's a fine morning,' said Mr Dicey. 'We'll have a fine day of it.'

'Unless it rains.' My father laughed until he was red in the face, and then abruptly ceased because no one was laughing with him. 'How're you, Dicey?' he more calmly inquired.

'I have an ache in my back,' replied Mr Dicey, handing my mother a letter.

Mr Dukelow nodded at him, greeting him in that way. Sometimes Mr Dukelow was so quiet in the kitchen that my father asked him if there was something awry with him.

'I was saying to the bucko here,' said my father, 'that when I was his age I used to deliver meat from the shop. Haven't times changed, Dicey?'

'They have not remained the same,' agreed Mr Dicey. 'You could not expect it.'

Bridget handed him a cup of tea. He stirred sugar into it, remarking to Bridget that he'd seen her out last night. It was said that Mr Dicey's curiosity was so great that he often steamed open a letter and delivered it a day late. He was interested in everyone in the town and was keen to know of fresh developments in people's lives.

'You didn't see me at all,' he said to Bridget. He paused, drinking his tea. 'You were engaged at the same time,' he said, 'with another person.'

'Oh, Bridie has her admirers all right,' said my father.

'From the Munster and Leinster Bank.' Mr Dicey laughed. 'There's a letter from your daughter,' he said to my mother. 'I know her little round-shaped writing.'

My mother, concerned with the letter, nodded.

'Bridie could claim the best,' said my father.

I looked at him and saw that he was glancing down the length of the table at my mother.

'Bridie could claim the best,' he repeated in a notably loud voice. 'Wouldn't you say that, Dicey? Isn't she a great-looking girl?'

'She is, of course,' said Mr Dicey. 'Why wouldn't she be?'

'It's a wonder she never claimed Henry Dukelow.' My father coughed and laughed. 'Amn't I right she could claim the best, Henry? Couldn't Bridie have any husband she put her eye on?'

'I'll carry over the chops to Mrs Ashe,' said Mr Dukelow, getting up from the table.

My father laughed. 'Henry Dukelow wouldn't be interested,' he said. 'D'you understand me, Dicey?'

'Oh, now, why wouldn't Henry be interested?' inquired Mr Dicey, interested himself.

Mr Dukelow washed his hands at the sink. He dried them on a towel that hung on the back of the kitchen door, a special towel that only he and my father used.

'He's not a marrying man,' said my father. 'Amn't I right, Henry?'

Mr Dukelow smiled at my father and left the kitchen without speaking. Mr Dicey began to say something, but my father interrupted him.

'He's not a marrying man,' he repeated. He pressed a piece of bread into the grease on his plate. He cleaned the plate with it, and then ate it and drank some tea. Mr Dicey put his cup and saucer on to the table, telling Bridget she was a marvel at making tea. There wasn't better tea in the town, Mr Dicey said, than the tea he drank in this kitchen. He wanted to remain, to hang around in case something happened: he was aware of a heavy atmosphere that morning and he was as puzzled as I was.

My mother was still reading the letter, my father was still staring at her head. Was he trying to hurt her? I wondered: was he attempting to upset her by saying that Bridget could have anyone she wanted as a husband?

She handed the letter to me, indicating that I should pass it on to him. I saw that it was from my sister Sheila, who had married, two Christmases before, a salesman of stationery. I gave it to my father and I watched him reading.

'Bedad,' he said. 'She's due for a baby.'

When I heard my father saying that I thought for only a moment about what the words signified. Bridget exclaimed appropriately, and then there was a silence while my father looked at my mother. She smiled at him in a half-hearted way, obliged by duty to do that, reluctant to share any greater emotion with him.

'Is it Sheila herself?' cried Mr Dicey in simulated excitement. 'God, you wouldn't believe it!' From the way he spoke it was evident that he had known the details of the letter. He went on to say that it seemed only yesterday that my sister was an infant herself. He continued to talk, his squinting eyes moving rapidly over all of us, and I could sense his interest in the calm way my mother had taken the news, not saying a word. There was a damper on the natural excitement, which no one could have failed to be aware of.

My father tried to make up for the lack of commotion by shouting out that for the first time in his life he would be a grandfather. My mother smiled again at him and then, like Mr Dukelow, she rose and left the kitchen. Reluctantly, Mr Dicey took his leave of us also.

Bridget collected the dishes from the table and conveyed them to the sink. My father lit a cigarette. He poured himself a cup of tea, humming a melody that often, tunelessly, he did hum. 'You're as quiet as Henry Dukelow this morning,' he said to me, and I wanted to reply that we were all quiet except himself, but I didn't say anything. Sometimes when he looked at me I remembered the time he'd said to me that he wondered when I was grown up if I'd take over his shop and be a butcher like he was. 'Your brothers didn't care for that,' he'd said, speaking without rancour but with a certain sorrow in his voice. 'They didn't fancy the trade.' He had smiled at me coaxingly, saying that he was a happy man and that he had built up the business and wouldn't want to see it die away. At the time I felt revulsion at the thought of cutting up dead animals all day long, knifing off slices of red steak and poking for kidneys. I had often watched him at work since he encouraged me to do that, even offering me the experience as a treat. 'Well, mister-me-buck,' he would shout at me, bustling about in his white apron, 'is there a nice piece of liver there for Mrs Bourke?' He would talk to his customers about me as he weighed their orders, remarking that I was growing well and was a good boy when I remembered to be. 'Will you be a butcher like your daddy?' a woman often asked me and I could feel the tension in him without at the time understanding it. It wasn't until I saw Mr Dukelow going about the business in his stylish way that I began to say to the women that I might be a butcher one day. Mr Dukelow didn't make me feel that he was cutting up dead animals at all: Mr Dukelow made it all seem civilized.

I didn't leave the kitchen that morning until my father had finished his cup of tea and was ready to go also, in case he'd kiss Bridget when they were alone together. He told me to hurry up and go and help my mother, but I delayed deliberately and in the end I shamed him into going before me. Bridget went on cleaning the dishes in the sink, standing there silently, as if she didn't know what was happening.

I went to my parents' bedroom, where my mother was making their bed. She asked me to take the end of a sheet and to pull it up so that she wouldn't have to walk around the bed and do it herself. She had taught me how to help her. I seized the end of the sheet and then the end of a blanket. I said:

'If you go away I will go with you.'

She looked at me. She asked me what I'd said and I said it again. She didn't reply. We went on making the bed together and when it was finished she said:

'It isn't me who's going away, love.'

'Is it Bridget?'

'There's no need for Bridget –'

'I saw him –'

'He didn't mean any harm.'

'Did you see him too?'

'It doesn't matter at all. Sheila's going to have a little baby. Isn't that grand?'

I couldn't understand why she was suddenly talking about my sister having a baby since it had nothing to do with my father kissing Bridget.

'It's not he who's going away?' I asked, knowing that for my father to go away would be the most unlikely development of all.

'Bridget was telling me yesterday,' my mother said, 'she's going to marry the porter at the Munster and Leinster Bank. It's a secret Bridget has: don't tell your father or Mr Dicey or anyone like that.'

'Mr Dukelow –'

'It is Mr Dukelow who will be going away.'

She covered the big bed with a candlewick bedspread. She pointed a finger at the side of the bedspread that was near me, indicating that I should aid her with it.

'Mr Dukelow?' I said. 'Why would –'

'He moves around from one place to another. He does different kinds of work.'

'Does he get the sack?'

My mother shrugged her shoulders. I went on asking questions, but she told me to be quiet. I followed her to the kitchen and watched her making potato-cakes, while Bridget went in and out. Occasionally they spoke, but they weren't unfriendly: it wasn't between them that there was anything wrong. I remembered Bridget saying to me one time that my mother was always very good to her, better than her own mother had ever been. She had a great fondness for my mother, she said, and I sensed it between them that morning because somehow it seemed greater than it had been in the past, even though the night before my father had been kissing Bridget in the hall. I kept looking at my mother, wanting her to explain whatever there was to explain to me, to tell me why Mr Dukelow, who'd said he never wanted to leave my father's shop, was going to leave now, after only six months. I couldn't imagine the house without Mr Dukelow. I couldn't imagine lying in my bed without anyone to come and tell me about Vasco da Gama. I couldn't imagine not seeing him lighting a Craven A cigarette with his little lighter.

'Well, isn't that terrible?' said my father when we were all sitting down again at the kitchen table for our dinner. 'Henry Dukelow's shifting on.'

Mr Dukelow looked nervous. He glanced from me to my mother, not knowing that my mother had guessed he would be going, not knowing she'd suggested it to me.

'We thought he might be,' my mother said. 'He's learnt the business.'

My father pressed potatoes into his mouth and remarked on the stew we were eating. His mood was wholly different now: he wagged his head at my mother, saying she'd cooked the meat well. There wasn't a woman in the country, he tediously continued, who could cook stew like my mother. He asked me if I agreed with that, and I said I did. 'You'll be back at school tomorrow,' he said, and I agreed with that also. 'Tell them they'll have an uncle in the class,' he advised, 'and give the teacher a few smiles.'

Releasing an obstreperous laugh, he pushed his plate away from him with the stumps of two fingers. 'Will we go down to Neenan's,' he suggested to Mr Dukelow, 'and have a talk about what you will do?'

'You can talk here,' said my mother with severity. I could see her saying to herself that it was the half-day and if my father entered Neenan's he'd remain there for the afternoon.

'Hurry up, Henry,' said my father, scraping his chair as he pushed it back on the flagged floor. 'A tip-top stew,' he repeated. He made a noise in his mouth, sucking through his teeth, a noise that was familiar to all of us. He told Mr Dukelow he'd be waiting for him in Neenan's.

'Keep an eye on him,' my mother murmured when he'd gone, and Mr Dukelow nodded.

'I would have told you that tonight,' he said to me. 'I didn't want to say a thing until I'd mentioned it to your father first.'

'Mr Dukelow'll be here a month yet.' My mother smiled at me. 'He can tell you a good few stories in that time.'

But Mr Dukelow in fact did not remain in our house for another month. When he returned with my father later that day, my father, in a better mood than ever, said:

'We've come to a good agreement. Henry's going to pack his traps. He'll catch the half-seven bus.'

But Mr Dukelow didn't say anything. He walked from the kitchen without swaying like my father was swaying.

My father had his hat on and he didn't take it off. He took his turnip watch from his waistcoat pocket and examined it. 'I can't see without my glasses,' he said to me. 'Will you take a gander at it, boy?'

He never wore glasses, but he often made the joke when he'd been down to Neenan's for a while. I told him it was twenty past six. He put the stumps of two fingers on my head and said I was a great boy. Did I know, he asked me, that in six months' time I'd be an uncle? He had a way of touching me with his stumps instead of with the fingers that remained with him, just as he had a way of pushing from him a plate from which he'd eaten a meal. 'Don't forget to tell the teacher,' he said. 'It's not every day he has an uncle to instruct.'

My mother took a barm brack from a tin and began to butter it for Mr Dukelow before he went. Bridget moved a kettle on to the hot area of the stove. It boiled at once. 'Will I fry him something?' she asked my mother.

'There's rashers there,' said my mother, 'and a bit of black pudding. Do him eggs, Bridget, and a few potato-cakes.'

'He's going,' repeated my father. His face, redder than usually it was, had sweat on the sides of it. 'He's going,' he said again.

I was sitting at the end of the table with a comic spread out in front of me. While I gazed at my father half my vision retained the confused mass of cartoon characters.

'Well, that's that,' said my father.

He stood there swaying, his feet rooted to the kitchen floor, like a statue about to topple in a wind. He was wearing the blue-striped suit that he always wore on the half-day; his hands were hanging by his sides.

'You should be bloody ashamed of yourself,' he said suddenly, and I thought he was talking to me. He wasn't looking at any of us; his eyes were turned upwards, regarding a corner of the ceiling. 'A chancer like that,' he said, 'that gives a young fellow two-bob pieces.' Instinctively I knew then that he was speaking to my mother, even though she did not acknowledge his remarks.

'Sent up from Satan,' he said. 'Sent up to make wickedness. I'm sorry about that thing, Bridget.'

Bridget shook her head, implying that it didn't matter, and I knew they were referring to what had happened in the hall last night.

'Tell Henry Dukelow I'll see him at the bus.' He moved to the back door, adding that he was returning to Neenan's until it was time to say goodbye to Mr Dukelow. 'He'll never make a butcher,' he said, 'or any other bloody thing either.'

I closed the comic and watched my mother and Bridget preparing Mr Dukelow's last meal in our house. They didn't speak and I was afraid to, now. I still couldn't understand why this series of events was taking place. I tried to connect one occurrence with another, but I failed. I felt forgotten in the house: I might have been dead at the table for all they considered me: they were assuming I had no mind.

Mr Dukelow came into the silence, carrying the suitcase he had first carried into the kitchen six months ago, bound up with what looked like the same piece of string. He ate in silence, and Bridget and my mother sat at the table, not saying anything either. I pretended to read the comic, but all the time I was thinking that I'd rather have Mr Dukelow for my father. I couldn't help thinking it and I began to imagine my father sitting on the Bantry bus and Mr Dukelow staying where he was, running the shop better than my father had ever run it, cutting the meat better. I thought of Mr Dukelow in the big bed with my mother, lying asleep beside her. I saw his hands on the white sheets, the thin clever hands instead of hands that made you turn your head away. I saw Mr Dukelow and my mother and myself going out for a walk together on a Sunday afternoon, and Mr Dukelow telling us about Vasco da Gama and Columbus. Mr Dukelow could spend the afternoon in Neenan's and not sway and lurch when he came back. There was no need for Mr Dukelow to go kissing the maid.

'I'm sorry I upset him,' said Mr Dukelow suddenly. 'He's a decent man.'

'It has nothing to do with anything,' said my mother. 'He's in a bad way with drink.'

'Yes,' said Mr Dukelow.

As out of a fog the truth came in pieces to me, and some of the pieces as yet were missing. In six months Mr Dukelow had become a better butcher than my father and my father was jealous of that. Jealousy had caused him to see Mr Dukelow as a monster; jealousy had spread from him in different directions until it wrapped my mother and myself, and tortured my father's pride until he felt he must get his own back and prove himself in some way.

'I'll say goodbye,' said Mr Dukelow, and I hated my father then for his silly pettiness. I wanted Mr Dukelow to go to my mother and kiss her as my father had kissed Bridget. I wanted him to kiss Bridget too, in a way more elegant than the way of my father.

But none of that happened, nor did I ask why, in the face of everything, my father was being described as a decent man. Mr Dukelow left the kitchen, having shaken hands with the three of us. I sat down again at the table while my mother and Bridget prepared the tea. They did not say anything, but I thought to myself that I could see in Bridget's flushed face a reflection of what was passing in her mind: that Mr Dukelow was a nicer man than the porter at the Munster and Leinster Bank. My mother's face was expressionless, but I thought to myself that I knew what expression would be there if my mother cared to permit its presence.

Again I pretended I was reading the comic, but all the time I was thinking about what had silently occurred in our house and how for no sensible reason at all my father's rumbustiousness had spoilt everything. No one but my father could not love Mr Dukelow: no one in the wide world, I thought, except that red-faced man with stumps on his hands, who fell over chairs when he'd been down in Neenan's, who swayed and couldn't read the time. I thought about the ugliness of my father's jealous nature and the gentleness it had taken exception to. 'Sent up from Satan,' his stumbling voice had ridiculously announced. 'Sent up to make wickedness.' How could it be, I wondered, that I was the child of one instead of the other?

'Well, mister-me-buck,' said my father, returning to the kitchen after a time. When I looked at him I began to cry and my mother took me up to bed, saying I was tired.

O Fat White Woman

Relaxing in the garden of her husband's boarding-school, Mrs Digby-Hunter could not help thinking that it was good to be alive. On the short grass of the lawn, tucked out of sight beneath her deck-chair, was a small box of Terry's All Gold chocolates, and on her lap, open at page eight, lay a paper-backed novel by her second-favourite writer of historical fiction. In the garden there was the pleasant sound of insects, and occasionally the buzzing of bees. No sound came from the house: the boys, beneath the alert tutelage of her husband and Mr Beade, were obediently labouring, the maids, Dympna and Barbara, were, Mrs Digby-Hunter hoped, washing themselves.

Not for the moment in the mood for reading, she surveyed the large, tidy garden that was her husband's pride, even though he never had a moment to work in it. Against high stone walls forsythia grew, and honeysuckle and little pear trees, and beneath them in rich, herbaceous borders the garden flowers of summer blossomed now in colourful variety. Four beech trees shaded patches of the lawn, and roses grew, and geraniums, in round beds symmetrically arranged. On either side of an archway in the wall ahead of Mrs Digby-Hunter were two yew trees and beyond the archway, in a wilder part, she could see the blooms of late rhododendrons. She could see as well, near one of the yew trees, the bent figure of Sergeant Wall, an ex-policeman employed on a part-time basis by her husband. He was weeding, his movements slow in the heat of that June afternoon, a stained white hat on his hairless head. It was pleasant to sit in the shade of a beech tree watching someone else working, having worked oneself all morning in a steamy kitchen. Although she always considered herself an easy-going woman, she had been very angry that morning because one of the girls had quite clearly omitted to make use of the deodorant she was at such pains to supply them with. She had accused each in turn and had got nowhere whatsoever, which didn't entirely surprise her. Dympna was just fifteen and Barbara only a month or two older; hardly the age at which to expect responsibility and truthfulness. Yet it was her duty to train them, as it was her husband's duty to train the boys. 'You'll strip wash, both of you,' she'd commanded snappishly in the end, 'immediately you've done the lunch dishes. From top to toe, please, every inch of you.' They had both, naturally, turned sulky.

Mrs Digby-Hunter, wearing that day a blue cotton dress with a pattern of pinkish lupins on it, was fifty-one. She had married her husband twenty-nine years ago, at a time when he'd been at the beginning of a career in the army. Her father, well-to-do and stern, had given her away and she'd been quite happy about his gesture, for love had then possessed her fully. Determined at all costs to make a success of her marriage and to come up to scratch as a wife, she had pursued a policy of agreeableness: she smiled instead of making a fuss, in her easy-going way she accepted what there was to accept, placing her faith in her husband as she believed a good wife should. In her own opinion she was not a clever person, but at least she could offer loyalty and devotion, instead of nagging and arguing. In a bedroom of a Welsh hotel she had disguised, on her wedding night, her puzzled disappointment when her husband had abruptly left her side, having lain there for only a matter of minutes.

Thus a pattern began in their marriage and as a result of it Mrs Digby-Hunter had never borne children although she had, gradually and at an increasing rate, put on weight. At first she had minded about this and had attempted to diet. She had deprived herself of what she most enjoyed until it occurred to her that caring in this way was making her bad-tempered and miserable: it didn't suit her, all the worrying about calories and extra ounces. She weighed now, although she didn't know it, thirteen stone.

Her husband was leaner, a tall man with strong fingers and smooth black hair, and eyes that stared at other people's eyes as if to imply shrewdness. He had a gaunt face and on it a well-kept though not extensive moustache. Shortly after their marriage he had abandoned his career in the army because, he said, he could see no future in it. Mrs Digby-Hunter was surprised but assumed that what was apparent to her husband was not apparent to her. She smiled and did not argue.

After the army her husband became involved with a firm that manufactured a new type of all-purpose, metal step-ladder. He explained to her the mechanism of this article, but it was complicated and she failed to understand: she smiled and nodded, murmuring that the ladder was indeed an ingenious one. Her husband, briskly businesslike in a herring-bone suit, became a director of the step-ladder company on the day before the company ran into financial difficulties and was obliged to cease all production.

'Your father could help,' he murmured, having imparted to her the unfortunate news, but her father, when invited to save the step-ladder firm, closed his eyes in boredom.

'I'm sorry,' she said, rather miserably, feeling she had failed to come up to scratch as a wife. He said it didn't matter, and a few days later he told her he'd become a vending-machine operator. He would have an area, he said, in which he would daily visit schools and swimming-pools, launderettes, factories, offices, wherever the company's vending-machines were sited. He would examine the machines to see that they were in good trim and would fill them full of powdered coffee and powdered milk and a form of tea, and minerals and biscuits and chocolate. She thought the work odd for an ex-army officer, but she did not say so. Instead, she listened while he told her that there was an expanding market for vending-machines, and that in the end they would make a considerable amount of money. His voice went on, quoting percentages and conversion rates. She was knitting him a blue pullover at the time. He held his arms up while she fitted it about his chest; she nodded while he spoke.

Then her father died and left her a sum of money.

'We could buy a country house,' her husband said, 'and open it up as a smart little hotel.' She agreed that that would be nice. She felt that perhaps neither of them was qualified to run an hotel, but it didn't seem worth making a fuss about that, especially since her husband had, without qualifications, joined a step-ladder firm and then, equally unskilled, had gone into the vending-machine business. In fact, their abilities as hoteliers were never put to the test because all of a sudden her husband had a better idea. Idling one evening in a saloon bar, he dropped into conversation with a man who was in a state of depression because his son appeared to be a dunce.

'If I was starting again,' said the man, 'I'd go into the cramming business. My God, you could coin it.' The man talked on, speaking of parents like himself who couldn't hold their heads up because their children's poor performances in the Common Entrance examination deprived them of an association with one of the great public schools of England. The next day Mrs Digby-Hunter's husband scrutinized bound volumes of the Common Entrance examination papers.

'A small boarding-school,' he later said to her, 'for temporarily backward boys; we might do quite nicely.' Mrs Digby-Hunter, who did not immediately take to the notion of being surrounded day and night by temporarily backward boys, said that the idea sounded an interesting one. 'There's a place for sale in Gloucestershire,' her husband said.

The school, begun as a small one, remained so because, as her husband explained, any school of this nature must be small. The turnover in boys was rapid, and it soon became part of the educational policy of Milton Grange to accept not more than twenty boys at any one time, the wisdom of which was reflected in results that parents and headmasters agreed were remarkable: the sons who had idled at the back of their preparatory school classrooms passed into the great public schools of England, and their parents paid the high fees of Milton Grange most gratefully.

At Milton Grange, part ivy-clad, turreted and baronial, Mrs Digby-Hunter was happy. She did not understand the ins and outs of the Common Entrance examination, for her province was the kitchen and the dormitories, but certainly life at Milton Grange as the headmaster's wife was much more like it than occupying half the ground floor of a semi-detached villa in Croydon, as the wife of a vending-machine operator.

'Christ, what a time we're having with that boy for Harrow,' her husband would say, and she would make a sighing noise to match the annoyance he felt, and smile to cheer him up. It was extraordinary what he had achieved with the dullards he took on, and she now and again wondered if one day he might even receive a small recognition, an OBE maybe. As for her, Milton Grange was recognition enough: an apt reward, she felt, for her marital agreeableness, for not being a nuisance, and coming up to scratch as a wife.

Just occasionally Mrs Digby-Hunter wondered what life would have been like if she'd married someone else. She wondered what it would have been like to have had children of her own and to have engaged in the activity that caused, eventually, children to be born. She imagined, once a year or so, as she lay alone in her room in the darkness, what it would be like to share a double bed night after night. She imagined a faceless man, a pale naked body beside hers, hands caressing her flesh. She imagined, occasionally, being married to a clergyman she'd known as a girl, a man who had once embraced her with intense passion, suddenly, after a dance in a church hall. She had experienced the pressure of his body against hers and she could recall still the smell of his clothes and the dampness of his mouth.

But Milton Grange was where she belonged now: she had chosen a man and married him and had ended up, for better or worse, in a turreted house in Gloucestershire. There was give and take in marriage, as always she had known, and where she was concerned there was everything to be thankful for. Once a year, on the last Saturday in July, the gardens of the school were given over to a Conservative fête, and more regularly she and her husband drove to other country houses, for dinner or cocktails. A local Boy Scout group once asked her to present trophies on a sports day because she was her husband's wife and he was well regarded. She had enjoyed the occasion and had bought new clothes specially for it.

In winter she put down bulbs, and in spring she watched the birds collecting twigs and straw for nests. She loved the gardens and often repeated to the maids in the kitchen that one was 'nearer God's Heart in a garden than anywhere else on earth'. It was a beautiful sentiment, she said, and very true.

On that June afternoon, while Mrs Digby-Hunter dropped into a doze beneath the beech trees and Sergeant Wall removed the weeds from a herbaceous border, the bearded Mr Beade walked between two rows of desks in a bare attic room. Six boys bent over the desks, writing speedily. In the room next door six other boys wrote also. They would not be idling, Mr Beade knew, any more than the boys in the room across the corridor would be idling.

'*Amavero, amaveris, amaverit,*' he said softly, his haired lips close to the ear of a boy called Timpson. '*Amaverimus,* Timpson, *amaveritis, amaverint.*' A thumb and forefinger of Mr Beade's seized and turned the flesh on the back of Timpson's left hand. '*Amaveritis,*' he said again, '*amaverint.*' While the flesh was twisted this way and that and while Timpson moaned in the quiet manner that Mr Beade preferred, Dympna and Barbara surveyed the sleeping form of Mrs Digby-Hunter in the garden. They had not washed themselves. They stood in the bedroom they shared, gazing through an open, diamond-paned window, smoking two Embassy tipped cigarettes. 'White fat slug,' said Barbara. 'Look at her.'

They looked a moment longer. Sergeant Wall in the far distance pushed himself from his knees on to his feet. 'He's coming in for his tea,' said Barbara. She held cigarette smoke in her mouth and then released it in short puffs. 'She can't think,' said Dympna. 'She's incapable of mental activity.' 'She's a dead white slug,' said Barbara.

They cupped their cigarettes in their hands for the journey down the back stairs to the kitchen. They both were thinking that the kettle would be boiling on the Aga: it would be pleasant to sit in the cool, big kitchen drinking tea with old Sergeant Wall, who gossiped about the village he lived in. It was Dympna's turn to make his sandwich, turkey paste left over from yesterday, the easy-to-spread margarine that Mrs Digby-Hunter said was better for you than butter. 'Dead white slug,' repeated Barbara, laughing on the stairs. 'Was she human once?'

Sergeant Wall passed by the sleeping Mrs Digby-Hunter and heard, just perceptibly, a soft snoring coming from her partially open mouth. She was tired, he thought; heat made women tired, he'd often heard. He removed his hat and wiped an accumulation of sweat from the crown of his head. He moved towards the house for his tea.

In his study Digby-Hunter sat with one boy, Marshalsea, listening while Marshalsea repeated recently acquired information about triangles.

'Then DEF,' said Marshalsea, 'must be equal in all respects to –'

'Why?' inquired Digby-Hunter.

His voice was dry and slightly high. His bony hands, on the desk between himself and Marshalsea, had minute fingernails.

'Because DEF –'

'Because the triangle DEF, Marshalsea.'

'Because the triangle DEF –'

'Yes, Marshalsea?'

'Because the triangle DEF has the two angles at the base and two sides equal to the two angles at the base and two sides of the triangle ABC –'

'You're talking bloody nonsense,' said Digby-Hunter quietly. 'Think about it, boy.'

He rose from his position behind his desk and crossed the room to the window. He moved quietly, a man with a slight stoop because of his height, a man who went well with the room he occupied, with shelves of textbooks, and an empty mantelpiece, and bare, pale walls. It was simple sense, as he often pointed out to parents, that in rooms where teaching took place there should be no diversions for the roving eyes of students.

Glancing from the window, Digby-Hunter observed his wife in her deck-chair beneath the beeches. He reflected that in their seventeen years at Milton Grange she had become expert at making shepherd's pie. Her bridge, on the other hand, had not improved and she still made tiresome remarks to parents. Once, briefly, he had loved her, a love that had begun to die in a bedroom in a Welsh hotel, on the night of their wedding-day. Her nakedness, which he had daily imagined in lush anticipation, had strangely repelled him. 'I'm sorry,' he'd murmured, and had slipped into the other twin bed, knowing then that this side of marriage was something he was not going to be able to manage. She had not said anything, and between them the matter had never been mentioned again.

It was extraordinary, he thought now, watching her in the garden, that she should lie in a deck-chair like that, unfastidiously asleep. Once at a dinner-party she had described a dream she'd had, and afterwards, in the car on the way back to Milton Grange, he'd had to tell her that no one had been interested in her dream. People had quietly sighed, he'd had to say, because that was the truth.

There was a knock on the door and Digby-Hunter moved from the window and called out peremptorily. A youth with spectacles and long, uncared-for hair entered the sombre room. He was thin, with a slight, thin mouth and a fragile nose; his eyes, magnified behind the tortoiseshell-rimmed discs, were palely nondescript, the colour of water in which vegetables have been boiled. His lengthy hair was lustreless.

'Wraggett,' said Digby-Hunter at once, as though challenging the youth to disclaim this title.

'Sir,' replied Wraggett.

'Why are you moving your head about like that?' Digby-Hunter demanded.

He turned to the other boy. 'Well?' he said.

'If the two angles at the base of DEF,' said Marshalsea, 'are equal to the two angles at the base of –'

'Open the book,' said Digby-Hunter. 'Learn it.'

He left the window and returned to his desk. He sat down. 'What d'you want, Wraggett?' he said.

'I think I'd better go to bed, sir.'

'Bed? What's the matter with you?'

'There's a pain in my neck, sir. At the back, sir. I can't seem to see properly.'

Digby-Hunter regarded Wraggett with irritation and dislike. He made a noise with his lips. He stared at Wraggett. He said:

'So you have lost your sight, Wraggett?'

'No, sir.'

'Why the damn hell are you bellyaching, then?'

'I keep seeing double, sir. I feel a bit sick, sir.'

'Are you malingering, Wraggett?'

'No, sir.'

'Then why are you saying you can't see?'

'Sir –'

'If you're not malingering, get on with the work you've been set, boy. The French verb to drink, the future conditional tense?'

'*Je boive* –'

'You're a cretin,' shouted Digby-Hunter. 'Get out of here at once.'

'I've a pain, sir –'

'Take your pain out with you, for God's sake. Get down to some honest work, Wraggett. Marshalsea?'

'If the two angles at the base of DEF,' said Marshalsea, 'are equal to the two angles at the base of ABC it means that the sides opposite the angles –'

His voice ceased abruptly. He closed his eyes. He felt the small fingers of Digby-Hunter briefly on his scalp before they grasped a clump of hair.

'Open your eyes,' said Digby-Hunter.

Marshalsea did so and saw pleasure in Digby-Hunter's face.

'You haven't listened,' said Digby-Hunter. His left hand pulled the hair, causing the boy to rise from his seat. His right hand moved slowly and then suddenly shot out, completing its journey, striking at Marshalsea's jaw-bone. Digby-Hunter always used the side of his hand, Mr Beade the ball of the thumb.

'Take two triangles, ABC and DEF,' said Digby-Hunter. Again the edge of his right hand struck Marshalsea's face and then, clenched into a fist, the hand struck repeatedly at Marshalsea's stomach.

'Take two triangles,' whispered Marshalsea, 'ABC and DEF.'

'In which the angle ABC equals the angle DEF.'

'In which the angle ABC equals the angle DEF.'

In her sleep Mrs Digby-Hunter heard a voice. She opened her eyes and saw a figure that might have been part of a dream. She closed her eyes again.

'Mrs Digby-Hunter.'

A boy whose name escaped her stood looking down at her. There were so many boys coming and going for a term or two, then passing on: this one was thin and tall, with spectacles. He had an unhealthy look, she thought, and then she remembered his mother, who had an unhealthy look also, a Mrs Wraggett.

'Mrs Digby-Hunter, I have a pain at the back of my neck.'

She blinked, looking at the boy. They'd do anything, her husband often said, in order to escape their studies, and although she sometimes felt sorry for them she quite understood that their studies must be completed since that was reason for their presence at Milton Grange. Still, the amount of work they had to do and their excessively long hours, half past eight until seven at night, caused her just occasionally to consider that she herself had been lucky to escape such pressures in her childhood. Every afternoon, immediately after lunch, all the boys set out with Mr Beade for a brisk walk, which was meant to be, in her husband's parlance, twenty minutes of freshening up. There was naturally no time for games.

'Mrs Digby-Hunter.'

The boy's head was moving about in an eccentric manner. She tried to remember if she had noticed it doing that before, and decided she hadn't. She'd have certainly noticed, for the movement made her dizzy. She reached beneath the deck-chair for the box of All Gold. She smiled at the boy. She said:

'Would you like a chocolate, Wraggett?'

'I feel sick, Mrs Digby-Hunter. I keep seeing double. I can't seem to keep my head steady.'

'You'd better tell the headmaster, old chap.'

He wasn't a boy she'd ever cared for, any more than she'd ever cared for his mother. She smiled at him again, trying to make up for being unable to like either himself or his mother. Again she pushed the box of chocolates at him, nudging a coconut caramel out of its rectangular bed. She always left the coconut caramels and the blackcurrant boats: the boy was more than welcome to them.

'I've told the headmaster, Mrs Digby-Hunter.'

'Have you been studying too hard?'

'No, Mrs Digby-Hunter.'

She withdrew her offer of chocolates, wondering how long he'd stand there waggling his head in the sunshine. He'd get into trouble if the loitering went on too long. She could say that she'd made him remain with her in order to hear further details about his pain, but there was naturally a limit to the amount of time he could hope to waste. She said:

'I think, you know, you should buzz along now, Wraggett –'

'Mrs Digby-Hunter –'

'There's a rule, you know: the headmaster must be informed when a boy is feeling under the weather. The headmaster comes to his own conclusions about who's malingering and who's not. When I was in charge of that side of things, Wraggett, the boys used to pull the wool over my eyes like nobody's business. Well, I didn't blame them, I'd have done the same myself. But the headmaster took another point of view. With a school like Milton Grange, every single second has a value of its own. Naturally, time can't be wasted.'

'They pull the hair out of your head,' Wraggett cried, his voice suddenly shrill. 'They hit you in a special way, so that it doesn't bruise you. They drive their fists into your stomach.'

'I think you should return to your classroom –'

'They enjoy it,' shouted Wraggett.

'Go along now, old chap.'

'Your husband half murdered me, Mrs Digby-Hunter.'

'Now that simply isn't true, Wraggett.'

'Mr Beade hit Mitchell in the groin. With a ruler. He poked the end of the ruler –'

'Be quiet, Wraggett.'

'Mrs Digby-Hunter –'

'Go along now, Wraggett.' She spoke for the first time sharply, but when the boy began to move she changed her mind about her command and called him back. He and all the other boys, she explained with less sharpness in her voice, were at Milton Grange for a purpose. They came because they had idled at their preparatory schools, playing noughts and crosses in the back row of a classroom, giggling and disturbing everyone. They came to Milton Grange so that, after the skilled teaching of the headmaster and

Mr Beade, they might succeed at an examination that would lead them to one of England's great public schools. Corporal punishment was part of the curriculum at Milton Grange, and all parents were apprised of that fact. If boys continued to idle as they had idled in the past they would suffer corporal punishment so that, beneath its influence, they might reconsider their behaviour. 'You understand, Wraggett?' said Mrs Digby-Hunter in the end.

Wraggett went away, and Mrs Digby-Hunter felt pleased. The little speech she had made to him was one she had heard her husband making on other occasions. 'We rap the occasional knuckle,' he said to prospective parents. 'Quite simply, we stand no nonsense.'

She was glad that it had come so easily to her to quote her husband, once again to come up to scratch as a wife. Boys who were malingering must naturally receive the occasional rap on the knuckles and her husband, over seventeen years, had proved that his ways were best. She remembered one time a woman coming and taking her son away on the grounds that the pace was too strenuous for him. As it happened, she had opened the door in answer to the woman's summons and had heard the woman say she'd had a letter from her son and thought it better that he should be taken away. It turned out that the child had written hysterically. He had said that Milton Grange was run by lunatics and criminals. Mrs Digby-Hunter, hearing that, had smiled and had quietly inquired if she herself resembled either a lunatic or a criminal. The woman shook her head, but the boy, who had been placed in Milton Grange so that he might pass on to the King's School in Canterbury, was taken away. 'To stagnate', her husband had predicted and she, knitting another pullover for him, had without much difficulty agreed.

Mrs Digby-Hunter selected a raspberry-and-honey cream. She returned the chocolate-box to the grass beneath her deck-chair and closed her eyes.

'What's the matter, son?' inquired Sergeant Wall on his way back to his weeding.

Wraggett said he had a pain at the back of his neck. He couldn't keep his head still, he said; he kept seeing double; he felt sick in the stomach. 'God almighty,' said Sergeant Wall. He led the boy back to the kitchen, which was the only interior part of Milton Grange that he knew. 'Here,' he said to the two maids, who were still sitting at the kitchen table, drinking tea. 'Here,' said Sergeant Wall, 'have a look at this.'

Wraggett sat down and took off his spectacles. As though seeking to control its wobbling motion, he attempted to shake his head, but the effort, so Barbara and Dympna afterwards said, appeared to be too much for him. His shoulders slipped forward, the side of his face struck the scrubbed surface of the kitchen table, and when the three of them settled him back on his chair in order to give him water in a cup they discovered that he was dead.

When Mrs Digby-Hunter entered the kitchen half an hour later she blinked her eyes several times because the glaring sunshine had affected them. 'Prick the sausages,' she automatically commanded, for today being a Tuesday it would be sausages for tea, a fact of which both Barbara and Dympna would, as always, have to be reminded. She was then aware that something was the matter.

She blinked again. The kitchen contained people other than Barbara and Dympna. Mr Beade, a man who rarely addressed her, was standing by the Aga. Sergeant Wall was endeavouring to comfort Barbara, who was noisily weeping.

'What's the matter, Barbara?' inquired Mrs Digby-Hunter, and she noticed as she spoke that Mr Beade turned more of his back to her. There was a smell of tobacco smoke in the air: Dympna, to Mrs Digby-Hunter's astonishment, was smoking a cigarette.

'There's been a tragedy, Mrs Digby-Hunter,' said Sergeant Wall. 'Young Wraggett.'

'What's the matter with Wraggett?'

'He's dead,' said Dympna. She released smoke through her nose, staring hard at Mrs Digby-Hunter. Barbara, who had looked up on hearing Mrs Digby-Hunter's voice, sobbed more quietly, gazing also, through tears, at Mrs Digby-Hunter.

'Dead?' As she spoke, her husband entered the kitchen. He addressed Mr Beade, who turned to face him. He said he had put the body of Wraggett on a bed in a bedroom that was never used. There was no doubt about it, he said, the boy was dead.

'Dead?' said Mrs Digby-Hunter again. '*Dead?*'

Mr Beade was mumbling by the Aga, asking her husband where Wraggett's parents lived. Barbara was wiping the tears from her face with a handkerchief. Beside her, Sergeant Wall, upright and serious, stood like a statue. 'In Worcestershire,' Mrs Digby-Hunter's husband said. 'A village called Pine.' She was aware that the two maids were still looking at her. She wanted to tell Dympna to stop smoking at once, but the words wouldn't come from her. She was asleep in the garden, she thought: Wraggett had come and stood by her chair, she had offered him a chocolate, now she was dreaming that he was dead, it was all ridiculous. Her husband's voice was quiet, still talking about the village called Pine and about Wraggett's mother and father.

Mr Beade asked a question that she couldn't hear: her husband replied that he didn't think they were that kind of people. He had sent for the school doctor, he told Mr Beade, since the cause of death had naturally to be ascertained as soon as possible.

'A heart attack,' said Mr Beade.

'Dead?' said Mrs Digby-Hunter for the fourth time.

Dympna held towards Barbara her packet of cigarettes. Barbara accepted one, and the eyes of the two girls ceased their observation of Mrs Digby-Hunter's face. Dympna struck a match. Wraggett had been all right earlier, Mr Beade said. Her husband's lips were pursed in a way that was familiar to her; there was anxiety in his eyes.

The kitchen was flagged, large grey flags that made it cool in summer and which sometimes sweated in damp weather. The boys' crockery, of hardened primrose-coloured plastic, was piled on a dresser and on a side table. Through huge, barred windows Mrs Digby-Hunter could see shrubs and a brick wall and an expanse of gravel. Everything was familiar and yet seemed not to be. 'So sudden,' her husband said. 'So wretchedly out of the blue.' He added that after the doctor had given the cause of death he himself would motor over to the village in Worcestershire and break the awful news to the parents.

She moved, and felt again the eyes of the maids following her. She would sack them, she thought, when all this was over. She filled a kettle at the sink, running water into it from the hot tap. Mr Beade remained where he was standing when she approached the Aga, appearing to be unaware that he was in her way. Her husband moved. She wanted to say that soon, at least, there'd be a cup of tea, but again the words failed to come from her. She heard Sergeant Wall asking her husband if there was anything he could do, and then her husband's voice said that he'd like Sergeant Wall to remain in the house until the doctor arrived so that he could repeat to the doctor what Wraggett had said about suddenly feeling unwell. Mr Beade spoke again, muttering to her husband that Wraggett in any case would never have passed into Lancing. 'I shouldn't mention that,' her husband said.

She sat down to wait for the kettle to boil, and Sergeant Wall and the girls sat down also, on chairs near to where they were standing, between the two windows. Her husband spoke in a low voice to Mr Beade, instructing him, it seemed: she couldn't hear the words he spoke. And then, without warning, Barbara cried out loudly. She threw her burning cigarette on the floor and jumped up from her chair. Tears were on her face, her teeth were widely revealed, though not in a smile. 'You're a fat white slug,' she shouted at Mrs Digby-Hunter.

Sergeant Wall attempted to quieten the girl, but her fingernails scratched at his face and her fingers gripped and tore at the beard of Mr Beade, who had come to Sergeant Wall's aid. Dympna did not move from her chair. She was looking at Mrs Digby-Hunter, smoking quietly, as though nothing at all was happening.

'It'll be in the newspapers,' shouted Barbara.

She was taken from the kitchen, and the Digby-Hunters could hear her sobbing in the passage and on the back stairs. 'She'll sell the story,' said Dympna.

Digby-Hunter looked at her. He attempted to smile at her, to suggest by his smile that he had a fondness for her. 'What story?' he said.

'The way the boys are beaten up.'

'Now look here, Dympna, you know nothing whatsoever about it. The boys at Milton Grange are here for a special purpose. They undergo special education – '

'You killed one, Mr Digby-Hunter.' Still puffing at her cigarette, Dympna left the kitchen, and Mrs Digby-Hunter spoke.

'My God,' she said.

'They're upset by death,' said her husband tetchily. 'Naturally enough. They'll both calm down.'

But Mr Beade, hearing those remarks as he returned to the kitchen, said that it was the end of Milton Grange. The girls would definitely pass on their falsehoods to a newspaper. They were telling Sergeant Wall now, he said. They were reminding him of lies they had apparently told him before, and of which he had taken no notice.

'What in the name of heaven,' Digby-Hunter angrily asked his wife, 'did you have to go engaging creatures like that for?'

They hated her, she thought: two girls who day by day had worked beside her in the kitchen, to whom she had taught useful skills. A boy had come and stood beside her in the sunshine and she had offered him a chocolate. He had complained of a pain, and she had pointed out that he must make his complaint to the headmaster, since that was the rule. She had explained as well that corporal punishment was part of the curriculum at Milton Grange. The boy was dead. The girls who hated her would drag her husband's boarding-school through the mud.

She heard the voice of Sergeant Wall saying that the girls, one of them hysterical but calming down, the other insolent, were out to make trouble. He'd tried to reason with them, but they hadn't even listened.

The girls had been in Milton Grange for two and a half months. She remembered the day they had arrived together, carrying cardboard suitcases. They'd come before that to be interviewed, and she'd walked them round the house, explaining about the school. She remembered saying in passing that once a year, at the end of every July, a Conservative fête was held, traditionally now, in the gardens. They hadn't seemed much interested.

'I've built this place up,' she heard her husband say. 'Month by month, year by year. It was a chicken farm when I bought it, Beade, and now I suppose it'll be a chicken farm again.'

She left the kitchen and walked along the kitchen passage and up the uncarpeted back stairs. She knocked on the door of their room. They called out together, saying she should come in. They were both packing their belongings into their cardboard suitcases, smoking fresh cigarettes. Barbara appeared to have recovered.

She tried to explain to them. No one knew yet, she said, why Wraggett had died. He'd had a heart attack most probably, like Mr Beade said. It was a terrible thing to have happened.

The girls continued to pack, not listening to her. They folded garments or pressed them, unfolded, into their suitcases.

'My husband's built the place up. Month by month, year by year, for seventeen years he has built it up.'

'The boys are waiting for their tea,' said Dympna. 'Mrs Digby-Hunter, you'd better prick the sausages.'

'Forget our wages,' said Barbara, and laughed in a way that was not hysterical.

'My husband –'

'Your husband,' said Dympna, 'derives sexual pleasure from inflicting pain on children. So does Beade. They are queer men.'

'Your husband,' said Barbara, 'will be jailed. He'll go to prison with a sack over his head so that he won't have to see the disgust on people's faces. Isn't that true, Mrs Digby-Hunter?'

'My husband –'

'Filth,' said Dympna.

She sat down on the edge of a bed and watched the two girls packing. She imagined the dead body in the bedroom that was never used, and then she imagined Sergeant Wall and Mr Beade and her husband in the kitchen, waiting for the school doctor to arrive, knowing that it didn't much matter what cause he offered for the death if these two girls were allowed to have their way.

'Why do you hate me?' she asked, quite calmly.

Neither replied. They went on packing and while they packed she talked, in desperation. She tried to speak the truth about Milton Grange, as she saw the truth, but they kept interrupting her. The bruises didn't show on the boys because the bruises were inflicted in an expert way, but sometimes hair was actually pulled out of the boys' scalps, small bunches of hair, she must have noticed that. She had noticed no such thing. 'Corporal punishment,' she began to say, but Barbara held out hairs that had been wrenched from the head of a boy called Bridle. She had found them in a wastepaper basket; Bridle had said they were his and had shown her the place they'd come from. She returned the hairs to a plastic bag that once had contained stockings. The hairs would be photographed, Barbara said; they would appear on the front page of a Sunday newspaper. They'd be side by side with the ex-headmaster, his head hidden beneath a sack, and Mr Beade skulking behind his beard. Milton Grange, turreted baronial, part ivy-clad, would be examined by Sunday readers as a torture chamber. And in the garden, beneath the beech trees, a man would photograph the deck-chair where a woman had slept while violence and death occurred. She and her husband might one day appear in a waxworks, and Mr Beade, too; a man who, like her husband, derived sexual pleasure from inflicting pain on children.

'You are doing this for profit,' she protested, trying to smile, to win them from the error of their ways.

'Yes,' they said together, and then confessed, sharing the conversation, that they had often considered telephoning a Sunday newspaper to say they had a story to tell. They had kept the hairs in the plastic bag because they'd had that in mind; in every detail they knew what they were going to say.

'You're making money out of –'

'Yes,' said Dympna. 'You've kept us short, Mrs Digby-Hunter.'

She saw their hatred of her in their faces and heard it in both their voices; like a vapour, it hung about the room.

'Why do you hate me?' she asked again.

They laughed, not answering, as though an answer wasn't necessary.

She remembered, although just now she didn't wish to, the clergyman who had kissed her with passion after a dance in a church hall, the dampness of his lips, his body pressed into hers. The smell of his clothes came back to her, across thirty years, seeming familiar because it had come before. She might have borne his children in some rectory somewhere. Would they have hated her then?

Underclothes, dresses, lipsticks, Woolworth's jewellery, unframed photographs of male singing stars were jumbled together in the two cardboard suitcases. The girls moved about the room, picking up their belongings, while Mrs Digby-Hunter, in greater misery than she had ever before experienced, watched them from the edge of the bed. How could human creatures be so cruel? How could they speak to her about being a figure in a waxworks tableau when she had done nothing at all? How could they so callously propose to tell lies to a newspaper about her husband and Mr Beade when the boy who had so tragically died was still warm with the memory of life?

She watched them, two girls so young that they were not yet fully developed. They had talked about her. In this room, night after night, they had wondered about her, and in the end had hated her. Had they said in their nightly gossiping that since the day of her marriage she had lived like a statue with another statue?

It was all her fault, she suddenly thought: Milton Grange would be a chicken farm again, her husband would be examined by a psychiatrist in a prison, she would live in a single room. It was all her fault. In twenty-nine years it had taken violence and death to make sense of facts that were as terrible.

The girls were saying they'd catch a bus on the main road. Without looking at her or addressing her again they left the bedroom they had shared. She heard their footsteps on the back stairs, and Dympna's voice asking Barbara if she was all right now and Barbara saying she was. A white slug, the girl had called her, a fat white slug.

She did not leave the room. She remained sitting on the edge of the bed, unable to think. Her husband's face appeared in her mind, with its well-kept moustache and shrewd-seeming dark eyes, a face in the bedroom of a Welsh hotel on the night of her wedding-day. She saw herself weeping, as she had not wept then. In a confused way she saw herself on that occasion and on others, protesting, shaking her head, not smiling.

'I'm leaving the army for a step-ladder firm,' he said to her, and she struck his face with her hands, tormented by the absurdity of what he said. She cried out in anger that she had married an army officer, not a step-ladder salesman who was after her father's money. She wept again when ridiculously he told her that he intended to spend his days filling machines full of powdered coffee. He had failed her, she shrilled at him, that night in the Welsh hotel and he had failed her ever since. In front of boys, she accused him of ill-treating those who had been placed in his care. If ever it happened again, she threatened, the police would be sent for. She turned to the boys and ordered them to run about the gardens for a while. It was ludicrous that they should be cooped up while the sun shone, it was ludicrous that they should strive so painfully simply to pass an examination into some school or other. She banged a desk with her hand after the boys had gone, she spat out words at him: they'd all be in the Sunday papers, she said, if he wasn't careful, and she added that she herself would leave Milton Grange for ever unless he pursued a gentler course with the boys who were sent to him, unless he at once dismissed the ill-mannered Mr Beade, who was clearly a sinister man.

In the room that had been the maids' room Mrs Digby-Hunter wept as her mind went back through the years of her marriage and then, still weeping, she left the room and descended the back stairs to the kitchen. To her husband she said that it was all her fault; she said she was sorry. She had knitted and put down bulbs, she said, and in the end a boy had died. Two girls had hated her because in her easy-going way she had held her peace, not wanting to know. Loyalty and devotion, said Mrs Digby-Hunter, and now a boy was dead, and her husband with a sack over his head would be taken from Milton Grange and later would have sessions with a prison psychiatrist. It was all her fault. She would say so to the reporters when they came. She would explain and take the blame, she would come up to scratch as a wife.

Her husband and Sergeant Wall and Mr Beade looked at Mrs Digby-Hunter. She stood in the centre of the kitchen, one hand on the table, a stout woman in a blue-and-pink dress, weeping. The tragedy had temporarily unhinged her, Sergeant Wall thought, and Mr Beade in irritation thought that if she could see herself she'd go somewhere else, and her husband thought that it was typical of her to be tiresomely stupid at a time like this.

She went on talking: you couldn't blame them for hating her, she said, for she might have prevented death and hadn't bothered herself. In a bedroom in Wales she should have wept, she said, or packed a suitcase and gone away. Her voice continued in the kitchen, the words pouring from it, repetitiously and in a hurry. The three men sighed and looked away, all of them thinking the same thing now, that she made no sense at all, with her talk about putting down bulbs and coming up to scratch.

Raymond Bamber and Mrs Fitch

For fifteen years, ever since he was twenty-seven, Raymond Bamber had attended the Tamberleys' autumn cocktail party. It was a function to which the Tamberleys inclined to invite their acquaintances rather than their friends, so that every year the faces changed a bit: no one except Raymond had been going along to the house in Eaton Square for as long as fifteen years. Raymond, the Tamberleys felt, was a special case, for they had known him since he was a boy, having been close friends of his father's.

Raymond was a tall man, six foot two inches, with spectacles and a small moustache. He was neat in all he did, and he lived what he himself referred to as a tidy life.

'I come here every year,' said Raymond at the Tamberleys', to a woman he had not met before, a woman who was tall too, with a white lean face and lips that were noticeably scarlet. 'It is an occasion for me almost, like Christmas or Easter. To some extent, I guide my life by the Tamberleys' autumn party, remembering on each occasion what has happened in the year gone by.'

'My name is Mrs Fitch,' said the woman, poking a hand out for a drink. 'Is that vermouth and gin?' she inquired of the Tamberleys' Maltese maid, and the maid agreed that it was. 'Good,' said Mrs Fitch.

'Raymond, Raymond,' cried the voice of Mrs Tamberley as Mrs Tamberley materialized suddenly beside them. 'How's Nanny Wilkinson?'

'She died,' murmured Raymond.

'Of course she did,' exclaimed Mrs Tamberley. 'How silly of me!'

'Oh no –'

'You put that sweet notice in *The Times*. His old nurse,' explained Mrs Tamberley to Mrs Fitch. 'Poor Nanny Wilkinson,' she said, and smiled and bustled off.

'What was all that?' asked Mrs Fitch.

'It's one of the things that happened to me during the year. The other was –'

'What's your name, anyway?' the woman interrupted. 'I don't think I ever caught it.'

Raymond told her his name. He saw that she was wearing a black dress with touches of white on it. Her shoulders were bare and bony; she had, Raymond said to himself, an aquiline face.

'The other thing was that an uncle died and left me a business in his will. That happened, actually, before the death of Nanny Wilkinson and to tell you the truth, Mrs Fitch, I just didn't know what to do. "What could I do with a business?" I said to myself. So I made my way to Streatham where the old lady lived. "Run a business, Raymond? You couldn't run a bath," she said.' Raymond laughed, and Mrs Fitch smiled frostily, looking about her for another drink. 'It rankled, that, as you may imagine. Why couldn't I run a business? I thought. And then, less than a week later, I heard that she had died in Streatham. I went to her funeral, and discovered that she'd left me a prayer-book in her will. All that happened in the last year. You see, Mrs Fitch?'

Mrs Fitch, her eyes on her husband, who was talking to a woman in yellow in a distant corner of the room, said vaguely:

'What about the business?'

'I sold the business. I live alone, Mrs Fitch, in a flat in Bayswater; I'm forty-two. I'm telling you that simply because I felt that I could never manage anything like taking on a business so suddenly. That's what I thought when I had considered the matter carefully. No good being emotional, I said to myself.'

'No,' said Mrs Fitch. She watched the woman move quite close to her husband and engage him in speech that had all the air of confidential talk. The woman wasn't young, Mrs Fitch noticed, but had succeeded in giving the impression of youth. She was probably forty-four, she reckoned; she looked thirty.

So Mrs Tamberley had seen the notice in *The Times*, Raymond thought. He had worded it simply and had stated in a straightforward manner the service that Nanny Wilkinson had given over the years to his family. He had felt it her due, a notice in *The Times*, and there was of course only he who might do it. He remembered her sitting regally in his nursery teaching him his tidiness. Orderliness was the most important thing in life, she said, after a belief in the Almighty.

'Get me a drink, dear,' said Mrs Fitch suddenly, holding out an empty glass and causing Raymond to note that this woman was consuming the Tamberleys' liquor at a faster rate than he.

'Gin and vermouth,' ordered Mrs Fitch. 'Dry,' she added. 'Not that red stuff.'

Raymond smiled and took her glass, while Mrs Fitch observed that her husband was listening with rapt care to what the woman in yellow was saying to him. In the taxi-cab on the way to the Tamberleys', he had remarked as usual that he was fatigued after his day's work. 'An early night,' he had suggested. And now he was listening carefully to a female: he wouldn't leave this party for another two hours at least.

'It was quite a blow to me,' said Raymond, handing Mrs Fitch a glass of gin and vermouth, 'hearing that she was dead. Having known her, you see, all my life –'

'Who's dead now?' asked Mrs Fitch, still watching her husband.

'Sorry,' said Raymond. 'How silly of me! No, I meant, you see, this old lady whom I had known as Nanny Wilkinson. I was saying it was a blow to me when she died, although of course I didn't see much of her these last few years. But the memories are there, if you see what I mean; and you cannot of course erase them.'

'No,' said Mrs Fitch.

'I was a particularly tall child, with my spectacles of course, and a longish upper lip. "When you're a big man," I remember her saying to me, "you'll have to grow a little moustache to cover up all that lip." And declare, Mrs Fitch, I did.'

'I never had a nanny,' said Mrs Fitch.

'"He'll be a tennis-player," people used to say – because of my height, you see. But in fact I turned out to be not much good on a tennis court.'

Mrs Fitch nodded. Raymond began to say something else, but Mrs Fitch, her eyes still fixed upon her husband, interrupted him. She said:

'Interesting about your uncle's business.'

'I think I was right. I've thought of it often since, of sitting down in an office and ordering people to do this and that, instead of remaining quietly in my flat in Bayswater. I do all my own cooking, actually, and cleaning and washing up. Well, you can't get people, you know. I couldn't even get a simple char, Mrs Fitch, not for love nor money. Of course it's easy having no coal fires to cope with: the flat is all-electric, which is what, really, I prefer.'

Raymond laughed nervously, having observed that Mrs Fitch was, for the first time since their conversation had commenced, observing him closely. She was looking into his face, at his nose and his moustache and his spectacles. Her eyes passed up to his forehead and down the line of his right cheek, down his neck until they arrived at Raymond's Adam's apple. He continued to speak to her, telling of the manner in which his flat in Bayswater was furnished, how he had visited the Sanderson showrooms in Berners Street to select materials for chair-covers and curtains. 'She made them for me,' said Raymond. 'She was almost ninety then.'

'What's that?' said Mrs Fitch. 'Your nurse made them?'

'I measured up for her and wrote everything down just as she had directed. Then I travelled out to Streatham with my scrap of paper.'

'On a bicycle.'

Raymond shook his head. He thought it odd of Mrs Fitch to suggest, for no logical reason, that he had cycled from Bayswater to Streatham. 'On a bus actually,' he explained. He paused, and then added: 'I could have had them made professionally, of course, but I preferred the other. I thought it would give her an interest, you see.'

'Instead of which it killed her.'

'No, no. No, you've got it confused. It was in 1964 that she made the curtains and the covers for me. As I was saying, she died only a matter of months ago.'

Raymond noticed that Mrs Fitch had ceased her perusal of his features and was again looking vacantly into the distance. He was glad that she had ceased to examine him because had she continued he would have felt obliged to move away from her, being a person who was embarrassed by such intent attention. He said, to make it quite clear about the covers and the curtains:

'She died in fact of pneumonia.'

'Stop,' said Mrs Fitch to the Tamberleys' Maltese maid who happened to be passing with a tray of drinks. She lifted a glass to her lips and consumed its contents while reaching out a hand for another. She repeated the procedure, drinking two glasses of the Tamberleys' liquor in a gulping way and retaining a third in her left hand.

'Nobody can be trusted,' said Mrs Fitch after all that. 'We come to these parties and everything's a sham.'

'What?' said Raymond.

'You know what I mean.'

Raymond laughed, thinking that Mrs Fitch was making some kind of joke. 'Of course,' he said, and laughed again, a noise that was more of a cough.

'You told me you were forty-two,' said Mrs Fitch. 'I in fact am fifty-one, and have been taken for sixty-five.'

Raymond thought he would move away from this woman in a moment. He had a feeling she might be drunk. She had listened pleasantly enough while he told her a thing or two about himself, yet here she was now speaking most peculiarly. He smiled at her and heard her say:

'Look over there, Mr Bamber. That man with the woman in yellow is my husband. We were born in the same year and in the same month, January 1915. Yet he could be in his thirties. That's what he's up to now; pretending the thirties with the female he's talking to. He's praying I'll not approach and give the game away. D'you see, Mr Bamber?'

'That's Mrs Anstey,' said Raymond. 'I've met her here before. The lady in yellow.'

'My husband has eternal youth,' said Mrs Fitch. She took a mouthful of her drink and reached out a hand to pick a fresh one from a passing tray. 'It's hard to bear.'

'You don't look fifty-one,' said Raymond. 'Not at all.'

'Are you mocking me?' cried Mrs Fitch. 'I do not look fifty-one. I've told you so: I've been taken for sixty-five.'

'I didn't mean that. I meant –'

'You were telling a lie, as well you know. My husband is telling lies too. He's all sweetness to that woman, yet it isn't his nature. My husband cares nothing for people, except when they're of use to him. Why do you think, Mr Bamber, he goes to cocktail parties?'

'Well –'

'So that he may make arrangements with other women. He desires their flesh and tells them so by looking at it.'

Raymond looked serious, frowning, thinking that that was expected of him.

'We look ridiculous together, my husband and I. Yet once we were a handsome couple. I am like an old crow while all he has is laughter lines about his eyes. It's an obsession with me.'

Raymond pursed his lips, sighing slightly.

'He's after women in this room,' said Mrs Fitch, eyeing her husband again.

'Oh, no, now –'

'Why not? How can you know better than I, Mr Bamber? I have had plenty of time to think about this matter. Why shouldn't he want to graze where the grass grows greener, or appears to grow greener? That Anstey woman is a walking confidence trick.'

'I think,' said Raymond, 'that I had best be moving on. I have friends to talk to.' He made a motion to go, but Mrs Fitch grasped part of his jacket in her right hand.

'What I say is true,' she said. 'He is practically a maniac. He has propositioned women in this very room before this. I've heard him at it.'

'I'm sure –'

'When I was a raving beauty he looked at me with his gleaming eye. Now he gleams for all the others. I'll tell you something, Mr Bamber.' Mrs Fitch paused. Raymond noticed that her eyes were staring over his shoulder, as though she had no interest in him beyond his being a person to talk at. 'I've gone down on my bended knees, Mr Bamber, in order to have this situation cleared up: I've prayed that that man might look again with tenderness on his elderly wife. But God has gone on,' said Mrs Fitch bitterly, 'in His mysterious way, not bothering Himself.'

Raymond did not reply to these observations. He said instead that he hadn't liked to mention it before but was Mrs Fitch aware that she was clutching in her right hand part of his clothes?

'He shall get to know your Anstey woman,' said Mrs Fitch. 'He shall come to know that her father was a bearlike man with a generous heart and that her mother, still alive in Guildford, is difficult to get on with. My husband shall come to know all the details about your Anstey woman: the plaster chipping in her bathroom, the way she cooks an egg. He shall know what her handbags look like, and how their clasps work – while I continue to wither away in the house we share.'

Raymond asked Mrs Fitch if she knew the Griegons, who were, he said, most pleasant people. He added that the Griegons were present tonight and that, in fact, he would like to introduce them to her.

'You are trying to avoid the facts. What have the Griegons to recommend them that we should move in their direction and end this conversation? Don't you see the situation, Mr Bamber? I am a woman who is obsessed because of the state of her marriage, how I have aged while he has not. I am obsessed by the fact that he is now incapable of love or tenderness. I have failed to keep all that alive because I lost my beauty. There are lines on my body too, Mr Bamber: I would show you if we were somewhere else.'

Raymond protested again, and felt tired of protesting. But Mrs Fitch, hearing him speak and thinking that he was not yet clear in his mind about the situation, supplied him with further details about her marriage and the manner in which, at cocktail parties, her husband made arrangements for the seduction of younger women, or women who on the face of it seemed younger. 'Obsessions are a disease,' said Mrs Fitch, drinking deeply from her glass.

Raymond explained then that he knew nothing whatsoever about marriage difficulties, to which Mrs Fitch replied that she was only telling him the truth. 'I do not for a moment imagine,' she said, 'that you are an angel come from God, Mr Bamber, in order to settle the unfortunateness. I didn't mean to imply that when I said I had prayed. Did you think I thought you were a messenger?' Mrs Fitch, still holding Raymond's jacket and glancing still at her husband and the woman in yellow, laughed shrilly. Raymond said:

'People are looking at us, the way you are pulling at my clothes. I'm a shy man –'

'Tell me about yourself. You know about me by now: how everything that once seemed rosy has worked out miserably.'

'Oh, come now,' said Raymond, causing Mrs Fitch to repeat her laughter and to call out for a further drink. The Tamberleys' maid hastened towards her. 'Now then,' said Mrs Fitch. 'Tell me.'

'What can I tell you?' asked Raymond.

'I drink a lot these days,' said Mrs Fitch, 'to help matters along. Cheers, Mr Bamber.'

'Actually I've told you quite a bit, you know. One thing and another –'

'You told me nothing except some nonsense about an old creature in Streatham. Who wants to hear that, for Christ's sake? Or is it relevant?'

'Well, I mean, it's true, Mrs Fitch. Relevant to what?'

'I remember you, believe it or not, in this very room on this same occasion last year. "Who's that man?" I said to the Tamberley woman and she replied that you were a bore. You were invited, year by year, so the woman said, because of some friendship between the Tamberleys and your father. In the distant past.'

'Look here,' said Raymond, glancing about him and noting to his relief that no one appeared to have heard what Mrs Fitch in her cups had said.

'What's the matter?' demanded Mrs Fitch. Her eyes were again upon her husband and Mrs Anstey. She saw them laugh together, and felt her unhappiness being added to as though it were a commodity within her body. 'Oh yes,' she said to Raymond, attempting to pass a bit of the unhappiness on. 'A grinding bore. Those were the words of Mrs Tamberley.'

Raymond shook his head. 'I've known Mrs Tamberley since I was a child,' he said.

'So the woman said. You were invited because of the old friendship: the Tamberleys and your father. I cannot tell a lie, Mr Bamber: she said you were a pathetic case. She said you hadn't learned how to grow up. I dare say you're a pervert.'

'My God!'

'I'm sorry I cannot tell lies,' said Mrs Fitch, and Raymond felt her grip tighten on his jacket. 'It's something that happens to you when you've been through what I've been through. That man up to his tricks with women while the beauty drains from my face. What's it like, d'you think?'

'I don't know,' said Raymond. 'How on earth could I know? Mrs Fitch, let's get one thing clear: I am not a pervert.'

'Not? Are you sure? They may think you are, you know,' said Mrs Fitch, glancing again at her husband. 'Mrs Tamberley has probably suggested that very thing to everyone in this room. Crueller, though, I would have thought, to say you were a grinding bore.'

'I am not a pervert —'

'I can see them sniggering over that all right. Unmentionable happenings between yourself and others. Elderly newspaper-vendors —'

'Stop!' cried Raymond. 'For God's sake, woman —'

'You're not a Jew, are you?'

Raymond did not reply. He stood beside Mrs Fitch, thinking that the woman appeared to be both drunk and not of her right mind. He did not wish to create a scene in the Tamberleys' drawing-room, and yet he recognized that by the look of her she intended to hold on to his jacket for the remainder of the evening. If he attempted to pull it away from her, she would not let go: she did not, somehow, seem to be the kind of woman who would. She wouldn't mind a scene at all.

'Why,' said Mrs Fitch, 'did you all of a sudden begin to tell me about that woman in Streatham, Mr Bamber, and the details about your chair-covers and curtains? Why did you tell me about your uncle dying and trying to leave you a business and your feeling that in your perverted condition you were unfit to run a business?'

Raymond's hands began to shake. He could feel an extra tug on his jacket, as though Mrs Fitch was now insisting that he stand closer to her. He pressed his teeth together, grinding his molars one upon another, and then opened his mouth and felt his teeth and his lips quivering. He knew that his voice would sound strange when he spoke. He said:

'You are being extremely offensive to me, Mrs Fitch. You are a woman who is a total stranger to me, yet you have seen fit to drive me into a corner at a cocktail party and hold me here by force. I must insist that you let go my jacket and allow me to walk away.'

'What about me, Mr Bamber? What about my husband and your Anstey woman? Already they are immoral on a narrow bed somewhere; in a fifth-class hotel near King's Cross station.'

'Your husband is still in this room, Mrs Fitch. As well you know. What your husband does is not my business.'

'Your business is your flat in Bayswater, is it? And curtains and covers from the Sanderson showrooms in Berners Street. Your world is people dying and leaving you stuff in wills – money and prayer-books and valuable jewellery that you wear when you dress yourself up in a nurse's uniform.'

'I must ask you to stop, Mrs Fitch.'

'I could let you have a few pairs of old stockings if they interest you. Or garments of my husband's.'

Mrs Fitch saw Raymond close his eyes. She watched the flesh on his face redden further and watched it twitch in answer to a pulse that throbbed in his neck. Her husband, a moment before, had reached out a hand and placed it briefly on the female's arm.

'So your nanny was a guide to you,' said Mrs Fitch. 'You hung on all her words, I dare say?'

Raymond did not reply. He turned his head away, trying to control the twitching in his face. Eventually he said, quietly and with the suspicion of a stammer:

'She was a good woman. She was kind in every way.'

'She taught you neatness.'

Raymond was aware, as Mrs Fitch spoke that sentence, that she had moved appreciably closer to him. He could feel her knee pressing against his. He felt a second knee, and felt next that his leg had been cleverly caught by her, between her own legs.

'Look here,' said Raymond.

'Yes?'

'Mrs Fitch, what are you trying to do?'

Mrs Fitch increased the pressure of her knees. Her right hand moved into Raymond's jacket pocket. 'I am a little the worse for wear,' she said, 'but I can still tell the truth.'

'You are embarrassing me.'

'What are your perversions? Tell me, Mr Bamber.'

'I have no perversions of any kind. I live a normal life.'

'Shall I come to you with a pram? I'm an unhappy woman, Mr Bamber. I'll wear black woollen stockings. I'll show you those lines on my body.'

'Please,' said Raymond, thinking he would cry in a moment.

Already people were glancing at Mrs Fitch's legs gripping his so strongly. Her white face and her scarlet lips were close to his eyes. He could see the lines on her cheeks, but he turned his glance away from them in case she mentioned again the lines on her body. She is a mad, drunken nymphomaniac, said Raymond to himself, and thought that never in all his life had anything so upsetting happened to him.

'Embrace me,' said Mrs Fitch.

'Please, I beg you,' said Raymond.

'You are a homosexual. A queer. I had forgotten that.'

'I'm not a homosexual,' shouted Raymond, aware that his voice was piercingly shrill. Heads turned and he felt the eyes of the Tamberleys' guests. He had been heard to cry that he was not a homosexual, and people had wished to see for themselves.

'Excuse me,' said a voice. 'I'm sorry about this.'

Raymond turned his head and saw Mrs Fitch's husband standing behind him. 'Come along now, Adelaide,' said Mrs Fitch's husband. 'I'm sorry,' he said again to Raymond. 'I didn't realize she'd had a tankful before she got here.'

'I've been telling him a thing or two,' said Mrs Fitch. 'We've exchanged life-stories.'

Raymond felt her legs slip away, and he felt her hand withdraw itself from the pocket of his jacket. He nodded in a worldly way at her husband and said in a low voice that he understood how it was.

'He's a most understanding chap,' said Mrs Fitch. 'He has a dead woman in Streatham.'

'Come along now,' ordered her husband in a rough voice, and Raymond saw that the man's hand gripped her arm in a stern manner.

'I was telling that man,' said Mrs Fitch again, seeming to be all of a sudden in an ever greater state of inebriation. Very slowly she said: 'I was telling him what I am and what you are, and what the Tamberleys think about him. It has been home-truths corner here, for the woman with an elderly face and for the chap who likes to dress himself out as a children's nurse and go with women in chauffeur's garb. Actually, my dear, he's a homosexual.'

'Come along now,' said Mrs Fitch's husband. 'I'm truly sorry,' he added to Raymond. 'It's a problem.'

Raymond saw that it was all being conducted in a most civilized manner. Nobody shouted in the Tamberleys' drawing-room, nobody noticed the three of them talking quite quietly in a corner. The Maltese maid in fact, not guessing for a moment that anything was amiss, came up with her tray of drinks and before anyone could prevent it, Mrs Fitch had lifted one to her lips. '*In vino veritas*,' she remarked.

Raymond felt his body cooling down. His shirt was damp with sweat, and he realized that he was panting slightly and he wondered how long that had been going on. He watched Mrs Fitch being aided through the room by her husband. No wonder, he thought, the man had been a little severe with her, if she put up a performance like that very often; no wonder he treated her like an infant. She was little more than an infant, Raymond considered, saying the first thing that came into her head, and going on about sex. He saw her lean form briefly again, through an opening in the crowded room, and he realized without knowing it that he had craned his neck for a last glimpse. She saw him too, as she smiled and bowed at Mrs Tamberley, appearing to be sober and collected. She shook her head at him, deploring him or suggesting, even, that he had been the one who had misbehaved. Her husband raised a hand in the air, thanking Raymond for his understanding.

Raymond edged his way through all the people and went to find a bathroom. He washed his face, taking his spectacles off and placing them beside a piece of lime-green soap. He was thinking that her husband was probably just like any other man at a cocktail party. How could the husband help it, Raymond thought, if he had not aged and if other women found him pleasant to talk to? Did she expect him to have all his hair plucked out and have an expert come to line his face?

Leaning against the wall of the bathroom, Raymond thought about Mrs Fitch. He thought at first that she was a fantastic woman given to fantastic statements, and then he embroidered on the thought and saw her as being more subtle than that. 'By heavens!' said Raymond aloud to himself. She was a woman, he saw, who was pathetic in what she did, transferring the truth about herself to other people. She it was, he guessed, who was the grinding bore, so well known for the fact that she had come to hear the opinion herself and in her unbalanced way sought to pretend that others were bores in order to push the thing away from her. She was probably even, he thought, a little perverted, the way in which she had behaved with her knees, and sought to imbue others with this characteristic too, so that she, for the moment, might feel rid of it: Mrs Fitch was clearly a case for a psychiatrist. She had said that her husband was a maniac where women were concerned; she had said that he had taken Mrs Anstey to a bed in King's Cross when Mrs Anstey was standing only yards away, in front of her eyes. *In vino veritas*, she had said, for no reason at all.

One morning, Raymond imagined, poor Mr Fitch had woken up to find his wife gabbling in that utterly crazy manner about her age and her hair and the lines on her body. Probably the woman was a nuisance with people who came to the door, the deliverers of coal and groceries, the milkman and the postman. He imagined the Express Dairy on the telephone to Mrs Fitch's husband, complaining that the entire milk-round was daily being disorganized because of the antics of Mrs Fitch, who was a bore with everyone.

It accounted for everything, Raymond thought, the simple fact that the woman was a psychological case. He closed his eyes and sighed with relief, and remembered then that he had read in newspapers about women like Mrs Fitch. He opened his eyes again and looked at himself in the mirror of the Tamberleys' smallest bathroom. He touched his neat moustache with his fingers and smiled at himself to ascertain that his teeth were not carrying a piece of cocktail food. 'You have a tea-leaf on your tooth,' said the voice of Nanny Wilkinson, and Raymond smiled, remembering her.

Raymond returned to the party and stood alone watching the people talking and laughing. His eyes passed from face to face, many of which were familiar to him. He looked for the Griegons with whom last year he had spent quite some time, interesting them in a small sideboard that he had just had french polished, having been left the sideboard in the will of a godmother. The man, a Mr French amusingly enough, had come to Raymond's flat to do the job there in the evenings, having explained that he had no real facilities or premises, being a postman during the day. 'Not that he wasn't an expert polisher,' Raymond had said. 'He did a most beautiful job. I heard of him through Mrs Adams who lives in the flat below. I thought it was reasonable, you know: seven guineas plus expenses. The sideboard came up wonderfully.'

'Hullo,' said Raymond to the Griegons.

'How d'you do?' said Mrs Griegon, a pleasant, smiling woman, not at all like Mrs Fitch. Her husband nodded at Raymond, and turned to a man who was talking busily.

'Our name is Griegon,' said Mrs Griegon. 'This is my husband, and this is Dr Oath.'

'I know,' said Raymond, surprised that Mrs Griegon should say who she was since they had all met so pleasantly a year ago. 'How do you do, Dr Oath?' he said, stretching out a hand.

'Yes,' said Dr Oath, shaking the hand rapidly while continuing his conversation.

Mrs Griegon said: 'You haven't told us your name.'

Raymond, puzzled and looking puzzled, said that his name was Raymond Bamber. 'But surely you remember our nice talk last year?' he said. 'I recall it all distinctly: I was telling you about Mr French who came to polish a sideboard, and how he charged only seven guineas.'

'Most reasonable,' said Mrs Griegon. '*Most* reasonable.'

'We stood over there,' explained Raymond, pointing. 'You and I and Mr Griegon. I remember I gave you my address and telephone number in case if you were ever in Bayswater you might like to pop in to see the sideboard. You said to your husband at the time, Mrs Griegon, that you had one or two pieces that could do with stripping down and polishing, and Mr French, who'll travel anywhere in the evenings and being, as you say, so reasonable –'

'Of course,' cried Mrs Griegon. 'Of course I remember you perfectly, and I'm sure Archie does too.' She looked at her husband, but her husband was listening carefully to Dr Oath.

Raymond smiled. 'It looks even better now that the initial shine has gone. I'm terribly pleased with it.' As he spoke, he saw the figure of Mrs Fitch's husband entering the room. He watched him glance about and saw him smile at someone he'd seen. Following the direction of this smile, Raymond saw Mrs Anstey smiling back at Mrs Fitch's husband, who at once made his way to her side.

'French polishing's an art,' said Mrs Griegon.

What on earth, Raymond wondered, was the man doing back at the Tamberleys' party? And where was Mrs Fitch? Nervously, Raymond glanced about the crowded room, looking for the black-and-white dress and the lean aquiline features of the woman who had tormented him. But although, among all the brightly coloured garments that the women wore there were a few that were black and white, none of them contained Mrs Fitch. 'We come to these parties and everything's a sham,' her voice seemed to say, close to him. 'Nobody can be trusted.' The voice came to him in just the same way as Nanny Wilkinson's had a quarter of an hour ago, when she'd been telling him that he had a tea-leaf on his tooth.

'Such jolly parties,' said Mrs Griegon. 'The Tamberleys are wonderful.'

'Do you know a woman called Mrs Fitch?' said Raymond. 'She was here tonight.'

'Mrs Fitch!' exclaimed Mrs Griegon with a laugh.

'D'you know her?'

'She's married to that man there,' said Mrs Griegon. She pointed at Mr Fitch and sniffed.

'Yes,' said Raymond. 'He's talking to Mrs Anstey.'

He was about to add that Mr Fitch was probably of a social inclination. He was thinking already that Mr Fitch probably had a perfectly sound reason for returning to the Tamberleys'. Probably he lived quite near and having seen his wife home had decided to return in order to say goodbye properly to his hosts. Mrs Anstey, Raymond had suddenly thought, was for all he knew Mr Fitch's sister: in her mentally depressed condition it would have been quite like Mrs Fitch to pretend that the woman in yellow was no relation whatsoever, to have invented a fantasy that was greater even than it appeared to be.

'He's always up to that kind of carry-on,' said Mrs Griegon. 'The man's famous for it.'

'Sorry?' said Raymond.

'Fitch. With women.'

'Oh but surely –'

'Really,' said Mrs Griegon.

'I was talking to Mrs Fitch earlier on and she persisted in speaking about her husband. Well, I felt she was going on rather. Exaggerating, you know. A bit of a bore.'

'He has said things to me, Mr Bamber, that would turn your stomach.'

'She has a funny way with her, Mrs Fitch has. She too said the oddest things –'

'She has a reputation,' said Mrs Griegon, 'for getting drunk and coming out with awkward truths. I've heard it said.'

'Not the truth,' Raymond corrected. 'She says things about herself, you see, and pretends she's talking about another person.'

'What?' said Mrs Griegon.

'Like maybe, you see, she was saying that she herself is a bore the way she goes on – well, Mrs Fitch wouldn't say it just like that. What Mrs Fitch would do is pretend some other person is the bore, the person she might be talking to. D'you see? She would transfer all her own qualities to the person she's talking to.'

Mrs Griegon raised her thin eyebrows and inclined her head. She said that what Raymond was saying sounded most interesting.

'An example is,' said Raymond, 'that Mrs Fitch might find herself unsteady on her feet through drink. Instead of saying that she was unsteady she'd say that you, Mrs Griegon, were the unsteady one. There's a name for it, actually. A medical name.'

'Medical?' said Mrs Griegon.

Glancing across the room, Raymond saw that Mr Fitch's right hand gripped Mrs Anstey's elbow. Mr Fitch murmured in her ear and together the two left the room. Raymond saw them wave at Mrs Tamberley, implying thanks with the gesture, implying that they had enjoyed themselves.

'I can't think what it is now,' said Raymond to Mrs Griegon, 'when people transfer the truth about themselves to others. It's some name beginning with an R, I think.'

'How nice of you,' said Mrs Tamberley, gushing up, 'to put that notice in *The Times*.' She turned to Mrs Griegon and said that, as Raymond had probably told her, a lifelong friend of his, old Nanny Wilkinson, had died a few months ago. 'Every year,' said Mrs Tamberley, 'Raymond told us all how she was bearing up. But now, alas, she's died.'

'Indeed,' said Mrs Griegon, and smiled and moved away.

Without any bidding, there arrived in Raymond's mind a picture of Mrs Fitch sitting alone in her house, refilling a glass from a bottle of Gordon's gin. '*In vino veritas*,' said Mrs Fitch, and began to weep.

'I was telling Mrs Griegon that I'd been chatting with Mrs Fitch,' said Raymond, and then he remembered that Mrs Tamberley had very briefly joined in that chat. 'I found her strange,' he added.

'Married to that man,' cried Mrs Tamberley. 'He drove her to it.'

'Her condition?' said Raymond, nodding.

'She ladles it into herself,' said Mrs Tamberley, 'and then tells you what she thinks of you. It can be disconcerting.'

'She really says anything that comes into her head,' said Raymond, and gave a light laugh.

'Not actually,' said Mrs Tamberley. 'She tells the truth.'

'Well, no, you see –'

'You haven't a drink,' cried Mrs Tamberley in alarm, and moved at speed towards her Maltese maid to direct the girl's attention to Raymond's empty glass.

Again the image of Mrs Fitch arrived in Raymond's mind. She sat as before, alone in a room, while her husband made off with a woman in yellow. She drank some gin.

'Sherry, sir?' said the Maltese maid, and Raymond smiled and thanked her, and then, in an eccentric way and entirely on an impulse, he said in a low voice:

'Do you know a woman called Mrs Fitch?'

The girl said that Mrs Fitch had been at the party earlier in the evening, and reminded Raymond that he had in fact been talking to her.

'She has a peculiar way with her,' explained Raymond. 'I just wondered if ever you had talked to her, or had listened to what she herself had to say.' But the Maltese maid shook her head, appearing not to understand.

'Mrs Fitch's a shocker,' said a voice behind Raymond's back, and added: 'That poor man.'

There was a crackle of laughter as a response, and Raymond, sipping his sherry, turned about and moved towards the group that had caused it. The person who had spoken was a small man with shiny grey hair. 'I'm Raymond Bamber,' said Raymond, smiling at him. 'By the sound of things, you saw my predicament earlier on.' He laughed, imitating the laughter that had come from the group. 'Extremely awkward.'

'She gets tight,' said the small man. 'She's liable to tell a home truth or two.' He began to laugh again. '*In vino veritas*,' he said.

Raymond looked at the people and opened his mouth to say that it wasn't quite so simple, the malaise of Mrs Fitch. 'It's all within her,' he wished to say. 'Everything she says is part of Mrs Fitch, since she's unhappy in a marriage and has lost her beauty.' But Raymond checked that speech, uttering in fact not a word of it. The people looked expectantly at him, and after a long pause the small man said:

'Mrs Fitch can be most embarrassing.'

Raymond heard the people laugh again with the same sharpness and saw their teeth for a moment harshly bared and noted that their eyes were like polished ice. They would not understand, he thought, the facts about

Mrs Fitch, any more than Mrs Griegon had seemed to understand, or Mrs Tamberley. It surprised Raymond, and saddened him, that neither Mrs Griegon nor Mrs Tamberley had cared to accept the truth about the woman. It was, he told himself, something of a revelation that Mrs Griegon, who had seemed so pleasant the year before, and Mrs Tamberley whom he had known almost all his life, should turn out to be no better than this group of hard-eyed people. Raymond murmured and walked away, still thinking of Mrs Griegon and Mrs Tamberley. He imagined them laughing with their husbands over Mrs Fitch, repeating that she was a bore and a drunk. Laughter was apparently the thing, a commodity that reflected the shallowness of minds too lazy to establish correctly the facts about people. And they were minds, as had been proved to Raymond, that didn't even bother to survey properly the simple explanations of eccentric conduct – as though even that constituted too much trouble.

Soon afterwards, Raymond left the party and walked through the autumn evening, considering everything. The air was cool on his face as he strode towards Bayswater, thinking that as he continued to live his quiet life Mrs Fitch would be attending parties that were similar to the Tamberleys', and she'd be telling the people she met there that they were grinding bores. The people might be offended, Raymond thought, if they didn't pause to think about it, if they didn't understand that everything was confused in poor Mrs Fitch's mind. And it would serve them right, he reflected, to be offended – a just reward for allowing their minds to become lazy and untidy in this modern manner. 'Orderliness,' said the voice of Nanny Wilkinson, and Raymond paused and smiled, and then walked on.

The Distant Past

In the town and beyond it they were regarded as harmlessly peculiar. Odd, people said, and in time this reference took on a burnish of affection.

They had always been thin, silent with one another, and similar in appearance: a brother and sister who shared a family face. It was a bony countenance, with pale blue eyes and a sharp, well-shaped nose and high cheekbones. Their father had had it too, but unlike them their father had been an irresponsible and careless man, with red flecks in his cheeks that they didn't have at all. The Middletons of Carraveagh the family had once been known as, but now the brother and sister were just the Middletons, for Carraveagh didn't count any more, except to them.

They owned four Herefords, a number of hens, and the house itself, three miles outside the town. It was a large house, built in the reign of George II, a monument that reflected in its glory and later decay the fortunes of a family. As the brother and sister aged, its roof increasingly ceased to afford protection, rust ate at its gutters, grass thrived in two thick channels all along its avenue. Their father had mortgaged his inherited estate, so local rumour claimed, in order to keep a Catholic Dublin woman in brandy and jewels. When he died, in 1924, his two children discovered that they possessed only a dozen acres. It was locally said also that this adversity hardened their will and that, because of it, they came to love the remains of Carraveagh more than they could ever have loved a husband or a wife. They blamed for their ill-fortune the Catholic Dublin woman whom they'd never met and they blamed as well the new national regime, contriving in their eccentric way to relate the two. In the days of the Union Jack such women would have known their place: wasn't it all part and parcel?

Twice a week, on Fridays and Sundays, the Middletons journeyed into the town, first of all in a trap and later in a Ford Anglia car. In the shops and elsewhere they made, quite gently, no secret of their continuing loyalty to the past. They attended on Sundays St Patrick's Protestant Church, a place that matched their mood, for prayers were still said there for the King whose sovereignty their country had denied. The revolutionary regime would not last, they quietly informed the Reverend Packham: what sense was there in green-painted pillar-boxes and a language that nobody understood?

On Fridays, when they took seven or eight dozen eggs to the town, they dressed in pressed tweeds and were accompanied over the years by a series of red setters, the breed there had always been at Carraveagh. They sold the eggs in Gerrity's grocery and then had a drink with Mrs Gerrity in the part of her shop that was devoted to the consumption of refreshment. Mr Middleton had whiskey and his sister Tio Pepe. They enjoyed the occasion, for they liked Mrs Gerrity and were liked by her in return. Afterwards they shopped, chatting to the shopkeepers about whatever news there was, and then they went to Healy's Hotel for a few more drinks before driving home.

Drink was their pleasure and it was through it that they built up, in spite of their loyalty to the past, such convivial relationships with the people of the town. Fat Cranley, who kept the butcher's shop, used even to joke about the past when he stood with them in Healy's Hotel or stood behind his own counter cutting their slender chops or thinly slicing their liver. 'Will you ever forget it, Mr Middleton? I'd ha' run like a rabbit if you'd lifted a finger at me.' Fat Cranley would laugh then, rocking back on his heels with a glass of stout in his hand or banging their meat on to his weighing-scales. Mr Middleton would smile. 'There was alarm in your eyes, Mr Cranley,' Miss Middleton would murmur, smiling also at the memory of the distant occasion.

Fat Cranley, with a farmer called Maguire and another called Breen, had stood in the hall of Carraveagh, each of them in charge of a shot-gun. The Middletons, children then, had been locked with their mother and father and an aunt into an upstairs room. Nothing else had happened: the expected British soldiers had not, after all, arrived and the men in the hall had eventually relaxed their vigil. 'A massacre they wanted,' the Middletons' father said after they'd gone. 'Damn bloody ruffians.'

The Second World War took place. Two Germans, a man and his wife called Winkelmann who ran a glove factory in the town, were suspected by the Middletons of being spies for the Third Reich. People laughed, for they knew the Winkelmanns well and could lend no credence to the Middletons' latest fantasy: typical of them, they explained to the Winkelmanns, who had been worried. Soon after the War the Reverend Packham died and was replaced by the Reverend Bradshaw, a younger man who laughed also and regarded the Middletons as an anachronism. They protested when prayers were no longer said for the Royal Family in St Patrick's, but the Reverend Bradshaw considered that their protests were as absurd as the prayers themselves had been. Why pray for the monarchy of a neighbouring island when their own island had its chosen President now? The Middletons didn't reply to that argument. In the Reverend Bradshaw's presence they rose to their feet when the BBC played 'God Save the King', and on the day of the coronation of Queen Elizabeth II they drove into the town with a small Union Jack propped up in the back window of their Ford Anglia. 'Bedad, you're a holy terror, Mr Middleton!' Fat Cranley laughingly exclaimed, noticing the flag as he lifted a tray of pork steaks from his display shelf. The Middletons smiled. It was a great day for the Commonwealth of Nations, they replied, a remark which further amused Fat Cranley and which he later repeated in Phelan's public house. 'Her Britannic Majesty,' guffawed his friend Mr Breen.

Situated in a valley that was noted for its beauty and with convenient access to rich rivers and bogs over which game-birds flew, the town benefited from post-war tourism. Healy's Hotel changed its title and became, overnight, the New Ormonde. Shopkeepers had their shop-fronts painted and Mr Healy organized an annual Salmon Festival. Even Canon Cotter, who had at first commented severely on the habits of the tourists, and in particular on the summertime dress of the women, was in the end obliged to confess that the morals of his flock remained unaffected. 'God and good sense', he proclaimed, meaning God and his own teaching. In time he even derived pride from the fact that people with other values came briefly to the town and that the values esteemed by his parishioners were in no way diminished.

The town's grocers now stocked foreign cheeses, brie and camembert and Port Salut, and wines were available to go with them. The plush Cocktail Room of the New Ormonde set a standard: the wife of a solicitor, a Mrs Duggan, began to give six o'clock parties once or twice a year, obliging her husband to mix gin and Martini in glass jugs and herself handing round a selection of nuts and small Japanese crackers. Canon Cotter looked in as a rule and satisfied himself that all was above board. He rejected, though, the mixture in the jugs, retaining his taste for a glass of John Jameson.

From the windows of their convent the Loreto nuns observed the long, sleek cars with GB plates; English and American accents drifted on the breeze to them. Mothers cleaned up their children and sent them to the Golf Club to seek employment as caddies. Sweet-shops sold holiday mementoes. The brown, soda and currant breads of Murphy-Flood's bakery were declared to be delicious. Mr Healy doubled the number of local girls who served as waitresses in his dining-room, and in the winter of 1961 he had the builders in again, working on an extension for which the Munster and Leinster Bank had lent him twenty-two thousand pounds.

But as the town increased its prosperity Carraveagh continued its decline. The Middletons were in their middle-sixties now and were reconciled to a life that became more uncomfortable with every passing year. Together they roved the vast lofts of their house, placing old paint tins and flowerpot saucers beneath the drips from the roof. At night they sat over their thin chops in a dining-room that had once been gracious and which in a way was gracious still, except for the faded appearance of furniture that was dry from lack of polish and of a wallpaper that time had rendered colourless. In the hall their father gazed down at them, framed in ebony and gilt, in the uniform of the Irish Guards. He had conversed with Queen Victoria, and even in their middle-sixties they could still hear him saying that God and Empire and Queen formed a trinity unique in any worthy soldier's heart. In the hall hung the family crest, and on ancient Irish linen the Cross of St George.

The dog that accompanied the Middletons now was called Turloch, an animal whose death they dreaded for they felt they couldn't manage the antics of another pup. Turloch, being thirteen, moved slowly and was blind and a little deaf. He was a reminder to them of their own advancing years and of the effort it had become to tend the Herefords and collect the weekly eggs. More and more they looked forward to Fridays, to the warm companionship of Mrs Gerrity and Mr Healy's chatter in the hotel. They stayed longer now with Mrs Gerrity and in the hotel, and idled longer in the shops, and drove home more slowly. Dimly, but with no less loyalty, they still recalled the distant past and were listened to without ill-feeling when they spoke of it and of Carraveagh as it had been, and of the Queen whose company their careless father had known.

The visitors who came to the town heard about the Middletons and were impressed. It was a pleasant wonder, more than one of them remarked, that old wounds could heal so completely, that the Middletons continued in their loyalty to the past and that, in spite of it, they were respected in the town. When Miss Middleton had been ill with a form of pneumonia in 1958 Canon Cotter had driven out to Carraveagh twice a week with pullets and young ducks that his housekeeper had dressed. 'An upright couple,' was the Canon's public opinion of the Middletons, and he had been known to add that eccentric views would hurt you less than malice. 'We can disagree without guns in this town,' Mr Healy pronounced in his Cocktail Room, and his visitors usually replied that as far as they could see this was the result of living in a Christian country. That the Middletons bought their meat from a man who had once locked them into an upstairs room and had then waited to shoot soldiers in their hall was a fact that amazed the seasonal visitors. You lived and learned, they remarked to Mr Healy.

The Middletons, privately, often considered that they led a strange life. Alone in their two beds at night they now and again wondered why they hadn't just sold Carraveagh forty-eight years ago when their father died: why had the tie been so strong and why had they in perversity encouraged it? They didn't fully know, nor did they attempt to discuss the matter in any way. Instinctively they had remained at Carraveagh, instinctively feeling that it would have been cowardly to go. Yet often it seemed to them now to be no more than a game they played, this worship of the distant past. And at other times it seemed as real and as important as the remaining acres of land, and the house itself.

'Isn't that shocking?' Mr Healy said one day in 1968. 'Did you hear about that, Mr Middleton, blowing up them post offices in Belfast?'

Mr Healy, red-faced and short-haired, spoke casually in his Cocktail Room, making midday conversation. He had commented in much the same way at breakfast-time, looking up from the *Irish Independent*. Everyone in the town had said it too: that the blowing up of sub-post offices in Belfast was a shocking matter.

'A bad business,' Fat Cranley remarked, wrapping the Middletons' meat. 'We don't want that old stuff all over again.'

'We didn't want it in the first place,' Miss Middleton reminded him. He laughed, and she laughed, and so did her brother. Yes, it was a game, she thought: how could any of it be as real or as important as the afflictions and problems of the old butcher himself, his rheumatism and his reluctance to retire? Did her brother, she wondered, privately think so too?

'Come on, old Turloch,' he said, stroking the flank of the red setter with the point of his shoe, and she reflected that you could never tell what he was thinking. Certainly it wasn't the kind of thing you wanted to talk about.

'I've put him in a bit of mince,' Fat Cranley said, which was something he often did these days, pretending the mince would otherwise be thrown away. There'd been a red setter about the place that night when he waited in the hall for the soldiers: Breen and Maguire had pushed it down into a cellar, frightened of it.

'There's a heart of gold in you, Mr Cranley,' Miss Middleton murmured, nodding and smiling at him. He was the same age as she was, sixty-six: he should have shut up shop years ago. He would have, he'd once told them, if there'd been a son to leave the business to. As it was, he'd have to sell it and when it came to the point he found it hard to make the necessary arrangements. 'Like us and Carraveagh,' she'd said, even though on the face of it it didn't seem the same at all.

Every evening they sat in the big old kitchen, hearing the news. It was only in Belfast and Derry, the wireless said; outside Belfast and Derry you wouldn't know anything was happening at all. On Fridays they listened to the talk in Mrs Gerrity's bar and in the hotel. 'Well, thank God it has nothing to do with the South,' Mr Healy said often, usually repeating the statement.

The first British soldiers landed in the North of Ireland, and soon people didn't so often say that outside Belfast and Derry you wouldn't know anything was happening. There were incidents in Fermanagh and Armagh, in Border villages and towns. One Prime Minister resigned and then another one. The troops were unpopular, the newspapers said; internment became part of the machinery of government. In the town, in St Patrick's Protestant Church and in the Church of the Holy Assumption, prayers for peace were offered, but no peace came.

'We're hit, Mr Middleton,' Mr Healy said one Friday morning. 'If there's a dozen visitors this summer it'll be God's own stroke of luck for us.'

'Luck?'

'Sure, who wants to come to a country with all that malarkey in it?'

'But it's only in the North.'

'Tell that to your tourists, Mr Middleton.'

The town's prosperity ebbed. The Border was more than sixty miles away, but over that distance had spread some wisps of the fog of war. As anger rose in the town at the loss of fortune so there rose also the kind of talk there had been in the distant past. There was talk of atrocities and counter-atrocities, and of guns and gelignite and the rights of people. There was bitterness suddenly in Mrs Gerrity's bar because of the lack of trade, and in the empty hotel there was bitterness also.

On Fridays, only sometimes at first, there was a silence when the Middletons appeared. It was as though, going back nearly twenty years, people remembered the Union Jack in the window of their car and saw it now in a different light. It wasn't something to laugh at any more, nor were certain words that the Middletons had gently spoken, nor were they themselves just an old, peculiar couple. Slowly the change crept about, all around them in the town, until Fat Cranley didn't wish it to be remembered that he had ever given them mince for their dog. He had stood with a gun in the enemy's house, waiting for soldiers so that soldiers might be killed: it was better that people should remember that.

One day Canon Cotter looked the other way when he saw the Middletons' car coming and they noticed this movement of his head, although he hadn't wished them to. And on another day Mrs Duggan, who had always been keen to talk to them in the hotel, didn't reply when they addressed her.

The Middletons naturally didn't discuss these rebuffs, but they each of them privately knew that there was no conversation they could have at this time with the people of the town. The stand they had taken and kept to for so many years no longer seemed ridiculous in the town. Had they driven with a Union Jack now they might, astoundingly, have been shot.

'It will never cease.' He spoke disconsolately one night, standing by the dresser where the wireless was.

She washed the dishes they'd eaten from, and the cutlery. 'Not in our time,' she said.

'It is worse than before.'

'Yes, it is worse than before.'

They took from the walls of the hall the portrait of their father in the uniform of the Irish Guards because it seemed wrong to them that at this time it should hang there. They took down also the crest of their family and the Cross of St George, and from a vase on the drawing-room mantel-piece they removed the small Union Jack that had been there since the Coronation of Queen Elizabeth II. They did not remove these articles in fear, but in mourning for the *modus vivendi* that had existed for so long between them and the people of the town. They had given their custom to a butcher who had planned to shoot down soldiers in their hall and he, in turn, had given them mince for their dog. For fifty years they had experi-enced, after suspicion had seeped away, a tolerance that never again in the years that were left to them would they know.

One November night their dog died and he said to her after he had buried it that they must not be depressed by all that was happening. They would die themselves and the house would become a ruin because there was no one to inherit it, and the distant past would be set to rest. But she disagreed: the *modus vivendi* had been easy for them, she pointed out, because they hadn't really minded the dwindling of their fortunes while the town prospered. It had given them a life, and a kind of dignity: you could take a pride out of living in peace.

He did not say anything and then, because of the emotion that both of them felt over the death of their dog, he said in a rushing way that they could no longer at their age hope to make a living out of the remains of Carraveagh. They must sell the hens and the four Herefords. As he spoke, he watched her nodding, agreeing with the sense of it. Now and again, he thought, he would drive slowly into the town, to buy groceries and meat with the money they had saved, and to face the silence that would sourly thicken as their own two deaths came closer and death increased in another part of their island. She felt him thinking that and she knew that he was right. Because of the distant past they would die friendless. It was worse than being murdered in their beds.

In Isfahan

They met in the most casual way, in the upstairs office of Chaharbagh Tours Inc. In the downstairs office a boy asked Normanton to go upstairs and wait: the tour would start a little later because they were having trouble with the engine of the minibus.

The upstairs office was more like a tiny waiting-room than an office, with chairs lined against two walls. The chairs were rudimentary: metal frames, and red plastic over foam rubber. There was a counter stacked with free guides to Isfahan in French and German, and guides to Shiraz and Persepolis in English as well. The walls had posters on them, issued by the Iranian Tourist Board: Mount Damavand, the Chalus road, native dancers from the Southern tribes, club-swinging, the Apadana Palace at Persepolis, the Theological School in Isfahan. The fees and conditions of Chaharbagh Tours were clearly stated: *Tours by De Lux microbus. Each Person Rls. 375 ($5). Tours in French and English language. Microbus comes to Hotel otherwise you'll come to Office. All Entrance Fees. No Shopping. Chaharbagh Tours Inc. wishes you the best.*

She was writing an air-mail letter with a ballpoint pen, leaning on a brochure which she'd spread out on her handbag. It was an awkward arrangement, but she didn't seem to mind. She wrote steadily, not looking up when he entered, not pausing to think about what each sentence might contain. There was no one else in the upstairs office.

He took some leaflets from the racks on the counter. *Isfahan était capitale de l'Iran sous les Seldjoukides et les Safavides. Sous le règne de ces deux dynasties l'art islamique de l'Iran avait atteint son apogée.*

'Are you going on the tour?'

He turned to look at her, surprised that she was English. She was thin and would probably not be very tall when she stood up, a woman in her thirties, without a wedding ring. In a pale face her eyes were hidden behind huge round sunglasses. Her mouth was sensuous, the lips rather thick, her hair soft and black. She was wearing a pink dress and white high-heeled sandals. Nothing about her was smart.

In turn she saw a man who seemed to her to be typically English. He was middle-aged and greying, dressed in a linen suit and carrying a linen hat that matched it. There were lines and wrinkles in his face, about the eyes especially, and the mouth. When he smiled more lines and wrinkles gathered. His skin was tanned, but with the look of skin that usually wasn't: he'd been in Persia only a few weeks, she reckoned.

'Yes, I'm going on the tour,' he said. 'They're having trouble with the minibus.'

'Are we the only two?'

He said he thought not. The minibus would go round the hotels collecting the people who'd bought tickets for the tour. He pointed at the notice on the wall.

She took her dark glasses off. Her eyes were her startling feature: brown, beautiful orbs, with endless depth, mysterious in her more ordinary face. Without the dark glasses she had an Indian look: lips, hair and eyes combined to give her that. But her voice was purely English, made uglier than it might have been by attempts to disguise a Cockney twang.

'I've been writing to my mother,' she said.

He smiled at her and nodded. She put her dark glasses on again and licked the edges of the air-mail letter-form.

'Microbus ready,' the boy from downstairs said. He was a smiling youth of about fifteen with black-rimmed spectacles and very white teeth. He wore a white shirt with tidily rolled-up sleeves, and brown cotton trousers. 'Tour commence please,' he said. 'I am Guide Hafiz.'

He led them to the minibus. 'You German two?' he inquired, and when they replied that they were English he said that not many English came to Persia. 'American,' he said. 'French. German people often.'

They got into the minibus. The driver turned his head to nod and smile at them. He spoke in Persian to Hafiz, and laughed.

'He commence a joke,' Hafiz said. 'He wish me the best. This is the first tour I make. Excuse me, please.' He perused leaflets and guidebooks, uneasily licking his lips.

'My name's Iris Smith,' she said.

His, he revealed, was Normanton.

They drove through blue Isfahan, past domes and minarets, and tourist shops in the Avenue Chaharbagh, with blue mosaic on surfaces everywhere, and blue taxi-cabs. Trees and grass had a precious look because of the arid earth. The sky was pale with the promise of heat.

The minibus called at the Park Hotel and at the Intercontinental and the Shah Abbas, where Normanton was staying. It didn't call at the Old Atlantic, which Iris Smith had been told at Teheran Airport was cheap and clean. It collected a French party and a German couple who were having trouble with sunburn, and two wholesome-faced American girls.

Hafiz continued to speak in English, explaining that it was the only foreign language he knew. 'Ladies-gentlemen, I am a student from Teheran,' he announced with pride, and then confessed: 'I do not know Isfahan well.'

The leader of the French party, a testy-looking man whom Normanton put down as a university professor, had already protested at their guide's inability to speak French. He protested again when Hafiz said he didn't know Isfahan well, complaining that he had been considerably deceived.

'No, no,' Hafiz replied. 'That is not my fault, sir, I am poor Persian student, sir. Last night I arrive in Isfahan the first time only. It is impossible my father send me to Isfahan before.' He smiled at the testy Frenchman. 'So listen please, ladies-gentlemen. This morning we commence happy tour, we see many curious scenes.' Again his smile flashed. He read in English from an Iran Air leaflet: '*Isfahan is the showpiece of Islamic Persia, but founded at least two thousand years ago!* Here we are, ladies-gentlemen, at the Chehel Sotun. This is pavilion of lyric beauty, palace of forty columns where Shah Abbas II entertain all royal guests. All please leave microbus.'

Normanton wandered alone among the forty columns of the palace. The American girls took photographs and the German couple did the same. A member of the French party operated a moving camera, although only tourists and their guides were moving. The girl called Iris Smith seemed out of place, Normanton thought, teetering on her high-heeled sandals.

'So now Masjed-e-Shah,' Hafiz cried, clapping his hands to collect his party together. The testy Frenchman continued to expostulate, complaining that time had been wasted in the Chehel Sotun. Hafiz smiled at him.

'*Masjed-e-Shah*,' he read from a leaflet as the minibus began again, '*is most outstanding and impressive mosque built by Shah Abbas the Great in early seventeenth century.*'

But when the minibus drew up outside the Masjed-e-Shah it was discovered that the Masjed-e-Shah was closed to tourists because of renovations. So, unfortunately, was the Sheikh Lotfollah.

'So commence to carpet-weaving,' Hafiz said, smiling and shaking his head at the protestations of the French professor.

The cameras moved among the carpet-weavers, women of all ages, producing at speed Isfahan carpets for export. 'Look now at once,' Hafiz commanded, pointing at a carpet that incorporated the features of the late President Kennedy. 'Look please on this skill, ladies-gentlemen.'

In the minibus he announced that the tour was now on its way to the Masjed-e-Jamé, the Friday Mosque. This, he reported after a consultation of his leaflets, displayed Persian architecture of the ninth to the eighteenth century. '*Oldest and largest in Isfahan*,' he read. '*Don't miss it! Many minarets in narrow lanes!* All leave microbus, ladies-gentlemen. All return to microbus in one hour.'

At this there was chatter from the French party. The tour was scheduled to be conducted, points of interest were scheduled to be indicated. The tour was costing three hundred and seventy-five rials.

'OK, ladies-gentlemen,' Hafiz said. 'Ladies-gentlemen come by me to commence informations. Other ladies-gentlemen come to microbus in one hour.'

An hour was a long time in the Friday Mosque. Normanton wandered away from it, through dusty crowded lanes, into market-places where letter-writers slept on their stools, waiting for illiterates with troubles. In hot, bright sunshine peasants with produce to sell bargained with deft-witted shopkeepers. Crouched on the dust, cobblers made shoes: on a wooden chair a man was shaved beneath a tree. Other men drank sherbet, arguing as vigorously as the heat allowed. Veiled women hurried, pausing to prod entrails at butchers' stalls or to finger rice.

'You're off the tourist track, Mr Normanton.'

Her white high-heeled sandals were covered with dust. She looked tired.

'So are you,' he said.

'I'm glad I ran into you. I wanted to ask how much that dress was.'

She pointed at a limp blue dress hanging on a stall. It was difficult when a woman on her own asked the price of something in this part of the world, she explained. She knew about that from living in Bombay.

He asked the stall-holder how much the dress was, but it turned out to be too expensive, although to Normanton it seemed cheap. The stall-holder followed them along the street offering to reduce the price, saying he had other goods, bags, lengths of cotton, pictures on ivory, all beautiful work-manship, all cheap bargains. Normanton told him to go away.

'Do you live in Bombay?' He wondered if she perhaps was Indian, brought up in London, or half-caste.

'Yes, I live in Bombay. And sometimes in England.'

It was the statement of a woman not at all like Iris Smith: it suggested a grandeur, a certain style, beauty, and some riches.

'I've never been in Bombay,' he said.

'Life can be good enough there. The social life's not bad.'

They had arrived back at the Friday Mosque.

'You've seen all this?' He gestured towards it.

She said she had, but he had the feeling that she hadn't bothered much with the mosque. He couldn't think what had drawn her to Isfahan.

'I love travelling,' she said.

The French party were already established again in the minibus, all except the man with the moving camera. They were talking loudly among themselves, complaining about Hafiz and Chaharbagh Tours. The German couple arrived, their sunburn pinker after their exertions. Hafiz arrived with the two American girls. He was laughing, beginning to flirt with them.

'So,' he said in the minibus, 'we commence the Shaking Minarets. *Two minarets able to shake*,' he read, '*eight kilometres outside the city*. Very famous, ladies-gentlemen, very curious.'

The driver started the bus, but the French party shrilly protested, declaring that the man with the moving camera had been left behind. '*Où est-ce qu'il est?*' a woman in red cried.

'I will tell you a Persian joke,' Hafiz said to the American girls. 'A Persian student commences at a party –'

'*Attention!*' the woman in red cried.

'*Imbécile!*' the professor shouted at Hafiz.

Hafiz smiled at them. He did not understand their trouble, he said, while they continued to shout at him. Slowly he took his spectacles off and wiped a sheen of dust from them. 'So a Persian student commences at a party,' he began again.

'I think you've left someone behind,' Normanton said. 'The man with the moving camera.'

The driver of the minibus laughed and then Hafiz, realizing his error, laughed also. He sat down on a seat beside the American girls and laughed unrestrainedly, beating his knees with a fist and flashing his very white teeth. The driver reversed the minibus, with his finger on the horn. 'Bad man!' Hafiz said to the Frenchman when he climbed into the bus, laughing again. 'Heh, heh, heh,' he cried, and the driver and the American girls laughed also.

'*Il est fou!*' one of the French party muttered crossly. '*Incroyable!*'

Normanton glanced across the minibus and discovered that Iris Smith, amused by all this foreign emotion, was already glancing at him. He smiled at her and she smiled back.

Hafiz paid two men to climb into the shaking minarets and shake them. The Frenchman took moving pictures of this motion. Hafiz announced that the mausoleum of a hermit was located near by. He pointed at the view from the roof where they stood. He read slowly from one of his leaflets, informing them that the view was fantastic. 'At the party,' he said to the American girls, 'the student watches an aeroplane on the breast of a beautiful girl. "Why watch you my aeroplane?" the girl commences. "Is it you like my aeroplane?" "It is not the aeroplane which I like," the student commences. "It is the aeroplane's airport which I like." That is a Persian joke.'

It was excessively hot on the roof with the shaking minarets. Normanton had put on his linen hat. Iris Smith tied a black chiffon scarf around her head.

'We commence to offices,' Hafiz said. 'This afternoon we visit Vank Church. Also curious Fire Temple.' He consulted his leaflets. 'An Armenian Museum. *Here you can see a nice collection of old manuscripts and paintings.*'

When the minibus drew up outside the offices of Chaharbagh Tours Hafiz said it was important for everyone to come inside. He led the way, through the downstairs office and up to the upstairs office. Tea was served. Hafiz handed round a basket of sweets, wrapped pieces of candy locally manufactured, very curious taste, he said. Several men in light-weight suits, the principals of Chaharbagh Tours, drank tea also. When the French professor complained that the tour was not satisfactory, the men smiled, denying that they understood either French or English, and in no way betraying that they could recognize any difference when the professor changed from one language to the other. It was likely, Normanton guessed, that they were fluent in both.

'Shall you continue after lunch?' he asked Iris Smith. 'The Vank Church, an Armenian museum? There's also the Theological School, which really is the most beautiful of all. No tour is complete without that.'

'You've been on the tour before?'

'I've walked about. I've got to know Isfahan.'

'Then why –'

'It's something to do. Tours are always rewarding. For a start, there are the other people on them.'

'I shall rest this afternoon.'

'The Theological School is easy to find. It's not far from the Shah Abbas Hotel.'

'Are you staying there?'

'Yes.'

She was curious about him. He could see it in her eyes, for she'd taken off her dark glasses. Yet he couldn't believe that he presented as puzzling an exterior as she did herself.

'I've heard it's beautiful,' she said. 'The hotel.'

'Yes, it is.'

'I think everything in Isfahan is beautiful.'

'Are you staying here for long?'

'Until tomorrow morning, the five o'clock bus back to Teheran. I came last night.'

'From London?'

'Yes.'

The tea-party came to an end. The men in the light-weight suits bowed. Hafiz told the American girls that he was looking forward to seeing them in the afternoon, at two o'clock. In the evening, if they were doing nothing else, they might meet again. He smiled at everyone else. They would continue to have a happy tour, he promised, at two o'clock. He would be honoured to give them the informations they desired.

Normanton said goodbye to Iris Smith. He wouldn't, he said, be on the afternoon tour either. The people of a morning tour, he did not add, were never amusing in the afternoon: it wouldn't be funny if the Frenchman with the moving camera got left behind again; the professor's testiness and Hafiz's pidgin English might easily become wearisome as the day wore on.

He advised her again not to miss the Theological School. There was a tourist bazaar beside it, with boutiques, where she might find a dress. But prices would be higher there. She shook her head: she liked collecting bargains.

He walked to the Shah Abbas. He forgot about Iris Smith.

She took a mild sleeping-pill and slept on her bed in the Old Atlantic. When she awoke it was a quarter to seven.

The room was almost dark because she'd pulled over the curtains. She'd taken off her pink dress and hung it up. She lay in her petticoat, staring sleepily at a ceiling she couldn't see. For a few moments before she'd slept her eyes had traversed its network of cracks and flaking paint. There'd been enough light then, even though the curtains had been drawn.

She slipped from the bed and crossed to the window. It was twilight outside, a light that seemed more than ordinarily different from the bright sunshine of the afternoon. Last night, at midnight when she'd arrived, it had been sharply different too: as black as pitch, totally silent in Isfahan.

It wasn't silent now. The blue taxis raced their motors as they paused in a traffic-jam outside the Old Atlantic. Tourists chattered in different languages. Bunches of children, returning from afternoon school, called out to one another on the pavements. Policemen blew their traffic whistles.

Neon lights were winking in the twilight, and in the far distance she could see the massive illuminated dome of the Theological School, a fat blue jewel that dominated everything.

She washed herself and dressed, opening a suitcase to find a black-and-white dress her mother had made her and a black frilled shawl that went with it. She rubbed the dust from her high-heeled sandals with a Kleenex tissue. It would be nicer to wear a different pair of shoes, more suitable for the evening, but that would mean more unpacking and anyway who was there to notice? She took some medicine because for months she'd had a nagging little cough, which usually came on in the evenings. It was always the same: whenever she returned to England she got a cough.

In his room he read that the Shah was in Moscow, negotiating a deal with the Russians. He closed his eyes, letting the newspaper fall on to the carpet.

At seven o'clock he would go downstairs and sit in the bar and watch the tourist parties. They knew him in the bar now. As soon as he entered one of the barmen would raise a finger and nod. A moment later he would receive his vodka lime, with crushed ice. 'You have good day, sir?' the barman would say to him, whichever barman it was.

Since the Chaharbagh tour of the morning he had eaten a chicken sandwich and walked, he estimated, ten miles. Exhausted, he had had a bath, delighting in the flow of warm water over his body, becoming drowsy until the water cooled and began to chill him. He'd stretched himself on his bed and then had slowly dressed, in a different linen suit.

His room in the Shah Abbas Hotel was enormous, with a balcony and blown-up photographs of domes and minarets, and a double bed as big as a night-club dance-floor. Ever since he'd first seen it he'd kept thinking that his bed was as big as a dance-floor. The room itself was large enough for a quite substantial family to live in.

He went downstairs at seven o'clock, using the staircase because he hated lifts and because, in any case, it was pleasant to walk through the luxurious hotel. In the hall a group of forty or so Swiss had arrived. He stood by a pillar for a moment, watching them. Their leader made arrangements at the desk, porters carried their luggage from the airport bus. Their faces looked happier when the luggage was identified. Swiss archaeologists, Normanton conjectured, a group tour of some Geneva society. And then, instead of going straight to the bar, he walked out of the hotel into the dusk.

They met in the tourist bazaar. She had bought a brooch, a square of coloured cotton, a canvas carrier-bag. When he saw her, he knew at once that he'd gone to the tourist bazaar because she might be there. They walked together, comparing the prices of ivory miniatures, the traditional polo-playing scene, variously interpreted. It was curiosity, nothing else, that made him want to renew their acquaintanceship.

'The Theological School is closed,' she said.

'You can get in.'

He led her from the bazaar and rang a bell outside the school. He gave the porter a few rials. He said they wouldn't be long.

She marvelled at the peace, the silence of the open courtyards, the blue mosaic walls, the blue water, men silently praying. She called it a grotto of heaven. She heard a sound which she said was a nightingale, and he said it might have been, although Shiraz was where the nightingales were. 'Wine and roses and nightingales,' he said because he knew it would please her. Shiraz was beautiful, too, but not as beautiful as Isfahan. The grass in the courtyards of the Theological School was not like ordinary grass, she said. Even the paving stones and the water gained a dimension in all the blueness. Blue was the colour of holiness: you could feel the holiness here.

'It's nicer than the Taj Mahal. It's pure enchantment.'

'Would you like a drink, Miss Smith? I could show you the enchantments of the Shah Abbas Hotel.'

'I'd love a drink.'

She wasn't wearing her dark glasses. The nasal twang of her voice continued to grate on him whenever she spoke, but her eyes seemed even more sumptuous than they'd been in the bright light of day. It was a shame he couldn't say to her that her eyes were just as beautiful as the architecture of the Theological School, but such a remark would naturally be mis-understood.

'What would you like?' he asked in the bar of the hotel. All around them the Swiss party spoke in French. A group of Texan oilmen and their wives, who had been in the bar the night before, were there again, occupying the same corner. The sunburnt German couple of the Chaharbagh tour were there, with other Germans they'd made friends with.

'I'd like some whisky,' she said. 'With soda. It's very kind of you.'

When their drinks came he suggested that he should take her on a conducted tour of the hotel. They could drink their way around it, he said. 'I shall be Guide Hafiz.'

He enjoyed showing her because all the time she made marvelling noises, catching her breath in marble corridors and fingering the endless mosaic of the walls, sinking her high-heeled sandals into the pile of carpets. Everything made it enchantment, she said: the gleam of gold and mirror-glass among the blues and reds of the mosaic, the beautifully finished furniture, the staircase, the chandeliers.

'This is my room,' he said, turning the key in the lock of a polished mahogany door.

'Gosh!'

'Sit down, Miss Smith.'

They sat and sipped at their drinks. They talked about the room. She walked out on to the balcony and then came and sat down again.

It had become quite cold, she remarked, shivering a little. She coughed.

'You've a cold.'

'England always gives me a cold.'

They sat in two dark, tweed-covered armchairs with a glass-topped table between them. A maid had been to turn down the bed. His green pyjamas lay ready for him on the pillow.

They talked about the people on the tour, Hafiz and the testy professor, and the Frenchman with the moving camera. She had seen Hafiz and the American girls in the tourist bazaar, in the tea-shop. The minibus had broken down that afternoon: he'd seen it outside the Armenian Museum, the driver and Hafiz examining its plugs.

'My mother would love that place,' she said.

'The Theological School?'

'My mother would feel its spirit. And its holiness.'

'Your mother is in England?'

'In Bournemouth.'

'And you yourself —'

'I have been on holiday with her. I came for six weeks and stayed a year. My husband is in Bombay.'

He glanced at her left hand, thinking he'd made a mistake.

'I haven't been wearing my wedding ring. I shall again, in Bombay.'

'Would you like to have dinner?'

She hesitated. She began to shake her head, then changed her mind. 'Are you sure?' she said. 'Here, in the hotel?'

'The food is the least impressive part.'

He'd asked her because, quite suddenly, he didn't like being in this enormous bedroom with her. It was pleasant showing her around, but he didn't want misunderstandings.

'Let's go downstairs,' he said.

In the bar they had another drink. The Swiss party had gone, so had the Germans. The Texans were noisier than they had been. 'Again, please,' he requested the barman, tapping their two glasses.

In Bournemouth she had worked as a shorthand typist for the year. In the past she had been a shorthand typist when she and her mother lived in London, before her marriage. 'My married name is Mrs Azann,' she said.

'When I saw you first I thought you had an Indian look.'

'Perhaps you get that when you marry an Indian.'

'And you're entirely English?'

'I've always felt drawn to the East. It's a spiritual affinity.'

Her conversation was like the conversation in a novelette. There was that and her voice, and her unsuitable shoes, and her cough, and not wearing enough for the chilly evening air: all of it went together, only her eyes remained different. And the more she talked about herself, the more her eyes appeared to belong to another person.

'I admire my husband very much,' she said. 'He's very fine. He's most intelligent. He's twenty-two years older than I am.'

She told the story then, while they were still in the bar. She had, although she did not say it, married for money. And though she clearly spoke the truth when she said she admired her husband, the marriage was not entirely happy. She could not, for one thing, have children, which neither of them had known at the time of the wedding and which displeased her husband when it was established as a fact. She had been displeased herself to discover that her husband was not as rich as he had appeared to be. He owned a furniture business, he'd said in the Regent Palace Hotel, where they'd met by chance when she was waiting for someone else: this was true, but he had omitted to add that the furniture business was doing badly. She had also been displeased to discover on the first night of her marriage that she disliked being touched by him. And there was yet another problem: in their bungalow in Bombay there lived, as well as her husband and herself, his mother and an aunt, his brother and his business manager. For a girl not used to such communal life, it was difficult in the bungalow in Bombay.

'It sounds more than difficult.'

'Sometimes.'

'He married you because you have an Indian look, while being the opposite of Indian in other ways. Your pale English skin. Your – your English voice.'

'In Bombay I give elocution lessons.'

He blinked, and then smiled to cover the rudeness that might have shown in his face.

'To Indian women,' she said, 'who come to the Club. My husband and I belong to a club. It's the best part of Bombay life, the social side.'

'It's strange to think of you in Bombay.'

'I thought I mightn't return. I thought I'd maybe stay on with my mother. But there's nothing much in England now.'

'I'm fond of England.'

'I thought you might be.' She coughed again, and took her medicine from her handbag and poured a little into her whisky. She drank a mouthful of the mixture, and then apologized, saying she wasn't being very ladylike. Such behaviour would be frowned upon in the Club.

'You should wear a cardigan with that cough.' He gestured at the barman and ordered further drinks.

'I'll be drunk,' she said, giggling.

He felt he'd been right to be curious. Her story was strange. He imagined the Indian women of the Club speaking English with her nasal intonation, twisting their lips to form the distorted sounds, dropping 'h's' because it was the thing to do. He imagined her in the bungalow, with her elderly husband who wasn't rich, and his relations and his business manager. It was a sour little fairy-story, a tale of Cinderella and a prince who wasn't a prince, and the carriage turned into an ice-cold pumpkin. Uneasiness overtook his curiosity, and he wondered again why she had come to Isfahan.

'Let's have dinner now,' he suggested in a slightly hasty voice.

But Mrs Azann, looking at him with her sumptuous eyes, said she couldn't eat a thing.

He would be married, she speculated. There was pain in the lines of his face, even though he smiled a lot and seemed lighthearted. She wondered if he'd once had a serious illness. When he'd brought her into his bedroom she wondered as they sat there if he was going to make a pass at her. But she knew a bit about people making passes, and he didn't seem the type. He was too attractive to have to make a pass. His manners were too elegant; he was too nice.

'I'll watch you having dinner,' she said. 'I don't mind in the least watching you if you're hungry. I couldn't deprive you of your dinner.'

'Well, I am rather hungry.'

His mouth curved when he said things like that, because of his smile. She wondered if he could be an architect. From the moment she'd had the idea of coming to Isfahan she'd known that it wasn't just an idea. She believed in destiny and always had.

They went to the restaurant, which was huge and luxurious like everywhere else in the hotel, dimly lit, with oil lamps on each table. She liked the way he explained to the waiters that she didn't wish to eat anything. For himself, he ordered a chicken kebab and salad.

'You'd like some wine?' he suggested, smiling in the same way. 'Persian wine's very pleasant.'

'I'd love a glass.'

He ordered the wine. She said:

'Do you always travel alone?'

'Yes.'

'But you're married?'

'Yes, I am.'

'And your wife's a home bird?'

'Yes.'

She imagined him in a house in a village, near Midhurst possibly, or Sevenoaks. She imagined his wife, a capable woman, good in the garden and on committees. She saw his wife quite clearly, a little on the heavy side but nice, cutting sweet-peas.

'You've told me nothing about yourself,' she said.

'There's very little to tell. I'm afraid I haven't a story like yours.'

'Why are you in Isfahan?'

'On holiday.'

'Is it always on your own?'

'I like being on my own. I like hotels. I like looking at people and walking about.'

'You're like me. You like travel.'

'Yes, I do.'

'I imagine you in a village house, in the Home Counties somewhere.'

'That's clever of you.'

'I can clearly see your wife.' She described the woman she could clearly see, without mentioning about her being on the heavy side. He nodded. She had second sight, he said with his smile.

'People have said I'm a little psychic. I'm glad I met you.'

'It's been a pleasure meeting you. Stories like yours are rare enough.'

'It's all true. Every word.'

'Oh, I know it is.'

'Are you an architect?'

'You're quite remarkable,' he said.

He finished his meal and between them they finished the wine. They had coffee and then she asked if he would kindly order more. The Swiss party had left the restaurant, and so had the German couple and their friends. Other diners had been and gone. The Texans were leaving just as Mrs Azann suggested more coffee. No other table was occupied.

'Of course,' he said.

He wished she'd go now. They had killed an evening together. Not for a long time would he forget either her ugly voice or her beautiful eyes. Nor would he easily forget the fairy-story that had gone sour on her. But that was that: the evening was over now.

The waiter brought their coffee, seeming greatly fatigued by the chore.

'D'you think,' she said, 'we should have another drink? D'you think they have cigarettes here?'

He had brandy and she more whisky. The waiter brought her American cigarettes.

'I don't really want to go back to Bombay,' she said.

'I'm sorry about that.'

'I'd like to stay in Isfahan for ever.'

'You'd be very bored. There's no club. No social life of any kind for an English person, I should think.'

'I do like a little social life.' She smiled at him, broadening her sensuous mouth. 'My father was a counter-hand,' she said. 'In a co-op. You wouldn't think it, would you?'

'Not at all,' he lied.

'It's my little secret. If I told the women in the Club that, or my husband's mother or his aunt, they'd have a fit. I've never even told my husband. Only my mother and I share that secret.'

'I see.'

'And now you.'

'Secrets are safe with strangers.'

'Why do you think I told you that secret?'

'Because we are ships that pass in the night.'

'Because you are sympathetic.'

The waiter hovered close and then approached them boldly. The bar was open for as long as they wished it to be. There were lots of other drinks in the bar. Cleverly, he removed the coffee-pot and their cups.

'He's like a magician,' she said. 'Everything in Isfahan is magical.'

'You're glad you came?'

'It's where I met you.'

He rose. He had to stand for a moment because she continued to sit there, her handbag on the table, her black frilled shawl on top of it. She hadn't finished her whisky but he expected that she'd lift the glass to her lips and drink what she wanted of it, or just leave it there. She rose and walked with him from the restaurant, taking her glass with her. Her other hand slipped beneath his arm.

'There's a discothèque downstairs,' she said.

'Oh, I'm afraid that's not really me.'

'Nor me, neither. Let's go back to our bar.'

She handed him her glass, saying she had to pay a visit. She'd love another whisky and soda, she said, even though she hadn't quite finished the one in her glass. Without ice, she said.

The bar was empty except for a single barman. Normanton ordered more brandy for himself and whisky for Mrs Azann. He much preferred her as Iris Smith, in her tatty pink dress and the dark glasses that hid her eyes: she could have been any little typist except that she'd married Mr Azann and had a story to tell.

'It's nice in spite of things,' she explained as she sat down. 'It's nice in spite of him wanting to you-know-what, and the women in the bungalow, and his brother and the business manager. They all disapprove because I'm English, especially his mother and his aunt. He doesn't disapprove because he's mad about me. The business manager doesn't much mind, I suppose. The dogs don't mind. D'you understand? In spite of everything, it's nice to have someone mad about you. And the Club, the social life. Even though we're short of the ready, it's better than England for a woman. There's servants, for a start.'

The whisky was affecting the way she put things. An hour ago she wouldn't have said 'wanting to you-know-what' or 'short of the ready'. It was odd that she had an awareness in this direction and yet could not hear the twang in her voice which instantly gave her away.

'But you don't love your husband.'

'I respect him. It's only that I hate having to you-know-what with him. I really do hate that. I've never actually loved him.'

He regretted saying she didn't love her husband: the remark had slipped out, and it was regrettable because it involved him in the conversation in a way he didn't wish to be.

'Maybe things will work out better when you get back.'

'I know what I'm going back to.' She paused, searching for his eyes with hers. 'I'll never till I die forget Isfahan.'

'It's very beautiful.'

'I'll never forget the Chaharbagh Tours, or Hafiz. I'll never forget that place you brought me to. Or the Shah Abbas Hotel.'

'I think it's time I saw you back to your own hotel.'

'I could sit in this bar for ever.'

'I'm afraid I'm not at all one for night-life.'

'I shall visualize you when I'm back in Bombay. I shall think of you in your village, with your wife, happy in England. I shall think of you working at your architectural plans. I shall often wonder about you travelling alone because your wife doesn't care for it.'

'I hope it's better in Bombay. Sometimes things are, when you least expect them to be.'

'It's been like a tonic. You've made me very happy.'

'It's kind of you to say that.'

'There's much that's unsaid between us. Will you remember me?'

'Oh yes, of course.'

Reluctantly, she drank the dregs of her whisky. She took her medicine from her handbag and poured a little into the glass and drank that, too. It helped the tickle in her throat, she said. She always had a tickle when the wretched cough came.

'Shall we walk back?'

They left the bar. She clung to him again, walking very slowly between the mosaiced columns. All the way back to the Old Atlantic Hotel she talked about the evening they had spent and how delightful it had been. Not for the world would she have missed Isfahan, she repeated several times.

When they said goodbye she kissed his cheek. Her beautiful eyes swallowed him up, and for a moment he had a feeling that her eyes were the real thing about her, reflecting her as she should be.

He woke at half past two and could not sleep. Dawn was already beginning to break. He lay there, watching the light increase in the gap he'd left between the curtains so that there'd be fresh air in the room. Another day had passed: he went through it piece by piece, from his early-morning walk to the moment when he'd put his green pyjamas on and got into bed. It was a regular night-time exercise with him. He closed his eyes, remembering in detail.

He turned again into the offices of Chaharbagh Tours and was told by Hafiz to go to the upstairs office. He saw her sitting there writing to her mother, and heard her voice asking him if he was going on the tour. He saw again the sunburnt faces of the German couple and the wholesome faces of the American girls, and faces in the French party. He went again on his afternoon walk, and after that there was his bath. She came towards him in the bazaar, with her dark glasses and her small purchases. There was her story as she had told it.

For his part, he had told her nothing. He had agreed with her novelette picture of him, living in a Home Counties village, a well-to-do architect married to a wife who gardened. Architects had become as romantic as doctors, there'd been no reason to disillusion her. She would for ever imagine him travelling to exotic places, on his own because he enjoyed it, because his wife was a home bird.

Why could he not have told her? Why could he not have exchanged one story for another? She had made a mess of things and did not seek to hide it. Life had let her down, she'd let herself down. Ridiculously, she gave elocution lessons to Indian women and did not see it as ridiculous. She had told him her secret, and he knew it was true that he shared it only with her mother and herself.

The hours went by. He should be lying with her in this bed, the size of a dance-floor. In the dawn he should be staring into her sumptuous eyes, in love with the mystery there. He should be telling her and asking for her sympathy, as she had asked for his. He should be telling her that he had walked into a room, not in a Home Counties village, but in harsh, ugly Hampstead, to find his second wife, as once he had found his first, in his bed with another man. He should in humility have asked her why it was that he was naturally a cuckold, why two women of different temperaments and characters had been inspired to have lovers at his expense. He should be telling her, with the warmth of her body warming his, that his second wife had confessed to greater sexual pleasure when she remembered that she was deceiving him.

It was a story no better than hers, certainly as unpleasant. Yet he hadn't had the courage to tell it because it cast him in a certain light. He travelled easily, moving over surfaces and revealing only surfaces himself. He was acceptable as a stranger: in two marriages he had not been forgiven for turning out to be different from what he seemed. To be a cuckold once was the luck of the game, but his double cuckoldry had a whiff of revenge about it. In all humility he might have asked her about that.

At half past four he stood by the window, looking out at the empty street below. She would be on her way to the bus station, to catch the five o'clock bus to Teheran. He could dress, he could even shave and still be there in time. He could pay, on her behalf, the extra air fare that would accrue. He could tell her his story and they could spend a few days. They could go together to Shiraz, city of wine and roses and nightingales.

He stood by the window, watching nothing happening in the street, knowing that if he stood there for ever he wouldn't find the courage. She had met a sympathetic man, more marvellous to her than all the marvels of Isfahan. She would carry that memory to the bungalow in Bombay, knowing nothing about a pettiness which brought out cruelty in people. And he would remember a woman who possessed, deep beneath her unprepossessing surface, the distinction that her eyes mysteriously claimed for her. In different circumstances, with a less unfortunate story to tell, it would have emerged. But in the early morning there was another truth, too. He was the stuff of fantasy. She had quality, he had none.

Angels at the Ritz

The game was played when the party, whichever party it happened to be, had thinned out. Those who stayed on beyond a certain point – beyond, usually, about one o'clock – knew that the game was on the cards and in fact had stayed for that reason. Often, as one o'clock approached, there were marital disagreements about whether or not to go home.

The game of swapping wives and husbands, with chance rather than choice dictating the formations, had been practised in this outer suburb since the mid-1950s. The swinging wives and husbands of that time were now passing into the first years of elderliness, but their party game continued. In the outer suburb it was most popular when the early struggles of marriage were over, after children had been born and were established at school, when there were signs of marital wilting that gin and tonic did not cure.

'I think it's awfully silly,' Polly Dillard pronounced, addressing her husband on the evening of the Ryders' party.

Her husband, whose first name was Gavin, pointed out that they'd known for years that the practice was prevalent at Saturday-night parties in the outer suburb. There'd been, he reminded her, the moment at the Meacocks' when they'd realized they'd stayed too late, when the remaining men threw their car-keys on to the Meacocks' carpet and Sylvia Meacock began to tie scarves over the eyes of the wives.

'I mean, it's silly Sue and Malcolm going in for it. All of a sudden, out of the blue like that.'

'They're just shuffling along with it, I suppose.'

Polly shook her head. Quietly, she said that in the past Sue and Malcolm Ryder hadn't been the kind to shuffle along with things. Sue had sounded like a silly schoolgirl, embarrassed and not looking her in the eye when she told her.

Gavin could see she was upset, but one of the things about Polly since she'd had their two children and had come to live in the outer suburb was that she was able to deal with being upset. She dealt with it now, keeping calm, not raising her voice. She'd have been the same when Sue Ryder averted her eyes and said that she and Malcolm had decided to go in, too, for the outer suburb's most popular party game. Polly would have been astonished and would have said so, and then she'd have attempted to become reconciled to the development. Before this evening came to an end she really would be reconciled, philosophically accepting the development as part of the Ryders' middle age, while denying that it could ever be part of hers.

'I suppose,' Gavin said, 'it's like a schoolgirl deciding to let herself be kissed for the first time. Don't you remember sounding silly then, Polly?'

She said it wasn't at all like that. Imagine, she suggested, finding yourself teamed up with a sweaty creature like Tim Gruffydd. Imagine any schoolgirl in her senses letting Tim Gruffydd within two million miles of her. She still couldn't believe that Sue and Malcolm Ryder were going in for stuff like that. What on earth happened to people? she asked Gavin, and Gavin said he didn't know.

Polly Dillard was thirty-six, her husband two years older. Her short fair hair had streaks of grey in it now. Her thin, rather long face wasn't pretty but did occasionally seem beautiful, the eyes deep blue, the mouth wide, becoming slanted when she smiled. She herself considered that nothing matched properly in her face and that her body was too lanky and her breasts too slight. But after thirty-six years she'd become used to all that, and other women envied her her figure and her looks.

On the evening of the Ryders' party she surveyed the features that did not in her opinion match, applying eye-shadow in her bedroom looking-glass and now and again glancing at the reflection of her husband, who was changing from his Saturday clothes into clothes more suitable for Saturday night at the Ryders': a blue corduroy suit, pink shirt and pinkish tie. Of medium height, fattening on lunches and alcohol, he was dark-haired and still handsome, for his chunky features were only just beginning to trail signs of this telltale plumpness. By profession Gavin Dillard was a director of promotional films for television, mainly in the soap and detergent field.

The hall doorbell rang as Polly rose from the chair in front of her looking-glass.

'I'll go,' he said, adding that it would be Estrella, their babysitter.

'Estrella couldn't come, I had to ring Problem. Some Irish-sounding girl it'll be.'

'Hannah McCarthy,' a round-faced girl at the door said. 'Are you Mr Dillard, sir?'

He smiled at her and said he was. He closed the door and took her coat. He led her through a white, spacious hall into a sitting-room that was spacious also, with pale blue walls and curtains. One child was already in bed, he told her, the other was still in his bath. Two boys, he explained: Paul and David. His wife would introduce her to them.

'Would you like a drink, Hannah?'

'Well, I wouldn't say no to that, Mr Dillard.' She smiled an extensive smile at him. 'A little sherry if you have it, sir.'

'And how's the old country, Hannah?' He spoke lightly, trying to be friendly, handing her a glass of sherry. He turned away and poured himself some gin and tonic, adding a sliver of lemon. 'Cheers, Hannah!'

'Cheers, sir! Ireland, d'you mean, sir? Oh, Ireland doesn't change.'

'You go back, do you?'

'Every holidays. I'm in teacher training, Mr Dillard.'

'I was at the Cork Film Festival once. A right old time we had.'

'I don't know Cork, actually. I'm from Listowel myself. Are you in films yourself, sir? You're not an actor, Mr Dillard?'

'Actually I'm a director.'

Polly entered the room. She said she was Mrs Dillard. She smiled, endeavouring to be as friendly as Gavin had been, in case the girl didn't feel at home. She thanked her for coming at such short notice and presumably so far. She was wearing a skirt that Gavin had helped her to buy in Fenwick's only last week, and a white lace blouse she'd had for years, and her jade beads. The skirt, made of velvet, was the same green as the jade. She took the babysitter away to introduce her to the two children.

Gavin stood with his back to the fire, sipping at his gin and tonic. He didn't find it puzzling that Polly should feel so strongly about the fact that Sue and Malcolm Ryder had reached a certain stage in their marriage. The Ryders were their oldest and closest friends. Polly and Sue had known one another since they'd gone together to the Misses Hamilton's nursery school in Putney. Perhaps it was this depth in the relationship that caused Polly to feel so disturbed by a new development in her friend's life. In his own view, being offered a free hand with an unselected woman in return for agreeing that some man should maul his wife about wasn't an attractive proposition. It surprised him that the Ryders had decided to go in for this particular party game, and it surprised him even more that Malcolm Ryder had never mentioned it to him. But it didn't upset him.

'All right?' Polly inquired from the doorway, with her coat on. The coat was brown and fur-trimmed and expensive: she looked beautiful in it, Gavin thought, calm and collected. Once, a long time ago, she had thrown a milk-jug across a room at him. At one time she had wept a lot, deploring her lankiness and her flat breasts. All that seemed strangely out of character now.

He finished his drink and put the glass down on the mantelpiece. He put the sherry bottle beside the babysitter's glass in case she should feel like some more, and then changed his mind and returned the bottle to the cabinet, remembering that they didn't know the girl: a drunk babysitter – an experience they'd once endured – was a great deal worse than no babysitter at all.

'She seems very nice,' Polly said in the car. 'She said she'd read to them for an hour.'

'An hour? The poor girl!'

'She loves children.'

It was dark, half past eight on a night in November. It was raining just enough to make it necessary to use the windscreen-wipers. Automatically, Gavin turned the car radio on: there was something pleasantly cosy about the glow of a car radio at night when it was raining, with the background whirr of the windscreen-wipers and the wave of warmth from the heater.

'Let's not stay long,' he said.

It pleased her that he said that. She wondered if they were dull not to wish to stay, but he said that was nonsense.

He drove through the sprawl of their outer suburb, all of it new, disguised now by the night. Orange street lighting made the façades of the carefully designed houses seem different, changing the colours, but the feeling of space remained, and the uncluttered effect of the unfenced front gardens. Roomy Volvo estate-cars went nicely with the detached houses. So did Vauxhall Victors, and big bus-like Volkswagens. Families were packed into such vehicles on summer Saturday mornings, for journeys to cottages in the Welsh hills or in Hampshire or Herts. The Dillards' cottage was in the New Forest.

Gavin parked the car in Sandiway Crescent, several doors away from the Ryders' house because other cars were already parked closer to it. He'd have much preferred to be going out to dinner in Tonino's with Malcolm and Sue, lasagne and peperonata and a carafe of Chianti Christina, a lazy kind of evening that would remind all of them of other lazy evenings. Ten years ago they'd all four gone regularly to Tonino's trattoria in Greek Street, and the branch that had opened in their outer suburb was very like the original, even down to the framed colour photographs of A.C. Milan.

'Come on *in*!' Sue cried jollily at Number Four Sandiway Crescent. Her face was flushed with party excitement, her large brown eyes flashed adventurously with party spirit. Her eyes were the only outsize thing about her: she was tiny and black-haired, as pretty as a rosebud.

'Gin?' Malcolm shouted at them from the depths of the crowded hall. 'Sherry, Polly? Burgundy?'

Gavin kissed the dimpled cheek that Sue Ryder pressed up to him. She was in red, a long red dress that suited her, with a red band in her hair and red shoes.

'Yes, wine please, Malcolm,' Polly said, and when she was close enough she slid her face towards his for the same kind of embrace as her husband had given his wife.

'You're looking edible, my love,' he said, a compliment he'd been paying her for seventeen years.

He was an enormous man, made to seem more so by the smallness of his wife. His features had a mushy look. His head, like a pink sponge, was perched jauntily on shoulders that had once been a force to reckon with in rugby scrums. Although he was exactly the same age as Gavin, his hair had balded away to almost nothing, a rim of fluff not quite encircling the sponge.

'You're looking very smart yourself,' Polly said, a statement that might or might not have been true: she couldn't see him properly because he was so big and she was so close to him, and she hadn't looked when she'd been further away. He was wearing a grey suit of some kind and a blue-striped shirt and the tie of the Harlequins' Rugby Club. Usually he looked smart: he probably did now.

'I'm feeling great,' he said. 'Nice little party we're having, Poll.'

It wasn't really little. Sixty or so people were in the Ryders' house, which was similar to the Dillards' house, well-designed and spacious. Most of the downstairs rooms, and the hall, had coffee-coloured walls, an experiment of Sue's which she believed had been successful. For the party, the bulkier furniture had been taken out of the coffee-coloured sitting-room, and all the rugs had been lifted from the parquet floor. Music came from a tape-recorder, but no one was dancing yet. People stood in small groups, smoking and talking and drinking. No one, so far, appeared to be drunk.

All the usual people were there: the Stubbses, the Burgesses, the Pedlars, the Thompsons, the Stevensons, Sylvia and Jack Meacock, Philip and June Mulally, Oliver and Olive Gramsmith, Tim and Mary-Ann Gruffydd and dozens of others. Not all of them lived in the outer suburb; and some were older, some younger, than the Ryders and the Dillards. But there was otherwise a similarity about the people at the party: they were men who had succeeded or were in the process of succeeding, and women who had kept pace with their husbands' advance. No one looked poor at the Ryders' party.

At ten o'clock there was food, smoked salmon rolled up and speared with cocktail sticks, chicken vol-au-vents or beef Stroganoff with rice, salads of different kinds, stilton and brie and Bel Paese, and meringues.

Wine flowed generously, white burgundy and red. Uncorked bottles were distributed on all convenient surfaces.

The dancing began when the first guests had eaten. To 'Love of the Loved', Polly danced with a man whose name she didn't know, who told her he was an estate agent with an office in Jermyn Street. He held her rather close for a man whose name she didn't know. He was older than Polly, about fifty, she reckoned, and smaller. He had a foxy moustache and foxy hair, and a round stomach, like a ball, which kept making itself felt. So did his knees.

In the room where the food was Gavin sat on the floor with Sylvia and Jack Meacock, and a woman in an orange trouser-suit, with orange lips.

'Stevie wouldn't come,' this woman said, balancing food in the hollow of a fork. 'He got cross with me last night.'

Gavin ate from his fingers a vol-au-vent full of chicken and mushrooms that had gone a little cold. Jack Meacock said nothing would hold him back from a party given by the Ryders. Or any party, he added, guffawing, given by anyone. Provided there was refreshment, his wife stipulated. Well naturally, Jack Meacock said.

'He wouldn't come,' the orange woman explained, 'because he thought I misbehaved in Olive Gramsmith's kitchen. A fortnight ago, for God's sake!'

Gavin calculated he'd had four glasses of gin and tonic. He corrected himself, remembering the one he'd had with the babysitter. He drank some wine. He wasn't entirely drunk, he said to himself, he hadn't turned a certain corner, but the corner was the next thing there was.

'If you want to kiss someone you kiss him,' the orange woman said. 'I mean, for God's sake, he'd no damn right to walk into Olive Gramsmith's kitchen. I didn't see you,' she said, looking closely at Gavin. 'You weren't there, were you?'

'We couldn't go.'

'You were there,' she said to the Meacocks. 'All over the place.'

'We certainly were!' Jack Meacock guffawed through his beef Stroganoff, scattering rice on to the coffee-coloured carpet.

'Hullo,' their hostess said, and sat down on the carpet beside Gavin, with a plate of cheese.

'You mean you've been married twelve years?' the estate agent said to Polly. 'You don't look it.'

'I'm thirty-six.'

'What's your better half in? Is here, is he?'

'He directs films. Advertisements for TV. Yes, he's here.'

'That's mine.' He indicated with his head a woman who wasn't dancing, in lime-green. She was going through a bad patch, he said: depressions. They danced to 'Sunporch Cha-Cha-Cha', Simon and Garfunkel.

'Feeling O K ?' the estate agent inquired, and Polly said yes, not understanding what he meant. He propelled her towards the mantelpiece and took from it the glass of white burgundy Polly had left there. He offered it to her and when she'd taken a mouthful he drank some from it himself. They danced again. He clutched her more tightly with his arms and flattened a cheek against one of hers, rasping her with his moustache. With dead eyes, the woman in lime-green watched.

At other outer-suburb parties Polly had been through it all before. She escaped from the estate agent and was caught by Tim Gruffydd, who had already begun to sweat. After that another man whose name she didn't know danced with her, and then Malcolm Ryder did.

'You're edible tonight,' he whispered, the warm mush of his lips damping her ear. 'You're really edible, my love.'

'Share my cheese,' Sue offered in the other room, pressing brie on Gavin.

'I need more wine,' the woman in orange said, and Jack Meacock pushed himself up from the carpet. They all needed more wine, he pointed out. The orange woman predicted that the next day she'd have a hangover and Sylvia Meacock, a masculine-looking woman, said she'd never had a hangover in forty-eight years of steady drinking.

'You going to stay a while?' Sue said to Gavin. 'You and Polly going to stay?' She laughed, taking one of his hands because it was near to her. Since they'd known one another for such a long time it was quite in order for her to do that.

'Our babysitter's unknown,' Gavin explained. 'From the bogs of Ireland.'

The orange woman said the Irish were bloody.

'Jack's Irish, actually,' Sylvia Meacock said.

She went on talking about that, about her husband's childhood in County Down, about an uncle of his who used to drink a bottle and a half of whiskey a day – on top of four glasses of stout, with porridge and bread, for his breakfast. If you drank at all you should drink steadily, she said.

Gavin felt uneasy, because all the time Sylvia Meacock was talking about the drinking habits of her husband's uncle in County Down Sue clung on to his hand. She held it lightly, moving her fingers in a caress that seemed to stray outside the realm of their long friendship. He was in love with Polly: he thought that deliberately, arraying the sentiment in his mind as a statement, seeing it suspended there. There was no one he'd ever known whom he'd been fonder of than Polly, or whom he respected more, or whom it would upset him more to hurt. Seventeen years ago he'd met her in the kitchens of the Hotel Belvedere, Penzance, where they had both gone to work for the summer. Five years later, having lived with one another in a flat in the cheaper part of Maida Vale, they'd got married because Polly wanted to have children. They'd moved to the outer suburb because the children needed space and fresh air, and because the Ryders, who'd lived on the floor above theirs in Maida Vale, had moved there a year before.

'She'll be all right,' Sue said, returning to the subject of the Irish baby-sitter. 'She could probably stay the night. She'd probably be delighted.'

'Oh, I don't think so, Sue.'

He imagined without difficulty the hands of men at the party unbuttoning Polly's lace blouse, the hands of Jack Meacock or the sweaty hands of Tim Gruffydd. He imagined Polly's clothes falling on to a bedroom carpet and then her thin, lanky nakedness, her small breasts and the faint mark of her appendix scar. 'Oh, I say!' she said in a way that wasn't like her when the man, whoever he was, took off his own clothes. Without difficulty either, Gavin imagined being in a room himself for the same purpose, with the orange woman or Sylvia Meacock. He'd walk out again if he found himself in a room with Sylvia Meacock and he'd rather be in a room with Sue than with the orange woman. Because he wasn't quite sober, he had a flash of panic when he thought of what might be revealed when the orange trouser-suit fell to the floor: for a brief, disturbing moment he felt it was actually happening, that in the bonhomie of drunkenness he'd somehow agreed to the situation.

'Why don't we dance?' Sue suggested, and Gavin agreed.

'I think I'd like a drink,' Polly said to Philip Mulally, an executive with Wolsey Menswear. He was a grey shadow of a man, not at all the kind to permit himself or his wife to be a party to sexual games. He nodded seriously when Polly interrupted their dance to say she'd like a drink. It was time in any case, he revealed, that he and June were making a move homewards.

'I love you in that lace thing,' Malcolm Ryder whispered boringly as soon as Polly stopped dancing with Philip Mulally. He was standing waiting for her.

'I was saying to Philip I'd like a drink.'

'Of course you must have a drink. Come and quaff a brandy with me, Poll.' He took her by the hand and led her away from the dancers. The brandy was in his den, he said.

She shook her head, following him because she had no option. Above the noise of Cilla Black singing 'Anyone Who Had a Heart' she shouted at him that she'd prefer some more white burgundy, that she was actually feeling thirsty. But he didn't hear her, or didn't wish to. 'Ain't misbehaving,' the foxy estate agent mouthed at her as they passed him, standing on his own in the hall. It was an expression that was often used, without much significance attaching to it, at parties in the outer suburb.

'Evening, all,' Malcolm said in the room he called his den, closing the door behind Polly. The only light in the room was from a desk-lamp. In the shadows, stretched on a mock-leather sofa, a man and a woman were kissing one another. They parted in some embarrassment at their host's jocular greeting, revealing themselves, predictably, as a husband and another husband's wife.

'Carry on, folks,' Malcolm said.

He poured Polly some brandy even though she had again said that what she wanted was a glass of burgundy. The couple on the sofa got up and went away, giggling. The man told Malcolm he was an old bastard.

'Here you are,' Malcolm said, and then to Polly's distaste he placed his mushy lips on hers and exerted some pressure. The brandy glass was in her right hand, between them: had it not been there, she knew the embrace would have been more intimate. As it was, it was possible for both of them to pretend that what had occurred was purely an expression of Malcolm Ryder's friendship for her, a special little detour to show that for all these years it hadn't been just a case of two wives being friends and the husbands tagging along. Once, in 1965, they'd all gone to the Italian Adriatic together and quite often Malcolm had given her a kiss and a hug while telling her how edible she was. But somehow – perhaps because his lips hadn't been so mushy in the past – it was different now.

'Cheers!' he said, smiling at her in the dimness. For an unpleasant moment she thought he might lock the door. What on earth did you do if an old friend tried to rape you on a sofa in his den?

With every step they made together, the orange woman increased her entwinement of Oliver Gramsmith. The estate agent was dancing with June Mulally, both of them ignoring the gestures of June Mulally's husband, Philip, who was still anxious to move homewards. The Thompsons, the Pedlars, the Stevensons, the Suttons, the Heeresmas and the Fultons were all maritally separated. Tim Gruffydd was clammily tightening his grasp of Olive Gramsmith, Sylvia Meacock's head lolled on the shoulder of a man called Thistlewine.

'Remember the Ritz?' Sue said to Gavin.

He did remember. It was a long time ago, years before they'd all gone together to the Italian Adriatic, when they'd just begun to live in Maida Vale, one flat above the other, none of them married. They'd gone to the Ritz because they couldn't afford it. The excuse had been Polly's birthday.

'March the 25th,' he said. '1961.' He could feel her breasts, like spikes because of the neat control of her brassière. He'd become too flabby, he thought, since March the 25th, 1961.

'What fun it was!' With her dark, petite head on one side, she smiled up at him. 'Remember it all, Gavin?'

'Yes, I remember.'

'I wanted to sing that song and no one would let me. Polly was horrified.'

'Well, it was Polly's birthday.'

'And of course we couldn't have spoiled that.' She was still smiling up at him, her eyes twinkling, the tone of her voice as light as a feather. Yet the words sounded like a criticism, as though she were saying now – fourteen years later – that Polly had been a spoilsport, which at the time hadn't seemed so in the least. Her arms tightened around his waist. Her face disappeared as she sank her head against his chest. All he could see was the red band in her hair and the hair itself. She smelt of some pleasant scent. He liked the sharpness of her breasts. He wanted to stroke her head.

'Sue fancies old Gavin, you know,' Malcolm said in his den.

Polly laughed. He had put a hand on her thigh and the fingers were now slightly massaging the green velvet of her skirt and the flesh beneath it. To have asked him to take his hand away or to have pushed it away herself would have been too positive, too much a reflection of his serious mood rather than her own determinedly casual one. A thickness had crept into his voice. He looked much older than thirty-eight; he'd worn less well than Gavin.

'Let's go back to the party, Malcolm.' She stood up, dislodging his hand as though by accident.

'Let's have another drink.'

He was a solicitor now, with Parker, Hille and Harper. He had been, in fact, a solicitor when they'd all lived in the cheaper part of Maida Vale. He'd still played rugby for the Harlequins then. She and Gavin and Sue used to watch him on Saturday afternoons, in matches against the London clubs, Rosslyn Park and Blackheath, Richmond, London Welsh, London Irish, and all the others. Malcolm had been a towering wing three-quarter, with a turn of speed that was surprising in so large a man: people repeatedly said, even newspaper commentators, that he should play for England.

Polly was aware that it was a cliché to compare Malcolm as he had been with the blubbery, rather tedious Malcolm beside whom it was unwise to sit on a sofa. Naturally he wasn't the same. It was probably a tedious life being a solicitor with Parker, Hille and Harper day after day. He probably did his best to combat the blubberiness, and no man could help being bald. When he was completely sober, and wasn't at a party, he could still be quite funny and nice, hardly tedious at all.

'I've always fancied you, Poll,' he said. 'You know that.'

'Oh, nonsense, Malcolm!'

She took the brandy glass from him, holding it between them in case he should make another lurch. He began to talk about sex. He asked her if she'd read, a few years ago, about a couple in an aeroplane, total strangers, who had performed the sexual act in full view of the other passengers. He told her a story about Mick Jagger on an aeroplane, at the time when Mick Jagger was making journeys with Marianne Faithfull. He said the springing system of Green Line buses had the same kind of effect on him. Sylvia Meacock was lesbian, he said. Olive Gramsmith was a slapparat. Philip Mulally had once been seen hanging about Shepherd Market, looking at the tarts. He hadn't been faithful to Sue, he said, but Sue knew about it and now they were going to approach all that side of things in a different way. Polly knew about it, too, because Sue had told her: a woman in Parker, Hille and Harper had wanted Malcolm to divorce Sue, and there'd been, as well, less serious relationships between Malcolm and other women.

'*Since you went away the days grow long,*' sang Nat King Cole in the coffee-coloured sitting-room, '*and soon I'll hear ole winter's song.*' Some guests, in conversation, raised their voices above the voice of Nat King Cole. Others swayed to his rhythm. In the sitting-room and the hall and the room where the food had been laid out there was a fog of cigarette smoke and the warm smell of burgundy. Men sat together on the stairs, talking about the election of Margaret Thatcher as leader of the Conservative party. Women had gathered in the kitchen and seemed quite happy there, with glasses of burgundy in their hands. In a bedroom the couple who had been surprised in Malcolm's den continued their embrace.

'So very good we were,' Sue said on the parquet dance-floor. She broke away from Gavin, seizing him by the hand as she did so. She led him across the room to a teak-faced cabinet that contained gramophone records. On top of it there was a gramophone and the tape-recorder that was relaying the music.

'Don't dare move,' she warned Gavin, releasing his hand in order to poke among the records. She found what she wanted and placed it on the turntable of the gramophone. The music began just before she turned the tape-recorder off. A cracked female voice sang: *That certain night, the night we met, there was magic abroad in the air . . .*

'Listen to it,' Sue said, taking Gavin's hand again and drawing him on to the dancing area.

'*There were angels dining at the Ritz, and a nightingale sang in Berkeley Square.*'

The other dancers, who'd been taken aback by the abrupt change of tempo, slipped into the new rhythm. The two spiky breasts again depressed Gavin's stomach.

'Angels of a kind we were,' Sue said. 'And fallen angels now, Gavin? D'you think we've fallen?'

Once in New York and once in Liverpool he'd made love since his marriage, to other girls. Chance encounters they'd been, irrelevant and unimportant at the time and more so now. He had suffered from guilt immediately afterwards, but the guilt had faded, with both girls' names. He could remeber their names if he tried: he once had, when suffering from a bout of indigestion in the night. He had remembered precisely their faces and their naked bodies and what each encounter had been like, but memories that required such effort hadn't seemed quite real. It would, of course, be different with Sue.

'Fancy Sue playing that,' her husband said, pausing outside the den with Polly. 'They've been talking about the Ritz, Poll.'

'Goodness!' With a vividness that was a welcome antidote to Malcolm's disclosure about the sex-life of his guests, the occasion at the Ritz returned to her. Malcolm said:

'It was my idea, you know. Old Gavin and I were boozing in the Hoop and he suddenly said, "It's Polly's birthday next week," and I said, "For God's sake! Let's all go down to the Ritz." '

'You had oysters, I remember.' She smiled at him, feeling better because they were no longer in the den, and stronger because of the brandy. Malcolm would have realized by now how she felt, he wouldn't pursue the matter.

'We weren't much more than kids.' He seized her hand in a way that might have been purely sentimental, as though he was inspired by the memory.

'My twenty-second birthday. What an extraordinary thing it was to do!'

In fact, it had been more than that. Sitting in the restaurant with people she liked, she'd thought it was the nicest thing that had ever happened to her on her birthday. It was absurd because none of them could afford it. It was absurd to go to the Ritz for a birthday treat: martinis in the Rivoli Bar because Malcolm said it was the thing, the gilt chairs and the ferns. But the absurdity hadn't mattered because in those days nothing much did. It was fun, they enjoyed being together, they had a lot to be happy about. Malcolm might yet play rugby for England. Gavin was about to make his breakthrough into films. Sue was pretty, and Polly that night felt beautiful. They had sat there carelessly laughing, while deferential waiters simulated the gaiety of their mood. They had drunk champagne because Malcolm said they must.

With Malcolm still holding her hand, she crossed the spacious hall of Number Four Sandiway Crescent. People were beginning to leave. Malcolm released his hold of her in order to bid them goodbye.

She stood in the doorway of the sitting-room watching Gavin and Sue dancing. She lifted her brandy glass to her lips and drank from it calmly. Her oldest friend was attempting to seduce her husband, and for the first time in her life she disliked her. Had they still been at the Misses Hamilton's nursery school she would have run at her and hit her with her fists. Had they still been in Maida Vale or on holiday on the Italian Adriatic she would have shouted and made a fuss. Had they been laughing in the Ritz she'd have got up and walked out.

They saw her standing there, both of them almost in the same moment. Sue smiled at her and called across the coffee-coloured sitting-room, as though nothing untoward were happening, 'D'you think we've fallen, Polly?' Her voice was full of laughter, just like it had been that night. Her eyes still had their party gleam, which probably had been there too.

'Let's dance, Poll,' Malcolm said, putting his arms around her waist from behind.

It made it worse when he did that because she knew by the way he touched her that she was wrong: he didn't realize. He probably thought she'd enjoyed hearing all that stuff about Philip Mulally hanging about after prostitutes and Olive Gramsmith being a slapparat, whatever a slapparat was.

She finished the brandy in her glass and moved with him on to the parquet. What had happened was that the Ryders had had a conversation about all this. They'd said to one another that this was how they wished – since it was the first time – to make a sexual swap. Polly and Gavin were to be of assistance to their friends because a woman in Parker, Hille and Harper had wanted Malcolm to get a divorce and because there'd been other relationships. Malcolm and Sue were approaching all that side of things in a different way now, following the fashion in the outer suburb since the fashion worked wonders with wilting marriages.

'Estrella babysitting, is she?' Malcolm asked. 'All right if you're late, is she? You're not going to buzz off, Poll?'

'Estrella couldn't come. We had to get a girl from Problem.'

He suggested, as though the arrangement were a natural one and had been practised before, that he should drive her home when she wanted to go. He'd drive the babysitter from Problem home also. 'Old Gavin won't want to go,' he pronounced, trying to make it all sound like part of his duties as host. To Polly it sounded preposterous, but she didn't say so. She just smiled as she danced with him.

They'd made these plans quite soberly presumably, over breakfast or when there was nothing to watch on television, or in bed at night. They'd discussed the game that people played with car-keys or playing cards, or by drawing lots in other ways. They'd agreed that neither of them cared for the idea of taking a chance. 'Different,' Malcolm had probably quite casually said, 'if we got the Dillards.' Sue wouldn't have said anything then. She might have laughed, or got up to make tea if they were watching the television, or turned over and gone to sleep. On some other occasion she might have drifted the conversation towards the subject again and Malcolm would have known that she was interested. They would then have worked out a way of interesting their oldest friends. Dancing with Malcolm, Polly watched while Gavin's mouth descended to touch the top of Sue's head. He and Sue were hardly moving on the dance-floor.

'Well, that's fixed up then,' Malcolm said. He didn't want to dance any more. He wanted to know that it was fixed up, that he could return to his party for an hour or so, with something to look forward to. He would drive her home and Gavin would remain. At half past one or two, when the men threw their car-keys on to the carpet and the blindfolded women each picked one out, Gavin and Sue would simply watch, not taking part. And when everyone went away Gavin and Sue would be alone with all the mess and the empty glasses. And she would be alone with Malcolm.

Polly smiled at him again, hoping he'd take the smile to mean that everything was fixed, because she didn't want to go on dancing with him. If one of them had said, that night in the Ritz, that for a couple of hours after dinner they should change partners there'd have been a most unpleasant silence.

Malcolm patted her possessively on the hip. He squeezed her forearm and went away, murmuring that people might be short of drink. A man whom she didn't know, excessively drunk, took her over, informing her that he loved her. As she swayed around the room with him, she wanted to say to Sue and Malcolm and Gavin that yes, they had fallen. Of course Malcolm hadn't done his best to combat his blubberiness, of course he didn't make efforts. Malcolm was awful, and Sue was treacherous. When people asked Gavin if he made films why didn't he ever reply that the films he made were television commercials? She must have fallen herself, for it was clearly in the nature of things, but she couldn't see how.

'It's time we went home, Sue,' Gavin said.

'Of course it isn't, Gavin.'

'Polly –'

'You're nice, Gavin.'

He shook his head. He whispered to her, explaining that Polly wouldn't ever be a party to what was being suggested. He said that perhaps they could meet some time, for a drink or for lunch. He would like to, he said; he wanted to.

She smiled. That night in the Ritz, she murmured, she hadn't wanted to be a blooming angel. 'I wanted you,' she murmured.

'That isn't true.' He said it harshly. He pushed her away from him, wrenching himself free of her arms. It shocked him that she had gone so far, spoiling the past when there wasn't any need to. 'You shouldn't have said that, Sue.'

'You're sentimental.'

He looked around for Polly and saw her dancing with a man who could hardly stand up. Some of the lights in the room had been switched off and the volume of the tape-recorder had been turned down. Simon and Garfunkel were whispering about Mrs Robinson. A woman laughed shrilly, kicking her shoes across the parquet.

Sue wasn't smiling any more. The face that looked up at him through the gloom was hard and accusing. Lines that weren't laughter-lines had developed round the eyes: lines of tension and probably fury, Gavin reckoned. He could see her thinking: he had led her on, he had kissed the top of her head. Now he was suggesting lunch some time, dealing out the future to her when the present was what mattered. He felt he'd been rude.

'I'm sorry, Sue.'

They were standing in the other dancers' way. He wanted to dance again himself, to feel the warmth of her small body, to feel her hands, and to smell her hair, and to bend down and touch it again with his lips. He turned away and extricated Polly from the grasp of the drunk who had claimed to love her. 'It's time to go home,' he said angrily.

'You're never going, old Gavin,' Malcolm protested in the hall. 'I'll run Poll home, you know.'

'I'll run her home myself.'

In the car Polly asked what had happened, but he didn't tell her the truth. He said he'd been rude to Sue because Sue had said something appalling about one of her guests and that for some silly reason he'd taken exception to it.

Polly did not believe him. He was making an excuse, but it didn't matter. He had rejected the game the Ryders had wanted to play and he had rejected it for her sake. He had stood by her and shown his respect for her, even though he had wanted to play the game himself. In the car she laid her head against the side of his shoulder. She thanked him, without specifying what she was grateful for.

'I feel terrible about being rude to Sue,' he said.

He stopped the car outside their house. The light was burning in the sitting-room window. The babysitter would be half asleep. Everything was as it should be.

'I'd no right to be rude,' Gavin said, still in the car.

'Sue'll understand.'

'I don't know that she will.'

She let the silence gather, hoping he'd break it by sighing or saying he'd telephone and apologize tomorrow, or simply saying he'd wait in the car for the babysitter. But he didn't sigh and he didn't speak.

'You could go back,' she said calmly, in the end, 'and say you're sorry. When you've driven the babysitter home.'

He didn't reply. He sat gloomily staring at the steering-wheel. She thought he began to shake his head, but she wasn't sure. Then he said:

'Yes, perhaps I should.'

They left the car and walked together on the short paved path that led to their hall door. She said that what she felt like was a cup of tea, and then thought how dull that sounded.

'Am I dull, Gavin?' she asked, whispering in case the words somehow carried in to the babysitter. Her calmness deserted her for a moment. 'Am I?' she repeated, not whispering any more, not caring about the babysitter.

'Of course you're not dull. Darling, of course you aren't.'

'Not to want to stay? Not to want to go darting into beds with people?'

'Oh, don't be silly, Polly. They're all dull except you, darling. Every single one of them.'

He put his arms around her and kissed her, and she knew that he believed what he was saying. He believed she hadn't fallen as he and the Ryders had, that middle age had dealt no awful blows. In a way that seemed true to Polly, for it had often occurred to her that she, more than the other three, had survived the outer suburb. She was aware of pretences but could not pretend herself. She knew every time they walked into the local Tonino's that the local Tonino's was just an Italian joke, a sham compared with the reality of the original in Greek Street. She knew the party they'd just been to was a squalid little mess. She knew that when Gavin enthused about a fifteen-second commercial for soap his enthusiasm was no cause for celebration. She knew the suburb for what it was, its Volvos and Vauxhalls, its paved paths in unfenced front gardens, its crescents and avenues and immature trees, and the games its people played.

'All right, Polly?' he said, his arms still about her, with tenderness in his voice.

'Yes, of course.' She wanted to thank him again, and to explain that she was thanking him because he had respected her feelings and stood by her.

She wanted to ask him not to go back and apologize, but she couldn't bring herself to do that because the request seemed fussy. 'Yes, of course I'm all right,' she said.

In the sitting-room the babysitter woke up and reported that the children had been as good as gold. 'Not a blink out of either of them, Mrs Dillard.'

'I'll run you home,' Gavin said.

'Oh, it's miles and miles.'

'It's our fault for living in such a godforsaken suburb.'

'Well, it's terribly nice of you, sir.'

Polly paid her and asked her again what her name was because she'd forgotten. The girl repeated that it was Hannah McCarthy. She gave Polly her telephone number in case Estrella shouldn't be available on another occasion. She didn't at all mind coming out so far, she said.

When they'd gone Polly made tea in the kitchen. She placed the teapot and a cup and saucer on a tray and carried the tray upstairs to their bedroom. She was still the same as she'd always been, they would say to one another, lying there, her husband and her friend. They'd admire her for that, they'd share their guilt and their remorse. But they'd be wrong to say she was the same.

She took her clothes off and got into bed. The outer suburb was what it was, so was the shell of middle age: she didn't complain because it would be silly to complain when you were fed and clothed and comfortable, when your children were cared for and warm, when you were loved and respected. You couldn't forever weep with anger, or loudly deplore yourself and other people. You couldn't hit out with your fists as though you were back at the Misses Hamilton's nursery school in Putney. You couldn't forever laugh among the waiters at the Ritz just because it was fun to be there.

In bed she poured herself a cup of tea, telling herself that what had happened tonight – and what was probably happening now – was reasonable and even fair. She had rejected what was distasteful to her, he had stood by her and had respected her feelings: his unfaithfulness seemed his due. In her middle-age calmness that was how she felt. She couldn't help it.

It was how she had fallen, she said to herself, but all that sounded silly now.

The Death of Peggy Meehan

Like all children, I led a double life. There was the ordinariness of dressing in the morning, putting on shoes and combing hair, stirring a spoon through porridge I didn't want, and going at ten to nine to the nuns' elementary school. And there was a world in which only the events I wished for happened, where boredom was not permitted and of which I was both God and King.

In my ordinary life I was the only child of parents who years before my birth had given up hope of ever having me. I remember them best as being different from other parents: they were elderly, it seemed to me, two greyly fussing people with grey hair and faces, in grey clothes, with spectacles. 'Oh, no, no,' they murmured regularly, rejecting on my behalf an invitation to tea or to play with some other child. They feared on my behalf the rain and the sea, and walls that might be walked along, and grass because grass was always damp. They rarely missed a service at the Church of the Holy Redeemer.

In the town where we lived, a seaside town thirty miles from Cork, my father was employed as a senior clerk in the offices of Cosgriff and McLoughlin, Solicitors and Commissioners for Oaths. With him on one side of me and my mother on the other, we walked up and down the brief promenade in winter, while the seagulls shrieked and my father worried in case it was going to rain. We never went for walks through fields or through the heathery wastelands that sloped gently upwards behind the town, or by the river where people said Sir Walter Ralegh had fished. In summer, when the visitors from Cork came, my mother didn't like to let me near the sands because the sands, she said, were full of fleas. In summer we didn't walk on the promenade but out along the main Cork road instead, past a house that appeared to me to move. It disappeared for several minutes as we approached it, a trick of nature, I afterwards discovered, caused by the undulations of the landscape. Every July, for a fortnight, we went to stay in Montenotte, high up above Cork city, in a boarding-house run by my mother's sister, my Aunt Isabella. She, too, had a grey look about her and was religious.

It was here, in my Aunt Isabella's Montenotte boarding-house, that this story begins: in the summer of 1936, when I was seven. It was a much larger house than the one we lived in ourselves, which was small and narrow and in a terrace. My Aunt Isabella's was rather grand in its way, a dark place with little unexpected half-landings, and badly lit corridors. It smelt of floor polish and of a mustiness that I have since associated with the religious life, a smell of old cassocks. Everywhere there were statues of the Virgin, and votive lights and black-framed pictures of the Holy Child. The residents were all priests, old and middle-aged and young, eleven of them usually, which was all the house would hold. A few were always away on their holidays when we stayed there in the summer.

In the summer of 1936 we left our own house in the usual way, my father fastening all the windows and the front and back doors and then examining the house from the outside to make sure he'd done the fastening and the locking properly. We walked to the railway station, each of us carrying something, my mother a brown cardboard suitcase and my father a larger one of the same kind. I carried the sandwiches we were to have on the train, and a flask of carefully made tea and three apples, all packed into a sixpenny fish basket.

In the house in Montenotte my Aunt Isabella told us that Canon McGrath and Father Quinn were on holiday, one in Tralee, the other in Galway. She led us to their rooms, Canon McGrath's for my father and Father Quinn's for my mother and myself. The familiar trestle-bed was erected at the foot of the bed in my mother's room. During the course of the year a curate called Father Lalor had repaired it, my aunt said, after it had been used by Canon McGrath's brother from America, who'd proved too much for the canvas.

'Ah, aren't you looking well, Mr Mahon!' the red-faced and jolly Father Smith said to my father in the dining-room that evening. 'And isn't our friend here getting big for himself?' He laughed loudly, gripping a portion of the back of my neck between a finger and a thumb. Did I know my catechism? he asked me. Was I being good with the nuns in the elementary school? 'Are you in health yourself, Mrs Mahon?' he inquired of my mother.

My mother said she was, and the red-faced priest went to join the other priests at the main dining-table. He left behind him a smell that was different from the smell of the house, and I noticed that he had difficulty in pulling the chair out from the table when he was about to sit down. He had to be assisted in this by a new young curate, a Father Parsloe. Father Smith had been drinking stout again, I said to myself.

Sometimes in my aunt's house there was nothing to do except to watch and to listen. Father Smith used to drink too much stout; Father Magennis, who was so thin you could hardly bear to look at him and whose flesh was the colour of whitewash, was not long for this world; Father Riordon would be a bishop if only he could have tidied himself up a bit; Canon McGrath had once refused to baptize a child; young Father Lalor was going places. For hours on end my Aunt Isabella would murmur to my parents about the priests, telling about the fate of one who had left the boarding-house during the year or supplying background information about a new one. My parents, so faultlessly regular in their church attendance and interested in all religious matters, were naturally pleased to listen. God and the organization of His Church were far more important than my father's duties in Cosgriff and McLoughlin, or my mother's housework, or my own desire to go walking through the heathery wastelands that sloped gently upwards behind our town. God and the priests in my Aunt Isabella's house, and the nuns of the convent elementary school and the priests of the Church of the Holy Redeemer, were at the centre of everything. 'Maybe it'll appeal to our friend,' Father Smith had once said in the dining-room, and I knew that he meant that maybe one day I might be attracted towards the priesthood. My parents had not said anything in reply, but as we ate our tea of sausages and potato-cakes I could feel them thinking that nothing would please them better.

Every year when we stayed with my aunt there was an afternoon when I was left in charge of whichever priests happened to be in, while my parents and my aunt made the journey across the city to visit my father's brother, who was a priest himself. There was some difficulty about bringing me: I had apparently gone to my uncle's house as a baby, when my presence had upset him. Years later I overheard my mother whispering to Father Riordon about this, suggesting – or so it seemed – that my father had once been intent on the priestly life but had at the last moment withdrawn. That he should afterwards have fathered a child was apparently an offence to his brother's feeling of propriety. I had the impression that my uncle was a severe man, who looked severely on my father and my mother and my Aunt Isabella on these visits, and was respected by them for being as he was. All three came back subdued, and that night my mother always prayed for much longer by the side of her bed.

'Father Parsloe's going to take you for a walk,' my Aunt Isabella said on the morning of the 1936 visit. 'He wants to get to know you.'

You walked all the way down from Montenotte, past the docks, over the river and into the city. The first few times it could have been interesting, but after that it was worse than walking on the concrete promenade at home. I'd have far preferred to have played by myself in my aunt's overgrown back garden, pretending to be grown up, talking to myself in a secret way, having wicked thoughts. At home and in my aunt's garden I became a man my father had read about in a newspaper and whom, he'd said, we must all pray for, a thief who broke the windows of jewellers' shops and lifted out watches and rings. I became Father Smith, drinking too much stout and missing the steps of the stairs. I became Father Magennis and would lie on the weeds at the bottom of the garden or under a table, confessing to gruesome crimes at the moment of death. In my mind I mocked the holiness of my parents and imitated their voices; I mocked the holiness of my Aunt Isabella; I talked back to my parents in a way I never would; I laughed and said disgraceful things about God and the religious life. Blasphemy was exciting.

'Are you ready so?' Father Parsloe asked when my parents and my aunt had left for the visit to my uncle. 'Will we take a bus?'

'A bus?'

'Down to the town.'

I'd never in my life done that before. The buses were for going longer distances in. It seemed extraordinary not to walk, the whole point of a walk was to walk.

'I haven't any money for the bus,' I said, and Father Parsloe laughed. On the upper deck he lit a cigarette. He was a slight young man, by far the youngest of the priests in my aunt's house, with reddish hair and a face that seemed to be on a slant. 'Will we have tea in Thompson's?' he said. 'Would that be a good thing to do?'

We had tea in Thompson's café, with buns and cakes and huge meringues such as I'd never tasted before. Father Parsloe smoked fourteen cigarettes and drank all the tea himself. I had three bottles of fizzy orangeade. 'Will we go to the pictures?' Father Parsloe said when he'd paid the bill at the cash desk. 'Will we chance the Pavilion?'

I had never, of course, been to the pictures before. My mother said that the Star Picture House, which was the only one in our town, was full of fleas.

'One and a half,' Father Parsloe said at the cash desk in the Pavilion and we were led away into the darkness. THE END it announced on the screen, and when I saw it I thought we were too late. 'Ah, aren't we in lovely time?' Father Parsloe said.

I didn't understand the film. It was about grown-ups kissing one another, and about an earthquake, and then a motor-car accident in which a woman who'd been kissed a lot was killed. The man who'd kissed her was married to another woman, and when the film ended he was sitting in a room with his wife, looking at her. She kept saying it was all right.

'God, wasn't that great?' Father Parsloe said as we stood in the lavatory of the Pavilion, the kind of lavatory where you stand up, like I'd never been in before. 'Wasn't it a good story?'

All the way back to Montenotte I kept remembering it. I kept seeing the face of the woman who'd been killed, and all the bodies lying on the streets after the earthquake, and the man at the end, sitting in a room with his wife. The swaying of the bus made me feel queasy because of the meringues and the orangeade, but I didn't care.

'Did you enjoy the afternoon?' Father Parsloe asked, and I told him I'd never enjoyed anything better. I asked him if the pictures were always as good. He assured me they were.

My parents, however, didn't seem pleased. My father got hold of a *Cork Examiner* and looked up the film that was on at the Pavilion and reported that it wasn't suitable for a child. My mother gave me a bath and examined my clothes for fleas. When Father Parsloe winked at me in the dining-room my parents pretended not to notice him.

That night my mother prayed for her extra long period, after the visit to my uncle. I lay in the dimly lit room, aware that she was kneeling there, but thinking of the film and the way the people had kissed, not like my parents ever kissed. At the convent elementary school there were girls in the higher classes who were pretty, far prettier than my mother. There was one called Claire, with fair hair and a softly freckled face, and another called Peggy Meehan, who was younger and black-haired. I had picked them out because they had spoken to me, asking me my name. I thought them very nice.

I opened my eyes and saw that my mother was rising from her knees. She stood for a moment at the edge of her bed, not smiling, her lips still moving, continuing her prayer. Then she got into bed and put out the light.

I listened to her breathing and heard it become the breathing which people have when they're asleep, but I couldn't sleep myself. I lay there, still remembering the film and remembering being in Thompson's and seeing Father Parsloe lighting one cigarette after another. For some reason, I began to imagine that I was in Thompson's with Father Parsloe and the two girls from the convent, and that we all went off to the Pavilion together, swinging along the street. 'Ah, isn't this the life for us?' Father Parsloe said as he led us into the darkness, and I told the girls I'd been to the Pavilion before and they said they never had.

I heard eleven o'clock chiming from a nearby church. I heard a stumbling on the stairs and then the laughter of Father Smith, and Father Riordon telling him to be quiet. I heard twelve chiming and half past twelve, and a quarter to one, and one.

After that I didn't want to sleep. I was standing in a classroom of the convent and Claire was smiling at me. It was nice being with her. I felt warm all over, and happy.

And then I was walking on the sands with Peggy Meehan. We ran, playing a game she'd made up, and then we walked again. She asked if I'd like to go on a picnic with her, next week perhaps.

I didn't know what to do. I wanted one of the girls to be my friend. I wanted to love one of them, like the people had loved in the film. I wanted to kiss one and be with one, just the two of us. In the darkness of the bedroom they both seemed close and real, closer than my mother, even though I could hear my mother breathing. 'Come on,' Peggy Meehan whispered, and then Claire whispered also, saying we'd always be best friends, saying we might run away. It was all wrong that there were two of them, yet both vividly remained. 'Tuesday,' Peggy Meehan said. 'We'll have the picnic on Tuesday.'

Her father drove us in his car, away from the town, out beyond the heathery wastelands, towards a hillside that was even nicer. But a door of the car, the back door against which Peggy Meehan was leaning, suddenly gave way. On the dust of the road she was as dead as the woman in the film.

'Poor Peggy,' Claire said at some later time, even though she hadn't known Peggy Meehan very well. 'Poor little Peggy.' And then she smiled and took my hand and we walked together through the heathery wastelands, in love with one another.

A few days later we left my Aunt Isabella's house in Montenotte and returned on the train to our seaside town. And a week after that a new term began at the convent elementary school. Peggy Meehan was dead, the Reverend Mother told us, all of us assembled together. She added that there was diphtheria in the town.

I didn't think about it at first; and I didn't connect the reality of the death with a fantasy that had been caused by my first visit to a cinema. Some part of my mind may passingly have paused over the coincidence, but that was all. There was the visit to the Pavilion itself to talk about in the convent, and the description of the film, and Father Parsloe's conversation and the way he'd smoked fourteen cigarettes in Thompson's. Diphtheria was a terrible disease, my mother said when I told her, and naturally we must all pray for the soul of poor Peggy Meehan.

But as weeks and months went by, I found myself increasingly remembering the story I had told myself on the night of the film, and remembering particularly how Peggy Meehan had fallen from the car, and how she'd looked when she was dead. I said to myself that that had been my wickedest thought, worse than my blasphemies and yet somehow part of them. At night I lay in bed, unable to sleep, trying hopelessly to pray for forgiveness. But no forgiveness came, for there was no respite to the images that recurred, her face in life and then in death, like the face of the woman in the film.

A year later, while lying awake in the same room in my aunt's boarding-house, I saw her. In the darkness there was a sudden patch of light and in the centre of it she was wearing a sailor-suit that I remembered. Her black plaits hung down her back. She smiled at me and went away. I knew instinctively then, as I watched her and after she'd gone, that the fantasy and the reality were part and parcel: I had caused this death to occur.

Looking back on it now, I can see, of course, that that feeling was a childish one. It was a childish fear, a superstition that occurring to an adult would cause only a shiver of horror. But, as a child, with no one to consult about the matter, I lived with the thought that my will was more potent than I knew. In stories I had learnt of witches and spells and evil spirits, and power locked up in people. In my games I had wickedly denied the religious life, and goodness, and holiness. In my games I had mocked Father Smith, I had pretended that the dying Father Magennis was a criminal. I had pretended to be a criminal myself, a man who broke jewellers' windows. I had imitated my parents when it said you should honour your father and your mother. I had mocked the holiness of my Aunt Isabella. I had murdered Peggy Meehan because there wasn't room for her in the story I was telling myself. I was possessed and evil: the nuns had told us about people being like that.

I thought at first I might seek advice from Father Parsloe. I thought of asking him if he remembered the day we'd gone on our outing, and then telling him how, in a story I was telling myself, I'd caused Peggy Meehan to be killed in a car accident like the woman in the film, and how she'd died in reality, of diphtheria. But Father Parsloe had an impatient kind of look about him this year, as if he had worries of his own. So I didn't tell him and I didn't tell anyone. I hoped that when we returned to our own house at the end of the stay in Montenotte I wouldn't see her again, but the very first day we were back I saw her at four o'clock in the afternoon, in the kitchen.

After that she came irregularly, sometimes not for a month and once not for a year. She continued to appear in the same sudden way but in different clothes, and growing up as I was growing up. Once, after I'd left the convent and gone on to the Christian Brother's, she appeared in the classroom, smiling near the blackboard.

She never spoke. Whether she appeared on the promenade or at school or in my aunt's house or our house, close to me or at a distance, she communicated only with her smile and with her eyes: I was possessed of the Devil, she came herself from God. In her eyes and her smile there was that simple message, a message which said also that my thoughts were always wicked, that I had never believed properly in God or the Virgin or Jesus who died for us.

I tried to pray. Like my mother, kneeling beside my bed. Like my aunt and her houseful of priests. Like the nuns and Christian Brothers, and other boys and girls of the town. But prayer would not come to me, and I realized that it never had. I had always pretended, going down on my knees at Mass, laughing and blaspheming in my mind. I hated the very thought of prayer. I hated my parents in an unnatural manner, and my Aunt Isabella and the priests in her house. But the dead Peggy Meehan fresh from God's heaven, was all forgiveness in her patch of light, smiling to rid me of my evil spirit.

She was there at my mother's funeral, and later at my father's. Claire, whom I had destroyed her for, married a man employed in the courthouse and became a Mrs Madden, prematurely fat. I naturally didn't marry anyone myself.

I am forty-six years old now and I live alone in the same seaside town. No one in the town knows why I am solitary. No one could guess that I have lived with a child's passionate companionship for half a lifetime. Being no longer a child, I naturally no longer believe that I was responsible for the death. In my passing, careless fantasy I wished for it and she, already dead, picked up my living thoughts. I should not have wished for it because in middle age she is a beautiful creature now, more beautiful by far than fat Mrs Madden.

And that is all there is. At forty-six I walk alone on the brief promenade, or by the edge of the sea or on the road to Cork, where the moving house is. I work, as my father worked, in the offices of Cosgriff and McLoughlin. I cook my own food. I sleep alone in a bed that has an iron bedstead. On Sundays I go hypocritically to Mass in the Church of the Holy Redeemer; I go to Confession and do not properly confess; I go to Men's Confraternity, and to Communion. And all the time she is there, appearing in her patch of light to remind me that she never leaves me. And all the time, on my knees at Mass, or receiving the Body and the Blood, or in my iron bed, I desire her. In the offices of Cosgriff and McLoughlin I dream of her nakedness. When we are old I shall desire her, too, with my shrunken, evil body.

In the town I am a solitary, peculiar man. I have been rendered so, people probably say, by my cloistered upbringing, and probably add that such an upbringing would naturally cultivate a morbid imagination. That may be so, and it doesn't really matter how things have come about. All I know is that she is more real for me than anything else is in this seaside town or beyond it. I live for her, living hopelessly, for I know I can never possess her as I wish to. I have a carnal desire for a shadow, which in turn is His mockery of me: His fitting punishment for my wickedest thought of all.

Mrs Silly

Michael couldn't remember a time when his father had been there. There'd always been the flat where he and his mother lived, poky and cluttered even though his mother tried so. Every Saturday his father came to collect him. He remembered a blue car and then a greenish one. The latest one was white, an Alfa-Romeo.

Saturday with his father was the highlight of the week. Unlike his mother's flat, his father's house was spacious and nicely carpeted. There was Gillian, his father's wife, who never seemed in a hurry, who smiled and didn't waste time. Her smile was cool, which matched the way she dressed. Her voice was quiet and reliable: Michael couldn't imagine it ever becoming shrill or weepy or furious, or in any other way getting out of control. It was a nice voice, as nice as Gillian herself.

His father and Gillian had two little girls, twins of six, two years younger than Michael. They lived near Cranleigh, in a half-timbered house in pretty wooded countryside. On Saturday mornings the drive from London took over an hour, but Michael never minded and on the way back he usually fell asleep. There was a room in the house that his father and Gillian had made his own, which the twins weren't allowed to enter in his absence. He had his Triang train circuit there, on a table that had been specially built into the wall for it.

It was in this house, one Saturday afternoon, that Michael's father brought up the subject of Elton Grange. 'You're nearly nine, you know,' his father said. 'It's high time, really, old chap.'

Elton Grange was a preparatory school in Wiltshire, which Michael's father had gone to himself. He'd mentioned it many times before and so had Michael's mother, but in Michael's mind it was a place that belonged to the distant future – with Radley, where his father had gone, also. He certainly knew that he wasn't going to stay at the primary school in Hammersmith for ever, and had always taken it for granted that he would move away from it when the rest of his class moved, at eleven. He felt, without actually being able to recall the relevant conversation, that his mother had quite definitely implied this. But it didn't work out like that. 'You should go in September,' his father said, and that was that.

'Oh, darling,' his mother murmured when the arrangements had all been made. 'Oh, Michael, I'll miss you.'

His father would pay the fees and his father would in future give him pocket-money, over and above what his mother gave him. He'd like it at Elton Grange, his father promised. 'Oh yes, you'll like it,' his mother said too.

She was a woman of medium height, five foot four, with a round, plump face and plump arms and legs. There was a soft prettiness about her, about her light-blue eyes and her wide, simple mouth and her fair, rather fluffy hair. Her hands were always warm, as if expressing the warmth of her nature. She wept easily and often said she was silly to weep so. She talked a lot, getting carried away when she didn't watch herself: for this failing, too, she regularly said she was silly. 'Mrs Silly', she used to say when Michael was younger, condemning herself playfully for the two small follies she found it hard to control.

She worked as a secretary for an Indian, a Mr Ashaf, who had an office-stationery business. There was the shop – more of a warehouse, really – with stacks of swivel chairs and filing-cabinets on top of one another and green metal desks, and cartons containing continuation paper and top-copy foolscap and flimsy, and printed invoices. There were other cartons full of envelopes, and packets of paper-clips, drawing-pins and staples. The carbon-paper supplies were kept in the office behind the shop, where Michael's mother sat in front of a typewriter, typing invoices mainly. Mr Ashaf, a small wiry man, was always on his feet, moving between the shop and the office, keeping an eye on Michael's mother and on Dolores Welsh who looked after the retail side. Before she'd married, Michael's mother had been a secretary in the Wedgwood Centre, but returning to work at the time of her divorce she'd found it more convenient to work for Mr Ashaf since his premises were only five minutes away from where she and Michael lived. Mr Ashaf was happy to employ her on the kind of part-time basis that meant she could be at home every afternoon by the time Michael got in from school. During the holidays Mr Ashaf permitted her to take the typewriter to her flat, to come in every morning to collect what work there was and hand over what she'd done the day before. When this arrangement wasn't convenient, due to the nature of the work, Michael accompanied her to Mr Ashaf's premises and sat in the office with her or with Dolores Welsh in the shop. Mr Ashaf used occasionally to give him a sweet.

'Perhaps I'll change my job,' Michael's mother said brightly, a week before he was due to become a boarder at Elton Grange. 'I could maybe go back to the West End. Nice to have a few more pennies.' She was cheering herself up – he could tell by the way she looked at him. She packed his belongings carefully, giving him many instructions about looking after himself, about keeping himself warm and changing any clothes that got wet. 'Oh, darling,' she said at Paddington on the afternoon of his departure. 'Oh, darling, I'll miss you so!'

He would miss her, too. Although his father and Gillian were in every way more fun than his mother, it was his mother he loved. Although she fussed and was a nuisance sometimes, there was always the warmth, the cosiness of climbing into her bed on Sunday mornings or watching Magic Roundabout together. He was too big for Magic Roundabout now, or so he considered, and he rather thought he was too big to go on climbing into her bed. But the memories of all this cosiness had become part of his relationship with her.

She wept as they stood together on the platform. She held him close to her, pressing his head against her breast. 'Oh, darling!' she said. 'Oh, my darling.'

Her tears damped his face. She sniffed and sobbed, whispering that she didn't know what she'd do. 'Poor thing!' someone passing said. She blew her nose. She apologized to Michael, trying to smile. 'Remember where your envelopes are,' she said. She'd addressed and stamped a dozen envelopes for him so that he could write to her. She wanted him to write at once, just to say he'd arrived safely.

'And don't be homesick now,' she said, her own voice trembling again. 'Big boy, Michael.'

The train left her behind. He waved from the corridor window, and she gestured at him, indicating that he shouldn't lean out. But because of the distances between them he couldn't understand what the gesture meant. When the train stopped at Reading he found his writing-paper and envelopes in his overnight bag and began to write to her.

At Elton Grange he was in the lowest form, Miss Brooks's form. Miss Brooks, grey-haired at sixty, was the only woman on the teaching staff. She did not share the men's common-room but sat instead in the matrons' room, where she smoked Senior Service cigarettes between lessons. There was pale tobacco-tinged hair on her face, and on Tuesday and Friday afternoons she wore jodhpurs, being in charge of the school's riding. Brookie she was known as.

The other women at Elton Grange were Sister and the undermatron Miss Trenchard, the headmaster's wife Mrs Lyng, the lady cook Miss Arland, and the maids. Mrs Lyng was a stout woman, known among the boys as Outsize Dorothy, and Sister was thin and brisk. Miss Trenchard and Miss Arland were both under twenty-three; Miss Arland was pretty and Miss Trenchard wasn't. Miss Arland went about a lot with the history and geography master, Cocky Marshall, and Miss Trenchard was occasionally seen with the P.T. instructor, a Welshman, who was also in charge of the carpentry shop. Among the older boys Miss Trenchard was sometimes known as Tampax.

Twice a week Michael wrote to his mother, and on Sundays he wrote to his father as well. He told them that the headmaster was known to everyone as A.J.L. and he told them about the rules, how no boy in the three lower forms was permitted to be seen with his hands in his pockets and how no boy was permitted to run through A.J.L.'s garden. He said the food was awful because that was what everyone else said, although he quite liked it really.

At half-term his father and Gillian came. They stayed in the Grand, and Michael had lunch and tea there on the Saturday and on the Sunday, and just lunch on the Monday because they had to leave in the afternoon. He told them about his friends, Carson and Tichbourne, and his father suggested that next half-term Carson and Tichbourne might like to have lunch or tea at the Grand. 'Or maybe Swagger Browne,' Michael said. Browne's people lived in Kenya and his grandmother, with whom he spent the holidays, wasn't always able to come at half-term. 'Hard up,' Michael said.

Tichbourne and Carson were in Michael's dormitory, and there was one other boy, called Andrews: they were all aged eight. At night, after lights out, they talked about most things: about their families and the houses they lived in and the other schools they'd been at. Carson told about the time he'd put stink-bombs under the chair-legs when people were coming to play bridge, and Andrews about the time he'd been caught, by a policeman, stealing strawberries.

'What's it like?' Andrews asked in the dormitory one night. 'What's it like, a divorce?'

'D'you see your mother?' Tichbourne asked, and Michael explained that it was his mother he lived with, not his father.

'Often wondered what it's like for the kids,' Andrews said. 'There's a woman in our village who's divorced. She ran off with another bloke, only the next thing was he ran off with someone else.'

'Who'd your mum run off with?' Carson asked.

'No one.'

'Your dad run off then?'

'Yes.'

His mother had told him that his father left her because they didn't get on any more. He hadn't left her because he knew Gillian. He hadn't met Gillian for years after that.

'D'you like her?' Andrews asked. 'Gillian?'

'She's all right. They've got twins now, my dad and Gillian. Girls.'

'I'd hate it if my mum and dad got divorced,' Tichbourne said.

'Mine quarrelled all last holidays,' Carson said, 'about having a room decorated.'

'Can't stand it when they quarrel,' Andrews said.

Intrigued by a situation that was strange to them, the other boys often asked after that about the divorce. How badly did people have to quarrel before they decided on one? Was Gillian different from Michael's mother? Did Michael's mother hate her? Did she hate his father?

'They never see one another,' Michael said. 'She's not like Gillian at all.'

At the end of the term the staff put on a show called Staff Laughs. Cocky Marshall was incarcerated all during one sketch in a wooden container that was meant to be a steam bath. Something had gone wrong with it. The steam was too hot and the catch had become jammed. Cocky Marshall was red in the face and nobody knew if he was putting it on or not until the end of the sketch, when he stepped out of the container in his underclothes. Mr Waydelin had to wear a kilt in another sketch and Miss Arland and Miss Trenchard were dressed up in rugby togs, with Cocky Marshall's and Mr Brine's scrum caps. The Reverend Green – mathematics and divinity – was enthusiastically applauded in his Mrs Wagstaffe sketch. A.J.L. did his magic, and as a grand finale the whole staff, including Miss Brooks, sang together, arm-in-arm, on the small stage. 'We're going home,' they sang. 'We're going home. We're on the way that leads to home. We've seen the good things and the bad and now we're absolutely mad. We're g-o-i-n-g home.' All the boys joined in the chorus, and that night in Michael's dormitory they ate Crunchie, Galaxy and Mars Bars and didn't wash their teeth afterwards. At half past twelve the next day Michael's mother was waiting for him at Paddington.

At home, nothing was different. On Saturdays his father came and drove him away to the house near Cranleigh. His mother talked about Dolores Welsh and Mr Ashaf. She hadn't returned to work in the West End. It was quite nice really, she said, at Mr Ashaf's.

Christmas came and went. His father gave him a new Triang locomotive and Gillian gave him a pogo-stick and the twins a magnet and a set of felt pens. His mother decorated the flat and put fairy-lights on a small Christmas tree. She filled his stocking on Christmas Eve when he was asleep and the next day, after they'd had their Christmas dinner, she gave him a football and a glove puppet and a jigsaw of Windsor Castle. He gave her a brooch he'd bought in Woolworth's. On January 14th he returned to Elton Grange.

Nothing was different at Elton Grange either, except that Cocky Marshall had left. Nobody had known he was going to leave, and some boys said he had been sacked. But others denied that, claiming that he'd gone of his own accord, without giving the required term's notice. They said A.J.L. was livid.

Three weeks passed, and then one morning Michael received a letter from his father saying that neither he nor Gillian would be able to come at half-term because he had to go to Tunisia on business and wanted to take Gillian with him. He sent some money to make up for the disappointment.

In a letter to his mother, not knowing what to say because nothing much was happening, Michael revealed that his father wouldn't be there at half-term. *Then I shall come*, his mother wrote back.

She stayed, not in the Grand, but in a boarding-house called Sans Souci, which had coloured gnomes fishing in a pond in the front garden, and a black gate with one hinge broken. They weren't able to have lunch there on the Saturday because the woman who ran it, Mrs Malone, didn't do lunches. They had lunch in the Copper Kettle, and since Mrs Malone didn't do teas either they had tea in the Copper Kettle as well. They walked around the town between lunch and tea, and after tea they sat together in his mother's bedroom until it was time to catch the bus back to school.

The next day she said she'd like to see over the school, so he brought her into the chapel, which once had been the gate-lodge, and into the classrooms and the gymnasium and the art-room and the changing-rooms. In the carpentry shop the P.T. instructor was making a cupboard. 'Who's that boy?' his mother whispered, unfortunately just loud enough for the P.T. instructor to hear. He smiled. Swagger Browne, who was standing about doing nothing, giggled.

'But how could he be a boy?' Michael asked dismally, leading the way on the cinder path that ran around the cricket pitch. 'Boys at Elton only go up to thirteen and a half.'

'Oh dear, of course,' his mother said. She began to talk of other things. She spoke quickly. Dolores Welsh, she thought, was going to get married, Mr Ashaf had wrenched his arm. She'd spoken to the landlord about the damp that kept coming in the bathroom, but the landlord had said that to cure it would mean a major upheaval for them.

All the time she was speaking, while they walked slowly on the cinder path, he kept thinking about the P.T. instructor, unable to understand how his mother could ever have mistaken him for a boy. It was a cold morning and rather damp, not raining heavily, not even drizzling, but misty in a particularly wetting kind of way. He wondered where they were going to go for lunch, since the woman in the Copper Kettle had said yesterday that the café didn't open on Sundays.

'Perhaps we could go and look at the dormitories?' his mother suggested when they came to the end of the cinder path.

He didn't want to, but for some reason he felt shy about saying so. If he said he didn't want to show her the dormitories, she'd ask him why and he wouldn't know what to say because he didn't know himself.

'All right,' he said.

They walked through the dank mist, back to the school buildings, which were mostly of red brick, some with a straggle of Virginia creeper on them. The new classrooms, presented a year ago by the father of a boy who had left, were of pinker brick than the rest. The old classrooms had been nicer, Michael's father said: they'd once been the stables.

There were several entrances to the house itself. The main one, approached from the cricket pitch by crossing A.J.L.'s lawns and then crossing a large, almost circular gravel expanse, was grandiose in the early Victorian style. Stone pillars supported a wide gothic arch through which, in a sizeable vestibule, further pillars framed a heavy oak front door. There were croquet mallets and hoops in a wooden box in this vestibule, and deck-chairs and two coloured golfing umbrellas. There was an elaborate wrought-iron scraper and a revolving brush for taking the mud from shoes and boots. On either side of the large hall door there was a round window, composed of circular, lead-encased panes. 'Well, at least they haven't got rid of those,' Michael's father had said, for these circular windows were a feature that boys who had been to Elton Grange often recalled with affection.

The other entrances to the house were at the back and it was through one of these, leading her in from the quadrangle and the squat new classrooms, past the kitchens and the staff lavatory, that Michael directed his mother on their way to the dormitories. All the other places they'd visited had been outside the house itself – the gymnasium and the changing-rooms were converted outbuildings, the carpentry shop was a wooden shed tucked neatly out of the way beside the garages, the art-room was an old conservatory, and the classroom block stood on its own, forming two sides of the quadrangle.

'What a nice smell!' Michael's mother whispered as they passed the kitchens, as Michael pressed himself against the wall to let Miss Brooks, in her jodhpurs, go by. Miss Brooks was carrying a riding stick and had a cigarette going. She didn't smile at Michael, nor at Michael's mother.

They went up the back stairs and Michael hoped they wouldn't meet anyone else. All the boys, except the ones like Swagger Browne whose people lived abroad, were out with their parents and usually the staff went away at half-term, if they possibly could. But A.J.L. and Outsize Dorothy never went away, nor did Sister, and Miss Trenchard had been there at prayers.

'How ever do you find your way through all these passages?' his mother whispered as he led her expertly towards his dormitory. He explained, in a low voice also, that you got used to the passages.

'Here it is,' he said, relieved to find that neither Sister nor Miss Trenchard was laying out clean towels. He closed the door behind them. 'That's my bed there,' he said.

He stood against the door with his ear cocked while she went to the bed and looked at it. She turned and smiled at him, her head a little on one side. She opened a locker and looked inside, but he explained that the locker she was looking in was Carson's. 'Where'd that nice rug come from?' she asked, and he said that he'd written to Gillian to say he'd been cold once or twice at night, and she'd sent him the rug immediately. 'Oh,' his mother said dispiritedly. 'Well, that was nice of Gillian,' she added.

She crossed to one of the windows and looked down over A.J.L.'s lawns to the chestnut trees that surrounded the playing-fields. It really was a beautiful place, she said.

She smiled at him again and he thought, what he'd never thought before, that her clothes were cheap-looking. Gillian's clothes were clothes you somehow didn't notice: it didn't occur to you to think they were cheap-looking or expensive. The women of Elton Grange all dressed differently, Outsize Dorothy in woollen things, Miss Brooks in suits, with a tie, and Sister and Miss Trenchard and Miss Arland always had white coats. The maids wore blue overalls most of the time but sometimes you saw them going home in the evenings in their ordinary clothes, which you never really thought about and certainly you never thought were cheap-looking.

'Really beautiful,' she said, still smiling, still at the window. She was wearing a headscarf and a maroon coat and another scarf at her neck. Her handbag was maroon also, but it was old, with something broken on one of the buckles: it was the handbag, he said to himself, that made you think she was cheaply dressed.

He left the door and went to her, taking her arm. He felt ashamed that he'd thought her clothes were cheap-looking. She'd been upset when he'd told her that the rug had been sent by Gillian. She'd been upset and he hadn't bothered.

'Oh, Mummy,' he said.

She hugged him to her, and when he looked up into her face he saw the mark of a tear on one of her cheeks. Her fluffy hair was sticking out a bit beneath the headscarf, her round, plump face was forcing itself to smile.

'I'm sorry,' he said.

'Sorry? Darling, there's no need.'

'I'm sorry you're left all alone there, Mummy.'

'Oh, but I'm not at all. I've got the office every day, and one of these days I really will see about going back to the West End. We've been awfully busy at the office, actually, masses to do.'

The sympathy he'd showed caused her to talk. Up to now – ever since they'd met the day before – she'd quite deliberately held herself back in this respect, knowing that to chatter on wouldn't be the thing at all. Yesterday she'd waited until she'd returned to Sans Souci before relaxing. She'd had a nice long chat with Mrs Malone on the landing, which unfortunately had been spoiled by a man in one of Mrs Malone's upper rooms poking his head out and asking for a bit of peace. 'Sorry about that,' she'd heard Mrs Malone saying to him later. 'Couldn't really stop her' – a statement that had spoiled things even more. 'I'm ever so sorry,' she'd said quietly to Mrs Malone at breakfast.

'Let's go down now,' Michael said.

But his mother didn't hear this remark, engaged as she was upon making a series of remarks herself. She was no longer discreetly whispering, but chattering on with even more abandon than she had displayed on Mrs Malone's stairs the night before. A flush had spread over her cheeks and around her mouth and on the portion of her neck which could be seen above her scarf. Michael could see she was happy.

'We'll have to go to Dolores' wedding,' she said. 'On the 8th. The 8th of May, a Thursday I think it is. They're coming round actually, Dolores and her young chap, Brian Haskins he's called. Mr Ashaf says he wouldn't trust him, but actually Dolores is no fool.'

'Let's go down now, Mum.'

She said she'd like to see the other dormitories. She'd like to see the senior dormitories, into one of which Michael would eventually be moving. She began to talk about Dolores Welsh and Brian Haskins again and then about Mrs Malone, and then about a woman Michael had never heard of before, a person called Peggy Urch.

He pointed out that the dormitories were called after imperial heroes. His was Drake, others were Ralegh, Nelson, Wellington, Marlborough and

Clive. 'I think I'll be moving to Nelson,' Michael said. 'Or Marlborough. Depends.' But he knew she wasn't listening, he knew she hadn't taken in the fact that the dormitories were named like that. She was talking about Peggy Urch when he led her into Marlborough. Outsize Dorothy was there with Miss Trenchard, taking stuff out of Verschoyle's locker because Verschoyle had just gone to the sanatorium.

'Very nice person,' Michael's mother was saying. 'She's taken on the Redmans' flat – the one above us, you know.'

It seemed to Michael that his mother didn't see Outsize Dorothy and Miss Trenchard. It seemed to him for a moment that his mother didn't quite know where she was.

'Looking for me?' Outsize Dorothy said. She smiled and waddled towards them. She looked at Michael, waiting for him to explain who this visitor was. Miss Trenchard looked, too.

'It's my mother,' he said, aware that these words were inept and inelegant.

'I'm Mrs Lyng,' Outsize Dorothy said. She held out her hand and Michael's mother took it.

'The Matron,' she said. 'I've heard of you, Mrs Lyng.'

'Well actually,' Outsize Dorothy contradicted with a laugh, 'I'm the headmaster's wife.' All the flesh on her body wobbled when she laughed. Tichbourne said he knew for a fact she was twenty stone.

'What a lovely place you have, Mrs Lyng. I was just saying to Michael. What a view from the windows!'

Outsize Dorothy told Miss Trenchard to go on getting Verschoyle's things together, in a voice that implied that Miss Trenchard wasn't paid to stand about doing nothing in the dormitories. All the women staff – the maids and Sister and Miss Arland and Miss Trenchard – hated Outsize Dorothy because she'd expect them, even Sister, to go on rooting in a locker while she talked to a parent. She wouldn't in a million years say: 'This is Miss Trenchard, the undermatron.'

'Oh, I'm afraid we don't have much time for views at Elton,' Outsize Dorothy said. She was looking puzzled, and Michael imagined she was thinking that his mother was surely another woman, a thinner, smarter, quieter person. But then Outsize Dorothy wasn't clever, as she often light-heartedly said herself, and was probably saying to herself that she must be confusing one boy's mother with another.

'Dorothy!' a voice called out, a voice which Michael instantly and to his horror recognized as A.J.L.'s.

'We had such a view at home!' Michael's mother said. 'Such a gorgeous view!' She was referring to her own home, a rectory in Somerset somewhere.

She'd often told Michael about the rectory and the view, and her parents, both dead now. Her father had received the call to the Church late in life: he'd been in the Customs and Excise before that.

'Here, dear,' Outsize Dorothy called out. 'In Marlborough.'

Michael knew he'd gone red in the face. His stomach felt hot also, the palms of his hands were clammy. He could hear the clatter of the headmaster's footsteps on the uncarpeted back stairs. He began to pray, asking for something to happen, anything at all, anything God could think of.

His mother was more animated than before. More fluffy hair had slipped out from beneath her headscarf, the flush had spread over a greater area of her face. She was talking about the lack of view from the flat where she and Michael lived in Hammersmith, and about Peggy Urch who'd come to live in the flat directly above them and whose view was better because she could see over the poplars.

'Hullo,' A.J.L. said, a stringy, sandy man, the opposite of Outsize Dorothy and in many ways the perfect complement. Tichbourne said he often imagined them naked in bed, A.J.L. winding his stringiness around her explosive bulk.

Hands were shaken again. 'Having a look round?' A.J.L. said. 'Staying at the Grand?'

Michael's mother said she wasn't staying at the Grand but at Sans Souci, did he know it? They'd been talking about views, she said, it was lovely to have a room with a view, she hoped Michael wasn't giving trouble, her husband of course – well, ex-husband now – had been to this school in his time, before going on to Radley. Michael would probably go to Radley too.

'Well, we hope so,' A.J.L. said, seizing the back of Michael's neck. 'Shown her the new classrooms, eh?'

'Yes, sir.'

'Shown her where we're going to have our swimming-pool?'

'Not yet, sir.'

'Well, then.'

His mother spoke of various diseases Michael had had, measles and whooping cough and chicken-pox, and of diseases he hadn't had, mumps in particular. Miss Trenchard was like a ghost, all in white, still sorting out the junk in Verschoyle's locker, not daring to say a word. She was crouched there, with her head inside the locker, listening to everything.

'Well, we mustn't keep you,' A.J.L. said, shaking hands again with Michael's mother. 'Always feel free to come.'

There was such finality about these statements, more in the headmaster's tone than in the words themselves, that Michael's mother was immediately silent. The statements had a physical effect on her, as though quite violently they had struck her across the face. When she spoke again it was in the whisper she had earlier employed.

'I'm sorry,' she said. 'I'm ever so sorry for going on so.'

A.J.L. and Outsize Dorothy laughed, pretending not to understand what she meant. Miss Trenchard would tell Miss Arland. Sister would hear and so would Brookie, and the P.T. instructor would say that this same woman had imagined him to be one of the boys. Mr Waydelin would hear, and Square-jaw Simpson – Cocky Marshall's successor – and Mr Brine and the Reverend Green.

'I have enjoyed it,' Michael's mother whispered. 'So nice to meet you.'

He went before her down the back stairs. His face was still red. They passed by the staff lavatory and the kitchens, out on to the concrete quadrangle. It was still misty and cold.

'I bought things for lunch,' she said, and for an awful moment he thought that she'd want to eat them somewhere in the school or in the grounds – in the art-room or the cricket pavilion. 'We could have a picnic in my room,' she said.

They walked down the short drive, past the chapel that once had been the gate-lodge. They caught a bus after a wait of half an hour, during which she began to talk again, telling him more about Peggy Urch, who reminded her of another friend she'd had once, a Margy Bassett. In her room in Sans Souci she went on talking, spreading out on the bed triangles of cheese, and tomatoes and rolls and biscuits and oranges. They sat in her room when they'd finished, eating Rollo. At six o'clock they caught a bus back to Elton Grange. She wept a little when she said goodbye.

Michael's mother did not, as it happened, ever arrive at Elton Grange at half-term again. There was no need for her to do so because his father and Gillian were always able to come themselves. For several terms he felt embarrassed in the presence of A.J.L. and Outsize Dorothy and Miss Trenchard, but no one at school mentioned the unfortunate visit, not even Swagger Browne, who had so delightedly overheard her assuming the P.T. instructor to be one of the boys. School continued as before and so did the holidays, Saturdays in Cranleigh and the rest of the week in Hammersmith, news of Mr Ashaf and Dolores Welsh, now Dolores Haskins. Peggy Urch, the woman in the flat upstairs, often came down for a chat.

Often, too, Michael and his mother would sit together in the evenings on the sofa in front of the electric fire. She'd tell him about the rectory in Somerset and her father who had received the call to the Church late in his life, who'd been in the Customs and Excise. She'd tell him about her own childhood, and even about the early days of her marriage. Sometimes she wept a little, hardly at all, and he would take her arm on the sofa and she would smile and laugh. When they sat together on the sofa or went out together, to the cinema, or for a walk by the river or to the teashop called the Maids of Honour near Kew Gardens, Michael felt that he would never want to marry because he'd prefer to be with his mother. Even when she chatted on to some stranger in the Maids of Honour he felt he loved her: everything was different from the time she'd come to Elton Grange because away from Elton Grange things didn't matter in the same way.

Then something unpleasant threatened. During his last term at Elton Grange Michael was to be confirmed. 'Oh, but of course I must come,' his mother said.

It promised to be worse than the previous occasion. After the service you were meant to bring your parents in to tea in the Great Hall and see that they had a cup of tea and sandwiches and cakes. You had to introduce them to the Bishop of Bath and Wells. Michael imagined all that. In bed at night he imagined his father and Gillian looking very smart, his father chatting easily to Mr Brine, Gillian smiling at Outsize Dorothy, and his mother's hair fluffing out from beneath her headscarf. He imagined his mother and his father and Gillian having to sit together in a pew in chapel, as naturally they'd be expected to, being members of the same party.

'There's no need to,' he said in the flat in Hammersmith. 'There's really no need to, Mum.'

She didn't mention his father and Gillian, although he'd repeatedly said that they'd be there. It was as if she didn't want to think about them, as if she was deliberately pretending that they'd decided not to attend. She'd stay in Sans Souci again, she said. They'd have a picnic in her room, since the newly confirmed were to be excused school tea on the evening of the service. 'Dinner at the Grand, old chap,' his father said. 'Bring Tichbourne if you want to.'

Michael returned to Elton Grange at the end of the Easter holidays, leaving his mother in a state of high excitement at Paddington Station because she'd be seeing him again within five weeks. He thought he might invent an illness a day or two before the confirmation, or say at the last moment that he had doubts. In fact, he did hint to the Reverend Green that he wasn't certain about being quite ready for the occasion, but the Reverend Green sharply told him not to be silly. Every time he went down on his knees at the end of a session with the Reverend Green he prayed that God might come to his rescue. But God did not, and all during the night before the confirmation service he lay awake. It wasn't just because she was weepy and embarrassing, he thought: it was because she dressed in that cheap way, it was because she was common, with a common voice that wasn't at all like Gillian's or Mrs Tichbourne's or Mrs Carson's or even Outsize Dorothy's. He couldn't prevent these thoughts from occurring. Why couldn't she do something about her fluffy hair? Why did she have to gabble like that? 'I think I have a temperature,' he said in the morning, but when Sister took it it was only 98.

Before the service the other candidates waited outside the chapel to greet their parents and godparents, but Michael went into the chapel early and took up a devout position. Through his fingers he saw the Reverend Green lighting the candles and preparing the altar. Occasionally, the Reverend Green glanced at Michael, somewhat suspiciously.

'Defend, O Lord, this Thy child,' said the Bishop of Bath and Wells, and when Michael walked back to his seat he kept his head down, not wanting to see his parents and Gillian. They sang Hymn 459. 'My God, accept,' sang Michael, 'my heart this day.'

He walked with Swagger Browne down the aisle, still with his eyes down. 'Fantastic,' said Swagger Browne outside the chapel, for want of anything better to say. 'Bloody fantastic.' They waited for the congregation to come out.

Michael had godparents, but his father had said that they wouldn't be able to attend. His godmother had sent him a prayer-book.

'Well done,' his father said. 'Well done, Mike.'

'What lovely singing!' Gillian murmured. She was wearing a white dress with a collar that was slightly turned up, and a white wide-rimmed hat. On the gravel outside the chapel she put on dark glasses against the afternoon sun.

'Your mother's here somewhere,' his father said. 'You'd better see to her, Mike.' He spoke quietly, with a hand resting for a moment on Michael's shoulder. 'We'll be all right,' he added.

Michael turned. She was standing alone, as he knew she would be. Unable to prevent himself, he wished she wouldn't always wear headscarves. 'Oh, darling,' she said.

She took his hands and pulled him towards her. She kissed him, apologizing for the embrace but saying that it was a special occasion. She wished her father were alive, she said.

'Tea in the Great Hall,' A.J.L. was booming, and Outsize Dorothy was waddling about in flowered yellow, smiling at the faces of parents and godparents. 'Do come and have tea,' she gushed.

'Oh, I'd love a cup of tea,' Michael's mother whispered.

The crowd was moving through the sunshine, suited men, the Reverend

Green in his cassock, the Bishop in crimson, women in their garden-party finery. They walked up the short drive from the chapel. They passed through the wide gothic arch that heralded the front door, through the vestibule where the croquet set was tidily in place and the deck-chairs neat against a wall. They entered what A.J.L. had years ago christened the Great Hall, where buttered buns and sandwiches and cakes and sausage-rolls were laid out on trestle tables. Miss Trenchard and Miss Arland were in charge of two silver-plated tea-urns.

'I'll get you something to eat,' Michael said to his mother, leaving her although he knew she didn't want to be left. 'Seems no time since I was getting done myself,' he heard his father saying to A.J.L.

Miss Arland poured a cup of tea for his mother and told him to offer her something to eat. He chose a plate of sausage-rolls. She smiled at him. 'Don't go away again,' she whispered.

But he had to go away again because he couldn't stand there holding the sausage-rolls. He darted back to the table and left the plate there, taking one for himself. When he returned to his mother she'd been joined by the Reverend Green and the Bishop.

The Bishop shook Michael's hand and said it had been a very great pleasure to confirm him.

'My father was in the Church,' Michael's mother said, and Michael knew that she wasn't going to stop now. He watched her struggling to hold the words back, crumbling the pastry of her sausage-roll beneath her fingers. The flush had come into her cheeks, there was a brightness in her eyes. The Bishop's face was kind: she couldn't help herself, when kindness like that was there.

'We really must be moving,' the Reverend Green said, but the Bishop only smiled, and on and on she went about her father and the call he'd received so late in life. 'I'm sure you knew him, my lord,' was one suggestion she made, and the Bishop kindly agreed that he probably had.

'Mrs Grainer would like to meet the Bishop,' Outsize Dorothy murmured to the Reverend Green. She looked at Michael's mother and Michael could see her remembering her and not caring for her.

'Well, if you'll excuse us,' the Reverend Green said, seizing the Bishop's arm.

'Oh Michael dear, isn't that a coincidence!'

There was happiness all over her face, bursting from her eyes, in her smile and her flushed cheeks and her fluffy hair. She turned to Mr and Mrs Tichbourne, who were talking to Mrs Carson, and said the Bishop had known her father, apparently quite well. She hadn't even been aware that it was to be this particular bishop today, it hadn't even occurred to her while she'd been at the confirmation service that such a coincidence could be possible. Her father had passed away fifteen years ago, he'd have been a contemporary of the Bishop's. 'He was in the Customs and Excise,' she said, 'before he received the call.'

They didn't turn away from her. They listened, putting in a word or two, about coincidences and the niceness of the Bishop. Tichbourne and Carson stood eating sandwiches, offering them to one another. Michael's face felt like a bonfire.

'We'll probably see you later,' Mr Tichbourne said, eventually edging his wife away. 'We're staying at the Grand.'

'Oh no, I'm at Sans Souci. Couldn't ever afford the Grand!' She laughed.

'Don't think we know the Sans Souci,' Mrs Tichbourne said.

'Darling, I'd love another cup of tea,' his mother said to Michael, and he went away to get her one, leaving her with Mrs Carson. When he returned she was referring to Peggy Urch.

It was then, while talking to Mrs Carson, that Michael's mother fell. Afterwards she said that she'd felt something slimy under one of her heels and had moved to rid herself of it. The next thing she knew she was lying on her back on the floor, soaked in tea.

Mrs Carson helped her to her feet. A.J.L. hovered solicitously. Outsize Dorothy picked up the cup and saucer.

'I'm quite all right,' Michael's mother kept repeating. 'There was something slippy on the floor, I'm quite all right.'

She was led to a chair by A.J.L. 'I think we'd best call on Sister,' he said. 'Just to be sure.'

But she insisted that she was all right, that there was no need to go bothering Sister. She was as white as a sheet.

Michael's father and Gillian came up to her and said they were sorry. Michael could see Tichbourne and Carson nudging one another, giggling. For a moment he thought of running away, hiding in the attics or something. Half a buttered bun had got stuck to the sleeve of his mother's maroon coat when she'd fallen. Her left leg was saturated with tea.

'We'll drive you into town,' his father said. 'Horrible thing to happen.'

'It's just my elbow,' his mother whispered. 'I came down on my elbow.'

Carson and Tichbourne would imitate it because Carson and Tichbourne imitated everything. They'd stand there, pretending to be holding a cup of tea, and suddenly they'd be lying flat on their backs. 'I think we'd best call on Sister,' Carson would say, imitating A.J.L.

His father and Gillian said goodbye to Outsize Dorothy and to A.J.L. His mother, reduced to humble silence again, seemed only to want to get away. In the car she didn't say anything at all and when they reached Sans

Souci she didn't seem to expect Michael to go in with her. She left the car, whispering her thanks, a little colour gathering in her face again.

That evening Michael had dinner with Gillian and his father in the Grand. Tichbourne was there also, and Carson, and several other boys, all with their parents. 'I can drive a few of them back,' his father said, 'save everyone getting a car out.' He crossed the dining-room floor and spoke to Mr Tichbourne and Mr Carson and the father of a boy called Mallabedeely. Michael ate minestrone soup and chicken with peas and roast potatoes. Gillian told him what the twins had been up to and said his father was going to have a swimming-pool put in. His father returned to the table and announced that he'd arranged to drive everyone back at nine o'clock.

Eating his chicken, he imagined his mother in Sans Souci, sitting on the edge of the bed, probably having a cry. He imagined her bringing back to London the stuff she'd bought for a picnic in her room. She'd never refer to any of that, she'd never upbraid him for going to the Grand for dinner when she'd wanted him to be with her. She'd consider it just that she should be punished.

As they got into the car, his father said he'd drive round by Sans Souci so that Michael could run in for a minute. 'We're meant to be back by a quarter past,' Michael said quickly. 'I've said goodbye to her,' he added, which wasn't quite true.

It would perhaps have been different if Tichbourne and Carson hadn't been in the car. He'd have gone in and paused with her for a minute because he felt pity for her. But the unattractive façade of Sans Souci, the broken gate of the small front garden and the fishermen gnomes would have caused further nudging and giggling in his father's white Alfa-Romeo.

'You're sure now?' his father said. 'I'll get you there by a quarter past.'

'No, it's all right.'

She wouldn't be expecting him. She wouldn't even have unpacked the picnic she'd brought.

'Hey, was that your godmother?' Tichbourne asked in the dormitory. 'The one who copped it on the floor?'

He began to shake his head and then he paused and went on shaking it. An aunt, he said, some kind of aunt, he wasn't sure what the relationship was. He hadn't thought of saying that before, yet it seemed so simple, and so right and so natural, that a distant aunt should come to a confirmation service and not stay, like everyone else, in the Grand. 'God, it was funny,' Carson said, and Tichbourne did his imitation, and Michael laughed with his friends. He was grateful to them for assuming that such a person could not be his mother. A.J.L. and Outsize Dorothy and Miss Trenchard knew she was his mother, and so did the Reverend Green, but for the remainder of his time at Elton Grange none of these people would have cause to refer to the fact in public. And if by chance A.J.L. did happen to say in class tomorrow that he hoped his mother was all right after her fall, Michael would say afterwards that A.J.L. had got it all wrong.

In the dark, he whispered to her in his mind. He said he was sorry, he said he loved her better than anyone.

A Complicated Nature

At a party once Attridge overheard a woman saying he gave her the shivers. 'Vicious-tongued,' this woman, a Mrs de Paul, had said. 'Forked like a serpent's.'

It was true, and he admitted it to himself without apology, though 'sharp' was how he preferred to describe the quality the woman had referred to. He couldn't help it if his quick eye had a way of rooting out other people's defects and didn't particularly bother to search for virtues.

Sharp about other people, he was sharp about himself as well: confessing his own defects, he found his virtues tedious. He was kind and generous to the people he chose as his friends, and took it for granted that he should be. He was a tidy man, but took no credit for that since being tidy was part of his nature. He was meticulous about his dress, and he was cultured, being particularly keen on opera – especially the operas of Wagner – and on Velázquez. He had developed his own good taste, and was proud of the job he had made of it.

A man of fifty, with hair that had greyed and spectacles with fine, colourless rims, he was given to slimming, for the weight he had gained in middle age rounded his face and made it pinker than he cared for: vanity was a weakness in him.

Attridge had once been married. In 1952 his parents had died, his father in February and his mother in November. Attridge had been their only child and had always lived with them. Disliking – or so he then considered – the solitude their death left him in, he married in 1953 a girl called Bernice Golder, but this most unfortunate conjunction had lasted only three months. 'Nasty dry old thing,' his ex-wife had screamed at him on their honeymoon in Siena, and he had enraged her further by pointing out that nasty and dry he might be but old he wasn't. 'You were never young,' she had replied more calmly than before. 'Even as a child you must have been like dust.' That wasn't so, he tried to explain; the truth was that he had a complicated nature. But she didn't listen to him.

Attridge lived alone now, existing comfortably on profits from the shares his parents had left him. He occupied a flat in a block, doing all his own cooking and taking pride in the small dinner parties he gave. His flat was just as his good taste wished it to be. The bathroom was tiled with blue Italian tiles, his bedroom severe and male, the hall warmly rust. His sitting-room, he privately judged, reflected a part of himself that did not come into the open, a mysterious element that even he knew little about and could only guess at. He'd saved up for the Egyptian rugs, scarlet and black and brown, on the waxed oak boards. He'd bought the first one in 1959 and each year subsequently had contrived to put aside his January and July Anglo-American Telegraph dividends until the floor was covered. He'd bought the last one a year ago.

On the walls of the room there was pale blue hessian, a background for his four tiny Velázquez drawings, and for the Toulouse-Lautrec drawing and the Degas, and the two brown charcoal studies, school of Michelangelo. There was a sofa and a sofa-table, authenticated Sheraton, and a Regency table in marble and gold that he had almost made up his mind to get rid of, and some Staffordshire figures. There was drama in the decoration and arrangement of the room, a quite flamboyant drama that Attridge felt was related to the latent element in himself, part of his complicated nature.

'I'm hopeless in an emergency,' he said in this room one afternoon, speaking with off-putting asperity into his ivory-coloured telephone. A woman called Mrs Matara, who lived in the flat above his, appeared not to hear him. 'Something has gone wrong, you see,' she explained in an upset voice, adding that she'd have to come down. She then abruptly replaced the receiver.

It was an afternoon in late November. It was raining, and already – at half past three – twilight had settled in. From a window of his sitting-room Attridge had been gazing at all this when his telephone rang. He'd been looking at the rain dismally falling and lights going on in other windows and at a man, five storeys down, sweeping sodden leaves from the concrete forecourt of the block of flats. When the phone rang he'd thought it might be his friend, old Mrs Harcourt-Egan. He and Mrs Harcourt-Egan were to go together to Persepolis in a fortnight's time and there were still some minor arrangements to be made, although the essential booking had naturally been completed long since. It had been a considerable surprise to hear himself addressed by name in a voice he had been quite unable to place. He'd greeted Mrs Matara once or twice in the lift and that was all: she and her husband had moved into the flats only a year ago.

'I do so apologize,' Mrs Matara said when he opened the door to her. Against his will he welcomed her into the hall and she, knowing the geography of the flat since it was the same as her own, made for the sitting-room. 'It's really terrible of me,' she said, 'only I honestly don't know where to turn.' She spoke in a rushed and agitated manner, and he sighed as he followed her, resolving to point out when she revealed what her trouble was that Chamberlain, the janitor, was employed to deal with tenants' difficulties. She was just the kind of woman to make a nuisance of herself with a neighbour, you could tell that by looking at her. It irritated him that he hadn't sized her up better when he'd met her in the lift.

She was a woman of about the same age as himself, he guessed, small and thin and black-haired, though the hair, he also guessed, was almost certainly dyed. He wondered if she might be Jewish, which would account for her emotional condition: she had a Jewish look, and the name was presumably foreign. Her husband, whom he had also only met in the lift, had a look about the eyes which Attridge now said to himself might well have been developed in the clothing business. Of Austrian origin, he hazarded, or possibly even Polish. Mrs Matara had an accent of some kind, although her English appeared otherwise to be perfect. She was not out of the top drawer, but then people of the Jewish race rarely were. His own ex-wife, Jewish also, had most certainly not been.

Mrs Matara sat on the edge of a chair he had bought for ninety guineas fifteen years ago. It was also certainly Sheraton, a high-back chair with slim arms in inlaid walnut. He'd had it resprung and upholstered and covered in striped pink, four different shades.

'A really ghastly thing,' Mrs Matara said, 'a terrible thing has happened in my flat, Mr Attridge.'

She'd fused the whole place. She couldn't turn a tap off. The garbage disposal unit had failed. His ex-wife had made a ridiculous fuss when, because of her own stupidity, she'd broken her electric hair-curling apparatus on their honeymoon. Grotesque she'd looked with the plastic objects in her hair; he'd been relieved that they didn't work.

'I really can't mend anything,' he said. 'Chamberlain is there for that, you know.'

She shook her head. She was like a small bird sitting there, a wren or an undersized sparrow. A Jewish sparrow, he said to himself, pleased with this analogy. She had a handkerchief between her fingers, a small piece of material, which she now raised to her face. She touched her eyes with it, one after the other. When she spoke again she said that a man had died in her flat.

'Good heavens!'

'It's terrible!' Mrs Matara cried. 'Oh, my God!'

He poured brandy from a Georgian decanter that Mrs Harcourt-Egan had given him three Christmases ago, after their trip to Sicily. She'd given him a pair, in appreciation of what she called his kindness on that holiday.

The gesture had been far too generous: the decanters were family heirlooms, and he'd done so little for her in Sicily apart from reading *Northanger Abbey* aloud when she'd had her stomach upset.

The man, he guessed, was not Mr Matara. No woman would say that a man had died, meaning her husband. Attridge imagined that a window-cleaner had fallen off a step-ladder. Quite clearly, he saw in his mind's eye a step-ladder standing at a window and the body of a man in white overalls huddled on the ground. He even saw Mrs Matara bending over the body, attempting to establish its condition.

'Drink it all,' he said, placing the brandy glass in Mrs Matara's right hand, hoping as he did so that she wasn't going to drop it.

She didn't drop it. She drank the brandy and then, to Attridge's surprise, held out the glass in a clear request for more.

'Oh, if only you would,' she said as he poured it, and he realised that while he'd been pouring the first glass, while his mind had been wandering back to the occasion in Sicily and the gift of the decanters, his guest had made some demand of him.

'You could say he was a friend,' Mrs Matara said.

She went on talking. The man who had died had died of a heart attack. The presence of his body in her flat was an embarrassment. She told a story of a love affair that had begun six years ago. She went into details: she had met the man at a party given by people called Morton, the man had been married, what point was there in hurting a dead man's wife? what point was there in upsetting her own husband, when he need never know? She rose and crossed the room to the brandy decanter. The man, she said, had died in the bed that was her husband's as well as hers.

'I wouldn't have come here – oh God, I wouldn't have come here if I hadn't been desperate.' Her voice was shrill. She was nearly hysterical. The brandy had brought out two patches of brightness in her cheeks. Her eyes were watering again, but she did not now touch them with the handkerchief. The water ran, over the bright patches, trailing mascara and other make-up with it.

'I sat for hours,' she cried. 'Well, it seemed like hours. I sat there looking at him. We were both without a stitch, Mr Attridge.'

'Good heavens!'

'I didn't feel anything at all. I didn't love him, you know. All I felt was, Oh God, what a thing to happen!'

Attridge poured himself some brandy, feeling the need for it. She reminded him quite strongly of his ex-wife, not just because of the Jewish thing or the nuisance she was making of herself but because of the way she had so casually said they'd been without a stitch. In Siena on their honeymoon his ex-wife had constantly been flaunting her nakedness, striding about their bedroom. 'The trouble with you,' she'd said, 'you like your nudes on canvas.'

'You could say he was a friend,' Mrs Matara said again. She wanted him to come with her to her flat. She wanted him to help her dress the man. In the name of humanity, she was suggesting, they should falsify the location of death.

He shook his head, outraged and considerably repelled. The images in his mind were most unpleasant. There was the naked male body, dead on a bed. There was Mrs Matara and himself pulling the man's clothes on to his body, struggling because *rigor mortis* was setting in.

'Oh God, what can I do?' cried Mrs Marata.

'I think you should telephone a doctor, Mrs Matara.'

'Oh, what use is a doctor, for God's sake? The man's dead.'

'It's usual –'

'Look, one minute we're having lunch – an omelette, just as usual, and salad and Pouilly Fuissé – and the next minute the poor man's dead.'

'I thought you said –'

'Oh, you know what I mean. "Lovely, oh darling, lovely," he said, and then he collapsed. Well, I didn't know he'd collapsed. I mean, I didn't know he was dead. He collapsed just like he always collapses. Post-coital –'

'I'd rather not hear –'

'Oh, for Jesus' sake!' She was shouting. She was on her feet, again approaching the decanter. Her hair had fallen out of the pins that held it and was now dishevelled. Her lipstick was blurred, some of it even smeared her chin. She looked most unattractive, he considered.

'I cannot help you in this matter, Mrs Matara,' he said as firmly as he could. 'I can telephone a doctor –'

'Will you for God's sake stop about a doctor!'

'I cannot assist you with your friend, Mrs Matara.'

'All I want you to do is to help me put his clothes back on. He's too heavy, I can't do it myself –'

'I'm very sorry, Mrs Matara.'

'And slip him down here. The lift is only a few yards –'

'That's quite impossible.'

She went close to him, with her glass considerably replenished. She pushed her face at his in a way that he considered predatory. He was aware of the smell of her scent, and of another smell that he couldn't prevent himself from thinking must be the smell of sexual intercourse: he had read of this odour in a book by Ernest Hemingway.

'My husband and I are a contentedly married couple,' she said, with her lips so near to his that they almost touched. 'That man upstairs has a wife who doesn't know a thing, an innocent woman. Don't you understand such things, Mr Attridge? Don't you see what will happen if the dead body of my lover is discovered in my husband's bed? Can't you visualize the pain it'll cause?'

He moved away. It was a long time since he had felt so angry and yet he was determined to control his anger. The woman knew nothing of civilized behaviour or she wouldn't have come bursting into the privacy of a stranger like this, with preposterous and unlawful suggestions. The woman, for all he knew, was unbalanced.

'I'm sorry,' he said in what he hoped was an icy voice. 'I'm sorry, but for a start I do not see how you and your husband could possibly be a contentedly married couple.'

'I'm telling you we are. I'm telling you my lover was contentedly married also. Listen, Mr Attridge.' She approached him again, closing in on him like an animal. 'Listen, Mr Attridge; we met for physical reasons, once a week at lunchtime. For five years ever since the Mortons' party, we've been meeting once a week, for an omelette and Pouilly Fuissé, and sex. It had nothing to do with our two marriages. But it will now: that woman will see her marriage as a failure now. She'll mourn it for the rest of her days, when she should be mourning her husband. I'll be divorced.'

'You should have thought of that –'

She hit him with her left hand. She hit him on the face, the palm of her hand stinging the pink, plump flesh.

'Mrs Matara!'

He had meant to shout her name, but instead his protest came from him in a shrill whisper. Since his honeymoon no one had struck him, and he recalled the fear he'd felt when he'd been struck then, in the bedroom in Siena. 'I could kill you,' his ex-wife had shouted at him. 'I'd kill you if you weren't dead already.'

'I must ask you to go, Mrs Matara,' he said in the same shrill whisper. He cleared his throat. 'At once,' he said, in a more successful voice.

She shook her head. She said he had no right to tell her what she should have thought of. She was upset as few women can ever be upset: in all decency and humanity it wasn't fair to say she should have thought of that. She cried out noisily in his sitting-room and he felt that he was in a nightmare. It had all the horror and absurdity and violence of a nightmare: the woman standing in front of him with water coming out of her eyes, drinking his brandy and hitting him.

She spoke softly then, not in her violent way. She placed the brandy glass on the marble surface of the Regency table and stood there with her head down. He knew she was still weeping even though he couldn't see her face and couldn't hear any noise coming from her. She whispered that she was sorry.

'Please forgive me, Mr Attridge. I'm very sorry.'

He nodded, implying that he accepted this apology. It was all very nasty, but for the woman it was naturally an upsetting thing to happen. He imagined, when a little time had passed, telling the story to Mrs Harcourt-Egan and to others, relating how a woman, to all intents and purposes a stranger to him, had telephoned him to say she was in need of assistance and then had come down from her flat with this awful tragedy to relate. He imagined himself describing Mrs Matara, how at first she'd seemed quite smart and then had become dishevelled, how she'd helped herself to his brandy and had suddenly struck him. He imagined Mrs Harcourt-Egan and others gasping when he said that. He seemed to see his own slight smile as he went on to say that the woman could not be blamed. He heard himself saying that the end of the matter was that Mrs Matara just went away.

But in fact Mrs Matara did not go away. Mrs Matara continued to stand, weeping quietly.

'I'm sorry too,' he said, feeling that the words, with the finality he'd slipped into them, would cause her to move to the door of the sitting-room.

'If you'd just help me,' she said, with her head still bent. 'Just to get his clothes on.'

He began to reply. He made a noise in his throat.

'I can't manage,' she said, 'on my own.'

She raised her head and looked across the room at him. Her face was blotched all over now, with make-up and tears. Her hair had fallen down a little more, and from where he stood Attridge thought he could see quite large areas of grey beneath the black. A rash of some kind, or it might have been flushing, had appeared on her neck.

'I wouldn't bother you,' she said, 'if I could manage on my own.' She would have telephoned a friend, she said, except there wouldn't be time for a friend to get to the block of flats. 'There's very little time, you see,' she said.

It was then, while she spoke those words, that Attridge felt the first hint of excitement. It was the same kind of excitement that he experienced just before the final curtain of *Tannhäuser*, or whenever, in the Uffizi, he looked upon Lorenzo di Credi's *Annunciation*. Mrs Matara was a wretched, unattractive creature who had been conducting a typical hole-in-corner affair and had received her just rewards. It was hard to feel sorry for her, and yet for some reason it was harder not to. The man who had died had got off scot-free, leaving her to face the music miserably on her own. 'You're inhuman,' his ex-wife had said in Siena. 'You're incapable of love. Or sympathy, or anything else.' She'd stood there in her underclothes, taunting him.

'I'll manage,' Mrs Matara said, moving towards the door.

He did not move himself. She'd been so impatient, all the time in Siena. She didn't even want to sit in the square and watch the people. She'd been lethargic in the cathedral. All she'd ever wanted was to try again in bed. 'You don't like women,' she'd said, sitting up with a glass of Brolio in her hand, smoking a cigarette.

He followed Mrs Matara into the hall, and an image entered his mind of the dead man's wife. He saw her as Mrs Matara had described her, as an innocent woman who believed herself faithfully loved. He saw her as a woman with fair hair, in a garden, simply dressed. She had borne the children of the man who now lay obscenely dead, she had made a home for him and had entertained his tedious business friends, and now she was destined to suffer. It was a lie to say he didn't like women, it was absurd to say he was incapable of sympathy.

Once more he felt a hint of excitement. It was a confused feeling now, belonging as much in his body as in his mind. In a dim kind of way he seemed again to be telling the story to Mrs Harcourt-Egan or to someone else. Telling it, his voice was quiet. It spoke of the compassion he had suddenly felt for the small, unattractive Jewish woman and for another woman, a total stranger whom he'd never even seen. 'A moment of truth,' his voice explained to Mrs Harcourt-Egan and others. 'I could not pass these women by.'

He knew it was true. The excitement he felt had to do with sympathy, and the compassion that had been engendered in it. His complicated nature worked in that way: there had to be drama, like the drama of a man dead in a bed, and the beauty of being unable to pass the women by, as real as the beauty of the Madonna of the Meadow. With her cigarette and her Brolio, his ex-wife wouldn't have understood that in a million years. In their bedroom in Siena she had expected something ordinary to take place, an act that rats performed.

Never in his entire life had Attridge felt as he felt now. It was the most extraordinary, and for all he knew the most important, occasion in his life. As though watching a play, he saw himself assisting the dead, naked man into his clothes. It would be enough to put his clothes on, no need to move the body from one flat to another, enough to move it from the bedroom.

'We put it in the lift and left it there,' his voice said, still telling the story. '"No need," I said to her, "to involve my flat at all." She agreed; she had no option. The man became a man who'd had a heart attack in a lift. A travelling salesman, God knows who he was.'

The story was beautiful. It was extravagant and flamboyant, incredible almost, like all good art. Who really believed in the Madonna of the Meadow, until jolted by the genius of Bellini? *The Magic Flute* was an impossible occasion, until Mozart's music charged you like an electric current.

'Yes, Mr Attridge?'

He moved towards her, fearing to speak lest his voice emerged from him in the shrill whisper that had possessed it before. He nodded at Mrs Matara, agreeing in this way to assist her.

Hurrying through the hall and hurrying up the stairs because one flight of stairs was quicker than the lift, he felt the excitement continuing in his body. Actually it would be many months before he could tell Mrs Harcourt-Egan or anyone else about any of it. It seemed, for the moment at least, to be entirely private.

'What was he?' he asked on the stairs in a whisper.

'Was?'

'Professionally.' He was impatient, more urgent now than she. 'Salesman or something, was he?'

She shook her head. Her friend had been a dealer in antiques, she said.

Another Jew, he thought. But he was pleased because the man could have been on his way to see him, since dealers in antiques did sometimes visit him. Mrs Matara might have said to the man, at another party given by the Mortons or anywhere else you liked, that Mr Attridge, a collector of pictures and Staffordshire china, lived in the flat below hers. She could have said to Attridge that she knew a man who might have stuff that would interest him and then the man might have telephoned him, and he'd have said come round one afternoon. And in the lift the man collapsed and died.

She had her latchkey in her hand, about to insert it into the lock of her flat door. Her hand was shaking. Surprising himself, he gripped her arm, preventing her from completing the action with the key.

'Will you promise me,' he said, 'to move away from these flats? As soon as you conveniently can?'

'Of course, of course! How could I stay?'

'I'd find it awkward, meeting you about the place, Mrs Matara. Is that a bargain?'

'Yes, yes.'

She turned the key in the lock. They entered a hall that was of the exact proportions of Attridge's but different in other ways. It was a most unpleasant hall, he considered, with bell chimes in it, and two oil paintings that appeared to be the work of some emergent African, one being of Negro children playing on crimson sand, the other of a Negro girl with a baby at her breast.

'Oh, God!' Mrs Matara cried, turning suddenly, unable to proceed. She pushed herself at him, her sharp head embedding itself in his chest, her hands grasping the jacket of his grey suit.

'Don't worry,' he said, dragging his eyes away from the painting of the children on the crimson sand. One of her hands had ceased to grasp his jacket and had fallen into one of his. It was cold and had a fleshless feel.

'We have to do it,' he said, and for a second he saw himself again as he would see himself in retrospect: standing with the Jewish woman in her hall, holding her hand to comfort her.

While they still stood there, just as he was about to propel her forward, there was a noise.

'My God!' whispered Mrs Matara.

He knew she was thinking that her husband had returned, and he thought the same himself. Her husband had come back sooner than he usually did. He had found a corpse and was about to find his wife holding hands with a neighbour in the hall.

'Hey!' a voice said.

'Oh no!' cried Mrs Matara, rushing forward into the room that Attridge knew was her sitting-room.

There was the mumble of another voice, and then the sound of Mrs Matara's tears. It was a man's voice, but the man was not her husband: the atmosphere which came from the scene wasn't right for that.

'There now,' the other voice was saying in the sitting-room. 'There now, there now.'

The noise of Mrs Matara's weeping continued, and the man appeared at the door of the sitting-room. He was fully dressed, a sallow man, tall and black-haired, with a beard. He'd guessed what had happened, he said, as soon as he heard voices in the hall: he'd guessed that Mrs Matara had gone to get help. In an extremely casual way he said he was really quite all right, just a little groggy due to the silly blackout he'd had. Mrs Matara was a customer of his, he explained, he was in the antique business. 'I just passed out,' he said. He smiled at Attridge. He'd had a few silly blackouts recently and despite what his doctor said about there being nothing to worry about he'd have to be more careful. Really embarrassing, it was, plopping out in a client's sitting-room.

Mrs Matara appeared in the sitting-room doorway. She leaned against it, as though requiring its support. She giggled through her tears and the man spoke sharply to her, forgetting she was meant to be his client. He warned her against becoming hysterical.

'My God, you'd be hysterical,' Mrs Matara cried, 'if you'd been through all that kerfuffle.'

'Now, now –'

'For Christ's sake, I thought you were a goner. Didn't I?' she cried, addressing Attridge without looking at him and not waiting for him to reply. 'I rushed downstairs to this man here. I was in a frightful state. Wasn't I?'

'Yes.'

'We were going to put your clothes on and dump you in his flat.'

Attridge shook his head, endeavouring to imply that that was not accurate, that he'd never have agreed to the use of his flat for this purpose. But neither of them was paying any attention to him. The man was looking embarrassed, Mrs Matara was grim.

'You should damn well have told me if you were having blackouts.'

'I'm sorry,' the man said. 'I'm sorry you were troubled,' he said to Attridge. 'Please forgive Mrs Matara.'

'Forgive *you*, you mean!' she cried. 'Forgive you for being such a damn fool!'

'Do try to pull yourself together, Miriam.'

'I tell you, I thought you were dead.'

'Well, I'm not. I had a little blackout –'

'Oh, for Christ's sake, stop about your wretched blackout!'

The way she said that reminded Attridge very much of his ex-wife. He'd had a headache once, he remembered, and she'd protested in just the same impatient tone of voice, employing almost the same words. She'd married again, of course – a man called Saunders in ICI.

'At least be civil,' the man said to Mrs Matara.

They were two of the most unpleasant people Attridge had ever come across. It was a pity the man hadn't died. He'd run to fat and was oily, there was a shower of dandruff on his jacket. You could see his stomach straining his shirt, one of the shirt-buttons had actually given way.

'Well, thank you,' Mrs Matara said, approaching Attridge with her right hand held out. She said it gracelessly, as a duty. The same hand had struck him on the face and later had slipped for comfort into one of his. It was hard and cold when he shook it, with the same fleshless feel as before. 'We still have a secret,' Mrs Matara said. She smiled at him in her dutiful way, without displaying interest in him.

The man had opened the hall door of the flat. He stood by it, smiling also, anxious for Attridge to go.

'This afternoon's a secret,' Mrs Matara murmured, dropping her eyes in a girlish pretence. 'All this,' she said, indicating her friend. 'I'm sorry I hit you.'

'Hit him?'

'When we were upset. Downstairs. I hit him.' She giggled, apparently unable to help herself.

'Great God!' The man giggled also.

'It doesn't matter,' Attridge said.

But it did matter. The secret she spoke of wasn't worth having because it was sordid and nothing else. It was hardly the kind of thing he'd wish to mull over in private, and certainly not the kind he'd wish to tell Mrs Harcourt-Egan or anyone else. Yet the other story might even have reached his ex-wife, it was not impossible. He imagined her hearing it, and her amazement that a man whom she'd once likened to dust had in the cause of compassion falsified the circumstances of a death. He couldn't imagine the man his ex-wife had married doing such a thing, or Mrs Matara's husband, or the dandruffy man who now stood by the door of the flat. Such men would have been frightened out of their wits.

'Goodbye,' she said.

'Goodbye,' the man said, smiling at the door.

Attridge wanted to say something. He wanted to linger for a moment longer and to mention his ex-wife. He wanted to tell them what he had never told another soul, that his ex-wife had done terrible things to him. He disliked all Jewish people, he wanted to say, because of his ex-wife and her lack of understanding. Marriage repelled him because of her. It was she who had made him vicious-tongued. It was she who had embittered him.

He looked from one face to the other. They would not understand and they would not be capable of making an effort, as he had when faced with the woman's predicament. He had always been a little on the cold side, he knew that well. But his ex-wife might have drawn on the other aspects of his nature and dispelled the coldness. Instead of displaying all that impatience, she might have cosseted him and accepted his complications. The love she sought would have come in its own good time, as sympathy and compassion had eventually come that afternoon. Warmth was buried deep in some people, he wanted to say to the two faces in the hall, but he knew that, like his ex-wife, the faces would not understand.

As he went he heard the click of the door behind him and imagined a hushed giggling in the hall. He would be feeling like a prince if the man had really died.

Teresa's Wedding

The remains of the wedding-cake were on top of the piano in Swanton's lounge-bar, beneath a framed advertisement for Power's whiskey. Chas Flynn, the best man, had opened two packets of confetti: it lay thickly on the remains of the wedding-cake, on the surface of the bar and the piano, on the table and the two small chairs that the lounge-bar contained, and on the tattered green-and-red linoleum.

The wedding guests, themselves covered in confetti, stood in groups. Father Hogan, who had conducted the service in the Church of the Immaculate Conception, stood with Mrs Atty, the mother of the bride, and Mrs Cornish, the mother of the bridegroom, and Mrs Tracy, a sister of Mrs Atty's.

Mrs Tracy was the stoutest of the three women, a farmer's widow who lived eight miles from the town. In spite of the jubilant nature of the occasion, she was dressed in black, a colour she had affected since the death of her husband three years ago. Mrs Atty, bespectacled, with her grey hair in a bun, wore a flowered dress – small yellow-and-blue blooms that blended easily with the confetti. Mrs Cornish was in pink, with a pink hat. Father Hogan, a big red-complexioned man, held a tumbler containing whiskey and water in equal measures; his companions sipped Winter's Tale sherry.

Artie Cornish, the bridegroom, drank stout with his friends Eddie Boland and Chas Flynn, who worked in the town's bacon factory, and Screw Doyle, so called because he served behind the counter in McQuaid's hardware shop. Artie, who worked in a shop himself – Driscoll's Provisions and Bar – was a freckled man of twenty-eight, six years older than his bride. He was heavily built, his bulk encased now in a suit of navy-blue serge, similar to the suits that all the other men were wearing that morning in Swanton's lounge-bar. In the opinion of Mr Driscoll, his employer, he was a conscientious shopman, with a good memory for where commodities were kept on the shelves. Customers occasionally found him slow.

The fathers of the bride and bridegroom, Mr Atty and Mr Cornish, were talking about greyhounds, keeping close to the bar. They shared a feeling of unease, caused by being in the lounge-bar of Swanton's, with women present, on a Saturday morning. 'Bring us two more big ones,' Mr Cornish requested of Kevin, a youth behind the bar, hoping that this addition to his consumption of whiskey would relax matters. They wore white carnations in the buttonholes of their suits, and stiff white collars which were reddening their necks. Unknown to one another, they shared the same thought: a wish that the bride and groom would soon decide to bring the occasion to an end by going to prepare themselves for their journey to Cork on the half-one bus. Mr Atty and Mr Cornish, bald-headed men of fifty-three and fifty-five, had it in mind to spend the remainder of the day in Swanton's lounge-bar, celebrating in their particular way the union of their children.

The bride, who had been Teresa Atty and was now Teresa Cornish, had a round, pretty face and black, pretty hair, and was a month and a half pregnant. She stood in the corner of the lounge with her friends, Philomena Morrissey and Kitty Roche, both of whom had been bridesmaids. All three of them were attired in their wedding finery, dresses they had feverishly worked on to get finished in time for the wedding. They planned to alter the dresses and have them dyed so that later on they could go to parties in them, even though parties were rare in the town.

'I hope you'll be happy, Teresa,' Kitty Roche whispered. 'I hope you'll be all right.' She couldn't help giggling, even though she didn't want to. She giggled because she'd drunk a glass of gin and Kia-Ora orange, which Screw Doyle had said would steady her. She'd been nervous in the church. She'd tripped twice on the walk down the aisle.

'You'll be marrying yourself one of these days,' Teresa whispered, her cheeks still glowing after the excitement of the ceremony. 'I hope you'll be happy too, Kit.'

But Kitty Roche, who was asthmatic, did not believe she'd ever marry. She'd be like Miss Levis, the Protestant woman on the Cork road, who'd never got married because of tuberculosis. Or old Hannah Flood, who had a bad hip. And it wasn't just that no one would want to be saddled with a diseased wife: there was also the fact that the asthma caused a recurrent skin complaint on her face and neck and hands.

Teresa and Philomena drank glasses of Babycham, and Kitty drank Kia-Ora with water instead of gin in it. They'd known each other all their lives. They'd been to the Presentation Nuns together, they'd taken First Communion together. Even when they'd left the Nuns, when Teresa had gone to work in the Medical Hall and Kitty Roche and Philomena in Keane's drapery, they'd continued to see each other almost every day.

'We'll think of you, Teresa,' Philomena said. 'We'll pray for you.' Philomena, plump and pale-haired, had every hope of marrying and had even planned her dress, in light lemony lace, with a Limerick veil. Twice in the last month she'd gone out with Des Foley the vet, and even if he was a few years older than he might be and had a car that smelt of cattle disinfectant, there was more to be said for Des Foley than for many another.

Teresa's two sisters, much older than Teresa, stood by the piano and the framed Power's advertisement, between the two windows of the lounge-bar. Agnes, in smart powder-blue, was tall and thin, the older of the two; Loretta, in brown, was small. Their own two marriages, eleven and nine years ago, had been consecrated by Father Hogan in the Church of the Immaculate Conception and celebrated afterwards in this same lounge-bar. Loretta had married a man who was no longer mentioned because he'd gone to England and had never come back. Agnes had married George Tobin, who was at present sitting outside the lounge-bar in a Ford Prefect, in charge of his and Agnes's three small children. The Tobins lived in Cork now, George being the manager of a shoe-shop there. Loretta lived with her parents, like an unmarried daughter again.

'Sickens you,' Agnes said 'She's only a kid, marrying a goop like that. She'll be stuck in this dump of a town for ever.'

Loretta didn't say anything. It was well known that Agnes's own marriage had turned out well: George Tobin was a teetotaller and had no interest in either horses or greyhounds. From where she stood Loretta could see him through the window, sitting patiently in the Ford Prefect, reading a comic to his children. Loretta's marriage had not been consummated.

'Well, though I've said it before I'll say it again,' said Father Hogan. 'It's a great day for a mother.'

Mrs Atty and Mrs Cornish politely agreed, without speaking. Mrs Tracy smiled.

'And for an aunt too, Mrs Tracy. Naturally enough.'

Mrs Tracy smiled again. 'A great day,' she said.

'Ah, I'm happy for Teresa,' Father Hogan said. 'And for Artie, too, Mrs Cornish; naturally enough. Aren't they as fine a couple as ever stepped out of this town?'

'Are they leaving the town?' Mrs Tracy asked, confusion breaking in her face. 'I thought Artie was fixed in Driscoll's.'

'It's a manner of speaking, Mrs Tracy,' Father Hogan explained. 'It's a way of putting the thing. When I was marrying them this morning I looked down at their two faces and I said to myself, "Isn't it great God gave them life?"'

The three women looked across the lounge, at Teresa standing with her friends Philomena Morrissey and Kitty Roche, and then at Artie, with Screw Doyle, Eddie Boland and Chas Flynn.

'He has a great career in front of him in Driscoll's,' Father Hogan pronounced. 'Will Teresa remain on in the Medical Hall, Mrs Atty?'

Mrs Atty replied that her daughter would remain for a while in the Medical Hall. It was Father Hogan who had persuaded Artie of his duty when Artie had hesitated. Mrs Atty and Teresa had gone to him for advice, he'd spoken to Artie and to Mr and Mrs Cornish, and the matter had naturally not been mentioned on either side since.

'Will I get you another glassful, Father?' inquired Mrs Tracy, holding out her hand for the priest's tumbler.

'Well, it isn't every day I'm honoured,' said Father Hogan with his smile, putting the tumbler into Mrs Tracy's hand.

At the bar Mr Atty and Mr Cornish drank steadily on. In their corner Teresa and her bridesmaids talked about weddings that had taken place in the Church of the Immaculate Conception in the past, how they had stood by the railings of the church when they were children, excited by the finery and the men in serge suits. Teresa's sisters whispered, Agnes continuing about the inadequacy of the man Teresa had just married. Loretta whispered without actually forming words. She wished her sister wouldn't go on so because she didn't want to think about any of it, about what had happened to Teresa, and what would happen to her again tonight, in a hotel in Cork. She'd fainted when it had happened to herself, when he'd come at her like a farm animal. She'd fought like a mad thing.

It was noisier in the lounge-bar than it had been. The voices of the bridegroom's friends were raised; behind the bar young Kevin had switched on the wireless. *'Don't get around much anymore,'* cooed a soft male voice.

'Bedad, there'll be no holding you tonight, Artie,' Eddie Boland whispered thickly into the bridegroom's ear. He nudged Artie in the stomach with his elbow, spilling some Guinness. He laughed uproariously.

'We're following you in two cars,' Screw Doyle said. 'We'll be waiting in the double bed for you.' Screw Doyle laughed also, striking the floor repeatedly with his left foot, which was a habit of his when excited. At a late hour the night before he'd told Artie that once, after a dance, he'd spent an hour in a field with the girl whom Artie had agreed to marry. 'I had a great bloody ride of her,' he'd confided.

'I'll have a word with Teresa,' said Father Hogan, moving away from Teresa's mother, her aunt and Mrs Cornish. He did not, however, cross the lounge immediately, but paused by the bar, where Mr Cornish and Mr

Atty were. He put his empty tumbler on the bar itself, and Mr Atty pushed it towards young Kevin, who at once refilled it.

'Well, it's a great day for a father,' said Father Hogan. 'Aren't they a tip-top credit to each other?'

'Who's that, Father?' inquired Mr Cornish, his eyes a little bleary, sweat hanging from his cheeks.

Father Hogan laughed. He put his tumbler on the bar again, and Mr Cornish pushed it towards young Kevin for another refill.

In their corner Philomena confided to Teresa and Kitty Roche that she wouldn't mind marrying Des Foley the vet. She'd had four glasses of Babycham. If he asked her this minute, she said, she'd probably say yes. 'Is Chas Flynn nice?' Kitty Roche asked, squinting across at him.

On the wireless Petula Clark was singing 'Downtown'. Eddie Boland was whistling 'Mother Macree'. 'Listen, Screw,' Artie said, keeping his voice low although it wasn't necessary. 'Is that true? Did you go into a field with Teresa?'

Loretta watched while George Tobin in his Ford Prefect turned a page of the comic he was reading to his children. Her sister's voice continued in its abuse of the town and its people, in particular the shopman who had got Teresa pregnant. Agnes hated the town and always had. She'd met George Tobin at a dance in Cork and had said to Loretta that in six months' time she'd be gone from the town for ever. Which was precisely what had happened, except that marriage had made her less nice than she'd been. She'd hated the town in a jolly way once, laughing over it. Now she hardly laughed at all.

'Look at him,' she was saying. 'I doubt he knows how to hold a knife and fork.'

Loretta ceased her observation of her sister's husband through the window and regarded Artie Cornish instead. She looked away from him immediately because his face, so quickly replacing the face of George Tobin, had caused in her mind a double image which now brutally persisted. She felt a sickness in her stomach, and closed her eyes and prayed. But the double image remained: George Tobin and Artie Cornish coming at her sisters like two farmyard animals and her sisters fighting to get away. 'Dear Jesus,' she whispered to herself. 'Dear Jesus, help me.'

'Sure it was only a bit of gas,' Screw Doyle assured Artie. 'Sure there was no harm done, Artie.'

In no way did Teresa love him. She had been aware of that when Father Hogan had arranged the marriage, and even before that, when she'd told her mother that she thought she was pregnant and had then mentioned

Artie Cornish's name. Artie Cornish was much the same as his friends: you could be walking along a road with Screw Doyle or Artie Cornish and you could hardly tell the difference. There was nothing special about Artie Cornish, except that he always added up the figures twice when he was serving you in Driscoll's. There was nothing bad about him either, any more than there was anything bad about Eddie Boland or Chas Flynn or even Screw Doyle. She'd said privately to Father Hogan that she didn't love him or feel anything for him one way or the other: Father Hogan had replied that in the circumstances all that line of talk was irrelevant.

When she was at the Presentation Convent Teresa had imagined her wedding, and even the celebration in this very lounge-bar. She had imagined everything that had happened that morning, and the things that were happening still. She had imagined herself standing with her bridesmaids as she was standing now, her mother and her aunt drinking sherry, Agnes and Loretta being there too, and other people, and music. Only the bridegroom had been mysterious, some faceless, bodiless presence, beyond imagination. From conversations she had had with Philomena and Kitty Roche, and with her sisters, she knew that they had imagined in a similar way. Yet Agnes had settled for George Tobin because George Tobin was employed in Cork and could take her away from the town. Loretta, who had been married for a matter of weeks, was going to become a nun.

Artie ordered more bottles of stout from young Kevin. He didn't want to catch the half-one bus and have to sit beside her all the way to Cork. He didn't want to go to the Lee Hotel when they could just as easily have remained in the town, when he could just as easily have gone in to Driscoll's tomorrow and continued as before. It would have been different if Screw Doyle hadn't said he'd been in a field with her: you could pretend a bit on the bus, and in the hotel, just to make the whole thing go. You could pretend like you'd been pretending ever since Father Hogan had laid down the law, you could make the best of it like Father Hogan had said.

He handed a bottle of stout to Chas Flynn and one to Screw Doyle and another to Eddie Boland. He'd ask her about it on the bus. He'd repeat what Screw Doyle had said and ask her if it was true. For all he knew the child she was carrying was Screw Doyle's child and would be born with Screw Doyle's thin nose, and everyone in the town would know when they looked at it. His mother had told him when he was sixteen never to trust a girl, never to get involved, because he'd be caught in the end. He'd get caught because he was easy-going, because he didn't possess the smartness of Screw Doyle and some of the others. 'Sure, you might as well marry Teresa as anyone else,' his father had said after Father Hogan had called to see them about the matter. His mother had said things would never be the same between them again.

Eddie Boland sat down at the piano and played 'Mother Macree', causing Agnes and Loretta to move to the other side of the lounge-bar. In the motor-car outside the Tobin children asked their father what the music was for.

'God go with you, girl,' Father Hogan said to Teresa, motioning Kitty Roche and Philomena away. 'Isn't it a grand thing that's happened, Teresa?' His red-skinned face, with the shiny false teeth so evenly arrayed in it, was close to hers. For a moment she thought he might kiss her, which of course was ridiculous, Father Hogan kissing anyone, even at a wedding celebration.

'It's a great day for all of us, girl.'

When she'd told her mother, her mother said it made her feel sick in her stomach. Her father hit her on the side of the face. Agnes came down specially from Cork to try and sort the matter out. It was then that Loretta had first mentioned becoming a nun.

'I want to say two words,' said Father Hogan, still standing beside her, but now addressing everyone in the lounge-bar. 'Come over here alongside us, Artie. Is there a drop in everyone's glass?'

Artie moved across the lounge-bar, with his glass of stout. Mr Cornish told young Kevin to pour out a few more measures. Eddie Boland stopped playing the piano.

'It's only this,' said Father Hogan. 'I want us all to lift our glasses to Artie and Teresa. May God go with you, the pair of you,' he said, lifting his own glass.

'Health, wealth and happiness,' proclaimed Mr Cornish from the bar.

'And an early night,' shouted Screw Doyle. 'Don't forget to draw the curtains, Artie.'

They stood awkwardly, not holding hands, not even touching. Teresa watched while her mother drank the remains of her sherry, and while her aunt drank and Mrs Cornish drank. Agnes's face was disdainful, a calculated reply to the coarseness of Screw Doyle's remarks. Loretta was staring ahead of her, concentrating her mind on her novitiate. A quick flush passed over the roughened countenance of Kitty Roche. Philomena laughed, and all the men in the lounge-bar, except Father Hogan, laughed.

'That's sufficient of that talk,' Father Hogan said with contrived severity. 'May you meet happiness halfway,' he added, suitably altering his intonation. 'The pair of you, Artie and Teresa.'

Noise broke out again after that. Father Hogan shook hands with Teresa and then with Artie. He had a funeral at half past two, he said: he'd better go and get his dinner inside him.

'Goodbye, Father,' Artie said. 'Thanks for doing the job.'

'God bless the pair of you,' said Father Hogan, and went away.

'We should be going for the bus,' Artie said to her. 'It wouldn't do to miss the old bus.'

'No, it wouldn't.'

'I'll see you down there. You'll have to change your clothes.'

'Yes.'

'I'll come the way I am.'

'You're fine the way you are, Artie.'

He looked at the stout in his glass and didn't raise his eyes from it when he spoke again. 'Did Screw Doyle take you into a field, Teresa?'

He hadn't meant to say it then. It was wrong to come out with it like that, in the lounge-bar, with the wedding-cake still there on the piano, and Teresa still in her wedding-dress, and confetti everywhere. He knew it was wrong even before the words came out; he knew that the stout had angered and befuddled him.

'Sorry,' he said. 'Sorry, Teresa.'

She shook her head. It didn't matter: it was only to be expected that a man you didn't love and who didn't love you would ask a question like that at your wedding celebration.

'Yes,' she said. 'Yes, he did.'

'He told me. I thought he was codding. I wanted to know.'

'It's your baby, Artie. The other thing was years ago.'

He looked at her. Her face was flushed, her eyes had tears in them.

'I had too much stout,' he said.

They stood where Father Hogan had left them, drawn away from their wedding guests. Not knowing where else to look, they looked together at Father Hogan's black back as he left the lounge-bar, and then at the perspiring, naked heads of Mr Cornish and Mr Atty by the bar.

At least they had no illusions, she thought. Nothing worse could happen than what had happened already, after Father Hogan had laid down the law. She wasn't going to get a shock like Loretta had got. She wasn't going to go sour like Agnes had gone when she'd discovered that it wasn't enough just to marry a man for a purpose, in order to escape from a town. Philomena was convincing herself that she'd fallen in love with an elderly vet, and if she got any encouragement Kitty Roche would convince herself that she was mad about anyone at all.

For a moment as Teresa stood there, the last moment before she left the lounge-bar, she felt that she and Artie might make some kind of marriage together because there was nothing that could be destroyed, no magic or anything else. He could ask her the question he had asked, while she stood there in her wedding-dress: he could ask her and she could truthfully reply, because there was nothing special about the occasion, or the lounge-bar all covered in confetti.

Office Romances

'Oh no, I couldn't,' Angela said in the outer office. 'Really, Mr Spelle. Thank you, though.'

'Don't you drink then, Miss Hosford? Nary a drop at all?' He laughed at his own way of putting it. He thought of winking at her as he laughed, but decided against it: girls like this were sometimes scared out of their wits by a wink.

'No, it's not that, Mr Spelle –'

'It's just that it's a way of getting to know people. Everyone else'll be down in the Arms, you know.'

Hearing that, she changed her mind and quite eagerly put the grey plastic cover on her Remington International. She'd refused his invitation to have a drink because she'd been flustered when he'd come into the outer office with his right hand poked out for her to shake, introducing himself as Gordon Spelle. He hadn't said anything about the other people from the office being there: in a matter of seconds he'd made the whole thing sound romantic, a tête-à-tête with a total stranger. Any girl's reaction would be to say she couldn't.

'Won't be a moment, Mr Spelle,' she said. She picked up her handbag from the floor beside her chair and walked with it from the office. Behind her, she heard the office silence broken by a soft whistling: Gordon Spelle essaying 'Smoke Gets in Your Eyes'.

Angela had started at C.S. & E. at half past nine that morning, having been interviewed a month ago by Miss Ivygale, her immediate employer. Miss Ivygale was a slender woman of fifty or thereabouts, her face meticulously made up. Her blue-grey hair was worked on daily by a hairdresser, a Mr Patric, whom twice that day she'd mentioned to Angela, deploring the fact that next March he was planning to leave the Elizabeth Salon. At C.S. & E. Miss Ivygale occupied an inner office that was more luxuriously appointed than the outer one where Angela sat with her filing cabinets and her Remington International. On the window-sill of the outer office Miss Ivygale's last secretary, whom she referred to as Sue, had left a Busy Lizzie in a blue-glazed pot. There was a calendar that showed Saturdays and Sundays in red, presented by the Michelin Tyre Company.

In a small lavatory Angela examined her face in the mirror over the wash-basin. She sighed at her complexion. Her eyes had a bulgy look because of her contact lenses. The optician had said the bulgy look would go when the lids became used to the contact lenses, but as far as she was concerned it never had. 'No, no, you're imagining it, Miss Hosford,' the optician had said when she'd gone back after a month to complain that the look was still there.

In the lavatory she touched one or two places on her cheeks with Pure Magic and powdered over it. She rubbed lipstick into her lips and then pressed a tissue between them. She ran a comb through her hair, which was fluffed up because she'd washed it the night before: it was her best feature, she considered, a pretty shade, soft and naturally curly.

'I like your dress, Miss Hosford,' he said when she returned to the outer office. 'Fresh as a flower it looks.' He laughed at his own description of the blue-and-white dress she was wearing. The blue parts were flowers of a kind, he supposed, a type of blue geranium they appeared to be, with blue leaves sprouting out of blue stems. Extraordinary, the tasteless stuff a girl like this would sometimes wear.

'Thank you,' she said.

'We don't bother much with surnames at C.S. & E.,' he told her as they walked along a green-carpeted corridor to a lift. 'All right to call you Angela, Miss Hosford?'

'Oh, yes, of course.'

He closed the lift doors. He smiled at her. He was a tall, sleek man who had something the matter with his left eye, a kind of droop in the upper lid and a glazed look in the eye itself, a suggestion of blindness. Another oddness about him, she thought in the lift, was his rather old-fashioned suit. It was a pepper-coloured suit with a waistcoat, cut in an Edwardian style. His manners were old-fashioned too, and the way he spoke had a pedantic air to it that recalled the past: Edwardian again perhaps, she didn't know. It seemed right that he had whistled 'Smoke Gets in Your Eyes' rather than a current pop song.

'I suppose it's your first job, Angela?'

'Oh, heavens, no!'

'I'd say you were twenty.'

'Twenty-six, actually.'

He laughed. 'I'm thirty-eight myself.'

They left the lift and walked together through the elegant reception area of C.S. & E. When she'd walked through it for her interview Angela had been reminded of the lounge of a large, new hotel: there were sofas and armchairs covered in white ersatz leather, and steel-framed reproductions of paintings by Paul Klee on rust-coloured walls, and magazines on steel-topped tables. When Angela had come for her interview, and again when she'd arrived at C.S. & E. that morning, there'd been a beautiful black-haired girl sitting at the large reception desk, which was upholstered here and there in the same ersatz leather as the sofas and the armchairs. But at this time of the evening, five to six, the beautiful black-haired girl was not there.

'I'd really have said it was your first job,' he said when they reached the street. He smiled at her. 'Something about you.'

She knew what he meant. She was often taken to be younger than she was, it had something to do with being small: five foot one she was, with thin, small arms that she particularly disliked. And of course there was her complexion, which was a schoolgirl complexion in the real sense, since schoolgirls rather than adults tended to be bothered with pimples. 'Attack them from inside, Miss Hosford,' her doctor had advised. 'Avoid all sweets and chocolate, avoid cakes and biscuits with your coffee. Lots of lemon juice, fresh fruit, salads.' She ate lots of fruit and salads anyway, just in case she'd get fat, which would have been the last straw. She naturally never ate sweet things.

'Horrid being new,' he said. 'Like your first day at school.'

The street, fashionably situated just off Grosvenor Square, was busy with people impatient to be home: it was a cold night in November, not a night for loitering. Girls in suede boots or platform shoes had turned up the collars of their coats. Some carried bundles of letters which had been signed too late to catch the afternoon dispatch boys. In the harsh artificial light their faces were pale, sometimes garish with make-up: the light drew the worst out of girls who were pretty, and killed the subtleties of carefully chosen lipstick and make-up shades. God alone knew, Angela said to herself, what it did to her. She sighed, experiencing the familiar feeling of her inferiority complex getting the upper hand.

'Hullo, Gordon,' a man in a black overcoat said to Gordon Spelle. The man had been walking behind them for some time, while Angela had been listening to Gordon Spelle going on about the first day he'd spent at school. Miserable beyond measure he'd been.

'God, it's chilly,' the man said, dropping into step with them and smiling at Angela.

'Angela Hosford,' Gordon Spelle said. 'She's come to work for Pam Ivygale.'

'Oh, Pam, dear Pam!' the man said. He laughed in much the same way as Gordon Spelle was given to laughing, or so it seemed to Angela. His black overcoat had a little rim of black fur on its collar. His hair was black also. His face in the distorting street-light had a purple tinge, and Angela guessed that in normal circumstances it was a reddish face.

'Tommy Blyth,' Gordon Spelle said.

They entered a public house at the corner of a street. It was warm there, and crowded, and quite attractively noisy. Fairy lights were draped on a Christmas tree just inside the door because Christmas was less than six weeks away. Men like Tommy Blyth, in overcoats with furred collars and with reddish faces, were standing by a coal fire with glasses in their hands. One of them had his right arm round the waist of C.S. & E.'s black-haired receptionist.

'What's your poison, Angela?' Gordon Spelle asked, and she said she'd like some sherry.

'Dry?'

'Oh, it doesn't matter – well, medium, actually.'

He didn't approach the bar but led her into a far corner and sat her down at a table. It was less crowded there and rather dimly lit. He said he wouldn't be a minute.

People were standing at the bar, animatedly talking. Some of the men had taken off their overcoats. All of them were wearing suits, most of them grey or blue but a few of a more extravagant shade, like Gordon Spelle's. Occasionally a particular man, older and stouter than his companions, laughed raucously, swaying backwards on his heels. On a bar-stool to this man's right, in a red wool dress with a chiffon scarf at her throat, sat Miss Ivygale. The red wool coat that had been hanging just inside the outer office door all day hung on the arm of the raucous man: Miss Ivygale, Angela deduced, was intent on staying a while, or at least as long as the man was agreeable to looking after her coat for her. 'You'll find it friendly at C.S. & E.,' Miss Ivygale had said. 'A generous firm.' Miss Ivygale looked as though she'd sat on her bar-stool every night for the past twenty-three years, which was the length of time she'd been at C.S. & E.

'Alec Hemp,' Gordon Spelle said, indicating the man who had Miss Ivygale's coat on his arm.

The name occurred on C.S. & E.'s stationery: *A. R. Hemp*. It was there with other names, all of them in discrete italics, strung out along the bottom of the writing paper that had *C.S. & E.* and the address at the top: *S. P. Bakewell, T. P. Cooke, N. N. E. Govier, A. R. Hemp, I. D. Jackson, A. F. Norris, P. Onniman*, the directors of the C.S. & E. board.

'That's been going on for years,' Gordon Spelle said. He handed her her sherry and placed on the table in front of him a glass of gin and Britvic orange juice. His droopy eye had closed, as if tired. His other, all on its own, looked a little beady.

'Sorry?'

'Pam Ivygale and Alec Hemp.'

'Oh.'

'It's why she never married anyone else.'

'I see.'

Miss Ivygale's brisk manner in the office and her efficient probing when she'd interviewed Angela had given the impression that she lived entirely for her work. There was no hint of a private life about Miss Ivygale, and certainly no hint of any love affair beyond a love affair with C.S. & E.

'Alec,' Gordon Spelle said, 'has a wife and four children in Brighton.'

'I see.'

'Office romance.' His droopy eye opened and gazed bleakly at her, contrasting oddly with the busyness of the other eye. He said it was disgraceful that all this should be so, that a woman should be messed up the way Mr Hemp for twenty-three years had messed up Miss Ivygale. Everyone knew, he said, that Alec Hemp had no intention of divorcing his wife: he was stringing Miss Ivygale along. 'Mind you, though,' he added, 'she's tricky.'

'She seems very nice —'

'Oh, Pam's all right. Now, tell me all about yourself.'

Angela lived in a flat with two other girls, a ground-floor flat in what had once been a private house in Putney. She'd lived there for three years, and before that she'd lived in a similar flat in another part of Putney, and before that in a hostel. Every six or seven weeks she went home for the weekend, to her parents in Exeter, Number 4 Carhampton Road. When she'd qualified as a shorthand typist at the City Commercial College in Exeter the College had found her a position in the offices of a firm that manufactured laminates. Three years later, after some months' discussion and argument with her parents, she'd moved to London, to the offices of a firm that imported and marketed German wine. From there, she'd moved to the firm called C.S. & E.

'You can hear it in your voice,' Gordon Spelle said. 'Exeter and all that.'

She laughed. 'I thought I'd lost it.'

'It's nice, a touch of the West Countries.'

The laminates firm had been a dull one, or at least a dull one for a girl to work in. But her parents hadn't understood that. Her parents, whom she liked and respected very much, had been frightened by the idea of her going to London, where there was loose living, so other parents had told them, and drinking and drugs, and girls spending every penny they had on clothes and rarely eating a decent meal. The German-wine firm had turned out to be a dull place for a girl to work in too, or so at least it seemed after a few years. Often, though, while finding it dull, Angela had felt that it suited her. With her poor complexion and her bulging contact lenses and her small, thin arms, it was a place to crouch away in. Besides herself, two elderly women were employed in the office, and there was Mr Franklin and Mr Snyder, elderly also. Economy was practised in the office, the windows seemed always to be dusty, electric lightbulbs were of a low wattage. On the mornings when a new pimple cruelly erupted on her neck or one of her cheeks, Angela had hurried from bus to tube and was glad when she reached the dingy office of the wine firm and lost herself in its shadows. Then a girl in the flat introduced her to Pure Magic, so good at disguising imperfections of the skin. But although it did not, as in an advertisement, change Angela's life and could do nothing at all for her thin arms, it did enough to draw her from the dinginess of the wine firm. A girl in the flat heard of the vacancy with Miss Ivygale at C.S. & E. and, not feeling like a change herself, persuaded Angela to apply for it. The shared opinion of the girls in the flat was that Angela needed drawing out. They liked her and were sorry for her; no joke at all, they often said to one another, to have an inferiority complex like Angela's. The inferiority complex caused nerviness in her, one of them diagnosed, and the nerviness caused her bad complexion. In actual fact, her figure and her arms were perfectly all right, and her hair was really pretty the way it curled. Now that she'd at last stopped wearing spectacles she looked quite presentable, even if her eyes did tend to bulge a little.

'Oh, you'll like it at C.S. & E.,' Gordon Spelle said. 'It's really friendly, you know. Sincerely so.'

He insisted on buying her another drink and while he was at the bar she wondered when, or if, she was going to meet the people he'd mentioned, the other employees of C.S. & E. Miss Ivygale had narrowed her eyes in her direction and then had looked away, as if she couldn't quite place her. The black-haired receptionist had naturally not remembered her face when she'd come into the bar with the two men. The only person Gordon Spelle had so far introduced her to was the man called Tommy Blyth, who had joined the group around the fire and was holding the hand of a girl.

'It's the C.S. & E. pub,' Gordon Spelle said when he returned with the drinks. 'There isn't a soul here who isn't on the strength.' He smiled at her, his bad eye twitching. 'I like you, you know.' She smiled back at him, not knowing how to reply. He picked up her left hand and briefly squeezed it.

'Don't trust that man, Angela,' Miss Ivygale said, passing their table on her way to the Ladies. She stroked the back of Gordon Spelle's neck. 'Terrible man,' she said.

Angela was pleased that Miss Ivygale had recognized her and had spoken to her. It occurred to her that her immediate employer was probably shortsighted and had seen no more than the outline of a familiar face when she'd peered across the bar at her.

'Come on, have a drink with us,' Miss Ivygale insisted on her way back from the Ladies.

'Oh, it's all right, Pam,' Gordon Spelle said quickly, but Miss Ivygale stood there, waiting for them to get up and accompany her. 'You watch your step, my boy,' she said to Gordon Spelle as they all three made their way together. Gordon Spelle told her she was drunk.

'This is my secretary, Alec,' Miss Ivygale said at the bar. 'Replacing Sue. Angela Hosford.'

Mr Hemp shook Angela's hand. He had folded Miss Ivygale's red coat and placed it on a bar-stool. He asked Angela what she was drinking and while she was murmuring that she wouldn't have another one Gordon Spelle said a medium sherry and a gin and Britvic orange for himself. Gordon Spelle was looking cross, Angela noticed. His bad eye closed again. He was glaring at Miss Ivygale with the other one.

'Cheers, Angela,' Mr Hemp said. 'Welcome to C.S. & E.'

'Thank you, Mr Hemp.'

People were leaving the bar, waving or calling out goodnight to the group she was with. A man paused to say something to Mr Hemp and then stayed to have another drink. By the fire the receptionist and another girl listened while Tommy Blyth told them about car radios, advising which kind to buy if they ever had to.

'I brought her in here to have a simple drink,' Gordon Spelle was protesting to Miss Ivygale, unsuccessfully attempting to keep his voice low. 'So's the poor girl could meet a few people.'

Miss Ivygale looked at Angela and Angela smiled at her uneasily, embarrassed because they were talking about her. Miss Ivygale didn't smile back, and it couldn't have been that Miss Ivygale didn't see her properly this time because the distance between them was less than a yard.

'You watch your little step, my boy,' Miss Ivygale warned again, and this time Gordon Spelle leaned forward and kissed her on the cheek. 'All right, my love?' he said.

Miss Ivygale ordered Mr Hemp another Bell's whisky and one for herself, reminding the barman that the measures they were drinking were double measures. 'What're you on, Dil?' she asked the man who was talking to Mr Hemp. 'No, no, must go,' he said.

'Bell's I think he's on,' the barman said, pouring a third large whisky.

'And a gin and Britvic for Gordon,' Miss Ivygale said. 'And a medium sherry.'

'Oh, really,' murmured Angela.

'Nonsense,' Miss Ivygale said.

In the lavatory Gordon Spelle swore as he urinated. Typical of bloody Pam Ivygale to go nosing in like that. He wouldn't have brought the girl to the Arms at all if he'd thought Ivygale would be soaked to the gills, hurling abuse about like bloody snowballs. God alone knew what kind of a type the girl thought he was now. Girls like that had a way of thinking you a sexual maniac if you so much as took their arm to cross a street. There'd been one he'd known before who'd come from the same kind of area, Plymouth or Bristol or somewhere. Bigger girl actually, five foot ten she must have been, fattish. 'Touch of the West Countries', he'd said when she'd opened her mouth, the first time he'd used the expression. Tamar Dymond she'd been called, messy bloody creature.

Gordon Spelle combed his hair and then decided that his tie needed to be reknotted. He removed his pepper-coloured jacket and his waistcoat and took the tie off, cocking up the collar of his striped blue shirt in order to make the operation easier. His wife, Ruth, would probably be reading a story to the younger of their two children, since she generally did so at about seven o'clock. As he reknotted his tie, he imagined his wife sitting by the child's bed reading a Topsy and Tim book.

'Oh, say you're going to Luton,' Miss Ivygale said. 'Tell her it's all just cropped up in the last fifteen minutes.'

Mr Hemp shook his head. He pointed out that rather often recently he'd telephoned his wife at seven o'clock to say that what had cropped up in the last fifteen minutes was the fact that unexpectedly he had to go to Luton. Mr Hemp had moved away from the man called Dil, closer to Miss Ivygale. They were speaking privately, Mr Hemp in a lower voice than Miss Ivygale. The man called Dil was talking to another man.

Standing by herself and not being spoken to by anyone, Angela was feeling happy. It didn't matter that no one was speaking to her, or paying her any other kind of attention. She felt warm and friendly, quite happy to be on her own while Gordon Spelle was in the Gents and Mr Hemp and Miss Ivygale talked to each other privately. She liked him, she thought as she stood there: she liked his old-fashioned manners and the way he'd whistled 'Smoke Gets in Your Eyes', and his sympathy over her being new. She smiled at him when he returned from the Gents. It was all much nicer than the German-wine firm, or the laminates firm.

'Hullo,' he said in a whisper, staring at her.

'It was nice of you to bring me here,' she said, whispering also.

'Nice for me, too,' said Gordon Spelle.

Mr Hemp went away to telephone his wife. The telephone was behind Angela, in a little booth against the wall. The booth was shaped like a sedan chair, except that it didn't have any shafts to carry it by. Angela had noticed it when she'd been sitting down with Gordon Spelle. She hadn't known then that it contained a telephone and had wondered at the presence of a sedan chair in a bar. But several times since then people had entered it and each time a light had come on, revealing a telephone and a pile of directories.

'Because they only told me ten minutes ago,' Mr Hemp was saying. 'Because the bloody fools couldn't make their minds up, if you can call them minds.'

Gordon Spelle squeezed her hand and Angela squeezed back because it seemed a friendly thing to do. She felt sorry for him because he had only one good eye. It was the single defect in his handsome face. It gave him a tired look, and suggested suffering.

'I wish you'd see it my way,' Mr Hemp was saying crossly in the sedan chair. 'God damn it, I don't *want* to go to the bloody place.'

'I really must go,' Angela murmured, but Gordon Spelle continued to hold her hand. She didn't want to go. 'I really must,' she said again.

In the Terrazza, where the waiters wore striped blue-and-white jerseys and looked like sailors at a regatta, Mr Hemp and Miss Ivygale were well known. So was Gordon Spelle. The striped waiters greeted them affectionately, and a man in a dark suit addressed all three of them by name. He bowed at Angela. 'How d'you do?' he said, handing her a menu.

'*Petto di pollo sorpresa,*' Gordon Spelle recommended. 'Chicken with garlic in it.'

'Garlic? Oh –'

'He always has it,' Miss Ivygale said, pointing with the menu at Gordon Spelle. 'You'll be all right, dear.'

'What're you having, darling?' Mr Hemp asked Miss Ivygale. In the taxi on the way to the Terrazza he had sat with his arm around her and once, as though they were in private, he'd kissed her on the mouth, making quite a lot of noise about it. Angela had been embarrassed and so, she imagined, had Gordon Spelle.

'*Gamberone al spiedo,*' Miss Ivygale ordered.

'Cheers,' Mr Hemp said, lifting a glass of white wine into the air.

'I think I'm a bit drunk,' Angela said to Gordon Spelle and he wagged his head approvingly. Mr Hemp said he was a bit drunk himself, and Miss Ivygale said she was drunk, and Gordon Spelle pointed out that you only live once.

'Welcome to C.S. & E.,' Mr Hemp said, lifting his glass again.

The next morning, in the flat in Putney, Angela told her flatmates about the delicious food at the Terrazza and how she couldn't really remember much else. There'd certainly been a conversation at the restaurant table, and in a taxi afterwards she remembered Gordon Spelle humming and then Gordon Spelle had kissed her. She seemed to remember him saying that he'd always wanted to be a dance-band leader, although she wasn't sure if she'd got that right. There were other memories of Gordon Spelle in the taxi, which she didn't relate to her flatmates. There'd been, abruptly, his cold hand on the flesh of one of her thighs, and her surprise that the hand could have got there without her noticing. At another point there'd been his cold hand on the flesh of her stomach. 'Look, you're not married or anything?' she remembered herself saying in sudden alarm. She remembered the noise of Gordon Spelle's breathing and his tongue penetrating her ear. 'Married?' he'd said at some other point, and had laughed.

Feeling unwell but not unhappy, Angela vividly recalled the face and clothes of Gordon Spelle. She recalled his hands, which tapered and were thin, and his sleek hair and droopy eye. She wondered how on earth she was going to face him after what had happened in the taxi, or how she was going to face Miss Ivygale because Miss Ivygale, she faintly remembered, had fallen against a table on their way out of the restaurant, upsetting plates of soup and a bottle of wine. When Angela had tried to help her to stand up again she'd used unpleasant language. Yet the dim memories didn't worry Angela in any real way, not like her poor complexion sometimes worried her, or her contact lenses. Even though she was feeling unwell, she only wanted to smile that morning. She wanted to write a letter to her parents in Carhampton Road, Exeter, and tell them she'd made a marvellous decision when she'd decided to leave the German-wine business and go to C.S. & E. She should have done it years ago, she wanted to tell them, because everyone at C.S. & E. was so friendly and because you only lived once. She wanted to tell them about Gordon Spelle, who had said in the taxi that he thought he was falling in love with her, which was of course an exaggeration.

She drank half a cup of Nescafé and caught a 37 bus. Sitting beside an Indian on the lower deck, she thought about Gordon Spelle. On the tube to Earl's Court she thought of him again, and on the Piccadilly line between Earl's Court and Green Park she went on thinking about him. When she closed her eyes, as she once or twice did, she seemed to be with him in some anonymous place, stroking his face and comforting him because of his bad eye. She walked from the tube station, past the Rootes' Group car showrooms and Thos Cook's in Berkeley Street, along Lansdowne Row with its pet shops and card shop and coffee shops, past the Gresham Arms, the C.S. & E. pub. It was a cold morning, but the cold air was pleasant. Pigeons waddled on the pavements, cars drew up at parking-meters. Fresh-faced and shaven, the men of the night before hurried to their offices. She wouldn't have recognized Tommy Blyth, she thought, or the man called Dil, or even Mr Hemp. Girls in suede boots hurried, also looking different in the morning light. She was being silly, she said to herself in Carlos Place: he probably said that to dozens of girls.

In Angela's life there had been a few other men. At the age of twelve she had been attracted by a youth who worked in a newsagent's. She'd liked him because he'd always been ready to chat to her and smile at her, two or three years older he'd been. At fourteen she'd developed a passion for an American actor called Don Ameche whom she'd seen in an old film on television. For several weeks she'd carried with her the memory of his face and had lain in bed at night imagining a life with him in a cliff-top house she'd invented, in California. She'd seen herself and Don Ameche running into the sea together, as he had run with an actress in the film. She'd seen them eating breakfast together, out in the open, on a sunny morning. But Don Ameche, she'd suddenly realized, was sixty or seventy now.

When Angela had first come to London a man who'd briefly been employed in the German-wine business used occasionally to invite her to have a cup of coffee with him at the end of the day, just as Gordon Spelle had invited her to have a drink. But being with this man wasn't like being with Gordon Spelle: the man was a shabby person who was employed in some lowly capacity, who seemed to Angela, after the third time they'd had coffee together, to be mentally deficient. One Monday morning he didn't turn up for work, and was never heard of again.

There'd been another man, more briefly, in Angela's life, a young man called Ted Apwell whom she'd met at a Saturday-night party given by a friend of one of her flatmates. She and Ted Apwell had paired off when the party, more or less at an end, had become uninhibited. At half past three in the morning she'd allowed herself to be driven home by Ted Apwell, knowing that it was to his home rather than hers they were going. He'd taken her clothes off and in a half-hearted, inebriated way had put an end to her virginity, on a hearth-rug in front of a gas-fire. He'd driven her on to her flat, promising – too often, she realized afterwards – that he'd telephone her on Monday. She'd found him hard to forget at first, not because she'd developed any great fondness for him but because of his nakedness and her own on the hearth-rug, the first time all that had happened. There hadn't, so far, been a second time.

Miss Ivygale did not come in that morning. Angela sat alone in the outer office, with nothing to do because there were no letters to type. A tea-lady arrived at a quarter past ten and poured milky coffee on to two lumps of sugar in a cup she'd earlier placed on Angela's desk. 'Pam not in this morning?' she said, and Angela said no, Miss Ivygale wasn't.

At ten past twelve Gordon Spelle entered the outer office. 'Red roses,' he lilted, 'for a blue lady. Oh, Mr Florist, please . . .' He laughed, standing by the door. He closed the door and crossed to her desk and kissed her. If anyone had asked her in that moment she'd have said that her inferiority complex was a thing of the past. She felt pretty when Gordon Spelle kissed her, not knowing what everyone else knew, that Gordon Spelle was notorious.

They had lunch in a place called the Coffee Bean, more modest than the Terrazza. Gordon Spelle told her about his childhood, which had not been happy. He told her about coming to C.S. & E. nine years ago, and about his earlier ambition to be a dance-band leader. 'Look,' he said when they'd drunk a carafe of Sicilian wine. 'I want to tell you, Angela: I'm actually married.'

She felt a coldness in her stomach, as though ice had somehow become lodged there. The coldness began to hurt her, like indigestion. All the warmth of her body had moved into her face and neck. She hated the flush that had come to her face and neck because she knew it made her look awful.

'Married?' she said.

He'd only laughed last night in the taxi, she remembered: he hadn't actually said he wasn't married, not that she could swear to it. He'd laughed and given the impression that married was the last thing he was, so that she'd woken up that morning with the firmly established thought that Gordon Spelle, a bachelor, had said he loved her and had embraced her with more passion than she'd ever permitted in another man or youth. In the moments of waking she'd even been aware of thinking that one day she and Gordon Spelle might be married, and had imagined her parents in their best clothes, her father awkward, giving her away. It was all amazing; incredible that Gordon Spelle should have picked her out when all around him, in C.S. & E. and in the other offices, there were beautiful girls.

'I didn't dare tell you,' he said. 'I tried to, Angela. All last night I tried to, but I couldn't. In case you'd go away.'

They left the Coffee Bean and walked about Grosvenor Square in bitter November sunshine. Men were tidying the flowerbeds. The people who had hurried from their offices last night and had hurried into them this morning, and out of them for lunch, were hurrying back to them again.

'I'm in love with you, Angela,' he said, and again she felt it was incredible. She might be dreaming, she thought, but knew she was not.

They walked hand in hand, and she suddenly remembered Mr Hemp telephoning in the sedan chair, cross and untruthful with his wife. She imagined Gordon Spelle's wife and saw her as a hard-faced woman who was particular about her house, who didn't let him smoke in certain rooms, who'd somehow prevented him from becoming a dance-band leader. She seemed to be older than Gordon Spelle, with hair that was quite grey and a face that Angela remembered from a book her father used to read her as a child, the face of a farmyard rat.

'She's a bit of an invalid, actually,' Gordon Spelle said. 'She isn't well most of the time and she's a ball of nerves anyway. She couldn't stand a separation, Angela, or anything like that: I wouldn't want to mislead you, Angela, like Alec Hemp –'

'Oh, Gordon.'

He looked away from her and with his face still averted he said he wasn't much of a person. It was all wrong, being in love with her like this, with a wife and children at home. He would never want her to go on waiting for him, as Pam Ivygale had waited for twenty-three years.

'Oh, love,' she said.

The ice had gone from her stomach, and her face had cooled again. He put his arms around her, one hand on her hair, the other pressing her body into his. He whispered, but she couldn't hear what he said and the words didn't seem important. The hurrying people glanced at them, surprised to witness a leisurely embrace, in daylight, on a path in Grosvenor Square.

'Oh, love,' she said again.

The cold had brought out the defects on her face: beneath heavily applied make-up he noticed that the skin was pimply and pitted. Affected by the cold also, her eyes were red-rimmed. She reminded him of Gwyneth Birkett, a girl who'd been at C.S. & E. three years ago.

They returned to the office. He released her hand and took her arm instead. He'd see her at half past five, he said in the lift. He kissed her in the lift because there was no one else in it. His mouth was moist and open. No one ever before had kissed her like he did, as though far more than kisses were involved, as though his whole being was passionate for hers. 'I love you terribly,' he said.

All afternoon, with no real work to do, she thought about it, continuing to be amazed. It was a mystery, a gorgeous mystery that became more gorgeous the more she surveyed the facts. The facts were gorgeous themselves: nicer, she considered, than any of the other facts of her life. In prettily coloured clothes the girls of C.S. & E. walked the green-carpeted corridors from office to office, their fingernails gleaming, their skins like porcelain, apparently without pores. In their suede boots or their platform shoes they queued for lunchtime tables in the Coffee Bean, or stood at five past six in the warm bar of the Gresham Arms. Their faces were nicer than her face, their bodies more lissom, their legs and arms more suavely elegant. Yet she had been chosen.

She leafed through files, acquainting herself further with the affairs of Miss Ivygale's office. She examined without interest the carbon copies of letters in buff-coloured folders. The faint, blurred type made no sense to her and the letters themselves seemed as unimportant as the flimsy paper they were duplicated on. In a daydream that was delicious his tapering hands again caressed her. 'I love you terribly, too,' she said.

At four o'clock Miss Ivygale arrived. She'd been working all day in her flat, she said, making notes for the letters she now wished to dictate. Her manner was businesslike, she didn't mention the evening before. 'Dear Sir,' she said. 'Further to yours of the 29th ...'

Angela made shorthand notes and then typed Miss Ivygale's letters. He did not love his wife; he had hinted that he did not love his wife; no one surely could kiss you like that, no one could put his arms around you in the broad daylight in Grosvenor Square, and still love a wife somewhere. She imagined being in a room with him, a room with an electric fire built into the wall, and two chintz-covered armchairs and a sofa covered in the same material, with pictures they had chosen together, and ornaments on the mantelpiece. 'No, I don't love her,' his voice said. 'Marry me, Angela,' his voice said.

'No, no, that's really badly done,' Miss Ivygale said. 'Type it again, please.'

You couldn't blame Miss Ivygale. Naturally Miss Ivygale was cross, having just had her share of Mr Hemp, one night out of so many empty ones. She smiled at Miss Ivygale when she handed her the retyped letter. Feeling generous and euphoric, she wanted to tell Miss Ivygale that she was still attractive at fifty, but naturally she could not do that.

'See they catch the post,' Miss Ivygale sourly ordered, handing her back the letters she'd signed.

'Yes, yes, of course, Miss Ivygale –'

'You'll need to hurry up.'

She took the letters to the dispatch-room in the basement and when she returned to the outer office she found that Miss Ivygale had already left the inner one. She put the grey plastic cover on her Remington International and went to the lavatory to put Pure Magic on her face. 'I wonder who's kissing her now,' Gordon Spelle was murmuring when she entered the outer office again. 'I wonder who's showing her how.'

He put his arms around her. His tongue crept between her teeth, his hands caressed the outline of her buttocks. He led her into Miss Ivygale's office, an arm around her waist, his lips damply on her right ear. He was whispering something about Miss Ivygale having left for the Gresham Arms and about having to lock the door because the cleaners would be coming round. She heard the door being locked. The light went out and the office was dark except for the glow of the street lamps coming through two uncurtained windows. His mouth was working on hers again, his fingers undid the zip at the side of her skirt. She closed her eyes, saturated by the gorgeousness of the mystery.

Take it easy, he said to himself when he had her on the floor, remembering the way Gwyneth Birkett had suddenly shouted out, in discomfort apparently although at the time he'd assumed it to be pleasure. A Nigerian cleaner had come knocking at the door when she'd shouted out the third or fourth time. 'Oh, God, I love you,' he whispered to Angela Hosford.

She had vodka and lime in the Gresham Arms because she felt she needed pulling together and one of the girls in the flat had said that vodka was great for that. It had been very painful on the floor of Miss Ivygale's office, and not even momentarily pleasurable, not once. It had been less painful the other time, with Ted Apwell on the hearth-rug. She wished it didn't always have to be on a floor, but even so it didn't matter – nor did the pain, nor the apprehension about doing it in Miss Ivygale's office. All the time he'd kept saying he loved her, and as often as she could manage it she'd said she loved him too.

'Must go,' he said now with sudden, awful abruptness. He buttoned the jacket of his pepper-coloured suit. He kissed her on the lips, in full view of everyone in the Gresham Arms. She wanted to go with him but felt she shouldn't because the drink he'd just bought her was scarcely touched. He'd drunk his own gin and Britvic in a couple of gulps.

'Sorry for being so grumpy,' Miss Ivygale said.

The Gresham Arms was warm and noisy, but somehow not the same at all. The men who'd been there last night were there again: Tommy Blyth and the man called Dil and all the other men – and the black-haired receptionist and all the other girls. Mr Hemp was not. Mr Hemp was hurrying back to his wife, and so was Gordon Spelle.

'What're you drinking?' Miss Ivygale asked her.

'Oh no, no. I haven't even started this one, thanks.'

But Miss Ivygale, whose own glass required refilling, insisted. 'Sit down, why don't you?' Miss Ivygale suggested indicating the bar-stool next to hers. 'Take off your coat. It's like a furnace in here.'

Slowly Angela took off her coat. She sat beside her immediate employer, still feeling painful and in other ways aware of what had occurred on Miss Ivygale's office floor. They drank together and in time they both became a little drunk. Angela felt sorry for Miss Ivygale then, and Miss Ivygale felt sorry for Angela, but neither of them said so. And in the end, when Angela asked Miss Ivygale why it was that Gordon Spelle had picked her out, Miss Ivygale replied that it was because Gordon Spelle loved her. What else could she say? Miss Ivygale asked herself. How could she say that everyone knew that Gordon Spelle chose girls who were unattractive because he believed such girls, deprived of sex for long periods at a time, were an easier bet? Gordon Spelle was notorious, but Miss Ivygale naturally couldn't say it, any more than she'd been able to say it to Gwyneth Birkett or Tamar Dymond or Sue, or any of the others.

'Oh, it's beautiful!' Angela cried suddenly, having drunk a little more. She was referring, not to her own situation, but to the fact that Miss Ivygale had wasted half a lifetime on a hopeless love. Feeling happy herself, she wanted Miss Ivygale to feel happy also.

Miss Ivygale did not say anything in reply. She was fifty and Angela was twenty-six: that made a difference where knowing what was beautiful was concerned. The thing about Gordon Spelle was that with the worst possible motives he performed an act of charity for the girls who were his victims. He gave them self-esteem, and memories to fall back on – for the truth was too devious for those closest to it to guess, and too cruel for other people ever to reveal to them. The victims of Gordon Spelle left C.S. & E. in the end because they believed the passion of his love for them put him under a strain, he being married to a wife who was ill. As soon as each had gone he looked around for someone else.

'And beautiful for you too, my dear,' Miss Ivygale murmured, thinking that in a way it was, compared with what she had herself. She'd been aware for twenty-three years of being used by the man she loved: self-esteem and memories were better than knowing that, no matter how falsely they came.

'Let's have two for the road,' murmured Miss Ivygale, and ordered further drinks.

Mr McNamara

'How was he?' my mother asked on the morning of my thirteenth birthday.

She spoke while pouring tea into my father's extra-large breakfast cup, the last remaining piece of a flowered set, Ville de Lyon clematis on a leafy ground. My father had a special knife and fork as well, the knife another relic of the past, the fork more ordinary, extra-strong because my father was always breaking forks.

'Oh, he's well enough,' he said on the morning of my thirteenth birthday, while I sat patiently. 'The old aunt's kicking up again.'

My mother, passing him his tea, nodded. She remarked that in her opinion Mr McNamara's aunt should be placed in an asylum, which was what she always said when the subject of Mr McNamara's aunt, reputedly alcoholic, cropped up.

My mother was tallish and slender, but softly so. There was nothing sharp or angular about my mother, nothing wiry or hard. She had misty blue eyes and she seemed always to be on the point of smiling. My father was even taller, a bulky man with a brown face and a brown forehead stretching back where hair once had been, with heavy brown-backed hands, and eyes the same shade of blue mist as my mother's. They were gentle with one another in a way that was similar also, and when they disagreed or argued their voices weren't ever raised. They could be angry with us, but not with one another. They meted out punishments for us jointly, sharing disapproval or disappointment. We felt doubly ashamed when our misdemeanours were uncovered.

'The train was like a Frigidaire,' my father said. 'Two hours late at the halt. Poor Flannagan nearly had pneumonia waiting.' The whole country had ivy growing over it, he said, like ivy on a gravestone. Eating bacon and sausages with his special knife and fork, he nodded in agreement with himself. 'Ivy-clad Ireland,' he said when his mouth was momentarily empty of food. 'Anthracite motor-cars, refrigerators on the Great Southern Railway. Another thing, Molly: it's the opinion in Dublin that six months' time will see foreign soldiers parading themselves on O'Connell Street. German or English, take your pick, and there's damn all Dev can do about it.'

My mother smiled at him and sighed. Then, as though to cheer us all up, my father told a story that Mr McNamara had told him, about a coal merchant whom Mr McNamara had apparently known in his youth. The story had to do with the ill-fitting nature of the coal merchant's artificial teeth, and the loss of the teeth when he'd once been swimming at Ringsend. Whenever my father returned from a meeting with Mr McNamara he brought us back such stories, as well as the current opinion of Mr Mc-Namara on the state of the nation and the likelihood of the nation becoming involved in the war. 'The opinion in Dublin' was the opinion of Mr McNamara, as we all knew. Mr McNamara drove a motor-car powered by gas because there wasn't much petrol to be had. The gas, so my father said, was manufactured by anthracite in a burner stuck on to the back of Mr McNamara's Ford V-8.

Returning each time from Dublin, my father bore messages and gifts from Mr McNamara, a tin of Jacob's biscuits or bars of chocolate. He was a man who'd never married and who lived on inherited means, in a house in Palmerston Road, with members of his family – the elderly alcoholic aunt who should have been in an asylum, a sister and a brother-in-law. The sister, now Mrs Matchette, had earlier had theatrical ambitions, but her husband, employed in the National Bank, had persuaded her away from them. My father had never actually met Mr McNamara's insane aunt or Mrs Matchette or her husband: they lived through Mr McNamara for him, at second hand, and for us they lived through my father, at a further remove. We had a vivid image of all of them, Mrs Matchette thin as a blade of grass, endlessly smoking and playing patience, her husband small and solemn, neatly moustached, with dark neat hair combed straight back from what Mr McNamara had called a 'squashed forehead'. Mr McNamara himself we imagined as something of a presence: prematurely white-haired, portly, ponderous in speech and motion. Mr McNamara used to frequent the bar of a hotel called Fleming's, an old-fashioned place where you could get snuff as well as tobacco, and tea, coffee and Bovril as well as alcoholic drinks. It was here that my father met him on his visits to Dublin. It was a comfort to go there, my father said, when his business for the day was done, to sit in a leather chair and listen to the chit-chat of his old companion. The bar would fill with smoke from their Sweet Afton cigarettes, while my father listened to the latest about the people in the house in Palmerston Road, and the dog they had, a spaniel called Wolfe Tone, and a maid called Kate O'Shea, from Skibbereen. There was ritual about it, my father smoking and listening, just as a day or so later he'd smoke and we'd listen ourselves, at breakfast-time in our house in the country.

There were my three sisters and myself: I was the oldest, the only boy.

We lived in a house that had been in the family for several generations, three miles from Curransbridge, where the Dublin train halted if anyone wanted it to, and where my father's granary and mill were. Because of the shortage of petrol, my father used to walk the three miles there and back every day. Sometimes he'd persuade Flannagan, who worked in the garden for us, to collect him in the dog-cart in the evening, and always when he went to Dublin he arranged for Flannagan to meet the train he returned on. In the early hours of the morning I'd sometimes hear the rattle of the dog-cart on the avenue and then the wheels on the gravel outside the front of the house. At breakfast-time the next morning my father would say he was glad to be back again, and kiss my mother with the rest of us. The whole thing occurred once every month or so, the going away in the first place, the small packed suitcase in the hall, my father in his best tweed suit, Flannagan and the dog-cart. And the returning a few days later: breakfast with Mr McNamara, my sister Charlotte used to say.

As a family we belonged to the past. We were Protestants in what had become Catholic Ireland. We'd once been part of an ascendancy, but now it was not so. Now there was the income from the granary and the mill, and the house we lived in: we sold grain and flour, we wielded no power. 'Proddy-woddy green-guts,' the Catholic children cried at us in Currans-bridge. 'Catty, Catty, going to Mass,' we whispered back, 'riding on the devil's ass.' They were as good as we were. It had not always been assumed so, and it sometimes seemed part of all the changing and the shifting of this and that, that Mr McNamara, so honoured in our house, was a Catholic himself. 'A liberal, tolerant man,' my father used to say. 'No trace of the bigot in him.' In time, my father used to say, religious differences in Ireland wouldn't exist. The war would sort the whole matter out, even though as yet Ireland wasn't involved in it. When the war was over, and whether there was involvement or not, there wouldn't be any patience with religious differences. So, at least, Mr McNamara appeared to argue.

Childhood was all that: my sisters, Charlotte, Amelia and Frances, and my parents gentle with each other, and Flannagan in the garden and Bridget our maid, and the avuncular spirit of Mr McNamara. There was Miss Sheil as well, who arrived every morning on an old Raleigh bicycle, to teach the four of us, since the school at Curransbridge was not highly thought of by my parents.

The house itself was a Georgian rectangle when you looked straight at it, spaciously set against lawns which ran back to the curved brick of the kitchen-garden wall, with a gravel sweep in front, and an avenue running straight as a die for a mile and a half through fields where sheep grazed.

My sisters had some world of their own which I knew I could not properly share. Charlotte, the oldest of them, was five years younger than I was, Amelia was six and Frances five.

'Ah, he was in great form,' my father said on the morning of my thirteenth birthday. 'After a day listening to rubbish it's a pleasure to take a ball of malt with him.'

Frances giggled. When my father called a glass of whiskey a ball of malt Frances always giggled, and besides it was a giggly occasion. All my presents were sitting there on the sideboard, waiting for my father to finish his breakfast and to finish telling us about Mr McNamara. But my father naturally took precedence: after all, he'd been away from the house for three days, he'd been cold and delayed on the train home, and attending to business in Dublin was something he disliked in any case. This time, though, as well as his business and the visit to Fleming's Hotel to see Mr McNamara, I knew he'd bought the birthday present that he and my mother would jointly give me. Twenty minutes ago he'd walked into the dining-room with the wrapped parcel under his arm. 'Happy birthday, boy,' he'd said, placing the parcel on the sideboard beside the other three, from my sisters. It was the tradition in our house – a rule of my father's – that breakfast must be over and done with, every scrap eaten, before anyone opened a birthday present or a Christmas present.

'It was McNamara said that,' my father continued. 'Ivy-clad Ireland. It's the neutral condition of us.'

It was my father's opinion, though not my mother's, that Ireland should have acceded to Winston Churchill's desire to man the Irish ports with English soldiers in case the Germans got in there first. Hitler had sent a telegram to de Valera apologizing for the accidental bombing of a creamery, which was a suspicious gesture in itself. Mr McNamara, who also believed that de Valera should hand over the ports to Churchill, said that any gentlemanly gesture on the part of the German Führer was invariably followed by an act of savagery. Mr McNamara, in spite of being a Catholic, was a keen admirer of the House of Windsor and of the English people. There was no aristocracy in the world to touch the English, he used to say, and no people, intent on elegance, succeeded as the English upper classes did. Class-consciousness in England was no bad thing, Mr McNamara used to argue.

My father took from the side pocket of his jacket a small wrapped object. As he did so, my sisters rose from the breakfast table and marched to the sideboard. One by one my presents were placed before me, my parents' brought from the sideboard by my mother. It was a package about two and a half feet long, a few inches in width. It felt like a bundle of twigs and was in fact the various parts of a box-kite. Charlotte had bought me a book called *Dickon the Impossible*, Amelia a kaleidoscope. 'Open mine exceedingly carefully,' Frances said. I did, and at first I thought it was a pot of jam. It was a goldfish in a jar.

'From Mr McNamara,' my father said, pointing at the smallest package. I'd forgotten it, because already the people who normally gave me presents were accounted for. 'I happened to mention,' my father said, 'that today was a certain day.'

It was so heavy that I thought it might be a lead soldier, or a horseman. In fact it was a dragon. It was tiny and complicated, and it appeared to be made of gold, but my father assured me it was brass. It had two green eyes that Frances said were emeralds, and small pieces let into its back which she said looked like rubies. 'Priceless,' she whispered jealously. My father laughed and shook his head. The eyes and the pieces in the brass back were glass, he said.

I had never owned so beautiful an object. I watched it being passed from hand to hand around the breakfast table, impatient to feel it again myself. 'You must write at once to Mr McNamara,' my mother said. 'It's far too generous of him,' she added, regarding my father with some slight disapproval, as though implying that my father shouldn't have accepted the gift. He vaguely shook his head, lighting a Sweet Afton. 'Give me the letter when you've done it,' he said. 'I have to go up again in a fortnight.'

I showed the dragon to Flannagan, who was thinning beetroot in the garden. I showed it to Bridget, our maid. 'Aren't you the lucky young hero?' Flannagan said, taking the dragon in a soil-caked hand. 'You'd get a five-pound note for that fellow, anywhere you cared to try.' Bridget polished it with Brasso for me.

That day I had a chocolate birthday cake, and sardine sandwiches, which were my favourite, and brown bread and greengage jam, a favourite also. After tea all the family watched while my father and I tried to fly the kite, running with it from one end of a lawn to the other. It was Flannagan who got it up for us in the end, and I remember the excitement of the string tugging at my fingers, and Bridget crying out that she'd never seen a thing like that before, wanting to know what it was for. 'Don't forget, dear, to write to Mr McNamara first thing in the morning,' my mother reminded me when she kissed me good-night. I wouldn't forget, I promised, and didn't add that of all my presents, including the beautiful green and yellow kite, I liked the dragon best.

But I never did write to Mr McNamara. The reason was that the next day was a grim nightmare of a day, during all of which someone in the house was weeping, and often several of us together. My father, so affectionate towards all of us, was no longer alive.

The war continued and Ireland continued to play no part in it. Further accidental German bombs were dropped and further apologies were sent to de Valera by the German Führer. Winston Churchill continued to fulminate about the ports, but the prophecy of Mr McNamara that foreign soldiers would parade in O'Connell Street did not come true.

Knitting or sewing, my mother listened to the BBC news with a sadness in her eyes, unhappy that elsewhere death was occurring also. It was no help to any of us to be reminded that people in Britain and Europe were dying all the time now, with the same sudden awfulness as my father had.

Everything was different after my father died. My mother and I began to go for walks together. I'd take her arm, and sometimes her hand, knowing she was lonely. She talked about him to me, telling me about their honeymoon in Venice, the huge square where they'd sat drinking chocolate, listening to the bands that played there. She told me about my own birth, and how my father had given her a ring set with amber which he'd bought in Louis Wine's in Dublin. She would smile at me on our walks and tell me that even though I was only thirteen I was already taking his place. One day the house would be mine, she pointed out, and the granary and the mill. I'd marry, she said, and have children of my own, but I didn't want even to think about that. I didn't want to marry; I wanted my mother always to be there with me, going on walks and telling me about the person we all missed so much. We were still a family, my sisters and my mother and myself, Flannagan in the garden, and Bridget. I didn't want anything to change.

After the death of my father Mr McNamara lived on, though in a different kind of way. The house in Palmerston Road, with Mr McNamara's aunt drinking in an upstairs room, and the paper-thin Mrs Matchette playing patience instead of being successful in the theatre, and Mr Matchette with his squashed forehead, and Kate O'Shea from Skibbereen, and the spaniel called Wolfe Tone: all of them remained quite vividly alive after my father's death, as part of our memory of him. Fleming's Hotel remained also, and all the talk there'd been there of the eccentric household in Palmerston Road. For almost as long as I could remember, and certainly as long as my sisters could remember, our own household had regularly been invaded by the other one, and after my father's death my sisters and I often recalled specific incidents retailed in Fleming's Hotel and later at our breakfast table. There'd been the time when Mr McNamara's aunt had sold the house to a man she'd met outside a public house. And the time when Mrs Matchette appeared to have fallen in love with Garda Molloy, who used to call in at the kitchen for Kate O'Shea every night. And the time the spaniel was run over by a van and didn't die. All of it was preserved, with Mr McNamara himself, white-haired and portly in the smoke-brown bar of Fleming's Hotel, where snuff could be bought, and Bovril as well as whiskey.

A few months after the death my mother remarked one breakfast-time that no doubt Mr McNamara had seen the obituary notice in the *Irish Times*. 'Oh, but you should write,' my sister Frances cried out in her excitable manner. My mother shook her head. My father and Mr Mc-Namara had been bar-room friends, she pointed out: letters in either direction would not be in order. Charlotte and Amelia agreed with this opinion, but Frances still protested. I couldn't see that it mattered. 'He gave us all that chocolate,' Frances cried, 'and the biscuits.' My mother said again that Mr McNamara was not the kind of man to write to about a death, nor the kind who would write himself. The letter that I was to have written thanking him for the dragon was not mentioned. Disliking the writing of letters, I didn't raise the subject myself.

At the end of that year I was sent to a boarding-school in the Dublin mountains. Miss Sheil continued to come to the house on her Raleigh to teach my sisters, and I'd have far preferred to have remained at home with her. It could not be: the boarding-school in the Dublin mountains, a renowned Protestant monument, had been my father's chosen destiny for me and that was that. If he hadn't died, leaving home might perhaps have been more painful, but the death had brought with it practical complications and troubles, mainly concerned with the running of the granary and the mill: going away to school was slight compared with all that, or so my mother convinced me.

The headmaster of the renowned school was a small, red-skinned English cleric. With other new boys, I had tea with him and his wife in the drawing-room some days after term began. We ate small ham-paste sandwiches and Battenburg cake. The headmaster's wife, a cold woman in grey, asked me what I intended to do – 'in life', as she put it. I said I'd run a granary and a mill at Curransbridge; she didn't seem interested. The headmaster told us he was in *Who's Who*. Otherwise the talk was of the war.

Miss Sheil had not prepared me well. 'Dear boy, whoever taught you French?' a man with a pipe asked me, and did not stay to hear my answer. 'Your Latin, really!' another man exclaimed, and the man who taught me mathematics warned me never to set my sights on a profession that involved an understanding of figures. I sat in the back row of the class with other boys who had been ill-prepared for the renowned school.

I don't know when it was – a year, perhaps, or eighteen months after my first term – that I developed an inquisitiveness about my father. Had he, I wondered, been as bad at everything as I was? Had some other man with a pipe scorned his inadequacy when it came to French? Had he felt, as I did, a kind of desperation when faced with algebra? You'd *have* to know a bit about figures, I used, almost miserably, to say to myself: you'd have to if you hoped to run a granary and a mill. Had he been good at mathematics?

I asked my mother these questions, and other questions like them. But my mother was vague in her replies and said she believed, although perhaps she was wrong, that my father had not been good at mathematics. She laughed when I asked the questions. She told me to do my best.

But the more I thought about the future, and about myself in terms of the man whose place I was to take, the more curious I became about him. In the holidays my mother and I still went on our walks together, through the garden and then into the fields that stretched behind it, along the banks of the river that flowed through Curransbridge. But my mother spoke less and less about my father because increasingly there was less to say, except with repetition. I imagined the huge square in Venice and the cathedral and the bands playing outside the cafés. I imagined hundreds of other scenes, her own varied memories of their relationship and their marriage. We often walked in silence now, or I talked more myself, drawing her into a world of cross-country runs, and odorous changing-rooms, and the small headmaster's repeated claim that the food we ate had a high calorific value. School was ordinarily dreary: I told her how we smoked wartime American cigarettes in mud huts specially constructed for the purpose and how we relished the bizarre when, now and again, it broke the monotony. There was a master called Mr Dingle, whose practice it was to inquire of new boys the colour and nature of their mother's night-dresses. In the oak-panelled dining-hall that smelt of mince and the butter that generations had flicked on to the ceiling, Mr Dingle's eye would glaze as he sat at the end of a Junior House table while one boy after another fuelled him with the stuff of fantasies. On occasions when parents visited the school he would observe through cigarette smoke the mothers of these new boys, stripping them of their skirts and blouses in favour of the night-clothes that their sons had described for him. There was another master, known as Nipper Achen, who was reputed to take a sensual interest in the sheep that roamed the mountainsides, and a boy called Testane-Hackett who was possessed of the conviction that he was the second son of God. In the dining-hall a gaunt black-clad figure, a butler called Toland, hovered about the high table where the headmaster and the prefects sat, assisted by a maid, said to be his daughter, who was known to us as the Bicycle. There was Fisher Major, who never washed, and Strapping, who disastrously attempted to treat some kind of foot ailment with mild acid. My mother listened appreciatively, and I often saw in her eyes the same look that had been there at breakfast-time when my father spoke of Fleming's Hotel and Mr McNamara. 'How like him you are!' she now and again murmured, smiling at me.

At Curransbridge I stood in his office above the mill, a tiny room now occupied by the man my mother had chosen to look after things, a Mr Myers. In the house I rooted through the belongings he'd left behind; I stared at photographs of him. With Flannagan and my sisters I flew the kite he'd bought me that last time he'd been to Dublin. I polished the small brass dragon that his bar-room companion had given him to give to me. 'It's the boy's birthday,' I imagined him saying in the brown bar of Fleming's Hotel, and I imagined the slow movement of Mr McNamara's hand as he drew the dragon from his pocket. It was inevitable, I suppose, that sooner or later I should seek out Fleming's Hotel.

'An uncle,' I said to the small headmaster. 'Passing through Dublin, sir.'

'Passing? Passing?' He had a Home Counties accent and a hard nasal intonation. 'Passing?' he said again, giving the word an extra vowel sound.

'On his way to Galway, sir. He's in the RAF, sir. I think he'd like to see me, sir, because my father —'

'Ah, yes, yes. Back in time for Chapel, please.'

Fleming's Hotel, it said in the telephone directory, *21 Wheeler Street*. As I cycled down from the mountains, I didn't know what I was going to do when I got there.

It was a narrow, four-storey building in a terrace with others, a bleak-looking stone façade. The white woodwork of the windows needed a coat of paint, the glass portico over the entrance doors had a dusty look. It was on this dusty glass that the name *Fleming's Hotel* was picked out in white enamel letters stuck to the glass itself. I cycled past the hotel twice, glancing at the windows — a dozen of them, the four at the top much smaller than the others — and at the entrance doors. No one left or entered. I propped the bicycle against the edge of the pavement some distance away from the hotel, outside what seemed to be the street's only shop, a greengrocer's. There were pears in the window. I went in and bought one.

I wheeled the bicycle away from the shop and came, at the end of the street, to a canal. Slowly I ate the pear, and then I took my red-and-green school cap from my head and wheeled my bicycle slowly back to Fleming's

Hotel. I pushed open one of the entrance doors and for a split second I heard my father's voice again, describing what I now saw: the smokiness of the low-ceilinged hall, a coal fire burning, and a high reception counter with the hotel's register open on it, and a brass bell beside the register. There were brown leather armchairs in the hall and a brown leather bench running along one wall. Gas lamps were lit but even so, and in spite of the fact that it was four o'clock in the afternoon, the hall was dim. It was empty of other people and quiet. A tall grandfather clock ticked, the fire occasionally hissed. There was a smell of some kind of soup. It was the nicest, most comfortable hall I'd ever been in.

Beyond it, I could see another coal fire, through an archway. That was the bar where they used to sit, where for all I knew Mr McNamara was sitting now. I imagined my father crossing the hall as I crossed it myself. The bar was the same as the hall, with the same kind of leather chairs, and a leather bench and gas lamps and a low ceiling. There were net curtains pulled across the two windows, and one wall was taken up with a counter, with bottles on shelves behind it, and leather-topped stools in front of it. There was a woman sitting by the fire drinking orange-coloured liquid from a small glass. Behind the bar a man in a white jacket was reading the *Irish Independent*.

I paused in the archway that divided the bar from the hall. I was under age. I had no right to take a further step and I didn't know what to do or to say if I did. I didn't know what drink to order. I didn't know if in the dim gaslight I looked a child.

I went to the bar and stood there. The man didn't look up from his newspaper. *Smithwick's Ale* were words on the labels of bottles: I would ask for a Smithwick's Ale. All I wanted was to be allowed to remain, to sit down with the beer and to think about my father. If Mr McNamara did not come today he'd come another day. Frances had been right: he should have been written to. I should have written to him myself, to thank my father's friend for his present.

'Good evening,' the barman said.

'Smithwick's, please,' I said as casually as I could. Not knowing how much the drink might be, I placed a ten-shilling note on the bar.

'Drop of lime in it, sir?'

'Lime? Oh, yes. Yes, please. Thanks very much.'

'Choppy kind of day,' the barman said.

I took the glass and my change, and sat down as far as possible from where the woman was sitting. I sat so that I was facing both the bar and the archway, so that if Mr McNamara came in I'd see him at once. I'd have to leave at six o'clock in order to be safely back for Chapel at seven.

I finished the beer. I took an envelope out of my pocket and drew pieces of holly on the back of it, a simple art-form that Miss Sheil had taught all of us. I took my glass to the bar and asked for another Smithwick's. The barman had a pale, unhealthy-seeming face, and wire-rimmed glasses, and a very thin neck. 'You do want the best, don't you?' he said in a joky kind of voice, imitating someone. 'Bird's Custard,' he said in the same joky way, 'and Bird's Jelly de Luxe.' My father had mentioned this barman: he was repeating the advertisements of Radio Eireann. 'You do want the best, don't you?' he said again, pushing the glass of beer towards me. By the fire, the woman made a noise, a slight, tired titter of amusement. I laughed myself, politely too.

When I returned to my armchair I found the woman was looking at me. I wondered if she could be a prostitute, alone in a hotel bar like that. A boy at school called Yeats claimed that prostitutes hung about railway stations mostly, and on quays. But there was of course no reason why you shouldn't come across one in a bar.

Yet she seemed too quietly dressed to be a prostitute. She was wearing a green suit and a green hat, and there was a coat made of some kind of fur draped over a chair near the chair she sat on. She was a dark-haired woman with an oval face. I'd no idea what age she was: somewhere between thirty and forty, I imagined: I wasn't good at guessing people's ages.

The Smithwick's Ale was having an effect on me. I wanted to giggle. How extraordinary it would be, I thought, if a prostitute tried to sell herself to me in my father's and Mr McNamara's hotel. After all, there was no reason at all why some prostitutes shouldn't be quietly dressed, probably the more expensive ones were. I could feel myself smiling, holding back the giggle. Naturally enough, I thought, my father hadn't mentioned the presence of prostitutes in Fleming's Hotel. And then I thought that perhaps, if he'd lived, he would have told me one day, when my sisters and my mother weren't in the room. It was the kind of thing, surely, that fathers did tell sons.

I took the envelope I'd drawn the holly on out of my pocket and read the letter it contained. They were managing, my mother said. Miss Sheil had had a dose of flu, Charlotte and Amelia wanted to breed horses, Frances didn't know what she wanted to do. His rheumatics were slowing Flannagan down a bit in the garden. Bridget was insisting on sweeping the drawing-room chimney. *It'll be lovely at Christmas*, she wrote. *So nice being all together again.*

The oval-faced woman put on her fur coat, and on her way from the bar she passed close to where I was sitting. She looked down and smiled at me.

'Hills of the North, rejoice!' we sang in chapel that night. 'Valley and lowland, sing!'

I smelt of Smithwick's Ale. I knew I did because as we'd stood in line in Cloisters several other boys had remarked on it. As I sang, I knew I was puffing the smell all over everyone else. 'Like a bloody brewery,' Gahan Minor said afterwards.

'... this night,' intoned the small headmaster nasally, 'and for ever more.'

'Amen,' we all replied.

Saturday night was a pleasant time. After Chapel there were two and a half hours during which you could do more or less what you liked, provided the master on duty knew where you were. You could work in the printing shop or read in the library, or take part in a debate, such as that this school is an outpost of the British Empire, or play billiards or do carpentry, or go to the model-railway club or the music-rooms. At half past nine there was some even freer time, during which the master on duty didn't have to know where you were. Most boys went for a smoke then.

After Chapel on the Saturday night after I'd visited Fleming's Hotel I read in the library. I read *Jane Eyre*, but all the time the oval face of the woman in the hotel kept appearing in my mind. It would stay there for a few seconds and then fade, and then return. Again and again, as I read *Jane Eyre*, she passed close to my chair in the bar of Fleming's Hotel, and looked down and smiled at me.

The end of that term came. The Sixth Form and Remove did *Macbeth* on the last two nights, A. McC. P. Jackson giving what was generally regarded as a fine performance as Banquo. Someone stole the secondhand Penguin I'd bought from Grace Major to read on the train, *Why Didn't They Ask Evans?* Drumgoole and Montgomery were found conversing in the shower-room in the middle of the night.

On the journey home I was unable to stop thinking about Fleming's Hotel. A man in the carriage lent me a copy of *Barrack Variety*, but the jokes didn't seem funny. It was at moments like these that the truth most harshly mocked me. Ever since I'd found the hotel, ever since the woman had stared at me, it had been a part of every day, and for whole nights in my long, cheerless dormitory I had been unable to sleep. My father's voice had returned to me there, telling again the stories of his friend, and reminding me of his friend's opinions. My father had disagreed with my mother in her view that de Valera should not hand over the ports to Churchill, preferring to share the view of his friend. At school and on the train, and most of all when I returned home, the truth made me feel ill, as though I had flu.

That Christmas morning we handed each other our presents, after we'd eaten, still observing my father's rule. We thought of him then, they in one way, I in another. 'Oh, my dear, how lovely!' my mother whispered over some ornament I'd bought her in a Dublin shop. I had thrown the dragon with the green glass eyes far into a lake near the school, unable to understand how my father had ever brought it to the house, or brought bars of chocolate or tins of Jacob's biscuits. To pass to his children beneath my mother's eyes the gifts of another woman seemed as awful a sin as any father could commit, yet somehow it was not as great as the sin of sharing with all of us this other woman's eccentric household, her sister and her sister's husband, her alcoholic aunt, a maid and a dog. 'That's Nora McNamara,' the barman's voice seemed to say again at our breakfast table, and I imagined them sitting there, my father and she, in that comfortable bar, and my father listening to her talk of the house in Palmerston Road and of how she admired the English aristocracy. I watched my mother smile that Christmas morning, and I wanted to tell the truth because the truth was neat and without hypocrisy: I wanted carefully to say that I was glad my father was dead.

Instead I left the breakfast table and went to my bedroom. I wept there, and then washed my face in cold water from the jug on my wash-stand. I hated the memory of him and how he would have been that Christmas morning; I hated him for destroying everything. It was no consolation to me then that he had tried to share with us a person he loved in a way that was different from the way he loved us. I could neither forgive nor understand. I felt only bitterness that I, who had taken his place, must now continue his deception, and keep the secret of his lies and his hypocrisy.

Afternoon Dancing

Every summer since the war the two couples had gone to Southend in September, staying in Mrs Roope's Prospect Hotel. They'd known each other since childhood: Poppy and Albert, Alice and Lenny. They'd been to the same schools, they'd all been married in the summer of 1938. They rented houses in the same street, Paper Street, SE4, Poppy and Albert Number 10, and Alice and Lenny Number 41. They were all in their mid-fifties now, and except for Poppy they'd all run to fat a bit. Len was a printer, Albert was employed by the London Electricity Board, as a cable-layer. Every night the two men had a few drinks together in the Cardinal Wolsey in Northbert Road, round the corner from Paper Street. Twice a week, on Wednesdays and Fridays, the wives went to Bingo. Alice's children – Beryl and Ron – were now married and had children of their own. Poppy's son, Mervyn, married also, had gone to Canada in 1969.

Poppy was very different from Alice. Alice was timid, she'd never had Poppy's confidence. In middle age Poppy was a small, wiry woman with glasses, the worrying kind you might think to look at her, only Poppy didn't worry at all. Poppy was always laughing, nudging Alice when they were together on a bus, drawing attention to some person who amused her. 'Poppy Edwards, you're a holy terror!' Miss Curry of Tatterall Elementary School had pronounced forty years ago, and in lots of ways Poppy was a holy terror still. She'd been a slaphappy mother and was a slaphappy wife, not caring much what people thought if her child wasn't as meticulously turned out as other children, or if Albert's sandwiches were carelessly made. Once, back in 1941 when Albert was in the army, she'd begun to keep company with a man who was an air-raid warden, whose bad health had prevented him from joining one of the armed forces. When the war came to an end she was still involved with this man and it had seemed likely then that she and Albert would not continue to live together. Alice had been worried about it all, but then, a month before Albert was due to be demobbed, the man had been knocked down by an army truck in Holborn and had instantly died. Albert remained in ignorance of everything, even though most people in Paper Street knew just what had been going on and how close Albert had come to finding himself wifeless. In those days Poppy had been a slim, small girl in her twenties, with yellow hair that looked as though it had been peroxided but which in fact hadn't, and light-blue mischievous eyes. Alice had been plumper, dark-haired and reliable-looking, pretty in her nice-girl way. Beryl and Ron had not been born yet.

During the war, with their two husbands serving in Italy and Africa together, Poppy had repeatedly urged Alice to let her hair down a bit, as she herself was doing with the air-raid warden. They were all going to be blown up, she argued, and if Alice thought that Lenny and Albert weren't chancing their arms with the local talent in Italy and Africa then Alice definitely had another think coming. But Alice, even after Lenny confessed that he'd once chanced his arm through physical desperation, couldn't bring herself to emulate the easy attitudes of her friend. The air-raid warden was always producing friends for her, men whose health wasn't good either, but Alice chatted politely to each of them and made it clear that she didn't wish for a closer relationship. With peace and the death of the air-raid warden, Poppy calmed down a bit, and the birth of her child eighteen months later calmed her down further.

But even so she was still the same Poppy, and in late middle age when she suggested that she and Alice should take up dancing again the idea seemed to Alice to be just like all the other ideas Poppy had had in the past: when they were seven, to take Mrs Grounds' washing off her line and peg it up on Mrs Bond's; when they were ten, to go to Woolworth's with Davie Rickard and slip packets of carrots from the counter into the pockets of his jacket; at fifteen, to write anonymous letters to every teacher who'd ever had anything to do with them; at sixteen, to cut the hair of people in the row in front of them in the Regal cinema. 'Dancing?' Alice said. 'Oh, Poppy, whatever would they say?'

Whatever would the two husbands say, she meant, and the other wives of Paper Street, and Beryl and Ron? Going to Bingo was one thing and quite accepted. Going dancing at fifty-four was a different kettle of fish altogether. Before their marriages they had often gone dancing: they had been taken to dance-halls on Saturday nights by the men they later married, and by other men. Every June, all four of them went dancing once or twice in Southend, even though the husbands increasingly complained that it made them feel ridiculous. But what Poppy had in mind now wasn't the Grand Palais in Southend or the humbler floors of thirty years ago, or embarrassed husbands, or youths treading over your feet: what Poppy had in mind was afternoon dancing in a place in the West End, without the husbands or anyone else knowing a thing about it. 'Teatime foxtrots,' Poppy said. 'The Tottenham Court Dance-Rooms. All the rage, they are.' And in the end Alice agreed.

They went quite regularly to the Tottenham Court Dance-Rooms, almost every Tuesday. They dressed up as they used to dress up years ago; with discretion they applied rouge and eye-shadow. Alice put on a peach-coloured corset in an effort to trim down her figure a bit, and curled the hair that had once been fair and now was grey. It looked a bit frizzy when she curled it now, the way it had never done when she was a girl, but although the sight of it sometimes depressed her she accepted the middle-aged frizziness because there was nothing she could do about it. Poppy's hair had become rather thin on the top of her head, but she didn't seem to notice and Alice naturally didn't mention the fact. In middle age Poppy always kept her grey hair dyed a brightish shade of chestnut, and when Alice once read in a magazine that excessive dying eventually caused a degree of baldness she didn't mention it either, fearing that in Poppy's case the damage was already done. On their dancing afternoons they put on headscarves and pulled their coats carefully about them, to hide the finery beneath. Poppy wore spectacles with gold-coloured trim on the orange frames, her special-occasion spectacles she called them. They always walked quickly away from Paper Street.

In the dance-rooms they had tea on the balcony as soon as they arrived, at about a quarter to three. There was a lot of scarlet plush on the balcony, and scarlet lights. There were little round tables with paper covers on them, for convenience. When they'd had tea and Danish pastries, and a few slices of Swiss roll, they descended one of the staircases that led to the dance-floor and stood chatting by a pillar. Sometimes men came up to them and asked if one or other would like to dance. They didn't mind if men came up or not, or at least they didn't mind particularly. What they enjoyed was the band, usually Leo Ritz and his Band, and looking at the other dancers and the scarlet plush and having tea. Years ago they'd have danced together, just for the fun of it, but somehow they felt too old for that, at fifty-four. An elderly man with rather long grey hair once danced too intimately with Alice and she'd had to ask him to release her. Another time a middle-aged man, not quite sober, kept following them about, trying to buy them Coca-Cola. He was from Birmingham, he told them; he was in London on business and had had lunch with people who were making a cartoon film for his firm. He described the film so that they could look out for it on their television screens: it was an advertisement for wallpaper paste, which was what his firm manufactured. They were glad when this man didn't appear the following Tuesday.

Other men were nicer. There was one who said his name was Sidney, who was lonely because his wife had left him for a younger man; and another who was delicate, a Mr Hawke. There was a silent, bald-headed man whom they both liked dancing with because he was so good at it, and there was Grantly Palmer, who was said to have won awards for dancing in the West Indies.

Grantly Palmer was a Jamaican, a man whom neither of them had agreed to dance with when he'd first asked them because of his colour. He worked as a barman in a club, he told them later, and because of that he rarely had the opportunity to dance at night. He'd often thought of changing his job since dancing meant so much to him, but bar work was all he knew. In the end they became quite friendly with Grantly Palmer, so much so that whenever they entered the dance-rooms he'd hurry up to them smiling, neat as a new pin. He'd dance with one and then the other. Tea had to wait, and when eventually they sat down to it he sat with them and insisted on paying. He was always attentive, pressing Swiss roll on both of them and getting them cigarettes from the coin machine. He talked about the club where he worked, the Rumba Rendezvous in Notting Hill Gate, and often tried to persuade them to give it a try. They giggled quite girlishly at that, wondering what their husbands would say about their attending the Rumba Rendezvous, a West Indian Club. Their husbands would have been astonished enough if they knew they went afternoon tea-dancing in the Tottenham Court Dance-Rooms.

Grantly Palmer was a man of forty-two who had never married, who lived alone in a room in Maida Vale. He was a born bachelor, he told the two wives, and would not have appreciated home life, with children and all that it otherwise implied. In his youth he had played the pins, he informed them with an elaborate, white smile, meaning by this that he'd had romantic associations. He would laugh loudly when he said it. He'd been naughty in his time, he said.

Whenever he talked like that, with his eyes blazing excitedly and his teeth flashing, Alice couldn't help thinking that Grantly Palmer was a holy terror just like Poppy had been and still in a way was, the male equivalent. She once said this to Poppy and immediately regretted it, fearing that Poppy would take offence at being likened to a black man, but Poppy hadn't minded at all. Poppy had puffed at a tipped Embassy and had made Alice blush all over her neck by saying that in her opinion Grantly Palmer fancied her. 'Skin and bone he'd think me,' Poppy said. 'Blacks like a girl they can get their teeth into.' They were on the upper deck of a bus at the time and Poppy had laughed shrilly into her cigarette smoke, causing people to glance amusedly at her. She peered through her gold-trimmed spectacles at the people who looked at her, smiling at them. 'My friend has a fella in love with her,' she said to the conductor, shouting after him as he clattered down the stairs. 'A holy terror she says he is.'

He was cheeky, Alice said, the way he always insisted on walking off the dance-floor hand in hand with you, the way he'd pinch your arm sometimes. But her complaints were half-hearted because the liberties Grantly Palmer took were never offensive: it wasn't at all the same as having a drunk pulling you too close to him and slobbering into your hair. 'You'll lose him, Alice,' Poppy cried now and again in shrill mock-alarm as they watched him paying attentions to some woman who was new to the dance-rooms. Once he'd referred to such a person, asking them if they'd noticed her, a stout woman in pink, an unmarried shorthand typist he said she was. 'My, my,' he said in his Jamaican drawl, shaking his head. 'My, my.' They never saw the unmarried shorthand typist again, but Poppy said he'd definitely been implying something, that he'd probably enticed her to his room in Maida Vale. 'Making you jealous,' Poppy said.

The men whom Alice and Poppy had married weren't at all like Grantly Palmer. They were quiet men, rather similar in appearance and certainly similar in outlook. Both were of medium build, getting rather bald in their fifties, Alice's Lenny with a moustache, Poppy's Albert without. They were keen supporters of Crystal Palace Football Club, and neither of them, according to Poppy, knew anything about women. The air-raid warden had known about women, Poppy said, and so did Grantly Palmer. 'He wants you to go out with him,' she said to Alice. 'You can see it in his eyes.' One afternoon when he was dancing with Alice he asked her if she'd consider having a drink on her own with him, some evening when she wasn't doing anything better. She shook her head when he said that, and he didn't ever bring the subject up again. 'He's mad for you,' Poppy said when she heard of this invitation. 'He's head over heels, love.' But Alice laughed, unable to believe that Grantly Palmer could possibly be mad for a corseted grandmother of fifty-four with unmanageable grey hair.

Without much warning, Poppy died. During a summer holiday at Mrs Roope's Prospect Hotel she'd complained of pains, though not much, because that was not her way. 'First day back you'll see Dr Pace,' Albert commanded. Two months later she died one night, without waking up.

After the death Alice was at a loss. For almost fifty years Poppy had been her friend. The affection between them had increased as they'd watched one another age and as their companionship yielded more memories they could share. Their children – Alice's Beryl and Ron, and Poppy's Mervyn – had played together. There'd been the business of Mervyn's emigration to Canada, and Alice's comforting of Poppy because of it. There'd been the marriage of Ron and then of Beryl, and Poppy's expression of Alice's unspoken thought, that Ron's Hilda wasn't good enough for him, too bossy for any man really, and Poppy's approval of Beryl's Tony, an approval that Alice shared.

Alice had missed her children when they'd gone, just as Poppy had missed Mervyn. 'Oh Lord, I know, dear!' Poppy cried when Alice wept the day after Beryl's wedding. Beryl had lived at home until then, as Ron had until his marriage. It was a help, being able to talk to Poppy about it, and Poppy so accurately understanding what Alice felt.

After Poppy's death the silence she'd prevented when Alice's children had grown up fell with a vengeance. It icily surrounded Alice and she found it hard to adapt herself to a life that was greyer and quieter, to days going by without Poppy dropping in or she herself dropping in on Poppy, without the cups of Maxwell House coffee they'd had together, and the cups of tea, and the biscuits and raspberry-jam sandwich cake, which Poppy had been fond of. Once, awake in the middle of the night, she found herself thinking that if Lenny had died she mightn't have missed him so much. She hated that thought and tried, unsuccessfully, to dispel it from her mind. It was because she and Poppy had told one another everything, she kept saying to herself, the way you couldn't really tell Lenny. But all this sounded rather lame, and when she said to herself instead that it was because she and Poppy had known one another all their lives it didn't sound much better: she and Lenny had known one another all their lives, too. For six months after the death she didn't go to Bingo, unable to face going on her own. It didn't even occur to her to go afternoon dancing.

The first summer after the death, Alice and Lenny and Albert went as usual to the Prospect Hotel in Southend. There seemed to the two men to be no good reason why they shouldn't, although when they arrived there Albert was suddenly silent and Alice could see that he was more upset than he'd imagined he would be. But after a day he was quite himself again, and when it wasn't necessary to cheer him up any more she began to feel miserable herself. It wasn't so much because of the death, but because she felt superfluous without Poppy. She realized gradually, and the two men realized even more gradually, that on previous holidays there had been no conversation that was general to all four of them: the men had talked to each other and so had their wives. The men did their best now to include Alice, but it was difficult and awkward.

She took to going for walks by herself, along the front and down the piers, out to the sea and back again. It was then, that summer at Southend, that Alice began to think about Grantly Palmer. It had never occurred to her before that he didn't even know that Poppy had died, even though they'd all three been such good friends on Tuesday afternoons at the Tottenham Court Dance-Rooms. She wondered what he thought, if he'd been puzzled by their sudden absence, or if he still attended the dance-rooms himself. One night in the Prospect Hotel, listening to the throaty breathing of her husband, she suddenly and quite urgently wanted to tell Grantly Palmer about Poppy's death. She suddenly felt that it was his due, that she'd been unkind not ever to have informed him. Poppy would wish him to know, she said to herself; it was bad that she'd let down her friend in this small way. In the middle of that night, while still listening to Lenny's breathing, she resolved to return to the Tottenham Court Dance-Rooms and found herself wondering if Leo Ritz and his Band would still be playing there.

'Breakfasts've gone down a bit,' Albert said on the way back to London, and Lenny reminded him that Mrs Roope had had a bit of family trouble. 'Dropped Charlie Cooke, I see,' Lenny said, referring to a Crystal Palace player. He handed Albert the *Daily Mirror*, open at the sports page. 'Dare say they'll be back to normal next year,' Albert said, still referring to the breakfasts.

In Paper Street, a week after their return, she put on her peach-coloured corset and the dress she'd worn the first time they'd gone afternoon dancing – blue-green satin, with a small array of sequins at the shoulders and the breast. It felt more silent than ever in the house in Paper Street, because in the past Poppy used to chat and giggle in just the same way as she had as a girl, lavishly spraying scent on herself, a habit she'd always had also. Alice closed the door of Number 41 behind her and walked quickly in Paper Street, feeling guiltier than she had when the guilt could be shared. She'd tell some lie if someone she knew said she was looking smart. She'd probably say she was going to Bingo, which was what they'd both said once when Mrs Tedman had looked them up and down, as though suspecting the finery beneath. You could see that Mrs Tedman hadn't believed that they were going to Bingo, but Poppy said it didn't matter what Mrs Tedman thought. It was all a bit frightening without Poppy, but then everything was something else without Poppy, dull or silent or frightening. Alice caught a bus, and at a quarter to three she entered the dance-rooms.

'Well, well!' Grantly Palmer said, smiling his bright smile. 'Well, well, stranger lady!'

'Hullo, Mr Palmer.'

'Oh, child, child!'

'Hullo, Grantly.'

It had always been a joke, the business of Christian names between the three of them. 'Alice and Poppy!' he'd said the first time they'd had tea together. 'My, my, what charmin' names!' They'd just begun to use his own Christian name when Poppy had died. 'Funny name, Grantly,' Poppy had remarked on the bus after he'd first told them, but soon it had become impossible to think of him as anything else.

'Where's Poppy, dear?'

'Poppy died, Grantly.'

She told him all about it, about last year's holiday at Southend and the development of the illness and then the funeral. 'My God!' he said, staring into her eyes. 'My God, Alice.'

The band was playing 'Lullaby of Broadway': middle-aged women, in twos or on their own, stood about, sizing up the men who approached them, in the same expert way as she and Poppy had sized men up in their time. 'Let's have a cup of tea,' Grantly Palmer said.

They had tea and Swiss-roll slices and Danish pastries. They talked about Poppy. 'Was she happy?' he asked. And Alice said her friend had been happy enough.

In silence on the balcony they watched the dancers rotating below them. He wasn't going to dance with her, she thought, because Poppy had died, because the occasion was a solemn one. She was aware of disappointment. Poppy had been dead for more than a year, after all.

'It's a horrible thing,' he said. 'A friend dying. In the prime of her life.'

'I miss her.'

'Of course, Alice.'

He reached across the tea-table and seized one of her hands. He held it for a moment and then let it go. It was a gesture that reminded her of being a girl. On television men touched girls' hands in that way. How nice, she suddenly thought, the chap called Ashley was in *Gone with the Wind*. She'd seen the film with Poppy, revived a few years back, Leslie Howard playing Ashley.

He went away and returned with another pot of tea and a plate of Swiss-roll slices. Leo Ritz and his Band were playing 'September Love'.

'I thought I'd never lay eyes on you again, Alice.'

He regarded her solemnly. He didn't smile when he said that the very first time he'd met her he'd considered her a very nice person. He was wearing a suit made of fine, black corduroy. His two grey hands were gripping his teacup, nursing it.

'I came back to tell you about Poppy, Grantly.'

'I kept on hoping you'd come back. I kept on thinking about you.' He nodded, lending emphasis to this statement. Without drinking from it, he placed his teacup on the table and pulled his chair in a bit, nearer to hers. She could feel some part of his legs, an ankle-bone it felt like. Then she felt one of his hands, beneath the table, touching her right knee and then touching the left one.

She didn't move. She gazed ahead of her, feeling through the material of her dress the warmth of his flesh. The first time they'd had tea with him he'd told a joke about three Jamaican clergymen on a desert island and she and Poppy had laughed their heads off. Even when it had become clear to Poppy and herself that what he was after was sex and not love, Poppy had still insisted that she should chance her arm with him. It was as though Poppy wanted her to go out with Grantly Palmer because she herself had gone out with the air-raid warden.

His hand remained on her left knee. She imagined it there, the thin grey hand on the blue satin material of her dress. It moved, pushing back the satin, the palm caressing, the tip of the thumb pressing into her thigh.

She withdrew her leg, smiling to cover the unfriendliness of this decision. She could feel warmth all over her neck and her cheeks and around her eyes. She could feel her eyes beginning to water. On her back and high up on her forehead, beneath the grey frizz of her hair, she felt the moisture of perspiration.

He looked away from her. 'I always liked you, Alice,' he said. 'You know? I liked you better than Poppy, even though I liked Poppy too.'

It was different, a man putting his hand on your knee: it was different altogether from the natural intimacy of dancing, when anything might have been accidental. She wanted to go away now; she didn't want him to ask her to dance with him. She imagined him with the pink woman, fondling her knees under a table before taking her to Maida Vale. She saw herself in the room in Maida Vale, a room in which there were lilies growing in pots, although she couldn't remember that he'd ever said he had lilies. There was a thing like a bedspread hanging on one of the walls, brightly coloured, red and blue and yellow. There was a gas-fire glowing and a standard lamp such as she'd seen in the British Home Stores, and a bed with a similar brightly coloured cloth covering it, and a table and two upright chairs, and a tattered green screen behind which there'd be a sink and a cooking stove. In the room he came to her and took her coat off and then undid the buttons of her dress. He lifted her petticoat over her head and unhooked her peach-coloured corset and her brassière.

'Will you dance with me, Alice?'

She shook her head. Her clothes were sticking to her now. Her armpits were clammy.

'Won't you dance, dear?'

She said she'd rather not, not today. Her voice shivered and drily crackled. She'd just come to tell him about Poppy, she said again.

'I'd like to be friends with you, Alice. Now that Poppy has –'

'I have to go home, Grantly. I have to.'

'Don't go, darling.'

His hands had crossed the table again. They held her wrists; his teeth and his eyes flashed at her, though not in a smiling way. She shouldn't have come, her own voice kept protesting in the depths of her mind, like an echo. It had all been different when there were three of them, all harmless flirtation, with Poppy giggling and pretending, just fun.

There was excitement in his face. He released her wrists, and again, beneath the table, she felt one of his legs against hers. He pushed his chair closer to the table, a hand moved on her thigh again.

'No, no,' she said.

'I looked for you. I don't know your other name, you know. I didn't know Poppy's either. I didn't know where you lived. But I looked for you, Alice.'

He didn't say how he'd looked for her, but repeated that he had, nodding emphatically.

'I thought if I found you we'd maybe have a drink one night. I have records in my room I'd like you to hear, Alice. I'd like to have your opinion.'

'I couldn't go to your room –'

'It would be just like sitting here, Alice. It would be quite all right.'

'I couldn't ever, Grantly.'

What would Beryl and Ron say if they could see her now, if they could hear the conversation she was having, and see his hand on her leg? She remembered them suddenly as children, Beryl on the greedy side yet refusing to eat fish in any shape or form, Ron having his nails painted with Nail-Gro because he bit them. She remembered the birth of Ron and how it had been touch and go because he'd weighed so little. She remembered the time Beryl scalded herself on the electric kettle and how Lenny had rung 999 because he said it would be the quickest way to get attention. She remembered the first night she'd been married to Lenny, taking her clothes off under a wrap her mother had given her because she'd always been shy about everything. All she had to do, she said to herself, was to stand up and go.

His hands weren't touching her any more. He moved his body away from hers, and she looked at him and saw that the excitement had gone from his face. His eyes had a dead look. His mouth had a melancholy twist to it.

'I'm sorry,' she said.

'I fancied you that first day, Alice. I always fancied you, Alice.'

He was speaking the truth to her and it was strange to think of it as the truth, even though she had known that in some purely physical way he desired her. It was different from being mad for a person, and yet she felt that his desiring her was just as strange as being mad for her. If he didn't desire her she'd have been able to return to the dance-rooms, they'd have been able to sit here on the balcony, again and again, she telling him more about Poppy and he telling her more about himself, making one another laugh. Yet if he didn't desire her he wouldn't want to be bothered with any of that.

'Can't fancy black girls,' he said, with his head turned well away from her. 'White women, over sixty if it's possible. Thirteen stone or so. That's why I go to the dance-rooms.' He turned to face her and gazed morosely at her eyes. 'I'm queer that way,' he said. 'I'm a nasty kind of black man.'

She could feel sickness in her stomach, and the skin of her back, which had been so damp with sweat, was now cold. She picked up her handbag and held it awkwardly for a moment, not knowing what to say. 'I must go,' she said eventually, and her legs felt shaky when she stood on them.

He remained at the table, all his politeness gone. He looked bitter and angry and truculent. She thought he might insult her. She thought he might shout loudly at her in the dance-rooms, calling her names and abusing her. But he didn't. He didn't say anything at all to her. He sat there in the dim, tinted light, seeming to slump from one degree of disappointment to a deeper one. He looked crude and pathetic. He looked another person.

Again, as she stood there awkwardly, she thought about the room in Maida Vale, which she'd furnished with lilies and brightly coloured cloths. Again his grey hands undid her corset and her brassière, and just for a moment it seemed that there wouldn't have been much wrong in letting him admire her in whatever way he wanted to. It was something that would disgust people if they knew; Beryl and Ron would be disgusted, and Lenny and Albert naturally enough. Grantly Palmer would disgust them, and she herself, a grandmother, would disgust them for permitting his attentions. There was something wrong with Grantly Palmer, they'd all say: he was sick and dirty, as he even admitted himself. Yet there were always things wrong with people, things you didn't much care for and even were disgusted by, like Beryl being greedy and Ron biting his nails, like the way Lenny would sometimes blow his nose without using a handkerchief or a tissue. Even Poppy hadn't been perfect: on a bus it had sometimes been too much, her shrillness and her rushy ways, so clearly distasteful to other people sitting there.

Alice wanted to tell Grantly Palmer all that. Desperately she tried to form an argument in her mind, a conversation with herself that had as its elements the greediness of her daughter and her son's bitten nails and her husband clearing the mucus from his nose at the sink, and she herself agreeing to be the object of perversion. But the elements would not connect, and she felt instinctively that she could not transform them into coherent argument. The elements spun dizzily in her mind, the sense she sought from them did not materialize.

'Goodbye,' she said, knowing he would not answer. He was ashamed of himself; he wanted her to go. 'Goodbye,' she said again. 'Goodbye, Grantly.'

She moved away from him, forcing herself to think about the house in Paper Street, about entering it and changing her clothes before Lenny returned. She'd bought two chops that morning and there was part of a packet of frozen beans in the fridge. She saw herself peeling potatoes at the sink, but at the same time she could feel Grantly Palmer behind her, still sitting at the table, ashamed when he need not be. She felt ashamed herself for having tea with him, for going to see him when she shouldn't, just because Poppy was dead and there was no one else who was fun to be with.

Leo Ritz and his Band were playing 'Scatterbrain' as she left the dance-rooms. The middle-aged dancers smiled as they danced, some of them humming the tune.

Last Wishes

In the neighbourhood Mrs Abercrombie was a talking point. Strangers who asked at Miss Dobbs' Post Office and Village Stores or at the Royal Oak were told that the wide entrance gates on the Castle Cary road were the gates to Rews Manor, where Mrs Abercrombie lived in the past, with servants. No one from the village except old Dr Ripley and a window-cleaner had seen her since 1947, the year of her husband's death. According to Dr Ripley, she'd become a hypochondriac.

But even if she had, and in spite of her desire to live as a recluse, Mrs Abercrombie continued to foster the grandeur that made Rews Manor, nowadays, seem old-fashioned. Strangers were told that the interior of the house had to be seen to be believed. The staircase alone, in white rose-veined marble, was reckoned to be worth thousands; the faded carpets had come from Persia; all the furniture had been in the Abercrombie family for four or five generations. On every second Sunday in the summer the garden was open to visitors and the admission charges went to the Nurses.

Once a week Plunkett, the most important of Mrs Abercrombie's servants, being her butler, drove into the village and bought stamps and cigarettes in the post office and stores. It was a gesture more than anything else, Miss Dobbs considered, because the bulk of the Rews Manor shopping was done in one or other of the nearby towns. Plunkett was about fifty, a man with a sandy appearance who drove a pre-war Wolseley and had a pleasant, easy-going smile. The window-cleaner reported that there was a Mrs Plunkett, a uniformed housemaid, but old Dr Ripley said the uniformed maid was a person called Tindall. There were five servants at Rews Manor, Dr Ripley said, if you counted the two gardeners, Mr Apse and Miss Bell, and all of them were happy. He often repeated that Mrs Abercrombie's servants were happy, as though making a point: they were pleasant people to know, he said, because of their contentment. Those who had met Plunkett in the village agreed, and strangers who had come across Mr Apse and Miss Bell in the gardens of Rews Manor found them pleasant also, and often envied them their dispositions.

In the village it was told how there'd always been Abercrombies at Rews Manor, how the present Mrs Abercrombie's husband had lived there alone when he'd inherited it – until he married at forty-one, having previously not intended to marry at all because he suffered from a blood disease that had killed his father and his grandfather early in their lives. It was told how the marriage had been a brief and a happy one, and how there'd been no children. Mrs Abercrombie's husband had died within five years and had been buried in the grounds of Rews Manor, near the azaleas.

'So beautifully kept, the garden,' visitors to the neighbourhood would marvel. 'That gravel in front, not a stone out of place! Those lawns and rose-bushes!' And then, intrigued by the old-fashioned quality of the place, they'd hear the story of this woman whose husband had inopportunely died, who existed now only in the world of her house and gardens, who lived in the past because she did not care for the present. People wove fantasies around this house and its people; to those who were outside it, it touched on fantasy itself. It was real because it was there and you could see it, because you could see the man called Plunkett buying stamps in the post office, but its reality was strange, as exotic as a coloured orchid. In the 1960s and 1970s, when life often had a grey look, the story of Rews Manor cheered people up, both those who told it and those who listened. It created images in minds and it affected imaginations. The holidaymakers who walked through the beautifully kept garden, through beds of begonias and roses, among blue hydrangeas and potentilla and witch-hazel and fuchsia, were grateful. They were grateful for the garden and for the story that went with it, and later they told the story themselves, with conjectured variations.

At closer quarters, Rews Manor was very much a world of its own. In 1947, at the time of Mr Abercrombie's death, Mr Apse, the gardener, worked under the eighty-year-old Mr Marriott, and when Mr Marriott died Mrs Abercrombie promoted Mr Apse and advertised for an assistant. There seemed no reason why a woman should not be as suitable as a man and so Miss Bell, being the only applicant, was given the post. Plunkett had also been advertised for when his predecessor, Stubbins, had become too old to carry on. The housemaid, Tindall, had been employed a few years after the arrival of Plunkett, as had Mrs Pope, who cooked.

The servants all lived in, Mr Apse where he had always lived, in a room over the garage, Miss Bell next door to him. The other three had rooms in a wing of the house which servants, in the days when servants were more the thing, had entirely occupied. They met for meals in the kitchen and sometimes they would sit there in the evenings. The room which once had been the servants' sitting-room had a dreariness about it: in 1956 Plunkett moved the television set into the kitchen.

Mr Apse was sixty-three now and Miss Bell was forty-five. Mrs Pope was fifty-nine, Tindall forty-three. Plunkett, reckoned in the village to be about fifty, was in fact precisely that. Plunkett, who had authority over the indoor servants and over Mr Apse and Miss Bell when they were in the kitchen, had at the time of Mrs Abercrombie's advertisement held a position in a *nouveau-riche* household in Warwickshire. He might slowly have climbed the ladder and found himself, when death or age had made a gap for him, in charge of its servants. He might have married and had children. He might have found himself for the rest of his life in the butler's bungalow, tucked out of sight on the grounds, growing vegetables in his spare time. But for Plunkett these prospects hadn't seemed quite right. He didn't want to marry, nor did he wish to father children. He wanted to continue being a servant because being a servant made him happy, yet the stuffiness of some households was more than he could bear and he didn't like having to wait for years before being in charge. He looked around, and as soon as he set foot in Rews Manor he knew it was exactly what he wanted, a small world in which he had only himself to blame if the food and wine weren't more than up to scratch. He assisted Mrs Abercrombie in her choosing of Mrs Pope as cook, recognizing in Mrs Pope the long-latent talents of a woman who sought the opportunity to make food her religion. He also assisted in the employing of Tindall, a fact he had often recalled since, on the nights he spent in her bed.

Mrs Pope had cooked in a YWCA until she answered the advertisement. The raw materials she was provided with had offered her little opportunity for the culinary experiments she would have liked to attempt. For twenty years she had remained in the kitchens of the YWCA because her husband, now dead, had been the janitor. In the flat attached to the place she had brought up two children, a boy and a girl, both of them now married. She'd wanted to move to somewhere nicer when Winnie, the girl, had married a traveller in stationery, but her husband had refused point-blank, claiming that the YWCA had become his home. When he died, she hadn't hesitated.

Miss Bell had been a teacher of geography, but had been advised for health considerations to take on outdoor work. Having always enjoyed gardening and knowing quite a bit about it, she'd answered Mrs Abercrombie's advertisement in *The Times*. She'd become used to living in, in a succession of boarding-schools, so that living in somewhere else suited her quite well. Mr Apse was a silent individual, which suited her also. For long hours they would work side by side in the vegetable garden or among the blue hydrangeas and the azaleas that formed a shrubbery around the house, neither of them saying anything at all.

Tindall had worked as a packer in a frozen-foods factory. There'd been trouble in her life in that the man she'd been engaged to when she was twenty-two, another employee in the factory, had made her pregnant and had then, without warning, disappeared. He was a man called Bert Fask, considerate in every possible way, quiet and seemingly reliable. Everyone said she was lucky to be engaged to Bert Fask and she had imagined quite a happy future. 'Don't matter a thing,' he said when she told him she was pregnant, and he fixed it that they could get married six months sooner than they'd intended. Then he disappeared. She'd later heard that he'd done the same thing with other girls, and when it became clear that he didn't intend to return she began to feel bitter. Her only consolation was the baby, which she still intended to have even though she didn't know how on earth she was going to manage. She loved her unborn child and she longed for its birth so that she herself could feel loved again. But the child, two months premature, lived for only sixteen hours. That blow was a terrible one, and it was when endeavouring to get over it that she'd come across Mrs Abercrombie's advertisement, on a page of a newspaper that a greengrocer had wrapped a beetroot in. That chance led her to a contentment she hadn't known before, to a happiness that was different only in detail from the happinesses of the other servants.

On the morning July 12th 1974, a Friday, Tindall knocked on Mrs Abercrombie's bedroom door at her usual time of eight forty-five. She carried into the room Mrs Abercrombie's breakfast tray and the morning mail, and placed the tray on the Queen Anne table just inside the door. She pulled back the bedroom's six curtains. 'A cloudy day,' she said.

Mrs Abercrombie, who had been reading Butler's *Lives of the Saints*, extinguished her bedside light. She remarked that the wireless the night before had predicted that the weather would be unsettled: rain would do the garden good.

Tindall carried the tray to the bed, placed it on the mahogany bed-table and settled the bed-table into position. Mrs Abercrombie picked up her letters. Tindall left the room.

Letters were usually bills, which were later passed to Plunkett to deal with. Plunkett had a housekeeping account, into which a sum of money was automatically transferred once a month. Mrs Abercrombie's personal requirements were purchased from this same account, negligible since she had ceased to buy clothes. It was Tindall who noticed when she needed a lipstick refill or lavender-water or more hairpins. Tindall made a list and handed it to Plunkett. For years Mrs Abercrombie herself hadn't had the bother of having to remember, or having to sign a cheque.

This morning there was the monthly account from the International Stores and one from the South Western Electricity Board. The pale brown envelopes were identification enough: she put them aside unopened. The third envelope contained a letter from her solicitors about her will.

In the kitchen, over breakfast, the talk turned to white raspberries. Mr Apse said that in the old days white raspberries had been specially cultivated in the garden. Tindall, who had never heard of white raspberries before, remarked that the very idea of them gave her the creeps. 'More flavour really,' Miss Bell said quietly.

Plunkett, engrossed in the *Daily Telegraph*, did not say anything. Mrs Pope said she'd never had white raspberries and would like to try them. She'd be more than grateful, she added, if Mr Apse could see his way to putting in a few canes. But Mr Apse had relapsed into his more familiar mood of silence. He was a big man, slow of movement, with a brown bald head and tufts of grey hair about his ears. He ate bacon and mushrooms and an egg in a slow and careful manner, occasionally between mouthfuls drinking tea. Miss Bell nodded at Mrs Pope, an indication that Mr Apse had heard the request about the raspberries and would act upon it.

'Like slugs they sound,' Tindall said.

Miss Bell, who had small tortoiseshell glasses and was small herself, with a weather-beaten face, said that they did not taste like slugs. Her father had grown white raspberries, her mother had made a delicious dish with them, mixing them with loganberries and baking them with a meringue top. Mrs Pope nodded. She'd read a recipe like that once, in Mrs Beeton it might have been; she'd like to try it out.

In the *Daily Telegraph* Plunkett read that there was a strike of television technicians and a strike of petrol hauliers. The sugar shortage was to continue and there was likely to be a shortage of bread. He sighed without making a sound. Staring at print he didn't feel like reading, he recalled the warmth of Tindall's body the night before. He glanced round the edge of the newspaper at her: there was a brightness in her eyes, which was always there the morning after he'd visited her in bed. She'd wept twice during the four hours he'd spent: tears of fulfilment he'd learnt they were, but all the same he could never prevent himself from comforting her. Few words passed between them when they came together in the night; his comforting consisted of stroking her hair and kissing her damp cheeks. She had narrow cheeks, and jet-black hair which she wore done up in a knot during the day but which tumbled all over the pillows when she was in bed. Her body was bony, which he appreciated. He didn't know about the tragedy in her life because she'd never told him; in his eyes she was a good and efficient servant and a generous woman, very different from the sorrowful creature who'd come looking for employment twenty years ago. She had never once hinted at marriage, leaving him to deduce that for her their arrangement was as satisfactory as it was for him.

'Moussaka for dinner,' Mrs Pope said, rising from the breakfast table. 'She asked for it special.'

'No wonder, after your last one,' Miss Bell murmured. The food at the schools where she'd taught geography had always been appalling: grey-coloured mince and soup that smelt, huge sausage-rolls for Sunday tea, cold scrambled egg.

'Secret is, cook it gently,' Mrs Pope said, piling dishes into the sink. 'That's all there's to it if you ask me.'

'Oh no, no,' Miss Bell murmured, implying that there was a great deal more to moussaka than that. She carried her own dishes to the sink. Mrs Pope had a way with moussaka, she added in her same quiet way, which was why Mrs Abercrombie had asked for it again.

Tindall chewed her last corner of toast and marmalade. She felt just slightly sore, pleasantly so, as she always did after a visit from Plunkett. Quite remarkable he sometimes was in the middle of the night, yet who'd have thought he'd know a thing about any of it?

Mr Apse left the kitchen and Miss Bell followed him. Tindall carried her dishes to the sink and assisted Mrs Pope with the washing up. At the table Plunkett lit his first cigarette of the day, lingering over a last cup of tea.

As she did every morning after breakfast, Mrs Abercrombie recalled her husband's death. It had taken place on a fine day in March, a day with a frost in the early morning and afterwards becoming sunny, though still cold. He'd had a touch of flu but was almost better; Dr Ripley had suggested his getting up in time for lunch. But by lunchtime he was dead, with the awful suddenness that had marked the deaths of his father and his grandfather, nothing to do with flu at all. She'd come into their bedroom, with the clothes she'd aired for him to get up into.

Mrs Abercrombie was sixty-one now; she'd been thirty-four at the time of the death. Her life for twenty-seven years had been a memorial to her brief marriage, but death had not cast unduly gloomy shadows, for after the passion of her sorrow there was some joy at least in her sentimental memories. Her own death preoccupied her now: she was going to die because with every day that passed she felt more weary. She felt herself slipping away and even experienced slight pains in her body, as if some ailment had developed in order to hurry her along. She'd told Dr Ripley, wondering if her gallstones were playing up, but Dr Ripley said there was nothing the matter with her. It didn't comfort her that he said it because she didn't in the least mind dying. She had a belief that after death she would meet again the man who had himself died so abruptly, that the interrupted marriage would somehow continue. For twenty-seven years this hope had been the consolation that kept her going. That and the fact that she had provided a home for Mr Apse and Miss Bell, and Mrs Pope and Tindall and Plunkett, all of whom had grown older with her and had shared with her the beauty of her husband's house.

'I shall not get up today,' she murmured on the morning of July 12th. She did not, and in fact did not ever again get up.

They were thrown into confusion. They stood in the kitchen looking at one another, only Plunkett looking elsewhere, at the Aga that for so long now had been Mrs Pope's delight. No one had expected Mrs Abercrombie to die, having been repeatedly assured by Dr Ripley that there was nothing the matter with her. The way she lived, so carefully and so well looked after, there had seemed no reason why she shouldn't last for another twenty years at the very least, into her eighties. In bed at night, on the occasions when he didn't visit Tindall's bed, Plunkett had worked out that if Mrs Abercrombie lived until she was eighty, Miss Bell would be sixty-four and Mrs Pope seventy-eight. Tindall, at sixty-two, would presumably be beyond the age of desire, as he himself would no doubt be, at sixty-nine. Mr Apse, so grizzled and healthy did he sometimes seem, might still be able to be useful in the garden, at eighty-two. It seemed absurd to Plunkett on the morning of July 12th that Mrs Abercrombie had died twenty years too soon. It also seemed unfair.

It seemed particularly unfair because, according to the letter which Mrs Abercrombie had that morning received from her solicitors, she had been in the process of altering her will. Mrs Abercrombie had once revealed to Plunkett that it had been her husband's wish, in view of the fact that there were no children, that Rews Manor should eventually pass into the possession of a body which was engaged in the study of rare grasses. It was a subject that had interested him and which he had studied in considerable detail himself. 'There'll be legacies of course,' Mrs Abercrombie had reassured Plunkett, 'for all of you.' She'd smiled when she'd said that and Plunkett had bowed and murmured in a way that, years ago, he'd picked up from Hollywood films that featured English butlers.

But in the last few weeks Mrs Abercrombie had apparently had second thoughts. Reading between the lines of the letter from her solicitors, it was clear to Plunkett that she'd come to consider that legacies for her servants weren't enough. *We assume your wish to be,* the letter read, *that after your death your servants should remain in Rews Manor, retaining the house as it is and keeping the gardens open to the public. That this should be so*

*until such time as Mr Plunkett should have reached retirement age, i.e.
sixty-five years or, in the event of Mr Plunkett's previous death, that this
arrangement should continue until the year 1990. At either time, the house
and gardens should be disposed of as in your current will and the servants
remaining should receive the legacies as previously laid down. We would
be grateful if you would confirm at your convenience that we are correct
in this interpretation of your wishes: in which case we will draw up at
once the necessary papers.* But her convenience had never come because
she had left it all too late. With the typewritten sheet in his hand, Plunkett
had felt a shiver of bitterness. He'd felt it again, with anger, when he'd
looked at her dead face.

'Grass,' he said in the kitchen. 'They'll be studying grass here.'

The others knew what he was talking about. They, like he, believing
that Mrs Abercrombie would live for a long time yet, had never paused to
visualize Rews Manor in that far-off future. They did so now, since the
future was bewilderingly at hand. Contemporary life closed in upon the
house and garden that had belonged to the past. They saw the house
without its furniture since such furniture would be unsuitable in a centre
for the studying of grasses. They saw, in a vague way, men in shirtsleeves,
smoking pipes and carrying papers. Tindall saw grasses laid out for examination on a long trestle table in the hall. Mr Apse saw roses uprooted
from the garden, the blue hydrangeas disposed of, and small seed-beds
neatly laid out, for the cultivation of special grass. Miss Bell had a vision
of men with a bulldozer, but she could not establish their activity with
more precision. Mrs Pope saw caterers' packs on the kitchen table and in
the cold room and the store cupboards: transparent plastic bags containing
powdered potatoes in enormous quantities, fourteen-pound tins of instant
coffee, dried mushrooms and dried all-purpose soup. Plunkett saw a laboratory in the drawing-room.

'I must telephone Dr Ripley,' Plunkett said, and the others thought, but
did not say it, that it was too late for Dr Ripley to be of use.

'You have to,' Plunkett said, 'when a person dies.'

He left the kitchen, and Mrs Pope began to make coffee. The others sat
down at the table, even though it was half past eleven in the morning.
There were other houses, Tindall said to herself, other country houses
where life would be quiet and more agreeable than life in a frozen-foods
firm. And yet other houses would not have him coming to her bedroom,
for she could never imagine his suggesting that they should go somewhere
together. That wasn't his way; it would be too binding, too formal, like a
proposal of marriage. And she wouldn't have cared to be Mrs Plunkett,
for she didn't in the least love him.

'Poor thing,' Mrs Pope said, pouring her boiling water on to the coffee she had ground, and for a moment Tindall thought the reference was to her.

'Yes,' Miss Bell whispered, 'poor old thing.' She spoke in a kind way, but her words, sincerely meant, did not sound so in the kitchen. Somewhere in the atmosphere that the death had engendered there was resentment, a reflection of the bitterness it had engendered in Plunkett. There was a feeling that Mrs Abercrombie, so considerate in her lifetime, had let them down by dying. Even while she called her a poor old thing, Miss Bell wondered what she should do now. Many employers might consider the idea of a woman gardener eccentric, and certainly other men, more set in their ways than Mr Apse, mightn't welcome a female assistant.

Mrs Pope thought along similar lines. You became used to a place, she was reflecting as she poured the coffee into cups, and there'd be few other places where you could cook so grandly for a single palate, where you were appreciated every day of your life. 'Bloody inedible,' she'd heard a girl exclaim in a corridor of the YWCA, referring to carefully poached haddock in a cream sauce.

'The doctor'll be here at twelve,' Plunkett sombrely announced, re-entering the kitchen from the back hall. 'I left a message; I didn't say she'd died.'

He sat down at the table and waited while Mrs Pope filled his coffee-cup. Tindall placed the jug of hot milk beside him and for a moment the image of her fingers on the flowered surface of the china caused him to remember the caressing of those fingers the night before. He added two lumps of sugar and poured the milk. He felt quite urgent about Tindall, which he never usually did at half past eleven on a morning after. He put it down to the upset of the death, and the fact that he was idle when normally on a Friday morning he'd be going through the stores with Mrs Pope.

'Doctor'll sign a death warrant,' Mrs Pope said. 'There'll be the funeral.'

Plunkett nodded. Mrs Abercrombie had a cousin in Lincolnshire and another in London, two old men who once, twelve years ago, had spent a weekend in Rews Manor. Mrs Abercrombie hadn't corresponded with them after that, not caring for them, Plunkett imagined. The chances were they were dead by now.

'No one much to tell,' Mrs Pope said, and Miss Bell mentioned the two cousins. He'd see if they were alive, Plunkett said.

It was while saying that, and realizing as he said it the pointlessness of summoning these two ancient men to a funeral, that he had his idea: why should not Mrs Abercrombie's last wishes be honoured, even if she hadn't managed to make them legal? The idea occurred quickly and vividly to him, and immediately he regretted his telephoning of Dr Ripley. But as soon as he regretted it he realized that the telephoning had been essential. Dr Ripley was a line of communication with the outside world and had been one for so long that it would seem strange to other people if a woman, designated a hypochondriac, failed to demand as regularly as before the attentions of her doctor. It would seem stranger still to Dr Ripley.

Yet there was no reason why Mrs Abercrombie should not be quietly buried beside the husband she had loved, where she was scheduled to be buried anyway. There was no reason that Plunkett could see why the household should not then proceed as it had in the past. The curtains of the drawing room would be drawn when next the window-cleaner came, Dr Ripley would play his part because he'd have no option.

'I see no harm in it,' Plunkett said.

'In what?' Mrs Pope inquired, and then, speaking slowly to break the shock of his idea, he told them. He told them about the letter Mrs Abercrombie had received that morning from her solicitors. He took it from an inside pocket and showed it to them. They at first thought it strange that he should be carrying Mrs Abercrombie's correspondence on his person, but as the letter passed among them, they understood.

'Oh no,' Miss Bell murmured, her small brown face screwed up in distaste. Mrs Pope shook her head and said she couldn't be a party to deception. Mr Apse did not say anything. Tindall half shook her head.

'It was what she clearly wished,' Plunkett explained. 'She had no intention of dying until she'd made this stipulation.'

'Death waits for no one's wishes,' Mr Apse pointed out in a ponderous voice.

'All we are doing,' Plunkett said, 'is to make it wait.'

'But there's Dr Ripley,' Tindall said, and Mrs Pope added that a doctor couldn't ever lend himself to anything shady. It surprised Mrs Pope that Plunkett had made such an extraordinary suggestion, just as it surprised Miss Bell. Tindall and Mr Apse were surprised also, but more at themselves for thinking that what Plunkett was suggesting was only a postponement of the facts, not a suppression.

'But, Plunkett, what exactly are you wanting to do?' Mrs Pope cried out, suddenly shrill.

'She must be buried as she said. She spoke to us all of it, that she wished to be laid down by Mr Abercrombie in the garden.'

'But you have to inform the authorities,' Miss Bell whispered, and Mrs Pope, still shrill, said there had to be a coffin and a funeral.

'I'd make a coffin,' Plunkett replied swiftly. 'There's the timber left over from the drawing-room floorboards. Beautiful oak, plenty of it.'

They knew he could. They'd seen him making other things, a step-ladder and bird-boxes, and shelves for the store-room.

'I was with her one day,' Plunkett said, not telling the truth now. 'We were standing in the garage looking at the timber. "You could make a coffin out of that," she said. "I don't suppose you've ever made a coffin, Plunkett." Those were her exact words. Then she turned and went away: I knew what she meant.'

They believed this lie because to their knowledge he had never lied before. They believed that Mrs Abercrombie had spoken of a coffin, but Miss Bell and Mrs Pope considered that she had only spoken in passing, without significance. Mr Apse and Tindall, wishing to believe that the old woman had been giving a hint to Plunkett, saw no reason to doubt that she had.

'I really couldn't,' Miss Bell said, 'be a party to anything like that.'

For the first time in their association Plunkett disliked Miss Bell. He'd always thought her a little field-mouse of a thing, all brown creases he imagined her body would be, like her face. Mrs Abercrombie had asked him what he'd thought when Miss Bell had answered the advertisement for an assistant gardener. 'She's been a teacher,' Mrs Abercrombie had said, handing him Miss Bell's letter, in which it was stated that Miss Bell was qualified to teach geography but had been medically advised to seek outdoor work. 'No harm in seeing her,' he'd said, and had promised to give Mrs Abercrombie his own opinion after he'd opened the hall door to the applicant and received her into the hall.

'You would not be here, Miss Bell,' he said now, 'if I hadn't urged Mrs Abercrombie that it wasn't peculiar to employ a woman in the garden. She was dead against it.'

'But that's no reason to go against the law,' Mrs Pope cried, shrill again. 'Just because she took a woman into the garden doesn't mean anything.'

'You would not be here yourself, Mrs Pope. She was extremely reluctant to have a woman whose only experience in the cooking line was in a hostel. It was I who had an instinct about your letter, Mrs Pope.'

'There's still Dr Ripley,' Miss Bell said, feeling that all the protestation and argument were anyway in vain because Dr Ripley was shortly due in the house and would put an end to all this absurdity. Dr Ripley would issue a death certificate and would probably himself inform a firm of undertakers. The death of Mrs Abercrombie had temporarily affected Plunkett, Miss Bell considered. She'd once read in the *Daily Telegraph* of a woman who'd wished to keep the dead body of her husband under glass.

'Of course there's Dr Ripley,' Mrs Pope said. She spoke sharply and with a trace of disdain in her voice. If Mrs Abercrombie had let them down by dying before her time, then Plunkett was letting them down even more. Plunkett had always been in charge, taking decisions about everything, never at a loss. It was ironic that he should be the one to lose his head now.

'It is Dr Ripley I'm thinking about,' Plunkett said. 'People will say he neglected her.'

There was a silence then in the kitchen. Mrs Pope had begun to lick her lips, a habit with her when she was about to speak. She changed her mind and somehow, because of what had been said about Dr Ripley, found herself less angry. Everyone liked the old doctor, even though they'd often agreed in the kitchen that he was beyond it.

When Plunkett said that Dr Ripley might have neglected Mrs Abercrombie, guilt nibbled at Miss Bell. There was a time two years ago when she'd cut her hand on a piece of metal embedded in soil. She'd gone to Dr Ripley with it and although he'd chatted to her and been extremely kind his treatment hadn't been successful. A week later her whole arm had swelled up and Plunkett had insisted on driving her to the out-patients' department of a hospital. She was lucky to keep the arm, an Indian doctor had pronounced, adding that someone had been careless.

Mrs Pope recalled the affair of Miss Bell's hand, and Mr Apse recalled the occasion, and so did Tindall. In the snow once Dr Ripley's old Vauxhall had skidded on the drive and Mr Apse had had to put gravel under the back wheels to get it out of the ditch. It had puzzled Mr Apse that the skid had occurred because, as far as he could see, there'd been no cause for Dr Ripley to apply his brakes. It had occurred to him afterwards that the doctor hadn't quite known what he was doing.

'It's a terrible thing for a doctor to be disgraced,' Plunkett said. 'She thought the world of him, you know.'

The confusion in the kitchen was now considerable. The shock of the death still lingered and with it, though less than before, the feeling of resentment. There was the varying reaction to Plunkett's proposal that Mrs Abercrombie's remains should be quietly disposed of. There was concern for Dr Ripley, and a mounting uneasiness that caused the concern to give way to a more complicated emotion: it wasn't simply that the negligence of Dr Ripley had brought about a patient's death, it seemed that his negligence must be shared, since they had known he wasn't up to it and had not spoken out.

'Her death will cause unhappiness all round,' Plunkett said. 'Which she didn't wish at all. He'd be struck off.'

Dr Ripley had attended Miss Bell on a previous occasion, a few months after her arrival in Rews Manor. She'd come out in spots which Dr Ripley had diagnosed as German measles. He had been called in when Tindall had influenza in 1960. He'd been considerate and efficient about a tiresome complaint of Mrs Pope's.

The two images of Dr Ripley hovered in the kitchen: a man firm of purpose and skilful in his heyday, moustached and smart but always sympathetic, a saviour who had become a medical menace.

'She died of gallstones,' Plunkett said, 'which for eight or nine years she suffered from, a fact he always denied. She'd be still alive if he'd treated her.'

'We don't know it was gallstones,' Miss Bell protested quietly.

'We would have to say. We would have to say that she complained of gallstones.' Plunkett looked severe. 'If he puts down pneumonia on the death certificate we would have to disagree. After all,' he continued, his severity increasing with each word, 'he could kill other people too.'

He looked from one face to another and saw that the mind behind each was lost in the confusion he had created. He, though, could see his way through the murk of it. Out of the necessary chaos he could already see the order he desired, and it seemed to him now that everything else he had ever experienced paled beside the excitement of the idea he'd been visited by.

'We must bargain with Dr Ripley,' he said, 'for his own sake. She would not have wished him to be punished for his negligence, any more than she would wish us to suffer through her unnecessary death. We must put it all to Dr Ripley. He must sign a death certificate in her room this morning and forget to hand it in. I would be satisfied with that.'

'Forget?' Miss Bell repeated, aghast and totally astonished.

'Or leave it behind here and forget that he has left it behind. Any elderly behaviour like that, it's all of a piece. I'm sure there's no law that says she can't be quietly put away in the garden, and the poor old chap'll be long since dead before anyone thinks to ask a question. We would have saved his bacon for him and be looked after ourselves, just as she wished. No one would bother about any of it in a few years' time, and we'd have done no wrong by burying her where she wished to be. Only the old chap would be a bit amiss by keeping quiet about a death, but he'd be safely out of business by then.'

Mr Apse remembered a lifetime's association with the garden of Rews Manor, and Mrs Pope recalled the cheerless kitchens of the YWCA, and Miss Bell saw herself kneeling in a flower-bed on an autumn evening, taking begonia tubers from the earth. There could be no other garden for Mr Apse, and for Miss Bell no other garden either, and no other kitchen for Mrs Pope. Plunkett might propose to her, Tindall said to herself, just in order to go on sharing beds with her, but the marriage would not be happy because it was not what they wanted.

'There's the will,' Miss Bell said, whispering so low that her words were almost incomprehensible. 'There's the will she has signed.'

'In time,' Plunkett said, 'the will shall naturally come into its own. That is what she intended. We should all be properly looked after, and then the grass merchants will take over, as laid down. When the place is no longer of use to us.' He added that he felt he had been visited, that the idea had quite definitely come from outside himself rather than from within. Regretful in death, he said, Mrs Abercrombie had expressed herself to him because she was cross with herself, because she was worried for her servants and for the old doctor.

'He let her die of neglected gallstones,' Plunkett repeated with firm conviction. 'A most obvious complaint.'

In the hall the doorbell rang, a clanging sound, for the bell was of an old-fashioned kind.

'Well?' Plunkett said, looking from one face to another.

'We don't know that it was gallstones,' Miss Bell protested again. 'She only mentioned gallstones. Dr Ripley said –'

'Oh, for heaven's sake, Miss Bell!'

He glared at Miss Bell with dislike in his face. They'd been through all that, he said: gallstones or something else, what did it matter? The woman was dead.

'It's perfectly clear to all of us, Miss Bell, that Mrs Abercrombie would not have wished her death to cause all this fuss. That's the only point I'm making. In my opinion, apparently not shared by you, Mrs Abercrombie was a woman of remarkable sensitivity. And kindness, Miss Bell. Do you really believe that she would have wished to inflict this misery on a harmless old doctor?' He paused, staring at Miss Bell, aware that the dislike in his face was upsetting her. 'Do you really believe she wished to deprive us of our home? Do you believe that Mrs Abercrombie was unkind?'

Miss Bell did not say anything, and in the silence the doorbell pealed again. Mrs Pope was aware that her head had begun to ache. Mr Apse took his pipe from his pocket and put it on the table. He cut slivers from a plug of tobacco and rubbed them together in the palm of his left hand. Tindall watched him, thinking that she had never seen him preparing his pipe in the kitchen before.

'You're mad!' Miss Bell suddenly cried. 'The whole thing has affected you, Plunkett. It's ridiculous what you're saying.' The blood had gone to her face and neck, and showed in dark blotches beneath her weathered skin. Her eyes, usually so tranquil, shone fierily in her anger. She didn't move, but continued to stand at the corner of the kitchen table, just behind Mr Apse, who was looking up at her, astonished.

'How can we possibly do such a thing?' Miss Bell shrieked. 'It's a disgusting, filthy kind of thing to suggest. Her body's still warm and you can stand there saying that everything should be falsified. You don't care tuppence for Dr Ripley, it's not Dr Ripley who matters to you. They could hang him for murder –'

'I did not say Dr Ripley would be hanged.'

'You implied it. You implied the most terrible things.'

The power left her voice as she uttered the last three words. Her eyes closed for a moment and when she opened them again she was weeping.

'Now, now, my dear,' Mrs Pope said, going to her and putting a hand on her arm.

'I am only thinking of Mrs Abercrombie's wishes,' Plunkett said, unmoved and still severe. 'Her wishes didn't say the old doctor should be hounded.'

Mrs Pope continued to murmur consolation. She sat Miss Bell down at the table. Tindall went to a drawer in the dresser and took from it a number of household tissues which she placed in front of Miss Bell. Mr Apse pressed the shredded tobacco into his pipe.

'I see no reason at all not to have a private household funeral,' Plunkett said. He spoke slowly, emphasizing the repetition in his statement, summing everything up. What right had the stupid little creature to create a ridiculous fuss when the other three would easily now have left everything in his hands? It wasn't she who mattered, or she who had the casting vote: it was old Ripley, still standing on the doorstep.

'No,' Miss Bell whispered. 'No, no.'

It was a nightmare. It was a nightmare to be crouched over the kitchen table, with Mrs Pope's hand on her shoulder and tissues laid out in front of her. It was a nightmare to think that Mr Apse wouldn't have cared what they did with Mrs Abercrombie, that Tindall wouldn't have cared, that Mrs Pope was coming round to Plunkett's horrible suggestions. It was a nightmare to think of the doctor being blackmailed by Plunkett's oily tongue. Plunkett was like an animal, some creature out of which a devil of hell had come.

'Best maybe to have a chat with the doctor,' Miss Bell heard Mrs Pope's voice say, and heard the agreement of Tindall, soothing, like a murmur. She was aware of Mr Apse nodding his head. Plunkett said:

'I think that's fair.'

'No. No, no,' Miss Bell cried.

'Then what is fair, Miss Bell?' Mrs Pope, quite sharply, asked.

'Mrs Abercrombie is dead. It must be reported.'

'That's the doctor's job,' Plunkett pointed out. 'It don't concern us.'

'The doctor'll know,' Tindall said, considering it odd that Plunkett had all of a sudden used bad grammar, a lapse she had never before heard from him.

Without saying anything else, Plunkett left the kitchen.

Dr Ripley, who had pulled the bell four times, was pulling it again when Plunkett opened the hall door. The butler, Dr Ripley thought, was looking dishevelled and somewhat flushed. Blood pressure, he automatically said to himself, while commenting on the weather.

'She died,' Plunkett said. 'I wanted to tell you in person, Doctor.'

They stood for a moment while Plunkett explained the circumstances, giving the time of death as nine thirty or thereabouts.

'I'm really sorry,' Dr Ripley said. 'Poor dear.'

He mounted the stairs, with Plunkett behind him. Never again would he do so, he said to himself, since he, too, knew that the house was to pass into the possession of an organization which studied grasses. In the bedroom he examined the body and noted that death was due to simple heart failure, a brief little attack, he reckoned, judging by her countenance and the unflustered arrangement of her body. He sighed over the corpse, although he was used to corpses. It seemed a lifetime, and indeed it was, since he had attended her for a throat infection when she was a bride.

'Heart,' Dr Ripley said on the landing outside the bedroom. 'She was very beautiful, you know. In her day, Plunkett.'

Plunkett nodded. He stood aside to allow the doctor to precede him downstairs.

'She'll be happy,' Dr Ripley said. 'Being still in love with her husband.'

Again Plunkett nodded, even though the doctor couldn't see him. 'We wondered what best to do,' he said.

'Do?'

'You'll be issuing a certificate?'

'Well yes, of course.'

'It was that we were wondering about. The others and myself.'

'Wondering?'

'I'd like a chat with you, Doctor.'

Dr Ripley, who hadn't turned his head while having this conversation, reached the hall. Plunkett stepped round him and led the way to the drawing-room.

'A glass of sherry?' Plunkett suggested.

'Well, that's most kind of you, Plunkett. In the circumstances –'

'I think she'd have wished you to have one, sir.'

'Yes, maybe she would.'

Plunkett poured from a decanter and handed Dr Ripley the glass. He waited for the doctor to sip before he spoke.

'She sent a message to you, Doctor. Late last night she rang her bell and asked for me. She said she had a feeling she might die in the night. "If I do," she said, "I don't want him blamed." '

'Blamed? Who blamed? I don't understand you, Plunkett.'

'I asked her that myself. "Who blamed?" I said, and she said: "Dr Ripley." '

Plunkett watched while a mouthful of sherry was consumed. He moved to the decanter and carried it to Dr Ripley's glass. Mrs Abercrombie had had a heart attack, Dr Ripley said. He couldn't have saved her even if he'd been called in time.

'Naturally, we didn't send for you last night, sir, even though she said that. On account of your attitude, Doctor.'

'Attitude?'

'You considered her a hypochondriac, sir.'

'Mrs Abercrombie was.'

'No, sir. She was a sick woman.'

Dr Ripley finished his second glass of sherry and crossed the drawing-room to the decanter. He poured some more, filling the glass to the brim.

'I'm afraid,' he said, 'I've no idea what you're talking about, Plunkett.'

It the kitchen they did not speak. Mrs Pope made more coffee and put pieces of shortbread on a plate. No one ate the shortbread, and Miss Bell shook her head when Mrs Pope began to refill her coffee-cup.

'Bovril, dear?' Mrs Pope suggested, but Miss Bell rejected Bovril also.

The garden had an atmosphere, different scents came out at different times of year, varying also from season to season. It was in the garden that she'd realized how unhappy she'd been, for eleven years, teaching geography. Yet even if the garden were Paradise itself you couldn't just bury a dead woman in it and pretend she hadn't died. Every day of your life you'd pass the mound, your whole existence would be a lie.

'I'll go away,' Miss Bell said shakily, in a whisper. 'I'll pack and go. I promise you, I'll never tell a thing.'

To Dr Ripley's astonishment, Mrs Abercrombie's butler accused him of negligence and added that it would have been Mrs Abercrombie's desire to hush the matter up. He said that Mrs Abercrombie would never have wished to disgrace an old man.

'What I'm suggesting,' Plunkett said, 'is that you give the cause of death to suit yourself and then become forgetful.'

'Forgetful?'

'Leave the certificate behind you, sir, as if in error.'

'But it has to be handed in, Plunkett. Look here, there's no disgrace involved, or negligence or anything else. You haven't been drinking, have you?'

'It's a decision we came to in the kitchen, Doctor. We're all agreed.'

'But for heaven's sake, man –'

'Mrs Abercrombie's wish was that her body should be buried in the shrubbery, beside her husband's. That can be quietly done. Your good name would continue, Doctor, without a stain. Whether or not you take on further patients is your own affair.'

Dr Ripley sat down. He stared through wire-rimmed spectacles at a man he had always considered pleasant. Yet this same man was now clearly implying that he was more of an undertaker than a doctor.

'What I am saying, sir, is that Rews Manor shall continue as Mrs Abercrombie wished it to. What I am saying is that you and we shall enter into the small conspiracy that Mrs Abercrombie is guiding us towards.'

'Guiding?'

'Since her death she has been making herself felt all over the house. Read that, sir.'

He handed Dr Ripley the letter from Mrs Abercrombie's solicitors, which Dr Ripley slowly read and handed back. Plunkett said:

'It would be disgraceful to go against the wishes of the recently dead, especially those of a person like Mrs Abercrombie, who was kindness itself – to all of us, and to you, sir.'

'You're suggesting that her death should be suppressed, Plunkett? So that you and the others may remain here?'

'So that you may not face charges, sir.'

'But, for the Lord's sake, man, I'd face no charges. I've done nothing at all.'

'A doctor can be in trouble for doing nothing, when he should be doing everything, when he should be prolonging life instead of saying his patients are imagining things.'

'But Mrs Abercrombie did –'

'In the kitchen we're all agreed, sir. We remember, Doctor. We remember Miss Bell's hand a few years ago, that she nearly died of. Criminal neglect, they said in the out-patients'. Another thing, we remember the time we had to get your car out of the ditch.'

'I skidded. There was ice –'

'I have seen you drunk, Doctor,' Plunkett said, 'at half past ten in the morning.'

Dr Ripley stared harder at Plunkett, believing him now to be insane. He didn't say anything for a moment and then, recovering from his bewilderment, he spoke quietly and slowly. There was a perfectly good explanation for the skid on the icy snow of the drive: he'd braked to avoid a blackbird that was limping about in front of him. He'd never in his life been drunk at half past ten in the morning.

'You know as well as I do,' Plunkett continued, as though he were deaf or as though the doctor hadn't spoken, 'you know as well as I do that Mrs Abercrombie wouldn't rest if she was responsible for getting you into the Sunday papers.'

In the kitchen they did not reply when Miss Bell said she'd pack and go. They didn't look at her, and she knew they were thinking that she wouldn't be able to keep her word. They were thinking she was hysterical and frightened, and that the weight of so eccentric a secret would prove too much for her.

'It's just that Mrs Abercrombie wanted to change her will, dear,' Mrs Pope said.

'Yes,' said Mr Apse.

They spoke gently, in soft tones like Miss Bell's own. They looked at her in a gentle way, and Tindall smiled at her, gently also. They'd be going against Mrs Abercrombie as soon as she was dead, Tindall said, speaking as softly as the others had spoken. They must abide by what had been in Mrs Abercrombie's heart, Mr Apse said.

Again Miss Bell wondered what she would do when she left the garden, and wondered then if she had the right to plunge these people into unhappiness. With their faces so gently disposed before her, and with Plunkett out of the room, she saw for the first time their point of view. She said to herself that Plunkett would return to normal, since all her other knowledge of him seemed to prove that he was not a wicked man. Certainly there was no wickedness in Mrs Pope or Mr Apse, or in Tindall; and was it really so terrible, she found herself wondering then, to take from Mrs Abercombie what she had wished to give? Did it make sense to quibble now when you had never quibbled over Dr Ripley's diagnosis of hypochondria?

Miss Bell imagined the mound in the shrubbery beside the other mound, and meals in the kitchen, the same as ever, and visitors in the garden on a Sunday, and the admission charges still passed on to the Nurses. She imagined, as often she had, growing quite old in the setting she had come to love.

'A quiet little funeral,' Mrs Pope said. 'She'd have wanted that.'

'Yes,' Mr Apse said.

In her quiet voice, not looking at anyone, Miss Bell apologized for making a fuss.

To Dr Ripley's surprise, Plunkett took a packet of cigarettes from his pocket and lit one. He blew out smoke. He said:

'Neglected gallstones: don't wriggle out of it, Doctor.' His voice was cool and ungracious. He regarded Dr Ripley contemptuously. 'What about Bell's hand? That woman near died as well.'

For a moment Dr Ripley felt incapable of a reply. He remembered the scratch on Miss Bell's hand, a perfectly clean little wound. He'd put some iodine on it and a sticking-plaster dressing. He'd told her on no account to go poking it into her flower-beds, but of course she'd taken no notice.

'Miss Bell was extremely foolish,' he said at length, speaking quietly. 'She should have returned to me the moment the complication began.'

'You weren't to be found, Doctor. You were in the bar of the Clarence Hotel or down in the Royal Oak, or the Rogues' Arms –'

'I am not a drunkard, Plunkett. I was not negligent in the matter of Miss Bell's hand. Nor was I negligent over Mrs Abercrombie. Mrs Abercrombie suffered in no way whatsoever from gallstone trouble. Her heart was a little tired; she had a will to die and she died.'

'That isn't true, Doctor. She had a will to live, as this letter proves. She had a will to get matters sorted out –'

'If I were you, Plunkett, I'd go and lie down for a while.'

Dr Ripley spoke firmly. The astonishment that the butler had caused in him had vanished, leaving him unflustered and professional. His eyes behind their spectacles stared steadily into Plunkett's. He didn't seem at all beyond the work he did.

'Your car skidded,' Plunkett said, though without his previous confidence. 'You were whistled to the gills on Christmas booze that day –'

'That's offensive and untrue, Plunkett.'

'All I'm saying, sir, is that it'd be better for all concerned –'

'I'd be obliged if you didn't speak to me in that manner, Plunkett.'

To Plunkett's horror, Dr Ripley began to go. He placed his empty sherry glass on the table beside the decanter. He buttoned his jacket.

'Please, sir,' Plunkett said, changing his tone a little and hastening towards the sherry decanter. 'Have another glassful, sir.'

Dr Ripley ignored the invitation. 'I would just like to speak to the others,' he said, 'before I go.'

'Of course. Of course, sir.'

It was, Dr Ripley recognized afterwards, curiosity that caused him to make that request. Were the others in the same state as Plunkett? Had they, too, changed in a matter of hours from being agreeable people to being creatures you could neither like nor respect nor even take seriously? Would they, too, accuse him to his face of negligence and drunkenness?

In the kitchen the others rose to their feet when he entered.

'Doctor's here to have a word,' Plunkett said. He added that Dr Ripley had come to see their point of view, a statement that Dr Ripley didn't contradict immediately. He said instead that he was sorry that Mrs Abercrombie had died.

'Oh, so are we, sir,' Mrs Pope cried. 'We're sorry and shaken, sir.'

But in the kitchen Dr Ripley didn't feel their sorrow, any more than he had felt sorrow emanating from Plunkett in the drawing-room. In the kitchen there appeared to be fear in the eyes of quiet Mr Apse and in the eyes of Mrs Pope and the softly-spoken Miss Bell, and in the eyes of Tindall. It was fear, Dr Ripley suddenly realized, that had distorted Plunkett and continued to distort him, though differently now. Fear had bred greed in them, fear had made them desperate, and had turned them into fools.

'Dr Ripley'll see us through,' Plunkett said.

When he told the truth, they didn't say anything at all. Not even Plunkett spoke, and for a moment the only sound in the kitchen was the soft weeping of Miss Bell.

'Her wishes were clear,' Dr Ripley said. 'She died when she knew she'd made them so, when she received the letter this morning. Her wishes would have been honoured in law, even though they weren't in a will.'

They stood like statues in the kitchen. The weeping of Miss Bell ceased; there was no sound at all. They would none of them remain in the house now, Dr Ripley thought, because of their exposure one to another. In guilt and deception they had imagined they would remain, held together by their aberration. But now, with the memory of their greed and the irony of their error, there would be hatred and shame among them.

He wanted to comfort them, but could not. He wanted to say that they should forget what had taken place since Mrs Abercrombie's death, that they should attempt to carry out her wishes. But he knew it was too late for any of that. He turned and went away, leaving them still standing like statues. It was strange, he thought as he made his way through the house, that a happiness which had been so rich should have trailed such a snare behind it. And yet it seemed cruelly fitting that the loss of so much should wreak such damage in pleasant, harmless people.

Mrs Acland's Ghosts

Mr Mockler was a tailor. He carried on his business in a house that after twenty-five years of mortgage arrangements had finally become his: 22 Juniper Street, S W 17. He had never married and since he was now sixty-three it seemed likely that he never would. In an old public house, the Charles the First, he had a drink every evening with his friends Mr Uprichard and Mr Tile, who were tailors also. He lived in his house in Juniper Street with his cat Sam, and did his own cooking and washing and cleaning: he was not unhappy.

On the morning of 19 October 1972, Mr Mockler received a letter that astonished him. It was neatly written in a pleasantly rounded script that wasn't difficult to decipher. It did not address him as 'Dear Mr Mockler', nor was it signed, nor conventionally concluded. But his name was used repeatedly, and from its contents it seemed to Mr Mockler that the author of the letter was a Mrs Acland. He read the letter in amazement and then read it again and then, more slowly, a third time:

Dr Scott-Rowe is dead, Mr Mockler. I know he is dead because a new man is here, a smaller, younger man, called Dr Friendman. He looks at us, smiling, with his unblinking eyes. Miss Acheson says you can tell at a glance that he has practised hypnosis.

They're so sure of themselves, Mr Mockler: beyond the limits of their white-coated world they can accept nothing. I am a woman imprisoned because I once saw ghosts. I am paid for by the man who was my husband, who writes out monthly cheques for the peaches they bring to my room, and the beef olives and the marrons glacés. *'She must above all things be happy,' I can imagine the stout man who was my husband saying, walking with Dr Scott-Rowe over the sunny lawns and among the rose-beds. In this house there are twenty disturbed people in private rooms, cosseted by luxury because other people feel guilty. And when we walk ourselves on the lawns and among the rose-beds we murmur at the folly of those who have so expensively committed us, and at the greater folly of the medical profession: you can be disturbed without being mad. Is this the letter of a lunatic, Mr Mockler?*

I said this afternoon to Miss Acheson that Dr Scott-Rowe was dead. She said she knew. All of us would have Dr Friendman now, she said, with his smile and his tape-recorders. 'May Dr Scott-Rowe rest in peace,' said Miss Acheson: it was better to be dead than to be like Dr Friendman. Miss Acheson is a very old lady, twice my age exactly: I am thirty-nine and she is seventy-eight. She was committed when she was eighteen, in 1913, a year before the First World War. Miss Acheson was disturbed by visions of St Olaf of Norway and she still is. Such visions were an embarrassment to Miss Acheson's family in 1913 and so they quietly slipped her away. No one comes to see her now, no one has since 1927.

'You must write it all down,' Miss Acheson said to me when I told her, years ago, that I'd been committed because I'd seen ghosts and that I could prove the ghosts were real because the Rachels had seen them too. The Rachels are living some normal existence somewhere, yet they were terrified half out of their wits at the time and I wasn't frightened at all. The trouble nowadays, Miss Acheson says and I quite agree, is that if you like having ghosts near you people think you're round the bend.

I was talking to Miss Acheson about all this yesterday and she said why didn't I do what Sarah Crookham used to do? There's nothing the matter with Sarah Crookham, any more than there is with Miss Acheson or myself: all that Sarah Crookham suffers from is a broken heart. 'You must write it all down,' Miss Acheson said to her when she first came here, weeping, poor thing, every minute of the day. So she wrote it down and posted it to A. J. Rawson, a person she found in the telephone directory. But Mr Rawson never came, nor another person Sarah Crookham wrote to. I have looked you up in the telephone directory, Mr Mockler. It is nice to have a visitor.

'You must begin at the beginning,' Miss Acheson says, and so I am doing that. The beginning is back a bit, in January 1949, when I was fifteen. We lived in Richmond then, my parents and one brother, George, and my sisters Alice and Isabel. On Sundays, after lunch, we used to walk all together in Richmond Park with our dog, a Dalmatian called Salmon. I was the oldest and Alice was next, two years younger, and George was eleven and Isabel eight. It was lovely walking together in Richmond Park and then going home to Sunday tea. I remember the autumns and winters best, the cosiness of the coal fire, hot sponge cake and special Sunday sandwiches, and little buns that Alice and I always helped to make on Sunday mornings. We played Monopoly by the fire, and George would always have the ship and Anna the hat and Isabel the racing-car and Mummy the dog. Daddy and I would share the old boot. I really loved it.

I loved the house: 17 Lorelei Avenue, an ordinary suburban house built some time in the early 1920s, when Miss Acheson was still quite young.

There were bits of stained glass on either side of the hall door and a single stained-glass pane, Moses in the bulrushes, in one of the landing windows. At Christmas especially it was lovely: we'd have the Christmas tree in the hall and always on Christmas Eve, as long as I can remember, there'd be a party. I can remember the parties quite vividly. There'd be people standing round drinking punch and the children would play hide-and-seek upstairs, and nobody could ever find George. It's George, Mr Mockler, that all this is about. And Alice, of course, and Isabel.

When I first described them to Dr Scott-Rowe he said they sounded marvellous, and I said I thought they probably were, but I suppose a person can be prejudiced in family matters of that kind. Because they were, after all, my brother and my two sisters and because, of course, they're dead now. I mean, they were probably ordinary, just like any children. Well, you can see what you think, Mr Mockler.

George was small for his age, very wiry, dark-haired, a darting kind of boy who was always laughing, who had often to be reprimanded by my father because his teachers said he was the most mischievous boy in his class. Alice, being two years older, was just the opposite: demure and silent, but happy in her quiet way, and beautiful, far more beautiful than I was. Isabel wasn't beautiful at all. She was all freckles, with long pale plaits and long legs that sometimes could run as fast as George's. She and George were as close as two persons can get, but in a way we were all close: there was a lot of love in 17 Lorelei Avenue.

I had a cold the day it happened, a Saturday it was. I was cross because they kept worrying about leaving me in the house on my own. They'd bring me back Black Magic chocolates, they said, and my mother said she'd buy a bunch of daffodils if she saw any. I heard the car crunching over the gravel outside the garage, and then their voices telling Salmon not to put his paws on the upholstery. My father blew the horn, saying goodbye to me, and after that the silence began. I must have known even then, long before it happened, that nothing would be the same again.

When I was twenty-two, Mr Mockler, I married a man called Acland, who helped me to get over the tragedy. George would have been eighteen, and Anna twenty and Isabel fifteen. They would have liked my husband because he was a good-humoured and generous man. He was very plump, many years older than I was, with a fondness for all food. 'You're like a child,' I used to say to him and we'd laugh together. Cheese in particular he liked, and ham and every kind of root vegetable, parsnips, turnips, celeriac, carrots, leeks, potatoes. He used to come back to the house and take four or five pounds of gammon from the car, and chops, and blocks of ice-cream, and biscuits, and two or even three McVitie's fruitcakes. He was very partial to McVitie's fruitcakes. At night, at nine or ten o'clock, he'd make cocoa for both of us and we'd have it while we were watching the television, with a slice or two of fruitcake. He was such a kind man in those days. I got quite fat myself, which might surprise you, Mr Mockler, because I'm on the thin side now.

My husband was, and still is, both clever and rich. One led to the other: he made a fortune designing metal fasteners for the aeroplane industry. Once, in May 1960, he drove me to a house in Worcestershire. 'I wanted it to be a surprise,' he said, stopping his mustard-coloured Alfa-Romeo in front of this quite extensive Victorian façade. 'There,' he said, embracing me, reminding me that it was my birthday. Two months later we went to live there.

We had no children. In the large Victorian house I made my life with the man I'd married and once again, as in 17 Lorelei Avenue, I was happy. The house was near a village but otherwise remote. My husband went away from it by day, to the place where his aeroplane fasteners were manufactured and tested. There were – and still are – aeroplanes in the air which would have fallen to pieces if they hadn't been securely fastened by the genius of my husband.

The house had many rooms. There was a large square drawing-room with a metal ceiling – beaten tin, I believe it was. It had patterns like wedding-cake icing on it. It was painted white and blue, and gave, as well as the impression of a wedding-cake, a Wedgwood effect. People remarked on this ceiling and my husband used to explain that metal ceilings had once been very popular, especially in the large houses of Australia. Well-to-do Australians, apparently, would have them shipped from Birmingham in colonial imitation of an English fashion. My husband and I, arm in arm, would lead people about the house, pointing out the ceiling or the green wallpaper in our bedroom or the portraits hung on the stairs.

The lighting was bad in the house. The long first-floor landing was a gloomy place by day and lit by a single wall-light at night. At the end of this landing another flight of stairs, less grand than the stairs that led from the hall, wound upwards to the small rooms that had once upon a time been servants' quarters, and another flight continued above them to attics and store-rooms. The bathroom was on the first floor, tiled in green Victorian tiles, and there was a lavatory next door to it, encased in mahogany.

In the small rooms that had once been the servants' quarters lived Mr and Mrs Rachels. My husband had had a kitchen and a bathroom put in for them so that their rooms were quite self-contained. Mr Rachels worked

*in the garden and his wife cleaned the house. It wasn't really necessary to
have them at all: I could have cleaned the house myself and even done the
gardening, but my husband insisted in his generous way. At night I could
hear the Rachels moving about above me. I didn't like this and my husband
asked them to move more quietly.*

*In 1962 my husband was asked to go to Germany, to explain his
aeroplane fasteners to the German aircraft industry. It was to be a prolonged trip, three months at least, and I was naturally unhappy when he
told me. He was unhappy himself, but on March 4th he flew to Hamburg,
leaving me with the Rachels.*

*They were a pleasant enough couple, somewhere in their fifties I would
think, he rather silent, she inclined to talk. The only thing that worried me
about them was the way they used to move about at night above my head.
After my husband had gone to Germany I gave Mrs Rachels money to buy
slippers, but I don't think she ever did because the sounds continued just
as before. I naturally didn't make a fuss about it.*

*On the night of March 7th I was awakened by a band playing in the
house. The tune was an old tune of the fifties called, I believe, 'Looking
for Henry Lee'. The noise was very loud in my bedroom and I lay there
frightened, not knowing why this noise should be coming to me like this,
Victor Silvester in strict dance tempo. Then a voice spoke, a long babble
of French, and I realized that I was listening to a radio programme. The
wireless was across the room, on a table by the windows. I put on my
bedside light and got up and switched it off. I drank some orange juice
and went back to sleep. It didn't even occur to me to wonder who had
turned it on.*

*The next day I told Mrs Rachels about it, and it was she, in fact, who
made me think that it was all rather stranger than it seemed. I definitely
remembered turning the wireless off myself before going to bed, and in
any case I was not in the habit of listening to French stations, so that even
if the wireless had somehow come on of its own accord it should not have
been tuned in to a French station.*

*Two days later I found the bath half-filled with water and the towels all
rumpled and damp, thrown about on the floor. The water in the bath was
tepid and dirty: someone, an hour or so ago, had had a bath.*

*I climbed the stairs to the Rachels' flat and knocked on their door. 'Is
your bathroom out of order?' I said when Mr Rachels came to the door,
not wearing the slippers I'd given them money for. I said I didn't at all
mind their using mine, only I'd be grateful if they'd remember to let the
water out and to bring down their own towels. Mr Rachels looked at me
in the way people have sometimes, as though you're insane. He called his*

wife and all three of us went down to look at my bathroom. They denied emphatically that either of them had had a bath.

When I came downstairs the next morning, having slept badly, I found the kitchen table had been laid for four. There was a tablecloth on the table, which was something I never bothered about, and a kettle was boiling on the Aga. Beside it, a large brown teapot, not the one I normally used, was heating. I made some tea and sat down, thinking about the Rachels. Why should they behave like this? Why should they creep into my bedroom in the middle of the night and turn the wireless on? Why should they have a bath in my bathroom and deny it? Why should they lay the breakfast table as though we had overnight guests? I left the table just as it was. Butter had been rolled into pats. Marmalade had been placed in two china dishes. A silver toast-rack that an aunt of my husband had given us as a wedding present was waiting for toast.

'Thank you for laying the table,' I said to Mrs Rachels when she entered the kitchen an hour later.

She shook her head. She began to say that she hadn't laid the table but then she changed her mind. I could see from her face that she and her husband had been discussing the matter of the bath the night before. She could hardly wait to tell him about the breakfast table. I smiled at her.

'A funny thing happened the other night,' I said. 'I woke up to find Victor Silvester playing a tune called "Looking for Henry Lee".'

'Henry Lee?' Mrs Rachels said, turning around from the sink. Her face, usually blotched with pink, like the skin of an apple, was white.

'It's an old song of the fifties.'

It was while saying that that I realized what was happening in the house. I naturally didn't say anything to Mrs Rachels, and I at once began to regret that I'd said anything in the first place. It had frightened me, finding the bathroom like that, and clearly it must have frightened the Rachels. I didn't want them to be frightened because naturally there was nothing to be frightened about. George and Alice and Isabel wouldn't hurt anyone, not unless death had changed them enormously. But even so I knew I couldn't ever explain that to the Rachels.

'Well, I suppose I'm just getting absent-minded,' I said. 'People do, so they say, when they live alone.' I laughed to show I wasn't worried or frightened, to make it all seem ordinary.

'You mean, you laid the table yourself?' Mrs Rachels said. 'And had a bath?'

'And didn't turn the wireless off properly. Funny,' I said, 'how these things go in threes. Funny, how there's always an explanation.' I laughed again and Mrs Rachels had to laugh too.

After that it was lovely, just like being back in 17 Lorelei Avenue. I bought Black Magic chocolates and bars of Fry's and Cadbury's Milk, all the things we'd liked. I often found bathwater left in and the towels crumpled, and now and again I came down in the morning to find the breakfast table laid. On the first-floor landing, on the evening of March 11th, I caught a glimpse of George, and in the garden, three days later, I saw Isabel and Alice.

On March 15th the Rachels left. I hadn't said a word to them about finding the bathroom used again or the breakfast laid or actually seeing the children. I'd been cheerful and smiling whenever I met them. I'd talked about how Brasso wasn't as good as it used to be to Mrs Rachels, and had asked her husband about the best kinds of soil for bulbs.

'We can't stay a minute more,' Mrs Rachels said, her face all white and tight in the hall, and then to my astonishment they attempted to persuade me to go also.

'The house isn't fit to live in,' Mr Rachels said.

'Oh now, that's nonsense,' I began to say, but they both shook their heads.

'There's children here,' Mrs Rachels said. 'There's three children appearing all over the place.'

'Come right up to you,' Mr Rachels said. 'Laugh at you sometimes.'

They were trembling, both of them. They were so terrified I thought they might die, that their hearts would give out there in the hall and they'd just drop down. But they didn't. They walked out of the hall door with their three suitcases, down the drive to catch a bus. I never saw them again.

I suppose, Mr Mockler, you have to be frightened of ghosts: I suppose that's their way of communicating. I mean, it's no good being like me, delighting in it all, being happy because I wasn't lonely in that house any more. You have to be like the Rachels, terrified half out of your wits. I think I knew that as I watched the Rachels go: I think I knew that George and Isabel and Alice would go with them, that I was only a kind of go-between, that the Rachels were what George and Isabel and Alice could really have fun with. I almost ran after the Rachels, but I knew it would be no good.

Without the Rachels and my brother and my two sisters, I was frightened myself in that big house. I moved everything into the kitchen: the television set and the plants I kept in the drawing-room, and a camp-bed to sleep on. I was there, asleep in the camp-bed, when my husband returned from Germany; he had changed completely. He raved at me, not listening to a word I said. There were cups of tea all over the house, he said, and bits of bread and biscuits and cake and chocolates. There were notes in envelopes, and messages scrawled in my hand-writing on the wallpaper in various rooms. Everywhere was dusty. Where, he wanted to know, were the Rachels?

He stood there with a canvas bag in his left hand, an airline bag that had the word Lufthansa *on it. He'd put on at least a stone, I remember thinking, and his hair was shorter than before.*

'Listen,' I said, 'I would like to tell you.' And I tried to tell him, as I've told you, Mr Mockler, about George and Isabel and Alice in 17 Lorelei Avenue and how we all went together for a walk with our dog, every Sunday afternoon in Richmond Park, and how on Christmas Eve my mother always gave a party. I told him about the stained-glass pane in the window, Moses in the bulrushes, and the hide-and-seek we played, and how my father and I always shared the old boot in Monopoly. I told him about the day of the accident, how the tyre on the lorry suddenly exploded and how the lorry went whizzing around on the road and then just tumbled over on top of them. I'd put out cups of tea, I said, and biscuits and cake and the little messages, just in case they came back again – not for them to eat or to read particularly, but just as a sign. They'd given me a sign first, I explained: George had turned on my wireless in the middle of the night and Isabel had had baths and Alice had laid the breakfast table. But then they'd gone because they'd been more interested in annoying the Rachels than in comforting me. I began to weep, telling him how lonely I'd been without them, how lonely I'd been ever since the day of the accident, how the silence had been everywhere. I couldn't control myself: tears came out of my eyes as though they'd never stop. I felt sickness all over my body, paining me in my head and my chest, sour in my stomach. I wanted to die because the loneliness was too much. Loneliness was the worst thing in the world, I said, gasping out words, with spit and tears going cold on my face. People were only shadows, I tried to explain, when you had loneliness and silence like that, like a shroud around you. You couldn't reach out of the shroud sometimes, you couldn't connect because shadows are hard to connect with and it's frightening when you try because everyone is looking at you. But it was lovely, I whispered, when the children came back to annoy the Rachels. My husband replied by telling me I was insane.

The letter finished there, and Mr Mockler was more astonished each time he read it. He had never in his life received such a document before, nor did he in fact very often receive letters of any kind, apart from bills and, if he was fortunate, cheques in settlement. He shook his head over the letter and placed it in the inside pocket of his jacket.

That day, as he stitched and measured, he imagined the place Mrs Acland wrote of, the secluded house with twenty female inmates, and the lawn and the rose-beds. He imagined the other house, 17 Lorelei Avenue in Richmond, and the third house, the Victorian residence in the Worcester-shire countryside. He imagined Mrs Acland's obese husband with his short hair and his aeroplane fasteners, and the children who had been killed in a motor-car accident, and Mr and Mrs Rachels whom they had haunted. All day long the faces of these people flitted through Mr Mockler's mind, with old Miss Acheson and Sarah Crookham and Dr Scott-Rowe and Dr Friendman. In the evening, when he met his friends Mr Tile and Mr Uprichard in the Charles the First, he showed them the letter before even ordering them drinks.

'Well, I'm beggared,' remarked Mr Uprichard, a man known locally for his gentle nature. 'That poor creature.'

Mr Tile, who was not given to expressing himself, shook his head.

Mr Mockler asked Mr Uprichard if he should visit this Mrs Acland. 'Poor creature,' Mr Uprichard said again, and added that without a doubt Mrs Acland had written to a stranger because of the loneliness she men-tioned, the loneliness like a shroud around her.

Some weeks later Mr Mockler, having given the matter further thought and continuing to be affected by the contents of the letter, took a Green Line bus out of London to the address that Mrs Acland had given him. He made inquiries, feeling quite adventurous, and was told that the house was three-quarters of a mile from where the bus had dropped him, down a side road. He found it without further difficulty. It was a house surrounded by a high brick wall in which large, black wrought-iron gates were backed with sheets of tin so that no one could look through the ornamental scrollwork. The gates were locked. Mr Mockler rang a bell in the wall.

'Yes?' a man said, opening the gate that was on Mr Mockler's left.

'Well,' said Mr Mockler and found it difficult to proceed.

'Yes?' the man said.

'Well, I've had a letter. Asking me to come, I think. My name's Mockler.'

The man opened the gate a little more and Mr Mockler stepped through.

The man walked ahead of him and Mr Mockler saw the lawns that had been described, and the rose-beds. The house he considered most attractive: a high Georgian building with beautiful windows. An old woman was walking slowly by herself with the assistance of a stick: Miss Acheson, Mr Mockler guessed. In the distance he saw other women, walking slowly on leaf-strewn paths.

Autumn was Mr Mockler's favourite season and he was glad to be in the country on this pleasantly autumnal day. He thought of remarking on this to the man who led him towards the house, but since the man did not incline towards conversation he did not do so.

In the yellow waiting-room there were no magazines and no pictures on the walls and no flowers. It was not a room in which Mr Mockler would have cared to wait for long, and in fact he did not have to. A woman dressed as a nurse except that she wore a green cardigan came in. She smiled briskly at him and said that Dr Friendman would see him. She asked Mr Mockler to follow her.

'How very good of you to come,' Dr Friendman said, smiling at Mr Mockler in the way that Mrs Acland had described in her letter. 'How very humane,' said Dr Friendman.

'I had a letter, from a Mrs Acland.'

'Quite so, Mr Mockler. Mr Mockler, could I press you towards a glass of sherry?'

Mr Mockler, surprised at this line of talk, accepted the sherry, saying it was good of Dr Friendman. He drank the sherry while Dr Friendman read the letter. When he'd finished, Dr Friendman crossed to the window of the room and pulled aside a curtain and asked Mr Mockler if he'd mind looking out.

There was a courtyard, small and cobbled, in which a gardener was sweeping leaves into a pile. At the far end of it, sitting on a tapestry-backed dining-chair in the autumn sunshine, was a woman in a blue dress. 'Try these,' said Dr Friendman and handed Mr Mockler a pair of binoculars.

It was a beautiful face, thin and seeming fragile, with large blue eyes and lips that were now slightly parted, smiling in the sunshine. Hair the colour of corn was simply arranged, hanging on either side of the face and curling in around it. The hair shone in the sunlight, as though it was for ever being brushed.

'I find them useful,' Dr Friendman said, taking the binoculars from Mr Mockler's hands. 'You have to keep an eye, you know.'

'That's Mrs Acland?' Mr Mockler asked.

'That's the lady who wrote to you: the letter's a bit inaccurate, Mr Mockler. It wasn't quite like that in 17 Lorelei Avenue.'

'Not quite like it?'

'She cannot forget Lorelei Avenue. I'm afraid she never will. That beautiful woman, Mr Mockler, was a beautiful girl, yet she married the first man who asked her, a widower thirty years older than her, a fat designer of aircraft fasteners. He pays her bills just as she says in her letter, and even when he's dead they'll go on being paid. He used to visit her at first, but he found it too painful. He stood in this very room one day, Mr Mockler, and said to Dr Scott-Rowe that no man had ever been appreciated by a woman as much as he had by her. And all because he'd been kind to her in the most ordinary ways.'

Mr Mockler said he was afraid that he didn't know what Dr Friendman was talking about. As though he hadn't heard this quiet protest, Dr Friendman smiled and said:

'But it was, unfortunately, too late for kindness. 17 Lorelei Avenue had done its damage, like a cancer in her mind: she could not forget her childhood.'

'Yes, she says in her letter. George and Alice and Isabel –'

'All her childhood, Mr Mockler, her parents did not speak to one another. They didn't quarrel, they didn't address each other in any way whatsoever. When she was five they'd come to an agreement: that they should both remain in 17 Lorelei Avenue because neither would ever have agreed to give up an inch of the child they'd between them caused to be born. In the house there was nothing, Mr Mockler, for all her childhood years: nothing except silence.'

'But there was George and Alice and Isabel –'

'No, Mr Mockler. There was no George and no Alice and no Isabel. No hide-and-seek or parties on Christmas Eve, no Monopoly on Sundays by the fire. Can you imagine 17 Lorelei Avenue, Mr Mockler, as she is now incapable of imagining it? Two people so cruel to one another that they knew that either of them could be parted from the child in some divorce court. A woman bitterly hating the man whom once she'd loved, and he returning each evening, hurrying back from an office in case his wife and the child were having a conversation. She would sit, Mr Mockler, in a room with them, with the silence heavy in the air, and their hatred for one another. All three of them would sit down to a meal and no one would speak. No other children came to that house, no other people. She used to hide on the way back from school: she'd go down the area steps of other houses and crouch beside dustbins.'

'Dustbins?' repeated Mr Mockler, more astonished than ever. *'Dustbins?'*

'Other children didn't take to her. She couldn't talk to them. She'd never learned to talk to anyone. He was a patient man, Mr Acland, when he came along, a good and patient man.'

Mr Mockler said that the child's parents must have been monsters, but Dr Friendman shook his head. No one was a monster, Dr Friendman said in a professional manner, and in the circumstances Mr Mockler didn't feel he could argue with him. But the people called Rachels were real, he did point out, as real as the fat designer of aircraft fasteners. Had they left the house, he asked, as it said in the letter? And if they had, what had they been frightened of?

Dr Friendman smiled again. 'I don't believe in ghosts,' he said, and he explained at great length to Mr Mockler that it was Mrs Acland herself who had frightened the Rachels, turning on a wireless in the middle of the night and running baths and laying tables for people who weren't there. Mr Mockler listened and was interested to note that Dr Friendman used words that were not easy to understand, and quoted from experts who were in Dr Friendman's line of business but whose names meant nothing to Mr Mockler.

Mr Mockler, listening to all of it, nodded but was not convinced. The Rachels had left the house, just as the letter said: he knew that, he felt it in his bones and it felt like the truth. The Rachels had been frightened of Mrs Acland's ghosts even though they'd been artificial ghosts. They'd been real to her, and they'd been real to the Rachels because she'd made them so. Shadows had stepped out of her mind because in her loneliness she'd wished them to. They'd laughed and played, and frightened the Rachels half out of their wits.

'There's always an explanation,' said Dr Friendman.

Mr Mockler nodded, profoundly disagreeing.

'She'll think you're Mr Rachels,' said Dr Friendman, 'come to say he saw the ghosts. If you wouldn't mind saying you did, it keeps her happy.'

'But it's the truth,' Mr Mockler cried with passion in his voice. 'Of course it's the truth: there can be ghosts like that, just as there can be in any other way.'

'Oh, come now,' murmured Dr Friendman with his sad, humane smile.

Mr Mockler followed Dr Friendman from the room. They crossed a landing and descended a back staircase, passing near a kitchen in which a chef with a tall chef's hat was beating pieces of meat. 'Ah, Wiener schnitzel,' said Dr Friendman.

In the cobbled courtyard the gardener had finished sweeping up the leaves and was wheeling them away in a wheelbarrow. The woman was still sitting on the tapestry-backed chair, still smiling in the autumn sunshine.

'Look,' said Dr Friendman, 'a visitor.'

The woman rose and went close to Mr Mockler. 'They didn't mean to frighten you,' she said, 'even though it's the only way ghosts can communicate. They were only having fun, Mr Rachels.'

'I think Mr Rachels realizes that now,' Dr Friendman said.

'Yes, of course,' said Mr Mockler.

'No one ever believed me, and I kept on saying, "When the Rachels come back, they'll tell the truth about poor George and Alice and Isabel." You saw them, didn't you, Mr Rachels?'

'Yes,' Mr Mockler said. 'We saw them.'

She turned and walked away, leaving the tapestry-backed chair behind her.

'You're a humane person,' Dr Friendman said, holding out his right hand, which Mr Mockler shook. The same man led him back through the lawns and the rose-beds, to the gates.

It was an experience that Mr Mockler found impossible to forget. He measured and stitched, and talked to his friends Mr Uprichard and Mr Tile in the Charles the First; he went for a walk morning and evening, and no day passed during which he did not think of the woman whom people looked at through binoculars. Somewhere in England, or at least somewhere in the world, the Rachels were probably still alive, and had Mr Mockler been a younger man he might even have set about looking for them. He would have liked to bring them to the secluded house where the woman now lived, to have been there himself when they told the truth to Dr Friendman. It seemed a sadness, as he once remarked to Mr Uprichard, that on top of everything else a woman's artificial ghosts should not be honoured, since she had brought them into being and given them life, as other women give children life.

Another Christmas

You always looked back, she thought. You looked back at other years, other Christmas cards arriving, the children younger. There was the year Patrick had cried, disliking the holly she was decorating the living-room with. There was the year Bridget had got a speck of coke in her eye on Christmas Eve and had to be taken to the hospital at Hammersmith in the middle of the night. There was the first year of their marriage, when she and Dermot were still in Waterford. And ever since they'd come to London there was the presence on Christmas Day of their landlord, Mr Joyce, a man whom they had watched becoming elderly.

She was middle-aged now, with touches of grey in her curly dark hair, a woman known for her cheerfulness, running a bit to fat. Her husband was the opposite: thin and seeming ascetic, with more than a hint of the priest in him, a good man. 'Will we get married, Norah?' he'd said one night in the Tara Ballroom in Waterford, 6 November 1953. The proposal had astonished her: it was his brother Ned, heavy and fresh-faced, a different kettle of fish altogether, whom she'd been expecting to make it.

Patiently he held a chair for her while she strung paper-chains across the room, from one picture-rail to another. He warned her to be careful about attaching anything to the electric light. He still held the chair while she put sprigs of holly behind the pictures. He was cautious by nature and alarmed by little things, particularly anxious in case she fell off chairs. He'd never mount a chair himself, to put up decorations or anything else: he'd be useless at it in his opinion and it was his opinion that mattered. He'd never been able to do a thing about the house, but it didn't matter because since the boys had grown up they'd attended to whatever she couldn't manage herself. You wouldn't dream of remarking on it: he was the way he was, considerate and thoughtful in what he did do, teetotal, clever, full of fondness for herself and for the family they'd reared, full of respect for her also.

'Isn't it remarkable how quick it comes round, Norah?' he said while he held the chair. 'Isn't it no time since last year?'

'No time at all.'

'Though a lot happened in the year, Norah.'

'An awful lot happened.'

Two of the pictures she decorated were scenes of Waterford: the quays and a man driving sheep past the Bank of Ireland. Her mother had given them to her, taking them down from the hall of the farmhouse.

There was a picture of the Virgin and Child, and other, smaller pictures. She placed her last sprig of holly, a piece with berries on it, above the Virgin's halo.

'I'll make a cup of tea,' she said, descending from the chair and smiling at him.

'A cup of tea'd be great, Norah.'

The living-room, containing three brown armchairs and a table with upright chairs around it, and a sideboard with a television set on it, was crowded by this furniture and seemed even smaller than it was because of the decorations that had been added. On the mantelpiece, above a built-in gas-fire, Christmas cards were arrayed on either side of an ornate green clock.

The house was in a terrace in Fulham. It had always been too small for the family, but now that Patrick and Brendan no longer lived there things were easier. Patrick had married a girl called Pearl six months ago, almost as soon as his period of training with the Midland Bank had ended. Brendan was training in Liverpool, with a firm of computer manufacturers. The three remaining children were still at school, Bridget at the nearby convent, Cathal and Tom at the Sacred Heart Primary. When Patrick and Brendan had moved out the room they'd always shared had become Bridget's. Until then Bridget had slept in her parents' room and she'd have to return there this Christmas because Brendan would be back for three nights. Patrick and Pearl would just come for Christmas Day. They'd be going to Pearl's people, in Croydon, on Boxing Day – St Stephen's Day, as Norah and Dermot always called it, in the Irish manner.

'It'll be great, having them all,' he said. 'A family again, Norah.'

'And Pearl.'

'She's part of us now, Norah.'

'Will you have biscuits with your tea? I have a packet of Nice.'

He said he would, thanking her. He was a meter-reader with North Thames Gas, a position he had held for twenty-one years, ever since he'd emigrated. In Waterford he'd worked as a clerk in the Customs, not earning very much and not much caring for the stuffy, smoke-laden office he shared with half a dozen other clerks. He had come to England because Norah had thought it was a good idea, because she'd always wanted to work in a London shop. She'd been given a job in Dickins & Jones, in the household linens department, and he'd been taken on as a meter-reader, cycling from door to door, remembering the different houses and where the meters were situated in each, being agreeable to householders: all of it suited him from the start. He devoted time to thought while he rode about, and in particular to religious matters.

In her small kitchen she made the tea and carried it on a tray into the living-room. She'd been late this year with the decorations. She always liked to get them up a week in advance because they set the mood, making everyone feel right for Christmas. She'd been busy with stuff for a stall Father Malley had asked her to run for his Christmas Sale. A fashion stall he'd called it, but not quite knowing what he meant she'd just asked people for any old clothes they had, jumble really. Because of the time it had taken she hadn't had a minute to see to the decorations until this afternoon, two days before Christmas Eve. But that, as it turned out, had been all for the best. Bridget and Cathal and Tom had gone up to Putney to the pictures, Dermot didn't work on a Monday afternoon: it was convenient that they'd have an hour or two alone together because there was the matter of Mr Joyce to bring up. Not that she wanted to bring it up, but it couldn't be just left there.

'The cup that cheers,' he said, breaking a biscuit in half. Deliberately she put off raising the subject she had in mind. She watched him nibbling the biscuit and then dropping three heaped spoons of sugar into his tea and stirring it. He loved tea. The first time he'd taken her out, to the Savoy cinema in Waterford, they'd had tea afterwards in the cinema café and they'd talked about the film and about people they knew. He'd come to live in Waterford from the country, from the farm his brother had inherited, quite close to her father's farm. He reckoned he'd settled, he told her that night: Waterford wasn't sensational, but it suited him in a lot of ways. If he hadn't married her he'd still be there, working eight hours a day in the Customs and not caring for it, yet managing to get by because he had his religion to assist him.

'Did we get a card from Father Jack yet?' he inquired, referring to a distant cousin, a priest in Chicago.

'Not yet. But it's always on the late side, Father Jack's. It was February last year.'

She sipped her tea, sitting in one of the other brown armchairs, on the other side of the gas-fire. It was pleasant being there alone with him in the decorated room, the green clock ticking on the mantelpiece, the Christmas cards, dusk gathering outside. She smiled and laughed, taking another biscuit while he lit a cigarette. 'Isn't this great?' she said. 'A bit of peace for ourselves?'

Solemnly he nodded.

'Peace comes dropping slow,' he said, and she knew he was quoting from some book or other. Quite often he said things she didn't understand. 'Peace and goodwill,' he added, and she understood that all right.

He tapped the ash from his cigarette into an ashtray which was kept for his use, beside the gas-fire. All his movements were slow. He was a slow thinker, even though he was clever. He arrived at a conclusion, having thought long and carefully; he balanced everything in his mind. 'We must think about that, Norah,' he said that day, twenty-two years ago, when she'd suggested that they should move to England. A week later he'd said that if she really wanted to he'd agree.

They talked about Bridget and Cathal and Tom. When they came in from the cinema they'd only just have time to change their clothes before setting out again for the Christmas party at Bridget's convent.

'It's a big day for them. Let them lie in in the morning, Norah.'

'They could lie in for ever,' she said, laughing in case there might seem to be harshness in this recommendation. With Christmas excitement running high, the less she heard from them the better.

'Did you get Cathal the gadgets he wanted?'

'Chemistry stuff. A set in a box.'

'You're great the way you manage, Norah.'

She denied that. She poured more tea for both of them. She said, as casually as she could:

'Mr Joyce won't come. I'm not counting him in for Christmas Day.'

'He hasn't failed us yet, Norah.'

'He won't come this year.' She smiled through the gloom at him. 'I think we'd best warn the children about it.'

'Where would he go if he didn't come here? Where'd he get his dinner?'

'Lyons used to be open in the old days.'

'He'd never do that.'

'The Bulrush Café has a turkey dinner advertised. There's a lot of people go in for that now. If you have a mother doing a job she maybe hasn't the time for the cooking. They go out to a hotel or a café, three or four pounds a head –'

'Mr Joyce wouldn't go to a café. No one could go into a café on their own on Christmas Day.'

'He won't come here, dear.'

It had to be said: it was no good just pretending, laying a place for the old man on an assumption that had no basis to it. Mr Joyce would not come because Mr Joyce, last August, had ceased to visit them. Every Friday night he used to come, for a cup of tea and a chat, to watch the nine o'clock news with them. Every Christmas Day he'd brought carefully chosen presents for the children, and chocolates and nuts and cigarettes. He'd given Patrick and Pearl a radio as a wedding present.

'I think he'll come all right. I think maybe he hasn't been too well. God help him, it's a great age, Norah.'

'He hasn't been ill, Dermot.'

Every Friday Mr Joyce had sat there in the third of the brown armchairs, watching the television, his bald head inclined so that his good ear was closer to the screen. He was tallish, rather bent now, frail and bony, with a modest white moustache. In his time he'd been a builder, which was how he had come to own property in Fulham, a self-made man who'd never married. That evening in August he had been quite as usual. Bridget had kissed him good-night because for as long as she could remember she'd always done that when he came on Friday evenings. He'd asked Cathal how he was getting on with his afternoon paper round.

There had never been any difficulties over the house. They considered that he was fair in his dealings with them; they were his tenants and his friends. When it seemed that the Irish had bombed English people to death in Birmingham and Guildford he did not cease to arrive every Friday evening and on Christmas Day. The bombings were discussed after the news, the Tower of London bomb, the bomb in the bus, and all the others. 'Maniacs,' Mr Joyce said and nobody contradicted him.

'He would never forget the children, Norah. Not at Christmas-time.'

His voice addressed her from the shadows. She felt the warmth of the gas-fire reflected in her face and knew if she looked in a mirror she'd see that she was quite flushed. Dermot's face never reddened. Even though he was nervy, he never displayed emotion. On all occasions his face retained its paleness, his eyes acquired no glimmer of passion. No wife could have a better husband, yet in the matter of Mr Joyce he was so wrong it almost frightened her.

'Is it tomorrow I call in for the turkey?' he said.

She nodded, hoping he'd ask her if anything was the matter because as a rule she never just nodded in reply to a question. But he didn't say anything. He stubbed his cigarette out. He asked if there was another cup of tea in the pot.

'Dermot, would you take something round to Mr Joyce?'

'A message, is it?'

'I have a tartan tie for him.'

'Wouldn't you give it to him on the day, Norah? Like you always do.' He spoke softly, still insisting. She shook her head.

It was all her fault. If she hadn't said they should go to England, if she hadn't wanted to work in a London shop, they wouldn't be caught in the trap they'd made for themselves. Their children spoke with London accents.

Patrick and Brendan worked for English firms and would make their homes in England. Patrick had married an English girl. They were Catholics and they had Irish names, yet home for them was not Waterford.

'Could you make it up with Mr Joyce, Dermot? Could you go round with the tie and say you were sorry?'

'Sorry?'

'You know what I mean.' In spite of herself her voice had acquired a trace of impatience, an edginess that was unusual in it. She did not ever speak to him like that. It was the way she occasionally spoke to the children.

'What would I say I was sorry for, Norah?'

'For what you said that night.' She smiled, calming her agitation. He lit another cigarette, the flame of the match briefly illuminating his face. Nothing had changed in his face. He said:

'I don't think Mr Joyce and I had any disagreement, Norah.'

'I know, Dermot. You didn't mean anything –'

'There was no disagreement, girl.'

There had been no disagreement, but on that evening in August something else had happened. On the nine o'clock news there had been a report of another outrage and afterwards, when Dermot had turned the television off, there'd been the familiar comment on it. He couldn't understand the mentality of people like that, Mr Joyce said yet again, killing just anyone, destroying life for no reason. Dermot had shaken his head over it, she herself had said it was uncivilized. Then Dermot had added that they mustn't of course forget what the Catholics in the North had suffered. The bombs were a crime but it didn't do to forget that the crime would not be there if generations of Catholics in the North had not been treated as animals. There'd been a silence then, a difficult kind of silence which she'd broken herself. All that was in the past, she'd said hastily, in a rush, nothing in the past or the present or anywhere else could justify the killing of innocent people. Even so, Dermot had added, it didn't do to avoid the truth. Mr Joyce had not said anything.

'I'd say there was no need to go round with the tie, Norah. I'd say he'd make the effort on Christmas Day.'

'Of course he won't.' Her voice was raised, with more than impatience in it now. But her anger was controlled. 'Of course he won't come.'

'It's a time for goodwill, Norah. Another Christmas: to remind us.'

He spoke slowly, the words prompted by some interpretation of God's voice in answer to a prayer. She recognized that in his deliberate tone.

'It isn't just another Christmas. It's an awful kind of Christmas. It's a Christmas to be ashamed, and you're making it worse, Dermot.' Her lips were trembling in a way that was uncomfortable. If she tried to calm herself she'd become jittery instead, she might even begin to cry. Mr Joyce had been generous and tactful, she said loudly. It made no difference to Mr Joyce that they were Irish people, that their children went to school with the children of I.R.A. men. Yet his generosity and his tact had been thrown back in his face. Everyone knew that the Catholics in the North had suffered, that generations of injustice had been twisted into the shape of a cause. But you couldn't say it to an old man who had hardly been outside Fulham in his life. You couldn't say it because when you did it sounded like an excuse for murder.

'You have to state the truth, Norah. It's there to be told.'

'I never yet cared for a North of Ireland person, Catholic or Protestant. Let them fight it out and not bother us.'

'You shouldn't say that, Norah.'

'It's more of your truth for you.'

He didn't reply. There was the gleam of his face for a moment as he drew on his cigarette. In all their married life they had never had a quarrel that was in any way serious, yet she felt herself now in the presence of a seriousness that was too much for her. She had told him that whenever a new bombing took place she prayed it might be the work of the Angry Brigade, or any group that wasn't Irish. She'd told him that in shops she'd begun to feel embarrassed because of her Waterford accent. He'd said she must have courage, and she realized now that he had drawn on courage himself when he'd made the remark to Mr Joyce. He would have prayed and considered before making it. He would have seen it in the end as his Catholic duty.

'He thinks you don't condemn people being killed.' She spoke quietly even though she felt a wildness inside her. She felt she should be out on the streets, shouting in her Waterford accent, violently stating that the bombers were more despicable with every breath they drew, that hatred and death were all they deserved. She saw herself on Fulham Broadway, haranguing the passers-by, her greying hair blown in the wind, her voice more passionate than it had ever been before. But none of it was the kind of thing she could do because she was not that kind of woman. She hadn't the courage, any more than she had the courage to urge her anger to explode in their living-room. For all the years of her marriage there had never been the need of such courage before: she was aware of that, but found no consolation in it.

'I think he's maybe seen it by now,' he said. 'How one thing leads to another.'

She felt insulted by the words. She willed herself the strength to shout, to pour out a torrent of fury at him, but the strength did not come. Standing up, she stumbled in the gloom and felt a piece of holly under the sole of her shoe. She turned the light on.

'I'll pray that Mr Joyce will come,' he said.

She looked at him, pale and thin, with his priestly face. For the first time since he had asked her to marry him in the Tara Ballroom she did not love him. He was cleverer than she was, yet he seemed half blind. He was good, yet he seemed hard in his goodness, as though he'd be better without it. Up to the very last moment on Christmas Day there would be the pretence that their landlord might arrive, that God would answer a prayer because His truth had been honoured. She considered it hypocrisy, unable to help herself in that opinion.

He talked but she did not listen. He spoke of keeping faith with their own, of being a Catholic. Crime begot crime, he said, God wanted it to be known that one evil led to another. She continued to look at him while he spoke, pretending to listen but wondering instead if in twelve months' time, when another Christmas came, he would still be cycling from house to house to read gas meters. Or would people have objected, requesting a meter-reader who was not Irish? An objection to a man with an Irish accent was down-to-earth and ordinary. It didn't belong in the same grand category as crime begetting crime or God wanting something to be known, or in the category of truth and conscience. In the present circumstances the objection would be understandable and fair. It seemed even right that it should be made, for it was a man with an Irish accent in whom the worst had been brought out by the troubles that had come, who was guilty of a cruelty no one would have believed him capable of. Their harmless elderly landlord might die in the course of that same year, a friendship he had valued lost, his last Christmas lonely. Grand though it might seem in one way, all of it was petty.

Once, as a girl, she might have cried, but her contented marriage had caused her to lose that habit. She cleared up the tea things, reflecting that the bombers would be pleased if they could note the victory they'd scored in a living-room in Fulham. And on Christmas Day, when a family sat down to a conventional meal, the victory would be greater. There would be crackers and chatter and excitement, the Queen and the Pope would deliver speeches. Dermot would discuss these Christmas messages with Patrick and Brendan, as he'd discussed them in the past with Mr Joyce. He would be as kind as ever. He would console Bridget and Cathal and Tom by saying that Mr Joyce hadn't been up to the journey. And whenever she looked at him she would remember the Christmases of the past. She would feel ashamed of him, and of herself.

Broken Homes

'I really think you're marvellous,' the man said.

He was small and plump, with a plump face that had a greyness about it where he shaved; his hair was grey also, falling into a fringe on his forehead. He was untidily dressed, a turtlenecked red jersey beneath a jacket that had a ballpoint pen and a pencil sticking out of the breast pocket. When he stood up his black corduroy trousers developed concertina creases. Nowadays you saw a lot of men like this, Mrs Malby said to herself.

'We're trying to help them,' he said, 'and of course we're trying to help you. The policy is to foster a deeper understanding.' He smiled, displaying small, evenly arranged teeth. 'Between the generations,' he added.

'Well, of course it's very kind,' Mrs Malby said.

He shook his head. He sipped the instant coffee she'd made for him and nibbled the edge of a pink wafer biscuit. As if driven by a compulsion, he dipped the biscuit into the coffee. He said:

'What age actually are you, Mrs Malby?'

'I'm eighty-seven.'

'You really are splendid for eighty-seven.'

He went on talking. He said he hoped he'd be as good himself at eighty-seven. He hoped he'd even be in the land of the living. 'Which I doubt,' he said with a laugh. 'Knowing me.'

Mrs Malby didn't know what he meant by that. She was sure she'd heard him quite correctly, but she could recall nothing he'd previously stated which indicated ill-health. She thought carefully while he continued to sip at his coffee and attend to the mush of biscuit. What he had said suggested that a knowledge of him would cause you to doubt that he'd live to old age. Had he already supplied further knowledge of himself which, due to her slight deafness, she had not heard? If he hadn't, why had he left everything hanging in the air like that? It was difficult to know how best to react, whether to smile or to display concern.

'So what I thought,' he said, 'was that we could send the kids on Tuesday. Say start the job Tuesday morning, eh, Mrs Malby?'

'It's extremely kind of you.'

'They're good kids.'

He stood up. He remarked on her two budgerigars and the geraniums on her window-sill. Her sitting-room was as warm as toast, he said; it was freezing outside.

'It's just that I wondered,' she said, having made up her mind to say it, 'if you could possibly have come to the wrong house?'

'Wrong? *Wrong?* You're Mrs Malby, aren't you?' He raised his voice. 'You're Mrs Malby, love?'

'Oh, yes, it's just that my kitchen isn't really in need of decoration.'

He nodded. His head moved slowly and when it stopped his dark eyes stared at her from beneath his grey fringe. He said, quite softly, what she'd dreaded he might say: that she hadn't understood.

'I'm thinking of the community, Mrs Malby. I'm thinking of you here on your own above a greengrocer's shop with your two budgies. You can benefit my kids, Mrs Malby; they can benefit you. There's no charge of any kind whatsoever. Put it like this, Mrs Malby: it's an experiment in community relations.' He paused. He reminded her of a picture there'd been in a history book, a long time ago, History with Miss Deacon, a picture of a Roundhead. 'So you see, Mrs Malby,' he said, having said something else while he was reminding her of a Roundhead.

'It's just that my kitchen is really quite nice.'

'Let's have a little look, shall we?'

She led the way. He glanced at the kitchen's shell-pink walls, and at the white paintwork. It would cost her nearly a hundred pounds to have it done, he said; and then, to her horror, he began all over again, as if she hadn't heard a thing he'd been saying. He repeated that he was a teacher, from the school called the Tite Comprehensive. He appeared to assume that she wouldn't know the Tite Comprehensive, but she did: an ugly sprawl of glass-and-concrete buildings, children swinging along the pavements, shouting obscenities. The man repeated what he had said before about these children: that some of them came from broken homes. The ones he wished to send to her on Tuesday morning came from broken homes, which was no joke for them. He felt, he repeated, that we all had a special duty where such children were concerned.

Mrs Malby again agreed that broken homes were to be deplored. It was just, she explained, that she was thinking of the cost of decorating a kitchen which didn't need decorating. Paint and brushes were expensive, she pointed out.

'Freshen it over for you,' the man said, raising his voice. 'First thing Tuesday, Mrs Malby.'

He went away, and she realized that he hadn't told her his name. Thinking she might be wrong about that, she went over their encounter in her mind, going back to the moment when her doorbell had sounded. 'I'm from Tite Comprehensive,' was what he'd said. No name had been mentioned, of that she was positive.

In her elderliness Mrs Malby liked to be sure of such details. You had to work quite hard sometimes at eighty-seven, straining to hear, concentrating carefully in order to be sure of things. You had to make it clear you understood because people often imagined you didn't. Communication was what it was called nowadays, rather than conversation.

Mrs Malby was wearing a blue dress with a pattern of darker blue flowers on it. She was a woman who had been tall but had shrunk a little with age and had become slightly bent. Scant white hair crowned a face that was touched with elderly freckling. Large brown eyes, once her most striking feature, were quieter than they had been, tired behind spectacles now. Her husband, Ernest, the owner of the greengrocer's shop over which she lived, had died five years ago; her two sons, Derek and Roy, had been killed in the same month – June 1942 – in the same desert retreat.

The greengrocer's shop was unpretentious, in an unpretentious street in Fulham called Catherine Street. The people who owned it now, Jewish people called King, kept an eye on Mrs Malby. They watched for her coming and going and if they missed her one day they'd ring her doorbell to see that she was all right. She had a niece in Ealing who looked in twice a year, and another niece in Islington, who was crippled with arthritis. Once a week Mrs Grove and Mrs Halbert came round with Meals on Wheels. A social worker, Miss Tingle, called; and the Reverend Bush called. Men came to read the meters.

In her elderliness, living where she'd lived since her marriage in 1920, Mrs Malby was happy. The tragedy in her life – the death of her sons – was no longer a nightmare, and the time that had passed since her husband's death had allowed her to come to terms with being on her own. All she wished for was to continue in these same circumstances until she died, and she did not fear death. She did not believe she would be reunited with her sons and her husband, not at least in a specific sense, but she could not believe, either, that she would entirely cease to exist the moment she ceased to breathe. Having thought about death, it seemed likely to Mrs Malby that after it came she'd dream, as in sleep. Heaven and hell were surely no more than flickers of such pleasant dreaming, or flickers of a nightmare from which there was no waking release. No loving omnipotent God, in Mrs Malby's view, doled out punishments and reward: human conscience, the last survivor, did that. The idea of a God, which had puzzled Mrs Malby for most of her life, made sense when she thought of it in terms like these, when she forgot about the mystic qualities claimed for a Church and for Jesus Christ. Yet fearful of offending the Reverend Bush, she kept such conclusions to herself when he came to see her.

All Mrs Malby dreaded now was becoming senile and being forced to enter the Sunset Home in Richmond, of which the Reverend Bush and Miss Tingle warmly spoke. The thought of a communal existence, surrounded by other elderly people, with sing-songs and card-games, was anathema to her. All her life she had hated anything that smacked of communal jolliness, refusing even to go on coach trips. She loved the house above the greengrocer's shop. She loved walking down the stairs and out on to the street, nodding at the Kings as she went by the shop, buying birdseed and eggs and fire-lighters, and fresh bread from Bob Skipps, a man of sixty-two whom she'd remembered being born.

The dread of having to leave Catherine Street ordered her life. With all her visitors she was careful, constantly on the lookout for signs in their eyes which might mean they were diagnosing her as senile. It was for this reason that she listened so intently to all that was said to her, that she concentrated, determined to let nothing slip by. It was for this reason that she smiled and endeavoured to appear agreeable and cooperative at all times. She was well aware that it wasn't going to be up to her to state that she was senile, or to argue that she wasn't, when the moment came.

After the teacher from Tite Comprehensive School had left, Mrs Malby continued to worry. The visit from this grey-haired man had bewildered her from the start. There was the oddity of his not giving his name, and then the way he'd placed a cigarette in his mouth and had taken it out again, putting it back in the packet. Had he imagined cigarette smoke would offend her? He could have asked, but in fact he hadn't even referred to the cigarette. Nor had he said where he'd heard about her: he hadn't mentioned the Reverend Bush, for instance, or Mrs Grove and Mrs Halbert, or Miss Tingle. He might have been a customer in the greengrocer's shop, but he hadn't given any indication that that was so. Added to which, and most of all, there was the consideration that her kitchen wasn't in the least in need of attention. She went to look at it again, beginning to wonder if there were things about it she couldn't see. She went over in her mind what the man had said about community relations. It was difficult to resist men like that, you had to go on repeating yourself and after a while you had to assess if you were sounding senile or not. There was also the consideration that the man was trying to do good, helping children from broken homes.

'Hi,' a boy with long blond hair said to her on the Tuesday morning. There were two other boys with him, one with a fuzz of dark curls all round his head, the other red-haired, a greased shock that hung to his shoulders. There was a girl as well, thin and beaky-faced, chewing something. Between them they carried tins of paint, brushes, cloths, a blue plastic bucket and a transistor radio. 'We come to do your kitchen out,' the blond boy said. 'You Mrs Wheeler then?'

'No, no. I'm Mrs Malby.'

'That's right, Billo,' the girl said. 'Malby.'

'I thought he says Wheeler.'

'Wheeler's the geyser in the paint shop,' the fuzzy-haired boy said.

'Typical Billo,' the girl said.

She let them in, saying it was very kind of them. She led them to the kitchen, remarking on the way that strictly speaking it wasn't in need of decoration, as they could see for themselves. She'd been thinking it over, she added: she wondered if they'd just like to wash the walls down, which was a task she found difficult to do herself?

They'd do whatever she wanted, they said, no problem. They put their paint tins on the table. The red-haired boy turned on the radio. 'Welcome back to Open House', a cheery voice said and then reminded its listeners that it was the voice of Pete Murray. It said that a record was about to be played for someone in Upminster.

'Would you like some coffee?' Mrs Malby suggested above the noise of the transistor.

'Great,' the blond boy said.

They all wore blue jeans with patches on them. The girl had a T-shirt with the words *I Lay Down With Jesus* on it. The others wore T-shirts of different colours, the blond boy's orange, the fuzzy one's light blue, the red-haired one's red. *Hot Jam-roll* a badge on the chest of the blond boy said; *Jaws* and *Bay City Rollers* other badges said.

Mrs Malby made them Nescafé while they listened to the music. They lit cigarettes, leaning about against the electric stove and against the edge of the table and against a wall. They didn't say anything because they were listening. 'That's a load of crap,' the red-haired boy pronounced eventually, and the others agreed. Even so they went on listening. 'Pete Murray's crappy,' the girl said.

Mrs Malby handed them the cups of coffee, drawing their attention to the sugar she'd put out for them on the table, and to the milk. She smiled at the girl. She said again that it was a job she couldn't manage any more, washing walls.

'Get that, Billo?' the fuzzy-haired boy said. 'Washing walls.'

'Who loves ya, baby?' Billo replied.

Mrs Malby closed the kitchen door on them, hoping they wouldn't take too long because the noise of the transistor was so loud. She listened to it for a quarter of an hour and then she decided to go out and do her shopping.

In Bob Skipps' she said that four children from the Tite Comprehensive had arrived in her house and were at present washing her kitchen walls. She said it again to the man in the fish shop and the man was surprised. It suddenly occurred to her that of course they couldn't have done any painting because she hadn't discussed colours with the teacher. She thought it odd that the teacher hadn't mentioned colours and wondered what colour the paint tins contained. It worried her a little that all that hadn't occurred to her before.

'Hi, Mrs Wheeler,' the boy called Billo said to her in her hall. He was standing there combing his hair, looking at himself in the mirror of the hall-stand. Music was coming from upstairs.

There were yellowish smears on the stair-carpet, which upset Mrs Malby very much. There were similar smears on the landing carpet. 'Oh, but please,' Mrs Malby cried, standing in the kitchen doorway. 'Oh, please, no!' she cried.

Yellow emulsion paint partially covered the shell-pink of one wall. Some had spilt from the tin on to the black-and-white vinyl of the floor and had been walked through. The boy with fuzzy hair was standing on a draining board applying the same paint to the ceiling. He was the only person in the kitchen.

He smiled at Mrs Malby, looking down at her. 'Hi, Mrs Wheeler,' he said.

'But I said only to wash them,' she cried.

She felt tired, saying that. The upset of finding the smears on the carpets and of seeing the hideous yellow plastered over the quiet shell-pink had already taken a toll. Her emotional outburst had caused her face and neck to become warm. She felt she'd like to lie down.

'Eh, Mrs Wheeler?' The boy smiled at her again, continuing to slap paint on to the ceiling. A lot of it dripped back on top of him, on to the draining board and on to cups and saucers and cutlery, and on to the floor. 'D'you fancy the colour, Mrs Wheeler?' he asked her.

All the time the transistor continued to blare, a voice inexpertly singing, a tuneless twanging. The boy referred to this sound, pointing at the transistor with his paintbrush, saying it was great. Unsteadily she crossed the kitchen and turned the transistor off. 'Hey, sod it, missus,' the boy protested angrily.

'I said to wash the walls. I didn't even choose that colour.'

The boy, still annoyed because she'd turned off the radio, was gesturing crossly with the brush. There was paint in the fuzz of his hair and on his

T-shirt and his face. Every time he moved the brush about paint flew off it. It speckled the windows, and the small dresser, and the electric stove and the taps and the sink.

'Where's the sound gone?' the boy called Billo demanded, coming into the kitchen and going straight to the transistor.

'I didn't want the kitchen painted,' Mrs Malby said again. 'I told you.'

The singing from the transistor recommenced, louder than before. On the draining board the fuzzy-haired boy began to sway, throwing his body and his head about.

'Please stop him painting,' Mrs Malby shouted as shrilly as she could.

'Here,' the boy called Billo said, bundling her out on to the landing and closing the kitchen door. 'Can't hear myself think in there.'

'I don't want it painted.'

'What's that, Mrs Wheeler?'

'My name isn't Wheeler. I don't want my kitchen painted. I told you.'

'Are we in the wrong house? Only we was told –'

'Will you please wash that paint off?'

'If we come to the wrong house –'

'You haven't come to the wrong house. Please tell that boy to wash off the paint he's put on.'

'Did a bloke from the Comp come in to see you, Mrs Wheeler? Fat bloke?'

'Yes, yes, he did.'

'Only he give instructions –'

'Please would you tell that boy?'

'Whatever you say, Mrs Wheeler.'

'And wipe up the paint where it's spilt on the floor. It's been trampled out, all over my carpets.'

'No problem, Mrs Wheeler.'

Not wishing to return to the kitchen herself, she ran the hot tap in the bathroom on to the sponge-cloth she kept for cleaning the bath. She found that if she rubbed hard enough at the paint on the stair-carpet and on the landing carpet it began to disappear. But the rubbing tired her. As she put away the sponge-cloth, Mrs Malby had a feeling of not quite knowing what was what. Everything that had happened in the last few hours felt like a dream; it also had the feeling of plays she had seen on television; the one thing it wasn't like was reality. As she paused in her bathroom, having placed the sponge-cloth on a ledge under the hand-basin, Mrs Malby saw herself standing there, as she often did in a dream: she saw her body hunched within the same blue dress she'd been wearing when the teacher called, and two touches of red in her pale face, and her white hair tidy on her head, and her fingers seeming fragile. In a dream anything could happen next: she might suddenly find herself forty years younger, Derek and Roy might be alive. She might be even younger; Dr Ramsey might be telling her she was pregnant. In a television play it would be different: the children who had come to her house might kill her. What she hoped for from reality was that order would be restored in her kitchen, that all the paint would be washed away from her walls as she had wiped it from her carpets, that the misunderstanding would be over. For an instant she saw herself in her kitchen, making tea for the children, saying it didn't matter. She even heard herself adding that in a life as long as hers you became used to everything.

She left the bathroom; the blare of the transistor still persisted. She didn't want to sit in her sitting-room, having to listen to it. She climbed the stairs to her bedroom, imagining the coolness there, and the quietness.

'Hey,' the girl protested when Mrs Malby opened her bedroom door.

'Sod off, you guys,' the boy with the red hair ordered.

They were in her bed. Their clothes were all over the floor. Her two budgerigars were flying about the room. Protruding from sheets and blankets she could see the boy's naked shoulders and the back of his head. The girl poked her face up from under him. She gazed at Mrs Malby. 'It's not them,' she whispered to the boy. 'It's the woman.'

'Hi there, missus.' The boy twisted his head round. From the kitchen, still loudly, came the noise of the transistor.

'Sorry,' the girl said.

'Why are they up here? Why have you let my birds out? You've no right to behave like this.'

'We needed sex,' the girl explained.

The budgerigars were perched on the looking-glass on the dressing-table, beadily surveying the scene.

'They're really great, them budgies,' the boy said.

Mrs Malby stepped through their garments. The budgerigars remained where they were. They fluttered when she seized them but they didn't offer any resistance. She returned with them to the door.

'You had no right,' she began to say to the two in her bed, but her voice had become weak. It quivered into a useless whisper, and once more she thought that what was happening couldn't be happening. She saw herself again, standing unhappily with the budgerigars.

In her sitting-room she wept. She returned the budgerigars to their cage and sat in an armchair by the window that looked out over Catherine Street. She sat in sunshine, feeling its warmth but not, as she might have done, delighting in it. She wept because she had intensely disliked finding the boy and girl in her bed. Images from the bedroom remained vivid in her mind. On the floor the boy's boots were heavy and black, composed of leather that did not shine. The girl's shoes were green, with huge heels and soles. The girl's underclothes were purple, the boy's dirty. There'd been an unpleasant smell of sweat in her bedroom.

Mrs Malby waited, her head beginning to ache. She dried away her tears, wiping at her eyes and cheeks with a handkerchief. In Catherine Street people passed by on bicycles, girls from the polish factory returning home to lunch, men from the brickworks. People came out of the greengrocer's with leeks and cabbages in baskets, some carrying paper bags. Watching these people in Catherine Street made her feel better, even though her headache was becoming worse. She felt more composed, and more in control of herself.

'We're sorry,' the girl said again, suddenly appearing, teetering on her clumsy shoes. 'We didn't think you'd come up to the bedroom.'

She tried to smile at the girl, but found it hard to do so. She nodded instead.

'The others put the birds in,' the girl said. 'Meant to be a joke, that was.'

She nodded again. She couldn't see how it could be a joke to take two budgerigars from their cage, but she didn't say that.

'We're getting on with the painting now,' the girl said. 'Sorry about that.'

She went away and Mrs Malby continued to watch the people in Catherine Street. The girl had made a mistake when she'd said they were getting on with the painting: what she'd meant was that they were getting on with washing it off. The girl had come straight downstairs to say she was sorry; she hadn't been told by the boys in the kitchen that the paint had been applied in error. When they'd gone, Mrs Malby said to herself, she'd open her bedroom window wide in order to get rid of the odour of sweat. She'd put clean sheets on her bed.

From the kitchen, above the noise of the transistor, came the clatter of raised voices. There was laughter and a crash, and then louder laughter. Singing began, attaching itself to the singing from the transistor.

She sat for twenty minutes and then she went and knocked on the kitchen door, not wishing to push the door open in case it knocked someone off a chair. There was no reply. She opened the door gingerly.

More yellow paint had been applied. The whole wall around the window was covered with it, and most of the wall behind the sink. Half of the ceiling had it on it; the woodwork that had been white was now a glossy dark blue. All four of the children were working with brushes. A tin of paint had been upset on the floor.

She wept again, standing there watching them, unable to prevent her tears. She felt them running warmly on her cheeks and then becoming cold. It was in this kitchen that she had cried first of all when the two telegrams had come in 1942, believing when the second one arrived that she would never cease to cry. It would have seemed ridiculous at the time, to cry just because her kitchen was all yellow.

They didn't see her standing there. They went on singing, slapping the paintbrushes back and forth. There'd been neat straight lines where the shell-pink met the white of the woodwork, but now the lines were any old how. The boy with the red hair was applying the dark-blue gloss.

Again the feeling that it wasn't happening possessed Mrs Malby. She'd had a dream a week ago, a particularly vivid dream in which the Prime Minister had stated on television that the Germans had been invited to invade England since England couldn't manage to look after herself any more. That dream had been most troublesome because when she'd woken up in the morning she'd thought it was something she'd seen on television, that she'd actually been sitting in her sitting-room the night before listening to the Prime Minister saying that he and the Leader of the Opposition had decided the best for Britain was invasion. After thinking about it, she'd established that of course it hadn't been true; but even so she'd glanced at the headlines of newspapers when she went out shopping.

'How d'you fancy it?' the boy called Billo called out to her, smiling across the kitchen at her, not noticing that she was upset. 'Neat, Mrs Wheeler?'

She didn't answer. She went downstairs and walked out of her hall door, into Catherine Street and into the greengrocer's that had been her husband's. It never closed in the middle of the day; it never had. She waited and Mr King appeared, wiping his mouth. 'Well then, Mrs Malby?' he said.

He was a big man with a well-kept black moustache and Jewish eyes. He didn't smile much because smiling wasn't his way, but he was in no way morose, rather the opposite.

'So what can I do for you?' he said.

She told him. He shook his head and repeatedly frowned as he listened. His expressive eyes widened. He called his wife.

While the three of them hurried along the pavement to Mrs Malby's open hall door it seemed to her that the Kings doubted her. She could feel them thinking that she must have got it all wrong, that she'd somehow imagined all this stuff about yellow paint and pop music on a radio, and her birds flying around her bedroom while two children were lying in her bed. She didn't blame them; she knew exactly how they felt. But when they entered her house the noise from the transistor could at once be heard.

The carpet of the landing was smeared again with the paint. Yellow footprints led to her sitting-room and out again, back to the kitchen.

'You bloody young hooligans,' Mr King shouted at them. He snapped the switch on the transistor. He told them to stop applying the paint immediately. 'What the hell d'you think you're up to?' he demanded furiously.

'We come to paint out the old ma's kitchen,' the boy called Billo explained, unruffled by Mr King's tone. 'We was carrying out instructions, mister.'

'So it was instructions to spill the blooming paint all over the floor? So it was instructions to cover the windows with it and every knife and fork in the place? So it was instructions to frighten the life out of a poor woman by messing about in her bedroom?'

'No one frightens her, mister.'

'You know what I mean, son.'

Mrs Malby returned with Mrs King and sat in the cubbyhole behind the shop, leaving Mr King to do his best. At three o'clock he arrived back, saying that the children had gone. He telephoned the school and after a delay was put in touch with the teacher who'd been to see Mrs Malby. He made this telephone call in the shop but Mrs Malby could hear him saying that what had happened was a disgrace. 'A woman of eighty-seven,' Mr King protested, 'thrown into a state of misery. There'll be something to pay on this, you know.'

There was some further discussion on the telephone, and then Mr King replaced the receiver. He put his head into the cubbyhole and announced that the teacher was coming round immediately to inspect the damage. 'What can I entice you to?' Mrs Malby heard him asking a customer, and a woman's voice replied that she needed tomatoes, a cauliflower, potatoes and Bramleys. She heard Mr King telling the woman what had happened, saying that it had wasted two hours of his time.

She drank the sweet milky tea which Mrs King had poured her. She tried not to think of the yellow paint and the dark-blue gloss. She tried not to remember the scene in the bedroom and the smell there'd been, and the new marks that had appeared on her carpets after she'd wiped off the original ones. She wanted to ask Mr King if these marks had been washed out before the paint had had a chance to dry, but she didn't like to ask this because Mr King had been so kind and it might seem like pressing him.

'Kids nowadays,' Mrs King said. 'I just don't know.'

'Birched they should be,' Mr King said, coming into the cubbyhole and picking up a mug of the milky tea. 'I'd birch the bottoms off them.'

Someone arrived in the shop, Mr King hastened from the cubbyhole. 'What can I entice you to, sir?' Mrs Malby heard him politely inquiring and the voice of the teacher who'd been to see her replied. He said who he was and Mr King wasn't polite any more. An experience like that, Mr King declared thunderously, could have killed an eighty-seven-year-old stone dead.

Mrs Malby stood up and Mrs King came promptly forward to place a hand under her elbow. They went into the shop like that. 'Three and a half p,' Mr King was saying to a woman who'd asked the price of oranges. 'The larger ones at four.'

Mr King gave the woman four of the smaller size and accepted her money. He called out to a youth who was passing by on a bicycle, about to start an afternoon paper round. He was a youth who occasionally assisted him on Saturday mornings: Mr King asked him now if he would mind the shop for ten minutes since an emergency had arisen. Just for once, Mr King argued, it wouldn't matter if the evening papers were a little late.

'Well, you can't say they haven't brightened the place up, Mrs Malby,' the teacher said in her kitchen. He regarded her from beneath his grey fringe. He touched one of the walls with the tip of a finger. He nodded to himself, appearing to be satisfied.

The painting had been completed, the yellow and the dark-blue gloss. Where the colours met there were untidily jagged lines. All the paint that had been spilt on the floor had been wiped away, but the black-and-white vinyl had become dull and grubby in the process. The paint had also been wiped from the windows and from other surfaces, leaving them smeared. The dresser had been wiped down and was smeary also. The cutlery and the taps and the cups and saucers had all been washed or wiped.

'Well, you wouldn't believe it!' Mrs King exclaimed. She turned to her husband. However had he managed it all? she asked him. 'You should have seen the place!' she said to the teacher.

'It's just the carpets,' Mr King said. He led the way from the kitchen to the sitting-room, pointing at the yellow on the landing carpet and on the sitting-room one. 'The blooming stuff dried,' he explained, 'before we could get to it. That's where compensation comes in.' He spoke sternly, addressing the teacher. 'I'd say she has a bob or two owing.'

Mrs King nudged Mrs Malby, drawing attention to the fact that Mr King was doing his best for her. The nudge suggested that all would be well because a sum of money would be paid, possibly even a larger sum than was merited. It suggested also that Mrs Malby in the end might find herself doing rather well.

'Compensation?' the teacher said, bending down and scratching at the paint on the sitting-room carpet. 'I'm afraid compensation's out of the question.'

'She's had her carpets ruined,' Mr King snapped quickly. 'This woman's been put about, you know.'

'She got her kitchen done free,' the teacher snapped back at him.

'They released her pets. They got up to tricks in a bed. You'd no damn right –'

'These kids come from broken homes, sir. I'll do my best with your carpets, Mrs Malby.'

'But what about my kitchen?' she whispered. She cleared her throat because her whispering could hardly be heard. 'My kitchen?' she whispered again.

'What about it, Mrs Malby?'

'I didn't want it painted.'

'Oh, don't be silly now.'

The teacher took his jacket off and threw it impatiently on to a chair. He left the sitting-room. Mrs Malby heard him running a tap in the kitchen.

'It was best to finish the painting, Mrs Malby,' Mr King said. 'Otherwise the kitchen would have driven you mad, half done like that. I stood over them till they finished it.'

'You can't take paint off, dear,' Mrs King said, 'once it's on. You've done wonders, Leo,' she said to her husband. 'Young devils.'

'We'd best be getting back,' Mr King said.

'It's quite nice, you know,' his wife added. 'Your kitchen's quite cheerful, dear.'

The Kings went away and the teacher rubbed at the yellow on the carpets with her washing-up brush. The landing carpet was marked anyway, he pointed out, poking a finger at the stains left behind by the paint she'd removed herself with the sponge-cloth from the bathroom. She must be delighted with the kitchen, he said.

She knew she mustn't speak. She'd known she mustn't when the Kings had been there; she knew she mustn't now. She might have reminded the Kings that she'd chosen the original colours in the kitchen herself. She might have complained to the man as he rubbed at her carpets that the carpets would never be the same again. She watched him, not saying anything, not wishing to be regarded as a nuisance. The Kings would have considered her a nuisance too, agreeing to let children into her kitchen to paint it and then making a fuss. If she became a nuisance the teacher and the Kings would drift on to the same side, and the Reverend Bush would somehow be on that side also, and Miss Tingle, and even Mrs Grove and Mrs Halbert. They would agree among themselves that what had happened had to do with her elderliness, with her not understanding that children who brought paint into a kitchen were naturally going to use it.

'I defy anyone to notice that,' the teacher said, standing up, gesturing at the yellow blurs that remained on her carpets. He put his jacket on. He left the washing-up brush and the bowl of water he'd been using on the floor of her sitting-room. 'All's well that ends well,' he said. 'Thanks for your cooperation, Mrs Malby.'

She thought of her two sons, Derek and Roy, not knowing quite why she thought of them now. She descended the stairs with the teacher, who was cheerfully talking about community relations. You had to make allowances, he said, for kids like that; you had to try and understand; you couldn't just walk away.

Quite suddenly she wanted to tell him about Derek and Roy. In the desire to talk about them she imagined their bodies, as she used to in the past, soon after they'd been killed. They lay on desert sand, desert birds swooped down on them. Their four eyes were gone. She wanted to explain to the teacher that they'd been happy, a contented family in Catherine Street, until the war came and smashed everything to pieces. Nothing had been the same afterwards. It hadn't been easy to continue with nothing to continue for. Each room in the house had contained different memories of the two boys growing up. Cooking and cleaning had seemed pointless. The shop which would have been theirs would have to pass to someone else.

And yet time had soothed the awful double wound. The horror of the emptiness had been lived with, and if having the Kings in the shop now wasn't the same as having your sons there at least the Kings were kind. Thirty-four years after the destruction of your family you were happy in your elderliness because time had been merciful. She wanted to tell the teacher that also, she didn't know why, except that in some way it seemed relevant. But she didn't tell him because it would have been difficult to begin, because in the effort there'd be the danger of seeming senile. Instead she said goodbye, concentrating on that. She said she was sorry, saying it just to show she was aware that she hadn't made herself clear to the children. Conversation had broken down between the children and herself, she wanted him to know she knew it had.

He nodded vaguely, not listening to her. He was trying to make the world a better place, he said. 'For kids like that, Mrs Malby. Victims of broken homes.'

Matilda's England

1. The Tennis Court

Old Mrs Ashburton used to drive about the lanes in a governess cart drawn by a donkey she called Trot. We often met her as we cycled home from school, when my brother and my sister were at the Grammar School and I was still at the village school. Of the three of us I was Mrs Ashburton's favourite, and I don't know why that was except that I was the youngest. 'Hullo, my Matilda,' Mrs Ashburton would whisper in her throaty, crazy-sounding way. 'Matilda,' she'd repeat, lingering over the name I so disliked, drawing each syllable away from the next. 'Dear Matilda.' She was excessively thin, rather tall, and frail-looking. We made allowances for her because she was eighty-one.

Usually when we met her she was looking for wild flowers, or if it was winter or autumn just sitting in her governess cart in some farmer's gateway, letting the donkey graze the farmer's grass. In spring she used to root out plants from the hedges with a little trowel. Most of them were weeds, my brother said; and looking back on it now, I realize that it wasn't for wild flowers, or weeds, or grazing for her donkey that she drove about the lanes. It was in order to meet us cycling back from school.

'There's a tennis court at Challacombe Manor,' she said one day in May, 1939. 'Any time you ever wanted to play, Dick.' She stared at my brother with piercing black eyes that were the colour of quality coal. She was eccentric, standing there in a long, very old and bald fur coat, stroking the ears of her donkey while he nibbled a hedge. Her hat was attached to her grey hair by a number of brass hat-pins. The hat was of faded green felt, the hat-pins had quite large knobs at the ends of them, inlaid with pieces of green glass. Green, Mrs Ashburton often remarked, was her favourite colour, and she used to remove these hat-pins to show us the glass additions, emphasizing that they were valueless. Her bald fur coat was valueless also, she assured us, and not even in its heyday would it have fetched more than five pounds. In the same manner she remarked upon her summer hats and dresses, and her shoes, and the governess cart, and the donkey.

'I mean, Dick,' she said that day in 1939, 'it's not much of a tennis court, but it was once, of course. And there's a net stacked away in one of the outhouses. And a roller, and a marker. There's a lawn-mower, too, because naturally you'll need that.'

'You mean, we could play on your court, Mrs Ashburton?' my sister Betty said.

'Of course I mean that, my dear. That's just what I mean. You know, before the war we really did have marvellous tennis parties at Challacombe. Everyone came.'

'Oh, how lovely!' Betty was fourteen and Dick was a year older, and I was nine. Betty was fair-haired like the rest of us, but much prettier than me. She had very blue eyes and a wide smiling mouth that boys at the Grammar School were always trying to kiss, and a small nose, and freckles. Her hair was smooth and long, the colour of hay. It looked quite startling sometimes, shining in the sunlight. I used to feel proud of Betty and Dick when they came to collect me every afternoon at Mrs Pritchard's school. Dick was to leave the Grammar School in July, and on the afternoons of that warm May, as Betty and I cycled home with him, we felt sorry that he wouldn't be there next term. But Dick said he was glad. He was big, as tall as my father, and very shy. He'd begun to smoke, a habit not approved of by my father. On the way home from school we had to stop and go into a ruined cottage so that he could have a Woodbine. He was going to work on the farm; one day the farm would be his.

'It would be lovely to play tennis,' Betty said.

'Then you must, my dear. But if you want to play this summer you'll have to get the court into trim.' Mrs Ashburton smiled at Betty in a way that made her thin, elderly face seem beautiful. Then she smiled at Dick. 'I was passing the tennis court the other day, Dick, and I suddenly thought of it. Now why shouldn't those children get it into trim? I thought. Why shouldn't they come and play, and bring their friends?'

'Yes,' Dick said.

'Why ever don't you come over to Challacombe on Saturday? Matilda, too, of course. Come for tea, all three of you.'

Mrs Ashburton smiled at each of us in turn. She nodded at us and climbed into the governess cart. 'Saturday,' she repeated.

'Honestly, Betty!' Dick glared crossly at my sister, as though she were responsible for the invitation. 'I'm not going, you know.'

He cycled off, along the narrow, dusty lane, big and red-faced and muttering. We followed him more slowly, talking about Mrs Ashburton.

'Poor old thing!' Betty said, which was what people round about often said when Mrs Ashburton was mentioned, or when she was seen in her governess cart.

The first thing I remember in all my life was my father breaking a fountain-pen. It was a large black-and-white pen, like tortoiseshell or marble. That was the fashion for fountain-pens then: two or three colours marbled together, green and black, blue and white, red and black-and-white. Conway Stewart, Waterman's, Blackbird. Propelling pencils were called Eversharp.

The day my father broke his pen I didn't know all that: I learnt it afterwards, when I went to school. I was three the day he broke the pen. 'It's just a waste of blooming money!' he shouted. He smashed the pen across his knee while my mother anxiously watched. Waste of money or not, she said, it wouldn't help matters to break the thing. She fetched him the ink and a dip-pen from a drawer of the dresser. He was still angry, but after a minute or two he began to laugh. He kissed my mother, pulling her down on to the knee he'd broken the pen over. Dick, who must have been nine then, didn't even look up from his homework. Betty was there too, but I can't remember what she was doing.

The kitchen hasn't changed much. The old range has gone, but the big light-oak dresser is still there, with the same brass handles on its doors and drawers and the same Wedgwood-blue dinner-set on its shelves, and cups and jugs hanging on hooks. The ceiling is low, the kitchen itself large and rectangular, with the back stairs rising from the far end of it, and a door at the bottom of them. There are doors to the pantry and the scullery, and to the passage that leads to the rest of the house, and to the yard. There's a long narrow light-oak table, with brass handles on its drawers, like the dresser ones, and oak chairs that aren't as light as all the other oak because chairs darken with use. But the table isn't scrubbed once a week any more, and the brass doesn't gleam. I know, because now and again I visit the farmhouse.

I remember the kitchen with oil-lamps, and the time, the day after my fifth birthday, when the men came to wire the house for electricity. My mother used to talk about an Aga, and often when she took us shopping with her she'd bring us to Archers', the builders' merchants, to look at big cream-coloured Agas. After a time, Mr Gray of the Aga department didn't even bother to bustle up to her when he saw her coming. She'd stand there, plump and pink-cheeked, her reddish hair neat beneath the brim of her hat, touching the display models, opening the oven doors and lifting up the two big hot-plate covers. When we returned to the farmhouse my father would tease her, knowing she'd been to Archers' again. She'd blush, cutting ham at teatime or offering round salad. My father would then forget about it. 'Well, I'm damned,' he'd say, and he'd read out an item from the weekly paper, about some neighbouring farmer or new County Council plans. My mother would listen and then both of them would nod. They were very good friends, even though my father teased her. She blushed like a rose, he said: he teased her to see it.

Once, before the electricity came, I had a nightmare. It was probably only a few months before, because when I came crying down to the kitchen my father kept comforting me with the reminder that it would soon be my fifth birthday. 'You'll never cry then, Matilda,' he whispered to me, cuddling me to him. 'Big girls of five don't cry.' I fell asleep, but it's not that that I remember now, not the fear from the nightmare going away, or the tears stopping, or my father's caressing: it's the image of my parents in the kitchen as I stumbled down the back stairs. There were two oil-lamps lit and the fire in the range was glowing red-hot behind its curved bars, and the heavy black kettle wasn't quite singing. My father was asleep with last Saturday's weekly paper on his knees, my mother was reading one of the books from the bookcase in the dining-room we never used, probably *The Garden of Allah*, which was her favourite. The two sheepdogs were asleep under the table, and when I opened the door at the top of the stairs they both barked because they knew that at that particular time no one should be opening that door. 'Oh, now, now,' my mother said, coming to me, listening to me when I said that there were cows on my bedroom wall. I remember the image of the two of them because they looked so happy sitting there, even though my mother hadn't got her Aga, even though my father was sometimes worried about the farm.

Looking back on it now, there was a lot of happiness, although perhaps not more than many families experience. Everything seems either dismal or happy in retrospect, and the happiness in the farmhouse is what I think of first whenever I think now of that particular past. I remember my mother baking in the kitchen, flour all over her plump arms, and tiny beads of moisture on her forehead, because the kitchen was always hot. I remember my father's leathery skin and his smile, and the way he used to shout at the sheepdogs, and the men, Joe and Arthur, sitting on yellow stubble, drinking tea out of a bottle, on a day hay had been cut.

Our farm had once been the home-farm of Challacombe Manor, even though our farmhouse was two miles away from the manor house. There'd been servants and gardeners at Challacombe Manor then, and horses in the stables, and carriages coming and going. But the estate had fallen into rack and ruin after the First World War because Mr Ashburton hadn't been able to keep it going and in the end, in 1924, he'd taken out various mortgages. When he died, in 1929, the extent of his debts was so great that Mrs Ashburton had been obliged to let Lloyd's Bank foreclose on the mortgages, which is how it came about that my father bought Challacombe Farm. It was a tragedy, people round about used to say, and the real tragedy was that Mr Ashburton had come back from the war in such a strange state that he hadn't minded about everywhere falling into rack and ruin. According to my father, Lloyd's Bank owned Challacombe Manor itself and had granted Mrs Ashburton permission to live there in her lifetime. It wouldn't surprise him, my father said, if it turned out that Lloyd's Bank owned Mrs Ashburton as well. 'He drank himself to death,' people used to say about Mr Ashburton. 'She watched him and didn't have the heart to stop him.' Yet before the First World War Mr Ashburton had been a different kind of man, energetic and sharp. The Challacombe estate had been a showpiece.

To me in particular Mrs Ashburton talked about her husband. She was lucky that he'd come back from the war, even if he hadn't been able to manage very well. His mind had been affected, she explained, but that was better than being dead. She told me about the men who'd died, gardeners at Challacombe Manor, and farm workers on the estate, and men she and her husband had known in the town. 'I thanked God,' Mrs Ashburton said, 'when he came safely back here all in one piece. Everything fell to bits around us, but it didn't matter because at least he was still alive. You understand, Matilda?'

I always nodded, although I didn't really understand. And then she'd go on about the estate as it had been, and then about her husband and the conversations they used to have. Sometimes she didn't address me directly. She smiled and just talked, always returning to the men who had been killed and how lucky she was that her husband had at least come back. She'd prayed, she said, that he'd come back, and every time another man from the estate or from the neighbourhood had been reported dead she'd felt that there was a better chance that her husband wouldn't die also. 'By the law of averages,' she explained, 'some had to come back. Some men have always come back from wars, you convince yourself.'

At this point I would always nod again, and Mrs Ashburton would say that looking back on it now she felt ashamed that she had ever applied the law of averages to the survival or death of men. Doing so was as horrible as war itself: the women who were left at home became cruel in their fear and their selfishness. Cruelty was natural in war, Mrs Ashburton said.

At the time she'd hated the Germans and she was ashamed of that too, because the Germans were just people like other people. But when she talked about them the remains of the hatred were still in her voice, and I imagined the Germans from what she told me about them: people who ate black bread and didn't laugh much, who ate raw bacon, who were dour, grey and steely. She described the helmets they wore in wartime. She told me what a bayonet was, and I used to feel sick when I thought of one going into a man's stomach and being twisted in there to make sure the man would die. She told me about poison gas, and the trenches, and soldiers being buried alive. The way she spoke I knew she was repeating, word for word, the things her husband had told her, things that had maybe been the cause of his affected mind. Even her voice sounded unusual when she talked about the war, as though she was trying to imitate her husband's voice, and the terror that had been in it. He used to cry, she said, as he walked about the gardens, unable to stop the tears once they'd begun.

Dick didn't say anything while we rode the two miles over to Challacombe Manor that Saturday. He didn't even say anything when he suddenly dismounted and leaned his bicycle against a black gate, and climbed over the gate to have a smoke behind the hedge. If my father had come by he'd have known what was happening because he would have seen Betty and myself waiting in the lane, surrounded by the cloud of smoke that Dick always managed to make with his Woodbine. Our job was to warn him if we saw my father coming, but my father didn't come that afternoon and when Dick had finished we continued on our way.

We'd often been to tea at Challacombe Manor before. Mrs Ashburton said we were the only visitors she had because most of her friends were dead, which was something that happened, she explained, if you were eighty-one. We always had tea in the kitchen, a huge room that smelt of oil, with armchairs in it and a wireless, and an oil-stove on which Mrs Ashburton cooked, not wishing to have to keep the range going. There were oatcakes for tea, and buttered white and brown bread, and pots of jam that Mrs Ashburton bought in the town, and a cake she bought also, usually a fruitcake. Afterwards we'd walk through the house with her, while she pointed out the places where the roof had given way, and the dry rot, and windows that were broken. She hadn't lived in most of the house since the war, and had lived in even less of it since her husband had died in 1929. We knew these details by heart because she'd told us so many times. In one of the outhouses there was an old motor-car with flat tyres, and the gardens were now all overgrown with grass and weeds. Rhododendrons were choked, and buddleia and kerria and hydrangeas.

The house was grey and square with two small wings, a stone Georgian house with wide stone steps leading to a front door that had pillars on either side of it and a fanlight above it. The gravel expanse in front of it was grassy now, and slippery in wet weather because of moss that had accumulated. French windows opened on to it on either side of the hall door, from the rooms that had been the drawing-room and the dining-room. Lawns stretched around the house, with grass like a meadow on them now. The tennis court, which we'd never known about until Mrs Ashburton mentioned it, was hidden away, beyond the jungle of shrubbery.

'You see?' she said. 'You see, Dick?' She was wearing a long, old-fashioned dress and a wide-brimmed white hat, and sunglasses because the afternoon was fiercely bright.

The grass on the tennis court was a yard high, as high as the rusty iron posts that were there to support the net. 'Look,' Mrs Ashburton said.

She led us to the stable-yard, past the outhouse where the motor-car was, and into a smaller outhouse. There was a lawn-mower there, as rusty as the tennis posts, and a marker in the same condition, and an iron roller. Tucked into the beams above our heads was a rolled-up tennis net. 'He adored tennis,' she said. 'He really loved it.'

She turned and we followed her across the stable-yard, into the kitchen by the back door. She talked about her husband while she made tea.

We ate the bought fruitcake, listening to her. We'd heard it all before, but we always considered it was worth it because of the cake and the biscuits and the buttered bread and the pots of jam. And always before we left she gave us ginger beer and pieces of chocolate broken up on a saucer. She told us about the child which might have been born to her husband and herself, six months after the old queen died, but which had miscarried. 'Everything went wrong,' she said. She told us about the parties there'd been at Challacombe Manor. Champagne and strawberries and cream, and parties with games that she described, and fancy dress.

'No reason at all,' she said, 'why we shouldn't have a tennis party.'

Dick made a sighing sound, a soft, slight noise that Mrs Ashburton didn't hear.

'Tennis party?' Betty murmured.

'No reason, dear.'

That morning Dick and Betty had had an argument. Betty had said that of course he must go to tea with Mrs Ashburton, since he'd always gone in the past. And Dick had said that Mrs Ashburton had been cunning: all these years, he said, she'd been inviting us to tea so that when the time was ripe she could get us to clean up her old tennis court. 'Oh, don't be silly!' Betty had cried, and then had said that it would be the cruellest thing that Dick had ever done if he didn't go to tea with an old woman just because she'd mentioned her tennis court. I'd been cross with Dick myself, and none of us felt very happy because the matter of the tennis court had unattractively brought into the open the motive behind our putting up with Mrs Ashburton. I didn't like it when she called me her Matilda and put her arms around me, and said she was sure her child would have been a little girl, and that she was almost as sure that she'd have called her Matilda. I didn't like it when she went on and on about the war and her husband coming back a wreck, or about the champagne and the strawberries and cream. 'Poor Mrs Ashburton!' we'd always said, but it wasn't because she was poor Mrs Ashburton that we'd filled the emptiness of Saturday afternoons by cycling over to Challacombe Manor.

'Shall we go and have another look at it?' she said when we'd eaten all the food that was on the table. She smiled in her frail, almost beautiful way, and for a moment I wondered if Dick wasn't perhaps right about her cunning. She led the way back to the overgrown tennis court and we all four stood looking at it.

'It's quite all right to smoke, Dick,' Mrs Ashburton said, 'if you want to.'

Dick laughed because he didn't know how else to react. He'd gone as red as a sunset. He kicked at the rusty iron tennis post, and then as casually as he could he took a packet of squashed Woodbines from his pocket and began to fiddle with a box of matches. Betty poked him with her elbow, suggesting that he should offer Mrs Ashburton a cigarette.

'Would you like one, Mrs Ashburton?' Dick said, proffering the squashed packet.

'Well, you know, I think I would, Dick.' She laughed and took the cigarette, saying she hadn't smoked a cigarette since 1915. Dick lit it for her. Some of the matches fell from the matchbox on to the long grass. He picked them up and replaced them, his own cigarette cocked out of the corner of his mouth. They looked rather funny, the two of them, Mrs Ashburton in her big white hat and sunglasses.

'You'd need a scythe,' Dick said.

That was the beginning of the tennis party. When Dick walked over the next Saturday with a scythe, Mrs Ashburton had a packet of twenty Player's waiting for him. He scythed the grass and got the old hand-mower going. The stubble was coarse and by the time he'd cut it short there were quite large patches of naked earth, but Betty and Mrs Ashburton said they didn't matter. The court would do as it was for this summer, but in the spring, Dick said, he'd put down fresh grass-seed. It rained heavily a fortnight later, which was fortunate, because Dick was able to even out some of the bumps with the roller. Betty helped him, and later on she helped him mark the court out. Mrs Ashburton and I watched, Mrs Ashburton holding my hand and often seeming to imagine that I was the child which hadn't been born to her.

We took to going to Challacombe Manor on Sunday mornings as well as Saturdays. There were always packets of Craven A, and ginger beer and pieces of chocolate. 'Of course, it's not her property,' my father said whenever anyone mentioned the tennis court, or the net that Mrs Ashburton had found rolled up in an outhouse. At dinnertime on Sundays, when we all sat around the long table in the kitchen, my father would ask Dick how he'd got on with the court. He'd then point out that the tennis court and everything that went with it was the property of Lloyd's Bank. Every Sunday dinnertime we had the same: roast beef and roast potatoes and Yorkshire pudding, and carrots or brussels sprouts according to the seasonal variation, and apple pie and cream.

Dick didn't ever say much when my father asked him about the tennis court. 'You want to be careful, lad,' my father used to say, squashing roast potatoes into gravy. 'Lloyd's is strict, you know.' My father would go on for ages, talking about Lloyd's Bank or the Aga cooker my mother wanted, and you never quite knew whether he was being serious or not. He would sit there with his jacket on the back of his chair, not smiling as he ate and talked. Farmers were like that, my mother once told Betty when Betty was upset by him. Farmers were cautious and watchful and canny. He didn't at all disapprove of what Betty and Dick and Mrs Ashburton were doing with the tennis court, my mother explained, rather the opposite; but he was right when he reminded them that everything, including the house itself, was the property of Lloyd's Bank.

Mrs Ashburton found six tennis racquets in presses, which were doubtless the property of Lloyd's Bank also. Dick examined them and said they weren't too bad. They had an antiquated look, and the varnish had worn off the frames, but only two of them had broken strings. Even those two, so Dick said, could be played with. He and Mrs Ashburton handed the racquets to one another, blowing at the dust that had accumulated on the presses and the strings. They lit up their cigarettes, and Mrs Ashburton insisted on giving Dick ten shillings to buy tennis balls with.

I sat with Mrs Ashburton watching Dick and Betty playing their first game on the court. The balls bounced in a peculiar way because in spite of all the rolling there were still hollows and bumps on the surface. The grass wasn't green. It was a brownish yellow, except for the bare patches, which were ochre-coloured. Mrs Ashburton clapped every time there was a rally, and when Dick had beaten Betty 6–1, 6–4, he taught me how to hit the ball over the net, and how to volley it and keep it going. 'Marvellous,

Matilda!' Mrs Ashburton cried, in her throaty voice, applauding again. 'Marvellous!'

We played all that summer, every Saturday and Sunday until the end of term, and almost every evening when the holidays came. We had to play in the evenings because at the end of term Dick began to work on the farm. 'Smoke your cigarettes if you want to,' my father said the first morning of the holidays, at breakfast. 'No point in hiding it, boy.' Friends of Dick's and Betty's used to come to Challacombe Manor to play also, because that was what Mrs Ashburton wanted: Colin Gregg and Barbara Hosell and Peggy Goss and Simon Turner and Willie Beach.

Sometimes friends of mine came, and I'd show them how to do it, standing close to the net, holding the racquet handle in the middle of the shaft. Thursday, August 31st, was the day Mrs Ashburton set for the tennis party: Thursday because it was half-day in the town.

Looking back on it now, it really does seem that for years and years she'd been working towards her tennis party. She'd hung about the lanes in her governess cart waiting for us because we were the children from the farm, the nearest children to Challacombe Manor. And when Dick looked big and strong enough and Betty of an age to be interested, she'd made her bid, easing matters along with fruitcake and cigarettes. I can imagine her now, on her own in that ruin of a house, watching the grass grow on her tennis court and watching Dick and Betty growing up and dreaming of one more tennis party at Challacombe, a party like there used to be before her husband was affected in the head by the Kaiser's war.

'August the 31st,' Betty reminded my parents one Sunday at dinnertime. 'You'll both come,' she said fiercely, blushing when they laughed at her.

'I hear Lloyd's is on the rampage,' my father said laboriously. 'Short of funds. Calling everything in.'

Dick and Betty didn't say anything. They ate their roast beef, pretending to concentrate on it.

''Course they're not,' my mother said.

'They'll sell Challacombe to some building fellow, now that it's all improved with tennis courts.'

'Daddy, don't be silly,' Betty said, blushing even more. All three of us used to blush. We got it from my mother. If my father blushed you wouldn't notice.

'True as I'm sitting here, my dear. Nothing like tennis courts for adding a bit of style to a place.'

Neither my mother nor my father had ever seen the tennis court. My father wouldn't have considered it the thing, to go walking over to Challacombe Manor to examine a tennis court. My mother was always busy, cooking and polishing brass. Neither my father nor my mother knew the rules of tennis. When we first began to play Betty used to draw a tennis court on a piece of paper and explain.

'Of course we'll come to the tennis party,' my mother said quietly. 'Of course, Betty.'

In the middle of the tennis party, my father persisted, a man in a hard black hat from Lloyd's Bank would walk on to the court and tell everyone to go home.

'Oh, Giles, don't be silly now,' my mother said quite sharply, and added that there was such a thing as going on too much. My father laughed and winked at her.

Mrs Ashburton asked everyone she could think of to the tennis party, people from the farms round about and shopkeepers from the town. Dick and Betty asked their friends and their friends' parents, and I asked Belle Frye and the Gorrys and the Seatons. My mother and Betty made meringues and brandy-snaps and fruitcakes and Victoria sponge cakes and scones and buns and shortbread. They made sardine sandwiches and tomato sandwiches and egg sandwiches and ham sandwiches. I buttered the bread and whipped up cream and wrapped the plates of sandwiches in damp tea-cloths. Dick cleared a place in the shrubbery beside the tennis court and built a fire to boil kettles on. Milk was poured into bottles and left to keep cool in the larder. August 31st was a fine, hot day.

At dinnertime my father pretended that the truck which was to convey the food, and us too, to the tennis court had a broken carburettor. He and Joe had been working on it all morning, he said, but utterly without success. No one took any notice of him.

I remember, most of all, what they looked like. Mrs Ashburton thin as a rake in a long white dress and her wide-brimmed white hat and her sunglasses. My father in his Sunday clothes, a dark blue suit, his hair combed and his leathery brown face shining because he had shaved it and washed it specially. My mother had powder on her cheeks and her nose, and a touch of lipstick on her lips, although she didn't usually wear lipstick and must have borrowed Betty's. She was wearing a pale blue dress speckled with tiny white flowers. She'd spent a fortnight making it herself, for the occasion. Her reddish hair was soft and a little unruly, being freshly washed. My father was awkward in his Sunday suit, as he always was in it. His freckled hands lolled uneasily by his sides, or awkwardly held tea things, cup and saucer and plate. My mother blushed beneath her powder, and sometimes stammered, which she did when she was nervous.

Betty was beautiful that afternoon, in a white tennis dress that my mother had made her. Dick wore long white flannels that he'd been given by old Mr Bowe, a solicitor in the town who'd been to other tennis parties at Challacombe Manor but had no further use for white flannel trousers, being seventy-two now and too large for the trousers he'd kept for more than fifty years. My mother had made me a tennis dress, too, but I felt shy that day and didn't want to do anything except hand round plates of meringues and cake. I certainly didn't want to play, for the tennis was serious: mixed doubles, Betty and Colin Gregg against Dick and Peggy Goss, and Simon Turner and Edie Turner against Barbara Hosell and Willie Beach.

People were there whom my father said he hadn't seen for years, people who had no intention of playing tennis, any more than he had. Between them, Dick and Betty and Mrs Ashburton had cast a wide net, and my father's protests at the mounds of food that had been prepared met with their answer as car after car drew up, and dog-carts and pony and traps. Belle Frye and I passed around the plates of meringues, and people broke off in their conversations to ask us who we were. Mrs Ashburton had spread rugs on the grass around the court, and four white ornamental seats had been repainted by Dick the week before. 'Just like the old days,' a man called Mr Race said, a corn merchant from the town. My mother nervously fidgeted, and I could feel her thinking that perhaps my father's laborious joke would come true, that any moment now the man from Lloyd's Bank would arrive and ask people what on earth they thought they were doing, playing tennis without the Bank's permission.

But that didn't happen. The balls zipped to and fro across the net, pinging off the strings, throwing up dust towards the end of the afternoon. Voices called out in exasperation at missed shots, laughter came and went. The sun continued to shine warmly, the tennis players wiped their foreheads with increasing regularity, the rugs on the grass were in the shade. Belle Frye and I collected the balls and threw them back to the servers. Mr Bowe said that Dick had the makings of a fine player.

Mrs Ashburton walked among the guests with a packet of Player's in her hand, talking to everyone. She kept going up to my mother and thanking her for everything she'd done. Whenever she saw me she kissed me on the hair. Mr Race said she shook hands like a duchess. The rector, Mr Throataway, laughed jollily.

At six o'clock, just as people were thinking of going, my father surprised everyone by announcing that he had a barrel of beer and a barrel of cider in the truck. I went with him and there they were, two barrels keeping cool beneath a tarpaulin, and two wooden butter-boxes full of glasses that he'd borrowed from the Heart of Oak. He drove the truck out from beneath the shade of the trees and backed it close to the tennis court. He and Dick set the barrels up and other men handed round the beer and cider, whichever anyone wanted. 'Just like him,' I heard a woman called Mrs Garland saying. 'Now, that's just like him.'

It was a quarter to ten that evening before they stopped playing tennis. You could hardly see the ball as it swayed about from racquet to racquet, looping over the net, driven out of court. My father and Mr Race went on drinking beer, and Joe and Arthur, who'd arrived after milking, stood some distance away from them, drinking beer also. Mrs Garland and my mother and Miss Sweet and Mrs Tissard made more tea, and the remains of the sandwiches and cakes were passed around by Belle Frye and myself. Joe said he reckoned it was the greatest day in Mrs Ashburton's life. 'Don't go drinking that cider now,' Joe said to Belle Frye and myself.

We all sat around in the end, smacking at midges and finishing the sandwiches and cakes. Betty and Colin Gregg had cider, and you could see from the way Colin Gregg kept looking at Betty that he was in love with her. He was holding her left hand as they sat there, thinking that no one could see because of the gloom, but Belle Frye and I saw, all right. Just before we went home, Belle Frye and I were playing at being ghosts round at the front of the house and we came across Betty and Colin Gregg kissing behind a rhododendron bush. They were lying on the grass with their arms tightly encircling one another, kissing and kissing as though they were never going to stop. They didn't even know Belle Frye and I were there. 'Oh, Colin!' Betty kept saying. 'Oh, Colin, Colin!'

We wanted to say goodbye to Mrs Ashburton, but we couldn't find her. We ran around looking everywhere, and then Belle Frye suggested that she was probably in the house.

'Mrs Ashburton!' I called, opening the door that led from the stable-yard to the kitchen. 'Mrs Ashburton!'

It was darker in the kitchen than it was outside, almost pitch-dark because the windows were so dirty that even in daytime it was gloomy.

'Matilda,' Mrs Ashburton said. She was sitting in an armchair by the oil-stove. I knew she was because that was where her voice came from. We couldn't see her.

'We came to say goodbye, Mrs Ashburton.'

She told us to wait. She had a saucer of chocolate for us, she said, and we heard her rooting about on the table beside her. We heard the glass being removed from a lamp and then she struck a match. She lit the wick and put the glass back. In the glow of lamplight she looked exhausted. Her eyes seemed to have receded, the thinness of her face was almost sinister.

We ate our chocolate in the kitchen that smelt of oil, and Mrs Ashburton didn't speak. We said goodbye again, but she didn't say anything. She didn't even nod or shake her head. She didn't kiss me like she usually did, so I went and kissed her instead. The skin of her face felt like crinkled paper.

'I've had a very happy day,' she said when Belle Frye and I had reached the kitchen door. 'I've had a lovely day,' she said, not seeming to be talking to us but to herself. She was crying, and she smiled in the lamplight, looking straight ahead of her. 'It's all over,' she said. 'Yet again.'

We didn't know what she was talking about and presumed she meant the tennis party. 'Yet again,' Belle Frye repeated as we crossed the stable-yard. She spoke in a soppy voice because she was given to soppiness. 'Poor Mrs Ashburton!' she said, beginning to cry herself, or pretending to. 'Imagine being eighty-one,' she said. 'Imagine sitting in a kitchen and remembering all the other tennis parties, knowing you'd have to die soon. Race you,' Belle Frye said, forgetting to be soppy any more.

Going home, Joe and Arthur sat in the back of the truck with Dick and Betty. Colin Gregg had ridden off on his bicycle, and Mr Bowe had driven away with Mrs Tissard beside him and Mr Tissard and Miss Sweet in the dickey of his Morris Cowley. My mother, my father and myself were all squashed into the front of the truck, and there was so little room that my father couldn't change gear and had to drive all the way to the farm in first. In the back of the truck Joe and Arthur and Dick were singing, but Betty wasn't, and I could imagine Betty just sitting there, staring, thinking about Colin Gregg. In Betty's bedroom there were photographs of Clark Gable and Ronald Colman, and Claudette Colbert and the little Princesses. Betty was going to marry Colin, I kept saying to myself in the truck. There'd be other tennis parties and Betty would be older and would know her own mind, and Colin Gregg would ask her and she'd say yes. It was very beautiful, I thought, as the truck shuddered over the uneven back avenue of Challacombe Manor. It was as beautiful as the tennis party itself, the white dresses and Betty's long hair, and everyone sitting and watching in the sunshine, and evening slowly descending. 'Well, that's the end of that,' my father said, and he didn't seem to be talking about the tennis party because his voice was too serious for that. He repeated a conversation he'd had with Mr Bowe and one he'd had with Mr Race, but I didn't listen because his voice was so lugubrious, not at all like it had been at the tennis party. I was huddled on my mother's knees, falling asleep. I imagined my father was talking about Lloyd's Bank again, and I could hear my mother agreeing with him.

I woke up when my mother was taking off my dress in my bedroom.

'What is it?' I said. 'Is it because the tennis party's over? Why's everyone so sad?'

My mother shook her head, but I kept asking her because she was looking sorrowful herself and I wasn't sleepy any more. In the end she sat on the edge of my bed and said that people thought there was going to be another war against the Germans.

'Germans?' I said, thinking of the grey, steely people that Mrs Ashburton had so often told me about, the people who ate black bread.

It would be all right, my mother said, trying to smile. She told me that we'd have to make special curtains for the windows so that the German aeroplanes wouldn't see the lights at night. She told me there'd probably be sugar rationing.

I lay there listening to her, knowing now why Mrs Ashburton had said that yet again it was all over, and knowing what would happen next. I didn't want to think about it, but I couldn't help thinking about it: my father would go away, and Dick would go also, and Joe and Arthur and Betty's Colin Gregg. I would continue to attend Miss Pritchard's School and then I'd go on to the Grammar, and my father would be killed. A soldier would rush at my father with a bayonet and twist the bayonet in my father's stomach, and Dick would do the same to another soldier, and Joe and Arthur would be missing in the trenches, and Colin Gregg would be shot.

My mother kissed me and told me to say my prayers before I went to sleep. She told me to pray for the peace to continue, as she intended to do herself. There was just a chance, she said, that it might.

She went away and I lay awake, beginning to hate the Germans and not feeling ashamed of it, like Mrs Ashburton was. No German would ever have played tennis that day, I thought, no German would have stood around having tea and sandwiches and meringues, smacking away the midges when night came. No German would ever have tried to recapture the past, or would have helped an old woman to do so, like my mother and my father had done, and Mr Race and Mr Bowe and Mr Throataway and Mrs Garland, and Betty and Dick and Colin Gregg. The Germans weren't like that. The Germans wouldn't see the joke when my father said that for all he knew Lloyd's Bank owned Mrs Ashburton.

I didn't pray for the peace to continue, but prayed instead that my father and Dick might come back when the war was over. I didn't pray that Joe and Arthur and Colin Gregg should come back since that would be asking too much, because some men had to be killed, according to Mrs Ashburton's law of averages. I hadn't understood her when Mrs Ashburton had said that cruelty was natural in wartime, but I understood now. I understood her law of averages and her sitting alone in her dark kitchen, crying over the past. I cried myself, thinking of the grass growing on her tennis court, and the cruelty that was natural.

2. The Summer-house

My father came back twice to the farm, unexpectedly, without warning. He walked into the kitchen, the first time one Thursday morning when there was nobody there, the second time on a Thursday afternoon.

My mother told us how on the first occasion she'd been crossing the yard with four eggs, all that the hens had laid, and how she'd sensed that something was different. The sheepdogs weren't in the yard, where they usually were at this time. Vaguely she'd thought that that was unusual. Hours later, when Betty and Dick and I came in from school, our parents were sitting at the kitchen table, talking. He was still in his army uniform. The big brown teapot was on the table, and two cups with the dregs of tea in them, and bread on the bread-board, and butter and blackberry jam. There was a plate he'd eaten a fry from, with the marks of egg-yolk on it. Even now it seems like yesterday. He smiled a slow, teasing smile at us, as though mocking the emotion we felt at seeing him there, making a joke even of that. Then Betty ran over to him and hugged him. I hugged him too. Dick stood awkwardly.

The second time he returned he walked into the kitchen at half past four, just after I'd come in from school. I was alone, having my tea.

'Hullo, Matilda,' he said.

I was nearly eleven then. Betty was sixteen and Dick was seventeen. Dick wasn't there that second time: he'd gone into the army himself. Betty had left the Grammar School and was helping my mother to keep the farm going. I was still at Miss Pritchard's.

I was going to be pretty, people used to say, although I couldn't see it myself. My hair had a reddish tinge, like my mother's, but it was straight and uninteresting. I had freckles, which I hated, and my eyes were a shade of blue I didn't much care for either. I detested being called Matilda. Betty and Dick, I considered, were much nicer names, and Betty was beautiful now. My friend Belle Frye was getting to be beautiful also. She claimed to have Spanish blood in her, though it was never clear where it came from. Her hair was jet-black and her skin, even in the middle of winter, was almost as deeply brown as her eyes. I'd have loved to look like her and to be called Belle Frye, which I thought was a marvellous name.

I made my father tea that Thursday afternoon and I felt a bit shy because I hadn't seen him for so long. He didn't comment on my making the tea, although he might have said that I hadn't been able to before. Instead he said he hadn't had a decent cup of tea since he'd been home the last time. 'It's great to be home, Matilda,' he said.

A few weeks later my mother told me he was dead. She told me at that same time of day and on a Thursday also: a warm June afternoon that had been tiring to trudge home from school through.

'Belle Frye has to stay in for two hours,' I was saying as I came into the kitchen. My mother told me to sit down.

The repetition was extraordinary, the three Thursday afternoons. That night in bed I was aware of it, lying awake thinking about him, wondering if he'd actually been killed on a Thursday also.

All the days of the week had a special thing about them: they had different characters and even different colours. Monday was light brown, Tuesday black, Wednesday grey, Thursday orange, Friday yellow, Saturday purplish, Sunday white. Tuesday was a day I liked because we had double History, Friday was cosy, Saturday I liked best of all. Thursday would be special now: I thought that, marking the day with my grief, unable to cry any more. And then I remembered that it had been a Thursday afternoon when old Mrs Ashburton had invited everyone for miles round to her tennis party, when I had realized for the first time that there was going to be a war against the Germans: Thursday, 31 August 1939.

I would have liked there to be a funeral, and I kept thinking about one. I never mentioned it to my mother or to Betty, or asked them if my father had had a funeral in France. I knew he hadn't. I'd heard him saying they just had to leave you there. My mother would cry if I said anything about it.

Then Dick came back, the first time home since he'd joined the army. He'd been informed too, and time had passed, several months, so that we were all used to it by now. It was even quite like the two occasions when my father had returned, Dick telling stories about the army. We sat in the kitchen listening to him, huddled round the range, with the sheepdogs under the table, and when the time came for him to go away I felt as I'd felt when my father had gone back. I knew that Betty and my mother were thinking about Dick in that way, too: I could feel it, standing in the yard holding my mother's hand.

Colin Gregg, who'd kissed Betty at Mrs Ashburton's tennis party, came to the farm when he was home on leave. Joe and Arthur, who'd worked for my father on the farm, came also. At one time or another they all said they were sorry about my father's death, trying not to say it when I was listening, lowering their voices, speaking to my mother.

Two years went by like that. Dick still came back, and Colin Gregg and Joe and Arthur. I left Miss Pritchard's school and went to the Grammar School. I heard Betty confiding to my mother that she was in love with Colin Gregg, and you could see it was Colin Gregg being in the war that she thought about now, not Dick. Belle Frye's father had had his left arm amputated because of a wound, and had to stay at home after that. A boy who'd been at the Grammar School, Roger Laze, had an accident with a gun when he was shooting rabbits, losing half his left foot. People said it was a lie about the rabbit-shooting. They said his mother had shot his foot off so that he wouldn't have to go into the army.

At church on Sundays the Reverend Throataway used to pray for victory and peace, and at school there was talk about the Russians, and jokes about Hitler and Göring and most of all about Goebbels. I remembered how old Mrs Ashburton used to talk about the previous war, from which her husband had come back with some kind of shell-shock. She'd made me think of Germans as being grey and steely, and I hated them now, just as she had. Whenever I thought about them I could see their helmets, different from the helmets of English soldiers, protecting their necks as well as their heads. Whenever I thought of the time before the war I thought of Mrs Ashburton, who had died soon after she'd given her tennis party. On the way home from school I'd sometimes go into the garden of Challacombe Manor and stand there looking at the tall grass on the tennis court, remembering all the people who'd come that afternoon, and how they'd said it was just like my father to say the tennis party was a lot of nonsense and then to bring on beer and cider at the end of the day. The tennis party had been all mixed up with our family. It felt like the last thing that had happened before the war had begun. It was the end of our being as we had been in our farmhouse, just as in the past, after the previous war, there must have been another end: when the farm had ceased to be the home-farm of Challacombe Manor, when the estate had been divided up after Mrs Ashburton's husband hadn't been able to run it any more.

When I wandered about the overgrown garden of Challacombe Manor I wondered what Mr Ashburton had been like before the war had affected him, but I couldn't quite see him in my mind's eye: all I could see was the person Mrs Ashburton had told me about, the silent man who'd come back, who hadn't noticed that everything was falling into rack and ruin around him. And then that image would disappear and I'd see my father instead, as he'd been in the farmhouse. I remembered without an effort the brown skin of his arms and his brown, wide forehead and the way crinkles formed at the sides of his eyes. I remembered his hands on the kitchen table at mealtimes, or holding a newspaper. I remembered his voice saying there'd been frost. 'Jack Frost's been,' he used to say.

When I was twelve I began to pray a lot. I prayed that my father should be safe in heaven and not worried about us. I prayed that Dick should be safe in the war, and that the war would soon end. In Scripture lessons the Reverend Throataway used to explain to us that God was in the weeds and the insects, not just in butterflies and flowers. God was involved in the worst things we did as well as our virtues, he said, and we drove another thorn into His beloved son's head when we were wicked. I found that difficult to understand. I looked at weeds and insects, endeavouring to imagine God's presence in them but not succeeding. I asked Belle Frye if she could, but she giggled and said God was a carpenter called Joseph, the father of Jesus Christ. Belle Frye was silly and the Reverend Throataway so vague and complicated that his arguments about the nature of God seemed to me like foolish chatter. God was neither a carpenter nor a presence in weeds and insects. God was a figure in robes, with a beard and shreds of cloud around Him. The paradise that was mentioned in the Bible was a garden with tropical plants in it, through which people walked, Noah and Moses and Jesus Christ and old Mrs Ashburton. I could never help thinking that soon the Reverend Throataway would be there too: he was so old and frail, with chalk on the black material of his clothes, sometimes not properly shaved, as if he hadn't the energy for it. I found it was a consolation to imagine the paradise he told us about, with my own God in it, and to imagine Hitler and Göring and Goebbels, with flames all around them, in hell. The more I thought about it all and prayed, the closer I felt to my father. I didn't cry when I thought about him any more, and my mother's face wasn't all pulled down any more. His death was just a fact now, but I didn't ever want not to feel close to him. It was as if being close to him was being close to God also, and I wanted that so that God could answer my prayer about keeping Dick safe in the war. I remembered how Mrs Ashburton had worked it out that by the law of averages some men have to come back from a war, and I suggested to the robed figure in charge of the tropical paradise that in all fairness our family did not deserve another tragedy. With my eyes tightly closed, in bed at night or suddenly stopping on the journey to school, I repetitiously prayed that Dick would be alive to come back when the war was over. That was all I asked for in the end because I could feel that my father was safe in the eternal life that the Reverend Throataway spoke of, and I didn't ask any more that the war should be over soon in case I was asking too much. I never told anyone about my prayers and I was never caught standing still with my eyes closed on the way to school. My father used to smile at me when I did that and I could faintly hear his voice teasing Dick about his smoking or teasing my mother about the Aga cooker she wanted, or Betty about almost anything. I felt it was all right when he smiled like that and his voice came back. I felt he was explaining to me that God had agreed to look after us now, provided I prayed properly and often and did not for a single instant doubt that God existed and was in charge. Mrs Ashburton had been doubtful about that last point and had told me so a few times, quite frightening me. But Mrs Ashburton would be in possession of the truth now, and would be forgiven.

My thoughts and my prayers seemed like a kind of world to me, a world full of God, with my father and Mrs Ashburton in their eternal lives, and the happiness that was waiting for the Reverend Throataway in his. It was a world that gradually became as important as the reality around me. It affected everything. It made me different. Belle Frye was still my friend, but I didn't like her the way I once had.

One wet afternoon she and I clambered into Challacombe Manor through a window that someone had smashed. We hadn't been there since the night of the tennis party, when we'd found Mrs Ashburton crying and she'd given us pieces of chocolate. We'd run out into the night, whispering excitedly about an old woman crying just because a party was over. I wouldn't have believed it then if someone had said I'd ever think Belle Frye silly.

'Whoever's going to live here?' she whispered in the dank hall after we'd climbed through the window. 'D'you think it'll just fall down?'

'There's a mortgage on it. Lloyd's Bank have it.'

'What's that mean then?'

'When the war's finished they'll sell the house off to someone else.'

All the furniture in the drawing-room had been taken away, stored in the cellars until someone, some day, had time to attend to it. People had pulled off pieces of the striped red wallpaper, boys from the Grammar School probably. There were names and initials and dates scrawled on the plaster. Hearts with arrows through them had been drawn.

'Anyone could come and live here,' Belle Frye said.

'Nobody'd want to.'

We walked from room to room. The dining-room still had a sideboard in it. There was blue wallpaper on the walls: none of that had been torn off, but there were great dark blots of damp on it. There were bundled-up newspapers all over the floor, and empty cardboard boxes that would have been useless for anything because they'd gone soft due to the damp. Upstairs there was a pool of water on a landing and in one of the bedrooms half the ceiling had fallen down. Everywhere there was a musty smell.

'It's haunted,' Belle Frye said.

'Of course it isn't.'

'She died here, didn't she?'

'That doesn't make it haunted.'

'I can feel her ghost.'

I knew she couldn't. I thought she was silly to say it, pretending about ghosts just to set a bit of excitement going. She said it again and I didn't answer.

We crawled out again, through the broken window. We wandered about in the rain, looking in the outhouses and the stables. The old motor-car that used to be in one of them had been taken away. The iron roller that Dick had rolled the tennis court with was still there, beside the tennis court itself.

'Let's try in here,' Belle Frye said, opening the door of the summer-house.

All the times I'd come into the garden on my own I'd never gone into the summer-house. I'd never even looked through a window of Challacombe Manor itself, or poked about the outhouses. I'd have been a bit frightened, for even though I thought it was silly of Belle Frye to talk about ghosts it wouldn't have surprised me to see a figure moving in the empty house or to hear something in one of the stables, a tramp maybe or a prisoner escaped from the Italian prisoner-of-war camp five miles away. The Italians were black-haired men mostly, whom we often met being marched along a road to work in the fields. They always waved and were given to laughing and singing. But even so I wouldn't have cared to meet one on his own.

In the centre of the summer-house was the table that had been covered with a white cloth, with sandwiches and cakes and the tea-urn on it, for the tennis party. The tennis marker was in a corner, placed there by Dick, I suppose, after he'd marked the court. The net was beside it, and underneath it, almost hidden by it, were two rugs, one of them brown and white, a kind of Scottish tartan pattern, the other grey. Both of these rugs belonged in our farmhouse. Could they have been lying in the summer-house since the tennis party? I wondered. I couldn't remember when I'd seen them last.

Facing one another across the table were two chairs which I remembered being there on the day of the party. They were dining-room chairs with red plush seats, brought from the house with a dozen or so others and arrayed on one side of the tennis court so that people could watch the games in comfort. These two must have been left behind when the others had been returned. I was thinking about that when I remembered my father hurriedly putting them into the summer-house at the end of the day. 'It'll maybe rain,' he'd said.

'Hey, look,' Belle Frye said. She was pointing at an ashtray on the table, with cigarette-butts and burnt-out matches in it. 'There's people using this place,' she said, giggling. 'Maybe an escaped prisoner,' she suggested, giggling again.

'Maybe.' I said it quickly, not wanting to pursue the subject. I knew the summer-house wasn't being used by an escaped prisoner. Our rugs hadn't been there since the day of the tennis party. They were part of something else, together with the cigarette-butts and the burnt-out matches. And then, quite abruptly, it occurred to me that the summer-house was where Betty and Colin Gregg came when Colin Gregg was on leave: they came to kiss, to cuddle one another like they'd been cuddling in the rhododendrons after the tennis party. Betty had brought the rugs specially, so that they could be warm and comfortable.

'I bet you it's an Eye-tie,' Belle Frye said. 'I bet you there's one living here.'

'Could be.'

'I'm getting out of it.'

We ran away. We ran through the overgrown garden on that wet afternoon and along the lane that led to the Fryes' farm. I should have turned in the opposite direction after we'd left the garden, but I didn't: I went with her because I didn't want her silliness to spoil everything. I thought it was romantic, Betty and Colin Gregg going to the summer-house. I remembered a film called *First Love*, which Betty had gone on about. It had Deanna Durbin in it.

'I'm going to tell,' Belle Frye said, stopping for breath before we came to the Fryes' farmyard. Her eyes jangled with excitement. There were drops of moisture in her smooth black hair.

'Let's have it a secret, Belle.'

'He could murder you, a blooming Eye-tie.'

'It's where my sister and Colin Gregg go.' I had to say it because I knew she'd never be able to keep a secret that involved an Italian prisoner of war. I knew that even if no prisoner had escaped people would go to the summer-house to see for themselves. I knew for a fact, I said, that it was where Betty and Colin Gregg went, and if she mentioned it to anyone I'd tell about going into Challacombe Manor through a broken window. She'd said as we'd clambered through it that her father would murder her if he knew. He'd specifically told her that she mustn't go anywhere near the empty house because the floor-boards were rotten and the ceilings falling down.

'But why would you tell?' she cried, furious with me. 'What d'you want to tell for?'

'It's private about the summer-house. It's a private thing of Betty's.'

She began to giggle. We could watch, she whispered. We could watch through the window to see what they got up to. She went on giggling and whispering and I listened to her, not liking her. In the last year or so she'd become like that, repeating the stories she heard from the boys at school, all to do with undressing and peeping. There were rhymes and riddles and jokes that she repeated also, none of them funny. She'd have loved peeping through the summer-house window.

'No,' I said. 'No.'

'But we could. We could wait till he was home on leave. We needn't make a sound.' Her voice had become shrill. She was cross with me again, not giggling any more. Her eyes glared at me. She said I was stupid, and then she turned and ran off. I knew she'd never peep through the summer-house window on her own because it wasn't something you could giggle over when you were alone. And I knew she wouldn't try and persuade anyone to go with her because she believed me when I said I'd tell about breaking into Challacombe Manor. Her father was a severe man; she was, fortunately, terrified of him.

I thought about the summer-house that evening when I was meant to be learning a verse of 'The Lady of Shalott' and writing a composition, 'The Worst Nightmare I Ever Had'. I imagined Betty and Colin Gregg walking hand in hand through the overgrown garden and then slipping into the summer-house when it became dusky. A summer's evening it was, with pink in the sky, and the garden was scented with the blossoms of its shrubs. I imagined them sitting on the two dining-chairs at the table, Colin telling her about the war while he smoked his cigarettes, and Betty crying because he would be gone in twelve hours' time and Colin comforting her, and both of them lying down on the rugs so that they could be close enough to put their arms around each other.

In the kitchen while I tried to record the details of a nightmare all I could think about was the much pleasanter subject of my sister's romance. She was in the kitchen also. She'd changed from her farm-working clothes into a navy-blue skirt and a matching jersey. I thought she was more beautiful than usual. She and my mother were sitting on either side of the range, both of them knitting, my mother reading a book by A.J. Cronin at the same time, my sister occasionally becoming lost in a reverie. I knew what she was thinking about. She was wondering if Colin Gregg was still alive.

Months went by and neither he nor Dick came back. There were letters, but there were also periods when no letters arrived and you could feel the worry, for one of them or the other. The war was going to be longer than everyone had thought. People looked gloomy sometimes, and when I caught their gloom I imagined bodies lying unburied and men in aeroplanes, with goggles on, the aeroplanes on fire and the men in goggles burning to death. Ages ago France had been beaten, and I remembered that in a casual moment in a Scripture class the Reverend Throataway had said that that could never happen, that the French would never give in. We would never give in either, Winston Churchill said, but I imagined the Germans marching on the lanes and the roads and through the fields, not like the cheerful Italians. The Germans were cruel in their helmets and their grey steeliness. They never smiled. They knew you hated them.

Belle Frye would have thought I was mad if I'd told her any of that, just like she'd have thought I was mad if I'd mentioned about praying and keeping my father vivid in my mind. She was the first friend I'd ever had, but the declining of our friendship seemed almost natural now. We still sat next to one another in class, but we didn't always walk home together. Doing that had always meant that one of us had to go the long way round and avoiding this extra journey now became an excuse. Not having had Dick and Betty to walk home with for so long, I'd enjoyed Belle Frye's company, but now I found myself pretending to be in a hurry or just slipping away when she wasn't looking. She didn't seem to mind, and we still spent days together, at the weekends or in the holidays. We'd have tea in each other's kitchens, formally invited by our mothers, who didn't realize that we weren't such friends. And that was still quite nice.

Sometimes in the evenings my mother used to go to see a woman called Mrs Latham because Mrs Latham was all alone in the Burrow Farm, three miles away. On these occasions I always hoped Betty would talk to me about Colin Gregg, that she'd even mention the summer-house. But she never did. She'd sit there knitting, or else writing a letter to him. She'd hear me say any homework I had to learn by heart, a theorem or poetry or spelling. She'd make me go to bed, just like my mother did, and then she'd turn on the wireless and listen to *Monday Night at Eight* or *Waterlogged Spa* or *Itma*. She'd become very quiet, less impatient with me than she'd been when we were younger, more grown-up, I suppose. I often used to think about her on those nights when my mother was out, when she was left alone in the kitchen listening to the wireless. I used to feel sorry for her.

And then, in that familiar sudden way, Colin Gregg came back on leave.

That was the beginning of everything. The evening after he came back was a Saturday, an evening in May. I'd been at the Fryes' all afternoon and when we'd finished tea we played cards for an hour or so and then Mrs Frye said it was time for me to go home. Belle wanted to walk with me, even though we'd probably have walked in silence. I was glad when her father said no. It was too late and in any case he had to go out himself, to set his rabbit snares: he'd walk with me back to our farm. I said goodbye, remembering to thank Mrs Frye, and with his remaining arm Mr Frye pushed his bicycle on the road beside me. He didn't talk at all. He was completely different from my father, never making jokes or teasing. I was quite afraid of him because of his severity.

The sheepdogs barked as I ran across our yard and into the kitchen. My mother had said earlier that she intended to go over to see Mrs Latham that evening. By eight o'clock Betty and Colin Gregg were to be back from the half past four show at the pictures, so that I wouldn't be in the house alone. It was twenty past eight now, and they weren't there.

I ran back into the yard, wanting to tell Mr Frye, but already he'd cycled out of sight. I didn't at all like the idea of going to bed in the empty house.

I played with the dogs for a while and then I went to look at the hens, and then I decided that I'd walk along the road to meet Betty and Colin Gregg. I kept listening because at night you could always hear the voices of people cycling in the lanes. I kept saying to myself that my mother wouldn't want me to go to bed when there was no one in the farmhouse. It was very still, with bits of red in the sky. I took the short-cut through the garden of Challacombe Manor and I wasn't even thinking about Betty and Colin Gregg when I saw two bicycles in the shrubbery at the back of the summer-house. I didn't notice them at first because they were almost entirely hidden by rhododendron bushes. They reminded me of the rugs half hidden beneath the tennis net.

Colin Gregg was going away again on Monday. He was being sent somewhere dangerous, he didn't know where, but I'd heard Betty saying to my mother that she could feel in her bones it was dangerous. When my mother had revealed that she intended to visit Mrs Latham that evening I'd said to myself that she'd arranged the visit so that Colin Gregg and Betty could spend the evening on their own in our kitchen. But on the way back from the pictures they'd gone into the summer-house, their special place.

Even now I can't think why I behaved like Belle Frye, unable to resist something. It was silly curiosity, and yet at the time I think it may have seemed more than just that. In some vague way I wanted to have something nice to think about, not just my imagining the war, and my prayers for Dick's safety and my concern with people's eternal lives. I wanted to see Betty and Colin Gregg together. I wanted to feel their happiness, and to see it.

It was then, while I was actually thinking that, that I realized something was the matter. I realized I'd been stupid to assume they could take the short-cut through the garden: you couldn't take the short-cut if you were coming from the town on a bicycle because you had to go through fields. You'd come by the lanes, and if you wanted to go to the summer-house you'd have to turn back and go there specially. It seemed all wrong that they should do that when they were meant to be back in the farmhouse by eight o'clock.

I should have turned and gone away. In the evening light I was unable to see the bicycles clearly, but even so I was aware that neither of them was Betty's. They passed out of my sight as I approached one of the summer-house's two small windows.

I could see nothing. Voices murmured in the summer-house, not saying anything, just quietly making sounds. Then a man's voice spoke more loudly, but I still couldn't hear what was being said. A match was struck and in a sudden vividness I saw a man's hand and a packet of Gold Flake cigarettes on the table, and then I saw my mother's face. Her reddish hair was untidy and she was smiling. The hand that had been on the table put a cigarette between her lips and another hand held the match to it. I had never in my life seen my mother smoking a cigarette before.

The match went out and when another one was struck it lit up the face of a man who worked in Blow's drapery. My mother and he were sitting facing one another at the table, on the two chairs with the red plush seats.

Betty was frying eggs at the range when I returned to the kitchen. Colin Gregg had had a puncture in his back tyre. They hadn't even looked yet to see if I was upstairs. I said we'd all forgotten the time at the Fryes', playing cards.

In bed I kept remembering that my mother's eyes had been different, not like they'd been for a long time, two dark-blue sparks. I kept saying to myself that I should have recognized her bicycle in the bushes because its mudguards were shaped like a V, not rounded like the mudguards of modern bicycles.

I heard Colin and Betty whispering in the yard and then the sound of his bicycle as he rode away and then, almost immediately, the sound of my mother's bicycle and Betty saying something quietly and my mother quietly replying. I heard them coming to bed, Betty first and my mother twenty minutes later. I didn't sleep, and for the first time in my life I watched the sky becoming brighter when morning began to come. I heard my mother getting up and going out to do the milking.

At breakfast-time it was as though none of it had happened, as though she had never sat on the red plush chair in the summer-house, smoking cigarettes and smiling at a man from a shop. She ate porridge and brown bread, reading a book: *Victoria Four-Thirty* by Cecil Roberts. She reminded me to feed the hens and she asked Betty what time Colin Gregg was coming over. Betty said any minute now and began to do the washing up. When Colin Gregg came he mended one of the cow-house doors.

That day was horrible. Betty tried to be cheerful, upset because Colin Gregg was being sent to somewhere dangerous. But you could feel the effort of her trying and when she thought no one was looking, when my mother and Colin were talking to one another, her face became unhappy. I couldn't stop thinking about my father. Colin Gregg went back to the war.

A month went by. My mother continued to say she was going to see Mrs Latham and would leave Betty and me in the kitchen about once a week.

'Whatever's the matter with Matilda?' I heard Betty saying to her once, and later my mother asked me if I had a stomach ache. I used to sit there at the table trying to understand simultaneous equations, imagining my mother in the summer-house, the two bicycles half hidden in the bushes, the cigarettes and the ashtray.

'The capital of India,' I would say. 'Don't tell me; I know it.'

'Begins with a "D",' Betty would prompt.

He came to the kitchen one evening. He ate cabbage and baked potatoes and fish pie, chewing the cabbage so carefully you couldn't help noticing. He was scrawny, with a scrawny nose. His teeth were narrowly crowded, his whole face pulled out to an edge, like a chisel. His hair was parted in the middle and oiled. His hands were clean, with tapering fingers. I was told his name but I didn't listen, not wishing to know it.

'Where'd you get the fish?' he asked my mother in a casual way. His head was cocked a little to one side. He was smiling with his narrow teeth, making my mother flustered as she used to get in the past, when my father was alive. She was even beginning to blush, not that I could see a cause for it. She said:

'Betty, where did you get the cod?'

'Croker's,' Betty said.

Betty smiled at him and my mother said quickly that Croker's were always worth trying in case they'd got any fish in, although of course you could never tell. It sounded silly the way she said it.

'I like fish,' he said.

'We must remember that.'

'They say it's good for you,' Betty said.

'I always liked fish,' the man said. 'From a child I've enjoyed it.'

'Eat it up now,' my mother ordered me.

'Don't you like fish, Matilda?' he said.

Betty laughed. 'Matilda doesn't like lots of things. Fish, carrots, eggs. Semolina. Ground rice. Custard. Baked apples, gravy, cabbage.'

He laughed, and my mother laughed. I bent my head over the plate I was eating from. My face had gone as hot as a fire.

'Unfortunately there's a war on,' he said. 'Hard times, Matilda.'

I considered that rude. It was rude the way he'd asked where the fish had come from. He was stupid, as well. Who wanted to hear that he liked fish? He was a fool, like Stupid Miller, who'd been at Miss Pritchard's school. He was ridiculous-looking and ugly, with his pointed face and crushed-together teeth. He'd no right to say there was a war on since he wasn't fighting in it.

They listened to the news on the wireless and afterwards they listened to the national anthems of the countries which were fighting against Germany. He offered my mother and Betty cigarettes and they both took one. I'd never seen Betty smoking a cigarette before. He'd brought a bottle of some kind of drink with him. They drank it sitting by the range, still listening to the national anthems.

'Good-night, Matilda,' he said, standing up when my mother told me it was time to go to bed. He kissed me on the cheek and I could feel his damp teeth. I didn't move for a moment after he'd done that, standing quite close to him. I thought I was going to bring up the fish pie and if I did I wanted to cover his clothes with it. I wouldn't have cared. I wouldn't have been embarrassed.

I heard Betty coming to bed and then I lay for hours, waiting for the sound of his bicycle going away. I couldn't hear their voices downstairs, the way I'd been able to hear voices when Betty had been there. Betty's had become quite loud and she'd laugh repeatedly. I guessed they'd been playing cards, finishing off the bottle of drink he'd brought. When I'd been there Betty had suggested rummy and he'd said that not a drop of the drink must be left. He'd kept filling up Betty's and my mother's glasses, saying the stuff was good for you.

I crossed the landing to the top of the stairs that led straight down into the kitchen. I thought they must have fallen asleep by the range because when a board creaked beneath my feet no one called out. I stood at the turn of the narrow staircase, peering through the shadows at them.

Betty had taken one of the two lamps with her as she always did. The kitchen was dim, with only the glow from the other. On the table, close to the lamp, was the bottle and one of the glasses they'd drunk from. The two dogs were stretched in front of the range. My mother was huddled on the man's knee. I could see his tapering fingers, one hand on the black material of her dress, the other stroking her hair. While I watched he kissed her, bending his damp mouth down to her lips and keeping it there. Her eyes were closed but his were open, and when he finished kissing her he stared at her face.

I went on down the stairs, shuffling my bare feet to make a noise. The dogs growled, pricking up their ears. My mother was half-way across the kitchen, tidying her hair with both hands, murmuring at me.

'Can't you sleep, love?' she said. 'Have you had a dream?'

I shook my head. I wanted to walk forward, past her to the table. I wanted to pick up the bottle he'd brought and throw it on to the flags of the floor. I wanted to shout at him that he was ugly, no more than a half-wit, no better than Stupid Miller, who hadn't been allowed in the Grammar School. I wanted to say no one was interested in his preference for fish.

My mother put her arms around me. She felt warm from sitting by the range, but I hated the warmth because it had to do with him. I pushed by her and went to the sink. I drank some water even though I wasn't thirsty. Then I turned and went upstairs again.

'She's sleepy,' I heard my mother say. 'She often gets up for a drink when she's sleepy. You'd better go, dear.'

He muttered something else and my mother said that they must have patience.

'One day,' she said. 'After it's all over.'

'It'll never end.' He spoke loudly, not muttering any more. 'This bloody thing could last for ever.'

'No, no, my dear.'

'It's all I want, to be here with you.'

'It's what I want too. But there's a lot in the way.'

'I don't care what's in the way.'

'We have to care, dear.'

'I love you,' he said.

'My own darling,' my mother said.

*

She was the same as usual the next day, presumably imagining that being half-asleep I hadn't noticed her sitting on the man's knees and being kissed by his mouth. In the afternoon I went into the summer-house. I looked at the two plush-seated chairs, imagining the figures of my mother and the man on them. I carried the chairs, one by one, to an outhouse and up a ladder to a loft. I put the tennis net underneath some seed-boxes. I carried the two rugs to the well in the cobbled yard and dropped them down it. I returned to the summer-house, thinking of doing something else, I wasn't sure what. There was a smell of stale tobacco, coming from butts in the ashtray. On the floor I found a tie-pin with a greyhound's head on it and I thought the treacherous, ugly-looking dog suited him. I threw it into the rhododendron shrubbery.

'Poor chap,' I heard Betty saying that evening. 'It's a horrid thing to have.' She'd always noticed that he looked delicate, she added.

'He doesn't get enough to eat,' my mother said.

In spite of her sympathy, you could see that Betty wasn't much interested in the man: she was knitting and trying to listen to *Bandwagon*. As far as Betty was concerned he was just some half-sick man whom my mother felt sorry for, the way she was supposed to feel sorry for Mrs Latham of Burrow Farm. But my mother wanted to go on talking about him, with a pretended casualness. It wasn't the right work for a person who was tubercular, she said, serving in a shop.

I imagined him in Blow's, selling pins and knitting-needles and satin by the yard. I thought the work suited him in the same way as the greyhound's-head tie-pin did.

'What's it mean, tubercular?' I asked Belle Frye, and she said it meant you suffered from a disease in your lungs.

'I expect you could fake it.'

'What'd you want to do that for?'

'To get out of the war. Like Mrs Laze shot off Roger Laze's foot.'

'Who's faking it then?'

'That man in Blow's.'

I couldn't help myself: I wanted it to be known that he was faking a disease in his lungs. I wanted Belle Frye to tell people, to giggle at him in Blow's, pointing him out. But in fact she wasn't much interested. She nodded, and then shrugged in a jerky way she had, which meant she was impatient to be talking about something else. You could tell she didn't know the man in Blow's had become a friend of my mother's. She hadn't seen them on their bicycles; she wouldn't have wanted to change the subject if she'd looked through the summer-house window and seen them with their cigarettes. Before that I hadn't thought about her finding out, but now I wondered if perhaps she would some time, and if other people would. I imagined the giggling and the jokes made up by the boys in the Grammar School, and the severity of Mr Frye, and the astonishment of people who had liked my father.

I prayed that none of that would happen. I prayed that the man would go away, or die. I prayed that my mother would be upset again because my father had been killed in the war, that she would remember the time when he had been in the farmhouse with us. I prayed that whatever happened she would never discredit him by allowing the man from Blow's to be there in the farmhouse, wearing my father's clothes.

Every day I prayed in the summer-house, standing close to the table with my eyes closed, holding on to the edge of it. I went there specially, and more vividly than ever I could see my father in the tropical garden of his eternal life. I could see old Mrs Ashburton walking among the plants with her husband, happy to be with him again. I could see the bearded face of the Almighty I prayed to, not smiling but seeming kind.

'Oh, my God,' was all my mother could say, whispering it between her bursts of tears. 'Oh, my God.'

Betty was crying too, but crying would do no good. I stood there between them in the kitchen, feeling I would never cry again. The telegram was still on the table, its torn envelope beside it. It might have said that Dick was coming home on leave, or that Colin Gregg was. It looked sinister on the table because Dick was dead.

I might have said to my mother that it was my fault as well as hers. I might have said that I'd known I should pray only for Dick to be safe and yet hadn't been able to prevent myself from asking, also, that she'd be as she used to be, that she wouldn't ever marry the man from Blow's.

But I didn't say that. I didn't say I'd prayed about the man, I just said it was a Thursday again.

'Thursday?' my mother whispered, and when I explained she didn't understand. She hadn't even noticed that the two times my father had come home it had been a Thursday and that the tennis party had been on a Thursday and that the other telegram had come on a Thursday too. She shook her head, as if denying all this repetition, and I wanted to hurt her when she did that because the denial seemed to be part and parcel of the summer-house and the man from Blow's. More deliberately than a moment ago I again didn't confess that I had ceased to concentrate on Dick's safety in my prayers. Instead I said that in a war against the Germans you couldn't afford to take chances, you couldn't go kissing a man when your husband had been killed.

'Oh, my God,' my mother said again.

Betty was staring at her, tears still coming from her eyes, bewildered because she'd never guessed about my mother and the man.

'It has nothing to do with this,' my mother whispered. 'Nothing.'

I thought Betty was going to attack my mother, maybe hammer at her face with her fists, or scratch her cheeks. But she only cried out, shrieking like some animal caught in a trap. The man was even married, she shrieked, his wife was away in the Women's Army. It was horrible, worse than ever when you thought of that. She pointed at me and said I was right: Dick's death was a judgement, things happened like that.

My mother didn't say anything. She stood there, white-faced, and then she said the fact that the man was married didn't make anything worse.

She spoke to Betty, looking at her, not at me. Her voice was quiet. She said the man intended to divorce his wife when the war came to an end. Of course what had happened wasn't a judgement.

'You won't marry him now,' Betty said, speaking as quietly.

My mother didn't reply. She stood there by the table and there was a silence. Then she said again that Dick's death and the man were two different things. It was terrible, she said, to talk as we were talking at a time like this. Dick was dead: that was the only thing that mattered.

'They used to go to the summer-house,' I said. 'They had two of our rugs there.'

My mother turned her head away, and I wanted Betty to remember as I was remembering and I believe she did. I could sense her thinking of the days when my father was alive, when Dick used to smoke cigarettes on the way home from school, when we were all together in the farmhouse, not knowing we were happy. That time seemed to haunt the kitchen just then, as if my mother was thinking about it too, as if our remembering had willed it back.

'He could never come here now,' Betty said to my mother. 'You couldn't do it to Matilda.'

I didn't know why she should have particularly mentioned me since it concerned us all, and anyway I felt it was too late to bother about me. Too much had happened. I felt I'd been blown to pieces, as if I'd been in the war myself, as if I'd been defeated by it, as old Mrs Ashburton had been defeated by her war. The man would come to live in the farmhouse. He would wear my father's clothes. He would sit by the range, reading the newspaper. He would eat at the table, and smile at me with his narrow teeth.

My mother left the kitchen. She went upstairs and after a few minutes we heard her sobbing in her bedroom. Sobbing would do no good, I thought, any more than crying would.

I walked by myself through the fields. Dick's death wasn't the same as my father's. There was the same emptiness and the same feeling that I never wanted to eat anything again or to drink anything again, but it was different because this was the second time. Dick was dead and we'd get used to it: that was something I knew now.

I didn't cry and I didn't pray. Praying seemed nonsense as I walked through the fields; praying was as silly as Belle Frye's thinking that God was a carpenter or the Reverend Throataway saying God was in weeds. God wasn't like that in the least. He wasn't there to listen to what you prayed for. God was something else, something harder and more awful and more frightening.

I should have known that the man from Blow's would be married, that he'd have a wife who was helping in the war while he was going on about a disease. It was somehow all of a piece with Betty wanting to hit my mother, and Mrs Laze shooting off her son's foot so that he could stay alive, and God being frightening. Facts and images rattled in my mind, senselessly jumbled, without rhyme or reason. Dick was there too, dead and unburied in his uniform, something ordinary to get used to.

I sat in the sunshine on a bank that had primroses on it. I could have returned to the farmhouse and let my mother put her arms around me, but I continued to sit there, still not crying, remembering Mrs Ashburton saying that cruelty in wartime was natural. At the time I hadn't understood what she'd meant, but I could feel the cruelty she'd spoken of now. I could feel it in myself, in my wanting my mother to be more unhappy than I was. Dick's death was more bearable because she could be blamed, as Betty had blamed her in speaking of a judgement.

3. The Drawing-room

I am writing this in the drawing-room, in fact at Mrs Ashburton's writing-desk. I don't think of it as a story – and certainly not as a letter, for she can never read it – but as a record of what happened in her house after the war. If she hadn't talked to me so much when I was nine there would not be this record to keep, and I would not still feel her presence. I do not understand what has happened, but as I slowly move towards the age she was when she talked to me I slowly understand a little more. What she said has haunted me for thirty-nine years. It has made me old before my time, and for this I am glad. I feel like a woman of sixty; I'm only forty-eight.

In 1951 the house was bought by people called Gregary. 'Filthy rich,' my stepfather said.

My stepfather had just been made manager at Blow's drapery in the town. He used to drive off every day in a blue pre-war baby Ford, and I was always glad to see him go. I worked on the farm with Joe and Arthur, like my father had, like my brother Dick would have if he hadn't been killed in the desert offensive.

I thought it was typical of my stepfather to know that the Gregarys were rich. It was the kind of information he picked up in Blow's, conversing across his counter, the gossip enlivening his chisel face. He said Mr Gregary was a businessman involved in the manufacture of motor-car components. He'd made a killing during the war: my stepfather called him a post-war tycoon.

On my twenty-first birthday my mother insisted on giving a kind of party. We had it in the farmhouse kitchen. We cooked a turkey and a ham and my mother made a great fuss about the vegetables that had been my favourites when I was small: celery and parsnips and carrots, and roast potatoes. The carrots were to be in a parsley sauce, the parsnips roasted with the potatoes. We made trifle because trifle had been a childhood favourite also, and brandy-snaps. It was impossible not to recall the preparations for Mrs Ashburton's tennis party on the Thursday before the war, but of course I didn't mention that. My mother believed that I didn't want to live in the present. I often felt her looking at me and when I turned my head I could see for a moment, before she changed her expression, that she believed I dwelt far too much on times that were not our own.

Fifteen people came to my birthday party, not counting my mother and my stepfather and myself. My sister Betty, who had married Colin Gregg, came with her two children. Belle Frye had married Martin Draper, who'd inherited the mill at Bennett's Cross: they brought the baby that had made the marriage necessary. Mr and Mrs Frye were there, and Miss Pritchard, who'd taught us all at school. Joe and Arthur, and Joe's wife, Maudie, came; and Mrs Laze and her son Roger. The idea was, I believe, that I might one day marry Roger, but it wasn't a prospect I relished. He limped because of his foot, and he hardly ever spoke, being shy like his mother. I didn't dislike him, I just didn't want to marry him.

All the time I kept wishing my mother hadn't given this party. It made me think of my other birthdays. Not that there was any reason to avoid doing that, except that naturally the past seemed better, especially the distant past, before the war. Miss Pritchard was the only person I ever talked to about things like that. 'Come and talk to me whenever you want to, Matilda,' she'd said one day in 1944, and ever since I'd been visiting her in her tiny sitting-room, knowing she was lonely because she was retired now. In a way our conversations reminded me of my conversations with Mrs Ashburton, except that it was Mrs Ashburton, not I, who used to do the talking and half the time I hadn't understood her. It was I who'd suggested that Miss Pritchard should come to my birthday party. I'd heard my mother saying to my stepfather that she couldn't understand it: she thought it extraordinary that I didn't want to invite lots of the boys I'd been at the Grammar School with, that I didn't want to have a gramophone going and tables of whist. My stepfather said he didn't think people played whist like they used to. He stood up for me, the way he always did, even though he didn't know I was listening. He made such efforts and still I couldn't like him.

Seventeen of us sat down at the kitchen table at half past six and my stepfather poured out cider for us, and orangeade for Betty's children. Belle Frye's baby was put to sleep upstairs. I couldn't think of her as Belle Draper, and haven't ever been able to since. Martin Draper had been a silly kind of boy at school and he still was silly now.

My stepfather carved the turkey and my mother the ham. Everyone was talking about Challacombe Manor having been sold to the people called Gregary.

'The son's going to run the place,' my stepfather said. 'Tax fiddle, I dare say.'

You could see that Miss Pritchard didn't know what he was talking about, and you could see that she suspected he didn't know what he was talking about himself. In his gossipy way he was always referring to tax fiddles and how people had made a fortune and what price such and such a shop in the town would fetch. The fact that he'd mentioned income tax evasion in connection with the Gregarys didn't mean that there was any truth in the suggestion. Even so, the reference, coupled with the information that Mr Gregary was in the motor-components industry, established the Gregarys as people of a certain kind. Carving the turkey, my stepfather said that in his opinion Challacombe would be restored to its former splendour.

'They haven't the land,' Mr Frye pointed out, for he himself farmed eighty acres of what had once been the Challacombe estate.

'It couldn't never be the same,' Joe added.

Plates of turkey and ham were passed from hand to hand until everyone present was attended to. My mother said that people must take vegetables and start, else the food would get cold. A more lively chatter about the new people at Challacombe broke out as the cider was consumed. Two of the Gregary daughters were married and living in some other part of the country, a third one was at a university. The son was the apple of his parents' eye. The father owned a grey Daimler.

The old range which had been in our kitchen all during my childhood had only the week before been replaced by a cream-coloured Aga. The acquisition of an Aga had been my mother's dream for almost as long as I could remember. I think she'd grown to hate the range, lighting it every morning with sticks and paper, the struggles she'd had with it during the war, trying to burn wood instead of coal. But I'd been sorry to see it go. I tried to stop myself being like that about things, but I couldn't help it.

'To the birthday girl,' my stepfather said, raising his glass of cider. 'Many happy returns, my best.'

It was that that I didn't care for in him: I wasn't his best, my mother was. Yet he'd say it casually, wanting to pay a compliment but overdoing it so that you didn't believe him, so that you distrusted him.

'Matilda,' other people said, holding up their glasses also. 'To Matilda.'

'Oh, my love!' my mother cried out, getting up and running round the table to kiss me. 'Oh, little Matilda!' I could feel the warm dampness of tears as her cheek came into contact with mine, and the touch of her mouth, reminding me of childhood. It was a long time since my mother had kissed me.

Everyone made a fuss then, even Martin Draper and Joe and Arthur. I can still see the sunburnt face of Colin Gregg, and his pale smooth hair, his eyes seeming to laugh at me as he wished me many happy returns. For a split second he reminded me of my father.

Betty said the turkey was delicious because she could see I was embarrassed by all the attention. Belle Frye said the next thing after a twenty-first was getting married. She reminded us that she'd been married herself within a fortnight of becoming twenty-one. She giggled and Martin Draper went red because everyone knew they'd got married in a hurry. She'd been terrified at the time of what her father would say, but to her surprise he'd taken the whole thing calmly, pointing out that there were worse than Martin Draper, reminding her that he'd just inherited the Bennett's Cross mill. It was Mrs Frye who'd been upset, unable to find consolation in her son-in-law's inheritance of a mill. Belle deserved better, she'd said.

'There's that chap on the haberdashery counter,' my stepfather said, winking his good eye all round the table, resting it for a moment on Roger Laze in order to stir up rivalry. 'Keen as mustard, that chap is.'

I knew he'd say that. As soon as Belle Frye had mentioned that the next thing after a twenty-first was a wedding I knew he'd refer to the chap on the haberdashery counter, a pimpled youth with no roof to his mouth. It was typical of my stepfather that he'd notice a counter-hand's interest in me. He'd repeatedly mentioned it before. It was typical that he'd mention it now, in public, assuming I'd be pleased that everyone should know I had an admirer, not thinking to himself that no girl would want even remotely to be associated with an unattractive shop-boy. It wasn't teasing, even though he winked: it was an attempt to be kind. My father would just have teased. He'd have made me blush and I'd have been angry and would have complained to my mother afterwards. It seemed silly now that I'd ever minded.

'Delicious, this stuffing is,' Betty said. 'Eat every scrap of your ham,' she warned one of her children, with a threat in her voice.

'Tip-top ham,' my stepfather said.

'I'll always remember the day Matilda was born,' Joe said. 'I nearly got sacked for letting a heifer wander.'

'A beautiful autumn,' Miss Pritchard said quietly, '1930.'

I was six weeks early, my mother said, a fact she'd told me before. She'd been over to Bennett's Cross in the trap and had had to pull hard on the reins when the pony had taken fright at a piece of newspaper on the road. It was that that had brought me on.

'Old Ashburton's funeral the day before,' Arthur said.

'I never knew that.' I looked at him, interested at last in the conversation, for it wasn't important that I'd been six weeks early or that the autumn had been beautiful. But it did seem strange that in all my conversations

with Mrs Ashburton it had never become established that the man she
talked so much about had been buried the day before my birth.

'Big old funeral,' Arthur said.

Miss Pritchard nodded and I could see the memory of it in her face. She
wouldn't of course have attended it because the Ashburtons and she
wouldn't have been on any kind of terms, there being nothing to connect
them. She'd told me that when I'd asked her once; she'd explained that to
people like the Ashburtons she'd been just a schoolteacher, adding that
she'd only been invited to Mrs Ashburton's tennis party because everyone
else had. But she'd have drawn the blinds of the school-house and would
have waited in the gloom until the funeral had gone by.

I watched her as she ate her turkey and ham. I watched her thinking and
remembering, not taking part in the conversations around her. She was
slight and fragile-looking, wearing a brown suit with a necklace of beads
falling on to a brown jersey. She'd retired about eighteen months ago; it
was impossible to believe that we'd ever considered her unfair.

'You're looking lovely, dear,' Mrs Laze whispered across the table at
me, leaning and poking her head out so that no one else would hear, for
she was a woman who rarely spoke. The story was still told that she'd
shot off Roger's foot during the war so that he wouldn't be called up, but
now that the war was over it was increasingly difficult to visualize the
scene and I began to think the rumour wasn't true. They both still said
that an accident had happened when he was setting out to shoot rabbits.

'Thank you, Mrs Laze.'

I wasn't looking lovely, just ordinary in a lavender-coloured dress, my
hair straight and reddish, freckles everywhere. Betty and Belle Frye were
far prettier than I was, as they'd always been. And Betty's girls were prettier
than I'd been at their age. My face was uninteresting, not quite plain, but
too round, too lacking in special characteristics. I greatly disliked my hair
and always had.

'D'you remember the day you kept us all in, Miss Pritchard?' Colin
Gregg said, laughing. 'The entire top class?'

'*Long fields of barley and of rye*,' Martin Draper said, laughing also.
'*An abbot on an ambling pad.*'

Miss Pritchard laughed herself. She'd taught Joe and Arthur too. Roger
Laze had been a favourite of hers, she'd never liked Belle Frye. She used
to shout at Martin Draper because he couldn't understand things.

'Who's else for ham?' my stepfather cried out, on his feet again, waving
a carving knife about. 'Ham? Turkey? Orders taken now, please. Pass up
the plates, young Martin.'

'The builders moved in today,' I heard Roger Laze saying in his quiet voice, answering a question Miss Pritchard had asked him. He was referring to Challacombe Manor, and I imagined the builders shaking their heads over the place, over the broken windows and the leaking roof and the floorboards that gave way when you walked on them. 'D'you remember that day?' Belle Frye shouted down the table at me, and I smiled at her and said yes, knowing she meant the day we'd climbed in through a window.

'Go round with the cider, love,' my stepfather murmured at me because my mother and Betty were busy seeing to the vegetables.

'Oh, I'm sorry,' I whispered back at him apologetically, feeling I should have noticed that no one was attending to people's glasses.

'No matter,' he said.

I don't know what I wanted then. I don't know what birthday present I'd have awarded myself if I'd have been able to, October 2nd, 1951. When I'd left the Grammar School it seemed natural to work on the farm, and I preferred it to the other occupations people suggested to me. My stepfather said he could get me into Blow's and my mother wanted me to try for a position in the accounting department of the Electricity Board because she said I was good at figures, which I wasn't. She used also to say it might be nice to be a receptionist in the Hogarth Arms Hotel. Miss Pritchard said I should become a teacher.

But I liked our farm. I liked it all the year round, the cold dairy on icy mornings, the clatter of cans and churns, driving in the cattle on a warm afternoon, working the sheepdogs. I didn't mind when the yard was thick with muck. I didn't object to the smell of silage. I even liked the hens.

Joe did all the rough work, clearing drains and the hedging and muck-spreading. My mother helped, especially at hay-making. Everyone helped then, even my stepfather; Colin Gregg and Betty came over, and the Fryes and the Lazes. More than anything else, hay-making reminded me of the past. Belle Frye and I used to run about when we were children, trying to be useful but really being a nuisance. I remembered dinnertimes, pasties and meat sandwiches in the fields, and cider and tea. My father used to eye the sky, but it always seemed to be fine then, for just long enough. 'We can laugh at it now,' he used to say when rain came and the hay was safely in.

On my twenty-first birthday I kept thinking of my mother and my stepfather becoming older in the farmhouse, my stepfather retiring from Blow's and being around all during the day. It was the same resentment I'd had of him when I was a child, before he married my mother, but of course it wasn't so intense now and it wasn't so violent. Yet it felt all wrong when I contemplated remaining with them in the farmhouse. It felt as if I'd married him too.

I opened my presents when we'd had our trifle, and I felt that everyone had been generous. Miss Pritchard had given me a cameo brooch which she used to wear herself and which I'd often admired. There were even things from Betty's children. My mother and stepfather had bought me a sewing-machine and Betty a clock for beside my bed, and Belle Frye a framed photograph of Trevor Howard, which was a joke really and typical of Belle Frye. Joe and Maudie had brought honeycombs and Mrs Laze and Roger a set of make-up and scent. There was another parcel, wrapped in red tissue paper and tied with a bow. It contained an eggcup and a matching saucer, and my stepfather said they came from the youth in Blow's. I didn't believe they did. I believed my stepfather had wrapped up the eggcup and saucer, thinking I'd be pleased if he pretended the boy had sent them. I felt awkward and embarrassed; I'd no idea what to say.

We played games with Betty's children afterwards, Snap and Snakes and Ladders. Roger Laze sat next to me, too shy to say a word; I often wondered if he was in pain from his foot. At a quarter past nine Betty and Colin Gregg had to go because it was long past their children's bedtime, and Joe and Maudie said they must be getting along also.

'So must I,' Miss Pritchard said.

She refused a lift with Colin and Betty and I said I'd like to walk with her because the night was beautiful, glaring with moonlight. I could see my mother thought I was silly to want to walk a mile and a half with an old schoolteacher who was being silly herself not to accept a lift when a lift was going. It was typical of me, my mother was thinking, like not having a more suitable twenty-first birthday party. Yet that walk through the moonlit lanes was the happiest part of it.

'Well, Matilda?' Miss Pritchard asked.

I knew what she was talking about. I said I didn't know; just stay on at the farm, I supposed.

'You'd be quite good with children, you know.'

'No.'

'Oh, well, perhaps you'll become a farmer's wife. You could do worse, I suppose.'

'I don't want to marry anyone.' The square face of Roger Laze came into my mind, and the face of the youth in Blow's. 'I really don't.'

'People often don't until someone comes along. Mr Right he's called.' Miss Pritchard laughed, and then we talked about other things, in particular about the new people at Challacombe Manor and what a difference it would make having that big old house occupied again.

Mr Gregary was a stout man and his wife was exceedingly thin. Their son was much older than I'd thought he'd be, thirty-seven as it turned out. They called him Ralphie. His brown hair was balding, and as if to make up for that he had a moustache. It was extensive but orderly, like a trimmed brown hedge in the pinkness of his face. He was broad and quite tall, rather clumsy in his movements.

All three of them came over to the farm one morning. They'd driven down from London to see how the builders were getting on and they came over to introduce themselves. Neither my mother nor I liked them.

'Cooee!' Mrs Gregary called out in our yard, standing there in unsuitable shoes and clothes. Her husband and her son were poking about the outhouses, pointing things out to one another as if they owned the place. They were dressed in tweed suits which you could see had been put on specially for the occasion; Mr Gregary carried a shooting-stick.

'Forgive the intrusion!' Mrs Gregary shouted at me when I came out of the byre. Her voice was shrill, like a bird's. A smile broke her bony face in half. Her hair was very smart; her lipstick matched the maroon of the suit she was wearing.

'We're the Gregarys,' her husband said. 'Challacombe Manor.'

'This was the home-farm, wasn't it?' his son asked, more modestly than his parents might have, less casually.

I said it had been and brought them into the kitchen, not knowing what on earth else to do with them. I was wearing fawn corduroy trousers and a fawn jersey that was darned and dirty. My mother was covered in flour, making a cake at the kitchen table. She became as flustered as I'd ever seen her when I walked in with the three Gregarys.

They were totally unlike their predecessor at Challacombe Manor, seeming a different species from her. As my mother cleared away her cake-making stuff I kept imagining Mrs Ashburton frowning over the Gregarys, bewildered by them and their conversation. In a humble way that annoyed me my mother apologized because the sitting-room wasn't warm, giving the Gregarys to believe it just happened to be that on this one particular morning a fire hadn't been lit there. I don't ever remember a fire being lit in the sitting-room, which was a room that smelt of must. The only time I remember anyone sitting down in it was when my father entertained a man from the taxation authorities, going through papers with him and giving him whisky.

'Now please don't put yourselves out!' Mrs Gregary shrilled. 'Anything does for the Gregarys.'

'We've been pigging it up in the house all morning,' her husband added, and he and his wife laughed over this, finding it amusing. The son laughed less.

'You could do with tea, I'm sure,' my mother said. She was cross with me for bringing them into the kitchen to find her all red-faced and floury, but what could I have done? Her hair was untidy and she was wearing a pair of slippers. 'Put out the cups, Matilda,' she ordered, finding it hard to keep the displeasure out of her voice, worried in case the Gregarys thought it was directed at them.

'So you're a Matilda?' the woman said, smiling her bony smile. 'What an enchanting name!'

She'd sat down at the table. The two men were poking about the place, trying to work out what the kitchen had been like when the house had first been built. They murmured about an open fire and an oven in the wall. They glanced up the steep back stairs that led straight out of a corner of the kitchen. They even opened cupboards.

'There'd have been a wheel there,' the son said, pointing at the Aga, 'which you turned to operate the bellows.'

His father wasn't listening to him. 'Structurally in splendid nick,' he was saying. 'Not a dodgy wall, I'd say.'

'More than you could claim for the manor!' the woman cried, her sudden shrillness making my mother jump. 'My God, the damage!'

'It's been a long time empty,' my mother said.

'Dry rot, wet rot, you name it!' cried the woman. She had four rings on the fingers of her left hand and two on her right. It seemed a mistake of some kind that she was coming to live in Challacombe Manor, like an absurdity in a dream.

'We'll be interested in buying land,' Mr Gregary revealed. His head was very neat, with strands of hair brushed into its baldness. His face had a polished look, like faintly pink marble. The flesh of his chins didn't wobble, but was firm and polished too. His eyes had a flicker of amusement in them.

'It's Ralphie's venture really,' Mrs Gregary said. 'We'll only ever come on visits.'

'Oh no, no,' the son protested.

'Longish visits, darling.'

'We're all in love with Challacombe Manor actually,' Mr Gregary said. 'We can't resist it.'

I wanted to say I loved it too, just to make the statement and by making it to imply that my love was different from theirs. I wanted it to be clear that I had loved Challacombe Manor all my life, that I loved our farm, and the gardens of Challacombe and the lanes around it, and the meadow we used to walk through on the way home from school, a journey which had been boring at the time. I wanted to say that I loved the memory of the past, of the Challacombe Mrs Ashburton had told me about, as it had been before the first of the two wars, and the memory of our family as it had been before the second. I wanted to say all that to show them how silly it was to stand there in a tweed suit and to state you were in love with a house and couldn't resist it. I wanted to belittle what wasn't real.

Politely I offered them milk and sugar, not saying anything. My mother told me to get some biscuits and Mrs Gregary said not to bother, but I got them anyway. I put some on to a plate and handed them around while my mother talked about the farmhouse and the farm. The Gregarys' son smiled at me when I held the plate out to him, and all of a sudden I was aware of a pattern of events. It seemed right that Challacombe Manor had stood there empty for so long, and Mrs Ashburton's voice echoed in my mind, telling me something when I was nine. I didn't know what it was, but all the same I felt that sense was being woven into the confusion. An event had occurred that morning in the kitchen, and it seemed extraordinary that I hadn't guessed it might, that I hadn't known that this was how things were meant to be.

'They think we're peasants, finding us like this,' my mother said crossly when they'd gone.

'It doesn't matter what they think.'

A long time went by, more than a year. Challacombe Manor was put to rights. The garden was cleared of the brambles that choked it; for the second time in my memory the tennis court became a tennis court again; the masonry of the summer-house was repointed. I watched it all happening. I stood in the garden and sometimes Ralphie Gregary stood beside me, as if seeking my approval for what he was doing. I walked with him through the fields; I showed him the short-cut we'd taken every day from school, the walk through the meadow and then through the garden; I told him about the tennis party Mrs Ashburton had given on the Thursday afternoon before the second of the two wars.

One day we had a picnic, one Sunday morning. We had it in the garden, near a magnolia tree; there was white wine and chicken and tomatoes and chives, and then French cheese and grapes. He told me about the boarding-school he'd been to. When he left it he went into his father's motor-components business and then he had fought in the war. During the war he had slowly come to the conclusion that what he wanted to do when it was over was to live a quiet life. He had tried to return to his father's business but he hadn't cared for it in the least. 'This is what I like,' he said. I felt quite heady after the wine, wanting to lie down in the warmth of the noon sun. I told him how Dick and Betty and I had collected ladybirds for

Mrs Ashburton so that they could eat the aphids that attacked the roses. I showed him the table in the summer-house which had been laden with food on the day of the tennis party. I smiled at him and he smiled back at me, understanding my love of the past.

'You can't make it come back, you know,' Miss Pritchard pointed out to me that same day, in her tiny sitting-room.

'I hate the present.'

We ate the macaroons she'd made, and drank tea from flowered porcelain. It was all right for Miss Pritchard. Miss Pritchard was too old to belong in the present, she didn't have to worry about it.

'You mustn't hate it.' Her pale eyes were like ice, looking into mine. For a moment she was frightening, as she used to be when you didn't know something at school. But I knew she didn't mean to frighten me. 'You should love the man you marry, Matilda.'

She didn't know, she couldn't be expected to understand. Mrs Ashburton would have known at once what was in my mind.

'He says he loves me,' I said.

'That isn't the same.'

'Mrs Ashburton –'

'Oh, for heaven's sake forget her!'

I shook my head. 'It'll be all right, Miss Pritchard.' He wasn't like his parents, I tried to explain to her; he was thoughtful and much quieter than either his father or his mother. In all sorts of ways he had been kind to me; he considered me beautiful even though I was not; there was a goodness about him.

'You're doing something wrong,' Miss Pritchard said.

I shook my head again and smiled at her. Already I had persuaded Ralphie to have the drawing-room of Challacombe Manor redecorated as it had been in Mrs Ashburton's time, with the same striped red wallpaper, and brass lamps on the walls, connected now to the electricity he'd had put in. A lot of the furniture from the drawing-room was still there, stored in the cellars, locked in after Mrs Ashburton's death so that it wouldn't be stolen. It was the kind of thing that had happened in the war, a temporary measure until everyone had time to think again. No one knew who'd put it there, and some of it had suffered so much from damp that it had to be abandoned. But there were four upright armchairs, delicately inlaid, which needed only to be re-upholstered. I had them done as I remembered them, in crimson and pink stripes that matched the walls. There were the two small round mahogany tables I'd admired, and the pictures of local landscapes in heavy gilt frames, and the brass fire-irons, and Mrs Ashburton's writing-desk and the writing-desk that had been her husband's. The pale patterned carpet came from Persia, she had told me. A corner of it had been nibbled by rats, but Ralphie said we could put a piece of furniture over the damage.

He told me he'd loved me the moment he'd seen me in our farmyard. He had closed his eyes in that moment; he had thought he was going to faint. There was no girl in England who was loved as much as I was, he said shyly, and I wondered if it would sound any different if Roger Laze had said it, or the counter-hand in Blow's. When I'd handed him the biscuits, I said, I'd felt the same; because there didn't seem any harm in saying that, in telling a minor lie in order to be kind. His parents didn't like what was happening, and my mother and stepfather didn't either. But none of that mattered because Ralphie and I were both grown-up, because Ralphie was getting on for forty and had a right to make a choice. And I intended to be good to him, to cook nice food for him and listen to his worries.

The wedding reception took place in the Hogarth Arms, although the Gregarys suggested the Bower House Hotel, twelve miles away, because there was more room there. They wanted to pay for everything, but my mother wouldn't agree to that. I suppose, in a way, it was all a bit awkward. You could feel the Gregarys thinking that my stepfather worked in a shop, that it was ridiculous of Ralphie to imagine he could take a girl from a farmyard and put her into Challacombe Manor.

Miss Pritchard came to the service and to the Hogarth Arms afterwards. Betty and Belle Frye were my matrons of honour and someone I'd never seen before was best man. I asked all sorts of people, the Fryes of course and Mrs Laze and Roger, and other people I'd been at school with, and Mrs Latham from Burrow Farm. I asked people from the shops in the town, and the people from the Hare and Hounds at Bennett's Cross, and the man from the artificial insemination centre, and Joe and Maudie, and Arthur. The Gregarys asked lots of people also, people like themselves.

I kept wanting to close my eyes as I stood in the lounge of the Hogarth Arms. I wanted to float away on the bubbles of the champagne I'd drunk. I couldn't understand why Miss Pritchard didn't see that everything was all right, that strictly speaking everything was perfect: I was there in my wedding-dress, married to Ralphie, who wasn't unkind; Challacombe Manor was as it used to be in its heyday, it was as Mrs Ashburton had known it as a bride also. Going to live there and watching over it seemed to make up for everything, for all the bad things that had happened, my father's death, and Dick's, and the arm that Mr Frye had had blown off, and Roger Laze's foot. The Fryes had sold their land to Ralphie because farming hadn't been easy since the losing of the arm. They'd be tenants in their farmhouse now for the rest of their lives, with a couple of acres they rented back from Ralphie: the arrangement suited them because there was no son to leave the farm to and they could enter old age in comfort. With the passing of time our own farm would revert to being the home-farm again, when it became too much for my mother. I couldn't help feeling that Ralphie knew it was what I wanted, and in his thoughtful kindliness had quietly brought it all about.

'Bless you, child,' my stepfather said.

I smiled at him because it was the thing to do on my wedding-day, but when he drew away his narrow face from mine after he'd kissed me I could see in it a reflection of what Miss Pritchard had said: he believed I shouldn't have married a man I didn't love, not even Ralphie, who was good and kind. It was in my mother's face too when she kissed me, and in my sister's and Belle Frye's, but not in the Gregarys' because none of them knew me.

'I'm happy,' I kept saying, smiling.

We went away to a hotel and then we came back to Challacombe. I'd almost imagined there'd be servants waiting, but of course there weren't. Instead there were the people called Stritch, a man and his wife. I'd always known the Stritches. I remembered Belle Frye and myself singing as we went by their cottage, raising our voices in a song about a bad-tempered woman because that was what Mrs Stritch was. I didn't like finding them there when we came back from our honeymoon.

There were small, silly misunderstandings between Ralphie and myself. They didn't matter because Ralphie's goodness lapped over them, and when I think about them I can't even remember very clearly what some of them were. All I can remember was that Ralphie always listened to me: I think he believed he needed to be gentle with me because I was still almost a child. I couldn't understand why he hadn't married someone before. I asked him, but he only smiled and shook his head. I had the feeling that in his mind there was the house, and the estate, and me; that I was part of the whole; that he had fallen in love with everything. All that, of course, should have been a bond between us, because the house and the estate formed the island of common ground where both of us were happy. Our marriage had Challacombe at its heart, and I was only alarmed when Ralphie spoke about our children because I didn't see that there was a need for them. Children, it seemed to me, would be all wrong. They would distort the pattern I could so precisely sense. They felt particularly alien.

Ralphie was patient with me. 'Yes, I understand,' he had said on the evening of our marriage, standing in front of me in the bedroom of the hotel he'd brought me to. The walls of the room were papered with a pinkish paper; Ralphie was wearing a flannel suit. In the hotel restaurant, called the Elizabethan Room, we had had dinner and wine. I'd had a coupe Jacques and Ralphie some kind of apricot soufflé. 'Yes,' he said again in the pinkish bedroom, and I talked to him for ages, making him sit beside me on one of the two beds in the room, holding his hand and stroking it. 'Yes, I understand,' he said, and I really think he did; I really think he understood that there was no question of children at Challacombe. He kept saying he loved me; he would never not love me, he said.

On the evening when we returned from our honeymoon I brought up the subject of the Stritches straight away. I explained it all to Ralphie when we were having supper, but he replied that he'd told me ages ago the Stritches were going to be at Challacombe. The arrangement apparently was that Mrs Stritch would come to the house every day except Sunday, and her husband would work in the garden. Ralphie repeated most earnestly that he'd told me this before, that he'd quite often mentioned the Stritches, and had asked my opinion of them. I knew he was mistaken, but I didn't want to say so. Ralphie had a lot on his mind, buying the Fryes' land and negotiating to buy Mrs Laze's, and wondering how to go about buying my mother's. He didn't know much about farming, but he was keenly endeavouring to learn. All of it took time: he couldn't be blamed if he made little mistakes about what he'd said to me and what he hadn't.

'You see, it's awkward, Ralphie,' I explained again one night at supper, smiling at him. 'Belle Frye and I said terrible things to her.'

'Oh, Mrs Stritch'll have forgotten. Darling, it's donkeys' years ago.'

For some reason I didn't like him using that endearment, especially when he put the word at the beginning of a sentence, as he often for some reason did. I don't know why I objected so much to that. It was how it sounded, I think, a sort of casualness that seemed out of place in the house. There was another thing: he had a way of turning the pages of a newspaper, one page and then another, until finally he pored over the obituaries and the little advertisements. I didn't like the way he did that. And I didn't like the way he sometimes drummed the surface of a table with one hand when he was thinking, as if playing the piano. Another thing was, he wore leather gaiters.

'It's just that it's embarrassing for me,' I said, still smiling. 'Having her around.'

He ate beetroot and a sardine salad I had prepared because he'd told me he liked sardines. I'd made him wait that morning in the car while I went into a shop and bought several tins. I wouldn't let him see what they were, wanting it to be a surprise. He said:

'Actually, Mrs Stritch is very nice. And he's doing wonders with the garden.'

'We called her terrible names. She'd be hanging out her washing or something and we'd deliberately raise our voices. "Worst temper in Dorset," Belle would say and then we'd giggle. "Driven her husband to drink," I'd say. "Mrs Stritch is a – very nice lady," we used to call out in sing-song voices.'

'All children call people names.'

'Oh, Betty would never have let me do that. Going home from school with Betty and Dick was different. But then they left, you see. They left the Grammar when Belle and I were just finishing at Miss Pritchard's, the same time that –'

'Darling, the Stritches have to be here. We have to have help.'

'I wish you wouldn't do that, Ralphie.'

'Do what?'

'I wish you wouldn't begin a sentence like that.'

He frowned at my smile, not understanding what was in my mind even though he was an understanding person. He didn't understand when I explained that I could manage the house on my own, that I didn't need Mrs Stritch in the way. I explained to him that Mrs Stritch had once taken a pair of gloves from Blow's. 'Please let's try it,' he said, and of course I didn't want to be difficult. I wanted him to see that I was prepared to try what he wished to try.

'Yes,' I said, smiling at him.

Like a black shadow she was in the drawing-room. She leaned back in her chair, one hand stretched out to the round table in front of her. It was just a memory, not the ghost of Mrs Ashburton, nothing like that. But the memory would have been better if Mrs Stritch hadn't always been around when Ralphie wasn't. Ralphie would go off every morning in his gaiters, and then Mrs Stritch would arrive. She would dust and clean and carry buckets of soapy water about the house. Her husband would come to the kitchen to have lunch with her, and Ralphie and I would have lunch in the dining-room. All afternoon I'd continue to be aware of her in the house, making little noises as she did her work. When it was time for her to go Ralphie would be back again.

'We're buying the Lazes' land,' he said one evening, crossing the drawing-room and pouring some whisky for himself from a decanter. I could see that he was delighted. 'I think your mother'll want to sell too,' he said.

I knew she would. Joe and Arthur were getting old, my stepfather was always saying the day would come. He'd no interest in the farm himself, and my mother would be glad not to have the responsibility.

'But you'll let the Lazes stay on in the farmhouse?' I said, because it worried me that they should have to move away.

He shook his head. He said they didn't want to. They wanted to go and live nearer the town, like the Fryes did.

'The Fryes? But the Fryes don't want to move away. You said they were going to farm a couple of acres –'

'They've changed their minds.'

I didn't smile at him any more because I didn't like what he was saying. He'd explained quite clearly that the Fryes would stay in the farmhouse, and that the Lazes could if they wanted to. He had reassured me about that. Yet he said now:

'You wanted the estate to be all together again, Matilda.'

'I didn't want people driven off, Ralphie. Not the Fryes and the Lazes. And what about my mother? Will she go also?'

'It'll be your mother's choice, Matilda. As it was theirs.'

'You've bought them all out. You promised me one thing and –'

'We need the housing for our own men.'

I felt deceived. I imagined a discussion between Ralphie and the man he'd hired to look after the estate, a cold-faced man called Epstone. I imagined Epstone saying that if you were going to do the thing, do it properly, offer them enough and they'll go. I imagined a discussion between Ralphie and his father, Ralphie asking if he could have another loan in order to plan his estate correctly, and his father agreeing.

'Well, I dare say,' I said to Ralphie, smiling at him again, determined not to be cross.

'In the old days on the Challacombe estate,' he said, 'it would have happened less humanely.'

I didn't want to hear him going on about that so I didn't ask him what he meant. Even though he was considerate, I had begun to feel I was his property. It was an odd feeling, and I think it came from the other feeling I had, that he'd married me because I was part of an idea he'd fallen in love with. I used to look at the china vases on the drawing-room mantelpiece and feel like one of them, or like the carpets and the new wallpaper. I was part of something his money had created, and I don't think he noticed that the rattling of his newspaper or the clink of the decanter against his glass had a way of interrupting my thoughts. These noises, and his footsteps in the hall or in a room, were like the noises Mrs Stritch made with her buckets and the Electrolux, but of course I never told him that.

I have forgotten a little about all that time in the house with Ralphie. He didn't always tell me what was happening on the estate; in a way he talked more readily to Mrs Stritch, for I often heard him. He also talked to himself. He would pace up and down the lawns Mr Stritch had restored, wagging his head or nodding, while I watched him from a window of the house. As time went by, it was clear that he had done what he'd wanted. As he said, the estate was all of a piece again. He had bought our farm and the farmhouse, offering so much for both that it couldn't be resisted. Joe and Arthur worked for him now.

Years were passing. Sometimes I walked over to see Miss Pritchard, going by the meadow we'd gone through on our way to school. I can't quite recall what we talked about as we had tea; only bits from our conversations come back to me. There is my own cheerfulness, my smiling at Miss Pritchard, and Miss Pritchard's glumness. Now and again I walked down to our farm and sat for a while with my mother, getting up to go before my stepfather returned. I went to see Betty and Belle, but I did that less and less. I began to think that they were all a little jealous of me. I thought that because I sensed an atmosphere when I went on these visits. 'You're cruel, Matilda,' Miss Pritchard said once, seeming to be unable to control the ill-temper that had caused the remark to surface. She turned her head away from me when she'd spoken. 'Cruel,' she said again, and I laughed because of course that was nonsensical. I remember thinking it was extraordinary that Miss Pritchard should be jealous.

Ralphie, I believe, must have begun to live some kind of life of his own. He often went out in the evenings, all dressed up. He came back jovial and would come to my room to kiss me good-night, until eventually I asked him not to. When I inquired at breakfast about where he'd been the night before his answer was always the same, that he had been to a house in the neighbourhood for dinner. He always seemed surprised that I should ask the question, claiming on each occasion that he had told me these details beforehand and that I had, in fact, refused to accompany him. In all this I really do not think he can have been right.

I welcomed the occasions when Ralphie went out in the evenings. I drew the curtains in the drawing-room and sat by the fire, just happy to be there. I thought of the time when we were all together in the farmhouse, my father teasing Betty about Colin Gregg, Dick going as red as a sunset because my father mentioned an empty Woodbine packet he'd found. Every Sunday morning Ralphie went to church and, since Mrs Stritch didn't come on Sundays, that was another good time. Ralphie would return and sit opposite me in the dining-room, carving the beef I'd cooked him, looking at me now and again from his pink face, his teeth like chalk beneath the trim brown hedge of his moustache. I wanted to explain to him that I was happy in the house when Mrs Stritch wasn't there and when he wasn't there. I wanted to make him understand that old Mrs Ashburton had wanted me to be in her house, that that was why she had told me so much when I was a child, that everything had to do with the two wars there'd been. He didn't know as much about war as Mrs Ashburton had, even though he'd fought in one: I wanted to explain that to him, too. But I never did because his eyes would have begun to goggle, which they had a way of doing if something he couldn't comprehend was put to him. It was easier just to cook his meals and smile at him.

There was another thing Ralphie said I had forgotten: a conversation about a party he gave. When I asked him afterwards he repeatedly assured me we'd had a conversation about it, and in all honesty I believe it must have been his own memory that was at fault. Not that it matters in the least which way round it was. What mattered at the time was that the house was suddenly full of people. I was embroidering in the drawing-room, slowly stitching the eye of a peacock, and the next thing was that Ralphie's parents were embracing me, pretending they liked me. It seemed they had come for the weekend, so that they could be at the party, which was to be on the following night. They brought other people with them in their grey Daimler, people called Absom. Mrs Absom was thin, like Mrs Gregary, but younger than Mrs Gregary. Mr Absom was stout, like Mr Gregary, but not like polished marble, and younger also.

Mrs Stritch's daughter Nellie came to help on the Saturday morning and stayed all day. Apparently Ralphie had given Mrs Stritch money to buy navy-blue overalls for both of them so that they'd stand out from the guests at the party. They bought them in Blow's, Mrs Stritch told me, and it was quite funny to think that my stepfather might have served them, even fitted them with the overalls. Mr Stritch was there on the night of the party also, organizing the parking of cars.

It all took place in the drawing-room. People stood around with drinks in their hands. Ralphie introduced them to me, but I found it hard to know what to say to them. It was his mother, really, who gave the party, moving about the drawing-room as if she owned it. I realized then why she'd come for the weekend.

'So how you like Challacombe Manor, Mrs Gregary?' a man with very short hair asked me.

Politely I replied that I was fond of the house.

'Ralphie!' the man said, gesturing around him. 'Fantastic!' He added that he enjoyed life in the country, and told me the names of his dogs. He said he liked fishing and always had.

There were fifty-two people in the drawing-room, which had begun to smell of cigarette smoke and alcohol. It was hot because Mrs Gregary had asked Mrs Stritch to make up an enormous fire, and it was becoming noisier because as the party advanced people talked more loudly. A woman, wearing a coffee-coloured dress, appeared to be drunk. She had sleek black hair and kept dropping her cigarette on to Mrs Ashburton's Persian carpet. Once when she bent to pick it up she almost toppled over.

'Hullo,' a man said. 'You're Mrs Ralphie.'

He was younger than the short-haired man. He stood very close to me, pressing me into a corner. He told me his name but I didn't listen because listening was an effort in the noisy room.

'Ever been there?' this man shouted at me. 'Ferns magnificent, this time of year.'

He smiled at me, revealing jagged teeth. 'Ferns,' he shouted, and then he said that he, or someone, had a collection of stuffed birds. I could feel one of his knees pressing into the side of my leg. He asked me something and I shook my head again. Then he went away.

Mrs Stritch and her daughter had covered the dining-room table with food. All kinds of cold meats there were, and various salads, and tarts of different kinds, and huge bowls of whipped cream, and cheeses. They'd done it all at the direction of Mrs Gregary: just by looking at the table you could see Mrs Gregary's hand in it, Mrs Stritch wouldn't have known a thing about it. The sideboard was entirely taken up with bottles of wine and glasses. The electric light wasn't turned on: there were slender red candles everywhere, another touch of Mrs Gregary's, or even Mrs Absom's. I had crossed the hall to the dining-room in order to get away from the noise for a moment. I thought I'd sit there quietly for a little; I was surprised to see the food and the candles.

I was alone in the dining-room, as I'd guessed I would be. But it wasn't any longer a room you could be quiet in. Everything seemed garish, the red glitter of the wine bottles, the red candles, dish after dish of different food, the cheeses. It made me angry that Mrs Gregary and Mrs Absom should have come to Challacombe Manor in order to instruct Mrs Stritch, that Mrs Gregary should strut about in the drawing-room, telling people who she was.

I jumbled the food about, dropping pieces of meat into the bowls of cream, covering the tarts with salad. I emptied two wine bottles over everything, watching the red stain spreading on the tablecloth and on the cheeses. They had no right to be in the house, their Daimler had no right to be in the garage. I had asked years ago that Mrs Stritch should not be here.

In the drawing-room someone said to me:

'I enjoy to get out after pheasants, to tramp with my dogs.'

It was the short-haired man. I hadn't noticed that he was a foreigner. I knew before he told me that he was German.

'You have dogs, Mrs Gregary?'

I smiled at him and shook my head. It seemed extraordinary that there should be a German in this drawing-room. I remembered when Mrs Ashburton used to talk to me about the First World War that I'd imagined the Germans as grey and steel-like, endlessly consuming black bread. This man didn't seem in the least like that.

'Hasenfuss,' he said. 'The name, you know.'

For a moment the room was different. People were dancing there at some other party. A man was standing near the door, waiting for someone to arrive, seeming a little anxious. It was all just a flash, as if I had fallen asleep and for a moment had had a dream.

'We are enemies and then we are friends. I advise on British beer, I enjoy your British countryside. It is my profession to advise on British beer. I would not enjoy to live in Germany today, Mrs Gregary.'

'You are the first German I have ever met.'

'Oh, I hope not the last.'

Again the drawing-room was different. There was the music and the dancing and the man by the door. The girl he was waiting for arrived. It was Mrs Ashburton, as she was in the photographs she'd showed me when I was nine. And he was the man she'd married.

'Here I am standing,' said the short-haired German, 'in the house of the people who put Mr Hitler in his place.' He laughed loudly when he'd made that remark, displaying more gold fillings than I had ever before seen in anyone's mouth. 'Your father-in-law, you know, made a lot of difference to the war.'

I didn't know what he was talking about. I was thinking of the dining-room and what would happen when everyone walked into it. It was like something Belle Frye and I might have done together, only we'd never have had the courage. It was worse than singing songs outside Mrs Stritch's cottage.

'In that I mean,' the German said, 'the manufacturing of guns.'

I hadn't known that. My stepfather had said that the Gregarys had made a killing, but I hadn't thought about it. Ralphie had never told me that his father's motor-components business had made guns during the war, that the war had made him rich. It was the war that enabled Ralphie now to buy up all the land and set the Challacombe estate to rights again. It was the war that had restored this drawing-room.

'The world is strange,' the German said.

I went upstairs and came down with Ralphie's gaiters. I remember standing at the door of the drawing-room, looking at all the people drinking, and seeing again, for an instant, the dancers of the distant past. Mrs Ashburton and her husband were among them, smiling at one another.

I moved into the room and when I reached the fireplace I threw the gaiters on to the flames. Someone noticed me, Mrs Absom, I think it was. She seemed quite terrified as she watched me.

The German was again alone. He told me he enjoyed alcohol, emphasizing this point by reaching his glass out towards Mrs Stritch, who was passing with some mixture in a jug. I told him about Mrs Ashburton's husband, how he had returned from the first of the two wars suffering from shell-shock, how the estate had fallen to bits because of that, how everything had had to be mortgaged. I was telling her story, and I was even aware that my voice was quite like hers, that I felt quite like her as well. Everything had happened all over again, I told the German, the repetition was cloying. I told him about Mrs Ashburton's law of averages, how some men always came back from a war, how you had to pray it would be the men who were closest to you, how it would have been better if her own husband had been killed.

The smell of burning leather was unpleasant in the room. People noticed it. Ralphie poked at his smouldering gaiters with a poker, wondering why they were there. I saw his mother looking at me while I talked to the German. 'Mrs Ashburton did what she could,' I said. 'There's nothing wrong with living in the past.'

I went around from person to person then, asking them to go. The party had come to an end, I explained, but Mrs Gregary tried to contradict that. 'No, no, no,' she cried. 'We've scarcely started.' She ushered people into the dining-room and then, of course, she saw that I was right.

'I would like you to go as well,' I said to Mr Gregary in the hall, while the visitors were rooting for their coats. 'I would like you to go and take the Absoms with you. I did not invite the Absoms here any more than I invited you.' I said it while smiling at him, so that he could see I wasn't being quarrelsome. 'Oh now, look here, Matilda!' he protested.

In the kitchen I told Mrs Stritch that I'd rather she didn't return to the house. I could easily manage on my own, I explained to her, trying to be kind in how I put it. 'It's just that it's embarrassing,' I said, 'having you here.'

The Gregarys and the Absoms didn't go until the following day, a Sunday. They didn't say goodbye to me, and I only knew that they had finally departed because Ralphie told me. 'Why are you doing this?' he said, sitting down on the other side of the fire in the drawing-room, where I was embroidering my peacocks. 'Why, Matilda?' he said again.

'I don't understand you.'

'Yes, you do.'

He had never spoken like that before. All his considerateness had disappeared. His eyes were fiery and yet cold. His large hands looked as though they wanted to commit some act of violence. I shook my head at him. He said:

'You're pretending to be deranged.'

I laughed. I didn't like him sitting opposite me like that, with his eyes and his hands. Everything about him had been a pretence: all he wanted was his own way, to have his mother giving parties in my drawing-room, to have Mrs Stritch forever vacuuming the stairs, to own me as he owned the land and the farms and the house. It was horrible, making money out of war.

'You don't even cook for me,' he said to my astonishment. 'Half-raw potatoes, half-raw chops –'

'Oh, Ralphie, don't be silly. You know I cook for you.'

'The only food that is edible in this house is made by Mrs Stritch. You can cook if you want to, only you can't be bothered.'

'I do my best. In every way I do my best. I want our marriage to be –'

'It isn't a marriage,' he said. 'It's never been a marriage.'

'We were married in the church.'

'Stop talking like that!' He shouted at me again, suddenly on his feet, looking down at me. His face was red with fury; I thought he might pick something up and hit me with it.

'I'm sorry,' I said.

'You're as sane as I am. For God's sake, Matilda!'

'Of course I'm sane,' I said quietly. 'I could not be sitting here if I were not. I could not live a normal life.'

'You don't live a normal life.' He was shouting again, stamping about the room like an animal. 'Every second of every day is devoted to the impression you wish to give.'

'But, Ralphie, why should I wish to give an impression?'

'To cover up your cruelty.'

I laughed again, gently so as not to anger him further. I remembered Miss Pritchard saying I was cruel, and of course there was the cruelty Mrs Ashburton had spoken of, the cruelty that was natural in wartime. I had felt it in myself when my father had been killed, and when Dick had been killed. I had felt it when I had first seen my mother embracing the man who became my stepfather, too soon after my father had died. God, if He existed, I had thought in the end, was something to be frightened of.

'The war is over,' I said, and he looked at me, startled by that remark.

'It isn't for you,' he said. 'It'll never be for you. It's all we ever hear from you, the war and that foolish old woman –'

'It wasn't over for Mrs Ashburton either. How could it be when she lived to see it all beginning again?'

'Oh, for God's sake, stop talking about her. If it hadn't been for her, if she hadn't taken advantage of a nine-year-old child with her rubbish, you would be a normal human being now.' He stood above my chair again, pushing his red face down at me and speaking slowly. 'She twisted you, she filled you full of hate. Whatever you are now, that dead woman has done to you. Millions have suffered in war,' he suddenly shouted. 'Who's asking you to dwell on it, for God's sake?'

'There are people who find it hard to pick up the pieces. Because they're made like that.'

'You'd have picked them up if she hadn't prevented you. She didn't want you to, because she couldn't herself.' Furiously he added, 'Some kind of bloody monster she was.'

I didn't reply to any of that. He said, with a bitterness in his voice which had never been there before, 'All I know is that she has destroyed Challacombe for me.'

'It was never real for you, Ralphie. I shall never forget the happiness in our farmhouse. What memories of Challacombe can you have?'

But Ralphie wasn't interested in the happiness in our farmhouse, or in memories he couldn't have. All he wanted to do was wildly to castigate me.

'How can I live here with you?' he demanded in a rough, hard voice, pouring at the same time a glass of whisky for himself. 'You said you loved me once. Yet everything you do is calculated to let me see your hatred. What have I done,' he shouted at me, 'that you hate me, Matilda?'

I quietly replied that he was mistaken. I protested that I did not hate him, but even as I spoke I realized that that wasn't true. I hated him for being what he was, for walking with his parents into the farmyard that morning, for thinking he had a place in the past. I might have confided in him but I did not want to. I might have said that I remembered, years ago, Miss Pritchard coming to see my mother and what Miss Pritchard had said. I had eavesdropped on the stairs that led to the kitchen, while she said she believed there was something the matter with me. It was before the death of Dick, after I'd discovered about my mother and the man who was now my stepfather. 'She dwells on her father's death,' Miss Pritchard had said and she'd gone on to say that I dwelt as well on the conversations I'd had with old Mrs Ashburton. I remembered the feeling I'd had, standing there listening: the feeling that the shell-shock of Mr Ashburton, carried back to Challacombe from the trenches in 1917, had conveyed itself in some other form to his wife, that she, as much as he, had been a victim of violence. I felt it because Miss Pritchard was saying something like it to my mother. 'There are casualties in wars,' she said, 'thousands of miles from where the fighting is.' She was speaking about me. I'd caught a mood, she said, from old Mrs Ashburton, and when my mother replied that you couldn't catch a mood like you caught the measles Miss Pritchard sharply replied that you could. '*Folie à deux* the French call it,' she insisted, an expression I welcomed and have never since forgotten. There had been *folie à deux* all over this house, and in the garden too, when he came back with his mind in pieces. She had shared the horror with him and later she had shared it with me, as if guessing that I, too, would be a casualty. As long as I lived I would honour that *folie* in their house. I would honour her and her husband, and my father and Dick, and the times they had lived in. It was right that the cruelty was there.

'Of course I don't hate you,' I said again. 'Of course not, Ralphie.'

He did not reply. He stood in the centre of the drawing-room with his glass in his hand, seeming like a beast caught in a snare: he had all the beaten qualities of such an animal. His shoulders slouched, his eyes had lost their fire.

'I don't know what to do,' he said.

'You may stay here,' I said, 'with me.' Again I smiled, wishing to make the invitation seem kind. I could feel no pity for him.

'How could I?' he shouted. 'My God, how could I? I lose count of the years in this house. I look at you every day, I look at your eyes and your hair and your face, I look at your hands and your fingernails, and the arch of your neck. I love you; every single inch of you I love. How can I live here and love you like that, Matilda? I shared a dream with you, Matilda, a dream that no one else but you would have understood. I longed for my quiet life, with you and with our children. I married you out of passion and devotion. You give me back nothing.'

'You married me because I was part of something, part of the house and the estate –'

'That isn't true. That's a rubbishy fantasy; not a word of it is true.'

'I cannot help it if I believe it.' I wasn't smiling now. I let my feelings show in my eyes because there was no point in doing otherwise any more. Not in a million years would he understand. 'Yes, I despise you,' I said. 'I have never felt affection for you.'

I said it calmly and bent my head again over my embroidery. He poured more whisky and sat down in the chair on the other side of the fireplace.

I spoke while still embroidering, magenta thread in a feather of my peacock's tail.

'You must never again touch me,' I said. 'Not even in passing me by in a room. We shall live here just as we are, but do not address me with endearments. I shall cook and clean, but there shall be no parties. Your parents are not welcome. It is discourteous to me to give parties behind my back and to employ people I do not care for.'

'You were told, you know perfectly well you were told –'

'You will fatten and shamble about the rooms of this house. I shall not complain. You will drink more whisky, and perhaps lose heart in your dream. "His wife does not go out," people will say; "they have no children. He married beneath him, but it isn't that that cut him down to size."'

'Matilda, please. Please for a moment listen to me –'

'Why should I? And why should you not lose heart in your dream because isn't your dream ridiculous? If you think that your Challacombe estate is like it was, or that you in your vulgarity could ever make it so, then you're the one who is deranged.'

I had not taken my eyes from the peacock's tail. I imagined a patch of damp developing on the ceiling of an upstairs room. I imagined his lifting the heavy lead-lined hatch in the loft and stepping out on to the roof to find the missing tile. I stood with him on the roof and pointed to the tile, lodged in a gutter. I had removed it myself and slid it down the incline of the roof. He could reach it with an effort, by grasping the edge of the chimney-stack to be safe. I heard the thump of his body as it struck the cobbles below. I heard it in the drawing-room as I worked my stitches, while he drank more whisky and for a while was silent.

'Damn you,' he shouted in the end, once more on his feet and seething above me. 'Damn you to hell, Matilda.'

'No matter what you do,' I said, still sewing the magenta thread, 'I shall not leave this house.'

He sold everything he'd bought except the house and garden. He sold the land and the farmhouses, the Fryes' and the Lazes' and what had been ours. He didn't tell me about any of it until he'd done it. 'I'll be gone in a week,' he said one day, six or seven months after we'd had that quarrel, and I did not urge him to stay.

It is a long time ago now, that day. I can't quite remember Ralphie's going, even though with such vividness I remember so much else. There are new people in all the farmhouses now, whole families have grown up; again the tennis court is overgrown. Miss Pritchard died of course, and my mother and my stepfather. I never saw much of them after Ralphie went, and I never laid eyes on Ralphie or even had a line from him. But if Ralphie walked in now I would take his hand and say I was sorry for the cruelty that possessed me and would not go away, the cruelty she used to talk about, a natural thing in wartime. It lingered and I'm sorry it did, and perhaps after all this time Ralphie would understand and believe me, but Ralphie, I know, will never return.

I sit here now in her drawing-room, and may perhaps become as old as she was. Sometimes I walk up to the meadow where the path to school was, but the meadow isn't there any more. There are rows of coloured caravans, and motor-cars and shacks. In the garden I can hear the voices of people drifting down to me, and the sound of music from their wireless sets. Nothing is like it was.

Torridge

Perhaps nobody ever did wonder what Torridge would be like as a man –
or what Wiltshire or Mace-Hamilton or Arrowsmith would be like, come
to that. Torridge at thirteen had a face with a pudding look, matching the
sound of his name. He had small eyes and short hair like a mouse's. Within
the collar of his grey regulation shirt the knot of his House tie was formed
with care, a maroon triangle of just the right shape and bulk. His black
shoes were always shiny.

Torridge was unique in some way: perhaps only because he was beyond
the pale and appeared, irritatingly, to be unaware of it. He wasn't good at
games and had difficulty in understanding what was being explained in the
classroom. He would sit there frowning, half smiling, his head a little to
one side. Occasionally he would ask some question that caused an outburst
of groaning. His smile would increase then. He would glance around the
classroom, not flustered or embarrassed in the least, seeming to be pleased
that he had caused such a response. He was naïve to the point where it
was hard to believe he wasn't pretending, but his naïveté was real and was
in time universally recognized as such. A master called Buller Yeats reserved
his cruellest shafts of scorn for it, sighing whenever his eyes chanced to
fall on Torridge, pretending to believe his name was Porridge.

Of the same age as Torridge, but similar in no other way, were Wiltshire,
Mace-Hamilton and Arrowsmith. All three of them were blond-haired and
thin, with a common sharpness about their features. They wore, untidily,
the same clothes as Torridge, their House ties knotted any old how, the
laces in their scuffed shoes often tied in several places. They excelled at
different games and were quick to sense what was what. Attractive boys,
adults had more than once called them.

The friendship among the three of them developed because, in a way,
Torridge was what he was. From the first time they were aware of him –
on the first night of their first term – he appeared to be special. In the
darkness after lights-out someone was trying not to sob and Torridge's
voice was piping away, not homesick in the least. His father had a button
business was what he was saying: he'd probably be going into the button
business himself. In the morning he was identified, a boy in red-and-blue
striped pyjamas, still chattering in the wash-room. 'What's your father do,

Torridge?' Arrowsmith asked at breakfast, and that was the beginning. 'Dad's in the button business,' Torridge beamingly replied. 'Torridge's, you know.' But no one did know.

He didn't, as other new boys did, make a particular friend. For a while he attached himself to a small gang of homesick boys who had only their malady in common, but after a time this gang broke up and Torridge found himself on his own, though it seemed quite happily so. He was often to be found in the room of the kindly housemaster of Junior House, an ageing white-haired figure called Old Frosty, who listened sympathetically to complaints of injustice at the hands of other masters, always ready to agree that the world was a hard place. 'You should hear Buller Yeats on Torridge, sir,' Wiltshire used to say in Torridge's presence. 'You'd think Torridge had no feelings, sir.' Old Frosty would reply that Buller Yeats was a frightful man. 'Take no notice, Torridge,' he'd add in his kindly voice, and Torridge would smile, making it clear that he didn't mind in the least what Buller Yeats said. 'Torridge knows true happiness,' a new young master, known as Mad Wallace, said in an unguarded moment one day, a remark which caused immediate uproar in a geography class. It was afterwards much repeated, like 'Dad's in the button business' and 'Torridge's, you know.' The true happiness of Torridge became a joke, the particular property of Wiltshire and Mace-Hamilton and Arrowsmith. Furthering the joke, they claimed that knowing Torridge was a rare experience, that the private realm of his innocence and his happiness was even exotic. Wiltshire insisted that one day the school would be proud of him. The joke was worked to death.

At the school it was the habit of certain senior boys to 'take an interest in' juniors. This varied from glances and smiles across the dining-hall to written invitations to meet in some secluded spot at a stated time. Friendships, taking a variety of forms, were then initiated. It was flattering, and very often a temporary antidote for homesickness, when a new boy received the agreeable but bewildering attentions of an important fifth-former. A meeting behind Chapel led to the negotiating of a barbed-wire fence on a slope of gorse bushes, the older boy solicitous and knowledgeable. There were well-trodden paths and nooks among the gorse where smoking could take place with comparative safety. Farther afield, in the hills, there were crude shelters composed of stones and corrugated iron. Here, too, the emphasis was on smoking and romance.

New boys very soon became aware of the nature of older boys' interest in them. The flattery changed its shape, an adjustment was made – or the new boys retreated in panic from this area of school life. Andrews and Butler, Webb and Mace-Hamilton, Dillon and Pratt, Tothill and Goldfish

Stewart, Good and Wiltshire, Sainsbury Major and Arrowsmith, Brewitt and Whyte: the liaisons were renowned, the combinations of names sometimes seeming like a music-hall turn, a soft-shoe shuffle of entangled hearts. There was faithlessness, too: the Honourable Anthony Swain made the rounds of the senior boys, a fickle and tartish *bijou*, desired and yet despised.

Torridge's puddingy appearance did not suggest that he had *bijou* qualities, and glances did not readily come his way in the dining-hall. This was often the fate, or good fortune, of new boys and was not regarded as a sign of qualities lacking. Yet quite regularly an ill-endowed child would mysteriously become the object of fifth- and sixth-form desire. This remained a puzzle to the juniors until they themselves became fifth- or sixth-formers and desire was seen to have to do with something deeper than superficial good looks.

It was the apparent evidence of this truth that caused Torridge, first of all, to be aware of the world of *bijou* and protector. He received a note from a boy in the Upper Fifth who had previously eschewed the sexual life offered by the school. He was a big, black-haired youth with glasses and a protruding forehead, called Fisher.

'Hey, what's this mean?' Torridge inquired, finding the note under his pillow, tucked into his pyjamas. 'Here's a bloke wants to go for a walk.'

He read the invitation out: '*If you would like to come for a walk meet me by the electricity plant behind Chapel. Half past four Tuesday afternoon. R.A.J. Fisher.*'

'Jesus Christ!' said Armstrong.

'You've got an admirer, Porridge,' Mace-Hamilton said.

'Admirer?'

'He wants you to be his *bijou*,' Wiltshire explained.

'What's it mean, *bijou*?'

'Tart, it means, Porridge.'

'Tart?'

'Friend. He wants to be your protector.'

'What's it mean, protector?'

'He loves you, Porridge.'

'I don't even know the bloke.'

'He's the one with the big forehead. He's a half-wit actually.'

'Half-wit?'

'His mother let him drop on his head. Like yours did, Porridge.'

'My mum never.'

Everyone was crowding around Torridge's bed. The note was passed from hand to hand. 'What's your dad do, Porridge?' Wiltshire suddenly asked, and Torridge automatically replied that he was in the button business.

'You've got to write a note back to Fisher, you know,' Mace-Hamilton pointed out.

'Dear Fisher,' Wiltshire prompted, 'I love you.'

'But I don't even –'

'It doesn't matter not knowing him. You've got to write a letter and put it in his pyjamas.'

Torridge didn't say anything. He placed the note in the top pocket of his jacket and slowly began to undress. The other boys drifted back to their own beds, still amused by the development. In the wash-room the next morning Torridge said:

'I think he's quite nice, that Fisher.'

'Had a dream about him, did you, Porridge?' Mace-Hamilton inquired. 'Got up to tricks, did he?'

'No harm in going for a walk.'

'No harm at all, Porridge.'

In fact, a mistake had been made. Fisher, in his haste or his excitement, had placed the note under the wrong pillow. It was Arrowsmith, still allied with Sainsbury Major, whom he wished to attract.

That this error had occurred was borne in on Torridge when he turned up at the electricity plant on the following Tuesday. He had not considered it necessary to reply to Fisher's note, but he had, across the dining-hall, essayed a smile or two in the older boy's direction: it had surprised him to meet with no response. It surprised him rather more to meet with no response by the electricity plant. Fisher just looked at him and then turned his back, pretending to whistle.

'Hullo, Fisher,' Torridge said.

'Hop it, look. I'm waiting for someone.'

'I'm Torridge, Fisher.'

'I don't care who you are.'

'You wrote me that letter.' Torridge was still smiling. 'About a walk, Fisher.'

'Walk? What walk?'

'You put the letter under my pillow, Fisher.'

'Jesus!' said Fisher.

The encounter was observed by Arrowsmith, Mace-Hamilton and Wiltshire, who had earlier taken up crouched positions behind one of the chapel buttresses. Torridge heard the familiar hoots of laughter, and because it was his way he joined in. Fisher, white-faced, strode away.

'Poor old Porridge,' Arrowsmith commiserated, gasping and pretending to be contorted with mirth. Mace-Hamilton and Wiltshire were leaning against the buttress, issuing shrill noises.

'Gosh,' Torridge said, 'I don't care.'

He went away, still laughing a bit, and there the matter of Fisher's attempt at communication might have ended. In fact it didn't, because Fisher wrote a second time and this time he made certain that the right boy received his missive. But Arrowsmith, still firmly the property of Sainsbury Major, wished to have nothing to do with R.A.J. Fisher.

When he was told the details of Fisher's error, Torridge said he'd guessed it had been something like that. But Wiltshire, Mace-Hamilton and Arrowsmith claimed that a new sadness had overcome Torridge. Something beautiful had been going to happen to him, Wiltshire said: just as the petals of friendship were opening the flower had been crudely snatched away. Arrowsmith said Torridge reminded him of one of Picasso's sorrowful harlequins. One way or the other, it was agreed that the experience would be beneficial to Torridge's sensitivity. It was seen as his reason for turning to religion, which recently he had done, joining a band of similarly inclined boys who were inspired by the word of the chaplain, a figure known as God Harvey. God Harvey was ascetic, seeming dangerously thin, his face all edge and as pale as milk, his cassock odorous with incense. He conducted readings in his room, offering coffee and biscuits afterwards, though not himself partaking of these refreshments. 'God Harvey's linnets' his acolytes were called, for often a hymn was sung to round things off. Welcomed into this fold, Torridge regained his happiness.

R.A.J. Fisher, on the other hand, sank into greater gloom. Arrowsmith remained elusive, mockingly faithful to Sainsbury Major, haughty when Fisher glanced pleadingly, ignoring all his letters. Fisher developed a look of introspective misery. The notes that Arrowsmith delightedly showed around were full of longing, increasingly tinged with desperation. The following term, unexpectedly, Fisher did not return to the school.

There was a famous Assembly at the beginning of that term, with much speculation beforehand as to the trouble in the air. Rumour had it that once and for all an attempt was to be made to stamp out the smiles and the glances in the dining-hall, the whole business of *bijoux* and protectors, even the faithless behaviour of the Honourable Anthony Swain. The school waited and then the gowned staff arrived in the Assembly Hall and waited also, in grim anticipation on a raised dais. Public beatings for past offenders were scheduled, it was whispered: the Sergeant-major – the school's boxing instructor, who had himself told tales of public beatings in the past – would inflict the punishment at the headmaster's bidding. But that did not happen. Stout and pompous and red-skinned, the headmaster marched to the dais unaccompanied by the Sergeant-major. Twitching with anger that many afterwards declared had been simulated, he spoke at great length of the school's traditions. He stated that for fourteen years he had been proud to be its headmaster. He spoke of decency, and then of his own dismay. The school had been dishonoured; he would wish certain practices to cease. 'I stand before you ashamed,' he added, and paused for a moment. 'Let all this cease,' he commanded. He marched away, tugging at his gown in a familiar manner.

No one understood why the Assembly had taken place at that particular time, on the first day of a summer term. Only the masters looked knowing, as though labouring beneath some secret, but pressed and pleaded with they refused to reveal anything. Even Old Frosty, usually a most reliable source on such occasions, remained awesomely tight-lipped.

But the pronounced dismay and shame of the headmaster changed nothing. That term progressed and the world of *bijoux* and their protectors continued as before, the glances, the meetings, cigarettes and romance in the hillside huts. R.A.J. Fisher was soon forgotten, having never made much of a mark. But the story of his error in placing a note under Torridge's pillow passed into legend, as did the encounter by the electricity plant and Torridge's deprivation of a relationship. The story was repeated as further terms passed by; new boys heard it and viewed Torridge with greater interest, imagining what R.A.J. Fisher had been like. The liaisons of Wiltshire with Good, Mace-Hamilton with Webb, and Arrowsmith with Sainsbury Major continued until the three senior boys left the school. Wiltshire, Mace-Hamilton and Arrowsmith found fresh protectors then, and later these new liaisons came to an end in a similar manner. Later still, Wiltshire, Mace-Hamilton and Arrowsmith ceased to be *bijoux* and became protectors themselves.

Torridge pursued the religious side of things. He continued to be a frequent partaker of God Harvey's biscuits and spiritual uplift, and a useful presence among the chapel pews, where he voluntarily dusted, cleaned brass and kept the hymn-books in a state of repair with Sellotape. Wiltshire, Mace-Hamilton and Arrowsmith continued to circulate stories about him which were not true: that he was the product of virgin birth, that he possessed the gift of tongues but did not care to employ it, that he had three kidneys. In the end there emanated from them the claim that a liaison existed between Torridge and God Harvey. 'Love and the holy spirit', Wiltshire pronounced, suggesting an ambience of chapel fustiness and God Harvey's grey boniness. The swish of his cassock took on a new significance, as did his thin, dry fingers. In a holy way the fingers pressed themselves on to Torridge, and then their holiness became a passion that could not be imagined. It was all a joke because Torridge was Torridge, but the laughter it caused wasn't malicious because no one hated him. He was a figure of fun; no one sought his downfall because there was no downfall to seek.

The friendship between Wiltshire, Mace-Hamilton and Arrowsmith continued after they left the school, after all three had married and had families. Once a year they received the Old Boys' magazine, which told of the achievements of themselves and the more successful of their schoolfellows. There were Old Boys' cocktail parties and Old Boys' Day at the school every June and the Old Boys' cricket match. Some of these occasions, from time to time, they attended. Every so often they received the latest rebuilding programme, with the suggestion that they might like to contribute to the rebuilding fund. Occasionally they did.

As middle age closed in, the three friends met less often. Arrowsmith was an executive with Shell and stationed for longish periods in different countries abroad. Once every two years he brought his family back to England, which provided an opportunity for the three friends to meet. The wives met on these occasions also, and over the years the children. Often the men's distant schooldays were referred to, Buller Yeats and Old Frosty and the Sergeant-major, the stout headmaster, and above all Torridge. Within the three families, in fact, Torridge had become a myth. The joke that had begun when they were all new boys together continued, as if driven by its own impetus. In the minds of the wives and children the innocence of Torridge, his true happiness in the face of mockery and his fondness for the religious side of life all lived on. With some exactitude a physical image of the boy he'd been took root; his neatly knotted maroon House tie, his polished shoes, the hair that resembled a mouse's fur, the pudding face with two small eyes in it. 'My dad's in the button business,' Arrowsmith had only to say to cause instant laughter. 'Torridge's, you know.' The way Torridge ate, the way he ran, the way he smiled back at Buller Yeats, the rumour that he'd been dropped on his head as a baby, that he had three kidneys: all this was considerably appreciated, because Wiltshire and Mace-Hamilton and Arrowsmith related it well.

What was not related was R.A.J. Fisher's error in placing a note beneath Torridge's pillow, or the story that had laughingly been spread about concerning Torridge's relationship with God Harvey. This would have meant revelations that weren't seemly in family circles, the explanation of the world of *bijou* and protector, the romance and cigarettes in the hillside huts, the entangling of hearts. The subject had been touched upon among the three husbands and their wives in the normal course of private conversation, although not everything had been quite recalled. Listening, the wives had formed the impression that the relationships between older and younger boys at their husbands' school were similar to the platonic admiration a junior girl had so often harboured for a senior girl at their own schools. And so the subject had been left.

One evening in June, 1976, Wiltshire and Mace-Hamilton met in a bar called the Vine, in Piccadilly Place. They hadn't seen one another since the summer of 1974, the last time Arrowsmith and his family had been in England. Tonight they were to meet the Arrowsmiths again, for a family dinner in the Woodlands Hotel, Richmond. On the last occasion the three families had celebrated their reunion at the Wiltshires' house in Cobham and the time before with the Mace-Hamiltons in Ealing. Arrowsmith insisted that it was a question of turn and turn about and every third time he arranged for the family dinner to be held at his expense at the Woodlands. It was convenient because, although the Arrowsmiths spent the greater part of each biennial leave with Mrs Arrowsmith's parents in Somerset, they always stayed for a week at the Woodlands in order to see a bit of London life.

In the Vine in Piccadilly Place Wiltshire and Mace-Hamilton hurried over their second drinks. As always, they were pleased to see one another, and both were excited at the prospect of seeing Arrowsmith and his family again. They still looked faintly alike. Both had balded and run to fat. They wore inconspicuous blue suits with a discreet chalk stripe, Wiltshire's a little smarter than Mace-Hamilton's.

'We'll be late,' Wiltshire said, having just related how he'd made a small killing since the last time they'd met. Wiltshire operated in the import-export world; Mace-Hamilton was a chartered accountant.

They finished their drinks. 'Cheerio,' the barman called out to them as they slipped away. His voice was deferentially low, matching the softly lit surroundings. 'Cheerio, Gerry,' Wiltshire said.

They drove in Wiltshire's car to Hammersmith, over the bridge and on to Barnes and Richmond. It was a Friday evening; the traffic was heavy.

'He had a bit of trouble, you know,' Mace-Hamilton said.

'Arrows?'

'She took a shine to some guy in Mombasa.'

Wiltshire nodded, poking the car between a cyclist and a taxi. He wasn't surprised. One night six years ago Arrowsmith's wife and he had committed adultery together at her suggestion. A messy business it had been, and afterwards he'd felt terrible.

In the Woodlands Hotel Arrowsmith, in a grey flannel suit, was not entirely sober. He, too, had run a bit to fat although, unlike Wiltshire and Mace-Hamilton, he hadn't lost any of his hair. Instead, it had dramatically changed colour: what Old Frosty had once called 'Arrows' blond thatch' was grey now. Beneath it his face was pinker than it had been and he had taken to wearing spectacles, heavy and black-rimmed, making him look even more different from the boy he'd been.

In the bar of the Woodlands he drank whisky on his own, smiling occasionally to himself because tonight he had a surprise for everybody. After five weeks of being cooped up with his in-laws in Somerset he was feeling good. 'Have one yourself, dear,' he invited the barmaid, a girl with an excess of lipstick on a podgy mouth. He pushed his own glass towards her while she was saying she didn't mind if she did.

His wife and his three adolescent children, two boys and a girl, entered the bar with Mrs Mace-Hamilton. 'Hi, hi, hi,' Arrowsmith called out to them in a jocular manner, causing his wife and Mrs Mace-Hamilton to note that he was drunk again. They sat down while he quickly finished the whisky that had just been poured for him. 'Put another in that for a start,' he ordered the barmaid, and crossed the floor of the bar to find out what everyone else wanted.

Mrs Wiltshire and her twins, girls of twelve, arrived while drinks were being decided about. Arrowsmith kissed her, as he had kissed Mrs Mace-Hamilton. The barmaid, deciding that the accurate conveying of such a large order was going to be beyond him, came and stood by the two tables that the party now occupied. The order was given; an animated conversation began.

The three women were different in appearance and in manner. Mrs Arrowsmith was thin as a knife, fashionably dressed in a shade of ash-grey that reflected her ash-grey hair. She smoked perpetually, unable to abandon the habit. Mrs Wiltshire was small. Shyness caused her to coil herself up in the presence of other people so that she often resembled a ball. Tonight she was in pink, a faded shade. Mrs Mace-Hamilton was carelessly plump, a large woman attired in a carelessly chosen dress that had begonias on it. She rather frightened Mrs Wiltshire. Mrs Arrowsmith found her trying.

'Oh, heavenly little drink!' Mrs Arrowsmith said, briefly drooping her blue-tinged eyelids as she sipped her gin and tonic.

'It *is* good to see you,' Mrs Mace-Hamilton gushed, beaming at everyone and vaguely raising her glass. 'And how they've all grown!' Mrs Mace-Hamilton had not had children herself.

'Their boobs have grown, by God,' the older Arrowsmith boy murmured to his brother, a reference to the Wiltshire twins. Neither of the two Arrowsmith boys went to their father's school: one was at a preparatory school in Oxford, the other at Charterhouse. Being of an age to do so, they both drank sherry and intended to drink as much of it as they possibly could. They found these family occasions tedious. Their sister, about to go to university, had determined neither to speak nor to smile for the entire evening. The Wiltshire twins were quite looking forward to the food.

Arrowsmith sat beside Mrs Wiltshire. He didn't say anything but after a moment he stretched a hand over her two knees and squeezed them in what he intended to be a brotherly way. He said without conviction that it was great to see her. He didn't look at her while he spoke. He didn't much care for hanging about with the women and children.

In turn Mrs Wiltshire didn't much care for his hand on her knees and was relieved when he drew it away. 'Hi, hi, hi,' he suddenly called out, causing her to jump. Wiltshire and Mace-Hamilton had appeared.

The physical similarity that had been so pronounced when the three men were boys and had been only faintly noticeable between Wiltshire and Mace-Hamilton in the Vine was clearly there again, as if the addition of Arrowsmith had supplied missing reflections. The men had thickened in the same way; the pinkness of Arrowsmith's countenance was a pinkness that tinged the other faces too. Only Arrowsmith's grey thatch of hair seemed out of place, all wrong beside the baldness of the other two: in their presence it might have been a wig, an impression it did not otherwise give. His grey flannel suit, beside their pinstripes, looked like something put on by mistake. 'Hi, hi, hi,' he shouted, thumping their shoulders.

Further rounds of drinks were bought and consumed. The Arrowsmith boys declared to each other that they were drunk and made further *sotto voce* observations about the forming bodies of the Wiltshire twins. Mrs Wiltshire felt the occasion becoming easier as Cinzano Bianco coursed through her bloodstream. Mrs Arrowsmith was aware of a certain familiar edginess within her body, a desire to be elsewhere, alone with a man she did not know. Mrs Mace-Hamilton spoke loudly of her garden.

In time the party moved from the bar to the dining-room. 'Bring us another round at the table,' Arrowsmith commanded the lipsticked barmaid. 'Quick as you can, dear.'

In the large dim dining-room waiters settled them around a table with little vases of carnations on it, a long table beneath the chandelier in the centre of the room. Celery soup arrived at the table, and smoked salmon and pâté, and the extra round of drinks Arrowsmith had ordered, and bottles of Nuits St Georges, and bottles of Vouvray and Anjou Rosé, and sirloin of beef, chicken à la king and veal escalope. The Arrowsmith boys laughed shrilly, openly staring at the tops of the Wiltshire twins' bodies. Potatoes, peas, spinach and carrots were served. Mrs Arrowsmith waved the vegetables away and smoked between courses. It was after this dinner six years ago that she had made her suggestion to Wiltshire, both of them being the worse for wear and it seeming not to matter because of that. 'Oh, *isn't* this jolly?' the voice of Mrs Mace-Hamilton boomed above the general hubbub.

Over Chantilly trifle and Orange Surprise the name of Torridge was heard. The name was always mentioned just about now, though sometimes sooner. 'Poor old bean,' Wiltshire said, and everybody laughed because it was the one subject they all shared. No one really wanted to hear about the Mace-Hamiltons' garden; the comments of the Arrowsmith boys were only for each other; Mrs Arrowsmith's needs could naturally not be voiced; the shyness of Mrs Wiltshire was private too. But Torridge was different. Torridge in a way was like an old friend now, existing in everyone's mind, a family subject. The Wiltshire twins were quite amused to hear of some freshly remembered evidence of Torridge's naïveté; for the Arrowsmith girl it was better at least than being questioned by Mrs Mace-Hamilton; for her brothers it was an excuse to bellow with simulated mirth. Mrs Mace-Hamilton considered that the boy sounded frightful, Mrs Arrowsmith couldn't have cared less. Only Mrs Wiltshire had doubts: she thought the three men were hard on the memory of the boy, but of course had not ever said so. Tonight, after Wiltshire had recalled the time when Torridge had been convinced by Arrowsmith that Buller Yeats had dropped dead in his bath, the younger Arrowsmith boy told of a boy at his own school who'd been convinced that his sister's dog had died.

'Listen,' Arrowsmith suddenly shouted out. 'He's going to join us. Old Torridge.'

There was laughter, no one believing that Torridge was going to arrive, Mrs Arrowsmith saying to herself that her husband was pitiful when he became as drunk as this.

'I thought it would be a gesture,' Arrowsmith said. 'Honestly. He's looking in for coffee.'

'You bloody devil, Arrows,' Wiltshire said, smacking the table with the palm of his hand.

'He's in the button business,' Arrowsmith shouted. 'Torridge's, you know.'

As far as Wiltshire and Mace-Hamilton could remember, Torridge had never featured in an Old Boys' magazine. No news of his career had been printed, and certainly no obituary. It was typical, somehow, of Arrowsmith to have winkled him out. It was part and parcel of him to want to add another dimension to the joke, to recharge its batteries. For the sight of Torridge in middle age would surely make funnier the reported anecdotes.

'After all, what's wrong,' demanded Arrowsmith noisily, 'with old school pals meeting up? The more the merrier.'

He was a bully, Mrs Wiltshire thought: all three of them were bullies.

Torridge arrived at half past nine. The hair that had been like a mouse's fur was still like that. It hadn't greyed any more; the scalp hadn't balded. He hadn't run to fat; in middle age he'd thinned down a bit. There was even a lankiness about him now, which was reflected in his movements. At school he had moved slowly, as though with caution. Jauntily attired in a pale linen suit, he crossed the dining-room of the Woodlands Hotel with a step as nimble as a tap-dancer's.

No one recognized him. To the three men who'd been at school with him the man who approached their dinner table was a different person, quite unlike the figure that existed in the minds of the wives and children.

'My dear Arrows,' he said, smiling at Arrowsmith. The smile was different too, a brittle snap of a smile that came and went in a matter-of-fact way. The eyes that had been small didn't seem so in his thinner face. They flashed with a gleam of some kind, matching the snap of his smile.

'Good God, it's never old Porridge!' Arrowsmith's voice was slurred. His face had acquired the beginnings of an alcoholic crimson, sweat glistened on his forehead.

'Yes, it's old Porridge,' Torridge said quietly. He held his hand out towards Arrowsmith and then shook hands with Wiltshire and Mace-Hamilton. He was introduced to their wives, with whom he shook hands also. He was introduced to the children, which involved further hand-shaking. His hand was cool and rather hard: they felt it should have been damp.

'You're nicely in time for coffee, Mr Torridge,' Mrs Mace-Hamilton said.

'Brandy more like,' Arrowsmith suggested. 'Brandy, old chap?'

'Well, that's awfully kind of you, Arrows. Chartreuse I'd prefer, really.'

A waiter drew up a chair. Room was made for Torridge between Mrs Mace-Hamilton and the Arrowsmith boys. It was a frightful mistake, Wiltshire was thinking. It was mad of Arrowsmith.

Mace-Hamilton examined Torridge across the dinner table. The old Torridge would have said he'd rather not have anything alcoholic, that a cup of tea and a biscuit were more his line in the evenings. It was impossible to imagine this man saying his dad had a button business. There was a suavity about him that made Mace-Hamilton uneasy. Because of what had been related to his wife and the other wives and their children he felt he'd been caught out in a lie, yet in fact that wasn't the case.

The children stole glances at Torridge, trying to see him as the boy who'd been described to them, and failing to. Mrs Arrowsmith said to herself that all this stuff they'd been told over the years had clearly been rubbish. Mrs Mace-Hamilton was bewildered. Mrs Wiltshire was pleased.

'No one ever guessed,' Torridge said, 'what became of R.A.J. Fisher.' He raised the subject suddenly, without introduction.

'Oh God, Fisher,' Mace-Hamilton said.

'Who's Fisher?' the younger of the Arrowsmith boys inquired.

Torridge turned to flash his quick smile at the boy. 'He left,' he said. 'In unfortunate circumstances.'

'You've changed a lot, you know,' Arrowsmith said. 'Don't you think he's changed?' he asked Wiltshire and Mace-Hamilton.

'Out of recognition,' Wiltshire said.

Torridge laughed easily. 'I've become adventurous. I'm a late developer, I suppose.'

'What kind of unfortunate circumstances?' the younger Arrowsmith boy asked. 'Was Fisher expelled?'

'Oh no, not at all,' Mace-Hamilton said hurriedly.

'Actually,' Torridge said, 'Fisher's trouble all began with the writing of a note. Don't you remember? He put it in my pyjamas. But it wasn't for me at all.'

He smiled again. He turned to Mrs Wiltshire in a way that seemed polite, drawing her into the conversation. 'I was an innocent at school. But innocence slips away. I found my way about eventually.'

'Yes, of course,' she murmured. She didn't like him, even though she was glad he wasn't as he might have been. There was malevolence in him, a ruthlessness that seemed like a work of art. He seemed like a work of art himself, as though in losing the innocence he spoke of he had recreated himself.

'I often wonder about Fisher,' he remarked.

The Wiltshire twins giggled. 'What's so great about this bloody Fisher?' the older Arrowsmith boy murmured, nudging his brother with an elbow.

'What're you doing these days?' Wiltshire asked, interrupting Mace-Hamilton, who had also begun to say something.

'I make buttons,' Torridge replied. 'You may recall my father made buttons.'

'Ah, here're the drinks,' Arrowsmith rowdily observed.

'I don't much keep up with the school,' Torridge said as the waiter placed a glass of Chartreuse in front of him. 'I don't so much as think about it except for wondering about poor old Fisher. Our headmaster was a cretin,' he informed Mrs Wiltshire.

Again the Wiltshire twins giggled. The Arrowsmith girl yawned and her brothers giggled also, amused that the name of Fisher had come up again.

'You will have coffee, Mr Torridge?' Mrs Mace-Hamilton offered, for the waiter had brought a fresh pot to the table. She held it poised above a cup. Torridge smiled at her and nodded. She said:

'Pearl buttons d'you make?'

'No, not pearl.'

'Remember those awful packet peas we used to have?' Arrowsmith inquired. Wiltshire said:

'Use plastics at all? In your buttons, Porridge?'

'No, we don't use plastics. Leathers, various leathers. And horn. We specialize.'

'How very interesting!' Mrs Mace-Hamilton exclaimed.

'No, no. It's rather ordinary really.' He paused, and then added, 'Someone once told me that Fisher went into a timber business. But of course that was far from true.'

'A chap was expelled a year ago,' the younger Arrowsmith boy said, contributing this in order to cover up a fresh outburst of sniggering. 'For stealing a transistor.'

Torridge nodded, appearing to be interested. He asked the Arrowsmith boys where they were at school. The older one said Charterhouse and his brother gave the name of his preparatory school. Torridge nodded again and asked their sister and she said she was waiting to go to university. He had quite a chat with the Wiltshire twins about their school. They considered it pleasant the way he bothered, seeming genuinely to want to know. The giggling died away.

'I imagined Fisher wanted me for his *bijou*,' he said when all that was over, still addressing the children. 'Our place was riddled with fancy larks like that. Remember?' he added, turning to Mace-Hamilton.

'*Bijou*?' one of the twins asked before Mace-Hamilton could reply.

'A male tart,' Torridge explained.

The Arrowsmith boys gaped at him, the older one with his mouth actually open. The Wiltshire twins began to giggle again. The Arrowsmith girl frowned, unable to hide her interest.

'The Honourable Anthony Swain,' Torridge said, 'was no better than a whore.'

Mrs Arrowsmith, who for some minutes had been engaged with her own thoughts, was suddenly aware that the man who was in the button business was talking about sex. She gazed diagonally across the table at him, astonished that he should be talking in this way.

'Look here, Torridge,' Wiltshire said, frowning at him and shaking his head. With an almost imperceptible motion he gestured towards the wives and children.

'Andrews and Butler. Dillon and Pratt. Tothill and Goldfish Stewart. Your dad,' Torridge said to the Arrowsmith girl, 'was always very keen. Sainsbury Major in particular.'

'Now look here,' Arrowsmith shouted, beginning to get to his feet and then changing his mind.

'My gosh, how they broke chaps' hearts, those three!'

'Please don't talk like this.' It was Mrs Wiltshire who protested, to everyone's surprise, most of all her own. 'The children are quite young, Mr Torridge.'

Her voice had become a whisper. She could feel herself reddening with embarrassment, and a little twirl of sickness occurred in her stomach. Deferentially, as though appreciating the effort she had made, Torridge apologized.

'I think you'd better go,' Arrowsmith said.

'You were right about God Harvey, Arrows. Gay as a grig he was, beneath that cassock. So was Old Frosty, as a matter of fact.'

'Really!' Mrs Mace-Hamilton cried, her bewilderment turning into outrage. She glared at her husband, demanding with her eyes that instantly something should be done. But her husband and his two friends were briefly stunned by what Torridge had claimed for God Harvey. Their schooldays leapt back at them, possessing them for a vivid moment: the dormitory, the dining-hall, the glances and the invitations, the meetings behind Chapel. It was somehow in keeping with the school's hypocrisy that God Harvey had had inclinations himself, that a rumour begun as an outrageous joke should have contained the truth.

'As a matter of fact,' Torridge went on, 'I wouldn't be what I am if it hadn't been for God Harvey. I'm what they call queer,' he explained to the children. 'I perform sexual acts with men.'

'For God's sake, Torridge,' Arrowsmith shouted, on his feet, his face the colour of ripe strawberry, his watery eyes quivering with rage.

'It was nice of you to invite me tonight, Arrows. Our *alma mater* can't be too proud of chaps like me.'

People spoke at once, Mrs Mace-Hamilton and Mrs Wiltshire, all three men. Mrs Arrowsmith sat still. What she was thinking was that she had become quietly drunk while her husband had more boisterously reached the same condition. She was thinking, as well, that by the sound of things he'd possessed as a boy a sexual urge that was a lot livelier than the one he'd once exposed her to and now hardly ever did. With boys who had grown to be men he had had a whale of a time. Old Frosty had been a kind of Mr Chips, she'd been told. She'd never ever heard of Sainsbury Major or God Harvey.

'It's quite disgusting,' Mrs Mace-Hamilton's voice cried out above the other voices. She said the police should be called. It was scandalous to have to listen to unpleasant conversation like this. She began to say the children should leave the dining-room, but changed her mind because it appeared that Torridge himself was about to go. 'You're a most horrible man,' she cried.

Confusion gathered, like a fog around the table. Mrs Wiltshire, who knew that her husband had committed adultery with Mrs Arrowsmith, felt another bout of nerves in her stomach. 'Because she was starved, that's why,' her husband had almost violently confessed when she'd discovered. 'I was putting her out of her misery.' She had wept then and he had comforted her as best he could. She had not told him that he had never succeeded in arousing in her the desire to make love: she had always assumed that to be a failing in herself, but now for some reason she was not so sure. Nothing had been directly said that might have caused this doubt, but an instinct informed Mrs Wiltshire that the doubt should be there. The man beside her smiled his brittle, malevolent smile at her, as if in sympathy.

With his head bent over the table and his hands half hiding his face, the younger Arrowsmith boy examined his father by glancing through his fingers. There were men whom his parents warned him against, men who would sit beside you in buses or try to give you a lift in a car. This man who had come tonight, who had been such a joke up till now, was apparently one of these, not a joke at all. And the confusion was greater: at one time, it seemed, his father had been like that too.

The Arrowsmith girl considered her father also. Once she had walked into a room in Lagos to find her mother in the arms of an African clerk. Ever since she had felt sorry for her father. There'd been an unpleasant scene at the time, she'd screamed at her mother and later in a fury had told her father what she'd seen. He'd nodded, wearily seeming not to be surprised, while her mother had miserably wept. She'd put her arms around her father, comforting him; she'd felt no mercy for her mother, no sympathy or understanding. The scene formed vividly in her mind as she sat at the dinner table: it appeared to be relevant in the confusion and yet not clearly so. Her parents' marriage was messy, messier than it had looked. Across the table her mother grimly smoked, focusing her eyes with difficulty. She smiled at her daughter, a soft, inebriated smile.

The older Arrowsmith boy was also aware of the confusion. Being at a school where the practice which had been spoken of was common enough, he could easily believe the facts that had been thrown about. Against his will, he was forced to imagine what he had never imagined before: his father and his friends as schoolboys, engaged in passion with other boys. He might have been cynical about this image but he could not. Instead it made him want to gasp. It knocked away the smile that had been on his face all evening.

The Wiltshire twins unhappily stared at the white tablecloth, here and there stained with wine or gravy. They, too, found they'd lost the urge to smile and instead shakily blinked back tears.

'Yes, perhaps I'd better go,' Torridge said.

With impatience Mrs Mace-Hamilton looked at her husband, as if expecting him to hurry Torridge off or at least to say something. But Mace-Hamilton remained silent. Mrs Mace-Hamilton licked her lips, preparing to speak herself. She changed her mind.

'Fisher didn't go into a timber business,' Torridge said, 'because poor old Fisher was dead as a doornail. Which is why our cretin of a headmaster, Mrs Mace-Hamilton, had that Assembly.'

'Assembly?' she said. Her voice was weak, although she'd meant it to sound matter-of-fact and angry.

'There was an Assembly that no one understood. Poor old Fisher had strung himself up in a barn on his father's farm. I discovered that,' Torridge said, turning to Arrowsmith, 'years later: from God Harvey actually. The poor chap left a note but the parents didn't care to pass it on. I mean it was for you, Arrows.'

Arrowsmith was still standing, hanging over the table. 'Note?' he said. 'For me?'

'Another note. Why d'you think he did himself in, Arrows?'

Torridge smiled, at Arrowsmith and then around the table.

'None of that's true,' Wiltshire said.

'As a matter of fact it is.'

He went, and nobody spoke at the dinner table. A body of a schoolboy hung from a beam in a barn, a note on the straw below his dangling feet. It hung in the confusion that had been caused, increasing the confusion. Two waiters hovered by a sideboard, one passing the time by arranging sauce bottles, the other folding napkins into cone shapes. Slowly Arrowsmith sat down again. The silence continued as the conversation of Torridge continued to haunt the dinner table. He haunted it himself, with his brittle smile and his tap-dancer's elegance, still faithful to the past in which he had so signally failed, triumphant in his middle age.

Then Mrs Arrowsmith quite suddenly wept and the Wiltshire twins wept and Mrs Wiltshire comforted them. The Arrowsmith girl got up and walked away, and Mrs Mace-Hamilton turned to the three men and said they should be ashamed of themselves, allowing all this to happen.

Death in Jerusalem

'Till then,' Father Paul said, leaning out of the train window. 'Till Jerusalem, Francis.'

'Please God, Paul.' As he spoke the Dublin train began to move and his brother waved from the window and he waved back, a modest figure on the platform. Everyone said Francis might have been a priest as well, meaning that Francis's quietness and meditative disposition had an air of the cloister about them. But Francis contented himself with the running of Conary's hardware business, which his mother had run until she was too old for it. 'Are we game for the Holy Land next year?' Father Paul had asked that July. 'Will we go together, Francis?' He had brushed aside all Francis's protestations, all attempts to explain that the shop could not be left, that their mother would be confused by the absence of Francis from the house. Rumbustiously he'd pointed out that there was their sister Kitty, who was in charge of the household of which Francis and their mother were part and whose husband, Myles, could surely be trusted to look after the shop for a single fortnight. For thirty years, ever since he was seven, Francis had wanted to go to the Holy Land. He had savings which he'd never spent a penny of: you couldn't take them with you, Father Paul had more than once stated that July.

On the platform Francis watched until the train could no longer be seen, his thoughts still with his brother. The priest's ruddy countenance smiled again behind cigarette smoke; his bulk remained impressive in his clerical clothes, the collar pinching the flesh of his neck, his black shoes scrupulously polished. There were freckles on the backs of his large, strong hands; he had a fine head of hair, grey and crinkly. In an hour and a half's time the train would creep into Dublin, and he'd take a taxi. He'd spend a night in the Gresham Hotel, probably falling in with another priest, having a drink or two, maybe playing a game of bridge after his meal. That was his brother's way and always had been – an extravagant, easy kind of way, full of smiles and good humour. It was what had taken him to America and made him successful there. In order to raise money for the church that he and Father Steigmuller intended to build before 1980 he took parties of the well-to-do from San Francisco to Rome and Florence, to Chartres and Seville and the Holy Land. He was good at raising money, not just for the church but for the boys' home of which he was president, and for the Hospital of Our Saviour, and for St Mary's Old People's Home on the west side of the city. But every July he flew back to Ireland, to the town in Co. Tipperary where his mother and brother and sister still lived. He stayed in the house above the shop which he might have inherited himself on the death of his father, which he'd rejected in favour of the religious life. Mrs Conary was eighty now. In the shop she sat silently behind the counter, in a corner by the chicken-wire, wearing only clothes that were black. In the evenings she sat with Francis in the lace-curtained sitting-room, while the rest of the family occupied the kitchen. It was for her sake most of all that Father Paul made the journey every summer, considering it his duty.

Walking back to the town from the station, Francis was aware that he was missing his brother. Father Paul was fourteen years older and in childhood had often taken the place of their father, who had died when Francis was five. His brother had possessed an envied strength and knowledge; he'd been a hero, quite often worshipped, an example of success. In later life he had become an example of generosity as well: ten years ago he'd taken their mother to Rome, and their sister Kitty and her husband two years later; he'd paid the expenses when their sister Edna had gone to Canada; he'd assisted two nephews to make a start in America. In childhood Francis hadn't possessed his brother's healthy freckled face, just as in middle age he didn't have his ruddy complexion and his stoutness and his easiness with people. Francis was slight, his sandy hair receding, his face rather pale. His breathing was sometimes laboured because of wheeziness in the chest. In the ironmonger's shop he wore a brown cotton coat.

'Hullo, Mr Conary,' a woman said to him in the main street of the town. 'Father Paul's gone off, has he?'

'Yes, he's gone again.'

'I'll pray for his journey so,' the woman promised, and Francis thanked her.

A year went by. In San Francisco another wing of the boys' home was completed, another target was reached in Father Paul and Father Steigmuller's fund for the church they planned to have built by 1980. In the town in Co. Tipperary there were baptisms and burial services and First Communions. Old Loughlin, a farmer from Bansha, died in McSharry's grocery and bar, having gone there to celebrate a good price he'd got for a heifer. Clancy, from behind the counter in Doran's drapery, married Maureen Talbot; Mr Nolan's plasterer married Miss Carron; Johneen

Meagher married Seamus in the chip-shop, under pressure from her family to do so. A local horse, from the stables on the Limerick road, was said to be an entry for the Fairyhouse Grand National, but it turned out not to be true. Every evening of that year Francis sat with his mother in the lace-curtained sitting-room above the shop. Every weekday she sat in her corner by the chicken-wire, watching while he counted out screws and weighed staples, or advised about yard brushes or tap-washers. Occasionally, on a Saturday, he visited the three Christian Brothers who lodged with Mrs Shea and afterwards he'd tell his mother about how the authority was slipping these days from the nuns and the Christian Brothers, and how Mrs Shea's elderly maid, Ita, couldn't see to cook the food any more. His mother would nod and hardly ever speak. When he told a joke – what young Hogan had said when he'd found a nail in his egg or how Ita had put mint sauce into a jug with milk in it – she never laughed, and looked at him in surprise when he laughed himself. But Dr Foran said it was best to keep her cheered up.

All during that year Francis talked to her about his forthcoming visit to the Holy Land, endeavouring to make her understand that for a fortnight next spring he would be away from the house and the shop. He'd been away before for odd days, but that was when she'd been younger. He used to visit an aunt in Tralee, but three years ago the aunt had died and he hadn't left the town since.

Francis and his mother had always been close. Before his birth two daughters had died in infancy, and his very survival had often struck Mrs Conary as a gift. He had always been her favourite, the one among her children whom she often considered least able to stand on his own two feet. It was just like Paul to have gone blustering off to San Francisco instead of remaining in Co. Tipperary. It was just like Kitty to have married a useless man. 'There's not a girl in the town who'd touch him,' she'd said to her daughter at the time, but Kitty had been headstrong and adamant, and there was Myles now, doing nothing whatsoever except cleaning other people's windows for a pittance and placing bets in Donovan's the turf accountant's. It was the shop and the arrangement Kitty had with Francis and her mother that kept her and the children going, three of whom had already left the town, which in Mrs Conary's opinion they mightn't have done if they'd had a better type of father. Mrs Conary often wondered what her own two babies who'd died might have grown up into, and imagined they might have been like Francis, about whom she'd never had a moment's worry. Not in a million years would he give you the feeling that he was too big for his boots, like Paul sometimes did with his lavishness and his big talk of America. He wasn't silly like Kitty, or so sinful you couldn't forgive him, the way you couldn't forgive Edna, even though she was dead and buried in Toronto.

Francis understood how his mother felt about the family. She'd had a hard life, left a widow early on, trying to do the best she could for everyone. In turn he did his best to compensate for the struggles and disappointments she'd suffered, cheering her in the evenings while Kitty and Myles and the youngest of their children watched the television in the kitchen. His mother had ignored the existence of Myles for ten years, ever since the day he'd taken money out of the till to pick up the odds on Gusty Spirit at Phoenix Park. And although Francis got on well enough with Myles he quite understood that there should be a long aftermath to that day. There'd been a terrible row in the kitchen, Kitty screaming at Myles and Myles telling lies and Francis trying to keep them calm, saying they'd give the old woman a heart attack.

She didn't like upsets of any kind, so all during the year before he was to visit the Holy Land Francis read the New Testament to her in order to prepare her. He talked to her about Bethlehem and Nazareth and the miracle of the loaves and fishes and all the other miracles. She kept nodding, but he often wondered if she didn't assume he was just casually referring to episodes in the Bible. As a child he had listened to such talk himself, with awe and fascination, imagining the walking on the water and the temptation in the wilderness. He had imagined the cross carried to Calvary, and the rock rolled back from the tomb, and the rising from the dead on the third day. That he was now to walk in such places seemed extraordinary to him, and he wished his mother was younger so that she could appreciate his good fortune and share it with him when she received the postcards he intended, every day, to send her. But her eyes seemed always to tell him that he was making a mistake, that somehow he was making a fool of himself by doing such a showy thing as going to the Holy Land. *I have the entire itinerary mapped out*, his brother wrote from San Francisco. *There's nothing we'll miss*.

It was the first time Francis had been in an aeroplane. He flew by Aer Lingus from Dublin to London and then changed to an El Al flight to Tel Aviv. He was nervous and he found it exhausting. All the time he seemed to be eating, and it was strange being among so many people he didn't know. 'You will taste honey such as never before,' an Israeli businessman in the seat next to his assured him. 'And Galilean figs. Make certain to taste Galilean figs.' Make certain too, the businessman went on, to experience Jerusalem by night and in the early dawn. He urged Francis to see places he had never heard of, Yad Va-Shem, the treasures of the Shrine of the

Book. He urged him to honour the martyrs of Masada and to learn a few words of Hebrew as a token of respect. He told him of a shop where he could buy mementoes and warned him against Arab street traders.

'The hard man, how are you?' Father Paul said at Tel Aviv airport, having flown in from San Francisco the day before. Father Paul had had a drink or two and he suggested another when they arrived at the Plaza Hotel in Jerusalem. It was half past nine in the evening. 'A quick little nightcap,' Father Paul insisted, 'and then hop into bed with you, Francis.' They sat in an enormous open lounge with low, round tables and square modern armchairs. Father Paul said it was the bar.

They had said what had to be said in the car from Tel Aviv to Jerusalem. Father Paul had asked about their mother, and Kitty and Myles. He'd asked about other people in the town, old Canon Mahon and Sergeant Murray. He and Father Steigmuller had had a great year of it, he reported: as well as everything else, the boys' home had turned out two tip-top footballers. 'We'll start on a tour at half-nine in the morning,' he said. 'I'll be sitting having breakfast at eight.'

Francis went to bed and Father Paul ordered another whisky, with ice. To his great disappointment there was no Irish whiskey in the hotel so he'd had to content himself with Haig. He fell into conversation with an American couple, making them promise that if they were ever in Ireland they wouldn't miss out Co. Tipperary. At eleven o'clock the barman said he was wanted at the reception desk and when Father Paul went there and announced himself he was given a message in an envelope. It was a telegram that had come, the girl said in poor English. Then she shook her head, saying it was a telex. He opened the envelope and learnt that Mrs Conary had died.

Francis fell asleep immediately and dreamed that he was a boy again, out fishing with a friend whom he couldn't now identify.

On the telephone Father Paul ordered whisky and ice to be brought to his room. Before drinking it he took his jacket off and knelt by his bed to pray for his mother's salvation. When he'd completed the prayers he walked slowly up and down the length of the room, occasionally sipping at his whisky. He argued with himself and finally arrived at a decision.

For breakfast they had scrambled eggs that looked like yellow ice-cream, and orange juice that was delicious. Francis wondered about bacon, but Father Paul explained that bacon was not readily available in Israel.

'Did you sleep all right?' Father Paul inquired. 'Did you have the jet-lag?'

'Jet-lag?'

'A tiredness you get after jet flights. It'd knock you out for days.'

'Ah, I slept great, Paul.'

'Good man.'

They lingered over breakfast. Father Paul reported a little more of what had happened in his parish during the year, in particular about the two young footballers from the boys' home. Francis told about the decline in the cooking at Mrs Shea's boarding-house, as related to him by the three Christian Brothers. 'I have a car laid on,' Father Paul said, and twenty minutes later they walked out into the Jerusalem sunshine.

The hired car stopped on the way to the walls of the Old City. It drew into a lay-by at Father Paul's request and the two men got out and looked across a wide valley dotted with houses and olive trees. A road curled along the distant slope opposite. 'The Mount of Olives,' Father Paul said. 'And that's the road to Jericho.' He pointed more particularly. 'You see that group of eight big olives? Just off the road, where the church is?'

Francis thought he did, but was not sure. There were so many olive trees, and more than one church. He glanced at his brother's pointing finger and followed its direction with his glance.

'The Garden of Gethsemane,' Father Paul said.

Francis did not say anything. He continued to gaze at the distant church, with the clump of olive trees beside it. Wild flowers were profuse on the slopes of the valley, smears of orange and blue on land that looked poor. Two Arab women herded goats.

'Could we see it closer?' he asked, and his brother said that definitely they would. They returned to the waiting car and Father Paul ordered it to the Gate of St Stephen.

Tourists heavy with cameras thronged the Via Dolorosa. Brown, bare-foot children asked for alms. Stall-keepers pressed their different wares: cotton dresses, metal-ware, mementoes, sacred goods. 'Get out of the way,' Father Paul kept saying to them, genially laughing to show he wasn't being abrupt. Francis wanted to stand still and close his eyes, to visualize for a moment the carrying of the Cross. But the ceremony of the Stations, familiar to him for as long as he could remember, was unreal. Try as he would, Christ's journey refused to enter his imagination, and his own plain church seemed closer to the heart of the matter than the noisy lane he was now being jostled on. 'God damn it, of course it's genuine,' an angry American voice proclaimed, in reply to a shriller voice which insisted that cheating had taken place. The voices argued about a piece of wood, neat beneath plastic in a little box, a sample or not of the Cross that had been carried.

They arrived at the Church of the Holy Sepulchre, and at the Chapel of the Nailing to the Cross, where they prayed. They passed through the Chapel of the Angel, to the tomb of Christ. Nobody spoke in the marble cell, but when they left the church Francis overheard a quiet man with spectacles saying it was unlikely that a body would have been buried within the walls of the city. They walked to Hezekiah's Pool and out of the Old City at the Jaffa Gate, where their hired car was waiting for them. 'Are you peckish?' Father Paul asked, and although Francis said he wasn't they returned to the hotel.

Delay funeral till Monday was the telegram Father Paul had sent. There was an early flight on Sunday, in time for an afternoon one from London to Dublin. With luck there'd be a late train on Sunday evening and if there wasn't they'd have to fix a car. Today was Tuesday. It would give them four and a half days. *Funeral eleven Monday* the telegram at the reception desk now confirmed. 'Ah, isn't that great?' he said to himself, bundling the telegram up.

'Will we have a small one?' he suggested in the open area that was the bar. 'Or better still a big one.' He laughed. He was in good spirits in spite of the death that had taken place. He gestured at the barman, wagging his head and smiling jovially.

His face had reddened in the morning sun; there were specks of sweat on his forehead and his nose. 'Bethlehem this afternoon,' he laid down. 'Unless the jet-lag ...?'

'I haven't got the jet-lag.'

In the Nativity Boutique Francis bought for his mother a small metal plate with a fish on it. He had stood for a moment, scarcely able to believe it, on the spot where the manger had been, in the Church of the Nativity. As in the Via Dolorosa it had been difficult to clear his mind of the surroundings that now were present: the exotic Greek Orthodox trappings, the foreign-looking priests, the oriental smell. Gold, frankincense and myrrh, he'd kept thinking, for somehow the church seemed more the church of the kings than of Joseph and Mary and their child. Afterwards they returned to Jerusalem, to the Tomb of the Virgin and the Garden of Gethsemane. 'It could have been anywhere,' he heard the quiet, bespectacled sceptic remarking in Gethsemane. 'They're only guessing.'

Father Paul rested in the late afternoon, lying down on his bed with his jacket off. He slept from half past five until a quarter past seven and awoke refreshed. He picked up the telephone and asked for whisky and ice to be brought up and when it arrived he undressed and had a bath, relaxing in the warm water with the drink on a ledge in the tiled wall beside him.

There would be time to take in Nazareth and Galilee. He was particularly keen that his brother should see Galilee because Galilee had atmosphere and was beautiful. There wasn't, in his own opinion, very much to Nazareth but it would be a pity to miss it all the same. It was at the Sea of Galilee that he intended to tell his brother of their mother's death.

We've had a great day, Francis wrote on a postcard that showed an aerial view of Jerusalem. *The Church of the Holy Sepulchre, where Our Lord's tomb is, and Gethsemane and Bethlehem. Paul's in great form*. He addressed it to his mother, and then wrote other cards, to Kitty and Myles and to the three Christian Brothers in Mrs Shea's, and to Canon Mahon. He gave thanks that he was privileged to be in Jerusalem. He read St Mark and some of St Matthew. He said his rosary.

'Will we chance the wine?' Father Paul said at dinner, not that wine was something he went in for, but a waiter had come up and put a large padded wine-list into his hand.

'Ah, no, no,' Francis protested, but already Father Paul was running his eye down the listed bottles.

'Have you local wine?' he inquired of the waiter 'A nice red one?'

The waiter nodded and hurried away, and Francis hoped he wouldn't get drunk, the red wine on top of the whisky he'd had in the bar before the meal. He'd only had the one whisky, not being much used to it, making it last through his brother's three.

'I heard some gurriers in the bar,' Father Paul said, 'making a great song and dance about the local red wine.'

Wine made Francis think of the Holy Communion, but he didn't say so. He said the soup was delicious and he drew his brother's attention to the custom there was in the hotel of a porter ringing a bell and walking about with a person's name chalked on a little blackboard on the end of a rod.

'It's a way of paging you,' Father Paul explained. 'Isn't it nicer than bellowing out some fellow's name?' He smiled his easy smile, his eyes beginning to water as a result of the few drinks he'd had. He was beginning to feel the strain: he kept thinking of their mother lying there, of what she'd say if she knew what he'd done, how she'd savagely upbraid him for keeping the fact from Francis. Out of duty and humanity he had returned each year to see her because, after all, you only had the one mother. But he had never cared for her.

Francis went for a walk after dinner. There were young soldiers with what seemed to be toy guns on the streets, but he knew the guns were real. In the shop windows there were television sets for sale, and furniture and clothes, just like anywhere else. There were advertisements for some film or other, two writhing women without a stitch on them, the kind of thing you wouldn't see in Co. Tipperary. 'You want something, sir?' a girl said, smiling at him with broken front teeth. The siren of a police car or an ambulance shrilled urgently near by. He shook his head at the girl. 'No, I don't want anything,' he said, and then realized what she had meant. She was small and very dark, no more than a child. He hurried on, praying for her.

When he returned to the hotel he found his brother in the lounge with other people, two men and two women. Father Paul was ordering a round of drinks and called out to the barman to bring another whisky. 'Ah, no, no,' Francis protested, anxious to go to his room and to think about the day, to read the New Testament and perhaps to write a few more postcards. Music was playing, coming from speakers that could not be seen.

'My brother Francis,' Father Paul said to the people he was with, and the people all gave their names, adding that they came from New York. 'I was telling them about Tipp,' Father Paul said to his brother, offering his packet of cigarettes around.

'You like Jerusalem, Francis?' one of the American women asked him, and he replied that he hadn't been able to take it in yet. Then, feeling that didn't sound enthusiastic enough, he added that being there was the experience of a lifetime.

Father Paul went on talking about Co. Tipperary and then spoke of his parish in San Francisco, the boys' home and the two promising footballers, the plans for the new church. The Americans listened and in a moment the conversation drifted on to the subject of their travels in England, their visit to Istanbul and Athens, an argument they'd had with the Customs at Tel Aviv. 'Well, I think I'll hit the hay,' one of the men announced eventually, standing up.

The others stood up too and so did Francis. Father Paul remained where he was, gesturing again in the direction of the barman. 'Sit down for a nightcap,' he urged his brother.

'Ah, no, no –' Francis began.

'Bring us two more of those,' the priest ordered with a sudden abruptness, and the barman hurried away. 'Listen,' said Father Paul. 'I've something to tell you.'

After dinner, while Francis had been out on his walk, before he'd dropped into conversation with the Americans, Father Paul had said to himself that he couldn't stand the strain. It was the old woman stretched out above the hardware shop, as stiff as a board already, with the little lights burning in her room: he kept seeing all that, as if she wanted him to, as if she was trying to haunt him. Nice as the idea was, he didn't think he could continue with what he'd planned, with waiting until they got up to Galilee.

Francis didn't want to drink any more. He hadn't wanted the whisky his brother had ordered him earlier, nor the one the Americans had ordered for him. He didn't want the one that the barman now brought. He thought he'd just leave it there, hoping his brother wouldn't see it. He lifted the glass to his lips, but he managed not to drink any.

'A bad thing has happened,' Father Paul said.

'Bad? How d'you mean, Paul?'

'Are you ready for it?' He paused. Then he said, 'She died.'

Francis didn't know what he was talking about. He didn't know who was meant to be dead, or why his brother was behaving in an odd manner. He didn't like to think it but he had to: his brother wasn't fully sober.

'Our mother died,' Father Paul said. 'I'm after getting a telegram.'

The huge area that was the lounge of the Plaza Hotel, the endless tables and people sitting at them, the swiftly moving waiters and barmen, seemed suddenly a dream. Francis had a feeling that he was not where he appeared to be, that he wasn't sitting with his brother, who was wiping his lips with a handkerchief. For a moment he appeared in his confusion to be struggling his way up the Via Dolorosa again, and then in the Nativity Boutique.

'Take it easy, boy,' his brother was saying. 'Take a mouthful of whisky.'

Francis didn't obey that injunction. He asked his brother to repeat what he had said, and Father Paul repeated that their mother had died.

Francis closed his eyes and tried as well to shut away the sounds around them. He prayed for the salvation of his mother's soul. 'Blessed Virgin, intercede,' his own voice said in his mind. 'Dear Mary, let her few small sins be forgiven.'

Having rid himself of his secret, Father Paul felt instant relief. With the best of intentions, it had been a foolish idea to think he could maintain the secret until they arrived in a place that was perhaps the most suitable in the world to hear about the death of a person who'd been close to you. He took a gulp of his whisky and wiped his mouth with his handkerchief again. He watched his brother, waiting for his eyes to open.

'When did it happen?' Francis asked eventually.

'Yesterday.'

'And the telegram only came —'

'It came last night, Francis. I wanted to save you the pain.'

'Save me? How could you save me? I sent her a postcard, Paul.'

'Listen to me, Francis —'

'How could you save me the pain?'

'I wanted to tell you when we got up to Galilee.'

Again Francis felt he was caught in the middle of a dream. He couldn't understand his brother: he couldn't understand what he meant by saying a telegram had come last night, why at a moment like this he was talking about Galilee. He didn't know why he was sitting in this noisy place when he should be back in Ireland.

'I fixed the funeral for Monday,' Father Paul said.

Francis nodded, not grasping the significance of this arrangement. 'We'll be back there this time tomorrow,' he said.

'No need for that, Francis. Sunday morning's time enough.'

'But she's dead –'

'We'll be there in time for the funeral.'

'We can't stay here if she's dead.'

It was this, Father Paul realized, he'd been afraid of when he'd argued with himself and made his plan. If he had knocked on Francis's door the night before, Francis would have wanted to return immediately without seeing a single stone of the land he had come so far to be moved by.

'We could go straight up to Galilee in the morning,' Father Paul said quietly. 'You'll find comfort in Galilee, Francis.'

But Francis shook his head. 'I want to be with her,' he said.

Father Paul lit another cigarette. He nodded at a hovering waiter, indicating his need of another drink. He said to himself that he must keep his cool, an expression he was fond of.

'Take it easy, Francis,' he said.

'Is there a plane out in the morning? Can we make arrangements now?' He looked about him as if for a member of the hotel staff who might be helpful.

'No good'll be done by tearing off home, Francis. What's wrong with Sunday?'

'I want to be with her.'

Anger swelled within Father Paul. If he began to argue his words would become slurred: he knew that from experience. He must keep his cool and speak slowly and clearly, making a few simple points. It was typical of her, he thought, to die inconveniently.

'You've come all this way,' he said as slowly as he could without sounding peculiar. 'Why cut it any shorter than we need? We'll be losing a week anyway. She wouldn't want us to go back.'

'I think she would.'

He was right in that. Her possessiveness in her lifetime would have reached out across a dozen continents for Francis. She'd known what she was doing by dying when she had.

'I shouldn't have come,' Francis said. 'She didn't want me to come.'

'You're thirty-seven years of age, Francis.'

'I did wrong to come.'

'You did no such thing.'

The time he'd taken her to Rome she'd been difficult for the whole week, complaining about the food, saying everywhere was dirty. Whenever he'd spent anything she'd disapproved. All his life, Father Paul felt, he'd done his best for her. He had told her before anyone else when he'd decided to enter the priesthood, certain that she'd be pleased. 'I thought you'd take over the shop,' she'd said instead.

'What difference could it make to wait, Francis?'

'There's nothing to wait for.'

As long as he lived Francis knew he would never forgive himself. As long as he lived he would say to himself that he hadn't been able to wait a few years, until she'd passed quietly on. He might even have been in the room with her when it happened.

'It was a terrible thing not to tell me,' he said. 'I sat down and wrote her a postcard, Paul. I bought her a plate.'

'So you said.'

'You're drinking too much of that whisky.'

'Now, Francis, don't be silly.'

'You're half drunk and she's lying there.'

'She can't be brought back no matter what we do.'

'She never hurt anyone,' Francis said.

Father Paul didn't deny that, although it wasn't true. She had hurt their sister Kitty, constantly reproaching her for marrying the man she had, long after Kitty was aware she'd made a mistake. She'd driven Edna to Canada after Edna, still unmarried, had had a miscarriage that only the family knew about. She had made a shadow out of Francis although Francis didn't know it. Failing to hold on to her other children, she had grasped her youngest to her, as if she had borne him to destroy him.

'It'll be you who'll say a Mass for her?' Francis said.

'Yes, of course it will.'

'You should have told me.'

Francis realized why, all day, he'd been disappointed. From the moment when the hired car had pulled into the lay-by and his brother had pointed across the valley at the Garden of Gethsemane he'd been disappointed and had not admitted it. He'd been disappointed in the Via Dolorosa and in the Church of the Holy Sepulchre and in Bethlehem. He remembered the bespectacled man who'd kept saying that you couldn't be sure about anything. All the people with cameras made it impossible to think, all the jostling and pushing was distracting. When he'd said there'd been too much to take in he'd meant something different.

'Her death got in the way,' he said.

'What d'you mean, Francis?'

'It didn't feel like Jerusalem, it didn't feel like Bethlehem.'

'But it is, Francis, it is.'

'There are soldiers with guns all over the place. And a girl came up to me on the street. There was that man with a bit of the Cross. There's you, drinking and smoking in this place –'

'Now, listen to me, Francis –'

'Nazareth would be a disappointment. And the Sea of Galilee. And the Church of the Loaves and Fishes.' His voice had risen. He lowered it again. 'I couldn't believe in the Stations this morning. I couldn't see it happening the way I do at home.'

'That's nothing to do with her death, Francis. You've got a bit of jet-lag, you'll settle yourself up in Galilee. There's an atmosphere in Galilee that nobody misses.'

'I'm not going near Galilee.' He struck the surface of the table, and Father Paul told him to contain himself. People turned their heads, aware that anger had erupted in the pale-faced man with the priest.

'Quieten up,' Father Paul commanded sharply, but Francis didn't.

'She knew I'd be better at home,' he shouted, his voice shrill and reedy. 'She knew I was making a fool of myself, a man out of a shop trying to be big –'

'Will you keep your voice down? Of course you're not making a fool of yourself.'

'Will you find out about planes tomorrow morning?'

Father Paul sat for a moment longer, not saying anything, hoping his brother would say he was sorry. Naturally it was a shock, naturally he'd be emotional and feel guilty, in a moment it would be better. But it wasn't, and Francis didn't say he was sorry. Instead he began to weep.

'Let's go up to your room,' Father Paul said, 'and I'll fix about the plane.'

Francis nodded but did not move. His sobbing ceased, and then he said, 'I'll always hate the Holy Land now.'

'No need for that, Francis.'

But Francis felt there was and he felt he would hate, as well, the brother he had admired for as long as he could remember. In the lounge of the Plaza Hotel he felt mockery surfacing everywhere. His brother's deceit, and the endless whisky in his brother's glass, and his casualness after a death seemed like the scorning of a Church which honoured so steadfastly the mother of its founder. Vivid in his mind, his own mother's eyes reminded him that they'd told him he was making a mistake, and upbraided him for not heeding her. Of course there was mockery everywhere, in the splinter of wood beneath plastic, and in the soldiers with guns that were not toys, and the writhing nakedness in the Holy City. He'd become part of it himself, sending postcards to the dead. Not speaking again to his brother, he went to his room to pray.

'Eight a.m., sir,' the girl at the reception desk said, and Father Paul asked that arrangements should be made to book two seats on the plane, explaining that it was an emergency, that a death had occurred. 'It will be all right, sir,' the girl promised.

He went slowly downstairs to the bar. He sat in a corner and lit a cigarette and ordered two whiskys and ice, as if expecting a companion. He drank them both himself and ordered more. Francis would return to Co. Tipperary and after the funeral he would take up again the life she had ordained for him. In his brown cotton coat he would serve customers with nails and hinges and wire. He would regularly go to Mass and to Confession and to Men's Confraternity. He would sit alone in the lace-curtained sitting-room, lonely for the woman who had made him what he was, married forever to her memory.

Father Paul lit a fresh cigarette from the butt of the last one. He continued to order whisky in two glasses. Already he could sense the hatred that Francis had earlier felt taking root in himself. He wondered if he would ever again return in July to Co. Tipperary, and imagined he would not.

At midnight he rose to make the journey to bed and found himself unsteady on his feet. People looked at him, thinking it disgraceful for a priest to be drunk in Jerusalem, with cigarette ash all over his clerical clothes.

Lovers of Their Time

Looking back on it, it seemed to have to do with that particular decade in London. Could it have happened, he wondered, at any other time except the 1960s? That feeling was intensified, perhaps, because the whole thing had begun on New Year's Day, 1963, long before that day became a bank holiday in England. 'That'll be two and nine,' she'd said, smiling at him across her counter, handing him toothpaste and emery boards in a bag. 'Colgate's, remember,' his wife had called out as he was leaving the flat. 'The last stuff we had tasted awful.'

His name was Norman Britt. It said so on a small plastic name-plate in front of his position in the travel agency where he worked, Travel-Wide as it was called. *Marie* a badge on her light-blue shop-coat announced. His wife, who worked at home, assembling jewellery for a firm that paid her on a production basis, was called Hilda.

Green's the Chemist's and Travel-Wide were in Vincent Street, a street that was equidistant from Paddington Station and Edgware Road. The flat where Hilda worked all day was in Putney. Marie lived in Reading with her mother and her mother's friend Mrs Druk, both of them widows. She caught the 8.05 every morning to Paddington and usually the 6.30 back.

He was forty in 1963, as Hilda was; Marie was twenty-eight. He was tall and thin, with a David Niven moustache. Hilda was thin also, her dark hair beginning to grey, her sharply featured face pale. Marie was well-covered, carefully made up, her hair dyed blonde. She smiled a lot, a slack, half-crooked smile that made her eyes screw up and twinkle; she exuded laziness and generosity. She and her friend Mavis went dancing a lot in Reading and had a sizeable collection of men friends. 'Fellas' they called them.

Buying things from her now and again in Green's the Chemist's Norman had come to the conclusion that she was of a tartish disposition, and imagined that if ever he sat with her over a drink in the nearby Drummer Boy the occasion could easily lead to a hug on the street afterwards. He imagined her coral-coloured lips, like two tiny sausages, only softer, pressed upon his moustache and his abbreviated mouth. He imagined the warmth of her hand in his. For all that, she was a little outside reality: she was there to desire, to glow erotically in the heady atmosphere of the Drummer Boy, to light cigarettes for in a fantasy.

'Isn't it cold?' he said as she handed him the emery boards and the toothpaste.

'Shocking,' she agreed, and hesitated, clearly wanting to say something else. 'You're in that Travel-Wide,' she added in the end. 'Me and my friend want to go to Spain this year.'

'It's very popular. The Costa Brava?'

'That's right.' She handed him threepence change. 'In May.'

'Not too hot on the Costa in May. If you need any help –'

'Just the bookings.'

'I'd be happy to make them for you. Look in any time. Britt the name is. I'm on the counter.'

'If I may, Mr Britt. I could slip out maybe at four, or roundabout.'

'Today, you mean?'

'We want to fix it up.'

'Naturally. I'll keep an eye out for you.'

It was hard not to call her madam or miss, the way he'd normally do. He had heard himself saying that he'd be happy to make the bookings for her, knowing that that was business jargon, knowing that the unfussy voice he'd used was a business one also. Her friend was a man, he supposed, some snazzy tough in a car. 'See you later then,' he said, but already she was serving another customer, advising about lipstick refills.

She didn't appear in Travel-Wide at four o'clock; she hadn't come when the doors closed at five-thirty. He was aware of a sense of disappointment, combined with one of anticipation: for if she'd come at four, he reflected as he left the travel agency, their bit of business would be in the past rather than the future. She'd look in some other time and he'd just have to trust to luck that if he happened to be busy with another customer she'd be able to wait. There'd be a further occasion, when she called to collect the tickets themselves.

'Ever so sorry,' she said on the street, her voice coming from behind him. 'Couldn't get away, Mr Britt.'

He turned and smiled at her, feeling the movement of his moustache as he parted his lips. He knew only too well, he said. 'Some other time then?'

'Maybe tomorrow. Maybe lunchtime.'

'I'm off myself from twelve to one. Look, you wouldn't fancy a drink? I could advise you just as easily over a drink.'

'Oh, you wouldn't have the time. No, I mustn't take advantage –'

'You're not at all. If you've got ten minutes?'

'Well, it's awfully good of you, Mr Britt. But I really feel I'm taking advantage, I really do.'

'A New Year's drink.'

He pushed open the doors of the saloon bar of the Drummer Boy, a place he didn't often enter except for office drinks at Christmas or when someone leaving the agency was being given a send-off. Ron Stocks and Mr Blackstaffe were usually there in the evenings: he hoped they'd be there now to see him in the company of the girl from Green's the Chemist's. 'What would you like?' he asked her.

'Gin and peppermint's my poison, only honestly I should pay. No, let me ask you –'

'I wouldn't dream of it. We can sit over there, look.'

The Drummer Boy, so early in the evening, wasn't full. By six o'clock the advertising executives from the firm of Dalton, Dure and Higgins, just round the corner, would have arrived, and the architects from Frine and Knight. Now there was only Mrs Gregan, old and alcoholic, known to everyone, and a man called Bert, with his poodle, Jimmy. It was disappointing that Ron Stocks and Mr Blackstaffe weren't there.

'You were here lunchtime Christmas Eve,' she said.

'Yes, I was.' He paused, placing her gin and peppermint on a cardboard mat that advertised Guinness. 'I saw you too.'

He drank some of his Double Diamond and carefully wiped the traces of foam from his moustache. He realized now that it would, of course, be quite impossible to give her a hug on the street outside. That had been just imagination, wishful thinking as his mother would have said. And yet he knew that when he arrived home twenty-five or so minutes late he would not tell Hilda that he'd been advising an assistant from Green's the Chemist's about a holiday on the Costa Brava. He wouldn't even say he'd been in the Drummer Boy. He'd say Blackstaffe had kept everyone late, going through the new package that Eurotours were offering in Germany and Luxembourg this summer. Hilda wouldn't in a million years suspect that he'd been sitting in a public house with a younger woman who was quite an eyeful. As a kind of joke, she quite regularly suggested that his sexual drive left something to be desired.

'We were thinking about the last two weeks in May,' Marie said. 'It's when Mavis can get off too.'

'Mavis?'

'My friend, Mr Britt.'

Hilda was watching *Z-Cars* in the sitting-room, drinking V.P. wine. His stuff was in the oven, she told him. 'Thanks,' he said.

Sometimes she was out when he returned in the evenings. She went round to friends, a Mr and Mrs Fowler, with whom she drank V.P. and played bridge. On other occasions she went to the Club, which was a place with a licence, for card-players and billiard-players. She quite liked her social life, but always said beforehand when she'd be out and always made arrangements about leaving food in the oven. Often in the daytime she'd go and make jewellery with Violet Parkes, who also went in for this occupation; and often Violet Parkes spent the day with Hilda. The jewellery-making consisted for the most part of threading plastic beads on to a string or arranging plastic pieces in the settings provided. Hilda was quick at it and earned more than she would have if she went out every day, saving the fares for a start. She was better at it than Violet Parkes.

'All right then?' she said when he carried his tray of food into the sitting-room and sat down in front of the television set. 'Want some V.P., eh?'

Her eyes continued to watch the figures on the screen as she spoke. He knew she'd prefer to be in the Fowlers' house or at the Club, although now that they'd acquired a TV set the evenings passed easier when they were alone together.

'No, thanks,' he said in reply to her offer of wine and he began to eat something that appeared to be a rissole. There were two of them, round and brown in a tin-foil container that also contained gravy. He hoped she wasn't going to be demanding in their bedroom. He eyed her, for sometimes he could tell.

'Hi,' she said, noticing the glance. 'Feeling fruity, dear?' She laughed and winked, her suggestive voice seeming odd as it issued from her thin, rather dried-up face. She was always saying things like that, for no reason that Norman could see, always talking about feeling fruity or saying she could see he was keen when he wasn't in the least. Norman considered that she was unduly demanding and often wondered what it would be like to be married to someone who was not. Now and again, fatigued after the intensity of her love-making, he lay staring at the darkness, wondering if her bedroom appetites were related in some way to the fact that she was unable to bear children, if her abandon reflected a maternal frustration. Earlier in their married life she'd gone out every day to an office where she'd been a filing clerk; in the evenings they'd often gone to the cinema.

He lay that night, after she'd gone to sleep, listening to her heavy breathing, thinking of the girl in Green's the Chemist's. He went through the whole day in his mind, seeing himself leaving the flat in Putney, hearing Hilda calling out about the emery boards and the toothpaste, seeing himself reading the *Daily Telegraph* in the Tube. Slowly he went through the morning, deliciously anticipating the moment when she handed him his change. With her smile mistily hovering, he recalled the questions and demands of a number of the morning's customers. 'Fix us up Newcastle and back?' a couple inquired. 'Mid-week's cheaper, is it?' A man with a squashed-up face wanted a week in Holland for himself and his sister and his sister's husband. A woman asked about Greece, another about cruises on the Nile, a third about the Scilly Isles. Then he placed the Closed sign in front of his position at the counter and went out to have lunch in Bette's Sandwiches off the Edgware Road. 'Packet of emery boards,' he said again in Green's the Chemist's, 'and a small Colgate's.' After that there was the conversation they'd had, and then the afternoon with her smile still mistily hovering, as in fact it had, and then her presence beside him in the Drummer Boy. Endlessly she lifted the glass of gin and peppermint to her lips, endlessly she smiled. When he slept he dreamed of her. They were walking in Hyde Park and her shoe fell off. 'I could tell you were a deep one,' she said, and the next thing was Hilda was having one of her early-morning appetites.

'I don't know what it is about that chap,' Marie confided to Mavis. 'Something, though.'

'Married, is he?'

'Oh, he would be, chap like that.'

'Now, you be careful, girl.'

'He has Sinatra's eyes. That blue, you know.'

'Now, Marie –'

'I like an older fella. He's got a nice moustache.'

'So's that fella in the International.'

'Wet behind the ears. And my God, his dandruff!'

They left the train together and parted on the platform, Marie making for the Underground, Mavis hurrying for a bus. It was quite convenient, really, living in Reading and travelling to Paddington every day. It was only half an hour and chatting on the journey passed the time. They didn't travel back together in the evenings because Mavis nearly always did an hour's overtime. She was a computer programmer.

'I talked to Mavis. It's OK about the insurance,' Marie said in Travel-Wide at half past eleven that morning, having slipped out when the shop seemed slack. There'd been some details about insurance which he'd raised the evening before. He always advised insurance, but he'd quite understood when she'd made the point that she'd better discuss the matter with her friend before committing herself to the extra expenditure.

'So I'll go ahead and book you,' he said. 'There'll just be the deposit.'

Mavis wrote the cheque. She pushed the pink slip across the counter to him. 'Payable to Travel-Wide.'

'That's quite correct.' He glanced at it and wrote her a receipt. He said: 'I looked out another brochure or two. I'd quite like to go through them with you. So you can explain what's what to your friend.'

'Oh, that's very nice, Mr Britt. But I got to get back. I mean, I shouldn't be out in the middle of the morning.'

'Any chance of lunchtime?'

His suavity astounded him. He thought of Hilda, deftly working at her jewellery, stringing orange and yellow beads, listening to the Jimmy Young programme.

'Lunchtime, Mr Britt?'

'We'd maybe talk about the brochures.'

He fancied her, she said to herself. He was making a pass, talking about brochures and lunchtime. Well, she wasn't disagreeable. She'd meant what she'd said to Mavis: she liked an older fella and she liked his moustache, so smooth it looked as if he put something on it. She liked the name Norman.

'All right then,' she said.

He couldn't suggest Bette's Sandwiches because you stood up at a shelf on the wall and ate the sandwiches off a cardboard plate.

'We could go to the Drummer Boy,' he suggested instead. 'I'm off at twelve-fifteen.'

'Say half past, Mr Britt.'

'I'll be there with the brochures.'

Again he thought of Hilda. He thought of her wiry, pasty limbs and the way she had of snorting. Sometimes when they were watching the television she'd suddenly want to sit on his knee. She'd get worse as she grew older; she'd get scrawnier; her hair, already coarse, would get dry and grey. He enjoyed the evenings when she went out to the Club or to her friends the Fowlers. And yet he wasn't being fair because in very many ways she did her best. It was just that you didn't always feel like having someone on your knee after a day's work.

'Same?' he said in the Drummer Boy.

'Yes please, Mr Britt.' She'd meant to say that the drinks were definitely on her, after what he'd spent last night. But in her flurry she forgot. She picked up the brochures he'd left on the seat beside her. She pretended to read one, but all the time she was watching him as he stood by the bar. He smiled as he turned and came back with their drinks. He said something about it being a nice way to do business. He was drinking gin and peppermint himself.

'I meant to pay for the drinks. I meant to say I would. I'm sorry, Mr Britt.'

'Norman my name is.' He surprised himself again by the ease with which he was managing the situation. They'd have their drinks and then he'd suggest some of the shepherd's pie, or a ham-and-salad roll if she'd prefer it. He'd buy her another gin and peppermint to get her going. Eighteen years ago he used to buy Hilda further glasses of V.P. wine with the same thought in mind.

They finished with the brochures. She told him she lived in Reading; she talked about the town. She mentioned her mother and her mother's friend Mrs Druk, who lived with them, and Mavis. She told him a lot about Mavis. No man was mentioned, no boyfriend or fiancé.

'Honestly,' she said, 'I'm not hungry.' She couldn't have touched a thing. She just wanted to go on drinking gin with him. She wanted to get slightly squiffy, a thing she'd never done before in the middle of the day. She wanted to put her arm through his.

'It's been nice meeting you,' he said.

'A bit of luck.'

'I think so too, Marie.' He ran his forefinger between the bones on the back of her hand, so gently that it made her want to shiver. She didn't take her hand away, and when she continued not to he took her hand in his.

After that they had lunch together every day, always in the Drummer Boy. People saw them, Ron Stocks and Mr Blackstaffe from Travel-Wide, Mr Fineman, the pharmacist from Green's the Chemist's. Other people from the travel agency and from the chemist's saw them walking about the streets, usually hand in hand. They would look together into the shop windows of Edgware Road, drawn particularly to an antique shop full of brass. In the evenings he would walk with her to Paddington Station and have a drink in one of the bars. They'd embrace on the platform, as other people did.

Mavis continued to disapprove; Marie's mother and Mrs Druk remained ignorant of the affair. The holiday on the Costa Brava that May was not a success because all the time Marie kept wishing Norman Britt was with her. Occasionally, while Mavis read magazines on the beach, Marie wept and Mavis pretended not to notice. She was furious because Marie's low spirits meant that it was impossible for them to get to know fellas. For months they'd been looking forward to the holiday and now, just because of a clerk in a travel agency, it was a flop. 'I'm sorry, dear,' Marie kept saying, trying to smile; but when they returned to London the friendship declined. 'You're making a fool of yourself,' Mavis pronounced harshly, 'and it's dead boring having to hear about it.' After that they ceased to travel together in the mornings.

The affair remained unconsummated. In the hour and a quarter allotted to each of them for lunch there was nowhere they might have gone to let their passion for one another run its course. Everywhere was public: Travel-Wide and the chemist's shop, the Drummer Boy, the streets they walked. Neither could easily spend a night away from home. Her mother and Mrs Druk would guess that something untoward was in the air; Hilda, deprived of her bedroom mating, would no longer be nonchalant in front of the TV. It would all come out if they were rash, and they sensed some danger in that.

'Oh, darling,' she whispered one October evening at Paddington, huddling herself against him. It was foggy and cold. The fog was in her pale hair, tiny droplets that only he, being close to her, could see. People hurried through the lit-up station, weary faces anxious to be home.

'I know,' he said, feeling as inadequate as he always did at the station.

'I lie awake and think of you,' she whispered.

'You've made me live,' he whispered back.

'And you me. Oh, God, and you me.' She was gone before she finished speaking, swinging into the train as it moved away, her bulky red handbag the last thing he saw. It would be eighteen hours before they'd meet again.

He turned his back on her train and slowly made his way through the crowds, his reluctance to start the journey back to the flat in Putney seeming physical, like a pain, inside him. 'Oh, for God's sake!' a woman cried angrily at him, for he had been in her way and had moved in the same direction as she had in seeking to avoid her, causing a second collision. She dropped magazines on to the platform and he helped her to pick them up, vainly apologizing.

It was then, walking away from this woman, that he saw the sign. *Hotel Entrance* it said in red neon letters, beyond the station's main bookstall. It was the back of the Great Western Royal, a short-cut to its comforts for train travellers at the end of their journey. If only, he thought, they could share a room there. If only for one single night they were granted the privilege of being man and wife. People passed through the swing-doors beneath the glowing red sign, people hurrying, with newspapers or suitcases. Without quite knowing why, he passed through the swing-doors himself.

He walked up two brief flights of steps, through another set of doors, and paused in the enormous hall of the Great Western Royal Hotel. Ahead of him, to the left, was the long, curved reception counter and, to the right, the porter's desk. Small tables and armchairs were everywhere; it was carpeted underfoot. There were signs to lifts and to the bar and the restaurant. The stairway, gently rising to his left, was gracious, carpeted also.

They would sit for a moment in this hall, he imagined, as other people were sitting now, a few with drinks, others with pots of tea and plates half empty of assorted biscuits. He stood for a moment, watching these people, and then, as though he possessed a room in the hotel, he mounted the stairs, saying to himself that it must somehow be possible, that surely they could share a single night in the splendour of this place. There was a landing, made into a lounge, with armchairs and tables, as in the hall below. People conversed quietly; a foreign waiter, elderly and limping, collected silver-plated teapots; a Pekinese dog slept on a woman's lap.

The floor above was different. It was a long, wide corridor with bedroom doors on either side of it. Other corridors, exactly similar, led off it. Chambermaids passed him with lowered eyes; someone gently laughed in a room marked *Staff Only*; a waiter wheeled a trolley containing covered dishes, and a bottle of wine wrapped in a napkin. *Bathroom* a sign said, and he looked in, just to see what a bathroom in the Great Western Royal Hotel would be like. 'My God!' he whispered, possessed immediately with the idea that was, for him, to make the decade of the 1960s different. Looking back on it, he was for ever after unable to recall the first moment he beheld the bathroom on the second floor without experiencing the shiver of pleasure he'd experienced at the time. Slowly he entered. He locked the door and slowly sat down on the edge of the bath. The place was huge, as the bath itself was, like somewhere in a palace. The walls were marble, white veined delicately with grey. Two monstrous brass taps, the biggest bath taps he'd ever in his life seen, seemed to know already that he and Marie would come to the bathroom. They seemed almost to wink an invitation to him, to tell him that the bathroom was a comfortable place and not often in use since private bathrooms were now attached to most of the bedrooms. Sitting in his mackintosh coat on the edge of the bath, he wondered what Hilda would say if she could see him now.

He suggested it to Marie in the Drummer Boy. He led up to it slowly, describing the interior of the Great Western Royal Hotel and how he had wandered about it because he hadn't wanted to go home. 'Actually,' he said, 'I ended up in a bathroom.'

'You mean the toilet, dear? Taken short –'

'No, not the toilet. A bathroom on the second floor. Done out in marble, as a matter of fact.'

She replied that honestly he was a one, to go into a bathroom like that when he wasn't even staying in the place! He said:

'What I mean, Marie, it's somewhere we could go.'

'Go, dear?'

'It's empty half the time. Nearly all the time it must be. I mean, we could be there now. This minute if we wanted to.'

'But we're having our lunch, Norman.'

'That's what I mean. We could even be having it there.'

From the saloon bar's juke-box a lugubrious voice pleaded for a hand to be held. *Take my hand,* sang Elvis Presley, *take my whole life too.* The advertising executives from Dalton, Dure and Higgins were loudly talking about their hopes of gaining the Canadian Pacific account. Less noisily the architects from Frine and Knight complained about local planning regulations.

'In a bathroom, Norman? But we couldn't just go into a bathroom.'

'Why not?'

'Well, we couldn't. I mean, we *couldn't.*'

'What I'm saying is we could.'

'I want to marry you, Norman. I want us to be together. I don't want just going to a bathroom in some hotel.'

'I know; I want to marry you too. But we've got to work it out. You know we've got to work it out, Marie – getting married.'

'Yes, I know.'

It was a familiar topic of conversation between them. They took it for granted that one day, somehow, they would be married. They had talked about Hilda. He'd described Hilda to her, he'd drawn a picture in Marie's mind of Hilda bent over her jewellery-making in a Putney flat, or going out to drink V.P. with the Fowlers or at the Club. He hadn't presented a flattering picture of his wife, and when Marie had quite timidly said that she didn't much care for the sound of her he had agreed that naturally she wouldn't. The only aspect of Hilda he didn't touch upon was her bedroom appetite, night starvation as he privately dubbed it. He didn't mention it because he guessed it might be upsetting.

What they had to work out where Hilda was concerned were the economics of the matter. He would never, at Travel-Wide or anywhere else, earn a great deal of money. Familiar with Hilda's nature, he knew that as soon as a divorce was mooted she'd set out to claim as much alimony as she possibly could, which by law he would have to pay. She would state that she only made jewellery for pin-money and increasingly found it difficult to do so due to a developing tendency towards chilblains or arthritis, anything she could think of. She would hate him for rejecting her, for depriving her of a tame companion. Her own resentment at not being able to have children would somehow latch on to his unfaithfulness: she would see a pattern which wasn't really there, bitterness would come into her eyes.

Marie had said that she wanted to give him the children he had never had. She wanted to have children at once and she knew she could. He knew it too: having children was part of her, you'd only to look at her. Yet that would mean she'd have to give up her job, which she wanted to do when she married anyway, which in turn would mean that all three of them would have to subsist on his meagre salary. And not just all three, the children also.

It was a riddle that mocked him: he could find no answer, and yet he believed that the more he and Marie were together, the more they talked to one another and continued to be in love, the more chance there was of suddenly hitting upon a solution. Not that Marie always listened when he went on about it. She agreed they had to solve their problem, but now and again just pretended it wasn't there. She liked to forget about the existence of Hilda. For an hour or so when she was with him she liked to assume that quite soon, in July or even June, they'd be married. He always brought her back to earth.

'Look, let's just have a drink in the hotel,' he urged. 'Tonight, before the train. Instead of having one in the buffet.'

'But it's a hotel, Norman. I mean, it's for people to stay in –'

'Anyone can go into a hotel for a drink.'

That evening, after their drink in the hotel bar, he led her to the first-floor landing that was also a lounge. It was warm in the hotel. She said she'd like to sink down into one of the armchairs and fall asleep. He laughed at that; he didn't suggest an excursion to the bathroom, sensing that he shouldn't rush things. He saw her on to her train, abandoning her to her mother and Mrs Druk and Mavis. He knew that all during the journey she would be mulling over the splendours of the Great Western Royal.

December came. It was no longer foggy, but the weather was colder, with an icy wind. Every evening, before her train, they had their drink in the hotel. 'I'd love to show you that bathroom,' he said once. 'Just for fun.' He hadn't been pressing it in the least; it was the first time he'd mentioned the bathroom since he'd mentioned it originally. She giggled and said he was terrible. She said she'd miss her train if she went looking at bathrooms, but he said there'd easily be time. 'Gosh!' she whispered, standing in the doorway, looking in. He put his arm around her shoulders and drew her inside, fearful in case a chambermaid should see them loitering there. He locked the door and kissed her. In almost twelve months it was their first embrace in private.

They went to the bathroom during the lunch hour on New Year's Day, and he felt it was right that they should celebrate in this way the anniversary of their first real meeting. His early impression of her, that she was of a tartish disposition, had long since been dispelled. Voluptuous she might seem to the eye, but beneath that misleading surface she was prim and proper. It was odd that Hilda, who looked dried-up and wholly uninterested in the sensual life, should also belie her appearance. 'I've never done it before,' Marie confessed in the bathroom, and he loved her the more for that. He loved her simplicity in this matter, her desire to remain a virgin until her wedding. But since she repeatedly swore that she could marry no one else, their anticipating of their wedding-night did not matter. 'Oh, God, I love you,' she whispered, naked for the first time in the bathroom. 'Oh, Norman, you're so good to me.'

After that it became a regular thing. He would saunter from the hotel bar, across the huge entrance lounge, and take a lift to the second floor. Five minutes later she would follow, with a towel brought specially from Reading in her handbag. In the bathroom they always whispered, and would sit together in a warm bath after their love-making, still murmuring about the future, holding hands beneath the surface of the water. No one ever rapped on the door to ask what was going on in there. No one ever questioned them as they returned, separately, to the bar, with the towel they'd shared damping her compact and her handkerchief.

Years instead of months began to go by. On the juke-box in the Drummer Boy the voice of Elvis Presley was no longer heard. '*Why she had to go I don't know*,' sang the Beatles, '*she didn't say ... I believe in yesterday*.' And Eleanor Rigby entered people's lives, and Sergeant Pepper with her. The fantasies of secret agents, more fantastic than ever before, filled the screens of London's cinemas. Carnaby Street, like a jolly trash-can, overflowed with noise and colour. And in the bathroom of the Great Western Royal Hotel the love affair of Norman Britt and Marie was touched with the same preposterousness. They ate sandwiches in the bathroom; they drank wine. He whispered to her of the faraway places he knew about but had never been to: the Bahamas, Brazil, Peru, Seville at Easter, the Greek islands, the Nile, Shiraz, Persepolis, the Rocky Mountains. They should have been saving their money, not spending it on gin and peppermint in the bar of the hotel and in the Drummer Boy. They should have been racking their brains to find a solution to the problem of Hilda, but it was nicer to pretend that one day they would walk together in Venice or Tuscany. It was all so different from the activities that began with Hilda's bedroom appetites, and it was different from the coarseness that invariably surfaced when Mr Blackstaffe got going in the Drummer Boy on an evening when a Travel-Wide employee was being given a send-off. Mr Blackstaffe's great joke on such occasions was that he liked to have sexual intercourse with his wife at night and that she preferred the conjunction in the mornings. He was always going on about how difficult it was in the mornings, what with the children liable to interrupt you, and he usually went into details about certain other, more intimate preferences of his wife's. He had a powerful, waxy guffaw, which he brought regularly into play when he was engaged in this kind of conversation, allying it with a nudging motion of the elbow. Once his wife actually turned up in the Drummer Boy and Norman found it embarrassing even to look at her, knowing as he did so much about her private life. She was a stout middle-aged woman with decorated spectacles: her appearance, too, apparently belied much.

In the bathroom all such considerations, disliked equally by Norman Britt and Marie, were left behind. Romance ruled their brief sojourns, and love sanctified – or so they believed – the passion of their physical intimacy. Love excused their eccentricity, for only love could have found in them a willingness to engage in the deception of a hotel and the courage that went with it: that they believed most of all.

But afterwards, selling tickets to other people or putting Marie on her evening train, Norman sometimes felt depressed. And then gradually, as more time passed, the depression increased and intensified. 'I'm so sad,' he whispered in the bathroom once, 'when I'm not with you. I don't think I can stand it.' She dried herself on the towel brought specially from Reading in her large red handbag. 'You'll have to tell her,' she said, with an edge in her voice that hadn't ever been there before. 'I don't want to leave having babies too late.' She wasn't twenty-eight any more; she was thirty-one. 'I mean, it isn't fair on me,' she said.

He knew it wasn't fair on her, but going over the whole thing yet again in Travel-Wide that afternoon he also knew that poverty would destroy them. He'd never earn much more than he earned now. The babies Marie wanted, and which he wanted too, would soak up what there was like blotting-paper; they'd probably have to look for council accommodation. It made him weary to think about it, it gave him a headache. But he knew she was right: they couldn't go on for ever, living off a passing idyll, in the bathroom of a hotel. He even thought, quite seriously for a moment, of causing Hilda's death.

Instead he told her the truth, one Thursday evening after she'd been watching *The Avengers* on television. He just told her he'd met someone, a girl called Marie, he said, whom he had fallen in love with and wished to marry. 'I was hoping we could have a divorce,' he said.

Hilda turned the sound on the television set down without in any way dimming the picture, which she continued to watch. Her face did not register the hatred he had imagined in it when he rejected her; nor did bitterness suddenly enter her eyes. Instead she shook her head at him, and poured herself some more V.P. She said:

'You've gone barmy, Norman.'

'You can think that if you like.'

'Wherever'd you meet a girl, for God's sake?'

'At work. She's there in Vincent Street. In a shop.'

'And what's she think of you, may I ask?'

'She's in love with me, Hilda.'

She laughed. She told him to pull the other one, adding that it had bells on it.

'Hilda, I'm not making this up. I'm telling you the truth.'

She smiled into her V.P. She watched the screen for a moment, then she said:

'And how long's this charming stuff been going on, may I inquire?'

He didn't want to say for years. Vaguely, he said it had been going on for just a while.

'You're out of your tiny, Norman. Just because you fancy some piece in a shop doesn't mean you go getting hot under the collar. You're no tomcat, you know, old boy.'

'I didn't say I was.'

'You're no sexual mechanic.'

'Hilda –'

'All chaps fancy things in shops: didn't your mother tell you that? D'you think I haven't fancied stuff myself, the chap who came to do the blinds, that randy little postman with his rugby songs?'

'I'm telling you I want a divorce, Hilda.'

She laughed. She drank more V.P. wine. 'You're up a gum tree,' she said, and laughed again.

'Hilda –'

'Oh, for God's sake!' All of a sudden she was angry, but more, he felt, because he was going on, not because of what he was actually demanding. She thought him ridiculous and said so. And then she added all the things he'd thought himself: that people like them didn't get divorces, that unless his girlfriend was well-heeled the whole thing would be a sheer bloody nonsense, with bloody solicitors the only ones to benefit. 'They'll send you to the cleaners, your bloody solicitors will,' she loudly pointed out, anger still trembling in her voice. 'You'd be paying them back for years.'

'I don't care,' he began, although he did. 'I don't care about anything except –'

'Of course you do, you damn fool.'

'Hilda –'

'Look, get over her. Take her into a park after dark or something. It'll make no odds to you and me.'

She turned the sound on the television up and quite quickly finished the V.P. wine. Afterwards, in their bedroom, she turned to him with an excitement that was greater than usual. 'God, that switched me on,' she whispered in the darkness, gripping him with her limbs. 'The stuff we were talking about, that girl.' When she'd finished her love-making she said, 'I had it with that postman, you know. Swear to God. In the kitchen. And since we're on the subject, Fowler looks in here the odd time.'

He lay beside her in silence, not knowing whether or not to believe what she was saying. It seemed at first that she was keeping her end up because he'd mentioned Marie, but then he wasn't so sure. 'We had a foursome once,' she said, 'the Fowlers and me and a chap that used to be in the Club.'

She began to stroke his face with her fingers, the way he hated. She always seemed to think that if she stroked his face it would excite him. She said, 'Tell me more about this piece you fancy.'

He told her to keep her quiet and to make her stop stroking his face. It didn't seem to matter now if he told her how long it had been going on, not since she'd made her revelations about Fowler and the postman. He even enjoyed telling her, about the New Year's Day when he'd bought the emery boards and the Colgate's, and how he'd got to know Marie because she and Mavis were booking a holiday on the Costa Brava.

'But you've never actually?'

'Yes, we have.'

'For God's sake where? Doorways or something? In the park?'

'We go to a hotel.'

'You old devil!'

'Listen, Hilda –'

'For God's sake go on, love. Tell me about it.'

He told her about the bathroom and she kept asking him questions, making him tell her details, asking him to describe Marie to her. Dawn was breaking when they finished talking.

'Forget about the divorce stuff,' she said quite casually at breakfast. 'I wouldn't want to hear no more of that. I wouldn't want you ruined for my sake, dear.'

He didn't want to see Marie that day, although he had to because it was arranged. In any case she knew he'd been going to tell his wife the night before; she'd want to hear the outcome.

'Well?' she said in the Drummer Boy.

He shrugged. He shook his head. He said:

'I told her.'

'And what'd she say, Norman? What'd Hilda say?'

'She said I was barmy to be talking about divorce. She said what I said to you: that we wouldn't manage with the alimony.'

They sat in silence. Eventually Marie said:

'Then can't you leave her? Can't you just not go back? We could get a flat somewhere. We could put off kiddies, darling. Just walk out, couldn't you?'

'They'd find us. They'd make me pay.'

'We could try it. If I keep on working you could pay what they want.'

'It'll never pan out, Marie.'

'Oh, darling, just walk away from her.'

Which is what, to Hilda's astonishment, he did. One evening when she was at the Club he packed his clothes and went to two rooms in Kilburn that he and Marie had found. He didn't tell Hilda where he was going. He just left a note to say he wouldn't be back.

They lived as man and wife in Kilburn, sharing a lavatory and a bathroom with fifteen other people. In time he received a court summons, and in court was informed that he had behaved meanly and despicably to the woman he'd married. He agreed to pay regular maintenance.

The two rooms in Kilburn were dirty and uncomfortable, and life in them was rather different from the life they had known together in the Drummer Boy and the Great Western Royal Hotel. They planned to find somewhere better, but at a reasonable price that wasn't easy to find. A certain melancholy descended on them, for although they were together they seemed as far away as ever from their own small house, their children and their ordinary contentment.

'We could go to Reading,' Marie suggested.

'Reading?'

'To my mum's.'

'But your mum's nearly disowned you. Your mum's livid, you said yourself she was.'

'People come round.'

She was right. One Sunday afternoon they made the journey to Reading to have tea with Marie's mother and her friend Mrs Druk. Neither of these women addressed Norman, and once when he and Marie were in the kitchen he heard Mrs Druk saying it disgusted her, that he was old enough to be Marie's father. 'Don't think much of him,' Marie's mother replied. 'Pipsqueak really.'

Nevertheless, Marie's mother had missed her daughter's contribution to the household finances and before they returned to London that evening it was arranged that Norman and Marie should move in within a month, on the firm understanding that the very second it was feasible their marriage would take place. 'He's a boarder, mind,' Marie's mother warned. 'Nothing but a boarder in this house.' There were neighbours, Mrs Druk added, to be thought of.

Reading was worse than the two rooms in Kilburn. Marie's mother continued to make disparaging remarks about Norman, about the way he left the lavatory, or the thump of his feet on the stair-carpet, or his fingermarks around the light-switches. Marie would deny these accusations and then there'd be a row, with Mrs Druk joining in because she loved a row, and Marie's mother weeping and then Marie weeping. Norman had been to see a solicitor about divorcing Hilda, quoting her unfaithfulness with a postman and with Fowler. 'You have your evidence, Mr Britt?' the solicitor inquired, and pursed his lips when Norman said he hadn't.

He knew it was all going to be too difficult. He knew his instinct had been right: he shouldn't have told Hilda, he shouldn't have just walked out. The whole thing had always been unfair on Marie; it had to be when a girl got mixed up with a married man. 'Should think of things like that,' her mother had a way of saying loudly when he was passing an open door. 'Selfish type he is,' Mrs Druk would loudly add.

Marie argued when he said none of it was going to work. But she wasn't as broken-hearted as she might have been a year or so ago, for the strain had told on Marie too, especially the strain in Reading. She naturally wept when Norman said they'd been defeated, and so for a moment did he. He asked for a transfer to another branch of Travel-Wide and was sent to Ealing, far away from the Great Western Royal Hotel.

Eighteen months later Marie married a man in a brewery. Hilda, hearing on some grapevine that Norman was on his own, wrote to him and suggested that bygones should be allowed to be bygones. Lonely in a bed-sitting-room in Ealing, he agreed to talk the situation over with her and after that he agreed to return to their flat. 'No hard feelings,' Hilda said, 'and no deception: there's been a chap from the Club in here, the Woolworth's manager.' No hard feelings, he agreed.

For Norman Britt, as the decade of the 1960s passed, it trailed behind it the marvels of his love affair with Marie. Hilda's scorn when he had confessed had not devalued them, nor had the two dirty rooms in Kilburn, nor the equally unpleasant experience in Reading. Their walk to the Great Western Royal, the drinks they could not afford in the hotel bar, their studied nonchalance as they made their way separately upstairs, seemed to Norman to be a fantasy that had miraculously become real. The second-floor bathroom belonged in it perfectly, the bathroom full of whispers and caressing, where the faraway places of his daily work acquired a hint of magic when he spoke of them to a girl as voluptuous as any of James Bond's. Sometimes on the Tube he would close his eyes and with the greatest pleasure that remained to him he would recall the delicately veined marble and the great brass taps, and the bath that was big enough for two. And now and again he heard what appeared to be the strum of distant music, and the voices of the Beatles celebrating a bathroom love, as they had celebrated Eleanor Rigby and other people of that time.

The Raising of Elvira Tremlett

My mother preferred English goods to Irish, claiming that the quality was better. In particular she had a preference for English socks and vests, and would not be denied in her point of view. Irish motor-car assemblers made a rough-and-ready job of it, my father used to say, the Austins and Morrises and Vauxhalls that came direct from British factories were twice the cars. And my father was an expert in his way, being the town's single garage-owner. *Devlin Bros.* it said on a length of painted wood, black letters on peeling white. The sign was crooked on the red corrugated iron of the garage, falling down a bit on the left-hand side.

In all other ways my parents were intensely of the country that had borne them, of the province of Munster and of the town they had always known. When she left the convent my mother had immediately been found employment in the meat factory, working a machine that stuck labels on to tins. My father and his brother Jack, finishing at the Christian Brothers', had automatically passed into the family business. In those days the only sign on the corrugated façade had said *Raleigh Cycles*, for the business, founded by my grandfather, had once been a bicycle one. 'I think we'll make a change in that,' my father announced one day in 1933, when I was five, and six months or so later the rusty tin sheet that advertised bicycles was removed, leaving behind an island of grey in the corrugated red. 'Ah, that's grand,' my mother approved from the middle of the street, wiping her chapped hands on her apron. The new sign must have had a freshness and a gleam to it, but I don't recall that. In my memory there is only the peeling white behind the letters and the drooping down at the left-hand side where a rivet had fallen out. 'We'll paint that in and we'll be dandy,' my Uncle Jack said, referring to the island that remained, the contours of Sir Walter Raleigh's head and shoulders. But the job was never done.

We lived in a house next door to the garage, two storeys of cement that had a damp look, with green window-sashes and a green hall door. Inside, a wealth of polished brown linoleum, its pattern faded to nothing, was cheered here and there by the rugs my mother bought in Roche's Stores in Cork. The votive light of a crimson Sacred Heart gleamed day and night in the hall. Christ blessed us half-way up the stairs; on the landing the Virgin Mary was coy in garish robes. On either side of a narrow trodden carpet the staircase had been grained to make it seem like oak. In the dining-room, never used, there was a square table with six rexine-seated chairs around it, and over the mantelpiece a mirror with chromium decoration. The sitting-room smelt of must and had a picture of the Pope.

The kitchen was where everything happened. My father and Uncle Jack read the newspaper there. The old battery wireless, the only one in the house, stood on one of the window-sills. Our two nameless cats used to crouch by the door into the scullery because one of them had once caught a mouse there. Our terrier, Tom, mooched about under my mother's feet when she was cooking at the range. There was a big scrubbed table in the middle of the kitchen, and wooden chairs, and a huge clock, like the top bit of a grandfather clock, hanging between the two windows. The dresser had keys and bits of wire and labels hanging all over it. The china it contained was never used, being hidden behind bric-à-brac: broken ornaments left there in order to be repaired with Seccotine, worn-out parts from the engines of cars which my father and uncle had brought into the kitchen to examine at their leisure, bills on spikes, letters and Christmas cards. The kitchen was always rather dusky, even in the middle of the day: it was partially a basement, light penetrating from outside only through the upper panes of its two long windows. Its concrete floor had been reddened with Cardinal polish, which was renewed once a year, in spring. Its walls and ceiling were a sooty white.

The kitchen was where we did our homework, my two sisters and two brothers and myself. I was the youngest, my brother Brian the oldest. Brian and Liam were destined for the garage when they finished at the Christian Brothers', as my father and Uncle Jack had been. My sister Effie was good at arithmetic and the nuns had once or twice mentioned accountancy. There was a commercial college in Cork she could go to, the nuns said, the same place that Miss Callan, who did the books for Bolger's Medical Hall, had attended. Everyone said my sister Kitty was pretty: my father used to take her on his knee and tell her she'd break some fellow's heart, or a dozen hearts or maybe more. She didn't know what he was talking about at first, but later she understood and used to go red in the face. My father was like that with Kitty. He embarrassed her without meaning to, hauling her on to his knee when she was much too old for it, fondling her because he liked her best. On the other hand, he was quite harsh with my brothers, constantly suspicious that they were up to no good. Every evening he asked them if they'd been to school that day, suspecting that they might have tricked the Christian Brothers and would the next day present them with a note they had written themselves, saying they'd had stomach trouble after eating bad sausages. He and my Uncle Jack had often engaged in such ploys themselves, spending a whole day in the field behind the meat factory.

My father's attitude to my sister Effie was coloured by Effie's plainness. 'Ah, poor old Effie,' he used to say, and my mother would reprimand him. He took comfort from the fact that if the garage continued to thrive it would be necessary to have someone doing the increased book-work instead of himself and Uncle Jack trying to do it. For this reason he was in favour of Effie taking a commercial course: he saw a future in which she and my two brothers would live in the house and run the business between them. One or other of my brothers would marry and maybe move out of the house, leaving Effie and whichever one would still be a bachelor: it was my father's way of coming to terms with Effie's plainness. 'I wonder if Kitty'll end up with young Lacy?' I once heard him inquiring of my mother, the Lacy he referred to being the only child of another business in the town – Geo. Lacy and Sons, High-Class Drapers – who was about eight at the time. Kitty would do well, she'd marry whom she wanted to, and somehow or other she'd marry money: he really believed that.

For my part I fitted nowhere into my father's vision of the family's future. My performance at school was poor and there would be no place for me in the garage. I used to sit with the others at the kitchen table trying to understand algebra and Irish grammar, trying without any hope to learn verses from 'Ode to the West Wind' and to improve my handwriting by copying from a headline book. 'Slow,' Brother Cahey had reported. 'Slow as a dying snail, that boy is.'

That was the family we were. My father was bulky in his grey overalls, always with marks of grease or dirt on him, his fingernails rimmed with black, like fingers in mourning, I used to think. Uncle Jack wore similar overalls but he was thin and much smaller than my father, a ferrety little man who had a way of looking at the ground when he spoke to you. He, too, was marked with grime and had the same rimmed fingernails, even at weekends. They both brought the smell of the garage into the kitchen, an oily smell that mingled with the fumes of my uncle's pipe and my father's cigarettes.

My mother was red-cheeked and stout, with waxy dark hair and big arms and legs. She ruled the house, and was often cross: with my brothers when they behaved obstreperously, with my sisters and myself when her patience failed her. Sometimes my father would spend a long time on a Saturday night in Macklin's, which was the public house he favoured, and she would be cross with him also, noisily shouting in their bedroom, telling him to take off his clothes before he got into bed, telling him he was a fool. Uncle Jack was a teetotaller, a member of the Pioneer movement. He was a great help to Father Kiberd in the rectory and in the Church of the Holy Assumption, performing chores and repairing the electric light. Twice a year he spent a Saturday night in Cork in order to go to greyhound racing, but there was more than met the eye to these visits, for on his return there was always a great silence in the house, a fog of disapproval emanating from my father.

The first memories I have are of the garage, of watching my father and Uncle Jack at work, sparks flying from the welding apparatus, the dismantling of oil-caked engines. A car would be driven over the pit and my father or uncle would work underneath it, lit by an electric bulb in a wire casing on the end of a flex. Often, when he wasn't in the pit, my father would drift into conversation with a customer. He'd lean on the bonnet of a car, smoking continuously, talking about a hurling match that had taken place or about the dishonesties of the Government. He would also talk about his children, saying that Brian and Liam would fit easily into the business and referring to Effie's plans to study commerce, and Kitty's prettiness. 'And your man here?' the customer might remark, inclining his head in my direction. To this question my father always replied in the same way. The Lord, he said, would look after me.

As I grew up I became aware that I made both my father and my mother uneasy. I assumed that this was due to my slowness at school, an opinion that was justified by a conversation I once overheard coming from their bedroom: they appeared to regard me as mentally deficient. My father repeated twice that the Lord would look after me. It was something she prayed for, my mother replied, and I imagined her praying after she'd said it, kneeling down by their bed, as she'd taught all of us to kneel by ours. I stood with my bare feet on the linoleum of the landing, believing that a plea from my mother was rising from the house at that very moment, up into the sky, where God was. I had been on my way to the kitchen for a drink of water, but I returned to the bedroom I shared with Brian and Liam and lay awake thinking of the big brown-brick mansion on the Mallow road. Once it had been owned and lived in by a local family. Now it was the town's asylum.

The town itself was small and ordinary. Part of it was on a hill, the part where the slum cottages were, where three or four shops had nothing in their windows except pasteboard advertisements for tea and Bisto. The rest of the town was flat, a single street with one or two narrow streets running off it. Where they met there was a square of a kind, with a statue of Daniel O'Connell. The Munster and Leinster Bank was here, and the Bank of Ireland, and Lacy and Sons, and Bolger's Medical Hall, and the Home and Colonial. Our garage was at one end of the main street, opposite

Corrigan's Hotel. The Vista cinema was at the other, a stark white façade not far from the Church of the Holy Assumption. The Protestant church was at the top of the hill, beyond the slums.

When I think of the town now I can see it very clearly: cattle and pigs on a fair-day, always a Monday; Mrs Driscoll's vegetable shop, Vickery's hardware, McPadden's the barber's, Kilmartin's the turf accountant's, the convent and the Christian Brothers', twenty-nine public houses. The streets are empty on a sunny afternoon, there's a smell of bread. Brass plates gleam on the way home from school: Dr Thos. Garvey M.D., R.C.S.; Regan and Broe, Commissioners for Oaths; W. Drennan, Dental Surgeon.

But in my memory our house and our garage close in on everything else, shadowing and diminishing the town. The bedroom I shared with Brian and Liam had the same nondescript linoleum as the hall and the landing had. There was a dressing-table with a wash-stand in white-painted wood, and a wardrobe that matched. There was a flowery wallpaper on the walls, but the flowers had all faded to a uniform brown, except behind the bedroom's single picture, of an ox pulling a cart. Our three iron bedsteads were lined against one wall. Above the mantelpiece Christ on his cross had already given up the ghost.

I didn't in any way object to this bedroom and, familiar with no alternative, I didn't mind sharing it with my brothers. The house itself was somewhere I was used to also, accepted and taken for granted. But the garage was different. The garage was a kind of hell, its awful earth floor made black with sump oil, its huge indelicate vices, the chill of cast iron, the grunting of my father and my uncle as they heaved an engine out of a tractor, the astringent smell of petrol. It was there that my silence, my dumbness almost, must have begun. I sense that now, without being able accurately to remember. Looking back, I see myself silent in a classroom, taught first by nuns and later by Christian Brothers. In the kitchen, while the others chattered at mealtimes, I was silent too. I could take no interest in what my father and uncle reported about the difficulties they were having in getting spare parts or about some fault in a farmer's carburettor. My brothers listened to all that, and clearly found it easy to. Or they would talk about sport, or tease Uncle Jack about the money he lost on greyhounds and horses. My mother would repeat what she had heard in the shops, and Uncle Jack would listen intently because although he never himself indulged in gossip he loved to hear it. My sisters would retail news from the convent, the decline in the health of an elderly nun, or the inability of some family to buy Lacy's more expensive First Communion dresses. I often felt, listening at mealtimes, that I was scarcely there. I didn't belong and I sensed it was my fault; I felt I was a burden, being unpromising at school, unable to hold out hopes for the future. I felt I was a disgrace to them and might even become a person who was only fit to lift cans of paraffin about in the garage. I thought I could see that in my father's eyes, and in my uncle's sometimes, and in my mother's. A kind of shame it was, peering back at me.

I turned to Elvira Tremlett because everything about her was quiet. 'You great damn clown,' my mother would shout angrily at my father. He'd smile in the kitchen, smelling like a brewery, as she used to say. 'Mind that bloody tongue of yours,' he'd retort, and then he'd eye my uncle in a belligerent manner. 'Jeez, will you look at the cut of him?' he'd roar, laughing and throwing his head about. My uncle would usually be sitting in front of the range, a little to one side so as not to be in the way of my mother while she cooked. He'd been reading the *Independent* or *Ireland's Own*, or trying to mend something. 'You're the right eejit,' my father would say to him. 'And the right bloody hypocrite.'

It was always like that when he'd been in Macklin's on a Saturday evening and returned in time for his meal. My mother would slap the plates on to the table, my father would sing in order to annoy her. I used to feel that my uncle and my mother were allied on these occasions, just as she and my father were allied when my uncle spent a Saturday night in Cork after the greyhound racing. I much preferred it when my father didn't come back until some time in the middle of the night. 'Will you look at His Nibs?' he'd say in the kitchen, drawing attention to me. 'Haven't you a word in you, boy? Bedad, that fellow'll never make a lawyer.' He'd explode with laughter and then he'd tell Kitty that she was looking great and could marry the crowned King of England if she wanted to. He'd say to Effie she was getting fat with the toffees she ate; he'd tell my brothers they were lazy.

They didn't mind his talk the way I did; even Kitty's embarrassment used to evaporate quite quickly because for some reason she was fond of him. Effie was fond of my uncle, and my brothers of my mother. Yet in spite of all this family feeling, whenever there was quarrelling between our parents, or an atmosphere after my uncle had spent a night away, my brothers used to say the three of them would drive you mad. 'Wouldn't it make you sick, listening to it?' Brian would say in our bedroom, saying it to Liam. Then they'd laugh because they couldn't be bothered to concern themselves too much with other people's quarrels, or with atmospheres.

The fact was, my brothers and sisters were all part of it, whatever it was – the house, the garage, the family we were – and they could take everything in their stride. They were the same as our parents and our uncle, and Elvira Tremlett was different. She was a bit like Myrna Loy, whom I had seen in the Vista, in *Test Pilot* and *Too Hot to Handle* and *The Thin Man*. Only she was more beautiful than Myrna Loy, and her voice was nicer. Her voice, I still consider, was the nicest thing about Elvira Tremlett, next to her quietness.

'What do you want?' the sexton of the Protestant church said to me one Saturday afternoon. 'What're you doing here?'

He was an old, hunched man in black clothes. He had rheumy eyes, very red and bloody at the rims. It was said in the town that he gave his wife an awful time.

'It isn't your church,' he said.

I nodded, not wanting to speak to him. He said:

'It's a sin for you to be coming into a Protestant church. Are you wanting to be a Protestant, is that it?' He was laughing at me, even though his lips weren't smiling. He looked as if he'd never smiled in his life.

I shook my head at him, hoping he might think I was dumb.

'Stay if you want to,' he said, surprising me, even though I'd seen him coming to the conclusion that I wasn't going to commit some act of vandalism. I think he might even have decided to be pleased because a Catholic boy had chosen to wander among the pews and brasses of his church. He hobbled away to the vestry, breathing noisily because of his bent condition.

Several months before that Saturday I had wandered into the church for the first time. It was different from the Church of the Holy Assumption. It had a different smell, a smell that might have come from mothballs or from the tidy stacks of hymn-books and prayer-books, whereas the Church of the Holy Assumption smelt of people and candles. It was cosier, much smaller, with dark-coloured panelling and pews, and stained-glass windows that seemed old, and no cross on the altar. There were flags and banners that were covered with dust, all faded and in shreds, and a Bible spread out on the wings of an eagle.

The old sexton came back. I could feel him watching me as I read the tablets on the walls, moving from one to the next, pretending that each of them interested me. I might have asked him: I might have smiled at him and timidly inquired about Elvira Tremlett because I knew he was old enough to remember. But I didn't. I walked slowly up a side-aisle, away from the altar, to the back of the church. I wanted to linger there in the shadows, but I could feel his rheumy eyes on my back, wondering about me. As I slipped away from the church, down the short path that led through black iron gates to the street at the top of the hill, I knew that I would never return to the place.

'Well, it doesn't matter,' she said. 'You don't have to go back. There's nothing to go back for.'

I knew that was true. It was silly to keep on calling in at the Protestant church.

'It's curiosity that sends you there,' she said. 'You're much too curious.'

I knew I was: she had made me understand that. I was curious and my family weren't.

She smiled her slow smile, and her eyes filled with it. Her eyes were brown, the same colour as her long hair. I loved it when she smiled. I loved watching her fingers playing with the daisies in her lap, I loved her old-fashioned clothes, and her shoes and her two elaborate earrings. She laughed once when I asked her if they were gold. She'd never been rich, she said.

There was a place, a small field with boulders in it, hidden on the edge of a wood. I had gone there the first time, after I'd been in the Protestant church. What had happened was that in the church I had noticed the tablet on the wall, the left wall as you faced the altar, the last tablet on it, in dull grey marble.

> Near by this Stone
> Lies Interred the Body
> of Miss Elvira Tremlett
> Daughter of Wm. Tremlett
> of Tremlett Hall
> in the County of Dorset.
> She Departed this Life
> 30 August 1873
> Aged 18.

Why should an English girl die in our town? Had she been passing through? Had she died of poisoning? Had someone shot her? Eighteen was young to die.

On that day, the first day I read her tablet, I had walked from the Protestant church to the field beside the wood. I often went there because it was a lonely place, away from the town and from people. I sat on a boulder and felt hot sun on my face and head, and on my neck and the backs of my hands. I began to imagine her, Elvira Tremlett of Tremlett Hall in the county of Dorset, England. I gave her her long hair and her smile and her elaborate earrings, and I felt I was giving her gifts. I gave her her clothes, wondering if I had got them right. Her fingers were delicate as straws, lacing together the first of her daisy-chains. Her voice hadn't the edge that Myrna Loy's had, her neck was more elegant.

'Oh, love,' she said on the Saturday after the sexton had spoken to me. 'The tablet's only a stone. It's silly to go gazing at it.'

I knew it was and yet it was hard to prevent myself. The more I gazed at it the more I felt I might learn about her: I didn't know if I was getting her right. I was afraid even to begin to imagine her death because I thought I might be doing wrong to have her dying from some cause that wasn't the correct one. It seemed insulting to her memory not to get that perfectly correct.

'You mustn't want too much,' she said to me on that Saturday afternoon. 'It's as well you've finished with the tablet on the wall. Death doesn't matter, you know.'

I never went back to the Protestant church. I remember what my mother had said about the quality of English goods, and how cars assembled in England were twice the ones assembled in Dublin. I looked at the map of England in my atlas and there was Dorset. She'd been travelling, maybe staying in a house near by, and had died somehow: she was right, it didn't matter.

Tremlett Hall was by a river in the country, with Virginia creeper all over it, with long corridors and suits of armour in the hall, and a fireplace in the hall also. In *David Copperfield*, which I had seen in the Vista, there might have been a house like Tremlett Hall, or in *A Yank at Oxford*: I couldn't quite remember. The gardens were beautiful: you walked from one garden to another, to a special rose-garden with a sundial, to a vegetable garden with high walls around it. In the house someone was always playing a piano. 'Me,' Elvira said.

My brothers went to work in the garage, first Brian and then Liam. Effie went to Cork, to the commercial college. The boys at the Christian Brothers' began to whistle at Kitty and sometimes would give me notes to pass on to her. Even when other people were there I could feel Elvira's nearness, even her breath sometimes, and certainly the warmth of her hands. When Brother Cahey hit me one day she cheered me up. When my father came back from Macklin's in time for his Saturday tea her presence made it easier. The garage I hated, where I was certain now I would one day lift paraffin cans from one corner to another, was lightened by her. She was in Mrs Driscoll's vegetable shop when I bought cabbage and potatoes for my mother. She was there while I waited for the Vista to open, and when I walked through the animals on a fair-day. In the stony field the sunshine made her earrings glitter. It danced over a brooch she had not had when first I imagined her, a brooch with a scarlet jewel, in the shape of a spider. Mist caught in her hair, wind ruffled the skirts of her old-fashioned dress. She wore gloves when it was cold, and a green cloak that wrapped itself all around her. In spring she often carried daffodils, and once – one Sunday in June – she carried a little dog, a grey cairn that afterwards became part of her, like her earrings and her brooch.

I grew up but she was always eighteen, as petrified as her tablet on the wall. In the bedroom which I shared with Brian and Liam I came, in time, to take her dragon's brooch from her throat and to take her earrings from her pale ears and to lift her dress from her body. Her limbs were warm, and her smile was always there. Her slender fingers traced caresses on my cheeks. I told her that I loved her, as the people told one another in the Vista.

'You know why they're afraid of you?' she said one day in the field by the wood. 'You know why they hope that God will look after you?'

I had to think about it but I could come to no conclusion on my own, without her prompting. I think I wouldn't have dared; I'd have been frightened of whatever there was.

'You know what happens,' she said, 'when your uncle stays in Cork on a Saturday night? You know what happened once when your father came back from Macklin's too late for his meal, in the middle of the night?'

I knew before she told me. I guessed, but I wouldn't have if she hadn't been there. I made her tell me, listening to her quiet voice. My Uncle Jack went after women as well as greyhounds in Cork. It was his weakness, like going to Macklin's was my father's. And the two weaknesses had once combined, one Saturday night a long time ago, when my uncle hadn't gone to Cork and my father was a long time in Macklin's. I was the child of my Uncle Jack and my mother, born of his weakness and my mother's anger as she waited for the red bleariness of my father to return, footless in the middle of the night. It was why my father called my uncle a hypocrite. It was maybe why my uncle was always looking at the ground, and why he assisted Father Kiberd in the rectory and in the Church of the Holy Assumption. I was their sin, growing in front of them, for God to look after.

'They have made you,' Elvira said. 'The three of them have made you what you are.'

I imagined my father returning that night from Macklin's, stumbling on the stairs, and haste being made by my uncle to hide himself. In these images it was always my uncle who was anxious and in a hurry: my mother kept saying it didn't matter, pressing him back on to the pillows, wanting him to be found there.

My father was like a madman in the bedroom then, wild in his crumpled Saturday clothes. He struck at both of them, his befuddled eyes tormented while my mother screamed. She went back through all the years of their marriage, accusing him of cruelty and neglect. My uncle wept. 'I'm no more than an animal to you,' my mother screamed, half-naked between the two of them. 'I cook and clean and have children for you. You give me thanks by going out to Macklin's.' Brian was in the room, attracted by the noise. He stood by the open door, five years old, telling them to be quiet because they were waking the others.

'Don't ever tell a soul,' Brian would have said, years afterwards, retailing that scene for Liam and Effie and Kitty, letting them guess the truth. He had been sent back to bed, and my uncle had gone to his own bed, and in the morning there had begun the pretending that none of it had happened. There was confession and penance, and extra hours spent in Macklin's. There were my mother's prayers that I would not be born, and my uncle's prayers, and my father's bitterness when the prayers weren't answered.

On the evening of the day that Elvira shared all that with me I watched them as we ate in the kitchen, my father's hands still smeared with oil, his fingernails in mourning, my uncle's eyes bent over his fried eggs. My brothers and sisters talked about events that had taken place in the town; my mother listened without interest, her large round face seeming stupid to me now. It was a cause for celebration that I was outside the family circle. I was glad not to be part of the house and the garage, and not to be part of the town with its statue and its shops and its twenty-nine public houses. I belonged with a figment of my imagination: an English ghost who had acquired a dog, whose lips were soft, whose limbs were warm, Elvira Tremlett, who lay beneath the Protestant church.

'Oh, love,' I said in the kitchen, 'thank you.'

The conversation ceased, my father's head turned sharply. Brian and Liam looked at me, so did Effie and Kitty. My mother had a piece of fried bread on a fork, on the way to her mouth. She returned it to her plate. There was grease at the corner of her lips, a little shiny stream from some previous mouthful, running down to her chin. My uncle pushed his knife and fork together and stared at them.

I felt them believing with finality now, with proof, that I was not sane. I was fifteen years old, a boy who was backward in his ways, who was all of a sudden addressing someone who wasn't in the room.

My father cut himself a slice of bread, moving the bread-saw slowly through the loaf. My brothers were as valuable in the garage now as he or my uncle; Effie kept the books and sent out bills. My father took things easy, spending more time talking to his older customers. My uncle pursued the racing pages; my mother had had an operation for varicose veins, which she should have had years ago.

I could disgrace them in the town, in all the shops and public houses, in Bolger's Medical Hall, in the convent and the Christian Brothers' and the Church of the Holy Assumption. How could Brian and Liam carry on the business if they couldn't hold their heads up? How could Effie help with the petrol pumps at a busy time, standing in her wellington boots on a wet day, for all the town to see? Who would marry Kitty now?

I had spoken by mistake, and I didn't speak again. It was the first time I had said anything at a meal in the kitchen for as long as I could remember, for years and years. I had suddenly felt that she might grow tired of coming into my mind and want to be left alone, buried beneath the Protestant church. I had wanted to reassure her.

'They're afraid of you,' she said that night. 'All of them.'

She said it again when I walked in the sunshine to our field. She kept on saying it, as if to warn me, as if to tell me to be on the look-out. 'They have made you,' she repeated. 'You're the child of all of them.'

I wanted to go away, to escape from the truth we had both instinctively felt and had shared. I walked with her through the house called Tremlett Hall, haunting other people with our footsteps. We stood and watched while guests at a party laughed among the suits of armour in the hall, while there was waltzing in a ballroom. In the gardens dahlias bloomed, and sweet-pea clung to wires against a high stone wall. Low hedges of fuchsia bounded the paths among the flower-beds, the little dog ran on in front of us. She held my hand and said she loved me; she smiled at me in the sunshine. And then, just for a moment, she seemed to be different; she wasn't wearing the right clothes; she was wearing a tennis dress and had a racquet in her hand. She was standing in a conservatory, one foot on a cane chair. She looked like another girl, Susan Peters in *Random Harvest*.

I didn't like that. It was the same kind of thing as feeling I had to speak to her even though other people were in the kitchen. It was a muddle, and somewhere in it I could sense an unhappiness I didn't understand. I couldn't tell if it was hers or mine. I tried to say I was sorry, but I didn't know what I was sorry for.

In the middle of one night I woke up screaming. Brian and Liam were standing by my bed, cross with me for waking them. My mother came, and then my father. I was still screaming, unable to stop. 'He's had some type of nightmare,' Brian said.

It wasn't a nightmare because it continued when I was awake. She was there, Elvira Tremlett, born 1855. She didn't talk or smile: I couldn't make her. Something was failing in me: it was the same as Susan Peters suddenly appearing with a tennis racquet, the same as my desperation in wanting to show gratitude when we weren't in private.

My mother sat beside my bed. My brothers returned to theirs. The light remained on. I must have whispered, I must have talked about her because I remember my mother's nodding head and her voice assuring me that it was all a dream. I slept, and when I woke up it was light in the room and my mother had gone; my brothers were getting up. Elvira Tremlett was still there, one eye half-closed in blindness, the fingers that had been delicate misshapen now. When my brothers left the room she was more vivid, a figure by the window, turning her head to look at me, a gleam of fury in her face. She did not speak but I knew what she was saying. I had used her for purposes of my own, to bring solace. What right, for God's sake, had I to blow life into her decaying bones? Born 1855, eighty-nine years of age.

I closed my eyes, trying to imagine her as I had before, willing her young girl's voice and her face and hair. But even with my eyes closed the old woman moved about the room, from the window to the foot of Liam's bed, to the wardrobe, into a corner, where she stood still.

She was on the landing with me, and on the stairs and in the kitchen. She was in the stony field by the wood, accusing me of disturbing her and yet still not speaking. She was in pain from her eye and her arthritic hands: I had brought about that. Yet she was no ghost, I knew she was no ghost. She was a figment of my imagination, drawn from her dull grey tablet by my interest. She existed within me, I told myself, but it wasn't a help.

Every night I woke up screaming. The sheets of my bed were sodden with my sweat. I would shout at my brothers and my mother, begging them to take her away from me. It wasn't I who had committed the sin, I shouted, it wasn't I who deserved the punishment. All I had done was to talk to a figment. All I'd done was to pretend, as they had.

Father Kiberd talked to me in the kitchen. His voice came and went, and my mother's voice spoke of the sodden sheets every morning, and my father's voice said there was terror in my eyes. All I wanted to say was that I hadn't meant any harm in raising Elvira Tremlett from the dead in order to have an imaginary friend, or in travelling with her to the house with virginia creeper on it. She hadn't been real, she'd been no more than a flicker on the screen of the Vista cinema: I wanted to say all that. I wanted to be listened to, to be released of the shame that I felt like a shroud around me. I knew that if I could speak my imagination would be free of the woman who haunted it now. I tried, but they were afraid of me. They were afraid of what I was going to say and between them they somehow stopped me. 'Our Father,' said Father Kiberd, 'Who art in heaven, hallowed be Thy name ...'

Dr Garvey came and looked at me: in Cork another man looked at me. The man in Cork tried to talk to me, telling me to lie down, to take my shoes off if I wanted to. It wasn't any good, and it wasn't fair on them, having me there in the house, a person in some kind of nightmare. I quite see now that it wasn't fair on them, I quite see that.

Because of the unfairness I was brought, one Friday morning in a Ford car my father borrowed from a customer, to this brown-brick mansion, once the property of a local family. I have been here for thirty-four years. The clothes I wear are rough, but I have ceased to be visited by the woman who Elvira Tremlett became in my failing imagination. I ceased to be visited by her the moment I arrived here, for when that moment came I knew that this was the house she had been staying in when she died. She brought me here so that I could live in peace, even in the room that had been hers. I had disturbed her own peace so that we might come here together.

I have not told this story myself. It has been told by my weekly visitor, who has placed me at the centre of it because that, of course, is where I belong. Here, in the brown-red mansion, I have spoken without difficulty. I have spoken in the garden where I work in the daytime; I have spoken at all meals; I have spoken to my weekly visitor. I am different here. I do not need an imaginary friend, I could never again feel curious about a girl who died.

I have asked my visitor what they say in the town, and what the family say. He replies that in the bar of Corrigan's Hotel commercial travellers are told of a boy who was haunted, as a place or a house is. They are drawn across the bar to a window: Devlin Bros., the garage across the street, is pointed out to them. They listen in pleasurable astonishment to the story of nightmares, and hear the name of an English girl who died in the town in 1873, whose tablet is on the wall of the Protestant church. They are told of the final madness of the boy, which came about through his visions of this girl, Elvira Tremlett.

The story is famous in the town, the only story of its kind the town possesses. It is told as a mystery, and the strangers who hear it sometimes visit the Protestant church to look up at the tablet that commemorates a death in 1873. They leave the church in bewilderment, wondering why an uneasy spirit should have lighted on a boy so many years later. They never guess, not one of them, that the story as it happened wasn't a mystery in the least.

Flights of Fancy

In her middle age Sarah Machaen had developed the habit of nostalgically slipping back into her childhood. Often, on a bus or at a dinner party, she would find herself caught in a mesh of voices and events that had been real forty years ago. There were summer days in the garden of her father's rectory, her brothers building another tree-house, her father asleep in a brown-and-orange-striped deck-chair. In the cool untidy kitchen she helped her mother to make strawberry cake; she walked with the old spaniel, Dodge, to Mrs Rolleston's Post Office and Stores in the village, her shoes dusty as soon as she took a single step. On wet winter afternoons, cosy by the fire in the drawing-room, the family played consequences or card games, or listened to the wireless. The war brought black-out curtains and rationing, and two evacuees.

At forty-seven Sarah Machaen was reconciled to the fact that her plainness wasn't going to go away. As a child she had believed that growing up would put paid to the face she couldn't care for, that it would develop prettily in girlhood, as the ugly duckling had developed. 'Oh, it's quite common,' she heard a woman say to her mother. 'Many a beauty was as plain as a pikestaff to begin with.' But no beauty dawned in Sarah's face.

Her older brother became a clergyman like their father, her younger one an engineer. She herself, in 1955, found employment she enjoyed in the firm of Pollock-Brown Lighting. She became secretary to Mr Everend, who at that time was assistant to the director in charge of publicity, whom he subsequently succeeded. The office was a busy one, and although Sarah had earlier had ambitions to work in the more cultural ambience of a museum or a publishing house she soon found herself taking a genuine interest in Pollock-Brown's range of well-designed products: light fittings that were increasingly specified by architects of taste all over Britain and Europe. The leaflets that passed through the Pollock-Brown publicity department constantly drew attention to the quality and the elegance that placed Pollock-Brown ahead of the field; the photographs in trade advertisements made many of the Pollock-Brown fitments seem like works of art. Sarah could discover no reason to argue with these claims, and was content to let Pollock-Brown become her daytime world, as a museum or a publishing house might have been. Her status in the organization rose with the status of Mr Everend, who often stated that he wished to be served by no other secretary. The offices of the firm were in London, a large block of glass and concrete in Kingsway. Twenty miles away, in factories just beyond the Green Belt, the manufacture of the well-designed fitments took place.

Since 1960 Sarah had had a flat in Tufnell Park, which was quite convenient, the Northern line all the way to Tottenham Court Road, the Central on to Holborn. The brother who was a clergyman lived in Harrogate and did not often come to London; the one who was an engineer had spent his life building dams in Africa and returned to England only with reluctance. Sarah's parents, happily married for almost fifty years, had died within a month of one another in 1972, sharing a room in an old-persons' home that catered exclusively for the clergy and their wives.

But even so Sarah was not alone. She had many friends, made in Pollock-Brown and through the Bach choir in which she sang, and some that dated back to her schooldays. She was a popular choice as a godmother. She was invited to parties and went regularly to the theatre or to concerts, often with her friend Anne, whose marriage had failed six years ago. She lived on her own in the flat in Tufnell Park now: when first she'd lived there she'd shared it with a girl called Elizabeth, with whom she'd been at school. Elizabeth, a librarian, was bespectacled and rather fat, a chatterbox and a compulsive nibbler. She hadn't been all that easy to live with but Sarah knew her well and appreciated her kindness and her warmth. It had astonished her when Elizabeth began to go out with a man she'd met in her library, a man whom she later became engaged to. It seemed to Sarah that Elizabeth wasn't the kind of girl who became engaged, any more than she herself was, yet in the end Elizabeth married and went to live in Cricklewood, where she reared a family. Sarah took in another girl but this time the arrangement didn't work because the new girl, a stranger to Sarah, kept having men in her bedroom. Sarah asked her to go, and did not attempt to replace her.

Almost every weekend she made the journey to Cricklewood to see Elizabeth and her family. The children loved her and often said so. Elizabeth's husband enjoyed chatting to her, drinking gin and tonic, to which Sarah had become mildly addicted. It was a home-from-home, and it wasn't the only one. No husband disliked Sarah. No one found her a bore. She brought small presents when she visited. She struck the right note and fitted in.

Now and again these friends attempted to bring Sarah into contact with suitable men, but nothing ever came of such efforts. There'd been, while she was still at the secretarial college she'd attended, a man called George, who had taken her out, who had embraced her and had once, in his bed-sitting-room, begun to undress her. She had enjoyed these attentions even though their perpetrator was not a person she greatly cared for. She had been quite prepared to permit him to take her clothes off and then to proceed in whatever way he wished, but he had suddenly appeared to change his mind, to lose interest or to develop nerves, it wasn't clear which. She'd felt quite sick and shaky, sitting on his lap in an armchair, while his fingers fell away from the buttons he'd been undoing. Awkwardly she had nuzzled her nose into his neck, hoping this would induce him to continue, but his arms, which hung down on either side of the armchair, had remained where they were. A moment later he'd clambered to his feet and had filled a kettle for tea. As an experience, it was one that Sarah was destined never to forget. She recalled it often as she lay alone in bed at night, extending her companion's desire and sometimes changing his identity before she did so. In middle age his bed-sitting-room was still as vivid as it had ever been, and she could still recall the feel of the blood draining away from her face and the sickness that developed when he seemed suddenly to reject her.

Sarah was not obsessed by this and she made efforts not to dwell on it, but it often struck her that it was unfair that she should be deprived of a side of life which was clearly pleasant. There was an assumption that girls without much in the way of looks didn't possess the kind of desire that looks appeared to indicate, but this of course was not true. When politely dancing with men or even when just talking to them she had more than once experienced what privately she designated as a longing to be loved by them. Her expression on these occasions did not ever betray her, and her plainness trailed a modesty that prevented her from ever being forward. She learnt to live with her frustrations, wondering as she grew older if some elderly widower, no longer moved by physical desire but seeking only an agreeable companion, might not one day propose marriage to her. She might accept, she vaguely thought. She wasn't at all sure what it would be like being married to an elderly widower, but some instinct informed her that she'd prefer it to being on her own in the flat in Tufnell Park all through her middle age. Alone at night her thoughts went further, creating the widower as a blind man who could not even sense her plainness, whose fingers caressing her face felt a beauty that was not there. Other scenes took place in which the widower ended by finding a vigour he thought he'd lost. It often astonished her in the daytime that she had imagined this.

On the other hand, her friend Anne, the one whose marriage had failed, lived a rackety life with men and sometimes said she envied Sarah the quietness of hers. Now and again, having dinner together after a visit to the theatre or a concert, Anne would refer to the lovers she'd had, castigating most of them as selfish. 'How right you are,' she had a way of saying, 'to steer clear of all that.' Sarah always laughed when Anne said that, pointing out that it hadn't been her choice. 'Oh, choice or not, by God you're better off,' Anne would insist. 'I really swear.' Then Anne met a Canadian, who married her and took her off to Montreal.

That was another person to miss, as she had missed the people of her childhood and her friend Elizabeth – for it naturally wasn't the same after Elizabeth married. She had often thought of telling Anne about her longing for a relationship with a man, but shyness had always held her back. The shyness had to do with not knowing enough, with having so little experience, the very opposite of Anne. Yet once, when they'd both had quite a lot of wine to drink, she'd almost asked her what she should do. 'Just because I'm so wretchedly plain,' she'd almost said, 'doesn't mean I can do without things.' But she hadn't said that, and now Anne was gone and there was no one else who wouldn't have been just a little shocked to hear stuff like that. Not in a million years could she have said it to Elizabeth.

And so it remained. No widower, elderly or otherwise, proposed marriage; no blind man proclaimed love. What happened was rather different from all that. Once a year, as Christmas approached, Pollock-Brown held its annual staff party at the factories beyond the Green Belt. Executive and clerical staff from the building in Kingsway met the factory workers in their huge canteen, richly decorated now with Christmas hangings. Dancing took place. There was supper, and unlimited drinks at the firm's expense. The managing director made a speech and the present chairman, Sir Robert Willis, made a speech also, in the course of which he thanked his workers for their loyalty. A thousand Pollock-Brown employees let their hair down, typists and secretaries, directors, executives who would soon be directors, tea-women, mould-makers, van-drivers, lorry-drivers, warehousemen, finishers, polishers. In a formal manner Mr Everend always reserved the first dance for Sarah and she felt quite proud to be led on to the floor in the wake of Sir Robert and his secretary and the managing director and his secretary, a woman called Mrs Mykers. After that the Christmas spirit really got going. Paper hats were supplied to everyone, including Sir Robert Willis, Mr Everend and the managing director. One of the dispatch boys had once poured a little beer over Mr Everend, because Mr Everend always so entered into the spirit of things that horseplay with beer seemed quite in order. There were tales, many of them true, of sexual congress in out-of-the-way corners, particularly in store-rooms.

'Hullo,' a girl said, addressing Sarah in what for this one evening of the year was called the Ladies' Powder Room. *Female Staff* a painted sign more ordinarily stated, hidden now beneath the festive card that bore the grander title.

'Hullo,' Sarah replied, unable to place the girl. She was small, with short black hair that was smooth and hung severely straight on either side of her face. She was pretty: an oval face with eyes almost as black as her hair, and a mouth that slightly pouted, dimpling her cheeks. Sarah frowned as the dimples came and went. The girl smiled in a friendly way. She said her name was Sandra Pond.

'You're Everend's girl,' she added.

'Secretary,' Sarah said.

'I meant that.' She laughed and the dimples danced about. 'I didn't mean nothing suspect, Miss Machaen.'

'Suspect?'

'You know.'

She wore a black dress with lace at her neck and wrists. Her feet were neat, in shiny black shoes. Her legs were slim, black-clad also. How nice to be so attractive! Sarah thought, a familiar reflection when meeting such girls for the first time. It wouldn't even matter having a slack, lower-class accent, as this girl had. You'd give up a lot for looks like that.

'I'm in polishing,' the girl said. 'Your plastic lampshades.'

'You don't sound as if you like it.' Sarah laughed. She glanced at herself in the mirror above one of the two wash-basins. Hurriedly she looked away.

'It's clean,' Sandra Pond said. 'A polishing machine's quite clean to operate.'

'Yes, I suppose it would be.'

'Care for a drink at all, Miss Machaen?'

'A drink?'

'Don't you drink, Miss Machaen?'

'Well, yes, but –'

'We're meant to mix at a thing like this. The peasants and the privileged.' She gave a rasping, rather unattractive laugh. 'Come on,' she said.

Beneath the prettiness there was something hard about her. There were flashes of bitterness in the way she'd said 'the peasants and the privileged', and in the way she'd laughed and in the way she walked out of the Ladies' Powder Room. She walked impatiently, as if she disliked being at the Christmas party. She was a prickly girl, Sarah said to herself. She wasn't at all glad that she'd fallen into conversation with her.

They sat down at a small table at the edge of the dance-floor. 'What d'you drink?' the girl said, immediately getting to her feet again in an edgy way. 'Whisky?'

'I'd like a gin and tonic.'

The dimples came and went, cracking the brittleness. The smile seemed disposed to linger but did not. 'Don't go away now,' the slack voice commanded as she jerked quickly away herself.

'Someone looking after you?' Dancing with the wife of the dispatch manager, Mr Everend shouted jollily at Sarah. He wore a scarlet, cone-shaped paper hat. The wife of the dispatch manager was eyeing, over his shoulder, a sales executive called Chumm, with whom, whenever it was possible, she went to bed.

'Yes, thanks, Mr Everend,' Sarah answered, waving a hand to indicate that he mustn't feel responsible for her.

'Horrid brute, that man,' Sandra Pond said, returning with their drinks. 'Cheers,' she said, raising a glass of what looked like whisky and touching Sarah's glass with it.

'Cheers,' Sarah said, although it was a salutation she disliked.

'It began last year here,' Sandra said, pointing with her glass at the dispatch manager's wife. 'Her and Chumm.'

'I've never met her actually.'

'You didn't miss nothing. That Chumm's a villain.'

'He has that reputation.'

'He screwed her in a store-room. I walked in on top of them.'

'Oh.'

'Oh in-bloody-deed.' She laughed. 'You like gin and t, d'you? Your drink, Miss Machaen?'

'Please call me Sarah. Yes, I like it.'

'Whisky mac this is. I love booze. You like it, Sarah?'

'Yes, I do rather.'

'Birds of a feather.' She laughed, and paused. 'I seen you last year. Dancing with Everend and that. I noticed you.'

'I've been coming for a long time.'

'How long you been at P-B, then?'

'Since 1960.'

'Jesus!'

'I know.'

'I was only a nipper in 1960. What age'd you say I was, Sarah?'

'Twenty-five?'

'Thirty. Don't look it, do I?'

'No, indeed.'

'You live alone, do you, Sarah?'

'Yes, I do. In Tufnell Park.'

'Nice?'

'It is quite nice.'

Sandra Pond nodded repeatedly. Tufnell Park was very nice indeed, she said, extremely nice.

'You sit there, Sarah,' she said. 'I'm going to get you another drink.'

'Oh, no. Let me. Please.' She began to get to her feet, but Sandra Pond shot out a hand, a movement like a whip's, instantly restraining her. Her small fingers pressed into the flesh of Sarah's arm. 'Stay right where you are,' she said.

An extraordinary thought occurred to Sarah as she watched the girl moving rapidly away with their two empty glasses: Sandra Pond wanted to share her flat.

'Now, now, now,' Mr Priddy from Accounts admonished, large and perspiring, staring down at her through thick spectacles. He reached for her, seemingly unaware of her protestations. His knees pressed into hers, forcing them into waltztime.

'They do an awful lot of good, these things,' Mr Priddy confidently remarked. 'People really get a chance.' He added something else, something about people getting a chance to chew the rag. Sarah nodded. 'We've had a miracle of a year,' Mr Priddy said. 'In spite of everything.'

She could see Sandra Pond standing with two full glasses, looking furious. She tried to smile at her through the dancing couples, to make some indication with her eyes that she'd had no option about dancing with Mr Priddy. But Sandra Pond, glaring into the dancers, hadn't even noticed her yet.

'Mrs Priddy couldn't come,' Mr Priddy told her. 'Tummy trouble.'

She said she was sorry, trying to remember what Mrs Priddy looked like and failing in that.

'She gets it,' Mr Priddy said.

Sandra Pond had seen them and was looking aggrieved now, her head on one side. She sat down at the table and lit a cigarette. She crossed her thin legs.

'Thank you very much,' Sarah said, and Mr Priddy smiled graciously and went away to do his duty by some other lone woman.

'Can't stand him,' Sandra Pond said. 'Clammy blooming hands.'

Sarah drank some gin and tonic. 'I say, you know,' a man called out, 'it's a hell of a party, eh?'

He wasn't sober. He swayed, with a glass in one hand, peering down at them. He was in charge of some department or other, Sarah couldn't remember which. He spent a great deal of time in a pub near the Kingsway building, not going home until the last minute. He lived with a sister, someone had once told her.

'Hey, who's she?' he demanded, wagging his glass at Sandra. 'Who's this one, Sarah?'

'Sandra Pond,' Sarah said sharply. 'In the polishing department.'

'Polishing, eh? Nice party, Sandra?'

'If you like the type of thing.'

'The drink's good.'

'It's free, you mean.'

'That's what I mean, girlie.'

He went away. Sandra Pond laughed. She was a little drunk herself, she confessed. It took her like that, quite suddenly, after the fifth or sixth whisky mac. 'How about you, Sarah?'

'I'm just about right.'

'D'you know what I'd like to do?'

'What?'

'Oh, no.' She looked away, coyly pouting, the dimples in her cheeks working. 'No, I couldn't say,' she said. 'I couldn't tell you, Sarah.'

The notion that the girl wanted to share her flat had remained with Sarah while she'd danced with Mr Priddy and while the man had swayed in front of them, saying the party was nice. It was still there now, at the very front of her mind, beginning to dominate everything else. It seemed to be an unspoken thought between them, deliberately placed there by the girl while she'd been saying that Tufnell Park was nice.

'Actually I'm quite pissed,' the girl was saying now, giggling.

The expression grated on Sarah. She could never see why people had to converse in an obscene way. It didn't in any way whatsoever make sense for the girl to say she was urinated when she meant drunk.

'Sorry,' Sandra Pond said.

'It's all right.'

'I offended you. It showed in your face. I'm sorry, Sarah.'

'Actually, it's time for me to go home.'

'Oh, God, I've driven you away.'

'It's not that.'

'Have another drink. I've spoiled your evening.'

'No, not at all.'

'You know how it is: everything smooth and unruffled and then everything going bonk! You know, Sarah?'

Sarah frowned, shaking her head.

'Like if you looked down a well and then you dropped a stone in. Know what I mean? There'd be a disturbance. I had a friend said that to me once, we was very close. Hazel she was called.'

'Well, I do know what she meant of course –'

'D'you really, Sarah?'

'Yes, of course.'

'She was talking about people, see. What happens to people. Like you meet someone, Sarah.'

It was the kind of cliché that Sarah didn't care for, still water and someone throwing a stone. It was silly and half-baked, but typical in a way of what was said at an office party.

'She was like that,' Sandra Pond said. 'She talked like that, did Hazel.'

'I see.'

'When she met me, she meant. A disturbance.'

'Yes.'

'Merry Christmas then, Sarah.'

'Merry Christmas.'

As she edged her way around the dance-floor, she felt glad she'd escaped and was thinking that when Mr Everend collided with her almost. He always gave her a lift home after the Christmas party. He offered to now, sensing that she was ready to go. But he insisted on a last dance and while they danced he thanked her for all the work she'd done during the year, and for being patient with him, which she really hadn't had to. 'A last drink,' he said as they stepped off the dance-floor, just beside where the drinks table was. He found her a gin and tonic and had a tomato juice himself.

In the arms of a black-haired youth, Sandra Pond danced by while the band played 'Just One of Those Things'; her thin arms were around the youth's neck, her head lolled on his shoulder. Her eyes were blank, Sarah noticed in the moment it took the couple to dance by.

'Merry Christmas, Sarah,' Mr Everend said.

'Merry Christmas, Mr Everend.'

That night she lay in bed, feeling woozy after all the gin and tonic. Not really wishing to, and yet slowly and quite carefully, she went over everything that had happened since Sandra Pond had addressed her in the Ladies' Powder Room. She remembered the grip of the girl's fingers and the pout of her lips, and her bitterness when she spoke of Pollock-Brown and even when she didn't. Had she really walked in on the dispatch manager's wife and Chumm in a store-room? It was odd the way she'd spoken to her in the Ladies' Powder Room, odd the way she'd spoken of Tufnell Park. For some minutes she imagined Sandra Pond sharing her flat with her as Elizabeth had, sharing the things in the kitchen cupboards, the Special K and the marmalade and the sugar. The girl was seventeen years younger, she didn't have the same background or presumably the same interests. Sarah smiled a little in the darkness, thinking about what people would say if she began to share her flat with a polisher of plastic lampshades. People would think she was mad, her brother and his wife in their Harrogate rectory, her other brother and his wife in Africa, the friends whose parties she went to, the Bach choir, Elizabeth, Anne in Montreal. And of course they would all be right. She was well-to-do and middle-aged and plain. Side by side with Mr Everend she had found her way to the top of the firm. She would retire one day and that would be that. It didn't make sense to share a flat with someone like Sandra Pond, but she sensed that had she stayed in Sandra Pond's company the flat would have been openly mentioned. And yet surely it must be as clear to Sandra Pond as it would be to everyone else that they'd make a most ill-assorted couple? What was in the girl's mind, that she could see the picture so differently? Thinking about it, Sarah could find only a single piece of common ground between them. It wasn't even properly real, based neither on a process of deduction or indeed of observation. It was an instinct that Sandra Pond, unlike Elizabeth or Anne, wouldn't marry. And for some reason Sarah sensed that Sandra Pond wouldn't be difficult, as the girl she'd tried to share the flat with after Elizabeth's departure had been. Her mind rebelliously wandered, throwing up flights of fancy that she considered silly almost as soon as they came to her, flights of fancy in which she educated Sandra Pond and discovered in her an intelligence that was on a par with her own, in which slowly a real friendship developed, and why should it not? Clearly there was a lot that Sandra Pond didn't know. Sarah doubted that the girl had ever been inside a theatre in her life, except maybe to see something like the Black and White Minstrel Show or a Christmas pantomime. She wondered if she ever opened a book or listened to music or went to an art gallery.

For a week, at odd moments of the day, or at night, Sarah wondered about Sandra Pond. She half expected that she might hear from her, that the slack accents would drift over her telephone, suggesting a drink. But she didn't. Instead, with the flights of fancy that she considered silly, she saw herself persevering in her patience and finally rewarded as Sandra Pond, calling on a sensitivity that had remained unaired till now, responded. Something assured Sarah that such a sensitivity was there: increasingly unable to prevent herself, she went over the course of their conversation in search of signs of it. And then, as if rejecting the extravagances of a dream in the first moments of consciousness, she would reject the fantasies that had not required a surrender to sleep. But all of them returned.

Sarah spent Christmas that year with Elizabeth and her family in

Cricklewood. She relaxed with gin and tonic, listened to Elizabeth's husband complaining about his sister, from whom he had just bought a faulty car. She received presents and gave them, she helped to cook the Christmas dinner. Preparing stuffing for the turkey, she heard herself saying:

'It's the only thing that worries me, being alone when I'm old.'

Elizabeth, plumper than ever this Christmas, expressed surprise by wrinkling her nose, which was a habit with her.

'Oh, but you manage so well.'

'Actually the future looks a little bleak.'

'Oh, Sarah, what nonsense!'

It was, and Sarah knew it was: she had learnt how to live alone. There was nothing nicer than coming back to the flat and putting a record on, pouring herself a drink and just sitting there listening to Mozart. There was nothing nicer than not having to consider someone else. She'd only shared the flat with Elizabeth in the first place because it had been necessary financially. That period was past.

'It's just that whatever shall I do when I finish at Pollock-Brown?'

'But that's years away.'

'Not really. Thirteen years. When I'm sixty.'

'They'll keep you on, surely? If you want to stay?'

'Mr Everend will be gone. I don't think I'd want to work for anyone else. No, I'll retire at sixty. According to the book.'

'But, my dear, you'll be perfectly all right.'

'I keep thinking of the flat, alone in it.'

'You've been alone in it for years.'

'I know.'

She placed more stuffing in the turkey and pressed it down with a wooden spoon. Sandra Pond would be forty-three when she was sixty. She'd probably look much the same, a little grey in her hair perhaps; she'd never run to fat.

'How are things going?' Elizabeth's husband demanded, coming into the kitchen in a breezy mood. 'Drink for Sarah?'

She smiled at him as he took tonic bottles from the fridge. 'I think she's got the change,' she heard Elizabeth saying to him later. 'Poor thing's gone all jittery.'

Sarah didn't mention the subject of her flat again that Christmas.

Well Im a les and I thought you was as well, the letter said. *Im sorry Sarah I didnt' mean to ofend you I didnt' no a thing about you. Ive loved other girls but not like you not as much. I really do love you Sarah. Im going to leave bloody PB because I dont want reminding every time I walk into*

*that bloody canteen. What I wanted was to dance with you remember
when I said I wanted to do something? Thats what I ment when I said
that. Sandra Pond.*

Sarah tried not to think about the letter, which both upset and shocked
her. She tried to forget the whole thing, the meeting with Sandra Pond and
how she'd felt herself drawn towards having a friendship with the girl. It
made her shiver when she thought about all that the letter suggested, it
even made her feel a little sick.

Such relationships between women had been talked about at school and
often occurred in newspaper reports and in books, on the television even.
Sarah had occasionally wondered if this woman or that might possibly
possess lesbian tendencies, but she had done so without much real interest
and had certainly never wondered about such tendencies in relation to
herself. But now, just as she had been unable to prevent her mind from
engaging in flights of fancy after her meeting with Sandra Pond, she was
unable to prevent it from straying about in directions that were inspired
by the girl's letter. The man called George, who over the years had become
the root of many fantasies, lost his identity to that of Sandra Pond. Yet it
was all different because revulsion, not present before, seemed everywhere
now. Was it curiosity of a kind, Sarah wondered, that drove her on,
enslaving her to fancies she did not care for? No longer did she think of
them as silly; malicious rather, certainly malign, like the stuff of nightmares.
Grimly she watched while Sandra Pond crossed the floor of a room, coming
closer to her, smiling at her. As the man called George had, the hands of
the girl undid the buttons of her dress, and then it seemed that fear was
added to revulsion. 'I really do love you, Sarah,' the slack voice said, as it
had said in the letter, as no other voice had ever said. The passion had a
cloying kind of headiness about it, like drunkenness. It was adoration, the
girl said, whispering now: it was adoration for every inch of skin and every
single hair that grew from Sarah's body and every light in her eyes, and
the beauty of her plainness. The pouting lips came closer to her own, the
dimples danced. And Sarah, then, would find herself weeping.

She never knew why she wept and assumed it was simply an extension
of her revulsion. She felt no desire to have this kind of relationship with a
person of her own sex. She didn't want a girl's lips leaving lipstick on her
own, she didn't want to experience their softness or the softness of the
body that went with them. She didn't want to experience a smell of scent,
or painted fingernails.

In rational moments Sarah said to herself that as time passed this
nightmare would fog over, as other occurrences in her life had fogged over

with the passing of time. She had destroyed the letter almost as soon as she'd read it. She had made inquiries: Sandra Pond, as she'd promised, had left Pollock-Brown.

Sarah visited Elizabeth and her family more frequently, she spent a weekend with her brother and his wife in Harrogate, she wrote at length to her other brother, saying they must not lose touch. She forced her mind back into childhood, to which it had regularly and naturally drifted before its invasion by Sandra Pond. It was a deliberate journey now, requiring discipline and concentration, but it was possible to make. Her father ambled into the sitting-room of the rectory, the spaniel called Dodge ambling after him. The wood fire brightly burned as indoor games were played, no one sulky or out of temper. 'And the consequences were,' her brother who was an engineer said, 'fire over England.' In the sunny garden she read about the girls of the Chalet School. Her brothers, in short trousers and flannel shirts, ran about catching wasps in jam jars. 'The peace of God,' her father's voice murmured, drifting over his small congregation. 'Of course you'll grow up pretty,' her mother softly promised, wiping away her tears.

The passing of time did help. The face of Sandra Pond faded a little, the wording of the ill-written letter became jumbled and uncertain. She would never hear of the girl again, she said to herself, and with an effort that lessened as more months passed by she continued to conjure up the distant world of the rectory.

Then, one Saturday morning in November, nearly a year after the Christmas party, Sandra Pond was there in the flesh again. She was in the Express Dairy, where Sarah always did her Saturday-morning shopping, and as soon as she saw her Sarah knew the girl had followed her into the shop. She felt faint and sickish when Sandra Pond smiled her pouting smile and the two dimples danced. She felt the blood draining away from her face and a tightening in her throat.

'Sorry,' Sandra Pond said instead of saying hullo, just standing there.

Sarah had a tin of Crosse and Blackwell's soup in one hand and a wire shopping basket in the other. She didn't know what to say. She thought she probably couldn't say anything even if she tried.

'I just wanted to say I was sorry,' Sandra Pond said. 'I've had it on my mind, Miss Machaen.'

Sarah shook her head. She put the Crosse and Blackwell's soup back on the stack of tins.

'I shouldn't have written that letter's what I mean.'

The girl didn't look well. She seemed to have a cold. She didn't look as pretty as she had at the Christmas party. She wore a brown tweed coat which wasn't very smart. Her shoes were cheap-looking.

'I don't know why I did it, Miss Machaen.'

Sarah tried to smile because she didn't want to be unkind. She ran her tongue about the inside of her mouth, which was dry, as though she'd eaten salt. She said:

'It doesn't matter.'

'It does to me. I couldn't sleep nights.'

'It was just a misunderstanding.'

Sandra Pond didn't say anything. She let a silence gather, and Sarah realized that she was doing so deliberately. Sandra Pond had come back to see how things were, to discover if, with time, the idea appealed to Sarah now, if she'd come to terms with the strangeness of it. As she stood there with the wire basket, she was aware that Sandra Pond had waited for an answer to her letter, that even before that, at the Christmas party, she had hoped for some sign. The girl was staring down at the cream-coloured tiles of the floor, her hands awkwardly by her sides.

The flights of fancy tumbled into Sarah's mind, jogging each other for precedence. They came in flashes: she and Sandra Pond sitting down to a meal, and walking into the foyer of a theatre, and looking at the *Madonna of the Meadow* in the National Gallery, and then a scene like the scene with the man called George occurred.

Sandra Pond looked up and at once the flights of fancy snapped out, like lights extinguished. What would people say? Sarah thought again, as she had on the night of the party. What would her brothers say to see passion thumping at their sister from the eyes of Sandra Pond? What would Elizabeth say, or Anne, or Mr Everend, or her dead father and mother? Would they cry out, amazed and yet delighted, that her plainness should inspire all this, that her plainness at last was beauty? Or would they shudder with disgust?

'I can't help being,' Sandra Pond said, 'the way I am.'

Sarah shook her head, trying to make the gesture seem sympathetic. She wanted to explain that she knew the girl had come specially back, to see what passing time had done, but she could not bring herself to. To have mentioned passing time in that way would have begun another kind of conversation. It was all ridiculous, standing here in the Express Dairy.

'I just wanted to say that and to say I was sorry. Thank you for listening, Miss Machaen.'

She was moving away, the heels of her shoes making a clicking noise on the cream-tiled floor. The smooth back of her head was outlined against packets of breakfast cereals and then against stacks of Mother's Pride bread. Something about her shoulders suggested to Sarah that she was holding back tears.

'Excuse me, dear,' a woman said, poking around Sarah to reach for oxtail soup.

'Oh, sorry.' Mechanically she smiled. She felt shaky and wondered if her face had gone pale. She couldn't imagine eating any of the food she'd selected. She couldn't imagine opening a tin or unwrapping butter without being overcome by the memory of Sandra Pond's sudden advent in the shop. Her instinct was to replace the goods on the shelves and she almost did so. But it seemed too much of a gesture, and too silly. Instead she carried the wire basket to the cashier and paid for what she'd chosen, transferring everything into her shopping-bag.

She walked away from the Express Dairy, by the newsagent's and the butcher's and the Martinez Dry Cleaners, who were offering a bargain, three garments cleaned for the normal price of one. She felt, as she had when the man called George had suddenly lost interest in her body, a pain inside her somewhere.

There was a bus stop, but Sandra Pond was not standing by it. Nor was she on the pavements that stretched on either side of a road that was busy with Saturday-morning traffic. Nor did she emerge from the telephone box, nor from the newsagent's, nor from Walton's the fruiterer's.

Sarah waited, still looking about. Sandra Pond had been genuinely sorry; she'd meant it when she'd said she'd hated causing the upset. 'Please come and have coffee,' were the words Sarah had ready to say now. 'It's really quite all right.' But she did not say them, because Sandra Pond had not lingered. And in a million years, Sarah thought, she would not ever find her.

Attracta

Attracta read about Penelope Vade in a newspaper, an item that upset her. It caused her to wonder if all her life as a teacher she'd been saying the wrong things to the children in her care. It saddened her when she thought about the faces that had passed through her schoolroom, ever since 1937. She began to feel she should have told them about herself.

She taught in a single schoolroom that hadn't altered much since the days when she'd been a pupil in it herself. There were portraits of England's kings and queens around the walls, painted by some teacher in the past. There were other pictures, added at some later date, of Irish heroes: Niall of the Nine Hostages, Lord Edward FitzGerald, Wolfe Tone and Grattan. Maps of Europe and of Ireland and of England, Wales and Scotland hung side by side. A new blackboard, attached to the wall, had ten years ago replaced the old pedestal one. The globe had always been there in Attracta's time, but since it did not designate political boundaries it wasn't much out of date. The twenty-five wooden desks more urgently needed to be replaced.

In the schoolroom Attracta taught the sixteen Protestant children of the town. The numbers had been sometimes greater in the past, and often fewer; sixteen was an average, a number she found easy to manage when divided into the four classes that the different ages demanded. The room was large, the desks arranged in groups; discipline had never been a problem. The country children brought sandwiches for lunch, the children of the town went home at midday. Attracta went home herself, to the house in North Street which she'd inherited from her Aunt Emmeline and where now she lived alone. She possessed an old blue Morris Minor but she did not often drive it to and from her schoolroom, preferring to make the journey on foot in order to get fresh air and exercise. She was a familiar figure, the Protestant teacher with her basket of groceries or exercise-books. She had never married, though twice she'd been proposed to: by an exchange clerk in the Provincial Bank and by an English visitor who'd once spent the summer in the area with his parents. All that was a long time ago now, for Attracta was sixty-one. Her predecessor in the schoolroom, Mr Ayrie, hadn't retired until he was over seventy. She had always assumed she'd emulate him in that.

Looking back on it, Attracta didn't regret that she had not married. She hadn't much cared for either of the men who'd proposed to her and she didn't mind being alone at sixty-one in her house in North Street. She regularly went to church, she had friends among the people who had been her pupils in the past. Now and again in the holidays she drove her Morris Minor to Cork for a day's shopping and possibly a visit to the Savoy or the Pavilion, although the films they offered were not as good as they'd been in the past. Being on her own was something she'd always known, having been both an only child and an orphan. There'd been tragedy in her life but she considered that she had not suffered. People had been good to her.

English Girl's Suicide in Belfast the headline about Penelope Vade said, and below it there was a photograph, a girl with a slightly crooked smile and freckled cheeks. There was a photograph of her husband in army uniform, taken a few weeks before his death, and of the house in Belfast in which she had later rented a flat. *From the marks of blood on carpets and rugs*, the item said, *it is deduced that Mrs Vade dragged herself across the floors of two rooms. She appears repeatedly to have fainted before she reached a bottle of aspirins in a kitchen cupboard.* She had been twenty-three at the time of her death.

It was Penelope Vade's desire to make some kind of gesture, a gesture of courage and perhaps anger, that had caused her to leave her parents' home in Haslemere and to go to Belfast. Her husband, an army officer, had been murdered in Belfast; he'd been decapitated as well. His head, wrapped in cotton-wool to absorb the ooze of blood, secured within a plastic bag and packed in a biscuit-tin, had been posted to Penelope Vade. Layer by layer the parcel had been opened by her in Haslemere. She hadn't known that he was dead before his dead eyes stared into hers.

Her gesture was her mourning of him. She went to Belfast to join the Women's Peace Movement, to make the point that somehow neither he nor she had been defeated. But her gesture, publicly reported, had incensed the men who'd gone to the trouble of killing him. One after another, seven of them had committed acts of rape on her. It was after that that she had killed herself.

A fortnight after Attracta had first read the newspaper item it still upset her. It haunted her, and she knew why it did, though only imprecisely. Alone at night, almost catching her unawares, scenes from the tragedy established themselves in her mind: the opening of the biscuit-box, the smell of death, the eyes, blood turning brown. As if at a macabre slide-show, the scene would change: before people had wondered about her whereabouts Penelope Vade had been dead for four days; mice had left droppings on her body.

One afternoon, in order to think the matter over in peace and quiet, Attracta drove her Morris Minor to the sea at Cedarstrand, eight miles from the town. She clambered from the strand up to the headland and paused there, gazing down into the bay, at the solitary island it held. No one had ever lived on the island because its smallness would have made a self-supporting existence impossible. When she'd been growing up she'd often wondered what it would be like to live alone on the rocky fastness, in a wooden hut or a cottage built of stones. Not very agreeable, she'd thought, for she'd always been sociable. She thought it again as she turned abruptly from the sea and followed a path inland through wiry purple heather.

Two fishermen, approaching her on the path, recognized her as the Protestant teacher from the town eight miles away and stood aside for her to pass. She was thinking that nothing she might ever have said in her schoolroom could possibly have prevented the death of a girl in a city two hundred miles away. Yet in a way it seemed ridiculous that for so long she had been relating the details of Cromwell's desecration and the laws of Pythagoras, when she should have been talking about Mr Devereux and Geraldine Carey. And it was Mr Purce she should have recalled instead of the Battle of the Boyne.

The fishermen spoke to her as she passed them by but she didn't reply. It surprised them that she didn't, for they hadn't heard that the Protestant teacher had recently become deaf or odd. Just old, they supposed, as they watched her progressing slowly: an upright figure, spare and seeming fragile, a certain stiffness in her movement.

What made Attracta feel close to the girl in the newspaper item was the tragedy in her own life: the death of her mother and her father when she was three. Her parents had gone away, she had been told, and at first she had wept miserably and would not be comforted. But as days passed into weeks, and weeks into months, this unhappiness gradually left her. She ceased to ask about her parents and became used to living in her Aunt Emmeline's house in North Street. In time she no longer remembered the morning she'd woken up in this house in a bed that was strange to her; nor could she recollect her parents' faces. She grew up assuming they were no longer alive and when once she voiced this assumption her aunt did not contradict it. It wasn't until later in her childhood, when she was eleven, that she learnt the details of the tragedy from Mr Purce, a small man in a hard black hat, who was often to be seen on the streets of the town. He was one of the people she noticed in her childhood, like the elderly beggar-woman called Limerick Nancy and the wild-looking builder's labourer who could walk a hundred miles without stopping, who never wore a jersey or a coat over his open shirt even on the coldest winter days. There were other people too: priests going for a walk in pairs, out along the road that led to the golf-course and to Cedarstrand by the longer route. Strolling through the afternoon sunshine there were nuns in pairs also, and there was Redmond the solicitor hurrying about with his business papers, and Father Quinlan on his bicycle. At night there were the florid country bachelors tipsily smiling through cigarette smoke, lips glistening in the street-light outside Colgan's public house. At all times of day, at all the town's corners, the children of the poor waited for nothing in particular.

The town was everything in Attracta's childhood, and only some of it had changed in the fifty years that had passed. Without nostalgia she remembered now the horses and carts with milk-churns for the creamery, slowly progressing on narrow streets between colour-washed houses. On fair-days the pavements had been slithery with dung, and on fair-days they still were. Farmers stood by their animals, their shirts clean for the occasion, a stud at their throats, without collar or tie. Dogs slouched in a manner that was characteristic of the dogs of the town; there was a smell of stout and sawdust. In her childhood there had been O'Mara's Picture House, dour grey cement encasing the dreamland of Fred Astaire and Ginger Rogers. Built with pride in 1929, O'Mara's was a ruin now.

Within the world of the town there was for Attracta a smaller, Protestant world. Behind green railings there was Mr Ayrie's Protestant schoolroom. There was the Church of Ireland church, with its dusty flags of another age, and Archdeacon Flower's prayers for the English royal family. There were the Sunday-school classes of Mr and Mrs Dell, and the patience of her aunt, which seemed like a Protestant thing also – the Protestant duty of a woman who had never expected to find herself looking after a child. There was Mr Devereux, a Protestant who never went to church.

No one in the town, not even her aunt, was kinder to Attracta than Mr Devereux. On her birthday he came himself to the house in North Street with a present carefully wrapped, a doll's house once, so big he'd had to ask the man next door to help him out of the dickey of his motor-car with it. At Christmas he had a Christmas tree in his house, and other children in the town, her friends from school, were invited to a party. Every Saturday she spent the afternoon with him, eating his housekeeper's delicious orange cake for tea and sticking stamps into the album he'd given her, listening to his gramophone in the room he called his office. He loved getting a huge fire going in his office, banking up the coals so that they'd glow and redden her cheeks. In summer he sat in his back garden with her, sometimes reading *Coral Island* aloud. He made her run away to the raspberry canes and come back with a punnet of fruit, which they'd have at suppertime. He was different from her aunt and from Mr Ayrie and Archdeacon Flower. He smelt of the tobacco he smoked in his pipe. He wore tweed suits and a striped shirt with a white celluloid collar, and patterned brown shoes which Attracta greatly admired. His tie matched the tweed of his suit, a gold watch dangled from the lapel of his jacket into his top pocket. He was by trade a grain merchant.

His house was quiet and always a little mysterious. The drawing-room, full of looming furniture, was dark in the daytime. Behind layers of curtains that hung to the ground, blue blinds obscured the greater part of the light: sunshine would damage the furniture, Mr Devereux's housekeeper used to say. On a summer's afternoon this woman would light a paraffin lamp so that she could polish the mahogany surfaces of the tables and the grand piano. Her name was Geraldine Carey: she added to the house's mystery.

Mr Devereux's smile was slow. There was a laziness about it, both in its leisurely arrival and the way it lingered. His eyes had a weary look, quite out of keeping with all the efforts he made to promote his friendship with Attracta and her aunt. Yet the efforts seemed natural to Attracta, as were the efforts of Geraldine Carey, who was the quietest person Attracta had ever met. She spoke in a voice that was often hard to hear. Her hair was as black as coal, drawn back from her face and arranged in a coiled bun at the back of her head. Her eyes were startlingly alive, seeming to be black also, often cast down. She had the kind of beauty that Attracta would like one day to possess herself, but knew she would not. Geraldine Carey was like a nun because of the dark clothes she wore, and she had a nun's piety. In the town it was said she couldn't go to Mass often enough. 'Why weren't you a nun, Geraldine?' Attracta asked her once, watching her making bread in her big, cool kitchen. The habit would have suited her, she added, already imagining the housekeeper's face framed by the coif, and the black voluminous skirts. But Geraldine Carey replied that she'd never heard God calling her. 'Only the good are called,' she said.

There'd been a time, faintly remembered by Attracta, when her Aunt Emmeline hadn't been well disposed towards Mr Devereux and Geraldine Carey. There'd been suspicion of some kind, a frowning over the presents he brought, an agitation whenever Attracta was invited to tea. Because of her own excitement over the presents and the invitations Attracta hadn't paid much attention to the nature of her aunt's concern, and looking back on it years later could only speculate. Her Aunt Emmeline was a precise person, a tall woman who had never married, reputed to be delicate. Her house in North Street, very different from Mr Devereux's, reflected her: it was neat as a new pin, full of light, the windows of its small rooms invariably open at the top to let in fresh air. The fanlight above the hall door was always gleaming, filling the hall with morning sunlight. Attracta's Aunt Emmeline had a fear of dankness, of damp clothes and wet feet, and rain falling on the head. She worried about lots of things.

Clearly she had worried about Mr Devereux. There was an occasion when Archdeacon Flower had been specially invited to tea, when Attracta had listened at the sitting-room door because she'd sensed from her aunt's flustered manner that something important was to be discussed. 'Oh, have no worry in that direction at all,' she heard the Archdeacon say. 'Gentle as a lamb that man's become.' Her aunt asked a question Attracta could not hear because of the sound of a teacup being replaced on a saucer. 'He's doing the best he can,' the Archdeacon continued, 'according to his lights.' Her aunt mentioned Geraldine Carey, and again the Archdeacon reassured her. 'Bygones are bygones,' he said. 'Isn't it a remarkable thing when a man gets caught in his own snare?' He commented on the quality of her aunt's fruitcake, and then said that everyone should be charitably disposed towards Mr Devereux and Geraldine Carey. He believed, he said, that that was God's wish.

After that, slowly over the years, Attracta's aunt began to think more highly of Mr Devereux, until in the end there was no one in the entire town, with the possible exception of Archdeacon Flower, whom she held in greater esteem. Once when MacQuilly the coal merchant insisted that she hadn't paid for half a ton of coal and she recollected perfectly giving the money to the man who'd delivered it, Mr Devereux had come to her aid. 'A right old devil, MacQuilly is,' Attracta heard him saying in the hall, and that was the end her aunt had ever heard of the matter. On Saturday evenings, having kept Attracta company on her walk home, Mr Devereux might remain for a little while in the house in North Street. He sometimes brought lettuces or cuttings with him, or tomatoes or strawberries. He would take a glass of sherry in the trim little sitting-room with its delicate inlaid chairs that matched the delicacy of Attracta's aunt. Often he'd still be there, taking a second glass, when Attracta came down to say good-night. Her aunt's cat, Diggory, liked to climb up on to his knees, and as if in respect of some kind Mr Devereux never lit his pipe. He and her aunt would converse in low voices and generally they'd cease when Attracta entered the room. She would kiss him good-night after she'd kissed her aunt. She imagined it was what having a father was like.

At the town's approximate centre there stood a grey woman on a pedestal, a statue of the Maid of Erin. It was here, only yards from this monument, that Mr Purce told Attracta the truth about her parents' death, when she was eleven. She'd always had the feeling that Mr Purce wanted to speak to her, even that he was waiting until she could understand what it was he had to say. He was a man people didn't much like; he'd settled in the town, having come there from somewhere else. He was a clerk in the court-house.

'There's a place I know where there's greenfinches,' he said, as if introducing himself. 'Ten nests of them, maybe twelve, maybe more. D'you understand me, Attracta? Would you like me to show you?'

She was on her way home from school. She had to get back to do her homework, she said to Mr Purce. She didn't want to go looking for green-finches with him.

'Did Devereux tell you not to talk to Mr Purce?' he said, and she shook her head. As far as she could remember, Mr Devereux had never mentioned Mr Purce. 'I see you in church,' Mr Purce said.

She had seen him too, sitting in the front, over on the lefthand side. Her aunt had often remarked that the day Mr Purce didn't go to church it would be a miracle. It was like Geraldine Carey going to Mass.

'I'll walk out with you,' he said. 'I have a half day today for myself.'

They walked together, to her embarrassment. She glanced at shop-windows to catch a glimpse of their reflection, to see if they looked as awkward as she felt. He was only a head taller than she and part of that was made up by his hard black hat. His clerk's suit was double-breasted, navy-blue with a pale stripe in it, shiny here and there, in need of a good ironing. He wore black leather gloves and carried a walking-stick. He always had the gloves and the walking-stick in church, but his Sunday suit was superior to the one he wore now. Her own fair hair, pinned up under her green-brimmed hat, was what stood out between the two of them. The colour of good corn, Mr Devereux used to say, and she always considered that a compliment, coming from a grain merchant. Her face was thin and her eyes blue, but reflected in the shop-windows there was now only a blur of flesh, a thin shaft between her hat and the green coat that matched it.

'You've had misfortune, Attracta.' Solemnly he nodded, repeating the motion of his head until she wished he'd stop. 'It was a terrible thing to be killed by mistake.'

Attracta didn't know what he was talking about. They passed by the last of the shops in North Street, Shannon's grocery and bar, Banim's bakery, the hardware that years ago had run out of stock. The narrow street widened a bit. Mr Purce said:

'Has she made a Catholic girl out of you, Attracta?'

'Who, Mr Purce?'

'Devereux's woman. Has she tried anything on? Has she shown you rosary beads?'

She shook her head.

'Don't ever look at them if she does. Look away immediately if she gets them out of her apron or anything like that. Will you promise me that, girl?'

'I don't think she would. I don't think Mr Devereux —'

'You can never tell with that crowd. There isn't a trick in the book they won't hop on to. Will you promise me now? Have nothing to do with carry-on like that.'

'Yes, Mr Purce.'

As they walked he prodded at the litter on the pavement with his walking-stick. Cigarette packets and squashed matchboxes flew into the gutter, bits of the *Cork Examiner*, sodden paper bags. He was known for this activity in the town, and even when he was on his own his voice was often heard protesting at the untidiness.

'I'm surprised they never told you, Attracta,' he said. 'What are you now, girl?'

'I'm eleven.'

'A big girl should know things like that.'

'What things, Mr Purce?'

He nodded in his repetitious manner, and then he explained himself. The tragedy had occurred in darkness, at night: her parents had accidentally become involved with an ambush meant for the Black and Tan soldiers who were in force in the area at the time. She herself had long since been asleep at home, and as he spoke she remembered waking up to find herself in a bed in her aunt's house, without knowing how she got there. 'That's how they got killed, Attracta,' Mr Purce said, and then he said an extra-ordinary thing. 'You've got Devereux and his woman to thank for it.'

She knew that the Black and Tan soldiers had been camped near the town; she knew there'd been fighting. She realized that the truth about the death had been counted too terrible for a child to bear. But that her parents should have been shot, and shot in error, that the whole thing had somehow been the responsibility of Mr Devereux and Geraldine Carey, seemed inconceivable to Attracta.

'They destroyed a decent Protestant pair,' Mr Purce continued, still flicking litter from the pavement. 'Half-ten at night on a public road, destroyed like pests.'

The sun, obscured by clouds while Attracta and Mr Purce had made the journey from the centre of the town, was suddenly warm on Attracta's face. A woman in a horse and cart, attired in the black hooded cloak of the locality, passed slowly by. There were sacks of meal in the cart which had probably come from Mr Devereux's mill.

'Do you understand what I'm saying to you, Attracta? Devereux was organizing resistance up in the hills. He had explosives and booby traps, he was drilling men to go and kill people. Did nobody tell you about himself and Geraldine Carey?'

She shook her head. He nodded again, as if to indicate that little better could be expected.

'Listen to me, Attracta. Geraldine Carey was brought into this town by the man she got married to, who used to work at Devereux's mill. Six months later she'd joined up with Devereux in the type of dirty behaviour I wouldn't soil myself telling you about. Not only that, Attracta, she was gun-running with him. She was fixing explosives like a man would, dressed up like a man in uniform. Devereux was as wild as a savage. There was nothing Devereux wouldn't do, there was nothing the woman wouldn't do either. They'd put booby traps down and it didn't matter who got killed. They'd ambush the British soldiers when the soldiers didn't have a chance.'

It was impossible to believe him. It was impossible to visualize the housekeeper and Mr Devereux in the role he'd given them. No one with any sense could believe that Geraldine Carey would kill people. Was everything Mr Purce said a lie? He was a peculiar man: had he some reason for stating her mother and her father had met their deaths in this way?

'Your father was a decent man, Attracta. He was never drunk in his life. There was prayers for him in the chapel, but that was only a hypocrisy of the priests. Wouldn't the priest Quinlan like to see every Protestant in this town dead and buried? Wouldn't he like to see you and me six foot down with clay in our eye-sockets?'

Attracta didn't believe that, and more certainly now it seemed to her that everything Mr Purce said was untrue. Catholics were different; they crossed themselves when they passed their chapel; they went in for crosses and confession; they had Masses and candles. But it was hard to accept that Father Quinlan, a jovial red-haired man, would prefer it if she were dead. She'd heard her aunt's maid, Méta, saying that Father Fallon was cantankerous and that Father Martin wasn't worth his salt, but neither of them seemed to Attracta to be the kind of man who'd wish people dead. 'Proddy-woddy green-guts,' Catholic children would shout out sometimes and the Protestants would call back the familiar reply. But there was never much vindictiveness about any of it. The sides were unevenly matched: there were too few Protestants in the town to make a proper opposition; trouble was avoided.

'He was a traitor to his religion, Attracta. And I'll promise you this: if I was to tell you about that woman of his you wouldn't enter the house they have.' Abruptly he turned and walked away, back into the town, his walking-stick still frantically working, poking away any litter it could find.

The sun was hot now. Attracta felt sticky within her several layers of clothes. She had a chapter of her history book to read, about the Saxons coming to England. She had four long-division sums to do, and seven lines of poetry to learn. *What potions have I drunk of Syren tears*, the first one stated, a statement Attracta could make neither head nor tail of.

She didn't go straight home. Instead she turned off to the left and walked through a back street, out into the country. She passed fields of mangels and turnips, again trying to imagine the scenes Mr Purce had sketched for her, the ambush of men waiting for the soldiers, the firing of shots. It occurred to her that she had never asked anyone if her parents were buried in the Church of Ireland graveyard.

She passed by tinkers encamped on the verge of the road. A woman ran after her and asked for money, saying her husband had just died. She swore when Attracta said she hadn't any, and then her manner changed again. She developed a whine in her voice, she said she'd pray for Attracta if she'd bring her money, tomorrow or the next day.

Had Mr Purce only wished to turn her against Mr Devereux because Mr Devereux did not go to church? Was there no more to it than that? Did Mr Purce say the first thing that came into his head? As Attracta walked, the words of Archdeacon Flower came back to her: in stating that Mr Devereux was now as gentle as a lamb, was there the implication that once he hadn't been? And had her aunt, worried about Geraldine Carey, been reassured on that score also?

'It's all over now, dear,' her aunt said. She looked closely at Attracta and then put her arms round her, as if expecting tears. But tears didn't come, for Attracta was only amazed.

Fifty years later, walking through the heather by the sea, Attracta remembered vividly that moment of her childhood. She couldn't understand how Mr Devereux and Geraldine Carey had changed so. 'Maybe they bear the burden of guilt,' Archdeacon Flower had explained, summoned to the house the following day by her aunt. 'Maybe they look at you and feel responsible. It was an accident, but people can feel responsible for an accident.' What had happened was in the past, he reminded her, as her aunt had. She understood what they were implying, that it must all be forgotten, yet she couldn't help imagining Mr Devereux and his housekeeper laying booby traps on roads and drilling men in the hills. Geraldine

Carey's husband had left the town, Mr Purce told her on a later occasion: he'd gone to Co. Louth and hadn't been heard of since. 'Whore,' Mr Purce said. 'No better than a whore she is.' Attracta, looking the word up in a dictionary, was astonished.

Having started, Mr Purce went on and on. Mr Devereux's house wasn't suitable for an eleven-year-old girl to visit, since it was the house of a murderer. Wasn't it a disgrace that a Protestant girl should set foot in a house where the deaths of British soldiers and the Protestant Irish had been planned? One Saturday afternoon, unable to restrain himself, he arrived at the house himself. He shouted at Mr Devereux from the open hall door. 'Isn't it enough to have destroyed her father and mother without letting that woman steal her for the Pope?' His grey face was suffused beneath his hard hat, his walking-stick thrashed the air. Mr Devereux called him an Orange mason. 'I hate the bloody sight of you,' Mr Purce said in a quieter voice, and then in his abrupt way he walked off.

That, too, Attracta remembered as she continued her walk around the headland. Mr Devereux afterwards never referred to it, and Mr Purce never spoke to her again, as if deciding that there was nothing left to say. In the town, as she grew up, people would reluctantly answer her when she questioned them about her parents' tragedy in an effort to discover more than her aunt or Archdeacon Flower had revealed. But nothing new emerged, the people she asked only agreeing that Mr Devereux in those days had been as wild as Mr Purce suggested. He'd drilled the local men, he'd been assisted in every way by Geraldine Carey, whose husband had gone away to Louth. But everything had been different since the night of the tragedy.

Her aunt tried to explain to her the nature of Mr Purce's hatred of Mr Devereux. Mr Purce saw things in a certain light, she said, he could not help himself. He couldn't help believing that Father Quinlan would prefer the town's Protestants to be dead and buried. He couldn't help believing that immorality continued in the relationship between Mr Devereux and his housekeeper when clearly it did not. He found a spark and made a fire of it, he was a bigot and was unable to do anything about it. The Protestants of the town felt ashamed of him.

Mr Purce died, and was said to have continued in his hatred with his last remaining breaths. He mentioned the Protestant girl, his bleak, harsh voice weakening. She had been contaminated and infected, she was herself no better than the people who used her for their evil purposes. She was not fit to teach the Protestant children of the town, as she was now commencing to do. 'As I lie dying,' Mr Purce said to the clergyman who had succeeded Archdeacon Flower, 'I am telling you that, sir.' But afterwards, when the story of Mr Purce's death went round, the people of the town looked at Attracta with a certain admiration, seeming to suggest that for her the twisting of events had not been easy, neither the death of her parents nor the forgiveness asked of her by Mr Devereux, nor the bigotry of Mr Purce. She'd been caught in the middle of things, they seemed to suggest, and had survived unharmed.

Surviving, she was happy in the town. Too happy to marry the exchange clerk from the Provincial Bank or the young man who came on a holiday to Cedarstrand with his parents. *Pride goeth before destruction*, her pupils' headlines stated, and *Look before you leap*. Their fingers pressed hard on inky pens, knuckles jutting beneath the strain, tongue-tips aiding concentration. Ariadne, Finn MacCool, King Arthur's sword, Cathleen ni Houlihan: legends filled the schoolroom, with facts about the Romans and the Normans, square roots and the Gulf Stream. Children grew up and went away, returning sometimes to visit Attracta in her house in North Street. Others remained and in the town she watched them changing, grey coming into their hair, no longer moving as lithely as they had. She developed an affection for the town without knowing why, beyond the fact that it was part of her.

'Yet in all a lifetime I learnt nothing,' she said aloud to herself on the headland. 'And I taught nothing either.' She gazed out at the smooth blue Atlantic but did not see it clearly. She saw instead the brown-paper parcel that contained the biscuit-box she had read about, and the fingers of Penelope Vade undoing the string and the brown paper. She saw her lifting off the lid. She saw her frowning for a moment, before the eyes of the man she loved stared deadly into hers. Months later, all courage spent and defeated in her gesture, the body of Penelope Vade dragged itself across the floors of two different rooms. There was the bottle full of aspirins in a cupboard, and water drunk from a Wedgwood-patterned cup, like the cups Attracta drank from every day.

In her schoolroom, with its maps and printed pictures, the sixteen faces stared back at her, the older children at the back. She repeated her question.

'Now, what does anyone think of that?'

Again she read them the news item, reading it slowly because she wanted it to become as rooted in their minds as it was in hers. She lingered over the number of bullets that had been fired into the body of Penelope Vade's husband, and over the removal of his head.

'Can you see that girl? Can you imagine men putting a human head in a tin box and sending it through the post? Can you imagine her receiving it? The severed head of the man she loved?'

'Sure, isn't there stuff like that in the papers the whole time?' one of the children suggested.

She agreed that that was so. 'I've had a good life in this town,' she added, and the children looked at her as if she'd suddenly turned mad.

'I'm getting out of it,' one of them said after a pause. 'Back of beyond, miss.'

She began at the beginning. She tried to get into the children's minds an image of a baby sleeping while violence and death took place on the Cork road. She described her Aunt Emmeline's house in North Street, the neat feminine house it had been, her aunt's cat, Diggory, the small sitting-room, her aunt's maid, Méta. She spoke of her own very fair hair and her thin face, and the heavy old-fashioned clothes she'd worn in those days. She spoke of the piety of Geraldine Carey, and the grain merchant's tired face. The friendship they offered her was like Penelope Vade proclaiming peace in the city where her husband had been killed; it was a gesture, too.

'His house would smell of roses on a summer's day. She'd carry his meals to him, coming out of the shadows of her kitchen. As if in mourning, the blue blinds darkened the drawing-room. It was they who bore the tragedy, not I.'

She described Mr Purce's face and his grating voice. She tried to make of him a figure they could see among the houses and shops that were familiar to them: the hard black hat, the walking-stick poking away litter. He had done his best to rescue her, acting according to his beliefs. He wanted her not to forget, not realizing that there was nothing for her to remember.

'But I tried to imagine,' she said, 'as I am asking you to imagine now: my mother and father shot dead on the Cork road, and Mr Devereux and Geraldine Carey as two monstrous people, and arms being blown off soldiers, and vengeance breeding vengeance.'

A child raised a hand and asked to leave the room. Attracta gave permission and awaited the child's return before proceeding. She filled the time in by describing things that had changed in the town, the falling to pieces of O'Mara's Picture House, the closing of the tannery in 1938. When the child came back she told of Mr Purce's death, how he'd said she was not fit to teach Protestant children.

'I tried to imagine a night I'd heard about,' she said, 'when Mr Devereux's men found a man in Madden's public house whom they said had betrayed them, and how they took him out to Cedarstrand and hanged him in a barn. Were they pleased after they'd done that? Did they light cigarettes, saying the man was better dead? One of those other men must have gone to a post office with the wrapped biscuit-box. He must have watched it being weighed and paid the postage. Did he say to himself he was exceptional to have hoodwinked a post-office clerk?'

Obediently listening in their rows of worn desks, the children wondered what on earth all this was about. No geography or history lesson had ever been so bewildering; those who found arithmetic difficult would have settled for attempting to understand it now. They watched the lined face of their teacher, still thin as she'd said it had been in childhood, the fair hair grey now. The mouth twitched and rapidly moved, seeming sometimes to quiver as if it struggled against tears. What on earth had this person called Penelope Vade to do with anything?

'She died believing that hell had come already. She'd lost all faith in human life, and who can blame her? She might have stayed in Haslemere, like anyone else would have. Was she right to go to the city where her husband had been murdered, to show its other victims that her spirit had not been wholly crushed?'

No one answered, and Attracta was aware of the children's startled gaze. But the startled gaze was a natural reaction. She said to herself that it didn't matter.

'My story is one with hers,' she said. 'Horror stories, with different endings only. I think of her now and I can see quite clearly the flat she lived in in Belfast. I can see the details, correctly or not I've no idea. Wallpaper with a pattern of brownish-purple flowers on it, gaunt furniture casting shadows, a tea-caddy on the hired television set. I drag my body across the floors of two rooms, over a carpet that smells of dust and cigarette ash, over rugs and cool linoleum. I reach up in the kitchen, a hand on the edge of the sink: one by one I eat the aspirins until the bottle's empty.'

There was a silence. Feet were shuffled in the schoolroom. No one spoke.

'If only she had known,' Attracta said, 'that there was still a faith she might have had, that God does not forever withhold His mercy. Will those same men who exacted that vengeance on her one day keep bees and budgerigars? Will they serve in shops, and be kind to the blind and the deaf? Will they garden in the evenings and be good fathers? It is not impossible. Oh, can't you see,' she cried, 'what happened in this town? Here, at the back of beyond. Can't you appreciate it? And can't you see her lying there, mice nibbling her dried blood?'

The children still were quiet, their faces still not registering the comment she wished to make. It was because she'd been clumsy, she thought. All she'd meant to tell them was never to despair. All she had meant to do was to prepare them for a future that looked grim. She had been happy, she said again. The conversation of Mr Purce had been full of the truth but it hadn't made sense because the years had turned the truth around.

To the children she appeared to be talking now to herself. She was old, a few of them silently considered; that was it. She didn't appear to understand that almost every day there was the kind of vengeance she spoke of reported on the television. Bloodshed was wholesale, girls were tarred and left for dead, children no older than they were armed with guns.

'I only hope,' they heard her saying, 'she knows that strangers mourn her.'

Another silence lingered awkwardly and then she nodded at a particular child and the child rose and rang a hand-bell. The children filed away, well-mannered and docile as she had taught them to be. She watched them in the playground, standing in twos and threes, talking about her. It had meant nothing when she'd said that people change. The gleam of hope she'd offered had been too slight to be of use, irrelevant in the horror they took for granted, as part of life. Yet she could not help still believing that it mattered when monsters did not remain monsters for ever. It wasn't much to put against the last bleak moments of Penelope Vade, but it was something for all that. She wished she could have made her point.

Twenty minutes later, when the children returned to the schoolroom, her voice no longer quivered, nor did it seem to struggle against tears. The older children learnt about agriculture in Sweden, the younger ones about the Pyrenees, the youngest that Munster had six counties. The day came to an end at three o'clock and when all the children had gone Attracta locked the schoolroom and walked to the house she had inherited in North Street.

A week later Archdeacon Flower's successor came to see her, his visit interrupting further violence on the television news. He beat about the bush while he nibbled biscuits and drank cups of tea by the fire; then he suggested that perhaps she should consider retiring one of these days. She was over sixty, he pointed out with his clerical laugh, and she replied that Mr Ayrie had gone on until seventy. Sixty, the clergyman repeated with another laugh, was the post's retirement age. Children were a handful nowadays.

She smiled, thinking of her sixteen docile charges. They had chattered to their parents, and the parents had been shocked to hear that they'd been told of a man decapitated and a girl raped seven times. School was not for that, they had angrily protested to the clergyman, and he had had no option but to agree. At the end of the summer term there'd be a presentation of Waterford glass.

'Every day in my schoolroom I should have honoured the small, remarkable thing that happened in this town. It matters that she died in despair, with no faith left in human life.'

He was brisk. For as long as most people could remember she had been a remarkable teacher; in no way had she failed. He turned the conversation to more cheerful topics, he ate more biscuits and a slice of cake. He laughed and even made a joke. He retailed a little harmless gossip.

Eventually she stood up. She walked with her visitor to the hall, shook hands with him and saw him out. In the sitting-room she piled the tea things on to a tray and placed it on a table by the door. She turned the television on again but when the screen lit up she didn't notice it. The face of Penelope Vade came into her mind, the smile a little crooked, the freckled cheeks.

A Dream of Butterflies

Various people awoke with a sense of relief. Sleepily, Colin Rhodes wondered what there was to be relieved about. As he did in the moment of waking every morning, he encased with his left hand one of his wife's plump breasts and then remembered the outcome of last night's meeting. Miss Cogings, alone in her narrow bed and listening to a chorus of housemartins, remembered it with the same degree of satisfaction. So did the Poudards when their Teasmade roused them at a quarter to seven. So did the Reverend Feare, and Mr Mottershead and Mr and Mrs Tilzey, and the Blennerhassetts, who ran the Village Stores. Mrs Feare, up since dawn with an ailing child, was pleased because her husband was. There would be peace when there might have been war. A defeat had been inflicted.

The Allenbys, however, awoke in Luffnell Lodge with mixed feelings. What to do with the Lodge now that it remained unsold? How long would they have to wait for another buyer? For having made their minds up, they really wanted to move on as soon as possible. A bridging loan had been negotiated at one point but they'd decided against it because the interest was so high. They planned to buy a bungalow in a part of Cornwall that was noted for its warmth and dryness, both of which would ease Mrs Allenby's arthritis. Everything that had been said at the meeting made sense to Mr and Mrs Allenby; they quite understood the general point of view. But they wished, that morning, that things might have been different.

'That's really bizarre,' Hugh said in the Mansors' breakfast-room.

'Dreams often are.'

'But butterflies –'

'It has to do with the meeting.'

'Ah, of course, the meeting.'

He saw at once what had been happening. He traced quite easily the series of his wife's thoughts, one built upon the last, fact in the end becoming fantasy.

Emily buttered toast and reached for grapefruit marmalade. 'Silly,' she said, not believing that it was.

'A bit,' he agreed, smiling at her. He went on to talk of something else, an item in *The Times*, another airliner hijacked.

The sun filled their breakfast-room. It struck the bones of his compact features; it livened his calm grey hair. It found the strawberry mark, like a tulip, on her neck; it made her spectacles glint. They were the same age, fifty-two, not yet grandparents but soon to be. He dealt in property; she'd once been a teacher of Latin and Greek. She was small and given to putting on weight if she wasn't careful: dumpy, she considered herself.

'Don't let it worry you,' Hugh said, folding *The Times* for further perusal on the train. 'It's all over now.'

He was handsome in his thin way, and she was plain. Perhaps he had married her because he had not felt up to the glamour of a beautiful woman: as a young man, unproved in the world, he had had an inferiority complex, and success in middle age had not managed to shake it off. It wouldn't have surprised him if the heights he'd scaled in his business world all of a sudden turned out to be a wasteland. He specialized in property in distant places, Jamaica, Spain, the Bahamas: some economic jolt could shatter everything. The house they lived in, on the edge of a Sussex village, was the symbol of his good fortune over the years. It was also his due, for he had worked doggedly; only his inferiority complex prevented him from taking it for granted. It puzzled him that he, so unpromising as a boy at school, had done so well; and occasionally, but not often, it puzzled him that they'd made a success of their marriage in times when the failure rate was high. Perhaps they'd made a go of it because she was modest too: more than once he'd wondered if that could be true. Could it be that Emily, so much cleverer than he, had found a level with him because her lack of beauty kept her in her place, as his inferiority complex kept him? She had said that as a girl she'd imagined she would not marry, assuming that a strawberry mark and dumpiness, and glasses too, would be too much for any man. He often thought about her as she must have been, cleverest in the class; while he was being slow on the uptake. 'You're very kind' was what most often, in the way of compliments, Emily said to him.

'Have a good day' was what she said now, forcing cheerfulness on to her face, for the dream she'd had still saddened her and the memory of the meeting worried her.

'I'll be on the five o'clock.' He touched her cheek with his lips, and then was gone, the door of the breakfast-room opening and closing, the hall door banging. She listened to the starting of the car and the sound of the wheels on the tarmac, then the engine fading to nothing in the distance.

She felt as he did, that together they had not done badly in twenty-seven years of marriage. She'd been a Miss Forrest; becoming Mrs Mansor had seemed the nicest thing that yet had happened to her; and for all their married life – the worries during the lean years, the bringing up of their three children – she had regretted nothing, and in the end there'd been the reward of happiness in middle age. She missed their son and daughters, all of whom were now married themselves, but in compensation there was the contentment that the house and garden brought, and the unexacting life of the village. As well, there were the visits of their children and her memories of girls whom she had taught, some of whom kept up with her. It was still a pleasure to read Horace and the lesser Greek poets, to find in an experimental way a new interpretation in place of the standard, scholar's one.

Their house, in the style of Queen Anne though in fact of a later period, was hidden from the road and the surrounding fields by modest glades of silver birches. It was a compact house, easy to run and keep clean, modernized with gadgets, warm in winter. Alone in it in the mornings Emily often played Bach or Mozart on the sitting-room hi-fi system, the music drifting into the kitchen and the bedrooms and the breakfast-room, pursuing her agreeably wherever she went.

But this morning she was not in the mood for Bach or Mozart. She continued to sit as her husband had left her, saying to herself that she must come to terms with what had happened. She had raised her voice but no one had cared to listen to it. Only Golkorn had listened, his great tightly cropped head slowly nodding, his eyes occasionally piercing hers. At the meeting her voice had faltered; her cheeks had warmed; nothing had come out as she'd meant it to.

Unladylike assortment of calumnies. In the train on the way to Waterloo he couldn't think of a nine-lettered word. As a chore, he did *The Times* crossword every day, determined to do better with practice. *There's none of the Old Adam in a cardinal* (6). He sighed and put the paper down.

It worried him that she'd been so upset. He hadn't known what to say, or to do, when she'd stood up suddenly at the meeting to make her unsuccessful speech. He'd felt himself embarrassed, in sympathy or shame, he couldn't tell which. He hadn't been quite able to agree with her and had been surprised when she'd stood up because it wasn't like her to do anything in public, even though she'd been saying she was unhappy about the thing for months. But then she was so unemphatic as a person that quite often it was hard to guess when she felt strongly.

With other suited men, some carrying as he did a briefcase and a newspaper, he stepped from the train at Waterloo. He strode along the platform with them, one in an army, it often seemed. In spite of how she felt, he really couldn't help believing that the village had been saved. Their own house and garden, and the glades of silver birches, would in no way suffer. The value of the house would continue to rise with inflation instead of quite sharply declining. There would be calm again in the village instead of angry voices and personal remarks, instead of Colin Rhodes saying to Golkorn's face that he was a foreigner. Thank God it was all over.

'There's been a telex,' Miss Owen informed him in his office. 'That place in Gibraltar.'

In the breakfast-room Emily's thoughts had spread out, from her dream of butterflies and the meeting there had been the night before. She saw images of women as they might have been, skulking in the woods near the village, two of them sitting on the stone seat beside the horse-trough on the green, another in a lane with ragwort in her hand. They were harmless women, as Golkorn had kept insisting. It was just that their faces were strange and their movements not properly articulated; nothing, of course, that they said made sense. 'Anywhere but here,' snapped the voice of Colin Rhodes, as vividly she recalled the meeting. 'My God, you've got the world to choose from, Golkorn.'

Golkorn had smiled. Their village was beautiful, he had irritatingly stated, as if in reply. Repeatedly it had been said at the meeting last night, and at previous meetings, that the village was special because it was among the most beautiful in England. The Manor dated back to Saxon times, it had been said, and the cottages round the green were almost unique. But it was that very beauty, and the very peacefulness of the lanes and woods, that Golkorn had claimed would be a paradise for his afflicted women. It was why he had chosen Luffnell Lodge when it went up for sale. Luffnell Lodge was less impressive than the Manor, and certainly nothing like as old. It was larger and less convenient, colder and in worse repair, yet ideal apparently for Golkorn's purpose. In her dream Emily had been walking with him in a field and he had pointed at what at first she'd taken to be flowers but had turned out to be butterflies. 'You've never seen that before,' he'd said. 'Butterflies in mourning, Mrs Mansor.' They flew away as he spoke, a whole swarm of them, busily flapping their black wings.

She rose and cleared away the breakfast things. She carried them on a tray through the hall and into the kitchen. Her dog, an old Sealyham called Spratts, wagged his tail without getting out of his basket. On the window-sill in front of the sink, hot with morning sunshine, a butterfly was poised and she thought at once that that was a coincidence. Its wings were tightly closed; it might have been dead but she knew it wasn't, and when she touched it and the wings opened they were not sinister.

Of course it had been for the best when the Allenbys had realized that to sell Luffnell Lodge to Golkorn would have caused havoc: dealing with the telex about the place in Gibraltar, Hugh found himself yet again thinking that. Golkorn was a frightful person; it was Golkorn's presence rather than his sick women that one might reasonably object to. Luffnell Lodge would put the village on the map, Golkorn had confidently promised, once it was full of his patients: in medical terms he was making a breakthrough. And Hugh knew that what he had offered the Allenbys was more than they'd get otherwise. You couldn't blame them, elderly and wanting to get rid of what they'd come to think of as a white elephant, for listening to Golkorn's adroit arguments. The Allenbys had done nothing wrong and in the end had made the sacrifice. They'd sell the Lodge eventually, it stood to reason, even if they had to wait a bit. 'You see, we don't particularly want to wait,' old Mr Allenby had said. 'That's just the trouble. We've waited two years as it is.' The Allenbys had asked Hugh's advice because they thought that being in the international property market he might know a little more than Musgrove and Carter, who after all were only country estate agents. 'Dr Golkorn is offering you a most attractive proposition,' he'd had to admit, no way around that. 'It could be a while before anyone matched it.' Mr Allenby had asked if he'd care to handle the sale, in conjunction with Musgrove and Carter, but Hugh had had to explain that property in England was outside his firm's particular field. 'Oh, dear, it's all so difficult,' Mrs Allenby had disconsolately murmured, clearly most unhappy at the prospect of having to hang on in the Lodge for another couple of years. Hugh had always liked the Allenbys. In many ways, as a friend and as an expert, he should have told them to accept immediately Golkorn's offer. But he hadn't and that was that; it was all now best forgotten.

For Hugh that day passed as days did at the office. He dictated letters and received telephone calls. He lunched with a client in the Isola Bella, quite often he thought about his wife. Emily was unhappy because of everything that had happened. She felt, but had not said so, that he had let the Allenbys down. She felt that she herself had let the inmates of Golkorn's home down. Hugh tried not to think about it; but in his mind's eye he kept seeing her again, standing up at the meeting and saying that afflicted women have to live somewhere. Like mongol children, she had said, stammering; or the blind. 'That's quite appreciated, Mrs Mansor,' the Reverend Feare had murmured, and as if to come to her assistance Golkorn had asked if he might address the meeting. He had nodded his heavy razored head at Emily; he had repeated what she'd said, that afflicted women, like mongol children and the blind, have to go somewhere. He had smiled and spread his hands out, impatient with those who were protesting and yet oilily endeavouring to hide it. A woman present, he'd even suggested, might one day need the home he proposed for Luffnell Lodge. Hugh sighed, remembering it too clearly. He would take Emily out to dinner, to the Rowan House Hotel. He was about to pick up the telephone in order to ask to be put through to her when it rang. Odd, he thought as he picked up the receiver, that she had dreamed so strangely of butterflies.

'It's a Dr Golkorn,' his secretary's voice said. 'On the other line, Mr Mansor.'

He hesitated. There was no point in speaking to Golkorn; at half past ten last night Golkorn had lost his case; the matter was closed. Yet something – perhaps just politeness, he afterwards thought – made him pick up the other telephone. 'Yes?' he said.

'It's Golkorn,' Golkorn said. 'Look, Mr Mansor, could we talk?'

'About the Lodge? But that's all over, Dr Golkorn. The Allenbys –'

'Sir, they agreed beneath all this pressure not to let me have the house. But with respect, is that just, sir? At least agree to exchange another word or two with me, Mr Mansor.'

'It would be useless, I'm afraid.'

'Mr Mansor, do me a favour.'

'I would willingly do you a favour if I thought –'

'I ask you only for ten minutes. If I may come to see you for ten minutes, Mr Mansor, I would esteem it.'

'You mean, you want to come here?'

'I mean, sir, I would like to come to your very pleasant home. I would like to call in at seven tonight if that might be convenient. The reason I am suggesting this, Mr Mansor, is I am still in the neighbourhood of the village. I am still staying in the same hotel.'

'Well, yes, come over by all means, but I really must warn you –'

'I am used to everything, Mr Mansor.' Laughter accompanied this remark and then Golkorn said, 'I look forward to seeing you and your nice wife. I promise only to occupy ten minutes.'

Hugh telephoned Emily. 'Golkorn,' he said. 'He wants to come and see us.'

'But what for?'

'I really can't think. I couldn't say no.'

'Of course not.'

'He's coming at seven.'

She said goodbye and put the receiver down. The development astonished her. She thought at least they had finished with Golkorn.

The telephone rang again and Hugh suggested that they should go out to dinner, to Rowan House, where they often went. She knew he was suggesting it because she'd been upset. She appreciated that, but she said she'd rather make it another night, mainly because she had a stew in the oven. 'I'm sorry about that wretched man,' Hugh said. 'He wasn't easy to choke off.' She reassured him, making a joke of Golkorn's insistence, saying that of course it didn't matter.

In the garden she picked sweet-peas. She sat for a moment in the corner where she and Hugh often had coffee together on Saturday and Sunday mornings. She put the sweet-peas on the slatted garden table and let her glance wander over lupins and delphiniums, and the tree geranium that was Hugh's particular pride. On trellises and archways which he'd made roses trailed in profusion, Mermaid and Danse du Feu. She loved the garden, as she loved the house.

At her feet the Sealyham called Spratts settled down to rest for a while, but she warned him that she didn't intend to remain long in the secluded corner. In a moment she picked up the sweet-peas and took them to the kitchen, where she arranged them in a cut-glass vase. The dog followed her when she carried it to the sitting-room. Was it unusual, she wondered, to pick flowers specially for a person you didn't like? Yet it had seemed a natural thing to do; she always picked flowers when a visitor was coming.

'Ten minutes I promised,' Golkorn said at seven o'clock, having been notably prompt, 'so ten minutes it must be.' He laughed, as if he'd made a joke of some kind. 'No, no drink for me, please.'

Hugh poured Emily a glass of sherry, Harvey's Luncheon Dry, which was what she always had. He smeared a glass with Angostura drops and added gin and water to it for himself. Perhaps there was something in the fact that he had rescued her, he thought, wanting to think about her rather than their visitor. Even though she loved the subject, she had never been entirely happy as a teacher of Classics because she was shy. Until she came to know them she was nervous of the girls she taught: her glasses and her strawberry mark and her dumpiness, the very fact that she was a teacher, seemed to put her into a certain category, at a disadvantage. And perhaps his rescuing of her, if you could so grandly call it that, had in turn given him something he'd lacked before. Perhaps their marriage was indeed built on debts to one another.

'Orange juice, Mr Golkorn?' Emily suggested, already rising to get it for him.

He waved a hand, denying his need of orange juice. 'Look,' he said, 'I don't want to beat about the bush. I want to come to the point. Luffnell Lodge, Mr Mansor. You're a man of business, you know those people wouldn't ever get that price. They'll lose a lot. You know that.'

'We've been through all of it, Dr Golkorn. The Allenbys do not wish to sell their property to you.'

'They're elderly people –'

'That has nothing to do with it.'

'With respect, Mr Mansor, it may have. Our elderly friends could be sitting there in that barracks for winter after winter. They could freeze to death. The old lady's crippled with arthritis as it is.'

'Mrs Allenby's illness cannot enter into this. The Allenbys –'

'With respect, sir, they came to you for advice.'

'That is so.'

'With respect, sir, the advice you gave them was unfortunate.'

'If they'd sold the Lodge to you they'd be hated in the village.'

'But they'd be gone, Mr Mansor. They'd have kicked the dust off their heels. They'd be imbibing the sun on some island somewhere. As their doctor advised.'

'They've lived in this village for more than fifty years. It matters to them what the village thinks of them. We've been all through this, you know. I can't help you, Dr Golkorn.'

Golkorn bent his head for a moment over clasped hands, as if praying for patience. He was slightly smiling. When eventually he looked up there was a glint in his dark, clever eyes which suggested that, despite appearances, he held the more useful cards. His black pinstriped suit was uncreased, his smooth black shoes had a glassy glow. He wore a blue shirt and a blue bow tie with small white spots on it. The night before, at the meeting, he'd been similarly dressed except for his shirt and tie. The shirt had last night been pink and the tie a shade of deep crimson, though also with white spots.

'What do you think, Mrs Mansor?' he said in his soft, unhurried voice, still smiling a little. 'How do you see this unhappy business?' His manner suggested that they might have been his patients. Any moment now, Hugh thought, he might tell them to go out for a walk.

'I feel as my husband does,' Emily said. 'I feel the Allenbys have given you their answer.'

'I mean, madam, how do you feel about the people I wish to help? I do not mean the Allenbys, Mrs Mansor; I mean of course those who would one day be my patients in Luffnell Lodge.'

'You heard what my wife said last night, Dr Golkorn,' Hugh interjected quickly. 'She is sympathetic towards such people.'

'You would not yourself object to these patients in your village, Mrs Mansor? Did I understand you correctly when you spoke last night?'

'That is what I said. I would personally not object.'

'With respect, madam, you feel a certain guilt? Well, I assure you it is natural to feel a certain guilt. By that I mean it is natural for some people.' He laughed. 'Not Colin Rhodes of course, or Mr Mottershead, or Mr and Mrs Tilzey, or Miss Cogings. Not your clergyman, Mr Feare, even though he is keen to show his concern for the unwell. I think you're different, madam.'

'My wife –'

'Let us perhaps hear your wife, eh? Mrs Mansor, you do not believe the village would be a bear garden if a handful of unhappy women were added to it: that was what you implied last night?'

'Yes.'

'But the vote went against you.'

'No vote was taken,' Hugh said sharply. 'The meeting was simply to explain to you why the Allenbys had decided not to sell.'

'But there had been other meetings, eh? At which I naturally was not present. There have been six months of meetings, I think I'm correct in stating. You've argued back and forth among yourselves, and sides have naturally been taken. In the end, you know, the question we have to ask is should our elderly friends not be allowed to do what is best for them since they have done so much for the village in the past? The other question we have to ask is would it be the end of the universe to have a handful of mentally ill women in Luffnell Lodge? With respect, madam, you feel guilty now because you did not fight hard enough for justice and humanity. And you, sir, because in your efforts to see everyone's point of view you permitted yourself to be bulldozed by the majority and to become their tool.'

'Now look here, Dr Golkorn –'

'With respect, you misinformed the vendors, sir. They'll be in Luffnell Lodge till they die now.'

'The house will be sold to another buyer. It's only a matter of time.'

'It's what you call a white elephant, sir.'

'I think we'd rather you went, Dr Golkorn.'

Golkorn leaned back in his chair. He crossed one leg over the other. He smiled, turning his head a little so that the smile was directed first at Hugh and then at Emily. He said:

'You are both of you upset. In my profession, Mr Mansor, which has to do with the human heart as much as the human mind, I could sense last night that you were both upset. You were saying to yourself, sir, that you had made an error of judgement. Mrs Mansor was wanting to weep.'

'I admit to no error of judgement –'

'Shall we refer to it as a mistake then, sir? You have made a mistake

with which you will live until the white elephant is sold. And even then, if
ever it is sold in the lifetime of the vendors, the mistake will still be there
because of the amount they will have forfeited. In good faith they called
you in, sir, taking you to be an honest man –'

'You're being offensive, Dr Golkorn.'

'I apologize for that, sir. I was purely making a point. Let me make
another one. Your wife, as long as she has breath to keep her alive, will
never forgive herself.'

Emily tried not to look at him. She looked at the sweet-peas she'd
arranged. Through her shoes she could feel the warmth of the Sealyham,
who had a way of hugging her feet. She felt there was nothing she could
say.

Hugh rose and crossed the room. He noticed that Emily hadn't touched
her sherry. He shook the little bottle of Angostura bitters over his own
glass, and added gin and water.

'Actually, sir,' Golkorn said, 'all I am suggesting you should do is to
pick up the telephone. And you, madam, all that is necessary is to say how
you feel to Mrs Allenby. She, too, has humanitarian instincts.'

His beadiness had discovered that they were the weak links in the chain.
When he'd argued with the others the night before, trying to make them
see his point of view, opinion had hardened immediately. And when he'd
persisted, anger had developed. 'In blunt terms,' Colin Rhodes had shouted
at him, 'we don't want you here. If you're going to be a blot on the
landscape, we'd be obliged if you could be it somewhere else.' And Colin
Rhodes would say it even more forcibly now: there'd have been no point
in Golkorn's insinuating his way into the Rhodes's sitting-room, or the
sitting-room of the Reverend Feare, or the sitting-room of Mr Mottershead
or Miss Cogings. There'd have been no point in tackling the Poudards, or
taking on the Tilzeys, or making a fuss with Mr and Mrs Blennerhassett
in the Village Stores.

'My trouble is,' Golkorn said softly, laughing as if to dress the words
with delicacy, 'I cannot accept no for an answer.'

She imagined telling him now that she had dreamed of butterflies in
mourning. She imagined his cropped head carefully nodding, going slowly
up and down in unspoken delight. Eventually he would explain the dream,
relishing the terms he employed, telling her nothing she did not already
know. He was a master of the obvious. He took ordinary, blunt facts and
gave them a weapon's edge.

'Which comes first,' he inquired quite casually, 'the beauty of an English
village, like a picture on a calendar, or the happiness of the wretched?' He
went on talking, going over the same ground, mentioning again by name

the Poudards and the Tilzeys and the Blennerhassetts, Mr Mottershead, Miss Cogings, Colin Rhodes and the Reverend Feare and Mrs Feare, comparing these healthy, normal people with other people who were neither. He made them seem like monsters. He mentioned the Middle Ages and referred to the people of the village as belonging to an inferno of ignorance out of which the world had hauled itself by its own bootstraps. He himself, he threw in for some kind of good measure, had been a poor man once; he had worked his way through a foreign university, details of which he gave; he was devoted to humanity, he said.

But the Poudards and the Tilzeys were not monsters. The Blennerhassetts just felt strongly, as the others, varying in degree, did also. Mr Mottershead would do anything for you; the Feares had had children from Northern Ireland to stay for two summers running; Miss Cogings cleaned old Mrs Dugdall's windows for her because naturally old Mrs Dugdall couldn't do it herself any more. Having sherry with Colin Rhodes after church on Sundays was a civilized occasion; you couldn't in a million years say that Colin Rhodes and Daphne were a pair of monsters.

'Listen, you've got this all wrong, Dr Golkorn,' Hugh said.

'I wouldn't have said so, sir.'

'Your patients would be all over the neighbourhood. You admitted that yourself. They would be free to wander in the village –'

'I see now, sir, I should have told a lie. I should have said these unhappy people would be safely behind bars; I should have said that no suffering face would ever disturb the peace of your picture-postcard village.'

'Why didn't you?' Emily asked, unable to restrain curiosity.

'Because with respect, madam, it is not in my lifestyle to tell lies.'

They had to agree with that. In all he had said to the Allenbys and at the meeting last night he had been open and straightforward about what he had intended to do with Luffnell Lodge. He might easily have kept quiet and simply bought the place. It was almost as if he had wished to fight his battle according to the rules he laid down himself, for if lies were not his style deviousness made up for their absence. He knew that if they approached the Allenbys with the second thoughts he was proposing the Allenbys would not hesitate. Deliberately he had let the rowdier opposition burn itself out in righteous fury, and had accepted defeat while seeing victory in sight. His eyes had not strayed once to Emily's tulip-shaped birthmark, nor lingered on her spectacles or her dumpiness, as such eyes might so easily have done. He had not sought to humiliate Hugh with argument too fast and clever.

'I think,' he said, 'all three of us know. You are decent people. You cannot turn your backs.'

In Luffnell Lodge the women would be comforted, some even cured. Emily knew that. She knew he was not pretending, or claiming too much for himself. She knew his treatment of such women was successful. He was right when he said you could not turn your back. You could not build a wall around a pretty village and say that nothing unpleasant should be permitted within it. No wonder she had dreamed of butterflies mourning the human race. And yet she hated Golkorn. She hated his arrogance in assuming that because his cause was good no one could object. She hated his deviousness far more than the few simple lies he might have told. If he'd told a lie or two to the Allenbys all this might have been avoided.

Hugh wanted him to go. He didn't need Golkorn to tell him he had misled the Allenbys. In misleading them he had acted out of instincts that were not dishonourable, but Golkorn would not for a second understand that.

'I have my car,' Golkorn said. 'We could the three of us drive up to Luffnell Lodge now.'

Hugh shook his head.

'And you, Mrs Mansor?' Golkorn prompted.

'I would like to talk to my husband.'

'I was hoping to save you petrol, madam.' He spoke as if, at a time like this, with such an issue, the saving of petrol was still important.

'Yes, we'd like to talk,' Hugh said.

'Indeed, sir. If I may only phone you from the hotel in an hour or so? To see how you've got on.'

They knew he would. They knew he would not rest now until he had dragged their consciences out of them and set them profitably to work. If they did not go to Luffnell Lodge he would return to argue further.

'You understand that if we do as you suggest we'd have to leave the village,' Hugh pointed out. 'We couldn't stay here.'

Golkorn frowned, seeming genuinely perplexed. He gestured with his hands. 'But why, sir? Why leave this village? With respect, I do not understand you.'

'We'd have been disloyal to our friends. We'd be letting everyone down.'

'You're not letting me down, sir. You're not letting two elderly persons down, nor women in need of care and love –'

'Yes, we're aware of that, Dr Golkorn.'

'Sir, may I say that the people of this village will see it our way in time? They'll observe the good work all around them, and understand.'

'In fact, they won't.'

'Well, I would argue that, sir. With respect –'

'We would like to be alone now, Dr Golkorn.'

He went away and they were left with the dying moments of the storm he had brought with him. They did not say much but in time they walked together from the house, through the garden, to the car. They waved at Colin Rhodes, out with his retrievers on the green, and at Miss Cogings hurrying to the post-box with a letter. It wasn't until the car drew up at Luffnell Lodge, until they stood with the Allenbys in the hall, that they were grateful they'd been exploited.

The Bedroom Eyes of Mrs Vansittart

'You couldn't trust those eyes,' people on Cap Ferrat say, for they find it hard to be charitable where Mrs Vansittart is concerned. 'The Wife Whom Nobody Cares For,' Jasper remarks, attaching a tinselly jangle to the statement, which manages to suggest that Mrs Vansittart belongs in neon lights.

At fifty-four, so Jasper has remarked as well, she remains a winner and a taker, for in St Jean and Monte Carlo young men still glance a second time when the slim body passes by, their attention lingering usually on the rhythmic hips. Years ago in Sicily – so the story is told – a peasant woman spat at her. Mrs Vansittart had gone to see the Greek ruins at Segesta, but what outraged the peasant woman was to observe Mrs Vansittart half undressed on the grass, permitting a local man to have his way with her. And then, as though nothing untoward had happened, she waited at the railway station for the next train to Catania. It was then that the woman spat at her.

Mrs Vansittart is American, but when she divides her perfect lips the voice that drawls is almost that of an English duchess. Few intonations betray her origins as a dentist's daughter from Holland Falls, Virginia; no phrase sounds out of place. Her husband, Harry, shares with her that polished Englishness – commanded to, so it is said on Cap Ferrat, as he is commanded in so much else. Early in their marriage the Vansittarts spent ten years in London, where Mrs Vansittart is reported to have had three affairs and sundry casual conjunctions. Harry, even then, was writing his cycle of songs.

The Vansittarts live now in the Villa Teresa just off the Avenue du Sémaphore, and they do not intend to move again. Their childless marriage has drifted all over Europe, from the hotels of Florence and Berlin to those of Château d'Oex and Paris and Seville. To the Villa Teresa the people from the other villas come to play tennis twice a week. In the evening there is bridge, in one villa or another.

Riches have brought these people to Cap Ferrat, riches maintain them. They have come from almost all the European countries, from America and other continents. They have come for the sun and the bougainvillaea, purchasing villas that were created to immortalize the personalities of previous owners – or building for themselves in the same whimsical manner. The varying styles of architecture have romance and nostalgia in common: a cluster of stone animals to remind their owners of somewhere else, a cupola added because a precious visitor once suggested it. Terracotta roofs slope decoratively, the eyes of emperors are sightless in their niches. Mimosa and pale wistaria add fairy-tale colour; cypresses cool the midday sun. Against the alien outside world a mesh of steel lurks within the boundary hedges; stern warnings abound, of a *Chien Méchant* and the ferocious *Sécurité du Cap*.

In her middle age Mrs Vansittart's life is one of swimming pools that are bluer than the blue Mediterranean, and titles which recall forever a mistress or a lover, or someone else's road to success, or an obsession that remains mysterious: Villa Banana, Villa Magdalene, Morning Dew, Waikiki, Villa Glorietta, Villa Stephen, So What, My Way. The Daimlers and the Bentleys slide along the Boulevard Général de Gaulle, cocktails are taken on some special occasion in the green bar of the Grand-Hotel. The Blochs and the Cecils and the Borromeos, who play tennis on the court at the Villa Teresa, have never quarrelled with Mrs Vansittart, for quarrels would be a shame. Jasper is her partner: her husband plays neither tennis nor bridge. He cooks instead, and helps old Pierre in the garden. Harry is originally of Holland Falls also, the inheritor of a paper-mill.

The Villa Teresa is as the Vansittarts wish it to be now; and as the years go by nothing much will change. In the large room which they call the salon there is the timeless sculptured wall, a variety of colours and ceramic shapes. There are the great Italian urns, the flowers in their vases changed every day; the Persian rugs, the Seurat, and the paperweights which Harry has collected on his travels. Carola and Madame Spad come every morning, to dust and clean and take in groceries. The Villa Teresa, like the other villas, is its own small island.

'Ruby, don't you think it's ridiculous?' Mrs Vansittart said a month or so ago. 'Don't you, Jasper?'

Mrs Cecil inclined her head. Jasper said:

'I think that sign they've put up is temporary.'

'If they spell it incorrectly now they'll do it again.'

Two tables of bridge were going, Mrs Cecil and Signor Borromeo with Jasper and Mrs Vansittart at one, the Blochs, Signora Borromeo and Mr Cecil at the other. In the lull halfway through the evening, during which Harry served tea and little *pâtisseries* which he made himself, the conversation had turned to the honouring of Somerset Maugham: an avenue was to be named after him, a sign had gone up near the Villa

Mauresque, on which, unfortunately, his surname had been incorrectly spelt.

'Then you must tell them, my dear,' urged Jasper, who liked to make mischief when he could. 'You must go along and vigorously protest.'

'Oh, I have. I've talked to the most awful little prat.'

'Did he understand?'

'The stupid creature argued. Harry, that's a polished surface you've put your teapot on.'

Harry snatched up the offending teapot and at once looked apologetic, his eyes magnified behind his horn-rimmed spectacles. Harry isn't tall but has a certain bulkiness, especially around the waist. His hands and feet are tiny, his mouse-coloured hair neither greying nor receding. He has a ready smile, is nervous perhaps, so people think, not a great talker. Everyone who comes to the villa likes him, and sympathizes because his wife humiliates him so. To strangers he seems like a servant about the place, grubbily on his knees in the garden, emerging from the kitchen regions with flour on his face. Insult is constantly added to injury, strangers notice, but the regular tennis-companions and bridge-players have long since accepted that it goes rather further, that Harry is the creature of his wife. A saint, someone once said, a Swedish lady who lived in the Villa Glorietta until her death. Mrs Cecil and Mrs Bloch have often said so since.

'Oh, Harry, look, it *has* marked it.'

How could she tell? Mrs Cecil thought. How could it be even remotely possible to see half-way across the huge salon, to ascertain through the duskiness – beyond the pools of light demanded by the bridge tables – that the teapot had marked the top of an escritoire? Mrs Cecil was sitting closer to the escritoire than Mrs Vansittart and couldn't see a thing.

'I think it's all right,' Harry quietly said.

'Well, thank God for that, old thing.'

'Delicious, Harry,' Mrs Cecil murmured quickly, commenting upon the *pâtisseries*.

'Bravo! Bravo!' added Signor Borromeo, in whom a generous nature and obesity are matched. He sampled a second cherry tart, saying he should not.

'We were talking, Harry,' Mrs Vansittart said, 'of the Avenue Somerset Maugham.'

'Ah, yes.'

He pressed the silver tray of *pâtisseries* on Signora Borromeo and the Blochs, a wiry couple from South Africa. '*Al limone?*' Signora Borromeo questioned, an index finger poised. Signora Borromeo, though not as stout as her husband, is generously covered. She wears bright dresses that Mrs Vansittart regards with despair; and she has a way of becoming excited. Yes, that one was lemon, Harry said.

'I mean,' Mrs Vansittart went on, 'it wouldn't be the nicest thing in the world if someone decided to call an avenue after Harry and then got *his* name wrong.'

'If somebody –' Mr Cecil began, abruptly ceasing when his wife shook her head and frowned at him.

'No, no one's going to,' Mrs Vansittart continued in a dogged way, which is a characteristic of hers when her husband features in a conversation. 'No, no one's going to, but naturally it could happen. Harry being a creative person too.'

'Yes, of course,' said Mrs Cecil and Mrs Bloch swiftly and simultaneously.

'It's not outside the bounds of possibility,' added Mrs Vansittart, 'that Harry should become well known. His cycle is really most remarkable.'

'Indeed,' said Jasper.

No one except Mrs Vansittart had been permitted to hear the cycle. It was through her, not its author, that the people of the villas knew what they did: that, for instance, the current composition concerned a Red Indian called Foontimo.

'No reason whatsoever,' said Jasper, 'to suppose that there mightn't be an Avenue Harry Vansittart.'

He smiled encouragingly at Harry, as if urging him not to lose heart, or at least urging something. Jasper wears a bangle with his name on it, and a toupee that most remarkably matches the remainder of his cleverly dyed hair. Sharply glancing at his lip-salve, Mrs Vansittart said:

'Don't be snide, Jasper.'

'Someone's bought La Souco,' Mrs Cecil quickly intervened. 'Swiss, I hear.'

Harry gathered up the teacups, the bridge recommenced. While the cards at his table were being dealt, Jasper placed a hand lightly on the back of one of Mrs Vansittart's. He had not meant to be snide, he protested, he was extremely sorry if he had sounded so. The apology was a formality, its effect that which Jasper wished for: to make a little more of the incident. 'I wouldn't hurt poor Harry for the world,' he breathlessly whispered as he reached out for his cards.

It was then, as each hand of cards was being arranged and as Harry picked up his tray, that a bell sounded in the Villa Teresa. It was not the telephone; the ringing was caused by the agitating of a brass bell-pull, in the shape of a fish, by the gate of the villa.

'Good Lord!' said Mrs Vansittart, for unexpected visitors are not at all the thing at any of the villas.

'I would not answer,' advised Signor Borromeo. '*Un briccone!*'

The others laughed, as they always do when Signor Borromeo exaggerates. But when the bell sounded again, after only a pause of seconds, Signora Borromeo became excited. '*Un briccone!*' she cried. '*In nome di Dio! Un briccone!*'

Harry stood with his laden tray. His back was to the card-players. He did not move when the bell rang a third time, even though there was no servant to answer it. Old Pierre comes to the garden of the Villa Teresa every morning and leaves at midday. Carola and Madame Spad have gone by five.

'We'll go with you, Harry,' the wiry Mr Bloch suggested, already on his feet.

Mr Cecil stood up also, as did Jasper. Signor Borromeo remained where he was.

Harry placed the tray on a table with a painted surface – beneath glass – of a hunting scene at the time of Louis XIV. Nervously, he shifted his spectacles on his nose. 'Yes, perhaps,' he said, accepting the offer of companionship on his way through the garden to the gate. Signora Borromeo fussily fanned her face with her splayed cards.

It was Jasper who afterwards told of what happened next. Mr Bloch took charge. He said they should not talk in the garden just in case Signor Borromeo was right when he suggested that whoever sought entry was there with nefarious purpose. He'd had experience of intruders in South Africa. Each one caught was one less hazard to the whole community: the last thing they wanted was for a criminal to be frightened away, to bide his time for another attempt. So as the bell rang again in the villa the four marched stealthily, a hand occasionally raised to smack away a mosquito.

The man who stood at the gate was swarthy and very small. In the light that went on automatically when the gate was opened he looked from one face to the next, uncertain about which to address. His glance hovered longer on Harry's than on the others, Jasper reported afterwards, and Harry frowned, as if trying to place the man. Neither of them appeared to be in the least alarmed.

'It is arranged,' the man said eventually. 'I search for Madame.'

'Madame Spad is not here,' Harry replied.

'Not Madame Spad. The Madame of the villa.'

'Look here, my old chap,' Mr Cecil put in, 'I doubt that Madame Vansittart is expecting you.' Mr Cecil is not one to make concessions when the nature of an occasion bewilders him, but it was Jasper's opinion that the swarthy visitor did not look like anyone's old chap. He thought of saying so, *sotto voce*, to Mr Bloch, but changed his mind.

'Better,' he advised the man instead, 'to telephone in the morning.'

'My wife is playing bridge tonight,' Harry explained. 'It's no time to come calling.'

'It is arranged,' the man repeated.

In a troop, as though conveying a prisoner, they made their way back through the garden. The man, although questioned further by Mr Bloch, only shrugged his shoulders. No one spoke after that, but similar thoughts gathered in each man's mind. It was known that old Pierre would shortly be beyond it: after tennis one evening Mrs Vansittart had relayed that information to her friends, inquiring if any of them knew of a younger gardener. What would seem to have happened was that this present individual had telephoned the villa and been told by Mrs Vansittart to report for an interview, and now arrived at ten o'clock in the evening instead of the morning. When they reached the villa Mr Cecil began to voice these conclusions, but the man did not appear to understand him.

He was placed in the hall, Jasper and Mr Bloch guarding him just to be on the safe side. The others re-entered the salon and almost immediately Mrs Vansittart emerged. As she did so, Jasper took advantage of the continuing interruption in order to go to the lavatory. Mr Bloch returned to the salon, where Harry picked up his tray of tea things and proceeded with it to the kitchen.

'I told you not to come here,' Mrs Vansittart furiously whispered. 'I had no idea it could possibly be you.'

'I tell a little lie, Madame. I say to the men there is arrangement.'

'My God!'

'This morning I wait, Madame, and you do not appear.'

'Will you kindly keep your voice down.'

'We go in your kitchen?'

'My husband is in the kitchen. I could not come this morning because I did not wake up.'

'I am by the lighthouse. It is time to fix the tablecloths but I stand by the lighthouse. How I know you ever come?'

'You could have telephoned, for God's sake,' whispered Mrs Vansittart, more furiously than before. 'All you had to do was to pick up the damn telephone. I was waiting in all day.'

'Yes, I pick up the damn telephone, Madame. You husband answer, I pick it down again. All the time Monsieur Jean watch me. "It is no good this time to fix the tablecloths!" he shout when I come running from the lighthouse. My hand make sweat on the tablecloths. I am no good, he shout, I am bad waiter, no good for Grand-Hotel –'

'I cannot talk to you here. I will meet you in the morning.'

'This at the lighthouse, Madame?'

'Of course at the lighthouse.'

All this Jasper heard through the slightly open lavatory door. It was not, he recognized at once, a conversation that might normally occur between Mrs Vansittart and a prospective gardener. As he passed through the hall again his hostess was saying in a clenched voice that of course she would wake up. She would be at the lighthouse at half past six.

'He's a waiter from the Grand-Hotel,' Jasper reported softly in the salon, but not so softly that the information failed to reach anyone present. 'They're carrying on in the mornings at the lighthouse.'

Signor Borromeo won that night, and so did Mrs Cecil. At a quarter to twelve Harry carried in a tray with glasses on it, and another containing decanters of cognac and whisky, and bottles of Cointreau, cherry brandy and yellow Chartreuse. He drank some Cointreau himself, talking to Mrs Cecil and Mrs Bloch about azaleas.

'Harry dear, you've dribbled that stuff all over your jacket!' Mrs Vansittart cried. 'Oh, Harry, really!'

He went to the kitchen to wipe at the stain with a damp cloth. 'Hot water, Harry,' his wife called after him. 'Make sure it's really hot. And just a trace of soap.'

He'd had a bad day, she reported when he was out of earshot. In his Red Indian song Foontimo's child-wife – the wife who was not real but who appeared to Foontimo in dreams – continued to be elusive. Harry couldn't get her name right. He had written down upwards of four hundred names, but not one of them registered properly. For weeks poor Harry had been depressed over that.

While they listened they all of them in their different ways disliked Mrs Vansittart more than ever they had before. Even Jasper, who had so enjoyed eavesdropping at the lavatory door, considered it extravagantly awful that Mrs Vansittart's seedy love life should have been displayed in front of everyone, while Harry washed up the dishes. Mrs Bloch several times tightened her lips during Mrs Vansittart's speech about the difficulties Harry was having with his creation of an Indian child-wife; her husband frowned and looked peppery. It was really too much, Mrs Cecil said to herself, and resolved that on the way home she'd suggest dropping the Vansittarts. There were all kinds of people in this world, Signor Borromeo said to himself, but found that this reflection caused him to like Mrs

Vansittart no more. A *cornuto* was one thing, but a man humiliated *in pubblico* was an unforgivable shame. Harry was *buono*, Signora Borromeo said to herself, Harry was like a *bambino* sometimes. Mr Cecil did not say anything to himself, being confused.

At midnight the gathering broke up. The visitors remarked that the evening had been delightful. They smiled and thanked Mrs Vansittart.

'She has destroyed that man,' Mrs Cecil said with feeling as she and her husband entered their villa, the Villa Japhico.

Signora Borromeo wept in the Villa Good-Fun, and her husband, sustaining himself with a late-night sandwich and a glass of beer, sadly shook his head.

'She has destroyed that man,' Jasper said to his friend in El Dorado, using the words precisely a minute after Mrs Cecil had used them in the Villa Japhico. In the Villa Hadrian the Blochs undressed in silence.

Mrs Vansittart lit a cigarette. She sat down at her dressing-table and removed her make-up, occasionally pausing to draw on her cigarette. Her mind contained few thoughts.

Her mind was tired, afflicted with the same fatigue that deadened, just a little, the eyes that people are rude about.

Harry sat at the piano in the snug little room he called his den. It was full of things he liked, ornaments and pictures he'd picked up in Europe, bric-à-brac that was priceless or had a sentimental value only. The main lights of the room were not switched on; an ornate lamp lit his piano and the sheets of music paper on the small table beside him. He wore a cotton dressing-gown that was mainly orange, a Javanese pattern.

The child-wife who visited the dreams of Foontimo said her name was Soaring Cloud. She prepared a heaven for Foontimo. She would never leave him, nor would she ever grow old.

Harry smiled over that, his even white teeth moist with excitement. He had known she could not elude him for ever.

The following morning Jasper watched from the rocks near the lighthouse. He carried with him a small pair of binoculars, necessary because the lie of the land would prevent him from getting close enough to observe his quarry profitably. He had to wait for some minutes before Mrs Vansittart appeared. She looked around her before descending a path that led to a gap among the rocks from which, later in the day, people bathed. She sat down and lit a cigarette. A moment later the swarthy waiter from the Grand-Hotel hurried to where she was.

Jasper moved cautiously. He was slightly above the pair, but well obscured from their view. Unfortunately it would be impossible to overhear a word they said. Wedging himself uncomfortably, he raised his binoculars and adjusted them.

A conversation, apparently heated, took place. There were many gestures on the part of the swarthy man and at one point he began to go away but was recalled by Mrs Vansittart. She offered him a cigarette, which he accepted. Then Mrs Vansittart took a wallet from a pocket of her trousers and counted a large number of notes on the palm of her companion. 'My God,' said Jasper, aloud, 'she pays for it!'

The couple parted, the waiter hurrying back towards the Grand-Hotel. Mrs Vansittart sat for a moment where he had left her and then clambered slowly back to the coastal path. She disappeared from Jasper's view.

Privately, Mrs Vansittart keeps an account of her life. While Harry composes his songs she fills a number of hard-backed notebooks with the facts she does not wish to divulge to anyone now but which, one day after her death and after Harry's, she would like to be known. Of this particular day she wrote:

I paused now and again to watch the early-morning fishermen. I had paid ten thousand francs. At the end of the season the man might go and not return, as he had promised. But I could not be sure.

The morning was beautiful, not yet even faintly hot, the sky a perfect blue. The houses of Beaulieu seemed gracious across the glittering sea, yet the houses of Beaulieu are as ordinary as houses anywhere. A jogger glanced at me as I stood aside to let him pass, perspiration on his nose and chin. He did not speak or smile. I sometimes hate it on Cap Ferrat.

On the coastal path that morning I thought about Harry and myself when we were both eleven; I was in love with him even then. In Holland Falls he'd brought me to his mother's bedroom to show me the rings she crowded on to her plump fingers, her heavily stoppered scent bottles, her garish silk stockings. But I wasn't interested in his mother's things. Harry told me to take my clothes off, which I shyly did, wanting to because he'd asked me and yet keeping my head averted. Everyone knew that Harry loathed his mother, but no one thought about it or blamed him particularly, she being huge and pink and doting on her only child in a shaming way. 'God!' he remarked, looking at my scrawny nakedness among his mother's frills. 'God, *Jesus*!' I had wires on my teeth, and spindly arms and legs; I didn't have breasts of any size. I took off Harry's red windcheater, and after that the rest of his clothes and his shoes. We lay side by side between his mother's scented sheets, while two floors down she talked to Mrs

Gilliland. 'Now, that's just a damned lie!' she afterwards shrieked at Rose when Rose said what she'd seen. I'll never forget poor Rose's pretty black face in the bedroom doorway, her eyes as round as teacups, bulging from her head. Harry's mother got rid of her because of it, but the story ran all over Holland Falls and someone told my own mother, who sat down and cried. My father bawled at me, his fury a single crimson explosion of lips and tongue, his dotted necktie gulping up and down. It wasn't Harry's fault, I said, I'd tempted Harry because I loved him. Besides, I added, nothing had happened. 'At eleven years of age?' my father yelled. 'It's not the point, for God's sake, that nothing happened!'

On the coastal path that morning I told myself it wasn't fair to remember my father in the moment of his greatest rage. He'd been a gentle man, at his gentlest when operating his high-speed dentist's drill, white-jacketed and happy. Even so, he never forgave me.

We ran away from Holland Falls when we were twenty-two. Harry had already inherited the paper-mill but it was run by a manager, by whom it has been run ever since. We drove about for a year, from town to town, motel to motel. We occupied different rooms because Harry had begun to compose his cycle and liked to be alone with it at night. I loved him more than I could ever tell him but never again, for Harry, did I take my clothes off. Harry has never kissed me, though I, in passing, cannot even now resist bending down to touch the side of his face with my lips. A mother's kiss, I dare say you would call it, and yet when I think of Harry and me I think as well of Héloïse and Abelard, Beatrice and Dante, and all the others. Absurd, of course.

I left the coastal path and went down to the rocks again, gazing into the depths of the clear blue water. 'You're never cross enough,' Harry said, with childish petulance in the City Hotel, Harrisburg, when we were still twenty-two. I had come into my room to find the girl lying on my bed, as I had lain on his mother's with him. In my presence he paid her forty dollars, but I knew he had not laid a finger on her, any more than he had on me when I was her age.

We went to England because Harry was frightened when a police patrol stopped our car one day and asked us if we'd ever been in Harrisburg. I denied it and they let us go, but that was why Harry thought of England, which he took to greatly as soon as we arrived. It became one of the games in our marriage to use only English phrases and to speak in the English way: Harry enjoyed that enormously, almost as much as working on his cycle. And loving him so, I naturally did my best to please him. Any distraction a harmless little game could provide, any compensation: that was how I saw my duty, if in the circumstances that is not too absurd a word. Anyway, the games and the distractions worked, sometimes for years on end. A great deal of time went by, for instance, between the incident in Harrisburg and the first of the two in England. 'It's all right,' the poor child cried out in London when I entered my room. 'Please don't tell, Mrs Vansittart.' Harry paid her the money he had promised her, and when she had gone I broke down and wept. I didn't even want to look at Harry, I didn't want to hear him speak. In an hour or so he brought me up a cup of tea.

It was, heaven knows, simple enough on the surface of things: I could not leave Harry because I loved him too much. I loved his chubby white hands and tranquil smile, and the weakness in his eyes when he took his spectacles off. If I'd left him, he would have ended up in prison because Harry needs to be loved. And then, besides, there has been so much happiness, at least for me: our travelling together, the pictures and the furniture we've so fondly collected, and of course the Villa Teresa. It's the strangest thing in the world, all that.

A fisherman brought his boat near to the rocks where I was sitting. I had lit a cigarette and put my sunglasses on because the glare of daytime was beginning. I watched the fisherman unloading his modest catch, his brown fingers expertly arranging nets and hooks. How different, I thought, marriage would have been with that stranger. And yet could I, with anyone else, have experienced such feelings of passion as I have known?

'I'm sorry,' Harry began to say, a catch-phrase almost, in the 1950s. He's always sorry when he comes in from the flowerbeds with clay on his shoes, or puts the teapot on a polished surface, or breaks the promises he makes. In a way that's hard to communicate Harry likes being sorry.

'*Bonjour, madame*,' the fisherman said, going by with his baskets of sole or whatever fish it was.

'*Bonjour*,' I replied, smiling at him.

Harry would be still in bed, having worked on his cycle until three or four in the morning. Old Pierre and Carola and Madame Spad would not arrive for another hour, and in any case I did not have to be there when they did. But at the back of my mind there's always the terror that when I return to the Villa Teresa Harry will be dead.

I clambered back to the coastal path and continued on my way. In England, after the first occasion, there was the convent girl in her red gymslip, who wasn't docile like the other ones but shouted at me that she loved Harry more than I did. Sometimes she was there when I returned from shopping in the afternoons, sometimes there was only the rumpling of my bed to remind me of her visit. We had to leave England because of the scenes she made, and after the awful melancholy that had seized him Harry promised that none of it would ever happen again.

My presence at the lighthouse that morning had to do with a German girl in Switzerland eleven years ago. The waiter who is at the Grand-Hotel for the season was at the Bon Accueil in Château d'Oex. The German girl was given wine at dinnertime and suddenly burst into tears, hysterically flinging her accusations about. I simply laughed. I said it was ridiculous.

We were gone by breakfast-time and Harry has kept his promise since, frightened for eleven years. Dear, gentle Harry, who never laid a finger on any of those girls, who never would.

Later that morning Jasper's friend shopped in St Jean, with Jasper's terrier on a lead. When he had finished he sat down to rest at the café by the bus stop to have a *jus d'abricot*. He watched the tourists and the young people from the yachts. The terrier, elderly now, crept beneath his chair in search of shade.

'Ah, Mrs Bloch!' Jasper's friend called out after a little while, for the lean South African lady was shopping also. He persuaded her to join him – rather against her will, since Mrs Bloch does not at all care for Jasper's friend. He then related what Jasper had earlier related to him: that Mrs Vansittart now paid money for the intimate services she received from men. He described in detail, with some natural exaggeration, the transaction by the lighthouse. Repelled by the account, Mrs Bloch tightened her lips.

On the way back to the Villa Hadrian she called in at the Villa Japhico with two mouse-traps which she had promised last night she would purchase for Mrs Cecil. The Cecils, with neither gardener nor cleaning woman, do not easily find the time for daily shopping and the chandler's store in St Jean will not deliver mouse-traps. Mrs Bloch waited to be thanked and then began.

'To think that man came last night for money! With Harry there and everyone else!'

Mrs Cecil shook her head in horror. Jasper was a troublemaker and so was his rather unpleasant friend, yet neither would surely tell an outright lie. It was appalling to think of Mrs Vansittart conducting such business with a waiter. The satisfying of lust in a woman was most unpleasant.

'I really can't think why he doesn't leave her,' she said.

'Oh, he never would. That simply isn't Harry's style.'

'Yes, Harry's loyal.'

That morning the Cecils had discussed the dropping of the Vansittarts, but had in the end agreed that the result of such a course of action would be that Harry would suffer. So they had decided against it, a decision which Mrs Cecil now passed on to her friend.

Mrs Bloch gloomily agreed.

Mrs Vansittart plays an ace and wins the trick. It is autumn, the season is over, the swarthy waiter has gone.

Harry enters the salon with his tray of tea, and the *pâtisseries* he has made that morning. He is so quiet in the shadows of the room that Mrs Bloch recalls how strangers to the villa have occasionally taken him for a servant. Mrs Cecil throws a smile in his direction.

Mr Bloch and Mr Cecil and Signor Borromeo, all of whom know about the transaction that took place near the lighthouse, prefer not to think about it. Jasper hopes that Mrs Vansittart will commit some further enormity shortly, so that the gossip it trails may while away the winter. It would be awfully dull, he often remarks to his friend, if Mrs Vansittart was like Mrs Bloch and Mrs Cecil and Signora Borromeo.

'Oh, my dear, don't pour it yet!' she cries across the room, and then with some asperity, 'We really aren't quite ready, old thing.'

Harry apologizes, enjoying the wave of sympathy her protest engenders. He waits until the hand is played, knowing that then her voice will again command him. He can feel the stifled irritation in the room, and then the sympathy.

He pours the tea and hands the cups around. She lights a cigarette. Once, at the beginning of their time in the Villa Teresa, she had a way of getting up and helping him with the teacups, but then she sensed that that was wrong. She senses things in a clumsy kind of way. She is not clever.

'Oh, look, you've made marzipan ones again! You *know* no one likes marzipan, dear.'

But Mrs Cecil and Mrs Bloch both select the marzipan ones, and Harry is apologetic. He is not aware that people have ever said his wife had three affairs and sundry casual conjunctions when they lived in England; nor does he know it is categorically stated that a peasant woman once spat in her face. It would not upset him to hear all this because it's only gossip and its falsity doesn't matter. It is a long time now since she sensed his modest wish, and in answer to it developed the rhythmic swing of her hips and the look in her eyes. Unconsciously, of course, she developed them; not quite in the way she allows the English intonations to creep into her voice. When he looks at her in the company of these people it's enjoyable to imagine the swarthy waiter undressing her among the rocks, even Signor Borromeo trying something on beneath the bridge table.

Harry smiles. He goes around with the teapot, refilling the cups. He wishes she would say again that an avenue on Cap Ferrat would be called after him. It's enjoyable, the feeling in the room then, the people thinking she shouldn't have said it. It's enjoyable when they think she shouldn't swing her hips so, and when they come to conclusions about her made-up English voice. It's enjoyable when she listens to his saga of Soaring Cloud the child-wife, and when her face is worried because yet another song has a theme of self-inflicted death. Harry enjoys that most of all.

Mrs Vansittart loses, for her attention had briefly wandered, as it sometimes does just after he has brought the tea around. She tried not to love him when her father was so upset. She tried to forget him, but he was always there, wordlessly pleading from a distance, so passionately demanding the love she passionately felt. She'd felt it long before the day she took her clothes off for him, and she remembers perfectly how it was.

For a moment at the bridge table the thoughts that have slipped beneath her guard make her so light-headed that she wants to jump up and run after him to the kitchen. She sees herself, gazing at him from the doorway, enticing him with her eyes, as first of all she did in Holland Falls. He puts his arms around her, and she feels on hers the lips she never has felt.

'Diamonds,' someone says, for she has asked what trumps are. Her virginal longing still warms her as the daydream dissipates. From its fragments Harry thanks her for the companion she has been, and her love is calm again at the bridge table.

Downstairs at Fitzgerald's

Cecilia's father would sit there, slowly eating oysters. Cecilia would tell him about school and about her half-brothers, and of course she'd have to mention her mother because it was impossible to have a conversation without doing that. She'd mention Ronan also, but because of her father's attitude to her stepfather this was never an embarrassment.

'Aren't they good today?' Tom, the waiter at Fitzgerald's, would remark, always at the same moment, when placing in front of Cecilia's father his second pint of stout.

'Great, Tom,' her father would unhesitatingly reply, and then Tom would ask Cecilia how her bit of steak was and if the chips were crisp. He'd mention the name of a racehorse and Cecilia's father would give his opinion of it, drawing a swift breath of disapproval or thoughtfully pursing his lips.

These occasions in Fitzgerald's Oyster Bar – downstairs at the counter – were like a thread of similar beads that ran through Cecilia's childhood, never afterwards to be forgotten. Dublin in the 1940s was a different city from the city it later became; she'd been different herself. Cecilia was five when her father first took her to Fitzgerald's, the year after her parents were divorced.

'And tell me,' he said some time later, when she was growing up a bit, 'have you an idea at all about what you'll do with yourself?'

'When I leave school, d'you mean?'

'Well, there's no hurry, I'm not saying there is. Still and all, you're nearly thirteen these days.'

'In June.'

'Ah, I know it's June, Cecilia.' He laughed, with his glass half-way to his lips. He looked at her over the rim, his light-blue eyes twinkling in a way she was fond of. He was a burly man with a brown bald head and freckles on the back of his hands and all over his forehead and his nose.

'I don't know what I'll do,' she said.

'Some fellow'll snap you up. Don't worry about that.' He swallowed another oyster and wiped his mouth with his napkin. 'How's your mother?'

'She's fine.'

He never spoke disparagingly of her mother, nor she of him. When

Cecilia was younger he used to drive up the short avenue of the house in Chapelizod in his old sloping-backed Morris, and Cecilia would always be ready for him. Her mother would say hullo to him and they'd have a little chat, and if Ronan opened the door or happened to be in the garden her father would ask him how he was, as though nothing untoward had ever occurred between them. Cecilia couldn't understand any of it, but mistily there was the memory of her father living in the house in Chapelizod, and fragments from that time had lodged in her recollection. By the fire in the dining-room he read her a story she had now forgotten. 'Your jersey's inside out,' he said to her mother and then he laughed because it was April Fools' Day. Her father and Ronan had run a furniture-making business together, two large workshops in Chapelizod, not far from the house.

'Lucky,' he said in Fitzgerald's. 'Any fellow you'd accept.'

She blushed. At school a few of her friends talked of getting married, but in a way that wasn't serious. Maureen Finnegan was in love with James Stewart, Betsy Bloom with a boy called George O'Malley: silly, really, it all was.

'The hard case,' a man in a thick overcoat said to her father, pausing on his way to the other end of the bar. 'Would I chance money on Persian Gulf?'

Cecilia's father shook his head and the man, accepting this verdict, nodded his. He winked at Cecilia in the way her father's friends sometimes did after such an exchange, an acknowledgement of her father's race track wisdom. When he had gone her father told her that he was a very decent person who had come down in the world due to heavy drinking. Her father often had such titbits to impart and when he did so his tone was matter-of-fact, neither malicious nor pitying. In return, Cecilia would relate another fact or two about school, about Miss O'Shaughnessy or Mr Horan or the way Maureen Finnegan went on about James Stewart. Her father always listened attentively.

He hadn't married again. He lived on his own in a flat in Waterloo Road, his income accumulating from a variety of sources, several of them to do with horse-racing. He'd explained that to her when she'd asked him once about this, wondering if he went to an office every day. She had never been to his flat, but he had described it to her because she'd wondered about that too.

'We'll take the trifle?' he suggested, the only alternative offered by Fitzgerald's being something called Bonanza Cream, over which Tom the waiter had years ago strenuously shaken his head.

'Yes, please,' she said.

When they'd finished it her father had a glass of whiskey and Cecilia another orange soda, and then he lit the third of his afternoon's cigarettes. They never had lunch upstairs at Fitzgerald's, where the restaurant proper was. 'Now come and I'll show you,' her father had offered a year or so ago, and they had stared through a glass door that had the word *Fitzgerald's* in elaborate letters running diagonally across it. Men and women sat at tables covered with pink tablecloths and with scarlet-shaded electric lamps on them, the lamps alight even though it was the afternoon. 'Ah no, it's nicer downstairs,' her father had insisted, but Cecilia hadn't entirely agreed, for downstairs in Fitzgerald's possessed none of that cosiness. There were green tiles instead of the pink peacock wallpaper of the upper room, and stark rows of gin and whiskey bottles, and a workmanlike mahogany food-lift that banged up and down loaded with plates of oysters. Tom the waiter was really a barman, and the customers were all men. Cecilia had never seen a woman downstairs in Fitzgerald's.

'Bedad, isn't her ladyship growing up,' Tom said when her father had finished his whiskey and they both stood up. 'Sure, it's hardly a day ago she was a chiseler.'

'Hardly a day,' Cecilia's father agreed, and Cecilia blushed again, glancing down at her wrists because she didn't know where else to look. She didn't like her wrists. They were the thinnest in Class Three, which was a fact she knew because a week ago one of the boys had measured everyone's wrists with a piece of string. She didn't like the black hair that hung down on either side of her face because it wasn't curly like her mother's. She didn't like her eyes and she didn't like the shape of her mouth, but the boy who had measured her wrists said she was the prettiest girl in Class Three. Other people said that too.

'She's a credit to yourself, sir,' Tom said, scooping up notes and coins from the bar. 'Thanks very much.'

Her father held her coat for her, taking it from a peg by the door. It and the hat he handed her were part of her school uniform, both of them green, the hat with a pale blue band. He didn't put on his own overcoat, saying that the afternoon wasn't chilly. He never wore a hat.

They walked past Christ Church Cathedral, towards Grafton Street. Their lunchtime encounters always took place on a Saturday, and sometimes in the middle of one Cecilia's father would reveal that he had tickets for a rugby international at Lansdowne Road, or a taxi-driver would arrive in Fitzgerald's to take them to the races at Phoenix Park. Sometimes they'd walk over to the Museum or the National Gallery. Cecilia's father no longer drove a car.

'Will we go to the pictures?' he said today. '*Reap the Wild Wind* at the Grafton?'

He didn't wait for an answer because he knew she'd want to go. He walked a little ahead of her, tidy in his darkish suit, his overcoat over his arm. On the steps of the cinema he gave her some money to go up to Noblett's to buy chocolate and when she returned he was waiting with the tickets in his hand. She smiled at him, thanking him. She often wondered if he was lonely in his flat, and at the back of her mind she had an idea that what she'd like best when she left school would be to look after him there. It gave her a warm feeling in her stomach when she imagined the flat he had described and thought about cooking meals for him in its tiny kitchen.

After the cinema they had tea in Roberts' and then he walked with her to the bus stop in the centre of the city. On the way he told her about an elderly couple in the café who'd addressed him by name, people who lived out in Greystones and bred Great Danes. 'Till next time then,' he said as the bus drew in, and kissed her shyly, in the manner of someone not used to kissing people.

She waved to him from her seat by the window and watched him turn and become lost in the crowded street. He would call in at a few public houses on his way back to the flat in Waterloo Road, places he often referred to by name, Toner's and O'Donoghue's and the upstairs lounge of Mooney's, places where he met his friends and talked about racing. She imagined him there, with men like the man who'd asked if he should chance his money on Persian Gulf. But again she wondered if he was lonely.

It was already dark and had begun to rain by the time Cecilia reached the white house in Chapelizod where her father had once lived but which was occupied now by her mother and Ronan, and by Cecilia and her two half-brothers. A stove, with baskets of logs on either side of it, burned in the square, lofty hall where she took her coat and hat off. The brass door-plates and handles gleamed in the electric light. From the drawing-room came the sound of the wireless. 'Ah, the wanderer's returned,' Ronan murmured when she entered, smiling, making her welcome.

Her half-brothers were constructing a windmill out of Meccano on the floor. Her mother and Ronan were sitting close together, he in an armchair, she on the hearthrug. They were going out that night, Cecilia could tell because her mother's face was already made up: cerise lipstick and mascara, smudges of shadow beneath her eyes that accentuated their brownness, the same brown as her own. Her mother was petite and dark-haired – like Claudette Colbert, as Maureen Finnegan had once said.

'Hullo,' her mother said. 'Nice time?'

'Yes, thanks.'

She didn't say anything else because they were listening to the wireless. Her father would be drinking more stout, she thought, his overcoat on a chair beside him, a fresh cigarette in his mouth. There wasn't a public house between Stephen's Green and Waterloo Road in which he wouldn't know somebody. Of course he wasn't lonely.

The voices on the wireless told jokes, a girl sang a song about a nightingale. Cecilia glanced at her mother and Ronan, she snuggling against his legs, his hand on her shoulder. Ronan was very thin, with a craggy face and a smile that came languidly on to his lips and died away languidly also. He was never cross: in the family, anger didn't play the part it did in the households of several of Cecilia's school friends, where there was fear of a father or a mother. Every Sunday she went with Ronan to the workshops where the furniture was made and he showed her what had been begun or completed during the week. She loved the smell of wood-shavings and glue and French polish.

When the programme on the wireless came to an end her mother rose to go upstairs, to finish getting ready. Ronan muttered lazily that he supposed he'd have to get himself into a suit. He stacked logs on to the fire and set the fireguard in place. 'Your tweed one's ironed,' Cecilia's mother reminded him sternly before she left the room. He grimaced at the boys, who were showing him their completed windmill. Then he grimaced at Cecilia. It was a joke in the family that Ronan never wanted to put on a suit.

Cecilia went to a school across the city from Chapelizod, in Ranelagh. It was an unusual place in the Dublin of that time, catering for both boys and girls, for Catholics and Protestants and Jews, and for Mohammedans when that rare need arose. Overflowing from a large suburban house into the huts and prefabricated buildings that served as extra classrooms, it was run by a headmaster, assisted by a staff of both sexes. There were sixty-eight pupils.

In spite of the superficially exotic nature of this establishment Cecilia was the only child whose parents had been divorced, and in the kind of conversations she began to have when she was twelve the details of that were increasingly a subject of curiosity. Divorce had a whiff of Hollywood and wickedness. Betsy Bloom claimed to have observed her parents naked on their bed, engaged in the act of love; Enid Healy's father had run amok with a sofa leg. What had happened within the privacy of Cecilia's family belonged in that same realm, and Cecilia was questioned closely. Even though her parents' divorce had had to be obtained in England owing to the shortcomings of the Irish law, the events leading up to it must clearly have occurred in Chapelizod. Had Cecilia ever walked into a room and found her mother and her stepfather up to something? Was it true that her mother and her stepfather used to meet for cocktails in the Gresham Hotel? What exactly *were* cocktails? Had detectives been involved? Her mother and Ronan were glanced at with interest on the very few occasions when they put in an appearance at a school function, and it was agreed that they lived up to the roles they had been cast in. The clothes her mother wore were not like the all-purpose garments of Mrs O'Reilly-Hamilton or Kitty Benson's mother. 'Sophisticated,' Maureen Finnegan had pronounced. 'Chic.'

But in the end Cecilia was aware of her schoolfellows' disappointment. There had been no detectives that she could recall, and she didn't know if there had been meetings in the Gresham Hotel. She had never walked into a room to find something untoward taking place and she could remember no quarrels – nothing that was even faintly in the same category as Enid Healy's father brandishing a sofa leg. In America, so the newspapers said, kidnappings occasionally took place when the estranged couples of divorce could not accept the dictates of the law where their children were concerned. 'Your daddy never try that?' Maureen Finnegan hopefully prompted, and Cecilia had to laugh at the absurdity of it. A satisfactory arrangement had been made, she explained for the umpteenth time, knowing it sounded dreary: everyone was content.

The headmaster of the school once spoke to her of the divorce also, though only in passing. He was a massively proportioned man known as the Bull, who shambled about the huts and prefabricated buildings calling out names in the middle of a lesson, ticking his way down the columns of his enormous roll-book. Often he would pause as if he had forgotten what he was about and for a moment or two would whistle through his breath 'The British Grenadiers', the marching song of the regiment in which he had once served with distinction. The only tasks he had ever been known to perform were the calling out of names and the issuing of an occasional vague announcement at the morning assemblies which were conducted by Mr Horan. Otherwise he remained lodged in his own cloudlands, a faint, blue-suited presence, benignly unaware of the feuds that stormed among his staff or the nature of the sixty-eight children whose immediate destinies had been placed in his care.

To Cecilia's considerable surprise the Bull sent for her one morning, the summons interrupting one of Miss O'Shaughnessy's science periods. Miss O'Shaughnessy was displaying how a piece of litmus paper had impressively changed colour, and when Mickey, the odd-job boy, entered the classroom and said that the headmaster wanted Cecilia an immediate whispering broke out. The substance of this was that a death must have taken place.

'Ah,' the Bull said when Cecilia entered the study where he ate all his meals, read the *Irish Times* and interviewed prospective parents. His breakfast tray was still on his desk, a paper-backed Sexton Blake adventure story beside it. 'Ah,' he said again, and did not continue. His bachelor existence was nicely expressed by the bleak furnishings of the room, the row of pipes above a damply smouldering fire, the insignia of the Grenadier Guards scattered on darkly panelled walls.

'Is anything the matter, sir?' Cecilia eventually inquired, for the suggestion that a death might have occurred still echoed as she stood there.

The headmaster regarded her without severity. The breathy whistling of the marching song began as he reached for a pipe and slowly filled it with tobacco. The whistling ceased. He said:

'The fees are sometimes a little tardy. The circumstances are unusual, since you are not regularly in touch with your father. But I would be obliged, when next you see him, if you would just say that the fees have of late been tardy.'

A match was struck, the tobacco ignited. Cecilia was not formally dismissed, but the headmaster's immense hand seized the Sexton Blake adventure story, indicating that the interview was over. It had never occurred to her before that it was her father, not her mother and Ronan, who paid her school fees. Her father had never in his life visited the school, as her mother and Ronan had. It was strange that he should be responsible for the fees, and Cecilia resolved to thank him when next she saw him. It was also embarrassing that they were sometimes late.

'Ah,' the Bull said when she had reached the door. 'You're – ah – all right, are you? The – ah – family trouble . . .?'

'Oh, that's all over, sir.'

'So it is. So it is. And everything . . .?'

'Everything's fine, sir.'

'Good. Good.'

Interest in the divorce had dwindled and might even have dissipated entirely had not the odd behaviour of a boy called Abrahamson begun. Quite out of the blue, about a month after the Saturday on which Cecilia and her father had gone to see *Reap the Wild Wind*, Abrahamson began to stare at her.

In the big classroom where Mr Horan's morning assemblies were held his eyes repeatedly darted over her features, and whenever they met in a corridor or by the tennis courts he would glance at her sharply and then glance away again, trying to do so before she noticed. Abrahamson's father was the solicitor to the furniture-making business and because of that

Abrahamson occasionally turned up in the house in Chapelizod. No one else from the school did so, Chapelizod being too distant from the neighbourhoods where most of the school's sixty-eight pupils lived. Abrahamson was younger than Cecilia, a small olive-skinned boy whom Cecilia had many times entertained in the nursery while his parents sat downstairs, having a drink. He was an only child, self-effacing and anxious not to be a nuisance: when he came to Chapelizod now he obligingly played with Cecilia's half-brothers, humping them about the garden on his back or acting the unimportant parts in the playlets they composed.

At school he was always called by his surname and was famous for his brains. He was neither popular nor unpopular, content to remain on the perimeter of things. Because of this, Cecilia found it difficult to approach him about his staring, and the cleverness that was reflected in the liquid depths of his eyes induced a certain apprehension. But since his interest in her showed no sign of diminishing she decided she'd have to point out that she found it discomfiting. One showery afternoon, on the way down the shrubbed avenue of the school, she questioned him.

Being taller than the boy and his voice being softly pitched, Cecilia had to bend over him to catch his replies. He had a way of smiling when he spoke – a smile, so everyone said, that had to do with his thoughts rather than with any conversation he happened to be having at the time.

'I'm sorry,' he said. 'I'm really sorry, Cecilia. I didn't know I was doing it.'

'You've been doing it for weeks, Abrahamson.'

He nodded, obligingly accepting the truth of the accusation. And since an explanation was required, he obligingly offered one.

'It's just that when you reach a certain age the features of your face aren't those of a child any more. I read it in a book: a child's face disguises its real features, but at a certain age the disguise falls off. D'you understand, Cecilia?'

'No, I don't. And I don't know why you've picked on me just because of something you read in a book.'

'It happens to everyone, Cecilia.'

'You don't go round staring at everyone.'

'I'm sorry. I'm terribly sorry, Cecilia.'

Abrahamson stopped and opened the black case in which he carried his school-books. Cecilia thought that in some clever way he was going to produce from it an explanation that made more sense. She waited without pressing the matter. On the avenue boys kicked each other, throwing caps about. Miss O'Shaughnessy passed on her motorized bicycle. Mr Horan strode by with his violin.

'Like one?' Abrahamson had taken from his case a carton containing two small, garishly iced cakes. 'Go on, really.'

She took the raspberry-coloured one, after which Abrahamson meticulously closed the carton and returned it to his case. Every day he came to school with two of these cakes, supplied by his mother for consumption during the eleven o'clock break. He sold them to anyone who had a few pence to spare, and if he didn't sell them at school he did so to a girl in a newsagent's shop which he passed on his journey home.

'I don't want to tell you,' he said as they walked on. 'I'm sorry you noticed.'

'I couldn't help noticing.'

'Call it quits now, will we?' There was the slightest of gestures towards the remains of the cake, sticky in Cecilia's hand. Abrahamson's tone was softer than ever, his distant smile an echo from his private world. It was said that he played chess games in his head.

'I'd like to know, Abrahamson.'

His thin shoulders just perceptibly shifted up and down. He appeared to be stating that Cecilia was foolish to insist, and to be stating as well that if she continued to insist he did not intend to waste time and energy in argument. They had passed through the gates of the school and were standing on the street, waiting for a number 11 bus.

'It's odd,' he said, 'if you want to know. Your father and all that.'

'Odd?'

The bus drew up. They mounted to the upper deck. When they sat down Abrahamson stared out of the window. It was as if he had already said everything that was necessary, as if Cecilia should effortlessly be able to deduce the rest. She had to nudge him with her elbow, and then – politely and very swiftly – he glanced at her, silently apologizing for her inability to understand the obvious. A pity, his small face declared, a shame to have to carry this burden of stupidity.

'When people get divorced,' he said, carefully spacing the words, 'there's always a reason. You'll observe that in films. Or if you read in the paper about the divorce of, say, William Powell and Carole Lombard. They don't actually bother with divorce if they only dislike one another.'

The conductor came to take their fares. Again the conversation appeared to have reached its termination.

'But what on earth's that got to do with what we're talking about, Abrahamson?'

'Wouldn't there have been a reason why your parents got divorced? Wouldn't the reason be the man your mother married?'

She nodded vehemently, feeling hot and silly. Abrahamson said:

'They'd have had a love affair while your father was still around. In the end there would have been the divorce.'

'I know all that, Abrahamson.'

'Well, then.'

Impatiently, she began to protest again but broke off in the middle of a sentence and instead sat there frowning. She sensed that the last two words her companion had uttered contained some further declaration, but was unable to grasp it.

'Excuse me,' Abrahamson said, politely, before he went.

'Aren't you hungry?' her mother asked, looking across the lace-trimmed white cloth on the dining-room table. 'You haven't been gorging yourself, have you?'

Cecilia shook her head, and the hair she didn't like swung about. Her half-brothers giggled, a habit they had recently developed. They were years younger than Cecilia, yet the briskness in her mother's voice placed her in a category with them, and she suddenly wondered if her mother could somehow guess what had come into her mind and was telling her not to be silly. Her mother was wearing a green dress and her fingernails had been freshly tinted. Her black bobbed hair gleamed healthily in watery afternoon sunshine, her dimples came and went.

'How was the Latin?'

'All right.'

'Did you get the passive right?'

'More or less.'

'Why're you so grumpy, Cecilia?'

'I'm not.'

'Well, I think I'd disagree with that.'

Cecilia's cheeks had begun to burn, which caused her half-brothers to giggle again. She knew they were kicking one another beneath the table and to avoid their scrutiny she stared through the french windows, out into the garden. She'd slept in a pram beneath the apple tree and once had crawled about among the flowerbeds: she could just remember that, she could remember her father laughing as he picked her up.

Cecilia finished her cup of tea and rose, leaving half a piece of coffee-cake on her plate. Her mother called after her when she reached the door.

'I'm going to do my homework,' Cecilia said.

'But you haven't eaten your cake.'

'I don't want it.'

'That's rude, you know.'

She didn't say anything. She opened the door and closed it softly behind her. Locked in the bathroom, she examined in the looking-glass the features Abrahamson had spoken of. She made herself smile. She squinted, trying to see her profile. She didn't want to think about any of it, yet she couldn't help herself. She hated being here, with the door locked at five o'clock in the evening, yet she couldn't help that either. She stared at herself for minutes on end, performing further contortions, glancing and grimacing, catching herself unawares. But she couldn't see anywhere a look of her stepfather.

'Well, you wouldn't,' Abrahamson explained. 'It's difficult to analyse your own face.'

They walked together slowly, on the cinder-track that ran around the tennis courts and the school's single hockey pitch. She was wearing her summer uniform, a green-and-blue dress, short white socks. Abrahamson wore flannel shorts and the elaborate school blazer.

'Other people would have noticed, Abrahamson.'

He shook his head. Other people weren't so interested in things like that, he said. And other people weren't so familiar with her family.

'It isn't a likeness or anything, Cecilia. Not a strong resemblance, nothing startling. It's only a hint, Cecilia, an inkling you could call it.'

'I wish you hadn't told me.'

'You wanted me to.'

'Yes, I know.'

They had reached the end of the cinder-track. They turned and walked back towards the school buildings in silence. Girls were playing tennis. 'Love, forty,' called the elderly English master, No-teeth Carroll he was known as.

'I've looked and looked,' Cecilia said. 'I spend hours in the bathroom.'

'Even if I hadn't read about the development of the features I think I'd have stumbled on it for myself. "Now, what on earth is it about that girl?" I kept saying to myself. "Why's her face so interesting all of a sudden?"'

'I think you're imagining it.'

'Well, maybe I am.'

They watched the tennis-players. He wasn't someone who made mistakes, or made things up; he wasn't like that at all. She wished she had her father's freckles, just a couple, anywhere, on her forehead or her nose. 'Deuce,' No-teeth Carroll called. 'No, it's definitely deuce,' he insisted, but an argument continued. The poor old fellow was on a term's notice, Abrahamson said.

They walked on. She'd heard it too, she agreed, about the term's notice. Pity, because he wasn't bad, the way he let you do anything you liked provided you were quiet.

'Would you buy one of my cakes today?' Abrahamson asked.

'Please don't tell anyone, Abrahamson.'

'You could buy them *every* day, you know. I never eat them myself.'

A little time went by. On the 15th of June Cecilia became thirteen. A great fuss was made of the occasion, as was usual in the family whenever there was a birthday. Ronan gave her *A Tale of Two Cities*, her mother a dress which she had made herself, with rosebuds on it, and her half-brothers gave her a red bangle. There was chicken for her birthday lunch, with roast potatoes and peas, and then lemon meringue pie. All of them were favourites of hers.

'Happy birthday, darling,' Ronan whispered, finding a special moment to say it when everyone else was occupied. She knew he was fond of her, she knew that he enjoyed their Sunday mornings in the workshops. She liked him too. She'd never thought of not liking him.

'*Really* happy birthday,' he said and it was then, as he smiled and turned away, that something occurred to her which she hadn't thought of before, and which Abrahamson clearly hadn't thought of either: when you'd lived for most of your life in a house with the man whom your mother had married you could easily pick up some of his ways. You could pick them up without knowing it, like catching a cold, his smile or some other hint of himself. You might laugh the way he did, or say things with his voice. You'd never guess you were doing it.

'Oh, of course,' Abrahamson obligingly agreed when she put it to him. 'Of course, Cecilia.'

'But wouldn't that be it then? I mean, mightn't that account –'

'Indeed it might.'

His busy, unassuming eyes looked up into hers and then at the distant figure of No-teeth Carroll, who was standing dismally by the long-jump pit.

'Indeed,' Abrahamson said again.

'I'm *certain* that's it. I mean, I still can't see anything myself in my looks –'

'Oh, there's definitely something.' He interrupted sharply, his tone suggesting that it was illogical and ridiculous to question what had already been agreed upon. 'It's very interesting, what you're saying about growing like someone you live with and quite like. It's perfectly possible, just as the other is perfectly possible. If you asked your mother, Cecilia, she probably wouldn't know what's what any more than anyone else does. On account of the circumstances.'

He was bored by the subject. He had acceded to her request about not telling anyone. It was best to let the subject go.

'Chocolate and strawberry today,' he said, smiling again as he passed over the two small cakes.

There was another rendezvous in Fitzgerald's Oyster Bar. Cecilia wore her new rosebud dress and her red bangle. On her birthday a ten-shilling note had arrived from her father, which she now thanked him for.

'When I was thirteen myself,' he said, pulling the cellophane from a packet of Sweet Afton, 'I didn't know whether I was coming or going.'

Cecilia kept her head averted. At least the light wasn't strong. There was a certain amount of stained glass in the windows and only weak bulbs burned in the globe-topped brass lamps that were set at intervals along the mahogany bar. She tried not to smile in case the inkling in her face had something to do with that.

'Well, I see your man's going up in front of the stewards,' Tom the waiter remarked. 'Sure, isn't it time they laid down the law on that fellow?'

'Oh, a terrible chancer that fellow, Tom.'

Their order was taken, and shouted down the lift-shaft.

'We might indulge in a drop of wine, Tom. On account of her ladyship's birthday.'

'I have a great little French one, sir. Mâcon, sir.'

'That'll suit us fine, Tom.'

It was early, the bar was almost empty. Two men in camel-coloured coats were talking in low voices by the door. Cecilia had seen them before. They were bookies, her father had told her.

'Are you all right?' he inquired. 'You haven't got the toothache or anything?'

'No, I'm all right, thanks.'

The bar filled up. Men stopped to speak to her father and then sat at the small tables behind them or on stools by the bar itself. Her father lit another cigarette.

'I didn't realize you paid the fees,' she said.

'What fees do you mean?'

She told him in order to thank him, because she thought they could laugh over the business of the fees being late every term. But her father received the reprimand solemnly. He was at fault, he confessed: the head-master was quite right, and must be apologized to on his behalf.

'He's not someone you talk to,' Cecilia explained, realizing that although she'd so often spoken about school to her father she'd never properly described the place, the huts and prefabricated buildings that were its classrooms, the Bull going round every morning with his huge roll-book.

She watched Tom drawing the cork from the bottle of red wine. She said that only yesterday Miss O'Shaughnessy's motorized bicycle had given up the ghost and she repeated the rumour that poor old No-teeth Carroll was on a term's notice. She couldn't say that she'd struck a silent bargain with a boy called Abrahamson, who brought to the school each day two dainty little cakes in a carton. She'd have liked just to tell about the cakes because her father would have appreciated the oddity of it. It was strange that she hadn't done so before.

'Now,' said Tom, placing the oysters in front of her father and her steak in front of her. He filled up their wine-glasses and drew a surplus of foam from the surface of someone else's stout.

'Is your mother well, Cecilia?'

'Oh, yes.'

'And everyone in Chapelizod?'

'They're all well.'

He looked at her. He had an oyster on the way to his mouth and he glanced at her and then he ate the oyster. He took a mouthful of wine to wash it down.

'Well, that's great,' he said.

Slowly he continued to consume his oysters. 'If we felt like it,' he said, 'we could catch the races at the Park.'

He had been through all of it, just as she had. Ever since the divorce he must have wondered, looking at her as he had looked at her just now, for tell-tale signs. 'They'd have had a love affair while your father was still around,' came the echo of Abrahamson's confident voice, out of place in the oyster bar. Her father had seen Abrahamson's inkling and had felt as miserable as she had. He had probably even comforted himself with the theory about two people in the same house, she picking up her stepfather's characteristics. He had probably said all that to himself over and over again but the doubt had lingered, as it had lingered with her. Married to one man, her mother had performed with another the same act of passion which Betty Bloom had witnessed in her parents' bedroom. As Abrahamson had fairly pointed out, in confused circumstances such as these no one would ever know what was what.

'We'll take the trifle, will we?' her father said.

'Two trifle,' Tom shouted down the lift-shaft.

'You're getting prettier all the time, girl.'

'I don't like my looks at all.'

'Nonsense, girl. You're lovely.'

His eyes, pinched a bit because he was laughing, twinkled. He was much older than her mother, Cecilia suddenly realized, something which had never struck her before.

Were the fees not paid on time because he didn't always have the money? Was that why he had sold his car?

'Will we settle for the races, or something else? You're the birthday lady today.'

'The races would be lovely.'

'Could you ever put that on for me, sir?' Tom requested in a whisper, passing a pound note across the bar. 'Amazon Girl, the last race.'

'I will of course, Tom.'

His voice betrayed nothing of the pain which Cecilia now knew must mark these Saturday occasions for him. The car that was due to collect them was late, he said, and as he spoke the taxi man entered.

'Step on it,' her father said, 'like a good man.'

He gave her money and advised her which horses to gamble on. He led her by the hand when they went to find a good place to watch from. It was a clear, sunny day, the sky without a cloud in it, and in the noise and bustle no one seemed unhappy.

'There's a boy at school,' she said, 'who brings two little cakes for the eleven o'clock lunch. He sells them to me every day.'

He wagged his head and smiled. But in a serious voice he said he hoped she didn't pay too much for the cakes, and she explained that she didn't.

It was odd the way Maureen Finnegan and all the others, even the Bull, had suspected the tidy settlement there'd been. It would be ridiculous, now, ever to look after him in his flat.

'I hate to lose poor Tom's money for him.'

'Won't Amazon Girl win?'

'Never a hope.'

Women in brightly coloured dresses passed by as Cecilia's father paused for a moment by a bookmaker's stand to examine the offered odds. He ran a hand over his jaw, considering. A woman with red hair and sunglasses came up. She said it was good to see him and then passed on.

'We'll take a small little flutter on Gillian's Choice,' he finally said. 'D'you like the sound of that, Cecilia?'

She said she did. She put some of the money he had given her on the horse and waited for him while he transacted with another bookmaker. He approached a third one with Tom's pound for Amazon Girl. It was a habit of his to bet with different bookmakers.

'That red-haired woman's from Carlow,' he said as they set off to their vantage point. 'The widow of the county surveyor.'

'Yes,' she said, not caring much about the red-haired woman.

'Gillian's Choice is the one with the golden hoops,' he said. 'Poor Tom's old nag is the grey one.'

The horses went under starter's orders and then, abruptly, were off. In the usual surprisingly short space of time the race was over.

'What did I tell you?' He laughed down at her as they went to collect the winnings from their two different bookmakers. He had won more than three hundred pounds, she fourteen and sixpence. They always counted at the end; they never lost when they went together. He said she brought him luck, but she knew it was the other way round.

'You'll find your way to the bus, Cecilia?'

'Yes, I will. Thanks very much.'

He nodded. He kissed her in his awkward way and then disappeared into the crowd, as he always seemed to do when they parted. It was standing about in the sun, she thought, that caused him to have so many freckles. She imagined him at other race-courses, idling between races without her, sunning himself while considering a race-card. She imagined him in his flat in Waterloo Road and wondered if he ever cried.

She walked slowly away, the money clenched in her hand because the rosebud dress had no pockets. He did cry, she thought: on the Saturdays when they met, when he was on his own again. It was easy to imagine him because she wanted to cry herself, because on all their occasions in the future there would be the doubt. Neither of them would ever really know what being together meant, downstairs at Fitzgerald's or anywhere else.

Mulvihill's Memorial

The man, naked himself, slowly removed the woman's clothes: a striped red-and-black dress, a petticoat, stockings, further underclothes. In an armchair he took the woman on to his knees, nuzzling her neck with his mouth.

A second man entered the room and divested himself of his clothes. A second woman, in a grey skirt and jersey, was divested of hers. The four sprawled together on the armchair and the floor. Complex sexual union took place.

The film ended; a square of bright light replaced the sexual antics on the sheet of cartridge paper which Mulvihill had attached to the back of his drawing-office door. He switched on a green-shaded desk light, removed the cartridge paper and the drawing-pins that had held it in place. Packing away his projector in the bottom drawer of his filing-cabinet, he hummed beneath his breath an old tune from his childhood, 'Who's Sorry Now?'. The projector and Mulvihill's films were naturally kept under lock and key. Some of his films he could project at home and often did so; others he did not feel he could. 'Whatever are you doing, dear?' his sister some-times called through the door of the garden shed where now and again he did a bit of carpentry, and of course it would be terrible if ever she discovered the stuff. So every Friday evening, when everyone else had left the Ygnis and Ygnis building – and before the West Indian cleaners arrived in the corridor where his office was – Mulvihill locked the door and turned the lights out. He'd been doing it for years.

He was a man with glasses, middle-aged, of medium height, neither fat nor thin. Given to wearing Harris tweed jackets and looking not unlike an advertisement for the Four Square tobacco he smoked, he travelled every day to the centre of London from the suburb of Purley, where his relation-ship with his slightly older sister was cemented by the presence in their lives of a Scotch terrier called Pasco. By trade Mulvihill was a designer of labels – labels for soup-tins and coffee in plastic packets, for seed-packets and sachets of shampoo. The drawing-office he shared with a Hungarian display artist called Wilkinski reflected the work of both of them. The walls were covered with enlarged versions of designs that had in the past been used to assist in the selling of a variety of products; cardboard point-of-sale material stood on all the office's surfaces except the two sloping drawing-boards, each with its green-shaded light. Paintbrushes and pencils filled jam jars, different-coloured papers were stored in a corner. In different colours also, sheaves of cellophane hung from bulldog-clips. Tins of Cow paper adhesive were everywhere.

Being at the ordinary end of things, neither Mulvihill nor Wilkinski created the Ygnis and Ygnis glamour that appeared on the television screen and in the colour supplements: their labels and display material were merely echoes of people made marvellous with a red aperitif on the way to their lips, of women enriched by the lather of a scented soap, and men invigorated by the smooth operation of a razor-blade. From Ygnis and Ygnis came images lined always with a promise, of happiness or ecstasy. Girls stood aloof by castle walls, beautiful in silk. Children laughed as they played, full of the beans that did them good. Ygnis and Ygnis was of the present, but the past was never forgotten: the hot days of summer before the worst of the wars, brown bread and jam, and faded flowered dresses. The future was simple with plain white furniture and stainless steel and Japanese titbits. In the world of wonders that was Ygnis and Ygnis's, empresses ate Turkish Delight and men raced speedboats. For ever and for ever there was falling in love.

Mulvihill took his mackintosh from a peg on the wall, and picked up the two short pieces of timber he'd purchased during the lunch hour and with which, that weekend, he hoped to repair a bookcase. He didn't light his pipe, although while watching 'Confessions of a Housewife' he had filled it with Four Square, ready to ignite it in the lift. 'Evening, Violet,' he said to the big West Indian lady who was just beginning to clean the offices of the corridor. He listened for a moment while she continued what she had been telling him last Friday, about a weakness her son had developed in his stomach. He nodded repeatedly and several times spoke sympathetically before moving on. He would call in at the Trumpet Major for a glass of red wine, as he did every Friday evening, and chat for a quarter of an hour to the usual people. It was all part of the weekend, but this time it wasn't to be. In the lift which Mulvihill always took – the one at the back of the building, which carried him to the garage and the mews – he died as he was lighting his pipe.

In the Trumpet Major nobody missed Mulvihill. His regular presence on Friday evenings was too brief to cause a vacuum when it did not occur. Insisting that a single glass of wine was all he required, he never became involved in rounds of drinks, and it was accepted that that was his way. R.B. Strathers was in the lounge bar, as always on Friday, with Tip Dainty and Capstick and Lilia. Other employees of Ygnis and Ygnis were there also, two of the post-boys in the public bar, Fred Stein the art buyer. At a quarter past eight Ox-Banham joined Strathers and his companions, who had made a place for themselves in a corner. Like Mulvihill, Ox-Banham was known to work late on Fridays, presumed to be finishing anything that had become outstanding during the week. In fact, like Mulvihill, he indulged a private hobby: the seduction, on the floor of his office, of his secretary, Rowena.

'Well, how are we all?' Ox-Banham demanded. 'And, more to the point, what are we having?'

Everyone was having the same as usual. Lilia, the firm's most important woman copywriter, was drunk, as she had been since lunchtime. R.B. Strathers, who had once almost played rugby for South Africa and was now the managing director of Ygnis and Ygnis, was hoping to be drunk shortly. Tip Dainty occasionally swayed.

Ox-Banham took a long gulp of his whisky and water and gave a little gasp of satisfaction. Rowena would be leaving the building about now, since the arrangement was that she stayed behind for ten minutes or so after he'd left her so that they wouldn't be seen together. In normal circumstances it didn't matter being seen together, an executive and his secretary, but just after sexual congress had taken place it might well be foolish: some tell-tale detail in their manner with one another might easily be still floating about on the surface. 'Point taken of course,' Rowena had said, being given to speaking in that masculine way. Hard as glass she was, in Ox-Banham's view.

'The confectionery boys first thing Monday,' he said now. 'Neat little campaign we've got for them, I think.'

Lilia, who was middle-aged and untidy, talked about shoes. She was clutching a bundle of papers in her left hand, pressing it tightly against her breast as if she feared someone might snatch it from her. Her grey hair had loosened, her eyes were glazed. 'How about Cliff Hangers?' she said to Tip Dainty, offering the term as a name for a new range of sandals.

Lilia's bundle of papers was full of such attempts to find a title for the new range. The sandals were well designed, so Ygnis and Ygnis had been told, with a definite no-nonsense look. Tip Dainty said Cliff Hangers sounded as if something dreadful might happen to you if you wore the things, and Lilia grinned extravagantly, her lean face opening until it seemed entirely composed of teeth. 'Hangers?' she suggested. 'Just Hangers?' But Tip Dainty said Hangers would make people think of death.

Ox-Banham talked to Capstick and R.B. Strathers about the confectionery people and the preparations that had been made by Ygnis and

Ygnis to gain the advertising of a new chocolate bar. Again there had been the question of a name and Ygnis and Ygnis in the end had settled for Go. It was Mulvihill who had designed the wrapper and the various cartons in which the bar would be delivered to the shops, as well as window-stickers and other point-of-sale material.

'I like that Go idea,' Ox-Banham said, 'and I like the moody feel of that scene in the cornfield.' His back was a little painful because Rowena had a way of digging her fingernails into whatever flesh she could find, but of course it was worth it. Rowena had been foisted on him by her father, Bloody Smithson, the awful advertising manager of McCulloch Paints, and when Ox-Banham had first seduced her he'd imagined he was getting his own back for years of Smithson's awkwardness. But in no time at all he'd realized Rowena was using him as much as he was using her: she wanted him to get her into the copywriting department.

'How about Strollers?' Lilia was asking, and Tip Dainty pointed out that Clark's were using it already. 'Cliff Hangers, Strath?' Lilia repeated, but in his blunt, rugby-playing way R.B. Strathers said Cliff Hangers was useless.

Mulvihill's sister, who was the manageress of a mini-market, was surprised when Mulvihill didn't put in an appearance at a quarter to nine, his usual time on Fridays. Every other evening he was back by ten past seven, in time for most of the Archers, but on Fridays he liked to finish off his week's work so as to have a clean plate on Monday. He smelt a little of the wine he drank in the Trumpet Major, but since he always told her the gossip he'd picked up she never minded in the least having to keep their supper back. She knew it wasn't really for the gossip he went to the public house but in order to pass a few moments with Ox-Banham and R.B. Strathers, to whom he owed his position at Ygnis and Ygnis. Not that either Ox-Banham or R.B. Strathers had employed him in the first place – neither had actually been at Ygnis and Ygnis in those days – but Ox-Banham had since become the executive to whom Mulvihill was mainly responsible and R.B. Strathers was naturally important, being the managing director. Miss Mulvihill had never met these men, but imagined them easily enough from the descriptions that had been passed on to her: Ox-Banham tight-faced in a striped dark suit, R.B. Strathers big, given to talking about rugby matches he had played in. Lilia was peculiar by the sound of her, and Capstick, who designed the best advertisements in Ygnis and Ygnis, was a bearded little creature with a tendency to become insulting when he reached a certain stage in drunkenness. Tip Dainty became genial.

Miss Mulvihill missed these people, her Friday people as she thought of them: she felt deprived as she impatiently waited, she even felt a little cross. Her brother had said he was going to pick up the timber pieces for the bookcase, but he'd have done that in his lunchtime. Never in a million years would he just stay on drinking, he didn't even like the taste. Shortly after ten o'clock the Scotch terrier, Pasco, became agitated, and at eleven Miss Mulvihill noticed that her crossness had turned to fear. But it wasn't until the early hours of the morning that she telephoned the police.

On the following Monday morning the employees of Ygnis and Ygnis arrived at the office building variously refreshed after their weekend. The body had been removed from the back lift, no trace of the death remained. The Hungarian, Wilkinski, was surprised that Mulvihill was not already in the office they shared, for normally he was the first of the two to arrive. He was still pondering the cause of this when the tea-woman, Edith, told him she'd heard Mulvihill had died. She handed Wilkinski his tea, with two lumps of sugar in the saucer, and even while she released the news she poured from her huge, brown enamel teapot a cup for the deceased. 'Oh, stupid thing!' she chided herself.

'But however dead, Edith? However he die, my God?'

Edith shook her head. It was terrible, she said, placing the edge of the teapot on Mulvihill's drawing-board because it was heavy to hold. She still couldn't believe it, she said, laughing and joking he'd been Friday, right as rain. 'Well, it just goes to show,' she said. 'Poor man!'

'Are you sure of this, Edith?' The fat on Wilkinski's face was puckered in mystification, his thick spectacles magnifying the confusion in his eyes. 'Dead?' he said again.

'Definitely,' Edith added, and moved on to spread the news.

My God, dead! Wilkinski continued to reflect, for several minutes unable to drink his tea and finding it cold when he did so. Mulvihill had been the easiest man in the world to share an office with, neither broody nor a bore, a pleasant unassuming fellow, perhaps a little over-worried about the safety of his job, but then who doesn't have faults in this world? He'd been happy, as far as Wilkinski had ever made out, with his sister and their dog in Purley, a few friends in on a Saturday night to cheese and wine, old films on the television. Anything to do with films had interested him, photography being as much of a hobby as his do-it-yourself stuff. In 1971, when Wilkinski's elder daughter married, Mulvihill had recorded the occasion with the camera he'd just bought. He'd made an excellent job of it, with titles he'd lettered himself, and a really impressive shot of the happy couple coming down the steps of the reception place. Unfortunately the marriage had broken up a year ago, and the film was no longer of interest. As dead as poor old Mulvihill, Wilkinski thought sadly: my God, it just goes to show. Ernie Taplow, the art buyer's assistant, came in at that point, shaking his head over the shock of it. And then Len Billings came in, and Harry Plant, and Carol Trotter the typographer.

Elsewhere in the building life continued normally that morning. The confectionery manufacturers arrived to see the proposals Ygnis and Ygnis had to put to them concerning the promotion of their new chocolate bar. Ox-Banham displayed posters and advertisements, and the labels and window-stickers Mulvihill had designed. 'Go,' one of the confectionery men said. 'Yes, I like that.' Ox-Banham took them down to the television theatre and showed them a series of commercials in which children were dressed up as cowboys and Indians. Afterwards his secretary, Rowena, poured them all drinks in his office, smiling at them and murmuring because it was part of her duty to be charming. Just occasionally as she did so she recalled the conjunction that had taken place in the office on Friday evening, Ox-Banham's wiry body as brown as a nut in places, the smell of his underarm-odour preventive. She liked it to take place in the dark, but he preferred the lights on and had more than once mentioned mirrors, although there were no mirrors in the office. They took it in turns, his way one week, hers the next. The only trouble was that personally she didn't much care for him. 'I want you to fix it immediately,' she'd said in her no-nonsense voice on Friday, and this morning he'd arranged for her to be moved into the copy department at the end of the month. 'I'll need a new girl,' he'd said, meaning a secretary. 'I'll leave that to you.'

Ox-Banham introduced the confectionery men to R.B. Strathers, in whose office they had another drink. He then took them to lunch, referring in the taxi to the four times Strathers had been a reserve for the South African rugby team: often a would-be client was impressed by this fact. He didn't mention Mulvihill's death, even though there might have been a talking point in the fact that the chap who'd designed the wrapper for the Go bar had had a heart attack in a lift. But it might also have cast a gloom, you never could tell, so he concentrated instead on making sure that each of the confectionery men had precisely what he wished to have in the way of meat and vegetables, solicitously filling up the wine-glass of the one who drank more than the others. He saw that cigars and brandy were at hand when the moment came, and in the end the most important man said, 'I think we buy it.' All the others agreed: the image that had been devised for the chocolate bar was an apt one, its future safe in the skilful hands of Ygnis and Ygnis.

'Wednesday,' said Miss Mulvihill on the telephone to people who rang with messages of sympathy. 'Eleven-thirty, Putney Vale Crematorium.'

As the next few weeks went by so life continued smoothly in the Ygnis and Ygnis building. Happy in the copywriting department, Rowena practised the composition of slogans and thought up trade names for shoes, underwear and garden seeds. She wrote a television commercial for furniture polish, and explained to Ox-Banham that there would now be no more Friday evenings. She began to spend her lunchtimes with a new young man in market research. Unlike Ox-Banham, he was a bachelor.

Bloody Smithson telephoned Strathers to say he was dissatisfied with Ygnis and Ygnis's latest efforts for McCulloch Paints. Typical, Ox-Banham said when Strathers sent for him: as soon as little Rowena's home and dry the old bugger starts doing his nut again. 'Let us just look into all that,' he murmured delicately to Bloody Smithson on the telephone.

'There are private possessions,' Wilkinski said to Mulvihill's sister, on the telephone also. 'Maybe we send a messenger to your house with them?'

'That's very kind, Mr Wilkinski.'

'No, no. But the filing-cabinet he had is locked. Maybe the key was on his person?'

'Yes, I have his bunch of keys. If I may, I'll post it to you, Mr Wilkinski.'

Everything else Wilkinski had tidied up: Mulvihill's paintbrushes and his pencils, his paints and his felt pens. Strictly speaking, they were the property of Ygnis and Ygnis, but Wilkinski thought Miss Mulvihill should have them. The filing-cabinet itself, the drawing-board and the green-shaded light, would pass on to Mulvihill's successor.

When the keys arrived, Wilkinski found that Mulvihill had retained samples of every label and sticker and wrapper, every packet and point-of-sale item he had ever designed. The samples were stuck on to sheets of white card, one to a sheet, and the sheets neatly documented and filed. Wilkinski decided that Mulvihill's sister would wish to have this collection, as well as the old Four Square tobacco tins containing drawing-pins and rubber bands, a pair of small brass hinges, several broken pipes, some dental fixative and two pairs of spectacles. Mulvihill's camera was there, side by side with his projector. And in the bottom drawer, beneath ideas for the lettering on a toothpaste tube, were his films.

Pleased to have an excuse to walk about the building, Wilkinski made his way to the basement and asked Mr Betts, the office maintenance man, for a large, strong cardboard carton, explaining why he wanted it. Mr Betts did his best to supply what was necessary and Wilkinski returned to his office with it. He packed the projector and the camera with great care and when he came to the vast assortment of neatly titled films, all in metal containers, he looked out for one that Carol Trotter wanted, to do with her father's retirement party. 'A Day in the Life of a Scotch Terrier', he read, and then 'A Scotch Terrier Has His Say' and 'A Scotch Terrier at Three'. A note was attached to the label, 'Mr Trotter's Retirement Occasion', a reminder that the film still needed some editing. Wilkinski put it aside for Carol Trotter and then, to his surprise, noticed that the label on the next tin said, 'Confessions of a Housewife'. He examined some of the others and was even more surprised to read, 'Virgins' Delight', 'Naughty Nell' and 'Bedtime with Bunny'.

Closer examination of the metal film-containers convinced Wilkinski that while most of the more exotic titles were not Mulvihill's own work, two or three of them were. 'Easy Lady', for instance, had a reminder stuck to it indicating that editing was necessary; 'Let's Go, Lover' and two untitled containers had a note about splicing. 'My God!' Wilkinski said.

He didn't know what to think. He imagined Mulvihill wandering about Soho in his lunch hour, examining the pictures that advertised the strip joints, entering the pornographic shops where blue films were discreetly for sale. None of that fitted Mulvihill, none of it was like him. Quite often Wilkinski had accompanied him and his camera to Green Park, to catch the autumn, or the ducks in springtime.

Wilkinski sat down. He ran the tip of his tongue over his rather thick lips. They had shared an office since 1960, yet he had never known a thing about this man. Clearly Mulvihill had bought 'Virgins' Delight' and 'Bedtime with Bunny' to see how it was done, and then he had begun to make blue films himself. Being in terror of losing his job, he had every day passed humbly through the huge reception area of Ygnis and Ygnis, its walls enriched by pictures of shoes and seed-packets and ironworks, and biscuits and whisky bottles. Humbly he had walked the corridors that rattled with the busyness of typewriters and voices in trivial conversation; humbly he had done his duty by the words and images that were daily created. Wilkinski recalled his saying that he'd always wanted to be a photographer: had he decided in the end to attempt to escape from his treadmill by becoming a pornographer instead? It was a sad thing to have happened to a man. It was an ugly thing as well.

Still, Wilkinski had a job to do and he knew that in the carton destined for Purley he must not include such items as 'Let's Go, Lover' and 'Confessions of a Housewife' because of the embarrassment they would cause. His first thought was that he should simply throw the pornographic films away, but even though he had emigrated from Hungary in 1955 Wilkinski was still aware that he had to be careful in a foreign country. Assiduously he avoided all trouble and was notably polite in tube trains and on the street: it seemed a doubtful procedure, to destroy the possessions of a dead man.

'Films?' Ox-Banham said on the telephone. 'You mean they're dirty?'

'Some you might call domestic. Others I think they could offend a lady.'

'I'll come and have a look.'

'Some are of a dog.'

Later that day Ox-Banham arrived in Wilkinski's small office and took charge of the films, including the ones of the dog. He locked them away in his own office, for he was personally not in the least interested in pornography and certainly not curious to investigate this private world of a label-designer who had remotely been in his charge. He didn't destroy the films because you never could tell: an occasion might quite easily arise when some client or would-be client would reveal, even without meaning to, an interest in such material. Topless waitresses, gambling clubs, or just getting drunk: where his clients were concerned, Ox-Banham was endlessly solicitous, a guide and a listener. It was unbecoming that Mulvihill should have titillated himself in this way, he reflected as he stood that evening in the Trumpet Major, getting more than a little drunk himself. Nasty he must have been, in spite of his pipe and his Harris tweed jackets.

In time the carton containing Mulvihill's effects was delivered to Purley. Miss Mulvihill returned from the mini-market one evening to find it on the doorstep. In the hall, where she opened it, she discovered that her brother's keys had been returned to her, Sellotaped on to one of the carton's flaps; only the key of the filing-cabinet had been removed, but Miss Mulvihill didn't even notice that. She looked through the white cards on which her brother had mounted the items he had designed at Ygnis and Ygnis; she wondered what to do with his old pipes. In the end she put everything back into the carton and hauled it into the cubbyhole beneath the stairs. Pasco bustled about at her feet, delighted to be able to make a foray into a cupboard that was normally kept locked.

An hour or so later, scrambling an egg for herself in the kitchen, Miss Mulvihill reflected that this was truly the end of her brother. The carton in the cubbyhole reminded her of the coffin that had slid away towards the fawn-coloured curtains in the chapel of the crematorium. She'd been through her brother's clothes, setting most of them aside for Help the Aged. She'd told the man next door that he could have the contents of the workshed in the garden, asking him to leave her only a screwdriver and a hammer and a pair of pliers.

She had always been fond of her brother; being the older one, she had looked after him as a child, taking him by the hand when they crossed a street together, answering his questions. Their mother had died when he was eight, and when their father died thirty years later it had seemed natural that they should continue to live together in the house in Purley. 'Let's have a dog,' her brother had said one Saturday morning nine years ago, and soon after that Pasco had entered their lives. The only animal the house had known before was Miss Muffin, their father's cat, but they'd agreed immediately about Pasco. Never once in their lives had they quarrelled, her brother being too nervous and she too even-tempered. Neither had ever wished to marry.

She'd put a rose in, she thought as she ate her scrambled egg, the way you could in the grounds of the crematorium, a living thing to remember him by.

A year went by in Ygnis and Ygnis. The new man who shared Wilkinski's office was young and given to whistling. On the telephone he addressed his wife as 'chick', which began to grate on Wilkinski's nerves. He possessed a 1951 Fiat, which he talked about; and a caravan, which he talked about also.

Established now in the copy department, Rowena Smithson was responsible for a slogan which won a prize. She had been put in charge of a frozen foods account and had devised a television campaign which displayed an ordinary family's preference for a packet of fish to a banquet. In Ygnis and Ygnis it was said more than once that Rowena Smithson was going places. Foolish in her dishevelled middle age, Lilia was said to be slipping.

During the course of that year Ox-Banham interested himself in one of Ygnis and Ygnis's three receptionists, a girl who wanted to get into the art department. The Trumpet Major continued to profit from the drinking requirements of Capstick, Lilia, Tip Dainty and R.B. Strathers. Several office parties took place during the year and at the end of it the Ygnis and Ygnis chairman was awarded an OBE.

'Well, I quite appreciate that of course,' Ox-Banham said on the telephone one morning after that year had passed. He was speaking to Bloody Smithson, who had not ceased to give him a bad time, forgetful of all that had been arranged in the matter of placing his daughter in her chosen career. Rowena was shortly to marry the man she'd begun to go out with, from the market research department. The man was welcome to her as far as Ox-Banham was concerned, but when her father was disagreeable it gave him no satisfaction whatsoever to recall how he'd repeatedly pleasured himself with her on the floor of his office. 'Let's iron it out over lunch,' he urged Bloody Smithson.

The lunch that look place was a sticky one, bitter with Bloody Smithson's acrimony. Only when coffee and glasses of Hine arrived on the table did the man from McCulloch Paints desist and Ox-Banham cease inwardly to swear. Then, quite unexpectedly, Bloody Smithson mentioned blue films. His mood was good by now, for he'd enjoyed being a bully for two hours; he described at length some material he'd been shown on a trip to Sweden. 'Awfully ripe,' he said, his large blood-red face inches from his companion's.

Until that moment Ox-Banham had forgotten about the metal containers he had locked away after Mulvihill's death. He didn't mention them, but that evening he read through their neatly labelled titles, and a week later he borrowed a projector. He found what he saw distasteful, as he'd known he would, but was aware that his own opinion didn't matter in the least. 'I've got hold of a few ripe ones that might interest you,' he said on the telephone to Bloody Smithson when he next had occasion to speak to him.

In the comfort of the television theatre they watched 'Confessions of a Housewife', 'Virgins' Delight' and 'Naughty Nell'. Bloody Smithson liked 'Virgins' Delight' best. Ox-Banham explained how the cache had fallen into his hands and how some of the films were apparently the late Mulvihill's own work. 'Let's try this "Day in the Life of a Scotch Terrier",' he suggested. 'Goodness knows what all *that's* about.' But Bloody Smithson said he'd rather have another showing of 'Virgins' Delight'.

Ox-Banham told the story in the Trumpet Major. 'Not a word to my daughter, mind,' Bloody Smithson had insisted, chortling in a way that was quite unlike him. The next day all of it went around the Ygnis and Ygnis building, but it naturally never reached the ears of Rowena because no one liked to tell her that her father had a penchant for obscene films. Mulvihill's name was used again, his face and clothing recalled, a description supplied to newcomers at Ygnis and Ygnis. Wilkinski heard the story and it hurt him that Mulvihill should be remembered in this way. It was improper, Wilkinski considered, and it made him feel guilty himself: he should have thrown the films away, as his first instinct had been. 'Mulvihill's Memorial' the pornography came to be called, and the employees of Ygnis and Ygnis laughed when they thought of an overweight advertising manager being shown 'Virgins' Delight' in the television theatre. It seemed to Wilkinski that the dead face of Mulvihill was being rubbed in the dirt he had left behind him. It worried Wilkinski, and eventually he plucked up his courage and went to speak to Ox-Banham.

'We shared the office since 1960,' he said, and Ox-Banham looked at him in astonishment. 'It isn't very nice to call it "Mulvihill's Memorial".'

'Mulvihill's dead and gone. What d'you expect us to do with his goodies?'

'Maybe put them down Mr Betts' incinerator.'

Ox-Banham laughed and suggested that Wilkinski was being a bit Hungarian about the matter. The smile that appeared on his face was designed to be reassuring, but Wilkinski found this reference to his origins offensive. It seemed that if Mulvihill's wretched pornography brought solace to a recalcitrant advertising manager, then Mulvihill had not died in vain. The employees had to be paid, profits had to be made. 'It isn't very nice,' Wilkinski said again, quietly in the middle of one night. No one heard him, for though he addressed his wife she was dreaming at the time of something else.

Then two things happened at once. Wilkinski had a telephone call from Miss Mulvihill, and Ox-Banham made a mistake.

'It's just that I was wondering,' Miss Mulvihill said. 'I mean, he definitely made these little films and there's absolutely no trace of them.'

'About a dog maybe?'

'And a little one about the scouts. Then again one concerning Purley.'

'Leave the matter with me, Miss Mulvihill.'

The telephone call came late in the day, and when Wilkinski tried to see Ox-Banham it was suggested that he should try again in the morning. It pleased him that Miss Mulvihill had phoned, that she had sought to have returned to her what was rightfully hers. He'd considered it high-handed at the time that Ox-Banham hadn't bothered to divide the films into two groups, as he had done himself. 'Oh, let's not bother with all that,' Ox-Banham had said with a note of impatience in his voice.

Wilkinski hurried to catch his train on the evening of Miss Mulvihill's call; Ox-Banham entertained Bloody Smithson in the television theatre. 'No, no, no,' Bloody Smithson protested. 'We'll stick with our Virgins, Ox.'

But Ox-Banham was heartily sick of 'Virgins' Delight', which he had seen by now probably sixty times. He thought he'd die if he had to watch, yet again, the three schoolgirls putting down their hockey sticks and beginning to take off their gymslips. 'I thought we were maybe wearing it out,' he said. 'I thought I'd better have a copy made.'

'You mean it's not here?'

'Back in a week or so, Smithy.'

They began to go through the others. 'Let's try this "Day in the Life of a Scotch Terrier",' Ox-Banham suggested, and shortly afterwards a dog appeared on the screen, ambling about a kitchen. Then the dog was put on a lead and taken for a walk around a suburb by a middle-aged woman. Back in the kitchen again, the dog begged with its head on one side and was given a titbit. There was another walk, a bus shelter, the dog smelling at bits of paper on the ground. 'Well, for God's sake!' Bloody Smithson protested when the animal was finally given a meal to eat and put to bed.

'Sorry, Smithy.'

'I thought she and the dog –'

'I know. So did I.'

'Some bloody nut made that one.'

Ox-Banham then showed 'Naughty Nell', followed by 'Country Fun', 'Oh Boy!' and 'Girlie'. But Bloody Smithson wasn't in the least impressed. He didn't care for 'Confessions of a Housewife' any more than he had the first time he'd seen it. He didn't care for 'Nothing on Tonight' and wasn't much impressed by anything else. Ox-Banham regretted that he'd said 'Virgins' Delight' was being copied. This tedious search for excitement could go on all night, for even though Smithson continued to say that everything was less good than 'Virgins' Delight' Ox-Banham had a feeling that some enjoyment at least was being derived from the continuous picture show.

'You're sure there isn't another reel or something to that dog stuff?' the advertising manager even inquired. 'I wouldn't mind seeing that dame with her undies off.' He gave a loud laugh, draining his glass of whisky and poking it out at Ox-Banham for a refill.

'I think that's the bloke's sister actually. I don't think she takes anything off.' Ox-Banham laughed himself, busy with glasses and ice. 'Call it a day after this one, shall we?'

'Might as well run through the lot, Ox.'

They saw 'Come and Get It', 'Girls on the Rampage', 'A Scotch Terrier Has His Say', 'Street of Desire', a film of boy scouts camping, scenes on a golf course, 'Saturday Morning, Purley' and 'Flesh for Sale'. It was then, after a few moments of a film without a title, that Ox-Banham realized something was wrong. Unfortunately he realized it too late.

'Great God almighty,' said Bloody Smithson.

'You opened the filing-cabinet, Wilkinski, you took the films out. What did you do next?' Ox-Banham ground his teeth together, struggling with his impatience.

'I say myself it's not nice for the sister. The sister phoned up yesterday, I came down to see you –'

'You didn't project any of the films?'

'No, no. I think of Mulvihill lying dead and I think of the sister. What the sister wants is the ones about the dog, and anything else, maybe boy scouts, is there?'

'You are absolutely certain that you did not project any of the films? Not one called "Easy Lady" or another, "Let's Go, Lover"? Neither of the two untitled ones?'

'No, no. I have no interest in this. I get the box from Mr Betts –'

'Is it possible that someone else might have examined the films? Did you leave the filing-cabinet unlocked, for instance?'

'No, no. I get the box from Mr Betts, maybe ten minutes. The cabinet is closed and locked then. The property of a dead man, I say myself –'

'So no one could possibly have projected one of these films?'

'No, no. The sister rings me yesterday. She is anxious for the dog ones, also boy scouts and others.'

'Oh, for God's sake, Wilkinski!'

'I promise I find –'

'They've all been destroyed. Everything's been destroyed.'

'Destroyed? But I thought –'

'I destroyed them myself last night.'

Returning to his office, Wilkinski paused for a moment in a corridor, removed his spectacles and polished them with his handkerchief. People hurried by him with proofs of new advertisements and typewritten pages of copy, but it was easier to think in the corridor than it would be in the office because of the whistling of Mulvihill's successor. Ox-Banham had looked almost ill, his voice had been shaky. Wilkinski shook his head and slowly padded back to his drawing-board, baffled by the turn of events. He didn't know what he was going to say to Mulvihill's sister.

What happened next was that Bloody Smithson removed the McCulloch Paints account from Ygnis and Ygnis. Then Rowena Smithson walked out. She didn't hand in her notice, she simply didn't return after lunch one day. The man in market research to whom she was engaged let it be known that the engagement had been broken off, and made it clear that it was he who had done the breaking. A rumour went round that the big shoe account – a Quaker concern and one of Ygnis and Ygnis's mainstays – was about to go, and a week later it did. Questions were asked by the men of the chocolate account which Ox-Banham had gained a year ago, and by the toiletries people and by the men of Macclesfield Metals. Hasty lunches were arranged, explanations pressed home over afternoon brandy. *Ygnis and Ygnis in Trouble* a headline in a trade magazine was ready to state, but the headline – and the report that went with it – was abandoned at the eleventh hour because it appeared that Ygnis and Ygnis had weathered their storm.

Wilkinski tried to piece things together, and so did the other employees. In the Trumpet Major it was said that for reasons of his own Bloody

Smithson had sworn to bring Ygnis and Ygnis to its knees, but neither Wilkinski nor anyone else knew why he had become so enraged. Then, making a rare appearance in the Trumpet Major, the market research man to whom Rowena Smithson had been engaged drank an extra couple of Carlsbergs while waiting for the rain to cease. Idling at the bar, he told Tip Dainty in the strictest confidence of a scene which had taken place at the time of the crisis in the Smithsons' house in Wimbledon: how he'd been about to leave, having driven Rowena home, when Bloody Smithson had thundered his way into the sitting-room, 'literally like a bull'. Mrs Smithson had been drinking a cup of Ovaltine at the time, Rowena had not yet taken off her coat. 'You filthy young prostitute!' Bloody Smithson had roared at her. 'You cheap whore!' It apparently hadn't concerned him that his daughter's fiancé was present, he hadn't even noticed when the cup of Ovaltine fell from his wife's grasp. He had just stood there shouting, oaths and obscenities bursting out of him, his face the colour of ripe strawberries.

By half past ten the following morning the story was known to every Ygnis and Ygnis employee: Mulvihill had made a film of Ox-Banham and Rowena Smithson banging away on the floor of Ox-Banham's office. Mulvihill had apparently hidden himself behind the long blue Dralon curtains, which in the circumstances had naturally been drawn. The lights in the room had been on and neither protagonist in the proceedings had been wearing a stitch.

At lunchtime that day, passing through the large, chic reception area, the people of Ygnis and Ygnis hardly noticed the images displayed on its walls. The messages that murmured at them were rich in sexual innuendo, but the hard facts of a dead pornographer briefly interested them more. 'Mulvihill!' some exclaimed in uneasy admiration, for to a few at least it seemed that Mulvihill had dealt in an honesty that just for a moment made the glamour of the images and the messages appear to be a little soiled. Wilkinski thought so, and longed to telephone Mulvihill's sister to tell her of what had occurred, but of course it was impossible to do that. He wrote a letter instead, apologizing for taking so long in replying to her query and informing her that the films she'd mentioned had been destroyed in error. It was not exactly a lie, and seemed less of one as the day wore on, as the glamour glittered again, undefeated when it came to the point.

Beyond the Pale

We always went to Ireland in June.

Ever since the four of us began to go on holidays together, in 1965 it must have been, we had spent the first fortnight of the month at Glencorn Lodge in Co. Antrim. Perfection, as Dekko put it once, and none of us disagreed. It's a Georgian house by the sea, not far from the village of Ardbeag. It's quite majestic in its rather elegant way, a garden running to the very edge of a cliff, a long rhododendron drive – or avenue, as they say in Ireland. The English couple who bought the house in the early sixties, the Malseeds, have had to build on quite a bit but it's all been discreetly done, the Georgian style preserved throughout. Figs grow in the sheltered gardens, and apricots, and peaches in the greenhouses which old Mr Saxton presides over. He's Mrs Malseed's father actually. They brought him with them from Surrey, and their Dalmatians, Charger and Snooze.

It was Strafe who found Glencorn for us. He'd come across an advertisement in the *Lady* in the days when the Malseeds still felt the need to advertise. 'How about this?' he said one evening at the end of the second rubber, and then read out the details. We had gone away together the summer before, to a hotel that had been recommended on the Costa del Sol, but it hadn't been a success because the food was so appalling. 'We could try this Irish one,' Dekko suggested cautiously, which is what eventually we did.

The four of us have been playing bridge together for ages, Dekko, Strafe, Cynthia and myself. They call me Milly, though strictly speaking my name is Dorothy Milson. Dekko picked up his nickname at school, Dekko Deakin sounding rather good, I dare say. He and Strafe were in fact at school together, which must be why we all call Strafe by his surname: Major R.B. Strafe he is, the initials standing for Robert Buchanan. We're of an age, the four of us, all in the early fifties: the prime of life, so Dekko insists. We live quite close to Leatherhead, where the Malseeds were before they decided to make the change from Surrey to Co. Antrim. Quite a coincidence, we always think.

'How *very* nice,' Mrs Malseed said, smiling her welcome again this year. Some instinct seems to tell her when guests are about to arrive, for she's rarely not waiting in the large, low-ceilinged hall that always smells of flowers. She dresses beautifully, differently every day, and changing of course in the evening. Her blouse on this occasion was scarlet and silver, in stripes, her skirt black. This choice gave her a brisk look, which was fitting because being so busy she often has to be a little on the brisk side. She has smooth grey hair which she once told me she entirely looks after herself, and she almost always wears a black velvet band in it. Her face is well made up, and for one who arranges so many vases of flowers and otherwise has to use her hands she manages to keep them marvellously in condition. Her fingernails are varnished a soft pink, and a small gold bangle always adorns her right wrist, a wedding present from her husband.

'Arthur, take the party's luggage,' she commanded the old porter, who doubles as odd-job man. 'Rose, Geranium, Hydrangea, Fuchsia.' She referred to the titles of the rooms reserved for us: in winter, when no one much comes to Glencorn Lodge, pleasant little details like that are seen to. Mrs Malseed herself painted the flower-plaques that are attached to the doors of the hotel instead of numbers; her husband sees to redecoration and repairs.

'Well, well, well,' Mr Malseed said now, entering the hall through the door that leads to the kitchen regions. 'A hundred thousand welcomes,' he greeted us in the Irish manner. He's rather shorter than Mrs Malseed, who's handsomely tall. He wears Donegal tweed suits and is brown as a berry, including his head, which is bald. His dark brown eyes twinkle at you, making you feel rather more than just another hotel guest. They run the place like a country house, really.

'Good trip?' Mr Malseed inquired.

'Super,' Dekko said. 'Not a worry all the way.'

'Splendid.'

'The wretched boat sailed an hour early one day last week,' Mrs Malseed said. 'Quite a little band were left stranded at Stranraer.'

Strafe laughed. Typical of that steamship company, he said. 'Catching the tide, I dare say?'

'They caught a rocket from me,' Mrs Malseed replied good-humouredly. 'A couple of old dears were due with us on Tuesday and had to spend the night in some awful Scottish lodging-house. It nearly finished them.'

Everyone laughed, and I could feel the others thinking that our holiday had truly begun. Nothing had changed at Glencorn Lodge, all was well with its Irish world. Kitty from the dining-room came out to greet us, spotless in her uniform. 'Ach, you're looking younger,' she said, paying the compliment to all four of us, causing everyone in the hall to laugh again. Kitty's a bit of a card.

Arthur led the way to the rooms called Rose, Geranium, Hydrangea and Fuchsia, carrying as much of our luggage as he could manage and returning for the remainder. Arthur has a beaten, fisherman's face and short grey hair. He wears a green baize apron, and a white shirt with an imitation-silk scarf tucked into it at the neck. The scarf, in different swirling greens which blend nicely with the green of his apron, is an idea of Mrs Malseed's and one appreciates the effort, if not at a uniform, at least at tidiness.

'Thank you very much,' I said to Arthur in my room, smiling and finding him a coin.

We played a couple of rubbers after dinner as usual, but not of course going on for as long as we might have because we were still quite tired after the journey. In the lounge there was a French family, two girls and their parents, and a honeymoon couple – or so we had speculated during dinner – and a man on his own. There had been other people at dinner of course, because in June Glencorn Lodge is always full: from where we sat in the window we could see some of them strolling about the lawns, a few taking the cliff path down to the seashore. In the morning we'd do the same: we'd walk along the sands to Ardbeag and have coffee in the hotel there, back in time for lunch. In the afternoon we'd drive somewhere.

I knew all that because over the years this kind of pattern had developed. We had our walks and our drives, tweed to buy in Cushendall, Strafe's and Dekko's fishing day when Cynthia and I just sat on the beach, our visit to the Giant's Causeway and one to Donegal perhaps, though that meant an early start and taking pot-luck for dinner somewhere. We'd come to adore Co. Antrim, its glens and coastline, Rathlin Island and Tievebulliagh. Since first we got to know it, in 1965, we'd all four fallen hopelessly in love with every variation of this remarkable landscape. People in England thought us mad of course: they see so much of the troubles on television that it's naturally difficult for them to realize that most places are just as they've always been. Yet coming as we did, taking the road along the coast, dawdling through Ballygally, it was impossible to believe that somewhere else the unpleasantness was going on. We'd never seen a thing, nor even heard people talking about incidents that might have taken place. It's true that after a particularly nasty carry-on a few winters ago we did consider finding somewhere else, in Scotland perhaps, or Wales. But as Strafe put it at the time, we felt we owed a certain loyalty to the Malseeds and indeed to everyone we'd come to know round about, people who'd always been glad to welcome us back. It seemed silly to lose our heads, and when we returned the following summer we knew immediately we'd been right. Dekko said that nothing could be further away from all the violence than Glencorn Lodge, and though his remark could hardly be taken literally I think we all knew what he meant.

'Cynthia's tired,' I said because she'd been stifling yawns. 'I think we should call it a day.'

'Oh, not at all,' Cynthia protested. 'No, please.'

But Dekko agreed with me that she was tired, and Strafe said he didn't mind stopping now. He suggested a nightcap, as he always does, and as we always do also, Cynthia and I declined. Dekko said he'd like a Cointreau.

The conversation drifted about. Dekko told us an Irish joke about a drunk who couldn't find his way out of a telephone box, and then Strafe remembered an incident at school concerning his and Dekko's housemaster, A.D. Cowley-Stubbs, and the house wag, Thrive Major. A.D. Cowley-Stubbs had been known as Cows and often featured in our after-bridge reminiscing. So did Thrive Major.

'Perhaps I *am* sleepy,' Cynthia said. 'I don't think I closed my eyes once last night.'

She never does on a sea crossing. Personally I'm out like a light the moment my head touches the pillow; I often think it must be the salt in the air because normally I'm an uneasy sleeper at the best of times.

'You run along, old girl,' Strafe advised.

'Brekky at nine,' Dekko said.

Cynthia said good-night and went, and we didn't remark on her tiredness because as a kind of unwritten rule we never comment on one another. We're four people who play bridge. The companionship it offers, and the holidays we have together, are all part of that. We share everything: the cost of petrol, the cups of coffee or drinks we have; we even each make a contribution towards the use of Strafe's car because it's always his we go on holiday in, a Rover it was on this occasion.

'Funny, being here on your own,' Strafe said, glancing across what the Malseeds call the After-Dinner Lounge at the man who didn't have a companion. He was a red-haired man of about thirty, not wearing a tie, his collar open at the neck and folded back over the jacket of his blue serge suit. He was uncouth-looking, though it's a hard thing to say, not at all the kind of person one usually sees at Glencorn Lodge. He sat in the After-Dinner Lounge as he had in the dining-room, lost in some concentration of his own, as if calculating sums in his mind. There had been a folded newspaper on his table in the dining-room. It now reposed tidily on the arm of his chair, still unopened.

'Commercial gent,' Dekko said. 'Fertilizers.'

'Good heavens, never. You wouldn't get a rep in here.'

I took no part in the argument. The lone man didn't much interest me, but I felt that Strafe was probably right: if there was anything dubious about the man's credentials he might have found it difficult to secure a room. In the hall of Glencorn Lodge there's a notice which reads: *We prefer not to feature in hotel guides, and we would be grateful to our guests if they did not seek to include Glencorn Lodge in the Good Food Guide, the Good Hotel Guide, the Michelin, Egon Ronay or any others. We have not advertised Glencorn since our early days, and prefer our recommendations to be by word of mouth.*

'Ah, thank you,' Strafe said when Kitty brought his whisky and Dekko's Cointreau. 'Sure you won't have something?' he said to me, although he knew I never did.

Strafe is on the stout side, I suppose you could say, with a gingery moustache and gingery hair, hardly touched at all by grey. He left the Army years ago, I suppose because of me in a sense, because he didn't want to be posted abroad again. He's in the Ministry of Defence now.

I'm still quite pretty in my way, though nothing like as striking as Mrs Malseed, for I've never been that kind of woman. I've put on weight, and wouldn't have allowed myself to do so if Strafe hadn't kept saying he can't stand a bag of bones. I'm careful about my hair and, unlike Mrs Malseed, I have it very regularly seen to because if I don't it gets a salt-and-pepper look, which I hate. My husband, Terence, who died of food-poisoning when we were still quite young, used to say I wouldn't lose a single look in middle age, and to some extent that's true. We were still putting off having children when he died, which is why I haven't any. Then I met Strafe, which meant I didn't marry again.

Strafe is married himself, to Cynthia. She's small and ineffectual, I suppose you'd say without being untruthful or unkind. Not that Cynthia and I don't get on or anything like that, in fact we get on extremely well. It's Strafe and Cynthia who don't seem quite to hit it off, and I often think how much happier all round it would have been if Cynthia had married someone completely different, someone like Dekko in a way, except that that mightn't quite have worked out either. The Strafes have two sons, both very like their father, both of them in the Army. And the very sad thing is they think nothing of poor Cynthia.

'Who's that chap?' Dekko asked Mr Malseed, who'd come over to wish us good-night.

'Awfully sorry about that, Mr Deakin. My fault entirely, a booking that came over the phone.'

'Good heavens, not at all,' Strafe protested, and Dekko looked horrified in case it should be thought he was objecting to the locals. 'Splendid-looking fellow,' he said, overdoing it.

Mr Malseed murmured that the man had only booked in for a single night, and I smiled the whole thing away, reassuring him with a nod. It's one of the pleasantest of the traditions at Glencorn Lodge that every evening Mr Malseed makes the rounds of his guests just to say good-night. It's because of little touches like that that I, too, wished Dekko hadn't questioned Mr Malseed about the man because it's the kind of thing one doesn't do at Glencorn Lodge. But Dekko is a law unto himself, very tall and gangling, always immaculately suited, a beaky face beneath mousy hair in which flecks of grey add a certain distinction. Dekko has money of his own and though he takes out girls who are half his age he has never managed to get around to marriage. The uncharitable might say he has a rather gormless laugh; certainly it's sometimes on the loud side.

We watched while Mr Malseed bade the lone man good-night. The man didn't respond, but just sat gazing. It was ill-mannered, but this lack of courtesy didn't appear to be intentional: the man was clearly in a mood of some kind, miles away.

'Well, I'll go up,' I said. 'Good-night, you two.'

'Cheery-bye, Milly,' Dekko said. 'Brekky at nine, remember.'

'Good-night, Milly,' Strafe said.

The Strafes always occupy different rooms on holidays, and at home also. This time he was in Geranium and she in Fuchsia. I was in Rose, and in a little while Strafe would come to see me. He stays with her out of kindness, because he fears for her on her own. He's a sentimental, good-hearted man, easily moved to tears: he simply cannot bear the thought of Cynthia with no one to talk to in the evenings, with no one to make her life around. 'And besides,' he often says when he's being jocular, 'it would break up our bridge four.' Naturally we never discuss her shortcomings or in any way analyse the marriage. The unwritten rule that exists among the four of us seems to extend as far as that.

He slipped into my room after he'd had another drink or two, and I was waiting for him as he likes me to wait, in bed but not quite undressed. He has never said so, but I know that that is something Cynthia would not understand in him, or ever attempt to comply with. Terence, of course, would not have understood either; poor old Terence would have been shocked. Actually it's all rather sweet, Strafe and his little ways.

'I love you, dear,' I whispered to him in the darkness, but just then he didn't wish to speak of love and referred instead to my body.

If Cynthia hadn't decided to remain in the hotel the next morning instead of accompanying us on our walk to Ardbeag everything might have been different. As it happened, when she said at breakfast she thought she'd just potter about the garden and sit with her book out of the wind somewhere, I can't say I was displeased. For a moment I hoped Dekko might say he'd stay with her, allowing Strafe and myself to go off on our own, but Dekko – who doesn't go in for saying what you want him to say – didn't. 'Poor old sausage,' he said instead, examining Cynthia with a solicitude that suggested she was close to the grave, rather than just a little lowered by the change of life or whatever it was.

'I'll be perfectly all right,' Cynthia assured him. 'Honestly.'

'Cynthia likes to mooch, you know,' Strafe pointed out, which of course is only the truth. She reads too much, I always think. You often see her putting down a book with the most melancholy look in her eyes, which can't be good for her. She's an imaginative woman, I suppose you would say, and of course her habit of reading so much is often useful on our holidays: over the years she has read her way through dozens of Irish guidebooks. 'That's where the garrison pushed the natives over the cliffs,' she once remarked on a drive. 'Those rocks are known as the Maidens,' she remarked on another occasion. She has led us to places of interest which we had no idea existed: Garron Tower on Garron Point, the mausoleum at Bonamargy, the Devil's Backbone. As well as which, Cynthia is extremely knowledgeable about all matters relating to Irish history. Again she has read endlessly: biographies and autobiographies, long accounts of the centuries of battling and politics there've been. There's hardly a town or village we ever pass through that hasn't some significance for Cynthia, although I'm afraid her impressive fund of information doesn't always receive the attention it deserves. Not that Cynthia ever minds; it doesn't seem to worry her when no one listens. My own opinion is that she'd have made a much better job of her relationship with Strafe and her sons if she could have somehow developed a bit more character.

We left her in the garden and proceeded down the cliff path to the shingle beneath. I was wearing slacks and a blouse, with the arms of a cardigan looped round my neck in case it turned chilly: the outfit was new, specially bought for the holiday, in shades of tangerine. Strafe never cares how he dresses and of course she doesn't keep him up to the mark: that morning, as far as I remember, he wore rather shapeless corduroy trousers, the kind men sometimes garden in, and a navy-blue fisherman's jersey. Dekko as usual was a fashion plate: a pale-green linen suit with pleated jacket pockets, a maroon shirt open at the neck, revealing a medallion on a fine gold chain. We didn't converse as we crossed the rather difficult shingle, but when we reached the sand Dekko began to talk about some girl or other, someone called Juliet who had apparently proposed marriage to him just before we'd left Surrey. He'd told her, so he said, that he'd think about it while on holiday and he wondered now about dispatching a telegram from Ardbeag saying, *Still thinking*. Strafe, who has a simple sense of humour, considered this hugely funny and spent most of the walk persuading Dekko that the telegram must certainly be sent, and other telegrams later on, all with the same message. Dekko kept laughing, throwing his head back in a way that always reminds me of an Australian bird I once saw in a nature film on television. I could see this was going to become one of those jokes that would accompany us all through the holiday, a man's thing really, but of course I didn't mind. The girl called Juliet was nearly thirty years younger than Dekko. I supposed she knew what she was doing.

Since the subject of telegrams had come up, Strafe recalled the occasion when Thrive Major had sent one to A.D. Cowley-Stubbs: *Darling regret three months gone love Beulah*. Carefully timed, it had arrived during one of Cows' Thursday evening coffee sessions. Beulah was a maid who had been sacked the previous term, and old Cows had something of a reputation as a misogynist. When he read the message he apparently went white and collapsed into an armchair. Warrington P.J. managed to read it too, and after that the fat was in the fire. The consequences went on rather, but I never minded listening when Strafe and Dekko drifted back to their school-days. I just wish I'd known Strafe then, before either of us had gone and got married.

We had our coffee at Ardbeag, the telegram was sent off, and then Strafe and Dekko wanted to see a man called Henry O'Reilly whom we'd met on previous holidays, who organizes mackerel-fishing trips. I waited on my own, picking out postcards in the village shop that sells almost every-thing, and then I wandered down towards the shore. I knew that they would be having a drink with the boatman because a year had passed since they'd seen him last. They joined me after about twenty minutes, Dekko apologizing but Strafe not seeming to be aware that I'd had to wait because Strafe is not a man who notices little things. It was almost one o'clock when we reached Glencorn Lodge and were told by Mr Malseed that Cynthia needed looking after.

The hotel, in fact, was in a turmoil. I have never seen anyone as ashen-faced as Mr Malseed; his wife, in a forget-me-not dress, was limp. It wasn't explained to us immediately what had happened, because in the middle of telling us that Cynthia needed looking after Mr Malseed was summoned to the telephone. I could see through the half-open door of their little office a glass of whiskey or brandy on the desk and Mrs Malseed's bangled arm reaching out for it. Not for ages did we realize that it all had to do with the lone man whom we'd speculated about the night before.

'He just wanted to talk to me,' Cynthia kept repeating hysterically in the hall. 'He sat with me by the magnolias.'

I made her lie down. Strafe and I stood on either side of her bed as she lay there with her shoes off, her rather unattractively cut plain pink dress crumpled and actually damp from her tears. I wanted to make her take it off and to slip under the bedclothes in her petticoat but somehow it seemed all wrong, in the circumstances, for Strafe's wife to do anything so intimate in my presence.

'I couldn't stop him,' Cynthia said, the rims of her eyes crimson by now, her nose beginning to run again. 'From half past ten till well after twelve. He had to talk to someone, he said.'

I could sense that Strafe was thinking precisely the same as I was: that the red-haired man had insinuated himself into Cynthia's company by talking about himself and had then put a hand on her knee. Instead of simply standing up and going away Cynthia would have stayed where she was, embarrassed or tongue-tied, at any rate unable to cope. And when the moment came she would have turned hysterical. I could picture her screaming in the garden, running across the lawn to the hotel, and then the pandemonium in the hall. I could sense Strafe picturing that also.

'My God, it's terrible,' Cynthia said.

'I think she should sleep,' I said quietly to Strafe. 'Try to sleep, dear,' I said to her, but she shook her head, tossing her jumble of hair about on the pillow.

'Milly's right,' Strafe urged. 'You'll feel much better after a little rest. We'll bring you a cup of tea later on.'

'My God!' she cried again. 'My God, how could I sleep?'

I went away to borrow a couple of mild sleeping pills from Dekko, who is never without them, relying on the things too much in my opinion. He was tidying himself in his room, but found the pills immediately. Strangely enough, Dekko's always sound in a crisis.

I gave them to her with water and she took them without asking what they were. She was in a kind of daze, one moment making a fuss and weeping, the next just peering ahead of her, as if frightened. In a way she was like someone who'd just had a bad nightmare and hadn't yet completely returned to reality. I remarked as much to Strafe while we made our way down to lunch, and he said he quite agreed.

'Poor old Cynth!' Dekko said when we'd all ordered lobster bisque and entrecôte béarnaise. 'Poor old sausage.'

You could see that the little waitress, a new girl this year, was bubbling over with excitement; but Kitty, serving the other half of the dining-room, was grim, which was most unusual. Everyone was talking in hushed tones and when Dekko said, 'Poor old Cynth!' a couple of heads were turned in our direction because he can never keep his voice down. The little vases of roses with which Mrs Malseed must have decorated each table before the fracas had occurred seemed strangely out of place in the atmosphere which had developed.

The waitress had just taken away our soup plates when Mr Malseed hurried into the dining-room and came straight to our table. The lobster bisque surprisingly hadn't been quite up to scratch, and in passing I couldn't help wondering if the fuss had caused the kitchen to go to pieces also.

'I wonder if I might have a word, Major Strafe,' Mr Malseed said, and Strafe rose at once and accompanied him from the dining-room. A total silence had fallen, everyone in the dining-room pretending to be intent on eating. I had an odd feeling that we had perhaps got it all wrong, that because we'd been out for our walk when it had happened all the other guests knew more of the details than Strafe and Dekko and I did. I began to wonder if poor Cynthia had been raped.

Afterwards Strafe told us what occurred in the Malseeds' office, how Mrs Malseed had been sitting there, slumped, as he put it, and how two policemen had questioned him. 'Look, what on earth's all this about?' he had demanded rather sharply.

'It concerns this incident that's taken place, sir,' one of the policemen explained in an unhurried voice. 'On account of your wife –'

'My wife's lying down. She must not be questioned or in any way disturbed.'

'Ach, we'd never do that, sir.'

Strafe does a good Co. Antrim brogue and in relating all this to us he couldn't resist making full use of it. The two policemen were in uniform and their natural slowness of intellect was rendered more noticeable by the lugubrious air the tragedy had inspired in the hotel. For tragedy was what it was: after talking to Cynthia for nearly two hours the lone man had walked down to the rocks and been drowned.

When Strafe finished speaking I placed my knife and fork together on my plate, unable to eat another mouthful. The facts appeared to be that the man, having left Cynthia by the magnolias, had clambered down the cliff to a place no one ever went to, on the other side of the hotel from the sands we had walked along to Ardbeag. No one had seen him except Cynthia, who from the cliff-top had apparently witnessed his battering by the treacherous waves. The tide had been coming in, but by the time old Arthur and Mr Malseed reached the rocks it had begun to turn, leaving behind it the fully dressed corpse. Mr Malseed's impression was that the man had lost his footing on the seaweed and accidentally stumbled into the depths, for the rocks were so slippery it was difficult to carry the corpse more than a matter of yards. But at least it had been placed out of view, while Mr Malseed hurried back to the hotel to telephone for assistance. He told Strafe that Cynthia had been most confused, insisting that the man had walked out among the rocks and then into the sea, knowing what he was doing.

Listening to it all, I no longer felt sorry for Cynthia. It was typical of her that she should so sillily have involved us in all this. Why on earth had she sat in the garden with a man of that kind instead of standing up and making a fuss the moment he'd begun to paw her? If she'd acted intelligently the whole unfortunate episode could clearly have been avoided. Since it hadn't, there was no point whatsoever in insisting that the man had committed suicide when at that distance no one could possibly be sure.

'It really does astonish me,' I said at the lunch table, unable to prevent myself from breaking our unwritten rule. 'Whatever came over her?'

'It can't be good for the hotel,' Dekko commented, and I was glad to see Strafe giving him a little glance of irritation.

'It's hardly the point,' I said coolly.

'What I meant was, hotels occasionally hush things like this up.'

'Well, they haven't this time.' It seemed an age since I had waited for them in Ardbeag, since we had been so happily laughing over the effect of Dekko's telegram. He'd included his address in it so that the girl could send a message back, and as we'd returned to the hotel along the seashore there'd been much speculation between the two men about the form this would take.

'I suppose what Cynthia's thinking,' Strafe said, 'is that after he'd tried something on with her he became depressed.'

'Oh, but he could just as easily have lost his footing. He'd have been on edge anyway, worried in case she reported him.'

'Dreadful kind of death,' Dekko said. His tone suggested that that was that, that the subject should now be closed, and so it was.

After lunch we went to our rooms, as we always do at Glencorn Lodge, to rest for an hour. I took my slacks and blouse off, hoping that Strafe would knock on my door, but he didn't and of course that was understandable. Oddly enough I found myself thinking of Dekko, picturing his long form stretched out in the room called Hydrangea, his beaky face in profile on his pillow. The precise nature of Dekko's relationship with these girls he picks up has always privately intrigued me: was it really possible that somewhere in London there was a girl called Juliet who was prepared to marry him for his not inconsiderable money?

I slept and briefly dreamed. Thrive Major and Warrington P.J. were running the post office in Ardbeag, sending telegrams to everyone they could think of, including Dekko's friend Juliet. Cynthia had been found dead beside the magnolias and people were waiting for Hercule Poirot to arrive. 'Promise me you didn't do it,' I whispered to Strafe, but when Strafe replied it was to say that Cynthia's body reminded him of a bag of old chicken bones.

Strafe and Dekko and I met for tea in the tea-lounge. Strafe had looked in to see if Cynthia had woken, but apparently she hadn't. The police officers had left the hotel, Dekko said, because he'd noticed their car wasn't parked at the front any more. None of the three of us said, but I think we presumed, that the man's body had been removed from the rocks during the quietness of the afternoon. From where we sat I caught a glimpse of Mrs Malseed passing quite briskly through the hall, seeming almost herself again. Certainly our holiday would be affected, but it might not be totally ruined. All that remained to hope for was Cynthia's recovery, and then everyone could set about forgetting the unpleasantness. The nicest thing would be if a jolly young couple turned up and occupied the man's room, exorcising the incident, as newcomers would.

The family from France – the two little girls and their parents – were chattering away in the tea-lounge, and an elderly trio who'd arrived that morning were speaking in American accents. The honeymoon couple appeared, looking rather shy, and began to whisper and giggle in a corner. People who occupied the table next to ours in the dining-room, a Wing-Commander Orfell and his wife, from Guildford, nodded and smiled as they passed. Everyone was making an effort, and I knew it would help matters further if Cynthia felt up to a rubber or two before dinner. That life should continue as normally as possible was essential for Glencorn Lodge, the example already set by Mrs Malseed.

Because of our interrupted lunch I felt quite hungry, and the Malseeds pride themselves on their teas. The chef, Mr McBride, whom of course we've met, has the lightest touch I know with sponge-cakes and little curranty scones. I was, in fact, buttering a scone when Strafe said:

'Here she is.'

And there indeed she was. By the look of her she had simply pushed herself off her bed and come straight down. Her pink dress was even more crumpled than it had been. She hadn't so much as run a comb through her hair, her face was puffy and unpowdered. For a moment I really thought she was walking in her sleep.

Strafe and Dekko stood up. 'Feeling better, dear?' Strafe said, but she didn't answer.

'Sit down, Cynth,' Dekko urged, pushing back a chair to make room for her.

'He told me a story I can never forget. I've dreamed about it all over again.' Cynthia swayed in front of us, not even attempting to sit down. To tell the truth, she sounded inane.

'Story, dear?' Strafe inquired, humouring her.

She said it was the story of two children who had apparently ridden bicycles through the streets of Belfast, out into Co. Antrim. The bicycles were dilapidated, she said; she didn't know if they were stolen or not. She didn't know about the children's homes because the man hadn't spoken of them, but she claimed to know instinctively that they had ridden away from poverty and unhappiness. 'From the clatter and the quarrelling,' Cynthia said. 'Two children who later fell in love.'

'Horrid old dream,' Strafe said. 'Horrid for you, dear.'

She shook her head, and then sat down. I poured another cup of tea. 'I had the oddest dream myself,' I said. 'Thrive Major was running the post office in Ardbeag.'

Strafe smiled and Dekko gave his laugh, but Cynthia didn't in any way acknowledge what I'd said.

'A fragile thing the girl was, with depths of mystery in her wide brown eyes. Red-haired of course he was himself, thin as a rake in those days. Glencorn Lodge was derelict then.'

'You've had a bit of a shock, old thing,' Dekko said.

Strafe agreed, kindly adding, 'Look, dear, if the chap actually interfered with you –'

'Why on earth should he do that?' Her voice was shrill in the tea-lounge, edged with a note of hysteria. I glanced at Strafe, who was frowning into his teacup. Dekko began to say something, but broke off before his meaning emerged. Rather more calmly Cynthia said:

'It was summer when they came here. Honeysuckle he described. And mother of thyme. He didn't know the name of either.'

No one attempted any kind of reply, not that it was necessary, for Cynthia just continued.

'At school there were the facts of geography and arithmetic. And the legends of scholars and of heroes, of Queen Maeve and Finn MacCool. There was the coming of St Patrick to a heathen people. History was full of kings and high-kings, and Silken Thomas and Wolfe Tone, the Flight of the Earls, the Siege of Limerick.'

When Cynthia said that, it was impossible not to believe that the unfortunate events of the morning had touched her with some kind of madness. It seemed astonishing that she had walked into the tea-lounge without having combed her hair, and that she'd stood there swaying before sitting down, that out of the blue she had started on about two children. None of it made an iota of sense, and surely she could see that the nasty experience she'd suffered should not be dwelt upon? I offered her the plate of scones, hoping that if she began to eat she would stop talking, but she took no notice of my gesture.

'Look, dear,' Strafe said, 'there's not one of us who knows what you're talking about.'

'I'm talking about a children's story, I'm talking about a girl and a boy who visited this place we visit also. He hadn't been here for years, but he returned last night, making one final effort to understand. And then he walked out into the sea.'

She had taken a piece of her dress and was agitatedly crumpling it between the finger and thumb of her left hand. It was dreadful really, having her so grubby-looking. For some odd reason I suddenly thought of her cooking, how she wasn't in the least interested in it or in anything about the house. She certainly hadn't succeeded in making a home for Strafe.

'They rode those worn-out bicycles through a hot afternoon. Can you feel all that? A newly surfaced road, the snap of chippings beneath their tyres, the smell of tar? Dust from a passing car, the city they left behind?'

'Cynthia dear,' I said, 'drink your tea, and why not have a scone?'

'They swam and sunbathed on the beach you walked along today. They went to a spring for water. There were no magnolias then. There was no garden, no neat little cliff paths to the beach. Surely you can see it clearly?'

'No,' Strafe said. 'No, we really cannot, dear.'

'This place that is an idyll for us was an idyll for them too: the trees, the ferns, the wild roses near the water spring, the very sea and sun they shared. There was a cottage lost in the middle of the woods: they sometimes looked for that. They played a game, a kind of hide-and-seek. People in a white farmhouse gave them milk.'

For the second time I offered Cynthia the plate of scones and for the second time she pointedly ignored me. Her cup of tea hadn't been touched. Dekko took a scone and cheerfully said:

'All's well that's over.'

But Cynthia appeared to have drifted back into a daze, and I wondered again if it could really be possible that the experience had unhinged her. Unable to help myself, I saw her being led away from the hotel, helped into the back of a blue van, something like an ambulance. She was talking about the children again, how they had planned to marry and keep a sweet-shop.

'Take it easy, dear,' Strafe said, which I followed up by suggesting for the second time that she should make an effort to drink her tea.

'Has it to do with the streets they came from? Or the history they learnt, he from his Christian Brothers, she from her nuns? History is unfinished in this island; long since it has come to a stop in Surrey.'

Dekko said, and I really had to hand it to him:

'Cynth, we have to put it behind us.'

It didn't do any good. Cynthia just went rambling on, speaking again of the girl being taught by nuns, and the boy by Christian Brothers. She began to recite the history they might have learnt, the way she sometimes did when we were driving through an area that had historical connections. 'Can you imagine,' she embarrassingly asked, 'our very favourite places bitter with disaffection, with plotting and revenge? Can you imagine the treacherous murder of Shane O'Neill the Proud?'

Dekko made a little sideways gesture of his head, politely marvelling. Strafe seemed about to say something, but changed his mind. Confusion ran through Irish history, Cynthia said, like convolvulus in a hedgerow. On 24 May 1487, a boy of ten called Lambert Simnel, brought to Dublin by a priest from Oxford, was declared Edward VI of all England and Ireland, crowned with a golden circlet taken from a statue of the Virgin Mary. On 24 May 1798, here in Antrim, Presbyterian farmers fought for a common cause with their Catholic labourers. She paused and looked at Strafe. Chaos and contradiction, she informed him, were hidden every-where beneath nice-sounding names. 'The Battle of the Yellow Ford,' she suddenly chanted in a singsong way that sounded thoroughly peculiar, 'the Statutes of Kilkenny. The Battle of Glenmama, the Convention of Drumceat. The Act of Settlement, the Renunciation Act. The Act of Union, the Toleration Act. Just so much history it sounds like now, yet people starved or died while other people watched. A language was lost, a faith forbidden. Famine followed revolt, plantation followed that. But it was people who were struck into the soil of other people's land, not forests of new trees; and it was greed and treachery that spread as a disease among them all. No wonder unease clings to these shreds of history and shots ring out in answer to the mockery of drums. No wonder the air is nervy with suspicion.'

There was an extremely awkward silence when she ceased to speak.

Dekko nodded, doing his best to be companionable. Strafe nodded also. I simply examined the pattern of roses on our teatime china, not knowing what else to do. Eventually Dekko said: 'What an awful lot you know, Cynth!'

'Cynthia's always been interested,' Strafe said. 'Always had a first-rate memory.'

'Those children of the streets are part of the battles and the Acts,' she went on, seeming quite unaware that her talk was literally almost crazy. 'They're part of the blood that flowed around those nice-sounding names.' She paused, and for a moment seemed disinclined to continue. Then she said:

'The second time they came here the house was being rebuilt. There were concrete-mixers, and lorries drawn up on the grass, noise and scaffolding everywhere. They watched all through another afternoon and then they went their different ways: their childhood was over, lost with their idyll. He became a dockyard clerk. She went to London, to work in a betting shop.'

'My dear,' Strafe said very gently, 'it's interesting, everything you say, but it really hardly concerns us.'

'No, of course not.' Quite emphatically Cynthia shook her head, appearing wholly to agree. 'They were degenerate, awful creatures. They must have been.'

'No one's saying that, my dear.'

'Their story should have ended there, he in the docklands of Belfast, she recording bets. Their complicated childhood love should just have dissipated, as such love often does. But somehow nothing was as neat as that.'

Dekko, in an effort to lighten the conversation, mentioned a boy called Gollsol who'd been at school with Strafe and himself, who'd formed a romantic attachment for the daughter of one of the groundsmen and had later actually married her. There was a silence for a moment, then Cynthia, without emotion, said:

'You none of you care. You sit there not caring that two people are dead.'

'Two people, Cynthia?' I said.

'For God's sake, I'm telling you!' she cried. 'That girl was murdered in a room in Maida Vale.'

Although there is something between Strafe and myself, I do try my best to be at peace about it. I go to church and take communion, and I know Strafe occasionally does too, though not as often as perhaps he might. Cynthia has no interest in that side of life, and it rankled with me now to hear her blaspheming so casually, and so casually speaking about death in Maida Vale on top of all this stuff about history and children. Strafe was shaking his head, clearly believing that Cynthia didn't know what she was talking about.

'Cynthia dear,' I began, 'are you sure you're not muddling something up here? You've been upset, you've had a nightmare: don't you think your imagination, or something you've been reading –'

'Bombs don't go off on their own. Death doesn't just happen to occur in Derry and Belfast, in London and Amsterdam and Dublin, in Berlin and Jerusalem. There are people who are murderers: that is what this children's story is about.'

A silence fell, no one knowing what to say. It didn't matter of course because without any prompting Cynthia continued.

'We drink our gin with Angostura bitters, there's lamb or chicken Kiev. Old Kitty's kind to us in the dining-room and old Arthur in the hall. Flowers are everywhere, we have our special table.'

'Please let us take you to your room now,' Strafe begged, and as he spoke I reached out a hand in friendship and placed it on her arm. 'Come on, old thing,' Dekko said.

'The limbless are left on the streets, blood spatters the car-parks. *Brits Out* it says on a rockface, but we know it doesn't mean us.'

I spoke quietly then, measuring my words, measuring the pause between each so that its effect might be registered. I felt the statement had to be made, whether it was my place to make it or not. I said:

'You are very confused, Cynthia.'

The French family left the tea-lounge. The two Dalmatians, Charger and Snooze, ambled in and sniffed and went away again. Kitty came to clear the French family's tea things. I could hear her speaking to the honeymoon couple, saying the weather forecast was good.

'Cynthia,' Strafe said, standing up, 'we've been very patient with you but this is now becoming silly.'

I nodded just a little. 'I really think,' I softly said, but Cynthia didn't permit me to go on.

'Someone told him about her. Someone mentioned her name, and he couldn't believe it. She sat alone in Maida Vale, putting together the mechanisms of her bombs: this girl who had laughed on the seashore, whom he had loved.'

'Cynthia,' Strafe began, but he wasn't permitted to continue either. Hopelessly, he just sat down again.

'Whenever he heard of bombs exploding he thought of her, and couldn't understand. He wept when he said that; her violence haunted him, he said.

He couldn't work, he couldn't sleep at night. His mind filled up with images of her, their awkward childhood kisses, her fingers working neatly now. He saw her with a carrier-bag, hurrying it through a crowd, leaving it where it could cause most death. In front of the mouldering old house that had once been Glencorn Lodge they'd made a fire and cooked their food. They'd lain for ages on the grass. They'd cycled home to their city streets.'

It suddenly dawned on me that Cynthia was knitting this whole fantasy out of nothing. It all worked backwards from the moment when she'd had the misfortune to witness the man's death in the sea. A few minutes before he'd been chatting quite normally to her, he'd probably even mentioned a holiday in his childhood and some girl there'd been: all of it would have been natural in the circumstances, possibly even the holiday had taken place at Glencorn. He'd said goodbye and then unfortunately he'd had his accident. Watching from the cliff edge, something had cracked in poor Cynthia's brain, she having always been a prey to melancholy. I suppose it must be hard having two sons who don't think much of you, and a marriage not offering you a great deal, bridge and holidays probably the best part of it. For some odd reason of her own she'd created her fantasy about a child turning into a terrorist. The violence of the man's death had clearly filled her imagination with Irish violence, so regularly seen on television. If we'd been on holiday in Suffolk I wondered how it would have seemed to the poor creature.

I could feel Strafe and Dekko beginning to put all that together also, beginning to realize that the whole story of the red-haired man and the girl was clearly Cynthia's invention. 'Poor creature,' I wanted to say, but did not do so.

'For months he searched for her, pushing his way among the people of London, the people who were her victims. When he found her she just looked at him, as if the past hadn't even existed. She didn't smile, as if incapable of smiling. He wanted to take her away, back to where they came from, but she didn't reply when he suggested that. Bitterness was like a disease in her, and when he left her he felt the bitterness in himself.'

Again Strafe and Dekko nodded, and I could feel Strafe thinking that there really was no point in protesting further. All we could hope for was that the end of the saga was in sight.

'He remained in London, working on the railways. But in the same way as before he was haunted by the person she'd become, and the haunting was more awful now. He bought a gun from a man he'd been told about and kept it hidden in a shoe-box in his rented room. Now and again he took it out and looked at it, then put it back. He hated the violence that possessed her, yet he was full of it himself: he knew he couldn't betray her with anything but death. Humanity had left both of them when he visited her again in Maida Vale.'

To my enormous relief and, I could feel, to Strafe's and Dekko's too, Mr and Mrs Malseed appeared beside us. Like his wife, Mr Malseed had considerably recovered. He spoke in an even voice, clearly wishing to dispose of the matter. It was just the diversion we needed.

'I must apologize, Mrs Strafe,' he said. 'I cannot say how sorry we are that you were bothered by that man.'

'My wife is still a little dicky,' Strafe explained, 'but after a decent night's rest I think we can say she'll be as right as rain again.'

'I only wish, Mrs Strafe, you had made contact with my wife or myself when he first approached you.' There was a spark of irritation in Mr Malseed's eyes, but his voice was still controlled. 'I mean, the unpleasantness you suffered might just have been averted.'

'Nothing would have been averted, Mr Malseed, and certainly not the horror we are left with. Can you see her as the girl she became, seated at a chipped white table, her wires and fuses spread around her? What were her thoughts in that room, Mr Malseed? What happens in the mind of anyone who wishes to destroy? In a back street he bought his gun for too much money. When did it first occur to him to kill her?'

'We really are a bit at sea,' Mr Malseed replied without the slightest hesitation. He humoured Cynthia by displaying no surprise, by speaking very quietly.

'All I am saying, Mr Malseed, is that we should root our heads out of the sand and wonder about two people who are beyond the pale.'

'My dear,' Strafe said, 'Mr Malseed is a busy man.'

Still quietly, still perfectly in control of every intonation, without a single glance around the tea-lounge to ascertain where his guests' attention was, Mr Malseed said:

'There is unrest here, Mrs Strafe, but we do our best to live with it.'

'All I am saying is that perhaps there can be regret when two children end like this.'

Mr Malseed did not reply. His wife did her best to smile away the awkwardness. Strafe murmured privately to Cynthia, no doubt beseeching her to come to her senses. Again I imagined a blue van drawn up in front of Glencorn Lodge, for it was quite understandable now that an imaginative woman should go mad, affected by the ugliness of death. The garbled speculation about the man and the girl, the jumble in the poor thing's mind – a children's story as she called it – all somehow hung together when you realized they didn't have to make any sense whatsoever.

'Murderers are beyond the pale, Mr Malseed, and England has always had its pales. The one in Ireland began in 1395.'

'Dear,' I said, 'what has happened has nothing whatsoever to do with calling people murderers and placing them beyond some pale or other. You witnessed a most unpleasant accident, dear, and it's only to be expected that you've become just a little lost. The man had a chat with you when you were sitting by the magnolias and then the shock of seeing him slip on the seaweed –'

'He didn't slip on the seaweed,' she suddenly screamed. 'My God, he didn't slip on the seaweed.'

Strafe closed his eyes. The other guests in the tea-lounge had fallen silent ages ago, openly listening. Arthur was standing near the door and was listening also. Kitty was waiting to clear away our tea things, but didn't like to because of what was happening.

'I must request you to take Mrs Strafe to her room, Major,' Mr Malseed said. 'And I must make it clear that we cannot tolerate further upset in Glencorn Lodge.'

Strafe reached for her arm, but Cynthia took no notice.

'An Irish joke,' she said, and then she stared at Mr and Mrs Malseed, her eyes passing over each feature of their faces. She stared at Dekko and Strafe, and last of all at me. She said eventually:

'An Irish joke, an unbecoming tale: of course it can't be true. Ridiculous, that a man returned here. Ridiculous, that he walked again by the seashore and through the woods, hoping to understand where a woman's cruelty had come from.'

'This talk is most offensive,' Mr Malseed protested, his calmness slipping just a little. The ashen look that had earlier been in his face returned. I could see he was beside himself with rage. 'You are trying to bring something to our doorstep which most certainly does not belong there.'

'On your doorstep they talked about a sweetshop: Cadbury's bars and different-flavoured creams, nut-milk toffee, Aero and Crunchie.'

'For God's sake pull yourself together,' I clearly heard Strafe whispering, and Mrs Malseed attempted to smile. 'Come along now, Mrs Strafe,' she said, making a gesture. 'Just to please us, dear. Kitty wants to clear away the dishes. Kitty!' she called out, endeavouring to bring matters down to earth.

Kitty crossed the lounge with her tray and gathered up the cups and saucers. The Malseeds, naturally still anxious, hovered. No one was surprised when Cynthia began all over again, by crazily asking Kitty what she thought of us.

'I think, dear,' Mrs Malseed began, 'Kitty's quite busy really.'

'Stop this at once,' Strafe quietly ordered.

'For fourteen years, Kitty, you've served us with food and cleared away the teacups we've drunk from. For fourteen years we've played our bridge and walked about the garden. We've gone for drives, we've bought our tweed, we've bathed as those children did.'

'Stop it,' Strafe said again, a little louder. Bewildered and getting red in the face, Kitty hastily bundled china on to her tray. I made a sign at Strafe because for some reason I felt that the end was really in sight. I wanted him to retain his patience, but what Cynthia said next was almost unbelievable.

'In Surrey we while away the time, we clip our hedges. On a bridge night there's coffee at nine o'clock, with macaroons or *petits fours*. Last thing of all we watch the late-night News, packing away our cards and scoring-pads, our sharpened pencils. There's been an incident in Armagh, one soldier's had his head shot off, another's run amok. Our lovely Glens of Antrim, we all four think, our coastal drives: we hope that nothing disturbs the peace. We think of Mr Malseed, still busy in Glencorn Lodge, and Mrs Malseed finishing her flower-plaques for the rooms of the completed annexe.'

'Will you for God's sake shut up?' Strafe suddenly shouted. I could see him struggling with himself, but it didn't do any good. He called Cynthia a bloody spectacle, sitting there talking rubbish. I don't believe she even heard him.

'Through honey-tinted glasses we love you and we love your island, Kitty. We love the lilt of your racy history, we love your earls and heroes. Yet we made a sensible pale here once, as civilized people create a garden, pretty as a picture.'

Strafe's outburst had been quite noisy and I could sense him being ashamed of it. He muttered that he was sorry, but Cynthia simply took advantage of his generosity, continuing about a pale.

'Beyond it lie the bleak untouchables, best kept as dots on the horizon, too terrible to contemplate. How can we be blamed if we make neither head nor tail of anything, Kitty, your past and your present, those battles and Acts of Parliament? We people of Surrey: how can we know? Yet I stupidly thought, you see, that the tragedy of two children could at least be understood. He didn't discover where her cruelty had come from because perhaps you never can: evil breeds evil in a mysterious way. That's the story the red-haired stranger passed on to me, the story you huddle away from.'

Poor Strafe was pulling at Cynthia, pleading with her, still saying he was sorry.

'Mrs Strafe,' Mr Malseed tried to say, but got no further. To my horror Cynthia abruptly pointed at me.

'That woman,' she said, 'is my husband's mistress, a fact I am supposed to be unaware of, Kitty.'

'My God!' Strafe said.

'My husband is perverted in his sexual desires. His friend, who shared his schooldays, has never quite recovered from that time. I myself am a pathetic creature who has closed her eyes to a husband's infidelity and his mistress's viciousness. I am dragged into the days of Thrive Major and A.D. Cowley-Stubbs: mechanically I smile. I hardly exist, Kitty.'

There was a most unpleasant silence, and then Strafe said:

'None of that's true. For God's sake, Cynthia,' he suddenly shouted, 'go and lie down.'

Cynthia shook her head and continued to address the waitress. She'd had a rest, she told her. 'But it didn't do any good, Kitty, because hell has invaded the paradise of Glencorn, as so often it has invaded your island. And we, who have so often brought it, pretend it isn't there. Who cares about children made into murderers?'

Strafe shouted again. 'You fleshless ugly bitch!' he cried. 'You bloody old fool!' He was on his feet, trying to get her on to, hers. The blood was thumping in his bronzed face, his eyes had a fury in them I'd never seen before. 'Fleshless!' he shouted at her, not caring that so many people were listening. He closed his eyes in misery and in shame again, and I wanted to reach out and take his hand but of course I could not. You could see the Malseeds didn't blame him, you could see them thinking that everything was ruined for us. I wanted to shout at Cynthia too, to batter the silliness out of her, but of course I could not do that. I could feel the tears behind my eyes, and I couldn't help noticing that Dekko's hands were shaking. He's quite sensitive behind his joky manner, and had quite obviously taken to heart her statement that he had never recovered from his schooldays. Nor had it been pleasant, hearing myself described as vicious.

'No one cares,' Cynthia said in the same unbalanced way, as if she hadn't just been called ugly and a bitch. 'No one cares, and on our journey home we shall all four be silent. Yet is the truth about ourselves at least a beginning? Will we wonder in the end about the hell that frightens us?'

Strafe still looked wretched, his face deliberately turned away from us. Mrs Malseed gave a little sigh and raised the fingers of her left hand to her cheek, as if something tickled it. Her husband breathed heavily. Dekko seemed on the point of tears.

Cynthia stumbled off, leaving a silence behind her. Before it was broken I knew she was right when she said we would just go home, away from this country we had come to love. And I knew as well that neither here nor at home would she be led to a blue van that was not quite an ambulance. Strafe would stay with her because Strafe is made like that, honourable in his own particular way. I felt a pain where perhaps my heart is, and again I wanted to cry. Why couldn't it have been she who had gone down to the rocks and slipped on the seaweed or just walked into the sea, it didn't matter which? Her awful rigmarole hung about us as the last of the tea things were gathered up – the earls who'd fled, the famine and the people planted. The children were there too, grown up into murdering riff-raff.

The Blue Dress

My cinder-grey room has a window, but I have never in all my time here looked out of it. It's easier to remember, to conjure up this scene or that, to eavesdrop. Americans give arms away, Russians promise tanks. In Brussels an English politician breakfasts with his mistress; a pornographer pretends he's selling Christmas cards. Carefully I listen, as in childhood I listened to the hushed conversation of my parents.

I stand in the cathedral at Vézelay, whose bishops once claimed it possessed the mortal remains of Mary Magdalene, a falseness which was exposed by Pope Boniface VIII. I wonder about that Pope, and then the scene is different.

I sit in the Piazza San Marco on the day when I discovered a sea of corruption among the local Communists. The music plays, visitors remark upon the pigeons.

Scenes coalesce: Miss Batchelor passes along the promenade, Major Trubstall lies, the blue dress flutters and is still. In Rotterdam I have a nameless woman. '*Feest wezen vieren?*' she says. '*Gedronken?*' In Corniglia the wine is purple, the path by the coast is marked as a lover's lane. I am silly, Dorothea says, the dress is just a dress. She laughs, like water running over pebbles.

I must try, they tell me; it will help to write it down. I do not argue, I do precisely as they say. Carefully, I remember. Carefully, I write it down.

It was Bath, not Corniglia, not Rotterdam or Venice, not Vézelay: it was in Bath where Dorothea and I first met, by chance in the Pump Room. 'I'm sorry,' I said, actually bumping into her.

She shook her head, saying that of course I hadn't hurt her. She blamed the crowds, tourists pushing like mad things, always in a hurry. But nothing could keep her out of the Pump Room because of its Jane Austen associations.

'I've never been here before.'

'Goodness! You poor thing!'

'I was on the way to have some coffee. Would you like some?'

'I always have coffee when I come.'

She was small and very young – twenty-one or -two, I guessed – in a plain white dress without sleeves. She carried a basket, and had very fair hair, quite straight and cut quite short. Her oval face was perfect, her eyes intense, the blue of a washed-out sky. She smiled when she told me about herself, as though she found the subject a little absurd. She was studying the history of art but when she finished that she didn't know what on earth she was going to do next. I said I was in Bath because my ex-wife's mother, who'd only come to live there six months ago, had died. The funeral had taken place that morning and my ex-wife, Felicity, had been furious that I'd attended it. But I'd always been fond of her mother, fonder in fact than Felicity had ever been. I'd known of course that I would have to meet her at the funeral. She'd married again, a man who ran a wine business: he had been there too.

'Is it horrible, a divorce?' the girl asked me while we drank our weak, cool coffee. 'I can never think of my parents divorcing.'

'It's nice you can't. Yes, it's horrible.'

'Did you have children?'

'No.'

'There's that at least. But isn't it odd, to make such a very rudimentary mistake?'

'Extraordinary.'

I don't know what it was about her manner that first morning, but something seemed to tell me that this beautiful creature would not be outraged if I said   which I did – that we might go somewhere else in search of a better cup of coffee. And when I said, 'Let's have a drink,' I said it confidently. She telephoned her parents' house. We had lunch together in the Francis Hotel.

'I went to a boarding-school I didn't like,' she told me. 'Called after St Catherine but without her charity. I was bad at maths and French and geography. I didn't like a girl called Angela Tate and I didn't like the breakfasts. I missed my brothers. What about you? What was your wife like?'

'Fond of clothes. Very fine tweed, a certain shade of scarlet, scarves of every possible variation. She hated being abroad, trailing after me.' I didn't add that Felicity had been unfaithful with anyone she had a fancy for; I didn't even want to think about that.

The waiter brought Dorothea veal escalope and steak *au poivre* for me. It was very like being in a dream. The funeral of my ex-mother-in-law had taken place at ten o'clock, there had been Felicity's furious glances and her husband's disdain, my walking away when the ceremony was over without a word to anyone. I'd felt wound up, like a watch-spring, seeing vividly in my mind's eye an old, grey woman who'd always entertained me with her gossip, who'd written to me when Felicity went to say how sorry she was, adding in a postscript that Felicity had always been a handful. She and I had shared the truth about her daughter, and it was that I'd honoured by making the journey to her funeral.

'They say I am compulsively naughty,' Dorothea said, as if guessing that I wondered what she had said to her parents on the telephone. I suspected she had not confessed the truth. There'd been some excuse to account for her delay, and already that fitted in with what I knew of her. Certainly she would not have said that she'd been picked up by a middle-aged journalist who had come to Bath to attend a funeral. She spoke again of Jane Austen, of Elizabeth Bennet, and Emma and Elinor. She spoke as though these fictional characters were real. She almost loved them, she said, but that of course could not have been quite true.

'Who were encumbered with low connections and gave themselves airs? Who bestowed their consent with a most joyful alacrity?'

I laughed, and waited for her to tell me. I walked with her to a parked car, a white Mini that had collected a traffic warden's ticket. Formally we shook hands and all the way to London on the train I thought of her. I sat in the bar drinking one after another of those miniature bottles of whisky that trains go in for, while her face jumped about in my imagination, unnerving me. Again and again her white, even teeth smiled at me.

Within a day or two I was in Belfast, sending reports to a Washington newspaper and to a syndicate in Australia. As always, I posted photocopies of everything I wrote to Stoyckov, who operates a news bureau in Prague. Stoyckov used to pay me when he saw me, quite handsomely in a sense, but it was never the money that mattered: it was simply that I saw no reason why the truth about Northern Ireland should not be told behind the Iron Curtain as well as in Washington and Adelaide.

I had agreed to do a two-months stint – no longer, because from experience I knew that Belfast becomes depressing. Immediately afterwards I was to spend three days in Madrid, trying to discover if there was truth in the persistent rumour that the Pope was to visit Spain next year. 'Great Christ alive,' Felicity used to scream at me, 'call this a marriage?'

In Belfast the army was doing its best to hush up a rape case. I interviewed a man called Ruairi O Baoill, whom I'd last seen drilling a gang of terrorists in the Syrian desert. 'My dear fellow, you can hardly call this rape,' a Major Trubstall insisted. 'The girl was yelling her head off for it.' But the girl had been doing no such thing; the girl was whey-faced, unable to stop crying; the girl was still in pain, she'd been rushed to hospital to have stitches. 'Listen,' Major Trubstall said, pushing a great crimson face into mine, 'if a girl goes out drinking with four soldiers, d'you think she isn't after something?' The Red Hand of Ulster meant what it said, O Baoill told me: the hand was waiting to grasp the hammer and the sickle. He didn't say it to his followers, and later he denied that he had said it at all.

Ruairi O Baoill is a sham, I wrote. *And so, it would appear, is a man called Major Trubstall. Fantasy rules*, I wrote, knowing it was the truth.

All the time in Northern Ireland and for three days in Spain Dorothea's voice continued about Emma and Elinor and Elizabeth Bennet, and Mrs Elton and Mr Woodhouse. I kept imagining us together in a clean, empty house that appeared to be our home. Like smoke evaporating, my failed marriage wasn't there any more. And my unhappy childhood slipped away also, as though by magic.

'Dorothea?'

'No, this is her mother. Please hold on. I'll fetch her.'

I waited for so long I began to fear that this was Mrs Lysarth's way of dealing with unwelcome telephone callers. I felt that perhaps the single word I'd spoken had been enough to convey an image of my unsuitableness, and my presumption.

'Yes?' Dorothea's voice said.

'It's Terris. Do you remember?'

'Of course I remember. Are you in Bath again?'

'No. But at least I've returned from Northern Ireland. I'm in London. How are you, Dorothea?'

'I'm very well. Are you well?'

'Yes.' I paused, not knowing how to put it.

'It's kind of you to ring, Terris.'

'D'you think we might meet?'

'Meet?'

'It would be nice to see you.'

She didn't answer. I felt I had proposed marriage already, that it was that she was considering. 'It doesn't matter,' I began to say.

'Of course we must meet. Would Thursday do? I have to be in London then.'

'We could have lunch again.'

'That would be lovely.'

And so it was. We sat in the bow window of an Italian restaurant in Romilly Street, and when anyone glanced in I felt inordinately proud. It was early September, a warm, clear day without a hint of autumn. Afterwards we strolled through Leicester Square and along Piccadilly. We were still in Green Park at six o'clock. 'I love you, Terris,' Dorothea said.

*

Her mother smiled a slanting smile at me, head a little on one side. She laid down an embroidery on a round, cane frame. She held a hand out.

'We've heard so much,' she said, still smiling, and then she introduced her sons. While we were drinking sherry Dorothea's father appeared, a thin, tall man, with spectacles on a length of leather, dancing on a tweed waistcoat.

'My dear fellow.' Vaguely he smiled and held a hand out: an amateur archaeologist, though by profession a medical doctor. That I was the divorced middle-aged man whom his young daughter wished to marry was not a fact that registered in his face. Dorothea had shown me a photograph of him, dusty in a crumpled linen suit, holding between finger and thumb a piece of glazed terracotta. 'A pleasure,' he continued as vaguely as before. 'A real pleasure.'

'A pleasure to meet *you*, Dr Lysarth.'

'Oh, not at all.'

'More sherry?' Dorothea suggested, pouring me whisky because she knew I probably needed it.

'That's whisky in that decanter, Dorothea,' her brother Adam pointed out and while I was saying it didn't matter, that whisky actually was what I preferred, her other brother, Jonathan, laughed.

'I'm sure Mr Terris knows what he wants,' Mrs Lysarth remarked, and Dorothea said:

'Terris is his Christian name.'

'Oh, I'm so sorry.'

'You must call him Terris, Mother. You cannot address a prospective son-in-law as Mister.'

'Please do,' I urged, feeling a word from me was necessary.

'Terris?' Adam said.

'Yes, it is an odd name.'

The brothers stood on either side of Dorothea's chair in that flowery drawing-room. There were pale blue delphiniums in two vases on the mantelpiece, and roses and sweet-peas in little vases everywhere. The mingled scent was delicious, and the room and the flowers seemed part of the family the Lysarths were, as did the way in which Adam and Jonathan stood, protectively, by their sister.

They were twins, both still at Cambridge. They had their mother's oval face, the pale blue eyes their parents shared, their father's languid tallness. I was aware that however protective they might seem they were not protecting Dorothea from me: I was not an interloper, they did not resent me. But their youth made me feel even older than I was, more knocked about and less suitable than ever for the role I wished to play.

'You've travelled a great deal,' Mrs Lysarth said. 'So Dorothea says.'

'Yes, I have.'

I didn't say I'd been an only child. I didn't mention the seaside town where I'd spent my childhood, or reveal that we'd lived in a kind of disgrace really, that my father worked ignominiously in the offices of the trawling business which the family had once owned. Our name remained on the warehouses and the fish-boxes, a daily reminder that we'd slipped down in the world. I'd told Dorothea, but I didn't really think all that would interest the other Lysarths.

'Fascinating, to travel so,' Mrs Lysarth remarked, politely smiling.

After dinner Dr Lysarth and I were left alone in the dining-room. We drank port in a manner which suggested that had I not been present Dr Lysarth would have sat there drinking it alone. He talked about a Roman pavement, twenty feet below the surface somewhere. Quite suddenly he said:

'Dorothea wants to marry you.'

'We both actually –'

'Yes, so she's told us.'

I hesitated. I said:

'I'm – I'm closer to your age, in a way, than to hers.'

'Yes, you probably are. I'm glad you like her.'

'I love her.'

'Of course.'

'I hope,' I began.

'My dear fellow, we're delighted.'

'I'm a correspondent, Dr Lysarth, as Dorothea, I think, has told you. I move about a bit, but for the next two years I'll be in Scandinavia.'

'Ah, yes.' He pushed the decanter towards me. 'She's a special girl, you know.'

'Yes, I do know, Dr Lysarth.'

'We're awfully fond of her. We're a tightly bound family – well, you may have noticed. We're very *much* a family.'

'Yes, indeed.'

'But of course we've always known that Dorothea would one day wish to marry.'

'I know I'm not what you must have imagined, Dr Lysarth, when you thought of Dorothea's husband. I assure you I'm aware of that.'

'It's just that she's more vulnerable than she seems to be: I just want to say that. She's really a very vulnerable girl.'

The decanter was again moved in my direction. The tone of voice closed the subject of Dr Lysarth's daughter. We returned to archaeological matters.

I spent that night at Wistaria Lodge and noticed at breakfast-time how right Dr Lysarth had been when he'd said that the family was a tightly bound one. Conversation drifted from one Lysarth to the next in a way that was almost artificial, as though the domestic scenes I witnessed belonged in the theatre. I formed the impression that the Lysarths invariably knew what was coming next, as though their lines had been learnt. My presence was accommodated through a telepathy that was certainly as impressive, another piece of practised theatre.

'Yes, we're like that,' Dorothea said in the garden after breakfast. 'We never seem to quarrel.'

She taught me how to play croquet and when we'd finished one game we were joined by her brothers. Adam was the best of the three and he, partnering Dorothea, easily beat Jonathan and myself. Mrs Lysarth brought a tray of drinks to a white table beside the lawn and we sat and sipped in the sunshine, while I was told of other games of croquet there had been, famous occasions when the tempers of visitors had become a little ragged.

'It's a perfect training for life,' Mrs Lysarth said, 'the game of croquet.'

'Cunning pays,' Adam continued. 'Generosity must know its place.'

'Not that we are against generosity, Terris,' Adam said. 'Not that we're on the side of cunning.'

'What a family poor Terris is marrying into!' Dorothea cried, and on cue her mother smiled and added:

'Terris is a natural croquet-player. He will one day put you all to shame.'

'I doubt that very much.' And as I spoke I felt I said precisely what was expected of me.

'You must teach the Scandinavians, Dorothea,' Adam said. 'Whatever else, you must flatten out a lawn in your little Scandinavian garden.'

'Oh yes, of course we shall. So there.'

After lunch Dorothea and I went for a walk. We had to say goodbye because the next day I was to go away; when I returned it would almost be the day we'd set for our wedding. We walked slowly through the village and out into the country. We left the road and passed along a track by the side of a cornfield. We rested by a stream which Dorothea had often told me about, a place she'd come to with her brothers as a child. We sat there, our backs against the same ivy-covered tree-stump. We talked about being married, of beginning our life together in Copenhagen. I made love to Dorothea by her stream, and it was afterwards that she told me the story of Agnes Kemp. She began it as we lay there, and continued while we washed and tidied ourselves and began the journey back to Wistaria Lodge.

'She was twelve at the time, staying with us while her parents were abroad. She fell from the beech tree. Her neck was broken.'

I only nodded because there isn't much anyone can say when a fact like that is related.

'I had always wanted to climb that tree, I had been told I never must. "I dare you," she said. "I dare you, Dorothea." I was frightened, but when no one was looking we climbed it together, racing one another to the top.'

She spoke of the funeral of Agnes Kemp, how the dead child's parents had not been present because it had been impossible to contact them in time. 'We don't much hear of them now,' Dorothea said. 'A card at Christmas. Agnes was an only child.'

We walked a little in silence. Then I said:

'What was she like?'

'Oh, she was really awfully spoilt. The kind of person who made you furious.'

I suppose it was that last remark that started everything off, that and the feeling that Wistaria Lodge was a kind of theatre. The remark passed unnoticed at the time, for even as she made it Dorothea turned round, and smiled and kissed me. 'It's all forgotten now,' she said when that was over, 'but of course I had to tell you.'

It was certainly forgotten, for when we arrived in the garden the white table had been moved beneath the beech tree out of the glare of the sun, and tea with scones and sandwiches and cake was spread all over it. I felt a dryness in my mouth that was not dispelled when I drank. I found it hard to eat, or even to smile in unison with the smiling faces around me. I kept seeing the spoilt child on the grass and Dr Lysarth bending over her, saying she was dead, as no doubt he must have. I kept thinking that the beech tree should have been cut down years ago, no matter how beautiful it was.

'You're mad,' Felicity shouted at me more than once. 'You're actually mad.' Her voice in its endless repetition is always a reminder of my parents' faces, that worry in their eyes. All I had wanted to know was the truth about ourselves: why did the offices and the warehouses still bear our name, what had my grandfather done? 'Best just left,' my mother said. 'Best not bothered with.' But in the end they told me because naturally I persisted – at eight and twelve and eighteen: naturally I persisted. My grandfather had been a criminal and that was that: a drunkard and an embezzler, a gambler who had run through a fortune in a handful of years:

I'd guessed, of course, by the time they told me. I didn't know why they'd been so reluctant, or why they'd displayed concern when I persisted about Miss Batchelor: why did she weep when she walked along the promenade? I had to guess again, because all my childhood Miss Batchelor's tears possessed me so: she wept for the music teacher, who was married and had a family, and I did not forgive my parents for wishing to keep that covered up. Passionately I did not forgive them, although my mother begged me, saying I made myself unhappy. 'You sound so noble,' Felicity snapped at me. 'Yet what's so marvellous about exposing a brothel-keeper for peddling drugs? Or a grimy pederast and a government minister?' Felicity's mother called her 'a tricky kind of customer'. And tricky was just the word. Tricky, no doubt, with bank tellers and men met idly in bars. Tricky in beds all over the place, when I was so often away, having to be away.

I crossed the bedroom to the window. The beech tree was lit by moonlight now. Gazing at it, I heard the voices that had haunted me ever since Dorothea told me the story.

'Then I dare you to,' Dorothea angrily shouts, stopping suddenly and confronting the other girl.

'You're frightened of it, Dorothea. You're frightened of a tree.'

'Of course I'm not.'

'Then I dare you to.'

In the garden the boys, delighted, listen. Their sister's cheeks have reddened. Agnes Kemp is standing on one foot and then the other, balancing in a way she has, a way that infuriates Dorothea.

'You're a horrid person,' Dorothea says. 'You aren't even pretty. You're stupid and spoilt and greedy. You always have two helpings. There's something the matter with your eyes.'

'There isn't, Dorothea Lysarth. You're jealous, that's all.'

'They're pig's eyes.'

'You're just afraid of a tree, Dorothea.'

They climb it, both at the same time, from different sides. There's a forked branch near the top, a sprawling knobbly crutch, easily distinguishable from the ground: they race to that.

The boys watch, expecting any moment that an adult voice will cry out in horror from the house, but no voice does. The blue dress of Agnes Kemp and the white one of Dorothea disappear into a mass of leaves, the boys stand further back, the dresses reappear. Agnes Kemp is in front, but their sister has chosen a different route to the top, a shorter one it seems. The boys long for their sister to win because if she does Agnes Kemp will at least be quiet for a day or two. They don't call out, although they want to: they want to advise Dorothea that in a moment she will have overtaken her challenger; they don't because their voices might attract attention from the house. From where they stand they can hear the grandfather clock in the hall striking ten. Most of the windows are open.

Dorothea slips and almost falls. Her shoes aren't right for climbing and when she glances to her left she can see that Agnes's are: Agnes has put on tennis shoes, knowing she will succeed that morning in goading Dorothea. This is typical of her, and when it is all over Dorothea will be blamed because of course Agnes will blurt it out, in triumph if she wins, in revenge if she doesn't.

The blue dress reaches the fork and then advances along one of its prongs, further than is necessary. Dorothea is a yard behind. She waits, crouched at the knobbly juncture, for Agnes Kemp's return. The boys don't understand that. They stare, wondering why their sister doesn't climb down again so that they can all three run away from Agnes Kemp, since it is running away from her that has been in their minds since breakfast-time. They watch while Agnes Kemp reaches a point at which to pose triumphantly. They watch while slowly she creeps backwards along the branch. Their sister's hand reaches out, pulling at the blue dress, at the child who has been such a nuisance all summer, who'll be worse than ever after her victory. There is a clattering among the leaves and branches. Like a stone, the body strikes the ground.

'Now what did anyone dream?' Mrs Lysarth inquired at breakfast. Knives rattled on plates, toast crackled, Dr Lysarth read *The Times*. It was a family thing to talk about dreams. I had been told that there were dreaming seasons, a period when dreams could be remembered easily and a time when they could not be. It was all another Lysarth game.

'I'd been skipping French classes again,' Adam said. 'For a year or even longer I'd been keeping so low a profile that Monsieur Bertain didn't even know I existed. And then some examination or other loomed.'

'Adam often has that dream,' Dorothea confided to me.

'I was in Istanbul,' Jonathan said, 'or at least it seemed like Istanbul. A man was selling me a stolen picture. A kind of goat, by Marc Chagall.'

'I had only a wisp of a thing,' Mrs Lysarth contributed. 'A bit out of Dorothea's birth.'

'I dreamed that Terris's wife was picking scallions in the garden,' Dorothea said. ' "You're wrong to think there's been a divorce," she said.'

'Did you dream, Terris?' Mrs Lysarth asked, buttering toast, but I was so confused about the night that had passed that I thought it better to say I hadn't.

'What's the criterion for *As You Like It*, ten letters, beginning with "T"?' Dr Lysarth asked.

'Touchstone,' Dorothea said, and another Lysarth game began. 'Lord of Eden End' was 'North', 'poet's black tie ruined by vulcanized rubber' was 'ebonite'. Within ten minutes the crossword puzzle was complete.

The faces laughed and smiled around the breakfast table, the conversation ran about. Especially for my benefit a description of Monsieur Bertain, Adam's French master, was engaged upon. His accent was imitated, his war wound designated as the cause of his short temper. Dr Lysarth looked forward to a dig in Derbyshire in the autumn; his wife was to accompany him and would, as always on archaeological occasions, spend her time walking and reading. Jonathan said he intended to visit us in Scandinavia. Dorothea pressed him and I found myself doing the same.

In the sunny room, while marmalade was passed and the flowered china had all the prettiness of a cottage garden, the horror was nonsensical. Mrs Lysarth's elegance, her perfect features and her burnished hair, would surely not be as they were. No wrinkles creased her face; the doctor's eyes were honestly untroubled, forget-me-not blue, a darker shade than Dorothea's. And Dorothea's hands would surely be less beautiful? The fingers clawing at the blue dress would have acquired some sign, a joint arthritic, a single bitten nail. The faces of the boys could not have shed all traces of the awful ugliness. 'Dear, it isn't our affair, why Miss Batchelor is troubled,' my mother agitatedly protested. 'Senseless,' Felicity shouted. 'You frighten me with your senseless talk.'

On Tuesday afternoon, three days away, we would marry and the car would take us to the station at Bath after the champagne on the lawn. Our flight to Paris was at five past seven, we would have dinner in the Chez les Anges. We would visit Versailles and Rouen, and the Jeu de Paume because Dorothea had never been there. I may for a moment have closed my eyes at the breakfast table, so lost was I in speculation and imaginings.

'Well, I have a surgery,' Dr Lysarth announced, folding the newspaper as he rose from the table.

'And I have Castlereagh to wonder about,' Adam said. 'That fascinating figure.'

For a moment in the sunny room the brothers again stood by Dorothea, an accidental conjunction or perhaps telepathy came into play: perhaps they guessed the contents of my mind. There was defiance in their stance, or so I thought, a reason for it now.

'When I was little I used to ride here on my ponies. On Jess first. Later on Adonis.'

We walked as we had on the day we'd made love, through a spinney, along the track by the cornfield. Poppies, not in bloom before, were everywhere now, cow-parsley whitened the hedges.

'The first thing I remember,' Dorothea said, 'is that bits of grass had got into my pram.'

I told myself that I should mention Agnes Kemp, but I did not do so. And when we reached the stream I did not embrace the girl who was to be my bride in a few days' time. We sat with our backs against the tree-trunk, watching the ripple of the water.

'I was lifted up,' Dorothea said, 'and there was a great tutting while the grass cuttings were removed. Years went by before I can remember anything else.'

Murder was not like stealing a pencil-sharpener at school, or spilling something. Agnes Kemp had been detested, a secret had afterwards become a way of life. Few words had perhaps been spoken within the family, Dr Lysarth's giving the cause of death as a broken neck being perhaps the only announcement as to how the future was to be. The faces of the boys on the lawn returned to me, and Dorothea's face as she looked down at the still body. Had she afterwards ridden her pony, Jess or Adonis, whichever it happened to be, by the cornfield and the poppies? 'I dreamed of Agnes,' was what she didn't say at breakfast any more, because the family had exorcised the ghost.

Alone, Miss Batchelor walks; the winter waves tumble about. 'Sea-spray,' my mother lies. 'Sea-spray on her cheeks, dear.' How can my father, morning after morning, leave our gaunt house in order to perform his ignominious work, pretending it is work like any other? How can he hope that I will not scratch away the falsehoods they tell? My father is caught like a creature in a trap, for ever paying back the debts his own father has incurred. It isn't nice, Miss Batchelor and a music teacher; it isn't nice, the truth in Northern Ireland. None of it is nice. 'No, no,' they tell me, 'you must be quiet, Terris.' But I am always quiet. I make no noise in the small grey room where I have to be alone because, so they say, it is better so. The room is full of falseness: then I must write it down, they tell me, quite triumphantly; it will be easier if I write it down.

Americans give arms away, Russians promise tanks. I stand again in the cathedral at Vézelay, pleased that Pope Boniface exposed the pretence about Mary Magdalene. Felicity passes me a drink, smiling with ersatz affection. Our fingers touch, I know how she has spent that afternoon. 'Poor Dorothea,' Mrs Lysarth comforts, and the boys are angry because Dorothea has always needed looking after, ever since the day of the accident, the wretched death of a nuisance. I know I am right, as that Pope knew also. They hold me and buckle the thing on to me, but still I know I am right. Flowers are arranged in vases, croquet played beneath the beech tree. Ruairi O Baoill adopts a hero's voice to proclaim his pretence of a cause, Major Trubstall's smile is loaded with hypocrisy. The blue dress flutters and is still, telling me again that I am right.

The Teddy-bears' Picnic

'I simply don't believe it,' Edwin said. 'Grown-up people?'

'Well, grown-up now, darling. We weren't always grown-up.'

'But *teddy-bears*, Deborah?'

'I'm sure I've told you dozens of times before.'

Edwin shook his head, frowning and staring at his wife. They'd been married six months: he was twenty-nine, swiftly making his way in a stockbroker's office, Deborah was twenty-six and intended to continue being Mr Harridance's secretary until a family began to come along. They lived in Wimbledon, in a block of flats called The Zodiac. 23 The Zodiac their address was and friends thought the title amusing and lively, making jokes about Gemini and Taurus and Capricorn when they came to drinks. A Dane had designed The Zodiac in 1968.

'I'll absolutely tell you this,' Edwin said, 'I'm not attending this thing.'

'But darling –'

'Oh, don't be bloody silly, Deborah.'

Edwin's mother had called Deborah 'a pretty little thing', implying for those who cared to be perceptive a certain reservation. She'd been more direct with Edwin himself, in a private conversation they'd had after Edwin had said he and Deborah wanted to get married. 'Remember, dear,' was how Mrs Chalm had put it then, 'she's not always going to be a pretty little thing. This really isn't a very sensible marriage, Edwin.' Mrs Chalm was known to be a woman who didn't go in for cant when dealing with the lives of the children she had borne and brought up; she made no bones about it and often said so. Her husband, on the other hand, kept out of things.

Yet in the end Edwin and Deborah had married, one Tuesday afternoon in December, and Mrs Chalm resolved to make the best of it. She advised Deborah about this and that, she gave her potted plants for 23 The Zodiac, and in fact was kind. If Deborah had known about her mother-in-law's doubts she'd have been surprised.

'But we've always done it, Edwin. All of us.'

'All of who, for heaven's sake?'

'Well, Angela for one. And Holly and Jeremy of course.'

'*Jeremy*? My God!'

'And Peter. And Enid and Pansy and Harriet.'

'You've never told me a word about this, Deborah.'

'I'm really sure I have.'

The sitting-room where this argument took place had a single huge window with a distant view of Wimbledon Common. The walls were covered with plum-coloured hessian, the floor with a plum-coloured carpet. The Chalms were still acquiring furniture: what there was, reflecting the style of The Zodiac's architecture, was in bent steel and glass. There was a single picture, of a field of thistles, revealed to be a photograph on closer examination. Bottles of alcohol stood on a glass-topped table, their colourful labels cheering that corner up. Had the Chalms lived in a Victorian flat, or a cottage in a mews, their sitting-room would have been different, fussier and more ornate, dictated by the architectural environment. Their choice of decor and furniture was the choice of newlyweds who hadn't yet discovered a confidence of their own.

'You mean you all sit round with your teddies,' Edwin said, 'having a picnic? And you'll still be doing that at eighty?'

'What d'you mean, eighty?'

'When you're eighty years of age, for God's sake. You're trying to tell me you'll still be going to this garden when you're stumbling about and hard of hearing, a gang of O.A.P.s squatting out on the grass with teddy-bears?'

'I didn't say anything about when we're old.'

'You said it's a tradition, for God's sake.'

He poured some whisky into a glass and added a squirt of soda from a Sparklets syphon. Normally he would have poured a gin and dry vermouth for his wife, but this evening he felt too cross to bother. He hadn't had the easiest of days. There'd been an error in the office about the B.A.T. shares a client had wished to buy, and he hadn't managed to have any lunch because as soon as the B.A.T. thing was sorted out a crisis had blown up over sugar speculation. It was almost eight o'clock when he'd got back to The Zodiac and instead of preparing a meal Deborah had been on the telephone to her friend Angela, talking about teddy-bears.

Edwin was an agile young man with shortish black hair and a face that had a very slight look of an alligator about it. He was vigorous and athletic, sound on the tennis court, fond of squash and recently of golf. His mother had once stated that Edwin could not bear to lose and would go to ruthless lengths to ensure that he never did. She had even remarked to her husband that she hoped this quality would not one day cause trouble, but her husband replied it was probably just what a stockbroker needed. Mrs Chalm had been thinking more of personal relationships, where losing couldn't be avoided. It was that she'd had on her mind when she'd had doubts about the marriage, for the doubts were not there simply because Deborah was a pretty little thing: it was the conjunction Mrs Chalm was alarmed about.

'I didn't happen to get any lunch,' Edwin snappishly said now. 'I've had a long unpleasant day and when I get back here –'

'I'm sorry, dear.'

Deborah immediately rose from among the plum-coloured cushions of the sofa and went to the kitchen, where she took two pork chops from a Marks and Spencer's carrier-bag and placed them under the grill of the electric cooker. She took a packet of frozen broccoli spears from the carrier-bag as well, and two Marks and Spencer's trifles. While typing letters that afternoon she'd planned to have fried noodles with the chops and broccoli spears, just for a change. A week ago they'd had fried noodles in the new Mexican place they'd found and Edwin said they were lovely. Deborah had kicked off her shoes as soon as she'd come into the flat and hadn't put them on since. She was wearing a dress with scarlet petunias on it. Dark-haired, with a heart-shaped face and blue eyes that occasionally acquired a bewildered look, she seemed several years younger than twenty-six, more like eighteen.

She put on water to boil for the broccoli spears even though the chops would not be ready for some time. She prepared a saucepan of oil for the noodles, hoping that this was the way to go about frying them. She couldn't understand why Edwin was making such a fuss just because Angela had telephoned, and put it down to his not having managed to get any lunch.

In the sitting-room Edwin stood by the huge window, surveying the tops of trees and, in the distance, Wimbledon Common. She must have been on the phone to Angela for an hour and a half, probably longer. He'd tried to ring himself to say he'd be late but each time the line had been engaged. He searched his mind carefully, going back through the three years he'd known Deborah, but no reference to a teddy-bears' picnic came to him. He'd said very positively that she had never mentioned it, but he'd said that in anger, just to make his point: reviewing their many conversations now, he saw he had been right and felt triumphant. Of course he'd have remembered such a thing, any man would.

Far down below, a car turned into the wide courtyard of The Zodiac, a Rover it looked like, a discreet shade of green. It wouldn't be all that long before they had a Rover themselves, even allowing for the fact that the children they hoped for would be arriving any time now. Edwin had not objected to Deborah continuing her work after their marriage, but family life would naturally be much tidier when she no longer could, when the children were born. Eventually they'd have to move into a house with a garden because it was natural that Deborah would want that, and he had no intention of disagreeing with her.

'Another thing is,' he said, moving from the window to the open doorway of the kitchen, 'how come you haven't had a reunion all the years I've known you? If it's an annual thing –'

'It isn't an annual thing, Edwin. We haven't had a picnic since 1975 and before that 1971. It's just when someone feels like it, I suppose. It's just a bit of fun, darling.'

'You call sitting down with teddy-bears a bit of fun? Grown-up people?'

'I wish you wouldn't keep on about grown-ups. I know we're grown-ups. That's the whole point. When we were little we all vowed –'

'Jesus Christ!'

He turned and went to pour himself another drink. She'd never mentioned it because she knew it was silly. She was ashamed of it, which was something she would discover when she grew up a bit.

'You know I've got Binky,' she said, following him to where the drinks were and pouring herself some gin. 'I've told you hundreds of times how I took him everywhere. If you don't like him in the bedroom I'll put him away. I didn't know you didn't like him.'

'I didn't say that, Deborah. It's completely different, what you're saying. It's private for a start. I mean, it's your teddy-bear and you've told me how fond you were of it. That's completely different from sitting down with a crowd of idiots –'

'They're not idiots, Edwin, actually.'

'Well, they certainly don't sound like anything else. D'you mean Jeremy and Peter are going to arrive clutching teddy-bears and then sit down on the grass pretending to feed them biscuit crumbs? For God's sake, Jeremy's a medical *doctor*!'

'Actually, nobody'll sit on the grass because the grass will probably be damp. Everyone brought rugs last time. It's really because of the garden, you know. It's probably the nicest garden in South Bucks, and then there're the Ainley-Foxletons. I mean, they do so love it all.'

He'd actually been in the garden, and he'd once actually met the Ainley-Foxletons. One Saturday afternoon during his engagement to Deborah there had been tea on a raised lawn. Laburnum and broom were out, a mass of yellow everywhere. Quite pleasant old sticks the Ainley-Foxletons had been, but neither of them had mentioned a teddy-bears' picnic.

'I think she did as a matter of fact,' Deborah mildly insisted. 'I remember because I said it hadn't really been so long since the last one – eighteen months ago would it be when I took you to see them? Well, 1975 wasn't all that long before that, and she said it seemed like aeons. I remember her saying that, I remember "aeons" and thinking it just like her to come out with a word people don't use any more.'

'And you never thought to point out the famous picnic site? For hours we walked round and round that garden and yet it never occurred to you –'

'We didn't walk round and round. I'm sorry you were bored, Edwin.'

'I didn't say I was bored.'

'I know the Ainley-Foxletons can't hear properly and it's a strain, but you said you wanted to meet them –'

'I didn't say anything of the kind. You kept telling me about these people and their house and garden, but I can assure you I wasn't crying out to meet them in any way whatsoever. In fact, I rather wanted to play tennis that afternoon.'

'You didn't say so at the time.'

'Of course I didn't say so.'

'Well, then.'

'What I'm trying to get through to you is that we walked round and round that garden even though it had begun to rain. And not once did you say, "That's where we used to have our famous teddy-bears' picnic."'

'As a matter of fact I think I did. And it isn't famous. I wish you wouldn't keep on about it being famous.'

Deborah poured herself more gin and added the same amount of dry vermouth to the glass. She considered it rude of Edwin to stalk about the room just because he'd had a bad day, drinking himself and not bothering about her. If he hadn't liked the poor old Ainley-Foxletons he should have said so. If he'd wanted to play tennis that afternoon he should have said so too.

'Well, be all that as it may,' he was saying now, rather pompously in Deborah's opinion, 'I do not intend to take part in any of this nonsense.'

'But everybody's husband will, and the wives too. It's only fun, darling.'

'Oh, do stop saying it's fun. You sound like a half-wit. And something's smelling in the kitchen.'

'I don't think that's very nice, Edwin. I don't see why you should call me a half-wit.'

'Listen, I've had an extremely unpleasant day –'

'Oh, do stop about your stupid old day.'

She carried her glass to the kitchen with her and removed the chops from beneath the grill. They were fairly black, and serve him right for upsetting her. Why on earth did he have to make such a fuss, why couldn't he be like everyone else? It was something to giggle over, not take so seriously, a single Sunday afternoon when they wouldn't be doing anything anyway. She dropped a handful of noodles into the hot oil, and then a second handful.

In the sitting-room the telephone rang just as Edwin was squirting soda into another drink. 'Yes?' he said, and Angela's voice came lilting over the line, saying she didn't want to bother Debbie but the date had just been fixed: June 17th. 'Honestly, you'll split your sides, Edwin.'

'Yes, all right, I'll tell her,' he said as coldly as he could. He replaced the receiver without saying goodbye. He'd never cared for Angela, patronizing kind of creature.

Deborah knew it had been Angela on the telephone and she knew she would have given Edwin the date she had arranged with Pansy and Peter, who'd been the doubtful ones about the first date, suggested by Jeremy. Angela had said she was going to ring back with this information, but when the Chalms sat down to their chops and broccoli spears and noodles Edwin hadn't yet passed the information on.

'Christ, what are these?' he said, poking at a brown noodle with his fork and then poking at the burnt chop.

'The little things are fried noodles, which you enjoyed so much the other night. The larger thing is a pork chop, which wouldn't have got overcooked if you hadn't started an argument.'

'Oh, for God's sake!'

He pushed his chair back and stood up. He returned to the sitting-room and Deborah heard the squirting of the soda syphon. She stood up herself, followed him to the sitting-room and poured herself another gin and vermouth. Neither of them spoke. Deborah returned to the kitchen and ate her share of the broccoli spears. The sound of television came from the sitting-room. 'Listen, buster, you give this bread to the hit or don't you?' a voice demanded. 'OK, I give the bread,' a second voice replied.

They'd had quarrels before. They'd quarrelled on their honeymoon in Greece for no reason whatsoever. They'd quarrelled because she'd once left the ignition of the car turned on, causing a flat battery. They'd quarrelled because of Enid's boring party just before Christmas. The present quarrel was just the same kind of thing, Deborah knew: Edwin would sit and sulk, she'd wash the dishes up feeling miserable, and he'd probably eat the chop and the broccoli when they were cold. She couldn't blame him for not wanting the noodles because she didn't seem to have cooked them correctly. Then she thought: what if he doesn't come to the picnic, what if he just goes on being stubborn, which he could be when he wanted to? Everyone would know. 'Where's Edwin?' they would ask, and she'd tell some lie and everyone would know it was a lie, and everyone would know they weren't getting on. Only six months had passed, everyone would say, and he wouldn't join in a bit of fun.

But to Deborah's relief that didn't happen. Later that night Edwin ate the cold pork chop, eating it from his fingers because he couldn't manage to stick a fork into it. He ate the cold broccoli spears as well, but he left the noodles. She made him tea and gave him a Danish pastry and in the morning he said he was sorry.

'So if we could it would be lovely,' Deborah said on her office telephone. She'd told her mother there was to be another teddy-bears' picnic, Angela and Jeremy had arranged it mainly, and the Ainley-Foxletons would love it of course, possibly the last they'd see.

'My dear, you're always welcome, as you know.' The voice of Deborah's mother came all the way from South Bucks, from the village where the Ainley-Foxletons' house and garden were, where Deborah and Angela, Jeremy, Pansy, Harriet, Enid, Peter and Holly had been children together. The plan was that Edwin and Deborah should spend the weekend of June 17th with Deborah's parents, and Deborah's mother had even promised to lay on some tennis for Edwin on the Saturday. Deborah herself wasn't much good at tennis.

'Thanks, Mummy,' she managed to say just as Mr Harridance returned from lunch.

'No, spending the whole weekend actually,' Edwin informed his mother. 'There's this teddy-bear thing Deborah has to go to.'

'What teddy-bear thing?'

Edwin went into details, explaining how the children who'd been friends in a South Bucks village nearly twenty years ago met from time to time to have a teddy-bears' picnic because that was what they'd done then.

'But they're adults surely now,' Mrs Chalm pointed out.

'Yes, I know.'

'Well, I hope you have a lovely time, dear.'

'Delightful, I'm sure.'

'It's odd when they're adults, I'd have thought.'

Between themselves, Edwin and Deborah did not again discuss the subject of the teddy-bears' picnic. During the quarrel Edwin had felt bewildered, never quite knowing how to proceed, and he hoped that on some future occasion he would be better able to cope. It made him angry when he wasn't able to cope, and the anger still hung about him. On the other hand, six months wasn't long in a marriage which he hoped would go on for ever: the marriage hadn't had a chance to settle into the shape that suited it, any more than he and Deborah had had time to develop their own taste in furniture and decoration. It was only to be expected that there should be problems and uncertainty.

As for Deborah, she knew nothing about marriages settling into shape: she wasn't aware that rules and tacit understandings, arrangements of give and take, were what made marriage possible when the first gloss had worn off. Marriage for Deborah was the continuation of a love affair, and as yet she had few complaints. She knew that of course they had to have quarrels.

They had met at a party. Edwin had left a group of people he was listening to and had crossed to the corner where she was being bored by a man in computers. 'Hullo,' Edwin just said. All three of them were eating plates of paella.

Finding a consideration of the past pleasanter than speculation about the future, Deborah often recalled that moment: Edwin's eager face smiling at her, the computer man discomfited, a sour taste in the paella. 'You're not Fiona's sister?' Edwin said, and when ages afterwards she'd asked him who Fiona was he confessed he'd made her up. 'I shouldn't eat much more of this stuff,' he said, taking the paella away from her. Deborah had been impressed by that: she and the computer man had been fiddling at the paella with their forks, both of them too polite to say that there was something the matter with it. 'What do you do?' Edwin said a few minutes later, which was more than the computer man had asked.

In the weeks that followed they told one another all about themselves, about their parents and the houses they'd lived in as children, the schools they'd gone to, the friends they'd made. Edwin was a daring person, he was successful, he liked to be in charge of things. Without in any way sounding boastful, he told her of episodes in his childhood, of risks taken at school. Once he'd dismantled the elderly music master's bed, causing it to collapse when the music master later lay down on it. He'd removed the carburettor from some other master's car, he'd stolen an egg-beater from an ironmonger's shop. All of them were dares, and by the end of his schooldays he had acquired the reputation of being fearless: there was nothing, people said, he wouldn't do.

It was easy for Deborah to love him, and everything he told her, self-deprecatingly couched, was clearly the truth. But Deborah in love naturally didn't wonder how this side of Edwin would seem in marriage, nor how it might develop as Edwin moved into middle age. She couldn't think of anything nicer than having him there every day, and in no way did she feel let down on their honeymoon in Greece or by the couple of false starts they made with flats before they eventually ended up in 23 The Zodiac. Edwin went to his office every day and Deborah went to hers. That he told her more about share prices than she told him about the letters she typed for Mr Harridance was because share prices were more important. It was true that she would often have quite liked to pass on details of this or that, for instance of the correspondence with Flitts, Hay and Co. concerning nearly eighteen thousand defective chair castors. The correspondence was interesting because it had continued for two years and had become vituperative. But when she mentioned it Edwin just agreeably nodded. There was also the business about Miss Royal's scratches, which everyone in the office had been conjecturing about: how on earth had a woman like Miss Royal acquired four long scratches on her face and neck between five-thirty one Monday evening and nine-thirty the following morning? 'Oh yes?' Edwin had said, and gone on to talk about the Mercantile Investment Trust.

Deborah did not recognize these telltale signs. She did not remember that when first she and Edwin exchanged information about one another's childhoods Edwin had sometimes just smiled, as if his mind had drifted away. It was only a slight disappointment that he didn't wish to hear about Flitts, Hay and Co., and Miss Royal's scratches: no one could possibly get into a state about things like that. Deborah saw little significance in the silly quarrel they'd had about the teddy-bears' picnic, which was silly itself of course. She didn't see that it had had to do with friends who were hers and not Edwin's; nor did it occur to her that when they really began to think about the decoration of 23 The Zodiac it would be Edwin who would make the decisions. They shared things, Deborah would have said: after all, in spite of the quarrel they were going to go to the teddy-bears' picnic. Edwin loved her and was kind and really rather marvellous. It was purely for her sake that he'd agreed to give up a whole weekend.

So on a warm Friday afternoon, as they drove from London in their Saab, Deborah was feeling happy. She listened while Edwin talked about a killing a man called Dupree had made by selling out his International Asphalt holding. 'James James Morrison Morrison Weatherby George Dupree,' she said.

'What on earth's that?'

'It's by A.A. Milne, the man who wrote about Pooh Bear. Poor Pooh!'

Edwin didn't say anything.

'Jeremy's is called Pooh.'

'I see.'

In the back of the car, propped up in a corner, was the blue teddy-bear called Binky which Deborah had had since she was one.

The rhododendrons were in bloom in the Ainley-Foxletons' garden, late

that year because of the bad winter. So was the laburnum Edwin remembered, and the broom, and some yellow azaleas. 'My dear, we're so awfully
glad,' old Mrs Ainley-Foxleton said, kissing him because she imagined he
must be one of the children in her past. Her husband, tottering about on
the raised lawn which Edwin also remembered from his previous visit, had
developed the shakes. 'Darlings, Mrs Bright has ironed our tablecloth for
us!' Mrs Ainley-Foxleton announced with a flourish.

She imparted this fact because Mrs Bright, the Ainley-Foxletons' charwoman, was emerging at that moment from the house, with the ironed
tablecloth over one arm. She carried a tray on which there were glass jugs
of orange squash and lemon squash, a jug of milk, mugs with Beatrix
Potter characters on them, and two plates of sandwiches that weren't much
larger than postage stamps. She made her way down stone steps from
the raised lawn, crossed a more extensive lawn and disappeared into a
shrubbery. While everyone remained chatting to the Ainley-Foxletons –
nobody helping to lay the picnic out because that had never been part of
the proceedings – Mrs Bright reappeared from the shrubbery, returned to
the house and then made a second journey, her tray laden this time with
cake and biscuits.

Before lunch Edwin had sat for a long time with Deborah's father in the
summer-house, drinking. This was something Deborah's father enjoyed
on Sunday mornings, permitting himself a degree of dozy inebriation which
only became noticeable when two bottles of claret were consumed at lunch.
Today Edwin had followed his example, twice getting to his feet to refill
their glasses and during the course of lunch managing to slip out to the
summer house for a fairly heavy tot of whisky, which mixed nicely with
the claret. He could think of no other condition in which to present
himself – with a teddy-bear Deborah's mother had pressed upon him – in
the Ainley-Foxletons' garden. 'Rather you than me, old chap,' Deborah's
father had said after lunch, subsiding into an armchair with a gurgle. At
the last moment Edwin had quickly returned to the summer-house and
had helped himself to a further intake of whisky, drinking from the cap of
the Teacher's bottle because the glasses had been collected up. He reckoned
that when Mrs Ainley-Foxleton had kissed him he must have smelt like a
distillery, and he was glad of that.

'Well, here we are,' Jeremy said in the glade where the picnic had first
taken place in 1957. He sat at the head of the tablecloth, cross-legged on
a tartan rug. He had glasses and was stout. Peter at the other end of the
tablecloth didn't seem to have grown much in the intervening years, but
Angela had shot up like a hollyhock and in fact resembled one. Enid was
dumpy, Pansy almost beautiful; Harriet had protruding teeth, Holly was

bouncy. Jeremy's wife and Peter's wife, and Pansy's husband – a man in Shell – all entered into the spirit of the occasion. So did Angela's husband, who came from Czechoslovakia and must have found the proceedings peculiar, everyone sitting there with a teddy-bear that had a name. Angela put a record on Mrs Ainley-Foxleton's old wind-up gramophone. 'Oh, don't go down to the woods today,' a voice screeched, 'without consulting me.' Mr and Mrs Ainley-Foxleton were due to arrive at the scene later, as was the tradition. They came with chocolates apparently, and bunches of buttercups for the teddy-bears.

'Thank you, Edwin,' Deborah whispered while the music and the song continued. She wanted him to remember the quarrel they'd had about the picnic; she wanted him to know that she now truly forgave him, and appreciated that in the end he'd seen the fun of it all.

'Listen, I have to go to the lav,' Edwin said. 'Excuse me for a minute.' Nobody except Deborah seemed to notice when he ambled off because everyone was talking so, exchanging news.

The anger which had hung about Edwin after the quarrel had never evaporated. It was in anger that he had telephoned his mother, and further anger had smacked at him when she'd said she hoped he would have a lovely time. What she had meant was that she'd told him so: marry a pretty little thing and before you can blink you're sitting down to tea with teddy-bears. You're a fool to put up with rubbish like this was what Deborah's father had meant when he'd said rather you than me.

Edwin did not lack brains and he had always been aware of it. It was his cleverness that was still offended by what he considered to be an embarrassment, a kind of gooey awfulness in an elderly couple's garden. At school he had always hated anything to do with dressing up, he'd even felt awkward when he'd had to read poetry aloud. What Edwin admired was solidity: he liked Westminster and the City, he liked trains moving smoothly, suits and clean shirts. When he'd married Deborah he'd known – without having to be told by his mother – that she was not a clever person, but in Edwin's view a clever wife was far from necessary. He had seen a future in which children were born and educated, in which Deborah developed various cooking and housekeeping skills, in which together they gave small dinner-parties. Yet instead of that, after only six months, there was this grotesque absurdity. Getting drunk wasn't a regular occurrence with Edwin: he drank when he was angry, as he had on the night of the quarrel.

Mr Ainley-Foxleton was pottering about with his stick on the raised lawn, but Edwin took no notice of him. The old man appeared to be looking for something, his head poked forward on his scrawny neck, bespectacled eyes examining the grass. Edwin passed into the house. From behind a closed door he could hear the voices of Mrs Ainley-Foxleton and Mrs Bright, talking about buttercups. He opened another door and entered the Ainley-Foxletons' dining-room. On the sideboard there was a row of decanters.

Edwin discovered that it wasn't easy to drink from a decanter, but he managed it none the less. Anger spurted in him all over again. It seemed incredible that he had married a girl who hadn't properly grown up. None of them had grown up, none of them desired to belong in the adult world, not even the husbands and wives who hadn't been involved in the first place. If Deborah had told him about any of it on that Sunday afternoon when they'd visited this house he wondered, even, if he would have married her.

Yet replacing the stopper of the decanter between mouthfuls in case anyone came in, Edwin found it impossible to admit that he had made a mistake in marrying Deborah: he loved her, he had never loved anyone else, and he doubted if he would ever love anyone else in the future. Often in an idle moment, between selling and buying in the office, he thought of her, seeing her in her different clothes and sometimes without any clothes at all. When he returned to 23 The Zodiac he sometimes put his arms around her and would not let her go until he had laid her gently down on their bed. Deborah thought the world of him, which was something she often said.

In spite of all that it was extremely annoying that the quarrel had caused him to feel out of his depth. He should have been able to sort out such nonsense within a few minutes; he deserved his mother's gibe and his father-in-law's as well. Even though they'd only been married six months, it was absurd that since Deborah loved him so he hadn't been able to make her see how foolish she was being. It was absurd to be standing here drunk.

The Ainley-Foxletons' dining-room, full of silver and polished furniture and dim oil paintings, shifted out of focus. The row of decanters became two rows and then one again. The heavily carpeted floor tilted beneath him, falling away to the left and then to the right. Deborah had let him down. She had brought him here so that he could be displayed in front of Angela and Jeremy and Pansy, Harriet, Holly, Enid, Peter, and the husbands and the wives. She was making the point that she had only to lift her little finger, that his cleverness was nothing compared with his love for her. The anger hammered at him now, hurting him almost. He wanted to walk away, to drive the Saab back to London and when Deborah followed him to state quite categorically that if she intended to be a fool there would have to be a divorce. But some part of Edwin's anger insisted that such a course of action would be an admission of failure and defeat. It was absurd that the marriage he had chosen to make should end before it had properly begun, due to silliness.

Edwin took a last mouthful of whisky and replaced the glass stopper. He remembered another social occasion, years ago, and he was struck by certain similarities with the present one. People had given a garden party in aid of some charity or other which his mother liked to support, to which he and his brother and sister, and his father, had been dragged along. It had been an excruciatingly boring afternoon, in the middle of a heatwave. He'd had to wear his floppy cotton hat, which he hated, and an awful tan-coloured summer suit, made of cotton also. There had been hours and hours of just standing while his mother talked to people, sometimes slowly giving them recipes, which they wrote down. Edwin's brother and sister didn't seem to mind that; his father did as he was told. So Edwin had wandered off, into a house that was larger and more handsome than the Ainley-Foxletons'. He'd strolled about in the downstairs rooms, eaten some jam he found in the kitchen, and then gone upstairs to the bedrooms. He'd rooted around for a while, opening drawers and wardrobes, and then he'd climbed a flight of uncarpeted stairs to a loft. From here he'd made his way out on to the roof. Edwin had almost forgotten this incident and certainly never dwelt on it, but with a vividness that surprised him it now returned.

He left the dining-room. In the hall he could still hear the voices of Mrs Ainley-Foxleton and Mrs Bright. Nobody had bothered with him that day; his mother, whose favourite he had always been, was even impatient when he said he had a toothache. Nobody had noticed when he'd slipped away. But from the parapet of the roof everything had been different. The faces of the people were pale, similar dots, all gazing up at him. The colours of the women's dresses were confused among the flowers. Arms waved frantically at him; someone shouted, ordering him to come down.

On the raised lawn the old man was still examining the grass, his head still poked down towards it, his stick prodding at it. From the glade where the picnic was taking place came a brief burst of applause, as if someone had just made a speech. '. . . today's the day the teddy-bears have their picnic,' sang the screeching voice, faintly.

A breeze had cooled Edwin's sunburnt arms as he crept along the parapet. He'd sensed his mother's first realization that it was he, and noticed his brother's and his sister's weeping. He had seen his father summoned from the car where he'd been dozing. Edwin had stretched his arms out, balancing like a tightrope performer. All the boredom, the tiresome heat, the cotton hat and suit, were easily made up for. Within minutes it had become his day.

'Well, it's certainly the weather for it,' Edwin said to the old man.

'Eh?'

'The weather's nice,' he shouted. 'It's a fine day.'

'There's fungus in this lawn, you know. Eaten up with it.' Mr Ainley-Foxleton investigated small black patches with his stick. 'Never knew there was fungus here,' he said.

They were close to the edge of the lawn. Below them there was a rockery full of veronica and sea-pinks and saponaria. The rockery was arranged in a semicircle, around a sundial.

'Looks like fungus there too,' Edwin said, pointing at the larger lawn that stretched away beyond this rockery.

'Eh?' The old man peered over the edge, not knowing what he was looking for because he hadn't properly heard. 'Eh?' he said again, and Edwin nudged him with his elbow. The stick went flying off at an angle, the old man's head struck the edge of the sundial with a sharp, clean crack. 'Oh, don't go down to the woods today,' the voice began again, drifting through the sunshine over the scented garden. Edwin glanced quickly over the windows of the house in case there should be a face at one of them. Not that it would matter: at that distance no one could see such a slight movement of an elbow.

They ate banana sandwiches and egg sandwiches, and biscuits with icing on them, chocolate cake and coffee cake. The teddy-bears' snouts were pressed over the Beatrix Potter mugs, each teddy-bear addressed by name. Edwin's was called Tomkin.

'Remember the day of the thunderstorm?' Enid said, screwing up her features in a way she had – like a twitch really, Edwin considered. The day he had walked along the parapet might even have been the day of the thunderstorm, and he smiled because somehow that was amusing. Angela was smiling too, and so were Jeremy and Enid, Pansy, Harriet and Holly, Peter and the husbands and the wives. Deborah in particular was smiling. When Edwin glanced from face to face he was reminded of the faces that had gazed up at him from so far below, except that there'd been panic instead of smiles.

'Remember the syrup?' Angela said. 'Poor Algernon had to be given a horrid bath.'

'Wasn't it Horatio, surely?' Deborah said.

'Yes, it was Horatio,' Enid confirmed, amusingly balancing Horatio on her shoulder.

'Today's the day the teddy-bears have their picnic,' suddenly sang everyone, taking a lead from the voice on the gramophone. Edwin smiled and even began to sing himself. When they returned to Deborah's parents' house the atmosphere would be sombre. 'Poor old chap was overlooked,' he'd probably be the one to explain, 'due to all that fuss.' And in 23 The Zodiac the atmosphere would be sombre also. 'I'm afraid you should get rid of it,' he'd suggest, arguing that the blue teddy-bear would be for ever a reminder. Grown up a bit because of what had happened, Deborah would of course agree. Like everything else, marriage had to settle into shape.

Pansy told a story of an adventure her Mikey had had when she'd taken him back to boarding-school, how a repulsive girl called Leonora Thorpe had stuck a skewer in him. Holly told of how she'd had to rescue her Percival from drowning when he'd toppled out of a motor-boat. Jeremy wound up the gramophone and the chatter jollily continued, the husbands and wives appearing to be as delighted as anyone. Harriet said how she'd only wanted to marry Peter and Peter how he'd determined to marry Deborah. 'Oh, don't go down to the woods today,' the voice began again, and then came Mrs Ainley-Foxleton's scream.

Everyone rushed, leaving the teddy-bears just anywhere and the gramophone still playing. Edwin was the first to bend over the splayed figure of the old man. He declared that Mr Ainley-Foxleton was dead, and then took charge of the proceedings.

The Time of Year

All that autumn, when they were both fourteen, they had talked about their Christmas swim. She'd had the idea: that on Christmas morning when everyone was still asleep they would meet by the boats on the strand at Ballyquin and afterwards quite casually say that they had been for a swim on Christmas Day. Whenever they met during that stormy October and November they wondered how fine the day might be, how cold or wet, and if the sea could possibly be frozen. They walked together on the cliffs, looking down at the breaking waves of the Atlantic, shivering in anticipation. They walked through the misty dusk of the town, lingering over the first signs of Christmas in the shops: coloured lights strung up, holly and Christmas trees and tinsel. They wondered if people guessed about them. They didn't want them to, they wanted it to be a secret. People would laugh because they were children. They were in love that autumn.

Six years later Valerie still remembered, poignantly, in November. Dublin, so different from Ballyquin, stirred up the past as autumn drifted into winter and winds bustled around the grey buildings of Trinity College, where she was now a student. The city's trees were bleakly bare, it seemed to Valerie; there was sadness, even, on the lawns of her hall of residence, scattered with finished leaves. In her small room, preparing herself one Friday evening for the Skullys' end-of-term party, she sensed quite easily the Christmas chill of the sea, the chilliness creeping slowly over her calves and knees. She paused with the memory, gazing at herself in the looking-glass attached to the inside of her cupboard door. She was a tall girl, standing now in a white silk petticoat, with a thin face and thin long fingers and an almost classical nose. Her black hair was straight, falling to her shoulders. She was pretty when she smiled and she did so at her reflection, endeavouring to overcome the melancholy that visited her at this time of year. She turned away and picked up a green corduroy dress which she had laid out on her bed. She was going to be late if she dawdled like this.

The parties given by Professor and Mrs Skully were renowned neither for the entertainment they provided nor for their elegance. They were, unfortunately, difficult to avoid, the Professor being persistent in the face of repeated excuses – a persistence it was deemed unwise to strain.

Bidden for half past seven, his history students came on bicycles, a few in Kilroy's Mini, Ruth Cusper on her motor-cycle, Bewley Joal on foot. Woodward, Whipp and Woolmer-Mills came cheerfully, being kindred spirits of the Professor's and in no way dismayed by the immediate prospect. Others were apprehensive or cross, trying not to let it show as smilingly they entered the Skullys' house in Rathgar.

'How very nice!' Mrs Skully murmured in a familiar manner in the hall. 'How jolly good of you to come.'

The hall was not yet decorated for Christmas, but the Professor had found the remains of last year's crackers and had stuck half a dozen behind the heavily framed scenes of Hanover that had been established in the hall since the early days of the Skullys' marriage. The gaudy crêpe paper protruded above the pictures in splurges of green, red and yellow, and cheered up the hall to a small extent. The coloured scarves and overcoats of the history students, already accumulating on the hall-stand, did so more effectively.

In the Skullys' sitting-room the Professor's record-player, old and in some way special, was in its usual place: on a mahogany table in front of the french windows, which were now obscured by brown curtains. Four identical rugs, their colour approximately matching that of the curtains, were precisely arranged on darker brown linoleum. Crimson-seated dining-chairs lined brownish walls.

The Professor's history students lent temporary character to this room, as their coats and scarves did to the hall. Kilroy was plump in a royal-blue suit. The O'Neill sisters' cluster of followers, jostling even now for promises of favours, wore carefully pressed denim or tweed. The O'Neill sisters themselves exuded a raffish, cocktail-time air. They were twins, from Lurgan, both of them blonde and both favouring an excess of eye-shadow, with lipstick that wetly gleamed, the same shade of pink as the trouser-suits that nudgingly hugged the protuberances of their bodies. Not far from where they now held court, the rimless spectacles of Bewley Joal had a busy look in the room's harsh light; the complexion of Yvonne Smith was displayed to disadvantage. So was the troublesome fair hair of Honor Hitchcock, who was engaged to a student known as the Reverend because of his declared intention one day to claim the title. Cosily in a corner she linked her arm with his, both of them seeming middle-aged before their time, inmates already of a draughty rectory in Co. Cork or Clare. 'I'll be the first,' Ruth Cusper vowed, 'to visit you in your parish. Wherever it is.' Ruth Cusper was a statuesque English girl, not yet divested of her motor-cycling gear.

The colours worn by the girls, and the denim and tweed, and the royal blue of Kilroy, contrasted sharply with the uncared-for garb of Woodward, Whipp and Woolmer-Mills, all of whom were expected to take Firsts. Stained and frayed, these three hung together without speaking, Woodward very tall, giving the impression of an etiolated newt, Whipp small, his glasses repaired with Sellotape, Woolmer-Mills for ever launching himself back and forth on the balls of his feet.

In a pocket of Kilroy's suit there was a miniature bottle of vodka, for only tea and what the Professor described as 'cup' were served in the course of the evening. Kilroy fingered it, smiling across the room at the Professor, endeavouring to give the impression that he was delighted to be present. He was a student who was fearful of academic failure, his terror being that he would not get a Third: he had set his sights on a Third, well aware that to have set them higher would not be wise. He brought his little bottles of vodka to the Professor's parties as an act of bravado, a gesture designed to display jauntiness, to show that he could take a chance. But the chances he took with his vodka were not great.

Bewley Joal, who would end up with a respectable Second, was laying down the law to Yvonne Smith, who would be grateful to end up with anything at all. Her natural urge to chatter was stifled, for no one could get a word in when the clanking voice of Bewley Joal was in full flow. 'Oh, it's far more than just a solution, dear girl,' he breezily pronounced, speaking of Moral Rearmament. Yvonne Smith nodded and agreed, trying to say that an aunt of hers thought most highly of Moral Rearmament, that she herself had always been meaning to look into it. But the voice of Bewley Joal cut all her sentences in half.

'I thought we'd start,' the Professor announced, having coughed and cleared his throat, 'with the "Pathétique".' He fiddled with the record-player while everyone sat down, Ruth Cusper on the floor. He was a biggish man in a grey suit that faintly recalled the clothes of Woodward, Whipp and Woolmer-Mills. On a large head hair was still in plentiful supply even though the Professor was fifty-eight. The hair was grey also, bushing out around his head in a manner that suggested professorial vagueness rather than a gesture in the direction of current fashion. His wife, who stood by his side while he placed a record on the turntable, wore a magenta skirt and twin-set, and a string of jade beads. In almost every way – including this lively choice of dress – she seemed naturally to complement her husband, to fill the gaps his personality couldn't be bothered with. Her nervous manner was the opposite of his confident one. He gave his parties out of duty, and having done so found it hard to take an interest in any students except those who had already proved themselves academically sound. Mrs Skully preferred to strike a lighter note. Now and again she made efforts to entice a few of the girls to join her on Saturday evenings, offering the suggestion that they might listen together to Saturday Night Theatre and afterwards sit around and discuss it. Because the Professor saw no point in television there was none in the Skullys' house.

Tchaikovsky filled the sitting-room. The Professor sat down and then Mrs Skully did. The doorbell rang.

'Ah, of course,' Mrs Skully said.

'Valerie Upcott,' Valerie said. 'Good evening, Mrs Skully.'

'Come in, come in, dear. The "Pathétique's" just started.' She remarked in the hall on the green corduroy dress that was revealed when Valerie took off her coat. The green was of so dark a shade that it might almost have been black. It had large green buttons all down the front. 'Oh, how really nice!' Mrs Skully said.

The crackers that decorated the scenes of Hanover looked sinister, Valerie thought: Christmas was on the way, soon there'd be the coloured lights and imitation snow. She smiled at Mrs Skully. She wondered about saying that her magenta outfit was nice also, but decided against it. 'We'll slip in quietly,' Mrs Skully said.

Valerie tried to forget the crackers as she entered the sitting-room and took her place on a chair, but in her mind the brash images remained. They did so while she acknowledged Kilroy's winking smile and while she glanced towards the Professor in case he chose to greet her. But the Professor, his head bent over clasped hands, did not look up.

Among the history students Valerie was an unknown quantity. During the two years they'd all known one another she'd established herself as a person who was particularly quiet. She had a private look even when she smiled, when the thin features of her face were startled out of tranquillity, as if an electric light had suddenly been turned on. Kilroy still tried to take her out, Ruth Cusper was pally. But Valerie's privacy, softened by her sudden smile, unfussily repelled these attentions.

For her part she was aware of the students' curiosity, and yet she could not have said to any one of them that a tragedy which had occurred was not properly in the past yet. She could not mention the tragedy to people who didn't know about it already. She couldn't tell it as a story because to her it didn't seem in the least like that. It was a fact you had to live with, half wanting to forget it, half feeling you could not. This time of year and the first faint signs of Christmas were enough to tease it brightly into life.

The second movement of the 'Pathétique' came to an end, the Professor rose to turn the record over, the students murmured. Mrs Skully slipped away, as she always did at this point, to attend to matters in the kitchen. While the Professor was bent over the record-player Kilroy waved his bottle of vodka about and then raised it to his lips. 'Hallo, Valerie,' Yvonne Smith whispered across the distance that separated them. She endeavoured to continue her communication by shaping words with her lips. Valerie smiled at her and at Ruth Cusper, who had turned her head when she'd heard Yvonne Smith's greeting. 'Hi,' Ruth Cusper said.

The music began again. The mouthing of Yvonne Smith continued for a moment and then ceased. Valerie didn't notice that, because in the room the students and the Professor were shadows of a kind, the music a distant piping. The swish of wind was in the room, and the shingle, cold on her bare feet; so were the two flat stones they'd placed on their clothes to keep them from blowing away. White flecks in the air were snow, she said: Christmas snow, what everyone wanted. But he said the flecks were flecks of foam.

He took her hand, dragging her a bit because the shingle hurt the soles of her feet and slowed her down. He hurried on the sand, calling back to her, reminding her that it was her idea, laughing at her hesitation. He called out something else as he ran into the breakers, but she couldn't hear because of the roar of the sea. She stood in the icy shallows and when she heard him shouting again she imagined he was still mocking her. She didn't even know he was struggling, she wasn't in the least aware of his death. It was his not being there she noticed, the feeling of being alone on the strand at Ballyquin.

'Cup, Miss Upcott?' the Professor offered in the dining-room. Poised above a glass, a jug contained a yellowish liquid. She said she'd rather have tea.

There were egg sandwiches and cakes, plates of crisps, biscuits and Twiglets. Mrs Skully poured tea, Ruth Cusper handed round the cups and saucers. The O'Neill sisters and their followers shared an obscene joke, which was a game that had grown up at the Skullys' parties: one student doing his best to make the others giggle too noisily. A point was gained if the Professor demanded to share the fun.

'Oh, but of course there isn't any argument,' Bewley Joal was insisting, still talking to Yvonne Smith about Moral Rearmament. Words had ceased to dribble from her lips. Instead she kept nodding her head. 'We live in times of decadence,' Bewley Joal pronounced.

Woodward, Whipp and Woolmer-Mills were still together, Woolmer-Mills launching himself endlessly on to the balls of his feet, Whipp sucking at his cheeks. No conversation was taking place among them: when the Professor finished going round with his jug of cup, talk of some kind would begin, probably about a mediaeval document Woodward had earlier mentioned. Or about a reference to *panni streit sine grano* which had puzzled Woolmer-Mills.

'Soon be Christmas,' Honor Hitchcock remarked to Valerie.

'Yes, it will.'

'I love it. I love the way you can imagine everyone doing just the same things on Christmas Eve, tying up presents, running around with holly, listening to the carols. And Christmas Day: that same meal in millions of houses, and the same prayers. All over the world.'

'Yes, there's that.'

'Oh, I think it's marvellous.'

'Christmas?' Kilroy said, suddenly beside them. He laughed, the fat on his face shaking a bit. 'Much overrated in my small view.' He glanced as he spoke at the Professor's profile, preparing himself in case the Professor should look in his direction. His expression changed, becoming solemn.

There were specks of what seemed like paint on a sleeve of the Professor's grey suit. She thought it odd that Mrs Skully hadn't drawn his attention to them. Valerie thought it odd that Kilroy was so determined about his Third. And that Yvonne Smith didn't just walk away from the clanking voice of Bewley Joal.

'Orange or coffee?' Ruth Cusper proffered two cakes that had been cut into slices. The fillings in Mrs Skully's cakes were famous, made with Trex and castor sugar. The cakes themselves had a flat appearance, like large biscuits.

'I wouldn't touch any of that stuff,' Kilroy advised, jocular again. 'I was up all night after it last year.'

'Oh, nonsense!' Ruth Cusper placed a slice of orange-cake on Valerie's plate, making a noise that indicated she found Kilroy's attempt at wit a failure. She passed on, and Kilroy without reason began to laugh.

Valerie looked at them, her eyes pausing on each face in the room. She was different from these people of her own age because of her autumn melancholy and the bitterness of Christmas. A solitude had been made for her, while they belonged to each other, separate yet part of a whole.

She thought about them, envying them their ordinary normality, the good fortune they accepted as their due. They trailed no horror, no ghosts or images that wouldn't go away: you could tell that by looking at them. Had she herself already been made peculiar by all of it, eccentric and strange and edgy? And would it never slip away, into the past where it belonged? Each year it was the same, no different from the year before, intent on hanging on to her. Each year she smiled and made an effort. She was brisk with it, she did her best. She told herself she had to live with it, agreeing with herself that of course she had to, as if wishing to be overheard. And yet to die so young, so pointlessly and so casually, seemed to be something you had to feel unhappy about. It dragged out tears from you; it made you hesitate again, standing in the icy water. Your idea it had been.

'Tea, you people?' Mrs Skully offered.

'Awfully kind of you, Mrs Skully,' Kilroy said. 'Splendid tea this is.'

'I should have thought you'd be keener on the Professor's cup, Mr Kilroy.'

'No, I'm not a cup man, Mrs Skully.'

Valerie wondered what it would be like to be Kilroy. She wondered about his private thoughts, even what he was thinking now as he said he wasn't a cup man. She imagined him in his bedroom, removing his royal-blue suit and meticulously placing it on a hanger, talking to himself about the party, wondering if he had done himself any damage in the Professor's eyes. She imagined him as a child, plump in bathing-trunks, building a sandcastle. She saw him in a kitchen, standing on a chair by an open cupboard, nibbling the corner of a crystallized orange.

She saw Ruth Cusper too, bossy at a children's party, friendlily bossy, towering over other children. She made them play a game and wasn't disappointed when they didn't like it. You couldn't hurt Ruth Cusper; she'd grown an extra skin beneath her motor-cycling gear. At night, she often said, she fell asleep as soon as her head touched the pillow.

You couldn't hurt Bewley Joal, either: a grasping child Valerie saw him as, watchful and charmless. Once he'd been hurt, she speculated: another child had told him that no one enjoyed playing with him, and he'd resolved from that moment not to care about stuff like that, to push his way through other people's opinion of him, not wishing to know it.

As children, the O'Neill sisters teased; their faithful tormentors pulled their hair. Woodward, Whipp and Woolmer-Mills read the *Children's Encyclopaedia*. Honor Hitchcock and the Reverend played mummies and daddies. 'Oh, listen to that chatterbox!' Yvonne Smith's father dotingly cried, affection that Yvonne Smith had missed ever since.

In the room the clanking of Bewley Joal punctuated the giggling in the corner where the O'Neill sisters were. More tea was poured and more of the Professor's cup, more cake was handed round. 'Ah, yes,' the Professor began. '*Panni streit sine grano*.' Woodward, Whipp and Woolmer-Mills bent their heads to listen.

*

The Professor, while waiting on his upstairs landing for Woolmer-Mills to use the lavatory, spoke of the tomatoes he grew. Similarly delayed downstairs, Mrs Skully suggested to the O'Neill sisters that they might like, one Saturday night next term, to listen to Saturday Night Theatre with her. It was something she enjoyed, she said, especially the discussion afterwards. 'Or you, Miss Upcott,' she said. 'You've never been to one of my evenings either.'

Valerie smiled politely, moving with Mrs Skully towards the sitting-room, where Tchaikovsky once more resounded powerfully. Again she examined the arrayed faces. Some eyes were closed in sleep, others were weary beneath a weight of tedium. Woodward's newt-like countenance had not altered, nor had Kilroy's fear dissipated. Frustration still tugged at Yvonne Smith. Nothing much was happening in the face of Mrs Skully.

Valerie continued to regard Mrs Skully's face and suddenly she found herself shivering. How could that mouth open and close, issuing invitations without knowing they were the subject of derision? How could this woman, in her late middle age, officiate at student parties in magenta and jade, or bake inedible cakes without knowing it? How could she daily permit herself to be taken for granted by a man who cared only for students with academic success behind them? How could she have married his pomposity in the first place? There was something wrong with Mrs Skully, there was something missing, as if some part of her had never come to life. The more Valerie examined her the more extraordinary Mrs Skully seemed, and then it seemed extraordinary that the Professor should be unaware that no one liked his parties. It was as if some part of him hadn't come to life either, as if they lived together in the dead wood of a relationship, together in this house because it was convenient.

She wondered if the other students had ever thought that, or if they'd be bothered to survey in any way whatsoever the Professor and his wife. She wondered if they saw a reflection of the Skullys' marriage in the brownness of the room they all sat in, or in the crunchy fillings of Mrs Skully's cakes, or in the upholstered dining-chairs that were not comfortable. You couldn't blame them for not wanting to think about the Skullys' marriage: what good could come of it? The other students were busy and more organized than she. They had aims in life. They had futures she could sense, as she had sensed their pasts. Honor Hitchcock and the Reverend would settle down as right as rain in a provincial rectory, the followers of the O'Neill sisters would enter various business worlds. Woodward, Whipp and Woolmer-Mills would be the same as the Professor, dandruff on the shoulders of three grey suits. Bewley Joal would rise to heights, Kilroy would not. Ruth Cusper would run a hall of residence, the O'Neill sisters would give two husbands hell in Lurgan. Yvonne Smith would live in hopes.

The music of Tchaikovsky gushed over these reflections, as if to soften some harshness in them. But to Valerie there was no harshness in her contemplation of these people's lives, only fact and a lacing of speculation. The Skullys would go on ageing and he might never turn to his wife and say he was sorry. The O'Neill sisters would lose their beauty and Bewley Joal his vigour. One day Woolmer-Mills would find that he could no longer launch himself on to the balls of his feet. Kilroy would enter a home for the senile. Death would shatter the cotton-wool cosiness of Honor Hitchcock and the Reverend.

She wondered what would happen if she revealed what she had thought, if she told them that in order to keep her melancholy in control she had played about with their lives, seeing them in childhood, visiting them with old age and death. Which of them would seek to stop her while she cited the arrogance of the Professor and the pusillanimity of his wife? She heard her own voice echoing in a silence, telling them finally, in explanation, of the tragedy in her own life.

'Please all have a jolly Christmas,' Mrs Skully urged in the hall as scarves and coats were lifted from the hall-stand. 'Please now.'

'We shall endeavour,' Kilroy promised, and the others made similar remarks, wishing Mrs Skully a happy Christmas herself, thanking her and the Professor for the party, Kilroy adding that it had been most enjoyable. There'd be another, the Professor promised, in May.

There was the roar of Ruth Cusper's motor-cycle, and the overloading of Kilroy's Mini, and the striding into the night of Bewley Joal, and others making off on bicycles. Valerie walked with Yvonne Smith through the suburban roads. 'I quite like Joal,' Yvonne Smith confided, releasing the first burst of her pent-up chatter. 'He's all right, isn't he? Quite nice, really, quite clever. I mean, if you care for a clever kind of person. I mean, I wouldn't mind going out with him if he asked me.'

Valerie agreed that Bewley Joal was all right if you cared for that kind of person. It was pleasant in the cold night air. It was good that the party was over.

Yvonne Smith said good-night, still chattering about Bewley Joal as she turned into the house where her lodgings were. Valerie walked on alone, a thin shadow in the gloom. Compulsively now, she thought about the party, seeing again the face of Mrs Skully and the Professor's face and the faces of the others. They formed, like a backdrop in her mind, an assembly as vivid as the tragedy that more grimly visited it. They seemed like the other side of the tragedy, as if she had for the first time managed to peer round a corner. The feeling puzzled her. It was odd to be left with it after the Skullys' end-of-term party.

In the garden of the hall of residence the fallen leaves were sodden beneath her feet as she crossed a lawn to shorten her journey. The bewilderment she felt lifted a little. She had been wrong to imagine she envied other people their normality and good fortune. She was as she wished to be. She paused in faint moonlight, repeating that to herself and then repeating it again. She did not quite add that the tragedy had made her what she was, that without it she would not possess her reflective introspection, or be sensitive to more than just the time of year. But the thought hovered with her as she moved towards the lights of the house, offering what appeared to be a hint of comfort.

Being Stolen From

'I mean I'm not like I used to be.'

She had married, Norma continued, she had settled down. A young man, sitting beside her on the sofa, agreed that this was so. He was soberly dressed, jolly of manner, not quite fat. His smiling blue eyes suggested that if Norma had ever been flighty and irresponsible she no longer was, due to the influence he had brought into her life.

'I mean in a way,' Norma said, 'things have changed for you too, Mrs Lacy.'

Bridget became flustered. Ever since childhood she had been embarrassed when she found herself the centre of attention, and even though she was forty nine now none of that had improved. She was plump and black-haired, her manner affected by her dislike of being in the limelight. It was true that things had changed for her also in the last six years, but how had Norma discovered it? Had neighbours been questioned?

'Yes, things have changed,' she said, quite cheerfully because she'd become used to the change.

Norma nodded, and so did her husband. Bridget could tell from their faces that although they might not know the details they certainly knew the truth of the matter. And the details weren't important because strangers wouldn't be interested in the countryside of Co. Cork where she and Liam had come from, or in the disappointment of their childless marriage. London had become their home, a small house in a terrace, with the *Cork Weekly Examiner* to keep them in touch. Liam had found a job in a newsagent's, the same shop he and the woman now owned between them.

'Your husband didn't seem the kind,' Norma began. 'I mean, not that I knew him.'

'No, he didn't seem like that.'

'I know what it feels like to be left, Mrs Lacy.'

'It feels like nothing now.'

She smiled again, but her cheeks had become hot because the conversation was about her. When Norma had phoned a week ago, to ask if they could have a chat, she hadn't known what to say. It would have been unpleasant simply to say no, nor was there any reason why she should take that attitude, but even so she'd been dreading their visit ever since.

She'd felt cross with herself for not managing to explain that Betty could easily be upset, which was why Betty wasn't in the house that afternoon. It was the first thing she'd said to them when she'd opened the hall door, not knowing if they were expecting to see the child or not. She'd sounded apologetic and was cross with herself for that, too.

All three of them drank tea while they talked. Bridget, who didn't make cakes because Liam hadn't liked them and she'd never since got into the way of it, had bought two kinds of biscuits and a Battenburg in Victor Value's. Alarmed at the last moment in case there wouldn't be enough and she'd be thought inhospitable, she had buttered some bread and put out a jar of apricot jam. She was glad she had because Norma's husband made quite a meal of it, taking most of the ginger-snaps and folding the sliced bread into sandwiches. Norma didn't eat anything.

'I can't have another baby, Mrs Lacy. That's the point, if you get what I mean? Like after Betty I had to have an abortion and then two more, horrible they were, the last one a bit of trouble really. I mean, it left my insides like this.'

'Oh dear, I'm sorry.'

Nodding, as if in gratitude for this sympathy, Norma's husband reached for a ginger-snap. He said they had a nice flat and there were other children living near by for Betty to play with. He glanced around the small living-room, which was choked with pieces of furniture and ornaments which Bridget was always resolving to weed out. In what he said, and in the way he looked, there was the implication that this room in a cramped house was an unsuitable habitat for a spirited four-year-old. There was also the implication that Bridget at forty-nine, and without a husband, belonged more naturally among the sacred pictures on the walls than she possibly could in a world of toys and children. It was Betty they had to think of, the young man's concerned expression insisted; it was Betty's well-being.

'We signed the papers at the time.' Bridget endeavoured, not successfully, to make her protest sound different from an apology. 'When a baby's adopted that's meant to be that.'

Norma's husband nodded, as if agreeing that that was a reasonable point of view also. Norma said:

'You were kindness itself to me, Mrs Lacy, you and your husband. Didn't I say so?' she added, turning to her companion, who nodded again.

The baby had been born when Norma was nineteen. There'd been an effort on her part to look after it, but within a month she'd found the task impossible. She'd been living at the time in the house across the road from the Lacys', in a bed-sitting-room. She'd had a bad reputation in the neighbourhood, even reputed to be a prostitute, which wasn't in fact true.

Bridget had always nodded to her in the street, and she'd always smiled back. Remembering all that when Norma had telephoned a day or two ago, Bridget found she had retained an impression of chipped red varnish on the girl's fingernails and her shrunken whey-white face. There'd been a prettiness about her too, though, and there still was. 'I don't know what to do,' she'd said four years ago. 'I don't know why I've had this kid.' She'd said it quite out of the blue, crossing the street to where Bridget had paused for a moment on the pavement to change the shopping she was carrying from one hand to the other. 'I often see you,' Norma had added, and Bridget, who noticed that she had recently been weeping and indeed looked quite ill, had invited her in for a cup of tea. Once or twice the sound of the baby's crying had drifted across the street, and of course she'd been quite interested to watch the progress of the pregnancy. Local opinion decreed that the pregnancy was what you'd expect of this girl, but Bridget didn't easily pass judgement. As Irish people in London, there was a politeness about the Lacys, a reluctance to condemn anyone who was English since they themselves were not. 'I've been a fool about this kid,' the girl had said: the father had let her down, as simple as that. He'd seemed as steady as a rock, but one night he hadn't been in the Queen's Arms and he hadn't been there the next night either, in fact not ever again.

'I couldn't let Betty go,' Bridget said, her face becoming hot again. 'I couldn't possibly. That's quite out of the question.'

A silence hung in the living-room for a moment. The air seemed heavier and stuffier, and Bridget wanted to open a window but did not. Betty was spending the afternoon with Mrs Haste, who was always good about having her on the rare occasions when it was necessary.

'No, it's not a question of letting her go,' the young man said. 'No one would think of it like that, Mrs Lacy.'

'We'd always like her to see you,' Norma explained. 'I mean, it stands to reason she'll have got fond of you.'

The young man again nodded, his features good-humouredly crinkled. There was no question, he repeated, of the relationship between the child and her adoptive mother being broken off. An arrangement that was suitable all round could easily be made, and any offer of babysitting would always be more than welcome. 'What's needed, Mrs Lacy, is for mother and child to be together. Now that the circumstances have altered.'

'It's two years since my husband left me.'

'I'm thinking of Norma's circumstances, Mrs Lacy.'

'I can't help wanting her,' Norma said, her lean cheeks working beneath her make-up. Her legs were crossed, the right one over the left. Her shoes, in soft pale leather, were a lot smarter than the shoes Bridget remembered from the past. So was her navy-blue shirt and her navy-blue corduroy jacket that zipped up the front. Her fingers were marked with nicotine, and Bridget knew she wanted to light a cigarette now, the way she had repeatedly done the first day she'd come to the sitting-room, six years ago.

'We made it all legal,' Bridget said, putting into different words what she had stated already. 'Everything was legal, Norma.'

'Yes, we do know that,' the young man replied, still patiently smiling, making her feel foolish. 'But there's the human side too, you see. Perhaps more important than legalities.'

He was better educated than Norma, Bridget noticed; and there was an honest decency in his eyes when he referred to the human side. There was justice above the ordinary justice of solicitors' documents and law courts, his decency insisted: Norma had been the victim of an unfair society and all they could do now was to see that the unfairness should not be perpetuated.

'I'm sorry,' Bridget said. 'I'm sorry I can't see it like that.'

Soon after that the visitors left, leaving behind them the feeling that they and Bridget would naturally be meeting again. She went to collect Betty from Mrs Haste and after tea they settled down to a familiar routine: Betty's bath and then bed, a few minutes of *The Tailor of Gloucester*. The rest of the evening stretched emptily ahead, with *Dallas* on the television, and a cardigan she was knitting. She quite liked *Dallas*, J.R. in particular, the most villainous TV figure she could think of, but while she watched his villainy now the conversation she'd had with her afternoon visitors kept recurring. Betty's round face, and the black hair that curved in smoothly on either side of it, appeared in her mind, and there was also the leanness of Norma and the sincerity of the man who wanted to become Betty's stepfather. The three faces went together as if they belonged, for though Betty's was differently shaped from the face of the woman who had given birth to her she had the same wide mouth and the same brown eyes.

At half past nine Miss Custle came into the house. She was an oldish woman who worked on the Underground and often had to keep odd hours, some days leaving the house shortly after dawn and on other days not until the late afternoon. 'Cup of tea, Miss Custle?' Bridget called out above the noise of the television.

'Well, thanks, Mrs Lacy,' Miss Custle replied, as she always did when this invitation came. She had a gas-stove and a sink in her room and did all her cooking there, but whenever Bridget heard her coming in as late as this she offered her a cup of tea. She'd been a lodger in the house ever since the break-up of the marriage, a help in making ends meet.

'Those people came,' Bridget said, offering Miss Custle what remained of the ginger-snaps. 'You know: Norma.'

'I told you to beware of them. Upset you, did they?'

'Well, talking about Betty like that. You know, Betty didn't even have a name when we adopted her. It was we thought of Betty.'

'You told me.'

Miss Custle was a powerful, grey-haired woman in a London Transport uniform which smelt of other people's cigarettes. Earlier in her life there'd been a romance with someone else on the Underground, but without warning the man had died. Shocked by the unexpectedness of it, Miss Custle had remained on her own for the next thirty years, and was given to gloom when she recalled the time of her loss. Among her colleagues on the Underground she was known for her gruffness and her devotion to the tasks she had performed for so much of her life. The London Underground, she occasionally stated in Bridget's living-room, had become her life, a substitute for what might have been. But tonight her mood was brisk.

'When a child's adopted, Mrs Lacy, there's no way it can be reversed. As I told you last evening, dear.'

'Yes, I do know that. I said it to them.'

'Trying it on, they was.'

With that, Miss Custle rose to her feet and said good-night. She never stayed long when she looked in for a cup of tea and a biscuit because she was usually tired. Her face took on a crumpled look, matching her crumpled uniform. She would iron her uniform before her next turn of duty, taking ages over it.

'Good-night, Miss Custle,' Bridget said, observing the weary passage of her lodger across the living-room and wondering just for a moment what the man who'd died had been like. One night, a year or so ago, she had told Miss Custle all about her own loss, not of course that it could be compared with death, although it had felt like it at the time. 'Horrible type of woman, that is,' Miss Custle had said.

Bridget cleared up the tea things and unplugged the television lead. She knew she wouldn't sleep properly: the visit of Norma and her husband had stirred everything up again, forcing her to travel backwards in time, to survey again all she had come to terms with. It was extraordinary that they'd thought she'd even consider handing Betty over to them.

In her bedroom she undressed and tidily arranged her clothes on a chair. She could hear Miss Custle moving about in her room next door, undressing also. Betty had murmured in her sleep when she'd kissed her good-night, and Bridget tried to imagine what life would be like not having Betty there to tuck up last thing, not having Betty's belongings about the house, her clothes to wash, toys to pick up. Sometimes Betty made her cross, but that was part of it too.

She lay in the darkness, her mind going back again. In the countryside of Co. Cork she had been one of a family of ten, and Liam had come from a large family also. It had astonished them when years later they had failed to have children of their own, but in no way had the disappointment impaired their marriage; and then Betty's presence had drawn them even closer together. 'I'm sorry,' Liam had said in the end, though, the greatest shock she'd ever had. 'I'm sorry, dear.'

Bridget had never seen the woman, but had imagined her: younger than she was, a Londoner, black hair like silk, predatory lips, and eyes that looked away from you. This woman and her mother had bought the newsagent's where Liam had worked for all his years in London, the manager more or less, under old Mr Vanish. The woman had been married before, an unhappy marriage according to Liam, a relationship that had left her wounded. 'Dear, it's serious,' he had said, trying to keep out of his voice a lightness that was natural in it, not realizing that he was opening a wound himself. In everything he said there was the implication that the love he'd felt for Bridget, though in no way false, hadn't been touched by the same kind of excitement.

The newsagent's shop was in another neighbourhood, miles across London, but in the days of old Mr Vanish, Bridget would just occasionally take Betty on a number 9 bus. When the woman and her mother took over the business some kind of shyness prevented the continuation of this habit, and after that some kind of fear. She had been ready to forgive Liam, to live in the hope that his infatuation would be washed away by time. She pleaded, but did not make scenes. She didn't scream at him or parade his treachery, or call the woman names. None of that came easily to Bridget, and all she could wonder was what life would be like if Liam stayed with her and went on loving the woman. It wasn't hard to imagine the bitterness that would develop in him, the hatred there would be in the end, yet she had continued to plead. Six weeks later he was gone.

For a moment in the darkness she wept. It was true what she'd said to her visitors that afternoon: that she felt nothing now. It was true, yet sometimes she wept when she remembered how together they had weathered the strangeness of their emigration or when she thought of Liam now, living in mortal sin with the woman and her mother above the newsagent's, not going to Confession or Mass any more. Every month money arrived from him, which with Miss Custle's rent and what she earned herself from cleaning the Winnards' flat three times a week was enough to manage on.

But Liam never came back, to see her or to see Betty, which implied the greatest change of all in him.

Memories were always difficult for her. Alone now, she too easily remembered the countryside she had grown up in, and the face of the Reverend Mother at the convent, and Mrs Barry's squat public house and grocery at a crossroads. Emir Ryall had stolen her Phillips' atlas, putting ink blots over her name and substituting her own. Madge Foley had curled her hair for her. Liam had always been in the neighbouring farm, but until after they'd both left school she'd hardly noticed him. He'd asked her to go for a walk with him, and in a field that was yellow with buttercups he had taken her hand and kissed her, causing her to blush. He'd laughed at her, saying the pink in her cheeks was lovely. He was the first person she'd ever danced with, in a nameless roadside dance-hall, ten miles away.

It was then, while she was still a round-faced girl, that Bridget had first become aware of fate. It was what you had to accept, what you couldn't kick against: God's will, the Reverend Mother or Father Keogh would have said, but for Bridget it began with the kind of person you were. Out of that, the circumstances of your life emerged: Bridget's shyness and her tendency to blush, her prettiness and her modesty, were the fate which had been waiting for her before she was born, and often she felt that Liam had been waiting for her also, that they were fated to fall in love because they complemented each other so well, he so bouncy and amusing, she so fond of the shadows. In those days it would have been impossible to imagine that he would ever go off with a woman in a newsagent's.

They were married on a Saturday in June, in a year when the foxgloves were profuse. She wore a veil of Limerick lace, borrowed from her grandmother. She carried scarlet roses. Liam was handsome, dark as a Spaniard in the Church of the Holy Virgin, his blue eyes jokily darting about. She had been glad when all of it was over, the reception in Kelly's Hotel, the car bedecked with ribbons. They'd gone away for three days, and soon after they'd returned they had had to emigrate to England because the sawmills where Liam had a job closed down. They'd been in London for more than twenty years when the woman came into his life.

Eventually Bridget slept, and dreamed of the countryside of her childhood. She sat on a cart beside her father, permitted to hold the reins of the horse while empty milk churns were rattled back from the creamery at the crossroads. Liam was suddenly there, trudging along in the dust, and her father drew up the reins in order to give him a lift. Liam was ten or eleven, a patch of sunburn on the back of his neck where his hair had been cut very short. It wasn't really a dream, because all of it had happened in the days when Liam hadn't been important.

Norma's husband came on his own. 'I hope you've no objection, Mrs Lacy,' he said, smiling in his wide-eyed way. There was a wave in his fairish hair, she noticed, a couple of curls hanging over his forehead. Everything about him was agreeable.

'Well, really I don't know.' She faltered, immediately feeling hot. 'I really think it's better if we don't go on about it.'

'I won't keep you ten minutes, Mrs Lacy. I promise.'

She held the hall door open and he walked into the hall. He stepped over a Weetabix packet which Betty had thrown down and strode away from. In the kitchen Betty was unpacking the rest of the shopping, making a kind of singing noise, which she often did.

'Sit down,' Bridget said in the living-room, as she would to any visitor.

'Thanks, Mrs Lacy,' he said politely.

'I won't be a minute.'

She had to see to Betty in the kitchen. There was flour among the shopping, and eggs, and other items in bags that might become perforated or would break when dropped from the kitchen table to the floor. Betty wasn't naughtier than any other child, but only a week ago, left on her own, she'd tried to make a cake.

'You go and get the Weetabix,' Bridget said, and Betty obediently marched into the hall to do so. Bridget hastily put the rest of the shopping out of reach. She took coloured pencils and a new colouring-book from a drawer and laid them out on the table. Betty didn't much care for filling already-drawn outlines with colour and generally just scrawled her name all over them: *Betty Lacy* in red, and again in blue and orange and green.

'Be a good big girl now,' Bridget said.

'Big,' Betty repeated.

In the sitting-room Norma's husband had picked up the *Cork Weekly Examiner*. As she entered, he replaced it on the pile of magazines near his armchair, saying that it appeared to be interesting.

'It's hard to know how to put this to you, Mrs Lacy.' He paused, his smile beginning to fade. Seriousness invaded his face as his eyes passed over the contents of the living-room, over the sacred pictures and the odds and ends that Bridget had been meaning to throw out. He said:

'Norma was in a bad way when I met up with her, Mrs Lacy. She'd been to the Samaritans; it was from them I heard about her. I'm employed by the council, actually. Social Services, counselling. That's my job, see.'

'Yes, I understand.'

'Norma was suffering from depression. Unhappiness, Mrs Lacy. She got in touch with the Samaritans and later she came round to us. I was able to help her. I won her confidence through the counselling I could give her. I love Norma now, Mrs Lacy.'

'Of course.'

'It doesn't often happen that way. A counsellor and a client.'

'No, I'm sure not.' She interrupted because she knew he was going to continue with that theme, to tell her more about a relationship that wasn't her business. She said that to herself. She said to herself that six years ago Norma had drifted into her life, leaving behind a child. She said to herself that the adoption of Betty had been at Norma's request. 'You're a lovely person, Mrs Lacy,' Norma had said at the time.

'I can't get to her at the moment,' Norma's husband explained. 'Ever since the other day she's hiding within herself. All the good that's been done, Mrs Lacy, all the care of our own relationship: it's going for nothing, you see.'

'I'm sorry.'

'She went to the Samaritans because she was suicidal. There was nothing left of the poor thing, Mrs Lacy. She was hardly a human person.'

'But Betty, you see – Betty has become my child.'

'I know, I know, Mrs Lacy.' He nodded earnestly, understandingly. 'The Samaritans gave Norma back her humanity, and then the council housed her. When she was making the recovery we fell in love. You understand, Mrs Lacy? Norma and I fell in love.'

'Yes, I do understand that.'

'We painted the flat out together. Saturdays we spent buying bits of furniture, month by month, what we could afford. We made a home because a home was what Norma had never had. She never knew her parents: I don't know if you were aware of that? Norma comes of a deprived background, she had no education, not to speak of. When I first met her, I had to help her read a newspaper.' Suddenly he smiled. 'She's much better now, of course.'

Bridget felt a silence gathering, the kind there'd been several of the other afternoon. She broke it herself, speaking as calmly as she could, trying to hold her visitor's eye but not succeeding because he was glancing round the living-room again.

'I'm sorry for Norma,' she said. 'I was sorry for her at the time, that is why I took in Betty. Only my husband and I insisted that it had to be legal and through the proper channels. We were advised about that, in case there was trouble later.'

'Trouble? Who advised you, Mrs Lacy?' He blinked and frowned. His voice sounded almost dense.

'We went to a solicitor,' she said, remembering that solicitor, small and moustached, recommended by Father Gogarty. He'd been very helpful; he'd explained everything.

'Mrs Lacy, I don't want to sound rude but there are two angles we can examine this case from. There is Norma's and there is your own. You've seen the change in Norma; you must take my word for it that she could easily revert. Then consider yourself, Mrs Lacy, as another person might see you, a person like myself for instance, a case-worker if you like, an outsider.'

'I don't think of it as a case, with angles or anything else. I really don't want to go on like this. Please.'

'I know it's difficult, and I'm sorry. But when the baby has become an adolescent you could find it hard to cope, Mrs Lacy. I see a lot of that in my work, a woman on her own, no father figure in the home. I know you have a caring relationship with Betty, Mrs Lacy, but the fact can't be altered that you're alone in this house with her, day in day out. All I'm saying is that another case-worker might comment on that.'

'There's Miss Custle too.'

'I beg your pardon, Mrs Lacy?'

'There's a lodger, Miss Custle.'

'You have a lodger? Another woman on her own?'

'Yes.'

'Young, is she?'

'No, Miss Custle isn't young.'

'An elderly woman, Mrs Lacy?'

'Miss Custle still works on the Underground.'

'The Underground?'

'Yes.'

'You see, Mrs Lacy, what might be commented upon is the lack of playmates. Just yourself, and a woman who is employed on the Underground. Again, Mrs Lacy, I'm not saying there isn't caring. I'm not saying that for an instant.'

'Betty is happy. Look, I'm afraid I'd rather you didn't come here again. I have things to do now –'

'I'm sorry to offend you, Mrs Lacy.'

She had stood up, making him stand up also. He nodded and smiled at her in his patient manner, which she now realized was professional, he being a counsellor. He said again he was sorry he'd offended her.

'I just thought you'd want to hear about Norma,' he said before he left, and on the doorstep he suddenly became awkward. The smile and the niceness vanished: solemnity replaced them. 'It's like putting a person together again. If you know what I mean, Mrs Lacy.'

In the kitchen Betty printed her name across the stomach of a whale. She heard voices in the hall, but paid them no attention. A moment later the door banged and then her mother came into the kitchen.

'Look,' Betty said, but to her surprise her mother didn't. Her mother hugged her, whispering her name. 'You've been washing your face,' Betty said. 'It's all cold.'

That afternoon Bridget cleaned the Winnards' flat, taking Betty with her, as she always did. She wondered about mentioning the trouble she was having with Norma and her husband to Mrs Winnard, who might suggest something for her to say so that the matter could be ended. Mrs Winnard was pretty and bespectacled, a kind young woman, full of sympathy, but that afternoon her two obstreperous boys, twins of two and a half, were giving her quite a time so Bridget didn't say anything. She hoovered the hallway and the bathroom and the four bedrooms, looking into the kitchen from time to time, where Betty was playing with the Winnard boys' bricks. She still hadn't said anything when the time came to pack up to go, and suddenly she was glad she hadn't because quite out of the blue she found herself imagining a look on Mrs Winnard's sympathetic face which suggested that the argument of Norma and her husband could not in all humanity be just dismissed. Bridget couldn't imagine Mrs Winnard actually saying so, but her intuition about the reaction remained.

In the park, watching Betty on a slide, she worried about that. Would the same thing happen if she talked to Father Gogarty? Would an instant of hesitation be reflected in his grey features as he, too, considered that Norma should not be passed by? Not everyone had experienced as awful a life as Norma had. On top of that, the regret of giving away the only child you had been able to have was probably a million times worse than simply being childless.

Not really wishing to, Bridget remembered how fate had seemed to her when she was a girl: that it began with the kind of person you were. 'We're greedy,' Liam had confessed, speaking of himself and the woman. 'I suppose we're made like that, we can't help it.' The woman was greedy, he had meant, making it cosier by saying he was too.

She watched Betty on the slide. She waved at her and Betty waved back. You couldn't call Norma greedy, not in the same way. Norma made a mess of things and then looked around for other people: someone to look after a child that had been carelessly born, the Samaritans, the man she'd married. In the end Norma was lucky because she'd survived, because all the good in her had been allowed to surface. It was the man's love that had done that, his gentleness and his sincerity. You couldn't begrudge her anything. Like Liam and the woman, fate had come up trumps for her because of the person she was.

'Watch, Mummy,' Betty shouted from the top of the slide, and again Bridget watched her sliding down it.

Eventually Bridget did speak to Mrs Winnard and to Father Gogarty because it was hard to keep the upset to herself, and because it worried her even more when she kept telling herself that she was being imaginative about what their reaction would be. Mrs Winnard said the couple's presumption was almost a matter for the police; Father Gogarty offered to go and see them, if they could easily be found. But before either Mrs Winnard or the priest spoke Bridget was certain that the brief flicker she'd been dreading had come into their faces. There had been the hesitation and the doubt and – far quicker than thought – the feeling that a child belonged more suitably with a young married couple than with a lone middle-aged woman and an ageing employee of the London Underground. In continuing to talk about it to Miss Custle herself, Bridget could swear she experienced the same intuition: beneath all Miss Custle's outrage and fury there was the same reasonable doubt.

The telephone rang one evening and the young man's voice said:

'Norma hasn't done anything silly. I just thought you'd like to know that, Mrs Lacy.'

'Yes, of course. I'm glad she's all right.'

'Well, she's not really all right of course. But she does take heart from your caring in the past.'

'I did what a lot of people would have done.'

'You did what was necessary, Mrs Lacy. You understood a cry for help. It's an unpleasant fact, but neither she nor Betty might be alive today if it hadn't been for you.'

'Oh, I can't believe that for an instant.'

'I think you have to, you know. There's only one small point, Mrs Lacy, if you could bear with me. I spoke to a colleague about this case – well, having a personal interest, I thought I better. You may remember I mentioned an outsider? Well, strangely enough my colleague raised an interesting question.'

'Look, I don't want to go on talking about any of this. I've told you I couldn't even begin to contemplate what you're suggesting.'

'My colleague pointed out that it isn't just Norma's circumstances which have changed, nor indeed your own. There's a third factor in all this, my colleague pointed out: this child is being brought up as the child of Irish parents. Well, fair enough you may say, Mrs Lacy, until you remember that the Irish are a different kettle of fish today from what they were ten years ago. How easy is it, you have to ask yourself, to be a child of Irish parents today, to bear an Irish name, to be a member of the Roman Catholic Church? That child will have to attend a London school, for instance, where there could easily be hostility. Increasingly we come across this in our work, Mrs Lacy.'

'Betty is my child –'

'Of course. That's quite understood, Mrs Lacy. But what my colleague pointed out is that sooner or later Norma is going to worry about the Irish thing as well. What will go through her mind is that it's not just a question of her baby being affected by a broken marriage, but of her baby being brought up in an atmosphere that isn't always pleasant. I'm sorry to mention it, Mrs Lacy, but, as my colleague says, no mother on earth would care to lie awake at night and worry about that.'

Her hand felt hot and damp on the telephone receiver. She imagined the young man sitting in an office, concerned and serious, and then smiling as he tried to find a bright side. She imagined Norma in their newly decorated flat, needing her child because everything was different now, hoping.

'I can't go on talking to you. I'm sorry.'

She replaced the receiver, and immediately found herself thinking about Liam. It was Liam's fault as well as hers that Betty had been adopted and was now to be regarded as the child of Irish parents. Liam had always firmly regarded himself as Betty's father, even if he never came near her now.

She didn't want to go and see him. She didn't want to make the journey on a number 9 bus, she didn't want to have to see the woman's predatory lips. But even as she thought that, she could hear herself asking Mrs Haste to have Betty for a couple of hours one afternoon. 'Hullo, Liam,' she said a few days later in the newsagent's.

She'd waited until there were no customers, and to her relief the woman wasn't there. The woman's old mother, very fat and dressed all in brown, was resting in an armchair in a little room behind the shop itself, a kind of store-room it seemed to be, with stacks of magazines tied with string, just as they'd come off the van.

'Heavens above!' Liam said.

'Liam, could I have a word?'

The old woman appeared to be asleep. She hadn't moved when Bridget had spoken. She was wearing a hat, and seemed a bit eccentric, sleeping there among the bundles of magazines.

'Of course you could, dear. How are you, Bridget?'

'I'm fine, Liam. And yourself?'

'I'm fine too, dear.'

She told him quickly. Customers hurried in for the *Evening Standard* or *Dalton's Weekly*, children paused on their way home from school. Liam looked for rubbers and ink cartridges, Yorkie bars and tubes of fruit pastilles. Twice he said that the *New Musical Express* didn't come out till Thursday. 'Extraordinary, how some of them forget that,' he said.

He listened to her carefully, picking up the thread of what she told him after each interruption. Because once they'd known one another so well, she mentioned the intuition she felt where Father Gogarty and Mrs Winnard and Miss Custle were concerned. She watched the expressions changing on his face, and she could feel him nodding inwardly: she felt him thinking that she was the same as she'd always been, nervous where other people were concerned, too modest and unsure of herself.

'I'll never forget how pretty you looked,' he said suddenly, and for no reason that Bridget could see. 'Wasn't everything great long ago, Bridie?'

'It's Betty we have to think of, Liam. The old days are over and done with.'

'I often go back to them. I'll never forget them, dear.'

He was trying to be nice, but it seemed to Bridget that he was saying she still belonged to the time he spoke of, that she had not managed to come to terms with life as it had been since. You had to be tougher to come to terms with a world that was tough itself, you had to get over being embarrassed when you were pulled out of the background. All that hadn't mattered long ago; when Emir Ryall had stolen her atlas she hadn't even complained. Being stolen from, she suddenly thought.

'I don't know what to say to them,' she said. 'The man keeps telephoning me.'

'Tell him to leave you alone, Bridget. Tell him he has no business bothering you.'

'I've tried saying that.'

'Tell him the thing was legally done and he hasn't a foot to stand on. Tell him he can be up for harassment.'

A child came into the shop and Liam had to look for drawing-pins. 'I'm afraid I have to shut up now,' he said when the child had gone, and as he spoke the old woman in the armchair stirred. She spoke his name. She said she'd fancy peaches for tea. 'There's a tin set aside for you, dear,' Liam said, winking at Bridget. He had raised his voice to address the old woman. He lowered it again to say goodbye. 'The best of luck with it,' he said, and Bridget knew he meant it.

'Thanks, Liam.' She tried to smile, and realized that she hadn't repeated the young man's remarks about Betty being brought up in a hostile atmosphere. She almost did so, standing at the door of the shop, imagining Liam angrily saying that the man needed putting in his place and offering to meet him. But as she walked away she knew all that was make-believe. Liam had his own life to live, peaches and a sort of mother-in-law. He couldn't be blamed for only wishing her luck.

She collected Betty from Mrs Haste and later in the evening, when she was watching television, the telephone rang. The young man said:

'I'm sorry, Mrs Lacy, I didn't mean to bring up that thing about your nationality. It's not your fault, Mrs Lacy, and please forget I mentioned it. I'm sorry.'

'Please don't telephone me again. That's all I ask. I've given you the only answer I can.'

'I know you have, Mrs Lacy. You've been kind to listen to me, and I know you're concerned for Norma, don't think I'm not aware of that. I love Norma, Mrs Lacy, which has made me a little unprofessional in my conversations with you, but I promise we'll neither of us bother you again. It was just that she felt she'd made a terrible mistake and all the poor thing wanted was to rectify it. But as my work so often shows me, Mrs Lacy, that is hardly ever possible. Are you there, Mrs Lacy?'

'Yes, I'm here.'

'I'll never stop loving Norma, Mrs Lacy. I promise you that also. No matter what happens to her now.'

She sat alone in her living-room watching the ten o'clock news, and when she heard Miss Custle in the hall she didn't offer her a cup of tea. Instead of Betty's rattling feet on the stairs there would be Miss Custle's aged panting as she propelled her bulk to her upstairs room. Instead of Betty's wondering questions there would be Miss Custle's gloom as still she mourned her long departed lover.

The television news came to an end, an advertisement for Australian margarine began. Soon after that the programmes ceased altogether, but Bridget continued to sit in her living-room, weeping without making a noise. Several times she went upstairs and stood with the light on by Betty's bed, gazing at the child, not wiping away her tears. For Betty's well-being, and for Norma's too, in all humanity the law would be reversed. No longer would she search the faces of Father Gogarty and Mrs Winnard and Miss

Custle for the signs of what they really believed. They would put that into words by saying she was good and had courage.

In the countryside of long ago her failure in marriage and motherhood might be easier to bear, but she would be a stranger there now. She belonged among her accumulated odds and ends, as Betty belonged with her mother, and Liam with the woman he loved. She would look after Miss Custle when Miss Custle retired from the Underground, as fate dictated.

Mr Tennyson

He had, romantically, a bad reputation. He had a wife and several children. His carry-on with Sarah Spence was a legend among a generation of girls, and the story was that none of it had stopped with Sarah Spence. His old red Ford Escort had been reported drawn up in quiet lay-bys; often he spent weekends away from home; Annie Green had come across him going somewhere on a train once, alone and morose in the buffet car. Nobody's parents were aware of the facts about him, nor were the other staff, nor even the boys at the school. His carry-on with Sarah Spence, and coming across him or his car, made a little tapestry of secrets that suddenly was yours when you became fifteen and a senior, a member of 2A. For the rest of your time at Foxton Comprehensive – for the rest of your life, preferably – you didn't breathe a word to people whose business it wasn't.

It was understandable when you looked at him that parents and staff didn't guess. It was also understandable that his activities were protected by the senior girls. He was forty years old. He had dark hair with a little grey in it, and a face that was boyish – like a French boy's, someone had once said, and the description had stuck, often to be repeated. There was a kind of ragamuffin innocence about his eyes. The cast of his lips suggested a melancholy nature and his smile, when it came, had sadness in it too. His name was Mr Tennyson. His subject was English.

Jenny, arriving one September in 2A, learnt all about him. She remembered Sarah Spence, a girl at the top of the school when she had been at the bottom, tall and beautiful. He carried on because he was unhappily married, she was informed. Consider where he lived even: trapped in a tiny gate-lodge on the Ilminster road because he couldn't afford anything better, trapped with a wife and children when he deserved freedom. Would he one day publish poetry as profound as his famous namesake's, though of course more up-to-date? Or was his talent lost for ever? One way or the other he was made for love.

It seemed to Jenny that the girls of 2A eyed one another, wondering which among them would become a successor to Sarah Spence. They eyed the older girls, of Class 1, 1A and 1B, wondering which of them was already her successor, discreetly taking her place in the red Ford Escort on dusky afternoons. He would never be coarse, you couldn't imagine coarseness in him. He'd never try anything unpleasant, he'd never in a million years fumble at you. He'd just be there, being himself, smelling faintly of fresh tobacco, the fingers of a hand perhaps brushing your arm by accident.

'Within the play,' he suggested in his soft voice, almost a whisper, 'order is represented by the royal house of Scotland. We must try and remember Shakespeare's point of view, how Shakespeare saw these things.'

They were studying *Macbeth* and *Huckleberry Finn* with him, but when he talked about Shakespeare it seemed more natural and suited to him than when he talked about Mark Twain.

'On Duncan's death,' he said, 'should the natural order continue, his son Malcolm would become king. Already Duncan has indicated – by making Malcolm Prince of Cumberland – that he considers him capable of ruling.'

Jenny had pale fair hair, the colour of ripened wheat. It fell from a divide at the centre of her head, two straight lines on either side of a thin face. Her eyes were large and of a faded blue. She was lanky, with legs she considered to be too long but which her mother said she'd be thankful for one day.

'Disruption is everywhere, remember,' he said. 'Disruption in nature as well as in the royal house. Shakespeare insinuates a comparison between what is happening in human terms and in terms of nature. On the night of Duncan's death there is a sudden storm in which chimneys are blown off and houses shaken. Mysterious screams are heard. Horses go wild. A falcon is killed by a mousing owl.'

Listening to him, it seemed to Jenny that she could listen for ever, no matter what he said. At night, lying in bed with her eyes closed, she delighted in leisurely fantasies, of having breakfast with him and ironing his clothes, of walking beside him on a seashore or sitting beside him in his old Ford Escort. There was a particular story she repeated to herself: that she was on the promenade at Lyme Regis and that he came up to her and asked her if she'd like to go for a walk. They walked up to the cliffs and then along the cliff-path, and everything was different from Foxton Comprehensive because they were alone together. His wife and he had been divorced, he told her, having agreed between themselves that they were incompatible. He was leaving Foxton Comprehensive because a play he'd written was going to be done on the radio and another one on the London stage. 'Oh, darling,' she said, daring to say it. 'Oh, Jenny,' he said.

Terms and holidays went by. Once, just before the Easter of that year, she met him with his wife, shopping in the International Stores in Ilminster. They had two of their four children with them, little boys with freckles. His wife had freckles also. She was a woman like a sack of something,

Jenny considered, with thick, unhealthy-looking legs. He was pushing a trolley full of breakfast cereals and wrapped bread, and tins. Although he didn't speak to her or even appear to see her, it was a stroke of luck to come across him in the town because he didn't often come into the village. Foxton had only half a dozen shops and the Bow and Arrow public house even though it was enormous, a sprawling dormitory village that had had the new Comprehensive added to all the other new building in 1969. Because of the position of the Tennysons' gate-lodge it was clearly more convenient for them to shop in Ilminster.

'Hullo, Mr Tennyson,' she said in the International Stores, and he turned and looked at her. He nodded and smiled.

Jenny moved into 1A at the end of that school year. She wondered if he'd noticed how her breasts had become bigger during the time she'd been in 2A, and how her complexion had definitely improved. Her breasts were quite presentable now, which was a relief because she'd had a fear that they weren't going to develop at all. She wondered if he'd noticed her Green Magic eye-shadow. Everyone said it suited her, except her father, who always blew up over things like that. Once she heard one of the new kids saying she was the prettiest girl in the school. Adam Swann and Chinny Martin from 1B kept hanging about, trying to chat her up. Chinny Martin even wrote her notes.

'You're mooning,' her father said. 'You don't take a pick of notice these days.'

'Exams,' her mother hastily interjected and afterwards, when Jenny was out of the room, quite sharply reminded her husband that adolescence was a difficult time for girls. It was best not to remark on things.

'I didn't mean a criticism, Ellie,' Jenny's father protested, aggrieved.

'They take it as a criticism. Every word. They're edgy, see.'

He sighed. He was a painter and decorator, with his own business. Jenny was their only child. There'd been four miscarriages, all of which might have been boys, which naturally were what he'd wanted, with the business. He'd have to sell it one day, but it didn't matter all that much when you thought about it. Having miscarriages was worse than selling a business, more depressing really. A woman's lot was harder than a man's, he'd decided long ago.

'Broody,' his wife diagnosed. 'Just normal broody. She'll see her way through it.'

Every evening her parents sat in their clean, neat sitting-room watching television. Her mother made tea at nine o'clock because it was nice to have a cup with the news. She always called upstairs to Jenny, but Jenny never wanted to have tea or see the news. She did her homework in her bedroom, a small room that was clean and neat also, with a pebbly cream wallpaper expertly hung by her father. At half past ten she usually went down to the kitchen and made herself some Ovaltine. She drank it at the table with the cat, Tinkle, on her lap. Her mother usually came in with the tea things to wash up, and they might chat, the conversation consisting mainly of gossip from Foxton Comprehensive, although never of course containing a reference to Mr Tennyson. Sometimes Jenny didn't feel like chatting and wouldn't, feigning sleepiness. If she sat there long enough her father would come in to fetch himself a cup of water because he always liked to have one near him in the night. He couldn't help glancing at her eye-shadow when he said good-night and she could see him making an effort not to mention it, having doubtless been told not to by her mother. They did their best. She liked them very much. She loved them, she supposed.

But not in the way she loved Mr Tennyson. 'Robert Tennyson,' she murmured to herself in bed. 'Oh, Robert dear.' Softly his lips were there, and the smell of fresh tobacco made her swoon, forcing her to close her eyes. 'Oh, yes,' she said. 'Oh, yes, yes.' He lifted the dress over her head. His hands were taut, charged with their shared passion. 'My love,' he said in his soft voice, almost a whisper. Every night before she went to sleep his was the face that entirely filled her mind. Had it once not been there she would have thought herself faithless. And every morning, in a ceremonial way, she conjured it up again, first thing, pride of place.

Coming out of Harper's the newsagent's one Saturday afternoon, she found waiting for her, not Mr Tennyson, but Chinny Martin, with his motor-cycle on its pedestal in the street. He asked her if she'd like to go for a spin into the country and offered to supply her with a crash helmet. He was wearing a crash helmet himself, a bulbous red object with a peak and a windshield that fitted over his eyes. He was also wearing heavy plastic gloves, red also, and a red windcheater. He was smiling at her, the spots on his pronounced chin more noticeable after exposure to the weather on his motor-cycle. His eyes were serious, closely fixed on hers.

She shook her head at him. There was hardly anything she'd have disliked more than a ride into the country with Chinny Martin, her arms half round his waist, a borrowed crash helmet making her feel silly. He'd stop the motor-cycle in a suitable place and he'd suggest something like a walk to the river or to some old ruin or into a wood. He'd suggest sitting down and then he'd begin to fumble at her, and his chin would be sticking into her face, cold and unpleasant. His fingernails would be ingrained, as the fingernails of boys who owned motor-cycles always were.

'Thanks all the same,' she said.

'Come on, Jenny.'

'No, I'm busy. Honestly. I'm working at home.'

It couldn't have been pleasant, being called Chinny just because you had a jutting chin. Nicknames were horrible: there was a boy called Nut Adams and another called Wet Small and a girl called Kisses. Chinny Martin's name was Clive, but she'd never heard anyone calling him that. She felt sorry for him, standing there in his crash helmet and his special clothes. He'd probably planned it all, working it out that she'd be impressed by his gear and his motor-cycle. But of course she wasn't. *Yamaha* it said on the petrol tank of the motor-cycle, and there was a girl in a swimsuit which he had presumably stuck on to the tank himself. The girl's swimsuit was yellow and so was her hair, which was streaming out behind her, as if caught in a wind. The petrol tank was black.

'Jenny,' he said, lowering his voice so that it became almost croaky. 'Listen, Jenny –'

'Sorry.'

She began to walk away, up the village street, but he walked beside her, pushing the Yamaha.

'I love you, Jenny,' he said.

She laughed because she felt embarrassed.

'I can't bear not seeing you, Jenny.'

'Oh, well –'

'Jenny.'

They were passing the petrol-pumps, the Orchard Garage. Mr Batten was on the pavement, wiping oil from his hands with a rag. 'How's he running?' he called out to Chinny Martin, referring to the Yamaha, but Chinny Martin ignored the question.

'I think of you all the time, Jenny.'

'Oh, Clive, don't be silly.' She felt silly herself, calling him by his proper name.

'D'you like me, Jenny?'

'Of course I like you.' She smiled at him, trying to cover up the lie: she didn't particularly like him, she didn't particularly not. She just felt sorry for him, with his noticeable chin and the nickname it had given him. His father worked in the powdered-milk factory. He'd do the same: you could guess that all too easily.

'Come for a ride with me, Jenny.'

'No, honestly.'

'Why not then?'

'It's better not to start anything, Clive. Look, don't write me notes.'

'Don't you like my notes?'

'I don't want to start anything.'

'There's someone else is there, Jenny? Adam Swann? Rick Hayes?'

He sounded like a character in a television serial; he sounded sloppy and stupid.

'If you knew how I feel about you,' he said, lowering his voice even more. 'I love you like anything. It's the real thing.'

'I like you too, Clive. Only not in that way,' she hastily added.

'Wouldn't you ever? Wouldn't you even try?'

'I've told you.'

'Rick Hayes's only after sex.'

'I don't like Rick Hayes.'

'Any girl with legs on her is all he wants.'

'Yes, I know.'

'I can't concentrate on things, Jenny. I think of you the entire time.'

'I'm sorry.'

'Oh God, Jenny.'

She turned into the Mace shop just to escape. She picked up a wire basket and pretended to be looking at tins of cat food. She heard the roar of the Yamaha as her admirer rode away, and it seemed all wrong that he should have gone like that, so noisily when he was so upset.

At home she thought about the incident. It didn't in the least displease her that a boy had passionately proclaimed love for her. It even made her feel quite elated. She felt pleasantly warm when she thought about it, and the feeling bewildered her. That she, so much in love with someone else, should be moved in the very least by the immature protestations of a youth from 1B was a mystery. She even considered telling her mother about the incident, but in the end decided not to. 'Quite sprightly, she seems,' she heard her father murmuring.

'In every line of that sonnet,' Mr Tennyson said the following Monday afternoon, 'there is evidence of the richness that makes Shakespeare not just our own greatest writer but the world's as well.'

She listened, enthralled, physically pleasured by the utterance of each syllable. There was a tiredness about his boyish eyes, as if he hadn't slept. His wife had probably been bothering him, wanting him to do jobs around the house when he should have been writing sonnets of his own. She imagined him unable to sleep, lying there worrying about things, about his life. She imagined his wife like a grampus beside him, her mouth open, her upper lip as coarse as a man's.

'When forty winters shall besiege thy brow,' he said, 'And dig deep trenches in thy beauty's field.'

Dear Jenny, a note that morning from Chinny Martin had protested. *I just want to be with you. I just want to talk to you. Please come out with me.*

'Jenny, stay a minute,' Mr Tennyson said when the bell went. 'Your essay.'

Immediately there was tension among the girls of 1A, as if the English master had caused threads all over the classroom to become taut. Unaware, the boys proceeded as they always did, throwing books into their briefcases and sauntering into the corridor. The girls lingered over anything they could think of. Jenny approached Mr Tennyson's desk.

'It's very good,' he said, opening her essay book. 'But you're getting too fond of using three little dots at the end of a sentence. The sentence should imply the dots. It's like underlining to suggest emphasis, a bad habit also.'

One by one the girls dribbled from the classroom, leaving behind them the shreds of their reluctance. Out of all of them he had chosen her: was she to be another Sarah Spence, or just some kind of stop-gap, like other girls since Sarah Spence were rumoured to have been? But as he continued to talk about her essay – called 'Belief in Ghosts' – she wondered if she'd even be a stop-gap. His fingers didn't once brush the back of her hand. His French boy's eyes didn't linger once on hers.

'I've kept you late,' he said in the end.

'That's all right, sir.'

'You will try to keep your sentences short? Your descriptions have a way of becoming too complicated.'

'I'll try, sir.'

'I really enjoyed that essay.'

He handed her the exercise book and then, without any doubt whatsoever, he smiled meaningfully into her eyes. She felt herself going hot. Her hands became clammy. She just stood there while his glance passed over her eye-shadow, over her nose and cheeks, over her mouth.

'You're very pretty,' he said.

'Thank you, sir.'

Her voice reminded her of the croak in Chinny Martin's when he'd been telling her he loved her. She tried to smile, but could not. She wanted his hand to reach out and push her gently away from him so that he could see her properly. But it didn't. He stared into her eyes again, as if endeavouring to ascertain their precise shade of blue.

'You look like a girl we had here once,' he said. 'Called Sarah Spence.'

'I remember Sarah Spence.'

'She was good at English too.'

She wanted something to happen, thunder to begin, or a torrent of rain, anything that would keep them in the classroom. She couldn't even bear the thought of walking to her desk and putting her essay book in her briefcase.

'Sarah went to Warwick University,' he said.

She nodded. She tried to smile again and this time the smile came. She said to herself that it was a brazen smile and she didn't care. She hoped it made her seem more than ever like Sarah Spence, sophisticated and able for anything. She wondered if he said to all the girls who were stop-gaps that they looked like Sarah Spence. She didn't care. His carry-on with Sarah Spence was over and done with, he didn't even see her any more. By all accounts Sarah Spence had let him down, but never in a million years would she. She would wait for him for ever, or until the divorce came through. When he was old she would look after him.

'You'd better be getting home, Jenny.'

'I don't want to, sir.'

She continued to stand there, the exercise book in her left hand. She watched while some kind of shadow passed over his face. For a moment his eyes closed.

'Why don't you want to go?' he said.

'Because I'm in love with you, sir.'

'You mustn't be, Jenny.'

'Why not?'

'You know why not.'

'What about Sarah Spence?'

'Sarah was different.'

'I don't care how many stop-gaps you've had. I don't care. I don't love you any less.'

'Stop-gaps, Jenny?'

'The ones you made do with.'

'Made do?' He was suddenly frowning at her, his face screwed up a little. 'Made do?' he said again.

'The other girls. The ones who reminded you of her.'

'There weren't any other girls.'

'You were seen, sir –'

'Only Sarah and I were seen.'

'Your car –'

'Give a dog a bad name, Jenny. There weren't any others.'

She felt iciness inside her, somewhere in her stomach. Other girls had formed an attachment for him, as she had. Other girls had probably stood on this very spot, telling him. It was that, and the reality of Sarah Spence, that had turned him into a schoolgirls' legend. Only Sarah Spence had gone with him in his old Ford Escort to quiet lay-bys, only Sarah Spence had felt his arms around her. Why shouldn't he be seen in the buffet car of a train, alone? The weekends he'd spent away from home were probably with a sick mother.

'I'm no Casanova, Jenny.'

'I had to tell you I'm in love with you, sir. I couldn't not.'

'It's no good loving me, I'm afraid.'

'You're the nicest person I'll ever know.'

'No, I'm not, Jenny. I'm just an English teacher who took advantage of a young girl's infatuation. Shabby, people would say.'

'You're not shabby. Oh God, you're not shabby!' She heard her own voice crying out shrilly, close to tears. It astonished her. It was unbelievable that she should be so violently protesting. It was unbelievable that he should have called himself shabby.

'She had an abortion in Warwick,' he said, 'after a weekend we spent in an hotel. I let that happen, Jenny.'

'You couldn't help it.'

'Of course I could have helped it.'

Without wanting to, she imagined them in the hotel he spoke of. She imagined them having a meal, sitting opposite each other at a table, and a waiter placing plates in front of them. She imagined them in their bedroom, a grimy room with a lace curtain drawn across the lower part of the single window and a wash-basin in a corner. The bedroom had featured in a film she'd seen, and Sarah Spence was even like the actress who had played the part of a shopgirl. She stood there in her underclothes just as the shopgirl had, awkwardly waiting while he smiled his love at her. 'Then let not winter's ragged hand deface,' he whispered, 'In thee thy summer, ere thou be distilled. Oh Sarah, love.' He took the underclothes from her body, as the actor in the film had, all the time whispering sonnets.

'It was messy and horrible,' he said. 'That's how it ended, Jenny.'

'I don't care how it ended. I'd go with you anywhere. I'd go to a thousand hotels.'

'No, no, Jenny.'

'I love you terribly.'

She wept, still standing there. He got down from the stool in front of his desk and came and put his arms about her, telling her to cry. He said that tears were good, not bad. He made her sit down at a desk and then he sat down beside her. His love affair with Sarah Spence sounded romantic, he said, and because of its romantic sheen girls fell in love with him. They fell in love with the unhappiness they sensed in him. He found it hard to stop them.

'I should move away from here,' he said, 'but I can't bring myself to do it. Because she'll always come back to see her family and whenever she does I can catch a glimpse of her.'

It was the same as she felt about him, like the glimpse that day in the International Stores. It was the same as Chinny Martin hanging about outside Harper's. And yet of course it wasn't the same as Chinny Martin. How could it possibly be? Chinny Martin was stupid and unprepossessing and ordinary.

'I'd be better to you,' she cried out in sudden desperation, unable to prevent herself. Clumsily she put a hand on his shoulder, and clumsily took it away again. 'I would wait for ever,' she said, sobbing, knowing she looked ugly.

He waited for her to calm down. He stood up and after a moment so did she. She walked with him from the classroom, down the corridor and out of the door that led to the car park.

'You can't just leave,' he said, 'a wife and four children. It was hard to explain that to Sarah. She hates me now.'

He unlocked the driver's door of the Ford Escort. He smiled at her. He said:

'There's no one else I can talk to about her. Except girls like you. You mustn't feel embarrassed in class, Jenny.'

He drove away, not offering her a lift, which he might have done, for their direction was the same. She didn't in the least look like Sarah Spence: he'd probably said the same thing to all the others, the infatuated girls he could talk to about the girl he loved. The little scenes in the classroom, the tears, the talk: all that brought him closer to Sarah Spence. The love of a girl he didn't care about warmed him, as Chinny Martin's love had warmed her too, even though Chinny Martin was ridiculous.

She walked across the car park, imagining him driving back to his gate-lodge with Sarah Spence alive again in his mind, loving her more than ever. 'Jenny,' the voice of Chinny Martin called out, coming from nowhere.

He was there, standing by his Yamaha, beside a car. She shook her head at him, and began to run. At home she would sit and eat in the kitchen with her parents, who wouldn't be any different. She would escape and lie on her bed in her small neat bedroom, longing to be where she'd never be now, beside him in his car, or on a train, or anywhere. 'Jenny,' the voice of Chinny Martin called out again, silly with his silly love.

Autumn Sunshine

The rectory was in County Wexford, eight miles from Enniscorthy. It was a handsome eighteenth-century house, with Virginia creeper covering three sides and a tangled garden full of buddleia and struggling japonica which had always been too much for its incumbents. It stood alone, seeming lonely even, approximately at the centre of the country parish it served. Its church – St Michael's Church of Ireland – was two miles away, in the village of Boharbawn.

For twenty-six years the Morans had lived there, not wishing to live anywhere else. Canon Moran had never been an ambitious man; his wife, Frances, had found contentment easy to attain in her lifetime. Their four girls had been born in the rectory, and had become a happy family there. They were grown up now, Frances's death was still recent: like the rectory itself, its remaining occupant was alone in the countryside. The death had occurred in the spring of the year, and the summer had somehow been bearable. The clergyman's eldest daughter had spent May and part of June at the rectory with her children. Another one had brought her family for most of August, and a third was to bring her newly married husband in the winter. At Christmas nearly all of them would gather at the rectory and some would come at Easter. But that September, as the days drew in, the season was melancholy.

Then, one Tuesday morning, Slattery brought a letter from Canon Moran's youngest daughter. There were two other letters as well, in unsealed buff envelopes which meant that they were either bills or receipts. Frail and grey-haired in his elderliness, Canon Moran had been wondering if he should give the lawn in front of the house a last cut when he heard the approach of Slattery's van. The lawn-mower was the kind that had to be pushed, and in the spring the job was always easier if the grass had been cropped close at the end of the previous summer.

'Isn't that a great bit of weather, Canon?' Slattery remarked, winding down the window of the van and passing out the three envelopes. 'We're set for a while, would you say?'

'I hope so, certainly.'

'Ah, we surely are, sir.'

The conversation continued for a few moments longer, as it did whenever

Slattery came to the rectory. The postman was young and easy-going, not long the successor to old Mr O'Brien, who'd been making the round on a bicycle when the Morans first came to the rectory in 1952. Mr O'Brien used to talk about his garden; Slattery talked about fishing, and often brought a share of his catch to the rectory.

'It's a great time of year for it,' he said now, 'except for the darkness coming in.'

Canon Moran smiled and nodded; the van turned round on the gravel, dust rising behind it as it moved swiftly down the avenue to the road. Everyone said Slattery drove too fast.

He carried the letters to a wooden seat on the edge of the lawn he'd been wondering about cutting. Deirdre's handwriting hadn't changed since she'd been a child; it was round and neat, not at all a reflection of the girl she was. The blue English stamp, the Queen in profile blotched a bit by the London postmark, wasn't on its side or half upside down, as you might possibly expect with Deirdre. Of all the Moran children, she'd grown up to be the only difficult one. She hadn't come to the funeral and hadn't written about her mother's death. She hadn't been to the rectory for three years.

I'm sorry, she wrote now. *I couldn't stop crying actually. I've never known anyone as nice or as generous as she was. For ages I didn't even want to believe she was dead. I went on imagining her in the rectory and doing the flowers in church and shopping in Enniscorthy.*

Deirdre was twenty-one now. He and Frances had hoped she'd go to Trinity and settle down, but although at school she'd seemed to be the cleverest of their children she'd had no desire to become a student. She'd taken the Rosslare boat to Fishguard one night, having said she was going to spend a week with her friend Maeve Coles in Cork. They hadn't known she'd gone to England until they received a picture postcard from London telling them not to worry, saying she'd found work in an egg-packing factory.

Well, I'm coming back for a little while now, she wrote, *if you could put up with me and if you wouldn't find it too much. I'll cross over to Rosslare on the 29th, the morning crossing, and then I'll come on to Enniscorthy on the bus. I don't know what time it will be but there's a pub just by where the bus drops you so could we meet in the small bar there at six o'clock and then I won't have to lug my cases too far? I hope you won't mind going into such a place. If you can't make it, or don't want to see me, it's understandable, so if you don't turn up by half six I'll see if I can get a bus on up to Dublin. Only I need to get back to Ireland for a while.*

It was, as he and Slattery had agreed, a lovely autumn. Gentle sunshine mellowed the old garden, casting an extra sheen of gold on leaves that were gold already. Roses that had been ebullient in June and July bloomed modestly now. Michaelmas daisies were just beginning to bud. Already the crab-apples were falling, hydrangeas had a forgotten look. Canon Moran carried the letter from his daughter into the walled vegetable garden and leaned against the side of the greenhouse, half sitting on a protruding ledge, reading the letter again. Panes of glass were broken in the greenhouse, white paint and putty needed to be renewed, but inside a vine still thrived, and was heavy now with black ripe fruit. Later that morning he would pick some and drive into Enniscorthy, to sell the grapes to Mrs Neary in Slaney Street.

Love, Deirdre: the letter was marvellous. Beyond the rectory the fields of wheat had been harvested, and the remaining stubble had the same tinge of gold in the autumn light; the beech trees and the chestnuts were triumphantly magnificent. But decay and rotting were only weeks away, and the letter from Deirdre was full of life. '*Love, Deirdre*' were words more beautiful than all the season's glories. He prayed as he leaned against the sunny greenhouse, thanking God for this salvation.

For all the years of their marriage Frances had been a help. As a younger man, Canon Moran hadn't known quite what to do. He'd been at a loss among his parishioners, hesitating in the face of this weakness or that: the pregnancy of Alice Pratt in 1954, the argument about grazing rights between Mr Willoughby and Eugene Dunlevy in 1960, the theft of an altar cloth from St Michael's and reports that Mrs Tobin had been seen wearing it as a skirt. Alice Pratt had been going out with a Catholic boy, one of Father Gowan's flock, which made the matter more difficult than ever. Eugene Dunlevy was one of Father Gowan's also, and so was Mrs Tobin.

'Father Gowan and I had a chat,' Frances had said, and she'd had a chat as well with Alice Pratt's mother. A month later Alice Pratt married the Catholic boy, but to this day attended St Michael's every Sunday, the children going to Father Gowan. Mrs Tobin was given Hail Marys to say by the priest; Mr Willoughby agreed that his father had years ago granted Eugene Dunlevy the grazing rights. Everything, in these cases and in many others, had come out all right in the end: order emerged from the confusion that Canon Moran so disliked, and it was Frances who had always begun the process, though no one ever said in the rectory that she understood the mystery of people as well as he understood the teachings of the New Testament. She'd been a freckle-faced girl when he'd married her, pretty in her way. He was the one with the brains.

Frances had seen human frailty everywhere: it was weakness in people, she said, that made them what they were as much as strength did. And she herself had her own share of such frailty, falling short in all sorts of ways of the God's image her husband preached about. With the small amount of housekeeping money she could be allowed she was a spendthrift, and she said she was lazy. She loved clothes and often overreached herself on visits to Dublin; she sat in the sun while the rectory gathered dust and the garden became rank; it was only where people were concerned that she was practical. But for what she was her husband had loved her with unobtrusive passion for fifty years, appreciating her conversation and the help she'd given him because she could so easily sense the truth. When he'd found her dead in the garden one morning he'd felt he had lost some part of himself.

Though many months had passed since then, the trouble was that Frances hadn't yet become a ghost. Her being alive was still too recent, the shock of her death too raw. He couldn't distance himself; the past refused to be the past. Often he thought that her fingerprints were still in the rectory, and when he picked the grapes or cut the grass of the lawn it was impossible not to pause and remember other years. Autumn had been her favourite time.

'Of course I'd come,' he said. 'Of course, dear. Of course.'

'I haven't treated you very well.'

'It's over and done with, Deirdre.'

She smiled, and it was nice to see her smile again, although it was strange to be sitting in the back bar of a public house in Enniscorthy. He saw her looking at him, her eyes passing over his clerical collar and black clothes, and his quiet face. He could feel her thinking that he had aged, and putting it down to the death of the wife he'd been so fond of.

'I'm sorry I didn't write,' she said.

'You explained in your letter, Deirdre.'

'It was ages before I knew about it. That was an old address you wrote to.'

'I guessed.'

In turn he examined her. Years ago she'd had her long hair cut. It was short now, like a black cap on her head. And her face had lost its chubbiness; hollows where her cheeks had been made her eyes more dominant, pools of seaweed green. He remembered her child's stocky body, and the uneasy adolescence that had spoilt the family's serenity. Her voice had lost its Irish intonation.

'I'd have met you off the boat, you know.'

'I didn't want to bother you with that.'

'Oh, now, it isn't far, Deirdre.'

She drank Irish whiskey, and smoked a brand of cigarettes called Three Castles. He'd asked for a mineral himself, and the woman serving them had brought him a bottle of something that looked like water but which fizzed up when she'd poured it. A kind of lemonade he imagined it was, and didn't much care for it.

'I have grapes for Mrs Neary,' he said.

'Who's that?'

'She has a shop in Slaney Street. We always sold her the grapes. You remember?'

She didn't, and he reminded her of the vine in the greenhouse. A shop surely wouldn't be open at this hour of the evening, she said, forgetting that in a country town of course it would be. She asked if the cinema was still the same in Enniscorthy, a cement building halfway up a hill. She said she remembered bicycling home from it at night with her sisters, not being able to keep up with them. She asked after her sisters and he told her about the two marriages that had taken place since she'd left: she had in-laws she'd never met, and nephews and a niece.

They left the bar, and he drove his dusty black Vauxhall straight to the small shop he'd spoken of. She remained in the car while he carried into the shop two large chip-baskets full of grapes. Afterwards Mrs Neary came to the door with him.

'Well, is that Deirdre?' she said as Deirdre wound down the window of the car. 'I'd never know you, Deirdre.'

'She's come back for a little while,' Canon Moran explained, raising his voice a little because he was walking round the car to the driver's seat as he spoke.

'Well, isn't that grand?' said Mrs Neary.

Everyone in Enniscorthy knew Deirdre had just gone off, but it didn't matter now. Mrs Neary's husband, who was a red-cheeked man with a cap, much smaller than his wife, appeared beside her in the shop doorway. He inclined his head in greeting, and Deirdre smiled and waved at both of them. Canon Moran thought it was pleasant when she went on waving while he drove off.

In the rectory he lay wakeful that night, his mind excited by Deirdre's presence. He would have loved Frances to know, and guessed that she probably did. He fell asleep at half past two and dreamed that he and Frances were young again, that Deirdre was still a baby. The freckles on Frances's face were out in profusion, for they were sitting in the sunshine in the garden, tea things spread about them, the children playing some game among the shrubs. It was autumn then also, the last of the September heat. But because he was younger in his dream he didn't feel part of the season himself, or sense its melancholy.

A week went by. The time passed slowly because a lot was happening, or so it seemed. Deirdre insisted on cooking all the meals and on doing the shopping in Boharbawn's single shop or in Enniscorthy. She still smoked her endless cigarettes, but the peakiness there had been in her face when she'd first arrived wasn't quite so pronounced – or perhaps, he thought, he'd become used to it. She told him about the different jobs she'd had in London and the different places she'd lived in, because on the postcards she'd occasionally sent there hadn't been room to go into detail. In the rectory they had always hoped she'd managed to get a training of some sort, though guessing she hadn't. In fact, her jobs had been of the most rudimentary kind: as well as her spell in the egg-packing factory, there'd been a factory that made plastic earphones, a cleaning job in a hotel near Euston, and a year working for the Use-Us Office Cleansing Service. 'But you can't have liked any of that work, Deirdre?' he suggested, and she agreed she hadn't.

From the way she spoke he felt that that period of her life was over: adolescence was done with, she had steadied and taken stock. He didn't suggest to her that any of this might be so, not wishing to seem either too anxious or too pleased, but he felt she had returned to the rectory in a very different frame of mind from the one in which she'd left it. He imagined she would remain for quite a while, still taking stock, and in a sense occupying her mother's place. He thought he recognized in her a loneliness that matched his own, and he wondered if it was a feeling that their loneliness might be shared which had brought her back at this particular time. Sitting in the drawing-room while she cooked or washed up, or gathering grapes in the greenhouse while she did the shopping, he warmed delightedly to this theme. It seemed like an act of God that their circumstances should interlace this autumn. By Christmas she would know what she wanted to do with her life, and in the spring that followed she would perhaps be ready to set forth again. A year would have passed since the death of Frances.

'I have a friend,' Deirdre said when they were having a cup of coffee together in the middle of one morning. 'Someone who's been good to me.'

She had carried a tray to where he was composing next week's sermon, sitting on the wooden seat by the lawn at the front of the house. He laid aside his exercise book, and a pencil and a rubber. 'Who's that?' he inquired.

'Someone called Harold.'

He nodded, stirring sugar into his coffee.

'I want to tell you about Harold, Father. I want you to meet him.'

'Yes, of course.'

She lit a cigarette. She said, 'We have a lot in common. I mean, he's the only person ...'

She faltered and then hesitated. She lifted her cigarette to her lips and drew on it.

He said, 'Are you fond of him, Deirdre?'

'Yes, I am.'

Another silence gathered. She smoked and drank her coffee. He added more sugar to his.

'Of course I'd like to meet him,' he said.

'Could he come to stay with us, Father? Would you mind? Would it be all right?'

'Of course I wouldn't mind. I'd be delighted.'

Harold was summoned, and arrived at Rosslare a few days later. In the meantime Deirdre had explained to her father that her friend was an electrician by trade and had let it fall that he was an intellectual kind of person. She borrowed the old Vauxhall and drove it to Rosslare to meet him, returning to the rectory in the early evening.

'How d'you do?' Canon Moran said, stretching out a hand in the direction of an angular youth with a birthmark on his face. His dark hair was cut very short, cropped almost. He was wearing a black leather jacket.

'I'm fine,' Harold said.

'You've had a good journey?'

'Lousy, 'smatter of fact, Mr Moran.'

Harold's voice was strongly Cockney, and Canon Moran wondered if Deirdre had perhaps picked up some of her English vowel sounds from it. But then he realized that most people in London would speak like that, as people did on the television and the wireless. It was just a little surprising that Harold and Deirdre should have so much in common, as they clearly had from the affectionate way they held one another's hand. None of the other Moran girls had gone in so much for holding hands in front of the family.

He was to sit in the drawing-room, they insisted, while they made supper in the kitchen, so he picked up the *Irish Times* and did as he was bidden. Half an hour later Harold appeared and said that the meal was ready: fried eggs and sausages and bacon, and some tinned beans. Canon Moran said grace.

Having stated that County Wexford looked great, Harold didn't say much else. He didn't smile much, either. His afflicted face bore an edgy look, as if he'd never become wholly reconciled to his birthmark. It was like a scarlet map on his left cheek, a shape that reminded Canon Moran of the toe of Italy. Poor fellow, he thought. And yet a birthmark was so much less to bear than other afflictions there could be.

'Harold's fascinated actually,' Deirdre said, 'by Ireland.'

Her friend didn't add anything to that remark for a moment, even though Canon Moran smiled and nodded interestedly. Eventually Harold said, 'The struggle of the Irish people.'

'I didn't know a thing about Irish history,' Deirdre said. 'I mean, not anything that made sense.'

The conversation lapsed at this point, leaving Canon Moran greatly puzzled. He began to say that Irish history had always been of considerable interest to him also, that it had a good story to it, its tragedy uncomplicated. But the other two didn't appear to understand what he was talking about and so he changed the subject. It was a particularly splendid autumn, he pointed out.

'Harold doesn't go in for anything like that,' Deirdre replied.

During the days that followed Harold began to talk more, surprising Canon Moran with almost everything he said. Deirdre had been right to say he was fascinated by Ireland, and it wasn't just a tourist's fascination. Harold had read widely: he spoke of ancient battles, and of the plantations of James I and Elizabeth, of Robert Emmet and the Mitchelstown martyrs, of Pearse and de Valera. 'The struggle of the Irish people' was the expression he most regularly employed. It seemed to Canon Moran that the relationship between Harold and Deirdre had a lot to do with Harold's fascination, as though his interest in Deirdre's native land had somehow caused him to become interested in Deirdre herself.

There was something else as well. Fascinated by Ireland, Harold hated his own country. A sneer whispered through his voice when he spoke of England: a degenerate place, he called it, destroyed by class-consciousness and the unjust distribution of wealth. He described in detail the city of Nottingham, to which he appeared to have a particular aversion. He spoke of unnecessary motorways and the stupidity of bureaucracy, the stifling presence of a Royal family. 'You could keep an Indian village,' he claimed, 'on what those corgis eat. You could house five hundred homeless in Buckingham Palace.' There was brainwashing by television and the newspaper barons. No ordinary person had a chance because pap was fed to the ordinary person, a deliberate policy going back into Victorian times when education and religion had been geared to the enslavement of minds. The English people had brought it on themselves, having lost their spunk, settling instead for consumer durables. 'What better can you expect,' Harold demanded, 'after the hypocrisy of that empire the bosses ran?'

Deirdre didn't appear to find anything specious in this line of talk, which surprised her father. 'Oh, I wonder about that,' he said himself from time to time, but he said it mildly, not wishing to cause an argument, and in any case his interjections were not acknowledged. Quite a few of the criticisms Harold levelled at his own country could be levelled at Ireland also and, Canon Moran guessed, at many countries throughout the world. It was strange that the two neighbouring islands had been so picked out, although once Germany was mentioned and the point made that developments beneath the surface there were a hopeful sign, that a big upset was on the way.

'We're taking a walk,' Harold said one afternoon. 'She's going to show me Kinsella's Barn.'

Canon Moran nodded, saying to himself that he disliked Harold. It was the first time he had admitted it, but the feeling was familiar. The less generous side of his nature had always emerged when his daughters brought to the rectory the men they'd become friendly with or even proposed to marry. Emma, the eldest girl, had brought several before settling in the end for Thomas. Linda had brought only John, already engaged to him. Una had married Carley not long after the death, and Carley had not yet visited the rectory: Canon Moran had met him in Dublin, where the wedding had taken place, for in the circumstances Una had not been married from home. Carley was an older man, an importer of tea and wine, stout and flushed, certainly not someone Canon Moran would have chosen for his second-youngest daughter. But, then, he had thought the same about Emma's Thomas and about Linda's John.

Thomas was a farmer, sharing a sizeable acreage with his father in Co. Meath. He always brought to mind the sarcasm of an old schoolmaster who in Canon Moran's distant schooldays used to refer to a gang of boys at the back of the classroom as 'farmers' sons', meaning that not much could be expected of them. It was an inaccurate assumption but even now, whenever Canon Moran found himself in the company of Thomas, he couldn't help recalling it. Thomas was mostly silent, with a good-natured smile that came slowly and lingered too long. According to his father, and there was no reason to doubt the claim, he was a good judge of beef cattle.

Linda's John was the opposite. Wiry and suave, he was making his way in the Bank of Ireland, at present stationed in Waterford. He had a tiny orange-coloured moustache and was good at golf. Linda's ambition for him was that he should become the Bank of Ireland's manager in Limerick or Galway, where the insurances that went with the position were particularly lucrative. Unlike Thomas, John talked all the time, telling jokes and stories about the Bank of Ireland's customers.

'Nothing is perfect,' Frances used to say, chiding her husband for an uncharitableness he did his best to combat. He disliked being so particular about the men his daughters chose, and he was aware that other people saw them differently: Thomas would do anything for you, John was fun, the middle-aged Carley laid his success at Una's feet. But whoever the husbands of his daughters had been, Canon Moran knew he'd have felt the same. He was jealous of the husbands because ever since his daughters had been born he had loved them unstintingly. When he had prayed after Frances's death he'd felt jealous of God, who had taken her from him.

'There's nothing much to see,' he pointed out when Harold announced that Deirdre was going to show him Kinsella's Barn. 'Just the ruin of a wall is all that's left.'

'Harold's interested, Father.'

They set off on their walk, leaving the old clergyman ashamed that he could not like Harold more. It wasn't just his griminess: there was something sinister about Harold, something furtive about the way he looked at you, peering at you cruelly out of his afflicted face, not meeting your eye. Why was he so fascinated about a country that wasn't his own? Why did he refer so often to 'Ireland's struggle' as if that struggle particularly concerned him? He hated walking, he had said, yet he'd just set out to walk six miles through woods and fields to examine a ruined wall.

Canon Moran had wondered as suspiciously about Thomas and John and Carley, privately questioning every statement they made, finding hidden motives everywhere. He'd hated the thought of his daughters being embraced or even touched, and had forced himself not to think about that. He'd prayed, ashamed of himself then, too. 'It's just a frailty in you,' Frances had said, her favourite way of cutting things down to size.

He sat for a while in the afternoon sunshine, letting all of it hang in his mind. It would be nice if they quarrelled on their walk. It would be nice if they didn't speak when they returned, if Harold simply went away. But that wouldn't happen, because they had come to the rectory with a purpose. He didn't know why he thought that, but he knew it was true: they had come for a reason, something that was all tied up with Harold's fascination and with the kind of person Harold was, with his cold eyes and his afflicted face.

In March 1798 an incident had taken place in Kinsella's Barn, which at that time had just been a barn. Twelve men and women, accused of harbouring insurgents, had been tied together with ropes at the command of a Sergeant James. They had been led through the village of Boharbawn, the Sergeant's soldiers on horseback on either side of the procession, the Sergeant himself bringing up the rear. Designed as an act of education, an example to the inhabitants of Boharbawn and the country people around, the twelve had been herded into a barn owned by a farmer called Kinsella and there burned to death. Kinsella, who had played no part either in the harbouring of insurgents or in the execution of the twelve, was afterwards murdered by his own farm labourers.

'Sergeant James was a Nottingham man,' Harold said that evening at supper. 'A soldier of fortune who didn't care what he did. Did you know he acquired great wealth, Mr Moran?'

'No, I wasn't at all aware of that,' Canon Moran replied.

'Harold found out about him,' Deirdre said.

'He used to boast he was responsible for the death of a thousand Irish people. It was in Boharbawn he reached the thousand. They rewarded him well for that.'

'Not much is known about Sergeant James locally. Just the legend of Kinsella's Barn.'

'No way it's a legend.'

Deirdre nodded; Canon Moran did not say anything. They were eating cooked ham and salad. On the table there was a cake which Deirdre had bought in McGovern's in Enniscorthy, and a pot of tea. There were several bunches of grapes from the greenhouse, and a plate of wafer biscuits. Harold was fond of salad cream, Canon Moran had noticed; he had a way of hitting the base of the jar with his hand, causing large dollops to spurt all over his ham. He didn't place his knife and fork together on the plate when he'd finished, but just left them anyhow. His fingernails were edged with black.

'You'd feel sick,' he was saying now, working the salad cream again. 'You'd stand there looking at that wall and you'd feel a revulsion in your stomach.'

'What I meant,' Canon Moran said, 'is that it has passed into local legend. No one doubts it took place; there's no question about that. But two centuries have almost passed.'

'And nothing has changed,' Harold interjected. 'The Irish people still share their bondage with the twelve in Kinsella's Barn.'

'Round here of course –'

'It's not round here that matters, Mr Moran. The struggle's world-wide; the sickness is everywhere actually.'

Again Deirdre nodded. She was like a zombie, her father thought. She was being used because she was an Irish girl; she was Harold's Irish connection, and in some almost frightening way she believed herself in love with him. Frances had once said they'd made a mistake with her. She had wondered if Deirdre had perhaps found all the love they'd offered her too much to bear. They were quite old when Deirdre was a child, the last expression of their own love. She was special because of that.

'At least Kinsella got his chips,' Harold pursued, his voice relentless. 'At least that's something.'

Canon Moran protested. The owner of the barn had been an innocent man, he pointed out. The barn had simply been a convenient one, large enough for the purpose, with heavy stones near it that could be piled up against the door before the conflagration. Kinsella, that day, had been miles away, ditching a field.

'It's too long ago to say where he was,' Harold retorted swiftly. 'And if he was keeping a low profile in a ditch it would have been by arrangement with the imperial forces.'

When Harold said that, there occurred in Canon Moran's mind a flash of what appeared to be the simple truth. Harold was an Englishman who had espoused a cause because it was one through which the status quo in his own country might be damaged. Similar such Englishmen, read about in newspapers, stirred in the clergyman's mind: men from Ealing and Liverpool and Wolverhampton who had changed their names to Irish names, who had even learned the Irish language, in order to ingratiate themselves with the new Irish revolutionaries. Such men dealt out death and chaos, announcing that their conscience insisted on it.

'Well, we'd better wash the dishes,' Deirdre said, and Harold rose obediently to help her.

The walk to Kinsella's Barn had taken place on a Saturday afternoon. The following morning Canon Moran conducted his services in St Michael's, addressing his small Protestant congregation, twelve at Holy Communion, eighteen at morning service. He had prepared a sermon about repentance, taking as his text St Luke, 15:32: ... *for this thy brother was dead, and is alive again; and was lost, and is found.* But at the last moment he changed his mind and spoke instead of the incident in Kinsella's Barn nearly two centuries ago. He tried to make the point that one horror should not fuel another, that passing time contained its own forgiveness. Deirdre and Harold were naturally not in the church, but they'd been present at breakfast, Harold frying eggs on the kitchen stove, Deirdre pouring tea. He had looked at them and tried to think of them as two young people on holiday. He had tried to tell himself they'd come to the rectory for a rest and for his blessing, that he should be grateful instead of fanciful. It was for his blessing that Emma had brought Thomas to the rectory, that Linda had brought John. Una would bring Carley in November. 'Now, don't be silly,' Frances would have said.

'The man Kinsella was innocent of everything,' he heard his voice insisting in his church. 'He should never have been murdered also.'

Harold would have delighted in the vengeance exacted on an innocent man. Harold wanted to inflict pain, to cause suffering and destruction. The end justified the means for Harold, even if the end was an artificial one, a pettiness grandly dressed up. In his sermon Canon Moran spoke of such matters without mentioning Harold's name. He spoke of how evil drained people of their humour and compassion, how people pretended even to themselves. It was worse than Frances's death, he thought as his voice continued in the church: it was worse that Deirdre should be part of wickedness.

He could tell that his parishioners found his sermon odd, and he didn't blame them. He was confused, and naturally distressed. In the rectory Deirdre and Harold would be waiting for him. They would all sit down to Sunday lunch while plans for atrocities filled Harold's mind, while Deirdre loved him.

'Are you well again, Mrs Davis?' he inquired at the church door of a woman who suffered from asthma.

'Not too bad, Canon. Not too bad, thank you.'

He spoke to all the others, inquiring about health, remarking on the beautiful autumn. They were farmers mostly and displayed a farmer's gratitude for the satisfactory season. He wondered suddenly who'd replace him among them when he retired or died. Father Gowan had had to give up a year ago. The young man, Father White, was always in a hurry.

'Goodbye so, Canon,' Mr Willoughby said, shaking hands as he always did, every Sunday. It was a long time since there'd been the trouble about Eugene Dunlevy's grazing rights; three years ago Mr Willoughby had been left a widower himself. 'You're managing all right, Canon?' he asked, as he also always did.

'Yes, I'm all right, thank you, Mr Willoughby.'

Someone else inquired if Deirdre was still at the rectory, and he said she was. Heads nodded, the unspoken thought being that that was nice for him, his youngest daughter at home again after all these years. There was forgiveness in several faces, forgiveness of Deirdre, who had been thoughtless to go off to an egg-packing factory. There was the feeling, also unexpressed, that the young were a bit like that.

'Goodbye,' he said in a general way. Car doors banged, engines started. In the vestry he removed his surplice and his cassock and hung them in a cupboard.

'We'll probably go tomorrow,' Deirdre said during lunch.

'Go?'

'We'll probably take the Dublin bus.'

'I'd like to see Dublin,' Harold said.

'And then you're returning to London?'

'We're easy about that,' Harold interjected before Deirdre could reply. 'I'm a tradesman, Mr Moran, an electrician.'

'I know you're an electrician, Harold.'

'What I mean is, I'm on my own; I'm not answerable to the bosses. There's always a bob or two waiting in London.'

For some reason Canon Moran felt that Harold was lying. There was a quickness about the way he'd said they were easy about their plans, and it didn't seem quite to make sense, the logic of not being answerable to bosses and a bob or two always waiting for him. Harold was being evasive about their movements, hiding the fact that they would probably remain in Dublin for longer than he implied, meeting other people like himself.

'It was good of you to have us,' Deirdre said that evening, all three of them sitting around the fire in the drawing-room because the evenings had just begun to get chilly. Harold was reading a book about Che Guevara and hadn't spoken for several hours. 'We've enjoyed it, Father.'

'It's been nice having you, Deirdre.'

'I'll write to you from London.'

It was safe to say that: he knew she wouldn't because she hadn't before, until she'd wanted something. She wouldn't write to thank him for the rectory's hospitality, and that would be quite in keeping. Harold was the same kind of man as Sergeant James had been: it didn't matter that they were on different sides. Sergeant James had maybe borne an affliction also, a humped back or a withered arm. He had ravaged a country that existed then for its spoils, and his most celebrated crime was neatly at hand so that another Englishman could make matters worse by attempting to make amends. In Harold's view the trouble had always been that these acts of war and murder died beneath the weight of print in history books, and were forgotten. But history could be rewritten, and for that Kinsella's Barn was an inspiration: Harold had journeyed to it as people make journeys to holy places.

'Yes?' Deirdre said, for while these reflections had passed through his mind he had spoken her name, wanting to ask her to tell him the truth about her friend.

He shook his head. 'I wish you could have seen your mother again,' he said instead. 'I wish she were here now.'

The faces of his three sons-in-law irrelevantly appeared in his mind: Carley's flushed cheeks, Thomas's slow good-natured smile, John's little moustache. It astonished him that he'd ever felt suspicious of their natures, for they would never let his daughters down. But Deirdre had turned her back on the rectory, and what could be expected when she came back with a man? She had never been like Emma or Linda or Una, none of whom smoked Three Castles cigarettes and wore clothes that didn't seem quite clean. It was impossible to imagine any of them becoming involved with a revolutionary, a man who wanted to commit atrocities.

'He was just a farmer, you know,' he heard himself saying. 'Kinsella.'

Surprise showed in Deirdre's face. 'It was Mother we were talking about,' she reminded him, and he could see her trying to connect her mother with a farmer who had died two hundred years ago, and not being able to. Elderliness, he could see her thinking. 'Only time he wandered,' she would probably say to her friend.

'It was good of you to come, Deirdre.'

He looked at her, far into her eyes, admitting to himself that she had always been his favourite. When the other girls were busily growing up she had still wanted to sit on his knee. She'd had a way of interrupting him no matter what he was doing, arriving beside him with a book she wanted him to read to her.

'Goodbye, Father,' she said the next morning while they waited in Enniscorthy for the Dublin bus. 'Thank you for everything.'

'Yeah, thanks a ton, Mr Moran,' Harold said.

'Goodbye, Harold. Goodbye, my dear.'

He watched them finding their seats when the bus arrived and then he drove the old Vauxhall back to Boharbawn, meeting Slattery in his postman's van and returning his salute. There was shopping he should have done, meat and potatoes, and tins of things to keep him going. But his mind was full of Harold's afflicted face and his black-rimmed fingernails, and Deirdre's hand in his. And then flames burst from the straw that had been packed around living people in Kinsella's Barn. They burned through the wood of the barn itself, revealing the writhing bodies. On his horse the man called Sergeant James laughed.

Canon Moran drove the car into the rectory's ramshackle garage, and walked around the house to the wooden seat on the front lawn. Frances should come now with two cups of coffee, appearing at the front door with the tray and then crossing the gravel and the lawn. He saw her as she had been when first they came to the rectory, when only Emma had been born; but the grey-haired Frances was somehow there as well, shadowing her youth. 'Funny little Deirdre,' she said, placing the tray on the seat between them.

It seemed to him that everything that had just happened in the rectory had to do with Frances, with meeting her for the first time when she was eighteen, with loving her and marrying her. He knew it was a trick of the autumn sunshine that again she crossed the gravel and the lawn, no more than pretence that she handed him a cup and saucer. 'Harold's just a talker,' she said. 'Not at all like Sergeant James.'

He sat for a while longer on the wooden seat, clinging to these words, knowing they were true. Of course it was cowardice that ran through Harold, inspiring the whisper of his sneer when he spoke of the England he hated so. In the presence of a befuddled girl and an old Irish clergyman England was an easy target, and Ireland's troubles a kind of target also.

Frances laughed, and for the first time her death seemed far away, as her life did too. In the rectory the visitors had blurred her fingerprints to nothing, and had made of her a ghost that could come back. The sunshine warmed him as he sat there, the garden was less melancholy than it had been.

Sunday Drinks

There was no one else about, not even a cat on the whole extent of the common. The early morning air hadn't yet been infected by the smell of London, houses were as silent as the houses of the dead. It was half past seven, a Sunday morning in June: on a weekday at this time voices would be calling out, figures already hurrying across the common to Barnes station; the buses would have started. On a weekday Malcolm would be lying for a last five minutes in bed, conserving his energy.

Not yet shaven, a fawn dressing-gown over striped red-and-blue pyjamas, he strolled on the cricket pitch, past the sight-screens and a small pavilion. He was middle-aged and balding, with glasses. Though no eccentric in other ways, he often walked on fine Sunday mornings across the common in his dressing-gown, as far as the poplars that grew in a line along one boundary.

Reaching them now, he turned and slowly made his way back to the house where he lived with Jessica, who was his wife. They'd lived there since he'd begun to be prosperous as a solicitor: an Edwardian house of pleasant brown brick, with some Virginia creeper on it, and bay trees in tubs on either side of the front door. They were a small family: quietly occupying an upstairs room, in many ways no trouble to anyone, there was Malcolm and Jessica's son.

In the kitchen Malcolm finished Chapter Eight of *Edwin Drood* and eventually heard the Sunday papers arrive. He went to fetch them, glanced through them, and then made coffee and toast. He took a tray and the newspapers up to his wife.

'I've brought you a cup of tea,' Jessica said later that morning, in their son's room. Sometimes he drank it, but often it was still there on the bedside table when she returned at lunchtime. He never carried the cup and saucer down to the kitchen himself and would apologize for that, wagging his head in irritation at his shortcomings.

He didn't reply when she spoke about the tea. He stared at her and smiled. One hand was clenched close to his bearded face, the fingernails bitten, the fingers gnawed here and there. The room smelt of his sweat because he couldn't bear to have the window open, nor indeed to have the blind up. He made his models with the electric light on, preferring that to daylight. In the room the models were everywhere: Hurricanes and Spitfires, sea-planes and Heinkel 178s, none of them finished. A month ago, on 25th May, they'd made an attempt to celebrate his twenty-fourth birthday.

She closed the door behind her. On the landing walls there was a wallpaper splashed with poppies and cornflowers, which ran down through the house. People often remarked on its pastoral freshness when Jessica opened the hall door to them, though others sometimes blinked. The hall had had a gloomy look before, the paintwork a shade of gravy. Doors and skirting-boards were brightly white now.

'Let's not go to the Morrishes',' Malcolm suggested in the kitchen, even though he'd put on his Sunday-morning-drinks clothes.

'Of course we must,' she said, not wanting to go to the Morrishes' either. 'I won't be a minute.'

In the downstairs lavatory she applied eye-shadow. Her thin face had a shallow look if she didn't make an effort with make-up; a bit of colour suited her, she reckoned, as it did the hall. She smeared on lipstick and pressed a tissue between her lips to clear away the surplus, continuing to examine her application of eye-shadow in the mirror above the wash-basin. Dark hair, greying now, curved around her face. Her deep blue eyes still managed a sparkle that spread beauty into her features, transforming her: nondescript little thing, someone once had said, catching her in a tired moment.

In the kitchen she turned on the extractor fan above the electric cooker; pork chops were cooking slowly in the oven. 'All right?' she said, and Malcolm, idling over an advertisement for photochromic lenses, nodded and stood up.

Their son was dreaming now: he was there, on the bank of the river. Birds with blue plumage swooped over the water; through the foliage came the strum of a guitar. All the friends there'd been were there, in different coloured sleeping-bags, lying as he was. They were happy by the river because India was where the truth was, wrapped up in gentleness and beauty. Someone said that, and everyone else agreed.

Anthea Chalmers was at the Morrishes', tall and elegant in green, long since divorced. She had a look of Bette Davis, eyes like soup-plates, that kind of mouth. The Livingstons were there also, and Susanna and David Maidstone, and the Unwins. So was Mr Fulmer, a sandy-complexioned man whom people were sorry for because his wife was a stick-in-the-mud and wouldn't go to parties. June and Tom Highband were there, and the

Taylor-Deeths, and Marcus Stire and his friend. There was a handful of faces that were unfamiliar to Jessica and Malcolm.

'Hullo, hullo,' their host called out, welcoming them with party joviality. The guests were passing from the sitting-room, through the french windows to the garden, all of them with glasses in their hands. The Morrishes – he pink and bluff, she pretty in a faded way – were busily making certain that these glasses contained precisely what people wanted. In the garden their French au pair boy was handing round bowls of nuts and shiny little biscuits from Japan. Children – the Morrishes' and others' – had congregated in a distant corner, by a tool-shed.

Jessica and Malcolm both asked for white wine, since chilled bottles of it stood there, inviting on a warm morning. They didn't say much to the Morrishes, who clearly wanted to get things going before indulging in chat. They stepped out into the garden, where a mass of flowers spectacularly bloomed and the lawns were closely shorn.

'Hi, Jessica,' Marcus Stire's friend said, a short, stout young man in a blue blazer. He'd made her black-bottom pie, he reported. He shook his head, implying disappointment with his version of the dish.

'Hullo, stranger,' Anthea Chalmers said to Malcolm.

She always seemed to pick him out. Ages ago he'd rejected the idea that a balding solicitor with glasses might possibly have some sensual attraction for her, even though all she ever talked to him about were sensual matters. She liked to get him into a corner, as she had done now, and had a way of turning interlopers away with a snakelike shift of her shoulders. She'd placed him with his back to the wall of the house, along which a creamy honeysuckle had been trained. A trellis to his right continued to support it; to his left, two old water-butts were swathed with purple clematis.

'A pig,' she said, referring to the man she'd once been married to. 'And I told him, Malcolm. I'd sooner share a bed with a farmyard pig was precisely what I said. Needless to say, he became violent.'

Jessica, having discussed the preparation of black-bottom pie with Marcus Stire's friend, smiled at the stout young man and passed on. The au pair boy offered her a Japanese biscuit and then a man she didn't know remarked upon the weather. Could anything be nicer, he asked her, than a drink or two on a Sunday morning in a sunny London garden? He was a man in brown suede, expensively cut to disguise a certain paunchiness. He had damp eyes and a damp-looking moustache. He had well-packed jowls, and a sun-browned head that matched the shade of his clothes. A businessman, Jessica speculated, excessively rich, a tough performer in his business world. He began to talk about a house he owned near Estepona.

*

On the surface of the tea which jessica had earlier brought her son a skin had formed, in which a small fly now struggled. Nothing else was happening in the room. The sound of breathing could hardly be heard, the dream about birds with blue plumage had abruptly ceased. Then – in that same abrupt manner, a repetition of the suddenness that in different ways affected this boy's life – his eyes snapped open.

Through the gloom, and seeming larger than reality, the Spitfires and the Heinkels greeted his consciousness. He was in a room with aeroplanes, he told himself, and while he lay there nothing more impinged on his mind. Eventually he rose and began to dress, his youthful beard scanty and soft, quite like a bearded lady's. Tears ran into it while slowly he pulled his clothes over his white flesh.

His T-shirt was pale blue, the paler message it bore almost washed away. *Wham!* it had said, the word noisily proclaimed against lightning flashes and the hooded figures of Batman and Robin. A joke all of it had been: those years had been full of jokes, with no one wanting to grow up, with that longing to be children for ever. Tears dripped from his beard to the T-shirt now; some fell on to his jeans. He turned the electric light on and then noticed the cup of tea by his bed. He drank it, swallowing the skin and the fly that had died in it. His tears did not distress him.

'Well, that was it, Malcolm,' Anthea Chalmers said. 'I mean, no one enjoys a bedroom more than I do, but for God's sake!'

Her soup-plate eyes rapidly blinked, her lips were held for a moment in a little knot. The man she'd married, she yet again revealed, had not been able to give her what she'd wanted and needed. Instead, intoxicated, he would return to their house at night and roar about from room to room. Often he armed himself with a bamboo cane. 'Which he bought,' she reminded Malcolm, 'quite openly in a garden shop.'

In the honeysuckle, suburban bees paused between moments of buzzing. A white butterfly fluttered beside Malcolm's face. 'You must be awfully glad to be rid of him,' he politely said.

'One's alone, Malcolm. It isn't easy, being alone.'

She went into details about how difficult it was, and how various frustrations could be eased. She lowered her voice, she said she spoke in confidence. Sexual fantasy flooded from her, tired and seeming soiled in the bright sunshine, with the scent of the honeysuckle so close to both of them. Malcolm listened, not moving away, not trying to think of other things. It was nearly two years since Anthea Chalmers had discovered that he would always listen at a party.

In the garden the voices had become louder as more alcohol was consumed. Laughter was shriller, cigarette smoke hung about. By the tool-shed in the far distance the children, organized by a girl who was a little older than the others, played a variation of Grandmother's Footsteps.

Tom Highband, who wrote under another name a column for the *Daily Telegraph*, told a joke that caused a burst of laughter. Sandy Mr Fulmer, whom nobody knew very well, listened to the Unwins exchanging gossip with Susanna Maidstone about the school their children all attended. 'Just a little slower,' Marcus Stire's friend pleaded, writing down a recipe for prune jelly on the back of a cheque-book. Taylor-Deeth was getting drunk.

'It has its own little beach of course,' the man with the damp-looking moustache informed Jessica. You went down a flight of steps and there you were. They adored the Spaniards, he added, Joan especially did.

And then Joan, who was his wife, was there beside them, in shades of pink. She was bulky, like her husband, with a smile so widely beaming that it seemed to run off her face into her greying hair. She had always had a thing about the Spanish, she agreed, the quality of Spanish life, their little churches. 'We have a maid of course,' her husband said, 'who keeps an eye on things. Old Violetta.'

Glasses were again refilled, the Morrishes together attending to that, as was their way at their parties. She did so quietly, he with more dash. People often remarked that they were like good servants, the way they complemented one another in this way. As well, they were said to be happily married.

Glancing between the couple who were talking to her, Jessica could see that Malcolm was still trapped. The Livingstons tried to cut in on the tête-à-tête but Anthea Chalmers's shoulder sharply edged them away. Together again after their separation, the Livingstons looked miserable.

'Violetta mothers us,' the man with the damp moustache said. 'We could never manage without old Violetta.'

'Another thing is Spanish dignity,' his wife continued, and the man added that old Violetta certainly had her share of that.

'Oh yes, indeed,' his wife agreed.

Marcus Stire arrived then, lanky and malicious. The couple with the house in Spain immediately moved away, as if they didn't like the look of him. He laughed. They were embarrassed, he explained, because at another party recently they'd all of a sudden quarrelled most violently in his presence. The man had even raised an arm to strike his wife, and Marcus Stire had had to restrain him.

'You'd never think it, would you, Jessica? All that guff about cosiness in Spain when more likely that smile of hers covers a multitude of sins.

What awful frauds people are!' He laughed again and then continued, his soft voice drawling, a cigarette between the rings on his fingers.

He ran through all the people in the garden. Susanna Maidstone had been seen with Taylor-Deeth in the Trat-West. The Livingstons' patched-up arrangement wouldn't of course last. The Unwins were edgy, frigidity was Anthea Chalmers's problem. 'Suburban middle age,' he said in his drawl. 'It's like a minefield.' The Morrishes had had a ghastly upset a month ago when a girl from his office had pursued him home one night, messily spilling the beans.

Jessica looked at the Morrishes, so neatly together as they saw to people's drinks, attending now to Mr Fulmer. It seemed astonishing that they, too, weren't quite as they appeared to be. 'Oh, heavens, yes,' Marcus Stire said, guessing at this doubt in her mind.

His malice was perceptive, and he didn't much exaggerate. He had a way of detecting trouble, and of accurately piecing together the fragments that came his way. Caught off her guard, she wondered what he said to other people about Malcolm and herself. She wondered just how he saw them and then immediately struggled to regain her concentration, knowing she should not wonder that.

He was commenting now on the girl who had persuaded the other children to play her version of Grandmother's Footsteps, a bossy handful he called her. How dreadful she'd be at forty-eight, her looks three-quarters gone, famous in some other suburb as a nagging wife. Jessica smiled, as if he had related a pleasant joke. Again she made the effort to concentrate.

You had to do that: to concentrate and to listen properly, as Malcolm was listening, as she had listened herself to the talk about a house in Spain. You had to have a bouncy wallpaper all over the house, and fresh white paint instead of gravy-brown. You mustn't forget your plan to get the garden as colourful as this one; you mustn't let your mind wander. Busily you must note the damp appearance of a man's moustache and the grey in a woman's hair, and the malevolence in the eyes that were piercing into you now.

'I've written off those years, Malcolm,' Anthea Chalmers said, and across the garden Malcolm saw that his wife had collapsed. He could tell at once, as if she'd fallen to the grass and lay there in a heap. Occasionally one or the other of them went under; impossible to anticipate which, or how it would happen.

He watched her face and saw that she was back in 1954, her pains developing a rhythm, a sweltering summer afternoon. A message had come to him in court, and when he'd returned to the house the midwife was smoking a cigarette in the hall. The midwife and the nurse had been up all night with a difficult delivery in Sheen. Afterwards, when the child had been born and everything tidied up, he'd given them a glass of whisky each.

Like an infection, all of it slipped across the garden, through the cigarette smoke and the people and the smartly casual Sunday clothes, from Jessica to Malcolm. Down their treacherous Memory Lane it dragged them, one after the other. The first day at the primary school, tears at the gate, the kindly dinner lady. The gang of four, their child and three others, at daggers drawn with other gangs. The winning of the high jump.

'Excuse me,' Malcolm said. It was worse for Jessica, he thought in a familiar way as he made his way to her. It was worse because after the birth she'd been told she must not have other babies: she blamed herself now for being obedient.

They left the party suddenly, while the children still played a version of Grandmother's Footsteps by the tool-shed, and the adults drank and went on talking to one another. People who knew them guessed that their abrupt departure might somehow have to do with their son, whom no one much mentioned these days, he being a registered drug addict. The couple who had spoken to Jessica about their Spanish house spoke of it now to their hosts, who did not listen as well as she had. Anthea Chalmers tried to explain to Marcus Stire's friend, but that was hopeless. Marcus Stire again surveyed the people in the garden.

Anger possessed Malcolm as they walked across the common that had been peaceful in the early morning. It was less so now. Cricket would be played that afternoon and preparations were being made, the square marked, the sight-screens wheeled into position. An ice-cream van was already trading briskly. People lay on the grass, youths kicked a football.

'I'm sorry,' Jessica said. Her voice was nervous; she felt ashamed of herself.

'It isn't you, Jessica.'

'Let's have a drink on our own, shall we?'

Neither of them wishing to return immediately to their house, they went to the Red Rover and sat outside. She guessed his thoughts, as earlier he had seen hers in her face. When people wondered where all of it had gone, all that love and all those flowers, he would have liked to have shown them their darkened upstairs room. The jolly sixties and those trips to wonderland were there, he'd once cried out, with half-made aeroplanes gathering a dust. Their son had a name, which was used when they addressed him; but when they thought of him he was nameless in their minds. Years ago they'd discovered that that was the same for both of them.

'Maybe,' she said, referring to the future, trying to cheer him up.

He made a gesture, half a nod: the speculation was impossible. And the consolation that families had always had children who were locked away and looked after wasn't a consolation in the least. They didn't have to live with a monstrous fact of nature, but with a form of accidental suicide, and that was worse.

They sat a little longer in the sunshine, both of them thinking about the house they'd left an hour or so ago. It would be as silent as if they'd never had a child, and then little noises would begin, like the noises of a ghost. The quiet descent of the stairs, the shuffling through the hall. He would be there in the kitchen, patiently sitting, when they returned. He would smile at them and during lunch a kind of conversation might develop, or it might not. A week ago he'd said, quite suddenly, that soon he intended to work in a garden somewhere, or a park. Occasionally he said things like that.

They didn't mention him as they sat there; they never did now. And it was easier for both of them to keep away from Memory Lane when they were together and alone. Instead of all that there was the gossip of Marcus Stire: Susanna Maidstone in the Trat-West, the girl from the office arriving in the Morrishes' house, the quarrel between the smiling woman and her suede-clad husband, Anthea Chalmers, lone Mr Fulmer, the Livingstons endeavouring to make a go of it. Easily, Malcolm imagined Marcus Stire's drawling tones and the sharpness of his eye, like a splinter of glass. He knew now how Jessica had been upset: a pair of shadows Marcus Stire would have called them, clinging to the periphery of life because that was where they felt safe, both of them a little destroyed.

They went on discussing the people they'd just left, wondering if some fresh drama had broken out, another explosion in the landscape of marriage that Marcus Stire had likened to a minefield. Finishing their drinks, they agreed that he'd certainly tell them if it had. They talked about him for a moment, and then the subject of the party drifted away from them and they talked of other things. Malcolm told her what was happening in *Edwin Drood*, because it was a book she would never read. His voice continued while they left the Red Rover and walked across the common, back to their house. It was odd, she reflected as she listened to it, that companionship had developed in their middle age, when luckier people made of their marriages such tales of woe.

The Paradise Lounge

On her high stool by the bar the old woman was as still as a statue. Perhaps her face is expressionless, Beatrice thought, because in repose it does not betray the extent of her years. The face itself was lavishly made up, eyes and mouth, rouge softening the wrinkles, a dusting of perfumed powder. The chin was held more than a little high, at an angle that tightened the loops of flesh beneath it. Grey hair was short beneath a black cloche hat that suggested a fashion of the past, as did the tight black skirt and black velvet coat. Eighty she'd be, Beatrice deduced, or eighty-two or -three.

'We can surely enjoy ourselves,' Beatrice's friend said, interrupting her scrutiny of the old woman. 'Surely we can, Bea?'

She turned her head. The closeness of his brick-coloured flesh and of the smile in his eyes caused her lips to tremble. She appeared to smile also, but what might have been taken for pleasure was a checking of her tears.

'Yes,' she said. 'Of course.'

They were married, though not to one another. Beatrice's friend, casually dressed for a summer weekend, was in early middle age, no longer slim yet far from bulky. Beatrice was thirty-two, petite and black-haired in a blue denim dress. Sunglasses disguised her deep-rust eyes, which was how – a long time ago now – her father had described them. She had wanted to be an actress then.

'It's best,' her friend said, repeating the brief statement for what might have been the hundredth time since they had settled into his car earlier that afternoon. The affair was over, the threat to their families averted. They had come away to say goodbye.

'Yes, I know it's best,' she said, a repetition also.

At the bar the old woman slowly raised a hand to her hat and touched it delicately with her fingers. Slowly the hand descended, and then lifted her cocktail glass. Her scarlet mouth was not quite misshapen, but age had harshly scored what once had been a perfect outline, lips pressed together like a rosebud on its side. Failure, Beatrice thought as casually she observed all this: in the end the affair was a failure. She didn't even love him any more, and long ago he'd ceased to love her. It was euphemism to call it saying goodbye: they were having a dirty weekend, there was nothing left to lift it higher than that.

'I'm sorry we couldn't manage longer,' he said. 'I'm sorry about Glengarriff.'

'It doesn't matter.'

'Even so.'

She ceased to watch the old woman at the bar. She smiled at him, again disguising tears but also wanting him to know that there were no hard feelings, for why on earth should there be?

'After all, we've been to Glengarriff,' she said, a joke because on the one occasion they'd visited the place they had nearly been discovered in their deceptions. She'd used her sister as an excuse for her absences from home: for a long time now her sister had been genuinely unwell in a farmhouse in Co. Meath, a house that fortunately for Beatrice's purpose didn't have a telephone.

'I'll never forget you,' he said, his large tanned hand suddenly on one of hers, the vein throbbing in his forehead. A line of freckles ran down beside the vein, five smudges on the redbrick skin. In winter you hardly noticed them.

'Nor I you.'

'Darling old Bea,' he said, as if they were back at the beginning.

The bar was a dim, square lounge with a scattering of small tables, one of which they occupied. Ashtrays advertised Guinness, beer-mats Heineken. Sunlight touched the darkened glass in one of two windows, drawing from it a glow that was not unlike the amber gleam of whiskey. Behind the bar itself the rows of bottles, spirits upside down above their global measures, glittered pleasantly as a centrepiece, their reflections gaudy in a cluttered mirror. The floor had a patterned carpet, further patterned with cigarette burns and a diversity of stains. The Paradise Lounge the bar had been titled in a moment of hyperbole by the grandfather of the present proprietor, a sign still proclaiming as much on the door that opened from the hotel's mahogany hall. Beatrice's friend had hesitated, for the place seemed hardly promising: Keegan's Railway Hotel in a town neither of them knew. They might have driven on, but he was tired and the sun had been in his eyes. 'It's all right,' she had reassured him.

He took their glasses to the bar and had to ring a bell because the man in charge had disappeared ten minutes ago. 'Nice evening,' he said to the old woman on the bar-stool, and she managed to indicate agreement without moving a muscle of her carefully held head. 'We'll have the same again,' he said to the barman, who apologized for his absence, saying he'd been mending a tap.

Left on her own, Beatrice sighed a little and took off her sunglasses. There was no need for this farewell, no need to see him for the last time in his pyjamas or to sit across a table from him at dinner and at breakfast, making conversation that once had come naturally. 'A final fling', he'd put it, and she'd thought of someone beating a cracked drum, trying to extract a sound that wasn't there any more. How could it have come to this? The Paradise Lounge of Keegan's Railway Hotel, Saturday night in a hilly provincial town, litter caught in the railings of the Christian Brothers': how *could* this be the end of what they once had had? Saying goodbye to her, he was just somebody else's husband: the lover had slipped away.

'Well, it's a terrible bloody tap we have,' the barman was saying. 'Come hell or high water, I can't get a washer into it.'

'It can be a difficult job.'

'You could come in and say that to the wife for me, sir.'

The drinks were paid for, the transaction terminated. Further gin and Martini were poured into the old woman's glass, and Beatrice watched again while like a zombie the old woman lit a cigarette.

Miss Doheny her name was: though beautiful once, she had never married. Every Saturday evening she met the Meldrums in the Paradise Lounge, where they spent a few hours going through the week that had passed, exchanging gossip and commenting on the world. Miss Doheny was always early and would sit up at the bar for twenty minutes on her own, having the extra couple of drinks that, for her, were always necessary. Before the Meldrums arrived she would make her way to a table in a corner, for that was where Mrs Meldrum liked to be.

It wasn't usual that other people were in the bar then. Occasionally it filled up later but at six o'clock, before her friends arrived, she nearly always had it to herself. Francis Keegan – the hotel's inheritor, who also acted as barman – spent a lot of time out in the back somewhere, attending to this or that. It didn't matter because after their initial greeting of one another, and a few remarks about the weather, there wasn't much conversation that Miss Doheny and he had to exchange. She enjoyed sitting up at the bar on her own, glancing at the reflections in the long mirror behind the bottles, provided the reflections were never of herself. On the other hand it was a pleasant enough diversion, having visitors.

Miss Doheny, who had looked twice at Beatrice and once at her companion, guessed at their wrong-doing. Tail-ends of conversation had drifted across the lounge, no effort being made to lower voices since more often than not the old turn out to be deaf. They were people from Dublin whose relationship was not that recorded in Francis Keegan's register in the hall. Without much comment, modern life permitted their sin; the light-brown motor-car parked in front of the hotel made their self-indulgence a simple matter.

How different it had been, Miss Doheny reflected, in 1933! Correctly she estimated that that would have been the year when she herself was the age the dark-haired girl was now. In 1933 adultery and divorce and light-brown motor-cars had belonged more in America and England, read about and alien to what already was being called the Irish way of life. 'Catholic Ireland,' Father Cully used to say. 'Decent Catholic Ireland.' The term was vague and yet had meaning: the emergent nation, seeking pillars on which to build itself, had plumped for holiness and the Irish language – natural choices in the circumstances. 'A certain class of woman,' old Father Cully used to say, 'constitutes an abhorrence.' The painted women of Clancy's Picture House – sound introduced in 1936 – were creatures who carried a terrible warning. Jezebel women, Father Cully called them, adding that the picture house should never have been permitted to exist. In his grave for a quarter of a century, he would hardly have believed his senses if he'd walked into the Paradise Lounge in Keegan's Railway Hotel to discover two adulterers, and one of his flock who had failed to heed his castigation of painted women. Yet for thirty-five years Miss Doheny had strolled through the town on Saturday evenings to this same lounge, past the statue of the 1798 rebel, down the sharp incline of Castle Street. On Sundays she covered the same ground again, on the way to and from Mass. Neither rain nor cold prevented her from making the journey to the Church of the Resurrection or to the hotel, and illness did not often afflict her. That she had become more painted as the years piled up seemed to Miss Doheny to be natural in the circumstances.

In the Paradise Lounge she felt particularly at home. In spring and summer the Meldrums brought plants for her, or bunches of chives or parsley, sometimes flowers. Not because she wished to balance the gesture with one of her own but because it simply pleased her to do so she brought for them a pot of jam if she had just made some, or pieces of shortbread. At Christmas, more formally, they exchanged gifts of a different kind. At Christmas the lounge was decorated by Francis Keegan, as was the hall of the hotel and the dining-room. Once a year, in April, a dance was held in the dining-room, in connection with a local point-to-point, and it was said in the town that Francis Keegan made enough in the bar during the course of that long night to last him for the next twelve months. The hotel ticked over from April to April, the Paradise Lounge becoming quite brisk with business when an occasional function was held in the dining-room, though never achieving the abandoned spending that distinguished the night of the point-to-point. Commercial travellers sometimes stayed briefly, taking pot-luck with Mrs Keegan's cooking, which at the best of times was modest in ambition and achievement. After dinner these men would sit on one of the high stools in the Paradise Lounge, conversing with Francis Keegan and drinking bottles of stout. Mrs Keegan would sometimes put in a late appearance and sip a glass of gin and water. She was a woman of slatternly appearance, with loose grey hair and slippers. Her husband complemented her in style and manner, his purplish complexion reflecting a dedication to the wares he traded in across his bar. They were an undemanding couple, charitable in their opinions, regarded as unfortunate in the town since their union had not produced children. Because of that, Keegan's Railway Hotel was nearing the end of its days as a family concern and in a sense it was fitting that that should be so, for the railway that gave it its title had been closed in 1951.

How I envy her! Miss Doheny thought. How fortunate she is to find herself in these easy times, not condemned because she loves a man! It seemed right to Miss Doheny that a real love affair was taking place in the Paradise Lounge and that no one questioned it. Francis Keegan knew perfectly well that the couple were not man and wife: the strictures of old Father Cully were as fusty by now as neglected mice droppings. The holiness that had accompanied the birth of a nation had at last begun to shed its first tight skin: liberation, Miss Doheny said to herself, marvelling over the word.

They walked about the town because it was too soon for dinner. Many shops were still open, greengrocers anxious to rid themselves of cabbage that had been limp for days and could not yet again be offered for sale after the weekend, chemists and sweetshops. Kevin Croady, Your Best for Hi-Fi, had arranged a loudspeaker in a window above his premises: Saturday-night music blared forth, punk harmonies and a tenor rendering of 'Kelly the Boy from Killann'. All tastes were catered for.

The streets were narrow, the traffic congested. Women picked over the greengrocers' offerings, having waited until this hour because prices would be reduced. Newly shaved men slipped into the public houses, youths and girls loitered outside Redmond's Café and on the steps of the 1798 statue. Two dogs half-heartedly fought outside the Bank of Ireland.

The visitors to the town inquired where the castle was, and then made their way up Castle Hill. 'Opposite Castle Motors,' the child they'd asked had said, and there it was: an ivy-covered ruin, more like the remains of a cowshed. Corrugated iron sealed off an archway, its torn bill-posters advertising Calor Gas and a rock group, Duffy's Circus and Fine Gael, and the annual point-to-point that kept Keegan's Railway Hotel going. Houses had been demolished in this deserted area, concrete replacements only just begun. The graveyard of the Protestant church was unkempt; *New Premises in Wolfe Tone Street*, said a placard in the window of Castle Motors. Litter was everywhere.

'Not exactly camera fodder,' he said with his easy laugh. 'A bloody disgrace, some of these towns are.'

'The people don't notice, I suppose.'

'They should maybe wake themselves up.'

The first time he'd seen her, he'd afterwards said, he had heard himself whispering that it was she he should have married. They'd sat together, talking over after-dinner coffee in someone else's house. He'd told her, lightly, that he was in the Irish rope business, almost making a joke of it because that was his way. A week later his car had drawn up beside her in Rathgar Road, where she'd lived since her marriage. 'I thought I recognized you,' he said, afterwards confessing that he'd looked up her husband's name in the telephone directory. 'Come in for a drink,' she invited, and of course he had. Her two children had been there, her husband had come in.

They made their way back to the town, she taking his arm as they descended the steep hill they'd climbed. A wind had gathered, cooling the evening air.

'It feels so long ago,' she said. 'The greater part of my life appears to have occurred since that day when you first came to the house.'

'I know, Bea.'

He'd seemed extraordinary and nice, and once when he'd smiled at her she'd found herself looking away. She wasn't unhappy in her marriage, only bored by the monotony of preparing food and seeing to the house and the children. She had, as well, a reluctant feeling that she wasn't appreciated, that she hadn't been properly loved for years.

'You don't regret it happened?' he said, stepping out into the street because the pavement was still crowded outside Redmond's Café.

She pitched her voice low so that he wouldn't hear her saying she wasn't sure. She didn't want to tell a lie, she wasn't certain of the truth.

He nodded, assuming her reassurance. Once, of course, he would never have let a mumbled reply slip by.

Miss Doheny had moved from the bar and was sitting at a table with the Meldrums when Beatrice and her friend returned to the Paradise Lounge after dinner. Mrs Meldrum was telling all about the visit last Sunday afternoon of her niece, Kathleen. 'Stones she's put on,' she reported, and then recalled that Kathleen's newly acquired husband had sat there for three hours hardly saying a word. Making a fortune he was, in the dry-goods business, dull but good-hearted.

Miss Doheny listened. Strangely, her mind was still on the visitors who had returned to the lounge. She'd heard the girl saying that a walk about the town would be nice, and as the Meldrums had entered the lounge an hour or so ago she'd heard the man's voice in the hall and had guessed they were then on their way to the dining-room. The dinner would not have been good, for Miss Doheny had often heard complaints about the nature of Mrs Keegan's cooking. And yet the dinner, naturally, would not have mattered in the least.

Mrs Meldrum's voice continued: Kathleen's four children by her first marriage were all grown up and off her hands, she was lucky to have married so late in life into a prosperous dry-goods business. Mr Meldrum inclined his head or nodded, but from time to time he would also issue a mild contradiction, setting the facts straight, regulating his wife's memory. He was a grey-haired man in a tweed jacket, very spare and stooped, his face as sharp as a blade, his grey moustache well cared-for. He smoked while he drank, allowing a precise ten minutes to elapse between the end of one cigarette and the lighting of the next. Mrs Meldrum was smaller than her companions by quite some inches, round and plump, with glasses and a black hat.

The strangers were drinking Drambuie now, Miss Doheny noticed. The man made a joke, probably about the food they'd eaten; the girl smiled. It was difficult to understand why it was that they were so clearly not man and wife. There was a wistfulness in the girl's face, but the wistfulness said nothing very much. In a surprising way Miss Doheny imagined herself crossing the lounge to where they were. 'You're lucky, you know,' she heard herself saying. 'Honestly, you're lucky, child.' She glanced again in the girl's direction and for a moment caught her eye. She almost mouthed the words, but changed her mind because as much as possible she liked to keep her face in repose.

Beatrice listened to her companion's efforts to cheer the occasion up. The town and the hotel — especially the meal they'd just consumed — combined to reflect the mood that the end of the affair had already generated. They were here, Beatrice informed herself again, not really to say goodbye to one another but to commit adultery for the last time. They would enjoy it as they always had, but the enjoyment would not be the same as that inspired by the love there had been. They might not have come, they might more elegantly have said goodbye, yet their presence in a bar ridiculously named the Paradise Lounge seemed suddenly apt. The bedroom where acts of mechanical passion would take place had a dingy wallpaper, its flattened pink soap already used by someone else. Dirty weekend, Beatrice thought again, for stripped of love all that was left was the mess of deception and lies there had been, of theft and this remaining, too ordinary desire. Her sister, slowly dying in the farmhouse, had been a bitter confidante and would never forgive her now. Tonight in a provincial bedroom a manufacturer of rope would have his way with her and she would have her way with him. There would be their nakedness and their mingled sweat.

'I thought that steak would walk away,' he spiritedly was continuing now. 'Being somebody's shoe-leather.'

She suddenly felt drunk, and wanted to be drunker. She held her glass toward him. 'Let's just drink,' she said.

She caught the eye of the old woman at the other table and for a moment sensed Miss Doheny's desire to communicate with her. It puzzled her that an elderly woman whom she did not know should wish to say something, yet she strongly felt that this was so. Then Miss Doheny returned her attention to what the other old woman was saying.

When they'd finished the drinks that Beatrice's companion had just fetched they moved from the table they were at and sat on two bar-stools, listening to Francis Keegan telling them about the annual liveliness in the hotel on the night of the April point-to-point. Mrs Keegan appeared at his side and recalled an occasion when Willie Kincart had ridden the horse he'd won the last race on into the hall of the hotel and how old Packy Briscoe had imagined he'd caught the d.t.'s when he looked down from the top of the stairs. And there was the story – before Mrs Keegan's time, as she was swift to point out – when Jack Doyle and Movita had stayed in Keegan's, when just for the hell of it Jack Doyle had chased a honeymoon couple up Castle Hill, half naked from their bed. After several further drinks, Beatrice began to laugh. She felt much less forlorn now that the faces of Francis Keegan and his wife were beginning to float agreeably in her vision. When she looked at the elderly trio in the corner, the only other people in the lounge, their faces floated also.

The thin old man came to the bar for more drinks and cigarettes. He nodded and smiled at Beatrice; he remarked upon the weather. 'Mr Meldrum,' said Francis Keegan by way of introduction. 'How d'you do,' Beatrice said.

Her companion yawned and appeared to be suggesting that they should go to bed. Beatrice took no notice. She pushed her glass at Francis Keegan, reaching for her handbag and announcing that it was her round. 'A drink for everyone,' she said, aware that when she gestured towards the Keegans and the elderly trio she almost lost her balance. She giggled. 'Definitely my round,' she slurred, giggling again.

Mrs Keegan told another story, about a commercial traveller called Artie Logan who had become drunk in his room and had sent down for so many trays of tea and buttered bread that every cup and saucer in the hotel had been carried up to him. 'They said to thank you,' her husband passed on, returning from the elderly trio's table. Beatrice turned her head. All three of them were looking at her, their faces still slipping about a bit. Their glasses were raised in her direction. 'Good luck,' the old man called out.

It was then that Beatrice realized. She looked from face to face, making herself smile to acknowledge the good wishes she was being offered, the truth she sensed seeming to emerge from a blur of features and clothes and three raised glasses. She nodded, and saw the heads turn away again. It had remained unstated: the love that was there had never in any way been exposed. In this claustrophobic town, in this very lounge, there had been the endless lingering of a silent passion, startlingly different from the instant requiting of her own.

Through the muzziness of inebriation Beatrice glanced again across the bar. Behind her the Keegans were laughing, and the man she'd once so intensely loved was loudly laughing also. She heard the sound of the laughter strangely, as if it echoed from a distance, and she thought for a moment that it did not belong in the Paradise Lounge, that only the two old women and the old man belonged there. He was loved, and in silence he returned that love. His plump, bespectacled wife had never had reason to feel betrayed; no shame nor guilt attached. In all the years a sister's dying had never been made use of. Nor had there been hasty afternoons in Rathgar Road, blinds drawn against neighbours who might guess, a bedroom set to rights before children came in from school. There hadn't been a single embrace.

Yet the love that had continued for so long would go on now until the grave: without even thinking, Beatrice knew that that was so. The old woman paraded for a purpose the remnants of her beauty, the man was elegant in his tweed. How lovely that was! Beatrice thought, still muzzily surveying the people at the table, the wife who had not been deceived quite contentedly chatting, the two who belonged together occupying their magic worlds.

How lovely that nothing had been destroyed: Beatrice wanted to tell someone that, but there was no one to tell. In Rathgar Road her children would be watching the television, their father sitting with them. Her sister would die before the year was finished. What cruelty there seemed to be, and more sharply now she recalled the afternoon bedroom set to rights and her sister's wasted face. She wanted to run away, to go backwards into time so that she might shake her head at her lover on the night they'd first met.

Miss Doheny passed through the darkened town, a familiar figure on a Saturday night. It had been the same as always, sitting there, close to him, the smoke drifting from the cigarette that lolled between his fingers. The girl by now would be close in a different way to the man who was somebody else's husband also. As in a film, their clothes would be scattered about the room that had been hired for love, their murmurs would break a silence. Tears ran through Miss Doheny's meticulous make-up, as often they did when she walked away from the Paradise Lounge on a Saturday night. It was difficult sometimes not to weep when she thought about the easy times that had come about in her lifetime, mocking the agony of her stifled love.

Mags

Neither Julia nor James could remember a time when Mags had not been there. She was part of the family, although neither a relation nor a connection. Long before either of them had been born she'd been, at school, their mother's best friend.

They were grown up now and had children of their own; the Memory Lane they travelled down at Mags's funeral was long; it was impossible not to recall the past there'd been with her. 'Our dear sister,' the clergyman in the crematorium murmured, and quite abruptly Julia's most vivid memory was of being on the beach at Rustington playing 'Mags's Game', a kind of Grandmother's Footsteps; and James remembered how Mags had interceded when his crime of taking unripe grapes from the greenhouse had been discovered. Imposing no character of its own upon the mourners, the crematorium filled easily with such moments, with summer jaunts and treats in teashops, with talk and stories and dressing up for nursery plays, with Mags's voice for ever reading the adventures of the Swallows and the Amazons.

Cicily, whose friend at school she'd been, remembered Miss Harper being harsh, accusing Mags of sloth and untidiness, and making Mags cry. There'd been a day when everyone had been made to learn 'The Voice and the Peak' and Miss Harper, because of her down on Mags, had made it seem that Mags had brought this communal punishment about by being the final straw in her ignorance of the verb *craindre*. There'd been, quite a few years later, Mags's ill-judged love affair with Robert Blakley, the callousness of Robert's eventual rejection of her, and Mags's scar as a result: her lifelong fear of ever again getting her fingers burnt in the same way. In 1948, when Cicily was having James, Mags had come to stay, to help and in particular to look after Julia, who was just beginning to toddle. That had been the beginning of helping with the children; in 1955 she'd moved in after a series of au pair girls had proved in various ways to be less than satisfactory. She'd taken over the garden; her coffee cake became a family favourite.

Cosmo, Cicily's husband, father of James and Julia, recalled at Mags's funeral his first meeting with her. He'd heard about her – rather a lot about her – ever since he'd known Cicily. The unfairness that had been meted out to Mags at school was something he had nodded sympathetically over; as well as over her ill-treatment at the hands of Robert Blakley, and the sudden and unexpected death of her mother, to whom she'd always been so devoted, and with whom, after the Robert Blakley affair, she had determined to make her life, her father having died when she was three. 'This is Mags,' Cicily had said one day in the Trocadero, where they were all about to lunch together, celebrating Cicily's and Cosmo's engagement. 'Hullo, Cosmo,' Mags had said, holding out a hand for him to shake. She did not much care for men he'd thought, gripping the hand and moving it slightly in a handshake. She was tall and rather angular, with black untidy hair and unplucked eyebrows. Her lips were a little chapped; she wore no make-up. It was because of Robert Blakley, he'd thought, that she did not take to men. 'I've heard an awful lot about you, Mags,' he said, laughing. She declined a drink, falling instead into excited chat with Cicily, whose cheeks had pinkened with pleasure at the reunion. They talked about girls they'd known, and the dreadful Miss Harper, and Miss Roforth the headmistress. At Mags's funeral he remembered that surreptitiously he had asked the waiter to bring him another gin and tonic.

They were a noticeably good-looking family. Cosmo and Cicily, in their middle fifties, were grey-haired but stylishly so, and both of them retained the spare figures of their youth. Cosmo's noticeably blue eyes and his chiselled face had been bequeathed to his son; and Cicily's smile, her slightly slanting mouth and perfect nose had come to Julia. They all looked a little similar, the men of a certain height, the two women complementing it, the same fair colouring in all four. There was a lack of awkwardness in their movements, a natural easiness that had often caused strangers to wonder where Mags came in.

The coffin began to move, sliding towards beige curtains, which obediently parted. Flames would devour it, they all four thought simultaneously, Mags would become a handful of dust: a part of the family had been torn away. How, Julia wondered, would her parents manage now? To be on their own after so long would surely be a little strange.

They returned to Tudors, the house near Maidenhead where the family had always lived. It was a pleasant house, half-timbered, black and white, more or less in the country. Cosmo had been left it by an aunt at just the right moment, when he'd been at the beginning of his career in the rare-books world; Julia and James had been born there. Seeing Tudors for the first time, Mags had said she'd fallen in love with it.

After the funeral service they stood around in the long low-ceilinged sitting-room, glad that it was over. They didn't say much, and soon moved

off in two directions, the men to the garden, Cicily and Julia to the room
that had been Mags's bedroom. In an efficiently drawn-up will some of
her jewellery had been left to Julia and an eighteenth-century clock to
James. There'd been bequests for Cicily and Cosmo too, and some clothes
and money for Mrs Forde, the daily woman at Tudors.

'Her mother had that,' Cicily said, picking up an amber brooch, a dragon
with a gold setting. 'I think it's rather valuable.'

Julia held it in the palm of her hand, gazing at it. 'It's lovely,' she said.
It had been Mags's favourite piece, worn only on special occasions. Julia
could remember it on a blue blouse, polka-dotted with white. It seemed
unfair that Mags, the same age as her mother, should have died; Mags
who had done no harm to anyone. Having never been married or known
children of her own, it seemed that the least she deserved was a longer life.

'Poor old Mags,' her mother said, as if divining these thoughts.

'You'll miss her terribly.'

'Yes, we shall.'

In the garden Cosmo walked with his son, who happened in that moment
to be saying the same thing.

'Yes, Cicily'll miss her,' Cosmo replied. 'Dreadfully.'

'So'll you, Father.'

'Yes, I shall too.'

The garden was as pleasant as the house, running down to the river,
with japonica and escallonia now in bloom on a meadow bank. It was
without herbaceous borders, sheltered by high stone walls. Magnolias and
acers added colour to the slope of grass that stretched from wall to wall.
Later there'd be roses and broom. It was Mags who had planned the
arrangement of all these shrubs, who had organized the removal of some
cherry trees that weren't to her liking, and had every week in summer cut
the grass with her Flymo. It was generally agreed that her good taste had
given the garden character.

'There'd been some man, hadn't there?' James asked his father as they
stood on the bank of the river, watching pleasure boats go by.

'Robert Blakley. Oh, a long time ago.'

'But it left a mark?'

'Yes, it left a mark.'

In the room that had been Mags's bedroom Cicily said:

'Misfortune came easily to her. It somehow seemed quite expected that
Robert Blakley should let her down.'

'What did he do?'

'Just said he'd made a mistake and walked away.'

'Perhaps it was as well if he was like that.'

'I never liked him.'

It seemed to Cicily, and always had, that though misfortune had come easily to her friend it had never been deserved. The world had sinned against her without allowing her the joy of sinning. Ready-made a victim, she'd been supplied with no weapons that Cicily could see as useful in her own defence. The best thing that had happened in Mags's life might well have been their long friendship and Mags's involvement with the family.

Before lunch they all had a glass or two of sherry because they felt they needed it. It cheered them up, as the lunch itself did. But even so, as Julia said goodbye to her parents, she wondered again how well they'd manage now. She said as much to James as they drove away together in his car, the French clock carefully propped on the back seat, the jewellery in Julia's handbag. When all these years there'd been a triangular quality about conversation in Tudors, how would conversation now continue?

It would not continue, Cosmo thought. There would be silences in Tudors, for already he could feel them gathering. On summer weekends he would start the Flymo for Cicily; they would go as usual to the Borders in July. But as they perused the menu in the bar of the Glenview Hotel they'd dread the moment when the waiter took it from them, when they could put off no longer the conversation that eluded them. At Christmas it would be all right because, as usual, Julia and James and the children would come to Tudors, but in the bleak hours after they'd left the emptiness would have an awful edge. Mags had chattered so.

Changing out of the sober clothes she'd worn for the funeral, Cicily recalled a visit with Mags to Fenwick's. It was she who had suggested it, 1969 it must have been. 'I insist,' she'd said. 'Absolutely no arguments.' The fact was, Mags hadn't bought herself so much as a new scarf for years. As a girl, she'd always done her best, but living in Tudors, spending most of her day in the garden, she'd stopped bothering. 'And if Fenwick's haven't anything then we go to Jaeger's,' Cicily had insisted. 'We're going to spend the whole day sorting you out.' Mags of course had protested, but in the end had agreed. She was quite well off, having inherited a useful income from her mother; she could easily afford to splash out.

But in the event she didn't. In Fenwick's the saleswoman was rude. She shook her head repeatedly when Mags stood in front of a looking-glass, first in yellow and then in blue. 'Not entirely madam's style,' she decreed. 'More yours, madam,' she suggested to Cicily. In the end they'd left the shop without anything and instead of going on to Jaeger's went to Dickins and Jones for coffee. Mags wept, not noisily, not making a fuss. She cried with her head bent forward so that people wouldn't see. She apologized and then confessed that she hated shopping for clothes: it was always the same, it always went wrong. Saleswomen sighed when they saw her coming. Almost before she could open her mouth she became the victim of their tired feet.

They went to D. H. Evans that day and bought a dreary wool dress in a shade of granite. It made Mags look like an old-age pensioner. 'Really nice,' the saleswoman assured them. 'Really suits the lady.'

That was the trouble, Cicily reflected as she hung up the coat she'd worn for the funeral: Mags had never had the confidence to fight back. She should have pointed out to the saleswoman in Fenwick's that the choice was hers, that she didn't need to be told what her style was. She should have protested that Miss Harper was being unfair. She should have told Robert Blakley to go to hell. Mags had been far better-looking than she'd ever known. With decent make-up and decent clothes she could have been quite striking in her way.

Cicily brushed her hair, glancing at her own face in her dressing-table looking-glass. No saleswoman had ever dared to patronize her; her beauty saw to that. It was all so wretchedly unfair.

Later that day Cosmo sat in the small room he called his study, its walls lined with old books. He had drawn the curtains and turned on the green-shaded desk light. In the kitchen Cicily was preparing their supper, cold ham and salad, and a vegetable soup to cheer it up. He'd passed the kitchen door and seen her at it, 'Any Questions' on the wireless. It was his fault; he knew it was; for twenty-seven years, ever since Mags had become part of the family, it had been his fault. He should have had the wisdom to know: he should have said over his dead body or something strong like that. 'I don't care who she is or how she's suffered,' he should have insisted, 'she's not going to come and live with us.' But of course it hadn't been like that, because Mags had just drifted into the family. Anyone would have thought him mad if he'd suggested that with the passing years she'd consume his marriage.

'Cosmo. Supper.'

He called back, saying he was coming, already putting the moment off. He turned the desk light out but when he left his study he didn't go directly to the kitchen. 'I'm making up the fire,' he announced from the sitting-room, pouring himself a glass of whisky and quickly drinking it.

'Julia seemed well,' Cicily said, pushing the wooden bowl of salad across the kitchen table at him.

'Yes, she did.' It was singular in a way, he thought, that he and Cicily should have taken to their hearts a person who was, physically, so very much the opposite of them. Mags had been like a cuckoo in the midst of the handsome family, and he wondered if she'd ever noticed it, if she'd ever said to herself that it was typical of her tendency to misfortune to find herself so dramatically shown up. He wanted to talk to Cicily about that. They had to talk about everything. They had to clear the air; certainly they had to agree that they were at a beginning, that they could not just go on.

'I suppose it was her looks,' he said, aware that he was putting it clumsily, 'that in the end didn't appeal to Robert Blakley. I mean, not as much as he'd imagined.'

'Oh, he was a horrid man.'

'No, but I mean, Cicily –'

'I don't want to talk about Robert Blakley.'

Neatly she arranged ham and salad on her fork. Any time she wanted to, he thought, she could pick up an affair. Men still found her as worth a second look as they always had: you could see it at cocktail parties and on trains, or even walking with her on the street. He felt proud of her, and glad that she hadn't let herself go.

'No, I meant she wasn't much to look at ever,' he said.

'Poor Mags had far more than looks. Let's not dwell on this, Cosmo.'

'I think we have to, dear.'

'She's dead. Nothing we can say will bring her back.'

'It's not that kind of thing we have to talk about.'

'She wanted her clothes to go to Oxfam. Except what she left to Mrs Forde. I'll see to that tonight.'

When, seven years ago, Cosmo had had an affair with a girl in his office the guilt he might have felt had failed to come about. His unfaithfulness – the only occasion of it in his marriage – had not caused him remorse and heart-searching, as he'd expected it would. He did not return to Tudors after an afternoon with the girl to find himself wanting at once to confess to Cicily. Nor did he walk into a room and find Cicily seeming to be forlorn because she was being wronged and did not know it. He did not think of her, alone and even lonely, while he was with the girl. Such thoughts were unnecessary because Cicily was always all right, because there was always Mags. It had even occasionally seemed to him that she had Mags and he the girl.

Cosmo had never in any way objected to the presence of Mags in his house. She had made things easier all round, it was a mutually satisfactory arrangement. Even at the time of his office affair it had not occurred to him that her presence could possibly be designated as an error; and in all honesty she had never been a source of irritation to him. It was her death, her absence, that had brought the facts to light.

'We have to talk, you know,' he said, still eating ham and salad. 'There are all sorts of things to come to terms with.'

'Talk, Cosmo? What things? What do you mean?'

'We could have made a mistake, you know, having Mags here all these years.'

She frowned. She shook her head, more in bewilderment than denial. He said, 'I think we need to talk about it now.'

But Cicily wanted to be quiet. Immediately after supper she'd go through the clothes, arranging them for Oxfam, keeping back the things for Mrs Forde. She wanted to get it done as soon as possible. She remembered being in the sanatorium one time with Mags, both of them with measles. They'd talked for hours about what they'd like to do with their lives. She herself had at that time wanted to be a nurse. 'I want to have babies,' Mags had said. 'I want to marry a decent kind of man and have a house in the country somewhere and bring up children.'

'You see,' Cosmo was saying, 'there'll be a certain adjustment.'

She nodded, not really listening. Half of Mags's desire had come about: at least she'd lived in a house in the country and at least she'd brought up children, even if the children weren't her own. There still was a school photograph, she and Mags and a girl called Evie Hopegood sitting in the sun outside the library. Just after it had been taken Miss Harper had come along and given Mags a row for sprawling in her chair.

'Incidentally,' Cicily said, 'the man's coming to mend that window-sash tomorrow.'

Cosmo didn't reply. Perhaps this wasn't the right moment to pursue the matter. Perhaps in a day or two, when she'd become more used to the empty house, he should try again.

They finished their meal. He helped her to wash up, something that hadn't been necessary in the past. She went upstairs, he watched the television in the sitting-room.

Young men and girls were playing a game with tractor tyres. They were dressed in running shorts and singlets, one team's red, the other's yellow. Points were scored, a man with a pork-pie hat grimaced into the camera and announced the score. Another man breezed up, trailing a microphone. He placed an arm around the first man's shoulders and said that things were really hotting up. Huge inflated ducks appeared, the beginning of another game. Cosmo turned the television off.

He poured himself another drink. He was aware that he wanted to be drunk, which was, in other circumstances, a condition he avoided. He knew that in a day or two the conversation he wished to have would be equally difficult. He'd go on trying to have it and every effort would fail. He drank steadily, walking up and down the long, low-ceiling sitting-room, glancing out into the garden, where dusk was already gathering. He turned the television on again and found the young men and girls playing a game with buckets of coloured water. He changed the channel. 'I can't help being a lotus-eater,' a man was saying, while an elderly woman wept. Elsewhere Shipham's paste was being promoted.

'It's no good putting it off,' Cosmo said, standing in the doorway of the room that had been Mags's. He had filled his glass almost to the brim and then had added a spurt of soda water. 'We have to talk about our marriage, Cicily.'

She dropped a tweed skirt on to Mrs Forde's pile on the floor. She frowned, thinking she must have misheard. It was unlike him to drink after supper, or indeed before. He'd brought a strong smell of alcohol into the room, which for some reason offended her.

'Our marriage,' he repeated.

'What about it?'

'I've been trying to say, Cicily. I want to talk about it. Now that Mags is dead.'

'Whatever had poor Mags to do with it? And now that she *is* dead, how on earth –?'

'Actually she consumed it.'

He knew he was not sober, but he knew as well that he was telling the truth. He had a feeling that had been trying to surface for days, which finally had succeeded in doing so while he was watching the athletes with the tractor tyres: deprived of a marriage herself, Mags had lived off theirs. Had she also, he wondered, avenged herself without knowing it?

These feelings about Mags had intensified since he'd been watching the television show, and it now seemed to Cosmo that everything had been turned inside out by her death. He wondered if James and Julia, looking back one day on their parents' marriage, would agree that the presence of Mags in the house had been a mistake; he wondered if Cicily ever would.

'Consumed?' Cicily said. 'I wasn't aware –'

'We were neither of us aware.'

'I don't know why you're drinking whisky.'

'Cicily, I want to tell you: I had an affair with a girl seven years ago.'

She stared at him, her lips slightly parted, her eyes unblinking. Then she puckered up her forehead, frowning again.

'You never told me,' she said, feeling the protest to be absurd as soon as she'd made it.

'I have to tell you now, Cicily.'

She sat down on the bed that had been her friend's. His voice went on speaking, saying something about Mags always being there, mentioning the Glenview Hotel for some reason, mentioning Robert Blakley and saying that Mags had probably intended no ill-will.

'But you liked her,' she whispered. 'You liked her and what on earth had poor Mags –'

'I'm trying to say I'm sorry, Cicily.'

'Sorry?'

'I'm sorry for being unfaithful.'

'But how could I not know? How could you go off with someone else and I not notice anything?'

'I think because Mags was here.'

She closed her eyes, not wanting to see him, in the doorway with his whisky. It didn't make sense what he was saying. Mags was their friend; Mags had never in her life said a thing against him. It was unfair to bring Mags into it. It was ludicrous and silly, like trying to find an excuse.

' The whole thing,' he said, 'from start to finish is all my fault. I shouldn't have allowed Mags to be here, I should have known.'

She opened her eyes and looked across the room at him. He was standing exactly as he had been before, wretchedness in his face. 'You're making this up,' she said, believing that he must be, believing that for some reason he'd been jealous of Mags all these years and now was trying to revenge himself by inventing a relationship with some girl. He was not the kind to go after girls; he wasn't the kind to hurt people.

'No,' he said. 'I'm making nothing up.' The girl had wept when, in the end, he'd decreed that for her there was too little in it to justify their continuing the association. He'd felt about the girl the way he'd wanted to feel about being unfaithful to Cicily: guilty and ashamed and miserable.

'I can't believe it of you,' Cicily whispered, weeping as the girl had wept. 'I feel I'm in an awful nightmare.'

'I'm sorry.'

'My God, what use is saying you're sorry? We had a perfectly good marriage, we were a happy family –'

'My dear, I'm not denying that. All I'm saying –'

'All you're saying,' she cried out bitterly, 'is that none of it meant anything to you. Did you hate me? Did I repel you? Was she marvellous, this girl? Did she make you feel young again? My God, you hypocrite!'

She picked up from the bed a summer dress that had been Mags's, a pattern of checks in several shades of blue. She twisted it between her hands, but Cosmo knew that the action was involuntary, that she was venting her misery on the first thing that came to hand.

'It's the usual thing,' she said more quietly, 'for men in middle age.'

'Cicily –'

'Girls are like prizes at a fun-fair. You shoot a row of ducks and there's your girl with her child's complexion still, and her rosebud lips and eager breasts –'

'Please, Cicily –'

'Why shouldn't she have eager breasts, for God's sake? At least don't deny her her breasts or her milky throat, or her eyes that melted with love. Like a creature in a Sunday supplement, was she? Advertising vodka or tipped cigarettes, discovering herself with an older man. You fell in love with all that and you manage to blame a woman who's dead. Why not blame yourself, Cosmo? Why not simply say you wanted a change?'

'I do blame myself. I've told you I do.'

'Why didn't you marry your girl? Because James and Julia would have despised you? Because she wouldn't have you?'

He didn't reply, and a reply wasn't really expected. She was right when she mentioned their children. He'd known at the time of the affair that they would have despised him for making what they'd have considered to be a fool of himself, going off with a girl who was young enough to be his daughter.

'I want you to understand about Mags,' he said. 'There's something we have to talk about, it's all connected, Cicily. I should have felt sorry for you, but there was always you and Mags, chatting. I kept saying you were all right because you had Mags. I couldn't help it, Cicily.'

'Mags has nothing to do with it. Mags was always blamed by people, ill-used behind her back –'

'I know. I'm sorry. It simply appears to be true, it's hard to understand.'

She sobbed, seeming not to have heard him, still twisting the dress between her fingers. She whispered something but he couldn't hear what it was. He said:

'I'm telling you because I love you, Cicily. Because it can't be between us.'

But even as he spoke he wasn't certain that he still loved Cicily. There was something stale in their relationship, even a whiff of tedium. A happy ending would be that Cicily would find another man and he a girl as different from Cicily as the girl in his office had been. Why should they sit for the rest of their days in Tudors or the bar of the Glenview Hotel trying to make bricks without straw? What was the point, in middle age, of such a dreary effort?

In the room that had been Mags's the weeping of Cicily grew louder
and eventually she flung her head on to the pillow and pressed her face
into its softness in an effort to stifle her sobs. He looked around at the
familiar clothes – dresses and hats and skirts and blouses, pairs of shoes
lined up on the floor. At this age happy endings with other people weren't
two a penny, and for a moment he wondered if perhaps they had the
strength and the patience to blow life into a marriage with which they had
lost touch. He shook his head, still standing by the door while Cicily wept.
It was asking too much of her; how could she suddenly look back at every
cut knee Mags had bandaged, every cake she'd baked, every word she'd
spoken, and see them differently? How could she come to consider that
Mags, an innocent predator, had got her own back simply by being in their
house? Yet Cosmo knew that that was the truth. He and Cicily would try
for a bit because they had no option, but the disruption that Mags's modest
presence had so meticulously denied would creep all through their marriage
now, a victim's legacy from her victim's world.

The News from Ireland

Poor Irish Protestants is what the Fogartys are: butler and cook. They have church connections, and conversing with Miss Fogarty people are occasionally left with the impression that their father was a rural dean who suffered some misfortune: in fact he was a sexton. Fogarty is the younger and the smaller of the pair, brought up by Miss Fogarty, their mother dying young. His life was saved by his sister's nursing the time he caught scarlatina, when he was only eight.

Dapper in his butler's clothes, a slight and unimposing man with a hazelnut face, Fogarty is at present fascinated by the newly arrived governess: Anna Maria Heddoe, from somewhere in England, a young woman of principle and sensibility, stranger and visitor to Ireland. Fogarty is an educated man, and thinks of other visitors there have been: the Celts, whose ramshackle gypsy empire expired in this same landscape, St Patrick with his holy shamrock, the outrageous Vikings preceding the wily Normans, the adventurers of the Virgin Queen. His present employers arrived here also, eight years ago, in 1839. The Pulvertafts of Ipswich, as Fogarty thinks of them, and wishes they had not bothered to make the journey after old Hugh Pulvertaft died. House and estate fell away under the old man, and in Fogarty's opinion it is a pity the process didn't continue until everything was driven back into the clay it came from. Instead of which along had come the Pulvertafts of Ipswich, taking on more staff, clearing the brambles from the garden in their endeavour to make the place what it had been in the past, long before the old man's time. The Pulvertafts of Ipswich belong here now. They make allowances for the natives, they come to terms, they learn to live with things. Fogarty has watched surprise and dismay fade from their faces. He has watched these people becoming important locally, and calling the place they have come to 'home'. Serving them in the dining-room, holding for them a plate of chops or hurrying to them a gravy dish, he wishes he might speak the truth as it appears to him: that their fresh, decent blood is the blood of the invader though they are not themselves invaders, that they perpetrate theft without being thieves. He does not dislike the Pulvertafts of Ipswich, he has nothing against them beyond the fact that they did not stay where they were. He and his sister might alone have attended the mouldering of the place, urging it back to the clay.

The governess is interesting to Fogarty because she is another of the strangers whom the new Pulvertafts have gathered around them in their advent. Such visitors, in the present and in the past, obsess the butler. He observes Miss Heddoe daily; he studies her closely and from a distance, but he does not reveal his obsession to his sister, who would consider it peculiar. He carries Miss Heddoe's meals to her room when normally this duty would be Cready's or Brigid's; he reads the letters she receives, and the diary she intermittently keeps.

October 15th, 1847. I look out of the window of my attic room, and in the early morning the men are already labouring on the road that is to encircle the estate. The estate manager, the one-armed Mr Erskine, oversees them from his horse. Mr Pulvertaft rides up, gesturing about some immediate necessity – how a particular shrub must be avoided, so his gestures suggest, or where best to construct a bridge. The estate manager listens and assents, his men do not cease in their work. Beyond the trees, beyond the high stone walls of the estate, women and children die of the hunger that God has seen fit to visit upon them. In my prayers I ask for mercy.

October 17th, 1847. Fogarty came in with my dinner on a tray and said that the marks of the stigmata had been discovered on a child.

'Is the child alive?' I demanded when he returned a half-hour later for the tray.

'Oh yes, miss. No doubt on that. The living child was brought to Father Horan.'

I was amazed but he seemed hardly surprised. I questioned him but he was vague; and the conversation continuing because he lingered, I told him the Legend of the True Cross, with which he was unfamiliar. He was delighted to hear of its elaborations, and said he would recount these in the kitchen. The stigmata on the child have been revealed on feet and hands only, but the priest has said that other parts of the body must be watched. The priest has cautiously given an opinion: that so clearly marked a stigma has never before been known in Ireland. The people consider it a miracle, a sign from God in these distressful times.

October 20th, 1847. I am not happy here. I do not understand this household, neither the family nor the servants. This is the middle of my third week, yet I am still in all ways at a loss. Yesterday, in the afternoon, I was for the first time summoned to the drawing-room to hear Adelaide play her pieces, and George Arthur's lessons being over for the day he sat by me, as naturally he should. Charlotte and her mother occupied the sofa,

Emily a chair in a recess. Mr Pulvertaft stood toasting his back at the fire, his riding-crop tapping time on the side of his polished boot. They made a handsome family picture – Emily beautiful, Charlotte petite and pretty, the plump motherliness of Mrs Pulvertaft, her husband's ruddy presence. I could not see George Arthur's features, for he was a little in front of me, but I knew them well from the hours I have surveyed them across our lessons-table. He is bright-faced, and dark like all the family except Mrs Pulvertaft, whose hair I would guess was red before becoming grey. Only Adelaide, bespectacled and seeming heavy for her age, does not share the family's gift of grace. Poor Adelaide is cumbersome; her movements are awkward at the piano and she really plays it most inelegantly.

Yet in the drawing-room no frown or wince betrayed the listeners' ennui. As though engrossed in a performance given by a fine musician, Mr Pulvertaft slightly raised and dropped his riding-crop, as he might a baton; similarly expressing absorption, his wife's lips were parted, the hurry and worry of her nature laid aside, her little eyes delighted. And Emily and Charlotte sat as girls more graciously endowed than a plain sister should, neither pouting nor otherwise recoiling from the halting cacophony. I too – I hope successfully – forced delight into an expression that constantly sought to betray me, while surreptitiously examining my surroundings. (I cannot be certain of what passed, or did not pass, over George Arthur's features: in the nursery, certainly, he is not slow to display displeasure.)

The drawing-room is lofty and more than usually spacious, with pleasant recesses, and french windows curving along a single wall. Two smaller windows flank the fireplace, which is of white marble that reflects, both in colour and in the pattern of its carving, the white plasterwork of the ceiling. Walls are of an apricot shade, crowded with landscape scenes and portraits of the Pulvertafts who belong to the past. Silks and velvets are mainly green; escritoires and occasional tables are cluttered with ornaments and porcelain pieces – too many for my own taste, but these are family heirlooms which it would be impolite to hide away. So Mrs Pulvertaft has explained, for the same degree of overcrowding obtains in the hall and dining-room, and on the day of my arrival she remarked upon it.

'*Most* charmingly rendered,' her husband pronounced when the music ceased. 'What fingers Adelaide is blessed with!'

Hands in the drawing-room were delicately clapped. Mr Pulvertaft applauded with his riding-crop. I pursed my lips at the back of George Arthur's head, for he was perhaps a little rumbustious in his response.

'Is not Adelaide talented, Miss Heddoe?' Mrs Pulvertaft suggested.

'Indeed, ma'am.'

Two maids, Cready and Brigid, brought in tea. I rose to go, imagining my visit to the drawing-room must surely now be concluded. But Mrs Pulvertaft begged me to remain.

'We must get to know you, Miss Heddoe,' she insisted in her bustling manner. (It is from his mother, I believe, that George Arthur inherits his occasional boisterousness.) 'And you,' she added, 'us.'

I felt, to tell the truth, that I knew the Pulvertafts fairly well already. I was not long here before I observed that families and events are often seen historically in Ireland – more so, for some reason, than in England. It surprised me when Mrs Pulvertaft went into details soon after I arrived, informing me that on the death of a distant relative Mr Pulvertaft had found himself the inheritor of this overseas estate. Though at first he had apparently resisted the move to another country, he ended by feeling it his bounden duty to accept the responsibility. 'It was a change of circumstances for us, I can tell you that,' Mrs Pulvertaft confessed. 'But had we remained in Ipswich these many acres would have continued to lose heart. There have been Pulvertafts here, you know, since Queen Elizabeth granted them the land.' I thought, but did not remark, that when Mr Pulvertaft first looked upon drawings of the house and gardens his unexpected inheritance must have seemed like a gift from heaven, which in a sense it was, for the distant relative had been by all accounts a good man.

'Much undergrowth has yet to be cleared and burnt,' Mr Pulvertaft was saying now, with reference to the estate road that was being built. 'The merry fires along the route will continue for a while to come. Next, stones must be chipped and laid, and by the lakeside the ground raised and strengthened. Here and there we must have ornamental seats.'

Cake was offered to us by Cready and by Brigid. It was not my place in the drawing-room to check the manners of George Arthur, but they do leave much to be desired. Old Miss Larvey, who was my predecessor and governess to all four children, had clearly become slack before her death. I smiled a little at George Arthur, and was unable to resist moving my fingers slightly in his direction, a gesture to indicate that a more delicate consuming of the cake would not be amiss. He pretended, mischievously, not to notice.

'Will the road go round Bright Purple Hill?' Emily inquired. 'It would be beautiful if it did.'

It could be made to do so, her father agreed. Yes, certainly it could go round the northern slopes at least. He would speak to Erskine.

'Now, what could be nicer,' he resumed, 'than a picnic of lunch by the lake, then a drive through the silver birches, another pause by the abbey, continuing by the river for a mile, and home by Bright Purple Hill? This road, Miss Heddoe, has become my pride.'

I smiled and nodded, acknowledging this attention in silence. I knew that there was more to the road than that: its construction was an act of charity, a way of employing the men for miles around, since the failure of their potato crops had again reduced them to poverty and idleness. In years to come the road would stand as a memorial to this awful time, and Mr Pulvertaft's magnanimity would be recalled with gratitude.

'Might copper beech trees mark the route?' suggested Adelaide, her dumpling countenance freshened by the excitement this thought induced. Her eyes bulged behind her spectacles and I noticed that her mother, in glancing at her, resisted the impulse to sigh.

'Beech trees indeed! Quite splendid!' enthused Mr Pulvertaft. 'And in future Pulvertaft generations they shall arch a roof, shading our road when need be. Yes, indeed there must be copper beech trees.'

The maids had left the drawing-room and returned now with lamps. They fastened the shutters and drew the curtains over. The velvets and silks changed colour in the lamplight, the faces of the portraits became as they truly were, the faces of ghosts.

A silence gathered after the talk of beech trees, and I found myself surprised at no one mentioning the wonder Fogarty had told me of, the marks of Christ on a peasant child. It seemed so strange and so remarkable, an occurrence of such import and magnitude, that I would hardly have believed it possible that any conversation could take place in the house without some astonished reference to it. Yet none had been made, and the faces and the voices in the drawing-room seemed as untouched by this visitation of the miraculous as they had been by Adelaide's labouring on the piano. In the silence I excused myself and left, taking George Arthur with me, for my time to do so had come.

October 23rd, 1847. I am homesick, I make no bones about it. I cannot help dwelling on all that I have left behind, on familiar sounds and places. First thing when I awake I still imagine I am in England: reality comes most harshly then.

While I write, Emily and George Arthur are conversing in a corner of the nursery. She has come here, as she does from time to time, to persuade him against a military career. I wish she would not do so in this manner, wandering in and standing by the window to await the end of a lesson. It is distracting for George Arthur, and after all this is my domain.

'What I mean, George Arthur, is that it is an uncomfortable life in a general sort of way.'

'Captain Coleborne does not seem uncomfortable. When you look at him he doesn't give that impression in the least.'

'Captain Coleborne hasn't lived in a barracks in India. That leaves a mark, so people say.'

'I should not mind a barracks. And India I should love.'

'I doubt it, actually. Flies carry disease in India, the water you drink is putrid. And you would mind a barracks because they're rough and ready places.'

'You'd drink something else if the water was putrid. You'd keep well away from the flies.'

'You cannot in India. No, George Arthur, I assure you you enjoy your creature comforts. You'd find the uniform rough on your skin and the food unappetizing. Besides, you have a family duty here.'

The nursery is a long, low-ceilinged room, with a fire at one end, close to which I sit as I write, for the weather has turned bitter. The big, square lessons-table occupies the centre of the room, and when Fogarty brings my tray he places it on the smaller table at which I'm writing now. There are pictures on the walls which I must say I find drab: one, in shades of brown, of St George and the Dragon; another of a tower; others of farmyard scenes. The nursery's two armchairs, occupied now by George Arthur and Emily, are at the other end with a rug between them. The floor is otherwise of polished board.

'Well, the truth is, George Arthur, I cannot bear the thought of your being killed.'

With that, Emily left the nursery. She smiled in her graceful manner at me, her head a little to one side, her dark, coiled hair gleaming for a moment in a shaft of afternoon sun. I had not thought a governess's position was difficult in a household, but somehow I am finding it so. I belong neither with the family nor the servants. Fogarty, in spite of calling me 'miss', addresses me more casually than he does the Pulvertafts; his sister is scarcely civil.

'Do they eat their babies, like in the South Seas?' George Arthur startled me by asking. He had crossed to where I sat and in a manner reminiscent of his father stood with his back to the fire, thereby blocking its warmth from me.

'Do who eat their babies, George Arthur?'

'The poor people.'

'Of course they don't.'

'But they are hungry. They have been hungry for ever so long. My mother and sisters give out soup at the back gate-lodge.'

'Hungry people do not eat their babies. And I think, you know, it's enemies, not babies, who are eaten in the South Seas.'

'But suppose a family's baby *did* die and suppose the family was hungry –'

'No, George Arthur, you must not talk like that.'

'Fogarty says he would not be surprised.'

'Well, she has settled down, I think,' Mrs Pulvertaft remarks to her husband in their bedroom, and when he asks her whom she refers to she says the governess.

'Pleasant enough, she seems,' he replies. 'I do prefer, you know, an English governess.'

'Oh yes, indeed.'

George Arthur's sisters have developed no thoughts about Miss Heddoe. They neither like nor dislike her; they do not know her; their days of assessing governesses are over.

But George Arthur's aren't. She is not as pretty as Emily or Charlotte, George Arthur considers, and she is very serious. When she smiles her smile is serious. The way she eats her food is serious, carefully cutting everything, carefully and slowly chewing. Often he comes into the nursery to find her eating from the tray that Fogarty carries up the back staircase for her, sitting all alone on one side of the fireplace, seeming very serious indeed. Miss Larvey had been different somehow, although she'd eaten her meals in much the same position, seated at the very same table, by the fire. Miss Larvey was untidy, her grey hair often working loose from its coils, her whole face untidy sometimes, her tray untidily left.

'Now it is transcription time,' Miss Heddoe says, interrupting these reflections. 'Carefully and slowly, please.'

Fogarty thinks about the governess, but hides such thoughts from his sister. Miss Heddoe will surely make a scene, exclaiming and protesting, saying to the Pulvertafts all the things a butler cannot. She will stand in the drawing-room or the hall, smacking out the truth at them, putting in a nutshell all that must be said. She will bring up the matter of the stigmata found on the child, and the useless folly of the road, and the wisdom of old Hugh Pulvertaft. She will be the voice of reason. Fogarty dwells upon these thoughts while conversing with his sister, adept at dividing his mind. His faith is in the governess.

'Declare to God,' remarks Miss Fogarty, 'Brigid'll be the death of me. Did you ever know a stupider girl?'

'There was a girl we had once who was stupider,' Fogarty replies. 'Fidelma was she called?'

They sit at the wide wooden table that is the pivot of kitchen activities. The preparation of food, the polishing of brass and silver, the stacking of dishes, the disposal of remains, the eating and drinking, all card-playing and ironing, all cutting out of patterns and cloth, the trimming of lamps: the table has as many uses as the people of the kitchen can devise. Tears have soaked into its grain, and blood from meat and accidents; the grease of generations polishes it, not quite scrubbed out by the efforts made, twice every day, with soap and water.

The Fogartys sit with their chairs turned a little away from the table, so that they partly face the range and in anticipation of the benefit they will shortly receive from the glow of dampened slack. It is their early evening pose, daily the same from October to May. In summer the sunlight penetrates to the kitchen in a way that at first seems alien but later is welcomed. It spreads over the surface of the table, drying it out. It warms the Fogartys, who move their chairs to catch its rays when they rest in the early evening.

'You would not credit,' remarks Miss Fogarty, 'that Brigid has been three years in this kitchen. More like three seconds.'

'There are some that are untrainable.' His teeth are less well preserved than his sister's. She is the thinner of the two, razorlike in face and figure.

'I said at the time I would prefer a man. A man is more trainable in my opinion. A man would be more use to yourself.'

'Ah, Cready knows the dining-room by now. I wouldn't want a change made there.'

'It's Cready we have to thank for Brigid. Wasn't it Cready who had you blackguarded until you took her on?'

'We had to take someone. To give Cready her due she said we'd find her slow.'

'I'll tell you this: Cready's no racehorse herself.'

'The slowness is in that family.'

'Whatever He did He forgot to put brains in them.'

'We live with His mistakes.'

Miss Fogarty frowns. She does not care for that remark. Her brother is sometimes indiscreet in his speech. It is his nature, it is part of his cleverness; but whenever she feels uneasy she draws his attention to the source of her uneasiness, as she does now. It is a dangerous remark, she says, better it had not been made.

Fogarty nods, knowing the nod will soothe her. He has no wish to have her flurried.

'The road is going great guns,' he says, deeming a change of subject wise. 'They were on about it in the dining-room.'

'Did they mention the ground rice pudding?'

'They ate it. Isn't it extraordinary, a road that goes round in a circle, not leading anywhere?'

'Heddoe left her ground rice. A pudding's good enough for the dining-room but not for Madam.'

'Was there an egg in it? Her stomach can't accept eggs.'

'Don't I know the woman can't take eggs? Isn't she on about it the entire time? There were four good turkey eggs in that pudding, and what harm did a turkey egg do anyone? Did eggs harm Larvey?'

'Oh true enough, Larvey ate anything. If you'd took a gate off its hinges she'd have ate it while you'd wink.'

'Larvey was a saint from heaven.'

Again Fogarty nods. In his wish not to cause flurry in his sister he refrains from saying that once upon a time Miss Larvey had been condemned as roundly as Miss Heddoe is now. When she'd been cold in her room she'd sent down to the kitchen for hot-water jars, a request that had not been popular. But when she died, as if to compensate for all this troublesomeness, Miss Larvey left the Fogartys a remembrance in her will.

'A while back I told Heddoe about that child. To see what she'd say for herself.'

Miss Fogarty's peaked face registers interest. Her eyes have narrowed into the slits that all his life have reminded Fogarty of cracks in a plate or a teacup.

'And what did the woman say?'

'She was struck silent, then she asked me questions. After that she told me an extraordinary thing: the Legend of the True Cross.'

As Fogarty speaks, the two maids enter the kitchen. Miss Fogarty regards them with asperity, telling Brigid she looks disgraceful and Cready that her cap is dirty. 'Get down to your work,' she snappishly commands. 'Brigid, push that kettle over the heat and stir a saucepan of milk for me.'

She is badly out of sorts because of Heddoe and the ground rice, Fogarty says to himself, and thinks to ease the atmosphere by relating the legend the governess has told him.

'Listen to me, girls,' he says, 'while I tell you the Legend of the True Cross.'

Cready, who is not a girl, appreciates the euphemism and displays appropriate pleasure as she sets to at the sink, washing parsnips. She is a woman of sixty-one, carelessly stout. Brigid, distantly related to her and thirty or so years younger, is of the same proportions.

'The Legend of the True Cross,' says Fogarty, 'has to do with a seed falling into Adam's mouth, some say his ear. It lay there until he died, and when the body decomposed a tree grew from the seed, which in time was felled to give timber for the beams of a bridge.'

'Well, I never heard that,' exclaims Cready in a loud, shrill voice, so fascinated by the revelation that she cannot continue with the parsnips.

'The Queen of Sheba crossed that bridge in her majesty. Later – well, you can guess – the Cross to which Our Lord was fastened was constructed from those very beams.'

'Is it true, Mr Fogarty?' cries Cready, her voice becoming still shriller in her excitement, her mouth hanging open.

'Control yourself, Cready,' Miss Fogarty admonishes her. 'You look ridiculous.'

'It's only I was never told it before, miss. I never knew the Cross grew out of Adam's ear. Did ever you hear it, Brigid?'

'I did not.'

'It's a legend,' Fogarty explains. 'It illustrates the truth. It does not tell it, Miss Fogarty and myself would say. Your own religion might take it differently.'

'Don't you live and learn?' says Cready.

There is a silence for some moments in the kitchen. Then Brigid, stirring the saucepan of milk on the range as Miss Fogarty has instructed her, says:

'I wonder does Father Horan know that?'

'God, I'd say he would all right.' Cready wags her head, lending emphasis to this opinion. There isn't much relating to theological matters that eludes Father Horan, she says.

'Oh, right enough,' agrees Fogarty. 'The priests will run this country yet. If it's not one crowd it's another.' He explains to the maids that the Legend of the True Cross has come into the house by way of the governess. It is a typical thing, he says, that a Protestant Englishwoman would pass the like of that on. Old Hugh wouldn't have considered it suitable; and the present Pulvertafts have been long enough away from England to consider it unsuitable also. He'd guess they have anyway; he'd consider that true.

Miss Fogarty, still idle in her chair by the range, nods her agreement. She states that, legend or not, she does not care for stuff like that. In lower tones, and privately to her brother, she says she is surprised that he repeated it.

'It's of interest to the girls,' he apologizes. 'To tell the truth, you could have knocked me down when she told me in the nursery.'

*

'The boulders from the ridge may be used for walls and chipping?' inquires Mr Pulvertaft of his estate manager.

'It is a distance to carry boulders, sir.'

'So it is, but we must continue to occupy these men, Erskine. Time is standing still for them.'

'Yes, sir.'

The two men pace together on a lawn in front of the house, walking from one circular rose-bed to the next, then turning and reversing the procedure. It is here that Mr Pulvertaft likes to discuss the estate with Erskine, strolling on the short grass in the mid-morning. When it rains or is too bitterly cold they converse instead in the great open porch of the house, both of them gazing out into the garden. The eyes of Mr Pulvertaft and Erksine never meet, as if by unspoken agreement. Mr Pulvertaft, though speaking warmly of Erskine's virtues, fears him; and Erskine does not trust his eye to meet his master's in case that conjunction, however brief, should reveal too much. Mr Pulvertaft has been a painless inheritor, in Erskine's view; his life has been without hardship, he takes too easily for granted the good fortune that came his way.

'The road,' he is saying now, seeming to Erskine to make his point for him, 'is our generation's contribution to the estate. You understand me, Erskine? A Pulvertaft planted Abbey Wood, another laid out these gardens. Swift came here, did you know that, Erskine? The Mad Dean assisted in the planning of all these lawns and shrubberies.'

'So you told me, sir.'

It is Erskine's left arm that is missing but he considers the loss as serious as if it had been his right. He is an Englishman, stoutly made and once of renowned strength, still in his middle age. His temper is short, his disposition unsentimental, his soldier's manner abrupt; nor is there, beneath that vigorous exterior, a gentler core. Leading nowhere, without a real purpose, the estate road is unnecessary and absurd, but he accepts his part in its creation. It is ill fortune that people have starved because a law of nature has failed them, it is ill fortune that he has lost a limb and seen a military career destroyed: all that must be accepted also. To be the manager of an estate of such size and importance is hardly recompense for the glories that might have been. He has ended up in a country that is not his own, employing men whose speech he at first found difficult to understand, collecting rents from tenants he does not trust, as he feels he might trust the people of Worcestershire or Durham. The Pulvertaft family – with the exception of Mr Pulvertaft himself – rarely seek to hold with him any kind of conversation beyond the formalities of greeting and leave-taking. Stoically he occupies his position, ashamed because he is a one-armed man, yet never indulging in melancholy, for this he would condemn as weakness.

'There is something concerning the men, sir.'

'Poor fellows, there is indeed.'

'Something other, sir. They have turned ungrateful, sir.'

'Ungrateful?'

'As well to keep an eye open for disaffection, sir.'

'Good God, those men are hardly fit for that.'

'They bite the hand that feeds them, sir. They're reared on it.'

He speaks in a matter-of-fact voice. It is the truth as he recognizes it; he sees no point in dissembling for politeness' sake. He watches while Mr Pulvertaft nods his reluctant agreement. He does not need to remind himself that this is a landowner who would have his estate a realm of heaven, who would have his family and his servants, his tenants and all who work for him, angels of goodness. This is a landowner who expects his own generosity of spirit to beget such generosity in others, his unstinted patronage to find a reflection in unstinted gratitude. But reality, as Erskine daily experiences, keeps shattering the dream, and may shatter it irrevocably in the end.

They speak of other matters, of immediate practicalities. Expert and informed on all the subjects raised, Erskine gives the conversation only part of his attention, devoting the greater part to the recently arrived governess. He has examined her in church on the four occasions there have been since she joined the household. Twenty-five or -six years old, he reckons, not pretty yet not as plain as the plain one among the Pulvertaft girls. Hair too severely done, features too nervous, clothes too dowdy; but all that might be altered. The hands that hold the hymn book open before her are pale as marble, the fingers slender; the lips that open and close have a hint of voluptuousness kept in check; the breast that rises and falls has caused him, once or twice, briefly to close his eyes. He would marry her if she would have him, and why should she not, despite the absence of an arm? As the estate manager's wife she would have a more significant life than as a governess for ever.

'Well, I must not detain you longer,' Mr Pulvertaft says. 'The men are simple people, remember, rough in their ways. They may find gratitude difficult and, you know, I do not expect it. I only wish to do what can be done.'

Erskine, who intends to permit no nonsense, does not say so. He strides off to where his horse is tethered in the paddocks, wondering again about the governess.

*

Stout and round, Mrs Pulvertaft lies on her bed with her eyes closed. She feels a familiar discomfort low down in her stomach, on the left side, a touch of indigestion. It is very slight, something she has become used to, arriving as it does every day in the afternoon and then going away.

Charlotte will accept Captain Coleborne; Adelaide will not marry; Emily wishes to travel. Perhaps if she travels she will meet someone suitable; she is most particular. Mrs Pulvertaft cannot understand her eldest daughter's desire to visit France and Austria and Italy. They are dangerous places, where war is waged when offence is taken. Only England is not like that: dear, safe, uncomplicated England, thinks Mrs Pulvertaft, and for a moment is nostalgic.

The afternoon discomfort departs from her stomach, but she does not notice because gradually it has become scarcely anything at all. George Arthur must learn the ways of the estate so that he can sensibly inherit when his own time comes. Emily is right: it would be far better if he did not seek a commission. After all, except to satisfy his romantic inclination, there is no need.

Mrs Pulvertaft sighs. She hopes Charlotte will be sensible. An officer's wife commands a considerable position when allied with means, and she has been assured that Captain Coleborne's family, established for generations in Meath, leave nothing whatsoever to be desired socially. It is most unlikely that Charlotte will be silly since everything between her and Captain Coleborne appears to be going swimmingly, but then you never know: girls, being girls, are naturally inexperienced.

Mrs Pulvertaft dozes, and wakes a moment later. The faces of the women who beg on Sundays have haunted a brief dream. She has heard the chiming of the church bell and in some confused way the Reverend Poole's cherub face was among the women's, his surplice flapping in the wind. She stepped from the carriage and went towards the church. 'Give something to the beggars,' her husband's voice commanded, as it does every Sunday while the bell still rings. The bell ceases only when the family are in their pew, with Mr Erskine in the Pulvertaft pew behind them and the Fogartys and Miss Heddoe in the estate pew in the south transept.

It is nobody's fault, Mrs Pulvertaft reflects, that for the second season the potatoes have rotted in the ground. No one can be blamed. It is a horror that so many families have died, that so many bloated, poisoned bodies are piled into the shared graves. But what more can be done than is already being done? Soup is given away in the yard of the gate-lodge; the estate road gives work; the Distress Board is greatly pleased. Just and sensible laws prevent the wholesale distribution of corn, for to flood the country with corn would have consequences as disastrous as the hunger itself: that has been explained to her. Every Sunday, led by the Reverend Poole, they repeat the prayer that takes precedence over all other prayers: that God's love should extend to the hungry at this time, that His wrath may be lifted.

Again Mrs Pulvertaft drifts into a doze. She dreams that she runs through unfamiliar landscape, although she has not run anywhere for many years. There are sand dunes and a flat expanse which is empty, except for tiny white shells, crackling beneath her feet. She seems to be naked, which is alarming, and worries her in her dream. Then everything changes and she is in the drawing-room, listening to Adelaide playing her pieces. Tea is brought in, and there is ordinary conversation.

Emily, alone, walks among the abbey ruins on the lake-shore. It is her favourite place. She imagines the chanting of the monks once upon a time and the simple life they led, transcribing Latin and worshipping God. They built where the landscape was beautiful; their view of Bright Purple Hill had been perfect.

There is a stillness among the ruins, the air is mild for late October. The monks would have fished from the shore, they would have cultivated a garden and induced bees to make honey for them. For many generations they would have buried their dead here, but their graveyards have been lost in the time that has passed.

Evening sun bronzes the heathery purple of the hill. In the spring, Emily reflects, she will begin her journeys. She will stay with her Aunt Margaret in Bath and her Aunt Tabby in Ipswich. Already she has persuaded her Aunt Margaret that it would be beneficial to both of them to visit Florence, and Vienna and Paris. She has persuaded her father that the expense of all the journeys would be money profitably spent, an education that would extend the education he has expended money on already. Emily believes this to be true; she is not prevaricating. She believes that after she has seen again the architecture of England – which she can scarcely remember – and visited the great cities of Europe, some anxious spirit within her will be assuaged. She will return to Ireland and accept a husband, as Charlotte is about to do; or not accept a husband and be content to live her life in her brother's house, as Adelaide's fate seems certainly to be. She will bear children; or walk among the abbey ruins a spinster, composing verse about the ancient times and the monks who fished in the lake.

A bird swoops over the water and comes to rest on the pebbled shore, not far from where Emily stands. It rises on spindly legs, stretches out its wings and pecks at itself. Then it staggers uncomfortably on the pebbles before settling into an attitude that pleases it, head drawn into its body, wings wrapped around like a cloak. Such creatures would not have changed since the time of the monks, and Emily imagines a cowled and roughly bearded figure admiring the bird from a window of the once gracious abbey. He whispers as he does so and Emily remembers enough from her lessons with Miss Larvey to know that the language he speaks is not known to her.

It is a pleasant fancy, one for verse or drawing, to be stored away and one day in the future dwelt upon, and in one way or the other transcribed to paper. She turns her back on the lake and walks slowly through the ruins, past the posts which mark the route of the estate road, by the birchwood and over the stone bridge where Jonathan Swift is said to have stood and ordered the felling of three elms that obscured the panorama which has the great house as its centre. In the far distance she can see the line of men labouring on the road, and the figure of Erskine on his horse. She passes on, following a track that is familiar to her, which skirts the estate beneath its high boundary wall. Beyond the wall lie the Pulvertaft acres of farmland, but they have no interest for Emily, being for the most part flat, a territory that is tediously passed over every Sunday on the journey to and from church.

She reaches the yard of a gate-lodge and speaks to the woman who lives there, reminding her that soup and bread will be brought again tomorrow, that the utensils left last week must be ready by eleven o'clock on the trestle tables. Everything will be waiting, the woman promises, and a high fire alight in the kitchen.

October 31st, 1847. Fogarty told me. He stood beside me while I ate my dinner by the fire: stew and rice, with cabbage; a baked apple, and sago pudding. The child with the stigmata has died and been buried.

'And who will know now,' he questioned, himself as much as me, 'exactly what was what?'

There is a kind of cunning in Fogarty's nutlike face. The eyes narrow, and the lips narrow, and he then looks like his sister. But he is more intelligent, I would say.

'And what *is* what, Mr Fogarty?' I inquired.

'The people are edgy, miss. At the soup canteen they are edgy, I'm to understand. And likewise on the road. There is a feeling among them that the child should not have died. It is unpleasant superstition, of course, but there is a feeling that Our Lord has been crucified again.'

'But that's ridiculous!'

'I am saying so, miss. Coolly ridiculous, everything back to front. The trouble is that starvation causes a lightness in the head.'

'Do the Pulvertafts know of this? No one but you has mentioned this child to me.'

'I heard the matter mentioned at the dinner table. Mr Pulvertaft said that Mr Erskine had passed on to him the news that there was some superstition about. "D'you know its nature, Fogarty?" Mr Pulvertaft said, and I replied that it was to do with the marks of Our Lord's stigmata being noticed on the feet and hands of a child.'

'And what did anyone say then?'

' "Well, what's the secret of it, Fogarty?" Mr Pulvertaft said, and I passed on to him the opinion of Miss Fogarty and myself: that the markings were inflicted at the time of birth. They had all of them reached that conclusion also: Mrs Pulvertaft and Miss Emily and Miss Charlotte and Miss Adelaide, even Master George Arthur, no doubt, although he was not present then. As soon as ever they heard the news they had come to that assumption. Same with Mr Erskine.'

I stared, astonished, at the butler. I could not believe what he was telling me: that all these people had independently dismissed, so calmly and so finally, what the people who were closer to the event took to be a miracle. I had known, from the manner in which Fogarty spoke after his introduction of the subject, that he was in some way dubious. But I had concluded that he doubted the existence of the marks, that he doubted the reliability of the priest. I had never seen Father Horan, so did not know what kind of man he was even in appearance, or what age. Fogarty had told me he'd never seen him either, but from what he gathered through the maids the priest was of advanced years. Fogarty said now:

'My sister and I only decided that that was the truth of it after Cready and Brigid had gone on about the thing for a long time, how the priest was giving out sermons on it, how the bishop had come on a special journey and how a letter had been sent to Rome. Our first view was that the old priest had been presented with the child after he'd had a good couple of glasses. And then oiled up again and shown the child a second time. He's half blind, I've heard it said, and if enough people raved over marks that didn't exist, sure wouldn't he agree instead of admitting he was drunk and couldn't see properly? But as soon as Miss Fogarty and myself heard that the bishop had stirred his stumps and a letter had gone to Rome we realized the affair was wearing a different pair of shoes. They're as wily as cockroaches, these old priests, and there isn't one among them who'd run a chance of showing himself up by giving out sermons and summoning his bishop. He'd have let the matter rest, he'd have kept it local if he was flummoxed. "No doubt at all," Miss Fogarty said. "They've put marks on the baby." '

I couldn't eat. I shivered even though I was warm from the fire. I found it difficult to speak, but in the end I said:

'But why on earth would this cruel and blasphemous thing be done? Surely it could have been real, truly there, as stigmata have occurred in the past?'

'I would doubt that, miss. And hunger would give cruelty and blasphemy a different look. That's all I'd say. Seven other children have been buried in that family, and the two sets of grandparents. There was only the father and the mother with the baby left. "Sure didn't they see the way things was turning?" was how Miss Fogarty put it. "Didn't they see an RIP all ready for them, and wouldn't they be a holy family with the baby the way they'd made it, and wouldn't they be sure of preservation because of it?"'

In his dark butler's clothes, the excitement that enlivened his small face lending him a faintly sinister look, Fogarty smiled at me. The smile was grisly; I did not forgive it, and from that moment I liked the butler as little as I liked his sister. His smile, revealing sharp, discoloured teeth, was related to the tragedy of a peasant family that had been almost extinguished, as, one by one, lamps are in a house at night. It was related to the desperation of survival, to an act so barbarous that one could not pass it by.

'A nine days' wonder,' Fogarty said. 'I'd say it wasn't a bad thing the child was buried. Imagine walking round with a lie like that on you for all your mortal days.'

He took the tray and went away. I heard him in the lavatory off the nursery landing, depositing the food I hadn't eaten down the WC so that he wouldn't have to listen to his sister's abuse of me. I sat until the fire sank low, without the heart to put more coal on it even though the coal was there. I kept seeing that faceless couple and their just-born child, the woman exhausted, in pain, tormented by hunger, with no milk to give her baby. Had they touched the tiny feet and hands with a hot coal? Had they torn the skin open, as Christ's had been on the Cross? Had either of them in that moment been even faintly sane? I saw the old priest, gazing in wonder at what they later showed him. I saw the Pulvertafts in their dining-room, accepting what had occurred as part of their existence in this house. Must not life go on lest all life cease? A confusion ran wildly in my head, a jumble without a pattern, all sense befogged. In a civilized manner nobody protested at the cacophony in the drawing-room when the piano was played, and nobody spoke to me of the stigmata because the subject was too terrible for conversation.

I wept before I went to bed. I wept again when I lay there, hating more than ever the place I am in, where people are driven back to savagery.

*

'The men have not arrived this morning,' Erskine reports. 'I suspected they might not from their demeanour last evening. They attach some omen to this death.'

'But surely to heavens they see the whole thing was a fraud?'

'They do not think so, sir. Any more than they believe that the worship of the Virgin Mary is a fraud perpetrated by the priests. Or that the Body and the Blood is. Fraud is grist to their mill.'

Mr Pulvertaft thanks Erskine for reporting the development to him. The men will return to their senses in time, the estate manager assures him. What has happened is only a little thing. Hunger is the master.

Emily packs for her travels, and vows she will not forget the lake, or the shadows and echoes of the monks. In Bath and Florence, in Vienna and Paris she will keep faith with her special corner, where the spirit of a gentler age lingers.

Mrs Pulvertaft dreams that the Reverend Poole ascends to the pulpit with a bath towel over his shoulder. From this day forth we must all carry bath towels wherever we go, and the feet of Jesus must be dried as well as washed. 'And the woman anointed the feet,' proclaims the Reverend Poole, 'and Jesus thanked her and blessed her and went upon his way.' But Mrs Pulvertaft is unhappy because she does not know which of the men is Jesus. They work with shovels on the estate road, and when she asks them they tell her, in a most unlikely manner, to go away.

Alone in front of the drawing-room piano, Adelaide sits stiffly upright, not wishing to play because she is not in the mood. Again, only minutes ago, Captain Coleborne has not noticed her. He did not notice her at lunch; he did not address a single word to her, he evaded her glance as if he could not bear to catch it. Charlotte thinks him dull; she has said so, yet she never spurns his attentions. And he isn't dull. His handsome face, surmounting his sturdily handsome body, twinkles with vigour and with life. He has done so much and when he talks about the places he has been he is so interesting she could listen to him for ages.

Adelaide's spectacles have misted. She takes them off and wipes them with her handkerchief. She must not go red when he comes again, or when his name is mentioned. Going red will give away her secret and Emily and Charlotte will guess and feel sorry for her, which she could not bear.

'Very well,' Charlotte says by the sundial in the fuchsia garden.

Captain Coleborne blinks his eyes in an ecstasy of delight, and Charlotte thinks that yes, it probably will be nice, knowing devotion like this for ever.

'Heddoe's gone broody,' Fogarty reports in the kitchen.

'Not sickness in the house! One thing you could say about Larvey, she was never sick for an hour.'

'I think Heddoe'll maybe leave.' Fogarty speaks with satisfaction. The governess might leave because she finds it too much that such a thing should happen to a baby, and that her employers do not remark on it because they expect no better of these people. Erskine might be knocked from his horse by the men in a fit of anger because the death has not been honoured in the house or by the family. Erskine might lie dead himself on the day of the governess's departure, and the two events, combining, would cause these Pulvertafts of Ipswich to see the error of their ways and return to their native land.

The china rattles on the tea-trays which the maids carry to the draining boards, and Fogarty lights the lamps which he has arrayed on the table, as he does every afternoon at this time in winter. He inspects each flame before satisfying himself that the trimming of the wick is precisely right, then one after another places the glasses in their brass supports and finally adjusts each light.

The maids unburden the trays at the sink, Miss Fogarty places a damp cloth around a fruitcake and lays aside sandwiches and scones, later to be eaten in the kitchen. Then the maids take the lamps that are ready and begin another journey through the house.

In the nursery Miss Heddoe reads from the history book Miss Larvey has used before her: 'In this manner the monasteries were lawfully dissolved, for the King believed they harboured vile and treacherous plots and were the breeding grounds for future disaffection. The King was privy, through counsellors and advisers, of the vengeance that was daily planned, but was wise and bade his time.'

George Arthur does not listen. He is thinking about the savages of the South Sea islands who eat their enemies. He has always thought it was their babies they ate, and wonders if he has misunderstood something Miss Larvey said on the subject. He wonders then if Emily could possibly be right in what she says about the discomfort of the regimental life. It is true that he enjoys being close to the fire, and likes the cosiness of the nursery in the evenings; and it is true that he doesn't much care for rough material next to his skin. He knows that in spite of what Emily says officers like Captain Coleborne would not be made to drink putrid water, and that flies can't kill you, but the real thing is that he is expected to stay here because he is the only son, because somebody will have to look after the place when his father isn't able to any more. 'Duty', Emily says, and it is that in the end that will steal from him his dream of military glory. Itchy and uneasy, like the bite of an insect, this duty already nags him.

January 12th, 1848. Today it snowed. The fall began after breakfast and continued until it was almost dark. Great drifts have piled up in the garden, and from my window the scene is beautiful. George Arthur has a cold and so remained in bed; he is too feverish for lessons.

January 18th, 1848. The snow is high on the ground. In the garden we break the ice on pools and urns so that the birds may drink. Scraps are thrown out of the scullery doors for them.

February 4th, 1848. It is five months since I arrived here, and all that I have learnt is distressing. There is nothing that is not so. Last night I could not sleep again. I lay there thinking of the starvation, of the faces of the silent women when they come to the gate lodge for food. There is a yellow-greyness in the flesh of their faces, they are themselves like obedient animals. Their babies die when they feed them grass and roots; in their arms at the gate-lodge the babies who survive are silent also, too weak to cry until the sustenance they receive revives them. Last night I lay thinking of the men who are turned away from the work on the road because they have not the strength that is necessary. I thought of the darkness in the cottages, of dawn bringing with it the glaring eyes of death. I thought of the graves again clawed open, the earth still loose, another carcass pushed on to the rotting heap. I thought of an infant tortured with Our Saviour's wounds.

The famine-fever descends like a rain of further retribution, and I wonder – for I cannot help it – what in His name these people have done to displease God so? It is true they have not been an easy people to govern; they have not abided by the laws which the rest of us must observe; their superstitious worship is a sin. But God is a forgiving God. I pray to understand His will.

February 5th, 1848. Charlotte Pulvertaft is not to be married until her sister's return. 'Will you still be with us for the wedding?' Fogarty impertinently inquired last night, for he knows the age of George Arthur and unless I am dismissed I must of course still be here. The work continues on the road, it having been abandoned during the period of snow.

March 6th, 1848. A singular thing has happened. Walking alone in the grounds, I was hailed by Mr Erskine from his horse. I paused, and watched while he dismounted. I thought he had some message for me from the house, but in this I was wrong. Mr Erskine walked beside me, his horse ambling obediently behind. He spoke of the sunshine we were enjoying, and of the estate road. Beyond saluting me at church on Sundays he has never before paid me any attention whatsoever. My surprise must have shown in my face, for he laughed at something that was displayed there. 'I have always liked you, Miss Heddoe,' he said to my astonishment.

I reddened, as any girl would, and felt extremely awkward. I made no attempt at a reply.

'And have you settled, Miss Heddoe?' he next inquired. 'Do you care for it here?'

No one has asked me that before: why should they? My inclination was to smile and with vague politeness to nod. I did so, for to have said that I did not care for this place would have seemed ill-mannered and offensive. Mr Erskine, after all, is part of it.

'Well, that is good.' He paused and then resumed: 'If ever on your walks, Miss Heddoe, you pass near my house you would be welcome to stroll about the garden.'

I thanked him.

'It is the house at the southernmost point of the estate. The only large house there is, nearly hidden in summer by sycamore trees.'

'That is very kind of you, Mr Erskine.'

'I reclaimed the little garden, as the estate was reclaimed.'

'I see.'

The subject of conversation changed. We spoke again of the time of year and the progress that was being achieved on the estate road. Mr Erskine told me something of his history, how a military career had been cut short before it had properly begun. In return, and because the subjects seemed related, I passed on the ambition George Arthur had had in this direction.

'He is reconciled now,' I said, and soon after that the estate manager and I parted company, he riding back along the way we'd walked, I turning toward the house.

The estate road is completed on June 9th, 1848. Soon after that a letter arrives for Mr Pulvertaft from the Distress Board, thanking him for supplying so many months of work for the impoverished men. Since the beginning of the year the families of the area – some of them tenants of Mr Pulvertaft, some not – have been moving away to the harbour towns, to fill the exile ships bound for America. At least, Fogarty overhears Mr Pulvertaft remark in the dining-room, there is somewhere for them to go.

*

In August of that year there is champagne at Charlotte's wedding. Guests arrive from miles around. Emily, returned from her travels, is a bridesmaid.

At the celebrations, which take place in the hall and the drawing-room and the dining-room, and spill over into the garden, Fogarty watches Miss Heddoe, even though he is constantly busy. She wears a dress he has not seen before, in light-blue material, with lace at the collar and the wrists, and little pearl buttons. Wherever she is, she is in the company of George Arthur in his sailor suit. They whisper together and seem, as always nowadays, to be the best of friends. Occasionally Miss Heddoe chides him because an observation he has made oversteps the mark or is delivered indiscreetly. When Mr Erskine arrives he goes straight to where they are.

September 24th, 1848. I have been here a year. The potatoes are not good this year but at least the crop has not failed as completely as hitherto. I have not given Mr Erskine his answer, but he is kind and displays no impatience. I am very silly in the matter, I know I am, but sometimes I lie awake at night and pretend I am already his wife. I repeat the name and title; I say it aloud. I think of the house, hidden among the sycamores. I think of sitting with him in church, in the pew behind the Pulvertafts, not at the side with the Fogartys.

September 25th, 1848. A Mr Ogilvie comes regularly to take tea, and often strolls with Emily to the ruined abbey. Emily has made some drawings of it, which show it as it used to be. 'Well?' Mr Erskine said quietly this afternoon, riding up when I was out on my walk. But I begged, again, for more time to consider.

November 1st, 1848. All Saints' Day. Fogarty frightened me tonight. He leaned against the mantelpiece and said:

'I would advise you not to take the step you are considering, miss.'

'What step, Fogarty?'

'To marry or not to marry Mr Erskine.'

I was flabbergasted at this. I felt myself colouring and stammered when I spoke, asking him what he meant.

'I mean only what I say, miss. I would say to you not to marry him.'

'Are you drunk, Fogarty?'

'No, miss. I am not drunk. Or if I am it is only slight. You have been going through in your mind whether or not to marry Mr Erskine. A while ago you said you could never settle in this troubled place. You said that to yourself, miss. You could not become, as the saying goes, more Irish than the Irish.'

'Fogarty —'

'I thought you would go. When I told you about the child I thought you would pack your bags. There is wickedness here: I thought you sensed it, miss.'

'I cannot have you speaking to me like this, Fogarty.'

'Because I am a servant? Well, you are right, of course. In the evenings, miss, I have always indulged myself with port: that has always been my way. I have enjoyed our conversations, but I am disappointed now.'

'You have been reading my diary.'

'I have, miss. I have been reading your diary and your letters, and I have been observing you. Since they came here I have observed the Pulvertafts of Ipswich also, and Mr Erskine, who has done such wonders all around. I have watched his big square head going about its business; I have listened when I could.'

'You had no right to read what was private. If I mentioned this to Mr Pulvertaft –'

'If you did, miss, my sister and I would be sent packing. Mr Pulvertaft is a fair and decent man and it is only just that disloyal servants should be dismissed. But you would have it on your conscience. I had hoped we might keep a secret between us.'

'I have no wish to share secrets with you, Fogarty.'

'A blind eye was turned, miss, you know that. The hunger was a plague: what use a few spoonfuls of soup, and a road that leads nowhere and only insults the pride of the men who built it? The hunger might have been halted, miss, you know that. The people were allowed to die: you said that to yourself. A man and his wife were driven to commit a barbarous act of cruelty: blasphemy you called it, miss.'

'What I called it is my own affair. I should be grateful, Fogarty, if you left me now.'

'If the estate had continued in its honest decline, if these Pulvertafts had not arrived, the people outside the walls would have travelled here from miles around. They would have eaten the wild raspberries and the apples from the trees, the peaches that still thrived on the brick-lined walls, the grapes and plums and greengages, the blackberries and mulberries. They would have fished the lake and snared the rabbits on Bright Purple Hill. There is pheasant and woodcock grown tame in the old man's time. There was his little herd of cows they might have had. I am not putting forth an argument, miss; I am not a humanitarian; I am only telling you.'

'You are taking liberties, Fogarty. If you do not go now I will most certainly mention this.'

'That was the picture, miss, that might have been. Instead we had to hear of Charlotte's marrying and of Emily's travelling, and of George Arthur's brave decision to follow in the footsteps of his father. Adelaide sulks in the drawing-room and is jealous of her sisters. Mrs Pulvertaft, good soul, lies harmlessly down in the afternoon, and you have put it well in calling her husband a fair and decent man.'

'I did not call him that.'

'You thought it long before I said it.'

'You are drunker than you think, Fogarty.'

'No, miss, I am not. The wickedness here is not intentional, miss. Well, you know about the wickedness, for you have acutely sensed it. So did Mr Pulvertaft at first, so did his wife. Charlotte did not, nor Adelaide, nor did the boy. Emily sensed it until a while ago. Emily would linger down by the old abbey, knowing that the men who lie dead there have never been dispossessed by all the visitors and the strangers there have been since. But now the old abbey is a lady's folly, a pretty ruin that pleases and amuses. Well, of course you know all this.'

'I know nothing of the sort. I would ask you to leave me now.'

'You have thought it would be better for the boy to have his military life, to perish for Queen and empire, and so extinguish this line. Listening to talk of the boy's romance, you have thought that would not be bad. So many perish anyway, all about us.'

'That is a wicked thing to say,' I cried, made furious by this. 'And it is quite untrue.'

'It is wicked, miss, but not untrue. It is wicked because it comes from wickedness, you know that. Your sharp fresh eye has needled all that out.'

'I do not know these things.' My voice was quieter now, even, and empty of emotion. 'I would ask you to leave this room at once.'

But Fogarty went on talking until I thought in the end he must surely be insane. He spoke again of Charlotte's marriage to Captain Coleborne, of Emily and Adelaide, of George Arthur taking the place of his father. He spoke again of the hungry passing without hindrance through the gates of the estate, to feed off what its trees and bushes offered. He spoke of his sister and himself left after the old man's death, he glad to see the decay continue, his sister persuaded that they must always remain.

'The past would have withered away, miss. Instead of which it is the future that's withering now.'

Did he mean the hunger and the endless death, the exile ships of those who had survived? I did not ask him. He frightened me more than ever, standing there, his eyes as dead as ice. He was no humanitarian, he repeated, he was no scholar. All he said came from a feeling he had, a servant's feeling which he'd always had in this house during the years the old man had let everything decline. Poor Protestants as they were, he and his sister belonged neither outside the estate gates with the people who had starved nor with a family as renowned as the Pulvertafts. They were servants in their very bones.

'You have felt you have no place either, miss. You can see more clearly for that.'

'Please go, Fogarty.'

He told me of a dream he'd had the night before or last week, I was too upset to note which. The descendants of the people who had been hungry were in the dream, and the son of George Arthur Pulvertaft was shot in the hall of the house, and no Pulvertaft lived in the place again. The road that had been laid in charity was overgrown through neglect, and the gardens were as they had been at the time of old Hugh Pulvertaft, their beauty strangled as they returned to wildness. Fogarty's voice quivered as his rigmarole ridiculously rambled on; an institution for corrected girls the house became, without carpets on the floors. The bones of the dogs that generations of Pulvertafts had buried in the grounds were dug up by the corrected girls when they were ordered by a Mother Superior to make vegetable beds. They threw the bones about, pretending to be frightened by them, pretending they were the bones of people.

'I don't wish to hear your dreams, Fogarty.'

'I have told you only the one, miss. It is a single dream I had. The house of the estate manager was burnt to the ground, and people burnt with it. The stone walls of the estate were broken down, pulled apart in places by the ivy that was let grow. In a continuation of the dream I was standing here talking to you like I'm talking now. I said to you not to perpetuate what has troubled you.'

He took my tray from me and went away. A moment later I heard him in the lavatory, depositing the food I had not eaten.

'Not a bad soul,' Miss Fogarty remarks, 'when you come to know her.'

'Her father was a solicitor's clerk.'

'Oh granted, there's not a pennyworth of background to the creature. But I'd hardly say she wasn't good enough for Erskine.'

Fogarty does not comment. His sister resumes:

'I would expect to be invited to the house for late tea. I would expect her to say: "Why not walk over on Wednesday, Miss Fogarty, if you have a fancy for it?" I would expect the both of us to walk over for cards with the Erskines of an evening.'

'She has pulled herself up by marrying him. She is hardly going to drop down again by playing cards with servants.'

'Friends,' corrects Miss Fogarty. 'I would prefer to say friends.'

'When a bit of time goes by they'll dine with the Pulvertafts, she and Erskine. You'll cook the food at the range, I'll serve it at the table.'

'Oh, I hardly believe that'll be the order of it.'

Fogarty considers it unwise to pursue his argument and so is silent. Anna Maria Heddoe, he thinks, who was outraged when two guileful peasants tried on a trick. Well, he did his best. It is she, not he, who is the scholar and humanitarian. It is she, not he, who came from England and was distressed. She has wept into her pillow, she has been sick at heart. Stranger and visitor, she has written in her diary the news from Ireland. Stranger and visitor, she has learnt to live with things.

On the Zattere

Without meaning to, Verity had taken her mother's place. Six months after her mother's death she had given up her flat and moved back to the house where she and her two brothers – both of them now married – had grown up. She had pretended, even to herself at times, that she was concerned about her father's loneliness, but the true reason was that she wished to make a change on her own account, to break a pattern in her life. She became, as her mother had been, her father's chief companion and was in time exposed to traits in his nature she had not known existed. Preserving within the family the exterior of a bluff and genial man, good-hearted, knowledgeable and wise, her father had successfully disguised the worst of himself; and had been assisted by his wife's loyalty. It was different for a daughter, and Verity found herself watching the old man in a way she would once not have believed possible, impatient with his weaknesses, judging him.

Mr Unwill, unaware of this development in his daughter, was greatly pleased with the turn events had taken. He was touched when Verity gave up her flat and returned to the family home, and he was proud to be seen in her company, believing that strangers might not take her for his daughter but assume instead that he was an older man to whom this beautiful woman was sentimentally attached. He dressed the part when they went on their first holiday together – to Venice, which every autumn in her lifetime he had visited with his wife. In swirls of green and red, a paisley scarf was knotted at his throat and matched the handkerchief that spilt from the top pocket of his navy-blue blazer. There was no reason why they should be taken as father and daughter, he argued to himself, since they were so very different in appearance. Verity, who was neither small nor tall, gave an impression of slightness because she was slim and was delicately made. The nearly perfect features of her face were set on the suspicion of a slant, turning ordinary beauty into the unusual and causing people who saw it for the first time to glance again. Her hair, clinging smoothly around the contours of classically high cheekbones, was the brown of chestnuts; her eyes, almost strangely, matched it. She dressed and made up with care, as if believing that beauty should be honoured.

In contrast, Mr Unwill was a large man in his advanced sixties, with a ruddy complexion and a bald head. People who knew him quite well had difficulty remembering, when no longer in his presence, if he had a moustache or not. The lingering impression of his face – the ruddiness, the tortoiseshell spectacles – seemed somehow to suggest another, taken-for-granted characteristic, and in fact there was one: a grey growth of bristle on his upper lip, unnoticeable because it so easily became one with the similar greyness that flanked the naked dome.

'Well, what shall you do today?' he asked in the pensione dining-room when they had finished breakfast on their third day. 'I'll be all right, you know. Don't spare a worry for me.'

'I thought I'd go to the Church of San Zaccaria.'

'Why not? You trot along, my dear. I'll sit and watch the boats go by.'

They were alone in the dining-room: in early November the pensione was not full. The American family had not come in to breakfast, presumably having it in their rooms. The German girls had been and gone; so had the French threesome and the lone Italian lady in her purple hat.

'Nice, those German girls,' Mr Unwill said. 'The pretty one made a most interesting observation last night.' He paused, tobacco-stained teeth bared, his eyes ruminative behind his spectacles. 'She said she wondered where waiters go between meals. *Most* unGermanic, I thought.'

Verity, who was thirty-eight and had recently come to believe that life was going to pass her by, reached across the table and took one of her father's cigarettes from the packet that was open beside his coffee cup. She acknowledged the observation of the German girl by briefly nodding. She lit her cigarette from the flame of a small, gold lighter, given to her by the man she'd been in Venice with before.

'The pretty one's from Munich,' her father said. 'The other – now, where on earth did they tell me the fat one came from?' Furrows of thought appeared on his forehead, then he gave up. Slowly he removed his spectacles and in the same unhurried manner proceeded to wipe them with his paisley handkerchief. It was a way of his, a hobby almost. The frames were polished first, then each lens; sometimes he went to work with his Swiss penknife, tightening the screws of the hinges with the screwdriver that was incorporated in one of the blades. 'The pretty one's a laboratory assistant,' he said, 'the other one works in a shop or something.'

The penknife had not, this morning, been taken from his blazer pocket. He held the spectacles up to the light. 'I'll probably sit outside at the Cucciolo,' he said.

'The coffee's better at Nico's. And cheaper.'

It was he – years ago, so he said – who had established that, and yesterday it had been confirmed. She'd sat outside the Cucciolo by mistake, forgetting what he'd told her, obliging him to join her when he emerged from the pensione after his afternoon sleep. He'd later pointed out that a cappuccino at the Cucciolo was fifteen hundred but only eleven at Nico's or Aldo's. Her father was mean about spending small sums of money, Verity had discovered since becoming his companion. He didn't like it when she reached out and helped herself to one of his cigarettes, but he hadn't yet learnt to put the packet away quickly.

'Oh, I don't know that I'm up to the walk to Nico's this morning,' he said.

It took less than a minute to stroll along the Zattere to Nico's, and he was never not up to things. She had discovered also that whenever he felt like it he told petty, unimportant lies, and as they left the dining-room she wondered what this latest one was all about.

Straining a white jacket, beads of perspiration glistening on his forehead, the pensione's bearded waiter used a battery-powered gadget to sweep the crumbs from the tablecloths in the dining-room. His colleague, similarly attired and resembling Fred Astaire, laid two tables for the guests who had chosen to have lunch rather than dinner.

The dining-room was low-ceilinged, with mirrors and sideboards set against the fawn silk on the walls, and windows of round green panes. The breathing of the bearded waiter and the slurping of the canal just outside these windows were the only sounds after the crumbs had been cleared and the tables laid. The waiters glanced over their domain and went away to spend their time mysteriously, justifying the German girl's curiosity.

In the hall of the pensione guests who were never seen in the dining-room, choosing to take no meals, awaited the attention of the smart receptionist, this morning all in red. A kitten played on her desk while patiently she gave directions to the Church of the Frari. She told the Italian lady with the purple hat that there was a dry cleaner's less than a minute away. '*Pronto?*' she said, picking up her telephone. The hall, which was not large, featured in the glass door of the telephone-box and the doors that led outside the same round green panes as the dining-room. There were faded prints on the walls, and by the reception desk a map of Venice and a list of the pensione's credit-card facilities. A second cat, grey and gross and bearing the marks of a lifetime's disputes, lay sleeping on the stairs.

'Enjoy yourself, my dear,' Mr Unwill said to his daughter, stepping over this animal. She didn't appear to hear so he said it again when they had passed through the round-paned doors and stood together for a moment on the quayside.

'Yes,' she said. 'I'll probably wander a bit after I've been to San Zaccaria.'

'Why not, old girl? I'll be as happy as a sandboy, you know.'

The fog that had earlier obscured the houses of the Giudecca on the other side of the canal was lifting; already the sun evaporated the dankness in the air. Verity wore a flecked suit of pinkish-orange, with a scarf that matched it loosely tied over a cream blouse. In one lapel there was a tiny pearl brooch, another gift from the man she'd been in Venice with before.

She turned into the *fondamenta* that ran along one side of the pensione. It was cold there, untouched by the November sunshine. She shivered, but felt it was not from this chilliness. She wished she was not alone, for an irony in her present circumstance was that she found the company of other people both tiresome and of use. She walked more quickly, endeavouring to keep certain insistent thoughts out of her mind. At the Accademia she bought her ticket for the vaporetto and waited on the landing-stage. Other people, no matter who they were, disrupted such thoughts, which was something she welcomed. The attention other people demanded, the conversations they began, their faces and their voices, clogged her communication with herself; and yet, so much of the time while in the company of other people, she wished she was not.

Odd, to have taken her mother's place in this old-fashioned way: on the vaporetto she saw again the tortoiseshell spectacles in her father's hands, his square, wide fingers working the paisley silk over the lens. Repetition had etched this image in some corner of her mind: she heard his early-morning cough, and then the lowered tone he used when talking to himself. Had it been panic that had caused her to use his loneliness as an excuse, to break the pattern she found so merciless? Love-making had been easy in the convenient flat, too much had been taken for granted. But even so, giving up the flat might have struck some people as extreme.

On the vaporetto the Italians glanced at her, women assessing her in some Italian way, the men desirous. Venice was different in November, less of a bauble than the summer city she remembered. The tourist crowds had gone, with the mosquitoes and the cruel Italian heat. The orchestras had ceased to play in the Piazza San Marco, the Riva degli Schiavoni was again the property of the Venetians. She imagined her parents walking arm in arm on the Riva, or going to Torcello and Burano. Had the warmth of their companionship been a pretence on his part? For if he'd loved his wife how could he so easily come back to the city he and she had discovered together and had affectionately made their own? Eleven months had passed since her death and already in the pensione they had come to know so well he was striking up acquaintanceships as though nothing of importance had occurred since last he'd been there. There had been a moment in the hall when he mumblingly spoke to the smartly dressed receptionist, who said that everyone at the pensione sympathized. The elderly maid who welcomed him upstairs had murmured in Italian, and in the dining-room the waiters' voices had been low at first. It was he himself who subsequently set the mood, his matter-of-fact manner brushing sentiment aside, summarily dismissing death. Had her mother loved him or had their companionship in this city been, on her part also, a pretence? Marriage was riddled with such falsity, Verity reflected, dressed up as loyalty or keeping faith.

Palaces loomed majestically on either side of her, the lion of St Mark disdainful on his column, St Theodore modest on his. Carpaccio would still have recognized his city in the tranquillity of November, the Virgins of Cima still crossed the city's bridges. It was her mother who had said all that to her, translating emotions she had felt. Verity went on thinking about her parents, not wishing to think about herself, not wishing to catch a glimpse of herself in the summer dresses she had worn when she'd been in Venice before. There had been many weekends spent faithfully with the same companion in many beautiful cities, but Venice that July had left behind a special meaning because hope had died there.

Mr Unwill settled himself on one of the Cucciolo Bar's orange plastic seats. Verity was right: the Cucciolo wasn't a patch on Nico's or Aldo's. Fewer people passed by for a start, and the one cappuccino he'd been served yesterday by the Cucciolo's dour waiter had tasted of the last person's sugar. But the trouble with sitting outside Nico's or Aldo's was that people often turned off the Zattere before they reached them, and he happened to know that the pretty little German girl was still in the pensione because he'd seen the fat one striding off on her own half an hour ago. Of course it could be that the pretty one had preceded her friend, in which case he'd be four hundred lire down, which would be annoying.

'Prego, signore?'

He ordered his coffee. He wished he spoke Italian so that he might draw the waiter's attention to the inadequately washed cup he'd been presented with yesterday. He'd have done so in England: one of the few good things about being old was that you could make a fuss. Another was that you could drop into conversation with people without their thinking it was peculiar of you. Last night he'd wandered in from his stroll after Verity had gone to her room, and had noticed the two girls in the lounge. He'd leafed through a pile of magazines that had to do with the work of the Venetian police, and then the girls had begun to giggle unrestrainedly. By way of a polite explanation, the pretty one had spoken to him in English, explaining that it was the remark about where waiters go between meals which had caused their merriment. After that the conversation had drifted on. He'd told them a thing or two about Venice, which he knew quite well in a professional way.

Mr Unwill was retired, having been employed for all his adult life in a shipping office. Ships and their cargoes, the building, sale and insuring of ships, were what he was most familiar with. It was this interest that had first brought him to Venice, as it had to many other great ports. While his three children were still growing up it had been necessary to limit such travel to the British Isles, but later he and his wife had travelled as far and as adventurously as funds permitted, always economizing so that journeys might be extended or prolonged. Venice had become their favourite.

'Hullo there!' he called out to the German girl as she stepped around the corner, shading her eyes against the sun. She was wearing a short dress that was almost the same colour as her very blonde hair.

'What a day!' Mr Unwill said, standing up so that she could not easily just walk by. 'Now, how about a coffee?'

Her teeth, when she smiled her appreciation of this invitation, glistened damply, large white teeth, each one perfectly shaped. But to his disappointment, while smiling she also shook her head. She was late already, she explained: she was to meet her friend at the Rialto Bridge.

He watched her hurrying along the Zattere, her sturdy legs nicely bronzed, a camera slung across her shoulder. She turned the corner by the Church of the Gesuati and Mr Unwill sighed.

In the Church of San Zaccaria Verity gazed at the Bellini altarpiece her mother had sent her postcards of. Perfectly, she still contained her thoughts, conjecturing again. Had her mother stood on this very spot? Had her father accompanied her to the churches she liked so much or in all their visits had he been concerned only with duller interests? Verity didn't know; it had never seemed important.

The lights that illuminated the picture abruptly went out. Verity felt in her purse for two hundred lire, but before she found the coins a man stepped forward and dropped his through the slot of the little grey box on one side of the altar. The Virgin and her saints, in sacred conversation, were there again. Verity looked for a few moments longer and then moved away.

She hadn't looked at pictures that July. For a second she saw herself and heard her laughter: in a dress with primroses on it, wearing sunglasses and laughing, although she had not felt like laughing. In the church she felt again the effort of that laughter and was angry because for a single second her concentration had faltered. She dropped some money into a poor-box by the door. She hadn't realized how fond she'd been of her mother until the very last moment, until the coffin had soundlessly slipped away behind a beige curtain in the chapel of the crematorium. The soundlessness was eerie and unpleasant; Verity had hated that moment.

She left the church and walked back to the Riva. Metal trestles supported planks of wood, like crude tabletops, on which people might walk if the tides rose and the floods of autumn began. These improvised bridges were called *passerelle*, her father had told her, pointing them out to her on the Zattere. 'Oh heavens, of course I'll manage,' he'd kept repeating on the afternoon of the funeral and all of them, her brothers and her sisters-in-law, she herself, had admired his urbanity and his resolve not to be a nuisance.

She rose and walked slowly along the Riva towards the Arsenale. Already the quayside hotels had a deserted look; the pink Gabrielli-Sandwirth had put up its shutters. 'No, absolutely not,' her father had said on some later occasion. 'You have your own life, Verity.' And of course she had: her own life, her own job, her own flat in which love might be made.

A fun-fair was being erected further along the quay, dodgem cars and a tunnel of fear, swing-boats and fruit machines. 'American Games' a garish announcement read; 'Central Park' proclaimed another. Two bespectacled old women washed down a rifle-range; hobby-horses were unloaded. Outside the Pensione Bucintoro a shirt-sleeved waiter smoked a cigarette and watched.

In the Via Garibaldi children with satchels or school books chased one another on their journey home from morning school; women jostled and pushed at the vegetable stalls. In the public park, tatty and forgotten in the low season, cats swarmed or huddled – mangy tomcats with ravenous eyes, pitiful kittens that seemed resentful of their recent birth, leanly slinking mothers. All of them were dirty; two weakly fought, a hissing, clawing ball of different-coloured fur. Verity bent down and tried to attract a dusty marmalade-coloured kitten, but alarmed by her attentions it darted off. She walked on, still determinedly dwelling upon her father's heartlessness in so casually returning to this city, to the pensione, to the Zattere. She dwelt again upon her mother's misplaced loyalty, which had kept the marriage going. But she herself, in her primrose-yellow dress and her sunglasses, crept through these irrelevant reflections so crudely forced upon her consciousness. Her parents arm-in-arm in Venice, loving or not loving, vanished into wisps of mist, and were replaced by the sound of her own ersatz laughter. There was an image of her face, strained with a smile that choked away the hopelessness she was frightened to surrender to. The ice tinkled in her well-chilled Soave; the orchestras played in the great, romantic square. 'Oh, I am happy!' came the echo of her lying voice, and in the dingy public park her beauty fled as swiftly as the marmalade kitten had leapt from her grasp. She wept, but it did not matter because no one was about.

Mr Unwill, deprived of a conversation with the German girl, left the Cucciolo Bar and strolled down the Zattere in the direction of the western Stazione Marittima. It was an interesting place, this particular Stazione Marittima, and he would like one day to find someone who would show him round it. He often loitered by the bridge that led almost directly into it, hoping to catch the eye of some official with an hour or two on his hands who would welcome the interest of an Englishman who had been concerned with maritime commerce for a lifetime. But the officials were always in a hurry, and usually in groups of three or four, which made matters difficult. Clerks of course they'd be, not quite right anyway. Once he'd noticed a man with gold braid on his cap and his uniform, but when Mr Unwill smilingly approached him the man expostulated wildly, alarmed presumably by the sound of a language he did not understand. Mr Unwill had thought it a strange reaction in a seafaring man, who should surely be used to the world's tongues.

A cargo boat called the *Allemagna Express*, registered in Venice in spite of its German-sounding name, and flying the Italian flag, was being painted. On planks suspended along the side of its hull men dipped long-handled rollers into giant paint-containers which dangled at a convenient drop below each man. A single painter used a brush, touching in the red outline on the letters of *Allemagna Express*. Cautiously he moved back and forth on his plank, often calling up to his colleagues on the deck to work one of the ropes or pulleys. A yellow stripe extended the length of the hull, separating the white of the ship's upper reaches from the brown beneath. The old girl was certainly beginning to look smart, Mr Unwill considered, and wondered if they'd still be in Venice when the job was completed. There was nothing as rewarding as a well-painted ship, nothing as satisfying even if your own contribution had only been to watch the men at work. Mr Unwill sat for a long time on a stone bench on the quayside, content in this unexacting role. He wondered why *Express* was spelt with an 'x' since the vessel was Italian. That morning from his bedroom window he'd noticed the *Espresso Egitto* chugging by.

At half past eleven he rose and walked to Nico's, where he bought a banana ice-cream and ate it sitting on a *passerella*.

'There was a time, you know, when the Venetians could build a warship in a day.'

For dinner they sat at a round table in a corner of the low-ceilinged dining-room of the pensione. The bearded waiter doled out salad on to side plates, and the one who looked like Fred Astaire went round with platters of chicken and fried potatoes.

'I passed near the Arsenale today,' Verity said, remembering that that was where such warships had been built. '*Grazie*.'

'*Prego, signorina*.'

'You called in at the Naval Museum, did you?'

'No, actually I didn't.'

Apart from the German girls, the people who'd been in the dining-room the night before were there again. The American woman, with a blue-and-white bow tie, sat with her husband and her daughter at the table closest to the Unwills'. The two thin Frenchwomen and the frail man were beside the screen that prevented draughts. The solitary Italian woman in the purple hat was by the door. Other Italians, a couple who had not been in the dining-room last night, were at a table next to the German girls.

'I remember going to the Naval Museum,' Mr Unwill said. 'Oh, years ago. When I was first in Venice with your mother.'

'Did she go too?'

'Your mother always liked to accompany me to places. Most interesting she found the Naval Museum. Well, anyone would.'

He went on talking, telling her about the Naval Museum; she didn't listen. That afternoon she'd gone across to the Lido because it was a part of Venice they hadn't visited that July. But instead of the escape she'd hoped for she'd caught a nostalgic mood from its windswept, shuttered emptiness and its dead casino. She'd sat in a bar drinking brandy she didn't like the taste of, and when she returned to the pensione she found herself not wanting to change out of the clothes she'd worn all day. She'd seen her father glancing in surprise at her tired orange suit and she'd felt, ridiculously, that she was letting him down.

'Ah, here they are!' he exclaimed, making a sudden noise as the German girls entered. '*Buona sera!*' he shouted at them eagerly.

The girls smiled, and Verity wondered what on earth they thought of him. One of the Frenchwomen was complaining that her gnocchi was cold. The waiter who resembled Fred Astaire looked worried. She could not eat cold gnocchi, the woman protested, throwing her fork down, marking the white tablecloth.

'Where have you been today?' Mr Unwill called across the dining-room to the German girls. 'Done something nice?'

'*Ja,*' the fat girl replied. 'We have been in a glass factory.'

'Very sensible,' said Mr Unwill.

Another plate of gnocchi replaced the cold one at the French table. The American woman told her daughter that on her wedding day in Nevada she had thrown a cushion out of a window because she'd felt joyful. 'I guess your momma'd been drinking,' the father said, laughing very noisily. The Italian couple talked about the Feast of St Martin.

There had been only one love-making weekend since she'd moved back to the family house: she'd told her father some lie, not caring if he guessed.

'It's an interesting thing,' he was saying to her now, 'this St Martin business. They have a week of it, you know. Old people and children get gifts. Have you seen the confections in the shop windows? San Martino on horseback?'

'Yes, I've noticed them.' Made of biscuit, she had presumed, sometimes chocolate-coated, sometimes not, icing decorated with sweets.

'And *cotognata,*' he went on. 'Have you seen the *cotognata?* Centuries old, that St Martin's sweetmeat is, far nicer than Turkish delight.'

She smiled, and nodded. She'd noticed the *cotognata* also. She often wondered how he came by his information, and guessed he was for ever dropping into conversation with strangers in the hope that they spoke English.

'The first ghetto was in Venice,' he said. 'Did you know that? It's an Italian word, called after the place where the Jewish settlement was.'

'No, I didn't know that.'

'Well, there you are. Something every day.'

The bearded waiter cleared their plates away and brought them each a bowl of fruit.

'I thought we might wander down the Zattere after dinner,' her father suggested, 'and take a glass of mandarinetto and perhaps a slice of cake. Feel up to that, old girl?'

If she didn't accompany him he'd bother the German girls. She said a glass of mandarinetto would be nice.

'They're painting the *Allemagna Express.* Fine-looking vessel.'

In her bedroom she tied a different scarf around her neck, and put her coat on because the nights were cold. When she returned to the hall her father was not there and when he did appear he came from the dining-room, not from upstairs. 'I told them we were going for a drink,' he said. 'They'll join us in a moment. You all right, old girl?'

He was smoking a cigarette and, like her, he had gone to his room for his overcoat. On the Zattere he put his hat on at a jaunty angle. There was a smell of creosote because they'd been repainting the rafts that afternoon. Sheets of newspaper were suspended from strings that were looped along the quayside to draw attention to the newly treated timbers. A terrier settled down for the night among the rubble on a builder's barge. Cats crept about. It was extraordinary, she suddenly thought, that just because she'd given up her flat she should find herself in Venice with this old man.

'Nice here, eh?' he said in the café, surveying the amber-coloured cloths on the tables, the busyness behind the bar. He took his hat and overcoat off, and sat down. He stubbed his cigarette out and lit a fresh one. 'Mandarinetto,' he said to the waiter who came up. '*Due.*'

'*Sì, signore. Subito.*'

She lit a cigarette herself, caressing her lighter with her fingers, then feeling angry and ashamed that she had done so.

'Ah, here they are!' Her father was on his feet, exclaiming like a schoolboy, waving his hat at the German girls. He shouted after the waiter, ordering two more mandarinettos. 'I really recommend it here,' he informed the German girls, flashing his tobacco-stained smile about and offering them cigarettes. He went on talking, telling them about the *Allemagna Express*. He mentioned the Stazione Marittima and asked them if they had noticed the biscuit horsemen and the *cotognata*. 'By the weekend the Votive Bridge will be complete,' he said. 'A temporary timber bridge, you know, erected as a token of thanksgiving. Every year, for three days, Venetians celebrate the passing of the Plague by making a pilgrimage across it, their children waving balloons about. Then it's taken down again.'

Verity smiled at the fatter German, who was receiving less attention than her friend. And a bridge of boats, her father continued, was temporarily established every summer. 'Again to give thanks. Another tradition since the Plague.'

The Americans who had been in the pensione came in and sat not far away. They ordered ice-creams, taking a long time about it, questioning the waiter in English as to whether they would come with added cream.

'Oh, I remember Venice forty years ago,' Mr Unwill said. 'Of course, it's greatly changed. The Yugoslavs come now, you know, in busloads.' He issued a polite little laugh. 'Not to mention the natives of your own fair land.'

'Too many, I think,' the prettier girl responded, grimacing.

'Ah, *ja*, too many,' agreed her companion.

'No, no, no. You Germans travel well, I always say. Besides, to the Venetian a tourist's a tourist, and tourists mean money. The trouble with the Yugoslavs, they apparently won't be parted from it.'

It wasn't usually his opinion that Germans travelled well; rather the opposite. He told the girls that at one time the Venetians had been capable of building a warship in a day. He explained about ghettoes, and said that in Venice it was the cats who feared the pigeons. He laughed in his genial way. He said:

'That was a very clever remark you made last night, Ingrid. About waiters.'

'It was Brigitta who said it first, I think.'

'Oh, was it? Well, it's quite amusing anyway. Now, what we really want to know is how long you're staying at the pensione?'

'*Ja*, just today,' Ingrid said. 'Tomorrow we have gone.'

'Oh dear me, now that's very sad.'

He would not, when the moment came, pay for the mandarinettos or the cake he was now pressing upon his guests. He would discover that he had left his wallet in some other pocket.

'You must not spoil your looks, eh?' he said when Ingrid refused the cake. His smile nudged her in a way he might have thought was intimate, but which Verity observed the girl registering as elderly. Brigitta had already been biting into a slice of cake when the remark was made about the losing of looks. Hastily she put it down. They must go, she said.

'Go? Oh, surely not? No, please don't go.'

But both girls were adamant. They had been too tired last night to see the Bridge of Sighs by lamplight and they must see that before they left. Each held out a hand, to Verity and then to her father. When they had gone Verity realized she hadn't addressed a single word to either of them. A silence followed their departure, then Mr Unwill said in a whisper:

'Those Americans seem rather nice, eh?'

He would hold forth to the Americans, as he had to the German girls, concentrating his attention on the daughter because she was the most attractive of the three. The mother was vulgarly dressed, the father shouted. In the presence of these people everything would be repeated, the painting of the *Allemagna Express*, the St Martin's confections, the temporary bridges.

'No,' Verity said. 'No, I don't want to become involved with those Americans.'

He was taken aback. His mouth remained open after he'd begun to say something. He stared at her, slowly overcoming his bewilderment. For the second time that evening, he asked her if she felt all right. She didn't reply. Time of the month, he supposed, this obvious explanation abruptly dawning on him, wretched for women. And then, to his very great surprise, he was aware that his daughter was talking about her decision, some months ago, to return to the family home.

' "My father's on his own now," I told him, "so I have given up the flat." As soon as I had spoken I felt afraid. "We must be together," is what I thought he'd say. He'd be alarmed and upset, I thought, because I'd broken the pattern of our love affair by causing this hiatus. But all he said was that he understood.'

They'd known, of course, about the wretched affair. Her mother had been depressed by it; so much time passing by, no sign of a resolution in whatever it was, no sign of marriage. Verity had steered all conversation away from it; when the subject was discreetly approached by her mother or her brothers she made it clear that they were trespassing on private property; he himself had made no forays in that direction, it not being his way. Astonishing it was, that she should wish to speak of it now.

'I didn't in the least,' she said, 'feel sorry for your loneliness. I felt sorry for myself. I couldn't bear for a moment longer the routine love-making in that convenient flat.'

Feeling himself becoming hot, Mr Unwill removed his glasses and searched in the pockets of his blazer for his handkerchief. He didn't know what to say, so he said nothing. He listened while Verity more or less repeated what she had said already. There had been sixteen years of routine love-making, ever since she was twenty-two. Her love affair had become her life, the routine punctuated by generous gifts and weekends in beautiful cities.

There was a silence. He polished one lens and then the other. He tightened the screws of the hinges with the useful little screwdriver in his penknife. Since the silence continued, eventually he said:

'If you made an error in coming back to the house it can easily be rectified, old girl.'

'Surely, I thought, those brief weekends would never be enough? Surely we would have to talk about everything again, now that there was no flat to go to?' She spoke of the cities where the weekends had been spent: Bruges, Berlin, Paris, Amsterdam, Venice. Bruges had been the first. In Bruges she had assumed, although he had not said so, that he would leave his wife. They had walked through chilly squares, they had sat for hours over dinner in the Hotel Duc du Bourgogne. In Paris, some time later, she had made the same assumption. He did not love his wife; when the children grew up he would leave her. By the time they visited Venice, the children had grown up. 'Only just grown up,' she said. 'The last one only just, that summer.'

He did not say anything; the conversation was beyond his reach. He saw his daughter as an infant, a nurse holding a bundle towards him, the screwed-up face and tiny hands. She'd been a happy child, happy at school, happy with her friends. Young men had hung about the house; she'd gone to tennis-club dances and winter parties. 'Love's a disease sometimes,' her mother had said, angrily, a year or so ago. Her mother had been cross because Verity always smiled so, pretending the happiness that was no longer there, determinedly optimistic. Because of the love affair, her mother had said also, Verity's beauty had been wasted, seeming to have been uselessly visited upon her.

'It wasn't just a dirty weekend, you know, here in Venice. It's never just that.'

'Please, Verity. Please, now ...'

'He can't bring himself to be unkind to his wife. He couldn't be bad to a woman if he tried. I promise you, he's a remarkable man.'

He began to expostulate but changed his mind. Everything he tried to say, even everything he felt, seemed clumsy. She stared beyond him, through the smoke from her cigarette, causing him to feel a stranger. Her silliness in love had made her carelessly harsh, selfish and insensitive because she had to think so much about herself. In a daughter who was not naturally silly, who had been gentle as a child, these qualities were painful to observe. Once she could have imagined what it was like for him to hear her refer so casually to dirty weekends; now she didn't care if that hurt him or not. It was insulting to expect him to accept that the man was remarkable. It dismissed his intellect and his sense.

'It was ridiculous,' she said eventually, 'to give up my flat.'

He made some protest when she asked the waiter for the bill, but she didn't listen, paying the bill instead. He felt exhausted. He had sat in this very café with a woman who was dead; the man his daughter spoke of was still alive. It almost seemed the other way round. He would not have claimed a great deal for the marriage there had been: two people rubbing along, forgiving each other for this and that, one left alone to miss the nourishment of affection. Yet when the coffin had slipped away behind the beige curtain his grief had been unbearable and had remained so afterwards, for weeks and months, each day a hell.

'I'm sorry for being a nuisance,' she said before they rose from the table, and he wanted to explain to her that melancholy would have become too much if he allowed a city and its holiday memories to defeat him, that memories were insidious. But he didn't say anything because he knew she would not listen to him properly. She could not help thinking badly of him; the harshness that had been bred in her prevented the allowances that old age demanded. Nor could he, because of anger, make allowances for her.

'Hi!' one of the Americans whom he'd thought it might be quite nice to know called out. They had finished their ice-creams and were preparing to leave also. All of them smiled but it was Verity, not he, who returned their greeting.

'It's I who should be sorry,' he said on the Zattere. He'd been more gently treated than she: you knew where you were with death, in no way was it a confidence trick. He began to say that but changed his mind, knowing she would not wish to hear.

'Heavens, how cold it has become!' She hurried through the gathering fog, and so did he. The conversation was over, its loose ends hanging; each knew they would never be picked up. '*Buona notte*,' the smart receptionist, all in green now, murmured in the hall of the pensione, and they bade her good-night in their different ways.

They lifted their keys from the rack beside the stairs and stepped over the sleeping cat on the bottom step. On the first-floor landing they said good-night, were briefly awkward because of what had passed between them, then entered their separate rooms. Slowly he prepared himself for bed, slowly undressing, slowly washing, folding his clothes with an old man's care. She sat by her window, staring at the lights across the water, until the fog thickened and there was nothing left to see.

The Wedding in the Garden

Ever since Dervla was nine the people of the hotel had fascinated her. Its proprietor, Mr Congreve, wore clothes that had a clerical sombreness about them, though they were of a lighter hue than Father Mahony's stern black. Mr Congreve was a smiling man with a quiet face, apparently not in the least put out by reports in the town that his wife, in allying herself with a hotel proprietor, had married beneath her. Ladylike and elegant, she appeared not to regret her choice. Mrs Congreve favoured in her dresses a distinctive blend of greens and blues, her stylishness combining with the hotel proprietor's tranquil presence to lend the couple a quality that was unique in the town. Their children, two girls and an older boy, were imbued with this through the accident of their birth, and so were different from the town's other children in ways that might be termed superficial. 'Breeding,' Dervla's father used to say. 'The Congreves have great breeding in them.'

She herself, when she was nine, was fair-haired and skinny, with a graze always healing on one knee or the other because she had a way of tripping on her shoelaces. 'Ah, will you tie up those things!' her mother used to shout at her: her mother, big-faced and red, blinking through the steam that rose from a bucket of water. Her brothers and sisters had all left the house in Thomas MacDonagh Street by the time Dervla was nine; they'd left the town and the district, two of them in America even, one in London. Dervla was more than just the baby of the family: she was an afterthought, catching everyone unawares, born when her mother was forty-two. 'Chance had a hand in that one,' her father liked to pronounce, regarding her affectionately, as if pleased by this intervention of fate. When his brother from Leitrim visited the house in Thomas MacDonagh Street the statement was made often, being of family interest. 'If her mother didn't possess the strength of an ox,' Dervla's father liked to add, 'God knows how the end of it would have been.' And Dervla's Leitrim uncle, refreshing himself with a bottle of stout, would yet again wag his head in admiration and wonder at his sister-in-law's robust constitution. He was employed on the roads up in Leitrim and only came to the town on a Sunday, drawn to it by a hurling match. Dervla's father was employed by O'Mara the builder.

Even after she went to work in the Royal Hotel and came to know the family, her first image of them remained: the Congreves in their motor-car, an old Renault as she afterwards established, its canvas hood folded back, slowly making the journey to the Protestant church on a sunny Sunday morning. St Peter's Church was at one end of the town, the Royal Hotel at the other. It had, before its days as an hotel, apparently been owned by Mrs Congreve's family, and then people in the grocery business had bought it and had not lived there, people who had nothing to do with the town, who were not well known. After that Mr Congreve had made an offer with, so it was said, his wife's money.

The motor-car in the sunlight crept down Draper's Street, the bell of St Peter's Church still monotonously chiming. The boy – no older than Dervla herself – sat between his sisters in the back; Mr Congreve turned his head and said something to his wife. Daddy Phelan, outside Mrs Ryan's bar, saluted them in his wild way; Mrs Congreve waved back at him. The boy wore a grey flannel suit, the girls had fawn-coloured coats and tiny bows in their pigtails. The motor-car passed from view, and a moment later the bell ceased to chime.

Christopher couldn't remember the first time he'd been aware of her. All he knew was that she worked in the kitchen of the hotel, walking out from the town every day. Playing with Molly and Margery-Jane in the shrubberies of the garden, he had noticed now and again a solitary figure in a black coat, with a headscarf. He didn't know her name or what her face was like. 'Count to ten, Chris,' Margery-Jane would shrilly insist. 'You're not counting to ten!' Some game, rules now forgotten, some private family game they had invented themselves, stalking one another among the bamboos and the mahonias, Molly creeping on her hands and knees, not making a sound, Margery-Jane unable to control her excited breathing. The girl passed through the yard near by, a child as they were, but they paid her no attention.

A year or so later Mary, the elderly maid whose particular realm was the dining-room, instructed her in the clearing of a table. 'Dervla,' his mother said when the older waitress had led her away with cutlery and plates piled on to her tray. 'Her name is Dervla.' After that she was always in the dining-room at mealtimes.

It was then, too, that she began to come to the hotel on a bicycle, her day longer now, arriving before breakfast, cycling home again in the late evening. Once there was talk about her living there, but nothing had come of that. Christopher didn't know where she did live, had never once noticed Thomas MacDonagh Street in his wanderings about the town. Returning from boarding-school in Dublin, he had taken to going for walks, along the quay of the river where the sawmills were, through the lanes behind Brabazon's Brewery. He preferred to be alone at that time of his growing up, finding the company of his sisters too chattery. The river wound away through fields and sometimes a dog from the lanes or the cottages near the electricity plant would follow him. There was one in particular, a short-tailed terrier, its smooth white coat soiled and uncared for, ears and head flashed with black. There was a mongrel sheepdog also, an animal that ceased its customary cringing as soon as it gained the freedom of the fields. When he returned to the town these animals no longer followed him, but were occasionally involved in fights with other dogs, as though their excursion into the country had turned them into aliens who were no longer to be trusted. He went on alone then, through darkening afternoons or spitting rain, lingering by the shops that sold fruit and confectionery. There'd been a time when he and Margery-Jane and Molly had come to these shops with their pocket-money, for Peggy's Leg or pink bon-bons. More affluent now, he bought *Our Boys* and *Film Fun* and saved up for the *Wide World*.

His sisters had been born in the Royal Hotel, but he – before his father owned the place – in Dublin, where his parents had then lived. He did not remember Dublin: the hotel had become his world. It was a white building, set back a little from the street, pillars and steps prefacing its entrance doors. Its plain façade was decorated with a yellow AA sign and a blue RIAC one; in spring tulips bloomed in window-boxes on the downstairs windowsills. The words *Royal Hotel* were painted in black on this white façade and repeated in smaller letters above the pillared porch. At the back, beyond the yard and the garden, there was a row of garages and an entrance to them from Old Lane. The hotel's four employees came and went this way, Mrs O'Connor the cook, whatever maids there were, and Artie the boots. There was a stone-flagged hallway with doors off it to the kitchen and the larders and the scullery, and one to the passage that led to the back staircase. It was a dim hallway, with moisture sometimes on its grey-distempered walls, a dimness that was repeated in the passage that led to the back staircase and on the staircase itself. Upstairs there was a particular smell, of polish and old soup, with a tang of porter drifting up from the bar. The first-floor landing – a sideboard stretching along one wall, leather armchairs by the windows, occasional tables piled with magazines, a gold-framed mirror above the fireplace – was the heart of the hotel. Off it were the better bedrooms and a billiard-room where the YMCA held a competition every March; above it there was a less impressive landing, little more than a corridor. On the ground floor the dining-room had glass swing-doors, twelve tables with white tablecloths, always set for dinner. The family occupied a corner one between the fire and the dumb-waiter, with its array of silver-plated sugar castors and salt and pepper and mustard containers, bottles of Yorkshire Relish, thick and thin, mint sauce in cut-glass jugs, and Worcester sauce, and jam and marmalade.

When Christopher was younger, before he went away to school, he and Margery-Jane and Molly used to play hide-and-seek in the small, cold bedrooms at the top of the house, skulking in the shadows on the uncarpeted stairs that led to the attics. Occasionally, if a visitor was staying in the hotel, their father would call up to them to make less noise, but this didn't happen often because a visitor was usually only in the hotel at night. They were mainly senior commercial travellers who stayed at the Royal, representatives of Wills or Horton's or Drummond's Seeds, once a year the Urney man; younger representatives lodged more modestly. Insurance men stayed at the hotel, and bank inspectors had been known to spend a fortnight or three weeks. Bord na Móna men came and went, and once in a while there was an English couple or a couple from the North, touring or on their honeymoon. When Miss Gilligan, who taught leatherwork at the technical college, first came to the town she spent nearly a month in the Royal before being satisfied with the lodging she was offered. Artie the boots, grey-haired but still in his forties, worked in the garden and the yard, disposed of empty bottles from the bar and often served there. Old Mary served there too, and at a busy time, which only rarely occurred, Mrs O'Connor would come up from the kitchen to assist. Dr Molloy drank at the Royal, and Hogarty the surveyor, and the agent at the Bank of Ireland, Mr McKibbin, and a few of the other bank men in the town. The bar was a quiet place, though, compared with the town's public houses; voices were never raised.

The main hall of the hotel was quiet also, except for the ticking of the grandfather clock and its chiming. There was the same agreeable smell there, of soup and polish, and porter from the bar. A barometer hung beneath a salmon in a glass case, notices of point-to-point races and the Dublin Spring Show and the Horse Show hung from hooks among coloured prints of Punchestown. The wooden floor was covered almost completely with faded rugs, and the upper half of the door to the bar was composed of frosted glass with a border of shamrocks. There were plants in brass pots on either side of a wide staircase with a greenish carpet, threadbare in parts.

'Your inheritance one day,' Christopher's father said.

It was very grand, Dervla considered, to have your initials on a green trunk, and on a wooden box with metal brackets fixed to its edges. These containers stood in the back hall, with a suitcase, at the beginning of each term, before they were taken to the railway station. They stood there again when Christopher returned, before Artie helped him to carry them upstairs. On his first day back from school there was always a great fuss. His sisters became very excited, a special meal was prepared, Mr Congreve would light cigarette after cigarette, standing in front of the fire on the first-floor landing, listening to Christopher's tale of the long journey from Dublin. He always arrived in the evening, sometimes as late as seven o'clock but usually about half past five. In the dining-room when the family had supper he would say he was famished and tell his sisters how disgraceful the food at the school was, the turnips only half mashed, the potatoes with bits of clay still clinging to their skins, and a custard pudding called Yellow Peril. His mother, laughing at him, would say he shouldn't exaggerate, and his father would ask him about the rugby he had played, or the cricket. 'Like the game of tennis it would be,' Artie told her when Dervla asked him what cricket was. 'The way they'd wear the same type of clothing for it.' Miss Gillespie, the matron, was a tartar and Willie the furnace man's assistant told stories that couldn't be repeated. Dervla imagined the big grey house with a curving avenue leading up to it, and bells always ringing, and morning assemblies, and the march through cloisters to the chapel, which so often she had heard described. She imagined the boys in their grey suits kneeling down to say their prayers, and the ice on the inside of the windows on cold days. The chemistry master had blown his hair off, it was reported once in the dining-room, and Dervla thought of Mr Jerety who made up the prescriptions in the Medical Hall. Mr Jerety had no hair either, except for a little at the sides of his head.

Dervla managed the dining-room on her own now. Mary had become too rheumaticky to make the journey at any speed from the kitchen and found it difficult to lift the heavier plates from the table. She helped Mrs O'Connor with the baking instead, kneading dough on the marble slab at the side table in the kitchen, making pastry and preparing vegetables. It took her half a day, Dervla had heard Mr Congreve say, to mount the stairs to her bedroom at the top of the hotel, and the other half to descend it. He was fond of her, and would try to make her rest by the fire on the first-floor landing but she never did. 'Sure, if I sat down there, sir, I'd maybe never get up again.' It was unseemly, Dervla had heard old Mary saying in the kitchen, for an employee to be occupying an armchair in the place where the visitors and the family sat. Mr Congreve was devil-may-care about matters like that, but what would a visitor say if he came out of his bedroom and found a uniformed maid in an armchair? What would Byrne from Horton's say, or Boylan the insurance man?

In the dining-room, when she'd learnt how everything should be, 'the formalities', as Mr Congreve put it, Dervla didn't find her duties difficult. She was swift on her feet, as it was necessary to be, in case the food got cold. She could stack a tray with dishes and plates so economically that two journeys to the kitchen became one. She was careful at listening to what the visitors ordered and without writing anything down was able to relay the message to the kitchen. The family were never given a choice.

Often Christopher found himself glancing up from the food Dervla placed in front of him, to follow with his eyes her progress across the dining-room, the movement of her hips beneath her black dress, her legs clad in stockings that were black also. Once he addressed her in the backyard. He spoke softly, just behind her in the yard. It was dark, after seven, an evening in early March when a bitter wind was blowing. 'I'll walk with you, Dervla,' he said.

She wheeled her bicycle in Old Lane and they walked in silence except that once he remarked upon the coldness of the weather and she said she disliked rain more. When they reached the end of the lane he went one way and she the other.

'Hullo, Dervla,' he said one afternoon in the garden. It was late in August. He was lying on a rug among the hydrangeas, reading. She had passed without noticing that he was there; she returned some minutes later with a bunch of parsley. It was then that he addressed her. He smiled, trying to find a different intonation, trying to make his greeting softer, less ordinary than usual. He wanted her to sit down on the brown checked rug, to enjoy the sun for a while, but of course that was impossible. He had wanted to wheel her bicycle for her that evening, as he would have done had she been another girl, Hazel Warren or Annie Warren, the coal merchant's daughters, or a girl he'd never even spoken to, someone's cousin, who used to visit the town every Christmas. But it hadn't seemed natural in any way at all to wheel the bicycle of the dining-room maid, any more than it would have been to ask a kitchen maid at school where she came from or if she had brothers and sisters.

'Hullo,' she said, replying to his greeting in the garden. She passed on with her bunch of parsley, seeming not to be in a hurry, the crisp white strings of her apron bobbing as she walked.

In her bedroom in the house in Thomas MacDonagh Street she thought of him every night before she went to sleep. She saw him as he was when he returned from his boarding-school, in his grey long-trousered suit, a green-and-white-striped tie knotted into the grey collar of his shirt. When she awoke in the morning she thought of him also, the first person to share the day with. In winter she lay there in the darkness, but in summer the dawn light lit the picture of the Virgin above the door, and when Dervla felt the Virgin's liquid eyes upon her she prayed, asking the Holy Mother for all sorts of things she afterwards felt she shouldn't have because they were trivial. She pleaded that he might smile when he thanked her for the rashers and sausages she put in front of him, that his little finger might accidentally touch her hand as only once it had. She pleaded that Mr Congreve wouldn't engage her in conversation at lunchtime, asking how her father was these days, because somehow – in front of him – it embarrassed her.

There was a nightmare she had, possessing her in varied forms: that he was in the house in Thomas MacDonagh Street and that her mother was on her knees, scrubbing the stone floor of the scullery. Her mother didn't seem to know who he was and would not stand up. Her father and her uncle from Leitrim sat drinking stout by the fire, and when she introduced him they remarked upon his clothes. Sometimes in the nightmare her uncle nudged him with his elbow and asked him if he had a song in him.

'That young Carroll has an eye for you,' her father said once or twice, drawing her attention to Buzzy Carroll who worked in Catigan's hardware. But she didn't want to spend Sunday afternoons walking out on the Ballydrim road with Buzzy Carroll, or to sit with his arms around her in the Excel cinema. One of the Christian Brothers had first called him Buzzy, something to do with the way his hair fluffed about his head, and after that no one could remember what Buzzy Carroll's real name was. There were others who would have liked to go out with her, on walks or to the pictures, or to the Tara Dance Hall on a Friday night. There was Flynn who worked in Maguire's timber yard, and Chappie Reagan, and Butty Delaney. There was the porter at the auction rooms who had something the matter with his feet, the toes joined together in such a peculiar way that he showed them to people. And there was Streak Dwyer. 'You're nothing only a streak of woe,' the same Christian Brother had years ago pronounced. Streak Dwyer had ever since retained the sobriquet, serving now in Rattray's grocery, sombrely weighing flour and sugar. Dervla had once or twice wondered what walking out on the Ballydrim road with this melancholy shopman would be like and if he would suggest turning into one of the lanes, as Butty Delaney or Buzzy Carroll would have. She wouldn't have cared for it in the Excel cinema with Streak Dwyer any more than she cared for the idea of being courted by a man who showed people his toes.

*

'Dervla.'

On a wet afternoon, a Tuesday in September, he whispered her name on the first-floor landing. He put his arm around her, and she was frightened in case someone would come.

'I'm fond of you, Dervla.'

He took her hand and led her upstairs to Room 14, a tiny bedroom that was only used when the hotel was full. Both of them were shy, and their shyness evaporated slowly. He kissed her, stroking her hair. He said again he was fond of her. 'I'm fond of you too,' she whispered.

After that first afternoon they met often to embrace in Room 14. They would marry, he said at the end of that holidays; they would live in the hotel, just like his parents. Over and over again in Room 14 the afternoon shadows gathered as sunlight slipped away. They whispered, clinging to one another, the warmth of their bodies becoming a single warmth. She sat huddled on his knee, holding tightly on to him in case they both fell off the rickety bedroom chair. He loved the curve of her neck, he whispered, and her soft fair hair, her lips and her eyes. He loved kissing her eyes.

Often there was silence in the bedroom, broken only by the faraway cries of Molly and Margery-Jane playing in the garden. Sometimes it became quite dark in the room, and she would have to go then because Mrs O'Connor would be wanting her in the kitchen.

'Not a bad fella at all,' her father said in Thomas MacDonagh Street. 'Young Carroll.' She wanted to laugh when her father said that, wondering what on earth he'd say if he knew about Room 14. He would probably say nothing; in silence he would take his belt to her. But the thought of his doing so didn't make her afraid.

'Oh, Dervla, how I wish the time would hurry up and pass!'

Over the years he had come to see the town as little better than a higgledy-piggledy conglomeration of dwellings, an ugly place except for the small bridge at the end of Mill Street. But it was Dervla's town, and it was his own; together they belonged there. He saw himself in middle age walking through its narrow streets, as he had walked during his childhood. He saw himself returning to the hotel and going at once to embrace the wife he loved with a passion that had not changed.

'Oh, Dervla,' he whispered in Room 14. 'Dervla, I'm so fond of you.'

'Well, now, I think we must have a little talk,' Mrs Congreve said.

They were alone in the dining-room; Dervla had been laying the tables for dinner. When Mrs Congreve spoke she felt herself reddening; the knives and forks felt suddenly cold in her hands.

'Finish the table, Dervla, and then we'll talk about it.'

She did as she was bidden. Mrs Congreve stood by a window, looking out at people passing on the street. When Dervla had finished she caught a glimpse of herself in the mirror over the fireplace. Her thin, pretty face had a frightened look, and seemed fragile, perhaps because she had paled. She averted her gaze almost as soon as the mirror reflected it. Mrs Congreve said:

'Mr Congreve and I are disappointed that this has happened. It's most unfortunate.'

Turning from the window, Mrs Congreve smiled a lingering, gracious smile. She was wearing one of her green-and-blue dresses, a flimsy, delicate garment with tiny blue buttons and a stylishly stiff white collar. Her dark hair was coiled silkily about her head.

'It is perhaps difficult for you to understand, Dervla, and certainly it is unpleasant for me to say. But there are differences between you and Christopher that cannot be overlooked or ignored.' Mrs Congreve paused and again looked out of the window, slightly drawing the net curtain aside. 'Christopher is not of your class, Dervla. He is not of your religion. You are a maid in this hotel. You have betrayed the trust that Mr Congreve and I placed in you. I'm putting it harshly, Dervla, but there's no point in pretending.'

Dervla did not say anything. She felt desolate and alone. She wished he wasn't away at school. She wished she could run out of the dining-room and find him somewhere, that he would help her in this terrifying conversation.

'Oh, Christopher has done wrong also. I can assure you we are aware of that. We are disappointed in Christopher, but we think it better to close the matter in his absence. He will not be back for another three months almost; we think it best to have everything finished and forgotten by then. Mr Congreve will explain to Christopher.'

Again there was the gracious smile. No note of anger had entered Mrs Congreve's voice, no shadow of displeasure disrupted the beauty of her features. She might have been talking about the annual bloodstock dinner, giving instructions about how the tables should be set.

'We would ask you to write a note now, to Christopher at school. Mr Congreve and I would like to see it, Dervla, before it goes on its way. That, then, would be the end of the matter.'

As she spoke, Mrs Congreve nodded sympathetically, honouring Dervla's unspoken protest: she understood, she said. She did not explain how the facts had come to be discovered, but suggested that in the note she spoke of Dervla should write that she felt in danger of losing her position in the Royal Hotel, that she was upset by what had taken place and would not wish any of it to take place again.

'That is the important aspect of it, Dervla. Neither Mr Congreve nor I wish to dismiss you. If we did, you – and we – would have to explain to your parents, even to Father Mahony, I suppose. If it's possible, Dervla, we would much rather avoid all that.'

But Dervla, crimson-faced, mentioned love. Her voice was weak, without substance and seeming to be without conviction, although this was not so. Mrs Congreve replied that that was penny-fiction talk.

'We want to get married, ma'am.' Dervla closed her eyes beneath the effort of finding the courage to say that. The palms of her hands, chilled a moment ago, were warmly moist now. She could feel pinpricks on her forehead.

'That's very silly, Dervla,' Mrs Congreve said in the same calm manner. 'I'm surprised you should be so silly.'

'I love him,' Dervla cried, all convention abruptly shattered. Her voice was shrill in the dining-room, tears ran from her eyes and she felt herself seized by a wildness that made her want to shriek out in fury. 'I love him,' she cried again. 'It isn't just a little thing.'

'Don't you feel you belong in the Royal, Dervla? We have trained you, you know. We have done a lot, Dervla.'

There was a silence then, except for Dervla's sobbing. She found a handkerchief in the pocket of her apron and wiped her eyes and nose with it. In such silly circumstances, Mrs Congreve said, Christopher would not inherit the hotel. The hotel would be sold, and Christopher would inherit nothing. It wasn't right that a little thing like this should ruin Christopher's life. 'So you see, you must go, Dervla. You must take your wages up to the end of the month and go this afternoon.'

The tranquillity of Mrs Congreve's manner was intensified by the sadness in her voice. She was on Dervla's side, her manner insisted; her admonitions were painful for her. Again she offered the alternative:

'Or simply write a few lines to him, and we shall continue in the hotel as though nothing has happened. That is possible, you know. I assure you of that, my dear.'

Miserably, Dervla asked what she could say in a letter. She would have to tell lies. She wouldn't know how to explain.

'No, don't tell lies. Explain the truth: that you realize the friendship must not continue, now that you and he are growing up. You've always been a sensible girl, Dervla. You must realize that what happened between you was for children only.'

Dervla shook her head, but Mrs Congreve didn't acknowledge the gesture.

'I can assure you, Dervla – I can actually promise you – that when Christopher has grown up a little more he will see the impossibility of continuing such a friendship. The hotel, even now, is everything to Christopher. I can actually promise you, also, that you will not be asked to leave. I know you value coming here.'

At school, when he received the letter, Christopher was astonished. In Dervla's rounded handwriting it said that they must not continue to meet in Room 14 because it was a sin. It would be best to bring everything to an end now, before she was dismissed. They had done wrong, but at least they could avoid the worst if they were sensible now.

It was so chilly a letter, as from a stranger, that Christopher could hardly believe what it so very clearly said. Why did she feel this now, when a few weeks ago they had sworn to love one another for as long as they lived? Were all girls as fickle and as strange? Or had the priests, somehow, got at her, all this stuff about sin?

He could not write back. His handwriting on the envelope would be recognized in the hotel, and he did not know her address since she had not included it in her letter. He had no choice but to wait, and as days and then weeks went by his bewilderment turned to anger. It was stupid that she should suddenly develop these scruples after all they'd said to one another. The love he continued to feel for her became tinged with doubt and with resentment, as though they'd had a quarrel.

'Now, I don't want to say anything more about this,' his father said at the beginning of the next holidays. 'But it doesn't do, you know, to go messing about with the maids.'

That was the end of the unfortunateness as far as his father was concerned. It was not something that should be talked about, no good could come of that.

'It wasn't messing about.'

'That girl was very upset, Christopher.'

Three months ago Christopher would have said he wanted to marry Dervla, forced into that admission by what had been discovered. He would have spoken of love. But his father had managed to draw him aside to have this conversation before he'd had an opportunity even to see her, let alone speak to her. He felt confused, and uncertain about his feelings.

'It would be hard on her to dismiss her. We naturally didn't want to do that. We want the girl to remain here, Christopher, since really it's a bit of a storm in a teacup.'

His father lit a cigarette and seemed more at ease once he had made that pronouncement. There was a lazier look about his face than there had been a moment ago; a smile drifted over his lips. 'Good term?' he said, and Christopher nodded.

'Is it the priests, Dervla?' They stood together in a doorway in Old Lane, her bicycle propped against the kerb. 'Did the priests get at you?'

She shook her head.

'Did my mother speak to you?'

'Your mother only said a few things.'

She went away, wheeling her bicycle for a while before mounting it. He watched her, not feeling as miserable as when her letter had arrived, for during the months that had passed since then he had become reconciled to the loss of their relationship: between the lines of her letter there had been a finality.

He returned to the hotel and Artie helped him to carry his trunk upstairs. He wished that none of it had ever happened.

Dervla was glad he made no further effort to talk to her, but standing between courses by the dumb-waiter in the dining-room, she often wondered what he was thinking. While the others talked he was at first affected by embarrassment because at mealtimes in the past there had been the thrill of surreptitious glances and forbidden smiles. But after a week or so he became less quiet, joining in the family conversation, and she became the dining-room maid again.

Yet for Dervla the moment of placing his food in front of him was as poignant as ever it had been, and in her private moments she permitted herself the luxury of dwelling in the past. In her bedroom in Thomas MacDonagh Street she closed her eyes and willed into her consciousness the afternoon sunlight of Room 14. Once more she was familiar with the quickening of his heart and the cool touch of his hands. Once more she clung to him, her body huddled into his on the rickety chair in the corner, the faraway cries of Molly and Margery-Jane gently disturbing the silence.

Dervla did not experience bitterness. She was fortunate that the Congreves had been above the pettiness of dismissing her, and when she prayed she gave thanks for that. When more time had gone by she found herself able to confess the sinning that had been so pleasurable in Room 14, and was duly burdened with a penance for both the misdemeanours and her long delay in confessing them. She had feared to lose what there had been through expiation, but the fear had been groundless: only reality had been lost. 'Young Carroll was asking for you,' her father reported in a bewildered way, unable to understand her reluctance even to consider Buzzy Carroll's interest.

Everything was easier when the green trunk and the box with the metal brackets stood in the back hall at the beginning of another term, and when a few more terms had come and gone he greeted her in the hotel as if all she had confessed to was a fantasy. Like his parents, she sensed, he was glad her dismissal had not been necessary, for that would have been unfair. 'Did my mother speak to you?' The quiet vehemence there had been in his voice was sweet to remember, but he himself would naturally wish to forget it now: for him, Room 14 must have come to seem like an adventure in indiscretion, as naturally his parents had seen it.

Two summers after he left school Dervla noticed signs in him that painfully echoed the past. An archdeacon's daughter sometimes had lunch with the family: he couldn't take his eyes off her. Serving the food and in her position by the dumb-waiter, Dervla watched him listening while the archdeacon's daughter talked about how she and her parents had moved from one rectory to another and how the furniture hadn't fitted the new rooms, how there hadn't been enough stair-carpet. The archdeacon's daughter was very beautiful. Her dark hair was drawn back from a centre parting; when she smiled a dimple came and went in one cheek only; her skin was like the porcelain of a doll's skin. Often in the dining-room she talked about her childhood in the seaside backwater where she had once lived. Every morning in summer and autumn she and her father had gone together to the strand to bathe. They piled their clothes up by a breakwater, putting stones on them if there was a wind, and then they would run down the sand to the edge of the sea. A man sometimes passed by on a horse, a retired lighthouse keeper, a lonely, widowed man. Christopher was entranced.

Dervla cleared away the dishes, expertly disposing of chop bones or bits of left-behind fat. Mary had years ago shown her how to flick the table refuse on to a single plate, a different one from the plate you gathered the used knives and forks on to. Doing so now, she too listened to everything the archdeacon's daughter said. Once upon a time the Pierrots had performed on the strand in August, and Hewitt's Travelling Fun Fair had come; regularly, June to September, summer visitors filled the promenade boarding-houses, arriving on excursion trains. Garish pictures were painted with coloured powders on the sand, castles and saints and gardens. 'I loved that place,' the archdeacon's daughter said.

Afterwards Dervla watched from an upstairs window, the window in fact of Room 14. The archdeacon's daughter sat with him in the garden, each of them in a deck-chair, laughing and conversing. They were always laughing: the archdeacon's daughter would say something and he would throw his head back with appreciation and delight. Long before the engagement was announced Dervla knew that this was the girl who was going to take her place, in his life and in the hotel.

The Archdeacon conducted the service in St Peter's, and then the guests made their way to the garden of the hotel. That the wedding reception was to be at the hotel was a business arrangement between the Archdeacon and Mr Congreve, for the expenses were to be the former's, as convention demanded. It was a day in June, a Thursday, in the middle of a heatwave.

Dervla and a new maid with spectacles handed round glasses of champagne. Artie saw to it that people had chairs to sit on if they wished to sit. The archdeacon's daughter wore a wedding-dress that had a faint shade of blue in it, and a Limerick lace veil. She was kissed by people in the garden, she smiled while helping to cut the wedding cake. Her four bridesmaids, Molly and Margery-Jane among them, kept saying she looked marvellous.

Speeches were made in the sunshine. Dr Molloy made one and so did the best man, Tom Gouvernet, and Mr Congreve. Dr Molloy remembered the day Christopher was born, and Mr Congreve remembered the first time he'd set eyes on the beauty of the Archdeacon's daughter, and Tom Gouvernet remembered Christopher at school. Other guests remembered other occasions; Christopher said he was the lucky man and kissed the archdeacon's daughter while people clapped their hands with delight. Tom Gouvernet fell backwards off the edge of a raised bed.

There was an excess of emotion in the garden, an excess of smiles and tears and happiness and love. The champagne glasses were held up endlessly, toast after toast. Christopher's mother moved among the guests with the plump wife of the archdeacon and the Archdeacon himself, who was as frail as a stalk of straw. In his easy-going way Christopher's father delighted in the champagne and the sunshine, and the excitement of a party. Mr McKibbin, the bank agent, was there, and Hogarty the surveyor, and an insurance man who happened to be staying at the hotel. There was nothing Mr Congreve liked better than standing about talking to these barroom companions.

'Thanks, Dervla.' Taking a glass from her tray, Christopher smiled at her because for ages that had been possible again.

'It's a lovely wedding, sir.'

'Yes, it is.'

He looked at her eyes, and was aware of the demanding steadiness of her gaze. He sensed what she was wondering and wondered it himself:

what would have happened if she'd been asked to leave the hotel? He guessed, as she did: they would have shared the resentment and the anger that both of them had separately experienced; defiantly they would have continued to meet in the town; she would have accompanied him on his walks, out into the country and the fields. There would have been talk in the town and scenes in the hotel, their relationship would again have been proscribed. They would have drawn closer to one another, their outraged feelings becoming an element in the forbidden friendship. In the end, together, they would have left the hotel and the town and neither of them would be standing here now. Both their lives would be quite different.

'You'll be getting married yourself one of these days, Dervla.'

'Ah, no no.'

She was still quite pretty. There was a simplicity about her freckled features that was pleasing; her soft fair hair was neat beneath her maid's white cap. But she was not beautiful. Once, not knowing much about it, he had imagined she was. It was something less palpable that distinguished her.

'Oh, surely? Surely, Dervla?'

'I don't see myself giving up the hotel, sir. My future's here, sir.'

He smiled again and passed on. But his smile, which remained while he listened to a story of Tom Gouvernet's about the hazards to be encountered on a honeymoon, was uneasy. An echo of the eyes that had gazed so steadily remained with him, as did the reference she had made to her future. That she had not been turned out of the hotel had seemed something to be proud of at the time: a crudity had been avoided. But while Tom Gouvernet's lowered voice continued, he found himself wishing she had been. She would indeed not ever marry, her eyes had stated, she would not wish to.

A hand of his wife's slipped into one of his; the voice of Tom Gouvernet ceased. The hand was as delicate as the petal of a flower, the fingers so tiny that involuntarily he lifted them to his lips. Had Dervla seen? he wondered, and he looked through the crowd for a glimpse of her but could not see her. Hogarty the surveyor was doing a trick with a handkerchief, entertaining the coal merchant's daughters. Mr McKibben was telling one of his stories.

'Ah, he's definitely the lucky man,' Tom Gouvernet said, playfully winking at the bride.

It had never occurred to Christopher before that while he and his parents could successfully bury a part of the past, Dervla could not. It had never occurred to him that because she was the girl she was she did not appreciate that some experiences were best forgotten. Ever since the Congreves had owned the Royal Hotel a way of life had obtained there, but its subtleties had naturally eluded the dining-room maid.

'When you get tired of him,' Tom Gouvernet went on in the same light manner, 'you know who to turn to.'

'Oh, indeed I do, Tom.'

He should have told her about Dervla. If he told her now she would want Dervla to go; any wife would, in perfect reasonableness. An excuse must be found, she would say, even though a promise had been made.

'But I won't become tired of him,' she was saying, smiling at Tom Gouvernet. 'He's actually quite nice, you know.'

In the far distance Dervla appeared, hurrying from the hotel with a freshly laden tray. Christopher watched her, while the banter continued between bride and best man.

'He had the shocking reputation at school,' Tom Gouvernet said.

'Oh? I didn't know that.' She was still smiling; she didn't believe it. It wasn't true.

'A right Lothario you've got yourself hitched to.'

He would not tell her. It was too late for that, it would bewilder her since he had not done so before. It wouldn't be fair to require her not to wish that Dervla, even now, should be asked to go; or to understand that a promise made to a dining-room maid must be honoured because that was the family way.

Across the garden the Archdeacon lifted a glass from Dervla's tray. He was still in the company of his plump wife and Christopher's mother. They, too, took more champagne and then Dervla walked towards where Christopher was standing with his bride and his best man. She moved quickly through the crowd, not offering her tray of glasses to the guests she passed, intent upon her destination.

'Thank you, Dervla,' his wife of an hour said.

'I think Mr Hogarty,' he said himself, 'could do with more champagne.'

He watched her walking away and was left again with the insistence in her eyes. As the dining-room maid, she would become part of another family growing up in the hotel. She would listen to a mother telling her children about the strand where once she'd bathed, where a retired lighthouse keeper had passed by on a horse. For all his life he would daily look upon hers, but no words would ever convey her undramatic revenge because the right to speak, once his gift to her, had been taken away. He had dealt in cruelty and so now did she: her gift to him, held over until his wedding day, was that afternoon shadows would gather for ever in Room 14, while she kept faith.

Lunch in Winter

Mrs Nancy Simpson – who did not at all care for that name and would have wished to be Nancy le Puys or Nancy du Maurier – awoke on a December morning. She had been dreaming of a time long past in her life, when her name had been Nancy Dawes, before she'd been married to anyone. The band had been playing 'You are my Honeysuckle' and in the wings of the Old Gaiety they had all been in line, smiles ready, waiting to come on. *You are my honey-honeysuckle, I am the bee* ... Was it called something else, known by some other title? 'Smoke Gets in your Eyes' had once been called something else, so Laurie Henderson had said, although, God knows, if Laurie'd said it it probably wasn't true. You could never tell with songs. 'If You were the Only Girl in the World', for instance: was that the full title or was it 'If You were the Only Girl in the World and I was the Only Boy'? She'd had an argument with Laurie about that, a ridiculous all-night argument in Mrs Tomer's digs, Macclesfield, 1949 or '50. '50 probably because soon afterwards Laurie went down to London, doing something – barman probably – for the Festival of Britain thing. He'd walked out of Mrs Tomer's and she hadn't seen him for nine years. '51 actually it must have been. Definitely the Festival had been 1951.

She rose, and before she did anything else applied make-up to her face with very great care. She often thought there was nothing she liked better than sitting in her petticoat in front of a looking-glass, putting another face on. She powdered her lipstick, then smiled at herself. She thought about Fitz because today was Thursday and they'd drifted into the way of having lunch on Thursdays. 'My God, it's Nancy!' he'd said when by extraordinary chance he'd come upon her six months ago gazing into the windows of Peter Jones. They'd had a cup of tea, and had told one another this and that. 'Of course, why ever not?' she'd said when he'd suggested that they might occasionally see one another. 'Old times' sake,' she'd probably said: she couldn't remember now.

Her flat in Putney was high in a red-brick Victorian block, overlooking the river. Near by was the big, old-fashioned Sceptre Hotel, where drinkers from the flats spent a few evening hours, where foreign commercial travellers stayed. During Wimbledon some of the up-and-coming players stayed there also, with the has-beens. She liked to sit in the Bayeux Lounge and watch them passing through the reception area, pausing for their keys. That German who'd got into the final about ten years ago she'd noticed once, and she liked to think that McEnroe had stayed in the Sceptre before he'd got going, but she hadn't actually seen him. Every year from the windows of her tiny flat she watched the Boat Race going by, but really had no interest in it. Nice, though, the way it always brought the crowds to Putney. Nice that Putney in the springtime, one Saturday in the year, was not forgotten.

Fitz would be on his train, she thought as she crossed Putney Bridge on her way to the Underground. The bridge was where Christie, who'd murdered so many prostitutes, had been arrested. He'd just had a meal in the Lacy Dining Rooms and perhaps he'd even been thinking of murdering another that very night when the plain clothes had scooped him up. He'd gone, apparently, without a word of protest.

'My, you're a romantic, Fitz!' she'd said all those years ago, and really he hadn't changed. Typical of him to want to make it a regular Thursday rendezvous. Typical to come up specially from the coast, catching a train and then another train back. During the war they'd been married for four years.

She sang for a moment, remembering that; and then wanting to forget it. His family had thought he was mad, you could see that immediately. He'd led her into a huge drawing-room in Warwickshire, with a grand piano in one corner, and his mother and sister had actually recoiled. 'But for God's sake, you can't!' she'd heard his sister's shrill, unpleasant voice exclaiming in the middle of that same night. 'You can't marry a chorus girl!' But he had married her; they'd had to stomach her in the end.

She'd been a sunflower on the stage of the Old Gaiety when he'd first picked her out; after that he'd come night after night. He'd said she had a flimsy quality and needed looking after. When they met again six months ago in Regent Street he'd said in just the same kind of way that she was far too thin. She'd seen him eyeing her hair, which had been light and fair and was a yellowish colour now, not as pretty as it had been. But he didn't remark on it because he was the kind to remark only on the good things, saying instead she hadn't changed a bit. He seemed boyishly delighted that she still laughed the way she always had, and often remarked that she still held the stem of a glass and her cigarette in her own particular way. 'You're cold,' he'd said a week ago, reminding her of how he'd always gone on in the past about her not wearing enough clothes. He'd never understood that heavy things didn't suit her.

In other ways he hadn't changed, either. Still with a military bearing and hardly grey at all, he had a sunburnt look about the face, as always he'd had. He had not run to fat or slackness, and the sunburnt look extended over his forehead and beyond where his hair had receded. He was all of a piece, his careful suits, his soldier's walk. He'd married someone else, but after twenty-three years she'd gone and died on him.

'Good week?' he inquired in the Trattoria San Michele. 'What have you got up to, Nancy?'

She smiled and shrugged her skimpy shoulders. Nothing much, she didn't say. There'd been a part she'd heard about and had hoped for, but she didn't want to talk about that; it was a long time since she'd had a part.

'The trout with almonds,' he suggested. 'Shall we both have that?'

She smiled again and nodded. She lived on alimony, not his but that of the man she had married last, the one called Simpson. She lit a cigarette; she liked to smoke at meals, sometimes between mouthfuls.

'They've started that thing on the TV again,' she said. 'That *Blankety Blank*. Hilarious.'

She didn't know why she'd been unfaithful to him. She'd thought he wouldn't guess, but when he'd come back on his first leave he'd known at once. She'd promised it would never happen again, swearing it was due to the topsy-turviness of the war, the worry because he was in danger. Several leaves later, when the war was almost over, she promised again. 'I couldn't love anyone else, Fitz,' she'd whimpered, meaning it, really and truly. But at the beginning of 1948 he divorced her.

She hated to remember that time, especially since he was here and being so nice to her. She wanted to pay him back and asked him if he remembered the theme from *State Fair*. 'Marvellous. And then of course "Spring Fever" in the same picture.' She sang for a moment. '... *and it isn't even Spring*. 'Member?'

Eventually she had gone to Canada with a man called Eddie Lush, whom later she had married. She had stayed there, and later in Philadelphia, for thirteen years, but when she returned to England two children who had been born, a boy and a girl, did not accompany her. They'd become more attached to Eddie Lush than to her, which had hurt her at the time, and there'd been accusations of neglect during the court case, which had been hurtful too. Once upon a time they'd written letters to her occasionally, but she wasn't sure now what they were doing.

'And "I'll Be Around". 'Member "I'll Be Around"?' She sang again, very softly. '*No matter how ... you treat me now ...* Who was it sang it, d'you 'member?'

He shook his head. The waiter brought their trout and Nancy smiled at him. The tedium that had just begun to creep into these Thursday lunches had evaporated as soon as she'd set eyes on the Trattoria's new waiter six or so weeks ago. On Thursday evenings, in her corner of the Bayeux Lounge, his courtesy and his handsome face haunted her. Yes, he was a little sad, she often said to herself in the Bayeux Lounge. Was there even a hint of pain in those steady Latin eyes?

'Oh, lovely-looking trout,' she said, continuing to smile. 'Thanks ever so, Cesare.'

The man she had been married to was saying something else, but she didn't hear what it was. She remembered a chap like Cesare during the war, an airman from the base whom she'd longed to be taken out by, although in fact he'd never invited her.

'What?' she murmured, becoming aware that she'd been asked a question. But the question, now repeated, was only the familiar one, so often asked on Thursdays: did she intend to remain in her Putney flat, was she quite settled there? It was asked because once she'd said – she didn't know why – that the flat was temporary, that her existence in Putney had a temporary feel to it. She couldn't tell all the truth, she couldn't – to Fitz of all people – reveal the hope that at long last old Mr Robin Right would come bob-bob-bobbing along. She believed in Mr R.R., always had, and for some reason she'd got it into her head that he might quite easily walk into the Bayeux Lounge of the Sceptre Hotel. In the evenings she watched television in her flat or in the Bayeux Lounge, sometimes feeling bored because she had no particular friend or confidante. But then she'd always had an inclination to feel a bit like that. Boredom was the devil in her, Laurie Henderson used to say.

'Thanks ever so,' she said again because Cesare had skilfully placed a little heap of peas beside the trout. Typical of her, of course, to go falling for a restaurant waiter: you set yourself out on a sensible course, all serious and determined, and the next thing was you were half in love with an unsuitable younger man. Not that she looked fifty-nine, of course, more like forty – even thirty-eight, as a chap in the Bayeux Lounge had said when she'd asked him to guess a month ago. Unfortunately the chap had definitely not been Mr R.R.

'I just wondered,' Fitz was saying.

She smiled and nodded. The waiter was aware of her attention, no doubt about it. There was a little wink she was gifted with, a slight little motion of the lids, nothing suggestive about it. 'Makes me laugh, your wink,' Eddie Lush used to say, and it was probably Simpson who had called it a gift. She couldn't think why she'd ever allowed herself to marry Simpson, irritating face he'd had, irritating ways.

'It's been enjoyable, making the garden, building that wall. I never thought I'd be able to build a wall.'

He'd told her a lot about his house by the sea, a perfect picture it sounded, with flowerbeds all around the edge, and rustic trellising with ivy disguising the outside sanitary arrangements. He was terribly proud of what he'd done, and every right he had to be, the way he'd made the garden out of nothing. Won some kind of award the garden had, best on the south coast or the world or something.

'I could sell it very well. I've begun to think of that.'

She nodded. Cesare was expertly gathering up the plates four businessmen had eaten from. The men were stout and flushed, all of them married: you could tell a married look at once. At another table a chap who was married also was taking out a girl less than half his age, and next to them a couple looked as though they were planning a dirty weekend. A party of six, men and women, were at the big central table, just beside where the salads and the bowls of fruit were all laid out and where the dessert trolley was. She'd seen that party here a couple of weeks ago; they'd been talking about *En Tout Cas* tennis courts.

'Once you've made something as you want it,' Fitz was saying, 'you tend to lose interest, I suppose.'

The head-waiter called out to the other, younger Italian, she didn't know what his name was, lumpy-looking boy. But Cesare, because he was less busy, answered. '*Pronto! Pronto!*'

'You're never selling up, Fitz?'

'Well, I'm wondering about it.'

He had told her about the woman he'd married, a responsible type of woman she sounded, but she'd been ill or something and hadn't been able to have children. Twenty-three years was really a very long time for any two people to keep going. But then the woman had died.

'You get itchy feet,' he said. 'Even when you're passing sixty.'

'My, you don't look it.' Automatically she responded, watching the waiter while he served the party at the central table with T-bone steaks, a San Michele speciality. He said something else, but it didn't impinge on her. Then she heard:

'I often think it would be nice to live in London.'

He was eyeing her, to catch her reaction to this. 'You've had a battered life,' he'd said to her, the second time they'd had lunch. He'd looked at her much as he was looking at her now, and had said it twice. That was being an actress, she'd explained: always living on your nerves, hoping for this part or that, the disappointment of don't-call-us. 'Well, I suppose it batters you in the end,' she'd agreed. 'The old Profession.'

He, on the other hand, had appeared to have had quite a cosy time in the intervening years. Certainly, the responsible-sounding woman hadn't battered him, far from it. They'd been as snug as anything in the house by the sea, a heavy type of woman, Nancy imagined she'd been, with this thing wrong with her, whatever it was. It was after she'd dropped off her twig that he'd begun to feel sorry for himself and of course you couldn't blame him, poor Fitz. It had upset him at first that people had led unattached women up to him at cocktail parties, widows and the like, who'd lost their figures or had let their hair go frizzy, or were old. He'd told her all that one lunchtime and on another occasion he'd confessed that after a year or so had passed he'd gone to a bureau place, an introduction agency, where much younger women were fixed up for him. But that hadn't worked either. He had met the first of them for tea in the Ceylon Centre, where she'd told him that her deceased husband had been an important figure in a chemicals firm and that her older daughter was married in Australia, that her son was in the Hong Kong Police and another daughter married to a dentist in Worcester. She had not ceased to talk the entire time she was with him, apparently, telling him that she suffered from the heat, especially her feet. He'd taken another woman to a revival of *Annie Get Your Gun*, and he'd met a third in a bar she had suggested, where she'd begun to slur her speech after half an hour. Poor Fitz! He'd always been a simple soldier. She could have told him a bureau place would be no good, stood to reason you'd only get the down-and-outs.

'Sorry?' she said.

'I don't suppose you'd ever think of giving it another go?'

'Darling Fitz! *Dear* darling Fitz!'

She smiled at him. How typical it was that he didn't know it was impossible to pick up pieces that had been lying about for forty years! The past was full of Simpson and Laurie Henderson and Eddie Lush, and the two children she'd borne, the girl the child of a fertilizer salesman, which was something Eddie Lush had never guessed. You couldn't keep going on journeys down Memory Lane, and the more you did the more you realized that it was just an ugly black tunnel. Time goes by, as the old song had it, a kiss and a sigh and that was that. She smiled again. '*The fundamental things of life*,' she sang softly, smiling again at her ex-husband.

'I just thought –' he began.

'You always said pretty things, Fitz.'

'I always meant them.'

It had been so romantic when he'd said she needed looking after. He'd called her winsome another time. He was far more romantic than any of the others had ever been, but unfortunately when being romantic went on for a while it could become a teeny bit dreary, no other word for it. Not of course that you'd ever call poor Fitz dreary, far from it.

'Where d'you come from, Cesare?' she asked the waiter, thinking it a good idea to cause a diversion – and besides, it was nice to make the waiter linger. He was better looking than the airman from the base. He had a better nose, a nicer chin. She'd never seen such eyes, nor hair she longed so much to touch. Delicate with the coffee flask, his hands were as brown as an Italian fir-cone. She'd been to Italy once, to Sestri Levante with a man called Jacob Fynne who'd said he was going to put on *Lilac Time*. She'd collected fir-cones because she'd been bored, because all Jacob Fynne had wanted was her body. The waiter said he came from somewhere she'd never heard of.

'D'you know Sestri Levante?' she asked in order to keep him at their table.

He said he didn't, so she told him about it. Supposing she ran into him on the street, like she'd run into Fitz six months ago? He'd be alone: restaurant waiters in a city that was foreign to them could not know many people. Would it be so strange to walk together for a little while and then maybe to go in somewhere for a drink? 'Are your lodgings adequate, Cesare?' She would ask the question, and he would reply that his lodgings were not good. He'd say so because it stood to reason that the kind of lodgings an Italian waiter would be put into would of course be abominable. 'I'll look out for somewhere for you': would it be so wrong to say that?

'Would you consider it, Nancy? I mean, is it beyond the pale?'

For a moment it seemed that the hand which had seized one of hers was the waiter's, but then she noticed that Cesare was hurrying away with his flask of coffee. The hand that was paying her attention was marked with age, a bigger, squarer hand than Cesare's.

'Oh Fitz, you are a dear!'

'Well . . .'

'D'you think we might be naughty and go for a brandy today?'

'Of course.'

He signalled the waiter back. She lit another cigarette. When the brandy came and more coffee was being poured she said:

'And how do you like England? London?'

'Very nice, *signora*.'

'When you've tired of London you've tired of life, Cesare. That's a famous saying we have.'

'*Si, signora*.'

'D'you know Berkeley Square, Cesare? There's a famous song we have about a nightingale in Berkeley Square. Whereabouts d'you live, Cesare?'

'Tooting Bec, *signora*.'

'Good heavens! Tooting's miles away.'

'Not too far, *signora*.'

'I'd rather have Naples any day. See Naples and die, eh?'

She sang a little from the song she'd referred to, and then she laughed and slapped Cesare lightly on the wrist, causing him to laugh also. He said the song was very nice.

'I'm sorry,' Fitz was saying. 'It was a silly thing to say.'

'You've never been silly in your life, Fitz.' She laughed again. 'Except when you married me.'

Gallantly, he shook his head.

'Thanks ever so,' she called after the waiter, who had moved with his coffee flask to the table with the business people. She thought of his being in Putney, in the room she'd found for him, much more convenient than Tooting. She thought of his coming to see her in the flat, of their sitting together with the windows open so that they could look out over the river. It was an unusual relationship, they both knew that, but he confessed that he had always liked the company of older women. He said so very quietly, not looking at her, speaking in a solemn tone. Nothing would change between them, he promised while they drank Campari sodas and she explained about the Boat Race.

'I shouldn't have said it. I'm sorry, Nancy.'

She hummed a snatch of something, smiling at him to show it didn't matter in the least. He'd made another proposal, just like he had when she'd been a sunflower at the Old Gaiety. It was a compliment, but she didn't say so because she was still thinking about sitting with the windows open in Putney.

'I must get back. I'll take an earlier train today,' he said.

'Just a teeny 'nother coffee, Fitz? And perhaps ...' She lifted her empty brandy glass, her head a little on one side, the way he'd so often said he liked. And when the waiter came again she said:

'And have you always been a waiter, Cesare?'

He said he had, leaving a plate with the bill on it on the table. She tried to think of something else to say to him, but could think of nothing.

When they left the restaurant they walked with a bitter wind in their faces and he didn't take her arm, the way he'd done last week and the week before. On a crowded street the hurrying people jostled them, not apologizing. Once they were separated and for a moment she couldn't see her ex-husband and thought that he had slipped away from her, punishing her because she had been embarrassing with the waiter. But that was not his way. 'I'm here,' his voice said.

His cold lips touched her cheeks, first one, then the other. His large, square fingers gripped her arm for just a moment. 'Well, goodbye, Nancy,' he said, as always he did on Thursday afternoons, but this time he did not mention next week and he was gone before she could remind him.

That evening she sat in her usual corner of the Bayeux Lounge, sipping vodka and tonic and thinking about the day. She'd been terrible; if she knew poor Fitz's number she'd ring him now from the booth in the passage and say she was sorry. 'Wine goes to your head, Nancy,' Laurie Henderson used to say and it was true. A few glasses of red wine in the Trattoria San Michele and she was pawing at a waiter who was young enough to be her son. And Fitz politely sat there, officer and gentleman still written all over him, saying he'd sell his house up and come to London. The waiter'd probably thought she was after his body.

Not that it mattered what he thought, because he and the Trattoria San Michele already belonged in Memory Lane. She'd never been there until that lunchtime six months ago when old Fitz had said, 'Let's turn in here.' No word would come from him, she sensed that also: never again on a Thursday would she hurry along to the Trattoria San Michele and say she was sorry she was late.

I'll be around, no matter how you treat me now ... She'd seen him first when they'd sung that number, the grand finale; she'd suddenly noticed him, three rows from the front. She'd seen him looking at her and had wondered while she danced if he was Mr R.R. Well, of course, he had been in a way. He'd stood up for her to his awful relations, he'd kissed away her tears, saying he would die for her. And then the first thing she'd done when he'd married her after all that fuss, when he'd gone back after his leave, was to imagine that that stupid boy with a tubercular chest was the be-all and end-all. And when the boy had proved beyond a shadow of doubt that he was no such thing there was the new one they'd taken on for his tap-dancing.

She smiled in the Bayeux Lounge, remembering the laughter and the applause when the back legs of Jack and the Beanstalk's Dobbin surprised everyone by breaking into that elegant tap-dance, and how Jack and his mother had stood there with their mouths comically open. She'd told Fitz about it a few lunches ago because, of course, she hadn't been able to tell him at the time on account of the thing she'd had with the back legs. He had nodded solemnly, poor Fitz, not really amused, you could see, but pleased because she was happy to remember. A right little troublemaker that tap-dancer had turned out to be, and a right little scrounge, begging every penny he could lay his hands on, with no intention of paying a farthing back.

If she'd run out of hope, she thought, she could have said yes, let's try again. She could have admitted, because it was only fair to, that she'd never be like the responsible woman who'd gone and died on him. She could have pointed out that she'd never acquire the class of his mother and his sister because she wasn't that sort of person. She'd thought all that out a few weeks ago, knowing what he was getting around to. She'd thought it was awful for him to be going to a bureau place and have women telling him about how the heat affected them. She'd imagined saying yes and then humming something special, probably 'Love is the Sweetest Thing', and leaning her face towards him across the table, waiting for his kiss again. But of course you couldn't live in fantasies, you couldn't just pretend.

'Ready for your second, Nancy?' the barmaid called across the empty lounge, and she said yes, she thought she was.

You gave up hope if you just agreed because it sounded cosy. When he'd swept her off her feet all those years ago everything had sounded lovely: being with him in some nice place when the war was over, never again being short, the flowers he brought her. 'No need to come to London, Fitz,' she might have said today. 'Let's just go and live in your house by the sea.' And he'd have been delighted and relieved, because he'd only mentioned selling up in order to show her that he would if she wanted him to. But all hope would be gone if she'd agreed.

She sighed, sorry for him, imagining him in the house he talked about. He'd have arrived there by now, and she imagined him turning the lights on and everything coming to life. You could tell from the way he talked that there were memories there for him, that the woman he'd married was still all over the place: it wasn't because he'd finished making a stone wall in the garden that he wanted to move on. He'd probably pour himself a drink and sit down to watch the television; he'd open a tin later on. She imagined him putting a match to the fire and pulling over the curtains. Probably in a drawer somewhere he had a photo of her as a sunflower. He'd maybe sit with it in his hand, with his drink and the television. 'Dear, it's a fantasy,' she murmured. 'It couldn't ever have worked second time round, no more'n it did before.'

'Warm your bones, Nancy,' the barmaid said, placing her second vodka and tonic on a cardboard mat on the table where she sat. 'Freeze you tonight, it would.'

'Yes, it's very cold.'

She hadn't returned to the flat after the visit to the Trattoria San Michele;

somehow she hadn't felt like it. She'd walked about during the couple of hours that had to pass before the Bayeux Lounge opened. She'd looked in the shop windows, and looked at the young people with their peculiarly coloured hair. Two boys in eastern robes, with no hair, had tried to sell her a record. She hadn't been keen to go back to the flat because she wanted to save up the hope that something might have come on the second post, an offer of a part. If she saved it up it would still hover in her mind while she sat in the Bayeux Lounge – just a chance in a million but that was how chances always were. It was more likely, when her luck changed, that the telephone would ring, but even so you could never rule out a letter. You never should. You should never rule out anything.

She wished now she'd tried to tell him that, even though he might not ever have understood. She wished she'd explained that it was all to do with not giving up hope. She'd felt the same when Eddie had got the children, even though one of them wasn't his, and when they'd gone on so about neglect. All she'd been doing was hoping then too, not wanting to be defeated, not wanting to give in to what they demanded where the children were concerned. Eddie had married someone else, some woman who probably thought she was an awful kind of person because she'd let her children go. But one day the children would write, she knew that inside her somewhere; one day there'd be that letter waiting for her, too.

She sipped more vodka and tonic. She knew as well that one day Mr R.R. would suddenly be there, to make up for every single thing. He'd make up for all the disappointment, for Simpson and Eddie and Laurie Henderson, for treating badly the one man who'd been good to you. He'd make up for scrounging tap-dancers and waiters you wanted to be with because there was sadness in their faces, and the dear old Trattoria San Michele gone for ever into Memory Lane. You couldn't give up on Mr R.R., might as well walk out and throw yourself down into the river; like giving up on yourself it would be.

'I think of you only,' she murmured in her soft whisper, feeling much better now because of the vodka and tonic, 'only wishing, wishing you were by my side.' When she'd come in at half past five she'd noticed a chap booking in at the reception, some kind of foreign commercial traveller since the tennis people naturally didn't come in winter; fiftyish, handsome-ish, not badly dressed. She was glad they hadn't turned on the television yet. From the corner where she sat she could see the stairs, where sooner or later the chap would appear. He'd buy a drink and then he'd look around and there she'd be.

The Property of Colette Nervi

Drumgawnie the crossroads was known as, and for miles around the land was called Drumgawnie also. There was a single shop at the crossroads, next to a pink house with its roof gone. There was an abandoned mill, with tall grain stores no longer used for any purpose. Drumgawnie Rath, a ring of standing stones that predated history, was half a mile across the fields where Odd Garvey grazed his cattle.

It was in 1959, an arbitrary date as far as the people who lived in and around Drumgawnie were concerned, that visitors began to take an interest in the stones, drawing their cars up by the mill and the grain stores. English or French people they usually were, spring or summertime tourists who always called in at the shop to inquire the way. Mrs Mullally, who owned the shop, had thought of erecting a small sign but in the end had abandoned the notion on the grounds that one day, perhaps, a visitor might glance about her premises and purchase something. None ever had.

'You have to cross the little stream,' she informed a French couple in the early summer of 1968. 'Continue on past where you've drawn your car in and then there's rocks you can step on to see you over the bit of water. Go neither right nor left after that until you'll strike the stones standing up in the grass.'

In her bedroom Dolores Mullally, then aged twenty-two, watched from her window, the lacy half-curtain pulled back at the edge. She had heard the car coming to a halt by the mill, and minutes later foreign voices had become louder as the visitors approached the shop. She had pushed herself up from her bed and limped across to the window. The woman was wearing a black leather coat, a thin woman with a smiling, slanted face, strange-looking and beautiful. The man had a moustache and a slender pipe.

Dolores imagined these foreign people asking her mother about the standing stones, and her mother telling them, using the same expressions she always did. When her mother wasn't there and Dolores gave the directions herself she never used expressions like 'to see you over the bit of water' or 'you'll strike the stones standing up in the grass'. All that was her mother's old-fashioned way of putting things. Dolores simply said that the visitors must cross the stream at a place they'd see and then keep straight on. Her father, no longer alive, had once carried her to see the standing stones and she hadn't found them much to look at. But a visitor who had spent the whole afternoon examining them and had afterwards returned to the shop to verify the way to the Rossaphin road had stated that they were the most extraordinary stones of their kind in the whole of Europe. 'I think he was maybe drunk,' Dolores's mother had commented, and her father had agreed.

As soon as they left the shop the Frenchman took the woman's arm affectionately, both of them laughing at something or other. Dolores watched them walking on the left-hand side of the road, towards the mill and the towering grain stores. There had been prosperity in the place once, her father and her mother had said, at the time when the mill operated. Its owner had lived in the pink-distempered house with the fallen-in roof, a man called Mr Hackett, who had grown some special kind of plums in his garden.

The French couple stood for a moment by their car, a small, bright red vehicle, hired in Dublin, Dolores guessed. A group of English people and an American woman, returning from the stones some years ago, had been unable to start theirs and had telephoned the Dan Ryan car-hire organization from the shop. It was then, for the first time, that Dolores had realized it was possible for visitors from other countries to hire motor-cars and to drive all over Ireland in them.

The Frenchman removed the pipe from his mouth and knocked it out on the edge of his shoe. He unlocked one of the car doors and took from it two pairs of short green gum-boots, which he and the woman put on. They stowed their shoes in the car and then the man put his arms about his companion. He bent her head backwards, leaning his body against her and pushing his lips on to hers, although Dolores could not quite see that detail of the embrace. He released the woman and she at once placed her hands, fingers splayed out, on his black hair, drawing his face down to hers again. After a moment they separated and set off, hand in hand, their arms stretched across the path they walked along. On either side of them nettles and docks grew in great profusion; daisy-heads and buttercups decorated the grass of the path; ragwort was everywhere. The afternoon was sunny, puffy little clouds were stationary in the sky. On the red roof of the car there was what appeared to be a shadow, small and rectangular and vividly black: it was an object, Dolores realized when she screwed her eyes up, not a shadow at all. Carelessly the two had left it there.

She dropped the edge of the half-curtain and limped back to her bed, where she had been reading *Holster in the Dust* by Tom K. Kane. She picked a cigarette from a packet of Afton Major, open on the candlewick counterpane. She lit it and inhaled. Because of her bad leg she lay down for an hour or so almost every afternoon, unless it was the time of year when the seed potatoes had to be put in on the slope at the back or the later time when the grown potatoes had to be gathered. Years ago, when Dolores was twelve, old Dr McDowell had suggested that a rest in the afternoon might be a relief. The leg, shrivelled to the bone as a result of infantile paralysis, necessitated the use of a crutch, although in making her way across her bedroom or the kitchen, or sometimes moving about in the shop, Dolores could manage without this aid, limping from one steadying surface to the next. *The evening sun-rays reddened the canyon*, she read. *Dust was acrid in One-Draw's nostrils and grimy on his cheeks*. Her father had bought these yellow-backed books of the Wild West Library, which were closely printed on absorbent paper, a perpendicular line down the centre of each page, separating the prose as in a newspaper. Their soft covers were tattered now, creases running through horses and riders and gun-smoke, limp spines bent and split. Her father had bought one in Mackie's the newsagent's every Friday, making the journey to Rossaphin in the horse and cart, taking Dolores with him. He had brought to the town the carrots and cabbages he grew on the slope, turnips and potatoes when he had them, plums from the forgotten garden next door. A waste of time, Dolores's mother had always maintained, because of the small profit there'd been, and when Mr Mullally died the practice had ceased and the horse had been sold. The cart was still in the yard at the back, its faded orange-painted wood just beginning to rot. Even though her father had died fourteen years ago, Dolores still missed those weekly journeys and the feeling of excitement their anticipation had engendered.

The shop, patronized by everyone in the neighbourhood, kept Mrs Mullally and her daughter going. The bus dropped off newspapers there, groceries and confectionery were stocked, and a rudimentary post office maintained. At the time of Drumgawnie's greater prosperity Mrs Mullally's father had run it profitably, with a public house as well. Dolores's own father, once employed in Mr Hackett's milling business, had married into the shop after the closing of the mill. In his lifetime it was still thought that Dolores's affliction might miraculously right itself as she grew up, but this had not happened. He died in the kitchen armchair, having complained for several months of pains in the chest which Dr McDowell had not taken seriously. 'Well, Mother of God, isn't it the most surprising thing in three decades of practising medicine?' Dolores remembered him saying in the kitchen, the body already covered with a bedsheet. 'McDowell was drunk as a fish,' her mother was afterwards to remark. 'His breath would've knocked you down.' Not used to that particular smell, Dolores had imagined it to be a variation of the disinfectant in Dr McDowell's house in Rossaphin.

One-Draw slid from the saddle. His eyes were slits, measuring the distance. 'Cassidy!' he shouted. 'Reach, Cassidy!' There was no reply, no movement. Not a sound in the canyon.

Dolores folded down the corner of the page to keep her place. She lit another Afton Major. There was never any pain in her leg; it was just the ugliness of it, the difficult, unattractive movement, the crutch she hated so. She'd become used over the years to all the cumbersome arrangements that had to be made for her, the school bus coming specially to the crossroads to take her to the convent in Rossaphin, the Crowleys calling in on a Sunday to take her and her mother to Mass in their Ford. Once a year, three weeks before Christmas, she and her mother went for the day to shop in Rossaphin, driven on that occasion also by the Crowleys. They had a meal in Love's Café and didn't return to the crossroads until six o'clock. Her mother had to get special permission to close the post-office counter, which was something Father Deane was able to arrange, just as it was he who persuaded the Crowleys to be kind in the way they were.

Now and again, between one December and the next, Dolores managed to get in to Rossaphin on the bus, but the journey home again had to be arranged carefully and in advance, with the cooperation of one of the drivers who called regularly at the shop. Sheedy, who brought the bread, was no good because he came out in the morning, but the Mitchelstown Cheese man always passed through Rossaphin in the late afternoon and then came on to the crossroads, and Jimmy Reilly, who brought the bacon, came in the afternoon also. Having chosen a particular day and made the arrangement to meet one or other of the delivery men at a time and a place, Dolores usually had three hours or a bit more on her own. Her mother didn't like it though; her mother worried in case the van men might forget. Neither of them ever had, but something once did go wrong with Jimmy Reilly's engine and Dolores was left waiting outside the Provincial Bank until five o'clock when she should have been collected at two. A boy had come up to her with a message, and then Father Deane had appeared on his bicycle. He rang the bell of the bank and the manager's wife had allowed Dolores to sit on a chair in the hall until the Crowleys arrived in their Ford. The tears were running down her mother's cheeks when eventually she arrived back at the crossroads, and after that Dolores never again went into Rossaphin on her own.

She squashed her cigarette-butt on the ashtray that lay beside *Holster in the Dust* on the candlewick counterpane. The ashtray was made of glass, with green letters advertising 7-Up on it, a free gift from one of the delivery men. She'd easily finish *Holster in the Dust* tonight, Dolores considered, she'd even start *Guns of the Apache Country*. She'd read both of them before, but not recently.

She tidied the counterpane, brushing the wrinkles from it. She paused for a moment by the looking-glass on her dressing-table to smear fresh lipstick on to her lips and to run a comb through her long black hair. Her face was round, her chin a pleasant curve. Her father had told her that her eyes were like a dog's he'd once owned, meaning it as a compliment. They were brown and serious, as if all the time Dolores was intent on thoughts she chose not to share with other people. But mostly what she thought about were the adventures of the Wild West Library.

'Are you rested, pet?' her mother inquired in the shop. 'You didn't smoke too much?'

'Only two,' Dolores lied.

'You're better off without, pet.'

Dolores nodded. 'That's a well-dressed pair went up to the stones.'

'Did you see them? You should stay lying down, pet.'

'I'll look after the shop now.'

Her mother said that Mrs Connell hadn't come in for her bread yet, nor Whelan for his *Independent*. 'French those people said they were.'

She sliced a couple of rashers as she spoke and took them away on the palm of her hand, through the small store-room at the back of the shop, into the kitchen. In a moment the smell of frying would drift through the store-room, as it did every evening at this time, and soon afterwards Dolores would put up the wire shutter on the post-office counter and lock the drawer where the postal orders and the stamps and the registration book were kept. She'd take the key into the kitchen with her when eventually she went to sit down to her tea. She would hang it on a hook on the dresser, but the shop itself would remain open and anyone who came into it would rap on the counter for attention, knowing that that was expected.

'Mademoiselle,' the Frenchman said, and went on talking. Dolores couldn't understand him. He wasn't smiling any more, and his thin companion in her leather coat wasn't smiling either. They were agitated: the man kept gesturing, moving his hands about; the woman frowned, muttering in French to herself. Dolores shook her head. '*Je ne sais pas*,' the Frenchman said. '*Peut-être ici*.'

He looked around the shop. The woman looked also, on the counter, on the post-office counter, on the cartons that had arrived yesterday and had not yet been opened, on the floor.

'I didn't catch what you said,' Dolores explained, but the woman continued to speak French.

'*Le sac. Le sac noir.*'

'The handbag of my friend,' the man said. 'We lose the handbag.'

'Lose?'

'I place it,' the woman said. 'It is that I place it.'

Dolores reached for her crutch. She lifted the flap of the counter and helped in the search. She called loudly to her mother and when her mother arrived, wiping her hands on her apron, she explained that a handbag had been lost, that it might have been left in the shop.

'I would have noticed,' Mrs Mullally said quickly.

'*Ah, oui, oui,*' the man agreed.

'She was carrying a handbag,' Mrs Mullally said, a defensive note entering her voice. 'She definitely walked out of the shop with it. A square handbag, under her arm.'

Dolores tried to remember: had the woman had a handbag when they walked together to the car? Had she had it when they'd embraced? And then she did remember: the square dark shadow on the red roof, too vivid to be just a shadow.

'She put it on top of the car,' she said, and as she spoke she seemed to see what at the time had passed unnoticed: the woman's arm raised in the moment just before the embrace, the handbag in her hand and then on the red metal that glittered in the sunlight. Dolores had been too intent on the embrace to have observed this properly, but she was certain it had happened.

'Oh, yes,' she said, nodding to lend emphasis to her claim. 'You put it on the roof of your car.'

'You observe?' the Frenchman asked.

'I saw from a window upstairs.'

'*Ah, merci, mademoiselle. Merci beaucoup.*' It was the woman who spoke. The man said they were grateful, thanking Dolores in English.

She watched, leaning against the doorway of the shop. Her mother accompanied the French couple across the road and then disappeared from sight because of the incline down to the mill. Dolores had sensed her mother's anxiety, the feeling there'd been in her mother's mind that an accusation was being made. She thought of going upstairs to her bedroom to watch again from the window, and was about to do so when the smell of burning bacon wafted from the kitchen. Hurriedly, she shuffled through the shop and the store-room.

'They never found it,' her mother said, returning ten minutes later. 'They moved the car to see if it had fallen off. They'd been up and down to the stones four times, they said, looking on the path in case she dropped it.'

'She put it on the car, she couldn't have dropped it.'

'Ah, sure, you can't watch them.'

'So it's gone, is it?'

'They wrote down an address for me in case it would surface some day. She was down in the mouth, that woman.'

Dolores saw the beautiful, slanted face pulled further to one side, the mouth dragged into a corner of itself, tears threatening. The man would put his arm around the smartly clad shoulders, so very slight beneath the leather. He would comfort his lover and promise her another handbag because people like that, who could hire a motor-car, who could come all the way from France to see some stones in a field, wouldn't have to bother about the expense.

'Did you tell them to go to the gardai at Rossaphin?'

'I didn't mention the gardai to them.' Mrs Mullally spoke firmly again, and Dolores knew that she hadn't suggested the police because she didn't want it to become known that a handbag had disappeared in this manner at the crossroads. 'Sure, won't they find the thing in their motor-car somewhere?'

Dolores nodded, silently agreeing that somehow or other this would be the outcome of the matter. When they had returned from the stones the woman must have taken the handbag from the roof without noticing what she was doing, and she must have bundled it into the car without noticing either. Dolores cut a piece of fried bread and dipped it into the little mound of salt on the side of her plate. She began to think about One-Draw Hagan and his enemy, Red Cassidy.

'Only Henry Garvey was about,' her mother continued, 'driving in the old man's heifers. He'd have been too far away to catch what was going on.'

Dolores nodded again. Perhaps when the lovers returned to the car there had been another embrace, which had driven everything from their minds – like in *Travellin' Saddles* when Big Daunty found his Indian love and both of them went into a swoon, lost to the world. *Colette Nervi*, it said on the piece of paper the French lovers had given her mother. *10 rue St Just, Toulouse, France.* They had insisted on giving her money also, so that she could send them a letter in case the handbag ever turned up.

Henry Garvey was a large, slow man of forty, known in the neighbourhood for his laziness and his easy-going nature. His uncle, Odd Garvey, had outlived both of Henry's parents, and the two lived together in the farm-house which the whole Garvey family had once occupied. Odd Garvey, small and wizened in his old age, had never married – due to meanness, so it was locally said. He was reputed to be affected in the head, though this impression which he gave was perhaps no more than another reflection of a miserly nature. The farmhouse he occupied with his nephew was in need of considerable repair, its roof leaky, its walls wet with rising damp. Henry spent as little time as he could there, preferring to ride his mother's ancient bicycle into Rossaphin every morning and to remain there until it was time to fetch the heifers in. He laid bets, and drank in a number of selected public houses while waiting for the afternoon's racing to begin. He bet on greyhounds as well as horses, and had been known in one bar or another to offer odds on a variety of propositions, including the year of his uncle's decease. A permanent smile split his sunburned face, the easy, lazy smile of a man who was never in a hurry. Sometimes in the evenings he rode back into Rossaphin again, to drink more stout and to talk about racehorses. His uncle owned the farmhouse and the heifers, Henry the fields and the brood of turkeys he fattened every year for Christmas. He received payment from his uncle for the grazing of the heifers and from two other farmers for the grass he let them have on an annual basis: with his turkey profits, this made him a living of a kind. His four sisters had long ago left the neighbourhood, only one of them remaining in Ireland.

'There was foreign people over at the stones,' he reported to his uncle on the evening the French couple had come. 'Jabbering away.'

'Did you approach them? Did you charge them a price for going over our fields?'

Henry vaguely wagged his head, and knowing that such a charge had not been made the old man continued to grumble, his empty gums squashing up baked beans before he swallowed them. Because he had difficulty with crusts, he tore pieces of bread from the centre of a slice and dipped the soft white lumps into the sauce that went with the beans. Mumbling through this food, he said that the number of people who nowadays crossed their land was a disgrace. It was a favourite mealtime topic: every day, whether there had been visitors to the standing stones or not, the old man urged Henry to protest to the police or the Board of Works, or somebody at the courthouse in Rossaphin. He was convinced that a substantial sum of money was owing to the Garvey family because no toll had ever been charged on the right of way to Drumgawnie Rath. Now, at eighty-six, he was too old to do anything about it. He hadn't been to Mass for ten years, nor spoken to anyone except his nephew for six. No one ever came to the farmhouse.

In Henry's view the old man could have kept himself normal by picking up the groceries and the newspaper every day in Mrs Mullally's shop. In a normal manner he could have whiled away his time with Mrs Mullally or the daughter instead of skulking behind the trees, looking out for visitors. But he wouldn't enter the shop because he couldn't bear to hand over money to anyone, so Henry had to see to everything like that. Not that he particularly minded. He had a basket which he hung from the handlebars of his bicycle and he actually enjoyed loitering in shops, Mrs Mullally's or anyone else's. He would light a cigarette and sometimes in Mullally's might have a bottle of lemonade. He would lean his back against the counter and listen to the Mullally girl going on about the Wild West stories she read. She was a decent enough looking creature in her way, the only pity was the leg she was afflicted with.

'Dressed up to the nines they were,' Henry continued in the kitchen. 'A useless type of person, I'd say.'

His uncle emitted a sucking noise. The footsteps made by the visitors wore the grass down. Another thing was, the Board of Works should be informed that cars were being left without charge on the piece of verge by the mill.

'I don't think it's a matter for the Board of Works.'

'Why wouldn't it be? Didn't the Board man come to see me in 1949? Wasn't it the Board drew attention to the stones before any stranger knew they were there?'

'If it's anyone's concern I'd say it was the County Council's.'

'Go into the courthouse in that case. Go into the head clerk and say we're deprived of grass for the cattle due to footsteps wearing it down.'

Henry promised that he would do as he was asked. He always promised when the subject came up. He ate his beans and bread and drank several cups of tea. He didn't say that there were other ways of charging for the use of the path through the fields. He didn't explain that you could get what was owing to you if you were sharp with your eyes and used the intelligence you were born with.

Four years after the Frenchwoman's mishap with her handbag Dolores became aware – in the late summer of 1972 – of Henry Garvey's interest in her. During that July and August his manner changed. He no longer stood with his back to her, for instance, smiling through the open door at the roadway outside while she told him the plot of another Wild West novel. Instead he faced her, leaning an elbow on the counter. He even lifted his eyes to her face and scrutinized it. Now and again his glance moved over her long dark hair and over her shoulders. Once she'd noticed him looking at her hands.

It had never occurred to Dolores, twenty-six now, that romance would come her way. One cold January day, ages ago, the Crowleys had driven her and her mother to the cinema in Ballyreddy, sixteen miles beyond Rossaphin, for the Sunday matinée. Father Deane had had a hand in the arrangement – had no doubt said that it would be an act of charity – and the Crowleys, seeking through his good offices a chance of heavenly life, had acceded easily to his wish. *From Here to Eternity* the film had been, and Dolores had never forgotten any of it, far richer in romance than anything in her father's Wild West Library. But that was as close as she had so far come to the world of love and passion, and what neither the intercession of Father Deane nor the kindness of the Crowleys could achieve for her was a place among the Friday-night dancers in Rossaphin. Dolores had never been inside the Rossaphin dance-hall and she guessed she never would. There would be no point: she knew that and accepted it. Yet sometimes she dreamed that miraculously she danced beneath fairyland lights to the music she'd heard on the radio, and was sad for a moment after she woke up.

'I had him backed both ways,' Henry Garvey said towards the end of that August. 'I was fortunate all right.'

He had been talking about the horse, Wonder Boy, a day or two before. It was running on some English race-course, destined to make him a fortune. He had told her about a greyhound called Trumpeter, which had won at Limerick, and another greyhound called Smasheroo. His uncle had died, nearly two years ago now, and she and her mother had gone to the funeral in Rossaphin, driven by the Crowleys. Afterwards they'd all had a cup of tea in Love's Café and Mrs Mullally had taken the opportunity to purchase some oilcloth in Buckley's.

Even though old Garvey had been poor company, it was apparent enough that Henry had become lonely in the farmhouse. He came more often to the shop and lingered there longer than he used to. And then, one morning when Dolores was in the middle of telling him the plot of *Kid Kelly*, she found him scrutinizing her even more closely than before. Her mother was present on that occasion and Dolores knew she had observed, and had understood, Henry Garvey's interest. After he'd gone her mother was beside herself with delight, although she didn't say a word. Dolores heard her humming in the kitchen, and her manner was so sprightly when

Jimmy Reilly delivered the bacon in the afternoon that he asked her if she'd won the sweep.

'D'you know what it is,' Henry Garvey said at the beginning of September, 'I'm uncertain what to do with myself.'

As he spoke, he pushed his cigarette packet across the counter at her. She was sitting on the black-topped stool which Father Deane had given her as a present, its legs cut down to just the right height. She could sit on it and lean on the counter, just like Henry Garvey was leaning now, on a level with him.

'The old farmhouse above is shook,' he said.

Her mother was not there. Her mother had taken to slipping out to the potato slope whenever Henry Garvey appeared, even if it was raining. Dolores knew that the news of the courtship had been passed on to the Crowleys and to the van men who called at the shop, to Father Deane and to all the people who came to the crossroads for their groceries. When she rested in the afternoons she could hear the excited tone of her mother's voice in the shop below. She was never able to make out the words but she knew that the latest of Henry Garvey's attentions was being retailed and exaggerated.

'I'm wondering,' he said at the beginning of September, 'would I sell the old fellow's heifers?'

She made a slight gesture with the hand that held the cigarette, a shrug of the fingers intended to imply that Henry Garvey was his own master, that he alone had the privilege of reaching a decision about his late uncle's heifers.

'I have the acres all right, but sure what use is the old house to me? Isn't it falling down on account of the old fellow wouldn't permit a bit of cement to be applied to it?'

Dolores, who had never seen the farmhouse, made the same gesture again.

'And sure you could hardly call them heifers any more. Wouldn't I be better without the trouble of those lassies?'

He turned his ample smile towards her, the red-brick flesh of his face screwed up into small bulges. She had only once seen him wearing a tie and that was at the funeral of his uncle. On Sundays he went to a later Mass than her mother and herself: she supposed he put the tie on for that also.

'Another factor is,' he continued, 'I need a new bicycle.'

In the shop, and in the rooms above it and behind it, on the slope out at the back, he could take her father's place. He could occupy the chair in which her father had so abruptly died. He could marry into the shop and the house just as her father had, and he would bring with him the rent for the grazing of his fields. Her father had brought nothing.

'What I'm wondering is,' he said, 'could I learn to drive a car?'

She did not reply. She did not even make the same gesture again. She saw herself stepping out of the car he spoke of, the point of the crutch secure on the pavement. She saw herself limping beside him towards the cinema at Ballyreddy, up the steps and down the long passage with framed photographs of film stars on the walls. She saw herself in Rossaphin, not having to wait outside the Provincial Bank for Jimmy Reilly and his van, but going at her leisure in and out of the shops. On a Sunday, Mass would be attended when it was convenient, no need to fit in with the Crowleys. And would there be any harm in going, just once, into the dance-hall and standing there for a while, looking at the dancers and listening to the music?

'I'm sure you could drive a car,' she said. 'If Sheedy can drive that bread van I'd say you could drive a car.'

'The old bike was a good machine in its day, but the mudguards is overtaken by the rust.'

'A car would be handy for you, Henry.'

'There's nothing I like better than talking about matters like that to you.'

He paid the compliment without looking at her, gazing as he used to out into the roadway. He was nearly twenty years older than she was, but no other man would ever come into this shop and say he liked talking to her about bicycles and cars. No other man would examine her hair and her hands – or if he did he'd stop it in a hurry, like the new young conductor on the long-distance bus had when he'd realized she was crippled and misshapen.

Henry Garvey left the shop after he'd paid the compliment, and when her mother came in from the back Dolores told her he was considering buying a car. Her mother would have already said prayers, begging Our Lady to make it all right, begging that a crippled woman should not one day find herself alone at the crossroads. The paralysis had been a shock out of nowhere: the attentions of Henry Garvey were just as unexpected, a surprise that came surely from God.

'A car?' her mother said. 'Ah, wouldn't that be grand, pet?'

The crossroads was nearer to the town than the farmhouse was, the journey would be shorter, and easier without the stony track that led down to the farm. Often, lounging in the shop, he'd smelt a bit of cooking going on in the kitchen; he remembered Mullally in his day, selling stamps and weighing out potatoes. He liked it when she told him about Kid Kelly and One-Draw Hagan, and she appeared to be interested when he outlined his chances in a race. When an animal didn't come in she appeared to be sympathetic.

'That's fixed so,' he said to her on the day they arranged the marriage. 'Sure, it'll be suitable for the pair of us.'

He gave her a present, a necklace he'd found in the handbag he'd taken years ago as payment for all the strangers who had walked across the fields. There were little blue jewels in it: twenty-two of them, she told him, because she counted them. A week or so later he pushed the handbag itself across the counter at her. He'd found it with the necklace, he said, among his mother's possessions. Tim Howley was teaching him to drive a car, he said.

Dolores knew when Henry Garvey gave her the necklace that Mrs Garvey had never possessed such a piece of jewellery. Her mother knew also, but did not say anything. It wasn't until the handbag appeared that both of them guessed Henry Garvey had stolen the Frenchwoman's property. They still did not say anything. In the drawer where the postal orders and the registration book were kept there remained the scrap of paper on which Colette Nervi had written down her address. It had been there for all the intervening time, together with the small sum of money for postage in case the handbag ever came to light. Mrs Mullally destroyed the scrap of paper after Dolores had received her presents, and looking in the drawer one day Dolores discovered that she had done so.

The wedding was to take place in June. Two girls Dolores had been at the convent with were to be bridesmaids, and one of Henry Garvey's bar-room companions had agreed to act as best man. Everyone for miles around Drumgawnie was invited, all the shop's customers, the same people who'd attended Mr Mullally's funeral nineteen years ago, and Odd Garvey's funeral. The Crowleys were invited, and some Rossaphin people, Jimmy Reilly and Sheedy the bread man. Some of the other van-drivers lived too far beyond the district but all of them, without exception, brought gifts for Dolores a week or so before the wedding-day.

Father Deane had a crutch painted white and asked Mrs Crowley to cover the arm-support in lace to match the wedding-dress. Dolores thought she'd never seen a crutch look so pretty, and wondered if it was a marriage tradition for crippled brides, but did not ask. Henry Garvey's farmhouse was up for sale, the cattle had already been sold. Mrs Mullally had arranged to move out of her room, into the one that had always been

Dolores's. 'The simplest thing,' she said, not dwelling upon the subject.

'I don't know will he ever communicate the knack of it,' Henry Garvey said, referring to Tim Howley's efforts to teach him to drive a motor-car. The car had a way of jumping about with him, juddering and stalling before he even got it started. He had heavy feet, Tim Howley explained: a man driving a car needed to be sensitive with the clutch and the accelerator. 'You'd think it would be easy,' Henry said to Dolores, and she softly encouraged him, urging him to persevere. There would be nothing nicer, she continued in the same soft voice, than having a car. The white crutch was in her bedroom, in a corner by the dressing-table, waiting for the day in June. She had covered the lace on the arm-support with a piece of brown paper from the shop in case it got dirty.

On the night before the wedding Dolores wondered what else there had been in the handbag. Money would have been bet on a horse or a greyhound, keys perhaps thrown away; somewhere in the unsold farmhouse there'd be a make-up compact. In a month's time there was to be an auction of the furniture and the few remaining bits of farm machinery: before that happened she would find the compact and hide it carefully away. She would not keep her money in the black handbag, nor her cigarettes and matches; she would not be seen in the shops with it. She would be careful with the gifts of Henry Garvey in case, after all, the lovers from France had reported the loss to the police. Henry Garvey would not notice that the necklace was never seen at her neck because he was not the kind to notice things; nor was he the kind to realize that you had to be careful. She felt drowsily comforted by knowing what she must do, but when she turned the light out and attempted to sleep a chilliness possessed her: what if Henry Garvey rode over in the morning on his mother's bicycle to say he'd made a mistake? What if he stood with his back to the counter the way he used to, gazing with his smile out into the roadway? He would not say that the folly of the marriage had at last been borne in upon him. He would not say that he had seen in his mind's eye the ugliness of his bride's body, the shrivelled limb distorting everything. He would not say it had suddenly occurred to him that the awkward, dragging movement when she walked without her crutch was more than he could look at for the remainder of his life. 'I gave you stolen presents,' he'd say instead. 'I'm too ashamed to marry you.' And then he'd mount the bicycle and ride away like one of the cowboys of the Wild West.

In the darkness she lit another cigarette, calming herself. If he'd rather, he could have this room on his own and she could share her mother's. Being a bachelor for so long, that might be a preference he'd have. She'd hate it, in with her mother, but there was an empty back room, never used, which one day might be fixed up for her. There would be a bed and a wardrobe up at the farm, there might even be a length of linoleum going.

She turned the light on and read. She finished *Silent Prairie* and began one she hadn't read for ages, *King Cann Strikes Gold!* by Chas. D. Wasser. Through a faint dawn the birds eventually began to sing. At half past six she heard her mother moving.

He made a cup of tea in the kitchen. No one would buy the place, the way the roof and the kitchen wall were. The wall would hardly last the winter, the crack had widened suddenly, nearly nine inches it must be now. The old furniture would fetch maybe a hundred pounds.

At the kitchen table he stirred sugar into his tea. He wondered if he'd ever manage the driving. And if he did, he wondered if Mrs Mullally would stand the price of a car. It was a matter he hadn't mentioned yet, but with all the trouble he was going to over the learning wouldn't she tumble to it that he had done his share? The three of them were in it together, with the farmhouse the way it was and the girl the way she was. It was only a pity there hadn't been a ring in the handbag he'd taken as payment for the use of the path across his fields. Still and all, he'd got seven to one on Derby Joan with the money there'd been in the purse, which easily covered the cost of the ring he'd had to buy.

He drank his tea and then moved over to the sink to shave himself. They stocked razor-blades in the shop, which would be useful too.

In front of the altar she leant on the white crutch, wishing she could manage without it but knowing that the effort would be too much. Father Deane's voice whispered at them, and she could sense the delight in it, the joy that he truly felt. Beside her, Henry Garvey was wearing a tie, as she had known he would. There was a carnation and a few shreds of fern in his buttonhole. He smelt of soap.

She had to kneel, which was always difficult, but in time the ceremony was over and she made her way down the aisle, careful on the tiles, one hand gripping the wooden cross-piece of the crutch, the other holding on to him. Hidden beneath her wedding-dress, the necklace that had been stolen from Colette Nervi was cool on the flesh of her neck, and in those moments on the aisle Dolores recalled the embrace. She saw the lovers as they had been that day, the woman's leather coat, the man knocking out his pipe. Sunlight glimmered on the red, polished car, and enriched the green of the nettles and the docks. The woman's fingers were splayed out on her lover's dark head; the two faces were pressed into each other like the faces of the man and the woman in *From Here to Eternity*.

Running Away

It is, Henrietta considers, ridiculous. Even so she feels sorry for the girl, that slack, wan face, the whine in her voice. And as if to add insult to injury, Sharon, as a name, is far from attractive.

'Now, I'm sure,' Henrietta says gently, 'you must simply forget all this. Sharon, why not go away for a little? To ... to ...' Where would a girl like Sharon Tamm want to go? Margate? Benidorm? 'I could help you if you'd like me to. We could call it a little loan.'

The girl shakes her head. Hair, in need of washing, flaps. She doesn't want to go away, her whine protests. She wants to stay since she feels she belongs here.

'It's only, Sharon, that I thought it might be easier. A change of scene for a week or two. I know it's hard for you.'

Again the head is shaken, the lank hair flaps. Granny spectacles are removed and wiped carefully on a patchwork skirt, or perhaps a skirt that is simply patched. Sharon's loose, soiled sandals have been kicked off, and she plays with them as she converses. She is sitting on the floor because she never sits on chairs.

'We understand each other, you see,' Henrietta continues softly. 'My dear, I do want you to realize that.'

'It's all over, the thing I had with the Orange People. I'm not like that any more. I'm perfectly responsible.'

'I know the Orange thing is over. I know you've got your feet quite on the ground, Sharon.'

'It was awful, 'smatter of fact, all that.'

The Orange People offer a form of Eastern mysticism about which Henrietta knows very little. Someone once told her that the mysticism is an excuse for sexual licence, but explained no further. The sect is apparently quite different from the Hare Krishna people, who sometimes wear orange also but who eat food of such poor quality that sexual excess is out of the question. The Orange People had camped in a field and upset the locals, but all that was ages ago.

'And I know you're working hard, my dear. I know you've turned over a new leaf.' The trouble is that the leaf has been turned, absurdly, in the direction of Henrietta's husband.

'I just want to stay here,' Sharon repeats. 'Ever since it happened I feel I don't belong anywhere else.'

'Well, strictly speaking, nothing *has* happened, dear.'

'It has to me, though, Henrietta.'

Sharon never smiles. Henrietta can't remember having ever seen a smile enlivening the slack features any more than a hint of make-up has ever freshened the pale skin that stretches over them. Henrietta, who dresses well and maintains with care the considerable good looks she possesses, can understand none of it. Unpresentable Sharon Tamm is certainly no floosie, and hardly a gold-digger. Perhaps such creatures do not exist, Henrietta speculates, one perhaps only reads about them.

'I thought I'd better tell you,' Sharon Tamm says. 'I thought it only fair, Henrietta.'

'Yes, I'm glad you did.'

'*He* never would.'

The girl stands up and puts her sandals on to her grimy feet. There is a little white plastic bow, a kind of clasp, in her hair: Henrietta hasn't noticed it before because the hair has covered it in a way it wasn't meant to. The girl sorts all that out now, shaking her head again, taking the bow out and replacing it.

'He can't hurt people,' she tells Henrietta, speaking of the man to whom Henrietta has been married for more than twenty years.

Sharon Tamm leaves the room then, and Henrietta, who has been sitting in a high-backed chair during the conversation, does not move from it. She is flabbergasted by the last two impertinent statements of the girl's. How dare she say he never would! How dare she imply some knowledge of him by coyly remarking that he cannot hurt people! For a moment she experiences a desire to hurry after the girl, to catch her in the hall and to smack her on the face with the open palm of her hand. But she is so taken aback, so outraged by the whole bizarre conversation, that she cannot move. The girl, at her own request – a whispery whine on the telephone – asked to come to see her 'about something urgent'. And although Henrietta intended to go out that afternoon she at once agreed to remain in, imagining that Sharon Tamm was in some kind of pickle.

The hall door bangs. Henrietta – forty-three last month, dressed now in a blue jersey and skirt, with a necklace of pink corals at her throat and several rings on the fingers of either hand, her hair touched with a preparation that brings out the reddish brown in it – still does not move. She stares at the place on the carpet where the girl has been crouched. There was a time when Sharon Tamm came quite often to the house, when she talked a lot about her family, when Henrietta first felt sorry for her.

She ceased to come rather abruptly, going off to the Orange People instead.

In the garden Henrietta's dog, a cairn called Ka-Ki, touches the glass of the french windows with her nose, asking to be let in. Henrietta's husband, Roy, has trained her to do that, but the training has not been difficult because the dog is intelligent. Henrietta crosses the room to open the french windows, not answering in her usual way the fuss the dog makes of her, scampering at her feet, offering some kind of gratitude. The awful thing is, the girl seemed genuinely to believe in the extraordinary fantasy that possesses her. She would have told Roy of course, and Roy being Roy wouldn't have known what to do.

They had married when Roy was at the very beginning of his career, seven years older than Henrietta, who at the time had been a secretary in the department. She'd been nervous because she didn't belong in the academic world, because she had not had a university education herself. 'Only a typist!' she used bitterly to cry in those early, headstrong quarrels they'd had. 'You can't expect a typist to be bright enough to understand you.' But Roy, urbane and placid even then, had kissed her crossly pouting lips and told her not to be so silly. She was cleverer, and prettier, and more attractive in all sorts of other ways, than one after another of his female colleagues: ever since he has been telling her that, and meaning it. Henrietta cannot accept the 'cleverer', but 'prettier' and 'more attractive' she believes to be true, and isn't ashamed when she admits it to herself. They dress appallingly for a start, most of the women in the department, a kind of arrogance, Henrietta considers.

She clears away the tea things, for she has naturally offered Sharon Tamm tea, and carries them to the kitchen. Only a little less shaky than she was in the sitting-room after the girl's final statements, she prepares a turkey breast for the oven. There isn't much to do to it, but she likes to spike it with herbs and to fold it round a celery heart, a recipe she devised herself. She slices parsnips to roast with it, and peels potatoes to roast also. It isn't a special meal in any way, but somehow she finds herself taking special care because Roy is going to hate it when she mentions the visit of the girl.

She makes a pineapple pudding he likes. He has schoolboy tastes, he says himself, and in Henrietta's view he has too great a fondness for dairy products. She has to watch him where cream is concerned, and she insists he does not take too much salt. Not having children of their own has affected their relationship in ways like this. They look after one another, he in turn insisting that she should not Hoover for too long because Hoovering brings on the strain in her back.

She turns the pudding out into a Pyrex dish, ready to go into the oven in twenty minutes. She hears her husband in the hall, her own name called, the welcoming bark of Ka-Ki. 'Let's have a drink,' she calls back. 'Let's take a drink to the garden.'

He is there, by the summer-house, when she arrives with the tray of sherry and gin and Cinzano. She has done her face again, although she knows it hardly needs it; she has tied a red chiffon scarf into her hair. 'There now,' she says. 'Dinner'll be a while.' He's back earlier than usual.

She pours gin and Cinzano for him, and sherry for herself. 'Well, then?' She smiles at him.

'Oh, nothing much. MacMelanie's being difficult.'

'That man should be shot.'

'I only wish we could find someone to do it.'

There is nothing else to report except that a student called Fosse has been found hallucinating by a park keeper. A pity, apparently, because the boy is bright and has always seemed to be mature and well-balanced.

'Roy, I've something to tell you.'

'Ah?'

He is a man who sprawls over chairs rather than sits in them. He has a sprawling walk, taking up more room than is his due on pavements; he sprawls in cinemas and buses, and over the wheel of his car. His grey hair, of which there is a lot, can never acquire a combed look even though he combs it regularly and in the normal way. His spectacles, thickly rimmed and large, move about on his reddish face and often, in fact, fall off. His suits become tousled as soon as he puts them on, gaps appearing, flesh revealed. The one he wears now is of dark brown corduroy, the suit he likes best. A spotted blue handkerchief cascades out of an upper pocket, matching a loose bow tie.

'Sharon Tamm was here,' Henrietta says.

'Ah.'

She watches while he gulps his gin and vermouth. His eyes behind the pebbly glass of his spectacles are without expression. His mind does not appear to be associated with what she is saying. She wonders if he is thinking that he is not a success in the department, that he should have left the university years ago. She knows he often thinks that when Mac-Melanie has been troublesome.

'Now, Roy, you have to listen.'

'Well then, I'm listening.'

'It's embarrassing,' she warns.

'What is?'

'This Sharon Tamm thing.'

'She's really pulled herself together, you know. She's very bright. *Really* bright, I mean.'

'She has developed a fantasy about you.'

He says nothing, as if he has not heard, or has heard and not understood.

'She imagines she's in love with you.'

He drinks a mouthful of his drink, and then another. He reaches out to the tray on the table between them and pours himself some more, mostly gin, she notices. He doesn't gesture towards her sherry. He doesn't say anything.

'It was such an awkward conversation.'

All she wants is that it should be known that the girl arrived and said what she did say, that there should be no secret between them about so absurd a matter.

'I had to tell you, Roy. I couldn't not.'

He drinks again, still gulping at the liquid rather than sipping. He is perturbed: knowing him so well she can see that, and she wonders how exactly it is that MacMelanie has been a nuisance again, or if he is depressed because of the boy, Fosse. His eyes have changed behind the glass of his spectacles, something clouds his expression. He is trying not to frown, an effort she is familiar with, a sign of emotion in him. The vein that comes and goes in his forehead will soon appear.

'Roy.'

'I'm sorry Sharon came.'

Attempting to lighten the atmosphere, she laughs slightly. 'She should wear a bra, you know, for a start.'

She pours herself more sherry since he does not intend to. It didn't work, saying the girl should wear a bra: her voice sounded silly. She has a poor head for alcohol of any kind.

'She said you can't hurt people.'

He pulls the spotted handkerchief out of his pocket and wipes sweat from his chin with it. He runs his tongue over his lips. Vaguely, he shakes his head, as if denying that he can't hurt people, but she knows the gesture doesn't mean that. He is upset by what has happened, as she herself has been. He is thinking, as she did, that Sharon Tamm was once taken under their wing. He brought her back with him one evening, encouraging her, as a stray dog might be encouraged into the warmth. Other students, too, have been like daughters or sons to them and have remained their friends, a surrogate family. It was painful when Sharon Tamm left them for the Orange People.

'Of course I know,' Henrietta says, 'that was something we didn't understand.'

Vaguely he offers her more sherry, not noticing that she has had some. He pours more of his mixture for himself.

'Yes, there was something wrong,' he says.

They have been through all that. They talked about it endlessly, sending themselves to sleep with it, lazing with it on a Sunday morning. Henrietta found it hard to forgive the girl for being ungrateful. Both of them, she considered, had helped her in so very many ways.

'Shall we forget it all now?' she suggests, knowing that her voice has become nervous. 'Everything about the wretched girl?'

'Forget?'

That is impossible, his tone suggests. They cannot forget all that Sharon Tamm has told them about her home in Daventry, about her father's mother who lives with the family and stirs up so much trouble, about her overweight sister Diane and her brother Leslie. The world of Sharon Tamm's family has entered theirs. They can see, even now, the grandmother in her special armchair in the kitchen, her face snagged with a sourness that has to do with her wastrel husband, long since dead. They can see the saucepans boiling over on the stove because Mrs Tamm can never catch them in time, and Leslie's motor-cycling gear on the kitchen table, and Diane's bulk. Mr Tamm shouts perpetually, at Leslie to take his motor-cycling clothes away, at Diane for being so fat, at his wife, at Sharon, making her jump. 'You are stupid to an extent,' is the statement he has coined specially for his wife and repeats for her benefit several times every evening. He speaks slowly when he makes this statement, giving the words air, floating them through tired exasperation. His noisy manner leaves him when he dispatches these words, for otherwise – when he tells his wife she is ugly or a bitch – he shouts, and bangs anything he can lay his hand on, a saucepan lid, a tin of mushy peas, a spoon. The only person he doesn't shout at is his mother, for whom he has an exaggerated regard, even, according to Sharon, loves. Every evening he takes her down to the Tapper's Arms, returning at closing time to the house that Sharon has so minutely described: rooms separated by walls through which all quarrels can be heard, cigarette burns on the edge of the bath, a picture of a black girl on the landing, a stair-carpet touched with Leslie's motor-cycling grease and worn away in places. To Henrietta's sitting-room – flowery in summer because the french windows bring the garden in, cheerful with a wood fire when it's cold – these images have been repeatedly conveyed, for Sharon Tamm derived considerable relief from talking.

'Well, she told me and I've told you. Please can we just put it all aside?'

She rises as she speaks and hurries to the kitchen. She opens the oven and places the pineapple pudding on the bottom shelf. She bastes the turkey breast and the potatoes and the parsnips. She washes some broccoli and puts it ready on the draining board. He has not said, as she hoped he would, that Sharon Tamm is really a bit pathetic. Ka-Ki sniffs about the kitchen, excited by the smell that has come from the oven. She trots behind Henrietta, back to the garden.

'She told you too, didn't she, Roy? You knew all this?'

She didn't mean to say that. While washing the broccoli she planned to mention MacMelanie, to change the subject firmly and with deliberation. But the nervousness that Sharon Tamm inspired in her when she said that Roy couldn't hurt people has suddenly returned, and she feels muzzy due to the sherry, not entirely in control of herself.

'Yes, she told me,' he says. 'Well, actually, it isn't quite like that.'

He has begun to sweat again, little beads breaking on his forehead and his chin. He pulls the dotted handkerchief from his pocket and wipes at his face. In a slow, unwilling voice he tells her what some intuition already insists is the unbelievable truth: it is not just that the girl has a silly crush on him but that a relationship of some kind exists between them. Listening, she feels physically sick. She feels she is asleep, trying to wake herself out of a nightmare because the sickness is heaving through her stomach. The face of the girl is vivid, a whitehead in the crease of her chin, the rims of her eyes pink. The girl is an insult to her, with her dirty feet and broken fingernails.

'Let's not mention it ever again,' she hears herself urging repetitiously. 'MacMelanie,' she begins, but does not continue. He is saying something, his voice stumbling, larded with embarrassment. She can't hear him properly.

There has never been an uneasiness about their loyalty to one another, about their love or their companionship. Roy is disappointed because, professionally, he hasn't got on, but that has nothing to do with the marriage. Roy doesn't understand ambition, he doesn't understand that advancement has to be pursued. She knows that but has never said it.

'I'm sorry, Henrietta,' he says, and she wants to laugh. She wants to stare at him in amazement as he sprawls there, sweating and fat. She wants to laugh into his face so that he can see how ridiculous it all is. How can it possibly be that he is telling her he loves an unattractive girl who is thirty years younger than him?

'I feel most awfully dejected,' he mutters, staring down at the paving stones where they sit. Her dog is obedient at his feet. High above them an aeroplane goes over.

Does he want to marry the girl? Will she lead him into the house in

Daventry to meet her family, into the kitchen where the awful grandmother is? Will he shake hands with stupid Mrs Tamm, with Leslie and Diane? Will he go down to the Tapper's Arms with Mr Tamm?

'I can't believe this, Roy.'

'I'm sorry.'

'Do you adore her?'

He doesn't answer.

'Have I been no good to you all these years, Roy?'

'Of course you have.'

They have made love, the girl and he. He tells Henrietta so, confessing awkwardly, mentioning the floor of his room in the department. He would have taken off the girl's granny glasses and put them on the fawn vinyl by the leg of his desk. He would have run his fingers through the lustreless hair.

'How could you do this, Roy?'

'It's a thing that happened. Nobody did anything.' Red-faced, shame-faced, he attempts to shrug, but the effort becomes lost in his sprawling flabbiness. He is as unattractive as the girl, she finds herself reflecting: a stranded jellyfish.

'It's ridiculous, Roy,' she shouts, at last losing control. 'It's madness all this.' They have had quarrels before, ordinary quarrels about ordinary matters. Mild insults were later taken back, apologized for, the heat of the moment blamed.

'Why should it be ridiculous,' he questions now, 'that someone should love me? Why should it be?'

'She's a child, you're a man of fifty. How could there possibly be a normal relationship between you? What have you in common?'

'We fell in love, Henrietta. Love has nothing to do with having things in common or normal relationships. Hesselmann in fact points out –'

'For God's sake, Roy, this is not a time for Hesselmann.'

'He does suggest that love abnormalizes –'

'So you're going to become a middle-aged hippy, are you, Roy? You're going to put on robes and dance and meditate in a field with the Orange People? The Orange People were phony, you said. You said that, Roy.'

'You know as well as I do that Sharon has nothing to do with the Orange People any more.'

'You'll love her grandmother. Not to mention Mr Tamm.'

'Sharon needs to be protected from her family. As a matter of fact, she doesn't want ever to go back to that house. You're being snide, you know.'

'I'm actually suffering from shock.'

'There are things we must work out.'

'Oh, for heaven's sake, Roy, have your menopausal fling with the girl. Take her off to a hotel in Margate or Benidorm.'

She pours herself more sherry, her hands shaking, a harsh fieriness darkening her face, reflecting the fury in her voice. She imagines the pair of them in the places she mentions, people looking at them, he getting to know the girl's intimate habits. He would become familiar with the contents of her handbag, the way she puts on and takes off her clothes, the way she wakes up. Nineteen years ago, on their honeymoon in La Grève, Roy spoke of this aspect of a close relationship. Henrietta's own particular way of doing things, and her possessions – her lipstick, her powder compact, her dark glasses, the leather suitcase with her pre-marriage initials on it, the buttoning of her skirts and dresses – were daily becoming as familiar to him as they had been for so long to her. Her childhood existed for him because of what, in passing, she told him of it.

'D'you remember La Grève?' she asks, her voice calm again. 'The woman who called you Professor, those walks in the snow?'

Impatiently he looks away. La Grève is irrelevant, all of it far too long ago. Again he mentions Hesselmann. Not understanding, she says:

'At least I shall not forget La Grève.'

'I've tried to get over her. I've tried not seeing her. None of it works.'

'She said you would not have told me. What did you intend, Roy?'

'I don't know.'

'She said it wasn't fair, did she?'

'Yes, she did.' He pauses. 'She's very fond of you, you know.'

In the oven the breast of turkey would be shrivelling, the pineapple pudding of which he was so boyishly fond would be a burnt mess. She says, and feels ashamed of admitting it: 'I've always had affection for her too, in spite of what I say.'

'I need to talk to her now. I need to tell her we've cleared the air.'

He stands up and drinks what remains of his drink. Tears ooze from beneath his spectacles as he looks down at Henrietta, staring at her. He says nothing else except, yet again, that he is sorry. He shuffles and blows his nose as he speaks. Then he turns and goes away, and a few minutes later she hears the bang of the hall door, as she heard it after Sharon Tamm had left the house also.

Henrietta shops in a greengrocer's that in the Italian small-town manner has no name, just *Fiori e Frutta* above the door. The shy woman who serves there, who has come to know her, adds up the cost of *fagiolini*, pears and spinach on a piece of paper.

'*Mille quattro cento.*' Henrietta counts out the money and gathers up her purchases.

'*Buon giorno, grazie,*' the woman murmurs, and Henrietta wishes her good-day and passes out into the street.

The fat barber sleeps in his customers' chair, his white overall as spotless as a surgeon's before an operation. In the window his wife knits, glancing up now and again at the women who come and go in the Malgri Moda. It is Tuesday and the Jollycaffè is closed. The men who usually sit outside it are nowhere to be seen.

Henrietta buys a slice of beef, enough for one. In the mini-market she buys eggs and a packet of *zuppa di verdura*, and *biscotti strudel 'cocktail di frutta'*, which have become her favourites. She climbs up through the town, to the *appartamento* in the Piazza Santa Lucia. She is dressed less formally than she thought suitable for middle age in England. She wears a denim skirt, blue canvas shoes, a blue shirt which she bought before the weekend from Signora Leici. Her Italian improves a little every day, due mainly to the lessons she has with the girl in the *Informazioni*. They are both determined that by the winter she will know enough to teach English to the youngest children in the orphanage. Sister Maria has said she would welcome that.

It is May. On the verges of the meadows and the wheat fields that stretch below the town pale roses are in bloom. Laburnum blossoms in the vineyards, wires for the vines stretching between the narrow trunks of the trees. It is the season of broom and clover, of poppies, and geraniums forgotten in the grass. Sleepy vipers emerge from crevices, no longer kept down by the animals that once grazed these hillsides. Because of them Henrietta has bought rubber boots for walking in the woods or up Monte Totona.

She is happy because she is alone. She is happy in the small *appartamento* lent to her by friends of her sister, who use it infrequently. She loves the town's steep, cool streets, its quietness, the grey stone of its buildings, quarried from the hill it is built upon. She is happy because the nightmare is distant now, a picture she can illuminate in her mind and calmly survey. She sees her husband sprawling on the chair in the garden, the girl in her granny glasses, and her own weeping face in the bathroom looking-glass. Time shrinks the order of events: she packs her clothes into three suitcases; she is in her sister's house in Hemel Hempstead. That was the worst of all, the passing of the days in Hemel Hempstead, the sympathy of her sister, her generous, patient brother-in-law, their children imagining she was ill. When she thinks of herself now she feels a child herself, not the Henrietta of the suburban sitting-room and the tray of drinks, with chiffon tidily in her hair. Her father makes a swing for her because she has begged so, ropes tied to the bough of an apple tree. Her mother once was cross because she climbed that tree. She cries and her sister comforts her, a sunny afternoon when she got tar on her dress. She skates on an icy pond, a birthday treat before her birthday tea when she was nine. 'I can't stay here,' she said in Hemel Hempstead, and then there was the stroke of good fortune, people she did not even know who had an *appartamento* in a Tuscan hill town.

In the *cantina* of the Contucci family the wine matures in oaken barrels of immense diameter, the iron hoops that bind them stylishly painted red. She has been shown the *cantina* and the palace of the Contucci. She has looked across the slopes of terracotta roof-tiles to Monticchiello and Pienza. She has drunk the water of the nearby spa and has sat in the sun outside the café by the bank, whiling away a morning with an Italian dictionary. *Frusta* means whip, and it's also the word for the bread she has with *Fontina* for lunch.

Her husband pays money into her bank account and she accepts it because she must. There are some investments her father left her: between the two sources there is enough to live on. But one day, when her Italian is good enough, she will reject the money her husband pays her. It is degrading to look for support from someone she no longer respects. And one day, too, she will revert to her maiden name, for why should she carry with her the name of a man who shrugged her off?

In the cool of the *appartamento* she lunches alone. With her *frusta* and *Fontina* she eats peppery radishes and drinks *acqua minerale*. Wine in the daytime makes her sleepy, and she is determined this afternoon to learn another thirty words and to do two exercises for the girl in the *Informazioni*. *Le Chiavi del Regno* by A.J. Cronin is open beside her, but for a moment she does not read it. A week ago, on the telephone to England, she described the four new villas of Signor Falconi to prospective tenants, Signora Falconi having asked her if she would. The Falconis had shown her the villas they had built near their *fattoria* in the hills, and she assured someone in Gloucester that any one of them would perfectly suit her requirements, which were sun and tranquillity and room enough for six.

Guilt once consumed her, Henrietta considers. She continued to be a secretary in the department for six years after her marriage but had given it up because she'd found it awkward, having to work not just for her husband but for his rivals and his enemies. He'd been pleased when she'd done so, and although she'd always intended to find a secretarial post outside the university she never had. She'd felt guilty about that, because she was contributing so little, a childless housewife.

'I want to stay here.' She says it aloud, pouring herself more *acqua minerale*, not eating for a moment. '*Voglio stare qui.*' She has known the worst of last winter's weather; she has watched spring coming; heat will not defeat her. How has she not guessed, through all those years of what seemed like a contented marriage, that solitude suits her better? It only seemed contented, she knows that now: she had talked herself into an artificial contentment, she had allowed herself to become a woman dulled by the monotony of a foolish man, his sprawling bigness and his sense of failure. It is bliss of a kind not to hear his laughter turned on for a television joke, not to look daily at his flamboyant ties and unpolished shoes. *Quella mattina il diario si aprì alla data Ottobre 1917:* how astonished he would be if he could see her now, childishly delighting in *The Keys of the Kingdom* in Italian.

It was her fault, she'd always believed, that they could not have children – yet something informs her now that it was probably more her husband's, that she'd been wrong to feel inadequate. As a vacuum-cleaner sucks in whatever it touches, he had drawn her into a world that was not her own; she had existed on territory where it was natural to be blind – where it was natural, too, to feel she must dutifully console a husband because he was not a success professionally. 'Born with a sense of duty,' her father once said, when she was ten or so. 'A good thing, Henrietta.' She is not so sure: guilt and duty seem now to belong together, different names for a single quality.

Later that day she walks to the Church of San Biagio, among the meadows below the walls of the town. Boys are playing football in the shade, girls lie on the grass. She goes over her vocabulary in her mind, passing by the church. She walks on white, dusty roads, between rows of slender pines. *Solivare* is the word she has invented – to do with wandering alone. *Piantare* means to plant; *piantamento* is planting, *piantagione* plantation. Determinedly she taxes her atrophied memory: *sulla via di casa* and *in modo da; un manovale* and *la briciola.*

In the August of that year, when the heat is at its height, Signora Falconi approaches Henrietta in the *macelleria*. She speaks in Italian, for Henrietta's Italian is better now than Signora Falconi's rudimentary English. There is something, Signora Falconi reveals – a request that has not to do with reassuring a would-be tenant on the telephone. There is some other proposition that Signor Falconi and his wife would like to put to her.

'*Verrò*,' Henrietta agrees. '*Verrò martedí coll'autobus.*'

The Falconis offer her coffee and a little *grappa*. Their four villas, clustered around their *fattoria*, are full of English tenants now. Every fortnight these tenants change, so dirty laundry must be gathered for the *lavanderia*, fresh sheets put on the beds, the villa cleaned. And the newcomers, when they arrive, must be shown where everything is, told about the windows and the shutters, warned about the mosquitoes and requested not to use too much water. They must have many other details explained to them, which the Falconis, up to now, have not quite succeeded in doing. There is a loggia in one of the villas that would be Henrietta's, a single room with a balcony and a bathroom, an outside staircase. And the Falconis would pay just a little for the cleaning and the changing of the sheets, the many details explained. The Falconis are apologetic, fearing that Henrietta may consider the work too humble. They are anxious she should know that women to clean and change sheets are not easy to come by since they find employment in the hotels of the nearby spa, and that there is more than enough for Signora Falconi herself to do at the *fattoria*.

It is not the work Henrietta has imagined when anticipating her future, but her future in her *appartamento* is uncertain, for she cannot live for ever on strangers' charity and one day the strangers will return.

'*Va bene,*' she says to the Falconis. '*Lo faccio.*'

She moves from the Piazza San Lucia. *La governante* Signora Falconi calls her, and the tenants of the villas become her temporary friends. Some take her out to Il Marzucco, the hotel of the town. Others drive her to the sulphur baths or to the abbey at Monte Oliveto, where doves flutter through the cloisters, as white as the dusty roads she loves to walk on. On either side of the pink brick archway are the masterpieces of Luca della Robbia and sometimes the doves alight on them. This abbey on the hill of Oliveto is the most beautiful place she has ever visited: she owes a debt to the girl with the granny glasses.

In the evening she sits on her balcony, drinking a glass of *vino nobile*, hearing the English voices, and the voices of the Italians in and around the *fattoria*. But by October the English voices have dwindled and the only customers of the *fattoria* are the Italians who come traditionally for lunch on Sundays. Henrietta cleans the villas then. She scours the saucepans and puts away the cutlery and the bed linen. The Falconis seem concerned that she should be on her own so much and invite her to their meals occasionally, but she explains that her discovery of solitude has made her happy. Sometimes she watches them making soap and candles, learning how that is done.

The girl, walking up and down the sitting-room that once was Henrietta's, is more matter-of-fact and assured than Henrietta remembers her, though her complexion has not improved. Her clothes – a black jersey and a black leather skirt – are of a better quality. There is a dusting of dandruff on the jersey, her long hair has been cut.

'It's the way things worked out,' she says, which is something she has said repeatedly before, during the time they have had to spend together.

Henrietta does not reply, as she has not on the previous occasions. Upstairs, in blue-and-brown-striped pyjamas, purchased by herself three years ago, the man of whom each has had a share rests. He is out of danger, recovering in an orderly way.

'As Roy himself said,' the girl repeats also, 'we live in a world of mistakes.'

Yet they belong together, he and the girl, with their academic brightness and Hesselmann to talk about. The dog is no longer in the house. Ka-Ki has eaten a plastic bag, attracted by slivers of meat adhering to it, and has died. Henrietta blames herself. No matter how upset she'd felt it had been cruel to walk out and leave that dog.

'I gave Roy up to you,' she says, 'since that was what you and he wanted.'

'Roy is ill.'

'He is ill, but at the same time he is well again. This house is yours and his now. You have changed things. You have let the place get dirty, the windows don't seem ever to have been opened. I gave the house up to you also. I'm not asking you to give it back.'

'Like I say, Henrietta, it was unfortunate about the dog. I'm sorry about that.'

'I chose to leave the dog behind, with everything else.'

'Look, Henrietta –'

'Roy will be able to work again, just as before: we've been quite assured about that. He is to lose some weight, he is to take care of his diet. He is to exercise himself properly, something he never bothered with. It was you, not me, they gave those instructions to.'

'They didn't seem to get the picture, Henrietta. Like I say, we broke up, I wasn't even living here. I've explained that to you, Henrietta. I haven't been here for the past five months, I'm down in London now.'

'Don't you feel you should get Roy on his feet again, since you had last use of him, as it were?'

'That way you're talking is unpleasant, Henrietta. You're getting at me, you're getting at poor Roy. Like you're jealous or something. There was love between us, there really was. Deep love. You know, Henrietta? You understand?'

'Roy explained it to me about the love, that evening.'

'But then it went. It just extinguished itself, like maybe there *was* something in the age-difference bit. I don't know. Perhaps we'll never know, Henrietta.'

'Perhaps not indeed.'

'We were happy for a long time, Roy and me. As happy as any two people could be.'

'I'm sure you were.'

'I'm sorry. I didn't mean to say that. Look, Henrietta, I'm with someone else now. It's different what I've got now. It's going to work out.'

A damp coldness, like the fog that hangs about the garden, touches Henrietta's flesh, insinuating itself beneath her clothes, icy on her stomach and her back. The girl had been at the hospital, called there because Roy had asked for her. She did not say then that she was with someone else.

'May I just, you know, say goodbye to Roy? May I be with him for just five minutes, Henrietta?'

She does not reply. The coldness has spread to her arms and legs. It oozes over her breasts; it reaches for her feet. In blurred vision she sees the steep cool streets of the town, the laburnums and the blaze of clover in the landscape she ran away to.

'I know it's terrible for you, Henrietta.'

Sharon Tamm leaves the room to have her last five minutes. The blur in Henrietta's vision is nothing now. She wonders if they have buried her dog somewhere.

'Goodbye, Henrietta. He's tons better, you know.'

She hears the hall door close as she heard it on the afternoon when the girl came to talk to her, and later when Roy left the house. It's odd, she reflects, that because there has been a marriage and because she bears his name, she should be less free than the girl. Yet is not the life she discovered for herself much the same as finding someone else? Perhaps not.

'I'm sorry,' he says, when she brings him a tray. 'Oh God, I'm sorry about all this mess.'

He cries and is unable to cease. The tears fall on to the egg she has poached for him and into his cup of Bovril. 'Sorry,' he says. 'Oh God, I'm sorry.'

Cocktails at Doney's

'You've forgotten me,' were the first words Mrs Faraday spoke to him in the Albergo San Lorenzo. She was a tall, black-haired woman, wearing a rust-red suede coat cut in an Italian style. She smiled. She had white, even teeth, and the shade of her lipstick appeared subtly to match the colour of her coat. Her accent was American, her voice soft, with a trace of huskiness. She was thirty-five, perhaps thirty-seven, certainly not older. 'We met a long time ago,' she said, smiling a little more. 'I don't know why I never forget a face.'

She was married to a man who managed a business in some town in America he'd never heard of. She was a beautiful woman, but he could remember neither her nor her husband. Her name meant nothing to him and when she prompted him with the information about her husband's business he could not remember any better. Her eyes were brown, dominating her classic features.

'Of course,' he lied politely.

She laughed, clearly guessing it was a lie. 'Well, anyway,' she said, 'hullo to you.'

It was after dinner, almost ten o'clock. They had a drink in the bar since it seemed the natural thing to do. She had to do with fashion; she was in Florence for the Pitti Donna; she always came in February.

'It's nice to see you again. The people at these trade shows can be tacky.'

'Don't you go to the museums as well? The churches?'

'Of course.'

When he asked if her husband accompanied her on her excursions to Florence she explained that the museums, the churches, and the Pitti Donna would tire her husband immensely. He was not a man for Europe, preferring local race-tracks.

'And your wife? Is she here with you?'

'I'm actually not married.'

He wished he had not met Mrs Faraday. He didn't care for being approached in this manner, and her condemnation of the people at the trade exhibitions she spoke of seemed out of place since they were, after all, the people of her business world. And that she was married to a man who preferred race-tracks to culture was hardly of interest to a stranger.

Before their conversation ended he was certain they had not ever met before.

'I have to say good-night,' he said, rising when she finished her drink. 'I tend to get up early.'

'Why, so do I!'

'Good-night, Mrs Faraday.'

In his bedroom he sat on the edge of his bed, thinking about nothing in particular. Then he undressed and brushed his teeth. He examined his face in the slightly tarnished looking-glass above the wash-basin. He was fifty-seven, but according to this reflection older. His face would seem younger if he put on a bit of weight; chubbiness could be made to cover a multitude of sins. But he didn't want that; he liked being thought of as beyond things.

He turned the looking-glass light out and got into bed. He read *Our Mutual Friend* and then lay for a moment in the darkness. He thought of Daphne and of Lucy – dark-haired, tiny Lucy who had said at first it didn't matter, Daphne with her trusting eyes. He had blamed Daphne, not himself, and then had taken that back and asked to be forgiven; they were both of them to blame for the awful mistake of a marriage that should never have taken place, although later he had said that neither of them was, for how could they have guessed they were not suited in that way? It was with Lucy he had begun to know the truth; poor Lucy had suffered more.

He slept, and dreamed he was in Padua with a friend of another time, walking in the Botanical Gardens and explaining to his friend that the tourist guides he composed were short-lived in their usefulness because each reflected a city ephemerally caught. 'You're ashamed of your tourist guides,' his friend of that time interrupted, Jeremy it was. 'Why *are* the impotent so full of shame, my dear? Why *is* it?' Then Rosie was in the dream and Jeremy was laughing, playfully, saying he'd been most amusingly led up the garden path. 'He led me up it too, my God,' Rosie cried out furiously. 'All he could do was weep.'

Linger over the Giambologna birds in the Bargello, and the marble reliefs of Mino da Fiesole. But that's enough for one day; you must return tomorrow.

He liked to lay down the law. He liked to take chances with the facts, and wait for letters of contradiction. *At the height of the season there are twelve times as many strangers as natives in this dusty, littered city. Cascades of graffiti welcome them – the male sexual organ stylized to a Florentine simplicity, belligerent swastikas, hammers and sickles in the streets of gentle Fra Angelico ...*

At lunchtime on the day after he had met her Mrs Faraday was in Doney's with some other Americans. Seeing her in that smart setting, he was surprised that she stayed in the Albergo San Lorenzo rather than the Savoy or the Excelsior. The San Lorenzo's grandeur all belonged to the past: the old hotel was threadbare now, its curtains creased, its telephones unresponsive. Not many Americans liked it.

'Hi!' she called across the restaurant, and smiled and waved a menu.

He nodded at her, not wishing to seem stand-offish. The people she was with were talking about the merchandise they had been inspecting at the Pitti Donna. Wisps of their conversation drifted from their table, references to profit margins and catching the imagination.

He ordered tagliatelle and the chef's salad, and then looked through the *Nazione*. The body of the missing schoolgirl, Gabriella, had been found in a park in Florence. Youths who'd been terrorizing the neighbourhood of Santa Croce had been identified and arrested. Two German girls, hitchhiking in the south, had been made drunk and raped in a village shed. The *Nazione* suggested that Gabriella – a quiet girl – had by chance been a witness to drug-trafficking in the park.

'I envy you your job,' Mrs Faraday said, pausing at his table as he was finishing his tagliatelle. Her companions had gone on ahead of her. She smiled, as at an old friend, and then sat down. 'I guess I want to lose those two.'

He offered her a glass of wine. She shook her head. 'I'd love another cappuccino.'

The coffee was ordered. He folded the newspaper and placed it on the empty chair beside him. Mrs Faraday, as though she intended to stay a while, had hung her red suede coat over the back of the chair.

'I envy you your job,' she said again. 'I'd love to travel all over.'

She was wearing pearls at her throat, above a black dress. Rings clustered her fingers, earrings made a jangling sound. Her nails were shaped and painted, her face as meticulously made up as it had been the night before.

'Did you mind,' she asked when the waiter had brought their coffee, 'my wondering if you were married?'

He said he hadn't minded.

'Marriage is no great shakes.'

She lit a cigarette. She had only ever been married to the man she was married to now. She had had one child, a daughter who had died after a week. She had not been able to have other children.

'I'm sorry,' he said.

She looked at him closely, cigarette smoke curling between them. The tip of her tongue picked a shred of tobacco from the corner of her mouth.

She said again that marriage was no great shakes. She added, as if to lend greater weight to this:

'I lay awake last night thinking I'd like this city to devour me.'

He did not comment, not knowing what she meant. But quite without wishing to he couldn't help thinking of this beautiful woman lying awake in her bedroom in the Albergo San Lorenzo. He imagined her staring into the darkness, the glow of her cigarette, the sound of her inhaling. She was looking for an affair, he supposed, and hoped she realized he wasn't the man for that.

'I wouldn't mind living the balance of my life here. I like it better every year.'

'Yes, it's a remarkable city.'

'There's a place called the Palazzo Ricasoli where you can hire apartments. I'd settle there.'

'I see.'

'I could tell you a secret about the Palazzo Ricasoli.'

'Mrs Faraday –'

'I spent a naughty week there once.'

He drank some coffee in order to avoid speaking. He sighed without making a sound.

'With a guy I met at the Pitti Donna. A countryman of yours. He came from somewhere called Horsham.'

'I've never been to Horsham.'

'Oh, my God, I'm embarrassing you!'

'No, not at all.'

'Gosh, I'm sorry! I really am! Please say it's all right.'

'I assure you, Mrs Faraday, I'm not easily shocked.'

'I'm an awful shady lady embarrassing a nice Englishman! Please say you forgive me.'

'There is absolutely nothing to forgive.'

'It was a flop, if you want to know.' She paused. 'Say, what do you plan to write in your guidebook about Florence?'

'Banalities mostly.'

'Oh, come *on*!'

He shrugged.

'I'll tell you a nicer kind of secret. You have the cleverest face I've seen in years!'

Still he did not respond. She stubbed her cigarette out and immediately lit another. She took a map out of her handbag and unfolded it. She said:

'Can you show me where Santo Spirito is?'

He pointed out the church and directed her to it, warning her against the motorists' signs which pursued a roundabout one-way route.

'You're very kind.' She smiled at him, lavishly exposing her dazzling, even teeth as if offering a reward for his help. 'You're a kind person,' she said. 'I can tell.'

He walked around the perimeter of the vast Cascine Park, past the fun-fair and the zoo and the race-track. It was pleasant in the February sunshine, the first green of spring colouring the twiggy hedges, birches delicate by the river. Lovers sprawled on the seats or in motor-cars, children carried balloons. Stalls sold meat and nuts, and Coca-Cola and 7-Up. Runners in training-suits jogged along the bicycle track. *Ho fame* a fat young man had scrawled on a piece of cardboard propped up in front of him, and slept while he waited for charity.

Rosie, when she'd been his friend, had said he wrote about Italian cities so that he could always be a stranger. Well, it was true, he thought in the Cascine Park, and in order to rid himself of a contemplation of his failed relationship with Rosie he allowed the beauty of Mrs Faraday again to invade his mind. Her beauty would have delighted him if her lipstick-stained cigarettes and her silly, repetitious chattering didn't endlessly dis-figure it. Her husband was a good man, she had explained, but a good man was not always what a woman wanted. And it had come to seem all of a piece that her daughter had lived for only a week, and all of a piece also that no other children had been born, since her marriage was not worthy of children. It was the Annunciations in Santo Spirito she wanted to see, she had explained, because she loved Annunciations.

'Would it be wrong of me to invite you to dinner?' She rose from a sofa in the hall of the Albergo San Lorenzo as soon as she saw him, making no effort to disguise the fact that she'd been waiting for him. 'I'd really appreciate it if you'd accept.'

He wanted to reply that he would prefer to be left alone. He wanted to state firmly, once and for all, that he had never met her in the past, that she had no claims on him.

'You choose somewhere,' she commanded, with the arrogance of the beautiful.

In the restaurant she ate pasta without ceasing to talk, explaining to him that her boutique had been bought for her by her husband to keep her occupied and happy. It hadn't worked, she said, implying that although her fashion shop had kept her busy it hadn't brought her contentment. Her face, drained of all expression, was lovelier than he had so far seen it, so sad and fragile that it seemed not to belong to the voice that rattled on.

He looked away. The restaurant was decorated with modern paintings and was not completely full. A squat, elderly man sat on his own, conversing occasionally with waiters. A German couple spoke in whispers. Two men and a woman, talking rapidly in Italian, deplored the death of the schoolgirl, Gabriella.

'It must have been extraordinary for the Virgin Mary,' Mrs Faraday was saying. 'One moment she's reading a book and the next there's a figure with wings swooping in on her.' That only made sense, she suggested, when you thought of it as the Virgin's dream. The angel was not really there, the Virgin herself was not really reading in such plush surroundings. 'Later I guess she dreamed another angel came,' Mrs Faraday continued, 'to warn her of her death.'

He didn't listen. The waiter brought them grilled salmon and salad. Mrs Faraday lit a cigarette. She said:

'The guy I shacked up with in the Palazzo Ricasoli was no better than a gigolo. I guess I don't know why I did that.'

He did not reply. She stubbed her cigarette out, appearing at last to notice that food had been placed in front of her. She asked him about the painters of the Florentine Renaissance, and the city's aristocrats and patrons. She asked him why Savonarola had been burnt and he said Savonarola had made people feel afraid. She was silent for a moment, then leaned forward and put a hand on his arm.

'Tell me more about yourself. Please.'

Her voice, eagerly insistent, irritated him more than before. He told her superficial things, about the other Italian cities for which he'd written guidebooks, about the hill towns of Tuscany, and the Cinque Terre. Because of his reticence she said when he ceased to speak:

'I don't entirely make you out.' She added that he was nicer to talk to than anyone she could think of. She might be drunk; it was impossible to say.

'My husband's never heard of the Medicis nor any stuff like this. He's never even heard of Masaccio, you appreciate that?'

'Yes, you've made it clear the kind of man your husband is.'

'I've ruined it, haven't I, telling you about the Palazzo Ricasoli?'

'Ruined what, Mrs Faraday?'

'Oh, I don't know.'

They sat for some time longer, finishing the wine and having coffee. Once she reached across the table and put her hand on one of his. She repeated what she had said before, that he was kind.

'It's late,' he said.

'I know, honey, I know. And you get up early.'

He paid the bill, although she protested that it was she who had invited him. She would insist on their having dinner together again so that she might have her turn. She took his arm on the street.

'Will you come with me to Maiano one day?'

'Maiano?'

'It isn't far. They say it's lovely to walk at Maiano.'

'I'm really rather occupied, you know.'

'Oh, God, I'm bothering you! I'm being a nuisance! Forget Maiano. I'm sorry.'

'I'm just trying to say, Mrs Faraday, that I don't think I can be much use to you.'

He was aware, to his embarrassment, that she was holding his hand. Her arm was entwined with his and the palms of their hands had somehow come together. Her fingers, playing with his now, kept time with her flattery.

'You've got the politest voice I ever heard! Say you'll meet me just once again? Just once? Cocktails tomorrow? Please.'

'Look, Mrs Faraday —'

'Say Doney's at six. I'll promise to say nothing if you like. We'll listen to the music.'

Her palm was cool. A finger made a circular motion on one of his. Rosie had said he limped through life. In the end Jeremy had been sorry for him. Both of them were right; others had said worse. He was a crippled object of pity.

'Well, all right.'

She thanked him in the Albergo San Lorenzo for listening to her, and for the dinner and the wine. 'Every year I hope to meet someone nice in Florence,' she said on the landing outside her bedroom, seeming to mean it. 'This is the first time it has happened.'

She leaned forward and kissed him on the cheek, then closed her door. In his looking-glass he examined the faint smear of lipstick and didn't wipe it off. He woke in the night and lay there thinking about her, wondering if her lipstick was still on his cheek.

Waiting in Doney's, he ordered a glass of chilled Orvieto wine. Someone on a tape, not Judy Garland, sang 'Over the Rainbow'; later there was lightly played Strauss and some rhythms of the thirties. By seven o'clock Mrs Farady had not arrived. He left at a quarter to eight.

*

The next day he wandered through the cloisters of Santa Maria Novella, thinking again about the beauty of Mrs Faraday. He had received no message from her, no note to explain or apologize for her absence in Doney's. Had she simply forgotten? Or had someone better materialized? Some younger man she again hadn't been able to resist, some guy who didn't know any more about Masaccio than her good husband did? She was a woman who was always falling in love, which was what she called it, confusing love with sensuality. Was she, he wondered, what people referred to as a nymphomaniac? Was that what made her unhappy?

He imagined her with some man she'd picked up. He imagined her, satisfied because of the man's attentions, tramping the halls of a gift market, noting which shade of green was to be the new season's excitement. She would be different after her love-making, preoccupied with her business, no time for silliness and Annunciations. Yet it still was odd that she hadn't left a message for him. She had not for a moment seemed as rude as that, or incapable of making up an excuse.

He left the cloisters and walked slowly across the piazza of Santa Maria Novella. In spite of what she'd said and the compliments she'd paid, had she guessed that he hadn't listened properly to her, that he'd been fascinated by her appearance but not by her? Or had she simply guessed the truth about him?

That evening she was not in the bar of the hotel. He looked in at Doney's, thinking he might have misunderstood about the day. He waited for a while, and then ate alone in the restaurant with the modern paintings.

'We pack the clothes, *signore*. Is the carabinieri which can promote the inquiries for *la signora. Mi dispiace, signore.*'

He nodded at the heavily moustached receptionist and made his way to the bar. If she was with some lover she would have surfaced again by now: it was hard to believe that she would so messily leave a hotel bill unpaid, especially since sooner or later she would have to return for her clothes. When she had so dramatically spoken of wishing Florence to devour her she surely hadn't meant something like this? He went back to the receptionist.

'Did Mrs Faraday have her passport?'

'*Si, signore. La signora* have the passport.'

He couldn't sleep that night. Her smile and her brown, languorous eyes invaded the blur he attempted to induce. She crossed and re-crossed her legs. She lifted another glass. Her ringed fingers stubbed another cigarette. Her earrings lightly jangled.

In the morning he asked again at the reception desk. The hotel bill wasn't important, a different receptionist generously allowed. If someone had to leave Italy in a hurry, because maybe there was sickness, even a deathbed, then a hotel bill might be overlooked for just a little while.

'*La signora* will post to us a cheque from the United States. This the carabinieri say.'

'Yes, I should imagine so.'

He looked up in the telephone directory the flats she had mentioned. The Palazzo Ricasoli was in Via Mantellate. He walked to it, up Borgo San Lorenzo and Via San Gallo. 'No,' a porter in a glass kiosk said and directed him to the office. 'No,' a pretty girl in the office said, shaking her head. She turned and asked another girl. 'No,' this girl repeated.

He walked back through the city, to the American Consulate on the Lungarno Amerigo. He sat in the office of a tall, lean man called Humber, who listened with a detached air and then telephoned the police. After nearly twenty minutes he replaced the receiver. He was dressed entirely in brown – suit, shirt, tie, shoes, handkerchief. He was evenly tanned, another shade of the colour. He drawled when he spoke; he had an old-world manner.

'They suggest she's gone somewhere,' he said. 'On some kind of jaunt.' He paused in order to allow a flicker of amusement to develop in his lean features. 'They think maybe she ran up her hotel bill and skipped it.'

'She's a respectable proprietor of a fashion shop.'

'The carabinieri say the respectable are always surprising them.'

'Can you try to find out if she went back to the States? According to the hotel people, that was another theory of the carabinieri.'

Mr Humber shrugged. 'Since you have told your tale I must try, of course, sir. Would six-thirty be an agreeable hour for you to return?'

He sat outside in the Piazza della Repubblica, eating tortellini and listening to the conversations. A deranged man had gone berserk in a school in Rome, taking children as hostages and killing a janitor; the mayor of Rome had intervened and the madman had given himself up. It was a terrible thing to have happened, the Italians were saying, as bad as the murder of Gabriella.

He paid for his tortellini and went away. He climbed up to the Belvedere, filling in time. Once he thought he saw her, but it was someone else in the same kind of red coat.

'She's not back home,' Mr Humber said with his old-world lack of concern. 'You've started something, sir. Faraday's flying out.'

In a room in a police station he explained that Mrs Faraday had simply been a fellow-guest at the Albergo San Lorenzo. They had had dinner one evening, and Mrs Faraday had not appeared to be dispirited. She knew other people who had come from America, for the same trade exhibitions. He had seen her with them in a restaurant.

'These people, sir, return already to the United States. They answer the American police at this time.'

He was five hours in the room at the police station and the next day he was summoned there again and asked the same questions. On his way out on this occasion he noticed a man who he thought might be her husband, a big blond-haired man, too worried even to glance at him. He was certain he had never met him, or even seen him before, as he'd been certain he'd never met Mrs Faraday before she'd come up to him in the hotel.

The police did not again seek to question him. His passport, which they had held for fifty-six hours, was returned to him. By the end of that week the newspaper references to a missing American woman ceased. He did not see Mr Faraday again.

'The Italian view,' said Mr Humber almost a month later, 'is that she went off on a sexual excursion and found it so much to her liking that she stayed where she was.'

'I thought the Italian view was that she skipped the hotel. Or that someone had fallen ill.'

'They revised their thinking somewhat. In the light of various matters.'

'What matters?'

'From what you said, Mrs Faraday was a gallivanting lady. Our Italian friends find some significance in that.' Mr Humber silently drummed the surface of his desk. 'You don't agree, sir?'

He shook his head. 'There was more to Mrs Faraday than that,' he said.

'Well, of course there was. The carabinieri are educated men, but they don't go in for subtleties, you know.'

'She's not a vulgar woman. From what I said to the police they may imagine she is. Of course she's in a vulgar business. They may have jumped too easily to conclusions.'

Mr Humber said he did not understand. 'Vulgar?' he repeated.

'Like me, she deals in surface dross.'

'You're into fashion yourself, sir?'

'No, I'm not. I write tourist guides.'

'Well, that's most interesting.'

Mr Humber flicked at the surface of his desk with a forefinger. It was clear that he wished his visitor would go. He turned a sheet of paper over.

'I remind sightseers that pictures like Pietro Perugino's *Agony in the Garden* are worth a second glance. I send them to the Boboli Gardens. That kind of thing.'

Mr Humber's bland face twitched with simulated interest. Tourists were a nuisance to him. They lost their passports, they locked their ignition keys into their hired cars, they were stolen from and made a fuss. The city lived off them, but resented them as well. These thoughts were for a moment openly reflected in Mr Humber's pale brown eyes and then were gone. Flicking at his desk again, he said:

'I'm puzzled about one detail in all this. May I ask you, please?'

'Yes, of course.'

'Were you, you know, ah, seeing Mrs Faraday?'

'Was I having an affair, you mean? No, I wasn't.'

'She was a beautiful woman. By all accounts – by yours, I mean – sir, she'd been most friendly.'

'Yes, she was friendly.'

She was naïve for an American, and she was careless. She wasn't fearful of strangers and foolishly she let her riches show. Vulnerability was an enticement.

'I did not mean to pry, sir,' Mr Humber apologized. 'It's simply that Mr Faraday's detectives arrived a while ago and the more they can be told the better.'

'They haven't approached me.'

'No doubt they conclude you cannot help them. Mr Faraday himself has returned to the States: a ransom note would be more likely sent to him there.'

'So Mr Faraday doesn't believe his wife went off on a sexual excursion?'

'No one can ignore the facts, sir. There is indiscriminate kidnapping in Italy.'

'Italians would have known her husband was well-to-do?'

'I guess it's surprising what can be ferreted out.' Mr Humber examined the neat tips of his fingers. He rearranged tranquillity in his face. No matter how the facts he spoke of changed there was not going to be panic in the American Consulate. 'There has been no demand, sir, but we have to bear in mind that kidnap attempts do often nowadays go wrong. In Italy as elsewhere.'

'Does Mr Faraday think it has gone wrong?'

'Faraday is naturally confused. And, of course, troubled.'

'Of course.' He nodded to emphasize his agreement. Her husband was the kind who would be troubled and confused, even though unhappiness had developed in the marriage. Clearly she'd given up on the marriage; more than anything, it was desperation that made her forthright. Without it, she might have been a different woman – and in that case, of course, there would not have been this passing relationship between them: her tiresomeness had cultivated that. 'Tell me more about yourself,' her voice echoed huskily, hungry for friendship. He had told her nothing – nothing of the shattered, destroyed relationships, and the regret and shame; nothing of the pathetic hope in hired rooms, or the anguish turning into bitterness. She had been given beauty, and he a lameness that people laughed at when they knew. Would her tiresomeness have dropped from her at once, like the shedding of a garment she had thought to be attractive, if he'd told her in the restaurant with the modern paintings? Would she, too, have angrily said he'd led her up the garden path?

'There is our own investigation also,' Mr Humber said, 'besides that of Faraday's detectives. Faraday, I assure you, has spared no expense; the carabinieri file is by no means closed. With such a concentration we'll find what there is to find, sir.'

'I'm sure you'll do your best, Mr Humber.'

'Yes, *sir*.'

He rose and Mr Humber rose also, holding out a brown, lean hand. He was glad they had met, Mr Humber said, even in such unhappy circumstances. Diplomacy was like oil in Mr Humber. It eased his movements and his words; his detachment floated in it, perfectly in place.

'Goodbye, Mr Humber.'

Ignoring the lift, he walked down the stairs of the Consulate. He knew that she was dead. He imagined her lying naked in a wood, her even teeth ugly in a rictus, her white flesh as lifeless as the virgin modesty of the schoolgirl in the park. She hadn't been like a nymphomaniac, or even a sophisticated woman, when she'd kissed his cheek good-night. Like a schoolgirl herself, she'd still been blind to the icy coldness that answered her naïveté. Inept and academic, words he had written about the city which had claimed her slipped through his mind. *In the church of Santa Croce you walk on tombs, searching for Giotto's* Life of St Francis. *In Savonarola's own piazza the grey stone features do not forgive the tumbling hair of pretty police girls or the tourists' easy ways.* Injustice and harsh ambition had made her city what it was, the violence of greed for centuries had been its bloodstream; beneath its tinsel skin there was an iron heart. *The Florentines, like true provincials, put work and money first. In the Piazza Signoria the pigeons breakfast off the excrement of the hackney horses: in Florence nothing is wasted.*

He left the American Consulate and slowly walked along the quay. The sun was hot, the traffic noisy. He crossed the street and looked down into the green water of the Arno, wondering if the dark shroud of Mrs Faraday's life had floated away through a night. In the galleries of the Uffizi he would move from Annunciation to Annunciation, Simone Martini's, Baldovinetti's, Lorenzo di Credi's, and all the others. He would catch a glimpse of her red coat in Santa Trinità, but the face would again be someone else's. She would call out from a *gelateria*, but the voice would be an echo in his memory.

He turned away from the river and at the same slow pace walked into the heart of the city. He sat outside a café in the Piazza della Repubblica, imagining her thoughts as she had lain in bed on that last night, smoking her cigarettes in the darkness. She had arrived at the happiest moment of love, when nothing was yet destroyed, when anticipation was a richness in itself. She'd thought about their walk in Maiano, how she'd bring the subject up again, how this time he'd say he'd be delighted. She'd thought about their being together in an apartment in the Palazzo Ricasoli, how this time it would be different. Already she had made up her mind: she would not ever return to the town where her husband managed a business. 'I have never loved anyone like this,' she whispered in the darkness.

In his hotel bedroom he shaved and had a bath and put on a suit that had just been pressed. In a way that had become a ceremony for him since the evening he had first waited for her there, he went at six o'clock to Doney's. He watched the Americans drinking cocktails, knowing it was safe to be there because she would not suddenly arrive. He listened to the music she'd said she liked, and mourned her as a lover might.

Her Mother's Daughter

Her mother considered it ill-bred to eat sweets on the street, and worse to eat fruit or ice-cream. Her mother was tidy, and required tidiness in others. She peeled an apple in a particular way, keeping the peel in one long piece, as though it were important to do so. Her mother rarely smiled.

Her father, now dead, had been a lexicographer: a small, abstracted man who would not have noticed the eating of food on the street, not even slices of meat or peas from their pods. Most of the time he hadn't noticed Helena either. He died on her eighth birthday.

Her mother had always ruled the household. Tall and greyly dressed, she had achieved her position of command without resort to anger or dictatorial speech; she did not say much, and what she did say she never found necessary to repeat. A look informed the miscreant, indicating a button undone, an unwashed hand. Helena, possessing neither brother nor sister, was the only miscreant.

The house where she and her mother lived was in a south-western suburb of London. Next door on one side there was a fat widow, Mrs Archingford, who dyed her hair a garish shade of red. On the other an elderly couple were for ever bickering in their garden. Helena's mother did not acknowledge the presence of Mrs Archingford, who arrived at the house next door when Helena was nine; but she had written a note to the elderly man to request him to keep his voice down, a plea that caused him to raise it even more.

Helena played mainly by herself. Beneath the heavy mahogany of the dining-room table she cut the hair of Samson while he slept, then closed her eyes while the table collapsed around her, its great ribbed legs and the polished surface from which all meals were eaten splintering into fragments. The multitude in the temple screamed, their robes wet with blood. Children died, women wept.

'What are you doing, Helena?' her mother questioned her. 'Why are you muttering?'

Helena told a lie, saying she'd been singing, because she felt ashamed: her mother would not easily understand if she mentioned Delilah. She played outside on a narrow concrete path that ran between the rockery and the wooden fence at the bottom of the garden, where no one could see her from the windows. 'Now, here's a book,' her mother said, finding her with snails arranged in a semicircle. Helena washed her hands, re-tied the ribbon in the hair, and sat in the sitting-room to read *Teddy's Button*.

Few people visited the house, for Helena's mother did not go in for friends. But once a year Helena was put in a taxi-cab which drove her to her grandparents on her father's side, the only grandparents she knew about. They were a grinning couple who made a fuss of her, small like her father had been, always jumping up and down at the tea-table, passing plates of buttered bread to her and telling her that tea tasted nicer with sugar in it, pressing meringues and cake on her. Helena's mother always put a bowl beside Helena's bed on the nights there'd been a visit to the grandparents.

Her mother was the first teacher Helena had. In the dining-room they would sit together at the table with reading-books and copy-books and history and geography books. When she began to go to school she found herself far in advance of other children of her age, who because of that regarded her with considerable suspicion. 'Our little genius,' Miss Random used to say, meaning it cheerfully but making Helena uncomfortable because she knew she wasn't clever in the least. 'I don't consider that woman can teach at all,' her mother said after Helena had been at the school for six weeks and hadn't learnt anything new. So the dining-room lessons began again, in conjunction with the efforts of Miss Random. 'Pathetic, we have to say': her mother invested this favourite opinion with an importance and a strength, condemning not just Miss Random but also the milkman who whistled while waiting on the doorstep, and Mrs Archingford's attempt at stylish hair. Her mother employed a series of charwomen but was maddened by their chatter and ended by doing the housework herself, even though she found anything like that exceedingly irksome. She far preferred to sit in the dark study, continuing the work that had been cut short by death. In the lifetime of Helena's father her mother had assisted in the study and Helena had imagined her parents endlessly finding words in books and dissecting them on paper. Before the death conversations at mealtimes usually had to do with words. 'Fluxion?' she remembered her father saying, and when she shrugged her mother tightened her lips, her glance lingering on the shrug long after its motion had ceased. 'A most interesting derivation,' her father had supplied, and then went on to speak about the Newtonian calculus. The words he liked to bring up at mealtimes had rare meanings, sometimes five or six, but these, though worthy of record, had often to be dismissed on what he called the journey to the centre of interest. 'Fluxion, Helena, is *the rate at which a flowing motion increases its magnitude*. The Latin *fluxionem*. Now *flux*, Helena, is different. The familiar expression, *to be in a state of flux*, we know of course. But there is interestingly a variation: in mathematical terms, a drawn line is the flux of a point. You understand that, Helena? You place a dot with your pencil in your exercise-book, but you change your mind and continue the dot so that it becomes a line. With *flux* remember our pleasant word, *flow*. Remember our good friend, *fluere*. A flowing out, a flowing in. With *fluxion*, we have the notion of measuring, of calculation.' Food became cold while he explained, but he did not notice. All that was her memory of him.

More interesting than Helena's own household were the households round about. The death that had taken place, the honouring of the unfinished work, her mother's seriousness, were far less fascinating than the gaudy hair and dresses of Mrs Archingford or the arguments of the elderly couple in the garden of the house next door. Sometimes a son visited this couple, an unkempt figure who intrigued Helena most of all. Now and again she noticed him in the neighbourhood, usually carrying a cage with a bird in it. On one occasion he sat in the garden next door with a cage on either side of him, and Helena watched from a window while he pointed out to his mother the features of the budgerigars these cages contained. His mother poured tea and his father read a newspaper or protested, in a voice loud enough to carry to Helena's window, that the conversation about budgerigars was inane. On another occasion Helena saw the unkempt son entering Mrs Archingford's house with a cage and later leaving empty-handed, having presumably made a successful sale. She would have liked to report these incidents to her mother, but when once she referred to the elderly couple's son her mother stared at her in astonishment.

When she was twelve, Helena brought a girl called Judy Smeeth back to tea. She had asked her mother if she might, since she had herself been to tea several times with Judy Smeeth, who was considered at school to be stupid. She was stout, with spectacles, and experienced difficulty in covering her large thighs with her gymslip. When teachers drew attention to this immodest display she laughed and said she did the best she could.

Helena's mother looked at Judy Smeeth blankly, and afterwards said she didn't think she'd ever met a more unattractive person.

'She's my friend at school,' Helena explained.

'Biscuit after biscuit. No wonder she's the size she is.'

'She invited me to her house five times.'

'You mean by that, do you, Helena, that when she comes here she must make up for all those visits by grabbing as much as she can, by filling herself with biscuits and Swiss roll? Is there not a more attractive girl you could have as a companion?'

'No, there isn't.'

'That was said roughly, Helena.'

'She's my best friend.'

Helena's mother vaguely shook her head. She never talked about friends, any more than she talked about her mother or her father. Helena didn't know if she'd had brothers or sisters, and certainly that was not a question she could ask. 'Gosh, *your mother*!' Judy Smeeth said in her amazed way. 'Didn't half give me the jitters, your mother.'

Many months later, in answer to Helena's repeated pleas, Judy Smeeth was permitted to come to the house again. On this occasion they played with a tennis ball in the garden, throwing it to one another. Unfortunately, due to a clumsy delivery of Judy's, it crossed the fence into Mrs Archingford's garden. 'Hey!' Judy cried, having climbed on to a pear tree that grew beside the fence. 'Hey, lady, could we have the ball back?'

Her plump hams, clad only partially in navy-blue school-regulation knickers, were considerably exposed as she balanced herself between the pear tree and the fence. She shouted again, endeavouring to catch the attention of Mrs Archingford, who was reading a magazine beneath her verandah.

'Hey! Yoo-hoo, lady!'

Mrs Archingford looked up and was surprised to see the beaming face of Judy Smeeth, bespectacled and crowned with frizzy hair. Hearing the sound, she had expected the tidier and less extrovert presence of the girl next door. She rose and crossed her garden.

'It's only the ball, missus. We knocked the ball a bit hard.'

'Oh, I *see*,' said Mrs Archingford. 'D'you know, dearie, for a minute I thought your appearance had changed *most* peculiarly.'

'Eh?'

Mrs Archingford smiled at Judy Smeeth, and asked her what her name was. She picked the tennis ball out of her lupins.

'Judy the name is. Smeeth.'

'Mine's Mrs Archingford. Nice to meet you, Judy. Come to tea, have you?'

'That's right. Thanks for the ball.'

'Tell you what, why don't you and what's-her-name climb over that fence and have a glass of orangeade? Like orangeade, do you?'

'Yeah. Sure.'

'Tell you what, I've got a few Danish pastries. Almond and apple. Like Danish pastries, Judy?'

'Hey, Helena, the woman wants us to go over her place.'

'No,' Helena said.

'Why not?'

'Just no.'

'Sorry, missus. Cheerio then.'

Judy descended, having first thrown the ball to Helena.

'Hey, look,' she said when she was standing on the lawn, 'that woman was on about pastries. Why couldn't we?'

'Let's go into the house.'

Her mother would have observed the incident. She would have noticed the flesh of Judy's thighs and Judy's tongue sticking out of the corner of her mouth as she struggled to retain her balance. Two of a kind, she'd probably say when Judy had gone, she and vulgar Mrs Archingford. Her lips would tighten, her whole face would look like iron.

'I don't want that girl here again, Helena,' was what in fact she did.say. 'She is far from suitable.'

Helena did not protest, nor attempt to argue. She had long since learnt that you could not win an argument with her mother because her mother refused to engage in arguments. 'Gor, she don't half frighten me,' Judy Smeeth remarked after that second visit to the house. Helena had realized a long time ago that she was frightened of her also.

'The completion of your father's work,' her mother announced one day, 'is taking a great deal longer than I had anticipated, even though he left such clear and copious notes. I am unworthy and ill-equipped, but it is a task that must be undertaken. So much begun, so much advanced. Someone must surely carry it to fruition.'

'Yes,' Helena said.

'I cannot manage you and the work together, child. I do not wish you to go away to school, I prefer to have you by me. But circumstances dictate. I have no choice.'

So Helena went to a boarding-school in Sussex, and it never at that time occurred to her to wonder how the fees at this expensive place were afforded, or indeed to wonder where any money at all came from. She returned at the end of that first term to find her mother more deeply involved in the unfinished work and also somewhat changed in her manner, as if affected by the lack of a companion. Sarcasm snapped more freely from her. Her voice had become like a whip. She hates me, Helena thought, because I am a nuisance.

The house had become even more exclusive than it had been, no friend from school could ever be invited there now. The wireless, which had occasionally been listened to, was silent. The telephone was used only to order food and household goods from Barker's of Kensington. Letters rarely came.

Then one afternoon just after Easter, when Helena was fifteen, a visitor arrived. She heard the doorbell from her bedroom and went to answer it because her mother wouldn't bother to. It would be an onion-seller, she thought, or one of those people who pressed the *Encyclopaedia Britannica* on you.

'Hullo,' a middle-aged man said, smiling at her from a sandy face. His short hair was sandy also. He wore a greenish suit. 'Are you Helena?'

'Yes.'

'Then I'm your uncle. One of your mother's brothers. Did you know you had uncles and an aunt?'

She shook her head. He laughed.

'I was the one who made up the games we used to play. Different games for different parts of the garden. Aren't you going to let me in?'

'I'm sorry.'

He stepped into the hall, that awful, fusty hall she hated so, its grim brown curtains looping in the archway at the bottom of the stairs, its grim hallstand, the four mezzotints of Australian landscape, the stained ceiling.

She led him into the sitting-room, which was awful also, cluttered with tawdry furniture her mother didn't notice had grown ugly with wear and time, the glass-fronted cabinets full of forgotten objects, the dreary books drearily filling bookcase after bookcase.

'I heard about your father's death, Helena. I'm sorry.'

'It's ages ago now. Seven years actually. He died on my birthday.'

'I only met your father once.' He paused. 'We've often wondered about you, you know.'

'Wondered?'

'The family have. We've known of course that your mother wouldn't be short, but even so.'

He smiled his easy smile at her. It was her mother who had supplied the money there had been, Helena intuitively realized. Something about the way he had mentioned the family and had said her mother wouldn't be short had given this clear impression. Not just obsessive in his scholarship, her father had been needy also.

'I thought I'd call,' he said. 'I've written of course, but even so I just thought I'd call one of these days.'

She left him and went to knock on the study door, as her mother liked her to do. There was no reply, and when she knocked a second time her mother called out in irritation.

'An uncle has come,' Helena said.

'Who?'

'Your brother.'

'Is here, you mean?' Her mother, wearing reading-glasses on a chain, which she had recently taken to, had a finger marking the point on a page at which she had been interrupted. She was seated at the desk, papers and books all around her, the desk light turned on even though it was the middle of the afternoon.

'He's downstairs.'

Her mother said nothing, nor did she display further surprise, or emotion. She stared at Helena, her scrutiny suggesting that Helena was somehow to blame for the presence of this person, which in a sense Helena was, having opened the hall door to him and permitted his entrance. Her mother drew a piece of paper towards her, at the same time releasing her finger from the place it marked. She picked up a fountain pen and then opened a drawer and found an envelope.

'Give him this,' she said, and returned to her books.

Helena carried the missive to the sitting-room. The man had pulled back an edge of the grubby lace curtain and was gazing out into the empty street. He took the envelope from Helena and opened it.

'Well, there you are,' he said when he had read the message, and sighed. He left the note behind when he went. Her mother had simply ordered him to go away. *Please me by not returning to this house*, her mother had added, signing her full name.

In the dormitory called the Upper Nightingale Helena retailed the excesses of her mother. How the elderly couple in the house next door had been written to and requested to make less noise. How Mrs Archingford had been snubbed. How Judy Smeeth had been forbidden the house, how her mother's sandy-faced brother had been summarily dismissed. She told how her mother had never visited the grinning little grandparents, and how they had never come to the house. She described the house – the Australian mezzotints, the fustiness, the dim lights and curtained windows, the dirtiness that was beginning to gather. In their beds, each with a pink cover, other girls of Upper Nightingale listened with delight. None of them had a mother whose tongue was like a whip. None feared a mother's sarcasm. None dreaded going home.

When she closed her eyes after lights-out Helena saw her mother in the dark study, listing words and derivations, finding new words or words no longer used, all in loving memory. 'Oh God,' pleaded Helena in those moments given up to private prayer at the beginning and end of church. 'Oh God, please make her different.'

Her mother supplied her with money so that at the end of each term she could make her way from the school by train and then across London in a taxi-cab. It was not her mother's way to stand waiting at a railway station; nor, indeed, when Helena did arrive, to answer the doorbell until it had been rung twice or three times. It was not her way to embrace Helena, but instead to frown a little as if she had forgotten that her advent was due on a particular day. 'Ah, Helena,' she would say eventually.

These holiday periods were spent by Helena in reading, cleaning the kitchen, cooking and walking about the avenues and crescents of the neighbourhood. When she painted the shelves in her bedroom, her mother objected to the smell of paint, causing Helena to lose her temper. In awkward, adolescent rage, unreasonably passionate, she shouted at her mother. The matter was petty, she was being made petty herself, yet she could not, as she stood there on the landing, bear for a second longer her mother's pretence that the smell of paint could not possibly be coming from within the house since no workman had been employed to paint anything. There was astonishment in her mother's face when Helena said she had been painting her shelves.

'I went out and bought paint,' she cried, red-faced and furious. 'Is there something sinful in that? I went into a shop and bought paint.'

'Of course there's nothing sinful, Helena.'

'Then why are you blaming me? What harm is there in painting the shelves in my bedroom? I'm seventeen. Surely I don't have to ask permission for every single action I take?'

'I merely wondered about the smell, child.'

'You didn't wonder. You knew about the smell.'

'I do not care for that, Helena.'

'Why do you hate me?'

'Now, Helena, please don't be tiresome. Naturally I do not hate you.'

'Everyone knows you hate me. Everyone at school, even Mrs Archingford.'

'Mrs Archingford? What on earth has Mrs Archingford to do with it?'

'She is a human being, that's all.'

'No one denies that Mrs Archingford is a human being.'

'You never think of her like that.'

'You are in a tiresome mood, Helena.'

Her mother turned and went away, descending the stairs to the study. Without a show of emotion, she closed the door behind her, quietly, as if there had not been an angry scene, or as if no importance could possibly attach to anything that had been said.

In her bedroom, that afternoon, Helena wept. She lay on her bed and pressed her face into her pillow, not caring how ugly she was making herself, for who was there to see? In waves of fury that came and calmed, and then came on again, she struck at her thighs with her fists until the repeated impact hurt and she guessed there would be black and blue marks. She wished she had reached out and struck her mother as she stood at the top of the stairs. She wished she had heard the snap of her mother's neck and had seen her body lifeless, empty of venom in the hall.

Twilight was gathering when she got up and washed her face in the bathroom. She held a sponge to each puffed-up eye in turn, and then immersed her whole face in a basin of cold water, holding it there for as long as she could. Her hair was bedraggled as a result, clinging to her damp face. She looked awful, she thought, her mouth pulled down with wretchedness, but she didn't care.

She walked along the crescents and the avenues, and down by the river, finding a common she'd only visited once before. She wished she could simply go on walking through the evening, and never return to her mother's house. She wished that some young man in a motor-car would call out to her and ask her where she was going and say jump in. She would have, she knew she would have.

Instead she turned around and found her way back to the house, her footsteps dawdling and reluctant the closer she came to it. It was ten past nine by the clock in the sitting-room. Her mother, sitting by the electric fire, did not ask where she'd been.

'He will be forgotten,' she said instead, 'if I cannot complete his work.'

She spoke in a voice so matter-of-fact, so dry and spiritless that she might have been reciting a grocery list. Vaguely, Helena had listened when once she'd been told that the work consisted of the completion of a scholarly book, an investigation into how, over centuries, the meanings of words had altered. 'Difficult as it is,' her mother vowed, still without emotion, 'it shall not go unfinished.'

Helena nodded, for some reason feeling sorry she'd been so cross. There was a silence. Her mother stared without interest at the electric fire.

'When you were little,' Helena dared to begin.

'Little?'

'A child.'

'I didn't much care for being a child.'

'I just wondered if –'

'When you don't much care for something you prefer not to dwell upon it, Helena.'

The conversation ended, as abruptly as other attempts to elicit information always had. 'Of course I shall endeavour,' her mother said. 'I intend to continue to make an effort. He would consider it pusillanimous if I did not.'

Helena tried to imagine her as a child and then as an older girl but in neither of these efforts was she successful. The only photograph in the house was of her mother and her father on their wedding-day, standing against an undefined background. Her father was smiling because, Helena had always guessed, the photographer had asked him to. But her mother had not heeded this request.

'I've cooked us moussaka,' Helena said the next day, wanting to make up for her outburst. 'A kind of shepherd's pie.'

'Good heavens, child, how very ambitious of you!'

Her mother left most of it on her plate and went away to find herself a slice of bread. Some time later they spoke again of cooking. Helena said:

'There's a course you can take.'

'A course, Helena?'

She explained, her mother carefully listened. Her mother said:

'But surely you can take a more interesting course? What would be at the end of this, for instance?'

'A job, if I am lucky.'

'You would cook in some kitchen, is that it? Other people's food? Food for mouths in a hotel – or a hospital or a school? Is that it?'

'Well, perhaps.'

'I can only call it pathetic, Helena, to cook food for people in an institution.'

'Cooking is something I like.'

'I do not understand that.'

Genuinely, Helena knew, her mother didn't. The meals they ate – which as a child she had assumed to be as all meals were – had never been prepared with interest. Meat and vegetables arrived from the food department of the Kensington store and had, with as scant attention as possible, found their way on to the mahogany surface of the dining-table.

'The course doesn't cost a lot.'

'Child, it doesn't matter what it costs. Your father would be disappointed is what matters.'

There was resentment in her mother's voice. There was astonished disbelief, as if Helena had confessed to a crime. 'I'm glad he's dead,' her mother said, 'so that he need not suffer to see his only child becoming a cook.'

'I'm sorry it's such a tragedy.'

'It makes no sense, child.'

Her mother turned away, leaving the sitting-room, where the brief conversation had taken place. Helena might have told the truth: that any course, in cooking, in typing and shorthand, in nursery management, in accountancy or gardening, would have fulfilled her need, which was to close the door of the house behind her and never to return.

She worked in the kitchens of Veitch and Company, paper manufacturers, helping to cook canteen food for two hundred employees. Braised steak, silverside, gammon, beef, roast potatoes or mashed, peas, carrots, Brussels sprouts, broad beans in season, trifle or Black Forest gâteau, stewed plums or custard tart: they were dishes and tastes which represented a world as distant as it could possibly be from her mother's and father's. 'Helena!' a voice shouted in the kitchens one day and there was Mrs Archingford on the telephone, talking about the police and how the name of Veitch and Company had been discovered on a postcard in the dark study, where Helena's mother had been found also. It was Mrs Archingford who had noticed the curtains not drawn back in the sitting-room of her mother's house, who had worried and had finally spoken to a policeman on the beat. Starvation was given as the cause of death on the death certificate: still struggling with the work in the study, Helena's mother had not bothered to eat. Not having visited her for more than three years, Helena had tried not to think about her while that time passed.

'You'll forgive me, dear, if I fail to attend the funeral,' Mrs Archingford requested. 'She didn't care for the look of me and no bones about it. Would be a trifle hypocritical, should we say?'

Helena was the only person who did attend the funeral. While a clergyman who had never known her mother spoke his conventional farewell she kept thinking of the busy kitchens of Veitch and Company – all that mound of food, while her mother had absentmindedly starved.

She cleared the house, taking a week off from the kitchens. She gathered together her mother's clothes – and her father's, which still remained – and placed them ready in the hall, to be collected by a charitable organization. She telephoned a firm which a girl in the kitchens had told her about, which purchased the contents of uninhabited houses. She telephoned a house agents' and put the house on the market.

She found nothing, in her mother's bedroom or the study, that belonged to the past, before the time of the marriage. There were no personal letters of any kind, no photographs privately kept, no diaries. There was dust everywhere, some of her mother's clothes were unwashed; the gas cooker in the kitchen, the refrigerator and the kitchen cupboards, were all filthy. But the order which was absent elsewhere dominated the study. The papers and notebooks dealing with lexicographic matters were arranged tidily on the long rectangular table beneath the window, and on the desk itself were two stacks of lined foolscap, one covered with the tiny handwriting of

Helena's father, the other with her mother's, larger and firmer. The pages were numbered: there were seven hundred and forty-six of them. *I do not know about a title for the work,* her mother had written in the draft of a letter she had clearly been intending to dispatch to a publisher. *My husband left no instruction, but some phrase may particularly strike you from what he has written himself, and a title thus emanate. The work is now complete, in the form my husband wished it.* Had her mother put aside all other form of life as the final pages were composed, pathetically clinging to the relationship her wealth had bought? Helena wondered if she had bothered to go to bed since she had not bothered with food. She might have died of exhaustion as well as of starvation. She might have lost track of day and night, afraid to leave the study in case the long task should by some awful mischance be lost when the end was so very close. She imagined her mother struggling with sleep, weak in her body, the clarity of her bold handwriting now the most important fragment of her existence. She imagined her blinking away a sudden dizziness, and then moving in the room, one hand still on the desk to balance her progress, another reaching out into the gloom. She imagined her dead, lying on the unclean carpet.

On the foolscap pages there were underlined words, printed in capital letters: *Nympholepsy. Disembogue. Graphotype. Imagist. Macle. Rambunctious.* The precision of alphabetical order, the endlessly repeated reflections of her mother's seriousness, the intensity of her devotion to the subject out of which she and the man she'd married had spun a life together: all that lingered in the study, alive in the conjoined handwriting on the foolscap pages and the notebooks. The explanations of the paragraphs were meaningless to Helena and the burden of reading them caused her head to ache. She didn't know what to do with all the paper and the writing that had been left so purposefully behind. She didn't know what to do about the letter to a publisher, probably the last effort her mother had made. She closed the study door on all of it.

She did not sleep in the house. Each evening she returned to her two-room flat near Shepherd's Bush, where she turned the television on immediately to drive the house out of her thoughts. She sat in front of the bustling little screen with a glass of whisky and water, hoping that it, too, would help to cloud the images of the day. She longed to be back in her noisy kitchens, surrounded by different kinds of food. Sometimes, when she'd had a second and a third glass of whisky, the catalogue of the food which had become her life reminded her in a wry way of the catalogue of words in the study, one so esoteric, one so down-to-earth. Toad-in-the-hole, cabinet pudding, plaice and chips, French onion soup, trifle, jelly surprise.

One morning she arrived at the house with a cardboard carton into which she packed the foolscap pages. She carried it upstairs and placed it in a corner of the bedroom that had been her parents', with a note to the effect that it should not be taken away by the firm she had employed to take everything else. The books in the study would go, of course. In her small flat she could not possibly store them, and since they were of no possible interest to her what was the point?

Mrs Archingford kept ringing the doorbell, to ask if she would like a cup of tea or if she could help with anything. Mrs Archingford was, not unnaturally after the years that had gone by, curious. She told Helena that at Number 10 the elderly couple's son had moved in, to look after them in their now extreme old age. Birds flew about the rooms, so Mrs Archingford reported; the son was odd in the extreme.

'I dare say you'll be relieved to turn your back on the house?' she probed. 'No place for a young person, I shouldn't wonder?'

'Well, I don't want to live here, certainly.'

'My dear, however could you?'

Mrs Archingford's tone implied a most distressful childhood. She wouldn't be surprised to hear, her tone suggested, that Helena had been beaten and locked in cupboards, just to teach her. 'Most severe, your mother was, I always thought.'

'It was her way.'

'Forgive a nosy neighbour, dear, but your mother didn't look happy. Her own worst enemy, as I said one time to the gas man. "Be brisk about it," she ordered him, really sharply, you know, when the poor fellow came to read the meter. Oh, years ago it must have been, but I often remember it. Imagine that said to a meter man, when all the time he has to go careful in case of errors! And of course if he had made an error she'd be the first –'

'Actually, my mother wouldn't have noticed.'

'Why don't you slip in for a Nescafé and a Danish, eh? Smells like a morgue this hall does – oh, there, what a clumsy I am! Now, take that as unsaid, dear!'

Helena replied that it was quite all right, as indeed it was. Mrs Archingford pressed her invitation.

'What about a warming cup, though? D'you know, I've never in all my days been inside this house? Not that I expected to, I mean why should I? But really it's interesting to see it.'

Mrs Archingford poked a finger into the dust on the hallstand, and as she did so the doorbell rang. Women from the charitable organization had come for the clothes, so Helena was saved from having to continue the conversation about Nescafé and Danish pastries. That morning, too, a man arrived to estimate the value of the house and its contents so that death duties might be calculated. Then a man who was to purchase the contents came. He looked them over and suggested a figure far below that of the death duties man, but he pointed out that he was offering a full removal service, that in some unexplained way Helena was saving a fortune. She didn't argue. In the afternoon Mrs Archingford rang the bell again to say the estate agents Helena had chosen were not the best ones, so the woman in the Corner Shop had told her when she'd happened to allude to the matter while buying smoked ham. But Helena replied that the choice had been made.

A few days later she watched the furniture being lifted away, the books and ornaments in tea-chests, the crockery and saucepans and cutlery, even the gas cooker and the refrigerator. When everything was gone she walked about the empty rooms. Why had she not asked the sandy-haired man who had come? Why had she not made tea for him and persuaded him to tell her anything at all? Through a blur of mistiness she saw her mother as a child, playing with her brother in the garden he had mentioned. Helena stood in the centre of the room that had been her mother's bedroom and it seemed to her then that there were other children in the garden also, and voices faintly echoing. Trees and shrubs defined themselves; a house had lawns in front of it. 'Come on!' the children good-naturedly cried, but her mother didn't want to. Her mother hated playing. She hated having to laugh and run about. She hated being exposed to a jolliness that made her feel afraid. She wanted peace, and the serious silence of her room, but they always came in search of her and they always found her. Laughing and shouting, they dragged her into their games, not understanding that she felt afraid. She stammered and her face went white, but still they did not notice. Nobody listened when she tried to explain, nobody bothered.

These shadows filled her mother's bedroom. Helena knew that the playing children were a figment without reality, yet some instinct informed her that such shadows had been her mother's torment, that their dreaded world had accompanied her even after she had hidden from them in a suburban house where the intolerable laughter was not allowed. Companions too ordinary to comprehend her mother's different nature had left her afraid of ordinariness, and fear was what she had passed on to an ordinary daughter. Helena knew she would never marry; as long as she lived she would be afraid to bring a child into the world, and reflecting on that now she could feel within her the bitterness that had been her mother's, and even the vengeful urge to destroy that had been hers also.

Curtains had been taken down, light-shades removed. Huge patches glared from ancient wallpaper where furniture had stood or pictures hung.

The bare boards echoed with Helena's footsteps. She bolted what it was necessary to bolt and saw that all the windows were secure. She banged the hall door behind her and for the last time walked through the avenues and crescents she knew so well, on her way to drop the keys through the estate agents' letter-box. The cardboard carton containing her father's work, and her mother's achievement in completing it, remained in a corner of an empty bedroom. When the house was sold and the particulars completed the estate agents would telephone her in the kitchens at Veitch and Company to point out that this carton had been overlooked. Busy with meat or custard tart, she'd say it didn't matter, and give the instruction that it should be thrown away.

Bodily Secrets

At fifty-nine, she was on her own, the widow of the O'Neill who had inherited the town's coal business, who had started, as an enterprise of his own, the toy factory. Her children had flown the nest, her parents and her parents-in-law were no longer alive. Her husband had been in his lifetime a smallish though heavily built man, with wide shoulders and an unrelenting, cropped head, like a battering wedge. His cautious eyes had been set well apart beneath woolly eyebrows; small veins had reddened his nose. He had died at the age of sixty-three, falling down in the big, airy hall of Arcangelo House and afterwards not regaining any real awareness of who he was or what had happened. He had built Arcangelo House after he and his wife had stayed in an Italian hotel of that name when they visited Rome on the occasion of Holy Year.

A beauty once, she was a handsome woman still, tall and imposing in her middle age, with a well-covered look that reflected her liking for sweet things. Her grey hair was shaded towards its original brown, and discreetly burnished; she bought clothes extravagantly. She made up her face with precision, taking her time over it; and attended similarly to her fingernails and, in season, her toenails. She had borne four children in all, two of her three daughters being married now, one in Dublin, the other in Trim; the third was a nurse in Philadelphia. Her son, married also, ran the coal business but was more interested in developing a thousand acres of turf-bog he had bought and which he saw as the beginning of an enterprise that he believed would in time outstrip his father's and his grandfather's already established empire. He had inherited their entrepreneur's spirit, and since he'd first been aware of the role laid down for him he had seen himself as their rival. He was married to Thelma, daughter of a Portarlington publican, a girl whom Mrs O'Neill did not care for, considering her common. Particularly she did not care for the thought that one day Thelma would take her own place in Arcangelo House.

From the garden and the upstairs windows the house offered, over fields, a view of the town that was interrupted only by the toy factory. When the wind blew from the south it carried sounds rendered faint over the distance: the cries of children, a car being started somewhere, the saws in the timber works, the grind of a heavy lorry on Daly's Hill. And no matter where the wind came from there was always the bell at the convent, and the bell of Our Lady in Glory, and the Protestant bell on Sundays. At night the street lights and the lights of houses were spread out prettily – the town seen at its best, as Mrs O'Neill often reflected. But increasingly in the vacuum that Arcangelo House had become she reflected also that she felt like a pebble in a drum, and said as much to her bridge companions. They urged her to sell it and build a bungalow, but privately she felt that a bungalow was not her style.

When her husband had died Mrs O'Neill had been fifty-six, and although they had regularly disagreed in their thirty-seven years of marriage they had more often been affectionate companions. They had shared two interests in particular: golf and their children. Together they had attended the occasional race-meeting; and while her husband had not played bridge, she in turn had not inclined to join him in the bar of the Commercial Hotel, where he liked to spend an evening or two a week. Every summer they went to Lahinch or Bundoran for the golf, and for several years after Holy Year they had returned to Rome, to the hotel which had given their house its character and its name. Often, on a night which wasn't a bridge night, Mrs O'Neill wondered about the future and whether she should indeed sell Arcangelo House. When the television came to an end she sat alone in the big open drawing-room, feeling just a little lonely and vaguely wishing that there was another interest in her life besides bridge and golf and her grown-up family. Time had dulled the loss that widowhood had brought, but in no way had it filled the vacuum that was somehow more apparent as time progressed. Once she'd been the centre of things in Arcangelo House, looking after everyone, in charge of other people's lives. 'Ah, come on now,' she'd said a thousand times to the husband who'd died on her. 'You're as big a baby as any of them.' In her days as a beauty she had more or less designed the house herself, standing over MacGuire the architect and endeavouring to picture for him a cool, well-organized hotel in Rome. It still pleased her that she had succeeded so well, not that Arcangelo House was to everyone's taste, she was well aware of that: it was too different, too modern, in a way too grand. But old Canon Kenny, the most educated man for miles about, said he would wager money that the house was the most interesting to be found outside Dublin. It had been featured in *Social and Personal* and MacGuire, who was inordinately proud of it, had asked if a German architect, on a motoring holiday, might come and see it. How could she just leave it all? The garden, once little better than waste-land, had gorgeously matured. The portico, with its clean white arches, was rich with different clematis from June to August. The patio was warm enough to have breakfast on in March. Yet the accomplishing of what she'd wanted in the house and in the garden belonged to the time when she'd been in charge, and was a reminder that nothing now was changing or taking shape due to her efforts.

Occasionally, pursuing such lines of thought, she wondered if she would marry again. She couldn't help herself; she had no desire to remarry, yet widows did so, it was something that quite often occurred. At the golf club there was Sweetman, a few years younger than herself, a bachelor all his life, pleasantly sociable but bleary when he had drink taken, and according to Dolores Fitzfynne a tightwad. There was Corkin, who was her own age, but it was hard to think of Corkin without thinking also of the Mrs Corkin there had been, a drear of a woman who had played neither golf nor bridge, who hadn't even had children: Corkin had been infected by her dreariness or else had infected her in the first place. There was no one else, except perhaps Agnew, with his sallow face and his hands, which were sallow also, gesturing in the air, and his faintly high-pitched voice. He was younger than the others, younger than she was herself by seven or eight years, yet she often thought of him in this connection. She thought about him in a different way on the morning her son, Cathal, decreed that the toy factory would have to go. For seventeen years Agnew had been its manager.

In a blue-and-yellow paisley dressing-gown which she'd had all her married life she sat on the edge of her bed, listening to her son on the telephone saying that the people at the toy factory could easily be absorbed elsewhere, that for a long time now he had systematically been running the business down. The toy factory had been profitable only in the immediate postwar years, unable ultimately to sustain the competition which had so ominously built up: long before his death her husband had threatened that it would sooner or later have to close. It was a tiny concern, the loss would not be great.

'All they're making now are the fox-terriers,' Cathal said on the telephone, referring to wooden dogs on wheels.

'The building?' she said. 'Best to have it down, wouldn't it?'

'I could bale garden peat there. I'm going into that, you know.'

She did not say anything. She did not trust this dark-faced son she'd given birth to. Ceasing to be a toy factory, the building would be expanded when it became the location for one of his enterprises. There might be noise, even a smell of chemicals. You simply couldn't guess what would come along in order that more money might be made. And why should it matter since only a lone woman lived near by?

'We'll have to see,' she said.

'Ah, of course, of course. No hurry at all.'

She did not ask about Agnew. She could not see him being absorbed into the turf business or the coal business, and in any case Cathal didn't like him. Cathal would have him out on the street while you'd wink.

Cathal had his father's wedge of a head, his forehead and wide-apart, narrow eyes. He was the first of their children to be born, the one who had received most attention because the others were girls. Heir to so much, he had been claimed by a thrusting entrepreneur's world from infancy. The girls, except for Siobhan in Philadelphia, had been more mundanely claimed by men.

She wouldn't have minded any of the others being in Arcangelo House, but Thelma had a greedy way of looking at her, as if she couldn't wait to get into the place. Mrs O'Neill dearly wished that her son hadn't married this girl, but he had and that was that. She sighed as she replaced the receiver, seeing Thelma's slightly puffy face, her nose too small for the rest of it. She sat for a moment longer, endeavouring to release her imagination of that face and in the end succeeding. Then she dressed herself and went down to the toy factory. Agnew was in the inner office, standing by the window, his back to her as she entered.

'Mr Agnew.'

'Ah, Mrs O'Neill. Come in, come in, Mrs O'Neill.' He moved so swiftly in turning to greet her that she was reminded of the assured way he danced the quickstep. He came every December to the Golf Club Dance even though he was not a club member and had once confided to her that he had never played the game. 'Croquet,' he'd confided also. 'I used to be quite snappy at croquet.' He had his own expressions, a way of putting things that sometimes sounded odd. Typical that he should mention an old-fashioned game like croquet.

'I hope you're not busy, Mr Agnew. I'm not disturbing you, am I?'

'Heavens above, why would you be? Won't you take a chair, Mrs O'Neill? A cup of tea now?'

There was always this formality. He offered it and seemed shyly to demand it. Her husband had always used his surname, and so did Cathal; at the Golf Club Dance she'd heard other men call him by his initials, B.J. She couldn't in a million years imagine him addressing her as Norah.

'No, I won't have tea, thank you.'

'A taste of sherry at all? I have a nice sweet little sherry –'

'No, thanks. Really, Mr Agnew.'

He smiled, gently closing a glass-fronted cabinet he had opened in expectation of her accepting his hospitality. He was wearing a brown suit chalked with a pinstripe, and a green silk tie. He said:

'Well, it seems we have come to the end of the road.'

'I know. I'm awfully sorry.'

'Mr O'Neill saw it coming years ago.'

'Yes, I'm afraid he did.'

He smiled again; his voice was unperturbed. 'The first day I came up to Arcangelo House I was terrified out of my wits. D'you remember, Mrs O'Neill? Your husband had an advertisement for the job in the *Irish Times*.'

'It seems an age ago.'

'Doesn't it, though? An age.'

His face had acquired a meditative expression. He drew a packet of cigarettes from a pocket of his jacket and opened it slowly, folding back the silver paper. He advanced a single cigarette by knocking the packet on the surface of his desk. He leaned towards her, offering it. His wrists were slim: she had never noticed his wrists before.

'Thank you, Mr Agnew.'

He leaned across the desk again, holding the flame of a cigarette-lighter to the tip of her cigarette. It gleamed with the dull patina of gold, as slender as a coin.

'No, I don't entirely know what I'll do.' He lit his own cigarette and then held it, dangling, in his long fingers.

'Cathal should have something for you. It was my husband's intention, you know, that everyone at the toy factory should be offered something.'

She wanted to make that clear; she wanted to record this unequivocal statement in the inner office so that later on, if necessary, she could quote herself to Cathal. She inhaled some smoke and released it luxuriously through her nostrils. She was fond of the occasional cigarette, although she never smoked when she was on her own.

'I'm not so sure I'd entirely fit in, Mrs O'Neill. I don't know anything about selling turf.'

She mentioned coal, which after all was the fuel that had made the O'Neills wealthy. There was still a thriving coal business, the biggest in the county.

He shook his head. His hair, once black, was almost completely grey now. 'I don't think,' he said, 'I'd be at home in coal.'

'Well, I only thought I'd mention it.'

'It's more than kind, Mrs O'Neill.'

'My husband wouldn't have wanted anyone not looked after.'

'Oh, indeed I know it.'

She stared at the lipstick mark on her cigarette and then raised the cigarette to her mouth again. It was awkward because she didn't want to walk out of the factory smoking a cigarette, yet it was too soon to crush it out on the ashtray in front of her.

'If there's any way the family can help, you'll say, Mr Agnew?'

'I suppose I'll go to Dublin.'

The remark was not accompanied by one of his glancing smiles; he gave no sign whatsoever that he'd touched upon a fascinating topic. No one knew why he spent weekends occasionally in Dublin, and a certain curiosity had gathered round the mystery of these visits. There was some secret which he kept, which he had not even confided to her husband in his lifetime. He came back melancholy was all her husband had ever reported, and once or twice with bloodshot eyes, as if he had spent the time drinking.

'Though I'd rather not end up in Dublin,' he added now. 'To tell you the full truth, Mrs O'Neill, it's not a city I entirely care for.'

She bent the remains of her cigarette in half, extinguishing it on the ashtray. She stood up, thinking it odd that he'd said Dublin wasn't somewhere he cared for since he visited it so regularly.

'The toy factory was a favourite of my husband's. It saddened him to see it decline.'

'It had its heyday.'

'Yes, it had its day.'

She went, walking with him from the office, through a shed full of unassembled terriers on wheels. The white cut-out bodies with a brown spot around the tail, the brown heads, the little platforms that carried the wheels, the wheels themselves: all these dislocated parts lay about in stacks, seeming unwanted. No one was working in the shed.

He walked with her through other deserted areas, out on to the gravel forecourt that stretched in a semicircle around the front of the small factory. A man loaded wired cartons on to a lorry. They were still meeting orders in England, Agnew told her. The paint shop was as active as ever, three girls on full time.

He held his hand out, his sallow features illuminated by another smile. His palm was cool, his grip gentle. He asked her not to worry about him. He assured her he'd be all right.

There were gusts of laughter in the clubhouse. Dessie Fitzfynne had told a Kerry joke, concerning eight Kerry gardai and a cow. Dolores Fitzfynne, who'd just gone round in eighty-two and wanted to talk about that instead, requested that he shouldn't tell another. Sweetman was talking about horses, arranging something about going to the Curragh. Sweetman loved getting parties together to go racing or to Lansdowne Road, or for a weekend down in Kelly's at Rosslare. Paunchy and rubicund, Flanagan kept saying it was his turn and what did anyone want?

'I heard the factory's winding up,' the solicitor, Butler-Regan, remarked in his rowdy voice and she nodded, suddenly feeling dismal. She had forgotten about the toy factory while she'd been on the golf-course, going round in ninety-one, taking three to get out of the rough at the eighth. She'd been playing with Dessie Fitzfynne, opposing Dolores and Flanagan. They'd been beaten, of course.

It was silly to feel dismal just because the facts of commerce dictated the closure of an unprofitable concern. As both Cathal and Agnew had intimated, the end had been a matter of anticipation for years. Only sentiment had prevented such a decision in the lifetime of her husband.

'Ah well, there you are,' Butler-Regan said noisily. ''Tis better let it go, Norah.'

Flanagan handed her another gin and French even though she hadn't asked for one. Overhearing the reference to the toy factory, he said:

'I hear Agnew's wondering what to do with himself.'

'The bold Agnew!' Butler-Regan laughed. He, too, was paunchy and rubicund. He added, laughing again, shouting through this laughter: 'Oh, Master Agnew'll fall on his feet, I'd say.'

They all liked Agnew even though he was so different. He was an easy companion for half an hour or so if you happened to run into him in the bar of the Commercial Hotel; he was always willing to drop into conversation with you on the street. He had digs with the Misses McShane in a house called St Kevin's, where he was regularly to be seen tending the front garden, behind silver-painted railings set in a low concrete wall. He also walked the Misses McShane's dog, Mandy, about the town, and on Sundays he attended the Protestant church unless he happened to be in Dublin.

'We'd all miss Agnew,' Flanagan said. 'That wild Protestant man.' He laughed, making much the same explosive sound that the solicitor did. Did any of them realize, she wondered, that Agnew's quickstep put them all to shame every December?

'Oh, wild is right,' Butler-Regan agreed. 'Wasn't he in the city again a week ago?'

The two men laughed in unison, the burst of noise causing Rita Flanagan to glance sharply across the bar to ascertain if her husband was already drunk. In dog's-tooth skirt and soft fawn golfing-jacket, Mrs O'Neill wondered what any of them would think if they knew that, quite involuntarily as she stood there, she had again begun to speculate on the possibility of not remaining for ever the widow she presently was. She sipped her gin and French, not taking part in a conversation about Sweetman's outing to the Curragh. In the same involuntary manner she found herself following a thread of thought that led her back to her wedding-day. The O'Neills had insisted on paying for the reception, since her own family were not well-to-do. Old Canon Kenny – neither old nor a canon then – had conducted the service, assisted by a curate called Colquhoun, who had later left the priesthood. They had gone to Bray for their honeymoon and on their first night in the International Hotel she had been jittery. She hadn't known how it should be, whether she should simply take her clothes off or wait for him to say something, whether or not there was going to be preliminary kissing. She'd gone as red as anything after they'd come up from the restaurant. 'I think that waiter knew,' she'd whispered on the stairs, not noticing there was a maid just behind them. He'd been jittery too, and in the end it was she who inaugurated the kissing and in fact had taken his tie off. What on earth would it be like being in a bedroom in Bray with Agnew? There was fat on her shoulders now, which hadn't been there before, and naturally her thighs and her hips were no longer the same. Her body had been forgotten in that particular way for many years before her husband's death, almost since the birth of Siobhan. They had come to occupy separate bedrooms in Arcangelo House, having reached the decision that Cathal and the three girls were enough. At first, when it was safe to do so, she had visited the other bedroom, but the habit had dwindled and then ceased. Would it be a form of unfaithfulness to resume it in different circumstances now? It wasn't easy to guess how such things stood at fifty-nine.

Corkin, the widower of the woman who'd been a drear, approached her with the usual sorrowful look in his eyes, as if he still mourned the wife who had played neither bridge nor golf. The eyes themselves, lurking in their despondent wateriness behind spectacles, had pinkish rims and were the only feature you noticed in Corkin's flat face, except possibly his teeth, which moved uncomfortably in his jaw when he ate. He was eating now, chewing crisps from a transparent Tayto bag. His hair was like smooth lead; his limbs jutted from his clothes. There was no doubt whatsoever that Corkin, the manager of a butter business, was looking for a housekeeper in the form of a second wife. There was always a nudge or two in the clubhouse when he approached Mrs O'Neill for a chat.

'Ah, didn't I have a terrible round? Did you see me in front of you, Norah? Wasn't I shocking?'

She denied that. She hadn't noticed his misfortunes, she said, which indeed she hadn't. She might have added that the butter manager couldn't be shocking if he tried for the rest of his life.

'I've been meaning to ask you,' he said. 'Would you be interested in a bunch of delphiniums from the garden, Norah?'

She drank more gin and French. She had plenty of delphiniums at Arcangelo House, she replied, though it was very good of him to offer her more.

'Or the asparagus fern? D'you grow that stuff?'

'I grow asparagus all right. Only I eat it before the fern comes.'

'Ah well, why wouldn't you, Norah.'

Sweetman, at the bar, was sweating like an animal. No woman in her senses would want to marry Sweetman. His trouble with perspiration ironically denied his name, and the caginess Dolores Fitzfynne claimed for him would hardly have been easy to live with. He had a tendency towards forgetfulness when his round came up in the clubhouse and, according to Dolores, the parties he organized for race-meetings or Lansdowne Road were done so to his own pecuniary advantage. 'Too mingy with himself to look sideways at a woman,' Dolores had said, and probably she was right. He was a surveyor with the county council; and if he gave you a lift in his car he had a way of mentioning the high price of petrol.

She watched Sweetman while Corkin continued in his tedious manner, offering her marigold plants. It had surprised her when Agnew had said he'd never in his life played golf. She'd thought afterwards that he would probably have been good. He had the look of someone who had been athletic in his time. His dancing suggested ball sense, she didn't know why.

'To tell you the honest truth, I don't much care for marigolds.'

'The wife loved them. Give Mrs Corkin a box of marigolds and she'd be pricking them out till Kingdom come.'

He wagged his head; she nodded hers. She allowed a silence to develop in the hope that he'd go away. He said eventually:

'D'you ever watch that thing they have, *Dynasty* is it called?'

'I watched it the odd time.'

'Will you tell me this, Norah: where do they get the stories?'

'I suppose they invent them.'

'Isn't America the shocking place though?'

'I have a daughter there.'

'Ah, sure, of course you have.'

At the bar Butler-Regan looked as though he might sing. Very occasionally he did, striking the bar rhythmically with his fist, trying to make people join in. The club secretary, Dr Walsh, had had to speak to him, explaining that it wasn't usual to sing in a golf club, even adding that he didn't think it quite the thing for a solicitor to sing anywhere. But Butler-Regan had done so again, and had again to be warned. It was said that his wife, who like the late Mrs Corkin played neither bridge nor golf, had a terrible time with him.

'Does your girl ever remark on the *Dynasty* thing to you?' Corkin was inquiring. 'I mean, if it might be accurate?'

'Siobhan has never mentioned *Dynasty*.'

'Well, isn't that extraordinary?'

Ten minutes later the drinking in the clubhouse broke up and Mrs O'Neill drove back to Arcangelo House. She made scrambled egg and watched a film about drug-running on the television. The police of several nations pursued a foursome of gangsters and finally ran the ringleader to earth in Los Angeles. She dozed off, and when she woke up a priest with a Cork accent was talking about the feast of Corpus Christi. She listened to him until he'd finished and then turned the television off.

In her bedroom she did something she had not done for ten years at least: before she slipped into her night-dress she paused in front of the long looking-glass of her wardrobe and surveyed her naked body. It was most certainly no longer her best feature, she said to herself, remembering it when she was a child, standing up in the bath to be dried. She remembered being naked at last in the bedroom of the International Hotel in Bray, and the awkward voluptuousness that had followed. The bearing of four children, her fondness for sweet things, the insidious nips of gin in the clubhouse – in combination they had taken a toll, making clothes as necessary as all that meticulous care with make-up and hair. The first time she'd been pregnant, with Cathal, she had looked at herself in this same looking-glass, assuring herself that the enormous swelling would simply go away, as indeed it had. But nothing would go away now. Flesh hung loosely, marked with pink imprints of straps or elastic. If she slimmed herself to the bone there would be scrawny, empty skin, loops and pockets, hollows as ugly as the bulges. She drew her night-dress over her head and a pattern of pink roses in tight little bunches hid what she preferred not to see, transforming her again into a handsome woman.

Agnew had sensitive skin, yet could not resist the quality of finely woven tweed. He chose the sober colours, the greys and browns and inconspicuous greens. He bought his Donegal tweed in Kevin and Howlin's in Dublin and had the suits made up by a tailor in Rathmines. Because of his sensitive skin he had the trousers lined.

Agnew had never worn these suits to his office in the toy factory, for they did not seem to him to be sufficiently matter-of-fact for business. He wore them at weekends, when he went to church and on Sunday afternoons when he drove out to Rathfarran and walked around the cliffs, ending up in Lynch's Bar down by the strand, where by arrangement he took his Sunday supper. He wore them also on the weekends when he went to Dublin.

He would miss the cliffs and the strand, he reflected at breakfast one morning, a few weeks after his visit from Mrs O'Neill. He would miss the toy factory too, of course, and the people he had come to know in a passing kind of way, without intimacy or closeness but yet agreeably. In the snug, overcrowded dining-room of the terraced house called St Kevin's he broke a piece of toast in half and poured himself more tea. He had been fortunate in St Kevin's, fortunate because he was the only lodger and because the Misses McShane had never sought to share a meal with him, fortunate that the house was clean and the cooking averagely good. He'd been fortunate that his interest had never flagged in the job at the toy factory. He would take away with him a sample of every single wooden toy that had been manufactured during his time there: the duck with the quivering bill, the kangaroos, the giraffes, the little red steam engines, the donkeys and carts, the bricks, the elephants, the fox-terriers on wheels, and all the others. He was proud of these toys and of his part in their production. They were finer in every possible way – more ingeniously designed, constructed with greater craftsmanship, more fondly finished – than the torrent of shoddiness that had flooded them out of existence.

'I'll miss you too,' he said aloud in the overcrowded dining-room, staring down at the spaniel, Mandy, who was wagging her tail in the hope of receiving a rind of bacon. She would eat rinds only if they were so brittle that they broke between her teeth. This morning, Agnew knew, what he had left would not satisfy her: the bacon had not been overdone. He lit a cigarette, folded the *Irish Times*, which earlier he had been reading, and left the dining-room, pursued by the dog. 'I'm off now, Miss McShane,' he called out in the hall, and one of the sisters called back to him from the kitchen. Mandy, as she always did, followed him through the town to the toy factory, turning back when he reached the forecourt.

A woman called Mrs Whelan, who came to the factory three mornings a week to attend to whatever typing there was and to keep the books up to date, was to finish at the end of the week. She was there this morning, a prim, trim presence in navy-blue, conscientiously tapping out the last of the invoices. The final delivery was due to be dispatched that afternoon, for Cathal O'Neill had already laid down the peremptory instruction that further orders must not be accepted.

'Good morning, Mrs Whelan.'

'Good morning, sir.'

Interrupted for the briefest of moments, she went on typing. She would be extremely useful to someone else, Agnew reflected, if she managed to find a position that suited her. 'I think I'm going to start clearing out the inner office,' he said, passing into it reluctantly, for it was not a task he anticipated with any pleasure. What on earth was he going to do with himself? Fifty-one was far too young simply to retire, even if he could afford to. It was all very well saying he couldn't see himself in the fuel business, either coal or turf, but what alternative was there going to be? In the failing toy factory he had had a position, he had been of some small importance, and he had often wondered if he himself – and the predicament he must find himself in when the factory closed – hadn't been an element in his late employer's sentiment. Had Mr O'Neill lived, the toy factory might have struggled on until a convenient moment was reached, when its manager might gracefully retire. Still, a father's sentiment rarely passed to a son, nor could it be expected to.

He took his jacket off and hung it up. As he did so the telephone rang and the widow of his late and sentimental employer invited him to what she described as a very small party on Friday evening. It would be in his honour, he said to himself after he had politely accepted. It was the kind of thing people did; there might even be a presentation, in the conventional way, of cutlery or Waterford glass or a clock.

'Now, this is bloody ridiculous!' Cathal glared at his mother, squinting in his extreme rage.

She remembered that squint in his pram. She remembered how his face would turn scarlet before exploding like a volcano, how he would beat his fists against her when she tried to lift him up. His father had had a bad temper also, though over the years she had learnt to ignore it.

'It isn't ridiculous at all, Cathal.'

'You are fifty-nine years of age.'

'I'm only too well aware of that.'

'Agnew's our employee, for God's sake!' He said something else and then broke off, his shout becoming an incomprehensible stutter. He began again, calming down and collecting himself. 'My God, when I think of Agnew!'

'I invited Basil Agnew –'

'Basil? *Basil?*'

'You knew his name was Basil. B.J. Agnew. It's on all the letters.'

'In no way did I know the man's name was Basil. I didn't know what his bloody name was.'

'Don't be violent, Cathal.'

'Aw, for God's sake now!' He turned away from her. He crossed the Italianate drawing-room and stood with his back to her, morosely looking out of the window.

'I invited Basil Agnew to a little evening I had and he stayed on afterwards to help me clear up a bit. The Flanagans were there, and the Fitzfynnes and a few others. It was all quite above board, Cathal. Father Doherty was there, quite happy with the arrangement.'

'You were seen out at Rathfarran with Agnew. You were in Lynch's with him.'

'That was later on, the following Sunday week it was. And of course we were in Lynch's. We had two glasses of whiskey each in Lynch's, and then we had our supper there.'

'Will you for God's sake examine what you're doing? You hardly know Agnew.'

'I've known him for seventeen years.'

Cathal mentioned his father, who, God rest him, would be disgusted if he knew, and probably he did know. He could not understand, Cathal repeated for the third time in this tempestuous conversation, how any sane woman could behave like this.

'Well, I have behaved like this, Cathal. I have been asked a question by Basil Agnew and I have answered in the affirmative. I wanted to tell you before I spoke a word to Father Doherty.'

'Agnew's a Protestant.'

'We'll be married by Father Doherty. Basil isn't the least particular about matters like that.'

'I bet he isn't. The bloody man –'

'I must ask you, Cathal, not to keep referring to Basil Agnew as a bloody man. I do not refer to Thelma as a bloody woman. When you informed me in this very room that you intended to marry her I held my peace.'

'The man's after your money and that's all there's to it.'

'You're being unpleasant, Cathal.'

He almost spat. As a child, he had had a most disagreeable habit of spitting. His eyes savaged her as he continued violently to upbraid her and to insult the man she had agreed to marry. He left eventually, barging his way out of the drawing-room, shouting back at her from the hall before he barged his way out of the house.

That evening her two married daughters, Eileen in Dublin and Rose in Trim, telephoned her. They were more diplomatic than Cathal, as they had always been. They beseeched her not to be hasty; both offered to come and talk it over with her. She had written to them, she said; she was sorry Cathal had taken it upon himself to get in touch also, since she had particularly asked him not to. 'It's all in my letter,' she assured her daughters in turn. 'Everything about how I feel and how I've thought it carefully over.' The two men they'd married themselves were, after all, no great shakes. If you were honest you had to say that, one of them little better than a commercial traveller, the other reputed to be the worst veterinary surgeon in Trim. Yet she hadn't made much of a fuss when Eileen first brought her mousy little Liam to Arcangelo House, nor over Rose's Eddie, a younger version of Dessie Fitzfynne, with the same stories about Kerrymen and the same dull bonhomie. 'It'll work out grand,' she said to her daughters in turn. 'Was I ever a fool in anything I did?'

The following morning Thelma came round and in her crude way said how flabbergasted she was. She sat there with her vacant expression and repeated three times that you could have knocked her down with a feather when Cathal had walked in the door and informed her that his mother was intending to marry Agnew. 'I couldn't close my mouth,' Thelma said. 'I was stirring custard in the kitchen and declare to God didn't the damn stuff burn on me. "She's after getting engaged to Agnew," he said, and if you'd given me a thousand pounds I couldn't go on with the stirring.'

Thelma's rigmarole continued, how Cathal had stormed about the kitchen, how he'd shouted at the children and knocked a pot of black-currant jam on to the floor with his elbow, how she'd had to sit down to recover herself. Then she lowered her voice as if there were other people in her mother-in-law's drawing-room. 'Isn't there a lot of talk, though, about what Agnew gets up to when he goes off to Dublin for the two days? Is it women he goes after?' While she spoke, Thelma nodded vehemently, answering her own question. She'd heard it for certain, she continued in the same subdued voice, that Agnew had women of a certain description up in Dublin.

'That's tittle-tattle, Thelma.'

'Ah sure, I'd say it was, all right. Still and all, Mrs O'Neill.'

'What Mr Agnew does with his own time is hardly the business of anyone except himself.'

'Ah sure, of course 'tisn't. It's only Cathal and myself was wondering.'

The moon that was Thelma's face, its saucer eyes and jammy red mouth, the nose that resembled putty, was suddenly closer than Mrs O'Neill found agreeable. It was a way that Thelma had when she was endeavouring to be sincere.

'I had an uncle married late. Sure, the poor man ended demented.'

You are the stupidest creature God ever put breath into, Mrs O'Neill reflected, drawing herself back from her daughter-in-law's advancing features. She did not comment on Thelma's uncle any more than she had commented on the burning of the custard or the loss of the pot of black-currant jam.

'You know what I mean, Mrs O'Neill?' The subdued tones became a whisper. 'A horse-trainer's widow in Portarlington that went after the poor old devil's few pence.'

'Well, I'm most certainly not after Mr Agnew's few pence.'

'Ah no, I'm not saying that at all. I'd never say a thing like that, Mrs O'Neill, what you'd be after or what he'd be after. Sure, where'd I find the right to make statements the like of that?'

Thelma eventually went away. She would have been sent by Cathal, who would also have written to Siobhan. But Siobhan had always possessed a mind of her own and in due course a letter arrived from Philadelphia. *I'm delighted altogether at the news. I kind of hoped you'd do something like this.*

It had never, in the past, occurred to Agnew to get married. Nor would he have suggested it to his late employer's wife if he hadn't become aware that she wished him to. Marriage, she had clearly decided, would be the rescuing of both of them: she from her solitariness in Arcangelo House, he from the awkwardness of being unemployed. She had said she would like him to oversee the demolition of the toy factory and the creation of an apple orchard in its place. This enterprise was her own and had nothing to do with Cathal.

The women she played bridge with still addressed him friendlily when he met them on the street or in a shop. Her golfing companions – especially Flanagan and Fitzfynne – had even been enthusiastic. Butler-Regan had slapped him on the shoulders in the bar of the Commercial Hotel and said he was glad it hadn't been Corkin she'd gone for. Only Corkin had looked grumpy, not replying to Agnew's greeting when they met in Lawlor's one morning, both of them buying cigarettes. Dolores Fitzfynne telephoned him at the toy factory and said she was delighted. It was a good idea to plant an apple orchard on the site of the factory – Cox's and Beauty of Bath, Russets and Bramleys and Worcesters. In the fullness of time the orchard would become her own particular interest, as the toys had been her husband's and the turf-bogs were her son's. It was a pity the family were almost all opposed to the match, but naturally such a reaction was to be expected.

She was aware of eyes upon them when they danced together in the clubhouse bedecked with Christmas decorations. What did these people really think? Did all of them share, while appearing not to, the family's disapproval? Did fat Butler-Regan and fat Flanagan think she was ridiculous, at fifty-nine years of age, to be allowing a man to marry her for her money? Did Dolores Fitzfynne think so? Mrs Whelan, who had been his secretary for so long at the toy factory, always attended the Golf Club Annual Dance with her husband; the Misses McShane, his landladies for the same period of time in the terraced house called St Kevin's, came to help with the catering. Did these three women consider her beneath contempt because she'd trapped a slightly younger, attractive man as a companion for her advancing years?

'I've always liked the way you dance the quickstep,' she whispered.

'Always?'

'Yes, always.'

The confession felt disgraceful. Cathal and Thelma, dancing only yards away, would talk all night about it if they knew. With Corkin, she wouldn't have had to be unfaithful in that way.

'You're not entirely devoid of rhythm yourself.'

'I've always loved dancing, actually.'

Corkin would have asked for more, and for less. Some hint of man's pride would have caused him scrupulously to avoid touching a penny of her money, nor would he have wanted to go planting apple trees under her direction. But Corkin would have entered her bedroom and staked his claim there, and she could not have borne that.

'We'll be married this time next week,' he said. 'Do you realize that?'

'Unless you decide to take to the hills.'

'No, I'll not do that, Norah.'

The Artie Furlong Band, new to the clubhouse this year and already reckoned to be a success, played an old tune she loved, 'Smoke Gets in Your Eyes'. His step changed easily, he scarcely touched her as he guided her through the other dancers. Sweetman was appalling to dance with because of his perspiration troubles, Dessie Fitzfynne's knees were always driving themselves into you, Butler-Regan held you far too tight. She'd go on playing bridge and golf after they were married, no reason not to. He'd said he intended to continue exercising the Misses McShane's spaniel.

'You're sure about this?' he whispered, bending his long face closer to hers, smiling a little. 'You're absolutely sure, Norah?'

She remembered thinking how she couldn't imagine him ever calling her Norah, and how strange his own Christian name had felt when first she'd used it. She would never know him, she was aware of that; nor could he ever fully know her. There would never be the passion of love between them; all that must be done without.

'I'm sure all right.'

The music ceased. They went to get a drink and were joined immediately by the Fitzfynnes and Rita Flanagan. Thelma came up and said one of the children had spots all over his stomach. Cathal kept his distance.

'We're drinking to the happy couple,' Dessie Fitzfynne shouted, raising his glass. Thelma scuttled away, as if frightened to be seen anywhere near such a toast.

'Cheers to the both of you,' Rita Flanagan shrilled, and in another part of the decorated clubhouse Butler-Regan began to sing.

She smiled at the glasses that were raised towards them. 'That's very kind of you,' he said quietly. 'We're touched.'

She would have liked to add something, to have sorted out falsity from the truth. He was indeed marrying her for her money. But he, in return, was giving her a role that money could not purchase. Within a week the family would no longer possess her. Cathal's far-apart eyes would no longer dismiss her as a remnant of the dead.

'We're going to have an orchard, you know, where the toy factory is now.'

They looked a bit surprised, at first not quite grasping her meaning and then wondering why she should mention an orchard just then.

'Our wedding present to one another,' he explained. 'Norah's trees and I shall tend them.'

The band struck up again, drowning the raucous singing of Butler-Regan. Cathal at last approached his mother and asked her to dance, as every year he did on this Christmas occasion. But he did not at last say that he hoped it would work out all right, Agnew and herself in Arcangelo House. She had paid some price, Cathal believed, apart from the financial one. But Cathal, really, was not right and for him, too, she would have liked to sort out falsity from the truth.

'Well, that is that,' he said, turning off the television on a Sunday night, after he had returned from Dublin. He lurched a little as he moved towards her, holding out his packet of cigarettes. He had said, before their marriage, that he often became intoxicated in the course of these weekends. He met his friends and they went from place to place, all of them men who enjoyed the company of men. Sometimes, left alone, or unlucky in the new companions he had met, he wandered the quaysides of the city, thinking about the sailors on the ships. On the strand at Rathfarran his face had been averted when he told her this, and when he finished she had not spoken. Dessie Fitzfynne and Sweetman liked men's company also, she had thought, and so had her husband in his lifetime. But that, of course, was not the same.

'I don't think I'll go back there.' He swayed, like Flanagan did in drink. 'God knows, I don't want to.'

He always said that. He always offered her a cigarette after turning off the Sunday television. A moment later he made the renunciatory statement.

'It doesn't matter.' She tried to smile, imagining him in the public houses he had told her about, his dignified presence mocked by a man who was once particularly his friend, a waiter who no longer liked him.

'I dread for your sake that someone will find out one of these days. I hadn't thought of that when we married.'

'I knew what I was doing. You told me the truth, and you're honourable for that.'

When he'd told her she had not confessed a truth as well: that clothes and make-up disguised a loss she found it hard to bear. She was haunted by herself, by the beauty that had been there in a hotel in Bray. Lingering in the clubhouse on these Sunday nights, she drank more gin and French than usual, knowing he would be tipsy, too, when he returned. Once they'd fallen asleep in their chairs, and she'd woken up at twenty past three and crept away to bed. He'd seemed like a child, one arm hanging down, fingers resting on the carpet. On the strand at Rathfarran he'd told her he never wanted to go to sleep on these Sunday nights because he hated waking up so. In his bedroom at St Kevin's, the door locked against indiscreet entrance by one or other of the Misses McShane, he had sat with the whiskey bottle he'd bought for the purpose in Dublin. She'd listened while he'd told her that; concerning herself, there'd been no need to say what she might have said because, being the man he was, he guessed.

They passed together through the hall of Arcangelo House and mounted the stairs to their separate bedrooms. They paused before they parted, offering in their tipsiness a vague, unstated reassurance. Tomorrow none of this would be mentioned; their common ground would not be traversed on a mundane Monday morning. For a moment on the landing outside their bedrooms they spoke of the orchard that would replace the toy factory, and the trees they would watch growing up.

Two More Gallants

You will not, I believe, find either Lenehan or Corley still parading the streets of Dublin, but often in the early evening a man called Heffernan may be found raising a glass of Paddy in Toner's public house; and FitzPatrick, on his bicycle, every working day makes the journey across the city, from Ranelagh to the offices of McGibbon, Tait & FitzPatrick, solicitors and commissioners for oaths. It is on his doctor's advice that he employs this mode of transport. It is against the advice of *his* that Heffernan continues to indulge himself in Toner's. The two men no longer know one another. They do not meet and, in order to avoid a confrontation, each has been known to cross a street.

Thirty or so years ago, when I first knew Heffernan and FitzPatrick, the relationship was different. The pair were closely attached, Heffernan the mentor, FitzPatrick ready with a laugh. All three of us were students, but Heffernan, a Kilkenny man, was different in the sense that he had been a student for as long as anyone could remember. The College porters said they recalled his presence over fifteen years and, though given to exaggeration, they may well have been accurate in that: certainly Heffernan was well over thirty, a small ferrety man, swift to take offence.

FitzPatrick was bigger and more amiable. An easy smile perpetually creased the bland ham of his face, causing people to believe, quite incorrectly, that he was stupid. His mouse-coloured hair was kept short enough not to require a parting, his eyes reflected so profound a degree of laziness that people occasionally professed surprise to find them open. Heffernan favoured pin-striped suits, FitzPatrick a commodious blue blazer. They drank in Kehoe's in Anne Street.

'He is one of those chancers,' Heffernan said, 'we could do without.'

'Oh, a right old bollocks,' agreed FitzPatrick.

' "Well, Mr Heffernan," ' he says, ' "I see you are still with us." '

'As though you might be dead.'

'If he had his way.'

In the snug of Kehoe's they spoke of Heffernan's *bête noire*, the aged Professor Flacks, a man from the North of Ireland.

' "I see you are still with us," ' Heffernan repeated. 'Did you ever hear the beat of that?'

'Sure, Flacks is senile.'

'The mots in the lecture giggle when he says it.'

'Oh, an ignorant bloody crowd.'

Heffernan became meditative. Slowly he lit a Sweet Afton. He was supported in his continuing studentship by the legacy left to him for that purpose by an uncle in Kilkenny, funds which would cease when he was a student no longer. He kept that tragedy at bay by regularly failing the Littlego examination, a test of proficiency in general studies to which all students were obliged to submit themselves.

'A fellow came up to me this morning,' he said now, 'a right eejit from Monasterevin. Was I looking for grinds in Little-go Logic? Five shillings an hour.'

FitzPatrick laughed. He lifted his glass of stout and drank from it, imposing on his upper lip a moustache of foam which was permitted to remain there.

'A minion of Flacks',' Heffernan continued. 'A Flacks boy and no mistake, I said to myself.'

'You can tell them a mile off.'

' "I know your father," I said to him. "Doesn't he deliver milk?" Well, he went the colour of a sunset. "Avoid conversation with Flacks," I told him. "He drove a wife and two sisters insane." '

'Did your man say anything?'

'Nothing, only "Cripes".'

'Oh, Flacks is definitely peculiar,' FitzPatrick agreed.

In point of fact, at that time FitzPatrick had never met Professor Flacks. It was his laziness that caused him to converse in a manner which suggested he had, and it was his laziness also which prevented him from noticing the intensity of Heffernan's grievance. Heffernan hated Professor Flacks with a fervour, but in his vague and unquestioning way FitzPatrick assumed that the old professor was no more than a passing thorn in his friend's flesh, a nuisance that could be exorcised by means of complaint and abuse. Heffernan's pride did not at that time appear to play a part; and FitzPatrick, who knew his friend as well as anyone did, would not have designated him as a possessor of that quality to an unusual degree. The opposite was rather implied by the nature of his upkeep and his efforts not to succeed in the Littlego examination. But pride, since its presence might indeed be questioned by these facts, came to its own support: when the story is told in Dublin today it is never forgotten that it has roots in Professor Flacks's causing girls to giggle because he repeatedly made a joke at Heffernan's expense.

Employed by the University to instruct in certain aspects of literature,

Professor Flacks concentrated his attention on the writings of James Joyce. Shakespeare, Tennyson, Shelley, Coleridge, Wilde, Swift, Dickens, Eliot, Trollope, and many another familiar name were all bundled away in favour of a Joycean scholarship that thirty or so years ago was second to none in Irish university life. Professor Flacks could tell you whom Joyce had described as a terrified YMCA man, and the date of the day on which he had written that his soul was full of decayed ambitions. He spoke knowledgeably of the stale smell of incense, like foul flowerwater; and of flushed eaves and stubble geese.

'Inane bloody show-off,' Heffernan said nastily in Kehoe's.

'You'll see him out, Heff.'

'A bogs like that would last for ever.'

Twelve months later, after he and Heffernan had parted company, FitzPatrick repeated all that to me. I didn't know either of them well, but was curious because a notable friendship had so abruptly come to an end. FitzPatrick, on his own, was inclined to talk to anyone.

We sat in College Park, watching the cricket while he endeavoured to remember the order of subsequent events. It was Heffernan who'd had the idea, as naturally it would be, since FitzPatrick still knew Professor Flacks only by repute and had not suffered the sarcasm which Heffernan found so offensive. But FitzPatrick played a vital part in the events which followed, because the elderly woman who played the main part of all was a general maid in FitzPatrick's digs.

'Has that one her slates on?' Heffernan inquired one night as they passed her by in the hall.

'Ah, she's only a bit quiet.'

'She has a docile expression all right.'

'She wouldn't damage a fly.'

Soon after that Heffernan took to calling in at FitzPatrick's digs in Donnybrook more often than he had in the past. Sometimes he was there when FitzPatrick arrived back in the evening, sitting in the kitchen while the elderly maid pricked sausages or cut up bread for the meal that would shortly be served. Mrs Maginn, the landlady, liked to lie down for a while at that time of day, so Heffernan and the maid had the kitchen to themselves. But finding him present on several occasions when she came downstairs, Mrs Maginn in passing mentioned the fact to her lodger. FitzPatrick, who didn't himself understand what Heffernan's interest in the general maid was, replied that his friend liked to await his return in the kitchen because it was warm. Being an easy-going woman, Mrs Maginn was appeased.

'There's no doubt in my mind at all,' Heffernan stated in Kehoe's after a few weeks of this behaviour. 'If old Flacks could hear it he'd have a tortoise's pup.'

FitzPatrick wagged his head, knowing that an explanation was in the air. Heffernan said: 'She's an interesting old lassie.'

He then told FitzPatrick a story which FitzPatrick had never heard before. It concerned a man called Corley who had persuaded a maid in a house in Baggot Street to do a small service for him. It concerned, as well, Corley's friend, Lenehan, who was something of a wit. At first FitzPatrick was confused by the story, imagining it to be about a couple of fellow-students whom he couldn't place.

'The pen of Jimmy Joyce,' Heffernan explained. 'That yarn is Flacks's favourite of the lot.'

'Well, I'd say there wasn't much to it. Sure, a skivvy never would.'

'She was gone on Corley.'

'But would she steal for him?'

'You're no romantic, Fitz.'

FitzPatrick laughed, agreeable to accepting this opinion. Then, to his astonishment, Heffernan said: 'It's the same skivvy Mrs Maginn has above in your digs.'

FitzPatrick shook his head. He told Heffernan to go on with himself, but Heffernan insisted.

'She told me the full story herself one night I was waiting for you – maybe the first night I ever addressed a word to her. "Come into the kitchen outa the cold, Mr Heffernan," she says. D'you remember the occasion it was? Late after tea, and you didn't turn up at all. She fried me an egg.'

'But, holy Christ, man –'

'It was the same night you did well with the nurse from Dundrum.'

FitzPatrick guffawed. A great girl, he said. He repeated a few details, but Heffernan didn't seem interested.

'I was told the whole works in the kitchen, like Jimmy Joyce had it out of her when she was still in her teens. A little gold sovereign was what she fecked for your man.'

'But the poor old creature is as honest as the day's long.'

'Oh, she took it all right and she still thinks Corley was top of the bill.'

'But Corley never existed –'

'Of course he did. Wasn't he for ever entertaining that fine little tart with the witticisms of Master Lenehan?'

The next thing that happened, according to FitzPatrick, was that a bizarre meeting took place. Heffernan approached Professor Flacks with the information that the model for the ill-used girl in Joyce's story 'Two

'Gallants' had come to light in a house in Donnybrook. The Professor displayed considerable excitement, and on a night when Mrs Maginn was safely at the pictures he was met by Heffernan at the bus stop and led to the kitchen.

He was a frail man in a tweed suit, not at all as FitzPatrick had imagined him. Mrs Maginn's servant, a woman of about the same age, was slightly deaf and moved slowly owing to rheumatism. Heffernan had bought half a pound of fig-roll biscuits which he arranged on a plate. The old woman poured tea.

Professor Flacks plied her with questions. He asked them gently, with courtesy and diplomacy, without any hint of the tetchiness described so often by Heffernan. It was a polite occasion in the kitchen, Heffernan handing round the fig-rolls, the maid appearing to delight in recalling a romance in her past.

'And later you told Mr Joyce about this?' prompted Professor Flacks.

'He used come to the house when I worked in North Frederick Street, sir. A dentist by the name of O'Riordan.'

'Mr Joyce came to get his teeth done?'

'He did, sir.'

'And you'd talk to him in the waiting-room, is that it?'

'I'd be lonesome, sir. I'd open the hall door when the bell rang and then there'd be a wait for maybe an hour before it'd ring again, sir. I recollect Mr Joyce well, sir.'

'He was interested in your — ah — association with the fellow you mentioned, was he?'

'It was only just after happening, sir. I was turned out of the place in Baggot Street on account of the bit of trouble. I was upset at the time I knew Mr Joyce, sir.'

'That's most understandable.'

'I'd often tell a patient what had happened to me.'

'But you've no hard feelings today? You were badly used by the fellow, yet —'

'Ah, it's long ago now, sir.'

Heffernan and FitzPatrick saw the Professor on to a bus and, according to FitzPatrick, he was quivering with pleasure. He clambered into a seat, delightedly talking to himself, not noticing when they waved from the pavement. They entered a convenient public house and ordered pints of stout.

'Did you put her up to it?' FitzPatrick inquired.

'The thing about that one, she'd do anything for a scrap of the ready. Didn't you ever notice that about her? She's a right old miser.'

It was that that Heffernan had recognized when first he'd paid a visit to Mrs Maginn's kitchen: the old maid was possessed of a meanness that had become obsessional with her. She spent no money whatsoever, and was clearly keen to add to what she had greedily accumulated. He had paid her a pound to repeat the story he had instructed her in.

'Didn't she say it well? Oh, top of the bill, I'd say she was.'

'You'd be sorry for old Flacks.'

'Oh, the devil take bloody Mr Flacks.'

Some months went by. Heffernan no longer visited the kitchen in Donnybrook, and he spoke hardly at all of Professor Flacks. In his lazy way FitzPatrick assumed that the falsehoods which had been perpetrated were the be-all and end-all of the affair, that Heffernan's pride – now clearly revealed to him – had somehow been satisfied. But then, one summer's afternoon while the two idled in Stephen's Green in the hope of picking up girls, Heffernan said: 'There's a thing on we might go to next Friday.'

'What's that?'

'Mr Flacks performing. The Society of the Friends of James Joyce.'

It was a public lecture, one of several that were to be delivered during a week devoted by the Society to the life and work of the author who was its *raison d'être*. The Society's members came from far afield: from the United States, Germany, Finland, Italy, Australia, France, England and Turkey. Learned academics mingled with less learned enthusiasts. Mr James Duffy's Chapelizod was visited, and Mr Power's Dublin Castle. Capel Street and Ely Place were investigated, visits were made to the renowned Martello Tower, to Howth and to Pim's. Betty Bellezza was mentioned, and Val from Skibbereen. The talk was all Joyce talk. For a lively week Joyce reigned in Dublin.

On the appointed evening FitzPatrick accompanied his friend to Professor Flacks's lecture, his premonitions suggesting that the occasion was certain to be tedious. He had no idea what Heffernan was up to, and wasn't prepared to devote energy to speculating. With a bit of luck, he hoped, he'd be able to have a sleep.

Before the main event a woman from the University of Washington spoke briefly about Joyce's use of misprints; a bearded German read a version of 'The Holy Office' that had only recently been discovered. Then the tweeded figure of Professor Flacks rose. He sipped at a tumbler of water, and spoke for almost an hour about the model for the servant girl in the story, 'Two Gallants'. His discovery of that same elderly servant, now employed in a house in Donnybrook, engendered in his audience a whisper of excitement that remained alive while he spoke, and exploded into applause when he finished. A light flush enlivened the paleness of his face as he sat down. It was, as Heffernan remarked to his dozy companion, the old man's finest hour.

It was then that FitzPatrick first became uneasy. The packed lecture-hall had accepted as fact all that had been stated, yet none of it was true. Notes had been taken, questions were now being asked. A voice just behind the two students exclaimed that this remarkable discovery was worth coming two thousand miles to hear about. Mental pictures of James Joyce in a dentist's waiting-room flashed about the hall. North Frederick Street would be visited tomorrow, if not tonight.

'I'd only like to ask,' Heffernan shouted above the hubbub, 'if I may, a simple little question.' He was on his feet. He had caught the attention of Professor Flacks, who was smiling benignly at him. 'I'd only like to inquire,' Heffernan continued, 'if that whole thing couldn't be a lot of baloney.'

'Baloney?' a foreign voice repeated.

'Baloney?' said Professor Flacks.

The buzz of interest hadn't died down. Nobody was much interested in the questions that were being asked except the people who were asking them. A woman near to FitzPatrick said it was extraordinarily moving that the ill-used servant girl, who had been so tellingly presented as an off-stage character by Joyce, should bear no grudge all these years later.

'What I mean, Professor Flacks,' said Heffernan, 'is I don't think James Joyce ever attended a dentist in North Frederick Street. What I'm suggesting to you, sir, is that the source of your information was only looking for a bit of limelight.'

FitzPatrick later described to me the expression that entered Professor Flacks's eyes. 'A lost kind of look,' he said, 'as though someone had poked the living daylights out of him.' The old man stared at Heffernan, frowning, not comprehending at first. His relationship with this student had been quite different since the night of the visit to Mrs Maginn's kitchen: it had been distinguished by a new friendliness, and what had seemed like mutual respect.

'Professor Flacks and myself,' continued Heffernan, 'heard the old lady together. Only I formed the impression that she was making the entire matter up. I thought, sir, you'd formed that opinion also.'

'Oh, but surely now, Mr Heffernan, the woman wouldn't do that.'

'There was never a dentist by the name of O'Riordan that practised in North Frederick Street, sir. That's a fact that can easily be checked.'

Heffernan sat down. An uneasy silence gripped the lecture-hall. Eyes turned upon Professor Flacks. Weakly, with a hoarseness in his voice, he said: 'But why, Mr Heffernan, would she have made all that up? A woman of that class would hardly have read the story, she'd hardly have known –'

'It's an unfortunate thing, sir,' interrupted Heffernan, standing up again, 'but that old one would do anything for a single pound note. She's of a miserly nature. I think what has happened,' he went on, his tone changing as he addressed the assembly, 'is that a student the Professor failed in an examination took a chance to get his own back. Our friend Jas Joyce,' he added, 'would definitely have relished that.'

In misery Professor Flacks lifted the tumbler of water to his lips, his eyes cast down. You could sense him thinking, FitzPatrick reported, that he was a fool and he had been shown to be a fool. You could sense him thinking that he suddenly appeared to be unreliable, asinine and ridiculous. In front of the people who mattered to him most of all he had been exposed as a fraud he did not feel himself to be. Never again could he hold his head up among the Friends of James Joyce. Within twenty-four hours his students would know what had occurred.

An embarrassed shuffling broke out in the lecture-hall. People murmured and began to make their way into the aisles. FitzPatrick recalled the occasion in Mrs Maginn's kitchen, the two elderly puppets on the end of Heffernan's string, the fig-rolls and the tea. He recalled the maid's voice retailing the story that he, because he knew Heffernan so well, had doubted with each word that was uttered. He felt guilty that he hadn't sought the old man out and told him it wasn't true. He glanced through the throng in the lecture-hall at the lone figure in porridgy tweeds, and unhappily reflected that suicide had been known to follow such wretched disgrace. Outside the lecture-hall he told Heffernan to go to hell when a drink in Anne Street was suggested – a remark for which Heffernan never forgave him.

'I mean,' FitzPatrick said as we sat in College Park a long time later, 'how could anyone be as petty? When all the poor old fellow ever said to him was "I see you are still with us?"'

I made some kind of reply. Professor Flacks had died a natural death a year after the delivery of his lecture on 'Two Gallants'. Earlier in his life he had not, as Heffernan had claimed, driven a wife and two sisters mad: he'd been an only child, the obituary said in the *Irish Times*, and a bachelor. It was an awkward kind of obituary, for the gaffe he'd made had become quite famous and was still fresh in Dubliners' minds.

We went on talking about him, FitzPatrick and I, as we watched the cricket in College Park. We spoke of his playful sarcasm and how so vehemently it had affected Heffernan's pride. We marvelled over the love that had caused a girl in a story to steal, and over the miserliness that had persuaded an old woman to be party to a trick. FitzPatrick touched upon his own inordinate laziness, finding a place for that also in our cobweb of human frailty.

The Smoke Trees of San Pietro

My father was a great horseman. My mother was the most beautiful woman I have ever seen. I was taken to watch my father jumping as a member of the military team in Linvik when I was five years old. The team did not win that afternoon but my father's performance was faultless and he himself received a personal award. I remember the applause and his saluting, and my mother's fingers tightening on my arm. 'Oh, how deserved that is!' she whispered, and when my father joined us later you could see that he was proud. He smelt of horses and of leather, as he always did when he'd been jumping: to this day, I can evoke that smell at will.

That is the most vivid memory of that early time in my childhood. We drove away from the stadium and then there was my first dinner in a restaurant, my mother and father on either side of me, red roses in a vase, a candle burning in a wooden candlestick that was painted blue and green. 'One day,' my father predicted, anticipating that in time I, too, would be a member of the military team. Already I was promising: so he insisted when he watched me cantering with my mother along the grassy path beside the birch woods. In the restaurant they touched their wine-glasses and my father requested the waiter to pour me just a little wine so that on this particular occasion I might have my first taste of it. Johan my father called the waiter, while I wondered which feature it was that in particular made my mother's beauty so remarkable. One moment it seemed to be the candlelight gleaming on her pale hair, the next the blue of her eyes, and then her lips and the tiny wrinkle on her forehead, and then the graceful way she held her head. My father's hand reached across the tablecloth for one of hers, and there that memory ceases.

There is another one. In his surgery Dr Edlund probed my eyes with the beam of a torch that was as slim as a pencil. The disc of his stethoscope lingered on my back and chest, my reflexes were tested, my throat examined, my blood gathered in a capsule, the cavities of my body sounded. And afterwards, when weeks had passed, it was declared that I was not strong. Tiredness in future was to be avoided; I must canter more gently; becoming hot was not good. 'He will be different from what we imagined,' my father said. 'That is all.' I did not, then, sense the disappointment in his voice.

It was because of my delicate constitution that my mother first took me to San Pietro al Mare, initiating a summer regime that was to continue throughout my childhood. We went by train and because of my delicate constitution more time was devoted to the journey than might otherwise have been considered necessary. A night was spent in Hamburg, at the Hotel Kronberg, then by day and night we went slowly on, the air noticeably warmer each time we stopped at a station. A final night was spent at Milan, at the Hotel Belvedere. We arrived at San Pietro al Mare in the early afternoon.

I think, that first evening, my mother was a little nervous. She addressed the hotel staff in English and was apprehensive lest she was not correctly understood. In the restaurant, at dinner, she spoke very slowly to the waiter and I did not entirely follow what was said because I did not yet understand much English. But the waiter, who was extremely rapid in all he did – flicking open our napkins and expertly covering our knees with them, running his finger down the menu to make a suggestion, noting my mother's order on his pad – did not once request her to repeat a word. When he had gone my mother asked me if I felt tired, but I was not in the least. From the moment the train had begun to slow down for San Pietro I'd felt exhilarated. I was supposed not to carry heavy luggage but I had done so none the less, assisting the porter at the station to pack our suitcases into the taxi while my mother was at the *Cambio*. We had driven by palm trees – the first time I had ever seen such trees – and beyond them the sea was a shimmer of blue, just like the sky. Then the taxi turned abruptly, leaving behind the strolling couples on the promenade – the men in white suits, women in beach dresses – and the coloured umbrellas that offered each café table a pool of shade. For a very short time, no more than half a minute perhaps, the taxi climbed a hill which became quite steep and then drew up at the Villa Parco. The palm trees and the promenade were far below, the limpid sea appeared to stretch for ever.

At dinner I said I had never been in such an exotic place. The diningroom where we sat was more elegant and gracious, and a great deal larger, than the restaurant my father had taken us to on the evening of his triumph with the military team. I had never before seen so many people dining at the same time, many of them in evening dress. Spirit stoves burned at each table. Glass doors which stretched from the ceiling to the floor were thrown wide open to a terrace with a decorated balustrade – coloured medallions set among its brief, grey pillars. Beyond that the garden of the Villa Parco was spread with flowers that were quite unfamiliar to me: burgeoning shrubs of oleander and bougainvillaea, and trees called smoke trees, so my mother said. In the hotel I loved the sound of Italian, the mysterious words and phrases the chambermaids and the waiters called out to one another. And I loved the hesitant English of my mother.

The next morning – and every morning after that – my mother and I bathed among the rocks because Dr Edlund had prescribed as advantageous the exercise of unhurried swimming. We took the lift that descended to the bathing place from the hotel garden and afterwards we lay for a short time in the sun, covered with protecting creams, before walking to a café for an *albicocca*. We watched the people sauntering by, remarking on them when they were unusual. In this connection my mother taught me English words: 'haughty', 'wan', 'abstracted', and made me say in English, 'Thank you very much', when the waitress brought our *albicocca*. Then we would return to the hotel garden where, until lunchtime, my mother read to me from *Kidnapped*. I drew the faces of the waiters and the hall-porters, and the façade of the Villa Parco, and the white-painted chairs among the smoke trees. A visitor at the hotel would take one of these iron chairs and carry it to a secluded place and later idly leave it there. Or a tête-à-tête would occur, two of the chairs drawn away in the same manner and then vacated, two empty glasses left on a table. After lunch we rested, then swam again, and again visited the town. 'We must complete our postcard,' my mother would say on the way in to dinner or during the meal itself, and afterwards we would do so before dropping the postcard into the letter-box in the hall. Sometimes I made a drawing on it for my father, a caricature of a face or the outline of a shell we'd found, and from my mother there would always be a reference to my health.

That pattern of our holiday, established during our first summer at San Pietro, remained to influence the subsequent years. We always left Linvik on a Tuesday and stayed, *en route*, at the Hotel Kronberg in Hamburg and the Belvedere in Milan: we always remained for July and August at San Pietro. But on the later occasions there were differences also: my mother was no longer nervous about her English; the staff at the Villa Parco remembered us and welcomed us with increasing warmth; some of the other visitors, familiar from previous years, would greet us when we arrived. This pleased my mother but, for myself, I preferred the novelty of strangers. I liked to watch the laden taxis draw up, the emergence of a man and woman or a family, an elderly person of either sex issuing orders to a younger companion, or the arrival of a solitary figure, always the most interesting from the point of view of speculation. Monsieur Paillez was one of these: he appeared at the Villa Parco for the first time during our third summer, to be assessed by us, and no doubt by other regulars as well, when he strolled down the terrace steps late one afternoon, a thin, tall, dark-haired man in a linen suit. He sat not far from where we were and a moment later a waiter brought him a tray of tea. He smoked while he drank it, taking no interest either in his surroundings or the other people in the garden.

'A town called Linvik,' my mother said, and two ladies in the garden listened while she described it. The ladies were Italian, Signora Binelli and her daughter Claudia. They came from Genoa, they told my mother, which was a city renowned for its trade associations and its cuisine. They spoke of formidable grey stone and formidable palaces, stirring in the false impression that the palaces had been carved out of the side of an immense grey mountain. A passenger lift went up and down all day long between the heights of Genoa and its depths, making its passage through the mountain rock. This information the Italian ladies repeated, remarking that the lift was a great deal larger and more powerful than the one that conveyed us from the garden of the Villa Parco to the bathing place. The palaces of Genoa were built of rectangular blocks and decoratively finished, they said, and the earlier imprecision was adjusted in my mind.

Signora Binelli was very stout. She had smooth white skin, very tight, that seemed to labour under as much strain as her silk dresses did. She knew, my mother murmured once as we walked away from the two Italian ladies, not to wear over-bright clothes. There was always some black in them – in the oak leaves that patterned dark maroon or green, behind swirls of blue or brown. The Italians knew about being fat, my mother said.

Signora Binelli's daughter, Claudia, was not at all like that. She was a film star we were told, and certainly she presented that appearance, many of her fingers displaying jewelled rings, her huge red lips perpetually parted to display a glistening flash of snowy teeth. Her eyes were huge also, shown off to best effect by the dark saucers beneath them. Her clothes were more colourful than Signora Binelli's, but discreetly so. My mother said Claudia had taste.

'*Buon giorno*,' Monsieur Paillez greeted my mother and these ladies one morning in the garden, inclining his head as he went on his way to the lift. We sat at one of the tables, shaded by its vast blue-and-grey umbrella. Claudia's swimming bag hung from the arm of her chair; sunglasses obscured her magnificent eyes. A yellow-backed book, *Itinerario Svizzero*, was on the table beside the ashtray; she smoked a cigarette. Signora Binelli wore a wide-brimmed white hat that protected the skin of her face from the sunshine. The sleeves of her dark dress were buttoned at her wrists; her shoulders and much of her neck were covered.

'Paillez,' Signora Binelli said. 'Is it in France a name to know? Count Paillez?' Bewildered by these questions, my mother only smiled in reply.

Claudia removed the cigarette from between her lips. She did not think Monsieur Paillez was a count, she said. She had not heard that in the hotel.

'We do not have counts in my country,' my mother contributed.

'In Italian we say *conte*,' Signora Binelli explained. 'So also *contessa*.'

'I take my swim,' Claudia said.

My mother said we would take ours soon. In prescribing this form of exercise for me Dr Edlund had reminded my mother that it must not be indulged in while food was in the early stages of digestion: we always permitted two hours at least for my breakfast of tea and brioche to settle itself before I entered the sea. Others, I noticed, were not so meticulous about such matters, but I had become used to being different where health was concerned. A day would come, Dr Edlund had confidently assured me, when I would look back on all this mollycoddling with amusement – and with gratitude also, he hastily added, for I would be the stronger for it. He was not telling the truth, as doctors sometimes cannot. My life was confined to childhood, was what he'd told my mother and my father: it would not reach beyond it. 'We do not speak much of this,' my father had said in a moment when he did not know I could hear. My grandmother had come to Linvik for a few days: it was she he told, and he'd been wise enough to keep the news from her until her departure was quite imminent. Care and attention saw to it that my childhood continued to advance without mishap, my father said, but even so my grandmother hugged me tearfully before she went, pressing me so tightly into her arms that I thought my end would come there and then. That was some time before my mother and I spent our first summer at San Pietro al Mare. I was eleven the summer Monsieur Paillez arrived at the Villa Parco.

'Well, we might go now,' my mother said, and we gathered up our things and descended the slope of the lawn to the lift that took us to the bathing place. Signora Binelli, in search of deeper shade, had moved to a table beneath the trees.

There is very little I have since liked better than swimming among the rocks at San Pietro. The water was of a tranquillity and a clear blueness that made it seem more like a lake than the sea. The rocks were washed white, like smooth, curved bones that blissfully held your body when you lay on them. Two small bathing huts – in blue-and-grey canvas similar to the lawn umbrellas – became a world, my mother's and mine, safely holding our belongings while we swam or floated.

'*T'amuses-tu?*' Monsieur Paillez slipped by me, his overarm strokes hardly rippling the surface. '*Ti diverti?*' And finally translating into the language I had become familiar with: 'You enjoy yourself?'

'Oh yes, of course. Yes, thank you.'

'*C'est bon,*' he called back, over his shoulder. 'We are here to enjoy ourselves, eh?'

An attendant supplied my mother with inflated cushions to lie on, but I myself preferred the bonelike rock. Claudia had made a personal territory of a narrow little cape, spreading on it her towels and various possessions from her bathing bag, then stretching herself prone, and slumbering. The other bathers disposed themselves in similar ways, oiling the skin of their legs and backs. Monsieur Paillez briskly dried himself and went away.

That same day, an hour before dinner, my mother and I were returning from our evening walk around the town when a taxi drew up beside us and Monsieur Paillez said:

'May I offer you a lift?'

When my mother explained that our walk was taken for pleasure the Frenchman paid the driver and fell into step with us. This was a considerable surprise. ('I was quite astounded,' my mother remarked later, as we went over the incident during dinner.)

'I have a little business to conduct in Triora,' Monsieur Paillez said. 'How cool it is now!'

It had been oppressive in Triora, he said. How pleasant it always was to return to San Pietro! 'I greatly admire the smoke trees of San Pietro. Do you not also, madame?'

My mother said she did, and a conversation ensued between them concerning shrubs and horticulture. After that my mother revealed that she and I had been coming to San Pietro al Mare for three years, and Monsieur Paillez confessed that he did not know it as well as we did, this being his first visit. He had decided he might prefer the sea and a good hotel to what Triora had to offer. Triora he knew particularly well.

'We have always been happy at the Villa Parco,' my mother said.

Monsieur Paillez asked questions in a polite manner: if our journey to San Pietro was a long one, how we made it, where we stayed *en route*. My mother answered, equally politely.

'You have travelled from Paris, Monsieur Paillez?'

'Ah, no. Not Paris. I travel from Lille. Have you by chance heard of Lille?'

My mother had and when he questioned her again she mentioned Linvik, repeating the name because Monsieur Paillez had difficulty in understanding it at first. He had not known of our town's existence.

'Well, quite like Lille maybe,' my mother said. 'With manufacturing interests.'

'Though less extensive in size I would suggest?'

'Oh yes, much less extensive.'

'The scent in the air is the evening scent of the smoke trees,' Monsieur Paillez said. (Afterwards — over dinner — my mother confessed to me that she had only been aware of the familiar scent of bougainvillaea, and had never before heard that smoke trees gave off a perfume of any kind.)

'Such a place!' Monsieur Paillez enthused as we passed through the gardens of the hotel. 'Such a place!'

That was the beginning of Monsieur Paillez's friendship with my mother. The following morning, when we were resting after breakfast on the lawn, he did not pass our table by but again dropped into conversation and then inquired if he might sit down. Signora Binelli and Claudia, emerging from the hotel ten minutes later and about to join us, as on other days, did not do so. Signora Binelli settled herself beneath the smoke trees, Claudia went straight to the lift. It was clear to me — though possibly not to my mother and Monsieur Paillez, who by now were exchanging views on Mozart's operas — that the Italian ladies were displeased.

'What fun *Così fan Tutte* is!' Monsieur Paillez later exclaimed in the lift. 'It is the fun of it I love.'

The excursion to the bathing place, and the routine that followed it, did not vary from day to day. Everything was the same: my mother and I swimming for twenty minutes or so, then lying in the sunshine before swimming again, Claudia claiming her private territory, other swimmers occupying their places of the day before, Monsieur Paillez briskly drying himself and going away, as if suddenly in a hurry.

'Business in Triora!' Signora Binelli remarked one evening when he did not return to the hotel at his usual time. It was not yet too cool for me to be permitted to remain on the terrace with my mother while she took her aperitif. Signora Binelli and Claudia occupied the table next to ours, as always they did. Since the evening Monsieur Paillez had halted his taxi it had become his habit to join my mother while she had her aperitif and he his. A general conversation then took place, the Binellis drawn into it because it was natural that they should be, I the only silent one.

'There is not much business, I would have thought, in Triora,' Claudia said, placing her cigarette on the table's ashtray in order to select an olive. 'Not business to attract a Frenchman.'

'Monsieur Paillez visits his wife,' my mother said. 'It is his manner of speech to call it business.'

'Wife!' Signora Binelli repeated sharply. '*Moglie*,' she translated, visibly annoying her daughter.

'I am not uneducated,' Claudia retorted. 'So Monsieur Paillez is married, *signora*?'

'His wife is an Italian lady.' My mother paused. 'She is in the care of nuns.'

'*Le suore*,' Signora Binelli supplied, and Claudia crossly sighed.

'An asylum for the afflicted in Triora,' my mother said. 'She being of Triora originally. I think aristocratic.'

Abruptly Signora Binelli changed the subject. She did so in a manner that suggested the one engaging our attention required thinking about before it might profitably be continued. 'Claudia is to have a part,' she announced. 'We hear today. A fine part, in *Il Marito in Collegio*.'

'It's just a possibility,' Claudia corrected, retaining the crossness in her voice. 'First the film must be financed.'

Monsieur Paillez did not join us that evening, nor did he appear in the dining-room. My mother did not remark on this, but when we left our table we had to pass close to the Binellis'. 'He would not surely have gone without saying goodbye?' Signora Binelli said. With small, beady eyes she peered from the fatness of her face, searching my mother's expression for the explanation she clearly believed her to possess. 'Monsieur Paillez said nothing to me,' my mother replied, but when we had reached my room she quietly murmured, almost to herself: 'His wife has not been well today.'

After breakfast the next morning he did not join us, nor did he arrive at the bathing place. My mother, I thought, became a little disconsolate, as if some flickering of doubt had crept into her mind, as if she'd begun to imagine that she was wrong in the explanation that had occurred to her. But if this doubt had indeed begun to haunt her it was soon dissipated.

'This has been a sorrowful time for me,' Monsieur Paillez said in the town that evening, appearing suddenly beside us as we left the pharmacy where one of my prescriptions had been renewed. 'Since yesterday at midday it has been unhappy.'

'Oh, I'm sorry.'

'From time to time this has to be.'

Monsieur Paillez had a mobile face. His expressions changed rapidly, his dark eyes conveying the mood that possessed him, even before the line of his lips did. His wife was mad, my mother had told me when I'd asked her the evening before, not quite understanding the exchanges with Signora Binelli. It was not easy for Monsieur Paillez, my mother had added.

He walked with us back to the hotel and then sat on the terrace, ordering the aperitifs for my mother and himself and an *albicocca* for me. He had bought a linen hat in Triora, to match his suit. The sun was always fierce in Triora, he said.

'You have returned to us!' Signora Binelli cried as soon as she saw him sitting there.

'Ah, *oui*,' he replied. 'I have returned.'

In English he had difficulty with his h's, but only when they came at the beginning of a word. Sometimes he repeated what he'd just said, in order to set that right. He nodded after he'd agreed he had returned. He listened while Signora Binelli said everyone had missed him.

'Monsieur Paillez is safely here again,' she pointed out to her daughter when she arrived on the terrace. 'He has not gone without farewells.'

'Never,' Monsieur Paillez protested. 'Never would I be guilty.'

That evening – no doubt because of his low spirits – Monsieur Paillez sat with us for dinner. 'I do not intrude?' he said. 'I would not wish to.' My mother assured him he did not, and I do not believe she once observed the staring of Signora Binelli across the crowded dining-room, or Claudia's pretence that she had not noticed.

'Tell me what you like best to draw,' Monsieur Paillez invited me, 'here in San Pietro.'

I could not think what to reply – the rocks where we bathed? the waiters? the promenade when we sat outside a café? Claudia or Signora Binelli? So I said:

'The smoke trees because they are so difficult.' It was true. Try as I would, I could not adequately represent the misty foliage or catch the subtlety of its colours.

'And no drawing of course,' my mother said, 'could ever convey the smoke trees' evening scent.'

She laughed, and Monsieur Paillez laughed: at some time or another, although I could not guess when, his error in imagining that the smoke trees gave off a night-time perfume had become a joke between them. Sitting there not saying anything further, I received the impression that my mother had come to know Monsieur Paillez better than the moments after breakfast on the lawn, and the whiling away of their aperitifs, allowed. I experienced the bewildering feeling that their exchanges – even those in which I had taken part – conveyed more than the words were called upon to communicate.

'My dear, go up,' my mother said. 'I'll follow in a moment.'

I was a little shy, having to leave the dining-room on my own, which I had never done before. People always looked at my mother and myself when we did so together, some of them inclining their heads as a way of bidding us good-night, others actually saying '*Buona notte*' or '*Bon nuit*'. No one bothered with me on my own, except of course Signora Binelli, who remarked: 'So they have packed you off!'

'*Buona notte, signora.*'

Claudia clapped together the tips of her fingers, pleased that I spoke in Italian because she had taught me a few phrases. I had said good evening beautifully, she complimented, calling after me that certainly I had an ear.

'That poor child,' her mother tartly deplored as I pushed at the dining-room's swing-doors. 'What a thing for a child!'

That night I had a nightmare. My father and I were in the rector's house in Linvik. The purpose of our being there was mysterious, but having eaten something with the rector we were taken to a small room which was full of the clocks he collected and repaired as a pastime. Here, while he and my father were in conversation, I stole a clock face, attempting to secrete it in my clothes. Then it seemed that I had stolen more than that: springs and cogs and wheels and hands had been lifted from the blue baize of the table and filled all my pockets. 'I insist on the police,' the rector said, and I was made to sit down on a chair to which my father tied me with a rope. But it was not the police who came, only the old man who delivered firewood to us. 'This is a new treatment,' he said, taking from the blue baize cover on the table the minute hand of a grandfather clock and inserting its point beneath one of my eyelids.

'Now, now,' my mother said. 'It's only a nightmare.'

Her embrace protected me; her lips were cool on my cheek. The garlic in the veal escalope had made it rich, she said, and begged me to tell her the dream. But already it seemed silly to have been frightened by such absurdity, and although I told her about the woodseller's punishment I was ashamed that in my dream I had not been able to recognize this for what it was.

Behind my mother as she bent over me there was an upright rectangle of light. It came from the open doorway of her bedroom: because of my delicate constitution we always had adjoining rooms in the hotels where we stayed. 'Shall we have it like that tonight?' she suggested, but I shook my head, and rejected also her suggestion that my bedside light should be left burning. It was cowardly to capitulate to the threat of fantasies: my father may once have said so, although if he had he would not have said it harshly, for that was not my father's way.

I believe I slept for a while, impossible to gauge how long. I awoke abruptly and recalled at once the rector's clock-room and the fear that had possessed me. Without my mother's consoling presence, I did not wish to return to sleep, cowardice notwithstanding, and was immediately more wide awake than I had been when she'd come to put her arms around me. I lay in the darkness, fearful only of closing my eyes.

I heard the murmur of voices. A crack of light showed beneath the door that led to my mother's room. I stared at it and listened: my mother was speaking to someone, and being spoken to in return. There would be a silence for a while and then the murmur would begin again.

When the door unexpectedly opened I closed my eyes, not wishing my mother to know I was frightened of sleeping. She came softly to my bedside, stood still, and then re-crossed the room. Before she closed the door she said: 'He is sleeping.' Monsieur Paillez's voice replied that that was good.

Their quiet exchanges began again. What did they say to one another? I wondered. Had she told him about my delicate constitution? Had she said that in spite of Dr Edlund's bluff pretence it was accepted by everyone that I would not live beyond my childhood? I imagined her telling him, and Monsieur Paillez commiserating, as my mother would have over his mad Italian wife. I was glad for her that she had found such a friend at San Pietro, for she was so very kind to me, travelling this great distance down through Europe just for my sake, with nothing much to do when she arrived except to read and swim and exchange politenesses. I was aware that it had not been possible for my mother to have other children, for once I had asked her about the brothers and sisters who were not there. I was aware that sacrifices had been made for me, and of the sadness there would one day be for both my mother and my father, when my life came to an end. I should feel no sadness myself, since of course I should not know; I expected nothing more, beyond what I'd been promised.

I slept and dreamed again, but this time pleasantly: my mother and father and I were in the restaurant I had been taken to after my father's success in the jumping ring. Around us people were laughing and talking, and so were my mother and father. There was no more to the dream, but I felt happy when I remembered it in the morning.

'There is a fine Deposition in Triora,' Monsieur Paillez said on the lawn after breakfast. 'You might find it worth the journey.'

My mother answered as though she'd been expecting the suggestion. She answered quickly, almost before Monsieur Paillez had ceased to speak, and then she turned to me to say a visit to Triora might make an outing.

'There is a pretty trattoria not far from that church,' Monsieur Paillez said. 'Its terrace is shaded by a vine. Once or twice I have had lunch there.'

And so, after our swim that day, my mother did not lie on the inflated cushions nor I on the white rock I had made my own, but dressed ourselves and were as swift as Monsieur Paillez about it. The taxi he took every day to Triora was waiting outside the hotel.

I enjoyed the change in our routine, though not the Deposition, nor the church which housed it. We didn't spend long there, hardly more than a minute, finding instead a café where we wrote our daily postcard to my father. *We have come today to Triora*, I wrote, *with Monsieur Paillez,*

who is visiting his mad Italian wife. We have seen a picture in a church.
At last there was something different to write and for once the words came
easily. I was smiling when I handed the postcard to my mother, anticipating
her surprise that I had completed my message so quickly. She read it
carefully, but did not immediately add her own few sentences. She would
do that later, she said, placing the postcard in her handbag. (I afterwards
found it, torn into little pieces, in the wastepaper basket in her room.)

'At peace today,' Monsieur Paillez reported in the trattoria with the
vine. 'Yes, more at peace today.'

It was usually so, he explained: when his wife had had a bad spell there
was often a period of tranquillity. Because of it he did not visit the asylum
in the afternoon, but returned with us to the Villa Parco and joined us
when we swam again.

'It is almost certain that Claudia has secured the part,' Signora Binelli
announced on the terrace before dinner. 'All day long the telephone has
been ringing for her.'

My mother and Monsieur Paillez smiled, though without exchanging a
look. Claudia, arriving on the terrace, said the part in *Il Marito in Collegio*
was far from certain. The telephone ringing was always a bad sign, implying
indecision.

Just for a moment on the way in to dinner Monsieur Paillez's hand
gently cupped my mother's elbow. Tonight he sat with us also, even though
his spirits were no longer low, and as he and my mother conversed I again
felt happy that she had a friend in San Pietro, one who could be called that
more than the Binellis or any of the other guests could. That night I woke
up once, and listened, and heard the murmuring.

On the way back to Linvik – in Hamburg, I believe it was – my mother
said:

'Let's forget about that day we went to Triora.'

'Forget it?'

'Well, I mean, let's have it as a secret.'

I asked her why we should do that. She did not hesitate but said that on
that day, passing a shop window, she had seen in it what she wished to
buy my father for Christmas. She had not bought it at the time, but had
asked Monsieur Paillez to do so when he was next in Triora.

'And did he?'

'Yes, he did.'

Monsieur Paillez was just my father's size, she said: whatever the garment
was (my mother didn't identify it), he had kindly tried it on. 'I shall not
say much about Monsieur Paillez,' my mother said, 'in case I stupidly

divulge that little secret. When you talk about a person you sometimes do so without thinking. So perhaps we should neither of us much mention Monsieur Paillez.'

As I listened, I knew that I had never before heard my mother say anything as silly. Every evening after the day of our excursion to Triora Monsieur Paillez had stepped out of his taxi in front of the hotel and had joined us on the terrace. On none of these occasions had he carried a parcel, let alone handed one to my mother. In Triora I could not recollect her pausing even once by a shop window that contained men's clothes.

'Yes, all right,' I said.

That was the moment my childhood ended. It is the most devious irony that Dr Edlund's bluff assurances – certainly not believed by him – anticipated the circumstance that allows me now to look back to those summers in San Pietro al Mare, and to that summer in particular. It is, of course, the same circumstance that allows me to remember the rest of each year in Linvik. I did not know in my childhood that my mother and father had ceased to love one another. I did not know that it was my delicate constitution that kept them tied to one another; a child who had not long to live should not, in fairness, have to tolerate a family's disruption as well as everything else.

At the Villa Parco, when we returned the following summer, Monsieur Paillez was already there, visiting his mad Italian wife. The very first night he shared our table, and after that we did everything together. Signora Binelli and her daughter were not at the hotel that year. (Nor were they again at the Villa Parco when we were. My mother and Monsieur Paillez were relieved about that, I think, although they often mentioned Signora Binelli and her daughter and seemed amused by the memory of them.)

'We had snow in Lille as early as October,' Monsieur Paillez said, and so the conversation was on this night, and on other nights – conducted in such a manner because my presence demanded it. Later my mother did not say that we should avoid mentioning Monsieur Paillez when we returned to Linvik. She knew it was not necessary to go through another palaver of silliness.

When I was sixteen and seventeen we still returned to San Pietro. What had begun for my mother as a duty, taking her weakling child down through Europe to the sun, became the very breath of her life. Long after it was necessary to do so we continued to make the journey, our roles reversed, I now being the one inspired by compassion. The mad wife of Monsieur Paillez, once visited in compassion, died; but Monsieur Paillez did not cease to return to the Villa Parco. In the dining-room I sometimes observed the waiters repeating what there was to repeat to younger waiters, newly arrived at the hotel. As I grew older, my mother and I no longer had adjoining rooms.

In Linvik my father had other women. After my childhood ended I noticed that sometimes in the evenings he was drunk. It won't be long, he and my mother must have so often thought, but they were steadfast in their honourable resolve.

Slow years of wondering washed the magic from my childhood recollections and left them ordinary, like pallid photographs that gracelessly record the facts. Yet what a memory it was for a while, his hand reaching across the tablecloth, the candlelight on her hair. What a memory the smoke trees were, and Signora Binelli, and Claudia, and the sea as blue as the sky! My father was a great horseman, my mother the most beautiful woman I have ever seen. *'Ti diverti?'* Monsieur Paillez's voice was hardly raised as he swam by: how pleased I was that he had chosen to address me!

In my borrowed time I take from an ebony box my smudged attempts to draw the smoke trees of San Pietro and reflect that my talent did not amount to much. Silly, it seems now, to have tried so hard to capture the elusive character of that extraordinary foliage.

Virgins

Like a wasp, Laura says to herself, as she invariably does in the cathedral of Siena, with its violent argument of stripes. An uneasy place, her husband had been remarking only the other night, informing some other tourists in the Palazzo Ravizza.

In several languages, guides draw attention to the pulpit and Pastorino's *Last Supper*. Wilting Americans rest on chairs, Germans work their cameras. An old Italian woman lights a candle, children chatter and are silenced. With dark glasses dangling from her fingers, Laura makes her way through the cathedral crowds, having quickly verified that Francesco Piccolomini became Pius III. She knew she'd been right; her husband had said it was Pius II. Her husband is often wrong, about all sorts of things.

'Laura? Is it Laura?'

She stares at the round face, flushed from the August heat. Hair, once coppery red, Laura guesses, is peppered now with grey; a dress is less elegantly striped than the architecture, in lettuce-green and blue. Laura smiles, but shakes her head. She passes her glance down the tired dress, to legs on which mosquitoes have feasted, to sandals whose shade of blue once matched the blue of the cotton above. She smiles again, knowing she knows this woman of fifty or so.

'You haven't changed a bit!' the woman says, and immediately Laura remembers because the voice is as it has always been. Polite to say she hasn't changed a bit; politely she lies herself.

'Nor you, now that I look, Margaretta.'

But her tone is nervous, and her confidence melts as they stand among the tourists and the angry stripes. How odd to meet here, she says, knowing it is not odd at all, since everyone's a tourist nowadays. She wishes they had not met like this; why could not Margaretta just have seen her and let her pass by?

'It's lovely to see you,' Margaretta says.

They continue to look at one another, and simultaneously, in their different moods, their distant friendship possesses them. Two marriages and their children are irrelevant.

The Heaslips' house was in a straggling grassy square, dusty in summer.

A brass plate announced the profession of Dr Heaslip; the oak-grained hall door was heavy and impressive, with brass that matched in weight and tone the nameplate. Near by, the Bank of Ireland was ivy-covered, less gaunt because of it than the Heaslips' grey stone façade. Other houses, each detached from its neighbour, were of grey stone also, or colour-washed in pink or cream or white. In the approximate centre of an extensive area of shorn grass, green railings protected an empty pedestal, which Queen Victoria in her day had dominated. A cinema – the De Luxe Picture House, as antique as its title – occupied a corner created by the edge of the square and the town's main street. Hogan's Hotel filled the corner opposite.

One day in June, during the Second World War, a day when the brass plate shimmered in warm sunshine, a day Laura for all her life did not forget, Mrs Heaslip said in the drawing-room of the house:

'Laura, this is Margaretta.'

Laura held out her hand, as she had been taught, but Margaretta giggled, finding it amusing that two small girls should be so formal.

'Margaretta! Really, what will Laura think? Now, do at once apologize.'

'We're all like that in Ireland,' Margaretta pronounced instead. 'Bog-trotters, y'know.'

'Indeed we're not,' protested Mrs Heaslip, a thin, tall woman in a flowery dress. With some panache she wore as well a straw hat with a faded purple ribbon on it. The skin of her face, and of her arms and legs, was deeply brown, as if she spent the greater part of her time outside. 'Indeed, indeed, we're not,' she repeated, most emphatically. 'And do not say "y'know", Margaretta.'

They were nine, the girls, in 1941. Laura had been sent from England because of the war, called in Ireland 'the emergency': there was more nourishment to be had in Ireland, and a feeling of safety in an Irish provincial town. Years before Laura had been born, her mother, living in Ireland then, had been at a boarding-school in Bray with Mrs Heaslip. 'I think you'll like it in Ireland,' her mother had promised. 'If I didn't have this wretched job I'd come with you like a shot.' They lived in Buckinghamshire, in a village called Anstey Rye. In December 1939, when the war had scarcely begun, Laura's father had been killed, the Spitfire he'd been piloting shot down over the sea. Her mother worked in the Anstey Rye clothes shop, where she was responsible for the accounts, for correspondence with wholesalers and for considerable formalities connected with clothing coupons. It was all very different from Ireland.

'That's what's called a monkey puzzle, y'know,' Margaretta said in the garden, and Laura quietly replied that she knew a monkey puzzle when she saw one.

Unlike Mrs Heaslip, Margaretta wasn't thin. Nor was she brown. She was pretty in a sleepy, careless kind of way: her eyes were sleepily blue, her cheeks carelessly dimpled, her red jumble of hair the most beautiful Laura had ever seen. Margaretta would be astonishing when she grew up – what, Laura imagined, looking at her on that first afternoon, Helen of Troy must have been like. She felt jealous of the promise that seemed to be in every movement of Margaretta's body, in every footstep that she took as she led the way through the garden and the house.

'I am to show you everything,' Margaretta said. 'Would you be enormously bored to see the town?'

'No, no, of course not. Thank you, Margaretta.'

'It isn't much, I'll tell you that.'

The girls walked slowly through the wide main street, Margaretta drawing attention to the shops. All of them were cluttered, Laura noticed, except one, connected with a bakery, which seemed to sell, not bread, but only flour and sugar. They passed Martell's Café, Jas. Ryan's drapery and Medical Hall, Clancy's grocery, which Margaretta said was a public house as well as a grocer's, the Home and Colonial, a hardware shop and a shoe shop, other public houses. They paused by a window full of exercise-books and bottles of Stephens' ink, which Margaretta said was her favourite shop of all. The window was strewn with packets of nibs and pencils, packets of rubber bands, rulers, pencil-sharpeners, and Waterman fountain pens in different marbled colours. There was an advertisement for Mellifont Books, and some of the books themselves, with garish paper covers: *Angela and the Pixies* in the Children's Series, *Murder from Beyond* in Crime and Detection. The shop, Margaretta said, was called Coffey's although the name over the door was T. MacCarthy. She liked it because it smelt so pleasantly of paper. Clancy's smelt of whiskey and sawdust, the butcher's of offal.

'How're you, Margaretta?' Mr Hearne greeted her from his doorway, a heavy man in a blood-stained apron.

'Laura's come from England,' Margaretta said by way of reply.

'How're you, Laura?' Mr Hearne said.

In the weeks and months that followed, Laura came to know Mr Hearne well, for she and Margaretta did all the shopping for the household. 'Meat and women,' the butcher had a way of saying, 'won't take squeezing.' He used to ask riddles, of which he did not know the answers. His wife, Mrs Heaslip said, was frequently pregnant.

The sweetshops of the town became familiar to Laura also, Murphy's,

O'Connor's, Eldon's, Morrissey's, Mrs Finney's. Different brands of ice-cream were sold: H.B., Lucan, Melville, and Eldon's own make, cheaper and yellower than the others. Murphy's sold fruit as well as confectionery, and was the smartest of the sweetshops. Margaretta said it smelt the nicest, a mixture of vanilla and grapes. They all sold scarlet money-balls, in which, if you were lucky, you got your money back, a brand-new ha'penny wrapped in a piece of paper. They all sold boxes of Urney chocolates, and liquorice pipes and strips, and Lemon's Nut-Milk Toffees and Rainbow Toffees. In their windows, boxes of Willwood's Dolly Mixtures were laid out, and slabs of Mickey Mouse Toffee, and jelly babies. Best value of all was the yellow lemonade powder, which Margaretta and Laura never waited to make lemonade with but ate on the street.

That first summer in Ireland was full of such novelty, but most fascinating of all was the Heaslip family itself. Dr Heaslip related solemn jokes in an unhurried voice, and his equally unhurried smile came to your rescue when you were flustered and didn't know whether it was a joke or not. Mrs Heaslip read in the garden – books that had their covers protected with brown paper, borrowed from the library the nuns ran. Margaretta's two younger brothers, six and five, were looked after by Francie, a cross-eyed girl of nineteen who came every day to the house. Eileen and Katie between them did the cooking and cleaning, Katie for ever up and down the basement stairs, answering the hall door to Dr Heaslip's patients. Eileen was quite old – Margaretta said sixty, but Mrs Heaslip, overhearing that, altered the estimation to forty-five – and made brown bread that Laura thought delicious. Katie was keeping company with Wiry Bohan from the hardware's. Margaretta said she'd seen them kissing.

Dr Heaslip's motor-car, unlike the others in the town, which for the most part were laid up because of the emergency, was driven every day out of the garage at the back by a man called Mattie Devlin. He parked it in front of the house so that Dr Heaslip could hasten to it and journey out into the country to attend a childbirth or to do his best when there'd been an accident on a farm. 'Ah, well, we'll do our best' was a much-employed expression of his, issued in a tone of voice that did not hold out much hope of success though in fact, as Laura learnt, he often saved a life. 'She's out there ready, Doctor,' Mattie Devlin every morning shouted up through the house at breakfast-time. He then began his day's work in the garden, where, to Mrs Heaslip's displeasure, he refused to grow peas, broad beans or spinach, claiming that the soil was unsuitable for them. He grew instead a great number of turnips, both swedes and white, potatoes, and a form of kale which nobody in the family liked. He was a man in a striped brown suit who wore both belt and braces and tucked the ends of his trousers into his socks when he worked in the garden. He never took off either his jacket or his hat.

Sometimes when Dr Heaslip was summoned on a call that involved a journey in his car he would invite the girls to accompany him, but he was insistent that they should make themselves as inconspicuous as possible on the back seat in case their presence should be regarded as a misuse of his petrol allowance. When they arrived at whatever house it was that required his skill he relaxed this severity and permitted them to emerge. 'Go and look at the chickens and cows,' he'd urge. 'Show Laura what a chicken is, Margaretta.' If the day was fine and the farmhouse not too far from the town, they'd ask if they might walk home. Later he would pass them on the road and would blow his horn, slowing down to give them a lift if they wanted one. But they usually walked on and no one particularly minded when they were late for whatever meal it was. Their plates of meat and vegetables would be taken from the oven and they'd eat at the kitchen table, gravy dried away to nothing, mashed potatoes brown. Or tea, at teatime, would have gone black almost, keeping hot on the range.

Headstrong and impetuous, Dr Heaslip described his daughter as. 'Not like yourself, Laura. You're the wise virgin of the two.' He repeated this comparison often, asking Mrs Heaslip and sometimes Katie or Eileen, even Mattie Devlin, if they agreed. Margaretta ignored it, Laura politely smiled. Nothing much upset the Heaslip household and nothing hurried it. Mrs Heaslip's only complaints were the manner in which her daughter spoke and Mattie Devlin's ways with vegetables.

'*The Rains Came*,' Margaretta said. 'All about India, y'know.'

They went to it, as they did to all the films at the De Luxe Picture House, which hadn't yet acquired Western Electric Sound, so that the voices were sometimes difficult to hear. Dr Heaslip and Mrs Heaslip attended the De Luxe almost as regularly as Margaretta and Laura, who went three times a week, every time there was a change of programme. At breakfast the next day the girls reported on what they'd seen; Dr and Mrs Heaslip then made up their minds. *Mr Deeds Goes to Town* had for years been Mrs Heaslip's favourite and *The House of Rothschild* her husband's. Margaretta thought *The House of Rothschild* the most enormously boring picture she'd ever seen in her life, worse even than *The Hunchback of Notre Dame*. For her, and for Laura, the highlights of that first summer were *Fast and Loose*, *Dodge City*, *His Butler's Sister* and *Naughty Marietta*; and best of all, they easily agreed, was *The Rains Came*. On Saturdays there was a serial called *Flaming Frontiers*, and there were travelogues and the news, and shorts with Charlie Chase or Leon Errol. 'Don't you love the *smell* of the De Luxe?' Margaretta used to say after they'd dwelt at length on a performance by Franchot Tone or Deanna Durbin, exhausting the subject and yet unwilling to leave it. 'Hot celluloid, I think it is, and cigarette-butts.'

The war ended in May 1945 and Laura brought back to England these memories of the family and the town, of the school she had attended with Margaretta, of the people and the shops. Margaretta wrote from time to time, a huge sprawling hand, words grotesquely misspelt: Mrs Hearne had called her latest baby Liam Pius, after the Pope; *Cry Havoc* was on at the De Luxe, *The Way to the Stars* was coming.

Laura wrote neatly, with nothing to say because Margaretta couldn't be expected to be interested in all the talk about building things up again and descriptions of utility clothes. Margaretta had become her best friend and she Margaretta's. They had decided it the night before she'd returned. They'd shared Margaretta's bed, talking in whispers from ten o'clock until the Donald Duck clock said it was twenty past two. 'We'd better go to sleep, y'know,' Margaretta had said, but Laura had wanted to continue talking, to make the time go slowly. After Margaretta put the light out she lay in the darkness thinking she'd never had a friend like Margaretta before, someone who found the same things as boring as you did, someone you didn't have to be careful with. A wash of moonlight for a moment lightened the gloom, catching the untidy mass of Margaretta's hair on the pillow. She was breathing heavily, already asleep, smiling a little as if from some amusing dream. Then a cloud slipped over the moon again and the room abruptly darkened.

It was that night that Laura afterwards remembered most. 'You can't find friends in a town the like of this,' Margaretta had said. 'Well, I mean you can, y'know. Only it's different.' And she mentioned the girls she knew in the town, whom Laura knew also. None of them would have been fascinated, as they were, by the way Mrs Eldon of the sweetshop made her lips seem larger with the outline of her lipstick. None of them would have wondered how it was that Mr Hearne always had the same amount of stubble on his face. 'One day's growth,' Dr Heaslip had said when they'd asked him. How could a man, every day, have one day's stubble? 'They want to be nuns and things,' Margaretta said. These girls went to the De Luxe also, but they didn't take much interest in the performances, nor in the trademarks of the films, the roaring lion, the searchlights, the statue with the torch, the snow-capped mountain, the radio aerial with electricity escaping from it. The girls of the town didn't go in for finding things funny. Sometimes Laura and Margaretta found a remark a shopkeeper had made so funny that they had to lean against some other shopkeeper's window, laughing so much it gave them a stitch. Sometimes the very sight of people made them laugh. Entranced, Margaretta listened when Laura had told her how her Uncle Gilbert had taken her on to his bony knee on her sixth birthday and softly spanked her for no reason whatsoever. Afterwards he'd given her a sweet and said it was their secret. 'Keep well away from that fellow,' Margaretta had sharply advised, and both of them had giggled, not quite knowing what they were giggling at. It was something Laura had never told anyone else.

It is so drab, Laura wrote. *As you would say, enormously drab. Everyone said at first, you know, that the war would be over by Christmas. I remember people saying Hitler was a knut and didn't know what he was doing. But now everything's so drab after Ireland that you'd think he had won the thing. I haven't had an egg for months.*

And so, for nourishment only, since safety wasn't in question any more, Laura's mother sent her to stay again with the Heaslips. Mrs Heaslip had pressed for this, had pressed that Laura's mother should accompany her.

'They can't spare her,' Laura explained when she arrived, reiterating what her mother had written. 'She'd really have loved to come.' The drab auoterity was as confining as the war there had been.

For Laura, that summer had the pleasure of familiarity revisited in place of the novelty there had been when she'd first arrived in the town. Mrs Hearne might possibly be pregnant again, Mrs Eldon's lipstick still generously recreated her lips, *Murder from Beyond*, with curling, yellowed edges, was still in the window among the nibs and rubber bands.

Margaretta had acquired a bicycle during the year, and the saddle of Mrs Heaslip's Humber was lowered for Laura. For mile after mile of flat, undramatic landscape they talked, as they cycled, of the past performances at the De Luxe Picture House: Claudette Colbert in *Boom Town*, William Powell and Myrna Loy in *The Shadow of the Thin Man*, Ray Milland in *The Doctor Takes a Wife*. They turned off the tarred roads that were so easy to go fast on and explored countryside that was hilly and more interesting. Eileen made them sandwiches, which they carried in Margaretta's saddle-bag, and they were given money for lemonade. They usually ate the sandwiches in a field, leaving their bicycles by the roadside and chattering for ages in the sunshine. Once they took their clothes off and bathed in a stream, shrieking because it was so cold. But what they liked best of all was to call in at some cottage and ask for a drink of water. They would be invited into the kitchen and two cups of water would be fetched from a bucket or a pump. On one occasion a very old woman insisted on giving them tea, with boiled eggs and bread, although they kept telling her they'd just eaten a lot of sandwiches. She showed them photographs of her son, who was in Chicago, and made them promise they would call at her cottage again. But even if all they received was the water they asked for there was always the excitement, afterwards, of talking about whoever had given it to them. Scrutinizing people, remembering every word that was spoken and every detail of a kitchen: that became a kind of game. If they were far enough away from the town they called themselves by names that were not their own. 'Annabella Colman,' Margaretta replied when asked, and Laura gave the name of a girl she knew in England, Isabel Batchelor-Tate. They were Dublin girls, Margaretta once added, on holiday in Hogan's Hotel. Her father was a hay merchant and Laura's a taster of teas. 'I shouldn't tell people stuff like that,' Dr Heaslip reprimanded them one lunchtime. 'I'm quite well known, you know.' He went on humming after he'd spoken and they were unable to hide their fiery red faces, made to feel foolish because he had not been cross. Afterwards Mrs Heaslip looked at them amusedly, and suggested they should visit the de Courcys if they were bored.

'Oh, but we're not, Mrs Heaslip,' Laura protested vehemently. 'Not in the very least.'

'Take her to the de Courcys, Margaretta. I don't know what we've been thinking of not to introduce Laura to the de Courcys before this.'

'But, God, they're miles away.'

'Do not say "God", Margaretta. There is an invalid in that house. Of course a visit must be made. Eileen will make you salad sandwiches.'

They went the next morning. They cycled for nine miles and then they turned into an avenue with a gate-lodge from which a man carefully eyed them, from their sandals and white socks to their straw hats. He stood in the doorway, seeming to be listening to their conversation about Wiry Bohan's courtship of Katie. He was wearing a Guard's uniform, the coarse navy-blue tunic open at the neck, a cigarette in the middle of his mouth. He had grey hair and a grey, mournful face. When Margaretta said hullo he wagged his head but did not speak. They began to giggle when they'd cycled on a bit.

The avenue was long, its surface badly broken, but pleasantly cool because the trees that lined it kept out the sun. Laura considered it romantic, like the avenue in *Rebecca*. But Margaretta said that was only wishful thinking: there hadn't been an avenue in *Rebecca* encased with trees and foliage. An argument began, which continued until the pink-washed house appeared, with white hydrangeas on either side of it, and tall windows, and an open hall door. The bicycles crunched over gravel that made cycling difficult. The girls dismounted and walked the last bit.

'I'm Margaretta Heaslip,' Margaretta informed a maid who was winding a clock in the hall. 'We've been sent to see the de Courcys.'

The maid stared, appearing to be alarmed. She continued to wind the clock, which was on a table at the bottom of the stairs, and then she closed the glass of its face and put the key on a brass hook in an alcove; the time was half past eleven.

Tapestries hung by the staircase, curving with it as it ascended. Rugs were scattered on the darkly stained boards of the floor, as threadbare as the stair carpet and the tapestries, which were so faded that whatever scenes they depicted had been lost. There was a smell in the hall, as Margaretta said afterwards, of flowers and bacon.

'Will you tell the de Courcys?' she suggested to the maid, since the maid appeared hesitant about how to proceed. 'Just say Margaretta Heaslip and a friend are here.'

'The de Courcys went up to Punchestown races, miss.'

'Is Ralph de Courcy here?'

'He is of course.'

'Will you tell him then?'

'He didn't go up to the races, miss, in case they'd strain him.'

'Will you tell him Margaretta Heaslip and a friend are here?'

The maid was as young as Katie, but not as pretty. She had protruding teeth and hair that was in disarray beneath her white cap. She hesitated again, and then visibly reached a decision.

'I'll tell him so, miss. Will ye sit in the drawing-room?'

She left them where they stood. One door they opened led to a panelled room, too small and businesslike for a drawing-room. Another, with blue blinds pulled down, had dining-chairs arranged around a long table, its other furniture shadowy in the gloom. The drawing-room itself had a fire, although the day was so exceedingly warm that the windows were open. There were vases of flowers on the mantelpiece and on tables and on a grand piano, and family portraits were close to one another on the walls. An old black-and-white dog was lying on the hearthrug and did not move when the girls entered. It was the most beautiful room, Laura considered, she had ever been in.

They sat cautiously on the edge of a sofa that was striped in two shades of faded pink. They spoke in whispers, discussing the maid: would she be keeping company with the uniformed man at the gate-lodge?

'Will ye wait a while?' the maid invited, appearing at the door.

Margaretta giggled and put her hand up to her mouth; Laura said they'd wait. 'I wonder what her name is,' she added when the maid had gone.

'Ludmilla, I'd say.'

The giggling began again, the dog snorted in his sleep. Through the open windows came the sound of pigeons.

'Well, this is an honour,' a voice said. 'How do you do?'

He was older than they were by maybe as much as three years. He was pale and dark-haired, his eyes brown. He was dressed in flannel trousers and a green tweed jacket.

'Margaretta Heaslip,' he continued, smiling extravagantly. 'I remember you when you were little.'

He spoke as if she still were, as if they were both not in the least grown up. His manner insisted that he himself belonged to the adult world, that he had long ago passed through theirs.

'My mother said to call,' Margaretta explained, disowning responsibility for their presence. 'To inquire how you were, and to introduce Laura.'

'How do you do, Laura?'

He held out a hand, which Laura received, allowing her own to be briefly clasped. His touch was cold. Like marble, she thought.

'Laura's English, y'know.'

'Well now, and whereabouts in England, Laura?'

'A village called Anstey Rye. In Buckinghamshire.'

'How attractive that sounds!'

'Dead as old mutton, Laura says. The war, y'know.'

'Ah, yes. The horrible war. But at least the Allies won. You're pleased, Laura?'

He had a precise way of speaking, his Irish accent drawling out his sentences, a smile rarely absent from his face. Set in hollows, his dark eyes were fixed on Laura's, insistent that his interest in all she had to say was genuine.

'Well yes, I am pleased.'

'I used to listen to Lord Haw-Haw. He's most amusing.'

The maid returned with a tray of teacups, a teapot and biscuits on a plate.

'Thank you, Mary.'

As he spoke, Margaretta put her hand up to her face. But already he had noticed.

'What's the joke?' he politely inquired.

The maid left the room, and because she knew that she, too, would begin to giggle if she did not speak Laura said:

'Margaretta thought her name was Ludmilla.'

'Ludmilla?'

It wasn't funny any more, as it hadn't been when Dr Heaslip had not been cross. Politely, Ralph de Courcy handed them their cups of tea. He was right: they were children and he was not.

'Have a Marietta biscuit?'

They each took one. They felt silly and ashamed. Margaretta said:

'Are you feeling better these days?'

'I never feel ill at all.' He turned to Laura. 'My heart was weakened when I stupidly caught rheumatic fever as a boy. I'm meant to go carefully in case I die.'

They wanted to gasp in wonder at this reference to death, but they did not do so. Margaretta said:

'Are you getting better all the time?'

'Indubitably. I'm reading Thomas Mann. *Buddenbrooks*. Do you like Thomas Mann?'

They had never heard of this German author. Vaguely, they shook their heads. They had not yet read, Laura admitted, the book called *Buddenbrooks*.

'Shall I show you about the garden when you've finished your Marietta biscuits?'

'Yes, please,' Laura said. 'If you don't think the strain –'

'Strain is just a word they use. Your father came here once or twice, Margaretta, when I was at death's door – called in to offer a second opinion. It wasn't as disagreeable as it sounds, you know, being at death's door. Though nicer, perhaps, to be a few footsteps further off.'

His conversation was extraordinary, Laura considered. In a way everything about him was extraordinary, not least his detached smile and his eyes. His eyes did not flit about. They were the steadiest eyes she had ever seen, especially when he spoke of death.

'Oh, yes,' he said, 'they make a frightful fuss. Do you play tennis? You could stay to lunch and then we might play tennis.'

'But surely –' Margaretta began.

'I may play a *little* tennis. If I agree, and promise, not to sit about afterwards without a sweater and a blazer, then I may play a little tennis. Or at least that's what I say.'

Suppose he dies? Laura thought. Suppose he falls down on the tennis court and is unable to get up again? Imagine having to tell about that! Imagine Dr Heaslip saying nothing, but thinking what fools they were and how much they were to blame!

He took them to the garden. He didn't appear to know the names of any plants or flowers, but with his pale, cold hands he pointed about. He led them through a glasshouse full of tomatoes and out the other end. He pointed again: peaches flourished on a brick-lined wall. '*A la* Dean Swift,' he said: they'd no idea what he was talking about.

He sat between them on a wooden seat. A lawn stretched all around, bounded by white hydrangeas in front of towering cedar trees. Another dog, a brown spaniel, ambled from some corner and sat with them. Margaretta said the garden was beautiful.

'Sergeant Barry does it. Did you see Sergeant Barry by the gate-lodge?' They said they had.

'He resigned from the force because he couldn't learn the Irish. He feared they might demote him and he couldn't bear the thought of that. So he resigned as sergeant.'

In the drawing-room, when she'd brought the tea and biscuits, he'd told the maid that they would stay to lunch. They hadn't dared to say that there were salad sandwiches in Margaretta's saddle-bag.

'You must be starving,' he said now, 'after such a journey. Heaven knows what they've managed to scrape together. Shall we go and see?'

He led the way back to the house and to the dining-room. The blinds had been raised, and places laid at the table. He pulled at a bell in the wall and some minutes later the maid brought in three soup plates on a tray.

'Crosse and Blackwell's,' he said. 'Leave it if you don't like kidneys.'

All through the meal he asked questions, about Buckinghamshire and Anstey Rye, and if bombs had fallen near by; about the De Luxe Picture House, which he had been to once. There was a larger town, nearer to the de Courcys' house than their own, which had a cinema called the Palace, with Western Electric Sound. He'd seen *Gone with the Wind* there, which he described as 'light'. He'd like to see some German films, which he'd read about, but he doubted that they'd ever come to the Palace or the De Luxe. He related the plot of one, to do with the crimes committed by a man who was not sane, and enthusiastically they both said it sounded interesting. Perhaps now that the war was over these German films might be on in England, Laura added, and he agreed that that might be so. Then, quite abruptly, when they had all three finished their sago and stewed gooseberries, he said he was feeling a little tired. His smile continued. He was supposed to rest after lunch, he explained. It would perhaps be asking for trouble not to, today.

They stood up. They thanked him and hoped he would be completely better soon. It was as though tennis had never been mentioned; it was as though he had never said that people made a fuss. He did not move from where he sat at the head of the long table, but said that he had enjoyed their visit, that they were good to come all this way to bore themselves with the company of an invalid. Would they come again? he almost meekly asked.

'Yes, of course,' Laura replied, her assurance only moments ahead of Margaretta's.

'Please be careful,' Margaretta said. 'Please take a good rest.'

They rode in silence down the avenue, past the gate-lodge, where Sergeant Barry was reading a newspaper in his garden. He looked up from it to scrutinize them, another cigarette in the middle of his mouth. Again he wagged his head at them but did not attempt to speak.

'God!' Margaretta said when they were out of earshot. 'God, did you ever!'

'I hope we didn't cause a strain.'

'God, I know! I thought of that.'

When they next saw Dr Heaslip they asked him. 'Oh no, no,' he said. 'Company probably does the poor fellow good.' But neither Laura nor Margaretta could think of Ralph de Courcy as a poor fellow. A fortnight later they rode over to the de Courcys' house again, and Sergeant Barry, apprehending them as they turned into the avenue, told them the de Courcys were all away in Dublin.

'When will they be back?' Margaretta asked.

'Ah, not for a while. Not till the end of the month.'

A week later Laura returned to England. This time among the images she carried with her were ones of the hours they had spent in the de Courcys' house and in their garden. The indistinct tapestries, the key of the clock hanging in the alcove in the hall, the black-and-white dog asleep on the hearthrug: such images came and went in her mind, giving way to the face of the maid, and the sergeant at the gate-lodge, and Ralph de Courcy in his flannels and green tweed jacket. She dreamed that she and Margaretta walked among the white hydrangeas and the cedar trees, that they sat again on the pink-striped sofa. In her dream the hands fell off the clock in the hall, which Dr Heaslip said sometimes happened, owing to strain.

Margaretta wrote to say that the de Courcys had returned from Dublin, so she'd heard, but on her own she naturally hadn't had the nerve to cycle over. The De Luxe had at last acquired Western Electric Sound and the difference was tremendous. Wiry Bohan had been to the house to see about marrying Katie, and when Mrs Heaslip suggested that they should wait a little longer he'd gone red in the face and said he thought waiting wasn't a good idea. Mr Hearne was dealing in black-market sugar and tea, making more than he'd ever made out of meat. But soon, so people said, he'd be arrested.

The following summer, to her great disappointment, and to Margaretta's, Laura did not visit Ireland. The reason for this was that her mother, suffering a bout of pneumonia in the early part of the year, did not recover quickly. She struggled back to her desk in the cubbyhole behind the Anstey

Rye clothes shop, but an exhaustion that the illness had left her with would not lift, and when Laura's summer holidays came Dr Farquhar advised that she should be responsible for all the housework and all the cooking, taking this burden at least from her mother. Had it not been for the postwar effort that was still required of everyone, he would have stipulated total rest for her mother, three months simply doing nothing. And he knew that ends had to be made to meet.

So Laura cooked her mother's meals and her own, and Hoovered the rooms of their cottage. She made her mother rest on Sundays, bringing her trays in bed. She was conscientious about taking the wet battery of the wireless to be recharged once a week, she weeded the garden and transplanted the lettuce plants. All the time she cherished the hope that at the end of the summer, even for a week, she might be permitted to visit Margaretta. Her mother was clearly regaining her strength. She stopped spending Sundays in bed and instead sat in the garden. By mid-August she began to do the cooking again.

Letters from Margaretta asked if there was any chance, but in Anstey Rye Ireland was not mentioned. Instead, Laura's mother spoke of their straitened circumstances this year: because of her pneumonia, she had not earned as much for those few months as she might have; ends had not yet begun to meet again. So Laura wrote to Margaretta, explaining.

Isn't it strange, Margaretta herself wrote, long after that summer had passed and Laura's mother had entirely recovered, *that there should have been two invalids, your mother and Ralph de Courcy?* Her handwriting was less wild than once it had been, her spelling much improved. *My father says he's only slowly mending.* And in a daydream Laura allowed herself to pretend that it was he she had looked after, carrying trays up the curving staircase, carrying cushions to a chair in the garden. She wondered if she'd ever see that house again, and Sergeant Barry at the gate-lodge. *Isn't Linda Darnell beautiful?* Margaretta wrote. *I'd love to look like that. Have you seen* Tortilla Flat?

In 1948 Laura went again to Ireland. Katie had married Wiry Bohan and had had a baby. There was a new maid with Eileen in the kitchen, Mattie Devlin's daughter, Josie. The shopkeepers said Laura was getting prettier all the time, but Laura knew that it was Margaretta who was the beautiful one and always would be, her marvellous hair and her headstrong manner that Laura admired so. She'd been going to a boarding-school ever since Laura had last visited the Heaslips, the one in Bray where Mrs Heaslip and Laura's mother had met. 'You're better looking than Linda Darnell,' Laura said, meaning it.

They were too shy to cycle to the de Courcys' house. They didn't realize at first that such a shyness had developed in them, but when they talked about that warm day two summers ago they realized that they could not attempt to repeat it. Two children, with white socks and straw hats, had cycled up the avenue, chattering and giggling: it would be awkward now. But one evening, watching *Thunder Rock* at the De Luxe, they saw Ralph de Courcy two rows in front of them, with a blonde-haired girl. 'You're never Margaretta and Laura?' he said when the film had come to an end and they met him face to face in the aisle.

'Yes,' Laura said, aware that she reddened as she spoke. When she glanced at Margaretta she saw that she had reddened also.

'This is a sister of mine,' he introduced. 'Hazel.'

Margaretta said:

'I think I met you, Hazel, years ago when we were kids.'

'Yes, you did.'

'This is my friend Laura.'

'I've heard about the day you both came to see us, when we were all at Punchestown except Ralph.'

'You never came again,' he chided, through the smile that was always there. 'You said you would, you know.'

'Laura didn't stay with us last year.'

'You could have come on your own.'

Margaretta laughed, blushing again.

'That was really an appalling film,' he said. 'A waste of money.'

'Yes,' Laura agreed, although she did not think so. 'Yes, it was.'

The de Courcys had driven to town in a car powered by propane gas, a relic of the emergency. To Laura and Margaretta it looked like any other car except for an attachment at the back. Although the night was warm, Ralph put on a muffler and an overcoat before taking his place at the driver's wheel. Unlike her mother, Laura thought, he was not totally well again.

'Come and play tennis one day,' his sister invited. 'Come in the morning and stay to lunch.'

'Come on Friday,' he said.

'My husband is an eye specialist,' Laura says in the cathedral.

'Mine makes radio components.'

Margaretta had remained in the town, marrying Shulmann, who had set up his factory there in 1955. Shulmann was with her in Siena, resting now in their pensione. Their three children are grown up.

'I guessed you would have married,' Laura says.

'And I you.'

What does the eye specialist look like? Is Shulmann thin or fat? Laura remembers Margaretta's hair on the pillow, spread out in the moonlight, and Margaretta saying that the smell in the De Luxe Picture House was of hot celluloid and cigarette-butts, and how they giggled because they'd considered Sergeant Barry comic. How different would their lives have been if the friendship had continued? Some instinct tells her as they stand there among the tourists that their friendship in its time went deeper than the marriages they have mentioned. She sees them on their bicycles, and the curiosity of Sergeant Barry passing from their sandals and their white socks to their beribboned straw hats. 'Ludmilla', Margaretta says on the pink-striped sofa. Is friendship more fragile, Laura wonders, the more precious it is? And Margaretta reflects that in the thirty-eight years that have passed the friendship might have made a difference in all sorts of ways. They are tourists like the others now, strangers among strangers.

They rode over early on the Friday of the tennis party, but as they arrived at the de Courcys' house rain began to fall. Other people were there, friends of Hazel de Courcy who had also come to play tennis but who now stood about forlornly because the rain persisted. Then someone suggested whist and the occasion became a different one from the occasion the visitors had anticipated. The fire blazed in the drawing-room, there was tea and Marietta biscuits at eleven o'clock, and lunch at one; there was tea and cake, with bread and butter and scones, at four. Ralph de Courcy rested after lunch, but soon appeared again. He talked to Margaretta alone, questioning her about the boarding-school at Bray, about the buildings and the playing-fields and the food. He asked her if she was happy there.

'Oh, it's all right,' Margaretta replied, and she described the big assembly hall that was known as the ballroom because that was what it had been before the house became a school. A draughty conservatory served as the senior lounge; cold, gaunt dormitories contained rows of beds, each with its narrow pine cupboard and wash-stand. The two headmistresses were sisters, in tweed skirts and jumpers on which necklaces bounced. The food was inedible.

'Poor Margaretta,' he murmured.

She was about to say it wasn't as awful as it sounded but changed her mind because his sympathy was pleasant. He said he would think of her at the school, eating the inedible food, being polite to the headmistresses. She felt a shiver of warmth, in her head or her body, she wasn't sure which: a delicious sensation that made her want to close her eyes.

'It'll be lovely for me,' Ralph de Courcy said, 'being able to imagine you there, Margaretta.'

The rain ceased after tea but the tennis court was too sodden by now to permit play that day, and soon afterwards the party broke up. Hardly speaking at all – not once commenting as they might have on Hazel de Courcy's friends – the girls cycled back to the town, and when Dr Heaslip asked at supper how Ralph de Courcy had seemed neither at first replied. Then Margaretta said that he was quite recovered from his illness, even though he'd had his usual rest. Every day he was recovering a little more. Soon he would be just like anyone else, she said.

Laura cut her ham and salad into tiny shreds, not wanting to hear anything in the dining-room in case it impinged on what the day already meant to her. The sun had been warm during their ride back from the de Courcys' house; the damp fields and hedges had acquired a beauty as if in celebration of what had happened. 'Shall we write to one another?' he had suggested in the moments when they'd been alone. He had asked her about England, about Anstey Rye and her mother. He smiled more than ever while he spoke, making her feel complimented, as if smiling was natural in her presence.

'I didn't know till now,' Margaretta said a few days later, 'that I fell in love with him the first time we rode out there.'

They were walking together on a dull road, just beyond the town. Margaretta did not add that he'd asked her about her school, that he had been interested in all that ordinary detail so that he could picture her there that autumn. She refrained from this revelation because she knew that Laura was in love with him also. Laura had not said so but you could see, and it would hurt her horribly to know that he had asked – passionately almost – about the gaunt dormitories and the ballroom that had become an assembly hall.

'Well, of course,' Laura said, 'he's very nice.'

There was nothing else she could say. Bidding her goodbye, he had clasped her hand as though he never wanted to let it go. His deep, brown eyes had held hers in a way she knew she would never forget; she was certain he had almost kissed her. 'Are you good at secrets?' he had asked. 'Are you, Laura?' She had only nodded in reply, but she'd known that what he meant was that all this should be kept between themselves, and she intended to honour that.

'I simply think he's a marvellous person,' Margaretta said, possessively.

'Oh, yes, of course.'

Already it was September, and they did not speak of him again. Laura within a week returned to England and a few days after that Margaretta began another term at the boarding-school in Bray.

I see you so very clearly, he wrote. *I think of you and wonder about you. I'll never forget our being in the garden that day, I sometimes imagine I can still taste the tinned soup we had for lunch. Whatever can you have thought of me, going away to rest like that? Was it rude? Please write and tell me it wasn't rude and that you didn't mind. I rested, actually, with your face beside me on the cushion.*

He did not beg for love in vain, and in Bray and Buckinghamshire they exulted in their giving of it, though both felt saddened that in their own communications, one to another, they did not mention Ralph de Courcy or his letters. *I was glad when it rained because, actually, I don't play much tennis. Oh, heavens, how I should love to be walking with you beneath the beech trees! Did you think I was at death's door that first day – the day when I said to myself you were an angel sent to me? When we met in the De Luxe it was marvellous. Was it for you? Please write. I love your letters.*

In Bray and Buckinghamshire they loved his letters also. They snatched at them impatiently: from the letter table in the senior lounge, from the hallstand in Anstey Rye. They bore them away to read in private, to savour and learn by heart. They kept them hidden but close at hand, so that when the yearning came they could raise them to their lips. *Shall I come and see you in the holidays?* Margaretta wrote. *Or could you drive over in your father's gas contraption and maybe we'd go to the De Luxe? I can't wait till the holidays, to tell the truth. December the 16th.*

These suggestions provoked a swift response. Their friendship was a secret. If Margaretta came to the de Courcys' house would they be able to disguise it beneath the eye of the family? Of all absurd things, the family might mention strain, and a visit to the picture house was out of the question. *Dear Margaretta, we must wait a little while yet. Please wait. Please let's just write our letters for the moment.*

But Margaretta, on the 18th of that December, was unable to prevent herself from cycling out of the town in the direction of the de Courcys' house. It was a cold morning, with frost heavy on the hedges and beautifully whitening the fields. All she wanted was a single glimpse of him.

I cannot tell you the confusion it caused, he wrote, weeks later, to Laura, *and how great the unhappiness has been for me. It was so sad because she looked bulky and ridiculous in the trousers she had put on for cycling. They thought she was a thief at least. Why on earth did she come?*

Sergeant Barry found her among the rhododendrons and led her, weeping, to the house. 'Goodness, Margaretta!' Hazel de Courcy exclaimed in the hall while Margaretta tried to pull herself together. She said she'd just been passing by.

She seemed a different person from the girl who'd first come here with you, but that was perhaps because you were with her then. No one knew what to say when she stood there in the hall. I turned away and went upstairs. What else could I do?

Margaretta rode miserably back to the house in the square. She wrote immediately, apologizing, trying to explain, but her letter elicited no reply. She was unable to eat properly all the holidays, unable in any way to comfort herself. No letter arrived at the boarding-school in Bray. No letter, ever again, arrived for Margaretta from Ralph de Courcy.

Oafish, my sister said, and although it's hard I thought the same. Not beautiful in the least, her cheeks all red and ugly. I had never thought Margaretta was stupid before.

Laura was hurt by this description of her friend, and she wished she might have sent her a line of consolation. Poor Margaretta had ridden out that day with no companion to lend her courage, and to everyone in the de Courcys' house it must have been obvious that she was a lovesick girl. But by the summer she would have recovered, and Laura could gently tell her then that she and Ralph loved one another, because secrets could not remain secrets for ever.

But the summer, when it came, was not like that. In the February of that year Laura had become upset because her letters from Ralph de Courcy had ceased. A month later she received a note from Margaretta. *I thought I'd better tell you. Ralph de Courcy died.*

That summer, Margaretta and Laura were sixteen; and Mr Hearne, who had survived his years as a black-marketeer, was once again an ordinary butcher. 'Women and meat won't take squeezing,' he said, eyeing the girls with lasciviousness now. At the De Luxe Picture House they saw *Blithe Spirit* and *Green for Danger*. Laura asked about Ralph de Courcy's grave.

'God knows where it is,' Margaretta replied. 'He could be buried under a road for all I care.'

'We liked him.'

'He was cheap.'

'He's dead, Margaretta.'

'I'm glad he's dead.'

Still Margaretta had not told her about her cycle ride on that bitter morning. She offered no explanation for this violent change of heart, so Laura asked her.

'Well, something happened if you must know.'

She related all of it, telling how she had begun to receive letters from Ralph de Courcy, how they had come, two and three a week sometimes, to the boarding-school at Bray.

'I didn't mean any harm, Laura. All I wanted was a glimpse of him. Of course I should have gone at night, but how could I? Nine miles there and nine miles back?'

Laura hardly heard. 'Letters?' she whispered in a silence that had gathered. 'Love letters, you mean?'

The conversation took place in Margaretta's bedroom. She unlocked a drawer in her dressing-table and produced the letters she spoke of, tied together with a piece of red string.

'You can read them,' she said. 'I don't mind.'

I rested, actually, with your face beside me on the cushion. In Laura's own bedroom, among the love letters she had so sadly and so fondly brought with her to Ireland, were those words also. *I said to myself you were an angel sent to me.*

'What kind of love was it,' Margaretta cried, 'that could evaporate in a second? Just because I made a mistake?'

The letters were returned to the dressing-table drawer, the key turned in the lock, the key itself secreted beneath a frilled cloth. Laura, catching a reflection of herself in the dressing-table looking-glass, saw that she had turned as white as powder. She felt weak, and imagined that if she stood up she would faint.

'I don't know why I keep his old letters,' Margaretta said. 'I honestly don't know.'

That it had been Margaretta and not she who had been foolish was no consolation for Laura. That it was she, not Margaretta, to whom he had written for longer, until the day before his death, was none either. His protestations of passion seemed like mockery now.

'Except I suppose,' said Margaretta, 'that I went on loving him. I always will.'

And I, too, thought Laura. She would love him in spite of the ugly pain she felt, in spite of not understanding why he had behaved so. Had two girls' longing simply been more fun than one's? Had he been as cruel as that?

'I have a headache,' she said. 'I think I'll lie down for a little.'

The days that followed were as unbearable for Laura as the days that followed her foolishness had been for Margaretta. Dr Heaslip said twice that their guest was looking peaky; she did her best to smile. 'It's all right, really,' Margaretta reassured her, assuming that Laura's lowness was a kind of sympathy. 'It's over now. He's dead and gone.'

He was buried in a country churchyard a mile or so from the de Courcys' house: that much at least Laura had elicited from Margaretta. One early morning, as dawn was just beginning to glimmer, she let herself out of the tall wooden doors through which Matt Devlin every day drove Dr Heaslip's car, and cycled out into the countryside. Trees that were at first only shadows acquired foliage as dawn advanced, hedges and fields softened into colour, stone walls and gates offered again the detail that night had claimed. Around the churchyard, rooks were noisy, and on the grave of Ralph de Courcy there were fresh flowers that Laura knew were Margaretta's, conveyed there secretly also. She picked honeysuckle and laid it on the earth above his head. She knelt and spoke his name; she repeated what so often she had written in her letters. She couldn't help loving him in spite of still not understanding.

'You went, didn't you?' Margaretta accused. 'You went in the middle of the night?'

'In the early morning.'

'He loved me, y'know, before I was so stupid. It was me he wrote letters to.'

The summer crept by. They talked much less than they had talked before. Politeness began between them, and smiles that were not meant. They missed the past but did not say so, and then – on the night before Laura was to return to England – Margaretta said:

'I've hated you this summer.'

'There is no reason to hate me, Margaretta.'

'It has to do with him. I don't know what it is.'

'Well, I don't hate you, Margaretta, and I never could.'

'That's nice.'

'Don't be unhappy, Margaretta.'

Why could she not have shared the truth? Why could she not have said that in the game he'd played he'd wanted to know all about Anstey Rye also? She might have pointed out that when you scraped away the superficialities of her early-morning journey – the peaceful dawn, the rooks, the honeysuckle – it had been less honourable and less courageous than Margaretta's. In her wise virgin way, she had taken no chances in visiting only the dead.

'Margaretta . . .'

She hesitated, unable to go on. And Margaretta said:

'I'll never forgive you for going to his grave.'

'I only went to say goodbye.'

'It was me he wrote to.'

Again Laura tried to say that she, as much as Margaretta, had been shamed. Sharing their folly, would they have laughed in the end over Ralph de Courcy, she wondered, as they had laughed over so much else? Would they have talked for half the night in Margaretta's bedroom, exorcizing that lingering pain?

'Margaretta,' Laura began, but still could not go on.

The De Luxe Picture House has gone. Mr Hearne is dead. So is Mrs Eldon, her lips trimmed down to size. But Coffey's still smells pleasantly of paper, and Murphy's of vanilla and grapes. Wiry Bohan and Katie are grandparents now.

'But oh, it's not much changed, y'know.'

Dr Heaslip and his wife might or might not be dead also: this is not mentioned in Margaretta's news. Her voice is spiritless, and Laura has to think as each name is mentioned. Margaretta's features mourn the loss: a conversation, through desuetude, has lost its savour. It was harsh, so casually and so swiftly to have considered her bland and fat, implying insensitivity. Laura should reach out and kiss her, but the gesture would be false.

Margaretta remembers the flowers that year after year she has placed on the grave, and the bitterness she felt when she thought of Laura. She cycled in that same secret way to the churchyard, not caring if the de Courcys guessed that it was she who had picked the weeds from the mound that marked his presence. When she ceased to make the journey she had at first felt faithless, but the feeling had worn away with time.

For Laura there is the memory of the guilt that had remained for so long, the letters she had tried to compose, her disappointment in herself. *Dear Margaretta*: so many times she had begun her message, certain that there were words to soften her treachery and then discovering that there were not. In time she ceased also, weary of the useless effort.

Regret passes without words between them; they smile a shrugging smile. If vain Ralph de Courcy had chosen their girlish passion as a memorial to himself he might have chosen as well this rendezvous for their middle age, a waspish cathedral to reflect a waspish triumph. Yet his triumph seems hollow now, robbed by time of its drama and the heady confusions of an accidental cruelty. Death's hostage he had been, a ghost who had offered them a sleight of hand because he hadn't the strength for love. They only smile again before they part.

Music

At thirty-three Justin Condon was a salesman of women's undergarments, regularly traversing five counties with his samples and his order book in a Ford Fiesta. He had obediently accepted this role, agreeing when his father had suggested it to him. His father in his day had been a commercial traveller also and every Friday Justin returned to the house his father had returned to, arriving at much the same hour and occupying a room he had in childhood shared with his three brothers. His mother and his father still lived in the house, in the Dublin suburb of Terenure, and were puzzled by their youngest son because he was so unlike their other children, both physically and in other ways. His dark-haired head was neat; remote, abstracted eyes made a spherical, ordinary face seem almost mysterious. At weekends Justin took long walks on his own, all the way from Terenure to the city, to St Stephen's Green, where he sat on a seat or strolled among the flowerbeds, to Herbert Park, where he lay in the sunshine on the grass: people had seen him and remarked upon it. He had never in his life been known to listen to the commentary on a hurling match or a Gaelic match, let alone attend such an event. When he was younger he had come back one Friday with a greyhound, an animal he had proceeded to rear as a pet, apparently not realizing that such creatures had been placed in the world for the purpose of racing one another. 'Ah, poor Justin's the queer old flute,' his father had more than once privately owned in McCauley's public house. His mother wished he'd get married.

Justin's reason for remaining in his parents' house had not been shared with them, although it was a simple one: he considered that any other dwelling would be of a temporary nature and not worth the nuisance of moving to because one day he would leave, not just the suburb of Terenure but Dublin, and Ireland, for ever. He would leave his samples in the Ford Fiesta; he would leave the Ford Fiesta in a lay-by. He was not truly a purveyor of garments in imitation silk, his destiny was not the eternal entering of drapers' shops. He would escape as others had escaped before him; James Joyce he thought of particularly in this respect, and Gauguin. He liked the photograph of James Joyce in the broad-brimmed black hat, with the black coat reaching to his ankles; Gauguin had been a businessman. When Joyce had left Ireland he'd had to borrow a pair of boots. Later he'd tried to sell tweed to the Italians.

Dwelling on such matters, Justin watched the light of a May morning from a bed in Co. Waterford. There wasn't much to see: streaks of brightness along the edges of the drawn curtains, the ceiling of the bedroom mistily illuminated through rosy fabric. A man called Fahy, travelling in fertilizers, had assured him that when he stayed in this house he occupied the bed of Mrs Keane, its widowed landlady. When Garda Bevan, who lodged on a more permanent basis in the house, drank his eleven o'clock Bournville and stated his intention of retiring for the night, Fahy would rise from the kitchen table also, saying he'd had a long day. He would mount the stairs a few paces behind Garda Bevan and in full view of the policeman would enter the bedroom known as the 'overnight room' because it was set aside by Mrs Keane for her casual trade among commercial travellers. Garda Bevan, long since retired from the force, a lifelong bachelor, was a moral presence in Mrs Keane's house, a man who could be relied upon by Father Grennan or Father Reedy, selflessly working behind the scenes for the Pioneer cause and organizing the tug of war at the Nore Fête every Whit. Fahy said he gave him a quarter of an hour and then listened on the landing to the depth of his snoring. He smoked a final cigarette in the overnight bedroom, taking a good ten minutes over it, before listening again at the panels of Garda Bevan's door. If the rhythm of sleep had not altered, he made his way to the bed of Mrs Keane.

Justin supposed it was true. With some precision, Fahy had described the body of the widow, a woman of fifteen stone and in her sixty-first year. The hair that was grey about her head sprouted blackly and abundantly, according to the traveller in fertilizers, on other areas of her. Buttocks and stomach were vast; Hail Marys were repeated after sinning.

In the overnight room Justin imagined without pleasure the scenes Fahy described. Fahy was a little runt of a Dublin man, married with five or six children, always sticking his elbow into you to make a point. Sometimes in his ramblings he mentioned Thomasina Durcan, the dentist, who was the only other lodger in Mrs Keane's house. She had a great notion of Justin, Fahy insisted, the implication being that Justin could easily arrive at the same arrangement with Thomasina Durcan as he himself had arrived at with Mrs Keane. No man was an island was a repeated observation of Fahy's.

Justin rose in order to break his train of thought, and crossed to the window. He drew back the curtains and stood in his pyjamas looking out at the line of houses across the street. No blind had yet been released, no curtain or shutter opened. A cat crept along the grey pavement, interested in the empty bottles outside each door. The houses themselves were colour-washed in pink or cream, in yellow, grey or blue, their hall doors painted in some contrasting shade, or grained. The street was wide, with lamp-posts between every second house, and a single visible telegraph pole. Just visible also, where the street met another as it curved away to the left, was Hayes's shop, which traded in newspapers, tobacco and confectionery. The sight of it, with its hanging *Players Please* sign, reminded Justin that he was in need of a cigarette himself. He left the window and crossed to the bedside table.

Inhaling, he slipped out of his pyjamas and dressed himself in shirt and trousers, preparatory to making his way to Mrs Keane's bathroom. Still intent on keeping Fahy's reports and innuendoes at bay, he dwelt upon his earliest memory, which was the leg of a chair. That same chair was still in the house in Terenure and he often found himself looking at it, his eye travelling down one particular leg, to the rings cut into the timber, the varnish worn partially away. With three brothers and three sisters, he had grown up the baby of the family, surrounded by people who shouted more than he did, who were for ever arguing and snatching. At school the textbooks were inkstained and dirty, the blackboards so pitted you could hardly read the chalk marks on them, the desk-tops slashed with messages and initials. 'Come here and I'll show you,' Shay McNamara used to whisper; and forcibly he'd insist, no choice about it, on displaying the promise of his sexuality. Ikey Breen had been paid a threepenny piece by a woman under cover of darkness in the Stella cinema. All Riordan's jokes had to do with excrement.

Justin shaved in Mrs Keane's bathroom, hurrying to finish before Garda Bevan came rattling at the door. Long before he began to go to school he remembered his father driving away from the house in Terenure on a Monday morning. His father had taught him how to strike a match, and would let him hold it over the tobacco in his pipe while he sucked at the smoke, making a bubbling noise. His father used to take him on to his knee and ask him if he'd been a good boy, but Justin always had to turn his head away because of the whiff on his father's breath. The stench of stout, his mother said it was, bottle after bottle of stout that made the whole house stink like a brewery. He associated his father particularly with Sundays, with leading the family into Mass, with saying he was starving on the walk home. Sunday dinner was different from ordinary dinner, always meat and a pudding. Afterwards his father had his bath, with the door of the bathroom open so that he could listen to whatever sporting commentary there was on the radio. Justin's sisters were forbidden to go upstairs at this time in case they'd catch a glimpse from the landing. His brothers roller-skated in the yard.

Justin washed the remains of the shaving foam from his face. It was on a Sunday that his Aunt Roche had first put a record on her gramophone: John Count McCormack singing 'The Rose of Tralee'. After that he had begun to visit her sitting-room regularly, a room full of ferns in pots and framed embroideries. It was she and Father Finn who had given him faith in himself and in his musical aptitude, who hadn't laughed when he'd hinted that Mahler was his hero.

He dried his face and left the bathroom. Somewhere in the house he could hear the heavy tread of Garda Bevan. The smell of frying rashers and the chatty voice of a radio disc-jockey drifted from the kitchen.

'Mr Condon!' called Thomasina Durcan. 'Mr Condon, Mrs Keane has the breakfast ready.'

In her tiny sitting-room she dusted the ornaments on the mantelpiece: the brass gondola, the tuskless elephants, the row of trinket containers, the framed photograph of Justin as a child, specially taken by Mr Boland the insurance man, whose hobby was photography. She was not really his aunt: when he was six he had stood by the railings of her front garden, staring at her while she cut the grass. 'What's your name?' she'd asked, and he'd said it was Justin Condon. 'Ah now, isn't that a great name?' She'd smiled at him, knowing he was shy. Her face had been damp with perspiration due to the exertion of pushing the lawn-mower. He had watched her closely while she took her glasses off and wiped them on her apron.

She was a slight, frail woman of seventy-nine, with thin hands, and hair the colour of the ashes she now carried in a cardboard box from her sitting-room. She moved slowly, suffering a little from arthritis in one of her knees and in her arms. 'I think I have some Mi-Wadi,' she'd said that first day. 'D'you like Mi-Wadi lemonade, Justin?'

He had followed her into the house and in the kitchen she had poured an inch or two of Mi-Wadi into two glasses and filled them with water from the cold tap. She'd found some biscuits, raspberry wafers she'd bought for the weekend. He had three brothers and three sisters, he said; his father was in business and was never at home during the week. When he was older he told her about the Christian Brothers' school, the white-painted windows and the rowdy, concrete playground. He said that Brother Walsh had picked him out as someone who was useless.

The Sunday when she'd wound up the gramophone and put on the record of John Count McCormack was a special memory for her because she always thought of the occasion as marking the beginning of his interest in music. Later she had played him her selected arias from *La Traviata* and *Carmen* and *Il Trovatore* – on the same Sunday in September when he had posed for Mr Boland in the garden. He'd had to stand in front of the laurel bushes but Mr Boland hadn't been happy with that so he'd had to sit on a chair on the front-door step. In the end the photograph had been taken against the rose trellis.

'Well, that's disgraceful!' Father Finn had said on another Sunday, when he heard how a Christian Brother had described the child as useless.

'That's a right bit of bacon,' Garda Bevan complimented Mrs Keane. 'Isn't bacon in this country a greatly improved commodity?'

Neat as a napkin across the table from him, Thomasina Durcan smiled shyly at Justin, as if they shared some private opinion. Justin pretended not to notice. He bent his head over the bacon on his plate, over the slices of black pudding and the fried bread and the egg. Garda Bevan would think Stravinsky was the name of a racehorse, and so would Mrs Keane. 'Ah, sure, I knew all right,' Thomasina Durcan would protest, lying because she couldn't help herself. Her two prominent front teeth were like an advertisement for her trade; her eyes were prominent also, her nose and chin slight. She wore clothes in pastel shades, pale blues and pinks and greens. Like himself, she returned every weekend to Dublin, to stay with her parents.

'It's a sign of the advance the country has made,' continued Garda Bevan, 'the way the bacon is better these days.'

'The price of it would murder you,' Mrs Keane reminded him.

He nodded and continued to nod, dwelling on that. 'Well, isn't it another sign in that case,' he suggested eventually, 'the way the people would have the means for it?'

'Nearly a pound a pound. Sure, it's a holy disgrace.'

Mrs Keane's dining-room was heavy with furniture: rexine-covered chairs, a large ornate sideboard, a great mahogany dining-table, wax fruit on occasional tables, armchairs with antimacassars, pictures of forest scenes. Bottles of sauce stood on the sideboard, and empty decanters, and a pile of tablemats. Shells decorated the mantelpiece, and small cups and saucers, gifts from Tramore and Youghal.

'Well, it's the same way that's in it with everything.' The policeman's delivery of this statement was ponderous, the words punctuated by the munching of his jaws. He was a match for Mrs Keane in size, his rounded hill of a stomach tightly engaging the buttons of his waistcoat. A bulbous nose was set carelessly in a crimson countenance, short hair was as spiky as a hedgehog's.

'Wouldn't you say the prices is shocking?' Mrs Keane inquired of Thomasina Durcan, in a voice that insisted women knew best.

'Ah, they are of course.'

Garda Bevan turned to Justin, a piece of egg, already dipped in mustard, on the end of his fork. 'Have they inflation beat? Fahy was here last week and said inflation was beat.'

Justin shook his head. He didn't know, he said. He'd heard somewhere that, far from being defeated, inflation was gaining ground.

'Has your father a word to say on it? I remember a thing about your father when he used to stay with us here. He had a keen sense of politics.'

'I don't think I heard him mention inflation.'

'Give him a message from me, will you? Tell him Garda Bevan was asking for him.'

'I will of course.'

'Oh, Mr Condon, I meant to tell you: I saw you in Stephen's Green on Sunday.' Thomasina Durcan's two large teeth announced interest in him; the eyes blinked rapidly. Her pastel-green suit was trim on her trim form; he imagined her fingers, trim also, in a patient's mouth.

'I'm often in Stephen's Green.'

'I thought you lived in Terenure, Mr Condon.'

'I walk into the city.'

'God, I love walking.'

The fingers, in a hurry, would layer a gum with cotton-wool; sharply, they'd jab a hypodermic needle home. She'd talk to you when your mouth was full of implements; she'd tell you to have a wash-out with the pink stuff, and say she was nearly finished. Fahy said she had an eye on a bungalow out on the Cappoquin road. 'Wouldn't the two of you be snug in a bed there?' Fahy had said.

'I have a few friends coming in, Saturday fortnight. Would you care to join us, Mr Condon?'

He felt a tightening in the atmosphere. Both Garda Bevan and Mrs Keane were aware of the implication of what had just been said. An attempt was being made to develop the casual acquaintanceship that existed between Justin and the dentist in Mrs Keane's house; the relationship was to be extended to Dublin. Fahy would be told; so would Father Grennan and Father Reedy. 'Sure, if some girl like Thomasina Durcan doesn't do something about it that fellow'll be a bachelor at seventy': he could hear Mrs Keane saying that, or his father or his mother. Fahy would put it differently.

'Saturday fortnight?'

'About a quarter to eight. You know Clontarf? 21 Dunlow Road. Just a few friends and a bit of dancing.'

'I don't dance at all.'

'I'm not much at it myself.'

Garda Bevan and Mrs Keane were pleased. They had enjoyed this flutter of excitement. They would think about the party at 21 Dunlow Road, and discuss it. They would be unpleasantly agog after it had taken place.

'21 Dunlow Road,' Thomasina Durcan repeated, writing it clearly on a piece of paper she'd found in her handbag.

'You might ask him that,' requested Garda Bevan. 'Does he consider inflation beat? If there's one man in Ireland would know, it's your father.'

Justin nodded again, finishing the fried food on his plate. He promised to discuss the matter with his father and to obtain his father's opinion. He wouldn't turn up at 21 Dunlow Road, he said to himself. When he next spent a night at Mrs Keane's he'd say he'd lost the address.

When he was ten she had asked him if he'd like to learn how to play the piano and when he'd said yes she'd arranged for Father Finn to give him lessons in her sitting-room. She had paid for them and when she'd asked him not to tell his family he had eagerly agreed because apparently his family would have laughed at the idea of a boy playing a musical instrument. 'It's a great thing for him,' Father Finn later reported. 'And hasn't he a rare aptitude for it?' In the circumstances Father Finn wasn't averse to keeping the knowledge of the lessons from the Condons, and after a while he refused to accept any fee for the tuition. 'Well, that's one thing at any rate he's not useless at,' he remarked, later still.

God had arranged it, she often thought during those years that went by. God had arranged for the child to come by her gate that first afternoon, and for the music she played him on her gramophone to delight him. God had arranged a way for the three of them, Father Finn and herself and Justin. When the Condons had eventually discovered about the piano lessons they'd been bewildered but not cross, mainly because it was Father Finn who was giving them. And as well as for the lessons every Wednesday, Father Finn began to come round on Sunday afternoons, when they all three listened to John Count McCormack or the operatic arias. It was a natural thing for the priest to do since everyone knew now of the musical aptitude of Justin Condon and how it needed to be fostered and encouraged.

The sun warmed his exposed chest; beside him his shirt was laid out on the grass; his eyes were closed. Faintly the sound of the river by which he lay penetrated his sleep.

He dreamed of the queen who had inspired the choral symphony he was attempting to write. In his dream she led wolfhounds on leather thongs through her garden and listened to the spirits of the otherworld. From among them one took visible form: a young girl rose from the mists and the flowers and warned the queen of her folly.

Two flies tormented Justin's plump chin. Their tickling silenced music that had the resonance of music composed by Mahler. He smacked at his face but already the flies had gone.

The symphony told of a journey from the royal palaces in the West to the territory of Cúchulainn in Ulster. The queen's great army, fattened with the soldiers of her allies, with the long line of camp followers, with druids and jesters, storytellers, soothsayers, military men and servitors, travelled into heroic battle, while the mystical hero awaited their arrival. Sometimes, on Saturdays, Justin hired a piano cubicle in a music shop and spent the morning there, advancing his composition. Shortly after the death of Father Finn the piano in his Aunt Roche's sitting-room had gone hopelessly out of tune and apparently couldn't be much improved.

Justin reached for his shirt. When he had buttoned it he neatly tightened the knot of his tie. Since breakfast-time in Mrs Keane's dining-room he had visited sixteen drapers in seven different towns. He had O'Leary's and Callaghan's to call on yet, and then that would be that for the day. He drove on and did the business he had to do. He spent the night in Dungarvan in a room above a fish-and-chip café. The smell of the frying wafted up and through his open window. From his bed he listened to people talking about the film they had been to, and to a drunk man who proclaimed that he intended to stand no nonsense from his wife. He fell asleep at half past eleven and dreamed of the journey in his symphony, of the queen in her magnificence, and the chorus of otherworld spirits.

'Wait now till I get the brother,' said Mr McGurk, the joint proprietor of McGurk's Arcade, the following day. He left the shop and called up through the house. In a moment the older Mr McGurk appeared.

Justin's samples were laid out on the counter. Some were familiar to the McGurks and presented no problem when it came to deciding the size of the order. Others, lines that were new this spring, had to be considered with care.

'Would a woman of this area dress herself in that?' inquired the younger Mr McGurk, poking at a black garment trimmed flimsily with lace of the same colour.

'I don't know would she.'

'The gusset is strong,' Justin pointed out, since it said so on his sales sheet. 'A man-made fibre.'

'It isn't the gusset would sell that article,' replied the older Mr McGurk. 'What I'm thinking is, is it too ritzy for this area?'

'Will we call down Elaine?' suggested his brother.

'I'd say we would.'

Elaine, wife of the older Mr McGurk, was summoned from the house. She picked up the garment in question and meticulously examined it.

'Would you wear it?' her husband demanded.

'I would in a shade of peach. Does it come in a peach?'

Justin said it did, and in a shade of coffee.

'Order it in the peach,' advised Mrs McGurk. 'Black's not the tone for stuff the like of that.'

'Too ritzy,' agreed her husband. 'I'm just after saying it.'

'How's your father?' Mrs McGurk asked Justin.

'He's grand.'

'Has he still got the hilarious way with him?'

Justin replied that he supposed his father had. One after the other, the McGurk brothers said they'd never laughed at any traveller's jokes the way they'd laughed at Justin's father's. Justin could feel them thinking that he himself wasn't half the man his father was, that he didn't enter into the spirit of things, that all he seemed concerned with was writing down orders in his book. 'I'll tell you a thing about Thomasina Durcan,' Fahy had said. 'She has a notion of making a man of you. There's women like that around.'

He left the McGurks' shop and drove out to the estuary. He walked by the green, seaweedy water, wondering if Mahler would have composed a note if he'd been incarcerated in a bungalow on the Cappoquin road, listening every night to talk about cavity linings.

'Now, there never was,' she remembered Father Finn saying when Justin was thirteen, 'a great man of music that came out of Ireland.'

He made the pronouncement while eating a slice of buttered toast she had prepared for him. She had loved doing that, toasting the bread and spreading the butter on it, arranging blackcurrant jam in a glass dish. Blackcurrant was Father Finn's favourite, raspberry was Justin's.

'We had singers and harpists. We had all classes of instrumentalists. We have a proud tradition, but we never yet had a composer that could rank with the Germans. To this day, Justin, we have to turn to Germany for musical composition.'

Pouring tea for both of them, she mentioned Italy and the priest agreed that the Italians had made a contribution. He told the story of Puccini's life. He referred to the burden of a musical gift and to the reward it brought in time. 'A precious freedom of the spirit. A most glorious thing.'

She had delighted in listening to him. She was never happier than on those Sunday afternoons when he and Justin sat together by her fire or on the Wednesdays when she made a cup of tea after the piano lesson. No admission of affection had ever been made by the priest or by herself; no admission could be. Until Justin arrived in her life there had been no way of creating a relationship that went beyond that of priest and parishioner.

'There's a little thing Justin composed for me,' Father Finn said one Sunday. 'A short little piece, but I'd say it displayed promise.'

'We had a complaint, Mr Condon,' Miss Murphy reported in Castlemartyr. 'We had this slip brought back to us after it fell into holes.'

Only Thomasina Durcan and Miss Murphy called him Mr Condon, Thomasina Durcan because any other mode of address might have sounded forward, Miss Murphy for reasons he had never been able to fathom.

'Would it be the way it was washed, Miss Murphy? Was it put into a machine?'

'Oh, it would have been washed all right, Mr Condon. Naturally you'd expect it to have been washed.'

'No, I mean in a machine though. Or maybe it got boiled in error. It's all tinged with blue, look. Some blue garment has run into it.'

'It would save an argument with the customer, Mr Condon, if you replaced it. It's good for business when something gets replaced.'

Justin made a note in his order book and said that Miss Murphy would have a replacement within a fortnight. He had a new line he wanted to show her, he added, and displayed for her the sample he had displayed for fifty-seven other drapers, including the McGurks, since he'd left Dublin. Miss Murphy picked it up gingerly.

'It comes in a peach, Miss Murphy, and a coffee. The gusset is guaranteed sturdy. Man-made fibre.'

'I never saw that type of cut before.'

'It's the fashion in Dublin.'

Miss Murphy shook her head. She folded the piece of clothing in a professional manner and Justin returned it to the suitcase in which he carried his samples. Miss Murphy ordered a supply of summer vests and made arrangements to replenish her stock of first-communion stockings. 'Is your father fit?' she asked as Justin closed his order book, and for the first time since he had known Miss Murphy it idly occurred to him that she and his father might have had the same relationship as Fahy claimed to have with Mrs Keane. Miss Murphy was elderly now, a woman with a face like an arrow, with spectacles on a chain. Once she might have been pretty; it was odd that she had never married.

'He's grand,' Justin said.

'Remember me to him, will you?'

Her tone was different from Garda Bevan's when he mentioned Justin's father, different from the McGurks' and all the other drapers'. Had there always been a hint of bitterness in Miss Murphy's voice when she sent this message to his father? He looked up from the suitcase he was fastening and found her eyes upon him. They held his own until he felt embarrassed. He had noticed before that there was a similarity between his father and Fahy. They were both small men, rotund, bald-headed, pink-skinned, given to banter. He snapped the clasps on his suitcase and Miss Murphy turned away to attend another customer.

She made a cake, the banana cake he liked. Usually she wrapped in tin-foil what remained of it after their Sunday tea and he took it away to eat during the week, on his travels. She enjoyed thinking of him eating the cake, sitting out in the sunshine as he liked to do, in some quiet place.

Slowly she chopped up two bananas. He had belonged to them as he never had to his parents. On Sunday afternoons and again on Wednesdays they had been a family. She left the kitchen and in her sitting-room she delicately placed the needle on the same worn record of John Count McCormack singing 'The Rose of Tralee'. Soon she would die, as the old priest had, six months ago. She would fall down, or she would die in her sleep. And before any of it happened she might become muzzy in her thoughts, unable to explain to Justin Condon and properly to ask for his forgiveness. Father Finn had known also in the end, death banishing his illusions. 'We did a terrible thing,' the old priest had said, sending for her specially.

The record came to an end and she sat there for a moment longer, listening to the scratchy sound of the needle. She had once, long before the child had come into her life, tried to become Father Finn's housekeeper. 'Ah no, no,' he had murmured, gently rejecting her because it wouldn't have done.

'And how were things in West Waterford?' his father inquired. 'Has Joe Bolger retired from Merrick's?'

Glistening, as if he had just scrubbed his face with a nailbrush, Mr Condon held a glass of whiskey in his right hand. As well as his face, the backs of his hands glistened, as did his glasses, his even false teeth, the dome of his hairless head. Justin imagined him with Miss Murphy in her shop, telling a joke, driving out into the country with Miss Murphy when it was dark, the way Fahy said he'd had to with some woman in Claremorris before he got going with Mrs Keane.

'I didn't see Joe Bolger,' Justin said. 'I think maybe he's retired.'

'I always liked West Waterford.'

They were in the sitting-room. His father was standing in front of a coal fire that was too hot for the time of year. In the kitchen Justin's mother was frying their evening meal. Recently Mr Condon had taken to giving himself a glass of whiskey at a quarter to six in the evening instead of making his usual journey to McCauley's at the corner. When he'd eaten his food he returned to the sitting-room and occupied the chair nearest the television, pouring himself another glass of whiskey at a quarter past seven. Justin's mother said the whiskey was bad for him but he said it was doctor's orders. 'It's ready for you,' she shouted from the kitchen, reminding Justin of Thomasina Durcan calling out in Mrs Keane's that the breakfast was ready.

'I could eat an elephant,' said Mr Condon, swallowing the last of his whiskey.

Between them, his brothers and sisters had brought thirty-seven children into existence: Justin often thought of that. At Christmas they all crowded into the house, shouting and quarrelling and reminding Justin of what the house had been like in his childhood. On Saturdays there were visits from one or another of those families, and on Sundays also.

'There was a time I was below in Dungarvan,' Mr Condon recalled in the kitchen, 'the day Golden Miller won at Fairyhouse. Joe Bolger was footless behind the counter.'

Mrs Condon cut slices of loaf bread, and pushed the butter past her husband in Justin's direction. Mr Condon had never been known to pass anyone anything.

'God, you'd have died laughing.' As if to lend greater verisimilitude to this claim, Mr Condon laughed rumbustiously himself, exposing egg and bread partially chewed. 'He was handing out skeins of wool and not charging for it. He gave a gross of safety-pins to a farmer's wife by the name of Mrs Quinn. "Sure, aren't they always handy," he said, "in case you'd have something falling down?"'

Mrs Condon, who did not always care for her husband's humour, asked what the weather had been like down the country. Justin replied that it had been fine.

'There was another time,' Mr Condon went on, 'when the boys in the digs took poor Joe's clothes when he was asleep in bed. I didn't see it myself but didn't he have to descend the stairs with the sheets on him?'

'It rained on Wednesday,' Mrs Condon said. 'It didn't cease the whole day.'

'There wasn't a drop down the country.'

'Well, isn't that strange?'

'It's often that way.'

'They say it's settled in Dublin for the weekend.'

Mrs Condon was as thin as his Aunt Roche, with a worried look that Justin couldn't remember her ever having been without. She wore flowered overalls even when she went shopping, beneath her black coat.

'The wildest lads in West Waterford was in Joe Bolger's digs,' continued Mr Condon. 'There wasn't a trick they didn't have knowledge of.'

Justin, who had heard about these exploits in West Waterford before, nodded. Mrs Condon poured more tea.

'They went into the Bay Hotel one night when a pile of boxes containing young chicks had just come off the bus. Your men had them released in the hall before anyone could lift a hand. They had them flying up and down the stairs and into the dining-room, knocking down the sauce bottles. The next thing is, didn't they have them fluttering about the bedrooms?'

'You told us, Ger,' Mrs Condon said.

'I did of course. Didn't I come back that Friday and go through the whole thing? It could kill you stone dead to wake up in your bedroom and find chickens squawking all over you.'

'It must have been unpleasant certainly.'

'Well, that's West Waterford for you. Are you still telling that story, Justin?'

Justin nodded again. He wouldn't have known how to begin telling such a story, and he had never attempted to. He thought about the symphony, hearing the theme that the queen and her consort in their palace bed had inspired. A slow movement, lyrical in tone.

'Is that girl still stopping at Mrs Keane's?' his mother inquired. 'The dentist.'

He'd once mentioned Thomasina Durcan in order to fill a gap in some conversation; he wished he hadn't because his mother had somehow sensed his apprehension and appeared to have mistaken it for interest.

'Yes, she's still there.'

'Sounds a nice type of girl.'

Fortunately, Mr Condon had begun to laugh in anticipation of some further antics on the part of the lodgers in Joe Bolger's digs. When his laughter ceased he retailed them, as he had many times done in the past. Obediently Justin and his mother laughed in turn.

'There was a curate from Milecross,' Mr Condon said, 'a Father Dolan. Well, the lads in the digs had him tied in knots.'

'You told us about Father Dolan, Ger.'

'He was down at his tea and when he went upstairs there wasn't a stick of furniture left in the room. They had the bed and the wardrobe carried out, and the pictures off the walls. They took the wash-stand, and the Holy Mother off of the mantelpiece. The poor man thought he'd gone insane.'

The music was different now: brassy and wild as the journey across Ireland began. While it echoed, Justin saw for a moment his favourite picture of James Joyce, in the broad-brimmed hat and the long black coat. He wondered what Mahler had been like.

'Another time those eejits drew a sideboard across the entrance to the Gents, the day of Slip Hennessy's wedding. There wasn't a man in the place knew what to do with himself.' Mr Condon threw his head back and laughed, permitting his teeth to move about in his open mouth. When he'd finished, Mrs Condon said:

'Didn't you say the dentist was a Dublin girl?'

'I think she is.'

'It's nice she's at Mrs Keane's.'

He did not reply. His father said again that you'd have died laughing, and his mother rose from the table. Justin began to gather up the dishes, resolving that tomorrow he would spend the morning in the piano cubicle of the music shop. Afterwards he'd walk out to Herbert Park and lie in the sun, with a new bit of music lingering the way it always did.

On Sunday afternoon he told her about his time in West Waterford and East Cork, about the McGurk brothers and all the other drapers he had visited. He mentioned Garda Bevan and Mrs Keane and Miss Murphy. He spoke of Thomasina Durcan's party at 21 Dunlow Road, but he didn't go into details and he didn't retail what had passed through his mind concerning any of these people. He'd spent four hours yesterday in the piano cubicle, he said, and he'd lain down in Herbert Park.

'It's nice to get the sun,' she said, offering him a piece of the banana cake.

'Sure, we don't get enough of it.'

She nodded and then, to his astonishment, she spoke of his simplicity. It was that, she said, that the priest and she should have pointed out to him; it was that that was notable.

He sipped his tea, wondering if she was rambling in her elderliness. She never had done so before, she'd always been as sharp as a needle.

'Simplicity?' he said. 'Are you feeling yourself?'

'Father Finn liked to come here on a Sunday. He liked it particularly and I liked it myself. With the piano lessons on a Wednesday it was the same.'

He frowned, then nodded. He'd watched the tennis-players in Herbert Park, he said, after it had become too chilly to go on lying on the grass. It would be a long time yet, he said, before the symphony was complete; there'd be years in the piano cubicle and years lying out in the sun, letting the music run through his head. It was no good being in a hurry; you knew instinctively the pace that suited you.

'You were like a child to us all those years, Justin.'

'Ah, sure, it was enjoyable all round.'

He reached for another slice of cake. His teacup was empty and he wondered why she didn't fill it. He looked at her closely and saw that she had begun to weep, something she had never done in his presence before.

'My father was telling us last night,' he said, 'about a time some lads let a crate of chickens loose in the Bay Hotel, Dungarvan.'

He spoke in desperation: he wanted to stop her talking about Father Finn and about his own simplicity, how he'd been a child to them all those years. Her voice had a peculiar note in it.

'It's gone now,' he said, 'the old Bay Hotel.'

He knew she had no interest in a hotel she'd never seen nor heard of before; why should she have? Yet he went on talking about it, about the barricading of the Gents at the time of Slip Hennessy's wedding, and the removal of the furniture from Father Dolan's bedroom while he was having his tea. He spoke hurriedly, his words tumbling and juddering. Urgently they rushed from him, preventing her from speaking. But when he paused for breath she said:

'We damaged you between us, Justin. We took advantage of your simplicity.'

'Ah no, no.'

Again he spoke swiftly, endeavouring to convey through his agitation that he did not want to hear; that once she had spoken, the words could not be undone. For a long time now he had known he could play the piano in a tidy, racy way, that possibly he possessed no greater gift. It was his longing to walk away from his Ford Fiesta, from his parents' house and from Ireland, that made him different from his father, not his modest musical aptitude. And yet his fantasy sprang from a lingering sliver of hope, from words that had once been spoken in his Aunt Roche's sitting-room. He had clutched at the straw they had offered him and it had kept him going. He had played his part, not knowing what it was, offering them a straw also: for the first time, he realized that.

'Father Finn couldn't die guilty,' she said. 'No more than I can. He asked me to tell you the truth before he went, Justin, and I have to do that. No harm or damage was ever intended.'

Justin put down his teacup and saucer on a round, glass-topped table as familiar to him as any piece of furniture in his parents' house. She was right to have mentioned his simplicity: she might as easily have called him a fool. He felt ashamed of being in the room with her since she knew so much about his foolishness; she might even have guessed that he had seen himself in the broad-brimmed hat and the long black overcoat, or on an island with Gauguin's dark-skinned girls.

'I'd have deprived you of the piano and the gramophone if I'd sent you away.'

He stared at her. She should have sent him away all the same, she said, she should have sent him off to play with other children; and in time she should have urged him to embark on a friendship with a girl.

He stood up. 'That's a nice little piece you composed for me,' Father Finn had said, and he saw again the priest's face as he spoke those words, seeing it differently now. He saw his Aunt Roche's differently also, with anxiety twitching in it as the priest murmured his praise and his encouragement, both of them fearful for the safety of their Wednesday and Sunday afternoons.

'Don't go, Justin. Don't go.'

But there was no point in staying, any more than there was a point in saying he would end by marrying Thomasina Durcan. His Aunt Roche, who had seemed to understand so much, wouldn't understand that such things happened when you had nothing to keep you going. He had thought the world of her, just as he had of Father Finn, but she wouldn't understand if he said that in time he would acquire his father's bonhomie, even his popularity with the drapers of the provinces. A woman like Miss Murphy might enter his life, or a woman like Mrs Keane.

He did not look again at the frail presence in the room he had come to know so well. She cried out at him, only repeating that she'd had to tell the truth, that the truth was more important than anything. She caught at the sleeve of his jacket, begging him to forgive her for the past. He pushed her hand away, and swore at her before he went.

Events at Drimaghleen

Nothing as appalling had happened before at Drimaghleen; its people had never been as shocked. They'd had their share of distress, like any people; there were memories of dramatic occurrences; stories from a more distant past were told. In the 1880s a woman known as the Captain's wife had run away with a hunchbacked pedlar. In 1798 there'd been resistance in the hills and fighting in Drimaghleen itself. During the Troubles a local man had been executed in a field by the Black and Tans. But no story, and no long memory, could match the horror of the tragedy that awaited the people of Drimaghleen on 22 May 1985, a Wednesday morning.

The McDowds, that morning, awoke in their farmhouse and began the day as they always did, McDowd pulling on his shirt and trousers and lifting down a black overcoat from the pegs beside the kitchen door. He fastened it with a length of string which he kept in one of its pockets, found his socks in his gum-boots and went out with his two sheepdogs to drive the cows in for milking. His wife washed herself, put the kettle on the stove, and knocked on her daughter's door. 'Maureen!' she called. 'Come on now, Maureen!'

It was not unusual that Maureen failed to reply. Mrs McDowd re-entered her bedroom and dressed herself. 'Get up out of that, Maureen!' she shouted, banging again on her daughter's door. 'Are you sick?' she inquired, puzzled now by the lack of movement from within the room: always at this second rousing Maureen yawned or spoke. 'Maureen!' she shouted again, and then opened the door.

McDowd, calling in the cattle, was aware that there had been something wrong in the yard as he'd passed through it, but an early-morning torpor hindered the progression of his thoughts when he endeavoured to establish what it was. His wife's voice shouting across the field at him, and his daughter's name used repeatedly in the information that was being inadequately conveyed to him, jolted him into an awareness that what had been wrong was that Maureen's bicycle had not been leaning against the kitchen window-sill. 'Maureen hasn't come back,' his wife repeated again when he was close enough to hear her. 'She's not been in her bed.'

The cows were milked because no matter what the reason for Maureen's absence they had to be. The breakfast was placed on the kitchen table because no good would come of not taking food. McDowd, in silence, ate with an appetite that was unaffected; his wife consumed less than usual. 'We will drive over,' he said when they had finished, anger thickening his voice.

She nodded. She'd known as soon as she'd seen the unused bed that they would have to do something. They could not just wait for a letter to arrive, or a telegram, or whatever it was their daughter had planned. They would drive over to the house where Lancy Butler lived with his mother, the house to which their daughter had cycled the evening before. They did not share the thought that possessed both of them: that their daughter had taken the law into her own hands and gone off with Lancy Butler, a spoilt and useless man.

McDowd was a tallish, spare man of sixty-two, his face almost gaunt, grey hair ragged on his head. His wife, two years younger, was thin also, with gnarled features and the hands of a woman who all her life had worked in the fields. They did not say much to one another, and never had; but they did not quarrel either. On the farm, discussion was rarely apt, there being no profit in it; it followed naturally that grounds for disagreement were limited. Five children had been born to the McDowds; Maureen was the youngest and the only one who had remained at home. Without a show of celebration, for that was not the family way, her twenty-fifth birthday had passed by a month ago.

'Put your decent trousers on,' Mrs McDowd urged. 'You can't go like that.'

'I'm all right the way I am.'

She knew he would not be persuaded and did not try, but instead hurried back to her bedroom to change her shoes. At least he wouldn't drive over in the overcoat with the string round it: that was only for getting the cows in from the field when the mornings were cold. He'd taken it off before he'd sat down to his breakfast and there would be no cause to put it on again. She covered up her own old skirt and jumper with her waterproof.

'The little bitch,' he said in the car, and she said nothing.

They both felt the same, anxious and cross at the same time, not wanting to believe the apparent truth. Their daughter had ungratefully deceived them: again in silence the thought was shared while he drove the four miles to the Butlers' house. When they turned off the tarred road into a lane, already passing between the Butlers' fields, they heard the dog barking. The window of the Volkswagen on Mrs McDowd's side wouldn't wind up, due to a defect that had developed a month ago: the shrill barking easily carried above the rattle of the engine.

That was that, they thought, listening to the dog. Maureen and Lancy
had gone the night before, and Mrs Butler couldn't manage the cows on
her own. No wonder the old dog was beside himself. Bitterly, McDowd
called his daughter a bitch again, though only to himself. Lancy Butler, he
thought, my God! Lancy Butler would lead her a dance, and lead her
astray, and lead her down into the gutters of some town. He'd warned her
a thousand times about Lancy Butler. He'd told her the kind of fool he
was.

'His father was a decent man,' he said, breaking at last the long silence.
'Never touched a drop.'

'The old mother ruined him.'

It wouldn't last long, they both thought. Lancy Butler might marry her,
or he might wriggle out of it. But however it turned out she'd be back in
six months' time or at any rate a year's. There'd probably be a baby to
bring up.

The car turned into the yard, and neither McDowd nor his wife immediately saw their daughter lying beside the pump. For the first few moments
of their arrival their attention was claimed by the distressed dog, a black-
and-white sheepdog like their own two. Dust had risen from beneath the
Volkswagen's wheels and was still thick in the air as they stepped from
the car. The dog was running wildly across a corner of the yard, back and
forth, and back and forth again. The dog's gone mad, Mrs McDowd
thought, something's after affecting it. Then she saw her daughter's body
lying by the pump, and a yard or so away her daughter's bicycle lying on
its side, as if she had fallen from it. Beside the bicycle were two dead
rabbits.

'My God,' McDowd said, and his wife knew from his voice that he
hadn't seen his daughter yet but was looking at something else. He had
walked to another part of the yard, where the dog was. He had gone there
instinctively, to try to calm the animal.

She knelt down, whispering to Maureen, thinking in her confusion that
her daughter had just this minute fallen off her bicycle. But Maureen's face
was as cold as stone, and her flesh had already stiffened. Mrs McDowd
screamed, and then she was aware that she was lying down herself, clasping
Maureen's dead body. A moment later she was aware that her husband
was weeping piteously, unable to control himself, that he was kneeling
down, his hands on the body also.

Mrs McDowd did not remember rising to her feet, or finding the energy
and the will to do so. 'Don't go over there,' she heard her husband saying
to her, and saw him wiping at his eyes with the arm of his jersey. But he
didn't try to stop her when she went to where the dog was; he remained

on his knees beside their daughter, calling out to her between his sobs, asking her not to be dead.

The dog was crouched in a doorway, not barking any more. A yard or so away Mrs Butler lay with one of her legs twisted under her, blood on the ground already turned brown, a pool of it still scarlet. Looking down at her, Mrs McDowd thought with abrupt lucidity: Maureen did not fall off her bicycle. She went back to where her daughter lay and behind the two tin barrels that stood by the pump she saw the body of Lancy Butler, and on the ground not far from it the shotgun that must have blown off Mrs Butler's face.

O'Kelly of the Garda arrived at a swift conclusion. Old Mrs Butler had been as adamant as the McDowds in her opposition to the match that her son and Maureen McDowd had planned for themselves. And there was more to it than that: Mrs Butler had been obsessively possessive, hiding from no one her determination that no other woman should ever take her son away from her. Lancy was her only child, the single one to survive years of miscarrying. His father had died when Lancy was two years old, leaving mother and child to lead a lonely life on a farm that was remote. O'Kelly knew that Mrs Butler had been reputed to be strange in the head, and given to furious jealousies where Lancy was concerned. In the kind of rage that people who'd known her were familiar with she had shot her son's sweetheart rather than suffer the theft of him. He had wrenched the shotgun from her and by accident or otherwise it had exploded. A weak man at the best of times, he had turned it upon himself rather than face the reality of what had happened. This deduction, borne out by the details in the yard, satisfied O'Kelly of the Garda; the people of Drimaghleen arrived themselves at the same conclusion. 'It was always trouble,' McDowd said on the day of the funerals. 'The minute she went out with Lancy Butler it was trouble written down for poor Maureen.'

Drimaghleen was a townland, with nothing to mark it except a crossroads that was known as Drimaghleen Crossroads. The modest farms that comprised it, each of thirty or so acres, were scattered among bogland, one separated from the next by several miles, as the McDowds' and the Butlers' were. The village of Kilmona was where the people of Drimaghleen went to Mass, and where they confessed to Father Sallins. The children of the farms went to school in the small town of Mountcroe, driven each morning in a yellow bus that drove them back to the end of their lanes or farm tracks in the afternoon. Milk churns were collected in much the same way by the creamery lorry. Bread and groceries were bought in the village; fresh meat in Mountcroe. When the men of Drimaghleen got drunk they did so in Mountcroe, never in the village, although often they took a few bottles of stout there, in the bar beside the grocery counter. Hardware and clothes were bought in Mountcroe, which had had a cinema called the Abbey Picture House until the advent of television closed it in the early 1960s. Drimaghleen, Kilmona and Mountcroe formed a world that bounded the lives of the people of the Drimaghleen farms. Rarely was there occasion to venture beyond it to the facilities of a town that was larger – unless the purpose happened to be a search for work or the first step on the way to exile.

The children of the McDowds, whose search for such work had taken them far from the townland, returned heartbroken for their sister's Mass. All four of them came, two with husbands, one with a wife, one on her own. The weddings which had taken place had been the last family occasions, two of them in Kilmona, the third in distant Skibbereen, the home of the girl whom the McDowds' son had married a year ago. That wedding was on their minds at Maureen's Mass – the long journey there had been in the Volkswagen, the night they had spent in Tierney's Hotel, the farewells the next day. Not in the wildest horror of a nightmare could any of the McDowds have guessed the nature of the occasion destined to bring them together next.

After the funeral the family returned to the farm. The younger McDowds had known of Maureen's and Lancy Butler's attachment, and of their parents' opposition to it. They had known as well of Mrs Butler's possessive affection for her son, having grown up with stories of this maternal eccentricity, and having witnessed Lancy himself, as a child and as a boy, affected by her indulgence. 'Oh, it can wait, Lancy, it can wait,' she would say a dozen times an hour, referring to some necessary chore on the farm. 'Ah, sure, we won't bother with school today,' she had said before that, when Lancy had complained of a difficulty he was experiencing with the seven-times table or Brother Martin's twenty weekend spellings. The people of Drimaghleen used to wonder whether the farm or Lancy would suffer more in the end.

'What did she see in him?' Mrs McDowd mused sadly at the funeral meal. 'Will anyone ever tell me what she saw in him?'

They shook their heads. The cheeks of all of them were still smeared with the tears they had shed at the service. Conversation was difficult.

'We will never recover from it,' the father said, with finality in his voice. It was all that could be said, it was all they knew with certainty: for as long as the older McDowds remained in this farmhouse – which would be until their own deaths – the vicious, ugly tragedy would haunt them. They knew that if Maureen had been knocked from her bicycle by a passing motor-car they could have borne her death with greater fortitude; or if she had died of an illness, or been the victim of incurable disease. The knife that turned in their pain was their memory of the Butlers' farmyard, the barking dog running back and forth, the three still bodies. There was nothing but the waste of a life to contemplate, and the cruelty of chance – for why should it have been simple, pretty Maureen whose fate it was to become mixed up with so peculiar a couple as that mother and son? There were other girls in the neighbourhood – underhand girls and girls of doubtful character – who somehow more readily belonged with the Butlers: anyone would tell you that.

'Why don't you drive over and see us?' one of the daughters invited. 'Can't we persuade you?'

Her father stared into the table without trying to reply. It was unnecessary to say that a drive of such a distance could only be contemplated when there was a wedding or a funeral. Such journeys had not been undertaken during Maureen's lifetime, when she might have looked after the farm for a day; in no way could they be considered now. Mrs McDowd tried to smile, making an effort to acknowledge the concern that had inspired the suggestion, but no smile came.

Being of a nature that might interest strangers, the deaths were reported in the newspapers. They were mentioned on the radio, and on the television news. Then everything became quiet again at Drimaghleen, and in the village and in the town. People wrote letters to the McDowds, expressing their sorrow. People came to see them but did not stay long. 'I am always there,' Father Sallins said. 'Kilmona 23. You have only to summon me. Or call up at the rectory.'

The McDowds didn't. They watched the summer going by, taking in their hay during the warm spell in June, keeping an eye on the field of potatoes and the ripening barley. It began to rain more than usual; they worried about the barley.

'Excuse me,' a man said in the yard one afternoon in October. 'Are you Mr McDowd?'

McDowd said he was, shouting at the dogs to behave themselves. The stranger would be a traveller in fertilizers, he said to himself, a replacement for Donoghue, who had been coming to the farm for years. Then he realized that it was the wrong time of year for Donoghue.

'Would it be possible to have a word, Mr McDowd?'

McDowd's scrawny features slowly puckered; slowly he frowned. He lifted a hand and scratched at his grey, ragged hair, which was a way he had when he wished to disguise bewilderment. Part of his countryman's wiliness was that he preferred outsiders not to know, or deduce, what was occurring in his mind.

'A word?' he said.

'Could we maybe step inside, sir?'

McDowd saw no reason to step inside his own house with this man. The visitor was florid-faced, untidily dressed in dark corduroy trousers and a gaberdine jacket. His hair was long and black, and grew coarsely down the sides of his face in two brushlike panels. He had a city voice; it wasn't difficult to guess he came from Dublin.

'What d'you want with me?'

'I was sorry to hear that thing about your daughter, Mr McDowd. That was a terrible business.'

'It's over and done with.'

'It is, sir. Over and done with.'

The red bonnet of a car edged its way into the yard. McDowd watched it, reminded of some cautious animal by the slow, creeping movement, the engine purring so lightly you could hardly hear it. When the car stopped by the milking shed nobody got out of it, but McDowd could see a figure wearing sunglasses at the wheel. This was a woman, with black hair also, smoking a cigarette.

'It could be to your advantage, Mr McDowd.'

'What could be? Does that car belong to you?'

'We drove down to see you, sir. That lady's a friend of mine, a colleague by the name of Hetty Fortune.'

The woman stepped out of the car. She was taller than the man, with a sombre face and blue trousers that matched her blue shirt. She dropped her cigarette on to the ground and carefully stubbed it out with the toe of her shoe. As slowly as she had driven the car she walked across the yard to where the two men were standing. The dogs growled at her, but she took no notice. 'I'm Hetty Fortune,' she said in an English accent.

'I didn't tell you my own name, Mr McDowd,' the man said. 'It's Jeremiah Tyler.'

'I hope Jeremiah has offered you our condolences, Mr McDowd. I hope both you and your wife will accept our deepest sympathy.'

'What do you want here?'

'We've been over at the Butlers' place, Mr McDowd. We spent a long time there. We've been talking to a few people. Could we talk to you, d'you think?'

'Are you the newspapers?'

'In a manner of speaking. Yes, in a manner of speaking we represent the media. And I'm perfectly sure,' the woman added hastily, 'you've had more than enough of all that. I believe you'll find what we have to say to you is different, Mr McDowd.'

'The wife and myself have nothing to say to the newspapers. We didn't say anything at the time, and we have nothing to say since. I have things to do about the place.'

'Mr McDowd, would you be good enough to give us five minutes of your time? Five minutes in your kitchen, talking to yourself and your wife? Would you give us an opportunity to explain?'

Attracted by the sound by voices, Mrs McDowd came out of the house. She stood in the doorway, not quite emerging from the kitchen porch, regarding the strangers even more distrustfully than her husband had. She didn't say anything when the woman approached her and held out a hand which she was obliged to shake.

'We are sorry to obtrude on your grief, Mrs McDowd. Mr Tyler and I have been keen to make that clear to your husband.'

Mrs McDowd did not acknowledge this. She didn't like the look of the sombre-faced woman or her unkempt companion. There was a seediness about him, a quality that city people seemed often to exude if they weren't smartly attired. The woman wasn't seedy but you could see she was insincere from the way her mouth was. You could hear the insincerity when she spoke.

'The full truth has not been established, Mrs McDowd. It is that we would like to discuss with you.'

'I've told you no,' McDowd said. 'I've told them to go away,' he said to his wife.

Mrs McDowd's eyes stared at the woman's sunglasses. She remained where she was, not quite coming into the yard. The man said:

'Would it break the ice if I took a snap? Would you mind that, sir? If I was to take a few snaps of yourself and the wife?'

He had spoken out of turn. A shadow of anger passed over the woman's face. The fingers of her left hand moved in an irritated wriggle. She said quickly:

'That's not necessary at this stage.'

'We've got to get the pictures, Hetty,' the man mumbled, hushing the words beneath his breath so that the McDowds wouldn't hear. But they guessed the nature of his protest, for it showed in his pink face. The woman snapped something at him.

'If you don't leave us alone we'll have to get the Guards,' McDowd said. 'You're trespassing on this land.'

'Is it fair on your daughter's memory that the truth should be hidden, Mr McDowd?'

'Another thing is, those dogs can be fierce if they want to be.'

'It isn't hidden,' Mrs McDowd said. 'We all know what happened. Detectives worked it out, but sure anyone could have told them.'

'No, Mrs McDowd, nothing was properly worked out at all. That's what I'm saying to you. The surface was scarcely disturbed. What seemed to be the truth wasn't.'

McDowd told his wife to lock the door. They would drive over to Mountcroe and get a Guard to come back with them. 'We don't want any truck with you,' he harshly informed their visitors. 'If the dogs eat the limbs off you after we've gone don't say it wasn't mentioned.'

Unmoved by these threats, her voice losing none of its confidence, the woman said that what was available was something in the region of three thousand pounds. 'For a conversation of brief duration you would naturally have to be correctly reimbursed. Already we have taken up your working time, and of course we're not happy about that. The photograph mentioned by Mr Tyler would naturally have the attachment of a fee. We're talking at the end of the day of something above a round three thousand.'

Afterwards the McDowds remembered that moment. They remembered the feeling they shared, that this was no kind of trick, that the money spoken of would be honestly paid. They remembered thinking that the sum was large, that they could do with thirty pounds never mind three thousand. Rain had destroyed the barley; they missed their daughter's help on the farm; the tragedy had aged and weakened them. If three thousand pounds could come out of it, they'd maybe think of selling up and buying a bungalow.

'Let them in,' McDowd said, and his wife led the way into the kitchen.

The scene of the mystery is repeated all over rural Ireland. From Cork to Cavan, from Roscommon to Rosslare you will come across small, tucked-away farms like the Butlers' and the McDowds'. Maureen McDowd had been gentle-natured and gentle-tempered. The sins of sloth and greed had not been hers; her parents called her a perfect daughter, close to a saint. A photograph, taken when Maureen McDowd was five, showed a smiling, freckled child; another showed her in her First Communion dress; a third, taken at the wedding of her brother, was of a healthy-looking girl, her face creased up in laughter, a cup of tea in her right hand. There was a photograph of her mother and father, standing in their kitchen. Italicized beneath it was the information that it had been taken by Jeremiah Tyler. *The Saint of Drimaghleen*, Hetty Fortune had written, *never once missed Mass in all her twenty-five years.*

The story was told in fashionably faded pictures. 'You know our Sunday supplement?' Hetty Fortune had said in the McDowds' kitchen, but they hadn't: newspapers from England had never played a part in their lives. They read the *Sunday Independent* themselves.

The Butlers' yard was brownly bleak in the pages of the supplement; the pump had acquired a quality not ordinarily noticed. A bicycle similar to Maureen's had been placed on the ground, a sheepdog similar to the Butlers' nosed about the doors of the cowshed. But the absence of the three bodies in the photographed yard, the dust still rising where the bicycle had fallen, the sniffing dog, lent the composition an eerie quality – horror conveyed without horror's presence. 'You used a local man?' the supplement's assistant editor inquired, and when informed that Jeremiah Tyler was a Dublin man he requested that a note be kept of the photographer's particulars.

The gardai – in particular Superintendent O'Kelly – saw only what was convenient to see. Of the three bodies that lay that morning in the May sunshine they chose that of Lancy Butler to become the victim of their sluggish imagination. Mrs Butler, answering her notoriously uncontrollable jealousy, shot her son's sweetheart rather than have him marry her. Her son, so Superintendent O'Kelly infers from no circumstantial evidence whatsoever, wrenched the shotgun out of her hands and fired on her in furious confusion. He then, within seconds, took his own life. The shotgun bore the fingerprints of all three victims: what O'Kelly has signally failed to explain is why this should be so. Why should the Butlers' shotgun bear the fingerprints of Maureen McDowd? O'Kelly declares that 'in the natural course of events' Maureen McDowd would have handled the shotgun, being a frequent visitor to the farm. Frequent visitors, in our experience, do not, 'in the natural course of events' or otherwise, meddle with a household's firearms. The Superintendent hedges the issue because he is himself bewildered. The shotgun was used for keeping down rabbits, he states, knowing that the shotgun's previous deployment by the Butlers is neither here nor there. He mentions rabbits because he still can offer no reasonable explanation why Maureen McDowd should ever have handled the death weapon. The fingerprints of all three victims were blurred and 'difficult', and had been found on several different areas of the weapon. Take it or leave it is what the Superintendent is saying. And wearily he is saying: does it matter?

We maintain it does matter. We maintain that this extraordinary crime – following, as it does, hard on the heels of the renowned Kerry Babies mystery, and the Flynn case – has not been investigated, but callously shelved. The people of Drimaghleen will tell you everything that O'Kelly laboured over in his reports: the two accounts are identical. Everyone knows that Lancy Butler's mother was a sharp-tongued, possessive woman. Everyone knows that Lancy was a ne'er-do-well. Everyone knows that Maureen McDowd was a deeply religious girl. Naturally it was the mother who sought to end an intrusion she could not bear. Naturally it was slow, stupid Lancy who didn't pause to think what the consequences would be after he'd turned the gun on his mother. Naturally it was he who could think of no more imaginative way out of his dilemma than to join the two women who had dominated his life.

The scenario that neither O'Kelly nor the Butlers' neighbours paused to consider is a vastly different one. A letter, apparently – and astonishingly – overlooked by the police, was discovered behind the drawer of a table which was once part of the furniture of Lancy Butler's bedroom and which was sold in the general auction after the tragedy – land, farmhouse and contents having by this time become the property of Allied Irish Banks, who held the mortgage on the Butlers' possessions. This letter, written by Maureen McDowd a week before the tragedy, reads:

Dear Lancy, Unless she stops I can't see any chance of marrying you. I want to, Lancy, but she never can let us alone. What would it be like for me in your place, and if I didn't come to you where would we be able to go because you know my father wouldn't accept you here. She has ruined the chance we had, Lancy, she'll never let go of you. I am always cycling over to face her insults and the way she has of looking at me. I think we have reached the end of it.

This being a direct admission by Maureen McDowd that the conclusion of the romance had been arrived at, why would the perceptive Mrs Butler – a woman who was said to 'know your thoughts before you knew them yourself' – decide to kill Lancy's girl? And the more the mental make-up of that old woman is dwelt upon the more absurd it seems that she would have destroyed everything she had by committing a wholly unnecessary murder. Mrs Butler was not the kind to act blindly, in the fury of the moment. Her jealousy and the anger that protected it smouldered cruelly within her, always present, never varying.

But Maureen McDowd – young, impetuous, bitterly deprived of the man she loved – a saint by nature and possessing a saint's fervour, on that fatal evening made up for all the sins she had ever resisted. Hell hath no fury like a woman scorned – except perhaps a woman unfairly defeated. The old woman turned the screw, aware that victory was in sight. The insults and 'the way of looking' became more open and more arrogant; Mrs Butler wanted Maureen McDowd out, she wanted her gone for ever, never to dare to return.

It is known that Lancy Butler found two rabbits in his snares that night.

It is known that he and Maureen often made the rounds of the snares when she visited him in the evenings. He would ride her bicycle to the field where they were, Maureen sitting side-saddle on the carrier at the back. Lancy had no bicycle of his own. It is our deduction that the reason the shotgun bore Maureen's fingerprints is because they had gone on a shooting expedition as well and when they returned to the yard she was carrying both the shotgun and the snared rabbits. It is known that Maureen McDowd wept shortly before her death. In the fields, as they stalked their prey, Lancy comforted her but Maureen knew that never again would they walk here together, that never again would she come over to see him in the evening. The hatred his mother bore her, and Lancy's weakness, had combined to destroy what most of all she wanted. Mrs Butler was standing in the yard shouting her usual abuse and Maureen shot her. The rabbits fell to the ground as she jumped off the bicycle, and her unexpectedly sudden movement caused the bicycle itself, and Lancy on it, to turn over. He called out to her when it was too late, and she realized she could never have him now. She blamed him for never once standing up to his mother, for never making it easier. If she couldn't have this weak man whom she so passionately loved no one else would either. She shot her lover, knowing that within seconds she must take her own life too. And that, of course, she did.

There was more about Maureen. In the pages of the colour supplement Mrs McDowd said her daughter had been a helpful child. Her father said she'd been his special child. When she was small she used to go out with him to the fields, watching how he planted the seed-potatoes. Later on, she would carry out his tea to him, and later still she would assist with whatever task he was engaged in. Father Sallins gave it as his opinion that she had been specially chosen. A nun at the convent in Mountcroe remembered her with lasting affection.

O'Kelly fell prey to this local feeling. Whether they knew what they were doing or not, the people of Drimaghleen were protecting the memory of Maureen McDowd, and the Superintendent went along with the tide. She was a local girl of unblemished virtue, who had been 'specially chosen'. Had he publicly arrived at any other conclusion Superintendent O'Kelly might never safely have set foot in the neighbourhood of Drimaghleen again, nor the village of Kilmona, nor the town of Mountcroe. The Irish do not easily forgive the purloining of their latter-day saints.

'I wanted to tell you this stuff had been written,' Father Sallins said. 'I wanted it to be myself that informed you before you'd get a shock from hearing it elsewhere.'

He'd driven over specially. As soon as the story in the paper had been brought to his own notice he'd felt it his duty to sit down with the McDowds. In his own opinion, what had been printed was nearly as bad as the tragedy itself, his whole parish maligned, a police superintendent made out to be no better than the criminals he daily pursued. He'd read the thing through twice; he'd looked at the photographs in astonishment. Hetty Fortune and Jeremiah Tyler had come to see him, but he'd advised them against poking about in what was over and done with. He'd explained that people wanted to try to forget the explosion of violence that had so suddenly occurred in their midst, that he himself still prayed for the souls of the Butlers and Maureen McDowd. The woman had nodded her head, as though persuaded by what he said. 'I have the camera here, Father,' the man had remarked as they were leaving. 'Will I take a snap of you?' Father Sallins had stood by the fuchsias, seeing no harm in having his photograph taken. 'I'll send it down to you when it's developed,' the man said, but the photograph had never arrived. The first he saw of it was in the Sunday magazine, a poor likeness of himself, eyelids drooped as though he had drink taken, dark stubble on his chin.

'This is a terrible thing,' he said in the McDowds' kitchen, remembering the photograph of that also: the cream-enamelled electric cooker, the Holy Child on the green-painted dresser, beside the alarm clock and the stack of clothes-pegs, the floor carpeted for cosiness, the blue, formica-topped table, the radio, the television set. In the photograph the kitchen had acquired an extraneous quality, just as the photograph of the Butlers' yard had. The harsh, ordinary colours, the soiled edges of the curtains, the chipped paintwork, seemed like part of a meticulous composition: the photograph was so much a picture that it invited questioning as a record.

'We never thought she was going to say that about Maureen,' Mrs McDowd said. 'It's lies, Father.'

'Of course it is, Mrs McDowd.'

'We all know what happened that night.'

'Of course we do.'

McDowd said nothing. They had taken the money. It was he who had said that the people should be allowed into the house. Three thousand, one hundred and fifty pounds was the sum the woman had written the cheque for, insisting that the extra money was owed.

'You never said she'd been specially chosen, Father?'

'Of course I didn't, Mrs McDowd.'

He'd heard that Superintendent O'Kelly had gone to see a solicitor to inquire if he'd been libelled, and although he was told he probably had been he was advised that recourse in the courts would be costly and might not be successful. The simple explanation of what had happened at the Butlers' farm had been easy for the people of Drimaghleen and for the police to accept because they had known Mrs Butler and they had known her son. There'd been no mystery, there'd been no doubt.

'Will we say a prayer together?' the priest suggested.

They knelt, and when they rose again Mrs McDowd began to cry. Everyone would know about it, she said, as if the priest had neither prayed nor spoken. The story would get about and people would believe it. '*Disadvantaged people*', she quoted from the newspaper. She frowned, still sobbing, over the words. 'It says the Butlers were disadvantaged people. It says we are disadvantaged ourselves.'

'That's only the way that woman has of writing it down, Mrs McDowd. It doesn't mean much.'

'*These simple farm folk*,' Mrs McDowd read, '*of Europe's most western island form limited rural communities that all too often turn in on themselves.*'

'Don't pay attention,' Father Sallins advised.

'Does disadvantaged mean we're poor?'

'The way that woman would see it, Mrs McDowd.'

There was confusion now in Drimaghleen, in Kilmona and Mountcroe; and confusion, Father Sallins believed, was insidious. People had been separated from their instinct, and other newspaper articles would follow upon this one. More strangers would come. Father Sallins imagined a film being made about Maureen McDowd, and the mystery that had been created becoming a legend. The nature of Maureen McDowd would be argued over, books would be written because all of it was fascinating. For ever until they died her mother and her father would blame themselves for taking the money their poverty had been unable to turn away.

'The family'll see the pictures.'

'Don't upset yourself, Mrs McDowd.'

'No one ever said she was close to being a saint. That was never said, Father.'

'I know, I know.'

Mrs McDowd covered her face with her hands. Her thin shoulders heaved beneath the pain of her distress; sobs wrenched at her body. Too much had happened to her, the priest thought; it was too much for any mother that her murdered daughter should be accused of murder herself in order to give newspaper-readers something to think about. Her husband had turned away from the table she sat at. He stood with his back to her, looking out into the yard. In a low, exhausted voice he said:

'What kind of people are they?'

The priest slowly shook his head, unable to answer that, and in the kitchen that looked different in Jeremiah Tyler's photograph Mrs McDowd screamed. She sat at the blue-topped table with her lips drawn back from her teeth, one short, shrill scream following fast upon another. Father Sallins did not again attempt to comfort her. McDowd remained by the window.

Family Sins

A telegram arrived out of the blue. *Come for the weekend*, Hubert's message read, and I remember the excitement I felt because I valued his friendship more than anyone else's. I had no money for the train journey and had to raise the matter with my father. 'It's hard to come by these days,' my father said, giving me only what he could easily spare. I increased it playing rummy with McCaddy the courthouse clerk, who had a passion for the game.

It was the summer of 1946. Long warm days cast an unobtrusive spell, one following another in what seemed like orderly obedience. The train I took crept through a landscape that was just beginning to lose its verdancy but was not yet parched. The railway for the last few miles of the journey ran by the sea, which twinkled brilliantly, sunlight dancing on it.

'There's someone called Pamela,' Hubert said, greeting me in no other way. 'Probably I mightn't have mentioned her.'

We walked from Templemairt railway station, away from the sea, into a tangle of small suburban roads. Everywhere there were boarding-houses, cheaper than those by the promenade, Hubert said. Bookies' families stayed there, he said: Sans Souci, Freshlea House, Cois na Farraige. We climbed a hill and passed through iron gates into a garden that was also on a hill, steep rockeries on either side of a path with occasional steps in it. I could see the house above us, through hollyhocks and shrubs, a glass veranda stretching the length of its façade.

'Who's Pamela?'

'She spends the summers here. My cousin.'

We entered the house and a voice at once called out. 'Hubert, I should like to meet your friend.'

'Hell,' Hubert muttered. He led me into a small room, its burnt-brown blinds half drawn against the sun. An old woman sat at a piano, turning on the stool as we entered. She was dressed severely, in long, old-fashioned black clothes; her grey hair was swept up and neatly rolled. You could tell she had once been beautiful; and in the wrinkled tiredness of her face her eyes were still young.

'You are very welcome,' she said. 'Hubert does not often invite a friend.'

'It's nice of you to have me, Mrs Plunkett.'

The piano stool swivelled again. The first notes of a Strauss waltz were played. I picked my suitcase up and followed Hubert from the room. In the hall he threw his eyes upwards, but did not speak. Silently we mounted the stairs, and when we reached the first-floor landing a woman's voice called up from some lower part of the house: 'Hubert, don't tell me you forgot the honeycomb?'

'Oh, *God!*' Hubert muttered crossly. 'Leave your case. We'll have to go back for the damn thing.'

I placed my suitcase on the bed of the room we'd entered: a small cell of a place, masculine in character. Just before we left it Hubert said:

'My grandfather had a stroke. You won't be bothered with him. He doesn't come downstairs.'

On a table in the hall there was a dark-framed photograph of the man he spoke of, taken earlier in his lifetime: a stern, blade-like face with a tidy grey moustache, hair brushed into smooth wings on either side of a conventional parting, pince-nez, a watch-chain looping across a black waistcoat. At school Hubert had spoken a lot about his grandfather.

'That was Lily who was on about the honeycomb,' Hubert said as we descended the path between the rockeries. 'A kind of general maid I think you call her. They work the poor old thing to the bone.'

We passed out of the garden and walked back the way we'd come. Hubert talked about boys we'd been at school with, in particular Ossie Richpatrick and Gale and Furney. He'd had news of all three of them: Ossie Richpatrick had become a medical student, Gale had joined the British army, Furney was in a handkerchief business.

'The Dublin Handkerchief Company,' Hubert said. 'He wrote me a letter on their writing-paper.'

'Does he make the handkerchiefs? I can't see Furney making handkerchiefs.'

'He sells them actually.'

Ossie Richpatrick and Gale and Furney had left school the previous summer; Hubert and I more recently, only a matter of weeks ago. It was now August; in October I was, like Ossie Richpatrick, to become a student, though not of medicine. Hubert was uncertain about his future.

'This is the place,' he said. We passed through high wooden doors into what appeared to be a builder's yard. Bricks were stacked, lengths of plumber's piping were tied together with cord. In a shed there was a circular saw. 'This woman sells honey,' Hubert said.

He knocked on a half-open door and a moment later a woman arrived with a honeycomb already in her hand. 'I saw you turning in,' she said. 'How are you, Hubert?'

'I'm all right. Are you well yourself, Mrs Hanrahan?'

'I am of course, Hubert.'

She examined me with curiosity, but Hubert made no attempt to introduce me. He gave the woman some money and received the honeycomb in return. 'I picked that comb out for them. It's good rich honey.'

'You can tell by the look of it.'

'Is your grandmother well? Mr Plunkett no worse, is he?'

'Well, he's still ga-ga, Mrs Hanrahan. No worse than that.'

The woman had placed her shoulder against the doorjamb so that she could lean on it. You could see she wanted to go on talking, and I sensed that had I not been there Hubert would have remained a little longer. As we made our way through the yard he said: 'She lives in ignorance of Hanrahan's evil ways. He died a while back.'

Hubert didn't elaborate on Mr Hanrahan's evil ways, but suggested instead that we go down to the sea. He led the way to a sandy lane that twisted and turned behind small back gardens and came out eventually among sand dunes. He held the honeycomb by one side of its wooden frame. Wind would have blown sand into it, but the day was still, late-afternoon sunshine lightening an empty sky. We walked by the edge of the sea; there was hardly anyone about.

'What's your cousin like?'

'You'll see soon enough.'

Hubert had a face to which a faintly melancholy expression seemed naturally to belong. But when he laughed, or smiled, its bony landscape changed dramatically, delight illuminating every crevice, eyes sparkling like excited sapphires. Hair the colour of wheat was smoothly brushed, never untidy. 'Fancies himself a dandy, does he?' a disagreeable teacher of Greek and Latin had once remarked.

'I'm thinking of going to Africa,' he revealed when we'd turned and begun to make our way back to the house.

Hubert's mother and father had been killed in a car accident in England. 'The last thing that happened before the war,' Hubert used to say, regaling us at school with the story of the tragedy. On Saturday September 2nd, 1939, late at night, they had driven away from a roadhouse near Virginia Water and unfortunately had had a head-on collision with a lorry belonging to a travelling zoo. There'd been a cage full of apes on the back of the lorry, Hubert subsequently reported, which the impact had caused to become unfastened. He himself had been ten at the time, at a preparatory school in the suburbs of Oxford, and he told how the headmaster had broken the news to him, introducing it with references to courage and manliness. These had failed to prepare him for the death of his parents, because he'd imagined that what was coming next was the news that he would have to be sent home on the grounds that, yet again, the fees hadn't been paid. Already there had been the wireless announcement about the declaration of war, the whole school assembled to hear it. 'You will know no blacker day, Hubert,' the headmaster had asserted before releasing the more personal tidings. 'Take strength at least from that.'

We delivered the honeycomb to the kitchen. 'Lily,' Hubert said, by way of introducing the wiry little woman who was kneading bread on a baking board at the table. 'Mrs Hanrahan says it's good rich honey.'

She nodded in acknowledgement, and nodded a greeting at me. She asked me what kind of a journey I'd had and when I said it had been unremarkable she vouchsafed the information that she didn't like trains. 'I always said it to Hubert,' she recalled, 'when he was going back to school. I suffer on a train.'

'Have you a fag, Lily?' Hubert asked, and she indicated with a gesture of her head a packet of Player's on the dresser. 'I'll pay you back,' he promised. 'I'm taking two.'

'That's seven you owe the kitchen, mind, and I don't want money. You go and buy a packet after supper.'

'I was going to say, Lily, could you lend me a pound?' As he spoke he opened a green purse beside the Player's packet. 'Till Tuesday that would be.'

'It's always till Tuesday with you. You'd think the kitchen was made of Her Ladyships.'

'If Lily was a few years younger,' Hubert said, addressing me, 'I'd marry her tomorrow.'

He removed a pound note from the purse and smoothed it out on the surface of the dresser, examined the romantic countenance of Lady Lavery, raised it to his lips, and then carefully secreted the note in an inside pocket. 'We're going dancing tonight,' he said. 'Did you ever dance in the Four Provinces Ballroom, Lily?'

'Oh, don't be annoying me.'

We smoked in Hubert's room, a tidily kept place with Leonardo da Vinci's *Annunciation* on the wall between the windows. Hubert wound up a gramophone and then lay on his bed. I sat on the only chair. Frank Sinatra sang.

'They're trying to grow groundnuts in Africa,' Hubert said. 'I think I'd be interested in that.'

'What are groundnuts?'

'The groundnut is a nut they have an idea about. I think they'll pay my fare.'

He was vague about which African country he referred to, replying when I asked him that it didn't matter. There was another scheme he'd heard about, to do with supplying telephone-boxes, and a third one that involved teaching selected Africans the rudiments of hydraulic engineering. 'You have to go on a course yourself, naturally enough,' Hubert explained. 'Personally I favour the nuts.'

He turned the record over. Sinatra sang 'Begin the Beguine'. Hubert said:

'We can go in on the half-seven train. We'll have to try for a lift back. Don't dawdle in the dining-room.'

At school Hubert had been thought of as 'wild', a reputation he had to some extent inherited from his father's renown at the same school twenty-five years before. For his own part, it was not that he was constantly in breach of the rules, but rather that he tended to go his own way. Short of funds, which regularly he was, he had been known to sell his clothes. The suit of 'sober colouring' which we were permitted to wear on weekend exeats, and for Chapel on Sunday evenings, with either a school, House or Colours tie, he sold in a Dublin secondhand-clothes shop and, never known to go out on exeats himself, managed for Sunday Chapel with the black serge jacket and trousers that was our normal everyday wear. He sold his bicycle to Ossie Richpatrick for eleven shillings, and a suitcase for eightpence. 'I don't understand why that should be,' Hubert had a way of saying in class, voicing what the rest of us felt but didn't always have the courage to say. He didn't mind not understanding; he didn't mind arguing with the Chaplain about the existence of the Deity; he didn't mind leaving an entire meal untouched and afterwards being harangued by the duty prefect for what was considered to be a form of insolence. But, most of all, what marked Hubert with the characteristics of a personality that was unusual were the stories he repeated about his relationship with his grandfather, which was not a happy one. Mr Plunkett's strictures and appearance were endlessly laid before us, a figure emerging of a tetchy elder statesman, wing-collared and humourless, steeped in the Christian morality of the previous century. Mr Plunkett said grace at mealtimes, much as it was said at school, only continuing for longer; he talked importantly of the managerial position he had reached, after a lifetime of devotion and toil, in Guinness's brewery. 'Never himself touches a drop of the stuff, you understand. Having been an abstainer since the age of seven or something. A clerky figure even as a child.' Since Hubert's reports allowed Mrs Plunkett so slight a place in the household, and Lily none at all, his home life sounded spiky and rather cold. At the beginning of each term he was always the first to arrive back at school, and had once returned a week early, claiming to have misread the commencing date on the previous term's report.

'OK, let's go,' he said when a gong sounded, and we swiftly descended the stairs, Hubert setting the pace. I caught a brief glimpse of a door opening and of a girl. In the hall Hubert struck the gong again as he passed.

'No need for that,' his grandmother gently reprimanded in the dining-room. 'We are all present and correct.'

The girl smiled at me, so shyly that I was made to feel shy myself. In the absence of her husband Mrs Plunkett said grace while we stood with our hands resting on the backs of our chairs. 'We are quite a houseful now,' she chattily remarked as she sat down. 'Pamela, please pass that salad along to our visitor.'

'Yes, of course.'

Pamela blushed as she spoke, her eyes flittering for a moment in my direction. Hubert, silent beside me, was relishing her discomfiture: I knew that, I could feel it. He and I and his cousin were aware that we had not met; the old woman imagined we had.

'I hope you are a salad-eater,' Mrs Plunkett smiled at me. 'Hubert does not much go in for salad. I'm not sure why.'

'Because Hubert doesn't like the taste,' Hubert replied. 'Lettuce does not seem to him to taste at all. The skin of tomatoes catches in his throat. Chives hang about on his breath. Radishes are nasty little things. And so on.'

His cousin laughed. She was a pretty girl, with dark bobbed hair and blue eyes: I didn't, that evening, notice much else about her except that she was wearing a pale pink dress with white buttons down the front. She became even prettier when she smiled, a dimple appearing in one of her cheeks, her nose wrinkling in a way that became her.

'Well, that's most interesting,' Mrs Plunkett said, a little stiffly, when Hubert ceased to talk about his dislikes.

There was corned beef with the salad. Hubert buttered two slices of brown bread to make a sandwich of his, and all the time he was preparing this his grandmother watched him. She did so uncomfortably, in an odd, dutiful kind of way, and I received the impression that she would have preferred not to. It was what her husband would have done, I suddenly realized: as if guided by his silent presence in an upstairs room she was honourably obeying him, keeping faith with his wishes. Mustard was spread on the corned beef, pepper was sprinkled. Mrs Plunkett made no comment. The slow movements of Hubert's knife, a faint whispering under his breath of one of the songs Frank Sinatra had sung, contributed to the considerable unease of both Hubert's cousin and myself. Pamela reddened when she accidentally knocked the little silver spoon out of the salt cellar.

'You're not in a public house, Hubert,' Mrs Plunkett said when he lifted the sandwich to his mouth. 'Pamela, please pour the tea.'

Hubert ignored the reference to a public house. 'Don't dawdle,' he reminded me. 'If we miss the seven-thirty we'll have to cadge a lift and that takes ages.'

Pamela poured the tea. Mrs Plunkett cut her lettuce into fine shreds. She added salad cream, meticulously mixing everything up. She said eventually:

'Are you going in to Dublin?'

'We're going dancing,' Hubert said. 'The Four Provinces Ballroom in Harcourt Street. Music tonight by Ken Mackintosh.'

'I don't think I've heard of Mr Mackintosh.'

'Celebrity spot, the Inkspots.'

'Inkspots?'

'They sing songs.'

On a large round breadboard beside Mrs Plunkett there were several kinds of bread, which she cut very slowly with a battered breadsaw. On the table there was plum jam and raspberry jam, and the honeycomb we had bought from Mrs Hanrahan. There was a fruitcake and a coffee cake, biscuits and shortbread, and when we'd finished our corned beef Lily came in and added to this array a plate of éclairs. She lifted away the plates and dishes we'd finished with. Mrs Plunkett thanked her.

'Mrs Hanrahan said she picked that honeycomb out for you,' Hubert said.

'Well, that was most kind of her.'

'She's lonely since Hanrahan died. She'd talk the legs off you.'

'It's hard for the poor woman. A builder's widow.' Mrs Plunkett explained to me what I already knew. 'He fell off a roof six weeks ago.'

'As a matter of fact,' Hubert said, 'she's better off without him.'

'What on earth d'you mean, Hubert?'

'Hanrahan went after shop girls. Famous for it.'

'Don't speak so coarsely, Hubert.'

'Is Pam shocked? Are you shocked, Pam?'

'No, no, not at all.' Pamela swiftly replied before her grandmother could answer for her. She had reddened again in her confusion, but being flustered made her more vivacious and was not unattractive.

'Mr Hanrahan was a perfectly decent man,' Mrs Plunkett insisted. 'You're repeating tittle-tattle, Hubert.'

'There's a girl serves in Binchy's, another in Edwards' the cake shop. Hanrahan took both of them to the dunes. D'you remember Hanrahan, Pam?'

She shook her head.

'He painted the drain-pipes one time.'

'You'll need to hurry if you wish to catch the train,' Mrs Plunkett said. As she spoke she drew back the cuff of her sleeve to consult a wristwatch that had not been visible before. She nodded in agreement with the statement she'd just made. Addressing her granddaughter, she said:

'It doesn't matter if you don't finish.'

Doubtfully, Pamela half smiled at Mrs Plunkett. She began to say something, then changed her mind. Vaguely, she shook her head.

'Is Pamela going in to Dublin too?' Hubert said. 'Going to the flicks, Pamela?'

'Isn't she accompanying you? Don't you want to go dancing with the boys, Pamela?'

'No, no.' She shook her head, more vehemently than before. She was going to wash her hair, she said.

'But surely you'd like to go dancing, Pamela?'

Hubert stood up, half a piece of shortbread in one hand. He jerked his head at me, indicating that I should hurry. Pamela said again that she wanted to wash her hair.

'Jesus Christ!' Hubert murmured in the hall. He stifled laughter. 'I'm bloody certain,' he said as we hurried through the garden, 'she remembers Hanrahan. The man made a pass at her.'

In the train he told me when I asked that she was the child of his father's sister. 'She comes over every summer from some back-of-beyond rectory in Roscommon.' He was vague when I asked further questions, or else impatiently brushed them aside. 'Pam's dreary,' was all he said.

'She doesn't seem dreary to me.'

'The old man worships her. Like he did her mother by all accounts.'

In the Four Provinces Ballroom we met girls who were quite different from Hubert's cousin. Hubert said they came from the slums, though this could not have been true since they were fashionably dressed and had money for soft drinks and cigarettes. Their legs were painted – the liquid stockings of that time – and their features were emphasized with lipstick and mascara. But each one I danced with was either stunted or lumpy, and I kept thinking of Pamela's slim figure and her pretty face. Her lips, in particular, I remembered.

We danced to 'As Time Goes By' and 'Autumn Leaves' and 'Falling in Love with Love'. The Inkspots sang. One of the partners I danced with said: 'Your friend's very handsome, isn't he?'

In the end Hubert picked up two girls who were agreeable to being seen home when the evening came to an end.

Ken Mackintosh and his band began to pack away their instruments. We walked a little way along Harcourt Street and caught a number 11 bus. The girls were nurses. The one allocated to me, being bouncy and talkative, wanted to know what it was like living in a provincial town, as I did, and what my plans were for getting out of it. When I told her she said: 'Maybe I'll run into you when you're a student,' but her voice wasn't exactly loaded with pleasurable anticipation. She was wearing a thick, green woollen coat even though it was August. Her face was flat and pale, her lips garish beneath a fresh coating of lipstick. She had to get up at five o'clock every morning, she said, in order to get to the ward on time. The Sister was a tartar.

When we arrived at the girls' flat Hubert suggested that we might be offered a cup of tea, but the girls would permit us no further than the doorstep of the house. 'I thought we were away,' he murmured disconsolately. His father would have got in, he said. They'd have cooked a meal for his father, anything he wanted. We walked to where we hoped to get a lift to Templemairt. Two hours later a lorry driver picked us up.

The next day being a Saturday, Hubert and I went to Phoenix Park races. We missed breakfast and due to pressure of time we missed lunch also – and, in fact, the first race. 'The old man'll have been livid,' Hubert said. 'You understand he takes in what's going on?' Mrs Plunkett and Pamela would have sat waiting for us in the dining-room, he said, then Pamela would have been sent up to see if we were still asleep, and after that Mrs Plunkett would have gone up herself. 'They'll have asked Lily and she'll have told them we've hooked it to the races.' He neither laughed nor smiled, even though he seemed amused. Another two pounds had been borrowed from Lily before we left.

'He'll be livid because he'll think we should have taken Pam with us.'

'Why don't you like Pamela?'

Hubert didn't reply. He said instead: 'I'd love to have heard Hanrahan putting a proposition to her.'

At school all of it would have sounded different. We'd have laughed – I more than anyone – at the report of the lively builder attempting to seduce Hubert's cousin. And somehow it would have been funnier because this had occurred in his grandfather's house, his grandfather being the sort he was. We would have imagined the embarrassment of Hubert's cousin, and Hanrahan saying what harm was a little kiss. We would have imagined the old man oblivious of it all, and would have laughed because Hubert's cousin couldn't bring herself to say anything about it afterwards. Hubert told his stories well.

'He may not,' I said, 'have had a go at her.'

'He couldn't leave them alone, that man. I'm going for this Summer Rain thing.'

We stood in the crowd, examining the list of runners. Announcements were made over loudspeakers; all around us people were talking furiously. Men were in shirt-sleeves, women and girls in summer dresses. It was another sunny day.

'Paddy's Pride no good?' I said.

'Could be.' But we both put our bets on Summer Rain and to my surprise the horse won at nine to one. 'Let's have a drink,' Hubert said. Without asking me what I wanted he ordered stout at the bar.

We won again with Sarah's Cottage, lost with Monaghan Lad and King of Them All. We drank further bottles of stout. 'Take Gay Girl for a place,' a man who had dropped into conversation with us in the bar advised. We did so and were again successful. Between us we were now almost seventeen pounds richer than when we started. We watched the last race in high spirits, grasping glasses of stout and urging on a horse called Marino. We hadn't backed it; we hadn't backed anything because Hubert said he could tell our luck had come to an end. Marino didn't win.

'We'll have something to eat and then go to the pictures,' Hubert said.

The grass beneath our feet was littered with discarded race tickets and programmes. The bookmakers were dismantling their stands. Pale evening sunlight slanted over the drifting crowds; voices were more subdued than they had been. I kept thinking of Pamela in the house in Templemairt, of Mrs Plunkett saying grace again in the dining-room, the old man sensing that we weren't present for yet another meal.

'What about *The Moon and Sixpence*?' Hubert suggested, having bought an *Evening Herald* as we left the racecourse. 'George Sanders?'

We ordered two mixed grills at the cinema restaurant, and tea and cakes. We both bought packets of cigarettes. When *The Moon and Sixpence* came to an end we went to an ice-cream parlour and then we caught a Saturday-night bus that brought us almost as far as Templemairt. We walked the last bit, Hubert talking about Africa. Before we reached the town he said:

'He disowned my father, you know. When my father got involved with my mother that was the end of that. My mother was a barmaid, you understand.'

I nodded, having been informed of that before. Hubert said:

'I didn't know that old man existed until I was told after the funeral. He didn't even come to it.'

I didn't say it must have been awful, having both your parents killed at once. We'd often thought so at school and had said it when Hubert wasn't there. We'd often considered it must have affected him, perhaps made him the way he was – careless, it seemed, of what people thought of him.

'You should have heard him when he could talk, laying into me because he thinks I'm like my father. A chip off the old block is what he thinks. My father lived on his wits. A con man, you understand.'

Hubert had often told us this also. His father had briefly been a racing correspondent, had managed a night-club, had apparently worked in a bank. But none of these forays into the realm of employment had lasted long; each had been swiftly terminated, either on the grounds of erratic service or for liberties taken with funds. Hubert, at school, had made no bones about his father's reprehensible tendencies, nor about his mother's background. On the contrary, he had taken a certain pride in the fact that his father, in later life, had lived up to the reputation he had established when a schoolboy himself. The apes that had escaped from the circus cage at the time of the tragedy had chattered with delight, scampering over the wreckage. His father would have appreciated that, he said.

A weak crescent moon lightened the darkness as we walked towards Templemairt. The stars were out in force. No car passed us, but even if we'd been aware of headlights behind us I doubt that we'd have bothered to try for a lift. We smoked one cigarette after another, still exhilarated by our triumphant afternoon, and in the circumstances it seemed natural that Hubert should talk about his parents, who had spent a lot of time on racecourses.

'They were drunk, of course, when they crashed that car.'

It was not difficult to believe they were, but none the less I did not feel that hearty agreement was in order. I nodded briefly. I said:

'Were you born in England?'

'I believe in the back row of a cinema.'

I had never heard that before, but there was something about Hubert's honesty in other matters that prevented me from suspecting invention. The photograph of his grandfather in the hall was precisely as Mr Plunkett had so often been described, down to his eyebrows being almost a single horizontal line, and the celluloid collar of his shirt.

'When the lights went up she couldn't move. They had to send for a doctor, but before the ambulance arrived she popped me.'

We entered the house quietly and went to our rooms without further conversation. I had hoped that Pamela might still be up since it wasn't as late as last night. I had even prepared a scene that I felt could easily take place: Pamela in the hall as we closed the front door behind us, Pamela offering us tea in the kitchen and Hubert declining while I politely accepted.

*

'Pam, do you want to play tennis?'

She was as astonished as I was to hear this. A startled look came into her face. She stammered slightly when she replied.

'Three of us?' she said.

'We'll show you how three can play.'

Sunday lunch had already taken place, a somewhat silent occasion because Hubert and I were more than ever out of favour. Mrs Plunkett said quietly, but in the firm tones of one conveying a message as a matter of trust, that her husband had been disappointed because we hadn't accompanied Pamela and herself to church. I did my best to apologize; Hubert ignored the revelation. 'We won a fortune at the races,' he said, which helped matters as little as it would have had the old man been present.

'Tennis would be lovely,' Pamela said.

She added that she'd change. Hubert said he'd lend me a pair of tennis shoes.

A remarkable transformation appeared to have overtaken him, and for a moment I thought that the frosty lunchtime and his grandfather's reported distress had actually stirred his conscience. It then occurred to me that since there was nothing else to do on a Sunday afternoon, tennis with Pamela was better than being bored. I knew what he meant when he said we'd show her how three could play: on the tennis court Hubert belonged in a class far more exalted than my own, and often at school Ossie Richpatrick and I had together played against him and still not managed to win. It delighted me that Pamela and I were to be partners.

Hubert's tennis shoes didn't fit me perfectly, but I succeeded in getting them on to my feet. There was no suggestion that he and I should change our clothes, as Pamela had said she intended to. Hubert offered me a choice of several racquets and when I'd selected one we made our way to the tennis court at the back of the house. We raised the net, measured its height, and knocked up while we waited.

'I'm afraid we can't,' Pamela said.

She was wearing a white dress and tennis shoes and socks of the same pristine freshness. There was a white band in her hair and she was wearing sunglasses. She wasn't carrying her tennis racquet.

'Can't what?' Hubert said, stroking a ball over the net. 'Can't what, Pam?'

'We're not allowed to play tennis.'

'Who says we're not allowed to? What d'you mean, allowed?'

'Grandmother says we mustn't play tennis.'

'Why on earth not?'

'Because it's Sunday, because you haven't been to church.'

'Oh, don't be so bloody silly.'

'He asked her what we were doing. She had to tell him.'

'The idiotic old brute.'

'I don't want to play, Hubert.'

Hubert stalked away. I wound the net down. I was glad he hadn't insisted that he and I should play on our own.

'Don't be upset by it.' I spoke apologetically. I didn't know what else to say.

'There won't be a quarrel,' she reassured me, and in fact there wasn't. The raised voices of Hubert and his grandmother, which I thought we'd hear coming from the house, didn't materialize. Pamela went to change her dress. I took off Hubert's tennis shoes. In the drawing-room at teatime Mrs Plunkett said:

'Hubert's turned his face to the wall, has he?'

'Shall I call him?' Pamela offered.

'Hubert knows the hour of Sunday tea, my dear.'

Lily brought more hot water. She, too, seemed affected by what had occurred, her mouth tightly clamped. But I received the impression that the atmosphere in the drawing-room was one she was familiar with.

'A pity to turn one's face to the wall on such a lovely day,' Mrs Plunkett remarked.

Silence took over then and was not broken until Mrs Plunkett rose and left the room. Strauss began on the piano, tinkling faintly through the wall. Lily came in to collect the tea things.

'Perhaps we should go for a walk,' Pamela said.

We descended the stepped path between the rockeries and strolled past Hanrahan's yard. We turned into the sandy lane that led to the dunes and made our way on to the strand. We didn't refer to what had occurred.

'Are you still at school?' I asked.

'I left in July.'

'What are you going to do now?'

'I'm hoping to study botany.'

She was shyer than I'd thought. Her voice was reticent when she said she hoped to study botany, as if the vaunting of this ambition constituted a presumption.

'What are you going to do?'

I told her. I envied Hubert going to Africa, I said, becoming garrulous in case she was bored by silence. I mentioned the cultivation of groundnuts.

'Africa?' she said. When she stopped she took me unawares and I had to walk back a pace or two. Too late, I realized I had inadvertently disclosed a confidence.

'It's just an idea he has.'

I tried to change the subject, but she didn't seem to hear, or wasn't interested. I watched while she drew a pattern on the sand with the toe of her shoe. More slowly than before, she walked on again.

'I don't know why,' I said, 'we don't have a bathe.'

She didn't reply. Children were running into and out of the sea. Two men were paddling, with their trousers rolled up to their knees. A girl was sunbathing on a li-lo, both hands in the water, resisting the tide that would have carried her away from the shore.

'My bathing-dress is in the house,' Pamela said at last. 'I could get it if you like.'

'Would *you* like?'

She shrugged. Perhaps not, she said, and I wondered if she was thinking that bathing, as much as tennis, might be frowned upon as a breach of the Sabbath.

'I don't think, actually,' she said, 'that Hubert will ever go to Africa.'

Lily stood beside my deck-chair, a bunch of mint she'd picked in one hand. I hadn't known what else to do, since Hubert had not come out of his room, so I'd wandered about the garden and had eventually found the deck-chair on a triangle of grass in a corner. 'I'm going to read for a while,' Pamela had said when we returned from our walk.

'It's understandable they never had to be so severe with Pamela,' Lily said. 'On account of her mother being sensible in her life. Different from Hubert's father.'

I guessed she was talking to me like this because she'd noticed I was bewildered. The pettiness I had witnessed in my friend was a shock more than a surprise. Affected by it, I'd even wondered as I'd walked with Pamela back from the strand if I'd been invited to the house in order to become an instrument in her isolation. I'd dismissed the thought as a ridiculous flight of fancy: now I was not so sure.

'It's understandable, Hubert being bad to her. When you think about it, it's understandable.'

Lily passed on, taking with her the slight scent of mint that had begun to waft towards me because she'd crushed a leaf or two. 'He tried to beat me with a walking-stick,' Hubert had reported at school, and I imagined the apprehension Lily hinted at – the father of the son who'd gone to the bad determined that history should not be repeated, the mother anxious and agreeing.

'I was looking for you,' Hubert said, sitting down on the grass beside me. 'Why don't we go down to the hotel?'

I looked at him, his lean face in profile. I remembered Pamela drawing the pattern on the sand, her silence the only intimation of her love. When had an intonation or a glance first betrayed it to him? I wondered.

Hubert pushed himself to his feet and we sauntered off to the lounge-bar of the hotel beside the railway station. Without asking me what I would like, Hubert ordered gin and orange. The tennis we hadn't played wasn't mentioned, nor did I say that Pamela and I had walked on the strand.

'No need to go tomorrow,' Hubert said. 'Stay on a bit.'

'I said I'd be back.'

'Send them a wire.'

'I don't want to over-stay, Hubert. It's good of your grandmother to have me.'

'That girl stays for three months.'

I'd never drunk gin before. The orange made it pleasantly sweet, with only a slight aftertaste. I liked it better than stout.

'My father's drink,' Hubert said. 'My mother preferred gimlets. A gimlet,' he added, 'is gin with lime in it. They drank an awful lot, you understand.'

He confided to me that he intended to slip away to England himself. He was softening Lily up, he said, with the intention of borrowing a hundred pounds from her. He knew she had it because she never spent a penny; a hundred pounds would last him for ages, while he found out more about the prospects in Africa.

'I'll pay her back. I'd never not.'

'Yes, of course.'

'Anything would be better than the Dublin Handkerchief Company. Imagine being in the Dublin Handkerchief Company when you were fifty years of age! A lifetime of people blowing their noses!'

We sat there, talking about school, remembering the time Fitzherbert had dressed himself up in the kind of woman's clothes he considered suitable for a streetwalker and demanded an interview with Farquie, the senior languages master; and the time the Kingsmill brothers had introduced a laxative into the High Table soup; and when Prunty and Tatchett had appropriated a visiting rugby team's clothes while they were in the showers. We recalled the days of our first term: how Hubert and I had occupied beds next to one another in the junior dormitory, how Miss Fanning, the common-room secretary, had been kind to us, thinking we were homesick.

'One *pour la route*,' Hubert said.

He held the man who served us in conversation, describing the same mixture of gin and orangeade as he'd had it once in some other bar. There had been iced sugar clinging to the rim of the glass; delicious, he said. The man just stared at him.

'I'll fix it up with Lily tonight,' Hubert said on the way back to the house. 'If she can't manage the hundred I'd settle for fifty.'

We were still talking loudly as we mounted the stepped path between the rockeries, and as we passed through the hall. In the dining-room Mrs Plunkett and Pamela had clearly been seated at the table for some time. When we entered the old woman rose without commenting on our lateness and repeated the grace she had already said. A weary expression froze Hubert's features while he waited for her voice to cease.

'We were down in the hotel,' he said when it did, 'drinking gin and orange. Have you ever wandered into the hotel, Pam?'

She shook her head, her attention appearing to be occupied with the chicken leg on her plate. Hubert said the hotel had a pleasant little lounge-bar, which wasn't the description I'd have chosen myself. A rendezvous for the discriminating, he said, even if one encountered difficulty there when it came to a correctly concocted gin and orange. He was pretending to be drunker than he was.

'A rather dirty place, Dowd's Hotel,' Mrs Plunkett interposed, echoing what I knew would have been her husband's view.

'Hanrahan used to drink there,' Hubert continued. 'Many's the time I saw him with a woman in the corner. I've forgotten if you said you remembered the late Hanrahan, Pam?'

She said she didn't. Mrs Plunkett held out her cup and saucer for more tea. Pamela poured it.

'Hanrahan painted the drain-pipes,' Hubert said. 'D'you remember that time, Pam?'

She shook her head. I wanted to tell him to stop. I wanted to remind him that he had already asked his cousin if she remembered Hanrahan painting the drain-pipes, to point out that it wasn't she who had caused the difficulty that afternoon, that it wasn't she who had made us stand there while grace was said again.

'I'm surprised you don't,' Hubert said. 'I'm really very surprised, Pam.'

Mrs Plunkett didn't understand the conversation. She smiled kindly at me, and briefly indicated dishes I might like to help myself to. She lifted a forkful of cold chicken to her mouth.

'It's only that he mentioned you once in Dowd's,' Hubert said. He laughed, his eyes sparkling, as if with delight. 'He asked how you were getting on one time. A very friendly man.'

Pamela turned away from the table, but she couldn't hide what she wished to hide and she couldn't control her emotions. Her cheeks were blazing now. She sobbed, and then she pushed her chair back and hurried from the room.

'What have you said to her?' Mrs Plunkett asked in astonishment.

I could not sleep that night. I kept thinking about Pamela, unhappy in her bedroom, and Hubert in his. I imagined Hubert's father and Pamela's mother, children in the house also, the bad son, the good daughter. I imagined the distress suffered in the house when Hubert's father was accused of some small theft at school, which Hubert said he had been. I imagined the misdemeanour forgotten, a new leaf turned, and some time later the miscreant dunned by a debt collector for a sum he could not pay. Letters came to the house from England, pleading for assistance, retailing details of hardship due to misfortune. When I closed my eyes, half dreaming though I was not yet asleep, Mrs Plunkett wept, as Pamela had. She dreaded the letters, she sobbed; for a day or two she was able to forget and then another letter came. 'I will write a cheque': the man I had not seen spoke blankly, taking a cheque-book from his pocket and, at the breakfast table, writing it immediately.

I opened my eyes; I murmured Pamela's name. 'Pamela,' I whispered because repeating it made her face more vivid in my mind. I might have told her that Hubert, at school, had been sought out and admired more than any other boy because he was not ordinary, that he'd been attractive and different in all sorts of ways. I might have begged her not to hate the memory of him when she ceased to love him.

I fell asleep. We played tennis and Hubert easily beat us. A car lay on its side, headlights beaming on the apes that scampered from the broken cage. On the bloody grass of the roadside verge the two dead faces still smiled. 'You will know no blacker day,' the voice of a schoolmaster promised.

In the morning, after breakfast, I packed my suitcase while Hubert sat smoking a cigarette in silence. I said goodbye to Lily in the kitchen, and to Mrs Plunkett. Pamela was in the hall when we passed through it.

'Goodbye,' she said. At breakfast she had seemed to have recovered her composure. She smiled at me now, saying she was sorry I was going.

'Goodbye, Pamela.'

Hubert stood by the open hall door, not looking at her, gazing out into the sunlit garden. On the way to the railway station we talked again about incidents at school. He mentioned the two nurses we'd accompanied to their doorstep and the luck we'd had at the races. 'A pity we wouldn't have time for a gin and orange,' he said as we passed the hotel.

On the slow train, close at first to the sea and then moving into the landscape that was just beginning to seem parched because of the heatwave, I knew that I would never see Hubert again. A friendship had come to an end because when a little more time went by he would be ashamed, knowing I would not easily forget how he had made his cousin a casualty of the war with his grandfather. There would always be an awkwardness now, and the memory of Hubert at home.

A Trinity

Their first holiday since their honeymoon was paid for by the elderly man they both called Uncle. In fact, he was related to neither of them: for eleven years he had been Dawne's employer, but the relationship was more truly that of benefactor and dependants. They lived with him and looked after him, but in another sense it was he who looked after them, demonstrating regularly that they required such care. 'What you need is a touch of the autumn sun,' he had said, ordering Keith to acquire as many holiday brochures as he could lay his hands on. 'The pair of you're as white as bedsheets.'

The old man lived vicariously through aspects of their lives, and listened carefully to all they said. Sharing their anticipation, he browsed delightedly through the pages of the colourful brochures and opened out on the kitchen table one glossy folder after another. He marvelled over the blue of the Aegean Sea and the flower markets of San Remo, over the Nile and the pyramids, the Costa del Sol, the treasures of Bavaria. But it was Venice that most instantly caught his imagination, and again and again he returned to the wonder of its bridges and canals, and the majesty of the Piazza San Marco.

'I am too old for Venice,' he remarked a little sadly. 'I am too old for anywhere now.'

They protested. They pressed him to accompany them. But as well as being old he had his paper-shop to think about. He could not leave Mrs Withers to cope on her own; it would not be fair.

'Send me one or two postcards,' he said. 'That will be sufficient.'

He chose for them a package holiday at a very reasonable price: an air flight from Gatwick Airport, twelve nights in the fairyland city, in the Pensione Concordia. When Keith and Dawne went together to the travel agency to make the booking the counter clerk explained that the other members of that particular package were an Italian class from Windsor, all of them learning the language under the tutelage of a Signor Bancini. 'It is up to you if you wish to take the guided tours of Signor Bancini,' the counter clerk explained. 'And naturally you have your own table for breakfast and for dinner.'

The old man, on being told about the party from Windsor, was well pleased. Mixing with such people and, for just a little extra, being able to avail themselves of the expertise of an Italian language teacher amounted to a bonus, he pointed out. 'Travel widens the mind,' he said. 'I deplore I never had the opportunity.'

But something went wrong. Either in the travel agency or at Gatwick Airport, or in some anonymous computer, a small calamity was conceived. Dawne and Keith ended up in a hotel called the Edelweiss, in Room 212, in Switzerland. At Gatwick they had handed their tickets to a girl in the yellow-and-red Your-Kind-of-Holiday uniform. She'd addressed them by name, had checked the details on their tickets and said that that was lovely. An hour later it had surprised them to hear elderly people on the plane talking in North of England accents when the counter clerk at the travel agency had so specifically stated that Signor Bancini's Italian class came from Windsor. Dawne had even remarked on it, but Keith said there must have been a cancellation, or possibly the Italian class was on a second plane. 'That'll be the name of the airport,' he confidently explained when the pilot referred over the communications system to a destination that didn't sound like Venice. 'Same as he'd say Gatwick. Or Heathrow.' They ordered two Drambuies, Dawne's favourite drink, and then two more. 'The coach'll take us on,' a stout woman with spectacles announced when the plane landed. 'Keep all together now.' There'd been no mention of an overnight stop in the brochure, but when the coach drew in at the Edelweiss Hotel Keith explained that that was clearly what this was. By air and then by coach was how these package firms kept the prices down, a colleague at work had told him. As they stepped out of the coach it was close on midnight: fatigued and travel-stained, they did not feel like questioning their right to the beds they were offered. But the next morning, when it became apparent that they were being offered them for the duration of their holiday, they became alarmed.

'We have the lake, and the water-birds,' the receptionist smilingly explained. 'And we may take the steamer to Interlaken.'

'An error has been made,' Keith informed the man, keeping the register of his voice even, for it was essential to be calm. He was aware of his wife's agitated breathing close beside him. She'd had to sit down when they realized that something was wrong, but now she was standing up again.

'We cannot change the room, sir,' the clerk swiftly countered. 'Each has been given a room. You accompany the group, sir?'

Keith shook his head. Not this group, he said, a different group; a group that was travelling on to another destination. Keith was not a tall man, and often suffered from what he considered to be arrogance in other people, from officials of one kind or another, and shop-assistants with a tendency to assume that his lack of stature reflected a diminutive personality. In a way Keith didn't care for, the receptionist repeated:

'This is the Edelweiss Hotel, sir.'

'We were meant to be in Venice. In the Pensione Concordia.'

'I do not know the name, sir. Here we have Switzerland.'

'A coach is to take us on. An official said so on the plane. She was here last night, that woman.'

'Tomorrow we have the *fondue* party,' the receptionist went on, having listened politely to this information about an official. 'On Tuesday there is the visit to a chocolate factory. On other days we may take the steamer to Interlaken, where we have teashops. In Interlaken mementoes may be bought at fair prices.'

Dawne had still not spoken. She, too, was a slight figure, her features pale beneath orange-ish powder. 'Mingy', the old man had a way of saying in his joky voice, and sometimes told her to lie down.

'Eeh, idn't it luvely?' a voice behind Keith enthused. 'Been out to feed them ducks, 'ave you?'

Keith did not turn round. Speaking slowly, giving each word space, he said to the receptionist: 'We have been booked on to the wrong holiday.'

'Your group is booked twelve nights in the Edelweiss Hotel. To make an alteration now, sir, if you have changed your minds –'

'We haven't changed our minds. There's been a mistake.'

The receptionist shook his head. He did not know about a mistake. He had not been told that. He would help if he could, but he did not see how help might best be offered.

'The man who made the booking,' Dawne interrupted, 'was bald, with glasses and a moustache.' She gave the name of the travel agency in London.

In reply, the receptionist smiled with professional sympathy. He fingered the edge of his register. 'Moustache?' he said.

Three aged women who had been on the plane passed through the reception area. Had anyone noticed, one of them remarked, that there were rubber linings under the sheets? Well, you couldn't be too careful, another agreeably responded, if you were running a hotel.

'Some problem, have we?' another woman said, beaming at Keith. She was the stout woman he had referred to as an official, flamboyantly attired this morning in a two-tone trouser-suit, green and blue. Her flesh-coloured spectacles were decorated with swirls of metal made to seem like gold; her grey hair was carefully waved. They'd seen her talking to the yellow-and-red girl at Gatwick. On the plane she'd walked up and down the aisle, smiling at people.

'My name is Franks,' she was saying now. 'I'm married to the man with the bad leg.'

'Are you in charge, Mrs Franks?' Dawne inquired. 'Only we're in the wrong hotel.' Again she gave the name of the travel agency and described the bald-headed counter clerk, mentioning his spectacles and his moustache. Keith interrupted her.

'It seems we got into the wrong group. We reported to the Your-Kind-of-Holiday girl and left it all to her.'

'We should have known when they weren't from Windsor,' Dawne contributed. 'We heard them talking about Darlington.'

Keith made an impatient sound. He wished she'd leave the talking to him. It was no good whatsoever going on about Darlington and the counter clerk's moustache, confusing everything even more.

'We noticed you at Gatwick,' he said to the stout woman. 'We knew you were in charge of things.'

'I noticed *you*. Well, of course I did, naturally I did. I counted you, although I dare say you didn't see me doing that. Monica checked the tickets and I did the counting. That's how I know everything's OK. Now, let me explain to you. There are many places Your-Kind-of-Holiday sends its clients to, many tours, many different holidays at different prices. You follow me? Something to suit every pocket, something for every taste. There are, for instance, villa holidays for the adventurous under-thirty-fives. There are treks to Turkey, and treks for singles to the Himalayas. There is self-catering in Portugal, November reductions in Casablanca, February in Biarritz. There's Culture-in-Tuscany and Sunshine-in-Sorrento. There's the Nile. There's Your-Kind-of-Safari in Kenya. Now, what I am endeavouring to say to you good people is that all tickets and labels are naturally similar, the yellow with the two red bands.' Mrs Franks suddenly laughed. 'So if you simply followed other people with the yellow-and-red label you might imagine you could end up in a wildlife park!' Mrs Franks' speech came hurriedly from her, the words tumbling over one another, gushing through her teeth. 'But of course,' she added soothingly, 'that couldn't happen in a million years.'

'We're not meant to be in Switzerland,' Keith doggedly persisted.

'Well, let's just see, shall we?'

Unexpectedly, Mrs Franks turned and went away, leaving them standing. The receptionist was no longer behind the reception desk. The sound of typing could be heard.

'She seems quite kind,' Dawne whispered, 'that woman.'

To Keith it seemed unnecessary to say that. Any consideration of Mrs Franks was, in the circumstances, as irrelevant as a description of the man in the travel agent's. He tried to go over in his mind every single thing that had occurred: handing the girl the tickets, sitting down to wait, and then the girl leading the way to the plane, and then the pilot's voice welcoming them aboard, and the air hostess with the smooth black hair going round to see that everyone's seat-belt was fastened.

'Snaith his name was,' Dawne was saying. 'It said *Snaith* on a plastic thing in front of him.'

'What are you talking about?'

'The man in the travel place was called Snaith. *G. Snaith* it said.'

'The man was just a clerk.'

'He booked us wrong, though. That man's responsible, Keith.'

'Be that as it may.'

Sooner or later, Dawne had guessed, he'd say 'Be that as it may'. He put her in her place with the phrase; he always had. You'd make an innocent remark, doing your best to be helpful, and out he'd come with 'Be that as it may'. You expected him to go on, to finish the sentence, but he never did. The phrase just hung there, making him sound uneducated.

'Are you going to phone up that man, Keith?'

'Which man is this?'

She didn't reply. He knew perfectly well which man she meant. All he had to do was to get through to Directory Inquiries and find out the number of the travel agency. It was no good complaining to a hotel receptionist who had nothing to do with it, nor to a woman in charge of a totally different package tour. No good putting the blame where it didn't belong.

'Nice to have some young people along,' an elderly man said. 'Nottage the name is.'

Dawne smiled, the way she did in the shop when someone was trying to be agreeable, but Keith didn't acknowledge the greeting because he didn't want to become involved.

'Seen the ducks, 'ave you? Right champion them ducks are.'

The old man's wife was with him, both of them looking as if they were in their eighties. She nodded when he said the ducks were right champion. They'd slept like logs, she said, best night's sleep they'd had for years, which of course would be due to the lakeside air.

'That's nice,' Dawne said.

Keith walked out of the reception area and Dawne followed him. On the gravel forecourt of the hotel they didn't say to one another that there was an irony in the catastrophe that had occurred. On their first holiday since their honeymoon they'd landed themselves in a package tour of elderly people when the whole point of the holiday was to escape the needs and demands of the elderly. In his bossy way Uncle had said so himself when they'd tried to persuade him to accompany them.

'You'll have to phone up Snaith,' Dawne repeated, irritating Keith further. What she did not understand was that if the error had occurred with the man she spoke of it would since have become compounded to such a degree that the man would claim to be able to do nothing about their immediate predicament. Keith, who sold insurance over the counter for the General Accident insurance company, knew something of the complications that followed when even the slightest uncertainty in a requirement was passed into the programme of a computer. Somewhere along the line that was what had happened, but to explain it to Dawne would take a very long time. Dawne could work a till as well as anyone; in the shop she knew by heart the price of Mars bars and the different kinds of cigarettes and tobacco, and the prices of all the newspapers and magazines, but otherwise Keith considered her slow on the uptake, often unable to follow simple argument.

'Hi, there!' Mrs Franks called out, and they turned and saw her picking her way across the gravel towards them. She had a piece of pink paper in her hand. 'I've been doing my homework!' she cried when she was a little closer. She waved the pink paper. 'Take a look at this.'

It was a list of names, a computer print-out, each name a series of tiny dots. *K. and H. Beale*, they read, *T. and G. Craven, P. and R. Feinman*. There were many others, including *B. and Y. Nottage*. In the correct alphabetical position they were there themselves, between *J. and A. Hines* and *C. and L. Mace*.

'The thing is,' Dawne began, and Keith looked away. His wife's voice quietly continued, telling Mrs Franks that their holiday had been very kindly paid for by the old man whom they lived with, who had been her employer before they ever moved in to live with him, who still was. They called him Uncle but he wasn't a relation, a friend really – well, more than that. The thing was, he would be angry because they were not in Venice, he having said it should be Venice. He'd be angry because they were in a package for the elderly when he wanted them to have a rest from the elderly, not that she minded looking after Uncle herself, not that she ever would. The person in the travel agency had said the Windsor people were quite young. 'I always remember things like that,' Dawne finished up. 'Snaith he was called. G. Snaith.'

'Well, that's most interesting,' Mrs Franks commented, and added after a pause: 'As a matter of fact, Dawne, Mr Franks and myself are still in our fifties.'

'Be that as it may,' Keith said. 'At no time did we book a holiday in Switzerland.'

'Well, there you are, you see. The ticket you handed to me at Gatwick is as clear as daylight, exactly the same as the Beales' and the Maces', the same as our own, come to that. Not a tither of difference, Keith.'

'We need to be conveyed to our correct destination. An arrangement has to be made.'

'The trouble is, Keith, I don't know if you know it but you're half a continent away from Venice. Another thing is, I'm not employed by Your-Kind, nothing like that. They just reduce our ticket a bit if I agree to keep an eye. On location we call it.' Mrs Franks went on to say that her husband had also scrutinized the piece of pink paper and was in complete agreement with her. She asked Keith if he had met her husband, and said again that he was the man with the bad leg. He'd been an accountant and still did a lot of accountancy work one way or another, in a private capacity. The Edelweiss Hotel was excellent, she said. Your-Kind would never choose an indifferent hotel.

'We are asking you to get in touch with your firm in London,' Keith said. 'We do not belong with your group.'

In silence, though smiling, Mrs Franks held out the pink list. Her expression insisted that it spoke for itself. No one could gainsay the dotted identification among the others.

'Our name is there by mistake.'

A man limped across the gravel towards them. He was a large man of shambling appearance, his navy-blue pin-striped jacket and waistcoat at odds with his brown trousers, his spectacles repaired with Sellotape. The sound of his breath could be heard as he approached. He blew it through half-pursed lips in a vague rendition of a Gilbert and Sullivan melody.

'These are the poor lost lambs,' Mrs Franks said. 'Keith and Dawne.'

'How do?' Mr Franks held a hand out. 'Silly thing to happen, eh?'

It was Mr Franks who eventually suggested that Keith should telephone Your-Kind-of-Holiday himself, and to Keith's surprise he got through to a number in Croydon without any difficulty. 'Excuse me a minute,' a girl said when he finished. He heard her talking to someone else and he heard the other person laughing. There was a trace of laughter in the girl's voice when she spoke again. You couldn't change your mind, she said, in the middle of a package. In no circumstances whatsoever could that be permitted. 'We're not changing our minds,' Keith protested, but while he was explaining all over again he was cut off because he hadn't any more coins. He cashed a traveller's cheque with the receptionist and was supplied with a number of five-franc pieces, but when he re-dialled the number the girl he'd spoken to couldn't be located so he explained everything to another girl. 'I'm sorry, sir,' this girl said, 'but if we allowed people to change their minds on account of they didn't like the look of a place we'd be out of business in no time.' Keith began to shout into the telephone, and Dawne rapped on the glass of the booth, holding up a piece of paper on which she'd written *G. Snaith the name was.* 'Some sort of loony,' Keith heard the girl say in Croydon, the mouthpiece being inadequately muffled. There was an outburst of giggling before he was cut off.

It was not the first time that Keith and Dawne had suffered in this way: they were familiar with defeat. There'd been the time, a couple of years after their marriage, when Keith had got into debt through purchasing materials for making ships in bottles; earlier – before they'd even met – there was the occasion when the Lamb and Flag had had to let Dawne go because she'd taken tips although the rules categorically forbade it. Once Keith had sawn through the wrong water pipe and the landlords had come along with a bill for nearly two hundred pounds when the ceiling of the flat below collapsed. It was Uncle who had given Dawne a job in his shop after the Lamb and Flag episode and who had put them on their feet by paying off the arrears of the handicraft debt. In the end he persuaded them to come and live with him, pointing out that the arrangement would suit all three of them. Since his sister's death he had found it troublesome, managing on his own.

In Interlaken they selected a postcard to send him: of a mountain that had featured in a James Bond film. But they didn't know what to write on it: if they told the truth they would receive the old man's unspoken scorn when they returned – a look that came into his eyes while he silently regarded them. Years ago he had openly said – once only – that they were accident-prone. They were unfortunate in their dealings with the world, he had explained when Dawne asked him; lame ducks, he supposed you could say, if they'd forgive the expression, victims by nature, no fault of their own. Ever since, such judgements had been expressed only through his eyes.

'You choose your piece of gâteau,' Dawne said, 'up at the counter. They put it on a plate for you. Then the waitress comes along and you order the tea. I've been watching how it's done.'

Keith chose a slice of glazed greengage cake and Dawne a portion of strawberry flan. As soon as they sat down a waitress came and stood smiling in front of them. 'Tea with milk in it,' Dawne ordered, because when she'd said they were going abroad someone who'd come into the shop had warned her that you had to ask for milk, otherwise the tea came just as it was, sometimes no more than a tea-bag and a glass of hot water.

'A strike?' Dawne suggested. 'You're always hearing of strikes in airports.'

But Keith continued to gaze at the blank postcard, not persuaded that an attempt at falsehood was wise. It wasn't easy to tell the old man a lie. He had a way of making such attempts feel clumsy, and in the end of winkling out the truth. Yet his scorn would continue for many months, especially since he had paid out what he would call – a couple of hundred times at least – 'good money' for their tickets. 'That's typical of Keith, that is,' he'd repeatedly inform his customers in Dawne's hearing, and she'd pass it on that night in bed, the way she always passed his comments on.

Keith ate his greengage slice, Dawne her strawberry flan. They did not share their thoughts, although their thoughts were similar. 'You've neither of you a head for business,' he'd said after the ships-in-bottles calamity, and again when Dawne unsuccessfully attempted to make a go of dressmaking alterations. 'You wouldn't last a week in charge of things downstairs.' He always referred to the shop as 'downstairs'. Every day of his life he rose at five o'clock in order to be downstairs for the newspapers when they arrived. He'd done so for fifty-three years.

The plane couldn't land at the Italian airport, Keith wrote, *owing to a strike. So it had to come down here instead. It's good in a way because we're seeing another country as well!* Hope your cold's cleared up, Dawne added. *It's really lovely here!* XXX

They imagined him showing the postcard to Mrs Withers. 'That's typical, that is,' they imagined him saying and Mrs Withers jollying him along, telling him not to be sarky. Mrs Withers was pleased about earning the extra; she'd been as keen as anything when he'd asked her to come in fulltime for a fortnight.

'Could happen to anyone, a strike,' Dawne said, voicing Mrs Withers' response.

Keith finished his greengage slice. 'Call in to Smith's for a will form,' he imagined the cross, tetchy voice instructing Mrs Withers, the postcard already tucked away on the Embassy Tipped shelf. And when she arrived with the will form the next morning he'd let it lie around all day but have it in his hand when she left, before he locked the shop door behind her. 'Silly really,' Mrs Withers would say when eventually she told Dawne about it.

'I'd just as soon be here,' Dawne whispered, leaning forward a bit, daring at last to say that. 'I'd just as soon be in Switzerland, Keithie.'

He didn't reply, but looked around the teashop: at the display of cake in the long glass cabinet that served also as a counter – apricot and plum and apple, carrot-cake and Black Forest gâteau, richly glazed fruitcake, marzipan slices, small lemon tarts, orange éclairs, coffee fondants. Irritated because his wife had made that statement and wishing to be unpleasant to her by not responding, he allowed his gaze to slip over the faces of the couples who sat sedately at round, prettily arranged tables. In a leisurely manner he examined the smiling waitresses, their crimson aprons matching the crimson of the frilled tablecloths. He endeavoured to give the impression that the waitresses attracted him.

'It's really nice,' Dawne said, her voice still shyly low.

He didn't disagree; there was nothing wrong with the place. People were speaking in German, but when you spoke in English they understood you. Enoch Melchor, in Claims, had gone to somewhere in Italy last year and had got into all sorts of difficulties with the language, including being given the head of a fish when he thought he'd ordered peas.

'We could say we liked it so much we decided to stay on,' Dawne suggested.

She didn't seem to understand that it wasn't up to them to decide anything. Twelve days in Venice had been chosen for them; twelve days in Venice had been paid for. 'No better'n a sewer,' Enoch Melchor had said, not that he'd ever been there. 'Stinks to high heaven,' he'd said, but that wasn't the point either. Memories of Venice had been ordered, memories that were to be transported back to London, with glass figurines for the mantelpiece because Venice was famous for its glass. The menus at the Pensione Concordia and the tunes played by the café orchestras were to be noted in Dawne's day-to-day diary. Venice was bathed in sunshine, its best autumn for years, according to the newspapers.

They left the teashop and walked about the streets, their eyes stinging at first, until they became used to the bitter breeze that had got up. They examined windows full of watches, and went from one to another of the souvenir shops because notices said that entrance was free. There was a clock that had a girl swinging on a swing every hour, and another that had a man and a woman employing a cross-saw, another that had a cow being milked. All sorts of tunes came out of different-shaped musical boxes: 'Lily Marlene', 'The Blue Danube', 'Lara's Theme' from *Doctor Zhivago*, the 'Destiny Waltz'. There were oven gloves with next year's calendar printed on them in English, and miniature arrangements of dried flowers, framed, on velvet. In the chocolate shops there were all the different brands, Lindt, Suchard, Nestlé, Cailler, and dozens of others. There was chocolate with nuts, and chocolate with raisins, with nougat and honey, white chocolate, milk or plain, chocolate with fudge filling, with cognac or whisky or chartreuse, chocolate mice and chocolate windmills.

'It's ever so enjoyable here,' Dawne remarked, with genuine enthusiasm. They went into another teashop, and this time Keith had a chestnut slice and Dawne a blackcurrant one, both with cream.

At dinner, in a dining-room tastefully panelled in grey-painted wood, they sat among the people from Darlington, at a table for two, as the clerk in the travel agency had promised. The chicken-noodle soup was quite what they were used to, and so was the pork chop that followed, with apple sauce and chipped potatoes. 'They know what we like,' the woman called Mrs Franks said, making a round of all the tables, saying the same thing at each.

'Really lovely,' Dawne agreed. She'd felt sick in her stomach when they'd first realized about the error; she'd wanted to go to the lavatory and just sit there, hoping it was all a nightmare. She'd blamed herself because it was she who'd wondered about so many elderly people on the plane after the man in the travel place had given the impression of young people, from Windsor. It was she who had frowned, just for a moment, when the name of the airport was mentioned. Keith had a habit of pooh-poohing her doubts, like when she'd been doubtful about the men who'd come to the door selling mattresses and he'd been persuaded to make a down-payment. The trouble with Keith was, he always sounded confident, as though he knew something she didn't, as though someone had told him. 'We'll just be here for the night,' he'd said, and she'd thought that was something he must have read in the brochure or that the clerk in the travel place had said. He couldn't help himself, of course; it was the way he was made. 'Cotton-wool in your brain-box, have you?' Uncle had rudely remarked, the August Bank Holiday poor Keith had got them on to the slow train to Brighton, the one that took an hour longer.

'Silver lining, Keithie.' She put her head on one side, her small features softening into a smile. They'd walked by the lakeside before dinner. Just by stooping down, she'd attracted the birds that were swimming on the water. Afterwards she'd changed into her new fawn dress, bought specially for the holiday.

'I'll try that number again tomorrow,' Keith said.

She could see he was still worried. He was terribly subdued, even though he was able to eat his food. It made him cross when she mentioned the place they'd bought the tickets, so she didn't do so, although she wanted to. Time enough to face the music when they got back, better to make the best of things really: she didn't say that either.

'If you want to, Keithie,' she said instead. 'You try it if you've a call to.'

Naturally he'd feel it more than she would; he'd get more of the blame, being a man. But in the end it mightn't be too bad, in the end the storm would be weathered. There'd be the *fondue* party to talk about, and the visit to the chocolate factory. There'd be the swimming birds, and the teashops, and the railway journey they'd seen advertised, up to the top of an alp.

'Banana split?' the waiter offered. 'You prefer meringue Williams?'

They hesitated. Meringue Williams was meringue with pears and ice-cream, the waiter explained. Very good. He himself would recommend the meringue Williams.

'Sounds lovely,' Dawne said, and Keith had it too. She thought of pointing out that everyone was being nice to them, that Mrs Franks was ever so sympathetic, that the man who came round to ask them if the dinner was all right had been ever so pleasant, and the waiter too. But she decided not to because often Keith just didn't want to cheer up. 'Droopy Drawers', Uncle sometimes called him, or 'Down-in-the-Dumps Donald'.

All around them the old people were chattering. They were older than Uncle, Dawne could see; some of them were ten years older, fifteen even. She wondered if Keith had noticed that, if it had added to his gloom. She could hear them talking about the mementoes they'd bought and the teashops they'd been to; hale and hearty they looked, still as full of vim as Uncle. 'Any day now I'll be dropping off my twig,' he had a way of saying, which was nonsense of course. Dawne watched the elderly mouths receiving spoonfuls of banana or meringue, the slow chewing, the savouring of the sweetness. A good twenty years Uncle could go on for, she suddenly thought.

'It's just bad luck,' she said.

'Be that as it may.'

'Don't say that, Keithie.'

'Say what?'

'Don't say "Be that as it may".'

'Why not?'

'Oh just because, Keithie.'

They had in common an institution background: they had not known their parents. Dawne could remember Keith when he was eleven and she was nine, although at that time they had not been drawn to one another. They'd met again later, revisiting their children's home for the annual dance, disco as it was called these days. 'I got work in this shop,' she'd said, not mentioning Uncle because he was only her employer then, in the days when his sister was alive. They'd been married for a while before he became an influence in their lives. Now they could anticipate, without thinking, his changes of heart and his whims, and see a mile off another quarrel with the Reverend Simms, whose church occasionally he attended. Once they'd tried to divert such quarrels, to brace themselves for changes of heart, to counter the whims that were troublesome. They no longer did so. Although he listened carefully, he took no notice of what they said because he held the upper hand. The Smith's will forms and an old billiard-room – 'the happiest place a man could spend an hour in' – were what he threatened them with. He met his friends in the billiard-room; he read the *Daily Express* there, drinking bottles of Double Diamond, which he said was the best bottled beer in the world. It would be a terrible thing if men of all ages could no longer play billiards in that room, terrible if funds weren't available to keep it going for ever.

Mrs Franks made an announcement. She called for silence, and then gave particulars of the next day's programme. There was to be a visit to the James Bond mountain, everyone to assemble on the forecourt at half past ten. Anyone who didn't want to go should please tell her tonight.

'We don't have to, Keithie,' Dawne whispered when Mrs Franks sat down. 'Not if we don't want to.'

The chatter began again, spoons excitedly waved in the air. False teeth, grey hair, glasses; Uncle might have been among them except that Uncle never would because he claimed to despise the elderly. 'You're telling *me*, are you? You're telling *me* you got yourselves entangled with a bunch of O.A.P's?' As clearly as if he were beside her Dawne could hear his voice, enriched with the pretence of amazement. 'You landed up in the wrong country and spent your holiday with a crowd of geriatrics! You're never telling me that?'

Sympathetic as she was, Mrs Franks had played it down. She knew that a young couple in their thirties weren't meant to be on a package with the elderly; she knew the error was not theirs. But it wouldn't be any use mentioning Mrs Franks to Uncle. It wouldn't be any use saying that Keith had got cross with the receptionist and with the people in Croydon. He'd listen and then there'd be a silence. After that he'd begin to talk about the billiard-room.

'Had a great day, did you?' Mrs Franks said on her way out of the dining-room. 'All's well that ends well, eh?'

Keith continued to eat his meringue Williams as if he had not been addressed. Mr Franks remarked on the meringue Williams, laughing about it, saying they'd all have to watch their figures. 'I must say,' Mrs Franks said, 'we're lucky with the weather. At least it isn't raining.' She was dressed in the same flamboyant clothes. She'd been able to buy some Madame Rochas, she said, awfully good value.

'We don't have to say about the old people,' Dawne whispered when the Frankses had passed on. 'We needn't mention that.'

Dawne dug into the deep glass for the ice-cream that lay beneath the slices of pear. She knew he was thinking she would let it slip about the old people. Every Saturday she washed Uncle's hair for him since he found it difficult to do it himself. Because he grumbled so about the tepid rinse that was necessary in case he caught a cold afterwards, she had to jolly him along. She'd always found it difficult to do two things at once, and it was while washing his hair that occasionally she'd forgotten what she was saying. But she was determined not to make that mistake again, just as she had ages ago resolved not to get into a flap if he suddenly asked her a question when she was in the middle of counting the newspapers that hadn't been sold.

'Did you find your friends from Windsor then?' an old woman with a walking frame inquired. 'Eeh, it were bad you lost your friends.'

Dawne explained, since no harm was meant. Other old people stood by to hear, but a few of them were deaf and asked to have what was being said repeated. Keith continued to eat his meringue Williams.

'Keithie, it isn't their fault,' she tentatively began when the people had passed on. '*They* can't help it, Keithie.'

'Be that as it may. No need to go attracting them.'

'I didn't attract them. They stopped by. Same as Mrs Franks.'

'Who's Mrs Franks?'

'You know who she is. That big woman. She gave us her name this morning, Keithie.'

'When I get back I'll institute proceedings.'

She could tell from his tone that that was what he'd been thinking about. All the time on the steamer they'd taken to Interlaken, all the time in the teashop, and on the cold streets and in the souvenir shops, all the time they'd been looking at the watch displays and the chocolate displays, all the time in the grey-panelled dining-room, he had been planning what he'd say, what he'd probably write on the very next postcard: that he intended to take legal proceedings. When they returned he would stand in the kitchen and state what he intended, very matter of fact. First thing on Monday he'd arrange to see a solicitor, he'd state, an appointment for his lunch hour. And Uncle would remain silent, not even occasionally inclining his head, or shaking it, knowing that solicitors cost money.

'They're liable for the full amount. Every penny of it.'

'Let's try to enjoy ourselves, Keithie. Why don't I tell Mrs Franks we'll go up the mountain?'

'What mountain's that?'

'The one she was on about, the one we sent him a postcard of.'

'I need to phone up Croydon in the morning.'

'You can do it before ten-thirty, Keithie.'

The last of the elderly people slowly made their way from the dining-room, saying good-night as they went. A day would come, Dawne thought, when they would go to Venice on their own initiative, with people like the Windsor people. She imagined the Windsor people in the Pensione Concordia, not one of them a day older than themselves. She imagined Signor Bancini passing among them, translating a word or two of Italian as he went. There was laughter in the dining-room of the Pensione Concordia, and bottles of red wine on the tables. The young people's names were Désirée and Rob, and Luke and Angélique, and Sean and Aimée. 'Uncle we used to call him,' her own voice said. 'He died a while back.'

Keith stood up. Skilful with the tablecloths, the waiter wished them good-night. In the reception area a different receptionist, a girl, smiled at them. Some of the old people were standing around, saying it was too cold to go for a walk. You'd miss the television, one of them remarked.

The warmth of their bodies was a familiar comfort. They had not had children because the rooms above the shop weren't suitable for children. The crying at night would have driven Uncle mad, and naturally you could see his point of view. There'd been an error when first they'd lived with him; they'd had to spend a bit terminating it.

They refrained from saying that their bodies were a comfort. They had never said so. What they said in their lives had to do with Keith's hoping for promotion, and the clothes Dawne coveted. What they said had to do with their efforts to make a little extra money, or paying their way by washing the woodwork of an old man's house and tacking down his threadbare carpets.

When he heard their news he would mention the savings in the Halifax Building Society and the goodwill of the shop and the valuation that had been carried out four years ago. He would mention again that men of all ages should have somewhere to go of an evening, or in the afternoons or the morning, a place to be at peace. He would remind them that a man who had benefited could not pass on without making provision for the rent and the heating and for the replacing of the billiard tables when the moment came. 'Memorial to a humble man', he would repeat. 'Shopkeeper of this neighbourhood'.

In the darkness they did not say to one another that if he hadn't insisted they needed a touch of the autumn sun they wouldn't again have been exposed to humiliation. It was as though, through knowing them, he had arranged their failure in order to indulge his scorn. Creatures of a shabby institution, his eyes had so often said, they could not manage on their own: they were not even capable of supplying one another's needs.

In the darkness they did not say that their greed for his money was much the same as his greed for their obedience, that greed nourished the trinity they had become. They did not say that the money, and the freedom it promised, was the galaxy in their lives, as his cruelty was the last pleasure in his. Scarcely aware that they held on to one another beneath the bedclothes, they heard his teasing little laugh while they were still awake, and again when they slept.

The Third Party

The two men met by arrangement in Buswell's Hotel. The time and place
had been suggested by the man who was slightly the older of the two; his
companion had agreed without seeking an adjustment. Half past eleven in
the bar: 'I think we'll probably spot one another all right,' the older man
had said. 'Well, she'll have told you what I look like.'

He was tall, acquiring bulkiness, a pinkish-brown sunburn darkening
his face, fair curly hair that was turning grey. The man he met was thinner,
with spectacles and a smooth black overcoat, a smaller man considerably.
Lairdman this smaller man was called; the other's name was Boland. Both
were in their early forties.

'Well, we're neither of us late,' Boland said in greeting, the more nervous
of the two. 'Fergus Boland. How are you?'

They shook hands. Boland pulled out his wallet. 'I'll have a Jameson
myself. What'll I get you?'

'Oh, only a mineral. This time of day, Fergus. A lemonade.'

'A Jameson and a lemonade,' Boland ordered.

'Sure,' the barman said.

They stood by the bar. Boland held out a packet of cigarettes. 'D'you
smoke?'

Lairdman shook his head. He cocked an elbow on to the bar, arranging
himself tidily. 'Sorry about this,' he said.

They were alone except for the barman, who set their two glasses in
front of them. They weren't going to sit down; there was no move to do
so. 'A pound and tenpence,' the barman said, and Boland paid him.
Boland's clothes – tweed jacket and corduroy trousers – were wrinkled:
he'd driven more than a hundred miles that morning.

'I mean I'm really sorry,' Lairdman went on, 'doing this to anyone.'

'Good luck.' Boland raised his glass. He had softened the colour of the
whiskey by adding twice as much water. 'You never drink this early in the
day, I suppose?' he said, constrainedly polite. 'Well, very wise. That's very
sensible: I always say it.'

'I thought it mightn't be a drinking occasion.'

'I couldn't face you without a drink in, Lairdman.'

'I'm sorry about that.'

'You've lifted my wife off me. That isn't an everyday occurrence, you know.'

'I'm sorry –'

'It would be better if you didn't keep saying that.'

Lairdman, who was in the timber business, acknowledged the rebuke with a sideways wag of his head. The whole thing was awkward, he confessed, he hadn't slept a wink the night before.

'You're a Dubliner, she tells me,' Boland said, the same politeness to the fore. 'You make blockboard: there's money in that, no doubt about it.'

Lairdman was offended. She'd described her husband as clumsy but had added that he wouldn't hurt a fly. Already, five minutes into the difficult encounter, Lairdman wasn't so sure about that.

'I don't like Dublin,' Boland continued. 'I'll be frank about it. I never have. I'm a small-town man, but of course you'll know.'

He imagined his wife feeding her lover with information about his provincialism. She liked to tell people things; she talked a great deal. Boland had inherited a bakery in the town he had referred to, one that was quite unconnected with the more renowned Dublin bakery of the same name. A few years ago it had been suggested to him that he should consider retitling his, calling it Ideal Bread and Cakes, or Ovenfresh, in order to avoid confusion, but he saw no need for that, believing, indeed, that if a change should come about it should be made by the Dublin firm.

'I want to thank you,' Lairdman said, 'for taking this so well. Annabella has told me.'

'I doubt I have an option.'

Lairdman's lips were notably thin, his mouth a narrow streak that smiled without apparent effort. He smiled a little now, but shook his head to dispel any misconception: he was not gloating, he was not agreeing that his mistress's husband had no option. Boland was surprised that he didn't have a little chopped-off moustache, as so many Dublin men had.

'I thought when we met you might hit me,' Lairdman said. 'I remarked that to Annabella, but she said that wasn't you at all.'

'No, it isn't me.'

'That's what I mean by taking it well.'

'All I want to know is what you have in mind. She doesn't seem to know herself.'

'In mind?'

'I'm not protesting at your intentions where my wife is concerned, only asking if you're thinking of marrying her, only asking if you have some kind of programme. I mean, have you a place up here that's suitable for her? You're not a married man, I understand? I'll have another J.J.,' Boland called out to the barman.

'No, I'm not a married man. What we were hoping was that – if you're agreeable – Annabella could move herself into my place more or less at once. It's suitable accommodation all right, a seven-room flat in Wellington Road. But in time we'll get a house.'

'Thanks,' Boland said to the barman, paying him more money.

'That was my turn,' Lairdman protested, just a little late.

She wouldn't care for meanness, Boland thought. She'd notice when it began to impinge on her, which in time it would: these things never mattered at first.

'But marriage?' he said. 'It isn't easy, you know, to marry another man's wife in Ireland.'

'Annabella and I would naturally like to be married one day.'

'That's what I wanted to put to you. How are you suggesting that a divorce is fixed? You're not a Catholic, I'm to understand?'

'No.'

'No more am I. No more is Annabella. But that hardly matters, one way or another. She's very vague on divorce. We talked about it for a long time.'

'I appreciate that. And I appreciated your suggestion that we should meet.'

'I have grounds for divorce, Lairdman, but a damn bit of use they are to me. A divorce'll take an age.'

'It could be hurried up if you had an address in England. If the whole thing could be filed over there we'd be home and dry in no time.'

'But I haven't an address in England.'

'It's only a thought, Fergus.'

'So she wasn't exaggerating when she said you wanted to marry her?'

'I don't think I've ever known Annabella to exaggerate,' Lairdman replied stiffly.

Then you don't know the most important thing about her, Boland confidently reflected – that being that she can't help telling lies, which you and I would politely refer to as exaggerations. He believed that his wife actually disliked the truth, a rare enough attribute, he imagined, in any human being.

'I'm surprised you never got married,' he said, genuinely surprised because in his experience cocky little men like this very often had a glamorous woman in tow. He wondered if his wife's lover could possibly be a widower: naturally Annabella would not have been reliable about that.

'I've known your wife a long time,' Lairdman retorted softly, and Boland saw him trying not to let his smile show. 'As soon as I laid eyes on Annabella I knew she was the only woman who would make sense for me in marriage.'

Boland gazed into his whiskey. He had to be careful about what he said. If he became angry for a moment he was quite likely to ruin everything. The last thing he wanted was that the man should change his mind. He lit a cigarette, again offering the packet to Lairdman, who again shook his head. Conversationally, friendlily, Boland said:

'Lairdman's an interesting name – I thought that when she told me.'

'It's not Irish. Huguenot maybe, or part of it anyway.'

'I thought Jewish when she told me.'

'Oh, undoubtedly a hint of that.'

'You know the way you're interested when you're told about a relationship like that? "What's his name?" It's not important, it doesn't matter in the least. But still you ask it.'

'I'm sure. I appreciate that.'

When she'd said his name was Lairdman, Boland had remembered the name from his schooldays. Vaguely, he'd guessed that the man she was telling him about was a boy he couldn't quite place. But knowing the name, he'd recognized in Buswell's bar the adult features immediately.

'"Where did you meet him?" That doesn't matter either. And yet you ask it.'

'Annabella and I –'

'I know, I know.'

At school Lairdman had been notorious for an unexpected reason: his head had been held down a lavatory while his hair was scrubbed with a lavatory brush. Roche and Dead Smith had done it, the kind of thing they tended to do if they suspected uppitiness. Roche and Dead Smith were the bullies of their time, doling out admonitions to new boys who arrived at the school in the summer or winter terms rather than the autumn one, or to boys whose faces they found irritating. Lairdman's head had been scrubbed with the lavatory brush because he kept his hair tidy with perfumed oil that was offensive to Dead Smith.

'I think we were at school together,' Boland said.

Lairdman almost gave a jump, and it was Boland, this time, who disguised his smile. His wife would not have remembered the name of the school in question, not being in the least interested: the coincidence had clearly not been established.

'I don't recollect a Boland,' Lairdman said.

'I'd have been a little senior to yourself.' Deliberately, Boland sounded apologetic. 'But when she said your name I wondered. I was one of the boarders. Up from the country, you know. Terrible bloody place.'

Thirteen boarders there'd been, among nearly a hundred day boys. The day boys used to come noisily up the short, suburban avenue on their bicycles, and later ride noisily away. They were envied because they were returning to warmth and comfort and decent food, because after the weekends they'd talk about how they'd been to the Savoy or the Adelphi or even to the Crystal Ballroom. The boarders in winter would crouch around a radiator in one of the classrooms; in summer they'd walk in twos and threes around the playing-fields. The school matron, a Mrs Porter, was also the cook, but regularly burnt both the breakfast porridge and the barley soup she was given to producing as the main source of sustenance in the evening. An old boy of the school, occupying an attic at the top of a flight of uncarpeted stairs that led out of one of the dormitories, was the junior master, but he appeared to have acquired neither privilege nor distinction through that role: he, too, sat by the radiator in the classroom and dreaded the cooking of Mrs Porter. The bachelor headmaster, a boxer in his time – reputed to have been known in ringside circles as the Belted Earl, an obscurely acquired sobriquet that had remained with him – was a Savonarola-like figure in a green suit, sadistically inclined.

'Oh, I quite liked the place,' Lairdman said.

'You were a day boy.'

'I suppose it made a difference.'

'Of course it did.'

For the first time Boland felt annoyed. Not only was the man she'd become involved with mean, he was stupid as well. All this stuff about an address in England, all this stuff about giving up a seven-room flat, when if he had an iota of common sense he'd realize you didn't go buying houses for the likes of Annabella because in no way whatsoever could you rely on her doing what she said she was going to do.

'I've always thought, actually, it supplied a sound education,' Lairdman was saying.

The awful little Frenchman who couldn't make himself understood. O'Reilly-Flood, whose method of teaching history was to give the class the textbook to read while he wrote letters. The mathematics man who couldn't solve the problems he set. The Belted Earl in his foul laboratory, prodding at your ears with the sharp end of a tweezers until you cried out in pain.

'Oh, a great place,' Boland agreed. 'A fine academy.'

'We'd probably send our children there. If we have boys.'

'Your children?'

'You'd have no objection? Lord no, why should you? I'm sorry, that's a silly thing to say.'

'I'll have another,' Boland requested of the barman. 'How about your mineral?'

'No, I'm OK, thanks.'

This time he did not mention, even too late, that he should pay. Instead he looked away, as if wishing to dissociate himself from an over-indulgence in whiskey on an occasion such as this, before it was yet midday. Boland lit another cigarette. So she hadn't told him? She'd let this poor devil imagine that in no time at all the seven-room flat in Wellington Road wouldn't be spacious enough to contain the family that would naturally come trotting along once she'd rid herself of her provincial husband. Of course there'd have to be a divorce, and of course it would have to be hurried up: no one wanted a litter of little bastards in a seven-room flat or anywhere else.

'Good man, yourself,' he said to the barman when his whiskey came. If he ended up having too much to drink, as indeed might happen, he'd spend the night in the hotel rather than drive back. But it was early yet, and it was surprising what a heavy lunch could do.

'I'm sorry about that,' Lairdman repeated, referring again to his slip of the tongue. 'I wasn't thinking.'

'Ah, for heaven's sake, man!'

Boland briefly touched him, a reassuring tap on the shoulder. He could hear her telling him that the reason for their childless marriage had long ago been established. 'Poor old fellow,' she'd probably said, that being her kind of expression. She'd known before their marriage that she couldn't have children; in a quarrel long after it she'd confessed that she'd known and hadn't said.

'Naturally,' Lairdman blandly continued, 'we'd like to have a family.'

'You would of course.'

'I'm sorry that side of things didn't go right for you.'

'I was sorry myself.'

'The thing is, Fergus, is it OK about the divorce?'

'Are you saying I should agree to be the guilty party?'

'It's the done thing, as a matter of fact.'

'The done thing?'

'If you find it distasteful –'

'Not at all, of course not. I'll agree to be the guilty party and we'll work it out from there.'

'You're being great, Fergus.'

The way he was talking, Boland thought, he might have been drinking.

There were people who became easy-going, who adopted that same kind of tone, even if they'd only been with someone else who was drinking: he'd often heard that but he'd never believed it. A sniff of someone else's glass, he'd heard, a vapour in the air.

'D'you remember the cokeman they used to have there? McArdle?'

'Where was that, Fergus?'

'At school.'

Lairdman shook his head. He didn't remember McArdle, he said. He doubted that he'd ever known anyone of that name. 'A cokeman?' he repeated. 'What kind of a cokeman? I don't think I know the word.'

'He looked after the furnace. We called him the cokeman.'

'I never knew that person at all.'

Other people came into the bar. A tall man in a gaberdine overcoat who opened an *Irish Times* and was poured a glass of stout without having to order it. An elderly woman and two men who appeared to be her sons. A priest who looked around the bar and went away again.

'You wouldn't have noticed McArdle because you weren't a boarder,' Boland said. 'When you're weekends in a place you notice more.'

'I'm sorry I don't remember you.'

'I wouldn't expect you to.'

She'd be imagining this conversation, Boland suddenly realized. It was she who had suggested this bar for their meeting, speaking as if she knew it and considered it suitable. 'I think I'll go up and see Phyllis,' she used to say, saying it more often as time went by. Phyllis was a friend she had in Terenure, whose own marriage had ended on the rocks and who was suffering from an internal complaint besides. But of course Phyllis had just been a name she'd used, a stalwart friend who would cover up for her if she needed it. For all he knew, Phyllis might never have been married, her internal system might be like iron. 'Phone me,' he used to say, and obediently and agreeably his wife would. She'd tell him how Dublin looked and how Phyllis was bearing up. No doubt she'd been sitting on the edge of a bed in the seven-room flat in Wellington Road.

'It's really good of you to come all this way,' Lairdman said with a hint of finality in his voice, an indication that quite soon now the encounter should be brought to an end. 'I really appreciate it. I'll ring Annabella this afternoon and tell her we know where we stand. You won't mind that, Fergus?'

'Not at all.'

Boland had often interrupted such a telephone conversation. He would walk into the hall and there she'd be, knees drawn up, on the second step of the stairs, the receiver strung through the banisters. She'd be talking quite normally in her slightly high-pitched voice, but when he stepped through the hall door she'd wave a greeting and begin to whisper, the hand that had waved to him now cupped around the mouthpiece. He'd often wondered what she imagined he thought, or if she achieved some tremor of satisfaction from the hushed twilight of this semi-surreptitious carry-on. The trouble with Annabella was that sooner or later everything in the world bored her. 'Now, I want to hear,' she would soon be saying to Lairdman, 'every single thing since the moment you left the house.' And the poor man would begin a long history about catching a bus and passing through the entrance doors of his blockboard business, how he had said good morning to the typist and listened to the foreman's complaint concerning a reprehensible employee, how he'd eaten a doughnut with his eleven o'clock coffee, not as good a doughnut as he'd eaten the day before. Later, in a quarrel, she'd fling it all back at him: who on earth wanted to know about his doughnuts? she'd screech at him, her fingers splayed out in the air so that her freshly applied crimson nail varnish would evenly dry. She had a way of quarrelling when she was doing her nails, because she found the task irksome and needed some distraction. Yet she'd have felt half undressed if her fingernails weren't properly painted, or if her make-up wasn't right or her hair just as she wanted it.

'I'll be able to say,' Lairdman was stating with what appeared to be pride, 'that there wasn't an acrimonious word between us. She'll be pleased about that.'

Boland smiled, nodding agreeably. He couldn't imagine his wife being pleased since she so rarely was. He wondered what it was in Lairdman that attracted her. She'd said, when he'd asked her, that her lover was fun; he liked to go abroad, she'd said, he appreciated food and painting; he possessed what she called a 'devastating' sense of humour. She hadn't mentioned his sexual prowess, since it wasn't her habit to talk in that way. 'Will you be taking those cats?' Boland had inquired. 'I don't want them here.' Her lover would willingly supply a home for her Siamese cats, she had replied, both of which she called 'Ciao'. Boland wondered if his successor even knew of their existence.

'I wonder what became,' he said, 'of Roche and Dead Smith?'

He didn't know why he said it, why he couldn't have accepted that the business between them was over. He should have shaken hands with Lairdman and left it at that, perhaps saying there were no hard feelings. He would never have to see the man again; once in a while he would feel sorry for the memory of him.

'Dead Smith?' Lairdman said.

'Big eejit with a funny eye. There's a barrister called Roche now; I often wonder if that's the same fellow.'

'I don't think I remember either of them.'

'Roche used to go round in a pin-striped blue suit. He looked like one of the masters.'

Lairdman shook his head. 'I'll say cheerio, Fergus. Again, my gratitude.'

'They were the bright sparks who washed your hair in a lavatory bowl.'

Boland had said to himself over and over again that Lairdman was welcome to her. He looked ahead to an easy widower's life, the house she had filled with her perversities and falsehoods for the last twelve years as silent as a peaceful sleep. He would clear out the memories of her because naturally she wouldn't do that herself – the hoarded magazines, the empty medicine bottles, the clothes she had no further use for, the cosmetics she'd pitched into the corners of cupboards, the curtains and chair-covers clawed by her cats. He would get Molloy in to paint out the rooms. He would cook his own meals, and Mrs Coughlan would still come every morning. Mrs Coughlan wouldn't be exactly sorry to see the back of her, either.

'I don't know why,' Lairdman said, 'you keep going on about your schooldays.'

'Let me get you a decent drink before you go. Bring us two big ones,' he called out to the barman, who was listening to an anecdote the man in the gaberdine coat was retailing at the far end of the bar.

'No, really,' Lairdman protested. 'Really now.'

'Oh, go on, man. We're both in need of it.'

Lairdman had buttoned his black overcoat and drawn on a pair of black leather gloves. Finger by finger he drew one of the gloves off again. Boland could feel him thinking that, for the sake of the woman who loved him, he must humour the cuckold.

'It takes it out of you,' Boland said. 'An emotional thing like this. Good luck to you.'

They drank, Lairdman seeming awkward now because of what had been said. He looked a bit like a priest, Boland thought, the black attire and the way he wore it. He tried to imagine the pair of them abroad, sitting down together in a French restaurant, Lairdman being pernickety about a plate of food he didn't like the look of. It didn't make sense, all this stuff about a devastating sense of humour.

'I only mentioned the school,' Boland said, 'because it was the other thing we had in common.'

'As a matter of fact, I'm a governor up there now.'

'Ah, go on!'

'That's why I said we'd maybe send the children there.'

'Well, doesn't that beat the band!'

'I'm pleased myself. I'm pleased they asked me.'

'Sure, anyone would be.'

Stupid he might be, Boland thought, but he was cute as well, the way he'd managed not to make a comment on the Roche and Dead Smith business. Cuteness was the one thing you could never get away from in Dublin. Cute as weasels they were.

'You don't remember it?' he prompted.

'What's that?'

'The lavatory thing.'

'Look here, Boland —'

'I've offended you. I didn't mean that at all.'

'Of course you haven't offended me. It's just that I see no point in harping on things like that.'

'We'll talk of something else.'

'Actually, I'm a bit on the late side.'

The second glove was again drawn on, the buttons of the smooth black overcoat checked to see that all was well for the street. The glove was taken off again when Lairdman remembered there'd have to be a handshake.

'Thanks for everything,' he said.

For the second time, Boland surprised himself by being unable to leave well alone. He wondered if it was the whiskey; the long drive and then the whiskey on top of an empty stomach because of course there hadn't been anything in the house for his breakfast when he'd gone to look, not even a slice of bread. 'I'll come down and do you scrambled eggs and a few rashers,' she'd said the night before. 'You'll need something inside you before you set off.'

'I'm interested in what you say about sending your children there,' was what he heard himself saying. 'Would these be your and Annabella's children you have in mind?'

Lairdman looked at him as if he'd gone out of his senses. His narrow mouth gaped in bewilderment. Boland didn't know if he was trying to smile or if some kind of rictus had set in.

'What other children are there?' Lairdman shook his head, still perplexed. He held his hand out, but Boland did not take it.

'I thought those might be the children you had in mind,' he said.

'I don't follow what you're saying.'

'She can't have children, Lairdman.'

'Ah now, look here —'

'That's a medical fact. The unfortunate woman is incapable of mothering children.'

'I think you're drunk. One after another you've had. I thought it a moment ago when you got maudlin about your schooldays. Annabella's told me a thing or two, you know.'

'She hasn't told you about the cats she's going to spring on you. She hasn't told you she can't give birth. She hasn't told you she gets so bored her face turns white with fury. It's best not to be around then, Lairdman. Take my tip on that.'

'She's told me you can't stay sober. She's told me you've been warned off every racecourse in Ireland.'

'I don't go racing, Lairdman, and apart from occasions like this I hardly drink at all. A lot less than our mutual friend, I can promise you that.'

'You have been unable to give Annabella children. She's sorry for you, she doesn't blame you.'

'Annabella was never sorry for anyone in her life.'

'Now look here, Boland –'

'Look nowhere, man. I've had twelve years of the woman. I'm obliging you by stepping aside. But there's no need for this talk of divorce, Lairdman, in England or anywhere else. I'm just telling you that. She'll come and live with you in your seven-room flat; she'll live in any house you care to buy, but if you wait till kingdom come you'll not find children trotting along. All you'll have is two Siamese cats clawing the skin off you.'

'You're being despicable, Boland.'

'I'm telling you the truth.'

'You seem to have forgotten that Annabella and myself have talked about all this. She knew you'd take it hard. She knew there'd be bitterness. Well, I understand that. I've said I'm sorry.'

'You're a mean little blockboard man, Lairdman. You belong with your head held down in a lavatory bowl. Were you wringing wet when they let go of you? I'd love to have seen it, Lairdman.'

'Will you keep your damn voice down? And will you stop trying to pick a quarrel? I came out this morning in good faith. I'm aware of the delicacy of the thing, and I'm not saying I've been a saint. But I'll not stand here and be insulted. And I'll not hear Annabella insulted.'

'I think Dead Smith became a vet.'

'I don't care what he became.'

Abruptly, Lairdman was gone. Boland didn't turn his head, or otherwise acknowledge his departure. He examined the row of bottles behind the bar, and in a moment he lit a fresh cigarette.

For half an hour he remained on his own where his usurper had left him. All he could think of was Lairdman as he remembered him, a boy who was pointed out because of what two bullies had done to him. The old cokeman, McArdle, used to laugh over the incident. Sometimes, when the classroom radiator wasn't hot enough, the boarders would go down to McArdle's cokehole and sit around his furnace. He'd tell them obscene stories, all of them to do with the matron and cook, or else he told them about Lairdman. The more Boland thought about it all the more clearly he remembered Lairdman: not much different in appearance, the same trap of a mouth, a propelling pencil and a fountain pen clipped into the pocket of his jacket. He had a bicycle, Boland could remember, a new one that had perhaps replaced an older one, a Golden Eagle. 'Oh, we met at a party Phyllis gave,' she had said, but there was no way of knowing how much truth there was in that, presumably none.

Boland ate his lunch in the dining-room of the hotel, among people he did not know, who gave the impression of lunching there regularly. He didn't have to say he'd take nothing to drink because the waitress didn't ask him. There was water in a glass jug on the table; he'd be all right for the journey home, he decided.

'The cod,' he ordered. 'Yes, I'll have the cod. And the cream of celery.'

He remembered a time when the thirteen boarders had smashed a window in an outhouse that no longer had a purpose. Most of the window-panes were broken already, the roof had long ago tumbled in, and one of the walls was so badly split that it had begun to disintegrate. It was forbidden for any boy to enter this small, crumbling building, and the boarders had not done so. They had stood twenty or so yards away throwing stones at the remaining window-panes, as they might have thrown stones at a cockshot. They had meant no harm, and did not realize that an outhouse which was so badly damaged already might be worthy of preservation. Ceremoniously the following morning the Belted Earl had taken his cane to them in the presence of the assembled day boys. Lairdman would have been watching, Boland reflected as he ate his soup: Lairdman might have brought it up just as he himself had brought up the other matter, but of course that wasn't Lairdman's way. Lairdman considered himself a sophisticate; even in the days of his Golden Eagle he would have considered himself that.

Boland crumbled the bread on his side plate, picking up bits of it between mouthfuls of soup. He saw himself, one day in the future, entering the silence of his house. He saw himself on a summer evening pushing open the french windows of the drawing-room and going out into the garden, strolling among its fuchsia bushes and apple trees. He'd known the house all his life; he'd actually been born in it. Opposite O'Connor Motors, it was the last one in the town, yellow-washed and ordinary, but a house he loved.

'Did you say the fish, sir?' the waitress inquired.

'Yes, I did.'

He'd been married in Dublin, she being the daughter of a Dublin wine merchant. The old man was still alive and so was her mother. 'You've taken on a handful,' the old man once had said, but he'd said it playfully because in those days Annabella had been a handful to delight in. What they thought of her now Boland had no idea.

'The plate's hot, sir,' the waitress warned.

'Thanks very much.'

People who'd known him in his childhood had been delighted when he brought her to live among them. They'd stopped him on the street and said he was lucky. They were happy for him: he'd come back from Dublin with a crown of jewels, which was how they saw it. And yet those same people would be delighted when she left. The terrible frustration that possessed her – the denial of children through some mischance within her – turned beauty into wanton eccentricity. It was that that had happened, nothing else.

Slowly he ate his cod, with parsley sauce and cabbage and potatoes. Nobody would mention it much; they'd know what had happened and they'd say to one another that one day, probably, he'd marry again. He wondered if he would. He'd spoken airily of divorce to Lairdman, but in truth he knew nothing of divorce in Ireland these days. A marriage should wither away, he somehow felt, it should rot and die; it didn't seem quite like a cancer, to be swiftly cut out.

He ordered apple tart and cream, and later coffee came. He was glad it was all over: the purpose of his visit to Dublin had been to set a seal on everything that had happened, and in the encounter that had taken place the seal had at some point been set. The air had been cleared, he had accepted the truth it had been necessary to hear from someone else besides his wife. When first she'd told him he'd wondered if she could possibly be making it all up, and he'd wondered it since. Even while he'd waited in Buswell's bar he'd said to himself he wouldn't be surprised if no one turned up.

On the way to the car park two tinker children begged from him. He knew it wasn't coppers they were after, but his wallet or whatever else they could get their fingers on. One held out a cardboard box, the other pressed close to him, with a rug folded over her hands. He'd seen the trick before; Dublin was like that now. 'Go on, along with you,' he ordered them as harshly as he could.

It was because there hadn't been enough for her to do: he thought that as he eased the car through the heavy city traffic. And from the very start she hadn't taken to provincial life. A childless woman in a provincial town had all the time in the world to study its limitations. She had changed the furniture around, and had chosen the wallpapers that her Siamese cats had later damaged. But she'd resisted bridge and tennis, and had deplored the absence of even a cinema café. He'd thought he'd understood; so well used to the limitations himself, he was nevertheless aware that the society he had plunged her into was hardly scintillating. He'd driven her as often as he could to Dublin, before she'd taken to going on her own to visit Phyllis. For years he'd known she wasn't happy, but until she told him he'd never suspected she'd become involved with a man.

He stopped in Mullingar and had a cup of tea. The Dublin evening papers had arrived before him. He read in the *Herald* that the Italian government had been successfully re-formed after the Achille Lauro incident; the dollar was slipping again; a meat-processing plant was to close in Cork. He dawdled over the paper, not wanting to go home. Lairdman would have telephoned her by now. 'Why don't you drive up this afternoon?' he might have said. Maybe she had been packing all day, knowing the encounter was only a formality. 'He won't stand in the way,' Lairdman would have said. 'He'll even supply grounds.' There'd be nothing to keep her, now that all three of them knew where they stood, and it was the kind of thing she'd do, pack up and go when she'd got him out of the way.

A coal fire was burning in the café. A rare welcome these days, he remarked to the woman who'd served him, and pulled a chair up close to it. 'I'd take another cup of tea,' he said.

The little white Volkswagen he'd bought her might be on the road to Dublin already. She wouldn't leave a note because she wouldn't consider it necessary. If the Volkswagen passed by now she would be puzzled at not meeting him on the road; she'd never notice his own car parked outside the café.

'Ah well, you'd need a fire,' the woman said, returning with his tea. 'A shocking foggy old month we're having.'

'I've known better certainly.'

He drove on after he'd had a third cup of tea, keeping an eye out for the Volkswagen. Would she greet him with a touch on the horn? Or would he greet her? He didn't know if he would. Better to wait for the moment.

But over the next fifty or so miles there was no sign of his wife's car. And of course, he told himself, there was no reason why there should be: it was pure conjecture that she'd depart that afternoon, and the amount she had to pack made it unlikely that she could manage to do so in a day. For the next few miles he speculated on how, otherwise, her departure would be. Would Lairdman drive down to assist her? That had not been agreed upon or even touched upon as a possibility: he would instantly put his foot down if it was suggested. Would Phyllis arrive to help her? He would naturally have no objection to that. Certainly, the more he thought about it, the less likely was it that she could be capable of completing the move on her own. She had a way of calling on other people when something difficult had to be undertaken. He imagined her sitting on the second step of the stairs, chattering on the telephone. 'Would you ever ...?' she had a way of beginning her demands and her requests.

His headlights caught the familiar sign, in English and Irish, indicating that the town which was his home was the next one. He turned the radio on. 'Dancing in the dark', a sensual female voice lilted, reminding him of the world he supposed his wife and Lairdman belonged to; the thrill of illicit love, tête-à-tête dancing, as the song implied. 'Poor Annabella', he said aloud, while the music still played. Poor girl, ever to have got herself married to the inheritor of a country-town bakery. Lucky, in all fairness, that cocky little Lairdman had turned up. The music continued, and he imagined them running towards one another along an empty street, like lovers in a film. He imagined their embrace, and then their shared smile before they embraced again. As the dull third party, not even a villain, he had no further part to play.

But as Boland reached the first few houses on this side of the town he knew that none of that was right. Not only had the white Volkswagen not conveyed her to Lairdman in his absence, it would not do so tomorrow or the next day, or next week. It would not do so next month, or after Christmas, or in February, or in the spring: it would not ever do so. It hadn't mattered reminding Lairdman of the ignominy he had suffered as a boy; it hadn't mattered reminding him that she was a liar, or insulting him by calling him mean. All that abuse was conventional in the circumstances, an expected element in the man-to-man confrontation, the courage for it engendered by an intake of John Jameson. Yet something had impelled him to go further: little men like Lairdman always wanted children. 'That's a total lie,' she'd have said already on the telephone, and Lairdman would have soothed her. But soothing wasn't going to be enough for either of them.

Boland turned the radio off. He drew the car up outside Donovan's public house and sat for a moment, swinging the keys between his thumb and forefinger before going in and ordering a bottle of Smithwick's with lime. At the bar he greeted men he knew and stood with them drinking, listening to talk of racehorses and politics. They drifted away when a few more drinks had been taken but Boland remained there for a long time, wondering why he hadn't been able to let Lairdman take her from him.

Honeymoon in Tramore

They stayed in a boarding-house, St Agnes's, run by a Mrs Hurley. 'You have it written all over you!' this woman said when she opened the door to them. She eyed a speck of confetti on the lapel of his navy-blue suit and then glanced briefly at the rounding of Kitty's stomach. It was the summer of 1948, a warm afternoon in July.

Mrs Hurley was a middle-aged landlady in a brown coat, who apologized for the wellington boots she was wearing: she'd been brushing down the yard. Her fingernails were enamelled a vivid shade of pink, her hair was contained by a tidy blue hairnet which partially disguised an arrangement of pins and curling papers. They would be very happy in St Agnes's, she said, they'd have the place to themselves because there was no one else stopping in the house at the moment. When they were carrying their two suitcases upstairs she said that marriage was a God-given institution and added that her husband went to Mass every morning of his life, on his way to work with the county council. 'Your tea'll be on the table at six on the dot,' she said.

On their own, they embraced. He put his hand under his wife's skirt and felt for the warm flesh at the top of her stockings. 'Jesus, you're terrible,' she murmured thickly at him, as she had on the bus when he'd pressed himself close against her. She was sweating because of her condition and the July heat. Her face was sticky with perspiration, and small patches of it had developed on her dress, beneath each armpit. 'Jesus,' she whispered again. 'Oh Jesus, go easy now.'

He didn't want to go easy. They were free of the farm, and of her father and her aunt and her Uncle Ned Cauley. He had a right to his desires.

'That woman'll be listening,' she whispered in the same slurred voice, but it didn't matter if the woman was listening. It didn't even matter if the woman opened the door and walked in. The bed made creaking sounds when she wriggled away from him, saying again that he was terrible, giggling as she said it. The bedroom smelt of flies, as if the windows hadn't been opened for a long time. 'God, you're great, Kitty,' he said, his own voice thickening also.

He was thirty-three, Kitty two years older. At fifteen he had been taken from the orphans' home in Cork by Kitty's father and her Uncle Ned

Cauley. The two men had let it be known that they could do with a young fellow on the farm, and Father Doran, who was their parish priest at that time, had made inquiries of Father Lyhane at the orphans' home on their behalf. 'Davy Toome's a good lad,' Father Lyhane had said, and a few weeks later, after the recommendation had been passed on to the farmers and after Father Doran had been assured that the candidate would be strong enough for farm-work, a label with that name on it had been attached to the boy and he'd been forwarded by train. 'And did you never do farm-work before?' Kitty's Uncle Ned Cauley had asked, sitting beside him in the cart as they slowly progressed on the road from the railway junction. But Davy had never even seen fields with corn in them before, let alone taken part in farm-work. 'I'm thinking,' said Kitty's uncle, who'd spent an hour in Doolin's public house at the railway junction, 'that it could be we bought a pig in a poke.' He said it again in the kitchen when they arrived, while his wife and his brother-in-law were examining Davy, silently agreeing that he was not as strong as the priest had claimed. 'Will you for God's sake take off that label!' the woman said to him, and then, in a gentler voice, asked him about his name. She'd never heard of Toome before, she said, so he told them that his name had been given to him when the orphans' home had taken him in as an infant, that there'd been a priest connected with it then who'd had an interest in naming the orphans. His first name was in memory of St David. Toome meant a burial mound. 'Is he right in the head?' he afterwards heard Kitty's father asking his brother-in-law and her uncle replying that you wouldn't know, the way he was talking about burial mounds.

'Will you come on now, for heaven's sake!' Kitty rebuked him in the bedroom at St Agnes's. 'And let me take off my hat.'

She pushed him away from her and told him to open the window. It was she who had chosen Tramore for the weekend of their honeymoon, saying she'd heard it was lovely, with a sandy little beach. Kitty knew what she wanted, her aunt used to say, and you couldn't budge her when she made up her mind. 'Would you accompany me to Cork?' she had suggested one day four months ago. 'I'm a stranger to the city, Davy.' He hadn't been back to Cork since he'd come to the farm, and he didn't really know his way around it; but it turned out that Kitty had never been there at all. 'We'll fix it to go on a Saturday,' she said, and on the bus he felt proud to be sitting there with her, a big handsome girl, the daughter of his employer: he hoped that on the streets they'd maybe meet someone from the orphans' home. She'd looked out the window most of the time, not saying very much to him, her round face pink with excitement. She was good-looking in a way he admired, better-looking than any of the other girls at Mass, or the tinker girls whom he'd caught once stealing turnips from the field, who'd shouted over a hedge at him that their sister would marry him. Her hair was very fine and very black, like a dark mist encircling her face. He'd heard her aunt calling her sullen, but he'd never noticed that himself, even though sometimes a blankness came into her face and stayed there till she roused herself. Her three brothers had all been born with something wrong with them and had died in childhood, before he had come to the farm. Nobody mentioned them; he hadn't even known about her brothers until one of the men who came to help with the harvest referred to them in passing. Her mother had died giving birth to the last of them.

'Are you OK, pet?' Kitty said, putting lipstick on at the dressing-table. 'Isn't it great we're on our own?'

He leaned against the window-frame, looking at her, seeing her in the looking-glass as well. She had to go to see a Mr Minogue, she'd said eventually on the bus, a chemist in McHenry Street.

'Great,' he said from the window.

'Can you hear the sea there?'

He shook his head. They'd found the chemist's shop, having had to ask for directions to McHenry Street. If her mother was alive she'd have accompanied her, she said all of a sudden, and then she said she couldn't go into the chemist's shop alone. Her voice became different. Her legs wouldn't have taken her, she said, and then she told him she was in trouble. Her aunt had found out about the chemist, she said, only she'd refused to accompany her. 'Take Toome to show you the way,' her aunt had said.

'Will we go down, pet?'

He moved to where she stood by the dressing-table but when he put his arms around her she said sharply that she didn't want to get messed up again. She'd spilt powder on the glass top of the dressing-table, the same peach shade that was on her cheeks. She'd put on perfume he could smell, a strong sweet smell that made him want to try again to put his arms around her. But already she had crossed the room to the door. She opened it and he followed her downstairs.

'I've done you black puddings,' Mrs Hurley said in the dining-room, placing before them plates of fried sausages and fried eggs and slices of the delicacy she spoke of.

'God, I love black pudding,' Kitty said, and he passed her his because as a boy in the orphans' home he had developed a revulsion for this dark composition of pig's blood and entrails. The table they sat at was empty of other guests, as Mrs Hurley had promised. He smiled at his bride across it. On the way downstairs she had kept repeating that this would be their first meal as husband and wife. She attached importance to the fact. She'd said it again as they sat down. Through the wooden hatch that opened into the kitchen the voice of Mrs Hurley could be heard raised in abuse, speaking about a greyhound.

'Are you hungry, pet?'

He wasn't; he shook his head.

'D'you know what it is,' Kitty said, cutting into a soda farl, 'I could eat the head off of a horse.'

A low mumble of protest had begun in the kitchen, which he guessed must emanate from Mrs Hurley's husband. 'Errah, have a pick of sense, will you?' the landlady stridently interrupted. 'Would any animal in its sane mind keep getting into a cement mixer?'

Kitty giggled. She'd nearly died, she said, when Mrs Kilfedder gave her a kiss at the wedding. 'One thing about Kilfedder,' she added, 'he keeps his hands to himself.'

At that moment a man in shirtsleeves entered the dining-room. He greeted them and introduced himself as Mr Hurley. He inquired if they'd like another pot of tea, already seizing the metal teapot and moving towards the hatch with it. They'd find St Agnes's restful, he said, no children for miles around. The hatch opened and Mrs Hurley's freshly rouged face appeared. She had removed her hairnet, and the hair it had controlled, now seen to be a shade of henna, fluffed elaborately about her head. 'Have they butter enough?' she demanded of her husband, in the same uncompromising tone she had employed when protesting about the activities of the greyhound. 'It's good country butter,' she shouted at her guests. 'Fresh as a daisy.'

'We have plenty,' Kitty replied. 'It's good butter all right, Mrs Hurley.'

The teapot was handed back through the hatch and placed on the table. 'There's a big attraction in Tramore tonight,' Mr Hurley said. 'Have you ever heard tell of the Carmodys?'

When they said they hadn't he told them that the Carmodys ran a Wall of Death that was reputed to be great entertainment. She had never seen a Wall of Death yet, Kitty said when he'd gone. 'D'you like the sausages, pet?'

He nodded, holding his cup out for tea. Under the table the calves of their legs were pressed together.

'Coddy Donnegan wanted to take me once, only I said I couldn't watch it.'

'Maybe we wouldn't bother in that case.'

'I'd watch anything with yourself, Davy. Maybe we'd walk down by the sea as well.'

He nodded again and she leaned forward to say she was feeling fine, a reference to the fact that she had recently been subject to bouts of sickness in her stomach. They'd have a few drinks after the Wall of Death and the walk, she suggested, in case it wouldn't look good, coming back to the bedroom too soon. She winked and nudged him with her knee. Under the table he put his hand on her lightly stockinged leg. 'Oh Jesus, lay off now,' she whispered.

It wasn't Coddy Donnegan, she'd told him in McHenry Street, standing outside the chemist's shop. She'd never been in love with Coddy Donnegan. She'd never been in love until the other thing happened, until there was a man taking her hand in a way Coddy Donnegan wouldn't do in a million years – a cousin of Father Tolan's, who was destined himself for the priesthood. He'd been about in the parish for the summer holidays; she'd have put down her life for him, she said. 'He'd marry me if he knew, Davy. He'd give up the priesthood, only I'd never tell him.'

They finished the meal Mrs Hurley had prepared for them. 'I'll just go upstairs a minute,' she said. 'I won't be a tick, pet.'

Waiting in the hall, Davy examined the pictures on the walls. A light burned beneath the Virgin and Child; there were reproductions of Victorian paintings, one of a match-seller, another of a shawled woman with a basket of lavender. He turned away from them, and the face of the chemist crept into his recollection: the jaw dark, the chin pimpled beneath a raw shave, eyes magnified behind heavily lensed spectacles, cheeks as pale as the white coat he wore. 'Come in,' Mr Minogue had welcomed them that day, knowing what they wanted although nothing had been said yet. It was the afternoon when his shop was closed, and he led them through the stillness of it into a room at the back, where there were no chairs to sit on, only a table with a rubber sheet on it. 'I take a grave risk,' Mr Minogue announced without preamble, his unsmiling countenance reflecting eloquently the gravity he spoke of. 'The assistance I offer you in your distress is offered for humanitarian reasons only. But the risk must be covered, you understand that? It is not of my own volition that I charge a fee.' While he spoke he did not remove his bulbously magnified eyes from their faces, revolving his stare in a circle around each, sliding it from one to the other. 'You may know the fee?' he said, and when Kitty placed the money before him his grey, closely barbered head bowed over the notes he counted. 'Yes, this is correct,' he said, speaking directly to Davy, clearly assuming him to be the father of the unwanted child and the source of the fee. He placed the notes in a wallet he'd taken out of the back pocket of his trousers, and jerked his head at Davy, indicating that he should return to the shop and wait there. But before Davy could do so both he and the abortionist were taken by surprise because without any warning whatsoever Kitty cried out that she couldn't do it. She would burn in hell for it, she shrieked in sudden, shrill, unexpected emotion; she could never confess it, there was no penance she could be given. 'I'd rather die as I stand, sir,' she said to Mr Minogue, and gave way to tears. They flooded on her flushed, round cheeks; the humane abortionist stood arrested, one hand still in the back pocket of his trousers. 'Hail Mary, Mother of God!' Kitty cried, shrill again. 'Sweet Mother, don't abandon me!' The money was handed back, no further word was spoken. Mr Minogue removed his white coat and led the way to the door of his shop, glancing before he opened it around the edge of an advertisement for liver salts pasted to its glass. The street was empty. As there had been no salutation, so there was no farewell.

'Are we right so?' Kitty said, descending the stairs.

He opened the hall door and they stepped out into the evening. It was warm and quiet on the terraced cul-de-sac, in which St Agnes's was the last house. They still couldn't hear the sea and Kitty said the waves wouldn't be big in that case. 'I'm sorry,' she'd said outside the chemist's shop, still sobbing, and then they'd walked for ages through the streets, before having a cup of tea in a café. She was calm by that time; it had never for a second occurred to her that she couldn't do it, she said, but the sin when she'd handed Mr Minogue the money had been like something alive in the room with them. 'I swear to God, Davy.' He'd said he understood, but in fact he didn't. He was confused because there was so much to take in – her being in trouble, the purpose of their journey being revealed, and then the episode with Mr Minogue. He was the man on the farm, the labourer who worked in the yard and the fields: it had been strange enough being asked to go to Cork with her. In the café, after she'd drunk two cups of tea, she said she was better. She ate a bun with currants in it, but he couldn't eat anything himself. Then he brought her to the orphans' home just to look at the outside of. 'God, Davy, what am I going to do?' she suddenly cried when they were standing there, as suddenly as she'd said in the back room of the chemist's that she couldn't go through with it.

'It's down at the strand,' a man told them when they asked about the Wall of Death. He pointed out the way, and soon they heard the music that accompanied it and the roar of the motor-cycle's engine. '... *to see again the moonlight over Clara*', moaned a tenor voice, robbed of its mellifluous quality by the scratching of a gramophone needle. '... *and to see the sun going down on Galway Bay*'. They paid the admission charge and climbed up rickety stairs, like a ladder, that led to the top of the circular wooden wall. A platform ran around the circumference, with a balustrade to prevent the jostling audience from falling into the pit below. 'God, it's great,' Kitty shouted above the noise, and Davy gave her arm a squeeze. A small, wizened man in red gaiters and black leather clothes, with a spotted red neckerchief, mounted the quivering motor-cycle that stood on its pedestal in the centre of the pit. He pushed it forward and ran it on to the incline at the bottom of the wall, gradually easing it on to the wall itself. Each circle he made increased the angle of his machine until in the end, close to the balustrade over which the audience leaned, he and his motor-cycle were horizontal. The timbers of the wall and of the platform shuddered, the roar of the engine was deafening. Waving above his head, the performer descended, the same circular motion in reverse. The audience clapped and threw coins into the pit. 'Are you O K?' Davy shouted, for in the excitement Kitty had closed her eyes. In the pit the motor-cycle was returned to its stand. The man bowed his gratitude for the money that still lay on the ground, and then threw out an arm in a sudden, dramatic gesture. He was joined immediately by a woman, dressed in red-and-black clothing also, who climbed on to the pillion of his motor-cycle and when it reached the centre of the wall clambered on to his back. She stood on his shoulders, with his spotted neckerchief streaming from between her teeth. Kitty screamed and closed her eyes again. More coins were thrown.

'Is she his wife, Davy?' Kitty asked as they walked away.

'I'd say she was.'

'Wouldn't it be shocking if she came off?'

'I'd say she wouldn't.'

'God, I love the smell of the sea, Davy.'

If she hadn't been wearing stockings she'd have paddled, she said, and he told her about a time they'd been taken from the orphans' home to the seaside at Courtmacsherry. He continued to tell her about this while they walked back to the town and went in search of a public house. They found one that was as quiet as St Agnes's, a murky place that Kitty said was cosy. Two elderly men sat at the counter, steadily drinking, not conversing. The publican was shifting sacks of meal in the grocery that adjoined the bar. Davy called out to him, ordering bottles of stout.

'Was it terrible in the orphans' home?' Kitty asked when he'd carried them to the table she was sitting at. 'Did you hate it the whole time?'

He said he hadn't. It hadn't been bad; he'd never known anywhere else until he came to the farm. 'Jeez, it looks like a prison,' she'd said that day, looking up at the orphans' home from the street.

'It's terrible, though, no family to turn to,' she said now. 'I have the half of it myself, with no mother.'

'You get used to the way it is.'

A week after their visit to Cork her aunt said to him in the yard that Kitty would marry him if he asked her. Her aunt stood there in the early-morning sunlight, a heavily made woman who was always dressed in black. She more than anyone, more than her husband or her brother or Kitty herself, knew that ever since he'd arrived at the farm with a label on him he'd had a notion of Kitty. The aunt was the sharpest of them, her eyes as black as her clothes, always watchful. She had noticed him looking at Kitty across the table when they all sat down to their dinner; he'd never been able to help looking at her, and it embarrassed him every time her aunt caught him. Did she guess that he lay in bed at night imagining Kitty's lips on his own, and the lovely white softness of her? They would have the farm between them was what she omitted to say in the yard because it was not necessary to say it: Kitty would inherit the farm since there was no one else, and if he married her he would no longer be the hired man, with the worst of the work always reserved for him. 'I'll ask her so,' he said, and because of the day there had been in Cork it was easier to pluck up the courage. Before that, Kitty had always ordered him about in the way her father and her uncle did when they all worked together at certain seasons, making hay or lifting the potatoes. He had never disliked her for it, any more than he'd ever felt he had a right to resent Coddy Donnegan's rusty old Vauxhall arriving in the yard and Coddy Donnegan waiting in it, and the way he'd push open a door of the car when he heard the sound of her heels tip-tapping across the concrete. Father Tolan's cousin had never come near the farm; all that was a mystery.

'Would there be anything to eat in here, pet? Would they have biscuits?'

At the bar he ordered two more bottles of stout and inquired if biscuits could be supplied. The publican said he had ginger-snaps and went to the grocery to weigh out half a pound.

'Oh, great,' Kitty said. She crumbled one in her mouth. He poured out the stout. The day before her aunt had made her suggestion in the yard he had noticed Kitty going up to Coddy Donnegan after Mass, and Coddy Donnegan had turned away from her as if they'd had a quarrel, which was understandable in view of her friendship with Father Tolan's cousin. After that, Coddy Donnegan's Vauxhall never again drove up to the farm.

'We'll never forget our honeymoon,' Kitty said. 'I wish we had a camera. I'd love to take snaps of Tramore.'

He knew what she meant. For the rest of their lives they'd be at the farm, milking every morning and evening, taking the churns down to the creamery, ploughing and sowing and ditching. No matter how you fixed it there was never enough time, except for the couple of hours you took to go to Mass. He always rode to Mass on his bicycle, and on Sunday afternoons he rode over to Doolin's at the old railway junction, where no trains came any more. A new road passed by Doolin's now and on Sunday afternoons there would always be bicycles propped up against its window, and the same dozen or so faces inside. 'I hear you're marrying in,' one of the men said to him on the Sunday after Kitty agreed. 'More power to your elbow, Davy!' No one was displeased at his good fortune, in Doolin's or anywhere else. Father Tolan came up to the farm specially and walked down to the mangold field to shake his hand and to congratulate him. Even Ned Cauley, who rarely had a good word to say on any subject, wagged his head at him in an approving way.

'I love the taste of ginger-snaps and stout,' Kitty said. 'Did you know ginger-snaps were my favourite?'

'They're all the man had.'

Suddenly she asked him if he was happy. She repeated the question, putting it differently, asking him if he was contented in himself. He said he was.

'Will you ever forget the day we went to Cork, Davy?'

From her voice, he thought she was maybe getting drunk, that her condition made the stout go to her head. She was looking at him, giggling. She leaned closer to him and said that on the bus that day she'd thought to herself she wouldn't mind being married to him.

'You were good to me that day, Davy, d'you know that?'

'I always had a notion of you, Kitty.'

'I never noticed it till that day, pet. That was the first time I knew it.'

He went to the bar for two further bottles of stout. He had wondered if the men in Doolin's knew the state she was in, and if they imagined he was the man involved. The same applied where her father and her uncle were concerned, and Father Tolan. He didn't know if there'd been talk or not.

'Didn't it work out OK, in the end?' she said when he returned with the stout. She asked if there were any more biscuits and he went back to buy another quarter pound. When he returned to where they sat she said:

'Were you ever jealous of Coddy, pet?'

He nodded, pouring his stout from the bottle, and she laughed because she'd made him feel awkward. He looked away, wishing she hadn't brought up Coddy Donnegan. Then he turned and clumsily attempted to kiss her on the lips, but found them gritty with biscuit crumbs.

'Oh, Coddy's the right romantic! It was maybe ten or eleven times he said would we get married.'

He frowned, feeling that something wasn't quite right, yet for the moment uncertain as to what it was.

'Did I tell you poor Coddy cried?' she said. 'The day I told him I was marrying yourself?'

After that the conversation became confused. Kitty again mentioned her surprise when Mrs Kilfedder had embraced her at the wedding. She counted up the wedding guests, and said it must have been the biggest wedding for a long time. Her father had had to sell two bullocks to pay for it. 'Did you see the cut of old Feehy, without a collar or tie?' She went through all the guests then, commenting or their dress and wondering why other women hadn't embraced her. 'Will we take back a few bottles?' she suggested, nudging him and winking. 'Hey!' she called out to the publican. 'Put a dozen stout in a bag for us, Mister.'

When Davy had paid for them they left the public house, Kitty talking about a girl called Rose she'd been at the national school with, wondering where she was now. She hung on to his arm; he listened vaguely. Turning into the cul-de-sac, they met Mr Hurley exercising a greyhound, a dejected animal which in the course of conversation Mr Hurley said was worth a fortune. 'Is it the one that gets into the cement mixer?' Kitty asked, and Mr Hurley explained that the greyhound only got into the cement mixer the odd time.

Kitty laughed shrilly. The trouble with a habit like that, she pointed out, was that the creature might get turned into concrete. 'Will you take a stout, Mr Hurley? We brought home a few bottles.'

Mr Hurley instantly fell into step with them and when they arrived at the house he led them round to the back, incarcerating the greyhound in a shed on the way. 'Sit down on a chair,' he said in the kitchen and his wife produced glasses, saying it was unusual to have guests bringing drink back to St Agnes's, but where was the harm in it? 'Good luck!' said Mr Hurley.

Details of the Wall of Death were given, and details of the wedding. The unexpected embrace of Mrs Kilfedder was retailed, and reference made to Kitty's father singing 'Lily of Laguna' and to old Feehy without his collar or tie. 'Poor Coddy Donnegan hadn't the heart to attend,' Kitty said. 'He's a fellow from the slaughterhouse, Mrs Hurley. I went out with poor Coddy for three years.'

'They take it hard,' agreed Mrs Hurley.

'He cried, poor Coddy.'

'I had a similar case myself. A fellow by the name of O'Gorman.'

'A chancer,' said Mr Hurley beneath his breath. 'A real oiler.'

'O'Gorman could have charmed the leaves off the trees. I heard him called the handsomest man in Tramore.'

'The story is told,' Mr Hurley said in the same low voice, 'that he fecked a crucifix off a nun.'

' "Well, I'll never marry now," was what poor Coddy came out with when I told him. "I'll keep myself by for you, Kitty." '

'Where'd the point be in that, though?' Mrs Hurley interposed. 'Is poor Coddy a bit slow?'

'It's only his way of putting the thing, Mrs Hurley.'

The dozen bottles took an hour to drink, during which time Mr Hurley gave Davy a number of racing tips. He talked about famous greyhounds he had known or had even had a hand in the breeding of, but Davy was more interested in what the two women were discussing and was unable to prevent himself from listening. He heard Kitty saying the husband she'd married would do anything for you. He watched her leaning closer to Mrs Hurley and heard her referring to the cousin of Father Tolan. 'Errah, go on, are you serious?' Mrs Hurley exclaimed, glancing across at him, and he guessed at once what she'd been told – that the lapse of the priest's cousin had determined him in his vocation, that God had gained in the end.

'Held back all summer,' Mr Hurley continued. 'Put every penny in your pocket on him.'

Davy promised he would, although he had never in his life backed a horse and hadn't heard what the one Mr Hurley recommended was called. Kitty stood up and was swaying back and forth, her eyes blearily staring. 'I don't know should I have eaten the ginger-snaps,' she muttered uneasily, but Mrs Hurley said a ginger-snap never did anyone any harm. Mr Hurley was talking about another horse, and Davy kept nodding.

'You're a good man,' the landlady whispered as he went by her. He had one arm around Kitty, holding her up. He shook his head, silently disclaiming the goodness Mrs Hurley imbued him with.

'Are you all right?' he asked Kitty on the stairs, and she didn't reply until they were in the bedroom, when she said she wasn't. He lifted the china jug out of the basin on the wash-stand and after she had finished being sick he carried the basin across the landing to the lavatory.

'God, I'm sorry, pet,' she managed to say before she fell asleep, lying across the bed.

Even though she couldn't hear him, he said it didn't matter. It had never occurred to him before that a cousin of Father Tolan's who came to the parish for his holidays must have attended Mass on Sundays, yet he had never seen him there. Nor had he ever heard anyone else but Kitty mention him. She had painted a picture of a saintly young man who had since become a priest, and in her befuddled state she'd wanted Mrs Hurley to know about him too. She had wanted Mrs Hurley to know that it wasn't anything crude that had occurred, like going with Coddy Donnegan in the back of a bloodstained Vauxhall.

'It's all right, Kitty.' He spoke aloud, sitting beside her on the bed, looking down into her face. In the bedroom there was the rancid smell of her vomit; her breath as he pulled the dress over her head was cloyed with it. Again he looked down into her face, understanding why she had told the lies. When she'd approached Coddy Donnegan after Mass that day he'd probably retorted that she'd let herself get into that condition in order to catch him.

Davy stood up and slowly took his clothes off. He was lucky that she had gone with Coddy Donnegan because if she hadn't she wouldn't now be sleeping on their honeymoon bed. Once more he looked down into her face: for eighteen years she had seemed like a queen to him and now, miraculously, he had the right to kiss her. He straightened her slackened body, moving her arms and legs until she was lying comfortably. Slowly he pulled the bed-clothes up and turned the light out; then he lay beside her and caressed her in the darkness. He had come to the farm with a label round his neck; he had come out of nowhere, from rooms and corridors that were as bleakly anonymous as the orphan home's foundling inmates. He had been known as her father's hired man, but now he would be known as her husband. That was how people would refer to him, and in the end it wouldn't matter when she talked about Coddy Donnegan, or lowered her voice to mention the priest's cousin. It was natural that she should do so since she had gained less than he had from their marriage.

The Printmaker

In the large room Charlotte hangs her prints to dry, like clothes on clothes lines. Three crows, framed by the legs and belly of a cow, have rested for an instant beneath its udder: all over the room this stark image is multiplied, in black and white and tones of green.

The reality was years ago, in France: Charlotte senses that confidently, without being able to recall the moment of observation. Familiar to her is the feeling that a glance from the window, or from a motor-car, has been retained for half a lifetime. 'This is still the Langevins' land,' Monsieur Langevin said in English, the first time he drove her in his white Citroën the fifteen kilometres from Massuery to St Cérase. Obediently she inspected the fields to her right, treeless and uninteresting, cattle grazing. Perhaps there were three crows also.

In the room the suspended sheets are scrutinized, and one in every seven or eight rejected. Fragile, tapering fingers loosen the tiny, variously coloured pegs that hold the prints in place; each inferior reproduction floats softly to the bare-wood floor. Intent upon her task, Charlotte moves silently in the room, seeming almost a ghost among the ubiquitous repetition of what she has created. At thirty-nine she is as slender as ever, her bones as apparent as her flesh. Bright azure eyes illuminate a face that is still a girl's. Shattered only twice in Charlotte's appearance is the illusion that time has been defeated; grey strands creep through hair that once was as pale as corn, and on the backs of her hands are the reminders that sun and weather do not pass gently by.

One by one, she picks up the rejected prints where they have dropped. She tears each in half and bundles it into the wooden box that is the room's repository for wastepaper. Then she examines one of the suspended sheets, holding it obliquely against the light to see if it has wholly dried. Satisfied that this is so, she releases the pegs and trims the paper in her guillotine. She signs it and writes in pencil *1/50*, then places it in a pale green portfolio. She repeats all this with each remaining print, then loosely ties the folder's tattered ribbons.

'To look at, there is *l'église* St Cérase,' Monsieur Langevin said, that first Wednesday afternoon. He stopped the car in the Place de la Paix and pointed out the way. There was nothing much else in the town, he warned.

A park beside the Maison de la Presse, tea-rooms and cafés, the Hostellerie de la Poste. But the church was quite impressive. 'Well, anyway, the façade,' Monsieur Langevin added.

Charlotte walked to it, admired the façade and went inside. There was a smell of candle grease and perhaps of incense: it was difficult precisely to identify the latter. Charlotte was seventeen then, her presence in the Langevin household arranged by her father, who set great store by what he referred to as 'perfect French'. Some acquaintance of his had a connection with a cousin of Madame Langevin; an arrangement had been made. 'I've been good about your drawing,' her father had earlier claimed, in the parental manner of that time. 'I'm only asking in return that you acquire the usefulness of perfect French.' Her father did not believe in her talent for drawing; a businessman himself, he anticipated for his only child a niche in some international commercial firm, where the French she had perfected would float her to desirable heights. Charlotte's father had her interests – as he divined them – at heart. A prosperous marriage would come latter. He was a conventional man.

In the church of St Cérase she walked by confessionals and the Stations of the Cross, taking no interest at seventeen, only wishing her father hadn't been insistent on sending her to Massuery. She had every Wednesday afternoon to herself, when Madame Langevin took her children riding. She had Sunday afternoons as well, and every evening when the children had gone to bed. But what on earth could she do on Sunday afternoons except go for a walk in the woods? And in the evenings the family seemed surprised if she did not sit with them. There were in all five children, the youngest still an infant. The twins were naughty and, though only six, knew how to tease. Colette sulked. Guy, a dark-haired boy of ten, was Charlotte's favourite.

This family's details were recorded in an unfinished letter in Charlotte's handbag: the sulking, the teasing, Guy's charm, the baby's podginess. Her mother would read between the lines, winkling out an unhappiness that had not been stated; her father would skip a lot. *Madame Langevin's sister is here on a visit. She is tall and languid, an incessant smoker, very painted up, beautifully dressed. Madame Langevin's quite different, smartly dressed too, and just as good-looking in her way, only nicer in the sense that she wants people to be all right. She smiles a lot and worries. Monsieur Langevin does not say much.*

Outside a café in the square she completed the letter, pausing often to make the task last. It was July and necessary to sit in the shade. *There hasn't been a cloud in the sky since I arrived.* She drank tea with lemon and when she'd sealed the envelope and written the address she watched the people going by. But there were few of them because of the heat of the afternoon – a woman in a blue dress, with sunglasses and a poodle, a child on a bicycle, a man delivering shoe-boxes from a van. Charlotte bought a stamp in a *tabac* and found the park by the Maison de la Presse. The seats were dusty, and whitened with bird droppings; sunlight didn't penetrate the foliage of the trees, but at least the place was cool and empty. She read the book she'd brought, *The Beautiful and Damned*.

Twenty-two years later Charlotte sees herself sitting there, and can even recall the illustration on the cover of the novel – a girl with a cigarette, a man in evening dress. *Madame Langevin's conscientious about speaking French to me*, a line in her letter reported. *Monsieur practises his English*. Charlotte was timid then, and innocent of almost all emotion. In her childhood she'd been aware of jealousy, and there'd always been the affection she felt for her father and her mother; but she had no greater experience of the vagaries of her heart, or even of its nature, and only loneliness concerned her at first at Massuery.

In the room set aside for her work Charlotte slips a green Loden overcoat from a coat-hanger and searches for her gloves, the park at St Cérase still vividly recurring. She might have wept that afternoon, protected by the human absence around her; she rather thought she had. After an hour she had gone to the museum, only to find it shut. Beneath a flamboyant female figure representing Eternal Peace she had waited in the Place de la Paix for the bus that would take her back to the gates of Massuery.

'Describe to me England,' Madame Langevin's sister requested that evening, practising her English also. 'Describe to me the house of your father. The food of England is not agreeable, *n'est-ce pas?*'

Replying, Charlotte spoke in French, but the tall, beautifully dressed woman stopped her. She wanted to hear the sound of English, it made a change. She yawned. The country was tedious, but so was Paris in July.

So Charlotte described the house where she lived, and her mother and her father. She explained how toast was made because Madame Langevin's sister particularly wanted to know that, and also how English butchers hung their beef. She wasn't sure herself about the beef and she didn't know the names of the various joints, but she did her best. Madame Langevin's sister lay listening on a sofa, her cigarette in a black holder, her green silk dress clinging to her legs.

'I have heard of Jackson's tea,' she said.

Charlotte had not. She said her parents did not have servants. She did not know much about the Royal Family, she confessed.

'Pimm's Number One,' Madame Langevin's sister prompted. *'Qu'est-ce que c'est que ça?'*

The Massuery estate was extensive. Beyond the gardens there were fields where sheep grazed, and beyond the fields there were plantations of young trees, no more than a foot high. On the slopes beyond them, firs grew in great profusion, and sometimes the chain-saws whirred all day long, an ugly sing-song that grated on Charlotte's nerves.

In front of the house, early every morning, gardeners raked the gravel. An old man and a boy, with rakes wider than Charlotte had ever seen before, worked for an hour, destroying every suspicion of a weed, smoothing away the marks of yesterday's wheels. The same boy brought vegetables to the house an hour or so before lunch, and again in the evening.

Marble nymphs flanked the front door at Massuery. A decorated balustrade accompanied the steps that rose to the left and right before continuing grandly on, as a single flight. The stone of the house was greyish-brown, the slatted shutters of its windows green. Everything at Massuery was well kept up, both inside and out. The silver, the furniture, the chandeliers, the tapestries of hunting scenes, the chessboard marble of the huge entrance hall, were all as lovingly attended to as the gravel. The long, slender stair-rods and the matching brass of the banister were regularly polished, the piano in the larger of the two salons kept tuned, the enamel of the dining-room peacocks never allowed to lose its brilliance. Yet in spite of all its grandeur, Massuery possessed only one telephone. This was in a small room on the ground floor, specially set aside for it. A striped wallpaper in red and blue covered the walls, matching the colours of an ornate ceiling. A blue-shaded light illuminated the telephone table and the chair in front of it. There were writing materials and paper for noting messages on. Madame Langevin's sister, with the door wide open, sat for hours in the telephone room, speaking to people in Paris or to those who, like herself, had left the city for the summer months.

'*Mon Dieu!*' Monsieur Langevin would sometimes murmur, passing the open door. Monsieur Langevin was grey at the temples. He was clean-shaven, of medium height, with brown eyes that became playful and indulgent in his children's presence. But the children, while agreeable to their father's spoiling of them, were equally fond of their mother, even though it was she who always punished them for their misdemeanours. There was the day the twins put the cat in the chimney, and the day the bough of the apricot tree collapsed beneath their weight, and the morning old Jules couldn't find his shoes, not a single pair. There were occasions when Colette refused to speak to anyone, especially to Charlotte, when she lay on her bed, her face turned to the wall, and picked at the wallpaper. Monsieur Langevin was as angry about that as he was about the cat in the chimney, but in each case it was Madame Langevin who arranged for whatever deprivation appeared to her to be just.

Madame Langevin's sister was having an affair. Her husband arrived at the house every Thursday night, long after dinner, close on midnight. He came on the Paris train and remained until Sunday evening, when he took a sleeper back again. He was a vivacious man, not as tall as his wife, with a reddish face and a small black moustache. After his first weekend Madame Langevin told Charlotte that her sister had married beneath her, but even so she spoke affectionately of her brother-in-law, her tone suggesting that she was relaying a simple fact. Madame Langevin would not speak ill of anyone, nor would she seek, maliciously, to wound: she was not that kind of woman. When she mentioned her sister's love affair, she did so with a shrug. On her sister's wedding-day she had guessed that there would be such a development: with some people it was a natural thing. 'Le monde,' Madame Langevin said, her tone neither condemning her sister nor disparaging her brother-in-law in his cuckold role.

Charlotte descends dimly lit stairs from her flat to the street, the green portfolio under her arm. The chill of a December morning has penetrated the house. The collar of her Loden overcoat is turned up, a black muffler several times wound round her neck. Does it happen, she wonders in other people's lives that a single event influences all subsequent time? When she was five she was gravely ill, and though she easily remembers the drama there was, and how she sensed a closeness to death and was even reconciled to it, the experience did not afterwards pursue her. She left it, snagged in its time and place, belonging there while she herself went lightly on. So, too, she had left behind other circumstances and occurrences, which had seemed as if they must surely cast perpetually haunting shadows: they had not done so. Only that summer at Massuery still insistently accompanies her, established at her very heart as part of her.

'It is the yellow wine of the Jura,' Monsieur Langevin said, in English still. 'Different from the other wines of France.'

From the windows of Massuery you could see the mountains of the Jura. Spring and early summer were sometimes cold because of wind that came from that direction. So they told her: the Jura was often a conversational topic.

'Is there a doctor at hand?' Madame Langevin's sister inquired, quoting from an English phrase-book she had made her husband bring her from Paris. 'What means "at hand"? *Un médicin sur la main? C'est impossible!*' With the precision of the bored, Madame Langevin's sister selected another cigarette and placed it in her holder.

'The lover is a younger man,' Madame Langevin passed on in slowly articulated French. 'Assistant to a pharmacist. One day of course he will wish to marry and that will be that.'

First thing in the morning, as soon as I open my eyes, the smell of coffee being made wafts through my open window. It is the servants' breakfast, I think. Later, at half past eight, ours is served in an arbour in the garden, and lunch is taken there too, though never dinner, no matter how warm the evening. On Sundays Monsieur Langevin's mother comes in a tiny motor-car she can scarcely steer. She lives alone except for a housekeeper, in a village thirty kilometres away. She is small and formidable, and does not address me. Sometimes a man comes with her, a Monsieur Ogé with a beard. He speaks to me in detail about his health, and afterwards I look up the words I do not know. Other relations occasionally come on Sundays also, Madame's cousin from Saulieu and her husband, and the widow of a general.

During the war, when there were only women and children at Massuery, a German soldier was discovered in the grounds. He had made himself a shelter and apparently lived on the remains of food thrown out from the house. He would not have been discovered had he not, in desperation, stolen cheese and bread from a larder. For more than a week the women lived with the knowledge of his presence, catching glimpses of him at night, not knowing what to do. They assumed him to be a deserter and yet were not certain, for he might as easily have been lost. In the end, fearing they were themselves being watched for a purpose they could not fathom, they shot him and buried him in the garden. '*Ici*,' Madame Langevin said, pointing at a spot in the middle of a great oval flowerbed where roses grew. '*C'était moi*,' she added, answering Charlotte's unasked question. On a wet night she and her mother-in-law and a maidservant had waited for the soldier to emerge. Her first two shots had missed him and he'd advanced, walking straight towards them. Her third shot made him stagger, and then she emptied both barrels into his body. She'd only been married a few months, not much older than Charlotte was now. *She seems so very gentle*, Charlotte wrote. *You can't imagine it.*

On 14 August, a date that was to become enshrined in Charlotte's consciousness, she was driven again to her Wednesday-afternoon freedom by Monsieur Langevin. But when they came to the Place de la Paix, instead of opening the car door as usual and driving on to his mid-week appointment, he said:

'I have nothing to do this afternoon.'

He spoke, this time, in French. He smiled. Like her, he said, he had hours on his hands. He had driven her to St Cérase specially, she realized then. On all previous Wednesday afternoons it had been convenient to give her a lift and, now, when it was not, he felt some kind of obligation had been established.

'I could have caught the bus at the gates,' she said.

He smiled again. 'That would have been a pity, Charlotte.'

This was the first intimation of his feelings for her. She didn't know how to reply. She felt confused, and knew that she had flushed. *He's such a charming man*, she'd written. *Both Monsieur and Madame are charming people. There's no other word for it.*

'Let me drive you some place, Charlotte. There's nothing to do here.'

She shook her head. She had a few things to buy, she said, after which she would return to Massuery as usual, on the bus. She would be all right.

'What will you do, Charlotte? Look at the front of the church again? The museum isn't much. It doesn't take long to drink a cup of coffee.'

The French her father wished her to perfect was far from perfect yet. Haltingly, she replied that she enjoyed her Wednesday afternoons. But even as she spoke she knew that what she'd come to enjoy most about them was the drive with Monsieur Langevin. Before, she hadn't dared to allow that thought to form. Now, she could not prevent it.

'I'll wait,' Monsieur Langevin said, 'while you do your shopping.'

When she returned to the car he drove to a country hotel, almost fifty kilometres away. It was ivy-covered, by a river, with doves in the garden and a stream near by. They sat at a table beneath a beech tree, but nobody came hurrying out to ask them what they'd like. The garden was deserted; the hotel seemed so too. Everyone was sleeping, Monsieur Langevin said.

'Are you happy at Massuery, Charlotte?'

She was three feet away from him, yet she could feel a fondness that made her faintly dizzy. Her flesh tingled, as though the tips of his fingers had touched her forearm and were sending reverberations through her body. Yet they hadn't. She tried to think of his children, endeavouring to imagine Colette and the twins at their most tiresome. She tried to think of Madame Langevin, to hear her soft, considerate voice. But nothing happened. All there was was the presence of the man she was with, his white car drawn up in the distance, the small round table at which they sat. A deception was taking place. Already they were sharing a deception.

'Yes, I am happy at Massuery now.'

'You were not at first?'

'I was a little lonely.'

Charlotte walks swiftly through the grey December streets with her portfolio. There was another print, a long time ago, of that round white table, and two faceless figures sitting at it. There was one of three women blurred by heavy rain, waiting among the dripping shrubs. There was one of Massuery caught in dappled sunlight, another of children playing, another of a white Citroën with nobody in it.

'They like you, Charlotte. Guy most of all perhaps.'

'I like them now too.'

They returned to the car when they had talked a while. Only, perhaps, an hour had passed: afterwards she calculated it was about an hour. No one had served them.

'Everyone is still asleep,' he said.

How had it happened that he put his arms around her? Had they stopped in their walk across the grass? Afterwards she realized they must have. But in her memory of the moment she was only aware that she had murmured protests, that the palms of both her hands had pressed against his chest. He hadn't kissed her, but the passion of the kiss was there. Afterwards she knew that too.

'Dear Charlotte,' he said, and then: 'Forgive me.'

She might have fainted and, as though he sensed it, he took her arm, his fingers lightly supporting her elbow, as a stranger on the street might have. He told her, as he drove, about his childhood at Massuery. The old gardener had been there, and nothing much had changed in the house. A forest of birches that had been sold for timber after the war had been replanted. In the fields where sunflowers were grown for their oil now there had been wheat before. He remembered carts and even oxen.

The white Citroën turned in at the gates and glided between the plane trees on the drive, its tyres disturbing the gravel. There'd been an oak close to the house, but its branches had spread too wide and it had been felled. He pointed at the place. They walked up the steps together, and into the hall.

That evening at dinner Madame Langevin's sister tried out a new phrase. 'My friend and I desire to attend a theatre,' she repeated several times, seeking guidance as to emphasis and pronunciation. No one remarked upon the fact that Charlotte had returned in the car with Monsieur Langevin, when always previously on Wednesdays she had arrived back on the bus. No one had noticed; no one was interested. It had been just a moment, she told herself, just the slightest thing. She hadn't been able to reply when he asked her to forgive him. He hadn't even taken her hand.

When Sunday came, Monsieur Langevin's mother brought the bearded Monsieur Ogé who talked about his health, and the widow of the general was there also. The deceived husband was in particularly good spirits that day. '*Mon chéri*,' Madame Langevin's sister murmured on the telephone after he'd left for the railway station in the evening. '*C'est trop cruel.*'

When Wednesday came Madame Langevin asked Charlotte if she'd mind taking the bus to St Cérase today because her husband was not going in that direction. And the following Wednesday, as though a precedent had been set by that, it seemed to be assumed that she would take the bus also. Had Madame Langevin somehow discovered? Her manner did not suggest it, but Charlotte remembered her philosophical tone when she'd first spoken of her sister's relationship with the pharmacist's assistant, her matter-of-fact acceptance of what clearly she considered to be an absurdity.

Sitting at the café where her solitary presence had become a Wednesday-afternoon feature, Charlotte tried to feel relieved that she'd been saved a decision. But would she really have said no if he'd offered, again, to drive her somewhere pleasant, or would her courage have failed her? Alone at the café, Charlotte shook her head. If he'd asked her, her longing to be with him would have quenched her conventional protests: courage did not come into it.

That day, she went again to the museum and sat in the dusty park. She sketched a hobby-horse that lay abandoned by a seat. The deception was still there, even though he'd changed his mind. Nothing could take it from them.

'*Tu es triste,*' Guy said when she bade him good-night that evening. '*Pourquoi es-tu triste, Charlotte?*' Only three weeks were left of her time at Massuery: that was why she was sad, she replied, which was the truth in part. '*Mais tu reviendras,*' Guy comforted, and she believed she would. It was impossible to accept that she would not see Massuery again.

The man nods appreciatively. He knows what he wants and what his clients like. The décor he supplies is enhanced by a pale-framed pleasantry above a minibar or a television set. In the bedrooms of fashionable hotels – and in boardrooms and directors' dining-rooms and the offices of industrial magnates – Charlotte's summer at Massuery hangs.

While her patron examines what she has brought him today, she sees herself walking in the Massuery woods, a lone, slight figure among the trees. What was it about her that had made a man of the world love her? She'd not been without a kind of beauty, she supposes, but often she'd been awkward in her manner and certainly ill-informed in conversation, naïve and credulous, an English schoolgirl whose clothes weren't smart, who hardly knew how to make up her face and sometimes didn't bother. Was it her very artlessness that had attracted his attention? Had he somehow delighted in the alarmed unease that must have been displayed in her face when he said he'd wait for her to finish her shopping? With long hindsight, Charlotte believes she had noticed his attention from the very first day she arrived at Massuery. There was a fondness in the amused glances he cast at her, which she had not understood and had not sought to. Yet as soon as he permitted the *frisson* between them, as soon as his manner and his words created it, she knew that being in his company was in every way different from being in Madame Langevin's, though, before, she had assumed she liked them equally. With that same long hindsight, Charlotte believes she came to love Monsieur Langevin because of his sense of honour and his strength, yet she knows as well that before she was aware of these qualities in him her own first stirrings of emotion had surfaced and, with unconscious propriety, been buried.

Madame Langevin's sister embraced her warmly the day Charlotte left Massuery. 'Farewell,' she wished her, and inquired if that was what was said on such occasions in England. The children gave her presents. Monsieur Langevin thanked her. He stood with his hands on Colette's shoulders, removing one briefly to shake one of Charlotte's. It was Madame Langevin who drove her to the railway station, and when Charlotte looked back from the car she saw in Monsieur Langevin's eyes what had not been there a moment before: the anguish of the sadness that already claimed their clandestine afternoon. His hands remained on his daughter's shoulders but even so it was as if, again, he'd spoken. At the railway station Madame Langevin embraced her, as her sister had.

Journeying through late September sunshine, Charlotte wept in a corner of her compartment. He respected Madame Langevin too much to betray her in the way her sister betrayed the husband she'd once chosen. Nor was he a man to cause his children pain in order to gratify a selfishness in himself. She knew all that, and in turn respected him. Her resignation was melancholy on that train journey, but with the balm of passing time it became more bearable.

'You're miles away, Charlotte,' young men would later amusedly accuse, and she'd apologize, already back at Massuery. Listening to the young men's chatter, she descended again the wide staircase, and walked in the woods. Such memories made it easier when with embarrassed gaucheness the young men seized her hand, or kissed her. When proposals came, her private reply was to see the white car waiting for her in the Place de la Paix, while aloud she apologized to whoever had got it into his head that she was free to love him.

'These'll ring the changes,' the man who has commissioned the new prints says. When a business-room or the bedrooms of a hotel are repainted he always likes to have fresh curtains and fresh prints as well; it's something that's expected. In six months' time, he says, he may be ready for another contribution from her. 'That's something to be thinking about, my love.' He always calls her that. He has mahogany-coloured hair with a spring in it; the stubble on his chin and neck grows so slightly and so softly that he hardly has to shave. 'We'll send a cheque,' he says.

Charlotte thanks him. There are other such men, and women too, who remember her when they want something new and unexacting for their décor. They admire her prints more than Charlotte does herself; for her the prints are by the way. What matters more is the certainty of her faith: even without thinking she knows that time, for her lover also, has failed to absorb the passion that was not allowed. For all the years that have passed she has thought of him as that; and dwelling on the nature of love during all that time she has long ago concluded that it's a mystery, appearing to come from nowhere, no rhyme nor reason to it. The truth will not yield: why did so unsuitably, so cruelly almost, two people love?

Daylight hasn't properly penetrated the December drabness. Fog shrouds the streets; the pavements are dampened by it. Busy with their assets and takeovers, the men of the business rooms have probably never noticed the prints that hang there. 'How charming that is!' a woman, half-dressed in a hotel bedroom, may have remarked after the scurry of afternoon love or in some idle moment during a weekend's deceit.

Charlotte sits for a while in the corner of a bar, her green portfolio empty beside her. No one else, except two barmen, are there so early in the day. She sips with pleasure the glass of red wine that has been brought to her; she lights a cigarette and with slow deliberation drops the spent match into the discoloured plastic ashtray in front of her. Then idly, on the cover of her folder, she sketches a funeral procession, sombre between two lines of plane trees. When eventually he sees it the man with the mahogany hair will display no curiosity, for he never does; in the rooms destined for her funeral scene no one will wonder either.

She finishes her wine and catches the eye of the taller barman. He brings her another glass. She remembers her father being angry, and her mother frowning in bewilderment. She never told them what she might have; but her father was angry because she had no ambition, because one young man after another was so summarily rejected. 'You're alone so,' her mother sadly observed. Charlotte did not attempt to explain, for how could happily married people understand that such flimsiness could become the heart of a human existence? Ambitions in this direction or that, and would-be husbands keenly persuading, seemed empty of seriousness, ludicrous almost, compared with what she had.

She has never seen Monsieur Langevin's handwriting, but imagines it is large and sloping, a little like Guy's was. She knows she'll never see it, for the thoughts that occur to her from time to time leave no illusions behind them: no letter will ever inform her that Madame Langevin, a month or so ago, was thrown from her horse – as once, unable to help herself, she dreamed. The funeral is not a hope, only another image from her printmaker's stock. Why should an honourable deception end in romance? Rewards for decency are not duly handed out.

Their love affair, for her, is there among the memories of a summer, with the people of a household, the town she visited, Guy saying she will return, the sound of the gravel raked, the early-morning smell of coffee. For Monsieur Langevin, the deception is lived with every day, pain blinked away, words bitten back. For both of them, the pattern of their lives has formed around a moment in an afternoon. It is not often so, her lover tells her in yet another silent conversation. He, too, is grateful.

In Love with Ariadne

Images cluster, fragments make up the whole. The first of Barney's memories is an upturned butter-box − that particular shape, narrower at the bottom. It's in a corner of the garden where the grass grows high, where there are poppies, and pinks among the stones that edge a flowerbed. A dog pants, its paws stretched out on the grass, its tongue trailing from its mouth. Barney picks the pinks and decorates the dog with them, sticking them into its brindle fur. 'Oh, you are bold!' The hem of the skirt is blue, the shoes black. The hat Barney has thrown off is placed again on his head. He has a stick shaped like a finger, bent in the middle. It is hard and shiny and he likes it because of that. The sunshine is hot on his skin. There is a baby's perspiration.

Barney's mother died three years after his birth, but even so his childhood was not unhappy. In the garden at Lisscrea there was Charlie Redmond to talk to, and Nuala was in the kitchen. *Dr G. T. Prenderville* the brass plate on the wall by the hall door said, and all over the neighbourhood Barney's father was known for his patience and his kindness − a big man in a tweed suit, his greying hair brushed straight back, his forehead tanned, a watch-chain looped across his waistcoat. Charlie Redmond made up doggerel, and twice a day came to the kitchen for cups of tea, leaving behind him a basket of peas, or beetroot, or whatever was in season. Because of the slanderous nature of his doggerel, Nuala called him a holy terror.

Lisscrea House, standing by the roadside, was covered with virginia creeper. There were fields on one side and on the other the Mulpatricks' cottage. Beyond that was the Edderys' cottage, and an iron gate which separated it from Walsh's public house − single-storeyed and whitewashed like the cottages. Opposite, across the road, were the ruins of a square tower, with brambles growing through them. A mile to the west was the Catholic church, behind white railings, with a shrine glorifying the Virgin just inside the gates. All the rooms at Lisscrea were long and narrow, each with a different, flowered wallpaper. In the hall the patients sat on a row of chairs that stretched between the front door and the stairs, waiting silently until Dr Prenderville was ready. Sometimes a man would draw up a cart or a trap outside, or dismount from a bicycle, and the doorbell would jangle urgently. 'Always listen carefully to what's said at the door,' Dr Prenderville instructed Nuala. 'If I'm out, write a message down.'

When Barney was seven he went to school in Ballinadra, waiting every morning on the road for Kilroy's cart on its way to Ballinadra creamery with churns of milk. The bread van brought him back in the afternoon, and none of that changed until he was allowed to cycle – on Dr Prenderville's old B.S.A. with its saddle and handle-bars lowered. '*Up the airy mountain,*' Miss Bone's thin voice enunciated in the schoolroom. Her features were pale, and slight; her fingers stained red with ink. *There goes Miss Bone*, Charlie Redmond's cruel doggerel recorded. *She's always alone.* Miss Bone was tender-hearted and said to be in love with Mr Gargan, the school's headmaster, a married man. *Quod erat demonstrandum*, Mr Gargan regularly repeated in gravelly tones.

On the Sunday before he made the journey to school on the B.S.A. for the first time Barney found his father listening to the wireless in the drawing-room, a thing he never did on a Sunday morning. Nuala was standing in the doorway with a dishcloth in her hand, listening also. They'd have to buy in tea, she said, because she'd heard it would be short, and Dr Prenderville said they'd have to keep the curtains drawn at night as a protection against being bombed from an aeroplane. Charlie Redmond had told Barney a few days before that the Germans were hard cases. The Germans were in league with the Italians, who ate stuff that looked like string. De Valera, Charlie Redmond said, would keep the country out of things.

The war that began then continued for the duration of Barney's time at school. Lisscrea was affected by the shortages that Nuala had anticipated; and de Valera did not surrender the will to remain at peace. It was during those years that Barney decided to follow in his father's and his grandfather's footsteps and become the doctor at Lisscrea.

'How're the digs?' Rouge Medlicott asked, and the Pole, Slovinski, again beckoned the waitress – not because he required more coffee but because he liked the look of her.

'Awful,' Barney said. 'I'm moving out.'

When he'd arrived in Dublin at the beginning of the term he found he had not been allocated a set of College rooms and had been obliged to settle for unsatisfactory lodgings in Dún Laoghaire. Greyhounds cluttered the stairs of this house, and broke into a general barking on imagined provocation. Two occupied a territory they had made their own beneath the dining-room table, their cold noses forever investigating whatever flesh they could find between the top of Barney's socks and the turn-ups of his trousers. Rouge Medlicott and Slovinski shared College rooms and at night pursued amorous adventures in O'Connell Street, picking up girls who'd been left in the lurch outside cinemas or ice-cream parlours.

'Why doesn't she come to me?' Slovinski demanded crossly, still waving at the waitress.

'Because you're bloody ugly,' Medlicott replied.

Students filled the café. They shouted to one another across plates of iced buns, their books on the floor beside their chairs, their gowns thrown anywhere. Long, trailing scarves in black and white indicated the extroverts of the Boat Club. Scholars were recognized by their earnest eyes, sizars by their poverty. Nigerians didn't mix. There were tablefuls of engineers and medical practitioners of the future, botanists and historians and linguists, geographers and eager divinity students. Rouge Medlicott and Slovinski were of an older generation, two of the many ex-servicemen of that time. Among these were G.I.s and Canadians and Czechs, a couple of Scots, a solitary Egyptian, and balding Englishmen who talked about Cecil Sharp or played bridge.

'You meet me tonight,' Slovinski suggested in a peremptory manner, having at last succeeded in summoning the waitress. 'What about tonight?'

'Tonight, sir?'

'We'll have oysters in Flynn's.'

'Oh God, you're shocking, sir!' cried the waitress, hurrying away.

Barney had got to know Slovinski and Rouge Medlicott through sitting next to them in biology lectures. He didn't think of them as friends exactly, but he enjoyed their company.

Medlicott had acquired his sobriquet because of the colour of his hair, a quiff of which trailed languorously over his forehead. There was a hint of flamboyance in his attire – usually a green velvet suit and waistcoat, a green shirt and a bulky green tie. His shoes were of soft, pale suede. He was English, and notably good-looking. Slovinski was small and bald, and still wore military uniform – a shade of blue – which Medlicott claimed he had bought in a Lost Property office. Slovinski could play part of Beethoven's Fifth Symphony on his teeth, with his thumbnails.

'I heard of digs,' Medlicott said. 'Out near the Zoo. That Dutch fellow was after them only he decided to go back to Holland instead.'

It was in this casual way that Barney first came to hear about Sinnott Street, and that evening he went out to inspect the lodgings. A woman with a carefully powdered face and waved black hair opened the door to him. A discreet smear of lipstick coloured her lips, and there was a hint of eye-shadow beneath her myopic-seeming eyes. She was wearing a flowered overall, which she removed in the hall. Beneath was a navy-blue skirt and a cream-coloured blouse that had a fox-terrier brooch pinned to it. She folded the overall and placed it on the hall-stand. Normally she would not take in boarders, she explained, but the house was too large, really, for herself and her mother and her daughter, just the three of them. A pity to have rooms and not use them, a pity to have them empty. The trouble was that smaller houses were usually not in districts she cared for. She led the way upstairs while still speaking about the house and household. 'It's a residence that's been in the Lenehan family for three generations,' she said. 'That's another consideration.'

The door of a room on the second floor was opened. 'Fusty,' Mrs Lenehan said, and crossed to the window. The bed was narrow, the bedstead of ornamental iron. There was a wash-stand with an enamel basin on it and a shaving mirror above it on the wall. There was a wardrobe, a chest of drawers, two holy pictures, and a chair. Patterned, worn linoleum partially covered the floor, leaving a darkly varnished surround. There were net curtains and a blind.

'The bathroom and W.C. are off the landing below,' Mrs Lenehan said. In Mr Lenehan's childhood there were two maids and a cook in this house, she went on, and in her own day there'd always been a single maid at least, and a scrubbing woman once a fortnight. Now you couldn't get a servant for love nor money. She noticed Barney glancing at the fireplace, which contained an arrangement of red tissue paper. She said that in the old days there'd have been a fire laid in the grate every morning and coal blazing cheerfully every evening. Now, of course, that was out of the question. 'Thirty shillings would be fair, would it? Breakfast and six p.m. tea, the extra meal on a Sunday.'

Barney said he thought thirty shillings was a reasonable rent for what was offered.

'Of a Friday evening, Mr Prenderville. In advance would be fair, I think.'
'Yes, it would.'

'Best to have a clear arrangement, I always say. No chance for mis-understandings.'

Two days later Barney moved in. When he'd unpacked his suitcases and was waiting for the gong which Mrs Lenehan had told him would sound at six o'clock there was a knock on his door. 'I'm Ariadne,' Mrs Lenehan's daughter said, standing in the doorway with a bar of yellow soap in her hand. 'My mother said give you this.' She was dark-haired, about the same age as Barney. The rather long mauve dress she wore was trimmed with black, and snowy-white beads were looped several times around her neck. Her lips were painted, her hands and wrists delicately slender. Large brown eyes surveyed Barney frankly and with curiosity.

'Thanks very much,' he said, taking the bar of soap from her.

She nodded vaguely, seeming to be no longer interested in him. Quietly she closed the door, and he listened to her footfall on the stairs. As light as gossamer, he said to himself. He was aware of a pleasurable sensation, a tingling on the skin of his head. The girl had brought to the room a whiff of perfume, and it remained after she'd gone. Barney wanted to close the window to keep it with him, but he also wanted just to stand there.

The sounding of the gong roused him from this pleasant reverie. He had never much cared for the appearance of the girls – women sometimes – whom Medlicott and Slovinski admired in cafés or on the streets. Ariadne was different. There was an old-fashioned air about her, and an unusualness. As well, Barney considered her beautiful.

'Fennerty's the name,' a small, jaunty old woman said in the dining-room. Wiry white hair grew tidily on a flat-looking head; eyes like beads peered at Barney. 'Fennerty's the name,' she repeated. 'Mrs Lenehan's mother.'

Barney told her who he was. The last occupant of his room had been employed in Clery's bed-linen department, she replied, a youth called Con Malley from Carlow. Now that someone had replaced him, the house would again be full. There had been difficulty in regularly extracting the rent from Con Malley. 'Mrs Lenehan won't tolerate anything less than promptness,' the old woman warned.

A man of about fifty, wearing a navy-blue belted overcoat and tan gloves, entered the dining-room. 'How're you, Mr Sheehy?' Mrs Fennerty inquired.

Divesting himself of his coat and gloves and placing them on the seat of a chair by the door, the man replied that he wasn't so good. He had a sharply receding chin, with features that had a receding look about them also, and closely clipped hair, nondescript as to colour. The removal of his coat revealed a brown pin-striped suit, with the corner of a handerkerchief peeping from the top pocket, and a tiny badge, hardly noticeable, in the left lapel. This proclaimed Mr Sheehy's teetotalism, the emblem of the Pioneer movement.

'I had a bad debt,' Mr Sheehy said, sitting down at the table. Mrs Fennerty vacated a sagging armchair by the fire and took her place also. Ariadne entered with a laden tray, and placed plates of fried food in front of the three diners. Mrs Fennerty said the thick Yorkshire Relish had been finished the evening before, and when Ariadne returned to the dining-room a minute or so later with a metal teapot she brought a bottle of Yorkshire Relish as well. Neither she nor her mother joined the others at the dining-table.

'Did you know Mattie Higgins?' Mr Sheehy inquired of Mrs Fennerty.

When he spoke he kept his teeth trapped behind his lips, as though nervous of their exposure. 'I sold him a wireless set. Three pounds fifteen. I had the price agreed with him, only when I brought it round all he had was a five-pound note. "I'll have that broken into tonight," he said. "Come back in the morning." Only didn't he die that night in his bed?'

Swiftly, the old woman crossed herself. 'You got caught with that one,' she said.

'I was round there at eight o'clock this morning, only the place was in the hands of five big daughters. When I mentioned the wireless they ate the face off of me. A good Pye wireless gone west.'

Mrs Fennerty, still consuming her food, glanced across the room at the radio on the dumb-waiter in a corner. 'Is it a Pye Mrs Lenehan has?'

'It is.'

'I heard the Pye's the best.'

'I told that to the daughters. The one I sold him had only a few fag burns on the cabinet. The five of them laughed at me.'

'I know the type.'

'Five fat vultures, and your man still warming the bed.'

'Strumpets.'

The rest of the meal was taken in a silence that wasn't broken until Ariadne came to clear the table. 'I meant to have told you,' she remarked to Barney. 'Your window gets stuck at the top.'

He said it didn't matter. He had noticed her mother opening the bottom sash in preference to the top one, he added conversationally. It didn't matter in the least, he said.

'The top's stuck with paint,' Ariadne said.

Mrs Fennerty returned to her place by the fire. Mr Sheehy put on his navy-blue overcoat and his gloves and sat on the chair by the door. Skilfully, with the glass held at an angle, Mrs Fennerty poured out a bottle of stout that had been placed in the fender to warm. On her invitation, accompanied by a warning concerning hasty digestion, Barney occupied the second fireside armchair, feeling too shy to disobey. Mrs Fennerty lit a cigarette. She was a boarder the same as Mr Sheehy, she said. She paid her way, Mrs Lenehan's mother or not. That was why she sat down in the dining-room with Mr Sheehy and whoever the third boarder happened to be.

'Are you at Dowding's?' She referred to a commercial college that offered courses in accountancy and book-keeping, preparing its students for the bank and brewery examinations.

'No. Not Dowding's.' He explained that he was a medical student.

'A doctor buries his mistakes. Did you ever hear that one?' Mrs Fennerty laughed shrilly, and in a sociable way Barney laughed himself. Mr Sheehy remained impassive by the door. Barney wondered why he had taken up a position there, with his coat and gloves on.

'Six feet under, no questions asked,' Mrs Fennerty remarked, again laughing noisily.

Dressed to go out, Mrs Lenehan entered the dining-room, and Mr Sheehy's behaviour was explained. He rose to his feet, and when the pair had gone Mrs Fennerty said:

'Those two are doing a line. Up to the McKee Barracks every evening. Sheehy wouldn't part with the price of anything else. Turn round at the barracks, back by the Guards' Depot. Then he's down in the kitchen with her. That's Ned Sheehy for you.'

Barney nodded, not much interested in Mr Sheehy's courtship of Mrs Lenehan. Nevertheless the subject was pursued. 'Ned Sheehy has a post with the Hibernian Insurance. That's how he'd be selling wireless sets to people. He calls in at houses a lot.'

'I see.'

'He's keen on houses all right. It's the house we're sitting in he has designs on, not Mrs Lenehan at all.'

'Oh, I'm sure –'

'If there's a man in Dublin that knows his bricks and mortar better than Ned Sheehy give me a gander at him.'

Barney said he didn't think he could supply the old woman with such a person, and she said that of course he couldn't. No flies on Ned Sheehy, she said, in spite of what you might think to look at him.

'She made a mistake the first time and she'll make another before she's finished. You could turn that one's head like the wind would turn a weather-cock.'

Ariadne came in with the *Evening Herald* and handed it to her grandmother. Barney smiled at her, but she didn't notice. Mrs Fennerty became engrossed in the newspaper. Barney went upstairs.

In time, he heard footsteps in the room above his, and knew they were Ariadne's. They crossed the room to the window. The blind was drawn down. Ariadne crossed the room again, back and forth, back and forth. He knew when she took her shoes off.

Handwritten notes clamoured for attention on the green baize of the board beside the porters' lodge: love letters, brief lines of rejection, relationships terminated, charges of treachery, a stranger's admiration confessed. The same envelope remained on the baize-covered board for months: *R.R. Woodley*, it said, but R.R. Woodley either did not exist or had long since ceased to be an undergraduate. *It is hard to find myself the way I am, and to be alone with not a soul to turn to*: a heart was laid bare within the dust-soiled envelope, its ache revealed to the general curiosity. But other notes, on torn half-sheets of exercise-paper, remained on the green board for only a few hours, disappearing for ever while they were still fresh.

Within their fire-warmed lodge the porters were a suspicious breed of men, well used to attempted circumvention of the law that began where their own rule did. They wore black velvet jockey caps; one carried a mace on ceremonial occasions. They saw to it that bicycles were wheeled through the vast archway they guarded, and that female undergraduates passed in and out during the permitted hours only, that their book was signed when this was necessary. In the archway itself, posters advertised dances and theatrical productions. Eminent visitors were announced. Societies' account sheets were published. There were reports of missionary work in Africa.

Beyond this entrance, dark façades loomed around a cobbled square. Loops of chain protected tidily shorn lawns. The Chapel stared stolidly at the pillars of the Examination Hall. Gold numerals lightened the blue face of the Dining Hall clock. A campanile rose fussily.

Barney attended the lectures of Bore McGusty and Professor Makepeace-Green and the elderly Dr Posse, who had been in the medical school in his father's time. Bore McGusty was a long-winded young man, Professor Makepeace-Green a tetchily severe woman, who particularly objected to Slovinski reading the *Daily Sketch* during her lectures. The students of Barney's age keenly took notes and paid attention, but the recent shedding of years of discipline by the ex-servicemen left them careless of their academic obligations. 'Listen,' Slovinski regularly invited, interrupting Bore McGusty's dissertation on the functioning of the bile-ducts by playing Beethoven on his teeth.

The medical students favoured certain public houses: the International Bar, Ryan's in Duke Street, McFadden's. After an evening's drinking they danced in the Crystal Ballroom, or sat around pots of tea in the café attached to the Green cinema, where the private lives of their mentors were breezily speculated upon, and for the most part scorned. On such occasions Slovinski spoke of his wartime liaisons, and Medlicott retailed the appetites of a baker's widow, a Mrs Claudia Rigg of Bournemouth. For Barney – years later – this time in his life was as minutely preserved as his childhood at Lisscrea. And always, at the heart of the memory, was Mrs Lenehan's household in Sinnott Street.

'You've maybe not come across the name Ariadne before,' Mrs Lenehan said one morning in the hall, adding that she'd found it in a story in *Model Housekeeping*. Had a son been born instead of a daughter he'd have been christened Paul, that being a family name on her own side. As soon as she'd seen *Ariadne* written down she'd settled for it.

Barney liked the name also. He thought it suited Mrs Lenehan's daughter, whom increasingly he found himself thinking about, particularly during the lectures of Bore McGusty and Professor Makepeace-Green. Ariadne, he soon discovered, didn't go out to work; her work was in her mother's house and it was there, during the lectures, that he imagined her. She assisted with the cleaning and the preparation of meals, and the washing-up afterwards. She was often on the stairs with a dust-pan and brush; she polished the brass on the front door. Every morning she set the dining-room fire, and lit it every evening. Once in a while she and her mother cleaned the windows.

Mrs Lenehan occasionally sang while she performed her household tasks. Ariadne didn't. There was no trace of reluctance in her expression, only a kind of vagueness: she had the look of a saint, Barney found himself thinking once, and the thought remained with him. In the dining-room he was usually the last to finish breakfast, deliberately dawdling. Ariadne came in with a tray and, seeing him still at the table, absorbed the time by damping the fire down with wet slack and picking up the mantelpiece ornaments and dusting them. Her elegant hands were as delicate as the porcelain she attended to, and her clothes never varied: the same shade of mauve combined repeatedly with mourner's black. 'Good evening, Mr Prenderville,' she sometimes whispered in the dusk of the hall, a fleeting figure passing from one closed door to another.

After he'd been in the lodgings a month Barney was familiar with every movement in the room above his. When Ariadne left it and did not return within a few minutes he said to himself that she was washing her hair, which he imagined wrapped in a towel, the way Nuala wrapped hers before she sat down to dry it at the range. He imagined the glow of an electric fire on Ariadne's long, damp tresses. Staring at a discoloured ceiling, he invaded her privacy, investing every sound she made with his speculations. Would she be sewing or embroidering, as Nuala did in the evening? Nuala pressed flowers between the pages of the medical encyclopaedia in the dining-room at Lisscrea, pansies and primulas she asked Charlie Redmond to bring from the garden. Barney wondered if Ariadne did that also. He guessed the moment when she lay down to sleep, and lay in the darkness himself, accompanying her to oblivion.

He didn't tell Rouge Medlicott and Slovinski, or anyone else, about Ariadne. In his letters to his father he mentioned Mrs Lenehan and Mrs

Fennerty and Mr Sheehy: Ariadne mightn't have existed. Yet in the noisy cafés and the lecture-halls he continued to feel haunted by her, and wished she was there also. He left the house in Sinnott Street reluctantly each morning, and hurried back to it in the evenings.

'Ariadne.'

He addressed her on the first-floor landing one Sunday afternoon. His voice was little more than a whisper; they were shadows in the dim afternoon light. 'Ariadne,' he said again, delighting, while they were alone, in this repetition of her name.

'Yes, Mr Prenderville?'

Mrs Lenehan and Mr Sheehy spent Sunday afternoons with Mrs Fennerty in the dining-room, listening to a radio commentary on a hurling or Gaelic football match, the only time the dining-room wireless was ever turned on. When it was over Mr Sheehy and Mrs Lenehan went to the kitchen.

'Would you like to come for a walk, Ariadne?'

She did not reply at once. He gazed through the gloom, hoping for the gleam of her smile. From the dining-room came the faint sound of the commentator's rapid, excited voice. Ariadne didn't smile. She said:

'This minute, Mr Prenderville?'

'If you are doing nothing better.'

'I will put on my coat.'

He thought of her mother and Mr Sheehy as he waited. He didn't know which direction the McKee Barracks and the Civic Guards' Depot lay in, but wherever these places were he didn't want even to see them in the distance. 'I'm ready,' Ariadne said, having delayed for no longer than a minute. Barney opened the front door softly, and softly closed it behind them. Damp autumn leaves lay thickly on the pavements, blown into mounds and heaps. When the wind gusted, more slipped from the branches above them and gently descended. Ariadne's coat was another shade of mauve, matching her headscarf. There'd been no need to leave the house in that secret way, but they had done so nonetheless, without exchanging a look.

'I love Sunday,' Ariadne said.

He said he liked the day also. He told her about Sundays at Lisscrea because he didn't know how else to interest her. His father and he would sit reading in the drawing-room on a winter's afternoon, or in the garden in the summer. Nuala would bring them tea, and a cake made the day before. His father read books that were sent to him by post from a lending library in Dublin, novels by A.E.W. Mason and E. Phillips Oppenheim and

Sapper. Once, laying one down when he had finished it, he changed his mind and handed it to Barney. 'Try this,' he said, and after that they shared the books that came by post. Barney was fourteen or fifteen then.

'Your mother is not there, Mr Prenderville?'

'My mother died.'

He described Lisscrea to her: the long, narrow rooms of the house, the garden where Charlie Redmond had worked for as long as Barney could remember, the patients in the hall. He mentioned the cottages next to Lisscrea House, and Walsh's public house, and the ruined tower he could see from his bedroom window. He repeated a piece of Charlie Redmond's doggerel, and described his prematurely wizened features and Nuala's countrywoman's looks. He told Ariadne about school at Ballinadra, the journey on the milk cart when he was small, the return by the bread van in the afternoon, and then the inheriting of his father's old B.S.A. bicycle. She'd never known a town like Ballinadra, Ariadne said; she only knew Dublin.

'It isn't much,' he said, but she wanted to know, and he tried to make a picture of the place for her: the single street and the square, O'Kevin's hardware, the grocers' shops that were bars as well, the statue of Father Mathew.

'A quiet place,' Ariadne said.

'Oh, a grave.'

She nodded solemnly. She could see the house, she said. She knew what he meant by virginia creeper. She could see his father clearly.

'What would you have done if I hadn't suggested a walk?'

'Stayed in my room.'

'Doing nothing, Ariadne?' He spoke lightly, almost teasing her. But she was still solemn and did not smile. Maybe tidying her drawers, she said. She called him Mr Prenderville again, and he asked her not to. 'My name's Barney.'

'Just Barney?'

'Barney Gregory.'

Again she nodded. They walked in silence. He said:

'Will you always help your mother in the house?'

'What else would I do?'

He didn't know. He wanted to suggest some work that was worthy of her, something better than carrying trays of food to the dining-room and sweeping the stair-carpet. Even work in a shop was more dignified than what she did, but he did not mention a shop. 'Perhaps a nurse.'

'I would be frightened to be a nurse. I'd be no good at it.'

'I'm sure you would, Ariadne.'

She would care tenderly. Her gentleness would be a blessing. Her beauty would cheer the low spirits of the ill.

'Nuns are better at all that,' she said.

'Did you go to a convent, Ariadne?'

She nodded, and for a moment seemed lost in the memory the question inspired. When she spoke again her voice, for the first time, was eager. 'Will we walk to the convent, Barney? It isn't far away.'

'If you would like to.'

'We have to turn right when we come to Prussia Street.'

No one was about. The front doors of the houses they walked by were tightly closed against the world. Their footsteps were deadened by the sodden leaves.

'I like that colour you wear,' he said.

'An aunt left me her clothes.'

'An aunt?'

'A great-aunt, Aunt Loretta. Half of them she never wore. She loved that colour.'

'It suits you.'

'She used to say that.'

That was why her dresses, and the coat she wore now, were rather long for her. It was her clothes that gave her her old-fashioned air. Had she no clothes of her own? he wondered, but did not ask.

The convent was a cement building with silver-coloured railings in front of it. The blinds were drawn down in several of its windows; lace curtains ensured privacy in the others. A brass letter-box and knocker gleamed on a green side-door.

'Did you walk here every morning?' he asked.

'When I was small my father used to take me. It wasn't out of his way.'

She went on talking about that, and he formed a picture of her childhood, just as, a few moments ago, she had of his. He saw her, hand in hand with her father, hurrying through the early-morning streets. Her father had worked in Maguire's coal office in Easter Street. Sometimes they'd call in at a shop for his tobacco, half an ounce of Digger.

When they crossed the street he wanted to take her arm, but he didn't have the courage. They could walk to a bus stop, he suggested, and wait for a bus to O'Connell Street. They could have tea somewhere, one of the cinema cafés that were open on a Sunday. But she shook her head. She'd have to be getting back, she said.

They turned and walked the way they'd come, past the silent houses. A drizzle began. They didn't say much else.

*

'God, there's talent for you!' Medlicott exclaimed in the Crystal Ballroom, surveying the girls who stood against the walls. Slovinski conveyed a willowy woman of uncertain age on to the dance-floor, from which, a few minutes later, they disappeared and did not return. Some of the girls who were standing about glanced back at Medlicott, clearly considering him handsome. He approached a lean-featured one with hair the colour of newly polished brass, not at all pretty, Barney considered.

Because he had no knowledge of dance-steps, the partners Barney chose usually excused themselves after a minute or two. 'What line are you in?' a plump one, more tolerant than the others, inquired. He said he worked in a dry-cleaner's, Slovinski having warned him not to mention being a student in case the girls took fright. 'You can't dance,' the plump girl observed, and commenced to teach him.

When the end of the evening came she was still doing so. Medlicott had remained attached to the lean-featured girl, whom he confidently reported he had 'got going'. Outside the dance-hall Barney heard him complimenting her on her eyes, and felt embarrassed because he didn't want to have to tell the plump girl that she, too, had lovely eyes, which wouldn't have been true. Instead, he asked her her name. 'May,' she said.

Medlicott suggested that they should go out to Goatstown in a taxi, since the city bars were closed by now. There were fields in Goatstown, he reminded his companions: after they'd had a couple of nightcaps they could go for a walk through the fields in the moonlight. But May said her father would skin her if she got in late. She took Barney's arm. Her father was fierce-tempered, she confided.

The lean-faced girl didn't want to make the journey to Goatstown either, so Medlicott led her into an alleyway. They kissed one another in a doorway while May and Barney stood some distance away. When her father went wild, May said, nothing could hold him. 'All right,' Barney heard the lean-faced girl say.

A battered Ford car was parked at the far end of the alleyway next to a skip full of builder's rubble. Medlicott and his companion approached it, she teetering on gold-coloured high heels. Medlicott opened one of the back doors. 'Come on in here, darling,' he invited.

It was difficult to know what to say to May, so Barney didn't say anything. She talked about her brothers and sisters; half listening, he imagined Ariadne at Lisscrea. He imagined being engaged to her, and introducing her to Nuala in the kitchen and Charlie Redmond in the garden. He saw himself walking along the road with her, and waiting while she attended Mass in the nearby church. He showed her Ballinadra – the rudimentary shops, the statue of Father Mathew in the square.

He glanced at the car and caught a glimpse of brassy hair through the back window. He would introduce her to the tender-hearted Miss Bone. He imagined Miss Bone dismounting from her bicycle outside O'Kevin's hardware. 'Welcome to Ballinadra, Ariadne,' she murmured in her gentle voice.

Three men had turned into the alleyway, and a moment later shouting began. A door of the car was wrenched open; clothing was seized and flung out. One of the lean girl's gold-coloured shoes bounced over the surface of the alleyway, coming to rest near the skip. 'Get that hooer out of my car,' a voice furiously commanded.

In spite of what was happening, Barney couldn't properly detach himself from his thoughts. He walked with Ariadne, from the town to Lisscrea House. On the way he showed her the Lackens' farm and the hay-shed where the Black and Tans had murdered a father and a son, and the ramshackle house at the end of a long avenue, where the bread van used to call every day when he got a lift in it back from school, where mad Mrs Boyce lived. Weeds flowered on the verges; it must have been summer.

'Get out of that bloody car!'

The garments that lay on the ground were pitched into the skip, with the shoe. Medlicott called out incomprehensibly, a humorous observation by the sound of it. 'D'you want your neck broken?' the same man shouted back at him. 'Get out of my property.'

'I'm off,' May said, and Barney walked with her to her bus stop, not properly listening while she told him that a girl who would enter a motor-car as easily as that would come to an unsavoury end. 'I'll look out for you in the Crystal,' she promised before they parted.

On the journey back to Sinnott Street Barney was accompanied by an impression, as from a fantasy, of May's plump body, breasts pressed against his chest, a knee touching one of his, the moist warmth of her palm. Such physical intimacy was not the kind he had ever associated with Ariadne, but as he approached his lodgings he knew he could not let the night pass without the greater reality of seeing her face, without – even for an instant – being again in her company.

When he arrived at Mrs Lenehan's house he continued to ascend the stairs after he'd reached the landing off which his room lay. Any moment a light might come on, he thought; any moment he would stand exposed and have to pretend he had made a mistake. But the darkness continued, and he switched on no lights himself. Softly, he turned the handle of the door above his, and closed it, standing with his back to the panels. He could see nothing, but so close did the unspoken relationship feel that he half expected to hear his name whispered. That did not happen; he could not hear even the sound of breathing. He remained where he stood, prepared to do so for however many hours might pass before streaks of light showed on either side of the window blinds. He gazed at where he knew the bed must be, confirmed in this conjecture by the creeping twilight. He waited, with all the passion he possessed pressed into a longing to glimpse the features he had come to love. He would go at once then. One day, in some happy future, he would tell Ariadne of this night of adoration.

But as the room took form – the wardrobe, the bed, the wash-stand, the chest of drawers – he sensed, even before he could discern more than these outlines, that he was alone. No sleeping face rewarded his patience, no dark hair lay on the pillow. The window blinds were not drawn down. The bed was orderly, and covered. The room was tidy, as though abandoned.

Before the arrival of Professor Makepeace-Green the following morning, the episode in the alleyway and Slovinski's swift spiriting away of the willowy woman from the dance-hall floor were retailed. Barney was commiserated with because he had failed to take his chances. Rouge Medlicott and Slovinski, and several other ex-servicemen, gave him advice as to amorous advancement in the future. His preoccupied mood went unnoticed.

That evening, it was the old woman who told him. When he remarked upon Ariadne's absence in the dining-room she said their future needs in this respect would be attended to by a maid called Biddy whom Mrs Lenehan was in the process of employing. When he asked her where Ariadne had gone she said that Ariadne had always been religious.

'Religious?'

'Ariadne's working in the kitchen of the convent.'

Mr Sheehy came into the dining-room and removed his navy-blue overcoat and his tan gloves. A few minutes later Mrs Lenehan placed the plates of fried food in front of her lodgers, and then returned with the metal teapot. Mr Sheehy spoke of the houses he had visited during the day, in his capacity as agent for the Hibernian Insurance Company. Mrs Lenehan put her mother's bottle of stout to warm in the fender.

'Is Ariadne not going to live here any more?' Barney asked Mrs Fennerty when Mr Sheehy and Mrs Lenehan had gone out for their walk to the McKee Barracks.

'I'd say she'll stop in the convent now. Ariadne always liked that convent.'

'I know.'

Mrs Fennerty lit her evening cigarette. It was to be expected, she said. It was not a surprise.

'That she should go there?'

'After you took Ariadne out, Barney. You follow what I mean?'

He said he didn't. She nodded, fresh thoughts agreeing with what she had already stated. She poured her stout. She had never called him Barney before.

'It's called going out, Barney. Even if it's nothing very much.'

'Yes, but what's that to do with her working in the convent?'

'She didn't tell you about Lenehan? She didn't mention her father, Barney?'

'Yes, she did.'

'She didn't tell you he took his life?' The old woman crossed herself, her gesture as swift as it always was when she made it. She continued to pour her stout, expertly draining it down the side of the glass.

'No, she didn't tell me that.'

'When Ariadne was ten years old her father took his life in an upstairs room.'

'Why did he do that, Mrs Fennerty?'

'He was not a man I ever liked.' Again she paused, as though to dwell privately upon her aversion to her late son-in-law. 'Shame is the state Ariadne lives in.'

'Shame?'

'Can you remember when you were ten, Barney?'

He nodded. It was something they had in common, he'd said to Ariadne, that for both of them a parent had died. Any child had affection for a father, Mrs Fennerty was saying.

'Why did Mr Lenehan take his life?'

Mrs Fennerty did not reply. She sipped her stout. She stared into the glow of the fire, then threw her cigarette end into it. She said Mr Lenehan had feared arrest.

'Arrest?' he repeated, stupidly.

'There was an incident on a tram.' Again the old woman blessed herself. Her jauntiness had left her. She repeated what she'd told him the first evening he sat with her: that her daughter was a fool where men were concerned. 'At that time people looked at Ariadne on the street. When the girls at the convent shunned her the nuns were nice to her. She's never forgotten that.'

'What kind of an incident, Mrs Fennerty?'

'A child on a tram. They have expressions for that kind of thing. I don't even like to know them.'

He felt cold, even though he was close to the fire. It was as though he had been told, not of the death of Ariadne's father but of her own. He wished he had taken her arm when they went for their walk. He wished she'd said yes when he'd suggested they should have tea in a cinema café. Not so long ago he hadn't even known she existed, yet now he couldn't imagine not loving her.

'It would have been no good, Barney.'

He asked her what she meant, but she didn't answer. He knew anyway. It would have been no good because what seemed like a marvel of strangeness in Ariadne was damage wrought by shame. She had sensed his love, and fear had come, possibly revulsion. She would have hated it if he'd taken her arm, even if he'd danced with her, as he had with May.

'Ariadne'll stay there always now,' the old woman said, sipping more of her stout. Delicately, she wiped a smear of foam from her lips. It was a silver lining that there'd been the convent kitchen to go to, that the same nuns were there to be good to her.

'She'd still be here if I hadn't taken the room.'

'You were the first young man, Barney. You couldn't be held to blame.'

When Barney returned to Dublin from Lisscrea at the beginning of his second term he found, unexpectedly, that he had been allocated College rooms. He explained that in Sinnott Street, and Mrs Lenehan said it couldn't be helped. 'Mr Sheehy and myself are getting married,' she added in the hall.

Barney said he was glad, which was not untrue. Mr Sheehy had been drawn towards a woman's property; for her part, Mrs Lenehan needed more than a man could offer her on walks to the McKee Barracks. Mrs Lenehan had survived the past; she had not been damaged; second time round, she had settled for Mr Sheehy.

In the dining-room he said goodbye to Mrs Fennerty. There was a new young clerk in Ned Sheehy's office who was looking for digs, she said. He would take the vacant room, it wouldn't be empty for long. A student called Browder had moved into Ariadne's a week or so after her going. It hadn't been empty for long either.

It was snowing that evening. Huge flakes clung to Barney's overcoat as he walked to the convent, alone in the silence of the streets. Since Ariadne's going he had endlessly loitered by the convent, but its windows were always blank, as they were on that Sunday afternoon. Tonight, a dim light burned above the green side-door, but no curtain twitched as he scanned the grey façade, no footsteps disturbed the white expanse beyond the railings. In the depths of the ugly building were the strangeness and the beauty as he had known them, and for a moment he experienced what was left of his passion: a useless longing to change the circumstances there had been.

While he was still in Mrs Lenehan's house he had thought that somehow he might rescue Ariadne. It was a romantic urge, potent before love began to turn into regret. He had imagined himself ringing the convent bell, and again seeing Ariadne's face. He had imagined himself smiling at her with all the gentleness he possessed, and walking again with her; and persuading her, when time had passed, that love was possible. 'You'll get over her,' his father had said in the holidays, guessing only that there had been some girl.

A bus creeps through the snow: years later, for Barney, there is that image, a fragment in the cluster that makes the whole. It belongs with the upturned butter-box in the grass and the pinks in the brindle hair of the dog, with Rouge Medlicott and Slovinski, and the jockey-capped porters, and the blue-faced Dining Hall clock. A lone figure stares out into the blurred night, hating the good sense that draws him away from loitering gloomily outside a convent.

A Husband's Return

As dawn lightened Maura Brigid's bedroom the eyes of the Virgin Mary surveyed her waking face dispassionately. Two fingers of the Holy Child blessed her from a tiny pedestal above the room's single window. Sleepily recollected, the routine of the day before passed unobtrusively through her thoughts, prefacing the daytime shadow of her desertion by the man she'd loved. This pall of distress reclaimed its potency in the first moments of every day, establishing itself afresh, as the sacred statues did. Then, this morning, Maura Brigid remembered that her sister Bernadette had died.

In his bedroom across the landing Maura Brigid's brother, Hiney, awoke with the occasion already alive in his consciousness. In the town the family had travelled to a banner had been suspended high up across a street, offering a welcome on behalf of a carnival in the future. Halfway between white iron railings and the church, on a hill, there was a shrine, a pietà, in white also. The yellow grain of the coffin was bright in the sunshine, the face of the priest wan and strained. Hiney pushed back the bedclothes, the action assisting him to dispel these recollections of a time spent unhappily in an unfamiliar place. Bernadette had run away from the farmhouse with her sister's husband: that sin had still been ugly at the funeral.

Affected also by the recent death, Mrs Colleary, the mother of Maura Brigid and Hiney, rose an hour later. She released the two blinds in her bedroom and dressed herself in the nondescript wear of a farmer's widow. He would have gone after Bernadette, she reflected, thinking of her husband; he would have brought her back, and the danger was that he might even have killed Lawless, for his anger had always been difficult to control. It was as well he'd been spared all of it, because nothing he might have done could have lessened the disgrace into which the family had been dragged. Mrs Colleary told her rosary, and prayed for the soul of her husband, and for her daughter's soul. It was the morning of a Tuesday in May, a month after the funeral.

In another bedroom an old man, distantly related to the family, remained in his bed. Of everyone in the farmhouse, only he no longer dwelt on the scandal that had occurred. He had been upset by it at the time, but with the passing years it had settled in his mind, as had so much else in a long life. He was a small, wizened man who had spent most of that life on this farm. His relationship to the remaining Collearys was vague.

The house where the family lived was large and square and white, facing a grassy hill, its back to the distant sea. The hall door had been nailed in place a long time ago, to keep out draughts; a slated roof, obtusely pitched, was scarcely visible. The gravel sweep that lay between the house and the hill was weedless; the windows that looked out on it were curtained heavily with net and velveteen. The front of the house was where appearances were kept up. At the back a cobbled yard, with a hay-barn and outhouses, and a feed-shed where potatoes and swill were boiled, was less tidy. A porch in need of repair led to sculleries and kitchen.

Weeding a field of mangolds that ran to the edge of the cliffs, Hiney heard in the distance the engine of the post van, and knew by the direction it came from that the van was on its way to the farmhouse. Would an abrupt, buff-enveloped notice announce the withdrawal of the tillage grant? Or was there at last a communication from the Appeal Commissioners? Sunshine warmed Hiney's shoulders and his head as he bent over the mangolds, the impassive solemnity of his countenance unaffected by speculation. His waistcoat hung loosely; his collarless shirt was held at the neck by a stud. More likely it was the bill for the diesel that brought the post van down the avenue, he guessed.

The old man was visited in his bedroom by Mrs Colleary. She spoke to him about the weather, reporting that it was a brightly sunny morning. But it was always uncertain whether or not he comprehended what was said to him, and this morning he gave no sign that he did. The old man's age was as mysterious as his relationship to the family; he was perhaps ninety-four or -five. Mrs Colleary visited him first thing every morning to make sure he was all right.

Maura Brigid fried bacon in the kitchen. She had set the table the night before, the last to leave the kitchen, as she always was. She pushed the bacon to one side of the pan and dropped slices of griddle bread into the fat. She heard her brother's footsteps in the yard, and for an instant imagined his slow walk and his wide, well-shaved face, his dark hair brushed flat on either side of its parting, his lips set dourly, his blue eyes expressionless. Work was what Hiney thought about, work that had been completed, work that had yet to be done. His life was the fields, and his tractor, and the weather.

The letter that had arrived lay on the stone floor of the scullery passage, just inside the door from the yard. When there was a letter the postman opened the back door and placed it on the passage floor, propped against the wall, since there was no letter-box and nowhere else to put it. Entering the house, Hiney picked up the communication that had just been delivered. It was not the bill for the diesel, nor was it about the tillage grant or the appeal that had been lodged with the tax commissioners. It was a white envelope, addressed in a sloping hand to Maura Brigid. Hiney was curious about it. He turned the envelope over, but nothing was written on the back.

In the kitchen Mrs Colleary said she thought the old man would get up today. She always knew if he intended to get up when she visited him first thing. The anticipation of his intentions might have shown as a glimpse in his eyes or in some variation of the sound he emitted when she spoke to him: she had no idea how the impression was conveyed, only that she received it.

'I have an egg ready to fry for him,' Maura Brigid said, that being what the old man had for breakfast. Bacon he couldn't manage.

Hiney placed the letter on the table beside his sister's knife and fork. He sat where he always sat, on the chair that had been his father's in his lifetime. 'Move into his place, Hiney,' Mrs Colleary had said a few weeks after her husband's death in 1969, when Hiney was still a boy.

'Did Paidín bring a letter?' Mrs Colleary did not question the delivery of a letter since the letter was clearly there and could have arrived by no other means than with the postman: her query was her way of expressing surprise. She could see that the letter was a personal one, and from where she stood she could see it was addressed to her daughter.

Maura Brigid, having placed three plates of food on the table, sat down herself. Mrs Colleary poured the tea. Maura Brigid examined the envelope much as her brother had done. She did not recognize the handwriting.

Dear Mrs Lawless, I am writing to you from my conscience. There is repentance in Michael, that's all I'm writing to say to you. There is sorrow in him also, left behind after the death. Poor Michael is tormented in his heart over the way he was tempted and the sin there was. He told me more times than once that he would endeavour to make recompense to you for the pain he inflicted on you. I am writing to advise you to pray to Our Lady for guidance at this time in your life. I am asking you to recollect the forgiveness She displayed in Her Own Life.

'It's from Father Mehegan,' Maura Brigid said, 'the priest that did the funeral.'

She handed the letter to her mother because all letters that came to the farm were read in that general way. Mrs Colleary noted without comment what Father Mehegan had written. Hiney read the letter in silence also.

'I hear him on the stairs,' Mrs Colleary said. A few moments later the old man entered the kitchen, his shirt not yet buttoned, his trousers hitched up with ragged braces. A vest that had been drained of its whiteness through washing was exposed, its two buttons not fastened either. He sat down in his usual place to await his breakfast. Maura Brigid rose to fry his egg.

'Is he off the hunger strike yet?' the old man inquired, lost in a confusion that evoked for him a distant past. 'Will MacSwiney go to the end, Hiney?'

'He will.' Hiney nodded in his solemn way. Indulging such dislocation of time was not unusual in the farmhouse.

'I was saying he would myself.'

Michael does not know I'm writing to you, the priest's letter ended. *That's in confidence between us.* It was three years since Michael Lawless and Bernadette had run off in the middle of a July night. Maura Brigid had been married for six months at the time and no particular lack of accord between husband and wife had warned of what was to occur. No hint as to the direction of her affections had ever slipped from Bernadette. No note had been left behind.

'Isn't it a terrible thing, Hiney, that they'd let poor MacSwiney go to the end?'

'It is all right.'

'I'd say they'd pay the price of it.'

'I'd say they would.'

Hiney folded the letter and returned it to its envelope. Bernadette had died of an internal infection; she'd been two days in hospital. A message had come to them through their own priest, Father Brennan, from a parish more than sixty miles away. They had not known that Bernadette and Michael Lawless had been living there. After their flight the two had not been spoken of.

'I put my faith in Collins to this day,' the old man said. 'Won't Collins have a word to say when Terry MacSwiney goes?'

Hiney nodded, and so did Mrs Colleary. It was she who had led the silence in the house, her anger and her pain eventually becoming creased into her features. She had offered Maura Brigid no comfort. That Lawless had shattered the lives of both her daughters was how she registered what had occurred. Nor was it any consolation that she had never liked Michael Lawless, believing at the time of his marriage to Maura Brigid that he was after what he could extract to his advantage from the farm, while comfortably living as a member of the household. His running away might have seemed to disprove such an intention, but not for Mrs Colleary. In the humiliation of the scandal there was little room for reason, and no desire to pursue it. The Collearys, and the family Mrs Colleary had come from herself, were well known and well respected in the neighbourhood.

They farmed their land, they did not miss Mass, there had never been talk of debts to shopkeepers or supply merchants. 'I would see Lawless hung,' Mrs Colleary had said, the last time she mentioned her son-in-law's name.

Maura Brigid tilted the frying pan and spooned fat on to the yolk of the egg. She wondered if Bernadette had been pregnant. Was that the cause of it, something going wrong inside her? At the funeral no details had been given because none had been asked for. Still wondering, she completed the frying of the old man's egg and scooped it on to a plate. She remembered playing in the yard when she and Bernadette were children, and Bernadette's doll being carried off to a hay-barn by one of the sheepdogs, and Bernadette crying. Sawdust had come out of the doll because the dog's tooth had pierced one of its legs. Margy it had been called.

'Are you out in the fields, Hiney?' the old man inquired, returning from his travels through remembered time. 'Will I lend you a hand?'

'I'm weeding the mangolds.'

'I'll come out so.'

The old man cut his egg into quarters. He removed the centre of a slice of bread and soaked some of the fat on his plate into it. He spooned sugar into his tea.

'I'm at the bottom of the cliff field,' Hiney said.

'It's a fine day for the cliff field.'

No more was said about the priest's letter. No more was necessary. The silence it had broken – that had been broken also by Bernadette's death – would knit together and be as it had been before. Nothing would be said to Father Brennan. The Mass for Bernadette had been offered in the distant town, which was where she would now lie for ever, well separated from the family she had disgraced. No one outside the farmhouse had been told about her death. No one need know, and no one would ask. After Father Brenann had conveyed the message, he had gone quickly away, and they knew he would remain silent on the subject.

Hiney spread sugar on to a piece of buttered bread. He was five years older than the sister who had married Michael Lawless, and older by another three than Bernadette. When they were younger he had looked after them, once lying in wait for the two boys who had taken to following them along the road on their way home from school. While he'd cuffed the boys and threatened them with worse Maura Brigid had been demure but Bernadette had laughed. The boys would never have bothered them if Bernadette hadn't encouraged them in the first place.

Mrs Colleary wondered if Lawless had been as bad to Bernadette as he had been to Maura Brigid. That thought had just come into her mind, suggested somehow by the priest's letter. A man who'd desert a wife would have other sins up his sleeve, other punishments to mete out before he'd be finished. That had never occurred to her before, not even on the day of the funeral. God's anger had been assuaged was what she'd thought, wiping her eyes with a sleeve of her black mourning coat.

Maura Brigid wanted to read the letter again, but did not do so. Occasionally during her marriage she had woken up in the middle of the night to find her husband not beside her, and when she'd asked him the next morning he'd said he'd gone out for a walk because he couldn't sleep. When they'd watched television in the kitchen he usually sat next to Bernadette, though not in any noticeable way at the time. It was the brevity of the marriage, the way it was still something new, with people still coming up to both of them after Mass to give them good wishes, that Maura Brigid hadn't been able to get out of her mind.

It was not Sunday, the old man was thinking. He knew it wasn't because she'd have reminded him, when she came into his bedroom, to put on different clothes. If it was a Sunday he'd be on the way to Mass now, sitting in the back of the car with the girl.

'They say a man'd be fit for nothing,' he said, 'after a hunger strike.'

Four months later Michael Lawless returned. It was September then, the shortening days pleasantly mild, the smell of the season in the woods and the fields. In the twilight of an evening Maura Brigid's husband advanced cautiously up the avenue on a bicycle. He dismounted before he came within sight of the house and wheeled the bicycle on to the grass verge. He leaned it against the wire of the avenue fence and continued on foot.

In the yard the sheepdogs barked. They licked the hand he held out to them from the shadows where he stood. Ignoring their noise, Hiney emerged from an outhouse with a new shaft fitted into a spade. He passed through the yard, and the sheepdogs ran after him. Ten minutes later Mrs Colleary came out of the house and scattered feed for the fowls.

'Hullo, Maura Brigid,' Lawless whispered when his wife appeared later still that evening. 'Shh, don't call out,' he begged when her hand went up to her mouth to stifle a cry. 'I'm sorry I frightened you, Maura Brigid.'

He'd stepped out of the shadows and she'd seen the movement from the corner of her eye. She'd only recognized him when she turned her head and even then she had to peer. But when her eyes grew accustomed to the gloom she saw her husband clearly: the broad face and the light-brown hair combed and parted, the collar and tie, the dark serge suit, its trouser ends held tidily in place with bicycle-clips.

'I've something I want to say to you, Maura Brigid.' He reached for her arm and gently guided her into the barn where the summer's hay was stacked. 'It wasn't my fault she died, Maura Brigid. She had an infection like anyone can have.'

'I don't want to talk to you. I don't know what you're doing here.'

'Maura Brigid –'

'Let go of my arm or I'll shout out.'

'Don't shout out, Maura Brigid. Please now. I'm sorry about everything that happened.'

'It's too late to be sorry now. You've no right to be here.'

'I only want to talk to you. I cycled the whole sixty miles of it.'

'We're troubled enough without you coming here.'

'I want to be with you, Maura Brigid.'

'What are you talking about?' she whispered, staring at him. She felt stupid, as though she had failed to comprehend what had been said to her, or had misunderstood it. She'd been on her way to the feed house to make sure the fire under the swill was damped down for the night, and the sudden presence of her husband both confused and alarmed her. She felt as she often did in a dream, plunged without warning into unreality, unable to escape.

'I want it to be like it was,' he said. 'I feel that way about you, Maura Brigid.'

'I'm going in now. Take your hand off of my arm and let me go. Don't ever come back here.'

'It was never right, Maura Brigid. We were never at ease, Bernadette and myself.' He paused, as though expecting a response. When none came he said: 'I wasn't the father.'

'Oh, my God!'

'Bernadette was that way. She led me a dance, Maura Brigid.'

Maura Brigid pulled her arm out of his grasp and ran across the yard. In the scullery passage she bolted the back door behind her. She didn't enter the kitchen but went straight up to her bedroom. She couldn't have faced her mother and Hiney, and they'd have known at once by the sight of her that something was the matter. They'd have asked her questions and she'd have told them in the end. Her mother would have sat there, tight-lipped. She knew, without even having to think, that the infection Bernadette had suffered had been due to an effort to prevent the birth. The nuns at the convent had called Bernadette wild.

'Dear Mother of God, help me,' Maura Brigid pleaded in her room, her voice distorted by agitation and tears she could no longer stifle. At the funeral she'd known he was trying to talk to her. She'd seen him looking at her, as though begging for mercy, but they'd driven straight off afterwards, not even stopping in a café for a cup of tea. Going away like that was what Hiney and her mother wanted. They'd hardly said thank you to the priest.

She mumbled through her rosary, sitting on the edge of the bed, the beads between her fingers. The first time she'd ever seen him he'd been a boy at the Christian Brothers', much quieter, more solitary, than the other boys. 'Who's that fellow with his eye on you?' Bernadette had said. He'd begun to turn up at the farm, asking Hiney for work, coming on a bicycle, as he had tonight. He'd done jobs for Hiney. He was better than Hiney at mending things.

Maura Brigid crossed to the window and slightly pulled aside the edge of the curtain. She had not yet turned on the light, fearful in case he was watching. Her room looked out over the gravel at the front of the house, and just for a moment she imagined she saw the movement of a figure on the avenue. 'Would you marry me?' was what he'd said. 'Am I good enough for you?'

She reached in among the curtains and pulled the blind down, separating herself further from what lay outside. She still did not light the room, but undressed in the darkness and crept into the bed she had shared with him. Her tears began again, a sobbing that was too soft for anyone passing by on the landing to hear.

The last of the potatoes were lifted. The old man and Maura Brigid and Mrs Colleary helped Hiney with them, and then Hiney ploughed the two potato fields. 'Is Lawless back?' the old man asked out of the blue, returning to the house with Maura Brigid and her mother.

When the old man walked he became bent, which made him seem even smaller. But he moved quickly, and would have been swifter over the stubble they crossed had he not slackened his pace in order to converse. His motion was a sideways one, the left shoulder hunched upwards and preceding the right, his grizzled head bent into his chest. 'Sure, a woman would want the man she has,' he remarked. 'Sure, why wouldn't she?'

Mrs Colleary ignored what he said, but Maura Brigid knew he must have seen her husband. He sometimes went wandering about the hill just before nightfall, setting snares. He would have looked down and recognized the familiar figure in the distance. His eyes were particularly sharp.

'Amn't I right, Maura Brigid?'

As though humouring him, she agreed that he was, and her mother paid no heed. Even if he'd stated that he'd spoken to her husband it wouldn't have mattered. Neither her mother nor Hiney would have placed any credence in the claim.

'He'll be a help for poor Hiney,' the old man said. 'It's hard going for Hiney sometimes.'

Maura Brigid knew she could write to the priest with a message for her husband. She could say she forgave him and was prepared to have him back. Whenever she thought about what he'd said concerning Bernadette, she had to repress her tears. When she'd known him well he'd never been untruthful. 'What d'you say that for?' Bernadette had crossly reprimanded her when she'd told Hiney that the boys who followed them on the road were a nuisance. Her sister's mood was quite different when she was scolded by the nuns: repentantly she would cast her eyes down. 'Sure, it was only a bit of fun, Sister,' she'd say, and probably she'd have made the same excuse to the man she'd led a dance. 'It won't happen again,' Maura Brigid could imagine her saying after she'd got pregnant with someone else. She had the ability to twist people round her little finger – their mother and Hiney and the old man, the nuns, someone in a shop she was bargaining with. She could wheedle her way with anyone.

'Leave off about him,' Mrs Colleary said snappishly when the old man again mentioned Michael Lawless. 'Don't speak that name, d'you hear?'

They reached the yard and for a moment Maura Brigid thought he might be there, hiding in the hay-barn until darkness came. She imagined his tidy hair and clothes. She remembered the strength of his arms when he put them around her, and the particular smell he had, a brackeny smell with a trace of tobacco in it. It had never occurred to her to say to herself that Bernadette wouldn't change just because she ran off with someone, just because she'd disgraced a whole family. She'd been the apple of their father's eye, and of their mother's until the scandal, and Hiney's favourite, and the old man's. She had been turned into a sinful woman by a man you couldn't mention: that was how they saw it.

Later that evening, when Maura Brigid crossed the yard to damp down the swill fire, no voice whispered her name. Later still, after she'd drawn down the blinds in her bedroom, she realized that her husband would not return unless she summoned him. He had come to make a case for his remorse; the priest had written from his conscience. Unless she chose to, she would hear no more from either of them.

Dear Father Mehegan, she wrote. *Thanks for writing to me. Would you tell Michael I will meet him halfway, in Cappoquin one Friday. Tell him I understand what he was saying to me.*

She addressed the envelope, but did not send the letter. She kept it in a drawer in her bedroom, saying she would post it the next Friday she went in to do the shopping. After that, she would be on the watch for a reply, ready to collect it from the scullery passage before Hiney found it. She'd drive on to Cappoquin on the Friday they arranged, making sure she put more petrol in the car, so that Hiney wouldn't notice how much had been used. They'd sit in the car in a car park.

'You'd need the fellow's assistance, Hiney,' the old man said. 'It's understandable you would.'

The old man sometimes sat in the dining-room, which was nowadays never used, under the impression that a land steward called Mahaffy was about to call to see him. Effortlessly he had created a world made up of random details from the past, and had peopled it as he wished. No one on the farm had ever heard of the land steward, Mahaffy. Terence MacSwiney, Mayor of Cork, had died on his hunger strike sixty-seven years ago.

'Ah, don't be silly now,' Hiney said when the assistance of Michael Lawless was referred to, Hiney as keen as his mother that the name should not be mentioned. The scandal Maura Brigid had inflicted on the family by bringing a scoundrel to the farm was too recent and too painful to be permitted in an old man's silliness. 'That man didn't come back,' Hiney shouted in the kitchen. 'D'you understand that now? He's gone for good.'

But the old man insisted. Michael Lawless had come back up the avenue on a bicycle. The sheepdogs had barked when he walked into the yard. 'We'll ask him about it when we see him,' the old man said. 'We'll ask him wasn't I right.'

All of it was her fault, Maura Brigid could feel her mother and Hiney thinking. If she had not married the man Bernadette would not have been ruined. Bernadette would still be alive. It was her fault that a scoundrel had come and gone, doing the worst that could be done to two sisters, duping them.

'He did come back,' she said. 'A while after the funeral he came back.'

She was on her feet when she spoke, giving them their food, as so often she did. She had fried chops and mashed turnips, and tumbled a saucepan of potatoes on to a sheet of newspaper, which would become accumulated with peelings as the meal progressed. Chops or fried steak, fish or boiled bacon, frozen peas or turnips or cabbage, and potatoes: that was the food she cooked and served for the main meal they ate every day. At half past twelve she placed the newspaper on the centre of the table. At a quarter past one she made tea. She and her mother washed up afterwards.

'What are you talking about?' Hiney said. 'Lawless never came back here.'

'He came back and told me Bernadette was pregnant, only it wasn't his child. She tried to get rid of it.'

Mrs Colleary crossed herself. Hiney's solemn face was unusually animated. 'That's a bloody lie,' he said.

'He couldn't control her, Hiney. She was like she always was.'

The old man asked them what they were talking about, something he
rarely did. Nobody answered him. Mrs Colleary said:

'He never told the truth.'

'Never in his life,' Hiney agreed with harsh vigour. 'We all know the
kind Lawless is.'

'You were always taken in, Maura Brigid. You were always soft.'

She knew that if she began to cry she wouldn't be able to stop. But the
tears she repressed kept making her blink and she turned her head away.
They were the same kind, she and the man who had married her. They'd
been companions the way he and her sister had never been, you could tell
that from how he spoke of Bernadette. Bernadette had hurt him, too.

'It's bad enough the way things are,' Hiney insisted. 'Keep it to yourself
he came back.'

When he'd first come to the farm to court her they used to walk in the
woods and climb down the cliffs to the strand. He'd always been shy, only
taking her hand and clumsily kissing her. After they were married there
had never been any question about his not coming on to the farm: Hiney
needed the assistance and Michael was employed on the roads, work he
didn't like. She remembered how she had wondered about a baby being
born, her own baby and his on the farm.

'There were girls at the convent,' she said, 'used call Bernadette a hooer.'

Again Mrs Colleary crossed herself. She drew her breath in and held it
for a moment. Her eyes were closed.

'What's the matter with you, Maura Brigid?' Hiney asked quietly.

'On account of the way she enticed the Christian Brothers' boys. That's
why they called her that.'

'If Lawless comes back here I'll take a gun to him,' Hiney said, still
without raising his voice. He stood up, leaving his food untouched. He
walked from the kitchen, and the sheepdogs who'd been lying under the
table followed him.

'You shouldn't ever have married that man,' Mrs Colleary said, opening
her eyes. Her face had gone pale. Her mouth was pulled down, as though
in weariness, as though she couldn't be bothered arranging it differently
any more. 'I told you at the time he was rotten to the core.'

Maura Brigid did not reply. It was not true to say the man she'd married
had never told the truth in his life. He was weak, and she was weak herself:
she didn't possess the courage to leave the farm, to run off with him as
Bernadette had. She would be frightened, and she was well-behaved by

nature. He hadn't come to the farm to ask her to run off, that wasn't his way; he'd come to the farm to tell her something, to see how she might feel about it. The priest had written to beg that there might be forgiveness.

'I'll go down and help them in the fields,' the old man said, finishing the cup of tea he'd poured himself. 'I think the pair of them are digging out ditches.'

The letter she had written would remain in her drawer. In the old man's senile fantasy her husband would continue to work on the cliff land, to cut timber in the woods, and help her with the Friday shopping, as he had once upon a time. In the old man's senile fantasy there was repentance, and forgiveness.

'Those are terrible things you said,' her mother whispered, still sitting at the table, her chop congealed in its fat. 'Enough has happened to us without that.'

When the old man died there would be no more talk of her husband, and when her mother died the task of making Hiney's bed would be hers, and there would only be Hiney and herself to cook for. Hiney would never marry because all Hiney was interested in was work. People would be sorry for her, but they would always say it was her foolishness that had dragged the family through disgrace, her fault for marrying a scoundrel. In the farmhouse and the neighbourhood that was the person she had become.

Coffee with Oliver

That is Deborah, Oliver said to himself: my daughter has come to see me. But at the pavement table of the café where he sat he did not move. He did not even smile. He had, after all, only caught a glimpse of a slight girl in a yellow dress, of fair hair, and sunglasses and a profile: it might not be she at all.

Yet, Oliver insisted to himself, you know a thing like that. You sense your flesh and blood. And why should Deborah be in Perugia unless she planned to visit him? The girl was alone. She had hurried into the hotel next to the café in a businesslike manner, not as a sightseer would.

Oliver was a handsome man of forty-seven, with greying hair, and open, guileless features. This morning he was dressed as always he was when he made the journey to Perugia. in a pale-cream linen suit, a pale shirt with a green stripe in it, and the tie of an English public school. His tan shoes shone; the socks that matched the cream of his suit were taut over his ankles.

'Signorina!'

He summoned the waitress who had just finished serving the people at the table next to his and ordered another cappuccino. This particular girl went off duty at eleven and the waitress who replaced her invariably made out the bill for one cappuccino only. It was fair enough, Oliver argued to himself, since he was a regular customer at the café and spent far more there than a tourist would.

'Sì, signore. Subito.'

What he had seen in the girl who'd gone into the hotel was a resemblance to Angelica, who was slight and fair-haired also, and had the same quick little walk and rather small face. If the girl had paused and for some reason taken off her dark glasses he would at once, with warm nostalgia, have recognized her mother's deep, dark eyes, of that he was certain. He wouldn't, of course, have been so sure had it not been for the resemblance. Since she'd grown up he'd only seen photographs of his daughter.

It was best to let whatever Deborah had planned just happen, best not to upset the way she wanted it. He could ask for her at the reception desk of the hotel. He could be waiting for her in the hall, and they could lunch together. He could show her about the town, put her into the picture gallery for an hour while he waited at the café across the street; afterwards they could sit over a drink. But that would be all his doing, not Deborah's, and it wouldn't be fair. Such a programme would also be expensive, for Deborah, in spite of being at a smart hotel, might well not be able to offer a contribution: it would not be unlike Angelica to keep her short. Oliver's own purpose in being in Perugia that morning was to visit the Credito Italiano, to make certain that the monthly amount from Angelica had come. He had cashed a cheque, but of course that had to be made to last.

'*Prego, signore,*' the waitress said, placing a fresh cup of coffee in front of him and changing his ashtray for an unused one.

He smiled and thanked her, then blew gently at the foam of his cappuccino and sipped a little of the coffee. He lit a cigarette. You could sit all day here, he reflected, while the red-haired Perugians went by, young men in twos and threes, and the foreign students from the language schools, and the tourists who toiled up, perspiring, from the car parks. Idling time away, just ruminating, was lovely.

Eventually Oliver paid for his coffee and left. He should perhaps buy some meat, in case his daughter arrived at his house at a mealtime. Because it was expensive he rarely did buy meat, once in a blue moon a packet of cooked turkey slices, which lasted for ages. There was a butcher's he often passed in a side street off the via dei Priori, but this morning it was full of women, all of them pressing for attention. Oliver couldn't face the clamour and the long wait he guessed there'd be. The butcher's in Betona might still be open when he arrived off the five past twelve bus. Probably best left till then in any case, meat being tricky in the heat.

He descended from the city centre by a steep short-cut, eventually arriving at the bus stop he favoured. He saved a little by using this particular fare-stage, and though he did not often make the journey to Perugia all such economies added up. What a marvellous thing to happen, that Deborah had come! Oliver smiled as he waited for his bus in the midday sunshine; the best things were always a surprise.

Deborah had a single memory of her father. He'd come to the flat one Sunday afternoon and she'd been at the top of the short flight of stairs that joined the flat's two floors. She hadn't known who he was but had watched and listened, sensing the charged atmosphere. At the door the man was smiling. He said her mother was looking well. He hoped she wouldn't mind, he said. Her mother was cross. Deborah had been five at the time.

'You know I mind,' she'd heard her mother say.

'I was passing. Unfriendly just to pass, I thought. We shouldn't not ever talk to one another again, Angelica.'

Her mother's voice was lowered then. She spoke more than she had already, but Deborah couldn't hear a word.

'Well, no point,' he said. 'No point in keeping you.'

Afterwards, when Deborah asked, her mother told her who the man was. Her mother was truthful and found deception difficult. When two people didn't get on any more, she said, it wasn't a good idea to try to keep some surface going.

He'd lit a cigarette while they'd been talking. Softly, he'd tried to interrupt her mother. He'd wanted to come in, but her mother hadn't permitted that.

'I'm here because of a mistake? Is that it?' Deborah pinned her mother down in a quarrel years after that Sunday afternoon. It was her mother's way of putting it when her marriage came up: two people had made a mistake. Mistakes were best forgotten, her mother said.

The dwelling Oliver occupied, in the hills above the village of Betona, was a stone building of undistinguished shape and proportions. It had once housed sheep during the frozen winter months, and wooden stairs, resembling a heavily constructed ladder, led to a single upstairs room, where shepherds had sought privacy from their animals. Efforts at conversion had been made. Electricity had been brought from the village; a kitchen, and a lavatory with a shower in it, had been fitted into the space below. But the conversion had an arrested air, reflecting a loss of interest on the part of Angelica who, years ago, had bought the place as it stood. At the time of the divorce she had made over to him the ramshackle habitation. She herself had visited it only once; soon after the divorce proceedings began she turned against the enterprise, and work on the conversion ceased. When Oliver returned on his own he found the corrugated roof still letting in rain, no water flowing from either the shower or the lavatory, the kitchen without a sink or a stove, and a cesspit not yet dug. He had come from England with his clothes and four ebony-framed pictures. 'Well, anyway it's somewhere to live,' he said aloud, looking around the downstairs room, which smelt of concrete. He sighed none the less, for he was not deft with his hands.

The place was furnished now, though modestly. Two folding garden chairs did service in the downstairs room. There was a table with a fawn formica surface, and a pitch-pine bookcase. Faded rugs covered most of the concrete floor. The four heavily framed pictures – scenes of Suffolk landscape – adorned the rough stone walls to some effect. Across a corner there was a television set.

The cesspit remained undug, but in other directions Oliver had had a bit of luck. He'd met an Englishman on one of his visits to the Credito Italiano and had helped with a language difficulty. The man, in gratitude, insisted on buying Oliver a cup of coffee and Oliver, sensing a usefulness in this acquaintanceship, suggested that they drive together in the man's car to Betona. In return for a summer's lodging – a sleeping-bag on the concrete floor – the man replaced the damaged corrugated iron of the roof, completed the piping that brought water to the shower and the lavatory, and installed a sink and an antique gas stove that someone had thrown out, adapting the stove to receive bottled gas. He liked to work like this, to keep himself occupied, being in some kind of distress. Whenever Oliver paused in the story of his marriage his companion had a way of starting up about the business world he'd once belonged to, how failure had led to bankruptcy: finding the interruption of his own narration discourteous, Oliver did not listen. Every evening at six o'clock the man walked down to the village and returned with a litre of red wine and whatever groceries he thought necessary. Oliver explained that since he himself would not have made these purchases he did not consider that he should make a contribution to their cost. His visitor was his guest in the matter of accommodation; in fairness, it seemed to follow, he should be his visitor's guest where the odd egg or glass of wine was concerned.

'Angelica was never easy,' Oliver explained, continuing the story of his marriage from one evening to the next. 'There was always jealousy.' His sojourn in the Betona hills was temporary, he stated with confidence. But he did not add that, with his sights fixed on something better, he often dropped into conversation with lone English or American women in the rooms of the picture gallery or at the café next to the hotel. He didn't bore his companion with this information because it didn't appear to have much relevance. He did his best only to be interesting about Angelica, and considered he succeeded. It was a dispute in quite a different area that ended the relationship, as abruptly as it had begun. As well as hospitality, the visitor claimed a sum of money had been agreed upon, but while conceding that a cash payment had indeed been mooted, Oliver was adamant that he had not promised it. He did not greatly care for the man in the end, and was glad to see him go.

When Angelica died two years ago Deborah was twenty. The death was not a shock because her mother had been ill, and increasingly in pain, for many months: death was a mercy. Nonetheless, Deborah felt the loss acutely. Although earlier, in her adolescence, there had been arguments and occasionally rows, she'd known no companion as constant as her mother; and as soon as the death occurred she realized how patient with her and how fond of her Angelica had been. She'd been larky too, amused by unexpected things, given to laughter that Deborah found infectious. In her distress at the time of her mother's death it never occurred to her that the man who'd come to the flat that Sunday afternoon might turn up at the funeral. In fact, he hadn't.

'You'll be all right,' Angelica had said before she died, meaning that there was provision for Deborah to undertake the post-graduate work she planned after she took her degree. 'Don't worry, darling.'

Deborah held her hand, ashamed when she remembered how years ago she'd been so touchy because Angelica once too often repeated that her marriage was a mistake. Her mother had never used the expression again.

'I was a horrid child,' Deborah cried forlornly before her mother died. 'A horrid little bully.'

'Darling, of course you weren't.'

At the funeral people said how much they'd always liked her mother, how nice she'd been. They invited Deborah to visit them at any time, just to turn up when she was feeling low.

When Oliver stepped off the bus in the village the butcher's shop was still open but he decided, after all, not to buy a pork chop, which was the choice he had contemplated when further considering the matter on the bus. A chop was suitable because, although it might cost as much as twenty thousand lire, it could be divided quite easily into two. But supposing it wasn't necessary to offer a meal at all? Supposing Deborah arrived in the early afternoon, which was not unlikely? He bought the bread he needed instead, and a packet of soup, and cigarettes.

He wondered if Deborah had come with a message. He did not know that Angelica had died and wondered if she was hoping he might be persuaded to return to the flat in the square. It was not unlikely. As he ascended the track that led to his property, these thoughts drifted pleasurably through Oliver's mind. 'Deborah, I'll have to think about that.' He saw himself sitting with his daughter in what the man who'd set the place to rights had called the patio — a yard really, with two car seats the man had rescued from a dump somewhere, and an old tabletop laid across concrete blocks. 'We'll see,' he heard himself saying, not wishing to dismiss the idea out of hand.

He had taken his jacket off, and carried it over his arm. '*E caldo!*' the woman he'd bought the bread from had exclaimed, which indicated that the heat was excessive, for in Betona references to the weather were only made when extremes were reached. Sweat gathered on Oliver's forehead and at the back of his neck. He could feel it becoming clammy beneath his shirt. Whatever the reason for Deborah's advent he was glad she had come because company was always cheerful.

In the upstairs room Oliver took his suit off and carefully placed it on a wire coat-hanger on the wall. He hung his tie over one linen shoulder, and changed his shirt. The trousers he put on were old corduroys, too heavy in the heat, but the best he could manage. In the kitchen he made tea and took it out to the patio, with the bread he'd bought and his cigarettes. He waited for his daughter.

After Angelica's death Deborah felt herself to be an orphan. Angelica's brother and his wife, a well-meaning couple she hardly knew, fussed about her a bit; and so did Angelica's friends. But Deborah had her own friends, and she didn't need looking after. She inherited the flat in London and went there in the university holidays. She spent a weekend in Norfolk with her uncle and his wife, but did not do so again. Angelica's brother was quite unlike her, a lumpish man who wore grey, uninteresting suits and had a pipe, and spectacles on a chain. His wife was wan and scatter-brained. They invited Deborah as a duty and were clearly thankful to find her independent.

Going through her mother's possessions, Deborah discovered neither photographs of, nor letters from, her father. She did not know that photographs of herself, unaccompanied by any other form of communication, had been sent to her father every so often, as a record of her growing up. She did not know of the financial agreement that years ago had been entered into. It did not occur to her that no one might have informed the man who'd come that Sunday afternoon of Angelica's death. It didn't occur to her to find some way of doing so herself. None of this entered Deborah's head because the shadowy figure who had smiled and lit a cigarette belonged as deeply in the grave as her mother did.

She had no curiosity about him, and her uncle did not mention him. Nor did any of Angelica's friends on the occasions when they invited Deborah to lunch or drinks, since she had not just turned up as they'd suggested at the funeral. In reply to some casual query by a stranger, she once replied that her father was probably dead. The happiness of her relationship with Angelica was what she thought about and moodily dwelt upon, regretting that she had taken it for granted.

The heat was at its most intense at three o'clock, but afterwards did not lose its fervour. The concrete blocks of Oliver's patio, the metal ribs of the car chairs, the scorching upholstery, the stone of the house itself, all cancelled the lessening of the sun's attack by exuding the heat that had been stored. By half past five a kind of coolness was beginning. By seven it had properly arrived. By half past eight there was pleasure in its relief.

Perhaps he had been wrong, Oliver thought later, not to approach the girl: thoughtfulness sometimes was misplaced. If she had waited for the day to cool she would have found herself too late for the last bus to Betona, and a taxi would have been outrageously expensive. Angelica would have taken a taxi, of course, though in other ways, as he well knew, she could be penny-pinching.

But Deborah didn't come that evening, nor the next day, nor the day after that. So Oliver made the journey into Perugia again, long before it was time for his next visit to the Credito Italiano. The only explanation was that the girl had not been Deborah at all. But he still felt she was, and was bewildered. He even wondered if his daughter was lying low because she'd been sent to spy on him.

'*Sì, signore?*' The clerk in the reception of the hotel smiled at him, and in slow Italian Oliver made his query. He wrote down Deborah's name on a piece of paper so that there could be no confusion. He remembered the date of the day he'd last sat at the café. From the photograph he had of her he described his daughter.

'*Momento, signore. Scusi.*' The clerk entered a small office to one side of the reception desk and returned some minutes later with a registration form. On it were Deborah's name and signature, and the address of the flat in London. She had stayed one night only in the hotel.

'Student,' a girl who had accompanied the clerk from the office said. 'She search a room in Perugia.'

'A room?'

'She ask.' The girl shrugged. 'I no have room.'

'Thank you.' Oliver smiled at both of them in turn. The clerk called after him in Italian. The girl had given Deborah the name of an agency, not twenty metres away, where rooms were rented to students. 'Thank you,' Oliver said again, but did not take the details of the agency. At the café he ordered a cappuccino.

Deborah had enrolled on a course – language or culture, or perhaps a combination. Perugia was famous for its courses; students came from all over the place. Sometimes they spent a year, or even longer, depending on the course they'd chosen. He knew that because now and again he dropped into conversation with one, and in return for a *grappa* or a cappuccino supplied some local information. Once he'd had lunch with a well-to-do young Iranian who'd clearly been grateful for his company.

'*Ecco, signore!*' The waitress who went off duty at eleven placed his coffee in front of him.

'*Grazie.*'

'*Prego, signore.*'

He lit a cigarette. Once he'd had a lighter and a silver cigarette case, given to him by a Mrs Dogsmith, whom he'd met in the Giardini Carducci. For a moment he saw again the slim, faintly embossed case, and the initials curling around one another at the bottom left-hand corner of the lighter. He'd sold both of them years ago.

A woman came out of the hotel and paused idly, glancing at the café tables. She was taller than Mrs Dogsmith and a great deal thinner. A widow or divorcee, Oliver guessed, but then a man came out of the hotel and took her arm.

'Your mother gave you so much.' Angelica's irrational chatter lurched at him suddenly. 'But still you had to steal from her.'

He felt himself broken into, set upon and violated, as he remembered feeling at the time. The unpleasant memory had come because of Deborah, because Deborah's presence put him in mind of Angelica, naturally enough. More agreeably, he recalled that it was he who'd chosen that name for their daughter. 'Deborah,' he'd suggested, and Angelica had not resisted it.

Not wishing to think about Angelica, he watched the waddling movement of a pigeon on the pavement, and then listened to a conversation in Italian between a darkly suited man and his companion, a woman in a striped tan dress. They were talking about swimwear; the man appeared to be the proprietor of a fashion shop. Young people in a group went by, and Oliver glanced swiftly from face to face, but his daughter was not among them. He ordered another cappuccino because in ten minutes or so the early-morning waitress would be going off duty.

It was a silliness of Angelica's to say he'd stolen from his mother. He more than anyone had regretted the sad delusions that had beset his mother. It was he who had watched her becoming vague, he who had suffered when she left all she possessed to a Barnardo's home. Angelica belonged to a later time; she'd hardly known his mother.

Slowly Oliver lit and smoked another cigarette, filling in time while he waited for the new waitress to arrive. As soon as he saw her he crumpled up the little slip that had accompanied his first cup of coffee, and placed on the table the money for the second. But this morning, when he'd gone only a few yards along the street, the waitress came hurrying after him, jabbering in Italian. He smiled and shook his head. She held out the money he'd left.

'Oh! *Mi dispiace!*' he apologized, paying her the extra.

*

'Deborah.'

She heard her name and turned. A middle-aged man was smiling at her. She smiled back, thinking he was one of the tutors whom she couldn't place.

'Don't you recognize me, Deborah?'

They were in the square. He had risen from the edge of a wooden stage that had been erected for some public meeting. The two girls Deborah was with were curious.

'My dear,' the man said, but seventeen years had passed since Deborah had caught her one glimpse of her father that Sunday afternoon. Neither features nor voice were familiar. 'It's really you!' the man said.

Bewildered, Deborah shook her head.

'I'm Oliver,' Oliver said. 'Your father.'

They sat outside, at the nearest café. She didn't take off her sunglasses. She'd spoken to the girls she'd been with and they'd walked on. She had a class at two, she'd said.

'Time at least for a coffee,' Oliver said.

She had a look of him, even though she was more like Angelica. It had been a disappointment, the deduction that she hadn't come here to seek him out. A disappointment that it was no more than a coincidence, her presence in Perugia.

'You knew of course?' he said. 'You did have my address?'

She shook her head. She'd had no idea. She hadn't even been aware that he was not in England.

'But, Deborah, surely Angelica –'

'No, she never did.'

Their coffee came. The waiter was young and unshaven, not neatly in a uniform like the girls at the café by the hotel. He glanced at Deborah with interest. Oliver thought he heard him making a sound with his lips, but he could not be sure.

'I often think of you and your mother in that flat.'

Deborah realized he didn't know Angelica had died, and found it difficult to break the news. She did so clumsily, or so she thought.

'My God!' he said.

Deborah dipped a finger into the foam of her coffee. She didn't like the encounter; she wished it hadn't taken place. She didn't like sitting here with a man she didn't know and didn't want to know. 'Apparently he's my father,' she'd said to her companions, momentarily enjoying the sophistication; but later, of course, all that would have to be explained.

'Poor Angelica!' he said.

Deborah wondered why nobody had warned her. Why hadn't her grey-suited uncle or one of Angelica's friends advised against this particular Italian city? Why hadn't her mother mentioned it?

Presumably they hadn't warned her because they didn't know. Her mother hadn't ever wanted to mention him; it wasn't Angelica's way to warn people against people.

'She used to send me a photograph of you every summer,' he said. 'I wondered why none came these last two years. I never guessed.'

She nodded meaninglessly.

'Why are you learning Italian, Deborah?'

'I took my degree in the history of art. It's necessary to improve my Italian now.'

'You're taking it up? The history of art?'

'Yes, I am.'

'It's lovely you're here.'

'Yes.'

She had chosen Perugia rather than Florence or Rome because the course was better. But if she'd known she wouldn't have.

'Not really a coincidence,' he was saying, very softly. 'These things never are.'

Just for a moment Deborah felt irritated. What had been the use of Angelica's being generous, unwilling to malign, bending over backwards to be decent, when this could happen as a result? What was the good of calling a marriage a mistake, and leaving it at that? But the moment passed; irritation with the dead was shameful.

'Is it far from here, where you live?' she asked, hoping that it was.

Oliver tore a cheque-stub from his cheque-book and wrote his address on it, then tore out another and drew a map. He wrote down the number of the Betona bus.

'It's lovely you're here,' he said again, giving his daughter the cheque-stubs. An excitement had begun in him. If he hadn't been outside the hotel that morning he'd never even have known she was in Perugia. She might have come and gone and he'd have been none the wiser. Angelica had died, the two of them were left; he wouldn't have known that, either.

'If you don't mind,' he heard his daughter saying and felt she was repeating something he hadn't heard the first time, 'I don't think I'll visit you.'

'You've been told unpleasant things, Deborah.'

'No, not at all.'

'We can be frank, you know.'

Angelica had been like that, he knew it to his cost. In his own case, she had laid down harsh conditions, believing that to be his due. The half-converted house and the monthly transfer of money carried the proviso that he should not come to the flat ever again, that he should not live in England. That wasn't pleasant, but since it was what she wanted he'd agreed. At least the money hadn't ceased when the woman died. Oliver smiled, feeling that to be a triumph.

'Angelica was always jealous. It was jealousy that spoilt things.'

'I never noticed that in her.'

He smiled again, knowing better. Heaven alone knew what this girl had been told about him, but today, now that she was here and Angelica was not, it didn't matter.

'A pity you feel you can't come out to Betona. The bus fare's quite a bit, else I'd come in oftener while you're here.'

'Actually, to tell the truth, I'd rather we didn't have to meet.' Deborah's tone was matter of fact and sharp. A note of impatience had entered it, reminding Oliver not of his wife, but strangely of his mother.

'I only come in once a month or so.' He slid a cigarette from his packet of MS. 'Angelica tried to keep us apart,' he said, 'all these years. She made the most elaborate arrangements.'

Deborah rooted in her handbag and found her own cigarettes and matches. Oliver said he'd have offered her one of his if he'd known she smoked. She said it didn't matter.

'I don't want any of this hassle,' she said.

'Hassle, Deborah? A cup of coffee now and again –'

'Look, honestly, not even that.'

Oliver smiled. It was always better not to argue. He'd never argued with Angelica. It was she who'd done the arguing, working herself up, making it sound as though she were angrily talking to herself. Deborah could easily sleep in the downstairs room; there were early-morning buses to Perugia. They could share the expenses of the household: the arrangement there'd been with the bankrupt man had been perfectly satisfactory.

'Sorry,' Deborah said, and to Oliver her voice sounded careless. She blew out smoke, looking over her shoulder, no doubt to see if her friends were still hanging around. He felt a little angry. He might have been just anyone, sitting there. He wanted to remind her that he had given her life.

'It's simple at Betona,' he said instead. 'I'm not well off. But I don't think you'd find it dreadful.'

'I'm sure I wouldn't. All the same —'

'Angelica was well off, you know. She never wanted me to be.'

Deborah missed her two o'clock lesson because it was harder than she'd anticipated to get away. She was told about all sorts of things, none of which she'd known about before. The Sunday afternoon she remembered was mentioned. 'I wasn't very well then,' Oliver said. It was after that occasion that a legal agreement had been drawn up: in return for financial assistance Oliver undertook not to come to the flat again, not ever to attempt to see his child. He was given the house near Betona, no more than a shack really. 'None of it was easy,' he said. He looked away, as if to hide emotion from her. The photographs he annually received were a legality also, the only one he had insisted on himself. Suddenly he stood up and said he had a bus to catch.

'It's understandable,' he said. 'Your not wanting to come to Betona. Of course you have your own life.'

He nodded and went away. Deborah watched him disappearing into the crowd that was again collecting, after the afternoon siesta.

Who on earth would have believed that he'd outlive Angelica? Extraordinary how things happen; though, perhaps, in a sense, there was a fairness in it. Angelica had said he always had to win. In her unpleasant moods she'd said he had to cheat people, that he could not help himself. As a gambler was in thrall to luck, or a dipsomaniac to drink, his flaw was having to show a gain in everything he did.

On the bus journey back to Betona Oliver did not feel angry when he recalled that side of Angelica, and supposed it was because she was dead. Naturally it was a relief to have the weight of anger lifted after all these years, no point in denying it. The trouble had been it wasn't easy to understand what she was getting at. When she'd found the three or four pieces among his things, she'd forgotten that they were his as much as his mother's, and didn't even try to understand that you couldn't have told his mother that, she being like she was. Instead Angelica chose to repeat that he hadn't been able to resist 'getting the better of' his mother. Angelica's favourite theme was that: what she called his pettiness and his meanness left him cruel. He had often thought she didn't care what she said; it never mattered how she hurt.

On the bus Angelica's face lolled about in Oliver's memory, with his mother's and – to Oliver's surprise – his daughter's. Angelica pleaded about something, tears dripped from the old woman's cheeks, Deborah simply shook her head. 'Like cancer in a person', Angelica said. Yet it was Angelica who had died, he thought again.

Deborah would come. She would come because she was his flesh and blood. One day he'd look down and see her on the path, bringing something with her because he wasn't well off. Solicitors had drawn up the stipulations that had kept them apart all these years; in ugly legal jargon all of it was written coldly down. When Deborah considered that, she would begin to understand. He'd sensed, before they parted, a shadow of unease: guilt on Angelica's behalf, which wasn't surprising in the circumstances.

The thought cheered Oliver considerably. In his house, as he changed his clothes, he reflected that it didn't really matter, the waitress running after him for the money. In all, over the months that had passed since this waitress had begun to work at the café, he'd probably had twenty, even thirty, second cups of coffee. He knew it didn't matter because after a little time it hadn't mattered that the bankrupt man had made a scene, since by then the roof was repaired and the plumbing completed. It hadn't mattered when Mrs Dogsmith turned nasty, since already she'd given him the lighter and the cigarette case. That was the kind of thing Angelica simply couldn't understand, any more than she'd understood the confusions of his mother, any more than, probably, she'd understood their daughter. You couldn't keep flesh and blood apart; you actually weren't meant to.

In the kitchen Oliver put the kettle on for tea. When it boiled he poured the water on to a tea-bag he'd already used before setting out for Perugia. He carried the glass out to the patio and lit a cigarette. The car seats were too hot to sit on, so he stood, waiting for them to cool. There'd been no reason why she shouldn't have paid for their coffee since she, after all, had been the cause of their having it. Eighteen thousand lire a cappuccino cost at that particular café, he'd noticed it on the bill.

August Saturday

'You don't remember me,' the man said.

His tone suggested a statement, not a question, but Grania did remember him. She had recognized him immediately, his face smiling above the glass he held. He was a man she had believed she would never see again. For sixteen years – since the summer of 1972 – she had tried not to think about him, and for the most part had succeeded.

'Yes, I do remember you,' she said. 'Of course.'

A slice of lemon floated on the surface of what she guessed was gin and tonic; there were cubes of ice and the little bubbles that came from tonic when it was freshly poured. It wouldn't be tonic on its own; it hadn't been the other time. 'I've drunk a bit too much,' he'd said.

'I used to wonder,' he went on now, 'if ever we'd meet again. The kind of thing you wonder when you can't sleep.'

'I didn't think we would.'

'I know. But it doesn't matter, does it?'

'Of course not.'

She wondered why he had come back. She wondered how long he intended to stay. He'd be staying with the Prendergasts, she supposed, as he had been before. For sixteen years she had avoided the road on which the avenue that led to the Prendergasts' house was, the curve of the green iron railings on either side of the open gates, the unoccupied gate-lodge.

'You weren't aware that Hetty Prendergast died?' he said.

'No, I wasn't.'

'Well, she did. Two days ago.'

The conversation took place in the bar of the Tara Hotel, where Grania and her husband, Desmond, dined once a month with other couples from the tennis club – an arrangement devised by the husbands so that the wives, just for a change, wouldn't have to cook.

'You don't mind my talking to you?' the man said. 'I'm on my own again.'

'Of course I don't.'

'When I was told about the death I came on over. I've just come in from the house to have a meal with the Quiltys.'

'Tonight, you mean?'

'When they turn up.'

Quilty was a solicitor. He and his wife, Helen, belonged to the tennis club and were usually present at the monthly dinners in the Rhett Butler Room of the Tara Hotel. The death of old Hetty Prendergast had clearly caught them unawares, and Grania could imagine Helen Quilty sulkily refusing to cancel a long-booked babysitter in order to remain at home to cook a meal for the stranger who had arrived from England, with whom her husband presumably had business to discuss. 'We'll take him with us,' Quilty would have said in his soothing voice, and Helen would have calmed down, as she always did when she got her way.

'Still playing tennis, Grania?'

'Pretty badly.'

'You've hardly aged, you know.'

This was so patently a lie that it wasn't worth protesting about. After the funeral of the old woman he would go away. He hadn't arrived for the other funeral, that of Mr Prendergast, which had taken place nearly ten years ago, and there wouldn't be another one because there was no other Prendergast left to die. She wondered what would happen to the house and to the couple who had looked after the old woman, driving in every Friday to shop for her. She didn't ask. She said:

'A group of us have dinner here now and again, the Quiltys too. I don't know if they told you that.'

'You mean tonight?'

'Yes.'

'No, that wasn't said.'

He smiled at her. He sipped a little gin. He had a long face, high cheekbones, greying hair brushed straight back from a sallow forehead. His blue-green eyes were steady, almost staring because he didn't blink much. She remembered the eyes particularly, now that she was again being scrutinized by them. She remembered asking who he was and being told a sort of nephew of the Prendergasts, an Englishman.

'I've often wondered about the tennis club, Grania.'

'It hasn't changed. Except that we've become the older generation.'

Desmond came up then and she introduced her companion, reminding Desmond that he'd met him before. She stumbled when she had to give him a name because she'd never known what it was. 'Prendergast,' she mumbled vaguely, not sure if he was called Prendergast or not. She'd never known that.

'Hetty died, I hear,' Desmond said.

'So I've been telling your wife. I've come over to do my stuff.'

'Well, of course.'

'The Quiltys have invited me to your dinner do.'

'You're very welcome.'

Desmond had a squashed pink face and receding hair that had years ago been sandy. As soon as he put his clothes on they became crumpled, no matter how carefully Grania ironed them. He was a man who never lost his temper, slow-moving except on a tennis court, where he was surprisingly subtle and cunning, quite unlike the person he otherwise was.

Grania moved away. Mavis Duddy insisted she owed her a drink from last time and led her to the bar, where she ordered two more Martinis. 'Who was that?' she asked, and Grania replied that the grey-haired man was someone from England, related to the Prendergasts, she wasn't entirely certain about his name. He'd come to the tennis club once, she said, an occasion when Mavis hadn't been there. 'Over for old Hetty's funeral, is he?' Mavis said and, accepting the drink, Grania agreed that was so.

They were a set in the small town; since the time they'd been teenagers the tennis club had been the pivot of their social lives. In winter some of them played bridge or golf, others chose not to. But all of them on summer afternoons and evenings looked in at the tennis club even if, like Francie MacGuinness and the Haddons, they didn't play much any more. They shared memories, and likes and dislikes, that had to do with the tennis club; there were photographs that once in a blue moon were sentimentally mulled over; friendships had grown closer or apart. Billy MacGuinness had always been the same, determinedly a winner at fourteen and determinedly a winner at forty-five. Francie, who'd married him when it had seemed that he might marry Trish, was a winner also: Trish had made do with Tom Crosbie. There'd been quarrels at the tennis club: a great row in 1961 when Desmond's father had wanted to raise money for a hard court and resigned in a huff when no one agreed; and nearly ten years later there had been the quarrel between Laverty and Dr Timothy Sweeney which had resulted in both their resignations, all to do with a dispute about a roller. There were jealousies and gossip, occasionally both envy and resentment. The years had been less kind to some while favouring others; the children born to the couples of the tennis club were often compared, though rarely openly, in terms of achievement or promise. Tea was taken, supplied by the wives, on Saturday afternoons from May to September. The men supplied drinks on that one day of the week also, and even washed up the glasses. The children of the tennis club tasted their first cocktails there, Billy MacGuinness's White Ladies and Sidecars.

A handful of the tennis-club wives were best friends, and had been since their convent days: Grania and Mavis, Francie, Helen, Trish. They trusted one another, doing so more easily now than they had when they'd been at the convent together or in the days when each of them might possibly have married one of the others' husbands. They told one another most things, confessing their errors and their blunders; they comforted and were a solace, jollying away feelings of inadequacy or guilt. Trish had worried at the convent because her breasts wouldn't grow, Helen because her face was scrawny and her lips too thin. Francie had almost died when a lorry had knocked her off her bicycle. Mavis had agonized for months before she said yes to Martin Duddy. As girls, they had united in their criticism of girls outside their circle; as wives they had not changed.

'I heard about that guy,' Mavis said. 'So that's what he looks like.'

That August Saturday in 1972 he'd come to the tennis club on a bicycle, in whites he had borrowed at the house where he was staying, a racquet tied with string to the crossbar. He'd told Grania afterwards that Hetty Prendergast had looked the whites out for him and had lent him the racquet as well. Hetty had mentioned the tennis club, to which she and her husband had years ago belonged themselves. 'Of course a different kind of lot these days,' she'd said. 'Like everywhere.' He'd pushed the bicycle through the gate and stood there watching a doubles game, not yet untying his racquet. 'Who on earth's that?' someone had said, and Grania approached him after about a quarter of an hour, since she was at that time the club's secretary and vaguely felt it to be her duty.

Sipping the Martini Mavis had claimed to owe her, Grania remembered the sudden turning of his profile in her direction when she spoke and then his smile. Nothing of what she subsequently planned had entered her head then; she would have been stunned by even the faintest inkling of it. 'I'm awfully sorry,' he'd said. 'I'm barging in.'

Grania had been twenty-seven then, married to Desmond for almost eight years. Now she was forty-three, and her cool brown eyes still strikingly complemented the lips that Desmond had once confessed he'd wanted to kiss ever since she was twelve. Her dark hair had been in plaits at twelve, later had been fashionably long, and now was short. She wasn't tall and had always wished she was, but at least she didn't have to slim. She hadn't become a mother yet, that Saturday afternoon when the stranger arrived at the tennis club. But she was happy, and in love with Desmond.

'Aisling's going out with some chartered accountant,' Mavis said, speaking about her daughter. 'Martin's hopping mad.'

The Quiltys arrived. Grania watched while they joined Desmond and their dinner guest. Desmond moved to the bar to buy them drinks. Quilty – a small man who reminded Grania of a monkey – lit a cigarette. Politely, Grania transferred her attention to her friend. Why should Martin be angry? she asked, genuinely not knowing. She could tell from Mavis's tone of voice that she was not displeased herself.

'Because he's nine years older. We had a letter from Aisling this morning. Martin's talking about going up to have it out with her.'

'That might make it worse, actually.'

'If he mentions it will you tell him that? He listens to you, you know.'

Grania said she would. She knew Martin Duddy would mention it, since he always seemed to want to talk to her about things that upset him. Once upon a time, just before she'd become engaged to Desmond, he'd tried to persuade her he loved her.

'They earn a fortune,' Mavis said. 'Chartered accountants.'

Soon after that they all began to move into the Rhett Butler Room. Grania could just remember the time when the hotel had been called O'Hara's Commercial, in the days of Mr and Mrs O'Hara. It wasn't all that long ago that their sons, giving the place another face-lift as soon as they inherited it, had decided to change the name to the Tara and to give the previously numbered bedrooms titles such as 'Ashley's' and 'Melanie's'. The bar was known as Scarlett's Lounge. There were regular discos in Belle's Place.

'Who's that fellow with the Quiltys?' Francie MacGuinness asked, and Grania told her.

'He's come back for Hetty Prendergast's funeral.'

'God, I didn't know she died.'

As always, several tables had been pushed together to form a single long one in the centre of the dining-room. At it, the couples who'd been drinking in the bar sat as they wished: there was no formality. Una Carty-Carroll, Trish Crosbie's sister, was unmarried but was usually partnered on these Saturday occasions by the surveyor from the waterworks. This was so tonight. At one end of the table a place remained unoccupied: Angela, outside the circle of best friends, as Una Carty-Carroll and Mary Ann Haddon were, invariably came late. In a distant corner of the Rhett Butler Room one other couple were dining. Another table, recently occupied, was being tidied.

'I think it's Monday,' Grania said when Francie asked her when the funeral was.

She hoped he'd go away again immediately. That other Saturday he'd said he found it appallingly dull at the Prendergasts', a call of duty, no reason in the world why he should ever return. His reassurances had in a way been neither here nor there at the time, but afterwards of course she'd recalled them. Afterwards, many times, she'd strained to establish every single word of the conversation they'd had.

'D'you remember poor old Hetty,' Francie said, 'coming in to the club for a cup of tea once? Ages ago.'

'Yes, I remember her.'

A small woman, they remembered, a frail look about her face. There was another occasion Francie recalled: when the old woman became agitated because one of Wm. Cole's meal lorries had backed into her Morris Minor. 'I thought she'd passed on years ago,' Francie said.

They separated. Helen was sitting next to him, Grania noticed, Quilty on his other side. Presumably they'd talk over whatever business there was, so that he wouldn't have to delay once the funeral had taken place.

'How're you doing, dear?' Martin Duddy said, occupying the chair on her left. Desmond was on her right; he nearly always chose to sit next to her.

'I'm all right,' she replied. 'Are you OK, Martin?'

'Far from it, as a matter of fact.' He twisted backwards and stretched an arm out, preventing the waitress who was attempting to pass by from doing so. 'Bring me a Crested Ten, will you? Aisling's in the family way,' he muttered into Grania's ear. 'Jesus Christ, Grania!'

He was an architect, responsible for the least attractive bungalows in the county, possibly in the province. He and Mavis had once spent a protracted winter holiday in Spain, the time he'd been endeavouring to find himself. He hadn't done so, but that period of his life had ever since influenced the local landscape. Also, people said, his lavatories didn't work as well as they might have.

'Do you mean it, Martin? Are you sure?'

'Some elderly Mr Bloody. I'll wring his damn neck for him.'

He was drunk to the extent that failing to listen to him wouldn't matter. No opportunity for comment would be offered. The advice sought, the plea for understanding, would not properly register in the brain that set in motion the requests. It was extremely unlikely that Aisling was pregnant.

'Old Hetty left him the house,' Desmond said on her other side. 'He's going to live in it. Nora,' he called out to the waitress, 'I need to order the wine.'

Martin Duddy gripped her elbow, demanding the return of her attention. His face came close to hers: the small, snub nose, the tightly bunched, heated cheeks, droplets of perspiration on forehead and chin. Grania looked away. Across the table, Mavis was better-looking than her husband in all sorts of ways, her lips prettily parted as she listened to whatever it was Billy MacGuinness was telling her about, her blue eyes sparkling with Saturday-evening vivacity. Francie was listening to the surveyor. Mary Ann Haddon was nervously playing with her fork, the way she did when she felt she was being ignored: she had a complex about her looks, which were not her strong point. Helen Quilty was talking to the man who'd come back for the funeral, her wide mouth swiftly opening and closing. Francie, who'd given up smoking a fortnight ago, lit a cigarette. Billy MacGuinness's round face crinkled with sudden laughter. Mavis laughed also.

The waitress hurried away with Desmond's wine order. Light caught one lens of Mary Ann's glasses. 'Oh, I don't *believe* you!' Francie cried, her voice for a single instant shrill above the buzz of conversation. The man who'd come back to attend the old woman's funeral still listened politely. Trish – the smallest, most demure of the wives – kept nodding while Kevy Haddon spoke in his dry voice, his features drily matching it.

There were other faces in the Rhett Butler Room, those of Clark Gable and Vivien Leigh reproduced on mirrored glass with bevelled edges, huge images that also included the shoulders of the film stars, the *décolletage* of one, the frilled evening shirt of the other. Clark Gable was subtly allowed the greater impact; in Scarlett's Lounge, together on a single mirror, the two appeared to be engaged in argument, he crossly pouting from a distance, she imperious in close-up.

'This man here, you mean?' Grania said to her husband when there was an opportunity. She knew he did; there was no one else he could mean. She didn't want to think about it, yet it had to be confirmed. She wanted to delay the knowledge, yet just as much she had to know quickly.

'So he's been saying,' Desmond said. 'You know, I'd forgotten who he was when you introduced us.'

'But what on earth does he want to come and live in that awful old house for?'

'He's on his uppers apparently.'

Often they talked together on these Saturday occasions, in much the same way as they did in their own kitchen while she finished cooking the dinner and he laid the table. In the kitchen they talked about people they'd run into during the day, the same people once a week or so, rarely strangers. When his father retired almost twenty years ago, Desmond had taken over the management of the town's laundry and later had inherited it. The Tara Hotel was his second most important customer, the Hospital of St Bernadette of Lourdes being his first. He brought back to Grania reports of demands for higher wages, and the domestic confidences of his staff. In return she passed on gossip, which both of them delighted in.

'How's Judith?' Martin Duddy inquired, finger and thumb again tightening on her elbow. 'No Mr Bloody yet?'

'Judith's still at the convent, remember.'

'You never know these days.'

'I think you've got it wrong about Aisling being pregnant.'

'I pray to God I have, dear.'

Desmond said he intended to go to Hetty Prendergast's funeral, but she saw no reason why she should go herself. Desmond went to lots of funerals, often of people she didn't know, business acquaintances who'd lived miles away. Going to funerals was different when there was a business reason, not that the Prendergasts had ever made much use of the laundry.

'I have a soft spot for Judith,' Martin Duddy said. 'She's getting to be a lovely girl.'

It was difficult to agree without sounding smug, yet it seemed disloyal to her daughter to deny what was claimed for her. Grania shrugged, a gesture that was vague enough to indicate whatever her companion wished to make of it. There was no one on Martin Duddy's other side because the table ended there. Angela, widow of a German businessman, had just sat down in the empty place opposite him. The most glamorous of all the wives, tall and slim, her hair the colour of very pale sand, Angela was said to be on the look-out for a second marriage. Her husband had settled in the neighbourhood after the war and had successfully begun a cheese-and-pâté business, supplying restaurants and hotels all over the country. With a flair he had cultivated in her, Angela ran it now. 'How's Martin?' She smiled seductively across the table, the way she'd smiled at men even in her husband's lifetime. Martin Duddy said he was all right, but Grania knew that only a desultory conversation would begin between the two because Martin Duddy didn't like Angela for some reason, or else was alarmed by her.

'Judith always has a word for you,' he said. 'Rare, God knows, in a young person these days.'

'Who's that?' Angela leaned forward, her eyes indicating the stranger.

She was told, and Grania watched her remembering him. Angela had been pregnant with the third of her sons that August afternoon. 'Uncomfortably warm,' she now recalled, nodding in recollection.

Martin Duddy displayed no interest. He'd been at the club that afternoon and he remembered the arrival of the stranger, but an irritated expression passed over his tightly made face while Grania and Angela agreed about the details of the afternoon in question: he resented the interruption and wished to return to the subject of daughters.

'What I'm endeavouring to get at, Grania, is what would you say if Judith came back with some fellow old enough to be her father?'

'Mavis didn't say Aisling's friend was as old as that.'

'Aisling wrote us a letter, Grania. There are lines to read between.'

'Well, naturally I'd prefer Judith to marry someone of her own age. But of course it all depends on the man.'

'D'you find a daughter easy, Grania? There's no one thinks more of Aisling than myself. The fonder you are the more worry there is. Would you say that was right, Grania?'

'Probably.'

'You're lucky in Judith, though. She has a great way with her.'

Angela was talking to Tom Crosbie about dairy products. The Crosbies were an example of a marriage in which there was a considerable age difference, yet it appeared not to have had an adverse effect. Trish had had four children, two girls and two boys; they were a happy, jolly family, even though when Trish married it had been widely assumed that she was not in love, was if anything still yearning after Billy MacGuinness. It was even rumoured that Trish had married for money, since Tom Crosbie owned Boyd Motors, the main Ford franchise in the neighbourhood. Trish's family had once been well-to-do but had somehow become penurious.

'What's Judith going to do for herself? Nursing, is it, Grania?'

'If it is she's never mentioned it.'

'I only thought it might be.'

'There's talk about college. She's not bad at languages.'

'Don't send her to Dublin, dear. Keep the girl by you. D'you hear what I'm saying, Desmond?' Martin Duddy raised his voice, shouting across Grania. He began all over again, saying he had a soft spot for Judith, explaining about the letter that had arrived from Aisling. Grania changed places with him. 'Martin's had a few,' Angela said.

'He's upset about Aisling. She's going out with an older man.'

She shouldn't have said it with Tom Crosbie sitting there. She made a face to herself and leaned across the table to tell him he was looking perky. As soon as she'd spoken she felt she'd made matters worse, that her remark could be taken to imply he was looking young for his years.

'There's a new place,' Angela said when Grania asked her about her dress. ' "Pursestrings". D'you know it?'

Ever since she'd become a widow Angela had gone to Dublin to buy something during the week before each Saturday dinner. Angela liked to be first, though often Francie ran her close. Mavis tried to keep up with them but couldn't quite. Grania sometimes tried too; Helen didn't mind what she wore.

'Is Desmond going to the funeral?' Tom Crosbie asked in his agreeable way – perhaps, Grania thought, to show that no offence had been taken.

'Yes, he is.'

'Desmond's very good.'

That was true. Desmond was good. He'd been the pick of the tennis club when she'd picked him herself, the pick of the town. Looking round the table – at Tom Crosbie's bald head and Kevy Haddon's joylessness, at the simian lines of Quilty's cheeks and Billy MacGuinness's tendency to glow, Martin Duddy's knotted features – she was aware that, on top of everything else, Desmond had worn better than any of them. He had acquired authority in middle age; the reticence of his youth had remained, but time had displayed that he was more often right than wrong, and his opinion was sought in a way it once had not been. Desmond was quietly obliging, a quality more appreciated in middle age than in youth. Mavis had called him a dear when he was still a bachelor.

They ate their prawn cocktails. The voices became louder. For a moment Grania's eye was held by the man who had said, at first, that she didn't remember him. A look was exchanged and persisted for a moment. Did he suspect that she had learnt already of his intention to live in the Prendergasts' house? Would he have told her himself if they hadn't been interrupted by Desmond?

'Hetty was a nice old thing,' Angela said. 'I feel I'd like to attend her funeral myself.'

She glanced again in the direction of the stranger. Tom Crosbie began to talk about a court case that was causing interest. Martin Duddy got up and ambled out of the dining-room, and Desmond moved to where he'd been sitting so that he was next to his wife again. The waitresses were collecting the prawn-cocktail glasses. 'Martin's being a bore about this Aisling business,' Desmond said.

'Desmond, did Prendergast mention being married now?'

He looked down the table, and across it. He shook his head. 'He hasn't the look of being married. Another thing is, I have a feeling he's called something else.'

'Angela says she's going to the funeral.'

One of the waitresses brought round plates of grilled salmon, the other offered vegetables. Martin Duddy returned with a glass of something he'd picked up in the bar, whiskey on ice it looked like. He sat between Desmond and Una Carty-Carroll, not seeming to notice that it wasn't where he'd been sitting before.

Mavis's back was reflected in the Rhett Butler mirror, the V of her black dress plunging deeply down her spine. Her movements, and those of Billy MacGuinness next to her, danced over the features of Clark Gable.

'He might suit Angela,' Desmond said. 'You never know.'

That August afternoon Billy MacGuinness, who was a doctor, had been called away from the club, some complication with a confinement. 'Damned woman,' he'd grumbled unfeelingly, predicting an all-night job. 'Come back to the house, Francie,' Grania had invited when the tennis came to an end, and it was then that Desmond had noticed the young man attaching his tennis racquet to the crossbar of his bicycle and had issued the same invitation. Desmond had said he'd drive him back to the Prendergasts' when they'd all had something to eat, and together they lifted his bicycle on to the boot of the car. 'I've something to confess,' Francie had said in the kitchen, cutting the rinds off rashers of bacon, and Grania knew what it would be because 'I've something to confess' was a kind of joke among the wives, a time-honoured way of announcing pregnancy. 'You're *not!*' Grania cried, disguising envy. 'Oh, Francie, how grand!' Desmond brought them drinks, but Francie didn't tell him, as Grania had guessed she wouldn't. 'February,' Francie said. 'Billy says it should be February.'

Billy telephoned while they were still in the kitchen, guessing where Francie was when there'd been no reply from his own number. He'd be late, as he'd predicted. 'Francie's pregnant,' Grania told Desmond while Francie was still on the phone. 'Don't tell her I said.'

In the sitting-room they had a few more drinks while in the kitchen the bacon cooked on a glimmer of heat. All of them were still in their tennis clothes and nobody was in a hurry. Francie wasn't because of the empty evening in front of her. Grania and Desmond weren't because they'd nothing to do that evening. The young man who was staying with the Prendergasts was like a schoolboy prolonging his leave. The sipping of their gin, the idle conversation – the young man told about the town and the tennis club, told who Angela was, and which the Duddys were: all of it took on the pleasurable feeling of a party happening by chance. Desmond picked up the telephone and rang the Crosbies but Trish said they wouldn't be able to get a babysitter or else of course they'd come over, love to. Eventually Desmond beat up eggs to scramble and Grania fried potato cakes and soda bread. 'We're none of us sober,' Desmond said, offering a choice of white or red wine as they sat down to eat. Eartha Kitt sang 'Just an Old-fashioned Girl'.

In the Rhett Butler Room Grania heard the tune again. '... and an old-fashioned millionaire', lisped the cool, sensuous voice, each emphasis strangely accented. They'd danced to it among the furniture of the sitting-room, Francie and the young man mostly, she and Desmond. 'I'm sorry, darling,' Desmond whispered, but she shook her head, refusing to concede that blame came into it. If it did, she might as well say she was sorry herself. 'I have to get back,' Francie said. 'Cook something for Billy.' Desmond said he'd drop her off on his way to the Prendergasts, but then he changed the record to 'Love Grows', and fell asleep as soon as the music began.

Francie didn't want a lift. She wanted to walk because the air would do her good. 'D'you trust me?' Grania asked the young man, and he laughed and said he'd have to because he didn't have a lamp on his bicycle. She'd hardly spoken to him, had been less aware of him than of Desmond's apparent liking of him. With strangers Desmond was often like that. 'What do you do?' she asked in the car, suddenly shy in spite of all the gin and wine there'd been. He'd held her rather close when he'd danced with her, but she'd noticed he'd held Francie close too. Francie had kissed him goodbye. 'Well, actually I've been working in a pub,' he said. 'Before that I made toast in the Marine Hotel in Bournemouth.'

She drove slowly, with extreme caution, through the narrow streets of the town. The public houses were closing; gaggles of men loitered near each, smoking or just standing. Youths thronged the pavement outside the Palm Grove fish-and-chip shop. Beyond the last of its lamp-posts the town straggled away to nothing, solitary cottages and bungalows gave way to fields. 'I haven't been to this house before,' Grania said in a silence that had developed. Her companion had vouchsafed no further information about himself beyond the reference to a pub and making toast in Bournemouth. 'They'll be in bed,' he said now. 'They go to bed at nine.'

The headlights picked out trunks of trees on the avenue, then urns, and steps leading up to a hall door. White wooden shutters flanked the downstairs windows, the paint peeling, as it was on the iron balustrade of the steps. All of it was swiftly there, then lost: the car lights isolated a rose-bed and a seat on a lawn. 'I won't be a minute,' he said, 'unshackling this bike.'

She turned the lights off. The last of the August day hadn't quite gone; a warm duskiness was scented with honeysuckle she could not see when she stepped out of the car. 'You've been awfully good to me,' he said, unknotting the strings that held the bicycle in place. 'You and Desmond.'

In the Rhett Butler Room, now rowdy with laughter and raised voices, she didn't want to look at him again, and yet she couldn't help herself: waiting for her were the unblinking eyes, the hair brushed back from the sallow forehead, the high cheekbones. Angela would stand at the graveside and afterwards would offer him sympathy. Quilty would be there, Helen wouldn't bother. 'I'd say we all need a drink': Grania could imagine Angela saying that, including Desmond in the invitation, gathering the three men around her. In the dark the bicycle had been wheeled away and propped against the steps. 'Come in for a minute,' he'd said, and she'd begun to protest that it was late, even though it wasn't. 'Oh, don't be silly,' he'd said.

She remembered in the garish hotel dining-room, the flash of his smile in the gloom, and how she'd felt his unblinking eyes caressing her. He reached out for her hand, and in a moment they were in a hall, the electric light turned on, a grandfather clock ticking at the bottom of the stairs. There was a hallstand, and square cream-and-terracotta tiles, brown engravings framed in oak, fish in glass cases. 'I shall offer you a nightcap,' he whispered, leading her into a flagged passage and then into a cavernous kitchen. 'Tullamore Dew is what they have,' he murmured. 'Give every man his dew.' She knew what he intended. She'd known it before they'd turned in at the avenue gates; she'd felt it in the car between them. He poured their drinks and then he kissed her, taking her into his arms as though that were simply a variation of their dancing together. 'Dearest,' he murmured, surprising her: she hadn't guessed that he intended, also, the delicacy of endearments.

Did she, before the car turned in at the avenue gates, decide herself what was to happen? Or was it later, even while still protesting that it was late? Or when he reached up to the high shelf of the dresser for the bottle? At some point she had said to herself: I am going to do this. She knew she had because the words still echoed. 'How extraordinary!' he murmured in the kitchen, all his talk as soft as that now. 'How extraordinary to find you at a tennis club in Ireland!' Her own arms held him to her; yet for some reason she didn't want to see his face, not that she found it unattractive.

The empty glasses laid down on the kitchen table, stairs without a carpet, a chest of drawers on a landing, towels in a pile on a chair, the door of his bedroom closing behind them: remembered images were like details from a dream. For a moment the light went on in his room: a pink china jug stood in a basin on a wash-stand, there was a wardrobe, a cigarette packet on the dressing-table, the shirt and trousers he'd changed from into his tennis clothes were thrown on to the floor. Then the light was extinguished and again he embraced her, his fingers already unbuttoning her tennis dress, which no one but Desmond had ever done in that particular way. Before her marriage she'd been kissed, twice, by Billy MacGuinness, and once by a boy who'd left the neighbourhood and gone to Canada. As all the tennis-club wives were when they married, she'd been a virgin. 'Oh God, Grania!' she heard him whispering, and her thoughts became worries when she lay, naked, on the covers of his bed. Her father's face was vivid in her mind, disposing of her with distaste. 'No, don't do that, dear,' her mother used to say, smacking with her tongue when Grania picked a scab on her knee or made a pattern on the raked gravel with a stick.

In the kitchen they ate raspberries and cream. She asked him again about himself but he hardly responded, questioning her instead and successfully extracting answers. The raspberries were delicious; he put a punnet on the seat beside the driving seat in the car. They were for Desmond, but he didn't say so. 'Don't feel awkward,' he said. 'I'm going back on Monday.'

A hare ran in front of the car on the avenue, bewildered by the lights. People would guess, she thought; they would see a solitary shadow in the car and they would know. It did not occur to her that if her expedition to the Prendergasts' house had been as innocent as its original purpose the people who observed her return would still have seen what they saw now. In fact, the streets were quite deserted when she came to them.

'God, I'm sorry,' Desmond said, sitting up on the sofa, his white clothes rumpled, the texture of a cushion-cover on his cheek, his hair untidy. She smiled, not trusting herself to speak or even to laugh, as in other circumstances she might have. She put the raspberries in the refrigerator and had a bath.

In the Rhett Butler Room they began to change places in the usual way, after the Black Forest gâteau. She sat by Francie and Mavis. 'Good for Aisling,' Francie insisted when Mavis described the chartered accountant; he did not seem old at all. 'I'll have it out with Martin when we get back,' Mavis said. 'There's no chance whatsoever she's been naughty. I can assure you I'd be the first to know.' They lowered their voices to remark on Angela's interest in the stranger. 'The house would suit her rightly,' Mavis said.

All the rooms would be done up. The slatted shutters that flanked the windows would be repainted, and the balustrade by the steps. There'd be new curtains and carpets; a gardener would be employed. Angela had never cared for the house her well-to-do husband had built her, and since his death had made no secret of the fact.

'I'll never forget that night, Grania.' Francie giggled, embarrassedly groping for a cigarette. 'Dancing with your man and Desmond going to sleep. Wasn't it the same night I told you Maureen was on the way?'

'Yes, it was.'

The three women talked of other matters. That week in the town an elderly clerk had been accused of embezzlement. Mavis observed that the surveyor from the waterworks was limbering up to propose to Una Carty-Carroll. 'And doesn't she know it!' Francie said. Grania laughed.

Sometimes she'd wondered if he was still working in a pub and told herself that of course he wouldn't be, that he'd have married and settled down ages ago. But when she saw him tonight she'd guessed immediately that he hadn't. She wasn't surprised when Desmond had said he was on his uppers. 'I am going to do this': the echo of her resolve came back to her as she sat there. 'I am going to do this because I want a child.'

'God, I'm exhausted,' Mavis said. 'Is it age or what?'

'Oh, it's age, it's age.' Francie sighed, stubbing out her cigarette. 'Damn things,' she muttered.

Mavis reached for the packet and flicked it across the table. 'Present for you, Kevy,' she said, but Francie pleaded with her eyes and he flicked it back again. Grania smiled because they'd have noticed if she didn't.

In the intervening years he would never have wondered about a child being born. But if Angela married him he would think about it; being close by would cause him to. He would wonder, and in the middle of a night, while he lay beside Angela in bed, it would be borne in upon him that Desmond and Grania had one child only. Grania considered that: the untidiness of someone else knowing, her secret shared. There'd been perpetually, every instant of the day it sometimes seemed, the longing to share – with Desmond and with her friends, with the child that had been born. But this was different.

The evening came to an end. Cars were started in the yard of the hotel; there were warnings of ice on the roads. 'Good-night, Grania,' the man who'd come for the funeral said. She buckled herself into her seat-belt. Desmond backed and then crawled forward into West Main Street. 'You're quiet,' he said, and immediately she began to talk about the possibility of Una Carty-Carroll being proposed to in case he connected her silence with the presence of the stranger. 'As a matter of fact,' he said when that subject was exhausted, 'I met that fellow of Aisling's once. He's only thirty-five.' She opened the garage door and he drove the car in. The air was refreshingly cold, sharper than it had been in the yard of the hotel.

They locked their house. Grania put things ready for the morning. It was a relief that a babysitter was no longer necessary, that she didn't have to wait with just a trace of anxiety while Desmond drove someone home. He'd gone upstairs and she knew that he'd done so in order to press open Judith's door and glance in at her while she slept. Whenever they came in at night he did that.

At the sink Grania poured glasses of water for him and for herself, and carried them upstairs. When she had placed them on either side of their bed she, too, went to look in at her daughter – a mass of brown hair untidy on the pillow, eyes lightly closed. 'I might play golf tomorrow,' Desmond said, settling his trousers into his electric press. Almost as soon as he'd clambered into bed he fell asleep. She switched out his bedside light and went downstairs.

Alone in the kitchen, sitting over a cup of tea, she returned again to the August Saturday. Two of Trish's children had already been born then, and two of Mavis's, and Helen's first. 'I wouldn't be surprised,' Billy MacGuinness had said, 'if Angela doesn't drop this one in a deck-chair.' Mary Ann Haddon had just started her second. Older children were sitting on the clubhouse steps.

Grania forced her thoughts through all the rest of it, through the party that had happened by chance, the headlights picking out the rose-bed. She savoured easily the solitude she had disguised during the years that had passed since then, the secret that had seemed so safe. In the quiet kitchen, when she had been over this familiar ground, she felt herself again possessed by the confusion that had come like a fog when she'd seen tonight the father of her child. Then slowly it lifted: she was incapable of regret.

Children of the Headmaster

The greater part of the house was shabby from use. The white paintwork of the corridors and the rooms had been chipped and soiled. Generations of feet had clattered against skirting-boards; fingers had darkened an area around door-handles; shoulders had worn patches on walls. The part of the house known as 'Private Side' was in better decorative repair, this being the wing occupied by the Headmaster's family – six people in contrast to the hundred and twenty-odd boys who comprised the boarding-school. In the holidays the house regained its unity, and the Headmaster's children were together again. Jonathan returned to his own room from whichever dormitory he had occupied during the term, and was glad to do so. Margery, Georgina and Harriet explored the forbidden territory of the last few months.

Mr Arbuary, the children's father, had bought the house with money left to his wife in a will. On learning about the legacy, the Arbuarys returned to England from Hong Kong, where Mr Arbuary had been a police officer. The legacy allowed them the first chance in their married life to 'do something', as they put it privately to one another. In those days Mrs Arbuary was on for anything, but had since developed a nervous condition that drained her energy. Only the two older children were born before the family's return to England, Jonathan and Margery.

Mr Arbuary was a tall, bespectacled man with a sandy moustache, increasing in stoutness as the years advanced, and balding at about the same rate. His wife, once stout herself, was skin and bone due to her nervous complaint, with lank fair hair and eyes as darting as a rabbit's. Their combination had produced children who were physically like neither of them except that they were blue-eyed and were not sallow-skinned or black-haired. Yet among the children there was a distinct family resemblance: a longish face in which the features were cut with a precision that lent them an aristocratic air, a tendency to stare. Margery and Georgina, when they were ten and nine respectively, were pretty. Harriet, at eight, gave little indication of how she would be in the future. Jonathan, the oldest, had already been told by the Classics master, Old Mudger, that he was not without good looks.

The house that was both school and home was on the outskirts of a seaside town, at the end of a brief, hydrangea-laden drive. In purchasing it and deciding to start a boarding-school, Mr Arbuary did his homework carefully. He recalled his own schooldays and all that had gone with them in the name of education and 'older values'. He believed in older values. At a time when the country he returned to appeared to be in the hands of football hooligans and trade unionists such values surely needed to be re-established, and when he thought about them Mr Arbuary was glad he had decided to invest his wife's legacy in a preparatory school rather than an hotel, which had been an alternative. He sought the assistance of an old schoolfellow who had spent the intervening years in the preparatory-school world and was familiar with the ropes. This was the Classics master whom generations of boys came to know as Old Mudger when Mr Arbuary had enticed him to the new establishment. Mrs Arbuary – presenting in those days a motherly front – took on the responsibility of catering and care of the boys' health. The boarding-school began with three pupils, increasing its intake slowly at first, later accelerating.

'Now,' Georgina prompted on the first afternoon of the Easter holidays in 1988. 'Anything good?'

The furniture-room, in the attics above the private part of the house, was the children's secret place. They crouched among the stored furniture that, ten years ago, their mother had inherited with the legacy. That morning the boys had gone, by car mostly, a few by train. In contrast to the bustle and the rush there'd been, the house was as silent as a tomb.

'Nothing much,' Jonathan said. 'Really.'

'Must have been *something*,' Harriet insisted.

Jonathan said that the winter term in the other side of the house had been bitterly cold. Everyone had chilblains. He recounted the itching of his own, and the huddling around the day-room fire, and his poor showing at algebra, geometry and Latin. His sisters were not much impressed. He said:

'Half Starving got hauled up. He nearly got the sack.'

Three times a year Jonathan brought to his sisters the excitement of the world they were protected from, for it was one of the Headmaster's rules that family life and school life should in no way impinge upon one another. The girls heard the great waves of noise and silence that came whenever the whole school congregated, a burst of general laughter sometimes, a master's voice raised to address the ranks of boys at hand-inspection times in the hall, the chatter of milk-and-biscuits time. They saw, from the high windows of the house, the boys in their games clothes setting off for the playing-fields. Sometimes, when an emergency arose, a senior boy would cross to Private Side to summon their father. He would glance at the three girls with curiosity, and they at him. On Sundays the girls came closer to the school, walking to church with their mother and the undermatron, Miss Mainwaring, behind the long crocodile of boys, and sitting five pews behind them.

'Why did Half Starving get hauled up?' Georgina asked.

The junior master was called Half Starving because of his unhealthily pallid appearance. As such, he had been known to the girls ever since their brother had passed the nickname on. By now they'd forgotten his real name.

'Because of something he said to Haxby,' Jonathan said. At lunch one day Half Starving had asked Haxby what the joke was, since the whole table had begun to snigger. 'No joke, sir,' Haxby replied, and Half Starving said: 'What age are you, Haxby?' When Haxby said nine, Half Starving said he'd never seen a boy of nine with grey hair before.

Georgina giggled, and so did Harriet. Margery said: 'What happened then?'

'Another boy said that wasn't a very nice thing to say because Haxby couldn't help his hair. The boy – Temple, I think it was – said it was a personal remark, and Half Starving said he hadn't meant to make a personal remark. Then he asked Haxby if he'd ever heard of the Elephant Man.'

'The *what?*' Harriet stared at Jonathan with her mouth open, the way her father said she never in any circumstances whatsoever should.

'A man in a peepshow who looked like an elephant. Someone asked Half Starving if Haxby reminded him of this elephant person and Half Starving said the elephant person had had grey hair when he was a boy also. Then someone said Haxby might be good in a peepshow and Half Starving asked Haxby if travelling about sounded like a life he'd enjoy. Everyone laughed and afterwards Cuthbert hauled Half Starving up because of the noise.'

Cuthbert was the school's nickname for the children's father. Jonathan had felt embarrassed about using it to his sisters at first, but he'd got over that years ago. For his own part, Mr Arbuary liked simply to be known as 'the Headmaster'.

'I think I know which Haxby is,' Margery said. 'Funny-looking fish. All the same, I doubt anyone would pay to see him in a peepshow. Anything else?'

'Spencer II puked in the dorm, first night of term. All the mint chocs he brought back and something that looked like turnips. Mange-coloured.'

'Ugh!' Harriet said.

Baddle, Thompson-Wright and Wardle had been caned for giving cheek.

Thompson-Wright had blubbed, the others hadn't. The piano master had been seen on the promenade with one of the maids, Reene.

Jonathan's sisters were interested in that. The piano master's head sloped at an angle from his shoulders. He dressed like an undertaker and did not strike the girls as the kind to take women on to the promenade.

'Who saw them?' Georgina asked.

'Pomeroy when he was going for Old Mudger's tobacco.'

'I don't like to think of it,' Margery said. 'Isn't the piano master meant to smell?'

Jonathan said the piano master himself didn't smell: more likely it was his clothes. 'Something gets singed when it's ironed.'

'A vest,' Harriet suggested.

'I don't know what it is.'

'I think a vest probably.'

Soon after that the children left the furniture-room. There was tea in the dining-room then, a daily ritual in the holidays, the long mahogany table with curved ends laid for six. The Headmaster liked it to be so. He liked Mrs Arbuary to make sandwiches: sardine and egg in winter, in summer cucumber and tomato. The Headmaster's favourite cake was fruit-cake, so there was fruitcake as well.

The dining-room was a darkish room, wallpaper in crimson-and-black stripes combining with two pairs of curtains – velvet, in crimson also, and net – to set this sombre tone. The grained paintwork was the same deep brown as the curlicued sideboard, on which were arrayed the silver teapots and water-jugs, the gravy boats and loving cups, that Mrs Arbuary had inherited at the same time as the furniture and her legacy. It was an aunt who had died.

The children took their places at the table. Mrs Arbuary poured tea. The maid who had been observed in the piano master's company brought in a plate of buttered toast. She and the other domestic staff – Monica and Mrs Hodge and Mrs Hodge's husband, who was the general handyman – continued to come daily to the school during the holidays, but for much shorter hours. That was the only way the Arbuarys could keep them.

'Thank you, Reene,' the Headmaster said, and the girls began to giggle, thinking about the piano master. He was a man who had never earned a nickname, and it was a tradition at the school not ever to employ his surname. Since Jonathan had passed that fact on to his sisters they had not, even in their thoughts, done so either.

'Well,' the Headmaster said next. 'We are *en famille*.'

Mrs Arbuary, who rarely instigated conversations and only occasionally contributed to them, did not do so now. She smeared raspberry jam on a finger of toast and raised it to her lips. The school was a triumph for her husband after a lustreless career in Hong Kong, but it had brought her low. Being answerable to often grumpy parents, organizing a kitchen and taking responsibility during epidemics did not suit her nature. She had been happier before.

'A good term,' the Headmaster said. 'I think we might compliment ourselves on a successful term. Eh, Jonathan?'

'I suppose so.' The tone was less ungracious than the sentiment. Jonathan drummed as much cheeriness into it as he could muster, yet felt the opinion must be expressed honestly in those words. He had no idea if the term had been successful or not; he supposed so if his father claimed so.

'A single defeat on the hockey field,' the Headmaster reminded him. 'And your own report's not half bad, old chap.'

'Georgina got a frightful one,' Harriet said.

The girls attended a day school in the town, St Beatrice's. When the time came they would be sent away to boarding-school, but at the preparatory stage funds could not be stretched. Once, years ago, Mrs Arbuary had suggested that the girls might receive their preparatory education at her husband's school, but this was before she appreciated that the older values did not permit this.

'Georgina,' Mr Arbuary said, in his Headmaster's rather than his father's voice, 'has much to mend this holidays. So, too, has Harriet.'

'My report wasn't too awful,' Harriet insisted in an unconvincing mutter meant mainly for herself.

'Speak clearly if you wish to be heard, Harriet. Reports are written to be assessed by parents. I would remind you of that.'

'I only meant –'

'You are a chatterbox, Harriet. What should be placed on chatterboxes?'

'Lids.'

'Precisely so.'

A silence fell around the table. Mrs Arbuary cut the fruitcake. The Headmaster passed his cup for more tea. Eventually he said:

'It is always a pity, I think, when Easter is as early as it is this year.'

He gave no reason for this view, but elicited none the less a general response – murmurs of agreement, nods. Neither Mrs Arbuary nor the children minded when Easter fell, but in the dining-room responses were required.

Increasingly, there was much that Jonathan did not pass on to his sisters. Mrs Arbuary's nickname, for instance, was the Hen because a boy called McAtters had said she was like a hen whose feathers had been drenched in a shower of rain – a reference to what McAtters, and others, considered to be a feeble manner. It had been noticed that Mrs Arbuary feared not just her husband, but Miss Mainwaring the undermatron and most of the assistant masters. It had been noticed that she played obsessively with one of her forefingers whenever parents engaged her in conversation. A boy called Windercrank said that once when she looked up from a flowerbed she was weeding there were soil-stained tears on her cheeks.

Jonathan had not passed on to his sisters the news that their father was generally despised. It had been easier to tell them about Old Mudger, how he sometimes came into the dorm if a boy had been sent to bed before prep because Miss Mainwaring thought he was looking peaky. 'Well, friendly, I suppose,' Jonathan had explained to Georgina and Harriet. 'Anyway, that's what we call it. Friendly.' Margery had an inkling: he'd seen it in her eyes. All three of them had laughed over the Mudger being friendly, Georgina and Harriet knowing it was funny because no one would particularly want to be friendly with their father's old schoolfellow. But they wouldn't laugh – nor would he – if he told them their mother was called the Hen. They wouldn't laugh if he told them their father was scorned for his pomposity, and mocked behind his back as a fearsome figure of fun.

And now – these Easter holidays – there was something else. A boy Jonathan did not like, who was a year older than he was, called Tottle, had sent a message to Margery. All term he had been bothering Jonathan with his messages, and Jonathan had explained that because of the Headmaster's rules he would have no opportunity to deliver one until the holidays. Tottle had doubted his trustworthiness in the matter, and two days before the term ended he pushed him into a corner in the lavatories and rammed his fist into Jonathan's stomach. He kept it there, pressing very hard, until Jonathan promised that he would deliver the message to Margery as soon as possible in the holidays. When Jonathan had first been a pupil in his father's school, when he was seven, no one had even seemed to notice his sisters, but during the last year or so – because they were older, he supposed – all that had changed. Boys he wasn't friends with asked questions about them, boys who'd never spoken to him before. Once, at lunch, Half Starving had warned a boy not to speak like that about the Headmaster's daughters. 'Fancy them yourself, sir?' someone else shouted down the table, and Half Starving went red, the way he always did when matters got out of hand.

'Tell her to meet me, first night of term,' Tottle's message was. 'Round by the carpentry hut. Seven.'

Tottle claimed that he had looked round and smiled at Margery in church. The third Sunday he'd done it she'd smiled back. Without any evidence to the contrary, Jonathan had denied that. 'You bloody little tit,' Tottle snapped, driving his fist further into Jonathan's stomach, hurting him considerably.

Tottle was due to leave at the end of next term, but Jonathan guessed that after Tottle there would be someone else, and that soon there would be messages for Georgina as well as Margery, and later for Harriet. He wouldn't have to be involved in that because he'd have left himself by then, but some other means of communication would be found, through Reene or Mrs Hodge or Hodge. Jonathan hated the thought of that; he hated his sisters being at the receiving end of dormitory coarseness. In the darkness there'd been guffaws when the unclothing of Reene by the piano master had been mooted – and sly tittering which he'd easily joined in himself. Not that he'd even believed Pomeroy when he said he'd seen them on the promenade. Pomeroy didn't often tell the truth.

But it wasn't the pursuit of his sisters that worried Jonathan most: it was what they would learn by the carpentry shed or in the seclusion of the hydrangeas. It stood to reason that their pursuers would let things slip. 'Cuthbert', Tottle would say, and Margery would laugh, saying she knew her father was called Cuthbert. Then, bit by bit, on similar occasions, all the rest of it would tumble out. You giggled when the Hen was imitated, the stutter she'd developed, her agitated playing with a forefinger. Cuthbert's walk was imitated, his catchphrases concerning the older values repeated in self-important tones. 'Bad taste' another catchphrase was. When the pomposity was laid aside and severity took its place he punished ruthlessly, his own appointed source of justice. When the rules were broken he showed no mercy. Other people's fathers were businessmen or doctors, Bakinghouse's was a deep-sea salvage operator. No one mentioned what they were like; no one knew.

'Margery,' Jonathan said in the furniture-room when Georgina and Harriet were receiving tuition from their father. 'Margery, do you know what a boy called Tottle looks like?'

Margery went pink. 'Tottle?' she said.

'He's one of the first three leading into church. There's Reece and Greated, then usually Tottle.'

'Yes, I know Tottle,' Margery admitted, and Jonathan knew from her casual tone that what Tottle had said about Margery smiling back was true.

'Tottle sent you a message,' Jonathan said.

'What kind of a message?' She turned her head away, trying to get her face into the shadows.

'He said to meet him by the carpentry shed next term. Seven o'clock the first evening.'

'Blooming cheek!'

'You won't, will you, Margery? He made me promise I'd tell you, otherwise I wouldn't have.'

'Of course I won't.'

'Tottle's not all that nice.'

'He's not bad-looking if he's the one I'm thinking of.'

Jonathan didn't say anything. Bakinghouse's father might turn into some kind of predator when he was at the bottom of the sea, quite different from the person Bakinghouse knew. A businessman mightn't be much liked by office people, but his family wouldn't know that either.

'Why d'you think Mummy's so nervy, Margery?'

'Nervy?'

'You know what I mean.'

Margery nodded. She didn't know why their mother was nervy, she said, sounding surprised. 'When did Tottle give you the message, Jonathan?'

'Two days before the end of term.'

Lying in bed the night before, he had made up his mind that he would pass the message on when Georgina and Harriet were occupied in one of the classrooms the next day. Best to get it over, he'd thought, and it was then that he began to wonder about their mother. He never had before and clearly Margery hadn't either. He remembered someone saying that the Hen was probably the way she was because of Cuthbert. 'Poor old Hen,' a voice in the dorm had sympathized.

'Don't tell the others,' Margery pleaded. 'Please.'

'Of course not.'

Their mother overheard things in the laundry-room when boys came for next week's sheet and clean pyjamas, and in the hall when she gave out the milk. As someone once said, it was easy to forget the poor old Hen was there.

'Don't meet him, Margery.'

'I told you I wouldn't.'

'Tottle's got a thing on you.'

Again Margery reddened. She told her brother not to be silly. Else why would Tottle want to meet her by the carpentry shed? he replied; it stood to reason. Tottle wasn't a prefect; he hadn't been made a prefect even though he was one of the oldest boys in the school. Had he been a prefect he wouldn't have been the third boy to enter the church on Sundays; he'd have led a battalion, as the five houses into which the school was divided were called. He wasn't a prefect because the Headmaster didn't consider him worthy and made no secret of the fact.

'It's nothing like that,' Margery persisted.

Jonathan didn't want to argue. He didn't even want to think about Tottle now that the message had been delivered. He changed the conversation; he asked Margery about Miss Mole, one of the mistresses who taught her, and about whom Margery was sometimes funny. But he hardly listened when she told him. It hadn't occurred to him before that Tottle was in some way attempting to avenge himself.

There was roast lamb for lunch. The Headmaster carved it. There was mint sauce, and carrots and mashed potatoes.

'I think we learned a thing or two this morning,' the Headmaster said. 'I hope we can compliment ourselves on that.'

Was he as bad as they said? Jonathan wondered. It was ridiculous to say he was like Mussolini, yet it had been said. 'Bully-boys are always a bit comic,' a boy called Piercey had suggested. 'Hitler. Mussolini. Cromwell. The Reverend Ian Paisley.'

'Jonathan.' His mother smiled at him, indicating that he should pass a dish to Harriet. By the end of the holidays she would be far less taut; that was always so. She and Mrs Hodge and Monica would launder blankets and clean the dormitory windows and polish the linoleum and wash down walls where it was necessary. Then all the beds had to be made and the dining-hall given a cleaning, the tables scrubbed and the serving range gone over with steel-wool. Hodge would clean the dining-hall windows because they were awkwardly placed. Crockery that had been broken during term would be replaced.

'Sorry,' Jonathan said, moving the dish of carrots towards his youngest sister. By the end of the holidays, though still subdued and jumpy, Mrs Arbuary would be more inclined to take part in mealtime conversation. Her hands would not quiver so much.

'Mrs Salkind telephoned in the middle of our labours,' the Headmaster reported. 'Apparently the Salkinds are being posted abroad. Did you know this, Jonathan? Did Salkind say?'

Jonathan shook his head.

'Apparently to Egypt. Some business thing.'

'Did Mrs Salkind give notice?' The hopeful note in his mother's tone caught in Jonathan's imagination. With a bit of luck all the other parents might give notice also. Again and again, that very afternoon, the telephone might ring and the news would be that father after father had been posted to distant parts. The school would close.

'On the contrary,' the Headmaster replied. 'No, quite the contrary. Our Master Salkind will be flown back and forth at the expense of some manufacturing company. Heavy-duty vehicle springs, I believe it is, that pay the piper where Salkind senior is concerned. I recall correctly, Jonathan?'

'I'm afraid I don't know.'

'No cause for fear, old chap. Heavy-duty vehicle springs, if I am not wildly astray, once featured long in a conversation with the senior Salkind. Buses, lorries, military transports. Now, it seems, the good man is to instruct the Egyptians in their manufacture, or else to set up a factory, or generally to liaise. The good Mrs Salkind did not reveal.'

While speaking, the Headmaster cut the meat on his plate, adding potatoes and carrots to each forkful. He paused to eat between sentences, so that what he said came slowly from him. When the children were younger they had fidgeted during their father's mealtime dissertations. They had since learned not to.

'No, the reason for the good lady's telephone call was to inquire if Master Salkind might have extra French.'

Not wishing to listen, Jonathan thought of Tottle again. The older boy's rather big, handsome face appeared clearly in his mind, a smile slung lazily across it. He glanced at Margery, seated opposite him. Was she, too, thinking about her admirer, visualizing him also? Was she wondering what it would be like to meet him as he'd suggested, what he'd say, how he'd act?

'French, apparently, is commercially *de rigueur* in Egypt, or at least in the Salkinds' corner of it.'

In the darkness of the dormitory there were confessions of desire. When one voice left off another began. Tales were told of what had been seen or heard. Intentions were declared, pretences aired.

'Though, truth to tell, I can hardly think of a reason why French should feature in any way whatsoever since the Egyptians have a perfectly good language of their own.'

The confessions of desire had to do with film stars usually, occasionally with Lady Di or Fergie, less often with Reene or Monica.

'Were you aware of that, old chap? French in Egypt?'

'No.'

'I think, you know, the good lady may have got it wrong.'

Tottle intended to try it on, and then to laugh in that way he had. He would put his big face close to Margery's, he'd put his big lips on to hers, and his hands would go all over her, just as though it wasn't real, just as though he was pretending. And later on, with someone else, it would be the same for Georgina, and for Harriet.

'But since Master Salkind's French is shaky an extra hour a week will hardly come amiss, eh?'

Everyone agreed.

The days of those Easter holidays went similarly by. The children of the Headmaster spent long afternoons on the grey sands that stretched beyond the shingle and the sea-front promenade. They sat in the Yew Tree Café sipping Coca-Cola and nibbling cheap biscuits. When their week's pocket-money ran out they crouched instead among the furniture of the furniture-room. Every morning Georgina and Harriet were given tuition by their father, and Jonathan and Margery read, alone in their rooms.

Tottle was not again mentioned, but as the weeks passed Jonathan found himself more and more dismayed by all that his imagination threw at him. It felt like that: as though heavy lumps of information were being lobbed in his direction, relentlessly and slowly. They dropped into the pond of his consciousness, creating little pictures. They nagged at him, and the intensity of colour in the pictures increased, and faces and expressions acquired greater distinctness.

Two nights before the holidays ended, restlessly awake, Jonathan arrived at a decision. The next afternoon he did not accompany his sisters to the sea-front and the Yew Tree Café, presenting them with the unlikely excuse that he had some history to read. He watched them set off from the window of his bedroom, delayed another twenty minutes, and then went slowly downstairs. He paused again, in doubt and trepidation, before he found the courage to knock on his father's study door. He had no idea how he might express himself.

'Yes?' the Headmaster responded.

Jonathan closed the door behind him. The study smelt, as always, of his father's pipe tobacco and a mustiness that could not be identified. Glass-paned cupboards were full of textbooks. There were supplies of chalk and geometrical instruments, globes of the world, cartridges for fountain pens, stacks of new exercise-books, blotting paper, pencils. His father sat behind his desk, a pipe in his mouth, the new term's timetables spread out before him.

'Well, old chap? Come to lend a hand?'

Beyond the geniality lay the ghost of the Headmaster's termtime self, of severity and suspicion. Pomposity wasn't what mattered most; talk of 'older values' and 'bad taste' was only tedious on its own. 'Bloody hypocrite', some boy – neither Tottle nor Piercey – had said once. 'Nasty brute'.

'Always tricky, the summer timetables.'

Jonathan nodded.

'Cricket's greedy,' the Headmaster said. 'Where time's concerned.'

'Yes, it is.'

His father knocked the ashes out of his pipe and drew a tin of tobacco towards him. All his life, Jonathan had been familiar with these tins: *Three Nuns* the tobacco was called, orange lettering on a creamy ground. He watched his father pressing the coiled shreds into the bowl of his pipe. His father knew: that was what Jonathan had at length deduced. His father had so determinedly separated Private Side from the school because he knew the girls must not be exposed to crudities. His father knew, but he didn't know enough. You couldn't insist there was a shutter that came down just because you pretended it did. You couldn't insist Old Mudger was a Mr Chips just because he looked like one.

'Girls out somewhere?' his father said.

'I think so.'

A match was struck, the tobacco caught. Jonathan watched it reddening, and smoke streaming from between his father's tightly clenched teeth. There was no conversation they could have. He could not mention the voices in the darkness of the dormitory, the confessions of desire, the declarations of intention. He could not tell his father he was despised for being the person he was, that boys were sorry for a woman they likened to a hen. He could not warn him of Tottle's revenge, nor suggest what lay ahead for Georgina and Harriet. Lying awake the night before, he had wanted to protect his sisters, and his mother also, because they were not to blame. And in a way he had even wanted to protect his father because he didn't know enough, because he blustered and was oppressive, and went about things stupidly.

'Well, I'd best get on, old chap,' his father said, applying himself once more to the sheets of paper that constituted the summer timetables. The balding head was bent again. Smoke eddied about it complacently.

Jonathan went away, softly closing the study door behind him. He ran through the empty corridors of the school, and down the hydrangea drive. He ran along the sea-front, looking for his sisters.

Kathleen's Field

'I'm after a field of land, sir.'

Hagerty's tone was modest to the bank agent, careful and cautious. He was aware that Mr Ensor would know what was coming next. He was aware that he constituted a risk, a word Mr Ensor had used a couple of times when endeavouring to discuss the overdraft Hagerty already had with the bank.

'I was wondering, sir ...' His voice trailed away when Mr Ensor's head began to shake. He'd like to say yes, the bank agent assured him. He would say yes this very instant, only what use would it be when Head Office wouldn't agree? 'They're bad times, Mr Hagerty.'

It was a Monday morning in 1948. Leaning on the counter, his right hand still grasping the stick he'd used to drive three bullocks the seven miles from his farm, Hagerty agreed that the times were as bad as ever he'd known them. He'd brought the bullocks in to see if he could get a price for them, but he hadn't been successful. All the way on his journey he'd been thinking about the field old Lally had spent his lifetime carting the rocks out of. The widow the old man had left behind had sold the nineteen acres on the other side of the hill, but the last of her fields was awkwardly placed for anyone except Hagerty. They both knew it would be convenient for him to have it; they both knew there'd be almost as much profit in that single pasture as there was in all the land he possessed already. Gently sloping, naturally drained, it was free of weeds and thistles, and the grass it grew would do you good to look at. Old Lally had known its value from the moment he'd inherited it. He had kept it ditched, with its gates and stone walls always cared for. And for miles around, no one had ever cleared away rocks like old Lally had.

'I'd help you if I could, Mr Hagerty,' the bank agent assured him. 'Only there's still a fair bit owing.'

'I know there is, sir.'

Every December Hagerty walked into the bank with a plucked turkey as a seasonal statement of gratitude: the overdraft had undramatically continued for seventeen years. It was less than it had been, but Hagerty was no longer young and he might yet be written off as a bad debt. He hadn't had much hope when he'd raised the subject of the field he coveted.

'I'm sorry, Mr Hagerty,' the bank agent said, stretching his hand across the width of the counter. 'I know that field well. I know you could make something of it, but there you are.'

'Ah well, you gave it your consideration, sir.'

He said it because it was his way to make matters easier for a man who had lent him money in the past: Hagerty was a humble man. He had a tired look about him, his spare figure stooped from the shoulders, a black hat always on his head. He hadn't removed it in the bank, nor did he in Shaughnessy's Provisions and Bar, where he sat in a corner by himself, with a bottle of stout to console him. He had left the bullocks in Cronin's yard in order to free himself for his business in the bank, and since Cronin made a small charge for this fair-day service he'd thought he might as well take full advantage of it by delaying a little longer.

He reflected as he drank that he hardly needed the bank agent's reminder about the times being bad. Seven of his ten children had emigrated, four to Canada and America, the three others to England. Kathleen, the youngest, now sixteen, was left, with Biddy, who wasn't herself, and Con, who would inherit the farm. But without the Lallys' field it wouldn't be easy for Con to keep going. Sooner or later he would want to marry the McKrill girl, and there'd always have to be a home for Biddy on the farm, and for a while at least an elderly mother and father would have to be accommodated also. Sometimes one or other of the exiled children sent back a cheque and Hagerty never objected to accepting it. But none of them could afford the price of a field, and he wasn't going to ask them. Nor would Con accept these little presents when his time came to take over the farm entirely, for how could the oldest brother be beholden like that in the prime of his life? It wasn't the same for Hagerty himself: he'd been barefoot on the farm as a child, which was when his humility had been learned.

'Are you keeping yourself well, Mr Hagerty?' Mrs Shaughnessy inquired, crossing the small bar to where he sat. She'd been busy with customers on the grocery side since soon after he'd come in; she'd drawn the cork out of his bottle, apologizing for her busyness when she gave it to him to pour himself.

'I am,' he said. 'And are you, Mrs Shaughnessy?'

'I have the winter rheumatism again. But thank God it's not severe.'

Mrs Shaughnessy was a tall, big-shouldered woman whom he remembered as a girl before she'd married into the shop. She wore a bit of make-up, and her clothes were more colourful than his wife's, although they were hidden now by her green shop overall. She had been flighty as a girl, so he remembered hearing, but in no way could you describe her as that in her late middle age; 'well-to-do' was the description that everything about Mrs Shaughnessy insisted upon.

'I was wanting to ask you, Mr Hagerty. I'm on the look-out for a country girl to assist me in the house. If they're any good they're like gold dust these days. Would you know of a country girl out your way?'

Hagerty began to shake his head and was at once reminded of the bank agent shaking his. It was then, while he was still actually engaged in that motion, that he recalled a fact which previously had been of no interest to him: Mrs Shaughnessy's husband lent people money. Mr Shaughnessy was a considerable businessman. As well as the Provisions and Bar, he owned a barber's shop and was an agent for the Property & Life Insurance Company; he had funds to spare. Hagerty had heard of people mortgaging an area of their land with Mr Shaughnessy, or maybe the farmhouse itself, and as a consequence being able to buy machinery or stock. He'd never yet heard of any unfairness or sharp practice on the part of Mr Shaughnessy after the deal had been agreed upon and had gone into operation.

'Haven't you a daughter yourself, Mr Hagerty? Pardon me now if I'm guilty of a presumption, but I always say if you don't ask you won't know. Haven't you a daughter not long left the nuns?'

Kathleen's round, open features came into his mind, momentarily softening his own. His youngest daughter was inclined to plumpness, but her wide, uncomplicated smile often radiated moments of prettiness in her face. She had always been his favourite, although Biddy, of course, had a special place also.

'No, she's not long left the convent.'

Her face slipped away, darkening to nothing in his imagination. He thought again of the Lallys' field, the curving shape of it like a tea-cloth thrown over a bush to dry. A stream ran among the few little ash trees at the bottom, the morning sun lingered on the heart of it.

'I'd never have another girl unless I knew the family, Mr Hagerty. Or unless she'd be vouched for by someone the like of yourself.'

'Are you thinking of Kathleen, Mrs Shaughnessy?'

'Well, I am. I'll be truthful with you, I am.'

At that moment someone rapped with a coin on the counter of the grocery and Mrs Shaughnessy hurried away. If Kathleen came to work in the house above the Provisions and Bar, he might be able to bring up the possibility of a mortgage. And the grass was so rich in the field that it wouldn't be too many years before a mortgage could be paid off. Con would be left secure, Biddy would be provided for.

Hagerty savoured a slow mouthful of stout. He didn't want Kathleen to go to England. *I can get her fixed up*, her sister, Mary Florence, had written in a letter not long ago. 'I'd rather Kilburn than Chicago,' he'd heard Kathleen herself saying to Con, and at the time he'd been relieved because Kilburn was nearer. Only Biddy would always be with them, for you couldn't count on Con not being tempted by Kilburn or Chicago the way things were at the present time. 'Sure, what choice have we in any of it?' their mother had said, but enough of them had gone, he'd thought. His father had struggled for the farm and he'd struggled for it himself.

'God, the cheek of some people!' Mrs Shaughnessy exclaimed, re-entering the bar. 'Tinned pears and ham, and her book unpaid since January! Would you credit that, Mr Hagerty?'

He wagged his head in an appropriate manner, denoting amazement. He'd been thinking over what she'd put to him, he said. There was no girl out his way who might be suitable, only his own Kathleen. 'You were right enough to mention Kathleen, Mrs Shaughnessy.' The nuns had never been displeased with her, he said as well.

'Of course, she would be raw, Mr Hagerty. I'd have to train every inch of her. Well, I have experience in that, all right. You train them, Mr Hagerty, and the next thing is they go off to get married. There's no sign of that, is there?'

'Ah, no, no.'

'You'd maybe spend a year training them and then they'd be off. Sure, where's the sense in it? I often wonder I bother.'

'Kathleen wouldn't go running off, no fear of that, Mrs Shaughnessy.'

'It's best to know the family. It's best to know a father like yourself.'

As Mrs Shaughnessy spoke, her husband appeared behind the bar. He was a medium-sized man, with grey hair brushed into spikes, and a map of broken veins dictating a warm redness in his complexion. He wore a collar and tie, which Mr Hagerty did not, and the waistcoat and trousers of a dark-blue suit. He carried a number of papers in his right hand and a packet of Sweet Afton cigarettes in his left. He spread the papers out on the bar and, having lit a cigarette, proceeded to scrutinize them. While he listened to Mrs Shaughnessy's further exposition of her theme, Hagerty was unable to take his eyes off him.

'You get in a country girl and you wouldn't know was she clean or maybe would she take things. We had a queer one once, she used eat a raw onion. You'd go into the kitchen and she'd be at it. "What are you chewing, Kitty?" you might say to her politely. And she'd open her mouth and you'd see the onion in it.'

'Kathleen wouldn't eat onions.'

'Ah, I'm not saying she would. Des, will you bring Mr Hagerty another bottle of stout? He has a girl for us.'

Looking up from his papers but keeping a finger in place on them, her husband asked her what she was talking about.

'Kathleen Hagerty would come in and assist me, Des.'

Mr Shaughnessy asked who Kathleen Hagerty was, and when it was revealed that her father was sitting in the bar with a bottle of stout, and in need of another one, he bundled his papers into a pocket and drew the corks from two further bottles. His wife winked at Hagerty. He liked to have a maid about the house, she said. He pretended he didn't, but he liked the style of it.

All the way back to the farm, driving home the bullocks, Hagerty reflected on that stroke of luck. In poor spirits he'd turned into Shaughnessy's, it being the nearest public house to the bank. If he hadn't done so, and if Mrs Shaughnessy hadn't mentioned her domestic needs, and if her husband hadn't come in when he had, there wouldn't have been one bit of good news to carry back. 'I'm after a field of land,' he'd said to Mr Shaughnessy, making no bones about it. They'd both listened to him, Mrs Shaughnessy only going away once, to pour herself half a glass of sherry. They'd understood immediately the thing about the field being valuable to him because of its position. 'Doesn't it sound a grand bit of land, Des?' Mrs Shaughnessy had remarked with enthusiasm. 'With a good hot sun on it?' He'd revealed the price old Lally's widow was asking; he'd laid every fact he knew down before them.

In the end, on top of four bottles of stout, he was poured a glass of Paddy, and then Mrs Shaughnessy made him a spreadable-cheese sandwich. He would send Kathleen in, he promised, and after that it would be up to Mrs Shaughnessy. 'But, sure, I think we'll do business,' she'd confidently predicted.

Biddy would see him coming, he said to himself as he urged the bullocks on. She'd see the bullocks and she'd run back into the house to say they hadn't been sold. There'd be long faces then, but he'd take it easy when he entered the kitchen and reached out for his tea. A bad old fair it had been, he'd report, which was nothing only the truth, and he'd go through the offers that had been made to him. He'd go through his conversation with Mr Ensor and then explain how he'd gone into Shaughnessy's to rest himself before the journey home.

On the road ahead he saw Biddy waving at him and then doing what he'd known she'd do: hurrying back to precede him with the news. As he murmured the words of a thanksgiving, his youngest daughter again filled Hagerty's mind. The day Kathleen was born it had rained from dawn till dusk. People said that was lucky for the family of an infant, and it might be they were right.

*

Kathleen was led from room to room and felt alarmed. She had never experienced a carpet beneath her feet before. There were boards or linoleum in the farmhouse, and linoleum in the Reverend Mother's room at the convent. She found the papered walls startling: flowers cascaded in the corners, and ran in a narrow band around the room, close to the ceiling. 'I see you admiring the frieze,' Mrs Shaughnessy said. 'I had the house redone a year ago.' She paused and then laughed, amused by the wonder in Kathleen's face. 'Those little borders,' she said. 'I think they call them friezes these days.'

When Mrs Shaughnessy laughed her chin became long and smooth, and the skin tightened on her forehead. Her very white false teeth – which Kathleen was later to learn she referred to as her 'delf' – shifted slightly behind her reddened lips. The laugh was a sedate whisper that quickly exhausted itself.

'You're a good riser, are you, Kathleen?'

'I'm used to getting up, ma'am.'

Always say ma'am, the Reverend Mother had adjured, for Kathleen had been summoned when it was known that Mrs Shaughnessy was interested in training her as a maid. The Reverend Mother liked to have a word with any girl who'd been to the convent when the question of local employment arose, or if emigration was mooted. The Reverend Mother liked to satisfy herself that a girl's future promised to be what she would herself have chosen for the girl; and she liked to point out certain hazards, feeling it her duty to do so. The Friday fast was not observed in Protestant households, where there would also be an absence of sacred reminders. Conditions met with after emigration left even more to be desired.

'Now, this would be your own room, Kathleen,' Mrs Shaughnessy said, leading her into a small bedroom at the top of the house. There was a white china wash-basin with a jug standing in it, and a bed with a mattress on it, and a cupboard. The stand the basin and the jug were on was painted white, and so was the cupboard. A net curtain covered the bottom half of a window and at the top there was a brown blind like the ones in the Reverend Mother's room. There wasn't a carpet on the floor and there wasn't linoleum either; but a rug stretched on the boards by the bed, and Kathleen couldn't help imagining her bare feet stepping on to its softness first thing every morning.

'There'll be the two uniforms the last girl had,' Mrs Shaughnessy said. 'They'd easily fit, although I'd say you were bigger on the chest. You wouldn't be be familiar with a uniform, Kathleen?'

'I didn't have one at the convent, ma'am.'

'You'll soon get used to the dresses.'

That was the first intimation that Mrs Shaughnessy considered her suitable for the post. The dresses were hanging in the cupboard, she said. There were sheets and blankets in the hot press.

'I'd rather call you Kitty,' Mrs Shaughnessy said. 'If you wouldn't object. The last girl was Kitty, and so was another we had.'

Kathleen said that was all right. She hadn't been called Kitty at the convent, and wasn't at home because it was the pet name of her eldest sister.

'Well, that's great,' Mrs Shaughnessy said, the tone of her voice implying that the arrangement had already been made.

'I was never better pleased with you,' her father said when Kathleen returned home. 'You're a great little girl.'

When she'd packed some of her clothes into a suitcase that Mary Florence had left behind after a visit one time, he said it was hardly like going away at all because she was only going seven miles. She'd return every Sunday afternoon; it wasn't like Kilburn or Chicago. She sat beside him on the cart and he explained that the Shaughnessys had been generous to a degree. The wages he had agreed with them would be held back and set against the debt: it was that that made the whole thing possible, reducing his monthly repayments to a figure he was confident he could manage, even with the bank overdraft. 'It isn't everyone would agree to the convenience of that, Kathleen.'

She said she understood. There was a new sprightliness about her father; the fatigue in his face had given way to an excited pleasure. His gratitude to the Shaughnessys, and her mother's gratitude, had made the farmhouse a different place during the last couple of weeks. Biddy and Con had been affected by it, and so had Kathleen, even though she had no idea what life would be like in the house above the Shaughnessys' Provisions and Bar. Mrs Shaughnessy had not outlined her duties beyond saying that every night when she went up to bed she should carry with her the alarm clock from the kitchen dresser, and carry it down again every morning. The most important thing of all appeared to be that she should rise promptly from her bed.

'You'll listen well to what Mrs Shaughnessy says,' her father begged her. 'You'll attend properly to all the work, Kathleen?'

'I will of course.'

'It'll be great seeing you on Sundays, girl.'

'It'll be great coming home.'

A bicycle, left behind also by Mary Florence, lay in the back of the cart. Kathleen had wanted to tie the suitcase on to the carrier and cycle in herself with it, but her father wouldn't let her. It was dangerous, he said; a suitcase attached like that could easily unbalance you.

'Kathleen's field is what we call it,' her father said on their journey together, and added after a moment: 'They're decent people, Kathleen. You're going to a decent house.'

'Oh, I know, I know.'

But after only half a day there Kathleen wished she was back in the farmhouse. She knew at once how much she was going to miss the comfort of the kitchen she had known all her life, and the room along the passage she shared with Biddy, where Mary Florence had slept also, and the dogs nosing up to her in the yard. She knew how much she would miss Con, and her father and her mother, and how she'd miss looking after Biddy.

'Now, I'll show you how to set a table,' Mrs Shaughnessy said. 'Listen to this carefully, Kitty.'

Cork mats were put down on the tablecloth so that the heat of the dishes wouldn't penetrate to the polished surface beneath. Small plates were placed on the left of each mat, to put the skins of potatoes on. A knife and a fork were arranged on each side of the mats and a spoon and a fork across the top. The pepper and salt were placed so that Mr Shaughnessy could easily reach them. Serving spoons were placed by the bigger mats in the middle. The breakfast table was set the night before, with the cups upside down on the saucers so that they wouldn't catch the dust when the ashes were taken from the fireplace.

'Can you cut kindling, Kitty? I'll show you how to do it with the little hatchet.'

She showed her, as well, how to sweep the carpet on the stairs with a stiff hand-brush, and how to use the dust-pan. She explained that every mantelpiece in the house had to be dusted every morning, and all the places where grime would gather. She showed her where saucepans and dishes were kept, and instructed her in how to light the range, the first task of the day. The backyard required brushing once a week, on Saturday between four o'clock and five. And every morning after breakfast water had to be pumped from the tank in the yard, fifteen minutes' work with the hand lever.

'That's the W.C. you'd use, Kitty,' Mrs Shaughnessy indicated, leading her to a privy in another part of the backyard. 'The maids always use this one.'

The dresses of the uniforms didn't fit. She looked at herself in the blue one and then in the black. The mirror on the dressing-table was tarnished, but she could tell that neither uniform enhanced her in any way whatsoever. She looked as fat as a fool, she thought, with the hems all crooked, and the sleeves too tight on her forearms. 'Oh now, that's really very good,' Mrs Shaughnessy said when Kathleen emerged from her bedroom in the black one. She demonstrated how the bodice of the apron was kept in place and how the afternoon cap should be worn.

'Is your father fit?' Mr Shaughnessy inquired when he came upstairs for his six o'clock tea.

'He is, sir.' Suddenly Kathleen had to choke back tears because without any warning the reference to her father had made her want to cry.

'He was shook the day I saw him,' Mr Shaughnessy said, 'on account he couldn't sell the bullocks.'

'He's all right now, sir.'

The Shaughnessys' son reappeared then too, a narrow-faced youth who hadn't addressed her when he'd arrived in the dining-room in the middle of the day and didn't address her now. There were just the three of them, two younger children having grown up and gone away. During the day Mrs Shaughnessy had often referred to her other son and her daughter, the son in business in Limerick, the daughter married to a county surveyor. The narrow-faced son would inherit the businesses, she'd said, the barber's shop and the Provisions and Bar, maybe even the insurances. With a bout of wretchedness, Kathleen was reminded of Con inheriting the farm. Before that he'd marry Angie McKrill, who wouldn't hesitate to accept him now that the farm was improved.

Kathleen finished laying the table and went back to the kitchen, where Mrs Shaughnessy was frying rashers and eggs and slices of soda bread. When they were ready she scooped them on to three plates and Kathleen carried the tray, with a teapot on it as well, into the dining-room. Her instructions were to return to the kitchen when she'd done so and to fry her own rasher and eggs, and soda bread if she wanted it. 'I don't know will we make much of that one,' she heard Mrs Shaughnessy saying as she closed the dining-room door.

That night she lay awake in the strange bed, not wanting to sleep because sleep would too swiftly bring the morning, and another day like the day there'd been. She couldn't stay here: she'd say that on Sunday. If they knew what it was like they wouldn't want her to. She sobbed, thinking again of the warm kitchen she had left behind, the sheepdogs lying by the fire and Biddy turning the wheel of the bellows, the only household task she could do. She thought of her mother and father sitting at the table as they always did, her mother knitting, her father pondering, with his hat still on his head. If they could see her in the dresses they'd understand. If they could see her standing there pumping up the water they'd surely be sorry for the way she felt. 'I haven't the time to tell you twice, Kitty,' Mrs Shaughnessy said over and over again, her long, painted face not smiling in the least way whatsoever. If anything was broken, she'd said, the cost of it would have to be stopped out of the wages, and she'd spoken as though the wages would actually change hands. In Kathleen's dreams Mrs Shaughnessy kept laughing, her chin going long and smooth and her large white teeth moving in her mouth. The dresses belonged to one of the King of England's daughters, she explained, which was why they didn't fit. And then Mary Florence came into the kitchen and said she was just back from Kilburn with a pair of shoes that belonged to someone else. The price of them could be stopped out of the wages, she suggested, and Mrs Shaughnessy agreed.

When Kathleen opened her eyes, roused by the alarm clock at half past six, she didn't know where she was. Then one after another the details of the previous day impinged on her waking consciousness: the cork mats, the shed where the kindling was cut, the narrow face of the Shaughnessys' son, the greasy doorknobs in the kitchen, the impatience in Mrs Shaughnessy's voice. The reality was worse than the confusion of her dreams, and there was nothing magical about the softness of the rug beneath her bare feet: she didn't even notice it. She lifted her night-dress over her head and for a moment caught a glimpse of her nakedness in the tarnished looking-glass – plumply rounded thighs and knees, the dimple in her stomach. She drew on stockings and underclothes, feeling even more lost than she had when she'd tried not to go to sleep. She knelt by her bed, and when she'd offered her usual prayers she asked that she might be taken away from the Shaughnessys' house. She asked that her father would understand when she told him.

'The master's waiting on his breakfast, Kitty.'

'I lit the range the minute I was down, ma'am.'

'If you don't get it going by twenty to seven it won't be hot in time. I told you that yesterday. Didn't you pull the dampers out?'

'The paper wouldn't catch, ma'am.'

'If the paper wouldn't catch you'll have used a damp bit. Or maybe paper out of a magazine. You can't light a fire with paper out of a magazine, Kitty.'

'If I'd had a drop of paraffin, ma'am –'

'My God, are you mad, child?'

'At home we'd throw on a half cup of paraffin if the fire was slow, ma'am.'

'Never bring paraffin near the range. If the master heard you he'd jump out of his skin.'

'I only thought it would hurry it, ma'am.'

'Set the alarm for six if you're going to be slow with the fire. If the breakfast's not on the table by a quarter to eight he'll raise the roof. Have you the plates in the bottom oven?'

When Kathleen opened the door of the bottom oven a black kitten darted out, scratching the back of her hand in its agitation.

'Great God Almighty!' exclaimed Mrs Shaughnessy. 'Are you trying to roast the poor cat?'

'I didn't know it was in there, ma'am.'

'You lit the fire with the poor creature inside there! What were you thinking of to do that, Kitty?'

'I didn't know, ma'am –'

'Always look in the two ovens before you light the range, child. Didn't you hear me telling you?'

After breakfast, when Kathleen went into the dining-room to clear the table, Mrs Shaughnessy was telling her son about the kitten in the oven. 'Haven't they brains like turnips?' she said, even though Kathleen was in the room. The son released a half-hearted smile, but when Kathleen asked him if he'd finished with the jam he didn't reply. 'Try and speak a bit more clearly, Kitty,' Mrs Shaughnessy said later. 'It's not everyone can understand a country accent.'

The day was similar to the day before except that at eleven o'clock Mrs Shaughnessy said:

'Go upstairs and take off your cap. Put on your coat and go down the street to Crawley's. A half pound of round steak, and suet. Take the book off the dresser. He'll know who you are when he sees it.'

So far, that was the pleasantest chore she had been asked to do. She had to wait in the shop because there were two other people before her, both of whom held the butcher in conversation. 'I know your father,' Mr Crawley said when he'd asked her name, and he held her in conversation also, wanting to know if her father was in good health and asking about her brothers and sisters. He'd heard about the buying of the Lallys' field. She was the last uniformed maid in the town, he said, now that Nellie Broderick at Maclure's had had to give up because of her legs.

'Are you mad?' Mrs Shaughnessy shouted at her on her return. 'I should be down in the shop and not waiting to put that meat on. Didn't I tell you yesterday not to be loitering in the mornings?'

'I'm sorry, ma'am, only Mr Crawley –'

'Go down to the shop and tell the master I'm delayed over cooking the dinner and can you assist him for ten minutes.'

But when Kathleen appeared in the grocery Mr Shaughnessy asked her if she'd got lost. The son was weighing sugar into grey paper bags and tying string round each of them. A murmur of voices came from the bar.

'Mrs Shaughnessy is delayed over cooking the dinner,' Kathleen said. 'She was thinking I could assist you for ten minutes.'

'Well, that's a good one!' Mr Shaughnessy threw back his head, exploding into laughter. A little shower of spittle damped Kathleen's face. The son gave his half-hearted smile. 'Can you make a spill, Kitty? D'you know what I mean by a spill?' Mr Shaughnessy demonstrated with a piece of brown paper on the counter. Kathleen shook her head. 'Would you know what to charge for a quarter pound of tea, Kitty? Can you weigh out sugar, Kitty? Go back to the missus, will you, and tell her to have sense.'

In the kitchen Kathleen put it differently, simply saying that Mr Shaughnessy hadn't required her services. 'Bring a scuttle of coal up to the dining-room,' Mrs Shaughnessy commanded. 'And get out the mustard. Can you make up mustard?'

Kathleen had never tasted mustard in her life; she had heard of it but did not precisely know what it was. She began to say she wasn't sure about making some, but even before she spoke Mrs Shaughnessy sighed and told her to wash down the front steps instead.

'I don't want to go back there,' Kathleen said on Sunday. 'I can't understand what she says to me. It's lonesome the entire time.'

Her mother was sympathetic, but even so she shook her head. 'There's people I used to know,' she said. 'People placed like ourselves whose farms failed on them. They're walking the roads now, no better than tinkers. I have ten children, Kathleen, and seven are gone from me. There's five of them I'll maybe never see again. It's that you have to think of, pet.'

'I cried the first night. I was that lonesome when I got into bed.'

'But isn't it a clean room you're in, pet? And aren't you given food to eat that's better than you'd get here? And don't the dresses she supplies save us an expense again? Wouldn't you think of all that, pet?'

A bargain had been struck, her mother also reminded her, and a bargain was a bargain. Biddy said it sounded great, going out into the town for messages. She'd give anything to see a house like that, Biddy said, with the coal fires and a stairs.

'I'd say they were well pleased with you,' Kathleen's father said when he came in from the yard later on. 'You'd have been back here inside a day if they weren't.'

She'd done her best, she thought as she rode away from the farmhouse on Mary Florence's bicycle; if she'd done everything badly she would have obtained her release. She wept because she wouldn't see Biddy and Con and her father and mother for another week. She dreaded the return to the

he couldn't understand how he could act normally with his son or with
is other children when they came on a visit. It was extraordinary to hear
Mrs Shaughnessy humming her songs about the house and calling him by
is Christian name.

'The Kenny girl's getting married,' Mrs Shaughnessy said on one of these
mealtime occasions. 'Tyson from the hardware.'

'I didn't know she was doing a line with him.'

'Oh, that's been going on a long time.'

'Is it the middle girl? The one with the peroxide?'

'Enid she's called.'

'I wonder Bob Crowe didn't hear that. There's not much Bob misses.'

'I never thought much of Tyson. But, sure, maybe they're well matched.'

'Did you hear that, Kitty? Enid Kenny's getting married. Don't go taking
ideas from her.' He laughed, and Mrs Shaughnessy laughed, and the son
smiled. There wasn't much chance of that, Kathleen thought. 'Are you
going dancing tonight?' Mr Crawley often asked her on a Friday, and she
would reply that she might, but she never did because it wasn't easy to go
alone. In the shops and at Mass no one displayed any interest in her
whatsoever, no one eyed her the way Mary Florence had been eyed, and
she supposed it was because her looks weren't up to much. But they were
good enough for Mr Shaughnessy, with his quivering breath and his face
on her hair. Bitterly, she dwelt on that; bitterly, she imagined herself turning
on him in the dining-room, accusing him to his wife and son.

'Did you forget to sweep the yard this week?' Mrs Shaughnessy asked
her. 'Only it's looking poor.'

She explained that the wind had blown in papers and debris from a
knocked-over dustbin. She'd sweep it again, she said.

'I hate a dirty backyard, Kitty.'

Was this why the other girls had left, she wondered, the girls whom Mrs
Shaughnessy had trained, and who'd then gone off? Those girls, whoever
they were, would see her, or would know about her. They'd imagine her
in one uniform or the other, obedient to him because she enjoyed his
attentions. That was how they'd think of her.

'Leave me alone, sir,' she said when she saw him approaching her the
next time, but he took no notice. She could see him guessing she wouldn't
scream.

'Please, sir,' she said. 'Please, sir. I don't like it.'

But after a time she ceased to make any protestation and remained as
silent as she had been at first. Twelve years or maybe fourteen, she said to
herself, lying awake in her bedroom: as long as that, or longer. In her two
different uniforms she would continue to be the outward sign of Mrs

desolate bedroom which her mother had reminded her was clean, and the
kitchen where there was no one to keep her company in the evenings. She
felt as if she could not bear it, more counting of the days until Sunday and
when Sunday came the few hours passing so swiftly. But she knew, by
now, that she would remain in the Shaughnessys' house for as long as was
necessary.

'I must have you back by half six, Kitty,' Mrs Shaughnessy said when
she saw her. 'It's closer to seven now.'

Kathleen said she was sorry. She'd had to stop to pump the back tyre
of her bicycle, she said, although in fact this was not true: what she'd
stopped for was to wipe away the signs of her crying and to blow her nose.
In the short time she had been part of Mrs Shaughnessy's household
she had developed the habit of making excuses, and of obscuring her
inadequacies beneath lies that were easier than the truth.

'Fry the bread like I showed you, Kitty. Get it brown on both sides. The
master likes it crisp.'

There was something Mr Shaughnessy liked also, which Kathleen discovered when seven of her free Sunday afternoons had gone by. She was
dusting the dining-room mantelpiece one morning when he came and stood
very close to her. She thought she was in his way, and moved out of it, but
a week or so later he stood close to her again, his breath warm on her
cheek. When it happened the third time she felt herself blushing.

It was in this manner that Mr Shaughnessy rather than his wife came to
occupy, for Kathleen, the central role in the household. The narrow-faced
son remained as he had been since the day of her arrival, a dour presence,
contributing little in the way of conversation and never revealing the
fruits of his brooding silence. Mrs Shaughnessy, having instructed, had
apparently played out the part she'd set herself. She came into the kitchen
at midday to cook meat and potatoes and one of the milk puddings her
husband was addicted to, but otherwise the kitchen was Kathleen's province now and it was she who was responsible for the frying of the food for
breakfast and for the six o'clock tea. Mrs Shaughnessy preferred to be in
the shop. She enjoyed the social side of that, she told Kathleen; and she
enjoyed the occasional half glass of sherry in the bar. 'That's me all over,
Kitty. I never took to housework.' She was more amiable in her manner,
and confessed that she always found training a country girl an exhausting
and irksome task and might therefore have been a little impatient. 'Kitty's
settled in grand,' she informed Kathleen's father when he looked into the
bar one fair-day to make a mortgage payment. He'd been delighted to hear
that, he told Kathleen the following Sunday.

Mr Shaughnessy never said anything when he came to stand close to her, although on other occasions he addressed her pleasantly enough, even complimenting her on her frying. He had an easy way with him, quite different from his son's. He was more like his two other children, the married daughter and the son who was in Limerick, both of whom Kathleen had met when they had returned to the house for an uncle's funeral. He occasionally repeated a joke he'd been told, and Mrs Shaughnessy would laugh, her chin becoming lengthy and the skin tightening on her forehead. On the occasion of the uncle's funeral his other son and his daughter laughed at the jokes also, but the son who'd remained at home only smiled. 'Wait till I tell you this one, Kitty,' he'd sometimes say, alone with her in the dining-room. He would tell her something Bob Crowe, who ran the barber's shop for him, had heard from a customer, making the most of the anecdote in a way that suggested he was anxious to entertain her. His manner and his tone of voice denied that it had ever been necessary for him to stand close to her, or else that his practice of doing so had been erased from his memory.

But the scarlet complexion of Mr Shaughnessy's face and the spiky grey hair, the odour of cigarette smoke that emanated from his clothes, could not be so easily forgotten by Kathleen. She no longer wept from loneliness in her bedroom, yet she was aware that the behaviour of Mr Shaughnessy lent the feeling of isolation an extra, vivid dimension, for in the farmhouse kitchen on Sundays the behaviour could not be mentioned.

Every evening Kathleen sat by the range, thinking about it. The black kitten that had darted out of the oven on her second morning had grown into a cat and sat blinking beside her chair. The alarm clock ticked loudly on the dresser. Was it something she should confess? Was it a sin to be as silent as she was when he came to stand beside her? Was it a sin to be unable to find the courage to tell him to leave her alone? Once, in the village where the convent was, another girl in her class had pointed out a boy who was loitering with some other boys by the sign-post. That boy was always trying to kiss you, the girl said; he would follow you about the place, whispering to you. But although Kathleen often went home alone the boy never came near her. He wasn't a bad-looking boy, she'd thought, she wouldn't have minded much. She'd wondered if she'd mind the boys her sisters had complained about, who tried to kiss you when they were dancing with you. Pests, her sisters had called them, but Kathleen thought it was nice that they wanted to.

Mr Shaughnessy was different. When he stood close to her his breathing would become loud and unsteady. He always moved away quite quickly, when she wasn't expecting him to. He walked off, never looking back, soundlessly almost.

Then one day, when Mrs Shaughnessy was buying a new s[...] son was in the shop, he came into the kitchen, where she w[...] the draining boards. He came straight to where she was, a[...] them there was some understanding that he should do so. H[...] slightly different position from usual, behind her rather than [...] and she felt for the first time his hands passing over her cloth[...]

'Mr Shaughnessy!' she whispered. 'Mr Shaughnessy, now.'

He took no notice. Some part of his face was touching h[...] rhythm of his breathing changed.

'Mr Shaughnessy, I don't like it.'

He seemed not to hear her; she sensed that his eyes wer[...] suddenly, and as quickly as always, he went away.

'Well, Bob Crowe told me a queer one this evening,' he sa[...] evening, while she was placing their plates of fried food in f[...] in the dining-room. 'It seems there's a woman asleep in [...] window above in Dublin.'

His wife expressed disbelief. Bob Crowe would tell you a[...] said.

'In a hypnotic trance, it seems. Advertising Odearest Mattr[...]

'Ah, go on now! He's pulling your leg, Des.'

'Not a bit of him. She'll stop there a week, it seems. The [...] to move the crowds on.'

Kathleen closed the dining-room door behind her. He h[...] look at her when he'd said there was a woman asleep in Cle[...] in an effort to include her in what he was retailing. His eyes [...] nothing of their surreptitious relationship, but Kathleen had [...] to meet them.

'We ploughed the field,' her father said the following Sund[...] turned up earth as good.'

She almost told him then. She longed to so much she [...] prevent herself. She longed to let her tears come and to [...] consoling her. When she was a child she'd loved that.

'You're a great girl,' he said.

Mr Shaughnessy took to attending an earlier Mass tha[...] son, and when they were out at theirs he would come i[...] When she hid in her bedroom he followed her there. Sh[...] herself in the outside W.C. if there'd been a latch on the [...]

'Well, Kitty and myself were quiet enough here,' he'd s[...] room later on, when the three of them were eating thei[...] She couldn't understand how he could bring himself to s[...] how he could so hungrily eat his food, as though noth[...]

Shaughnessy's well-to-do status, and her ordinary looks would continue to attract the attentions of a grey-haired man. Because of the field, the nature of the farm her father had once been barefoot on would change. 'Kathleen's field,' her father would often repeat, and her mother would say again that a bargain was a bargain.

Acknowledgements

These stories first appeared in the following publications: *Antaeus, Antioch Review, Atlantic Monthly, Best Irish Stories 2, A Book of Contemporary Nightmares, The Eighth Ghost Book, The Eleventh Ghost Book, Encounter, Good Housekeeping, Grand Street, Harper's, Irish Ghost Stories, Irish Press, Irish Times, James Joyce and Modern Literature, Listener, Literary Review, London Magazine, New Review, New Yorker, Nova, Observer, Penguin Modern Short Stories, The Real Thing: Seven Stories of Love* (The Bodley Head), *Redbook, Spectator, The Times, Town, Transatlantic Review, Voices 2* (Michael Joseph), *Winter's Tales* (Macmillan, London), *Winter's Tales from Ireland, Woman's Journal.*

'Going Home' and 'Attracta' first appeared as radio plays on BBC Radio Three.

Grateful acknowledgement is made to ATV Music Group for permission to quote from 'Yesterday' by John Lennon and Paul McCartney. Copyright © Maclen Music, Inc., 1965. ATV Music Corp., 6255 Sunset Boulevard, Los Angeles, CA 90028, for the USA, Canada, Mexico and the Philippines. Northern Songs Ltd for the rest of the world. Used by permission. All rights reserved.

READ MORE IN PENGUIN

In every corner of the world, on every subject under the sun, Penguin represents quality and variety – the very best in publishing today.

For complete information about books available from Penguin – including Puffins, Penguin Classics and Arkana – and how to order them, write to us at the appropriate address below. Please note that for copyright reasons the selection of books varies from country to country.

In the United Kingdom: Please write to *Dept. EP, Penguin Books Ltd, Bath Road, Harmondsworth, West Drayton, Middlesex UB7 0DA*

In the United States: Please write to *Consumer Sales, Penguin Putnam Inc., P.O. Box 12289 Dept. B, Newark, New Jersey 07101-5289.* VISA and MasterCard holders call 1-800-788-6262 to order Penguin titles

In Canada: Please write to *Penguin Books Canada Ltd, 10 Alcorn Avenue, Suite 300, Toronto, Ontario M4V 3B2*

In Australia: Please write to *Penguin Books Australia Ltd, P.O. Box 257, Ringwood, Victoria 3134*

In New Zealand: Please write to *Penguin Books (NZ) Ltd, Private Bag 102902, North Shore Mail Centre, Auckland 10*

In India: Please write to *Penguin Books India Pvt Ltd, 11 Community Centre, Panchsheel Park, New Delhi 110017*

In the Netherlands: Please write to *Penguin Books Netherlands bv, Postbus 3507, NL-1001 AH Amsterdam*

In Germany: Please write to *Penguin Books Deutschland GmbH, Metzlerstrasse 26, 60594 Frankfurt am Main*

In Spain: Please write to *Penguin Books S. A., Bravo Murillo 19, 1° B, 28015 Madrid*

In Italy: Please write to *Penguin Italia s.r.l., Via Benedetto Croce 2, 20094 Corsico, Milano*

In France: Please write to *Penguin France, Le Carré Wilson, 62 rue Benjamin Baillaud, 31500 Toulouse*

In Japan: Please write to *Penguin Books Japan Ltd, Kaneko Building, 2-3-25 Koraku, Bunkyo-Ku, Tokyo 112*

In South Africa: Please write to *Penguin Books South Africa (Pty) Ltd, Private Bag X14, Parkview, 2122 Johannesburg*

BY THE SAME AUTHOR

The Silence in the Garden

Winner of the *Yorkshire Post* Book of the Year Award

'The silence in the garden has hardened and grown cold before William Trevor's latest novel begins. It opens in 1971 when Sarah Pollexfen, the last witness to one family's secret tragedy, has died and her diary is about to be read ... Trevor's grave and lucid prose weaves recollections and the present together, and his measured compassion fuses the several narrations ... spare and moving' – Nicci Gerard in the *Observer*

Two Lives

'*Two Lives* offers two superb novels in one volume ... as rich and moving as anything I have read in years' – Glyn Hughes in the *Guardian*.

'*Reading Turgenev* is one of the most beautiful and memorable things he has written ... a drift of enchantment is evoked ... it stays in your memory – like Turgenev' – Hermione Lee in the *Independent on Sunday*.

'*My House in Umbria* is a brilliant examination of the mechanics of delusion, seen from within' – James Saynor in the *Observer*

BY THE SAME AUTHOR

Fools of Fortune

Willie Quinton lived a pleasant, cosseted life in County Cork, untouched by the troubles ... until the soldiers came and took a terrible revenge ... Spanning sixty years, William Trevor's tender and beautiful love story has at its centre a dark and violent act that spills over into the mutilated lives of generations to come.

'To my mind William Trevor's best novel and a very fine one'
– Graham Greene

The Love Department

Regal Lady Dolores ran the offices of the Love Department with a firm, bejewelled hand, resolving the heartaches of the lonely wives of Wimbledon with inimitable flourish and finesse. Now Lady Dolores's newest protégé, Edward Blakeston-Smith, was being sent on a mission – to learn the secrets of Septimus Tuam and to stop him in his tracks. Seductive and scheming, Septimus was irresistible to women. Many had succumbed to his charm and more had died of it ...

The Old Boys

Intrigue and skulduggery surround this year's election for the President of the Association. For the Old Boys, at seventy, the election revives the dormant conflicts that had tormented them as schoolboy adolescents. But now, being old, they possess a fiercer understanding of the things in life that matter   power, revenge, hatred, love and the failure of love.

BY THE SAME AUTHOR

The Children of Dynmouth

A small, pretty seaside town is harshly exposed by a young boy's curiosity. His prurient interest, oddly motivated, leaves few people unaffected – and the consequences cannot be ignored . . . 'A very fine novel. It is the work of a master craftsman and a deep creative talent . . . The bare bones of its structure are stark, simple, and stunningly subtle . . . simple yet brilliant . . . Without doubt he is one of Britain's finest novelists' – Peter Tiniswood in *The Times*

Other People's Worlds

Julia is very happy. Safe in her old stone house, drowsing in the sun, she is soon to be married to Francis. Doris is not happy. Sprawled among the grime of her Fulham flat, she gropes behind the breadbin for the vodka that keeps her going and waits endlessly for Francis. And Francis, dreaming of Constance Kent driving the knife deep into the child's throat, smiles . . .

The Boarding-House

By selecting carefully, William Wagner Bird filled his boarding-house with people that society would never miss – even if it noticed they were around. But then he made a fatal mistake. He died.

BY THE SAME AUTHOR

Elizabeth Alone

'He is a master of regret, betrayal and intimations that things will never again be as they were' – *Sunday Times*

'Comfortable, amiable Mrs Aidallbery – Elizabeth – is in hospital for a hysterectomy. So is Sylvia Clapper, with false teeth and bleached hair . . . she lives with a slippery Irishman: no children yet and now no chance. Likewise confined, devout Miss Sampson . . . and Lily Drucker, after repeated abortions, is in for childbirth . . . And there is William Trevor, taking relays from flies on a hundred walls, snipping, linking, shaping his material with delicate understanding, respect and a sparing trickle – just enough – of humour . . . A finely observed, gently sensitive comedy, delightful to read, like lived experience to remember' – *Daily Telegraph*

Mrs Eckdorf in O'Neill's Hotel

'A small work of art' – *The New York Times Book Review*

What was the tragedy that turned O'Neill's Hotel from a plush and prosperous establishment into a dingy house of disrepute? Ivy Eckdorf is determined to find out. Yet it is Mrs Eckdorf alone who is the victim of the truth she seeks to exploit, for the elusive mystery of O'Neill's Hotel turns out to be her own.

BY THE SAME AUTHOR

Death in Summer

The sudden death of Thaddeus Davenant's wife leaves him with the problem of childcare for baby Georgina. When none of the nannies interviewed is deemed suitable, Mrs Iveson, Thaddeus's mother-in-law, fulfils the position herself. But in rejecting one of the applicants, they have overlooked the beginnings of a fixed and unnatural obsession . . .

'Trevor can describe the most appalling things so evenly you only realize afterwards what's been said. Brilliant' – Ruth Padel, *Mail on Sunday*

After Rain

'Each of the twelve stories in William Trevor's glittering new collection, *After Rain*, surveys a quietly devastating little earthquake . . . Nothing escapes his eye, it seems; everything is caught with dazzling deftness by his pen' – Peter Kemp, *Sunday Times*

Miss Gomez and the Brethren

Miss Gomez lives for her postal correspondence with the Church of the Brethren of the Way in Jamaica. No one will believe her revelation of a hideous sex crime soon to be committed in the wasteland of Crow Street in South-West London, until Prudence Tuke disappears and the newspapers herald a 'Sex Crime Prophecy'. 'A tender and passionate book as well as a very funny one' – *Sunday Times*

Felicia's Journey
Winner of the 1994 Whitbread Book of the Year Award and the *Sunday Express* Book of the Year Award

'A book so brilliant that it compels you to stay up all night galloping through to the end . . . exquisitely crafted' Val Hennessy, *Daily Mail*. 'Immensely readable . . . The plot twist – a characteristic mix – is both sinister and affecting, and so skilfully done that you remember why authors had plot twists in the first place' – Philip Hensher, *Guardian*

Also published:

Ireland: Selected Stories
Outside Ireland: Selected Stories

Learning Resources
Centre